THE PLUM IN THE GOLDEN VASE

PRINCETON LIBRARY OF ASIAN TRANSLATIONS

The Plum in the Golden Vase

or, CHIN P'ING MEI

VOLUME FOUR: THE CLIMAX

Translated by David Tod Roy

PRINCETON UNIVERSITY PRESS
PRINCETON AND OXFORD

PRINCETON UNIVERSITY PRESS
PRINCETON AND OXFORD

Library of Congress Cataloging-in-Publication Data

Hsiao-hsiao-sheng

[Chin P'ing Mei. English]

  The plum in the golden vase, or, Chin P'ing Mei /

  translated by David Tod Roy.

        p. cm. —(Princeton library of Asian translations)

  Includes bibliographical references and index.

  Contents: v.   1. The gathering. v.   2. The rivals. v.   3. The aphrodisiac.

  ISBN-13: 978-0-691-15043-7

  ISBN-10: 0-691-15043-5

  1. Roy, David Tod 1933–.   II. Title   III. Series.

  PL2698.H73C4713 1993

  895.1'346–dc20 92-45054

British Library Cataloging-in-Publication Data is available

This book has been composed in ElectraLTstd

Printed on acid-free paper. ∞

Printed in the United States of America

10   9   8   7   6   5   4   3   2

To all those students, friends, and colleagues
WHO PARTICIPATED WITH ME IN THE EXCITEMENT

OF EXPLORING THE WORLD OF THE *CHIN P'ING MEI*

OVER THE PAST QUARTER CENTURY

CONTENTS

LIST OF ILLUSTRATIONS

ACKNOWLEDGMENTS

OF THOSE who have helped to make the appearance of this volume possible in innumerable ways, I wish particularly to thank Bill Alspaugh, James Cahill, Lois Fusek, Pieter Keulemans, Victor Mair, David Rolston, Charles Stone, and Richard G. Wang.

To my wife, Barbara Chew Roy, who urged me to embark on this interminable task, and who has lent me her unwavering support over the years despite the extent to which the work has preoccupied me, I owe a particular debt of gratitude. Without her encouragement I would have had neither the temerity to undertake it nor the stamina to continue it.

For indispensable technical advice and assistance concerning computers, printers, and word-processing programs, I continue to be indebted to Charles Stone.

The research that helped to make this work possible was materially assisted by a Grant for Research on Chinese Civilization from the American Council of Learned Societies in 1976–77, grants from the National Endowment for the Humanities in 1983–86 and 1995–96, a Residential Faculty Fellowship from the Chicago Humanities Institute in 1994–95, and gifts from the Norman and Carol Nie Foundation in 1995 and 2000. The Department of East Asian Languages and Civilizations and the Division of Humanities at the University of Chicago have also been generous in allowing me the time and space to devote to this project. For all of the above assistance, without which this venture could not have been contemplated, I am deeply grateful.

Needless to say, whatever infelicities and errors remain in the translation are solely my own.

CAST OF CHARACTERS

THE FOLLOWING list includes all characters who appear in the novel, listed alphabetically by surname. All characters with dates in parentheses after their names are historical figures from the Sung dynasty. Characters who bear the names of historical figures from the Ming dynasty are identified in the notes.

An Ch'en, winner of first place in the *chin-shih* examinations but displaced in favor of Ts'ai Yün because he is the younger brother of the proscribed figure, An Tun; becomes a protégé of Ts'ai Ching and is patronized by Hsi-men Ch'ing, later rising to the rank of secretary of the Bureau of Irrigation and Transportation in the Ministry of Works; rewarded for his part in facilitating the notorious Flower and Rock Convoys and the construction of the Mount Ken Imperial Park.

An Ch'en's second wife.

An, Consort. See Liu, Consort.

An Tun (1042–1104), elder brother of An Ch'en, a high official whose name has been proscribed for his role in the partisan political conflicts of the late eleventh century.

An-t'ung, page boy of Aunt Yang.

An-t'ung, page boy of Miao T'ien-hsiu who is rescued by a fisherman and does his utmost to see justice done for the murder of his master.

An-t'ung, page boy of Wang Hsüan.

Apricot Hermitage, Layman of. See Wang Hsüan.

Autumn Chrysanthemum. See Ch'iu-chü.

Barefaced Adept, Taoist master from the Fire Dragon Monastery in the Obdurate Grotto of the Vacuous Mountains from whom Yang Kuang-yen acquires the art of lying.

Bean curd-selling crone who identifies the home of Commander Yüan in Potter's Alley to Hsi-men Ch'ing.

"Beanpole, The." See Hui-ch'ing.

Black-robed lictor on the staff of Ho Hsin.

Black-robed lictor who announces the arrival of Chang Pang-ch'ang and Ts'ai Yu to congratulate Chu Mien.

Black Whirlwind. See Li K'uei.

Brocade Tiger. See Yen Shun.

Busybody who directs Ch'iao Yün-ko to Dame Wang's teashop when he is looking for Hsi-men Ch'ing.

Cassia. See Li Kuei-chieh.

Chai Ch'ien, majordomo of Ts'ai Ching's household in the Eastern Capital.

Chai Ch'ien's wife.

Chai Ching-erh, Sutra Chai, proprietor of a sutra printing shop in Ch'ing-ho.

Chai, Sutra. See Chai Ching-erh.

Ch'ai Chin, Little Whirlwind, Little Lord Meng-ch'ang, direct descendant of Ch'ai Jung (921–59), emperor Shih-tsung (r. 954–59) of the Later Chou dynasty (951–60).

Ch'ai Huang-ch'eng, paternal uncle of Ch'ai Chin.

Ch'an Master Snow Cave. See P'u-ching.

Chang An, caretaker of Hsi-men Ch'ing's ancestral graveyard outside Ch'ing-ho.

Chang, Auntie, go-between who helps arrange Ch'en Ching-chi's marriage to Ko Ts'ui-p'ing.

Chang Ch'eng, a neighborhood head in Ch'ing-ho.

Chang Ch'ing, a criminal innkeeper with whom Wu Sung seeks refuge after the murder of P'an Chin-lien.

Chang Ch'ing's wife.

Chang Ch'uan-erh, a garrulous chair-bearer in Ch'ing-ho, partner of Wei Ts'ung-erh.

Chang the Fourth. See Chang Ju-i.

Chang the Fourth. See Chang Lung.

Chang Hao-wen, Chang the Importunate, Chang the Second, proprietor of a paper shop in Ch'ing-ho, acquaintance of Han Tao-kuo.

Chang Hsi-ch'un, a ballad singer maintained at one time as a mistress by Hsi-men Ch'ing.

Chang Hsi-ts'un, an acquaintance of Hsi-men Ch'ing's who invites him to his home for a birthday party.

Chang Hsiao-hsien, Hsiao Chang-hsien, Trifler Chang, "ball clubber" in Ch'ing-ho who plays the tout to Wang Ts'ai on his visits to the licensed quarter and upon whom Hsi-men Ch'ing turns the tables by abusing the judicial system at the behest of Lady Lin.

Chang the Importunate. See Chang Hao-wen.

Chang Ju-i, Chang the Fourth, wife of Hsiung Wang, employed in Hsi-men Ch'ing's household as a wet nurse for Kuan-ko and later for Hsiao-ko, sexual partner of Hsi-men Ch'ing after the death of Li P'ing-erh, finally married to Lai-hsing.

Chang Ju-i's mother.

Chang Ko (1068–1113), promoted to the post of vice minister of the Ministry of Works for his part in facilitating the notorious Flower and Rock Convoys and the construction of the Mount Ken Imperial Park.

Chang Kuan, brother-in-law of Ch'en Hung and maternal uncle of Ch'en Ching-chi, militia commander of Ch'ing-ho.

Chang Kuan's sister. See Ch'en Hung's wife, née Chang.

Chang Kuan's wife.

Chang Lung, Chang the Fourth, maternal uncle of Meng Yü-lou's first husband Yang Tsung-hsi who unsuccessfully proposes that she remarry Shang Hsiao-t'ang and quarrels with Aunt Yang when she decides to marry Hsi-men Ch'ing instead.

Chang Lung, judicial commissioner of the Liang-Huai region.

Chang Lung's elder sister (Chang the Fourth's elder sister), mother of Yang Tsung-hsi and Yang Tsung-pao.

Chang Lung's wife (Chang the Fourth's wife).

Chang Mao-te, Chang the Second, nephew of Mr. Chang, the well-to-do merchant who first seduces P'an Chin-lien; a major rival of Hsi-men Ch'ing in the social world of Ch'ing-ho who, immediately after Hsi-men Ch'ing's death, bribes Cheng Chü-chung to intervene with Chu Mien and have him appointed to Hsi-men Ch'ing's former position as judicial commissioner so he can take over where Hsi-men Ch'ing left off.

Chang Mao-te's son, marries Eunuch Director Hsü's niece.

Chang Mei, professional actor of Hai-yen style drama.

Chang, Military Director-in-chief, official in Meng-chou.

Chang, Mr., a well-to-do merchant in Ch'ing-ho who first seduces P'an Chin-lien.

Chang, Mrs., wife of Mr. Chang, néeYü.

Chang, Old Mother, go-between who tries to sell two inexperienced country girls, Sheng-chin and Huo-pao, to P'ang Ch'un-mei.

Chang, Old Mother, proprietress of an inn next door to Auntie Hsüeh's residence.

Chang Pang-ch'ang (1081–1127), minister of rites, promoted to the position of grand guardian of the heir apparent for his part in facilitating the notorious Flower and Rock Convoys and the construction of the Mount Ken Imperial Park, puppet emperor of the short-lived state of Ch'u for thirty-two days in 1127.

Chang the Second. See Chang Hao-wen.

Chang the Second. See Chang Mao-te.

Chang Sheng, Street-skulking Rat, "knockabout" who, along with Lu Hua, shakes down Dr. Chiang Chu-shan at the behest of Hsi-men Ch'ing; later a servant in the household of Chou Hsiu, brother-in-law of Liu the Second; murders Ch'en Ching-chi when he overhears him plotting against him and is beaten to death by Chou Hsiu at the behest of P'ang Ch'un-mei.

Chang Sheng's reincarnation. See Kao family of the Ta-hsing Guard.

Chang Sheng's wife, née Liu, sister of Liu the Second.

Chang Shih-lien, Ch'en Hung's brother-in-law, related to Yang Chien by marriage, an official in the Eastern Capital.

Chang Shih-lien's wife, née Ch'en, Ch'en Hung's elder sister.

Chang Shu-yeh (1065–1127), prefect of Chi-chou in Shantung, later pacification commissioner of Shantung, responsible for the defeat of Sung Chiang and his acceptance of a government amnesty.

Chang Sung, Little. See Shu-t'ung.

Chang Ta (d. 1126), official who dies in the defense of T'ai-yüan against the invading Chin army.

Chang, Trifler. See Chang Hsiao-hsien.

Ch'ang, Cadger. See Ch'ang Shih-chieh.

Ch'ang the Second. See Ch'ang Shih-chieh.

Ch'ang Shih-chieh, Cadger Ch'ang, Ch'ang the Second, crony of Hsi-men Ch'ing, member of the brotherhood of ten.

Ch'ang Shih-chieh's wife.

Ch'ang Shih-chieh's wife's younger brother.

Ch'ang Yü, Commandant, officer rewarded for his part in facilitating the notorious Flower and Rock Convoys and the construction of the Mount Ken Imperial Park.

Chao, Auntie, go-between who sells Chin-erh to Wang Liu-erh.

Chao Chiao-erh, singing girl working out of My Own Tavern in Lin-ch'ing.

Chao, Dr.. See Chao Lung-kang.

Chao Hung-tao, domestic clerk on the staff of Yang Chien.

Chao I (fl. early 12th century), Duke of Chia, twenty-sixth son of Emperor Hui-tsung by Consort Liu.

Chao K'ai (d. c. 1129), Prince of Yün, third son of emperor Hui-tsung by Consort Wang.

Chao, Lama, head priest of the Pao-ch'ing Lamasery outside the west gate of Ch'ing-ho.

Chao Lung-kang, Dr. Chao, Chao the Quack, incompetent specialist in female disorders called in to diagnose Li P'ing-erh's fatal illness.

Chao Lung-kang's grandfather.

Chao Lung-kang's father.

Chao No, investigation commissioner for Shantung.

Chao the Quack. See Chao Lung-kang.

Chao, Tailor, artisan patronized by Hsi-men Ch'ing.

Chao-ti, servant in the household of Han Tao-kuo and Wang Liu-erh.

Chao T'ing (fl. early 12th century), prefect of Hang-chou, promoted to the post of chief minister of the Court of Judicial Review.

Chao, Widow, wealthy landowner from whom Hsi-men Ch'ing buys a country estate adjacent to his ancestral graveyard.

Chao Yu-lan, battalion commander rewarded for his part in facilitating the notorious Flower and Rock Convoys and the construction of the Mount Ken Imperial Park.

Ch'e, Hogwash. See Ch'e Tan.

Ch'e Tan, Hogwash Ch'e, a dissolute young scamp upon whom Hsi-men Ch'ing turns the tables by abusing the judicial system.

Ch'e Tan's father, proprietor of a wineshop in Ch'ing-ho.

Ch'en An, servant in Ch'en Ching-chi's household.

Ch'en, Battalion Commander, resident on Main Street in Ch'ing-ho from whom Hsi-men Ch'ing declines to buy a coffin after the death of Li P'ing-erh.

Ch'en Cheng-hui (fl. early 12th century), son of Ch'en Kuan, surveillance vice-commissioner of education for Shantung.

Ch'en Ching-chi, secondary male protagonist of the novel, son of Ch'en Hung, husband of Hsi-men Ta-chieh, son-in-law of Hsi-men Ch'ing who carries on a running pseudo-incestuous affair with P'an Chin-lien that is consummated after the death of Hsi-men Ch'ing; falls out with Wu Yüeh-niang and is evicted from the household; drives Hsi-men Ta-chieh to suicide; attempts unsuccessfully to shake down Meng Yü-lou in Yen-chou; squanders his patrimony and is reduced to beggary; accepts charity from his father's friend the philanthropist Wang Hsüan, who induces him to become a monk with the Taoist appellation Tsung-mei, the junior disciple of Abbot Jen of the Yen-kung Temple in Lin-ch'ing; is admitted to the household of Chou Hsiu as a pretended cousin of P'ang Ch'un-mei who carries on an affair with him under her husband's nose; also has affairs with Feng Chin-pao and Han Ai-chieh, marries Ko Ts'ui-p'ing, and is murdered by Chang Sheng when he is overheard plotting against him.

Ch'en Ching-chi's grandfather, a salt merchant.

Ch'en Ching-chi's reincarnation. See Wang family of the Eastern Capital.

Ch'en, Dr., resident of Ch'ing-ho.

Ch'en, Dr.'s son, conceived as a result of a fertility potion provided by Nun Hsüeh.

Ch'en, Dr.'s wife, conceives a son in middle age after taking a fertility potion provided by Nun Hsüeh.

Ch'en Hung, wealthy dealer in pine resin, father of Ch'en Ching-chi, related by marriage to Yang Chien.

Ch'en Hung's elder sister, wife of Chang Shih-lien.

Ch'en Hung's wife, née Chang, sister of Chang Kuan, mother of Ch'en Ching-chi.

Ch'en Kuan (1057–1122), a prominent remonstrance official, father of Ch'en Cheng-hui.

Ch'en Liang-huai, national university student, son of Vice Commissioner Ch'en, friend of Ting the Second.

Ch'en, Master, legal scribe who assists Wu Sung in drafting a formal complaint against Hsi-men Ch'ing.

Ch'en, Miss, daughter of the deceased Vice Commissioner Ch'en whose assignation with Juan the Third results in his death.

Ch'en, Miss's maidservant.

Ch'en, Mistress. See Hsi-men Ta-chieh.

Ch'en the Second, proprietor of an inn at Ch'ing-chiang P'u at which Ch'en Ching-chi puts up on his way to Yen-chou.

Ch'en Ssu-chen, right provincial administration commissioner of Shantung.

Ch'en the Third, "cribber" in the licensed quarter of Lin-ch'ing.

Ch'en the Third, criminal boatman who, along with his partner Weng the Eighth, murders Miao T'ien-hsiu.

Ch'en Ting, servant in Ch'en Hung's household.

Ch'en Ting's wife.

Ch'en Tsung-mei. See Ch'en Ching-chi.

Ch'en Tsung-shan, ward-inspecting commandant of the Eastern Capital.

Ch'en Tung (1086–1127), national university student who submits a memorial to the throne impeaching the Six Traitors.

Ch'en, Vice-Commissioner, deceased father of Miss Ch'en.

Ch'en, Vice-Commissioner, father of Ch'en Liang-huai.

Ch'en, Vice-Commissioner's wife, née Chang, mother of Miss Ch'en.

Ch'en Wen-chao, prefect of Tung-p'ing.

Cheng Ai-hsiang, Cheng Kuan-yin, Goddess of Mercy Cheng, singing girl from the Star of Joy Bordello in Ch'ing-ho patronized by Hua Tzu-hsü, elder sister of Cheng Ai-yüeh.

Cheng Ai-yüeh, singing girl from the Star of Joy Bordello in Ch'ing-ho patronized by Wang Ts'ai and Hsi-men Ch'ing, younger sister of Cheng Ai-hsiang.

Cheng, Auntie, madam of the Star of Joy Bordello in Ch'ing-ho.

Cheng, Battalion Commander's family in the Eastern Capital into which Hua Tzu-hsü is reincarnated as a son.

Cheng Chi, servant in Hsi-men Ch'ing's household.

Cheng Chiao-erh, singing girl in Ch'ing-ho, niece of Cheng Ai-hsiang and Cheng Ai-yüeh.

Cheng Chin-pao. See Feng Chin-pao.

Cheng Ch'un, professional actor in Ch'ing-ho, younger brother of Cheng Feng, Cheng Ai-hsiang, and Cheng Ai-yüeh.

Cheng Chü-chung (1059–1123), military affairs commissioner, cousin of Consort Cheng, granted the title of grand guardian for his part in facilitating the notorious Flower and Rock Convoys and the construction of the Mount Ken Imperial Park, accepts a bribe of a thousand taels of silver from Chang Mao-te to intervene with Chu Mien and have him appointed to the position of judicial commissioner left vacant by the death of Hsi-men Ch'ing.

Cheng, Consort, (1081–1132), a consort of Emperor Hui-tsung, niece of Madame Ch'iao.

Cheng Feng, professional actor in Ch'ing-ho, elder brother of Cheng Ai-Hsiang, Cheng Ai-yüeh, and Cheng Ch'un.

Cheng the Fifth, Auntie, madam of the Cheng Family Brothel in Lin-ch'ing.

Cheng the Fifth, Auntie's husband.

Cheng, Goddess of Mercy. See Cheng Ai-hsiang.

Cheng Kuan-yin. See Cheng Ai-hsiang.

Cheng, Third Sister, niece of Ch'iao Hung's wife, née Cheng, marries Wu K'ai's son Wu Shun-ch'en.

Cheng T'ien-shou, Palefaced Gentleman, third outlaw leader of the Ch'ing-feng Stronghold on Ch'ing-feng Mountain.

Cheng Wang. See Lai-wang.

Ch'eng-erh, younger daughter of Lai-hsing by Hui-hsiu.

Chi K'an, right administration vice commissioner of Shantung.

Chi-nan, old man from, who directs Wu Yüeh-niang to the Ling-pi Stockade in her dream.

Ch'i family brothel in Ch'ing-ho, madam of.

Ch'i Hsiang-erh, singing girl from the Ch'i family brothel in Ch'ing-ho.

Ch'i-t'ung, page boy in Hsi-men Ch'ing's household.

Chia, Duke of. See Chao I.

Chia Hsiang (fl. early 12th century), eunuch rewarded for his part in facilitating the notorious Flower and Rock Convoys and the construction of the Mount Ken Imperial Park.

Chia Hsiang's adopted son, granted the post of battalion vice commander of the Embroidered Uniform Guard by *yin* privilege as a reward for his father's part in facilitating the notorious Flower and Rock Convoys and the construction of the Mount Ken Imperial Park.

Chia Jen-ch'ing, False Feelings, neighbor of Hsi-men Ch'ing who intercedes unsuccessfully on Lai-wang's behalf.

Chia Lien, name to which Li Pang-yen alters Hsi-men Ch'ing's name on a bill of impeachment in return for a handsome bribe.

Chiang Chu-shan, Chiang Wen-hui, doctor who Li P'ing-erh marries on the rebound only to drive away ignominiously as soon as Hsi-men Ch'ing becomes available again.

Chiang Chu-shan's deceased first wife.

Chiang, Gate God. See Chiang Men-shen.

Chiang, Little, servant of Ch'en Ching-chi.

Chiang Men-shen, Gate God Chiang, elder brother of Chiang Yü-lan, gangster whose struggle with Shih En for control of the Happy Forest Tavern in Meng-chou results in his murder by Wu Sung.

Chiang Ts'ung, Sauce and Scallions, former husband of Sung Hui-lien, a cook in Ch'ing-ho who is stabbed to death in a brawl with a fellow cook over the division of their pay.

Chiang Ts'ung's assailant, convicted of a capital crime and executed as a result of Hsi-men Ch'ing's intervention.

Chiang Wen-hui. See Chiang Chu-shan.

Chiang Yü-lan, younger sister of Chiang Men-shen, concubine of Military Director-in-chief Chang of Meng-chou who assists her husband and brother in framing Wu Sung.

Ch'iao, distaff relative of the imperial family whose garden abuts on the back wall of Li P'ing-erh's house on Lion Street, assumes hereditary title of commander when Ch'iao the Fifth dies without issue.

Ch'iao Chang-chieh, infant daughter of Ch'iao Hung betrothed to Hsi-men Kuan-ko while both of them are still babes in arms.

Ch'iao, Consort, (fl. early 12th century), a consort of Emperor Hui-tsung, related to Ch'iao the Fifth.

Ch'iao the Fifth, deceased distaff relative of the imperial family through Consort Ch'iao whose hereditary title of commander passes to another branch of the family when he dies without issue.

Ch'iao the Fifth's widow. See Ch'iao, Madame.

Ch'iao Hung, uncle of Ts'ui Pen, wealthy neighbor and business partner of Hsi-men Ch'ing whose daughter, Ch'iao Chang-chieh, is betrothed to Hsi-men Ch'ing's son Kuan-ko while they are still babes in arms.

Ch'iao Hung's concubine, mother of Ch'iao Chang-chieh.

Ch'iao Hung's elder sister, Ts'ui Pen's mother.

Ch'iao Hung's wife, née Cheng.

Ch'iao, Madame, Ch'iao the Fifth's widow, née Cheng, aunt of Ch'iao Hung's wife, née Cheng, and of Consort Cheng.

Ch'iao T'ung, servant in Ch'iao Hung's household.

Ch'iao T'ung's wife.

Ch'iao Yün-ko, Little Yün, young fruit peddler in Ch'ing-ho who helps Wu Chih catch Hsi-men Ch'ing and P'an Chin-lien in adultery.

Ch'iao Yün-ko's father, retired soldier dependent on his son.

Ch'ien Ch'eng, vice magistrate of Ch'ing-ho district.

Ch'ien Ch'ing-ch'uan, traveling merchant entertained by Han Tao-kuo in Yang-chou.

Ch'ien Lao, clerk of the office of punishment in Ch'ing-ho.

Ch'ien Lung-yeh, secretary of the Ministry of Revenue in charge of collecting transit duties on shipping at the Lin-ch'ing customs house.

Ch'ien, Phlegm-fire. See Ch'ien T'an-huo.

Ch'ien T'an-huo, Phlegm-fire Ch'ien, Taoist healer called in to treat Hsi-men Kuan-ko.

Chih-yün, Abbot, head priest of Hsiang-kuo Temple in K'ai-feng visited by Hsi-men Ch'ing on his trip to the Eastern Capital.

Chin, Abbot, Taoist head priest of the Temple of the Eastern Peak on Mount T'ai.

Chin Ch'ien-erh, former maidservant in the household of Huang the Fourth's son purchased by P'ang Ch'un-mei as a servant for Ko Ts'ui-p'ing when she marries Ch'en Ching-chi.

Chin-erh, maidservant of Wang Liu-erh.

Chin-erh, singing girl in Longleg Lu's brothel on Butterfly Lane in Ch'ing-ho.

Chin-erh, singing girl working out of My Own Tavern in Lin-ch'ing.

Chin-erh's father, military patrolman whose horse is fatally injured in a fall and, for lack of replacement money, is forced to sell his daughter into domestic service.

Chin-kuei, employed in Chou Hsiu's household as a wet nurse for Chou Chin-ko.

Chin-lien. See P'an Chin-lien.

Chin-lien. See Sung Hui-lien.

Chin Ta-chieh, wife of Auntie Hsüeh's son Hsüeh Chi.

Chin-ts'ai, servant in the household of Han Tao-kuo and Wang Liu-erh.

Chin Tsung-ming, senior disciple of Abbot Jen of the Yen-kung Temple in Lin-ch'ing.

Ch'in-tsung, Emperor of the Sung dynasty (r. 1125–27), son of Emperor Hui-tsung who abdicated in his favor in 1125, taken into captivity together with his father by the Chin dynasty invaders in 1127.

Ch'in-t'ung, junior page boy in the household of Hua Tzu-hsü and Li P'ing-erh, originally named T'ien-fu but renamed when she marries into the household of Hsi-men Ch'ing.

Ch'in-t'ung, page boy of Meng Yü-lou who is seduced by P'an Chin-lien and driven out of the household when the affair is discovered.

Ch'in Yü-chih, singing girl in Ch'ing-ho patronized by Wang Ts'ai.

Ching-chi. See Ch'en Ching-chi.

Ching Chung, commander of the left battalion of the Ch'ing-ho Guard, later promoted to the post of military director-in-chief of Chi-chou, and finally to commander-general of the southeast and concurrently grain transport commander.

Ching Chung's daughter for whom he seeks a marriage alliance with Hsi-men Kuan-ko but is refused by Hsi-men Ch'ing.

Ching Chung's mother.

Ching Chung's wife.

Ch'iu-chü, Autumn Chrysanthemum, much abused junior maidservant of P'an Chin-lien.

Cho the Second. See Cho Tiu-erh.

Cho Tiu-erh, Cho the second, Toss-off Cho, unlicensed prostitute in Ch'ing-ho maintained as a mistress by Hsi-men Ch'ing and subsequently brought into his household as his Third Lady only to sicken and die soon thereafter.

Cho, Toss-off. See Cho Tiu-erh.

Chou, Censor, neighbor of Wu Yüeh-niang's when she was growing up, father of Miss Chou.

Chou Chin-ko, son of Chou Hsiu by P'ang Ch'un-mei the real father of which may have been Ch'en Ching-chi.

Chou Chung, senior servant in the household of Chou Hsiu, father of Chou Jen and Chou I.

Chou, Eunuch Director, resident of Ch'ing-ho whose invitation to a party Hsi-men Ch'ing declines not long before his death.

Chou Hsiao-erh, patron of Li Kuei-ch'ing and probably of Li Kuei-chieh also.

Chou Hsiu, commandant of the Regional Military Command, later appointed to other high military posts, colleague of Hsi-men Ch'ing after whose death he buys P'ang Ch'un-mei as a concubine and later promotes her to the position of principal wife when she bears him a son; commander-general of the Shantung region who leads the forces of Ch'ing-yen against the Chin invaders and dies at Kao-yang Pass of an arrow wound inflicted by the Chin commander Wan-yen Tsung-wang.

Chou Hsiu's first wife, blind in one eye, who dies not long after P'ang Ch'un-mei enters his household as a concubine.

Chou Hsiu's reincarnation. See Shen Shou-shan.

Chou Hsüan, cousin of Chou Hsiu's who looks after his affairs while he is at the front.

Chou I, servant in Chou Hsiu's household, son of Chou Chung and younger brother of Chou Jen, clandestine lover of P'ang Ch'un-mei who dies in the act of intercourse with him.

Chou I's paternal aunt with whom he seeks refuge after the death of P'ang Ch'un-mei.

Chou I's reincarnation. See Kao Liu-chu.

Chou Jen, servant in Chou Hsiu's household, son of Chou Chung and elder brother of Chou I.

Chou, Little, itinerant barber and masseur in Ch'ing-ho patronized by Hsi-men Ch'ing.

Chou, Miss, daughter of Censor Chou, neighbor of Wu Yüeh-niang's when she was growing up who broke her hymen by falling from a standing position onto the seat of a swing.

Chou, Ms., widowed second wife of Sung Te's father-in-law who commits adultery with him after her husband's death, for which Hsi-men Ch'ing sentences them both to death by strangulation.

Chou, Ms.'s maidservant.

Chou, Ms.'s mother.

Chou the Second, friend of Juan the Third.

Chou Shun, professional actor from Su-chou who specializes in playing female lead parts.

Chou Ts'ai, professional boy actor in Ch'ing-ho.

Chou Yü-chieh, daughter of Chou Hsiu by his concubine Sun Erh-niang.

Chu Ai-ai, Love, singing girl from Greenhorn Chu's brothel on Second Street in the licensed quarter of Ch'ing-ho, daughter of Greenhorn Chu.

Chu, Battalion Commander, resident of Ch'ing-ho, father of Miss Chu.

Chu, Battalion Commander's deceased wife, mother of Miss Chu.

Chu, Censor, resident of Ch'ing-ho, neighbor of Ch'iao Hung.

Chu, Censor's wife.

Chu family of the Eastern Capital, family into which Sung Hui-lien is reincarnated as a daughter.

Chu, Greenhorn, proprietor of a brothel on Second Street in the licensed
quarter of Ch'ing-ho situated next door to the Verdant Spring Bordello of
Auntie Li the Third.

Chu Jih-nien, Sticky Chu, Pockmarked Chu, crony of Hsi-men Ch'ing, member of the brotherhood of ten, plays the tout to Wang Ts'ai on his visits to
the licensed quarter.

Chu Mien (1075–1126), defender-in-chief of the Embroidered Uniform
Guard, an elite unit of the Imperial Bodyguard that performed secret police
functions; relative of Li Ta-t'ien, the district magistrate of Ch'ing-ho; chief
mover behind the notorious Flower and Rock Convoys and the construction of the Mount Ken Imperial Park, for which service to the throne he is
promoted to a series of high posts; one of the Six Traitors impeached by
Ch'en Tung.

Chu Mien's majordomo.

Chu Mien's son, granted the post of battalion commander of the Embroidered Uniform Guard by *yin* privilege as a reward for his father's part in facilitating the notorious Flower and Rock Convoys and the construction of
the Mount Ken Imperial Park.

Chu, Miss, daughter of Battalion Commander Chu.

Chu, Pockmarked. See Chu Jih-nien.

Chu, Sticky. See Chu Jih-nien.

Ch'u-yün, daughter of a battalion commander of the Yang-chou Guard purchased by Miao Ch'ing to send as a gift to Hsi-men Ch'ing.

Ch'u-yün's father, battalion commander of the Yang-chou Guard.

Ch'un-hsiang, maidservant in the household of Han Tao-kuo and Wang Liu-
erh.

Ch'un-hua, concubine of Ying Po-chüeh and mother of his younger son.

Ch'un-hung, page boy in Hsi-men Ch'ing's household.

Ch'un-mei. See P'ang Ch'un-mei.

Chung-ch'iu, junior maidservant in Hsi-men Ch'ing's household serving at
various times Hsi-men Ta-chieh, Sun Hsüeh-o, and Wu Yüeh-niang.

Chung Kuei, policeman from outside the city wall of the Eastern Capital into
whose family Hsi-men Ta-chieh is reincarnated as a daughter.

Ch'ung-hsi, maidservant purchased by Ch'en Ching-chi to serve Feng Chin-
pao.

Ch'ung Shih-tao (1051–1126), general-in-chief of the Sung armies defending
against the Chin invaders.

Ch'ü, Midwife, maternal aunt of Lai-wang in whose house on Polished Rice
Lane outside the east gate of Ch'ing-ho Lai-wang and Sun Hsüeh-o seek
refuge after absconding from the Hsi-men household.

Ch'ü T'ang, son of Midwife Ch'ü, cousin of Lai-wang.

Coal in the Snow. See P'an Chin-lien's cat.

Died-of-fright, Miss, wife of Yang Kuang-yen.

False Feelings. See Chia Jen-ch'ing.

Fan family of Hsü-chou, peasant family into which Wu Chih is reincarnated as a son.

Fan Hsün, battalion commander in the Ch'ing-ho Guard.

Fan, Hundred Customers. See Fan Pai-chia-nu.

Fan Kang, next-door neighbor of Ch'en Ching-chi in Ch'ing-ho.

Fan, Old Man, neighbor of the Hsieh Family Tavern in Lin-ch'ing.

Fan Pai-chia-nu, Hundred Customers Fan, singing girl from the Fan Family Brothel in Ch'ing-ho.

Fang Chen (fl. early 12th century), erudite of the Court of Imperial Sacrifices who reports that a brick in the Imperial Ancestral Temple is oozing blood.

Fang La (d. 1121), rebel who set up an independent regime in the southeast which was suppressed by government troops in 1121.

Feng Chin-pao, Cheng Chin-pao, singing girl from the Feng Family Brothel in Lin-ch'ing purchased as a concubine by Ch'en Ching-chi, later resold to the brothel of Auntie Cheng the Fifth who changes her name to Cheng Chin-pao.

Feng Chin-pao's mother, madam of the Feng Family Brothel in Lin-ch'ing.

Feng, Consort (fl. mid 11th-early 12th century), Consort Tuan, consort of Emperor Jen-tsung (r. 1022–63) who resided in the palace for five reigns.

Feng Family Brothel's servant.

Feng Huai, son of Feng the Second, son-in-law of Pai the Fifth, dies of injuries sustained in an affray with Sun Wen-hsiang.

Feng, Old Mother, waiting woman in Li P'ing-erh's family since she was a child, continues in her service when she is a concubine of Privy Councilor Liang Shih-chieh, wife of Hua Tzu-hsü, wife of Chiang Chu-shan, and after she marries Hsi-men Ch'ing, supplementing her income by working as a go-between on the side.

Feng the Second, employee of Sun Ch'ing, father of Feng Huai.

Feng T'ing-hu, left assistant administration commissioner of Shantung.

Fifth Lady. See P'an Chin-lien.

First Lady. See Wu Yüeh-niang.

Fisherman who rescues An-t'ung and helps him to locate the boatmen who had murdered his master.

Flying Demon. See Hou Lin.

Fourth Lady. See Sun Hsüeh-o.

Fu-jung, maidservant of Lady Lin.

Fu, Manager. See Fu Ming.

Fu Ming, Fu the Second, Manager Fu, manager of Hsi-men Ch'ing's pharmaceutical shop, pawnshop, and other businesses.

Fu Ming's wife.

Fu the Second. See Fu Ming.

Fu T'ien-tse, battalion commander rewarded for his part in facilitating the notorious Flower and Rock Convoys and the construction of the Mount Ken Imperial Park.

Golden Lotus. See P'an Chin-lien.

Good Deed. See Yin Chih.

Hai-t'ang, concubine of Chou Hsiu much abused by P'ang Ch'un-mei.

Han Ai-chieh, daughter of Han Tao-kuo and Wang Liu-erh, niece of Han the Second, concubine of Chai Ch'ien, mistress of Ch'en Ching-chi to whom she remains faithful after his death, ending her life as a Buddhist nun.

Han, Auntie, wife of Mohammedan Han, mother of Han Hsiao-yü.

Han, Baldy, father of Han Tao-kuo and Han the Second.

Han, Brother-in-law. See Han Ming-ch'uan.

Han Chin-ch'uan, singing girl in Ch'ing-ho, elder sister of Han Yü-ch'uan, younger sister of Han Pi.

Han Hsiao-ch'ou, singing girl in Ch'ing-ho, niece of Han Chin-ch'uan and Han Yü-ch'uan.

Han Hsiao-yü, son of Mohammedan Han and Auntie Han.

Han Lü (fl. early 12th century), vice-minister of the Ministry of Revenue, vice-minister of the Ministry of Personnel, brother-in-law of Ts'ai Ching's youngest son, Ts'ai T'ao, grants Hsi-men Ch'ing favorable treatment for his speculations in the salt trade.

Han, Master, formerly a court painter attached to the Hsüan-ho Academy, called upon by Hsi-men Ch'ing to paint two posthumous portraits of Li P'ing-erh.

Han Ming-ch'uan, Brother-in-law Han, husband of Meng Yü-lou's elder sister who lives outside the city gate of Ch'ing-ho; friend of Dr. Jen Hou-ch'i.

Han Ming-ch'uan's wife, née Meng, Mrs. Han, elder sister of Meng Yü-lou.

Han, Mohammedan, husband of Auntie Han, father of Han Hsiao-yü, renter of a room on the street front of Hsi-men Ch'ing's property next door to that of Pen Ti-ch'uan and his wife, employed on the staff of the eunuch director in charge of the local Imperial Stables.

Han, Mrs. See Han Ming-ch'uan's wife, née Meng.

Han Pang-ch'i, prefect of Hsü-chou.

Han Pi, professional boy actor in Ch'ing-ho, elder brother of Han Chin-ch'uan and Han Yü-ch'uan.

Han, Posturer. See Han Tao-kuo.

Han the Second, Trickster Han, younger brother of Han Tao-kuo, "knock-about" and gambler in Ch'ing-ho who carries on an intermittent affair with his sister-in-law, Wang Liu-erh, whom he marries after the death of Han Tao-kuo.

Han Tao-kuo, Posturer Han, husband of Wang Liu-erh, son of Baldy Han, elder brother of Han the Second, father of Han Ai-chieh, manager of Hsi-men Ch'ing's silk store on Lion Street who absconds with a thousand taels of his property on hearing of his death, content to live off the sexual earnings of his wife and daughter.

Han Tao-kuo's paternal uncle, elder brother of Baldy Han.

Han, Trickster. See Han the Second.

Han Tso, boy actor in Ch'ing-ho.

Han Tsung-jen, domestic clerk on the staff of Yang Chien.

Han Wen-kuang, investigation commissioner for Shantung.

Han Yü-ch'uan, singing girl in Ch'ing-ho, younger sister of Han Chin-ch'uan and Han Pi.

Hao Hsien, Idler Hao, a dissolute young scamp upon whom Hsi-men Ch'ing turns the tables by abusing the judicial system.

Hao, Idler. See Hao Hsien.

Ho Ch'i-kao, left administration vice commissioner of Shantung.

Ho Chin, assistant judicial commissioner of the Ch'ing-ho office of the Provincial Surveillance Commission, promoted to the post of commander of Hsin-p'ing Stockade and later to the post of judicial commissioner in the Huai-an office of the Provincial Surveillance Commission, thereby creating the vacancy filled by Hsi-men Ch'ing in return for the lavishness of his birthday presents to Ts'ai Ching.

Ho Chin-ch'an, singing girl from the Ho Family Bordello on Fourth Street in the licensed quarter of Ch'ing-ho.

Ho Ch'in, son of Ho the Ninth who succeeds to his position as head coroner's assistant of Ch'ing-ho.

Ho Ch'un-ch'üan, Dr. Ho, son of Old Man Ho, physician in Ch'ing-ho.

Ho, Dr. See Ho Ch'un-ch'üan.

Ho, Eunuch Director. See Ho Hsin.

Ho Hsin (fl. early 12th century), Eunuch Director Ho, attendant in the Yenning Palace, residence of Consort Feng, rewarded for his part in facilitating the notorious Flower and Rock Convoys and the construction of the Mount Ken Imperial Park, uncle of Ho Yung-shou, entertains Hsi-men Ch'ing on his visit to the Eastern Capital.

Ho-hua, maidservant of Chou Hsiu's concubine Sun Erh-niang.

Ho Liang-feng, younger brother of Magnate Ho.

Ho, Magnate, wealthy silk merchant from Hu-chou, elder brother of Ho Liang-feng, tries to buy P'an Chin-lien after the death of Hsi-men Ch'ing, patronizes Wang Liu-erh in Lin-ch'ing and takes her and Han Tao-kuo back to Hu-chou where they inherit his property.

Ho, Magnate's daughter.

Ho the Ninth, elder brother of Ho the Tenth, head coroner's assistant of Ch'ing-ho who accepts a bribe from Hsi-men Ch'ing to cover up the murder of Wu Chih.

Ho, Old Man, father of Ho Ch'un-ch'üan, aged physician in Ch'ing-ho.

Ho Pu-wei, clerk on the staff of the district magistrate of Ch'ing-ho, Li Ch'ang-ch'i, who assists his son Li Kung-pi in his courtship of Meng Yü-lou.

Ho the Tenth, younger brother of Ho the Ninth, let off the hook by Hsi-men Ch'ing when he is accused of fencing stolen goods.

Ho Yung-fu, nephew of Ho Hsin, younger brother of Ho Yung-shou.

Ho Yung-shou, nephew of Ho Hsin, elder brother of Ho Yung-fu, appointed to Hsi-men Ch'ing's former post as assistant judicial commissioner in the Ch'ing-ho office of the Provincial Surveillance Commission as a reward for Ho Hsin's part in facilitating the notorious Flower and Rock Convoys and the construction of the Mount Ken Imperial Park.

Ho Yung-shou's wife, née Lan, niece of Lan Ts'ung-hsi.

Hou Lin, Flying Demon, beggar boss in Ch'ing-ho who helps out Ch'en Ching-chi when he is reduced to beggary in return for his sexual favors.

Hou Meng (1054–1121), grand coordinator of Shantung, promoted to the post of chief minister of the Court of Imperial Sacrifices for his part in facilitating the notorious Flower and Rock Convoys and the construction of the Mount Ken Imperial Park.

Hsi-erh, page boy in the household of Chou Hsiu.

Hsi-men An. See Tai-an.

Hsi-men Ching-liang, Hsi-men Ch'ing's grandfather.

Hsi-men Ch'ing, principal male protagonist of the novel, father of Hsi-men Ta-chieh by his deceased first wife, née Ch'en, father of Hsi-men Kuan-ko by Li P'ing-erh, father of Hsi-men Hsiao-ko by Wu Yüeh-niang, decadent scion of a merchant family of some wealth from which he inherits a wholesale pharmaceutical business on the street in front of the district yamen of Ch'ing-ho, climbs in social status by means of a succession of corrupt sexual, economic, and political conquests only to die of sexual excess at the age of thirty-three.

Hsi-men Ch'ing's daughter. See Hsi-men Ta-chieh.

Hsi-men Ch'ing's first wife, née Ch'en, deceased mother of Hsi-men Ta-chieh.

Hsi-men Ch'ing's father. See Hsi-men Ta.

Hsi-men Ch'ing's grandfather. See Hsi-men Ching-liang.

Hsi-men Ch'ing's grandmother, née Li.

Hsi-men Ch'ing's mother, née Hsia.

Hsi-men Ch'ing's reincarnation. See Hsi-men Hsiao-ko and Shen Yüeh.

Hsi-men Ch'ing's sons. See Hsi-men Kuan-ko and Hsi-men Hsiao-ko.

Hsi-men Hsiao-ko, posthumous son of Hsi-men Ch'ing by Wu Yüeh-niang, born at the very moment of his death, betrothed while still a babe in arms to Yün Li-shou's daughter, claimed by the Buddhist monk P'u-ching to be the reincarnation of Hsi-men Ch'ing and spirited away by him at the end of the novel to become a celibate monk with the religious name Ming-wu.

Hsi-men Kuan-ko, son of Hsi-men Ch'ing by Li P'ing-erh, given the religious name Wu Ying-yüan by the Taoist priest Wu Tsung-che, betrothed while still a babe in arms to Ch'iao Chang-chieh, murdered by P'an Chin-lien out of jealousy of Li P'ing-erh.

Hsi-men Kuan-ko's reincarnation. See Wang family of Cheng-chou.

Hsi-men Ta, deceased father of Hsi-men Ch'ing whose business took him to many parts of China.

Hsi-men Ta-chieh, Mistress Ch'en, Hsi-men Ch'ing's daughter by his deceased first wife, née Ch'en, wife of Ch'en Ching-chi, so neglected and abused by her husband that she commits suicide.

Hsi-men Ta-chieh's reincarnation. See Chung Kuei.

Hsi-t'ung, page boy in the household of Wang Hsüan.

Hsiao-ko. See Hsi-men Hsiao-ko.

Hsia Ch'eng-en, son of Hsia Yen-ling, achieves status of military selectee by hiring a stand-in to take the qualifying examination for him.

Hsia-hua, junior maidservant of Li Chiao-erh who is caught trying to steal a gold bracelet.

Hsia Kung-chi, docket officer on the staff of the district yamen in Ch'ing-ho.

Hsia Shou, servant in the household of Hsia Yen-ling.

Hsia Yen-ling, judicial commissioner in the Ch'ing-ho office of the Provincial Surveillance Commission, colleague, superior, and rival of Hsi-men Ch'ing in his official career.

Hsia Yen-ling's son. See Hsia Ch'eng-en.

Hsia Yen-ling's wife.

Hsiang the Elder, deceased distaff relative of the imperial family through Empress Hsiang, consort of Emperor Shen-tsung (r. 1067–85), elder brother of Hsiang the fifth.

Hsiang, Empress, (1046–1101), consort of Emperor Shen-tsung (r. 1067–85).

Hsiang the Fifth, distaff relative of the imperial family through Empress Hsiang, consort of Emperor Shen-tsung (r. 1067–85), younger brother of Hsiang the Elder, sells part of his country estate outside Ch'ing-ho to Hsi-men Ch'ing.

Hsiao Chang-hsien. See Chang Hsiao-hsein.

Hsiao Ch'eng, resident of Oxhide Street and neighborhood head of the fourth neighborhood of the first subprecinct of Ch'ing-ho.

Hsiao-ko. See Hsi-men Hsiao-ko.

Hsiao-luan, junior maidservant of Meng Yü-lou.

Hsiao-yü, Little Jade, junior maidservant of Wu Yüeh-niang, married to Tai-an after Wu Yüeh-niang discovers them in flagrante delicto.

Hsiao-yüeh, Abbot, head priest of the Water Moon Monastery outside the south gate of Ch'ing-ho.

Hsieh En, assistant judicial commissioner of the Huai-ch'ing office of the Provincial Surveillance Commission.

Hsieh, Fatty. See Hsieh the Third.

Hsieh Hsi-ta, Tagalong Hsieh, crony of Hsi-men Ch'ing, member of the brotherhood of ten.

Hsieh Hsi-ta's father, deceased hereditary battalion commander in the Ch'ing-
ho Guard.

Hsieh Hsi-ta's mother.

Hsieh Hsi-ta's wife, née Liu.

Hsieh Ju-huang, What a Whopper, acquaintance of Han Tao-kuo who punc-
tures his balloon when he inflates his own importance.

Hsieh, Tagalong. See Hsieh Hsi-ta.

Hsieh the Third, Fatty Hsieh, manager of the Hsieh Family Tavern in Lin-
ch'ing.

Hsin Hsing-tsung (fl. early 12th century), commander-general of the Ho-nan
region who leads the forces of Chang-te against the Chin invaders.

Hsiu-ch'un, junior maidservant of Li P'ing-erh and later of Li Chiao-erh,
finally becoming a novice nun under the tutelage of Nun Wang.

Hsiung Wang, husband of Chang Ju-i, soldier forced by his lack of means to
sell his wife to Hsi-men Ch'ing as a wet nurse for Kuan-ko.

Hsiung Wang's son by Chang Ju-i.

Hsü, Assistant Administration Commissioner, of Yen-chou in Shantung.

Hsü-chou, old woman from, in whose house Han Ai-chieh encounters Han
the Second.

Hsü, Eunuch Director, wealthy eunuch speculator and moneylender, resident of Halfside Street in the northern quarter of Ch'ing-ho, landlord of
Crooked-head Sun and Aunt Yang, patron of Li Ming, original owner of
Hsia Yen-ling's residential compound, major rival of Hsi-men Ch'ing in the
social world of Ch'ing-ho whose niece marries Chang Mao-te's son.

Hsü, Eunuch Director's niece, marries Chang Mao-te's son.

Hsü Feng, prefect of Yen-chou in Chekiang who exposes Meng Yü-lou's and
Li Kung-pi's attempt to frame Ch'en Ching-chi.

Hsü Feng's trusted henchman who disguises himself as a convict in order to
elicit information from Ch'en Ching-chi.

Hsü Feng-hsiang, supervisor of the State Farm Battalion of the Ch'ing-ho
Guard, one of the officials who comes to Hsi-men Ch'ing's residence to
offer a sacrifice to the soul of Li P'ing-erh after her death.

Hsü the Fourth, shopkeeper outside the city wall of Ch'ing-ho who borrows
money from Hsi-men Ch'ing.

Hsü Hsiang, battalion commander rewarded for his part in facilitating the
notorious Flower and Rock Convoys and the construction of the Mount
Ken Imperial Park.

Hsü, Master, yin-yang master of Ch'ing-ho.

Hsü Nan-ch'i, military officer in Ch'ing-ho promoted to the post of commander of the Hsin-p'ing Stockade.

Hsü, Prefect, prefect of Ch'ing-chou, patron of Shih Po-ts'ai, the corrupt Taoist head priest of the Temple of the Goddess of Iridescent Clouds on the summit of Mout T'ai.

Hsü, Prefect's daughter.

Hsü, Prefect's son.

Hsü, Prefect's wife.

Hsü Pu-yü, Reneger Hsü, moneylender in Ch'ing-ho from whom Wang Ts'ai tries to borrow three hundred taels of silver in order to purchase a position in the Military School.

Hsü, Reneger. See Hsü Pu-yü.

Hsü Shun, professional actor of Hai-yen style drama.

Hsü Sung, prefect of Tung-ch'ang in Shantung.

Hsü Sung's concubine.

Hsü Sung's concubine's father.

Hsü, Tailor, artisan with a shop across the street from Han Tao-kuo's residence on Lion Street in Ch'ing-ho.

Hsü the Third, seller of date cakes in front of the district yamen in Ch'ing-ho.

Hsü Tsung-shun, junior disciple of Abbot Jen of the Yen-kung Temple in Linch'ing.

Hsüeh, Auntie, go-between in Ch'ing-ho who also peddles costume jewelry, mother of Hsüeh Chi, sells P'ang Ch'un-mei into Hsi-men Ch'ing's household, represents Hsi-men Ch'ing in the betrothal of his daughter Hsi-men Ta-chieh to Ch'en Ching-chi, proposes his match with Meng Yü-lou, arranges resale of P'ang Ch'un-mei to Chou Hsiu after she is forced to leave the Hsi-men household by Wu Yüeh-niang, arranges match between Ch'en Ching-chi and Ko Ts'ui-p'ing after Hsi-men Ta-chieh's suicide.

Hsüeh, Auntie's husband.

Hsüeh Chi, son of Auntie Hsüeh, husband of Chin Ta-chieh.

Hsüeh Chi's son by Chin Ta-chieh.

Hsüeh, Eunuch Director, supervisor of the imperial estates in the Ch'ing-ho region, despite his castration given to fondling and pinching the singing girls with whom he comes in contact.

Hsüeh Hsien-chung, official rewarded for his part in facilitating the notorious Flower and Rock Convoys and the construction of the Mount Ken Imperial Park.

Hsüeh, Nun, widow of a peddler of steamed wheat cakes living across the street from the Kuang-ch'eng Monastery in Ch'ing-ho who took the tonsure after the death of her husband and became abbess of the Ksitigarbha Nunnery, defrocked for her complicity in the death of Juan the Third, later rector of the Lotus Blossom Nunnery in the southern quarter of Ch'ing-ho who provides first Wu Yüeh-niang and then P'an Chin-lien with fertility potions, frequently invited to recite Buddhist "precious scrolls" to Wu Yüeh-niang and her guests.

Hsüeh, Nun's deceased husband, peddler of steamed wheat cakes living across the street from the Kuang-ch'eng Monastery in Ch'ing-ho.

Hsüeh-o. See Sun Hsüeh-o.

Hsüeh Ts'un-erh, unlicensed prostitute in Longfoot Wu's brothel in the Southern Entertainment Quarter of Ch'ing-ho patronized by P'ing-an after he absconds from the Hsi-men household with jewelry stolen from the pawnshop.

Hu, Dr., Old Man Hu, Hu the Quack, physician who lives in Eunuch Director Liu's house on East Street in Ch'ing-ho in the rear courtyard of which Hsi-men Ch'ing hides in order to evade Wu Sung, treats Hua Tzu-hsü, Li P'ing-erh, and Hsi-men Ch'ing without success, prescribes abortifacient for P'an Chin-lien when she becomes pregnant by Ch'en Ching-chi.

Hu, Dr's maidservant.

Hu the Fourth, impeached as a relative or adherent of Yang Chien.

Hu Hsiu, employee of Han Tao-kuo who spies on Hsi-men Ch'ing's lovemaking with Wang Liu-erh, accompanies his employer on his buying expeditions to the south, and tells him what he thinks about his private life in a drunken tirade in Yang-chou.

Hu, Old Man. See Hu, Dr.

Hu the Quack. See Hu, Dr.

Hu Shih-wen (fl. early 12th century), related to Ts'ai Ching by marriage, corrupt prefect of Tung-p'ing in Shantung who participates with Hsi-men Ch'ing and Hsia Yen-ling in getting Miao Ch'ing off the hook for murdering his master Miao T'ien-hsiu.

Hu Ts'ao, professional actor from Su-chou who specializes in playing young male lead roles.

Hua the Elder. See Hua Tzu-yu.

Hua, Eunuch Director, uncle of Hua Tzu-yu, Hua Tzu-hsü, Hua Tzu-kuang, and Hua Tzu-hua and adoptive father of Hua Tzu-hsü, member of the Imperial Bodyguard and director of the Firewood Office in the Imperial Palace, later promoted to the position of grand defender of Kuang-nan from which post he retires on account of illness to take up residence in his native place, Ch'ing-ho; despite his castration engaged in pseudo-incestuous hanky-panky with his daughter-in-law, Li P'ing-erh.

Hua the Fourth. See Hua Tzu-hua.

Hua Ho-lu, assistant magistrate of Ch'ing-ho.

Hua, Mistress. See Li P'ing-erh.

Hua, Mrs. See Li P'ing-erh.

Hua, Nobody. See Hua Tzu-hsü.

Hua the Second. See Hua Tzu-hsü.

Hua the Third. See Hua Tzu-kuang.

Hua-t'ung, page boy in Hsi-men Ch'ing's household sodomized by Wen Pi-ku.

Hua Tzu-hsü, Hua the Second, Nobody Hua, nephew and adopted son of Eunuch Director Hua, husband of Li P'ing-erh, next door neighbor of Hsi-men Ch'ing and member of the brotherhood of ten, patron of Wu Yin-erh and Cheng Ai-hsiang; cuckolded by Li P'ing-erh, who turns over much of his property to Hsi-men Ch'ing, he loses the rest in a lawsuit and dies of chagrin.

Hua Tzu-hsü's reincarnation. See Cheng, Battalion Commander's family in the Eastern Capital.

Hua Tzu-hua, Hua the Fourth, nephew of Eunuch Director Hua, brother of Hua Tzu-hsü.

Hua Tzu-hua's wife.

Hua Tzu-kuang, Hua the Third, nephew of Eunuch Director Hua, brother of Hua Tzu-hsü.

Hua Tzu-kuang's wife.

Hua Tzu-yu, Hua the Elder, nephew of Eunuch Director Hua, brother of Hua Tzu-hsü.

Hua Tzu-yu's wife.

Huai River region, merchant from, who employs Wang Ch'ao.

Huai Rvier region, merchant from, who patronizes Li Kuei-ch'ing.

Huang An, military commander involved with T'an Chen in defense of the northern frontier against the Chin army.

Huang, Buddhist Superior, monk of the Pao-en Temple in Ch'ing-ho.

Huang Chia, prefect of Teng-chou in Shantung.

Huang Ching-ch'en (d. 1126), defender-in-chief of the Palace Command, eunuch rewarded for his part in facilitating the notorious Flower and Rock Convoys and the construction of the Mount Ken Imperial Park, uncle of Wang Ts'ai's wife, née Huang, lavishly entertained by Hsi-men Ch'ing at the request of Sung Ch'iao-nien.

Huang Ching-ch'en's adopted son, granted the post of battalion commander of the Embroidered Uniform Guard by yin privilege as a reward for his father's part in facilitating the notorious Flower and Rock Convoys and the construction of the Mount Ken Imperial Park.

Huang the Fourth, merchant contractor in Ch'ing-ho, partner of Li Chih, ends up in prison for misappropriation of funds.

Huang the Fourth's son.

Huang the Fourth's wife, née Sun, daughter of Sun Ch'ing.

Huang-lung Temple, abbot of, entertains Hsi-men Ch'ing and Ho Yung-shou en route to Ch'ing-ho from the Eastern Capital.

Huang, Master, fortune teller residing outside the Chen-wu Temple in the northern quarter of Ch'ing-ho.

Huang Mei, assistant prefect of K'ai-feng, maternal cousin of Miao T'ien-hsiu who invites him to visit him in the capital and appeals to Tseng Hsiao-hsü on his behalf after his murder.

Huang Ning, page boy in the household of Huang the Fourth.

Huang Pao-kuang (fl. early 12th century), secretary of the Ministry of Works in charge of the Imperial Brickyard in Ch'ing-ho, provincial graduate of the same year as Shang Hsiao-t'ang.

Huang, Perfect Man. See Huang Yüan-pai.

Huang Yü, foreman on the staff of Wang Fu.

Huang Yüan-pai, Perfect Man Huang, Taoist priest sent by the court to officiate at a seven-day rite of cosmic renewal on Mount T'ai, also officiates at a rite of purification for the salvation of the soul of Li P'ing-erh.

Hui-ch'ing, "The Beanpole," wife of Lai-chao, mother of Little Iron Rod.

Hui-hsiang, wife of Lai-pao, née Liu, mother of Seng-pao.

Hui-hsiang's elder sister.

Hui-hsiang's mother.

Hui-hsiang's younger brother. See Liu Ts'ang.

Hui-hsiu, wife of Lai-hsing, mother of Nien-erh and Ch'eng-erh.

Hui-lien. See Sung Hui-lien.

Hui-tsung, Emperor of the Sung dynasty (r. 1100–25), father of Emperor Ch'in-tsung in whose favor he abdicated in 1125, taken into captivity together with his son by the Chin invaders in 1127.

Hui-yüan, wife of Lai-chüeh.

Hung, Auntie, madam of the Hung Family Brothel in Ch'ing-ho.

Hung the Fourth, singing girl from the Hung Family Brothel in Ch'ing-ho.

Hung-hua Temple in Ch'ing-ho, monk from, whom Hsi-men Ch'ing frames and executes in place of Ho the Tenth.

Huo-pao, eleven-year-old country girl offered to P'ang Ch'un-mei as a maid-servant but rejected for wetting her bed.

Huo-pao's parents.

Huo Ta-li, district magistrate of Ch'ing-ho who accepts Ch'en Ching-chi's bribe and lets him off the hook when accused of driving his wife, Hsi-men Ta-chieh, to suicide.

I Mien-tz'u, Ostensibly Benign, neighbor of Hsi-men Ch'ing who intercedes unsuccessfully on Lai-wang's behalf.

Imperial Stables in Ch'ing-ho, eunuch director of, employer of Mohammedan Han.

Indian monk. See Monk, Indian.

Iron Fingernail. See Yang Kuang-yen.

Iron Rod. See Little Iron Rod.

Itinerant acrobat called in by Chou Hsiu to distract P'ang Ch'un-mei from her grief over the death of P'an Chin-lien.

Jade Flute. See Yü-hsiao.

Jade Lotus. See Pai Yü-lien.

Jen, Abbot, Taoist priest of the Yen-kung Temple in Lin-ch'ing to whom Wang Hsüan recommends Ch'en Ching-chi as a disciple; dies of shock when threatened with arrest in connection with the latter's whoremongering.

Jen, Abbot's acolyte.

Jen Hou-ch'i, Dr. Jen, physician in Ch'ing-ho who treats Li P'ing-erh and Hsi-men Ch'ing without success, friend of Han Ming-ch'uan.

Jen T'ing-kuei, assistant magistrate of Ch'ing-ho.

Ju-i. See Chang Ju-i.

Juan the Third, dies of excitement in the act of making love to Miss Ch'en in the Ksitigarbha Nunnery during an assignation arranged by Nun Hsüeh.

Juan the Third's parents.

Jui-yün. See Pen Chang-chieh.

Jung Chiao-erh, singing girl in Ch'ing-ho patronized by Wang Ts'ai.

Jung Hai, employee of Hsi-men Ch'ing who accompanies Ts'ui Pen on a buy-ing trip to Hu-chou.

Kan Jun, resident of Stonebridge Alley in Ch'ing-ho, partner and manager of Hsi-men Ch'ing's silk dry goods store.

Kan Jun's wife.

Kan Lai-hsing. See Lai-hsing.

K'ang, Prince of. See Kao-tsung, Emperor.

Kao An, secondary majordomo of Ts'ai Ching's household in the Eastern Capital through whom Lai-pao gains access to Ts'ai Yu.

Kao Ch'iu (d. 1126), defender-in-chief of the Imperial Bodyguard, granted the title of grand guardian for his part in facilitating the notorious Flower and Rock Convoys and the construction of the Mount Ken Imperial Park; one of the Six Traitors impeached by Ch'en Tung.

Kao family from outside the city wall of the Eastern Capital, family into which Chou I is reincarnated as a son named Kao Liu-chu.

Kao family of the Ta-hsing Guard, family into which Chang Sheng is reincar-nated as a son.

Kao Lien, cousin of Kao Ch'iu, prefect of T'ai-an, brother-in-law of Yin T'ien-hsi.

Kao Lien's wife, née Yin, elder sister of Yin T'ien-hsi.

Kao Liu-chu, son of the Kao family from outside the city wall of the Eastern Capital, reincarnation of Chou I.

Kao-tsung, Emperor of the Southern Sung dynasty (r. 1127–1162), ninth son of Emperor Hui-tsung, Prince of K'ang; declares himself emperor in 1127 when the Chin invaders took emperors Hui-tsung and Ch'in-tsung into captivity; abdicates in favor of emperor Hsiao-tsung in 1162.

Ko Ts'ui-p'ing, wife of Ch'en Ching-chi in a marriage arranged by P'ang Ch'un-mei with whom he continues to carry on an intermittent affair; re-turns to her parents' family after Ch'en Ching-chi's death and the invasion by the Chin armies.

Ko Ts'ui-p'ing's father, wealthy silk dry goods dealer in Ch'ing-ho.

Ko Ts'ui-p'ing's mother.

Kou Tzu-hsiao, professional actor from Su-chou who specializes in playing male lead roles.

Ku, Silversmith, jeweler in Ch'ing-ho patronized by Li P'ing-erh and Hsi-men Ch'ing, employer of Lai-wang after he returns to Ch'ing-ho from exile in Hsü-chou.

Kuan, Busybody. See Kuan Shih-k'uan.

Kuan-ko. See Hsi-men Kuan-ko.

Kuan Shih-k'uan, Busybody Kuan, a dissolute young scamp upon whom Hsi-men Ch'ing turns the tables by abusing the judicial system.

Kuan-yin Nunnery, abbess of, superior of Nun Wang, frequent visitor in the Hsi-men household.

Kuang-yang, Commandery Prince of. See T'ung Kuan.

Kuei-chieh. See Li Kuei-chieh.

Kuei-ch'ing. See Li Kuei-ch'ing.

Kung Kuai (1057–1111), left provincial administration commissioner of Shantung.

K'ung, Auntie, go-between in Ch'ing-ho who represents Ch'iao Hung's family in arranging the betrothal of Ch'iao Chang-chieh to Hsi-men Kuan-ko.

K'ung family of the Eastern Capital, family into which P'ang Ch'un-mei is reincarnated as a daughter.

Kuo Shou-ch'ing, senior disciple of Shih Po-ts'ai, the corrupt Taoist head priest of the Temple of the Goddess of Iridescent Clouds on the summit of Mount T'ai.

Kuo Shou-li, junior disciple of Shih Po-ts'ai, the corrupt Taoist head priest of the Temple of the Goddess of Iridescent Clouds on the summit of Mount T'ai.

Kuo Yao-shih (d. after 1126), turncoat who accepts office under the Sung dynasty but goes over to the Chin side at a critical point and is instrumental in their conquest of north China.

La-mei, maidservant employed in the Wu Family Brothel in Ch'ing-ho.

Lai-an, servant in Hsi-men Ch'ing's household.

Lai-chao, Liu Chao, head servant in Hsi-men Ch'ing's household, husband of Hui-ch'ing, father of Little Iron Rod, helps Lai-wang to abscond with Sun Hsüeh-o.

Lai-chao's son. See Little Iron Rod.

Lai-chao's wife. See Hui-ch'ing.

Lai-chüeh, Lai-yu, husband of Hui-yüan, originally servant in the household of a distaff relative of the imperial family named Wang, loses his position on exposure of his wife's affair with her employer, recommended as a servant to Hsi-men Ch'ing by his friend Ying Pao, the son of Ying Po-chüeh.

Lai-chüeh's deceased parents.

Lai-chüeh's wife. See Hui-yüan.

Lai-hsing, Kan Lai-hsing, servant in Hsi-men Ch'ing's household, originally recruited by Hsi-men Ch'ing's father while traveling on business in Kan-chou, husband of Hui-hsiu, father of Nien-erh and Ch'eng-erh, helps to frame Lai-wang for attempted murder, married to Chang Ju-i after the death of Hui-hsiu.

Lai-pao, T'ang Pao, servant in Hsi-men Ch'ing's household often relied upon for important missions to the capital, husband of Hui-hsiang, father of Seng-pao, appointed to the post of commandant on the staff of the Prince of Yün in return for his part in delivering birthday presents from Hsi-men Ch'ing to Ts'ai Ching, embezzles Hsi-men Ch'ing's property after his death and makes unsuccessful sexual advances to Wu Yüeh-niang, ends up in prison for misappropriation of funds.

Lai-pao's son. See Seng-pao.

Lai-pao's wife. See Hui-hsiang.

Lai-ting, page boy in the household of Hua Tzu-yu.

Lai-ting, page boy in the household of Huang the Fourth.

Lai-ting, page boy in the household of Wu K'ai.

Lai-wang, Cheng Wang, native of Hsü-chou, servant in Hsi-men Ch'ing's household, husband of Sung Hui-lien, framed for attempted murder and driven out of the household in order to get him out of the way, carries on a clandestine affair with Sun Hsüeh-o before his exile and absconds with her when he returns to Ch'ing-ho after Hsi-men Ch'ing's death.

Lai-wang's first wife, dies of consumption.

Lai-wang's second wife. See Sung Hui-lien.

Lai-yu. See Lai-chüeh.

Lan-hsiang, senior maidservant of Meng Yü-lou.

Lan-hua, junior maidservant of P'ang Ch'un-mei after she becomes the wife of Chou Hsiu.

Lan-hua, elderly maidservant in the household of Wu K'ai.

Lan Ts'ung-hsi (fl. early 12th century), eunuch rewarded for his part in facilitating the notorious Flower and Rock Convoys and the construction of the Mount Ken Imperial Park, uncle of Ho Yung-shou's wife, née Lan.

Lan Ts'ung-hsi's adopted son, granted the post of battalion vice commander of the Embroidered Uniform Guard by yin privilege as a reward for his father's part in facilitating the notorious Flower and Rock Convoys and the construction of the Mount Ken Imperial Park.

Lan Ts'ung-hsi's niece. See Ho Yung-shou's wife, née Lan.

Lang, Buddhist Superior, monk of the Pao-en Temple in Ch'ing-ho.

Lei Ch'i-yüan, assistant commissioner of the Shantung Military Defense Circuit.

Li An, retainer in the household of Chou Hsiu who saves P'ang Ch'un-mei's life when she is threatened by Chang Sheng and resists her blandishments when she tries to seduce him.

Li An's father, deceased elder brother of Li Kuei.

Li An's mother, persuades Li An to avoid entanglement with P'ang Ch'un-mei by seeking refuge with his uncle Li Kuei in Ch'ing-chou.

Li, Barestick. See Li Kung-pi.

Li Ch'ang-ch'i, father of Li Kung-pi, district magistrate of Ch'ing-ho and later assistant prefect of Yen-chou in Chekiang.

Li Ch'ang-ch'i's wife, mother of Li Kung-pi.

Li Chiao-erh, Hsi-men Ch'ing's Second Lady, originally a singing girl from the Verdant Spring Bordello in Ch'ing-ho, aunt of Li Kuei-ch'ing and Li Kuei-chieh, enemy of P'an Chin-lien, tight-fisted manager of Hsi-men Ch'ing's household finances, engages in hanky-panky with Wu the Second, begins pilfering Hsi-men Ch'ing's property while his corpse is still warm, ends up as Chang Mao-te's Second Lady.

Li Chih, Li the Third, father of Li Huo, merchant contractor in Ch'ing-ho, partner of Huang the Fourth, ends up dying in prison for misappropriation of funds.

Li Chin, servant in the household of Li Chih.

Li Chung-yu, servant on the domestic staff of Ts'ai Ching.

Li, Eunuch Director. See Li Yen.

Li family of the Eastern Capital, family into which P'an Chin-lien is reincarnated as a daughter.

Li Huo, son of Li Chih.

Li Kang (1083–1140), minister of war under Emperor Ch'in-tsung who directs the defense against the Chin invaders.

Li Kuei, Shantung Yaksha, uncle of Li An, military instructor from Ch'ing-chou patronized by Li Kung-pi.

Li Kuei-chieh, Cassia, daughter of Auntie Li the Third, niece of Li Chiao-erh and Li Ming, younger sister of Li Kuei-ch'ing, singing girl from the Verdant Spring Bordello on Second Street in the licensed quarter of Ch'ing-ho, deflowered by Hsi-men Ch'ing, who maintains her as his mistress for twenty taels a month, adopted daughter of Wu Yüeh-niang, betrays Hsi-men Ch'ing with Ting the Second, Wang Ts'ai, and others.

Li Kuei-chieh's fifth maternal aunt.

Li Kuei-ch'ing, daughter of Auntie Li the Third, niece of Li Chiao-erh and Li Ming, elder sister of Li Kuei-chieh, singing girl from the Verdant Spring Bordello on Second Street in the licensed quarter of Ch'ing-ho.

Li K'uei, Black Whirlwind, bloodthirsty outlaw from Sung Chiang's band who massacres the household of Liang Shih-chieh and kills Yin T'ien-hsi.

Li Kung-pi, Bare Stick Li, only son of Li Ch'ang-ch'i, student at the Superior College of the National University, falls in love with Meng Yü-lou at first sight and arranges to marry her as his second wife, severely beaten by his father for his part in the abortive attempt to frame Ch'en Ching-chi, forced to return with his bride to his native place to resume his studies.

Li Kung-pi's deceased first wife.

Li Kung-pi's servant.

Li, Leaky. See Li Wai-ch'uan.

Li Ming, younger brother of Li Chiao-erh, uncle of Li Kuei-ch'ing and Li Kuei-chieh; actor and musician from the Verdant Spring Bordello on Second Street in the licensed quarter of Ch'ing-ho; employed by Hsi-men Ch'ing to teach Ch'un-mei, Yü-hsiao, Ying-ch'un, and Lan-hsiang to sing and play musical instruments; driven out of the house by Ch'un-mei for having the temerity to squeeze her hand during a lesson but allowed to return on many subsequent occasions; assists Li Chiao-erh, Li Kuei-ch'ing, and Li Kuei-chieh in despoiling Hsi-men Ch'ing's property after his death.

Li Pang-yen (d. 1130), minister of the right, grand academician of the Hall for Aid in Governance, and concurrently minister of rites, alters Hsi-men Ch'ing's name to Chia Lien on a bill of impeachment in return for a bribe of five hundred taels of silver, promoted to the ranks of pillar of state and grand preceptor of the heir apparent for his part in facilitating the notorious Flower and Rock Convoys and the construction of the Mount Ken Imperial Park, one of the Six Traitors impeached by Ch'en Tung.

Li P'ing-erh, Vase, Mrs. Hua, Mistress Hua, one of the three principal female protagonists of the novel, concubine of Liang Shih-chieh, wife of Hua Tzu-hsü, commits adultery with her husband's neighbor and sworn brother Hsi-men Ch'ing, wife of Dr. Chiang Chu-shan, Hsi-men Ch'ing's Sixth Lady, mother of Hsi-men Kuan-ko, dies of chronic hemorrhaging brought on by grief over the death of her son and Hsi-men Ch'ing's insistence on trying out his newly acquired aphrodisiac on her while she is in her menstrual period, commemorated in overly elaborate funeral observances that are prime examples of conspicuous consumption, haunts Hsi-men Ch'ing's dreams.

Li P'ing-erh's former incarnation. See Wang family of Pin-chou.

Li P'ing-erh's deceased parents.

Li P'ing-erh's reincarnation. See Yüan, Commander.

Li Ta-t'ien, district magistrate of Ch'ing-ho, relative of Chu Mien, appoints Wu Sung as police captain and later sends him to the Eastern Capital to stash his ill-gotten gains with his powerful relative, accepts Hsi-men Ch'ing's bribes to abuse the law in the cases of Wu Sung, Lai-wang, Sung Hui-lien, Miao T'ien-hsiu, and others.

Li the Third, seller of won-ton in front of the district yamen in Ch'ing-ho.

Li the Third. See Li Chih.

Li the Third, Auntie, madam of the Verdant Spring Bordello on Second Street in the licensed quarter of Ch'ing-ho, mother of Li Kuei-ch'ing and Li Kuei-chieh, partially paralyzed, prototypical procuress who milks her customers for all she can get.

Li, Vice Minister, employer of Licentiate Shui.

Li Wai-ch'uan, Leaky Li, influence peddling lictor on the staff of the district yamen in Ch'ing-ho who is mistakenly killed by Wu Sung in his abortive attempt to wreak vengeance on Hsi-men Ch'ing for the murder of his elder brother Wu Chih.

Li Yen (d. 1126), Eunuch Director Li, entertains Miao Ch'ing in his residence behind the Forbidden City in the Eastern Capital, rewarded for his
part in facilitating the notorious Flower and Rock Convoys and the construction of the Mount Ken Imperial Park, one of the Six Traitors impeached
by Ch'en Tung.

Li Yen's adopted son, granted the post of battalion vice commander of the
Embroidered Uniform Guard by *yin* privilege as a reward for his father's
part in facilitating the notorious Flower and Rock Convoys and the construction of the Mount Ken Imperial Park.

Liang, Privy Councilor. See Liang Shih-chieh.

Liang Shih-chieh, Privy Councilor Liang, regent of the Northern Capital at
Ta-ming prefecture in Hopei, son-in-law of Ts'ai Ching, first husband of Li
P'ing-erh, forced to flee for his life when his entire household is slaughtered
by Li K'uei.

Liang Shih-chieh's wife, née Ts'ai, daughter of Ts'ai Ching, extremely jealous
woman who beats numbers of maidservants and concubines of her husband
to death and buries them in the rear flower garden, forced to flee for her life
when her entire household is slaughtered by Li K'uei.

Liang To, professional boy actor in Ch'ing-ho.

Liang Ying-lung, commandant of security for the Eastern Capital.

Lin Ch'eng-hsün, judicial commissioner in the Huai-ch'ing office of the Provincial Surveillance Commission.

Lin Hsiao-hung, younger sister of Lin Ts'ai-hung, singing girl in Yang-chou
patronized by Lai-pao.

Lin, Lady, widow of Imperial Commissioner Wang I-hsüan, mother of Wang
Ts'ai, former mistress of P'an Chin-lien who learns to play musical instruments and to sing as a servant in her household, carries on an adulterous
affair with Hsi-men Ch'ing under the transparent pretext of asking him to
superintend the morals of her profligate son.

Lin Ling-su (d. c. 1125), Perfect Man Lin, Taoist priest who gains an ascen-
dancy over Emperor Hui-tsung for a time and is showered with high-sound-
ing titles, rewarded for his part in facilitating the notorious Flower and Rock
Convoys and the construction of the Mount Ken Imperial Park.

Lin, Perfect Man. See Lin Ling-su.

Lin Shu (d. c. 1126), minister of works rewarded with the title grand guardian
of the heir apparent for his part in facilitating the notorious Flower and
Rock Convoys and the construction of the Mount Ken Imperial Park.

Lin Ts'ai-hung, elder sister of Lin Hsiao-hung, singing girl in Yang-chou.

Ling, Master, fortune teller in Ch'ing-ho who interprets Meng Yü-lou's horoscope when she is about to marry Li Kung-pi.

Ling Yün-i, prefect of Yen-chou in Shantung.

Little Iron Rod, son of Lai-chao and his wife Hui-ch'ing.

Little Jade. See Hsiao-yü.

Little Whirlwind. See Ch'ai Chin.

Liu, Assistant Regional Commander, officer of the Hsi-hsia army who gives a horse to Chai Ch'ien, who in turn presents it to Hsi-men Ch'ing.

Liu Chao. See Lai-chao.

Liu Chü-chai, Dr., physician from Fen-chou in Shansi, friend of Ho Yung-shou who recommends him to Hsi-men Ch'ing when he is in extremis but whose treatment exacerbates his condition.

Liu, Company Commander, younger brother of Eunuch Director Liu, indicted for illicit use of imperial lumber in constructing a villa on a newly purchased estate at Wu-li Tien outside Ch'ing-ho, let off the hook by Hsi-men Ch'ing in response to a bribe proffered by Eunuch Director Liu.

Liu, Consort (1088–1121), Consort An, a favorite consort of Emperor Hui-tsung, mother of Chao I.

Liu, Dame, Stargazer Liu's wife, medical practitioner and shamaness frequently called upon by the women of Hsi-men Ch'ing's household.

Liu, Eunuch Director, elder brother of Company Commander Liu, manager of the Imperial Brickyard in Ch'ing-ho, resides on an estate outside the south gate of the city, intervenes with Hsi-men Ch'ing to get his younger brother off the hook when indicted for misappropriation of imperial lumber but supplies Hsi-men Ch'ing with bricks from the Imperial Brickyard for construction of his country estate.

Liu, Eunuch Director, landlord of Dr. Hu's house on East Street in Ch'ing-ho.

Liu, Eunuch Director, resides near Wine Vinegar Gate on the North Side of Ch'ing-ho, patron of Li Ming.

Liu Hui-hsiang. See Hui-hsiang.

Liu Kao, commander of An-p'ing Stockade, friend of Shih En who gives Wu Sung a hundred taels of silver and a letter of recommendation to him when he is sent there in military exile.

Liu, Mr., official serving in Huai-an who passed the *chin-shih* examinations the same year as Sung Ch'iao-nien.

Liu Pao, servant employed as a cook in Hsi-men Ch'ing's silk dry goods store.

Liu, School Official, native of Hang-chou, educational official in Ch'ing-ho who borrows money from Hsi-men Ch'ing.

Liu the Second, Turf-protecting Tiger, brother-in-law of Chang Sheng, proprietor of My Own Tavern west of the bridge in Lin-ch'ing, pimp and racketeer, boss of unlicensed prostitution in Lin-ch'ing, beaten to death by Chou Hsiu at the behest of P'ang Ch'un-mei after Chang Sheng's murder of Ch'en Ching-chi.

Liu the Second, Little, seller of ready-cooked food in front of the district yamen in Ch'ing-ho.

Liu Sheng, foreman on the domestic staff of Yang Chien.

Liu, Stargazer, husband of Dame Liu, blind fortune teller and necromancer who interprets P'an Chin-lien's horoscope, teaches her a method for working black magic on Hsi-men Ch'ing, and treats Hsi-men Kuan-ko ineffectually.

Liu the Third, servant of Company Commander Liu.

Liu Ts'ang, younger brother of Hui-hsiang, brother-in-law of Lai-pao with whom he cooperates in surreptitiously making off with eight hundred taels worth of Hsi-men Ch'ing's property after his death and using it to open a general store.

Liu Yen-ch'ing (1068–1127), commander-general of the Shensi region who leads the forces of Yen-sui against the Chin invaders.

Lo, Mohammedan, one of the "ball clubbers" patronized by Hsi-men Ch'ing.

Lo Ts'un-erh, singing girl of Ch'ing-ho patronized by Hsiang the Fifth.

Lo Wan-hsiang, prefect of Tung-p'ing.

Love. See Chu Ai-ai.

Lu Ch'ang-t'ui, Longleg Lu, madam of the brothel on Butterfly Lane in Ch'ing-ho where Chin-erh and Sai-erh work.

Lu Ch'ang-t'ui's husband.

Lu, Duke of. See Ts'ai Ching.

Lu Hu, clerical subofficial on the staff of Yang Chien.

Lu Hua, Snake-in-the-grass, "knockabout" who, along with Chang Sheng, shakes down Dr. Chiang Chu-shan at the behest of Hsi-men Ch'ing.

Lu, Longleg. See Lu Ch'ang-t'ui.

Lu Ping-i, Lu the Second, crony of Ch'en Ching-chi who suggests how he can recover his property from Yang Kuang-yen and goes into partnership with him as the manager of the Hsieh Family Tavern in Lin-ch'ing.

Lu the Second. See Lu Ping-i.

Lung-hsi, Duke of. See Wang Wei.

Lü Sai-erh, singing girl in Ch'ing-ho.

Ma Chen, professional boy actor in Ch'ing-ho.

Ma, Mrs., next-door neighbor of Ying Po-chüeh.

Man-t'ang, maidservant in the household of Li Kung-pi.

Mao-te, Princess (fl. early 12th century), fifth daughter of Emperor Hui-tsung, married to Ts'ai Ching's fourth son, Ts'ai T'iao.

Meng Ch'ang-ling (fl. early 12th century), eunuch rewarded for his part in facilitating the notorious Flower and Rock Convoys and the construction of the Mount Ken Imperial Park.

Meng Ch'ang-ling's adopted son, granted the post of battalion vice-commander of the Embroidered Uniform Guard by yin privilege as a reward for his father's part in facilitating the notorious Flower and Rock Convoys and the construction of the Mount Ken Imperial Park.

Meng-ch'ang, Little Lord. See Ch'ai Chin.

Meng the Elder, elder brother of Meng Yü-lou.

Meng the Elder's wife, Meng Yü-lou's sister-in-law.

Meng Jui, Meng the Second, younger brother of Meng Yü-lou, a traveling merchant constantly on the road.

Meng Jui's wife, Meng Yü-lou's sister-in-law.

Meng the Second. See Meng Jui.

Meng the Third. See Meng Yü-lou.

Meng Yü-lou, Tower of Jade, Meng the Third, one of the female protagonists of the novel, widow of the textile merchant Yang Tsung-hsi, Hsi-men Ch'ing's Third Lady, confidante of P'an Chin-lien, marries Li Kung-pi after the death of Hsi-men Ch'ing, forced to return with her husband to his native place in Hopei after their abortive attempt to frame Ch'en Ching-chi, bears a son to Li Kung-pi at the age of forty and lives to the age of sixty-seven.

Meng Yü-lou's elder brother. See Meng the Elder.

Meng Yü-lou's elder sister. See Han Ming-ch'uan's wife, née Meng.

Meng Yü-lou's son by Li Kung-pi.

Meng Yü-lou's younger brother. See Meng Jui.

Miao Ch'ing, servant of Miao T'ien-hsiu who conspires with the boatmen Ch'en the Third and Weng the Eighth to murder his master on a trip to the Eastern Capital, bribes Hsi-men Ch'ing to get him off the hook, and returns to Yang-chou where he assumes his former master's position in society and maintains relations with his benefactor Hsi-men Ch'ing.

Miao-ch'ü, teenage disciple of Nun Hsüeh.

Miao-feng, teenage disciple of Nun Hsüeh.

Miao Hsiu, servant in the household of Miao Ch'ing.

Miao Shih, servant in the household of Miao Ch'ing.

Miao T'ien-hsiu, a wealthy merchant of Yang-chou who is murdered by his servant Miao Ch'ing on a trip to the Eastern Capital.

Miao T'ien-hsiu's concubine. See Tiao the Seventh.

Miao T'ien-hsiu's daughter.

Miao T'ien-hsiu's wife, née Li.

Ming-wu. See Hsi-men Hsiao-ko.

Mirror polisher, elderly itinerant artisan in Ch'ing-ho who polishes mirrors for P'an Chin-lien, Meng Yü-lou, and P'ang Ch'un-mei and elicits their sympathy with a sob story.

Mirror polisher's deceased first wife.

Mirror polisher's second wife.

Mirror polisher's son.

Monk, Indian, foreign monk presented as the personification of a penis whom Hsi-men Ch'ing encounters in the Temple of Eternal Felicity and from whom he obtains the aphrodisiac an overdose of which eventually kills him.

Moon Lady. See Wu Yüeh-niang.

Ni, Familiar. See Ni P'eng.

Ni, Licentiate. See Ni P'eng.

Ni P'eng, Familiar Ni, Licentiate Ni, tutor employed in the household of Hsia Yen-ling as a tutor for his son, Hsia Ch'eng-en, who recommends his fellow licentiate Wen Pi-ku to Hsi-men Ch'ing.

Nieh Liang-hu, schoolmate of Shang Hsiao-t'ang employed in his household as a tutor for his son who writes two congratulatory scrolls for Hsi-men Ch'ing.

Nieh, Tiptoe. See Nieh Yüeh.

Nieh Yüeh, Tiptoe Nieh, one of the "cribbers" in the licensed quarter of Ch'ing-ho who plays the tout to Wang Ts'ai on his visits to the licensed quarter and upon whom Hsi-men Ch'ing turns the tables by abusing the judicial system at the behest of Lady Lin.

Nieh Yüeh's wife.

Nien-erh, elder daughter of Lai-hsing by Hui-hsiu.

Nien-mo-ho. See Wan-yen Tsung-han.

Niu, Ms., singing girl in the Great Tavern on Lion Street who witnesses Wu Sung's fatal assault on Li Wai-ch'uan.

Old woman who tells the fortunes of Wu Yüeh-niang, Meng Yü-lou, and Li P'ing-erh with the aid of a turtle.

Opportune Rain. See Sung Chiang.

Ostensibly Benign. See I Mien-tz'u.

Pai, Baldy. See Pai T'u-tzu.

Pai the Fifth, Moneybags Pai, father-in-law of Feng Huai, notorious local tyrant and fence for stolen goods in the area west of the Grand Canal.

Pai the Fourth, silversmith in Ch'ing-ho, acquaintance of Han Tao-kuo.

Pai Lai-ch'iang, Scrounger Pai, crony of Hsi-men Ch'ing, member of the brotherhood of ten.

Pai Lai-ch'iang's wife.

Pai, Mohammedan. See Pai T'u-tzu.

Pai, Moneyboys. See Pai the Fifth.

Pai, Scrounger. See Pai Lai-ch'iang.

Pai Shih-chung (d. 1127), right vice minister of rites rewarded with the title grand guardian of the heir apparent for his part in facilitating the notorious Flower and Rock Convoys and the construction of the Mount Ken Imperial Park.

Pai T'u-tzu, Baldy Pai, Mohammedan Pai, "ball-clubber" in Ch'ing-ho who plays the tout to Wang Ts'ai on his visits to the licensed quarter and upon whom Hsi-men Ch'ing turns the tables by abusing the judicial system at the behest of Lady Lin.

Pai Yü-lien, Jade Lotus, maidservant purchased by Mrs. Chang at the same time as P'an Chin-lien who dies shortly thereafter.

Palace foreman who plays the role of master of ceremonies at the imperial audience in the Hall for the Veneration of Governance.

Palefaced Gentleman. See Cheng T'ien-shou.

Pan-erh, unlicensed prostitute in Longfoot Wu's brothel in the Southern Entertainment Quarter of Ch'ing-ho patronized by P'ing-an after he absconds from the Hsi-men household with jewelry stolen from the pawnshop.

P'an Chi, one of the officials from the Ch'ing-ho Guard who comes to Hsi-men Ch'ing's residence to offer a sacrifice to the soul of Li P'ing-erh after her death.

P'an Chin-lien, Golden Lotus, P'an the Sixth, principal female protagonist of the novel, daughter of Tailor P'an from outside the South Gate of Ch'ing-ho who dies when she is only six years old; studies in a girls' school run by Licentiate Yü for three years where she learns to read and write; sold by her mother at the age of eight into the household of Imperial Commissioner Wang and Lady Lin where she is taught to play musical instruments and to sing; resold in her mid-teens, after the death of her master, into the house-hold of Mr. Chang who deflowers her and then gives her as a bride to his tenant, Wu Sung's elder brother, the dwarf Wu Chih; paramour of Hsi-men Ch'ing who collaborates with her in poisoning her husband and sub-sequently makes her his Fifth Lady; seduces her husband's page boy Ch'in-t'ung for which he is driven out of the household; carries on a running affair with her son-in-law, Ch'en Ching-chi, which is consummated after the death of Hsi-men Ch'ing; responsible, directly or indirectly, for the suicide of Sung Hui-lien, the death of Hsi-men Kuan-ko, and the demise of Hsi-men Ch'ing; aborts her son by Ch'en Ching-chi; is sold out of the house-hold by Wu Yüeh-niang, purchased by Wu Sung, and disemboweled by the latter in revenge for the death of his elder brother Wu Chih.

P'an Chin-lien's cat, Coal in the Snow, Snow Lion, Snow Bandit, long-haired white cat with a black streak on its forehead that P'an Chin-lien trains to attack Hsi-men Kuan-ko with fatal consequences.

P'an Chin-lien's father. See P'an, Tailor.

P'an Chin-lien's maternal aunt, younger sister of old Mrs. P'an.

P'an Chin-lien's maternal aunt's daughter, adopted by old Mrs. P'an to look after her in her old age.

P'an Chin-lien's mother. See P'an, old Mrs.

P'an Chin-lien's reincarnation. See Li Family of the Eastern Capital.

P'an, Demon-catcher. See P'an, Taoist Master.

P'an family prostitution ring operating out of My Own Tavern in Lin-ch'ing, madam of.

P'an the fifth, white slaver, masquerading as a cotton merchant from Shantung, who operates a prostitution ring out of My Own Tavern in Lin-ch'ing, buys Sun Hsüeh-o from Auntie Hsüeh, and forces her to become a singing girl.

P'an the Fifth's deceased first wife.

P'an the Fifth's mother.

P'an, old Mrs., widow of Tailor P'an, mother of P'an Chin-lien, sends her daughter to Licentiate Yü's girls' school for three years, sells her into the household of Imperial Commissioner Wang and Lady Lin at the age of eight, resells her in her mid-teens into the household of Mr. Chang, fre-quent visitor in Hsi-men Ch'ing's household where she is maltreated by

P'an Chin-lien who is ashamed of her low social status, adopts her younger sister's daughter to look after her in her old age, dies not long after the death of Hsi-men Ch'ing.

P'an the Sixth. See P'an Chin-lien.

P'an, Tailor, father of P'an Chin-lien, artisan from outside the South Gate of Ch'ing-ho who dies when P'an Chin-lien is only six years old.

P'an, Taoist Master, Demon-catcher P'an, Taoist exorcist from the Temple of the Five Peaks outside Ch'ing-ho who performs various rituals on Li P'ingerh's behalf but concludes that nothing can save her.

P'an, Taoist Master's acolyte.

P'ang Ch'un-mei, Spring Plum Blossom, one of the three principal female protagonists of the novel, originally purchased by Hsi-men Ch'ing from Auntie Hsüeh for sixteen taels of silver as a maidservant for Wu Yüeh-niang, reassigned as senior maidservant to P'an Chin-lien when she enters the household, becomes her chief ally and confidante; from the time that her mistress allows her to share the sexual favors of Hsi-men Ch'ing she remains loyal to her right up to and even after her death; after the demise of Hsi-men Ch'ing she aids and abets P'an Chin-lien's affair with Ch'en Ching-chi the discovery of which leads to her dismissal from the household; purchased as a concubine by Chou Hsiu, she bears him a son and is promoted to the status of principal wife, thereby rising higher in social status than any of the ladies she had formerly served as maidservant; comes to Wu Yüeh-niang's assistance when she is threatened by Wu Tien-en and condescends to pay a visit to her former mistress and to witness at first hand the signs of her relative decline; carries on an intermittent affair with Ch'en Ching-chi under her husband's nose and, after Chou Hsiu's death, dies in the act of sexual intercourse with his servant Chou I.

P'ang Ch'un-mei's deceased father who dies while she is still a child.

P'ang Ch'un-mei's deceased mother who dies a year after her birth.

P'ang Ch'un-mei's reincarnation. See K'ung family of the Eastern Capital.

P'ang Ch'un-mei's son. See Chou Chin-ko.

P'ang Hsüan, clerical subofficial on the staff of Yang Chien.

Pao, Dr., pediatric physician in Ch'ing-ho called in to treat Hsi-men Kuan-ko who declares the case to be hopeless.

Pao-en Temple in the Eastern Capital, monk from, tries unsuccessfully to warn Miao T'ien-hsiu against leaving home before his fatal trip to the Eastern Capital.

Pao, Ms., singing girl in the Great Tavern on Lion Street who witnesses Wu Sung's fatal assault on Li Wai-ch'uan.

Pen Chang-chieh, Jui-yün, daughter of Pen Ti-ch'uan and Yeh the Fifth, concubine of Hsia Yen-ling.

Pen the Fourth. See Pen Ti-ch'uan.

Pen, Scurry-about. See Pen Ti-ch'uan.

Pen Ti-ch'uan, Scurry-about Pen, Pen the Fourth, husband of Yeh the Fifth, father of Pen Chang-chieh, manager employed by Hsi-men Ch'ing in various capacities, member of the brotherhood of ten in which he replaces Hua Tzu-hsü after his death.

Pen Ti-ch'uan's daughter. See Pen Chang-chieh.

Pen Ti-ch'uan's wife. See Yeh the Fifth.

Pin-yang, Commandery Prince of. See Wang Ching-ch'ung.

P'ing-an, page boy in Hsi-men Ch'ing's household, absconds with jewelry stolen from the pawnshop after the death of Hsi-men Ch'ing, is caught, and allows himself to be coerced by the police chief Wu Tien-en into giving false testimony that Wu Yüeh-niang has been engaged in hanky-panky with Tai-an.

P'ing-erh. See Li P'ing-erh.

Prison guard on Chou Hsiu's staff.

Pu Chih-tao, No-account Pu, crony of Hsi-men Ch'ing, member of the brotherhood of ten whose place is taken after his death by Hua Tzu-hsü.

Pu, No-account. See Pu Chih-tao.

P'u-ching, Ch'an Master Snow Cave, mysterious Buddhist monk who provides Wu Yüeh-niang with a refuge in Snow Stream Cave on Mount T'ai when she is escaping attempted rape by Yin T'ien-hsi; at the end of the novel he conjures up a phantasmagoria in which all of the major protagonists describe themselves as being reborn in approximately the same social strata they had occupied in their previous incarnations; convinces Wu Yüeh-niang that her son Hsiao-ko is a reincarnation of Hsi-men Ch'ing, and spirits him away into a life of Buddhist celibacy as his disciple.

Sai-erh, singing girl in Longleg Lu's brothel on Butterfly Lane in Ch'ing-ho.

Sauce and Scallions. See Chiang Ts'ung.

Second Lady. See Li Chiao-erh.

Seng-pao, son of Lai-pao and Hui-hsiang, betrothed to Wang Liu-erh's niece, the daughter of Butcher Wang and Sow Wang.

Servant from the household of Chou Hsiu who is sent to fetch P'ang Ch'un-mei with a lantern.

Servant in the inn at the foot of Mount T'ai where Wu Yüeh-niang and Wu K'ai spend the night on their pilgrimage.

Servant from the Verdant Spring Bordello who runs errands for Li Kuei-chieh.

Sha San, Yokel Sha, one of the "cribbers" and "ball clubbers" in Ch'ing-ho who plays the tout to Wang Ts'ai on his visits to the licensed quarter and upon whom Hsi-men Ch'ing turns the tables by abusing the judicial system at the behest of Lady Lin.

Sha, Yokel. See Sha San.

Shamaness brought to the Hsi-men household by Dame Liu to burn paper money and perform a shamanistic dance on behalf of the sick Hsi-men Kuan-ko.

Shang Hsiao-t'ang, Provincial Graduate Shang, son of Shang Liu-t'ang, widower in Ch'ing-ho whom Chang Lung proposes unsuccessfully as a match for Meng Yü-lou, provincial graduate of the same year as Huang Pao-kuang, assisted by Hsi-men Ch'ing when he sets out for the Eastern Capital to compete in the *chin-shih* examinations.

Shang Hsiao-t'ang's second wife.

Shang Hsiao-t'ang's son.

Shang Liu-t'ang, Prefectural Judge Shang, father of Shang Hsiao-t'ang, formerly served as district magistrate of Huang Pao-kuang's district and prefectural judge of Ch'eng-tu in Szechwan, resident of Main Street in Ch'ing-ho from whom both Li P'ing-erh's and Hsi-men Ch'ing's coffins are purchased.

Shang Liu-t'ang's deceased wife, mother of Shang Hsiao-t'ang.

Shang, Prefectural Judge. See Shang Liu-t'ang.

Shang, Provincial Graduate. See Shang Hsiao-t'ang.

Shantung Yaksha. See Li Kuei.

Shao Ch'ien, boy actor in Ch'ing-ho.

Shen, Brother-in-law, Mr. Shen, husband of Wu Yüeh-niang's elder sister.

Shen Ching, resident of the Eastern Capital, father of Shen Shou-shan.

Shen, Mr. See Shen, Brother-in-law.

Shen, Second Sister, blind professional singer in Ch'ing-ho recommended to Hsi-men Ch'ing by Wang Liu-erh but driven out of his household by P'ang Ch'un-mei when she refuses to sing for her.

Shen Shou-shan, second son of Shen Ching, reincarnation of Chou Hsiu.

Shen Ting, servant in the household of Brother-in-law Shen.

Shen T'ung, wealthy resident of the Eastern Capital, father of Shen Yüeh.

Shen Yüeh, second son of Shen T'ung, reincarnation of Hsi-men Ch'ing.

Sheng-chin, ten-year-old country girl offered to P'ang Ch'un-mei as a maidservant but rejected for befouling her bed.

Sheng-chin's parents.

Shih Cho-kuei, Plastromancer Shih, shaman in Ch'ing-ho who prognosticates about the sick Hsi-men Kuan-ko through interpreting the cracks produced by applying heat to notches on the surface of the plastron of a tortoise shell.

Shih En, son of the warden of the prison camp at Meng-chou who befriends the exiled Wu Sung, obtains his assistance in his struggle with Chiang Men-shen for control of the Happy Forest Tavern, and gives him a hundred taels of silver and a letter of recommendation to Liu Kao when he is transferred to the An-p'ing Stockade.

Shih, Plastromancer. See Shih Cho-kuei.

Shih Po-ts'ai, corrupt Taoist head priest of the Temple of the Goddess of Iridescent Clouds on the summit of Mount T'ai.

Short-legged Tiger. See Wang Ying.

Shu-t'ung, Little Chang Sung, native of Su-chou, page boy catamite and transvestite presented to Hsi-men Ch'ing by Li Ta-t'ien, placed in charge of Hsi-men Ch'ing's studio where he handles his correspondence and caters to his polymorphous sexual tastes, becomes intimate with Yü-hsiao and when discovered in flagrante delicto by P'an Chin-lien purloins enough of Hsi-men Ch'ing's property to make good his escape to his native place.

Shui, Licentiate, scholar of problematic morals unsuccessfully recommended to Hsi-men Ch'ing as a social secretary by Ying Po-chüeh; after Hsi-men Ch'ing's death he is engaged by the remaining members of the brotherhood of ten to compose a funeral eulogy for Hsi-men Ch'ing in which he compares him to the male genitalia.

Shui, Licentiate's father, friend of Ying Po-chüeh's father.

Shui, Licentiate's grandfather, friend of Ying Po-chüeh's grandfather.

Shui, Licentiate's two sons, die of smallpox.

Shui, Licentiate's wife, elopes to the Eastern Capital with her lover.

Sick beggar whom Ch'en Ching-chi keeps alive with the warmth of his body when he is working as a night watchman.

Silver. See Wu Yin-erh.

Singing boys, two boy singers sent under escort all the way to Hsi-men Ch'ing's home in Ch'ing-ho by his host, Miao Ch'ing, after he expresses admiration for their singing at a banquet in the residence of Li Yen in the Eastern Capital.

Six Traitors, Ts'ai Ching, T'ung Kuan, Li Pang-yen, Chu Mien, Kao Ch'iu, and Li Yen.

Sixth Lady. See Li P'ing-erh.

Snake-in-the-grass. See Lu Hua.

Snow Bandit. See P'an Chin-lien's cat.

Snow Cave, Ch'an Master. See P'u-ching.

Snow Lion. See P'an Chin-lien's cat.

Snow Moth. See Sun Hsüeh-o.

Southerner who deflowers Cheng Ai-yüeh.

Spring Plum Blossom. See P'ang Ch'un-mei.

Ssu Feng-i, battalion commander rewarded for his part in facilitating the notorious Flower and Rock Convoys and the construction of the Mount Ken Imperial Park.

Stand-hard. See Tao-chien.

Star of Joy Bordello in Ch'ing-ho, cook from.

Storehouseman in charge of the local storehouse in Yen-chou Prefecture in Chekiang.

Street-skulking Rat. See Chang Sheng.

Sun, Blabbermouth. See Sun T'ien-hua.

Sun Chi, next door neighbor of Ch'en Ching-chi.

Sun Ch'ing, father-in-law of Huang the Fourth, father of Sun Wen-hsiang, employer of Feng the Second, merchant in Ch'ing-ho engaged in the cotton trade.

Sun Ch'ing's daughter. See Huang the Fourth's wife, née Sun.

Sun Ch'ing's son. See Sun Wen-hsiang.

Sun, Crooked-head, deceased husband of Aunt Yang.

Sun Erh-niang, concubine of Chou Hsiu, mother of Chou Yü-chieh.

Sun Erh-niang's maidservant.

Sun Erh-niang's maidservant's father.

Sun Hsüeh-o, Snow Moth, originally maidservant of Hsi-men Ch'ing's deceased first wife, née Ch'en, who enters his household as part of her dowry; Hsi-men Ch'ing's Fourth Lady but a second class citizen among his womenfolk whose responsibility is the kitchen; enemy of P'an Chin-lien and P'ang Ch'un-mei; carries on a clandestine affair with Lai-wang with whom she absconds when he returns to Ch'ing-ho after Hsi-men Ch'ing's death; apprehended by the authorities and sold into Chou Hsiu's household at the behest of P'ang Ch'un-mei who abuses her, beats her, and sells her into prostitution in order to get her out of the way when she wishes to pass off Ch'en Ching-chi as her cousin; renamed as the singing girl, Yü-erh, working out of My Own Tavern in Lin-ch'ing, she becomes the kept mistress of Chang Sheng until his death when she commits suicide.

Sun Hsüeh-o's reincarnation. See Yao family from outside the Eastern Capital.

Sun Jung, commandant of justice for the two townships of the Eastern Capital.

Sun Kua-tsui. See Sun T'ien-hua.

Sun T'ien-hua, Sun Kua-tsui, Blabbermouth Sun, crony of Hsi-men Ch'ing, member of the brotherhood of ten, plays the tout to Wang Ts'ai on his visits to the licensed quarter.

Sun T'ien-hua's wife.

Sun Wen-hsiang, son of Sun Ch'ing, brother-in-law of Huang the Fourth, involved in an affray with Feng Huai who dies of his injuries half a month later.

Sung Chiang (fl. 1117–21), Opportune Rain, chivalrous bandit chieftan, leader of a band of thirty-six outlaws in Liang-shan Marsh whose slogan is to "Carry out the Way on Heaven's behalf," slayer of Yen P'o-hsi, rescues Wu Yüeh-niang when she is captured by the bandits of Ch'ing-feng Stronghold and Wang Ying wants to make her his wife, eventually surrenders to Chang Shu-yeh and accepts the offer of a government amnesty.

Sung Ch'iao-nien (1047–1113), father-in-law of Ts'ai Yu, father of Sung Sheng-ch'ung, protégé of Ts'ai Ching, appointed regional investigating censor of Shantung to replace Tseng Hsiao-hsü, entertained by Hsi-men Ch'ing who presents him periodically with lavish bribes in return for which he gets Miao Ch'ing off the hook and does him numerous other illicit favors, rewarded for his part in facilitating the notorious Flower and Rock Convoys and the construction of the Mount Ken Imperial Park.

Sung Hui-lien, Chin-lien, daughter of Sung Jen, formerly maidservant in the household of Assistant Prefect Ts'ai who takes sexual advantage of her; sacked for colluding with her mistress in a case of adultery; marries the cook Chiang Ts'ung who is stabbed to death in a brawl; second wife of Lai-wang; carries on a clandestine affair with Hsi-men Ch'ing that soon becomes public knowledge; after Lai-wang is framed for attempted murder and driven out of the household she suffers from remorse and commits suicide.

Sung Hui-lien's reincarnation. See Chu family of the Eastern Capital.

Sung Hui-lien's maternal aunt.

Sung Jen, father of Sung Hui-lien, coffin seller in Ch'ing-ho who accuses Hsi-men Ch'ing of driving his daughter to suicide but is given such a beating by the corrupt magistrate Li Ta-t'ien that he dies of his wounds.

Sung Sheng-ch'ung (fl. early 12th century), son of Sung Ch'iao-nien, elder brother of Ts'ai Yu's wife, née Sung, regional investigating censor of Shensi suborned into traducing Tseng Hsiao-hsü by Ts'ai Ching.

Sung Te, commits adultery with Ms. Chou, the widowed second wife of his father-in-law, for which Hsi-men Ch'ing sentences them both to death by strangulation.

Sung Te's father-in-law, deceased husband of Ms. Chou.

Sung Te's mother-in-law, deceased mother of Sung Te's wife.

Sung Te's wife.

Sung T'ui, eunuch rewarded for his part in facilitating the notorious Flower and Rock Convoys and the construction of the Mount Ken Imperial Park.

Ta T'ien-tao, prefect of Tung-ch'ang.

Tai-an, Hsi-men An, favorite page boy of Hsi-men Ch'ing and his sedulous understudy in the arts of roguery and dissimulation; manages to stay on the right side of everyone with the exception of Wu Yüeh-niang who periodically berates him for his duplicity; married to Hsiao-yü after the death of Hsi-men Ch'ing when Wu Yüeh-niang discovers them in flagrante delicto; remains with Wu Yüeh-niang and supports her in her old age in return for which he is given the name Hsi-men An and inherits what is left of Hsi-men Ch'ing's property and social position.

T'ai-tsung, emperor of the Chin dynasty (r. 1123–35).

T'an Chen (fl. early 12th century), eunuch military commander with the concurrent rank of censor-in-chief, appointed to replace T'ung Kuan in command of the defense of the northern frontier against the Chin army.

T'ang Pao. See Lai-pao.

Tao-chien, Stand-hard, abbot of the Temple of Eternal Felicity at Wu-li Yüan outside the South Gate of Ch'ing-ho.

T'ao, Crud-crawler, an elderly resident of Ch'ing-ho who is renowned for having sexually molested all three of his daughters-in-law.

T'ao-hua, maidservant in the Star of Joy Bordello in Ch'ing-ho.

T'ao, Old Mother, licensed go-between in Ch'ing-ho who represents Li Kung-pi in his courtship of Meng Yü-lou.

Temple of the Jade Emperor outside the East Gate of Ch'ing-ho, lector of.

Teng, Midwife, called in by Ying Po-chüeh when his concubine, Ch'un-hua, bears him a son.

Third Lady. See Cho Tiu-erh and Meng Yü-lou.

Three-inch Mulberry-bark Manikin. See Wu Chih.

Ti Ssu-pin, Turbid Ti, vice-magistrate of Yang-ku district who locates the corpse of Miao T'ien-hsiu after his murder by Miao Ch'ing.

Ti, Turbid. See Ti Ssu-pin.

Tiao the Seventh, concubine of Miao T'ien-hsiu, formerly a singing girl from a brothel on the Yang-chou docks, carries on an affair with her husband's servant, Miao Ch'ing, the discovery of which leads to the beating of Miao Ch'ing and the murder of Miao T'ien-hsiu in revenge.

T'ien Chiu-kao, battalion commander rewarded for his part in facilitating the notorious Flower and Rock Convoys and the construction of the Mount Ken Imperial Park.

T'ien-fu. See Ch'in-t'ung.

T'ien-hsi, senior page boy in the household of Hua Tzu-hsü and Li P'ing-erh who absconds with five taels of silver when his master takes to his sickbed and vanishes without a trace.

T'ien Hu, bandit chieftan active in the Hopei area.

Ting, Director, Wu K'ai's predecessor as director of the State Farm Battalion in Ch'ing-ho, cashiered for corruption by Hou Meng.

Ting, Mr., father of Ting the Second, silk merchant from Hang-chou.

Ting the Second, Ting Shuang-ch'iao, son of Mr. Ting, friend of Ch'en Liang-huai, a silk merchant from Hang-chou who patronizes Li Kuei-chieh while on a visit to Ch'ing-ho and hides under the bed when Hsi-men Ch'ing discovers their liaison and smashes up the Verdant Spring Bordello.

Ting Shuang-ch'iao. See Ting the Second.

Ting the Southerner, wine merchant in Ch'ing-ho from whom Hsi-men Ch'ing buys forty jugs of Ho-ch'ing wine on credit.

Tou Chien (d. 1127), superintendant of the Capital Training Divisions and capital security commissioner.

Tower of Jade. See Meng Yü-lou.

Ts'ai, Assistant Prefect, resident of Ch'ing-ho from whose household Sung Hui-lien is expelled for colluding with her mistress in a case of adultery.

Ts'ai, Assistant Prefect's wife.

Ts'ai Ching (1046–1126), father of Ts'ai Yu, Ts'ai T'iao, Ts'ai T'ao, and Ts'ai Hsiu, father-in-law of Liang Shih-chieh, left grand councilor, grand academician of the Hall for Veneration of Governance, grand preceptor, minister of personnel, Duke of Lu, most powerful minister at the court of Emperor

Hui-tsung, impeached by Yü-wen Hsü-chung, patron and adoptive father of Ts'ai Yün and Hsi-men Ch'ing, first of the Six Traitors impeached by Ch'en Tung.

Ts'ai Ching's mansion in the Eastern Capital, gatekeepers of.

Ts'ai Ching's mansion in the Eastern Capital, page boy in.

Ts'ai Ching's wife.

Ts'ai family of Yen-chou in Shantung, family of which Hsi-men Hsiao-ko is alleged to have been a son in his previous incarnation.

Ts'ai Hsing (fl. early 12th century), son of Ts'ai Yu, appointed director of the Palace Administration as a reward for his father's part in facilitating the notorious Flower and Rock Convoys and the construction of the Mount Ken Imperial Park.

Ts'ai Hsiu, ninth son of Ts'ai Ching, prefect of Chiu-chiang.

Ts'ai, Midwife, presides over the deliveries of Li P'ing-erh's son, Hsi-men Kuan-ko, and Wu Yüeh-niang's son, Hsi-men Hsiao-ko.

Ts'ai T'ao (d. after 1147), fifth son of Ts'ai Ching.

Ts'ai T'iao (d. after 1137), fourth son of Ts'ai Ching, consort of Princess Mao-te.

Ts'ai Yu (1077–1126), eldest son of Ts'ai Ching, son-in-law of Sung Ch'iao-nien, brother-in-law of Sung Sheng-ch'ung, father of Ts'ai Hsing, academician of the Hall of Auspicious Harmony, minister of rites, superintendent of the Temple of Supreme Unity, rewarded with the title grand guardian of the heir apparent for his part in facilitating the notorious Flower and Rock Convoys and the construction of the Mount Ken Imperial Park, executed by order of Emperor Ch'in-tsung after the fall of Ts'ai Ching and his faction.

Ts'ai Yu's son. See Ts'ai Hsing.

Ts'ai Yu's wife, née Sung, daughter of Sung Ch'iao-nien, younger sister of Sung Sheng-ch'ung.

Ts'ai Yün, awarded first place in the *chin-shih* examinations in place of An Ch'en when the latter is displaced for being the younger brother of the proscribed An Tun, becomes a protégé and adopted son of Ts'ai Ching, appointed proofreader in the Palace Library, is patronized by Hsi-men Ch'ing; after being impeached by Ts'ao Ho he is appointed salt-control censor of the Liang-Huai region where his illicit favors to Hsi-men Ch'ing abet his profitable speculations in the salt trade.

Ts'ai Yün's mother.

Tsang Pu-hsi, docket officer on the staff of the district yamen in Ch'ing-ho.

Ts'ao Ho, censor who impeaches Ts'ai Yün and thirteen others from the Historiography Institute who had passed the *chin-shih* examinations in the same year.

Tseng Hsiao-hsü (1049–1127), son of Tseng Pu, regional investigating censor of Shantung, reopens the case of Miao T'ien-hsiu's murder at the request of Huang Mei and arrives at the truth only to have his memorial suppressed when Hsi-men Ch'ing and Hsia Yen-ling bribe Ts'ai Ching to intervene; submits a memorial to the throne criticizing the policies of Ts'ai Ching that so enrages the prime minister that he suborns his daughter-in-law's brother, Sung Sheng-ch'ung, into framing him on trumped up charges as a result of which he is deprived of his office and banished to the farthest southern extremity of the country.

Tseng Pu (1036–1107), father of Tseng Hsiao-hsü.

Tso Shun, professional boy actor in Ch'ing-ho.

Ts'ui-erh, maidservant of Sun Hsüeh-o.

Ts'ui-hua, junior maidservant of P'ang Ch'un-mei after she becomes the wife of Chou Hsiu.

Ts'ui Pen, nephew of Ch'iao Hung, husband of Big Sister Tuan, employee, manager, and partner in several of Hsi-men Ch'ing's enterprises.

Ts'ui Pen's mother, Ch'iao Hung's elder sister.

Ts'ui, Privy Councilor. See Ts'ui Shou-yü.

Ts'ui Shou-yü, Privy Councilor Ts'ui, relative of Hsia Yen-ling with whom he stays on his visit to the Eastern Capital.

Tsung-mei. See Ch'en Ching-chi.

Tsung-ming. See Chin Tsung-ming.

Tsung Tse (1059–1128), general-in-chief of the Southern Sung armies who retakes parts of Shantung and Hopei from the Chin invaders on behalf of Emperor Kao-tsung.

Tu the Third, maternal cousin of Ying Po-chüeh.

Tu the Third's page boy.

Tu the Third's wife.

Tu Tzu-ch'un, privy councilor under a previous reign living in retirement in the northern quarter of Ch'ing-ho, engaged by Hsi-men Ch'ing to indite the inscription on Li P'ing-erh's funeral banderole.

Tuan, Big Sister, wife of Ts'ui Pen.

Tuan, Big Sister's father.

Tuan, Consort. See Feng, Consort.

Tuan, Half-baked. See Tuan Mien.

Tuan Mien, Half-baked Tuan, one of the "cribbers" in the licensed quarter of Ch'ing-ho patronized by Hsi-men Ch'ing.

Tuan, Old Mother, waiting woman in Lady Lin's household whose residence in the rear of the compound is used as a rendezvous by her lovers.

Tung the Cat. See Tung Chin-erh.

Tung Chiao-erh, singing girl from the Tung Family Brothel on Second Street in the licensed quarter of Ch'ing-ho who spends the night with Ts'ai Yün at Hsi-men Ch'ing's behest.

Tung Chin-erh, Tung the Cat, singing girl from the Tung Family Brothel on Second Street in the licensed quarter of Ch'ing-ho, patronized by Chang Mao-te.

Tung Sheng, clerical subofficial on the staff of Wang Fu.

Tung Yü-hsien, singing girl from the Tung Family Brothel on Second Street in the licensed quarter of Ch'ing-ho.

T'ung Kuan (1054–1126), eunuch military officer beaten up by Wu Sung in a drunken brawl, uncle of T'ung T'ien-yin, military affairs commissioner, defender-in-chief of the Palace Command, Commandery Prince of Kuang-yang, one of the Six Traitors impeached by Ch'en Tung.

T'ung Kuan's nephew. See T'ung T'ien-yin.

T'ung, Prefectural Judge, prefectural judge of Tung-p'ing who conducts the preliminary hearing in the case of the affray between Feng Huai and Sun Wen-hsiang.

T'ung T'ien-yin, nephew of T'ung Kuan, commander of the guard, director of the Office of Herds in the Inner and Outer Imperial Demesnes of the Court of the Imperial Stud.

Turf-protecting Tiger. See Liu the Second.

Tutor employed in the household of Miao Ch'ing.

Tz'u-hui Temple, abbot of, recovers the corpse of the murdered Miao T'ien-hsiu and buries it on the bank of the river west of Ch'ing-ho where it is discovered by Ti Ssu-pin.

Vase. See Li P'ing-erh.

Waiter in My Own Tavern in Lin-ch'ing.

Wan-yen Tsung-han (1079–1136), Nien-mo-ho, nephew of Emperor T'ai-tsu (r. 1115–23) the founder of the Chin dynasty, commander of the Chin army that occupies K'ai-feng and takes Retired Emperor Hui-tsung and Emperor Ch'in-tsung into captivity.

Wan-yen Tsung-wang (d. 1127), Wo-li-pu, second son of Emperor T'ai-tsu (r. 1115–23) the founder of the Chin dynasty, associate commander of the Chin army that occupies K'ai-feng and takes Retired Emperor Hui-tsung and Emperor Ch'in-tsung into captivity, kills Chou Hsiu with an arrow through the throat.

Wang, Attendant, official on the staff of the Prince of Yün to whom Han Tao-kuo appeals through Hsi-men Ch'ing and Jen Hou-ch'i to be allowed to commute his hereditary corvée labor obligation to payments in money or goods.

Wang, Butcher, elder brother of Wang Liu-erh, husband of Sow Wang whose daughter is betrothed to Seng-pao.

Wang Ch'ao, son of Dame Wang, apprenticed to a merchant from the Huai River region from whom he steals a hundred taels entrusted to him for the purchase of stock, returns to Ch'ing-ho, and uses it as capital to buy two donkeys and set up a flour mill, becomes a casual lover of P'an Chin-lien while she is in Dame Wang's house awaiting purchase as a concubine.

Wang Chen, second son of Wang Hsüan, government student in the prefectural school.

Wang Ch'ien, eldest son of Wang Hsüan, hereditary battalion commander of the local Horse Pasturage Battalion of the Court of the Imperial Stud.

Wang Chin-ch'ing. See Wang Shen.

Wang Ching, younger brother of Wang Liu-erh, page boy employed in the household of Hsi-men Ch'ing as a replacement for Shu-t'ung after he absconds, sodomized by Hsi-men Ch'ing during his visit to the Eastern Capital, expelled from the household by Wu Yüeh-niang after the death of Hsi-men Ch'ing.

Wang Ching-ch'ung (d. 949), military commissioner of T'ai-yüan, Commandery Prince of Pin-yang, ancestor of Wang I-hsüan.

Wang Ch'ing, bandit chieftan active in the Huai-hsi area.

Wang Chu, elder brother of Wang Hsiang, professional boy actor in Ch'ing-ho.

Wang, Consort (d. 1117), a consort of Emperor Hui-tsung, mother of Chao K'ai, the Prince of Yün, related to Wang the Second.

Wang, Dame, mother of Wang Ch'ao, proprietress of a teahouse next door to Wu Chih's house on Amythest Street on the west side of the district yamen in Ch'ing-ho who is also active as a go-between and procuress; go-between who proposes the match between Hsi-men Ch'ing and Wu Yüeh-niang; inventor of the elaborate scheme by which Hsi-men Ch'ing seduces P'an Chin-lien; suggests the poisoning of her next door neighbor Wu Chih and helps P'an Chin-lien carry it out; intervenes on behalf of Ho the Tenth when he is accused of fencing stolen goods with the result that Hsi-men Ch'ing gets him off the hook and executes an innocent monk in his stead; after the death of Hsi-men Ch'ing, when Wu Yüeh-niang discovers P'an Chin-lien's affair with Ch'en Ching-chi, she expells her from the household and consigns her to Dame Wang, who entertains bids from Magnate Ho, Chang Mao-te, Ch'en Ching-chi, and Chou Hsiu before finally selling her to Wu Sung for a hundred taels of silver plus a five tael brokerage fee; that same night she is decapitated by Wu Sung after he has disemboweled P'an Chin-lien.

Wang, Dame's deceased husband, father of Wang Ch'ao, dies when she is thirty-five.

Wang, Dame's son. See Wang Ch'ao.

Wang, distaff relative of the imperial family. See Wang the Second.

Wang family of Cheng-chou, family into which Hsi-men Kuan-ko is reincarnated as a son.

Wang family of the Eastern Capital, family into which Ch'en Ching-chi is reincarnated as a son.

Wang family of Pin-chou, family in which Li P'ing-erh is alleged to have been formerly incarnated as a son.

Wang the First, Auntie, madam of the Wang Family Brothel in Yang-chou.

Wang Fu (1079–1126), minister of war impeached by Yü-wen Hsü-chung.

Wang Fu's wife and children.

Wang Hai-feng. See Wang Ssu-feng.

Wang Han, servant in the household of Han Tao-kuo and Wang Liu-erh.

Wang Hsiang, younger brother of Wang Chu, professional boy actor in Ch'ing-ho.

Wang Hsien, employee of Hsi-men Ch'ing who accompanies Lai-pao on a buying trip to Nan-ching.

Wang Hsüan, Layman of Apricot Hermitage, father of Wang Ch'ien and Wang Chen, friend of Ch'en Hung, retired philanthropist who provides aid to Ch'en Ching-chi three times after he is reduced to beggary and who recommends him to Abbot Jen of the Yen-kung Temple in Lin-ch'ing.

Wang Hsüan's manager, in charge of a pawnshop on the street front of his residence.

Wang Huan (fl. early 12th century), commander-general of the Hopei region who leads the forces of Wei-po against the Chin invaders.

Wang I-hsüan, Imperial Commissioner Wang, descendant of Wang Ching-ch'ung, deceased husband of Lady Lin, father of Wang Ts'ai.

Wang I-hsüan's wife. See Lady Lin.

Wang I-hsüan's son. See Wang Ts'ai.

Wang, Imperial Commissioner. See Wang I-hsüan.

Wang K'uan, head of the mutual security unit for Ch'en Ching-chi's residence in Ch'ing-ho.

Wang Lien, henchman on the domestic staff of Wang Fu.

Wang Liu-erh, Wang the Sixth, one of the female protagonists of the novel, younger sister of Butcher Wang, elder sister of Wang Ching, wife of Han Tao-kuo, mother of Han Ai-chieh; paramour of her brother-in-law, Han the Second, whom she marries after her husband's death, of Hsi-men Ch'ing, to whose death from sexual exhaustion she is a major contributor, and of Magnate Ho, whose property in Hu-chou she inherits.

Wang Liu-erh's niece, daughter of Butcher Wang and Sow Wang, betrothed to Seng-pao, the son of Lai-pao and Hui-hsiang.

Wang Luan, proprietor of the Great Tavern on Lion Street in Ch'ing-ho who witnesses Wu Sung's fatal attack on Li Wai-ch'uan.

Wang, Nun, Buddhist nun from the Kuan-yin Nunnery in Ch'ing-ho which is patronized by Wu Yüeh-niang, frequently invited to recite Buddhist "precious scrolls" to Wu Yüeh-niang and her guests, recommends Nun Hsüeh to Wu Yüeh-niang who takes her fertility potion and conceives Hsi-men Hsiao-ko, later quarrels with Nun Hsüeh over the division of alms from Li P'ing-erh and Wu Yüeh-niang.

Wang, Old Mrs., neighbor of Yün Li-shou in Chi-nan who appears in Wu Yüeh-niang's nightmare.

Wang, Old Sister, singing girl working out of My Own Tavern in Lin-ch'ing.

Wang Ping (d. 1126), commander-general of the Kuan-tung region who leads the forces of Fen-chiang against the Chin invaders.

Wang Po-ju, proprietor of an inn on the docks in Yang-chou recommended to Han Tao-kuo, Lai-pao, and Ts'ui Pen by Hsi-men Ch'ing as a good place to stay.

Wang Po-ju's father, friend of Hsi-men Ch'ing's father, Hsi-men Ta.

Wang Po-yen (1069–1141), right assistant administration commissioner of Shantung.

Wang the Second, distaff relative of the imperial family through Consort Wang, landlord of Wu Chih's residence on the west side of Amythest Street in Ch'ing-ho, purchaser of Eunuch Director Hua's mansion on Main Street in An-ch'ing ward of Ch'ing-ho, maintains a private troupe of twenty actors that he sometimes lends to Hsi-men Ch'ing to entertain his guests.

Wang Shen (c. 1048-c. 1103), Wang Chin-ch'ing, commandant-escort and director of the Court of the Imperial Clan, consort of the second daughter of Emperor Ying-tsung (r. 1063–67).

Wang Shih-ch'i, prefect of Ch'ing-chou in Shantung.

Wang the Sixth. See Wang Liu-erh.

Wang, Sow, wife of Butcher Wang whose daughter is betrothed to Seng-pao.

Wang Ssu-feng, Wang Hai-feng, salt merchant from Yang-chou who is set free from prison in Ts'ang-chou by Hou Meng, the grand coordinator of Shantung, as a result of Hsi-men Ch'ing's intervention with Ts'ai Ching.

Wang the Third. See Wang Ts'ai.

Wang Ts'ai (1078–1118), Wang the Third, feckless and dissolute third son of Wang I-hsüan and Lady Lin, married to the niece of Huang Ching-ch'en, tries unsuccessfully to borrow three hundred taels of silver from Hsü Pu-yü in order to purchase a position in the Military School, pawns his wife's possessions in order to pursue various singing girls in the licensed quarter including those patronized by Hsi-men Ch'ing, tricked into becoming the adopted son of Hsi-men Ch'ing during his intrigue with Lady Lin, continues his affair with Li Kuei-chieh after the death of Hsi-men Ch'ing.

Wang Ts'ai's wife, née Huang, niece of Huang Ching-ch'en.

Wang Tsu-tao (d. 1108), minister of personnel.

Wang Tung-ch'iao, traveling merchant entertained by Han Tao-kuo in Yang-chou.

Wang, Usher, official in the Court of State Ceremonial who offers the sixteen-year-old wife of his runaway retainer for sale as a maidservant through Old Mother Feng.

Wang, Usher's runaway retainer.

Wang, Usher's runaway retainer's wife.

Wang Wei, supreme commander of the Capital Training Divisions, Duke of Lung-hsi, granted the title of grand mentor for his part in facilitating the notorious Flower and Rock Convoys and the construction of the Mount Ken Imperial Park.

Wang Ying, Short-legged Tiger, second outlaw leader of the Ch'ing-feng Stronghold on Ch'ing-feng Mountain who wants to make Wu Yüeh-niang his wife when she is captured by his band but is prevented from doing so by Sung Chiang.

Wang Yu, commander of a training division rewarded for his part in facilitating the notorious Flower and Rock Convoys and the construction of the
Mount Ken Imperial Park.

Wang Yü, subofficial functionary on the domestic staff of Ts'ai Ching deputed
by Chai Ch'ien to carry a message of condolence to Hsi-men Ch'ing and a
personal letter from Han Ai-chieh to Han Tao-kuo and Wang Liu-erh.

Wang Yü-chih, singing girl from the Wang Family Brothel in Yang-chou patronized by Han Tao-kuo.

Wei Ch'eng-hsün, battalion commander rewarded for his part in facilitating
the notorious Flower and Rock Convoys and the construction of the Mount
Ken Imperial Park.

Wei Ts'ung-erh, a taciturn chair-bearer in Ch'ing-ho, partner of Chang
Ch'uan-erh.

Wen, Auntie, mother of Wen T'ang, go-between in Ch'ing-ho who represents
Ch'en Ching-chi's family at the time of his betrothal to Hsi-men Ta-chieh,
resident of Wang Family Alley on the South Side of town, active in promoting pilgrimages to Mount T'ai, patronized by Lady Lin for whom she acts
as a procuress in her adulterous affairs including that with Hsi-men Ch'ing,
involved with Auntie Hsüeh in arranging the betrothal between Chang
Mao-te's son and Eunuch Director Hsü's niece.

Wen Ch'en, one of the officials from the Ch'ing-ho Guard who comes to Hsi-
men Ch'ing's residence to offer a sacrifice to the soul of Li P'ing-erh after
her death.

Wen Hsi, military director-in-chief of Yen-chou in Shantung.

Wen, Licentiate. See Wen Pi-ku.

Wen, Pedant. See Wen Pi-ku.

Wen Pi-ku, Warm-buttocks Wen, Pedant Wen, Licentiate Wen, pederast recommended to Hsi-men Ch'ing by his fellow licentiate Ni P'eng to be his
social secretary, housed across the street from Hsi-men Ch'ing's residence
in the property formerly belonging to Ch'iao Hung, divulges Hsi-men
Ch'ing's private correspondence to Ni P'eng who shares it with Hsia Yen-
ling, sodomizes Hua-t'ung against his will and is expelled from the Hsi-men
household when his indiscretions are exposed.

Wen Pi-ku's mother-in-law.

Wen Pi-ku's wife.

Wen T'ang, son of Auntie Wen.

Wen T'ang's wife.

Wen, Warm-buttocks. See Wen Pi-ku.

Weng the Eighth, criminal boatman who, along with his partner Ch'en the
Third, murders Miao T'ien-hsiu.

What a Whopper. See Hsieh Ju-huang.

Wo-li-pu. See Wan-yen Tsung-wang.

Wu, Abbot. See Wu Tsung-che.

Wu, Battalion Commander, father of Wu K'ai, Wu the Second, Wu Yüeh-niang's elder sister, and Wu Yüeh-niang, hereditary battalion commander of the Ch'ing-ho Left Guard.

Wu, Captain. See Wu Sung.

Wu Ch'ang-chiao, Longfoot Wu, madam of the brothel in the Southern Entertainment Quarter of Ch'ing-ho patronized by P'ing-an after he absconds from the Hsi-men household with jewelry stolen from the pawnshop.

Wu Ch'ang-chiao's husband.

Wu Chih, Wu the Elder, Three-inch Mulberry-bark Manikin, elder brother of Wu Sung, father of Ying-erh by his deceased first wife, husband of P'an Chin-lien, simple-minded dwarf, native of Yang-ku district in Shantung who moves to the district town of Ch'ing-ho because of a famine and makes his living by peddling steamed wheat cakes on the street, cuckolded by P'an Chin-lien with his landlord, Mr. Chang, and then with Hsi-men Ch'ing, catches P'an Chin-lien and Hsi-men Ch'ing in flagrante delicto in Dame Wang's teahouse but suffers a near-fatal injury when Hsi-men Ch'ing kicks him in the solar plexus, poisoned by P'an Chin-lien with arsenic supplied by Hsi-men Ch'ing.

Wu Chih's daughter. See Ying-erh.

Wu Chih's deceased first wife, mother of Ying-erh.

Wu Chih's second wife. See P'an Chin-lien.

Wu the Elder. See Wu Chih.

Wu the Fourth, Auntie, madam of the Wu Family Bordello on the back alley in the licensed quarter of Ch'ing-ho.

Wu, Heartless. See Wu Tien-en.

Wu Hsün, secretary of the Bureau of Irrigation and Transportation in the Ministry of Works, rewarded for his part in facilitating the notorious Flower and Rock Convoys and the construction of the Mount Ken Imperial Park.

Wu Hui, younger brother of Wu Yin-erh, actor and musician from the Wu Family Bordello on the back alley in the licensed quarter of Ch'ing-ho.

Wu, Immortal. See Wu Shih.

Wu K'ai, eldest son of Battalion Commander Wu, elder brother of Wu the Second, Wu Yüeh-niang's elder sister, and Wu Yüeh-niang, father of Wu Shun-ch'en, brother-in-law of Hsi-men Ch'ing, inherits the position of battalion commander of the Ch'ing-ho Left Guard upon the death of his father, deputed to repair the local Charity Granary, promoted to the rank of assistant commander of the Ch'ing-ho Guard in charge of the local State Farm Battalion as a result of Hsi-men Ch'ing's influence with Sung Ch'iao-nien, accompanies Wu Yüeh-niang on her pilgrimage to Mount T'ai after the death of Hsi-men Ch'ing and is instrumental in rescuing her from attempted rape by Yin T'ien-hsi.

Wu K'ai's son. See Wu Shun-ch'en.

Wu K'ai's wife, Sister-in-law Wu, mother of Wu Shun-ch'en, sister-in-law of Hsi-men Ch'ing and a frequent guest in his household.

Wu, Longfoot. See Wu Ch'ang-chiao.

Wu the Second, second son of Battalion Commander Wu, younger brother of Wu K'ai, second elder brother of Wu Yüeh-niang, brother-in-law of Hsi-men Ch'ing and manager of his silk store on Lion Street; engages in hanky-panky with Li Chiao-erh for which he is denied access to the household by Wu Yüeh-niang when it is discovered after the death of Hsi-men Ch'ing although he continues to manage the silk store and later, along with Tai-an, the wholesale pharmaceutical business; accompanies Wu Yüeh-niang, Tai-an, Hsiao-yü, and Hsi-men Hsiao-ko when they flee the invading Chin armies to seek refuge with Yün Li-shou in Chi-nan; ten days after the climactic encounter with P'u-ching in the Temple of Eternal Felicity and Wu Yüeh-niang's relinquishment of Hsi-men Hsiao-ko to a life of Buddhist celibacy he accompanies Wu Yüeh-niang, Tai-an, and Hsiao-yü back to their now truncated household in Ch'ing-ho.

Wu the Second. See Wu Sung.

Wu the Second's wife, wife of Wu Yüeh-niang's second elder brother.

Wu Shih, Immortal Wu, Taoist physiognomist introduced to Hsi-men Ch'ing by Chou Hsiu who accurately foretells his fortune and those of his wife and concubines as well as Hsi-men Ta-chieh and P'ang Ch'un-mei; when Hsi-men Ch'ing is on his deathbed he is called in again and reports that there is no hope for him.

Wu Shih's servant boy.

Wu Shun-ch'en, son of Wu K'ai, husband of Third Sister Cheng.

Wu, Sister-in-law. See Wu K'ai's wife.

Wu Sung, Wu the Second, Captain Wu, younger brother of Wu Chih, brother-in-law of P'an Chin-lien; impulsive and implacable exponent of the code of honor; becomes a fugitive from the law for beating up T'ung Kuan in a drunken brawl; slays a tiger in single-handed combat while on his way to visit his brother and is made police captain in Ch'ing-ho for this feat; rejects attempted seduction by P'an Chin-lien and tells her off in no uncertain terms; delivers Li Ta-t'ien's illicit gains from his magistracy to the safe keeping of Chu Mien in the Eastern Capital; returns to Ch'ing-ho and mistakenly kills Li Wai-ch'uan while seeking to avenge the murder of his brother; is sentenced to military exile in Meng-chou where he is befriended by Shih En and helps him in his struggle with Chiang Men-shen for control of the Happy Forest Tavern; is framed by Military Director-in-chief Chang with the help of his concubine, Chiang Yü-lan, the younger sister of Chiang Men-shen, in revenge for which he murders his two guards and the entire households of Military Director-in-chief Chang and Chiang Men-shen; sets out for An-p'ing Stockade with a hundred taels of silver and a letter of recommendation from Shih En but is enabled by a general amnesty to return to Ch'ing-ho where he buys P'an Chin-lien from Dame Wang for a hundred taels of silver and disembowels her to avenge the death of his brother; once more a fugitive he disguises himself as a Buddhist ascetic with the help of the criminal innkeepers Chang Ch'ing and his wife and goes to join Sung Chiang's band of outlaws in Liang-shan Marsh.

Wu-t'ai, Mount, monk from, who solicits alms from Wu Yüeh-niang for the repair of his temple.

Wu Tien-en, Heartless Wu, originally a Yin-yang master on the staff of the district yamen in Ch'ing-ho who has been removed from his post for cause; makes his living by hanging around in front of the yamen and acting as a guarantor for loans to local officials and functionaries; crony of Hsi-men Ch'ing; member of the brotherhood of ten; manager employed by Hsi-men Ch'ing in various of his enterprises; misrepresents himself as Hsi-men Ch'ing's brother-in-law and is appointed to the post of station master of the Ch'ing-ho Postal Relay Station in return for his part in delivering birthday presents from Hsi-men Ch'ing to Ts'ai Ching; receives an interest-free loan of one hundred taels from Hsi-men Ch'ing to help cover the expenses of assuming office; promoted to the position of police chief of a suburb of Ch'ing-ho after the death of Hsi-men Ch'ing he apprehends the runaway P'ing-an and coerces him into giving false testimony that Wu Yüeh-niang has been engaged in hanky-panky with Tai-an, but when Wu Yüeh-niang appeals to P'ang Ch'un-mei he is dragged before Chou Hsiu's higher court and thoroughly humiliated.

Wu Tsung-che, Abbot Wu, head priest of the Taoist Temple of the Jade Emperor outside the East Gate of Ch'ing-ho, presides over the elaborate Taoist ceremony at which Hsi-men Kuan-ko is made an infant Taoist priest with the religious name Wu Ying-yüan, later officiates at funeral observances for Li P'ing-erh and Hsi-men Ch'ing.

Wu Yin-erh, Silver, elder sister of Wu Hui, singing girl from the Wu Family Bordello on the back alley of the licensed quarter in Ch'ing-ho, sweetheart of Hua Tzu-hsü, adopted daughter of Li P'ing-erh.

Wu Ying-yüan. See Hsi-men Kuan-ko.

Wu Yüeh-niang, Moon Lady, one of the female protagonists of the novel, daughter of Battalion Commander Wu, younger sister of Wu K'ai, Wu the Second, and an elder sister; second wife and First Lady of Hsi-men Ch'ing who marries her after the death of his first wife, née Ch'en, in a match proposed by Dame Wang; stepmother of Hsi-men Ta-chieh, mother of Hsi-men Hsiao-ko; a pious, credulous, and conventional Buddhist laywoman who constantly invites Nun Wang and Nun Hsüeh to the household to recite "precious scrolls" on the themes of salvation, retribution, and reincarnation, who has good intentions but is generally ineffectual at household management and is not a good judge of character; colludes with Hsi-men

Ch'ing in taking secret possession of Li P'ing-erh's ill-gotten property but quarrels with him over admitting her to the household; suffers a miscarriage but later takes Nun Hsüeh's fertility potion and conceives Hsi-men Hsiao-ko who is born at the very moment of Hsi-men Ch'ing's death; thoughtlessly betroths both Kuan-ko and Hsiao-ko to inappropriate partners while they are still babes in arms; makes a pilgrimage to Mount T'ai after Hsi-men Ch'ing's death and narrowly escapes an attempted rape by Yin T'ien-hsi and capture by the bandits on Ch'ing-feng Mountain; expels P'an Chin-lien, P'ang Ch'un-mei, and Ch'en Ching-chi from the household when she belatedly discovers their perfidy but is unable to cope effectively with the declining fortunes of the family; forced to seek the assistance of P'ang Ch'un-mei when she is threatened by Wu Tien-en she has no alternative but to accept the condescension of her former maidservant; while fleeing from the invading Chin armies to seek refuge with Yün Li-shou in Chi-nan she encounters P'u-ching and spends the night in the Temple of Eternal Felicity where she dreams that Yün Li-shou threatens her with rape if she refuses to marry him; still traumatized by this nightmare, she allows P'u-ching to persuade her that Hsiao-ko is the reincarnation of Hsi-men Ch'ing and relinquishes her teenage son to a life of Buddhist celibacy without so much as asking his opinion; on returning safely to Ch'ing-ho she adopts Tai-an as her husband's heir, renaming him Hsi-men An, and lives in reduced circumstances, presiding over a truncated household, until dying a natural death at the age of sixty-nine.

Wu Yüeh-niang's elder sister, wife of Brother-in-law Shen.

Yang, Aunt, widow of Crooked-head Sun, paternal aunt of Yang Tsung-hsi and Yang Tsung-pao, forceful advocate of Meng Yü-lou's remarriage to Hsi-men Ch'ing after the latter offers her a hundred taels of silver for her support, quarrels with Chang Lung when he tries to prevent this match.

Yang Chien (d. 1121), Commander Yang, eunuch military officer related to Ch'en Hung by marriage, commander in chief of the Imperial Guard in the Eastern Capital, bribed by Hsi-men Ch'ing to intervene on his behalf against Wu Sung and in favor of Hua Tzu-hsü, impeached by Yü-wen Hsü-chung, reported in a letter from Chai Ch'ien to Hsi-men Ch'ing to have died in prison in 1117.

Yang, Commander. See Yang Chien.

Yang the Elder. See Yang Kuang-yen.

Yang Erh-feng, second son of Yang Pu-lai and his wife, née Pai, younger brother of Yang Kuang-yen, a gambler and tough guy who scares off Ch'en Ching-chi when he tries to recover the half shipload of property that Yang Kuang-yen had stolen from him.

Yang Kuang-yen, Yang the Elder, Iron Fingernail, native of Nobottom ward in Carryoff village of Makebelieve district in Nonesuch subprefecture, son of

Yang Pu-lai and his wife, née Pai, disciple of the Barefaced Adept from whom he acquires the art of lying, husband of Miss Died-of-fright, con man employed by Ch'en Ching-chi who absconds with half a shipload of his property while he is in Yen-chou trying to shake down Meng Yü-lou and invests it in the Hsieh Family Tavern in Lin-ch'ing only to lose everything when Ch'en Ching-chi sues him with the backing of Chou Hsiu and takes over ownership of the tavern.

Yang Kuang-yen's father. See Yang Pu-lai.

Yang Kuang-yen's mother, née Pai.

Yang Kuang-yen's page boy.

Yang Kuang-yen's wife. See Died-of-fright, Miss.

Yang, Poor-parent. See Yang Pu-lai.

Yang, Prefect. See Yang Shih.

Yang Pu-lai, Poor-parent Yang, father of Yang Kuang-yen and Yang Erh-feng, brother-in-law of Yao the Second.

Yang Sheng, factotum on the domestic staff of Yang Chien.

Yang Shih (1053–1135), Prefect Yang, prefect of K'ai-feng, protégé of Ts'ai Ching, agrees under pressure from Ts'ai Ching and Yang Chien to treat Hua Tzu-hsü leniently when he is sued over the division of Eunuch Director Hua's property by his brothers Hua Tzu-yu, Hua Tzu-kuang, and Hua Tzu-hua.

Yang T'ing-p'ei, battalion commander rewarded for his part in facilitating the notorious Flower and Rock Convoys and the construction of the Mount Ken Imperial Park.

Yang Tsung-hsi, deceased first husband of Meng Yü-lou, elder brother of Yang Tsung-pao, nephew on his father's side of Aunt Yang and on his mother's side of Chang Lung, textile merchant residing on Stinkwater Lane outside the South Gate of Ch'ing-ho.

Yang Tsung-hsi's maternal uncle. See Chang Lung.

Yang Tsung-hsi's mother. See Chang Lung's elder sister.

Yang Tsung-hsi's paternal aunt. See Yang, Aunt.

Yang Tsung-pao, younger brother of Yang Tsung-hsi, nephew on his father's side of Aunt Yang and on his mother's side of Chang Lung, brother-in-law of Meng Yü-lou.

Yang Wei-chung (1067–1132), commander-general of the Shansi region who leads the forces of Tse-lu against the Chin invaders.

Yao family from outside the Eastern Capital, poor family into which Sun Hsüeh-o is reincarnated as a daughter.

Yao the Second, brother-in-law of Yang Pu-lai, neighbor of Wu Chih to whom Wu Sung entrusts his orphaned niece Ying-erh when he is condemned to military exile in Meng-chou; gives Ying-erh back to Wu Sung when he returns to Ch'ing-ho five years later only to repossess her after the inquest on

P'an Chin-lien's murder when Wu Sung once more becomes a fugitive; later arranges for her marriage.

Yeh the Ascetic, one-eyed illiterate Buddhist ascetic employed as a cook by Abbot Hsiao-yüeh of the Water Moon Monastery outside the South Gate of Ch'ing-ho, physiognomizes Ch'en Ching-chi when he is reduced to penury and working nearby as a day laborer.

Yeh Ch'ien, prefect of Lai-chou in Shantung.

Yeh the Fifth, wife of Pen Ti-ch'uan, mother of Pen Chang-chieh, originally a wet nurse who elopes with her fellow employee Pen Ti-ch'uan, carries on an intermittent affair with Tai-an while at the same time complaisantly accepting the sexual favors of Hsi-men Ch'ing.

Yen the Fourth, neighbor of Han Tao-kuo who informs him of Hsi-men Ch'ing's death when their boats pass each other on the Grand Canal at Lin-ch'ing.

Yen P'o-hsi, singing girl slain by Sung Chiang.

Yen Shun, Brocade Tiger, outlaw chieftan of the Ch'ing-feng Stronghold on Ch'ing-feng Mountain who is persuaded by Sung Chiang to let the captured Wu Yüeh-niang go rather than allowing Wang Ying to make her his wife.

Yin Chih, Good Deed, chief clerk in charge of the files in the Ch'ing-ho office of the Provincial Surveillance Commission who recognizes that Lai-wang has been framed by Hsi-men Ch'ing and manages to get his sentence reduced and to have him treated more leniently.

Yin Ching, vice-minister of the Ministry of Personnel.

Yin Ta-liang, regional investigating censor of Liang-che, rewarded for his part in facilitating the notorious Flower and Rock Convoys and the construction of the Mount Ken Imperial Park.

Yin T'ien-hsi, Year Star Yin, younger brother of Kao Lien's wife, née Yin, dissolute wastrel who takes advantage of his official connections to lord it over the Mount T'ai area with a gang of followers at his disposal, colludes with Shih Po-ts'ai, the corrupt head priest of the Temple of the Goddess of Iridescent Clouds on the summit of Mount T'ai, in attempting to rape Wu Yüeh-niang when she visits the temple on a pilgrimage after the death of Hsi-men Ch'ing; later killed at Sung Chiang's behest by the outlaw, Li K'uei.

Yin, Year Star. See Yin T'ien-hsi.

Ying, Beggar. See Ying Po-chüeh.

Ying-ch'un, disciple of Abbot Wu Tsung-che of the Temple of the Jade Emperor outside the East Gate of Ch'ing-ho.

Ying-ch'un, senior maidservant of Li P'ing-erh who after the death of Hsi-men Ch'ing agrees to be sent to the household of Chai Ch'ien in the Eastern Capital and is raped by Lai-pao on the way.

Ying the Elder, eldest son of the deceased silk merchant Master Ying, elder brother of Ying Po-chüeh, continues to operate his father's silk business in Ch'ing-ho.

Ying the Elder's wife.

Ying-erh, daughter of Wu Chih by his deceased first wife, niece of Wu Sung, much abused stepdaughter of P'an Chin-lien who turns her over to Dame Wang when she marries Hsi-men Ch'ing; repossessed by Wu Sung when he returns from the Eastern Capital after the death of her father; consigned to the care of his neighbor Yao the Second when he is condemned to military exile in Meng-chou after his first abortive attempt to avenge the murder of her father; taken back by Wu Sung on his return to Ch'ing-ho five years later and forced to witness his disembowelment of P'an Chin-lien and decapitation of Dame Wang; repossessed by Yao the Second after the inquest and provided by him with a husband.

Ying, Master, father of Ying the Elder and Ying Po-chüeh, deceased silk merchant of Ch'ing-ho.

Ying Pao, eldest son of Ying Po-chüeh, recommends his friend Lai-yu to Hsi-men Ch'ing who employs him as a servant and changes his name to Lai-chüeh.

Ying Po-chüeh, Ying the Second, Sponger Ying, Beggar Ying, son of the deceased silk merchant Master Ying, younger brother of Ying the Elder, father of Ying Pao and two daughters by his wife, née Tu, and a younger son by his concubine Ch'un-hua; having squandered his patrimony and fallen on hard times he has been reduced to squiring wealthy young rakes about the licensed quarters and living by his wits; boon companion and favorite crony of Hsi-men Ch'ing, member of the brotherhood of ten; a clever and amusing sycophant and opportunist he has the art to openly impose on Hsi-men Ch'ing and make him like it while he is alive and the gall to double-cross him without compunction as soon as he is dead.

Ying Po-chüeh's concubine. See Ch'un-hua.

Ying Po-chüeh's elder daughter, married with the financial assistance of Hsi-men Ch'ing.

Ying Po-chüeh's grandfather, friend of Licentiate Shui's grandfather.

Ying Po-chüeh's second daughter, after the death of her father she is proposed by Auntie Hsüeh as a match for Ch'en Ching-chi but turned down by P'ang Ch'un-mei for lack of a dowry.

Ying Po-chüeh's son by his concubine Ch'un-hua.

Ying Po-chüeh's wife, née Tu, mother of Ying Pao and two daughters.

Ying the Second. See Ying Po-chüeh.

Ying, Sponger. See Ying Po-chüeh.

Yu, Loafer. See Yu Shou.

Yu Shou, Loafer Yu, a dissolute young scamp upon whom Hsi-men Ch'ing turns the tables by abusing the judicial system.

Yung-ting, page boy in the household of Wang Ts'ai.

Yü, Big Sister, blind professional singer in Ch'ing-ho frequently invited into Hsi-men Ch'ing's household to entertain his womenfolk and their guests.

Yü Ch'un, Stupid Yü, one of the "cribbers" in the licensed quarter of Ch'ing-ho who plays the tout to Wang Ts'ai on his visits to the licensed quarter and upon whom Hsi-men Ch'ing turns the tables by abusing the judicial system at the behest of Lady Lin.

Yü-erh. See Sun Hsüeh-o.

Yü-hsiao, Jade Flute, senior maidservant of Wu Yüeh-niang, carries on an affair with Shu-t'ung the discovery of which by P'an Chin-lien leads him to abscond and return to his native Su-chou; after the death of Hsi-men Ch'ing agrees to be sent to the household of Chai Ch'ien in the Eastern Capital and is raped by Lai-pao on the way.

Yü, Licentiate, master of a girls' school in his home in Ch'ing-ho where P'an Chin-lien studies for three years as a child.

Yü-lou. See Meng Yü-lou.

Yü Shen (d. 1132), minister of war who suppresses Tseng Hsiao-hsü's memorial impeaching Hsia Yen-ling and Hsi-men Ch'ing for malfeasance in the case of Miao Ch'ing, rewarded with the title grand guardian of the heir apparent for his part in facilitating the notorious Flower and Rock Convoys and the construction of the Mount Ken Imperial Park.

Yü, Stupid. See Yü Ch'un.

Yü-t'ang, employed in Chou Hsiu's household as a wet nurse for Chou Chin-ko.

Yü-tsan, concubine of Li Kung-pi, originally maidservant of his deceased first wife, who enters his household as part of her dowry, reacts jealously to his marriage with Meng Yü-lou and is beaten by him and sold out of the household.

Yü-wen, Censor. See Yü-wen Hsü-chung.

Yü-wen Hsü-chung (1079–1146), Censor Yü-wen, supervising secretary of the Office of Scrutiny for War who submits a memorial to the throne impeaching Ts'ai Ching, Wang Fu, and Yang Chien.

Yüan, Commander, resident of Potter's Alley in the Eastern Capital into whose family Li P'ing-erh is reincarnated as a daughter.

Yüan-hsiao, senior maidservant of Li Chiao-erh who is transferred to the service of Hsi-men Ta-chieh at the request of Ch'en Ching-chi after her former mistress leaves the household, accompanies her new mistress through her many vicissitudes while also putting up with the capricious treatment of Ch'en Ching-chi in whose service she dies after he is reduced to penury.

Yüan Yen, professional actor from Su-chou who specializes in playing subsidiary female roles.

Yüeh Ho-an, vice-magistrate of Ch'ing-ho.

Yüeh-kuei, concubine of Chou Hsiu much abused by P'ang Ch'un-mei.

Yüeh-niang. See Wu Yüeh-niang.

Yüeh the Third, next door neighbor of Han Tao-kuo on Lion Street who fences Miao Ch'ing's stolen goods and suggests that he approach Hsi-men Ch'ing through Wang Liu-erh to get him off the hook for the murder of Miao T'ien-hsiu.

Yüeh the Third's wife, close friend of Wang Liu-erh who acts as an intermediary in Miao Ch'ing's approach to Hsi-men Ch'ing.

Yün, Assistant Regional Commander, elder brother of Yün Li-shou, hereditary military officer who dies at his post on the frontier.

Yün-ko. See Ch'iao Yün-ko.

Yün Li-shou, Welsher Yün, Yün the Second, younger brother of Assistant Regional Commander Yün, crony of Hsi-men Ch'ing, member of the brotherhood of ten, manager employed by Hsi-men Ch'ing in various of his enterprises, upon the death of his elder brother succeeds to his rank and the substantive post of vice commander of the Ch'ing-ho Left Guard, later appointed stockade commander of Ling-pi Stockade at Chi-nan where Wu Yüeh-niang seeks refuge with him from the invading Chin armies but dreams that he attempts to rape her.

Yün Li-shou's daughter, betrothed while still a babe in arms to Hsi-men Hsiao-ko.

Yün Li-shou's wife, née Su, proposes a marriage alliance to Wu Yüeh-niang while they are both pregnant and formally betroths her daughter to Hsi-men Hsiao-ko after the death of Hsi-men Ch'ing.

Yün, Little. See Ch'iao Yün-ko.

Yün, Prince of. See Chao K'ai.

Yün the Second. See Yün Li-shou.

Yün, Welsher. See Yün Li-shou.

THE PLUM IN THE GOLDEN VASE

Chapter 61

HAN TAO-KUO PREPARES AN ENTERTAINMENT

FOR HSI-MEN CH'ING;

LI P'ING-ERH PAINFULLY OBSERVES

THE DOUBLE YANG FESTIVAL

Last year on the Double Yang Festival
   my sorrow knew no limit;
When the memory arises in my mind I am
   ever more brokenhearted.
The autumn colors and the setting sun
   are both pallid and wan;
My tear-traces and my lonely thoughts
   are equally desolating.
The migrating geese fly in formation
   but bear me no letter;
The yellow chrysanthemums lack feeling
   but are still fragrant.
I am all too aware that recently I have
   become quite emaciated;
And often gaze into the phoenix mirror
   to examine my features.[1]

THE STORY GOES that one day in the evening, when Han Tao-kuo's job in the silk goods store was over, he went home and slept until the middle of the night, when his wife, Wang Liu-erh, opened a discussion with him.

"You and I have been patronized by him," she said. "And, on this occasion, we have made so much money out of it. Don't you think we should throw a party and invite him over for a visit? Not to mention the fact that he has just lost a child, and we ought to help him recover from his depression; it will hardly cost us a great deal to entertain him for half a day. Not only will it put us on a better footing with him, but our young employee, who will probably be headed south any day now, will observe that we are on more intimate terms with our employer than anyone else."

"I've been thinking along the same lines," said Han Tao-kuo. "Tomorrow is the fifth, which is an unlucky day.[2] But on the sixth we can hire a cook to prepare a feast, and engage the services of two singing girls. If we write out a formal invitation, I can go to his residence to deliver it in person, and invite His Honor to come for a visit and let us help him dispel his melancholy. In the evening I'll go to spend the night in the shop."

"What's the point of engaging any singing girls for no good reason?" said Wang Liu-erh. I'm afraid, after he's had something to drink, he may want to come into this room here for a visit, and they'll be in the way. There's a girl named Second Sister Shen who frequents the house of Yüeh the Third next door. She's a young woman, dresses stylishly, and can sing the songs that are popular these days. We ought to arrange for her to come sing for us. Then, in the evening, when the drinking is over, if His Honor comes back into this room, I can simply send her next door."

"That's a good suggestion," said Han Tao-kuo.

Of the events of that evening there is no more to tell.

The next day, Han Tao-kuo went to the shop, where he asked Licentiate Wen Pi-ku to write out an invitation for him, and then went across the street to see Hsi-men Ch'ing.

After greeting him with a bow, he said, "If Your Honor doesn't have any other engagements tomorrow, we've prepared a cup of watery wine at our place and would like to invite Your Honor, if you have nothing else to do, to deign to visit with us for a while in the hope of dissipating your melancholy."

He then handed the invitation to him.

When Hsi-men Ch'ing had read it, he said, "Why should you have put yourself to so much trouble? It happens that I have no other engagements tomorrow, so, after I come back from the yamen, I'll come to your place."

Han Tao-kuo took leave of him and went out the gate and over to the shop, where he carried on his business as usual.

The next morning, he took out some silver, gave it to his young employee, Hu Hsiu, and told him to take a basket and go out onto the street to buy some chicken feet, goose and duck, fresh fish, and other comestibles appropriate for a drinking party; and engaged a cook to take care of preparing the food in his home. He also sent a page boy ahead of time to hire a sedan chair and go to fetch Second Sister Shen. Wang Liu-erh, for her part, along with her maidservants, prepared a supply of:

Fine tea and fine water,

swept out the parlor, dusted the chairs and tables, and awaited Hsi-men Ch'ing's arrival.

She waited until the afternoon, when Ch'in-t'ung came to deliver a jug of grape wine. Only after that did Hsi-men Ch'ing show up, riding in an open sedan chair, accompanied by Tai-an and Wang Ching. When he arrived at the door and alighted from his sedan chair, he was wearing a "loyal and tranquil hat"[3] on his head, a long gown of jet moiré, and white-soled boots.

Han Tao-kuo ushered him into the parlor and, after exchanging the customary amenities, said, "We are most grateful to Your Honor for the wine you have bestowed upon us."

At the upper end of the room there was placed a single folding chair, upon which Hsi-men Ch'ing took his seat.

Before long, Wang Liu-erh came out, dressed in formal attire. On her head she wore a fret of silver filigree and a kingfisher blue crepe headband with purfled gold-spangled edging, held in place all around with gold-encrusted cricket-shaped stickpins. She was wearing a white blouse of Hang-chou chiffon that opened down the middle, with a vest of jade-colored moiré, over a gosling-yellow drawnwork skirt. On her feet she wore shoes of raven-black iridescent silk with high heels and gold-spangled toes. From her ears dangled a pair of clove-shaped pendant earrings. It was evident that she had taken pains to adorn herself as elegantly as possible.

Just as though inserting a taper in its holder,
she kowtowed to Hsi-men Ch'ing four times and then went back to the rear of the house to see to the tea.

Before long, Wang Ching came out carrying two teacups in raised saucers of red lacquer with gold tracery, containing tea steeped with osmanthus and cured green soybeans, further enhanced with eight precious ingredients. Han Tao-kuo first took one of the cups and, raising it up respectfully, presented it to Hsi-men Ch'ing, after which he took the other cup for himself and sat down to one side in order to keep him company. When they had finished drinking it, Wang Ching came in and took away the teacups.

Han Tao-kuo then initiated the conversation by saying, "Thanks to Your Honor's patronage:
My obligations to you are so great,
they cannot be described. I have been away from home for some time, during which you have favored my insignificant wife with your attentions and promoted Wang Ching to the position of a servant in your household.
My gratitude for your kindness is not shallow.[4]
Today, in consultation with my wife, although we have nothing adequate to express our filial respect, we have prepared a cup of watery wine and invited Your Honor for a visit. The other day, when our little brother passed away, although I was able to be there, my wife, because she was suffering from a cold, was unable to come to your residence to offer her condolences and feared that you might be annoyed with us. Today we have invited you over in the hope that we may be able to help dispel your grief, on the one hand, and that you may forgive our negligence, on the other."

"It doesn't amount to anything," said Hsi-men Ch'ing. "I fear I've put the two of you to a lot of trouble."

As he spoke, what should he see but Wang Liu-erh, who sat down on a low stool by his side and, turning to Han Tao-kuo, said, "Have you mentioned it to His Honor, or not?"

"No, I haven't mentioned it to him yet," said Han Tao-kuo.

"What is it?" asked Hsi-men Ch'ing.

"He thought that today we should engage the services of two girls from the licensed quarter to entertain Your Honor," she explained. "But we were afraid that Your Honor might not find them satisfactory, so we didn't venture to do so. However, there is a girl surnamed Shen, who goes by the name Second Sister Shen, who frequents the house of Yüeh the Third next door. Her repertory includes every kind of currently popular song, both long and short, and she can even perform *shu-lo*, or recitatives.[5] When I visited your residence on a former occasion, I had a chance to hear that performer named Big Sister Yü, but her singing was only mediocre, not as good as that of Second Sister Shen. For that reason, I've invited her to come sing for Your Honor today, but I don't know what you may think of the idea. If she meets with your approval, you can engage her to come to your residence and entertain your womenfolk. She is constantly busy performing at various houses, so if you wish to engage her services, you should do so several days in advance, and she will not presume to let you down."

"Since you've engaged the girl, that's fine," said Hsi-men Ch'ing. "Ask her to come out, so I can have a look at her."

At this juncture, Han Tao-kuo said to Tai-an, "Why don't you go over and help His Honor off with his formal clothes."

Meanwhile, a table was set up for their repast, and Hu Hsiu brought in the appetizers to go with their wine, which consisted of preserved duck, dried shrimp, seafood, spareribs, and the like.

Thereupon, Wang Liu-erh, who had opened the wine and heated it, stood to one side with flagon in hand, while Han Tao-kuo first proffered a cup to Hsi-men Ch'ing and then sat down to preside over the feast. Only after this was Second Sister Shen summoned into their presence.

Hsi-men Ch'ing opened his eyes wide and took a good look at her.

> Her cloudy locks were enclosed in a lofty chignon,[6]
> Held in place with a modest selection of ornaments,
> And an inconspicuous display of combs and hairpins.
> Underneath her green blouse and crimson skirt,
> Appeared the upturned points
>   of her golden lotuses;
> Atop her peach-colored cheeks and painted face,
> There were depicted a pair of
>   delicate spring peaks.
> A pair of lapis lazuli pendant earrings
>   dangled beneath her ears;

Silver teeth, as white as glutinous rice,
gleamed between her lips.

Facing in his direction:

Like a sprig of blossoms swaying in the breeze,

she kowtowed to Hsi-men Ch'ing four times.

"Please stand up," said Hsi-men Ch'ing. "May I ask how old you are at present?"

"I'm twenty years old," said Second Sister Shen.

"And how many songs are there in your repertory?" he went on to ask.

"I have committed to memory any number of songs and song suites," replied Second Sister Shen.

Hsi-men Ch'ing then directed Han Tao-kuo to provide her with a seat at their side. Second Sister Shen came forward and bowed once again before venturing to sit down.

She started out by taking up her psaltery and performing the song suite that begins with the tune "Decorous and Pretty," the first line of which is:

Just now I was enjoying myself in the
Autumn Fragrance Pavilion.[7]

When she had finished, a course of soup and rice was consumed and was replaced with another course, whereupon she went on to perform the song suite that begins with the tune "Powdery Butterflies," the first line of which is:

Five thousand rebel troops.[8]

By the time she finished, the wine had run out, and Hsi-men Ch'ing directed a servant to take away her psaltery and hand her the *p'i-p'a*, saying, "Have her sing a few current popular songs for me."

Second Sister Shen, who was only too happy to show off the fact that she was:

A practiced performer and an accomplished singer,

thereupon:

Lightly flaunted her silken sleeves,
Gently strummed the silken strings,

and:

Commencing to sing in full voice,

with her instrument tuned to a low pitch, performed a song to a medley version of the tune "Sheep on the Mountain Slope":

For some time now,
I have not met my lover face-to-face.
My innermost feelings,
Are hard to deliver, hard to transmit.
But, in my heart, I sincerely yearn for you.

On my account, you are totally preoccupied.
In our relations with each other,
We make no distinctions between us.[9]
Our promises to be as faithful as the hills and seas,
Are fixed firmly in our minds.
You are just like a reincarnation
    of Ts'ui Ying-ying,[10]
But, unfortunately, I am not in that
    temple in P'u-tung.[11]
I could not help myself after once having caught sight
    of your amorous glance.
Come!
Your jade features evoke an air of spring.
Your flowery countenance is beyond compare.
Once having heard the sound of your seductive voice,
I try to penetrate the eastern wall with my gaze,
And tire of loitering in the western bower.

To the same tune:

As for my loved one,
The two of us are totally preoccupied.
What obsesses me is that we are unable,
To exchange looks with eyes and eyebrows.
Once you departed, I have only my lonely pillow.
The pillow is cold, the coverlet remains;
Alone I confront my jasper-inlaid zither.
My sick body is like a stick of kindling;[12]
My waist has become emaciated.
I realize that it is difficult for you
    to leave your mother's side,
But this waiting only makes my heart
    feel the more inebriated.
I am all on tenterhooks as I keep company
    with this unfeeling lamp.
Come!
On hearing the sound of the wind rustling the bamboo,
I assume that my loved one has come,
And hastily step out of my study.
But it is only the gentle swaying of the flower shadows,[13]
In the moonlight that is as limpid as water.[14]

When she had finished singing these two songs to the tune "Sheep on the Mountain Slope," there was a call for something to drink, and Han Tao-kuo asked his wife to prepare some more wine.

After filling a cup to the brim and offering it to Hsi-men Ch'ing, he then
went on to say, "Second Sister Shen, you know some more good songs to the
tune 'Shrouding the Southern Branch.' Why don't you sing a couple of them
for His Honor?"

Second Sister Shen then switched modes and sang a song to the tune
"Shrouding the Southern Branch":

When we first met,
That girl of my dreams,
Was in the springtime of her youth,
   no more than twenty.
Her raven locks took shape as two black clouds;
Fragrant red defined a single daub of ruby lips.[15]
Her cheeks were like glowing peaches
   or tender bamboo shoots.
If she had been born into painted bowers
   or orchid-scented halls,[16]
She would surely have been fated
   to be a lady.
Alas, she has ended up in the licensed quarter,
Serving in a low-grade occupation.
If she were only able to marry
   out of her profession,
It would certainly be better than abandoning
   the old to welcome the new.[17]

To the same tune:

When we first met,
That captivating wench,
With her moonlike face and flowerlike countenance,[18]
   was a rare commodity in the demimonde.
The handful of her slender waist deserved a painting;
Her clever disposition was altogether inimitable.
My only regret is that I did not
   meet her sooner.
My only wish is that at the festive board,
   before the flowing cup,
We might sip wine and croon softly,[19]
   locked in each others' arms;
Each glance conveying true devotion,
Every look satisfying our hunger.
Though it should provide but half a moment
   of gratification,
It would suffice to dissipate melancholy
   and dispel sorrow.

As Hsi-men Ch'ing listened to these two songs to the tune "Shrouding the Southern Branch," he was reminded of his first visit to Cheng Ai-yüeh, and his heart was filled with delight. He was also impressed by the fact that his hosts had engaged a performer who understood music so well.

Wang Liu-erh, standing at his side, filled another cup of wine to the brim and offered it to him with an ingratiating smile, saying, "Father, enjoy the wine at your leisure. This sample of what Second Sister Shen can do is just a drop in the bucket. She knows a great many more songs than this. In the future, when you have the time, you can send a sedan chair for her, and let her entertain your womenfolk."

She then went on to say, "As for that singer that I've run into at your residence?"

"That would be Big Sister Yü," said Hsi-men Ch'ing. "She has been performing at my place for quite some years now."

"I guarantee," pronounced Wang Liu-erh, "that if Second Sister Shen were to sing at your place, she would be certain to outperform her. Father, if you wish to engage her services at some future date, let me know beforehand, and I can send a servant to pick her up with a sedan chair and deliver her to your residence."

Hsi-men Ch'ing then said, "Second Sister Shen, if I were to send someone for you on the Double Yang Festival, would you be able to come or not?"

"Your Honor," said Second Sister Shen, "how can you talk that way? You have but to call for me, and I would hardly dare to turn you down."

When Hsi-men Ch'ing saw that she had a way with words, he was utterly delighted.

Not long afterwards, while they were:
Exchanging cups as they drank,
Wang Liu-erh began to feel that they were not able to express themselves freely in her presence, so, after having her perform several more song suites, she quietly said to Han Tao-kuo, "Get our servant Chao-ti to escort her over to Yüeh the Third's place for the night."

As she was about to go, and respectfully took her leave of Hsi-men Ch'ing, he groped a packet containing three mace of silver out of his sleeve and gave it to her with which to buy replacement strings for her instruments. Second Sister Shen hastily responded:
Like a sprig of blossoms swaying in the breeze,
by kowtowing to him in order to express her gratitude.

Hsi-men Ch'ing reminded her of their agreement, saying, "On the eighth, I'll send someone to fetch you."

"Father," said Wang Liu-erh, "just send Wang Ching to speak to me about it, and I'll send my servant after her."

Second Sister Shen then bade farewell to Han Tao-kuo and his wife and, with Chao-ti escorting her, went next door. When Han Tao-kuo had seen

Second Sister Shen on her way, and informed his wife of the fact, he went off himself to spend the night at the shop, leaving his wife to keep Hsi-men Ch'ing company.

When they had played dice and continued drinking for a while, they began to hunger after each other. Hsi-men Ch'ing, on the pretext of the need to relieve himself, went into the woman's bedroom, where the two of them proceeded to lock the door and enjoy themselves. Wang Ching, thereupon, took the lamps and candles out to the side room in the front courtyard, where he fell to drinking with Tai-an and Ch'in-t'ung.

Meanwhile, at some point in the evening, the young man, Hu Hsiu, had gone back to the kitchen and stolen a few cups too many of wine. After the hired cook had been dismissed, he went into the anteroom for the display of Buddhist effigies and ancestral tablets that was adjacent to Wang Liu-erh's bedroom, put a mat down on the floor, and went to sleep. After sleeping there for a while, he got back to his feet.

It so happened that there was only a board partition between the room where he was and the bedroom next door. All of a sudden, he heard the woman in the other room making a commotion. Hu Hsiu noticed that there was lamplight visible through a crack in the partition and assumed that Hsi-men Ch'ing had left, and that Han Tao-kuo was in the bedroom sleeping with his wife. Surreptitiously extracting a hairpin from his head, he used it to poke a hole in the paper that had been pasted over the crack and proceeded to peek through it. He saw that the other room was brightly lit with lamps and candles, and that, unexpectedly, it was Hsi-men Ch'ing who was there with the woman, and that they were just in the thick of things.

Clearly and distinctly,[20]
he could see that the woman's two legs were suspended by her foot bindings from the top of the bed, and that Hsi-men Ch'ing was wearing only a satin jacket on the upper part of his body, while the lower part was completely exposed. The two of them were busy on the edge of the bed, where:

One comes, the other goes;
One moves, the other rests.[21]
As he slammed away at her:
The reiterated sounds reverberated loudly.
Everything conceivable in the way of:
Obscene noises and lascivious words,[22]
issued from her mouth as the two of them struggled to make themselves one.

After a while, he heard the woman say, "My own daddy! If you want to burn moxa on this whore of yours, you can burn me wherever you like. This whore of yours would not presume to stop you. After all, the body of this whore of yours is yours to command. What is there to worry about?"

"My only fear is that your husband might object," said Hsi-men Ch'ing.

"That cuckold!" the woman said. "How could he muster the:

Seven heads and eight galls,

to object to anything you did? Who does he depend on for his livelihood, after all?"

"Since you're so irrevocably committed to me," said Hsi-men Ch'ing, "after I've made enough silver off the existing consignment of goods, I'll send him, along with Lai-pao, for a long sojourn in the south, where he can set up an office and act as my purchasing agent. I've got Manager Kan Jun here at home to take care of sales, so all I lack is a buyer to take charge of acquiring the merchandise at that end."

"After he's come back from this second trip of his," said the woman, "send him off again by all means. What's the point of keeping him idle at home? He says himself that he's habituated to being away from home and would be happy to go on the road. He's been acquainted with life on the rivers and lakes since his childhood, and there's little he doesn't know about business and merchandising. If you choose to patronize him, that would be just fine. And when he returns, I'll find another bedmate for him. I don't need him anymore now that I've committed myself completely to you. You can stick him any-where you want as far as I'm concerned. If anything I say is false, may the worthless body of this whore of yours rot completely away!"

"My child," responded Hsi-men Ch'ing, "there's no need for you to swear oaths like that."

Who would have thought that every last thing that occurred between the two of them was so clearly overheard by Hu Hsiu that he might well have ejaculated:

"Is it not delightful?"

Earlier that evening, while Han Tao-kuo was still at home, he had been un-able to find Hu Hsiu and assumed that he had gone to the shop to sleep. When he arrived at the silk goods store and asked about it, the young employ-ees, Wang Hsien and Jung Hai, said that he had not come there. Han Tao-kuo, thereupon, returned home, called for someone to open the door, and looked everywhere for Hu Hsiu, without finding him, though he noticed that Wang Ching was drinking with Tai-an and Ch'in-t'ung in the front courtyard. When Hu Hsiu, recognizing his voice, realized that he had come home, he hastily lay down again on the mat and pretended to be asleep. In due course, Han Tao-kuo, having lit a lamp and made his way into the Buddhist chapel, found Hu Hsiu lying on the floor, where he was snoring loudly through his nostrils.

Kicking him awake with his foot, he cursed him, saying, "You lousy wild dog of a condemned jailbird! Why aren't you up and about? I assumed that you had already gone to the shop to sleep, but it turns out that you were here all the time, happily sacked out. Get up, and come along with me."

Hu Hsiu, thereupon, got to his feet, made a show of rubbing his eyes, and pretended to be stupefied with drink as he followed Han Tao-kuo back to the shop.

Meanwhile, Hsi-men Ch'ing's bout with the woman continued for nearly two hours before coming to a conclusion. In the process, he burnt moxa on the middle of Wang Liu-erh's chest, the top of her mons veneris, and her tailbone, three places in all.[23] The woman finally got up, put on her clothes, called for a maidservant to dish up some water, and washed her hands. Thereupon:

More warmed wine was served, and
Further dainties were provided,

as they continued to engage each other in flirtatious conversation.

Only after drinking a few more cups of wine did Hsi-men Ch'ing mount his horse and set off for home, attended by Tai-an, Wang Ching, and Ch'in-t'ung. By the time they arrived, it was already the second watch of the night, and Hsi-men Ch'ing went into Li P'ing-erh's quarters.

Li P'ing-erh was lying in her bed, and when she saw how drunk he was when he came in, she asked him, "Whose place have you been drinking at today?"

Hsi-men Ch'ing explained at length how, "Han Tao-kuo and his wife invited me to their place out of a desire to help dispel my depression over the loss of our child. With this end in view, they engaged the services of a professional female singer named Second Sister Shen, who's still a young woman, and really knows how to sing. In fact, she's better than Big Sister Yü. Tomorrow, on the eve of the Double Yang Festival, I'm going to send a servant with a sedan chair to bring her here so she can sing for all of you for a day or two, and help relieve your depression. Even though you may remain heartsick about it, you oughtn't to let it preoccupy your attention to such an extent."

When he had finished speaking, he wanted to call for Ying-ch'un to help him off with his clothes so he could sleep with Li P'ing-erh, but she said, "Don't you suggest any such thing. I am hemorrhaging all the time down below, and my maidservant is engaged in preparing my medicine over the fire. You go and spend the night in someone else's room. Haven't you noticed what a fine state I'm in all day long? I've hardly got a breath of life left in me, and you still want to pester me this way."

"My darling," said Hsi-men Ch'ing. "I can't do without you. What would you have me do?"

Li P'ing-erh gave him a sidelong glance and laughed, saying, "Who would believe that:

Specious mouth and throwaway tongue,

of yours? Do you expect me to believe that when I die in the near future, you won't be able to do without me?"

"In any case," she went on to say, "you can wait until I'm feeling better before coming to spend the night with me. It won't be any too late then."

After sitting with her a while longer, Hsi-men Ch'ing said, "That's enough of that! Since you don't want me to stay here, I'll go over and spend the night with P'an the Sixth."

Hsi-men Ch'ing While Drunk Burns Moxa on a Mons Veneris

"That's right," said Li P'ing-erh, "you go ahead and do that! It will spare you the need to sacrifice your desires. After all, she's burning up waiting for you over there, like:

A fire within a fire.[24]

Why should you neglect her by insisting upon barging into my place to pester me?"

"If that's the way you're going to talk about it," said Hsi-men Ch'ing, "I won't go."

"I was only kidding," said Li P'ing-erh with a smile. "You go ahead and go."

With that, she succeeded in sending Hsi-men Ch'ing on his way.

Li P'ing-erh then got up and sat on the edge of the bed, while Ying-ch'un helped her to take her medicine. As she took up the medicine, she couldn't prevent a cascade of tears from pouring, with a gush, over her fragrant cheeks, and she gave vent to a long sigh before downing the cup of medicine. Truly:

The unlimited tribulations that produced

the sorrow in her heart,[25]

Were all turned over to the yellow oriole

to express in its cries.

We will say no more, at present, about how Li P'ing-erh took her medicine and lay down to sleep, but return to the story of Hsi-men Ch'ing. When he arrived at the quarters of P'an Chin-lien, she had just told Ch'un-mei to cover the lamp and had gotten into bed to go to sleep.

Unexpectedly, Hsi-men Ch'ing pushed open the door and came in, saying, "My child, I see you've already gone to bed."

"Well, what a surprise!" exclaimed Chin-lien. "What wind has blown you into this room of mine?"

"And whose place have you been drinking at today?" she went on to ask.

"Manager Han Tao-kuo," Hsi-men Ch'ing said, "upon coming back from his trip to the South, and seeing that I had lost my child, on the one hand, in order to help relieve my depression, and, on the other hand, to express his gratitude for my patronage in sending him on this expedition, invited me over to his place for a visit."

"While he was abroad," remarked Chin-lien, "you certainly took advantage of the opportunity to patronize his wife."

"You're talking about the household of my own manager," protested Hsi-men Ch'ing. "How could there be any such thing?"

"Where the household of an employee is concerned," pronounced Chin-lien, "there could well be just such a thing. I suppose you've kept a cord wrapped around your waist, lest you might be tempted to violate that boundary! You think you can be up to your tricks, while keeping me in the dark, do you? I know all about it, and I'm fed up with you, to boot. During the celebration of your birthday, that lousy whore showed up here, didn't she? You had sur-reptitiously slipped her one of Li P'ing-erh's pins in the shape of the character for long life.

You may be a brown cat, but you've got a black tail.

By so doing, you enabled her to wear it here in order to show off where she stood. The First Lady, Meng the Third, and the whole household all noticed it. And when I interrogated her about it, her face turned crimson. Didn't she tell you about it? So today you found your way over there again, did you? Lousy, shameless, good-for-nothing that you are! The painted faces available to you in your own household aren't enough for you, are they? Instead, who knows why, you're taken by that overgrown pumpkin head of a long-faced whore. What with her:

Phony eyebrows and bogus airs,[26]

her temples adorned with long spit curls, the garish red color with which she daubs her lips, so her mouth looks like nothing so much as a bloody cunt, she's a fine woman indeed, nothing but a lanky, rosewood-complexioned, swarthy whore! I can't imagine what you see in her. No wonder you've taken that cuckold's brother-in-law, Wang Ching, under your wing, so you can use him to carry messages back and forth between you, early or late."

Hsi-men Ch'ing adamantly refused to acknowledge anything, but simply laughed, saying, "You crazy little slave! All you do is talk nonsense. How could any such thing have occurred? Today it was her husband who entertained me. She didn't even put in an appearance."

"You think you can fool me with that sort of talk, do you?" the woman said. "Who doesn't know that her husband is an open cuckold:

Grazing sheep on the one hand, while

Gathering kindling on the other?

He's simply turning his wife over to you as a means of getting a hand on your business and making money for himself out of it. You simpleminded good-for-nothing! You might just as well be:

Listening for the report of a blunderbuss

being fired forty li away."

Upon noticing that Hsi-men Ch'ing had taken off his outer clothes and was sitting on the edge of the bed, the woman stuck her hand out, pulled open his trousers, and groped out his organ, which was limp and flaccid, and still had a clasp fastened around it.

"There you go again," she said. "You're just like:

A preserved duck that's been put into

the pot to stew:

Its body has turned soft, but its beak

is as hard as ever.

The mute testimony is there for all to see.[27]

You ruffian! You've been fooling around with that whore all day before coming home, so that your organ is:

> As soft as driveling snot and thick as gravy,

yet you remain as hard-mouthed as ever. You can swear all you like. I'll get Ch'un-mei to bring a bottle of cold water, and if you dare drink it, I'll acknowledge that you've got guts. If you stop to consider it:

> This salt is just as salty;
> This vinegar just as sour.
> When a bald man puts a hairnet on his head;
> There's no need to brush it any further.

Enough is enough! If one were to believe what you say, you could seduce every woman in the world and get away with it. What a lousy shameless article you are! You're just a big good-for-nothing with too much fire in your eyes. It's a good thing you're a man. If you were a woman, you'd be:

> Laid by every man in the street, and
> Fucked by every guy in the alley.[28]
> You're in the same class as an itinerant shoemaker;
> Wherever two hides meet you'll cobble them together."[29]

These few lines of invective reduced Hsi-men Ch'ing to staring with wide-open eyes, as he made his way onto the bed. He then told Ch'un-mei to heat some distilled spirits for him, took a pill out of his cylindrical gold pillbox, put it in his mouth, and swallowed it.

Lying face up on the pillow, he then said to the woman, "My child, get down on your knees and suck your daddy off. If you can get it to stand up, it will be your good fortune."

The woman made a show of distaste, saying, "That filthy thing! You've been boring into that whore's hole with it, and now you want me to suck it off for you. That really shows how much you care for me!"

"You crazy little whore!" said Hsi-men Ch'ing. "All you ever do is talk nonsense. I never did any such thing."

"If you never did any such thing," the woman said, "you'll have to swear an oath on that fleshy body of yours before you can get me to believe it."

After bantering back and forth for a while, she tried to get Hsi-men Ch'ing to get out of bed and wash himself off with water, but he refused to get out of bed. The woman then pulled a figured handkerchief out of her sleeve and proceeded to wipe his organ off with it before engulfing it with her ruby lips and sucking it audibly for some time. In no time at all, she had manipulated it until:

> Its protuberances swelled and its head sprang up,

as it became engorged with rage.

He then positioned himself astride the woman's body and allowed his jade chowrie handle to penetrate her vagina from the rear, while he lifted up her thighs with his two hands, assumed a squatting position, and went to work. As he gave himself over to slamming away at her:

> The reiterated sounds reverberated loudly;
> In the light cast by the lamp,[30]

He savored the sight as it went in and out.

The woman knelt by the pillow side and raised her hips in response to his movements for some time. Hsi-men Ch'ing's ardor was still unslaked, so he had the woman turn over and face upwards, while he applied some of the pink aphrodisiac ointment to his organ, and plunged back into her. Taking her pair of feet in his hands, he arched his back and alternately submerged and exposed the knob of his glans, lifting her body into the air as he rammed away at her two or three hundred times.

The woman, finding his assault difficult to withstand, closed her eyes and cried out inarticulately in a trembling voice, "Daddy! On this occasion you'd better take it easy with me. You had no need to use that aphrodisiac."

"You little whore!" Hsi-men Ch'ing blurted out at her. "Are you afraid of me, or not? Will you ever dare to treat me so disrespectfully again?"

"My own daddy!" the woman cried out. "That's enough. If you'll only be a little easier on me, I'll never dare offend you again. Daddy, slow down a bit. You're mussing my hairdo."

The two of them:

> Tumbled and tossed like male and female phoenixes,

for half the night before tiring out and going to sleep.

To make a long story short, it was not long before the time came for the celebration of the Double Yang Festival.

Hsi-men Ch'ing said to Wu Yüeh-niang, "When Manager Han Tao-kuo invited me to his place the other day, we were entertained by a singer named Second Sister Shen. She is attractive and knows how to sing, as well as how to perform on both the *p'i-p'a* and the psaltery. I've sent a page boy to fetch her, and when she arrives, I propose that we keep her here for two days, so she can entertain the lot of you."

Thereupon, he ordered that the kitchen staff should prepare the appropriate wine, fruit, and other delicacies, and that in the great summerhouse in the garden, the Hall of Assembled Vistas, a large Eight Immortals table should be set up, and the bamboo blinds let down, so that the entire family could enjoy a feast there, in celebration of the Double Yang Festival.

It was not long before Wang Ching arrived, escorting Second Sister Shen in a sedan chair, and she was ushered into the rear compound, where she kowtowed to Yüeh-niang and the other ladies. Yüeh-niang saw that she was young, and good-looking, and, upon inquiry, was told that she was not able to perform too many song suites, but that when it came to the various kinds of independent songs, such as those to the tunes "Sheep on the Mountain Slope" and "Shrouding the Southern Branch," or recitatives, she could perform a fair number. After she had been provided with tea and something to eat, she sang two song suites for them in the rear compound, after which they adjourned to the garden, where the feast had been prepared.

That day, Hsi-men Ch'ing did not go to the yamen but stayed at home in order to supervise the planting of chrysanthemums. Wu Yüeh-niang, Li Chiao-erh, Meng Yü-lou, P'an Chin-lien, and Sun Hsüeh-o, as well as Hsi-men Ta-chieh, were all invited to take their places at the table, while Ch'un-mei, Yü-hsiao, Ying-ch'un, and Lan-hsiang stood in attendance at their side to serve the wine. Second Sister Shen also stood by with her *p'i-p'a* to entertain them. Li P'ing-erh was in her quarters, feeling poorly in her present condition, and had to be asked repeatedly before she made a belated appearance, looking for all the world like a tree that had been felled by the wind. It cost her a considerable effort to pull herself together sufficiently to come out and sit down by Hsi-men Ch'ing. Everyone urged her to drink, but she hardly drank anything at all.

Hsi-men Ch'ing and Yüeh-niang, noticing that:

> Her face exhibited a worried hue, and
> Her eyebrows remained contracted,[31]

said to her, "Sister Li, see if you can't relax. We'll have Second Sister Shen sing a song for you."

"Tell her what song you'd like to hear," said Meng Yü-lou, "so she can sing it for you."

But Li P'ing-erh remained adamantly silent.

As they were drinking, Wang Ching suddenly came in, and said, "Master Ying the Second and Uncle Ch'ang the Second have come."

"Invite Ying the Second and Ch'ang the Second to have a seat in the small summerhouse," said Hsi-men Ch'ing. "I'll be there directly."

"Uncle Ch'ang the Second has had a porter deliver two gift boxes, which are sitting outside," reported Wang Ching.

Hsi-men Ch'ing turned to Yüeh-niang and said, "These presents must be intended to express his gratitude for my help in closing the deal on that new house of his."

"We'll have to prepare something for their entertainment," said Yüeh-niang. "We can't let them go without an appropriate response. You go keep them company, while I arrange here to have some refreshments prepared for them."

Before leaving, Hsi-men Ch'ing said to Second Sister Shen, "Whatever you do, see that you sing a good song for the benefit of the Sixth Lady."

He then went straight out toward the front compound.

"I've never seen anything like it," Chin-lien said to Li P'ing-erh. "Why don't you simply mention any song you like so Second Sister Shen can sing it for you? You're disregarding Father's intentions. He invited her here on your account, and you won't even say what you'd like to hear."

At this point, Li P'ing-erh felt pressured to such an extent that she was compelled to comply and, after considering for some time, finally said, "Why don't you sing that song suite that begins with the words:

> The purple roads and red lanes,

for us."

"That's no problem," responded Second Sister Shen, "I know it."
Thereupon, picking up her psaltery, she:

> Adjusted the bridges ranged like wild geese,
> Retuned the icy strings,

and:

> Commencing to sing in full voice,

performed the song suite that begins with the tune "A Variation on A Sprig of Flowers":

> The purple roads and red lanes,
> Would be hard for even an expert painter[32]
>   to successfully depict.
> Eye-catching luxuriance is spread before me
>   like a brocade carpet.
> It is as though spring is out of tune with me;
> It is not I that am out of tune with spring.
> Simply on account of that one I've set my heart on,
> When I survey the scene it only augments my sorrow.

To the tune "Wen-chou Song":

> The blossoms lie scattered,
> The willows are umbrageous,
> The butterflies are jaded, the bees bemused,
>   and the orioles tired of singing.
> On first waking up,
> I had forgotten my longing,
> But the relentless twittering
>   of the swallows,
> Has stirred up my old resentment,
> And only served to reawaken it.
> In an endless pitter-patter,[33]
> My teardrops silently cascade.

To the tune "Spring Fills the Garden":

> The tranquil courtyard is secluded;
> Unspoken feelings entangle my heart.
> The cool pavilions and waterside retreats,[34]
> Are really suitable for feasting and drinking;

Li P'ing-erh While Ill Observes the Double Yang Festival

But I do not see my lover.
With whom is he sharing a flagon?
I could resume strumming the silken strings,
Or choose to pluck the *p'i-p'a*,
In order to dispel my melancholy;
But it seems I am tired of hearing them.[35]

To the tune "Wen-chou Song":

The pomegranate blossoms are ablaze,
Like clusters of scarlet brocade.
Their smokeless flames only succeed in
    incinerating my heart.
Bashfully, I move forward,
Thinking to pluck a blossom,
But I shilly-shally about
    wearing it,
Fearing that my flowery countenance,
Is no longer what it used to be.
When I am so lonesome and emaciated,[36]
It would not do to stick it in my hair.

To the tune "The Phoenix Tree":

The leaves of the phoenix tree are flying;
The metallic autumn wind has begun to blow.
As I gradually fall prey to lovesickness,
I feel as though I have fallen into a deep well.
Day after day, the nights grow longer,
But I find it hard to endure my lonely pillow.
Reluctantly I mount the lofty tower,[37]
In order to watch out for my lover.
It may be that the fickle fellow's heart
    is out of tune with mine.
Who knows where he may be, where he may be,
Pursuing pleasure and indulging in drink?[38]

To the tune "Wen-chou Song":

The chrysanthemums have blossomed,
The cassia flowers lie scattered.
Right now, the dew is chilly, and the wind cold,[39]
    as the autumnal feeling deepens.
Suddenly, outside the window, I hear,
The reiterated cries of a solitary wild goose,
As sorrowful and distressing[40]
    as a human lament.

I am most disturbed by the chirping of the crickets,
Under the flowers, beside the steps.
Their constant crick-crick chirp-chirp,[41]
Has utterly destroyed my peace of mind.

To the tune "Sands of Silk-washing Creek":

The wind has grown stronger,
The cold has become frigid.
When lovesick, what one dreads
    the most is dusk.
Listless and indifferent,[42] I confront
    my lonely lamp;
Repeatedly scanning the apertures
    in the window.
The sound of the bugle is prolonged,
    penetrating my ears;
Note after note is like a sob,
    difficult to hear.
In my depression, I force myself to pour
    another cup of wine,
But when it affects my melancholy bosom,
    the pearly tears cascade.

To the tune "Wen-chou Song":

Giving forth long sighs,
Two or three of them,
I lean against the standing screen,
    longing for that man.
Single-mindedly, I hope that in my dreams,
We may see each other once again.
In an endless pitter-patter, the snowflakes
    begin to fall.
The windblown chimes under the eaves,
Intrude upon my dreaming soul;
Their ding-ding dong-dong,
Shatter my peace of mind.

Coda:

On account of my loved one,
My heart is on tenterhooks.
I think of him by day and yearn for him at night,
    as my teardrops cascade.
How hateful it is that my talented lover won't
    even let me see his shadow.[43]

When the performance was finished, Wu Yüeh-niang said, "Sister Li, why don't you have a cup of this nice sweet wine?"

Li P'ing-erh, who was reluctant to refuse a request from Yüeh-niang, picked up her cup and swallowed a mouthful, before putting it back down again. She made an effort to continue sitting with the rest of the company, but, before long, she felt a surge of hot blood hemorrhaging from her lower body and had to return to her quarters. We will say no more, for the moment, about how the womenfolk entertained themselves, but return to the story of Hsi-men Ch'ing.

When he arrived at the small summerhouse, the Kingfisher Pavilion, he found that Ying Po-chüeh and Ch'ang Shih-chieh were standing beneath the Juniper Hedge admiring the chrysanthemums. It so happens that, on either side of the Juniper Hedge, there were arranged a total of twenty pots containing famous varieties of chrysanthemums, each of which was more than seven feet high. These included specimens of Great Crimson Robes, Principal Graduate Reds, Purple Robes with Gold Girdles, White Powdered Hsi-shihs,[44] Yellow Powdered Hsi-shihs, Skies Full of Stars, Drunken Yang Kuei-feis,[45] Jade Peonies, Goose Feather Chrysanthemums, Mandarin Duck Chrysanthemums, and the like.[46]

When Hsi-men Ch'ing came out, the two men stepped forward and bowed to him, after which Ch'ang Shih-chieh told the porter to bring in the two gift boxes.

Upon seeing them, Hsi-men Ch'ing asked, "What's all this?"

"Brother Ch'ang the Second," explained Ying Po-chüeh, "out of gratitude for your generosity in enabling him to close the deal on his new house, and having no other way to repay you, has asked his wife to prepare these fresh stuffed crabs, and these two smoked roast ducks, and invited me to join him in paying you a visit."

"Brother Ch'ang the Second," said Hsi-men Ch'ing, "what need was there for you to go to all this trouble? Your wife is still recuperating from her illness, and you have placed this additional burden upon her."

"That's exactly what I told him," said Ying Po-chüeh, "but he said that if he presented you with anything else, he feared you might not appreciate it."

Hsi-men Ch'ing told one of his attendants to open the boxes so they could have a look. There were forty large crabs, the shells of which had been scoured out and stuffed with crab meat, coated with a mixture of pepper, ginger, minced garlic, and starch, deep-fried in sesame oil, and flavored with soy sauce and vinegar, which rendered them fragrant and delectable. In addition, there were two oven-smoked ducks from the licensed quarter that had been roasted until they were succulent.

When Hsi-men Ch'ing had examined them, he told Ch'un-hung and Wang Ching to take them inside, and to reward the porter with fifty cash. He then expressed his thanks to Ch'ang Shih-chieh, at which point, Ch'in-t'ung lifted aside the portiere and invited them to come into the Kingfisher Pavilion and sit down.

Ying Po-chüeh could not stop lavishing praise upon the chrysanthemums and inquired, "Brother, where did you get them?"

"It was Eunuch Director Liu," said Hsi-men Ch'ing, "the manager of the Imperial Brickyard, that sent me these twenty pots of chrysanthemums."

"Including the pots?" asked Ying Po-chüeh.

"Yes, he sent everything to me, including the pots," replied Hsi-men Ch'ing.

"The flowers are nothing out of the ordinary," opined Ying Po-chüeh, "but these pots are double-banded wide-mouthed flowerpots, manufactured from the finest clay in the imperial kilns, and are both long-lasting and water-repellent. They are made from clay that has been strained through silken sieves and kneaded under foot until it becomes a thick paste, just like that used in the firing of the finest quality of bricks in Su-chou.⁴⁷ Where could one go to find articles of this quality these days?"

After Ying Po-chüeh had fulsomely praised them for a while, Hsi-men Ch'ing ordered that tea be served and, while they were drinking it, went on to ask, "When is Brother Ch'ang the Second going to move into his new house?"

"He moved in only three days after the silver was paid over," said Ying Po-chüeh. "The previous occupants had already located another place and moved out within two or three days. Yesterday being an auspicious day for such undertakings, he laid in some miscellaneous merchandise and opened his shop for business. Sister-in-law Ch'ang's younger brother is tending the store for him, and keeping track of the silver."

"We must get together soon, and purchase some congratulatory gifts," said Hsi-men Ch'ing. "We don't want too many people to be involved. We'll also invite Hsieh Hsi-ta; just the three or four of you. I'll have the refreshments prepared at my place and carried over there, so it won't cost Brother Ch'ang the Second anything at all. I'll engage the services of two singing girls so we can throw a housewarming party for him, and give ourselves over to enjoyment the whole day."

"I thought of inviting you over for a visit," said Ch'ang Shih-chieh, "but, after giving it some thought, did not presume to do so. The place is too cramped, and I feared you might feel imposed upon."

"Don't talk such rot!" said Hsi-men Ch'ing. "We don't intend to put you to any trouble. I'll send a page boy over right now to invite Hsieh Hsi-ta to join us, so we can tell him about it."

Then, turning to Ch'in-t'ung, he said, "Quickly, go and invite Master Hsieh over here."

"Brother," Ying Po-chüeh went on to ask, "which two singing girls do you plan to engage for this occasion?"

"I'll call upon Cheng Ai-yüeh and Hung the Fourth," said Hsi-men Ch'ing with a laugh. "Hung the Fourth can provide a drumbeat of accompaniment, while Cheng Ai-yüeh sings slow-tempoed songs to the tune "Sheep on the Mountain Slope."

"Brother," said Ying Po-chüeh, "what kind of a man are you, that you should have been patronizing Cheng Ai-yüeh without saying a word to me about it? How was I to know? As far as the breeze and the moonlight are concerned, how does she compare to Li Kuei-chieh?"

"Why:

'She's two under full four words'!"[48]

replied Hsi-men Ch'ing.

"Then why is it," said Ying Po-chüeh, "that, the other day, at your birthday party, she had hardly a word to say and pretended to be so demure? She's just a lousy, stiff-necked, sycophantic little whore!"

"When I go to see her again, sometime soon," said Hsi-men Ch'ing, "I'll take you along with me. Your mother, Ai-yüeh, can play a good game of backgammon, and you can play a couple of games with her."

"If I go with you," said Ying Po-chüeh, "I'll give that little whore a hard time. You mustn't spoil her."

"You perverted dog!" exclaimed Hsi-men Ch'ing. "You'd better not do anything to antagonize her."

As they were speaking, Hsieh Hsi-ta arrived, bowed to the company, and sat down.

"Brother Ch'ang the Second," explained Hsi-men Ch'ing, "thus and so, has acquired a new house for himself and has already moved in, without letting us know anything about it. Each of us ought to contribute something, whatever we can afford, so that it won't cost him anything, and I'll have some refreshments prepared at my place and carried over to his residence by a page boy, and also engage the services of two singing girls, so we can enjoy ourselves for a day. What do you think?"

"Brother," said Hsieh Hsi-ta, "just tell each of us what you think we should come up with, and we'll send it over to your place, that's all there is to it. Who else will be involved?"

"There won't be anyone else," said Hsi-men Ch'ing, "just the three or four of us. Two mace of silver apiece ought to suffice."

"If too many people are involved," explained Ying Po-chüeh, "he won't have room for us at his place."

As they were speaking, Ch'in-t'ung came in and reported, "Brother-in-law Wu K'ai has arrived."

"Tell Brother-in-law Wu to come in here and sit down," said Hsi-men Ch'ing.

Before long Wu K'ai came into the studio, where he first bowed to the other three guests, and then sat down, after exchanging the customary amenities with Hsi-men Ch'ing. A page boy provided another serving of tea, and they drank it together.

Wu K'ai then stood up and said, "May I ask my brother-in-law to accompany me back to the rear compound so I can have a word with him?"

Hsi-men Ch'ing promptly ushered Wu K'ai back to the rear compound, and into Wu Yüeh-niang's parlor. Yüeh-niang herself was still in the summerhouse drinking wine and listening to the singing with the other women of the household. When she heard a page boy say that her elder brother had come, and that her husband was chatting with him in the rear compound, she got up and went back to the master suite. Upon seeing her elder brother, she greeted him with a bow and ordered Hsiao-yü to provide a serving of tea.

Wu K'ai pulled ten taels of silver out of his sleeve and handed it to Yüehniang, saying, "Yesterday, I received only three ingots of silver from the prefectural office. If my brother-in-law will accept these ten taels of silver for the time being, I will pay back the remainder of what I owe him on another occasion."

"Brother-in-law," said Hsi-men Ch'ing, "there is no need to worry about it. Go ahead and spend it. What's the hurry?"

"I feared I might inconvenience my brother-in-law if I delayed," said Wu K'ai.

Hsi-men Ch'ing then went on to ask, "Is the repair work on the granary nearing completion?"

"It will be another month before it is done," said Wu K'ai.

"When the work is finished," said Hsi-men Ch'ing, "the office of the provincial regional inspector is sure to offer you a reward of some kind."

"This year's evaluation of military personnel is impending," said Wu K'ai. "I hope that my brother-in-law will continue to support me by speaking up on my behalf to the regional inspector."

"As far as that matter is concerned," said Hsi-men Ch'ing, "you can leave it to me."

When their conversation was over, Yüeh-niang said, "Will my elder brother not go back up front for a visit?"

"I'd better go," said Wu K'ai. "I fear those three gentlemen have some business to discuss."

"Not at all," said Hsi-men Ch'ing. "Brother Ch'ang the Second recently borrowed several taels of silver from me with which to buy a house of modest dimensions. He has already moved into it, and today he has brought some gifts to thank me for my help. In this festival season, I have asked them to stay for a visit. I didn't know that my brother-in-law would turn up, but you've arrived in the nick of time."

Thereupon, he ushered Wu K'ai back to the front compound in order to join the party, and Yüeh-niang promptly told the staff in the kitchen to send the refreshments up front. Ch'in-t'ung and Wang Ching had already finished setting up an Eight Immortals table, and they now brought out the appetizers, nuts, and wine. Hsi-men Ch'ing then ordered the storehouse to be opened, and a jug of the chrysanthemum wine that had been given to him by Hsia Yen-ling brought out for them. When they opened it, it turned out to be of a clear beryl-green color and exuded a pungent fragrance. Before straining it, they mixed it with a bottle of cold water, in order to reduce the sharpness of its flavor. After doing so, they poured it through a cheesecloth sieve, and when it had been strained, it turned out to be both mellow and delicious, superior to grape wine in these respects.

Hsi-men Ch'ing had Wang Ching fill a small gold goblet with it and offer it first to Wu K'ai to taste. After this, Ying Po-chüeh and the rest all tasted it:

Expressing the most fulsome admiration.

Before long, in:

Large platters and large bowls,

the appetizers and delicacies were brought in, filling the surface of the table. First there were two platters of steamed, rose-flavored, stuffed, glutinous rice cakes, to be dipped in white granulated sugar. The company made short work of them, grabbing them up while they were still hot. Only after that were the stuffed crabs brought out, along with two platters of roast duck.

Ying Po-chüeh offered a crab to Wu K'ai, and Hsieh Hsi-ta remarked, "I don't know how these were ever done to make them so flavorful, crisp, and delicious."

"They were sent over here from Brother Ch'ang the Second's place," explained Hsi-men Ch'ing.

"I have led a futile existence for fifty-one years," said Wu K'ai, "without knowing that crabs could be prepared in such a way. They really are delicious."

"Have our sisters-in-law in the rear compound had a chance to taste them?" asked Ying Po-chüeh.

"They've all had some," said Hsi-men Ch'ing.

"It's really put Sister-in-law Ch'ang to the test," remarked Ying Po-chüeh, "to demonstrate such culinary skill."

Ch'ang Shih-chieh laughed at this, saying, "My humble wife was only afraid that she had not made things tasty enough, and that you gentlemen would laugh at her."

When all the crabs had been eaten, the attendants came forward to replenish the wine, and Hsi-men Ch'ing told Ch'un-hung and Shu-t'ung to come up beside them and take turns entertaining them with southern-style songs.

At this point, Ying Po-chüeh suddenly noticed the sound of singing, accompanied by a psaltery, emanating from the great summerhouse and inquired, "Brother, is Li Kuei-chieh here today? If not, who is responsible for this music?"

"You keep listening," said Hsi-men Ch'ing, "and see if you think it's her, or not."

"If it's not Li Kuei-chieh," said Ying Po-chüeh, "it must be Wu Yin-erh."

"You beggar!" exclaimed Hsi-men Ch'ing. "All you ever do is talk blind nonsense. It's actually a professional female singer."

"Is it Big Sister Yü, then?" said Ying Po-chüeh.

"No, it's not her," said Hsi-men Ch'ing. "This one is called Second Sister Shen. She's young, has a good figure, and really knows how to sing."

"Really," said Ying Po-chüeh. "If she's as good as all that, why don't you drag her out here so we can have a look at her, and get her to sing something for us?"

"Today being a holiday," said Hsi-men Ch'ing, "I've engaged her to come and help the ladies of the household celebrate the Double Yang Festival. It would take the ears of a dog like you to pick her out."

"My senses are as sharp as those of Thousand Li Eyes and Wind-borne Ears,"[49] said Ying Po-chüeh.

"If a bee so much as buzzes forty li away,
    I can make it out."

The two of them continued chaffing each other for a while, after which Ying Po-chüeh said, "Brother, whatever you do, call her out here, so we can have a look at her. The rest of us may not matter, but you really ought to have her sing a song for your senior brother-in-law here. Enough is enough. Don't be so stubborn about it."

Unable to resist these importunities any longer, Hsi-men Ch'ing dispatched Wang Ching to bring Second Sister Shen out so she could sing something for Brother-in-law Wu K'ai. Before long, Second Sister Shen duly appeared, kow-towed to the company, and, after standing up again, sat down to one side on a folding chair that had been provided for her.

"Second Sister Shen," said Ying Po-chüeh, "may I ask how old you are?"

"I was born in the year of the ox," said Second Sister Shen, "so I'm twenty years old."

"And how many songs are there in your repertory?" he went on to ask.

"Accompanying myself with the *p'i-p'a* or the psaltery," said Second Sister Shen, "I can perform any number of songs and song suites."

"If you know as many as all that," said Ying Po-chüeh, "it ought to suffice."

"Second Sister Shen," said Hsi-men Ch'ing, "take your *p'i-p'a* and perform a few current popular songs for us. We don't want to burden you unduly. I hear that you can perform the piece called "The Four Dreams and Eight Nothings." Why don't you sing that for Brother-in-law Wu here?"

He then directed Wang Ching and Shu-t'ung to replenish the wine. Where-upon, Second Sister Shen:

Gently strummed the silken strings,
Lightly parted her sandalwood lips,[50]
and sang the set of songs to the tune "Lo River Lament":

Morbidly my indisposition grows worse;
When will it ever melt away?
I long for him in spring, yearn for him in summer,
    and do the same in autumn and winter.
With a breastful of sorrow,[51] I complain
    to the Lord of Heaven.
If Heaven possesses consciousness,
Why doesn't it show some kindness?
No matter how much kindness I show,
    it comes to nothing;
No matter how much feeling I show,
    it comes to nothing.
It all amounts to a Dream of the Southern Branch.[52]

He is in the East, I in the West;
When will we ever meet again?
Little by little, I fill the sheets of flowered paper,
    and seal them again and again.
I entrust these missives to the fish and
    wild geese as messengers,
But they are not trustworthy,
And fail to deliver my letters.
No matter how much I dote on him,
    it comes to nothing;
No matter how much I resent him,
    it comes to nothing.
It all amounts to a Dream of Witch's Mountain.[53]

My kindness evaporates like the morning breeze;
Leaving me languorous and depressed.
The way he carries on, he fails to finish
    that which he begins.
His promises to be as faithful as the hills and seas
    are no more than wind in my ears.
Does he not remember, in days of old,
How ardently he expressed his love?
No matter how much I may repine,
    it comes to nothing;
No matter how infatuated I may be,
    it comes to nothing.
It all amounts to only a Dream of a Butterfly.[54]

My brightness resembles stupidity;
I have fallen into his trap.[55]
In silence, all I can do is to secretly
   let my pearly tears well up.
Who would have thought that his mouth and
   heart were not in agreement?
My heart has been true to him,[56]
While he has played tricks on me.
No matter whether I gain the advantage,
   it comes to nothing;
No matter whether I lose the advantage,
   it comes to nothing.
It all amounts to a Dream of Radiant Terrace.[57]

We will say no more at present about the singing and drinking in the front compound.

To resume our story, when Li P'ing-erh got back to her room and sat down on the commode, the blood from her lower body flowed out as copiously as urine, and in no time at all, she started to black out. When she tried to get up and pull up her skirts, she suddenly suffered a spell of vertigo and fell face forward onto the ground. Luckily Ying-ch'un was at her side and was able to break her fall, but she had broken the skin on her forehead. Ying-ch'un and the wet nurse helped her onto the k'ang, but for some time she was:

   Oblivious to human affairs.

This threw Ying-ch'un into a panic, and she immediately told Hsiu-ch'un, "Quickly, go tell the First Lady what has happened."

Hsiu-ch'un went to the scene of the party and reported to Yüeh-niang and the others, "My mistress has fallen down in a faint in her quarters."

Yüeh-niang abruptly left the party and, accompanied by the other women-folk, hastened on her way to assess the situation. They found Ying-ch'un and the wet nurse holding her up in a sitting position on the k'ang, but she remained:

   Oblivious to human affairs.

"She seemed all right when she came back to her quarters," said Yüeh-niang. "What actually happened to bring her to this pass?"

Ying-ch'un took the lid off the commode and showed the contents to Yüeh-niang, which gave her quite a start.

"I fear," she said, "it must be the wine she drank just now that has brought on this copious flow of blood."

"But she hardly drank anything at all," both Meng Yü-lou and P'an Chin-lien exclaimed together.

Only some time after they had administered a decoction of bog rush and ginger to her did she gradually come back to her senses and recover her ability to speak.

"Sister Li," asked Yüeh-niang, "what happened to you?"

"It wasn't anything much," said Li P'ing-erh. "I sat down on the commode, but when I got up and started to pull up my skirts, a black patch appeared before my eyes and, before I knew it:

Heaven and Earth began to spin around,[58]

and I couldn't help falling down."

Yüeh-niang said, "I think I'd better send Lai-an to invite Father to come in here so we can explain the situation to him, and get him to send for Dr. Jen Hou-ch'i to come take a look at you."

Li P'ing-erh objected to sending for Hsi-men Ch'ing and said, "What's the need for:

Such a great show of consternation?

It will only disrupt his drinking party."

"Make up her bed then," Yüeh-niang said to Ying-ch'un, "and put your mistress to sleep."

Under the circumstances, Yüeh-niang had no wish to continue drinking, so she ordered that the utensils be cleared away, and they all went back to the rear compound.

Hsi-men Ch'ing continued to entertain Brother-in-law Wu K'ai and the others until evening, before returning to the master suite, where Yüeh-niang told him about Li P'ing-erh's fainting fit. Hsi-men Ch'ing hastily made his way back up front to see how she was and found Li P'ing-erh lying on the k'ang, with her face as sallow as wax.

Tugging at Hsi-men Ch'ing's sleeve, she started to weep, and when he asked her what it was about, Li P'ing-erh said, "When I went back to my room and sat down on the commode, somehow or other, I don't know why, the blood started to flow from my lower body, just as copiously as urine, and, before I knew it, a black patch appeared before my eyes. When I got up and started to pull up my skirts:

Heaven and Earth began to spin around,

and I fell down, no longer conscious of anything."

When Hsi-men Ch'ing saw that a strip of the cuticle on her forehead had been broken open by the fall, he said, "Where were your maidservants? Why weren't they looking after you? How did they let you fall down and wound your face that way?"

"Luckily," said Li P'ing-erh, "my senior maidservant was standing by and tried to break my fall. Together with the wet nurse, they were able to help me up. Otherwise, who knows how much worse a fall I might have taken?"

"Early tomorrow morning," said Hsi-men Ch'ing, "I'll send a page boy to ask Dr. Jen Hou-ch'i to come and have a look at you."

That night he slept in the bed across the room from where Li P'ing-erh was lying.

The next morning, he did not go to the yamen but sent Ch'in-t'ung, riding on a mule, to fetch Dr. Jen Hou-ch'i, who did not arrive until noontime. Hsi-men Ch'ing first shared a serving of tea with him in the main reception hall and then sent a page boy inside to announce the doctor's arrival. Li P'ing-erh spruced up her quarters, lit some incense, and then invited Dr. Jen Hou-ch'i to come in.

After palpating her pulse, he came back out to the reception hall and said to Hsi-men Ch'ing, "Your venerable consort's pulse is significantly more sluggish than it was the last time I examined her.

Her seven feelings have been wounded.[59]

The inflammation created by the element fire in her liver and lungs is excessive, with the result that the element wood is in the ascendant and the element earth is deficient, causing an abnormal circulation of her overheated blood. The resultant flooding is like the collapse of a mountain and cannot be regulated. Send your servant back to inquire. If the blood she has hemorrhaged is purple in color, her condition may be treated successfully. If it is bright red in color, it is fresh blood. In that case, if the medicine I prescribe abates the bleeding somewhat, there is hope. If not, it will be difficult to treat."

"I beseech you, venerable sir," said Hsi-men Ch'ing, "to take care in determining the dosage of the medications you prescribe. Your pupil will see that you are handsomely rewarded."

"What kind of talk is that?" said Dr. Jen. "You and I are on familiar terms with each other, as well as being mutual friends of Han Ming-ch'uan. Your pupil:

Will not fail to do his utmost on your behalf."[60]

After hosting another serving of tea, Hsi-men Ch'ing saw his guest out the door, immediately after which, he prepared a bolt of Hang-chou chiffon and two taels of silver and sent Ch'in-t'ung off with them to fetch the prescribed medication. It turned out to be a decoction for restoring the spleen, but when Li P'ing-erh took a dose of it after it had been heated, her hemorrhaging continued unabated.

Hsi-men Ch'ing became even more flustered than before and also invited Dr. Hu, who resided at the entrance to Main Street, to come and see her.

Dr. Hu said, "Anger has disrupted her blood vessels, causing an inflammation in her uterus."

He also prescribed a medication for her condition, but when she took it, it was no more efficacious than:

A stone sunk in the vast sea.

When Yüeh-niang realized that Hsi-men Ch'ing was preoccupied with consulting physicians in the front compound, she decided to keep Second Sister Shen for one night only, after which, she gave her five mace of silver, a vest of cloud-patterned damask, and some other trinkets, which she put into a gift box, and then sent her off in a sedan chair.

Hua Tzu-yu, who had been a guest at the party in celebration of the opening of Hsi-men Ch'ing's new silk goods store, upon hearing that Li P'ing-erh was unwell, had his wife purchase two gifts and go to pay her a visit. When she observed how emaciated and sallow she had become, and that her appearance was:

No longer what it used to be,[61]

the two of them had a good cry together in her room. After her visit, Yüeh-niang invited her to tea in the rear compound.

Han Tao-kuo, for his part, said to Hsi-men Ch'ing, "There is a Dr. Chao living outside the East Gate, who specializes in female disorders. He is adept at palpating the pulse and is an excellent diagnostician. Some years ago, when my wife was suffering from irregular menstruation, it was he who treated her. If Your Honor will send someone to invite him to come and examine the Sixth Lady, I am sure her condition will improve."

Hsi-men Ch'ing, thereupon, sent Ch'in-t'ung[62] and Wang Ching, the two of them riding tandem on a mule, to go outside the city gate and extend an invitation to Dr. Chao.

Hsi-men Ch'ing also invited Ying Po-chüeh to join him for a consultation in the anteroom in the front courtyard, saying, "My sixth consort has become seriously ill. What am I to do about it?"

Ying Po-chüeh expressed surprise, saying, "I understood that my sister-in-law's ailment was somewhat better. Why has it taken a turn for the worse?"

"Ever since her young son died," said Hsi-men Ch'ing, "she has been suffering from depression, which has resulted in a recurrence of her former ailment. Yesterday, in celebration of the Double Yang Festival, I proposed to invite Second Sister Shen, so that the women of the household could dispel their melancholy and have some fun together. She hardly drank anything at all on that occasion, but who would have expected that, no sooner had she returned to her quarters than she had a relapse, began to feel faint, and fell to the ground, breaking the skin on her face? I invited Dr. Jen Hou-ch'i to examine her, and he said that her pulse was more sluggish than before; but when she took the medication he prescribed, the flow of blood became more copious than ever."

"Brother," said Ying Po-chüeh, "when you invited Dr. Hu to examine her, what did he say?"

Hsi-men Ch'ing replied, "Dr. Hu said that anger had disrupted her blood vessels, but when she took the medication he prescribed, it produced no visible effect. Today, Han Tao-kuo recommended a certain Dr. Chao Lung-kang, who resides outside the city gate and is a specialist in female disorders. I have sent two page boys after him, and they have been gone for some time already. I'm as upset as can be about it. Simply because of what happened to the child, she is so preoccupied by it, day and night, that it has given rise to this ailment. She's just a woman after all and doesn't know how to put it behind her. No matter how much you admonish her, she doesn't pay any attention. I'm:

At a loss for what to do next."

As they were speaking, P'ing-an came in and reported, "Your kinsman Ch'iao Hung has come."

Hsi-men Ch'ing ushered him into the reception hall, where, after exchanging the customary amenities, they sat down together.

"I have heard," said Ch'iao Hung, "that my kinswoman, your Sixth Lady, is unwell. Yesterday, when my nephew, Ts'ui Pen, came home, he suggested that my wife should come pay her a visit."

"It's true," said Hsi-men Ch'ing. "For some time now, ever since our young son died, she has been suffering from depression. She had a physical indisposition to begin with, and this only served to exacerbate it. I appreciate your concern."

"Have you had anyone in to examine her?" asked Ch'iao Hung.

"She has been taking the medication prescribed by Dr. Jen Hou-ch'i," said Hsi-men Ch'ing, "and yesterday I also asked Dr. Hu from Main Street to examine her, but when she took the medication he prescribed, it only made her condition worse. Today, I have also sent for Dr. Chao Lung-kang, a specialist in female disorders who lives outside the city gate."

"The medical practitioner Old Man Ho," said Ch'iao Hung, "who lives outside the gate of the district yamen, is equally proficient at prescriptions, both great and small, and palpation of the pulse. His son, Ho Ch'un-ch'üan, has also recently set up practice as a licensed physician. Why don't you invite him to come and examine my kinswoman?"

"If he's as good as all that," said Hsi-men Ch'ing, "I'll wait until my servants have brought Dr. Chao Lung-kang to palpate her pulse, and see what he has to say. It won't be too late to invite Dr. Ho after that."

"Kinsman," said Ch'iao Hung, "in my ignorant view, the best thing to do would be to invite Old Man Ho to examine my kinswoman now and offer his diagnosis, after which you can have him sit in an antechamber. Then, after your servants have brought Dr. Chao Lung-kang here from outside the city gate to take her pulse, you can see what he has to say, and then get the two physicians to discuss it together, in the hope of ascertaining the origin of the ailment. If they can agree upon an appropriate prescription after that, it is unlikely to prove ineffective."

"Kinsman," said Hsi-men Ch'ing, "what you say makes sense."

He then turned to Tai-an and said, "Take my card and go with Ch'iao T'ung to invite the medical practitioner Old Man Ho who lives outside the gate of the district yamen to come here."

Tai-an and Ch'iao T'ung nodded in assent and departed on this errand. Hsi-men Ch'ing then invited Ying Po-chüeh to join them in the reception hall, where, after greeting Ch'iao Hung, he sat down with them for a cup of tea. It was not long before Old Man Ho arrived, came in the gate, bowed to Hsi-men Ch'ing and Ch'iao Hung, and was ushered to a seat in the place of honor.

Raising his hand in greeting, Hsi-men Ch'ing said, "It is some years since I have seen you, venerable sir, and your appearance is more impressive than ever, with your gray beard and white hair."

"And your distinguished son has been most successful in his career," chimed in Ch'iao Hung.

"The fact is," said Old Man Ho, "that he is so busy with his social responsibilities at the district yamen that he scarcely has time for anything else. It is my aged self who most often has to go out to examine the sick."

"For someone as old as you are, venerable sir," said Ying Po-chüeh, "you seem to be in remarkably good health."

"As of now," said Old Man Ho, "I have led a futile existence for eighty years."

When they had finished running through these amenities, tea was served, after which, a page boy was dispatched to let Li P'ing-erh know that the doctor was coming. Before long, he was invited into her quarters, where he approached her bed in order to palpate her pulse. She had been propped up into a sitting position on the k'ang, with the fragrant clouds of her hair concealing her bosom, and exhibited an extremely emaciated appearance. Behold:

> Her face is the hue of gilded paper;[63]
> Her body is thin as a bar of silver.
> By degrees her good looks have diminished;
> Imperceptibly her radiance has wasted away.
> Her breast is tight with anger;
> For days on end, neither water nor rice
>   has moistened her lips.
> Her five viscera are congested;
> All day long, it is difficult for pills
>   to get down to her stomach.
> With a constant din, the hollows of her ears
>   resound with the sound of chimes;
> Nebulously, as her eyesight becomes darker,
>   she seems to see fireflies flying.
> Her six pulses are weak and sluggish;[64]
> The Assessor of the Eastern Peak has
>   come to take away her life.
> Her numinous soul is drifting hazily;
> The Buddha of the Western Realm has
>   called her to accompany him.
> The baleful stars Death Knell and Condoler[65]
>   have already visited her;

Even the famous physician Pien Ch'üeh of Lu[66]
would find himself stumped.[67]

When Old Man Ho had finished palpating her pulse, he came outside to the reception hall and said to Hsi-men Ch'ing and Ch'iao Hung, "This lady's ailment originated from semen invading her menstrual blood vessels, after which she became afflicted with suppressed anger. When her anger and her blood came into conflict with each other, it resulted in copious hemorrhaging. Think carefully back to the time when her ailment began and see if this diagnosis is correct or not."

"Venerable sir," said Hsi-men Ch'ing, "how would you suggest that it be treated?"

As they were discussing the situation, it was suddenly reported that Ch'in-t'ung and Wang Ching had arrived back from outside the city gate with Dr. Chao.

"Who might that be?" asked Old Man Ho.

"It is another doctor who was recommended to me by my manager," said Hsi-men Ch'ing. "If you, venerable sir, will pretend to ignorance of the matter until after he comes back out from examining her pulse, the two of you can then discuss it together in the hope of agreeing upon an appropriate prescription."

Before long, he came in from outside, and Hsi-men Ch'ing, after exchanging greetings with him, introduced him to the others. The two venerable gentlemen, Old Man Ho and Ch'iao Hung, were seated in the center in the position of honor, the newcomer was offered a seat on the left, Ying Po-chüeh was seated on the right, while Hsi-men Ch'ing occupied the position of host. Lai-an brought in a serving of tea, and, after they had drunk it, took away the teacups in their raised saucers.

The newcomer then said, "May I ask what are the names of you two venerable gentlemen?"

Ch'iao Hung replied, "One of us is surnamed Ho and the other is surnamed Ch'iao."

"And my surname is Ying," said Ying Po-chüeh. "May I venture to ask, sir, what is your distinguished name; where do you reside; and what is your profession?"

"Unworthy as I am," the newcomer replied, "the dwelling of your humble servant is located outside the East Gate, on the First Alley, beyond the Temple of the Second Scion (Erh-lang Shen), across the Three Bends Bridge, in the Quarter of the Four Wells.[68] I am none other than the celebrated Chao the Quack and have practiced medicine all my life. My paternal grandfather was an administrative assistant in the Imperial Academy of Medicine, and my father is currently serving as a medical officer in the mansion of the Prince of Ju.[69] For three successive generations we have devoted ourselves to the study of the medical arts. Every day I pore over the works of Wang Shu-ho,[70] Li Kao,[71] and Wu-t'ing-tzu,[72] as well as such texts as the *Yao-hsing fu* (Rhapsody on the properties of drugs),[73] *Huang-ti nei-ching su-wen* (Essential questions regarding the Yellow Emperor's inner classic [of medicine]),[74] *Nan-ching* (The classic of difficult issues),[75] *Huo-jen shu* (The book on preserving human life),[76] *Tan-hsi tsuan-yao* (Essential teachings of Chu Chen-heng),[77] *Tan-hsi hsin-fa* (Quintessential methods of Chu Chen-heng),[78] *Chieh-ku lao mai-chüeh* (Chang Yüan-su's [commentary on Wang Shu-ho's] secrets of pulse diagnosis),[79] *Chia-chien shih-san fang* (Thirteen alterative prescriptions),[80] *Ch'ien-chin fang* (Prescriptions worth a thousand pieces of gold),[81] *Ch'i-hsiao liang-fang* (Beneficial prescriptions of unusual efficacy),[82] *Shou-yü shen-fang* (Divine prescriptions for the realm of longevity),[83] and *Hai-shang fang* (Overseas panaceas [from the Isles of the Blest]).[84]

> There is no text I have not perused;[85]
> There is not a text I have not read.
> In prescribing, I use the life-giving
>   methods stored in my breast;
> In pulse-taking, I clearly comprehend
>   the secrets under my fingers.
> The six conditions and the four seasons,
> Produce differences in the manifestations
>   of the Yin and the Yang.
> The seven outer and eight inner pulses,
> Determine whether blockage or repulsion
>   cause sinking or floating.
> As for the symptoms of wind, vacuity,
>   cold, and fever,
> I have mastered them all without exception.[86]
> With regard to thready, swollen, hollow,
>   and stony pulses,
> There are none I do not totally understand.
> With my awkward mouth and clumsy lips,[87]
> I may fail to explain myself in detail;
> But I have composed a few lines of verse,
> Which will lay out the general outline.

They go as follows:

> I'm a doctor whose surname is Chao,
> At my gate people constantly clamor.
> I sport placards and rattle my bell,[88]
> With no genuine article[89] to peddle.
> In healing, I abjure the best nostrums,
> In pulse taking, say what comes to mind.
> Incompetent at pharmacology and medicine,

I'm inept even at relieving constipation.
For headaches I use tightened headbands,
For eye ailments I rely on moxabustion.
For heart trouble I recommend surgery,
For deafness I would advise acupuncture.
For money I'm prepared to do anything,
I'm out for profit rather than results.
Those who consult me are less likely to be
    fortunate than unfortunate;[90]
Wherever I appear there is likely to be
    weeping rather than laughter.

Truly:
        Motivated only one half by benevolence
            and one half by self-interest;
        From of old, the pursuit of medicine is
            like the pursuit of immortality."[91]
When the company had heard him out, they all laughed uproariously.

Old Man Ho then asked him, "Did you acquire your expertise professionally, or acquire your expertise extra-professionally?"

Dr. Chao said, "What do you mean by the expressions 'acquire your expertise professionally,' or 'acquire your expertise extra-professionally'?"

"If you acquired your expertise professionally," responded Old Man Ho,
"you learned the proper techniques of pulse diagnosis from the example set by
your father. If you acquired your expertise extra-professionally, you can do no
more than:
        Ascertain the symptoms and prescribe accordingly,
that's all."

"Venerable sir," said Dr. Chao, "you don't understand. As the authorities of
yore have stated:
        Inspection, auscultation, interrogation, and palpation,
are the techniques that show a physician to be:
        Divine, sagely, craftsmanlike, or skilled.[92]
Since I have acquired my expertise professionally through three successive
generations, I know that in addition to first inquiring about the symptoms and
then examining the pulse, I must scrutinize the patient's coloration; just as the
practitioners of the Tzu-p'ing school of fortune-telling[93] combine it with the
astrological school of the Five Planets, and also resort to palmistry and physiognomy, in order to make sure that their predictions are reliable and unlikely
to be incorrect."

"In that case," said Old Man Ho, "Please go inside and examine the
patient."

Hsi-men Ch'ing thereupon told Ch'in-t'ung to go back and tell them that they were coming, and that he had also arranged for a visit by Dr. Chao.

Before long, Hsi-men Ch'ing escorted Dr. Chao into Li P'ing-erh's quarters. Li P'ing-erh, who had just lain down for a rest, was propped up into a sitting position once again, supported by her pillow and bedding.

Dr. Chao first palpated the pulse on her left wrist, and then that on her right, after which he said, "Venerable lady, please lift up your head so I can examine your coloration."

Li P'ing-erh actually lifted up her head, upon which, Dr. Chao said to Hsi-men Ch'ing, "Your Honor, ask your venerable lady who I am."

Hsi-men Ch'ing accordingly asked Li P'ing-erh, "Who do you thing this gentleman is?"

Li P'ing-erh raised her head to take a look at him, and then said in a low voice, "I imagine he must be a doctor."

"Your Honor," said Dr. Chao, "there is nothing to worry about. She is unlikely to die since she is able to recognize people."

Hsi-men Ch'ing laughed at this, and said, "Dr. Chao, do your best to examine her, and I will see that you are amply rewarded."

After examining her for some time, Dr. Chao said, "As for this ailment of your venerable lady's, pray don't take it amiss if I say so, but, after scrutinizing her coloration and palpating her pulse, I conclude that if it is not an externally contracted intestinal fever, it is an internally contracted miscellaneous disorder, and that if it did not develop postpartum, it must have done so prior to conception."

"That's not what it is," said Hsi-men Ch'ing. "Please be good enough to make another careful appraisal."[94]

"I venture to say," said Dr. Chao, "that it is a depression brought on by a dietary disorder resulting from overindulgence in food and drink."

"For days on end," responded Hsi-men Ch'ing, "she has hardly eaten any food at all."

"Perhaps it is a case of jaundice," opined Dr. Chao.

"That's not the case," said Hsi-men Ch'ing.

"If that's not the case," said Dr. Chao, "why is it that her face is so yellow?"

He then went on to say, "No doubt it is a case of spleen vacuity diarrhea."

"It is not a case of diarrhea," said Hsi-men Ch'ing.

"If it is not diarrhea, what can it be?" said Dr. Chao. "How can it be an ailment that one is at a loss to identify?"

After sitting in thought for some time, he said, "I've finally thought of something. If it isn't a case of swelling of the lymph nodes in the groin caused by venereal disease, it must be a case of irregular menstruation."

"Since she's a woman," said Hsi-men Ch'ing, "it's unlikely to be a case of swelling of the lymph nodes in the groin caused by venereal disease. But your suggestion that it might be a case of irregular menstruation is a little more reasonable."

"Amitābha be praised!" exclaimed Dr. Chao. "Somehow or other your humble servant has finally gotten something right."

"What kind of irregular menstruation might it be?" asked Hsi-men Ch'ing.

"If it is not due to debility arising from amenorrhea," opined Dr. Chao, "it must be a case of metrorrhagia like the collapse of a mountain."

"To tell you the truth, sir," said Hsi-men Ch'ing, "my spouse, thus and so, has been experiencing incessant hemorrhaging from her lower body, which has caused her figure to become emaciated. If you know of any fast-acting prescription that you can make up and give her to take, I will see that you are amply rewarded."

"That's no problem," said Dr. Chao. "I do possess such a prescription. After we return to the front reception hall, I will write it out, so you can have it made up."

Hsi-men Ch'ing then proceeded to accompany him back to the front reception hall. Ch'iao Hung and Old Man Ho were still there and asked him what he thought the origin of the ailment was.

"As I see it," said Dr. Chao, "it is only a case of menstrual flooding."

"What medicine would you use to treat it?" asked Old Man Ho.

"I've got a marvelous prescription," said Dr. Chao, "which contains a number of different ingredients. If she takes it, I can guarantee her recovery. Let me describe it for you." To the tune "Slavey Chu":

Take Radix Glycyrrhizae, Radix Euphorbiae,
    and Sal Ammoniacum,
Veratri Radix et Rhizoma, Crotonus Semen,
    and Daphnes Genkwa Flos;
Emulsify Arsenicum Trioxidum with fresh
    Rhizoma Pinelliae,
Use Radix Aconiti, Semen Pruni Armeniacae,
    and Semen Cannabis;
Combine all of these ingredients together;
Work them into a pill using honey mixed with
    Bulbus Allii Fistulosi,
And take it early in the morning with a draft
    of distilled spirits.[95]

"To treat her with drugs such as these," said Old Man Ho, "would only be to medicate her to death."

Dr. Chao responded, "It has always been true that:
        Toxic medications may be bitter to the taste
            but beneficial for an illness.[96]
After all:
        To bring the case to an early clear-cut conclusion,
        Is superior to letting things drag on interminably."

"This rascal is talking nothing but nonsense!" exclaimed Hsi-men Ch'ing. "Have the servants throw him out of here."

"Since your own manager recommended and vouched for him," said Ch'iao Hung, "you can hardly send the doctor off empty-handed."

"To comply with your suggestion," said Hsi-men Ch'ing, "I'll have someone in the shop up front weigh out two mace of silver for him and send him on his way."

Dr. Chao, accordingly, took the two mace of silver and headed for home:

> His one mind hastening like an arrow;
> His two legs racing as though flying.[97]

When Hsi-men Ch'ing saw that Dr. Chao was out of the way, he said to Ch'iao Hung, "This man turned out to be an ignoramus."

"Though I did not venture to say so just now," said Old Man Ho, "this fellow is well-known outside the East Gate as Chao the Quack. All he knows how to do is:

> Sport placards and rattle his bell,

on the streets, attempting to con the passersby. What does he know about pulse diagnosis or the etiology of disorders?"

"As for this ailment of your venerable lady's," he went on to say, "when I get home, I'll make up a couple of prescriptions for her in the hope that they will do the trick. After she has taken them, if her hemorrhaging is reduced, and her chest feels more comfortable, it will be expedient to prescribe further medication. I am afraid, however, that if the hemorrhaging does not stop, and her appetite does not improve, her condition will prove difficult to treat."

When he had finished speaking, he got up to go. Hsi-men Ch'ing sealed one tael of silver in a packet and sent Tai-an, with a gift box in hand, to pick up the prescribed medications. That evening they were administered to Li P'ing-erh, but they produced not the slightest change in her condition.

"You ought to be sparing in the medications you give her," said Wu Yüeh-niang. "She has already stopped eating and drinking, so what is there left in her stomach? If you insist on continuing to medicate her, it is likely to exhaust her vitality. Formerly, that Immortal Wu predicted that during her twenty-seventh year she would suffer a bloody catastrophe, and this just happens to be her twenty-seventh year. You ought to send someone to look for that Immortal Wu, and have him prognosticate on her behalf to see what the categories 'emolument' and 'horse' in her horoscope forebode for her.[98] If her fate should prove to be in conflict with some baleful star, he might be able to either avert the calamity or protect her against it."

Hsi-men Ch'ing, accordingly, sent a servant with his calling card in hand to the mansion of Commandant Chou Hsiu of the Regional Military Command to inquire as to the whereabouts of Immortal Wu.

The servant was told, "Immortal Wu is an itinerant priest who wanders like a cloud. His comings and goings are uncertain. When he comes here, he generally stays in the Temple of the Tutelary God south of the city. This year, in the fourth month, he left on a pilgrimage to Mount Wu-tang.[99] If you want someone to calculate a fortune, there is a Master Huang, who resides outside the Chen-wu Temple, who is good at calculating them. He charges only three mace of silver per calculation but will not make house calls. He can interpret the events of a lifetime, from beginning to end, as clearly as though he were seeing them with his own eyes."

Hsi-men Ch'ing, consequently, sent Ch'en Ching-chi, with three mace of silver, to seek out Master Huang's dwelling outside the Chen-wu Temple in the northern quarter of the city. He found a poster pasted on Master Huang's door, that read:

> Calculations concerning Anterior Heaven
>   based on the *Changes*;
> The charge for each prognostication is
>   three mace of silver.

Ch'en Ching-chi went inside, bowed respectfully, proffered the stipulated fee, and said, "I have someone's fortune that I would like to trouble you to calculate, sir."

He then told him the eight characters that determined Li P'ing-erh's horoscope, as well as the facts that she was a female, that she was currently in her twenty-seventh year, and that she was born at noon on the fifteenth day of the first month.

Master Huang performed some calculations on his abacus and then said, "This female's horoscope indicates that she was born in a *hsin-wei* year, in a *keng-yin* month, on a *hsin-mao* day, during the hour *jen-wu*, which calls for analysis of the horoscopic category 'seal ribbon.'[100] The first of her 'decennial periods of fate' began in her fourth year and was designated by the combination *chi-wei*, the second began in her fourteenth year and was designated by the combination *wu-wu*, the third began in her twenty-fourth year and was designated by the combination *ting-ssu*, the fourth will begin in her thirty-fourth year and be designated by the combination *ping-ch'en*. This year of her horoscope is a *ting-yu* year, which means that she will suffer from 'matched shoulders,' because the stem of this year, which corresponds to the element metal, will be injured by the stem of her day of birth, which corresponds to the element fire. During this year the planet Ketu[101] impinges on her fate, and it is also in conflict with the baleful stars known as Death Knell and the Five Devils, which will make trouble for her. Now Ketu is a dark star, the image of which resembles a tangle of threads without a head, the shape of which changes incessantly. If someone's decennial period of fate collides with it, it is likely to portend something ominous,[102] such as the development of disease. It indicates that in the first, second, and third, or the seventh, or ninth months a medical calamity may occur, involving the loss of property, the untimely death of a child, the scheming of petty people, and the spreading of malicious gossip,[103] intended to inflict material damage. If it is the horoscope of a female, it is very unpropitious. The judgment reads:

During this year when the planet Ketu encroaches,
Her destiny is like propelling a boat on dry land,[104]
Causing the head of the household to knit his brows.
In quietude, hesitating over the best thing to do,
In idleness, given over to sorrow without respite;
If you want to know why his woman is so afflicted,
And as unlikely to endure as a tangle of threads:
Ponder the events before conception and postpartum.[105]

Her fortune reads:

Aside from the fact that she entered into
    wedlock rather late,
It is also true that she lost her parents
    early on in life.
Her fragrant features and alluring beauty
    have bloomed of late,
Everything that she desired seemed to be
    there for the asking.
But no sooner was she happily wed than
    the dragon appeared,
And the congenial union of the sheep was
    menaced by the tiger.[106]
Sadly, when emotions are at their height
    feelings are lost,
When her fate enters the year of the cock[107]
    the leaves will fall."

When Master Huang had copied this information out, he sealed it and entrusted it to Ch'en Ching-chi to take home with him.

Hsi-men Ch'ing was sitting together with Ying Po-chüeh and Licentiate Wen Pi-ku when Ch'en Ching-chi came back with the copied fortune, and he took it back to the rear compound to explicate for Wu Yüeh-niang's benefit. It was apparent that the fortune was:

More likely to be unfortunate than fortunate.[108]

Nothing might have happened if Hsi-men Ch'ing had not heard about this, but having heard about it:

His brows became tightly knit, as though
    secured by a triple-spring lock;
His belly became overburdened, as though
    with ten thousand bushels of woe.[109]

Truly:

> The lofty and eminent in their youth
>   meet with calamity;
> While the clever and the intelligent
>   suffer in poverty.
> The year, month, day, and hour of birth
>   determine it all;
> However calculated, events are controlled
>   by fate rather than man.

> If you want to know the outcome of these events,
> Pray consult the story related in the following chapter.

Chapter 62

TAOIST MASTER P'AN PERFORMS AN EXORCISM ON THE LANTERN ALTAR;

HSI-MEN CH'ING LAMENTS EGREGIOUSLY ON BEHALF OF LI P'ING-ERH

Whether one's conduct is false or true
    is known only to oneself;
The causes of disaster or good fortune
    are not to be sought elsewhere.[1]
Good and evil acts inevitably bring
    their appropriate results;
The only question being whether they
    come early or come late.[2]
When one reexamines at one's leisure
    the deeds of one's lifetime,[3]
And ruminates in quietude about what
    one has done during the day;[4]
If one consistently practices rectitude
    with one's whole heart,
It is natural that Heaven's principles
    will not let one down.[5]

THE STORY GOES that when Hsi-men Ch'ing observed that the prescriptions Li P'ing-erh took, and the medical attention she received, were completely ineffectual; and that though:

    The gods were besought and diviners consulted,
the results of these prognostications were all:

    Ominous and inauspicious,
he was:

    At a loss for what to do next.

Initially, Li P'ing-erh still endeavored as best she could to comb her hair and wash her face, and she was still able to get off the k'ang by herself in order to sit on the commode. But afterwards, gradually:

    Her intake of food and drink diminished,[6]
    Her figure became increasingly emaciated,[7]

and the hemorrhaging from her lower body continued unabated. It did not take long for a woman as pretty as a flower to become so weak and emaciated that she did not bear looking at. She was no longer able to get off the k'ang to perform her natural functions, but simply lay on a pad that had been covered with a layer of absorbent grass paper. Fearing that anyone coming in might be offended by the foul odor, she had her maidservants keep incense burning in the room. Hsi-men Ch'ing, on observing that her arms were as thin as bars of silver, wept as he kept watch over her in her room and only went to the yamen every other day.

"My brother," protested Li P'ing-erh, "you really ought to report to the yamen, rather than letting my situation interfere with your responsibilities. My condition doesn't really matter. The only problem is the hemorrhaging down below. If it would only stop, I could open my mouth to eat and drink again, and should be all right. You're a man and can't afford to tie yourself down keeping vigil in somebody's room like this."

"My sister," wept Hsi-men Ch'ing, "I can't bear to relinquish you in my heart."

"Don't be a fool," said Li P'ing-erh. "If I don't die, that's that. But if I'm going to die, what can you do to prevent it?"

"I've been wanting to tell you, but haven't told you yet," she went on to say, "that whenever I'm alone in the room, I'm afraid. It seems, though vague and indistinct, that there is someone there in front of me. I constantly dream of him at night, looking just as he did when he was still alive:

Brandishing knives and flourishing weapons,

in the attempt to pick a quarrel with me, while holding the child in his arms. When I try to take the child, he pushes me roughly away. He says that he has purchased another house where he now is and demands over and over again that I should go join him there. But I've been reluctant to tell you about it."

When Hsi-men Ch'ing heard this, he said:

"A person's death is like the extinction of a lamp.[8]

During these several years, who knows where he has gone? This is all due to the fact that you have been ill for so long and have lost so much blood from hemorrhaging below. I doubt the existence of any such things as evil spirits or demons, or the ghosts of kinfolk or unrelated persons, bent on troubling you. But tomorrow I will send someone to Abbot Wu's temple to get a couple of written spells, and paste them on the door of your room. That way we can determine whether there are any evil influences at work, or not."

Before he had even finished speaking, he headed toward the front of the compound and deputed Tai-an to take a mount and ride to the Temple of the Jade Emperor in order to get the spells. When Tai-an got out onto the street, he ran into Ying Po-chüeh and Hsieh Hsi-ta and dismounted to speak to them.

"Is your master at home?" they inquired.

"Father is at home," reported Tai-an

"And where are you off to?" they went on to ask.

"I'm on my way to the Temple of the Jade Emperor to pick up some written spells," said Tai-an.

Ying Po-chüeh and Hsieh Hsi-ta then proceeded to Hsi-men Ch'ing's place, where Ying Po-chüeh said, "Hsieh Hsi-ta has heard that our sister-in-law is unwell, which gave him quite a start; so we have come to ask after her health."

"She's been a little better the last couple of days," said Hsi-men Ch'ing, "but I can tell you, her body has become so emaciated she is scarcely recognizable, which has left me entirely at a loss for what to do in any direction. Her child is dead, but why not leave it at that? All she does is cry all night long, and it is this excess of grief that has brought on her illness. If you try to talk her out of it, she won't pay you any attention, which leaves me completely at a loss for what to do next."

"Brother," asked Ying Po-chüeh, "what have you sent Tai-an to the temple for?"

Hsi-men Ch'ing told them all about how Li P'ing-erh was afraid whenever she was alone in her room. "She fears that there are evil influences at work, so I have sent the page boy to ask Abbot Wu for a couple of written spells which can be pasted up in her room with a view to suppressing them."

"Brother," said Hsieh Hsi-ta, "this is a result of the fact that my sister-in-law's vital spirits are at a low ebb. I doubt if there are any such things as evil spirits or demons involved."

"Brother," said Ying Po-chüeh, "if it's evil spirits that you want to dispel, that's no problem. Taoist Master P'an from the Temple of the Five Peaks outside the city gate is trained in the Five Thunder Rites of the Celestial Heart Sect[9] and is very adept at exorcising evil influences. He is popularly known as Demon-catcher P'an and constantly relieves people with his potions. Brother, if you will invite him to come here, he can examine my sister-in-law's room to see if there are any evil spirits lurking there. If there are, he will know it. If you then ask him to treat her ailment, he will be able to do so."

"After I get the written spells from Abbot Wu," said Hsi-men Ch'ing, "we can ascertain where he lives, and, if necessary, you can ride on a donkey with my page boy to invite him here."

"That's no problem," said Ying Po-chüeh. "I'm happy to go. And if Heaven takes pity on her so that my sister-in-law recovers, I'd be willing to kowtow every step of the way, if necessary."

After they had talked for a while, Ying Po-chüeh and Hsieh Hsi-ta, having finished their tea, stood up and went about their business.

When Tai-an returned with the written spells, they were pasted up in the sickroom, but that evening, Li P'ing-erh was still afraid and said to Hsi-men

Ch'ing, "Just now the deceased one, together with two other men, came to apprehend me, but when they saw you coming in, they hid themselves out of the way."

"You shouldn't believe in such evil spirits," said Hsi-men Ch'ing, "but it doesn't matter. Yesterday Brother Ying the Second remarked that these hallucinations are the result of your emaciated state. He said that outside the city gate, at the Temple of the Five Peaks, there is a Taoist Master P'an who is good at curing ailments with his potions, and also at exorcising evil spirits. Tomorrow morning I'll ask Brother Ying the Second to go invite him to come and see you. If there are any evil influences at work, we can get him to dispel them."

"My brother," said Li P'ing-erh, "get him to come as soon as possible. That wretch was angry when he went away just now. He's likely to come back to get me tomorrow. Send someone after the Taoist master as quickly as you can."

"If you're afraid," said Hsi-men Ch'ing, "I'll send a page boy with a sedan chair to bring Wu Yin-erh here to keep you company for a few days."

Li P'ing-erh shook her head, and said, "Don't impose on her. I'm afraid it would interfere with her business at home."

"How would it be," asked Hsi-men Ch'ing, "if I got Old Mother Feng to come and look after you for a couple of days?"

Li P'ing-erh nodded her head in assent. Hsi-men Ch'ing sent Lai-an to summon Old Mother Feng from the house on Lion Street, but she wasn't there, having locked her door and gone out.

Lai-an said to Lai-chao's wife, "The Beanpole," "As soon as she comes back, whatever you do, tell her to come over as quickly as possible. The Sixth Lady at the mansion is calling for her."

Hsi-men Ch'ing also instructed Tai-an, saying, "First thing tomorrow morning you must accompany Ying Po-chüeh to the Temple of the Five Peaks outside the city gate in order to invite Taoist Master P'an to come here." But no more of this.

The next day, who should appear but Nun Wang from the Kuan-yin Nunnery, who came to see Li P'ing-erh, carrying with her a box of nonglutinous rice, twenty large pieces of junket, and a small box of squash and eggplant julienne marinated with ten spices. When Li P'ing-erh saw that she had come, she hastily told Ying-ch'un to help her up into a sitting position to receive her. Nun Wang placed her palms together and saluted her in the Buddhist fashion, after which Li P'ing-erh invited her to take a seat.

"Reverend Wang," said Li P'ing-erh, "ever since you went off to arrange for the printing of that sutra, I haven't seen so much as your shadow. I've been as ill as this, and you haven't even bothered to come and see me."

"Mistress mine," said Nun Wang, "I was completely ignorant of the fact that you were unwell. I only found out about it when the First Lady sent a servant to the Nunnery the other day. And as for the printing of that sutra, you may not know it, but that old whore Nun Hsüeh and I have been engaged in quite a quarrel about it. By arranging for the printing of that sutra on your behalf all I was doing was driving the fish into the net for Nun Hsüeh, who connived with the printer to get a kickback of five taels, while I got off with not so much as a candareen. You may be bent on creating good fortune for yourself, but that old whore, in the future, will end up in the Avici Hell.[10] She has made me so angry that I'm not myself and even forgot to come by for the First Lady's birthday."

"Everyone creates his own karma," said Li P'ing-erh. "Let her do as she pleases. You shouldn't make an issue out of it."

"Who's making an issue out of it?" demanded Nun Wang.

"The First Lady is really annoyed with you," said Li P'ing-erh. "She says that you have even neglected to recite the *Shou-sheng ching*, or *Scripture on Incarnation*,[11] on her behalf."

"My bodhisattva!" protested Nun Wang. "However remiss I might be, I would never dare to neglect reciting a scripture for her. I have been reciting the *Shou-sheng ching* at my place for the last month and only finished doing so yesterday. On coming here today, I went first to the rear compound in order to see her and told her about my sense of grievance. When I told her, 'I didn't know that the Sixth Lady was unwell, and don't have anything to offer but this box of nonglutinous rice, some squash and eggplant julienne marinated with ten spices, and several pieces of junket that she can eat with her congee,' the First Lady told Sister Hsiao-yü to bring me here to see you."

When Hsiao-yü had opened the boxes to show her the contents, Li P'ing-erh said, "Thank you for your trouble."

"Sister Ying-ch'un," said Nun Wang, "take two pieces of this junket and steam them, so I can look on as your mistress eats them with some congee."

Ying-ch'un accordingly accepted the proffered gifts and put them away.

"Prepare some tea for Reverend Wang to drink," Li P'ing-erh instructed Ying-ch'un.

"I've just had some tea in the First Lady's room in the rear compound," said Nun Wang. "Have her boil up some congee so I can watch you eat it."

Before long, Ying-ch'un set up a table and laid out four varieties of snacks to go with the tea which she provided for Nun Wang. After this, she brought in the congee for Li P'ing-erh to eat. There were a saucer of squash and eggplant julienne served in a sweet sauce and marinated with ten spices, a saucer of junket steamed to a frosty brown, two cups of congee made from the nonglutinous rice, and a pair of miniature ivory chopsticks. Ying-ch'un deployed the chopsticks, while the wet nurse Ju-i stood to one side holding a cup, as they attempted to feed her for some time, but she was only able to swallow two or three mouthfuls of congee, and nibble on some junket, before she shook her head, stopped eating, and told them to take it away.

"For us human beings," said Nun Wang:

> It is food and water that sustain our lives.[12]

This is such good congee. Won't you have a little more?"

"What am I to do," said Li P'ing-erh, "if I'm unable to swallow it?"

Ying-ch'un then moved the tea table out of the way. Nun Wang lifted the coverlet aside, and when she saw that the flesh of Li P'ing-erh's body had wasted away to practically nothing, it gave her quite a start.

"Mistress mine!" she exclaimed. "When I left you the last time, you were getting better. Why have you taken such a turn for the worse, and become emaciated to such an extent?"

"She was indeed getting better," said Ju-i. "Her ailment originally began as a result of suppressed anger, and Father invited a doctor to come and examine her. She took the medicines he prescribed every day and was 70 or 80 percent on the way to recovery. But in the eighth month, her baby boy suffered a fright that left him in a bad way. The mistress was worried about him day and night and wore herself out so that she was not even able to get any sleep. Though she hoped against hope that the boy would recover, despite her expectations, he died. She can't help crying all day long, on top of which she is suffering from:

> Suppressed anger and suppressed resentment,

in her heart. Even someone forged out of iron or stone could hardly be expected to bear up under all these tribulations. It's not surprising that her ailment has taken a turn for the worse. When one is suffering from suppressed anger, it helps to discuss it with someone else, but the mistress won't let anything out. No matter how hard you press her on the subject, she won't say a word about it."

"What does she have to be angry about?" asked Nun Wang. "Your master loves her. The First Lady respects her. Of the five or six other ladies around her, who would actually give her cause for anger?"

"Reverend Wang," said the wet nurse, "are you really unaware of who has upset her?"

Turning to Hsiu-ch'un, she said, "Step outside and look around to see if the gate is shut, or not.

> Even if you only talk along the road,
> There may be someone lurking in the grass,

if you don't watch out."

She then went on to say, "It is the Fifth Lady next door who has upset our mistress. The cat from her place scratched the hand of her baby boy so badly that it caused him to go into convulsions. When the master came home, he interrogated her about it, but she refrained from telling him who was to blame. It was only later, after the First Lady had told him what happened, that he dashed the cat to death; but she still refused to acknowledge her guilt and vented her wrath on us. In the eighth month, after the little boy died, she took to:

>Pointing at the mulberry tree,
>But cursing the locust tree,

from her place next door, every day, expressing her gratification in a hundred different ways. Our mistress, in her room here, could hear everything she said perfectly clearly. How could she help being upset? In any case, although she was secretly perturbed, she didn't let the tears show. It's on account of this:

>Suppressed anger and suppressed resentment,

that she has developed this ailment. Heaven only knows, our mistress is possessed of an admirable disposition.

>The good things that take place she keeps to herself,
>The bad things that happen she also keeps to herself.

In her relations with her sister wives and concubines, she has never allowed herself to get:

>Red in the face with anger.[13]

If she has attractive clothes, she refrains from appearing in them until the others have something comparable to wear. In this entire household there is not a person who has not derived some benefit from their association with her. But, just as I said, despite having benefited from her generosity, there are those who don't have a good word to say for her behind her back."

"Why should they disapprove of her?" asked Nun Wang.

"For example," said Ju-i, "one time Old Mrs. P'an, the Fifth Lady's mother, was here on a visit when it happened that the master wanted to sleep in the Fifth Lady's room, so she came over here to spend the night with our mistress. When she was about to leave, our mistress gave her some shoe uppers, a jacket, and some money, in fact, there is hardly anything she wouldn't have given her, but the Fifth Lady still didn't have a good word to say for her."

When Li P'ing-erh heard this, she was annoyed at Ju-i and said, "Don't be such an old woman. Why should you criticize her for no good reason? I'm already as good as dead. Let her do as she pleases.

>Though Heaven does not speak, it is obvious
>   that it is high;
>Though Earth does not speak, it is apparent
>   that it is low."[14]

"My Lord Buddha!" Nun Wang exclaimed. "Who could have known that you have such a good heart?

>Heaven also has eyes, and
>Looks down from above.

You are sure to accrue benefits therefrom in the future."

"Reverend Wang," said Li P'ing-erh, "what benefits could there be for me? I haven't even been able to save the life of my only child, and now I'm not fated to live any longer myself. Suffering as I am from this ailment in my lower body, even if I were a ghost, I wouldn't be able to take a single step comfortably. I would like to give you some silver, Reverend Wang, in the hope that in the future, after I'm dead, you can arrange to have some nuns regularly recite the *Hsüeh-p'en ching*, or *Blood Pool Sutra*,[15] on my behalf. As for this evil karma of mine, there's no telling how much of it I may have accumulated."

"My bodhisattva!" exclaimed Nun Wang. "You are worrying far too much. Just see if you don't get better in the days to come. For someone as good-hearted as you are, the dragon kings and devas are sure to extend their protection."

As they were speaking, Ch'in-t'ung came in and said to Ying-ch'un, "Father has issued instructions that you should straighten up the room. Hua the Elder is about to come in to see how your mistress is. He is sitting outside in the front compound."

Nun Wang then stood up and said, "I'll go back to the rear compound for the time being."

"Reverend Wang," said Li P'ing-erh, "don't go home, but stay and keep me company for a few days. There are other things I want to discuss with you."

"Mistress mine," replied Nun Wang, "I won't go then."

Before long, Hsi-men Ch'ing ushered Hua the Elder in for a visit, but Li P'ing-erh remained lying on the k'ang and did not have anything to say.

"I didn't know anything about it," said Hua Tzu-yu, "until yesterday, when a servant from your place came to let me know. Tomorrow your sister-in-law will come to see how you are."

Li P'ing-erh merely responded by saying, "I'm putting you to a lot of trouble," and then turned over so that she was facing in the other direction.

Hua Tzu-yu sat with her for a while and then got up and returned to the front compound, where he said to Hsi-men Ch'ing, "When my deceased uncle, the old eunuch director, was serving as grand defender of Kuang-nan, he brought some medicinal notoginseng[16] back with him. Has she taken any of it, or not? No matter what sort of uterine bleeding a woman may suffer from, whether it be flooding or spotting, if five candareen's weight of this medication in powdered form is taken with wine, it will put a stop to it immediately. If my sister-in-law still retains any of this herbal medication, why doesn't she take some of it?"

"She has tried that medication," said Hsi-men Ch'ing. "The other day, Prefect Hu Shih-wen of Tung-p'ing prefecture came to pay a visit, and we discussed this medical problem. He also suggested a prescription, consisting of carbonized hemp palm fibers and white cockscomb flowers, decocted with wine, but it only stanched her bleeding for one day, after which the hemorrhaging continued more copiously than ever."

"In that case," said Hua Tzu-yu, "her condition will prove difficult to treat. Brother-in-law, you ought to look into getting a set of coffin boards for her as soon as possible, so they'll be ready when needed. Tomorrow, I'll have your sister-in-law come to see her."

When he had finished speaking, he stood up to go. Despite repeated attempts, Hsi-men Ch'ing could not persuade him to stay any longer, so he said goodbye and departed.

The wet nurse and Ying-ch'un were engaged in replacing the absorbent grass paper under Li P'ing-erh's body, when who should appear but Old Mother Feng, who came forward and saluted them with a bow.

"Old Mother Feng," said Ju-i, "you've been putting on the airs of a grande dame. Why haven't you come to look in on the mistress? Yesterday, Father sent Lai-an to fetch you, but he said you had locked your door and gone off somewhere."

"I can't tell you," said Old Mother Feng, "what a difficult time I've had, what with going to the temple to attend services all day long. I go out first thing in the morning, and then, no matter whether things go well or things go badly, I often don't get home until dark. And then I have to cope with Monk Chang, Monk Li, or Monk Wang."[17]

"However do you have the stamina to take on that many monks?" asked Ju-i. "It's a good thing Reverend Wang isn't here to hear you."

When Li P'ing-erh overheard this, she laughed lightly, saying, "This Old Mother never does anything but talk nonsense."

"Old Mother Feng," said Ju-i, "just when you're needed the most, you fail to show up. For the last several days, the mistress has not even swallowed a mouthful of congee, because she's been so depressed at heart. But you no sooner arrive than you induce her to laugh. If you would only consent to look after her for a few days, I'm sure that her ailment would take a turn for the better."

"I guess I'm just the sort of magician needed to fend off disaster for the mistress," said Old Mother Feng.

Everyone had a laugh at this.

Old Mother Feng then felt for Li P'ing-erh's body under the coverlet and said, "Mistress, everything will be all right if you can only get a little better."

She then went on to ask, "Can she get down to sit on the commode by herself?"

"It would be a good thing if she could," said Ying-ch'un. "The last two times she tried it, she struggled to do it and was just able to manage it with our support. For the last two days, however, she has remained on the k'ang. We put absorbent grass paper under her, and change it two or three times a day."

"The fact is," said Ju-i, "that she doesn't have the strength to eat anything much in the way of food, so how can her system withstand the effects of this hemorrhaging?"

As they were speaking, Hsi-men Ch'ing came in and, catching sight of Old Mother Feng, said, "Old Feng, you ought to be coming over here to see her all the time. How is it that after you leave you fail to come back?"

"Master," protested the old woman, "how could I fail to come back? The last several days have been the time of year for me to pickle vegetables in the hope of picking up a few candareens. As long as I've got some pickled vegetables in the house, when people bring their karmic encumbrances to me to find places for, I'll have something for them to eat. Otherwise, where would I find the idle money to buy vegetables for them to eat?"

"Why didn't you tell me?" said Hsi-men Ch'ing. "The other day they harvested the vegetables on my country estate. If I turn over the produce from two or three vegetable beds to you, that ought to suffice."

"I'd be much obliged to you once again," said the old woman.

When she had finished speaking, Old Mother Feng went over into an adjacent room. Hsi-men Ch'ing then sat down on the edge of the k'ang, beside which Ying-ch'un was burning some rue incense.

"How are you feeling at heart today?" Hsi-men Ch'ing inquired.

He then went on to ask Ying-ch'un, "Did your mistress eat any congee this morning, or not?"

"She did eat a little better than before," said Ying-ch'un. "Nun Wang brought her some pieces of junket, which I steamed for her, but she only nibbled at them. She was able to swallow no more than two mouthfuls of congee and broth, before she set them aside."

"Just now," said Hsi-men Ch'ing, "Brother Ying the Second and my page boy went outside the city gate to invite that Taoist Master P'an to come and see you, but he wasn't there. Tomorrow, I'll send Lai-pao on a donkey to go look for him again."

"Send someone after him as soon as possible," said Li P'ing-erh. "No sooner do I close my eyes than that wretch appears to harass me."

"That is only the result of your low spirits," said Hsi-men Ch'ing. "Just set your mind at rest, and stop imagining him. I'm sure that after we get that Taoist master here to dispel those evil influences for you, and after you've imbibed some of his medicine, you're bound to get better."

"My brother," said Li P'ing-erh, "since I've contracted this awkward illness, there's little chance of my recovery. The best I can hope for is that we might be together again in a life to come. Today, when there's no one else around, I can speak to you freely. I had hoped that I could remain by your side, so that we could share a life together for a number of years, after which, even if we died, we would have had the experience of living together as man and wife. Who could have known that now that I am in my twenty-seventh year, I should first lose my dear adversary of a son, and then have the bad luck to come down with this fatal disorder, and have to abandon you for good? If I am ever to run into you again, it will be in the Gateway to the Shades."

As she spoke, she grasped Hsi-men Ch'ing's hand firmly in her own, while the tears fell from her two eyes, until she choked up and could no longer utter a sound.

Hsi-men Ch'ing also was overcome by grief and wept, saying, "My sister, if you have anything to say, say it."

As the two of them were weeping together in her bedroom, Ch'in-t'ung suddenly came in and said, "An orderly has come to remind you, Master, that tomorrow is the fifteenth day of the month, when you will be expected to participate in the ceremonies of bowing before the imperial tablet, taking the formal roll call, and presiding over the general disposition of pending cases in the yamen. Will you be going, or not? The foreman needs to know so he can attend you."

"I won't be able to go tomorrow," said Hsi-men Ch'ing. "Take one of my cards and deliver it to His Honor Hsia Yen-ling, so he can take care of bowing before the imperial tablet without me."

Ch'in-t'ung nodded in assent and went out.

"My brother," said Li P'ing-erh, "if you do as I wish, you'll go to the yamen anyway. Don't let me interfere with your official responsibilities. They're important. Who knows when I'll die? It's early days yet."

"I'm going to stay at home and keep you company for a few days," said Hsi-men Ch'ing. "How could I bear to do otherwise? You must set your mind at rest, and stop worrying so much. Just now, Hua the Elder suggested to me that I look into getting a set of coffin boards for you, with a view to shocking you out of your indisposition. In that case, you'd surely get better."

Li P'ing-erh nodded in assent and said, "So be it; but you mustn't let yourself be talked into spending a foolish amount of money. It will suffice if you spend ten taels or so of silver in order to buy me a ready-made coffin, and then bury me beside the grave of your first wife. But don't have me cremated, if you care about our feelings for each other as man and wife. In that case, both early and late, it will be more convenient for me to partake of whatever offerings are made to the deceased. The members of your household are so numerous, you need to consider what it will take to support them in the future."

If Hsi-men Ch'ing had not heard these words nothing might have happened, but having heard them, he felt just as though:

A knife were slashing his liver and gall;
A sword were piercing his body and heart.

"My sister," he said with tears in his eyes, "how can you talk that way? I, Hsi-men Ch'ing, even though I were to become utterly impoverished, would never let you down."

As they were speaking, Yüeh-niang came in, with a small box of fresh apples in her hand, and said, "Sister Li, my elder brother's wife has sent these apples for you to eat."

She then instructed Ying-ch'un, saying, "Wash these clean, and then cut them into slices with a knife for your mistress to eat."

"Once again," said Li P'ing-erh, "I am indebted to your elder brother's wife for her solicitude on my behalf."

It did not take long for Ying-ch'un to peel the apples, cut them into slices, and put them in a bowl, after which, Hsi-men Ch'ing and Yüeh-niang, standing to either side of her, selected a slice to feed to her. They put it into her mouth, but after barely chewing enough of it to get the flavor, she spit it out. Yüeh-niang was afraid that they were tiring her, so she helped her into a supine position, with her face to the wall, and let her go to sleep. Hsi-men Ch'ing and Yüeh-niang then came outside to consult with each other about the situation.

"As for Sister Li," said Yüeh-niang, "it appears to me that her condition has reached a critical stage. You ought to look into obtaining a set of coffin boards for her as soon as possible, so that they will be available when needed. If you wait until the time for them is at hand, things will be in such an uproar that in scrambling to come up with a decent coffin, you'll be just like:

A horse trying to catch a rat.[18]

That's no way to handle the business."

"Today," responded Hsi-men Ch'ing, "Hua the Elder suggested the same thing. When I mentioned it to her just now, she enjoined me not to spend too much money and said that she would be content with a ready-made coffin. She went on to say, 'The members of your household are so numerous, you need to consider what it will take to support them in the future.' Her words have left me sore at heart ever since."

He then went on to say, "We might as well wait until Taoist Master P'an has come to consider her case before looking out for a coffin."

"Look here," said Yüeh-niang, "you don't know what you're saying. When a person is so emaciated she hardly retains her human shape, and when her esophagus is so stopped up that she can't even swallow a spoonful of water, you are still vainly expecting her to get well. We should be prepared for any contingency:

Beating the drum to sound an advance on the one hand,

And waving the flag to signal a retreat on the other.

If she is fortunate enough to recover, we can always donate the coffin to someone else. It won't cost us anything to speak of."

"I'll do as you say," said Hsi-men Ch'ing.

He then went back to the rear compound with Yüeh-niang and sent a page boy to summon Pen the Fourth.

When Pen the Fourth arrived in the reception hall, he asked him, "Who do you think has the best coffin boards available? I'd like you and my son-in-law to take some silver with you and see if you can find a good set."

"Battalion Commander Ch'en's place on Main Street," said Pen the Fourth, "has recently acquired several sets of good coffin boards."

"If he's got good coffin boards available," said Hsi-men Ch'ing, turning to Ch'en Ching-chi, "you go back to the rear compound and ask your mother-in-law for five large silver ingots, so the two of you can go look for a set."

Before long, Ch'en Ching-chi came back with five silver ingots of fifty taels weight each and then set off on this errand with Pen Ti-ch'uan. They did not return to report on their mission until mid-afternoon.

"What kept you so long?" asked Hsi-men Ch'ing.

"When we went to Battalion Commander Ch'en's place," the two of them replied, "we looked at several sets of coffin boards, but they were all of mediocre quality, and the price was not right. On our way home, however, we happened to run into your kinsman Ch'iao Hung in the street, who said that Provincial Graduate Shang has a fine set of coffin boards. They were originally brought back by his father from his tour of duty as prefectural judge of Ch'eng-tu in Szechwan and were intended for his wife. Initially there were two sets of coffin boards from Peach Blossom Cavern,[19] one of which has already been used, so this is the only set remaining. It is a complete set of five boards of different sizes, from which the side walls, bottom, lid, and end pieces can be fashioned,[20] and the asking price is 370 taels of silver. Ch'iao Hung went with us to look at these coffin boards, and they turned out to be of incomparably superior quality. Ch'iao Hung bargained over the price with Provincial Graduate Shang for some time, but he was only willing to reduce it by 50 taels. If it were not for the fact that he is planning to go to the capital to participate in the metropolitan examination next year, for which he needs the money, he would not be willing to part with this set of coffin boards. He also indicated that he is taking into consideration the fact that it is our household that wants them. If it were anyone else, he would insist on 350 taels."

"Since it is Ch'iao Hung who is acting as advocate," said Hsi-men Ch'ing, "we might as well pay out the 320 taels and have them carried here. But see that you do it quietly, without:

Ringing bells and beating drums."

"He has already accepted our 250 taels," said Ch'en Ching-chi, "so we only owe him another 70 taels of silver to close the deal."

He then went back to the rear compound and got Yüeh-niang to give him another 70 taels of "snowflake" silver, after which the two of them left to complete their errand.

At dusk that evening, who should appear but a crowd of idlers, who carried the coffin boards through the gate, wrapped in strips of red felt, put them down in the front courtyard, and unwrapped them for Hsi-men Ch'ing to look at. Sure enough, they turned out to be fine coffin boards. Artisans were promptly engaged to saw them open, and when they did, they exuded a pungent aroma. Each piece was five inches thick, two feet five inches wide, and seven feet five inches long.

Hsi-men Ch'ing's heart was filled with delight, and he showed them off to Ying Po-chüeh, saying, "These coffin boards will pass muster."

Ying Po-chüeh praised them unstintingly, saying, "It could be said that these coffin boards are fated to be hers.

Every object has its rightful owner.

Since my sister-in-law had the good fortune to marry you, Brother, it is only appropriate that she should end up in possession of these coffin boards."

Then, turning to the artisans, he said, "If you only take the pains to do a good job, your employer will reward you with five taels of silver."

"We understand," the artisans replied, and then proceeded, hugger-mugger, to go to work in the front reception hall, working all night to construct the coffin as quickly as possible. But no more of this.

Ying Po-chüeh then enjoined Lai-pao, "Early tomorrow morning, at the fifth watch, you should go to invite Taoist Master P'an. If he is willing to come, you should accompany him back here. This matter will brook no delay."

When he had finished speaking, he continued to keep Hsi-men Ch'ing company that evening in the front reception hall, looking on as the artisans worked on the construction of the coffin. It was not until the first watch that he got up to go home.

"Come back as soon as you can tomorrow morning," said Hsi-men Ch'ing. "I'm afraid that Taoist Master P'an may arrive rather early."

"I understand," responded Ying Po-chüeh, after which he said goodbye and went out the gate.

To resume our story, Old Mother Feng and Nun Wang were keeping Li P'ing-erh company in her room that night, when who should appear but Hsi-men Ch'ing, who came in to see her after the conclave in the front compound broke up and wanted to go to sleep there.

Li P'ing-erh objected to this, saying, "You mustn't think of it. This room is:
    Polluted and unclean,[21]
and the two of them are also here. It wouldn't be convenient. You go sleep somewhere else."

When Hsi-men Ch'ing saw that Nun Wang and Old Mother Feng were there, he went over to Chin-lien's quarters next door.

Li P'ing-erh told Ying-ch'un to close the postern gate and secure it with the crossbar, after which she told her to light a lamp, open her trunk, and get out several items of clothing and silver ornaments, and place them beside her.

First of all, she called Nun Wang over, gave her a five-tael ingot of silver, along with a bolt of silk, and said, "After I am dead, whatever you do, you must invite some fellow nuns to join you in recitations of the *Blood Pool Sutra* on my behalf."

"Mistress mine," expostulated Nun Wang, "you are worrying yourself over much. If Heaven only takes pity on you, you are likely to recover."

"You just put these things away," said Li P'ing-erh, "and don't tell the First Lady that I gave you any silver. Just say that I gave you this bolt of silk to compensate you for arranging the recitations of the sutra."

"I understand what you're saying," said Nun Wang, and she thereupon took possession of both the silver and the silk.

Li P'ing-erh then called over Old Mother Feng, picked up four taels of silver from beside her pillow, along with a white damask jacket, a yellow damask skirt, and a silver comb, and gave them to her, saying, "Old Feng, you're a familiar companion. You have served me from the time I was a child right up until the present time. Now, after I am dead, these articles of clothing and this ornamental comb can serve you as keepsakes, and you can use this silver to defray the cost of a coffin. And don't worry about the house. I'll talk to Father about it, so that you can continue to live there and act as a caretaker on his behalf, as it were. He's not about to evict you or anything like that."

Old Mother Feng accepted the silver and the clothing with one hand and knelt down to kowtow with tears in her eyes, saying, "It seems my luck is running out. As long as you remain alive I can count on you to look out for me. But if:

> Anything untoward should happen to you,[22]

what will become of me?"

Li P'ing-erh also called over the wet nurse Ju-i and gave her a purple damask jacket, a blue damask skirt, an old satin cloak, two hairpins with gold heads, and a silver cap ornament,[23] saying, "This is in recognition of the fact that you nursed my baby boy. Now, the boy has died, but, as I said, I didn't want you to bind up your breasts as though your job were over. It was my hope that as long as I remained alive, I might have further occasion to use you. Now, unexpectedly, it looks as though I am going to die, but I will talk to your master and the First Lady, and suggest that after my death, if the First Lady gives birth to a son, they should not get rid of you, but allow you to nurse her child. I am giving you these articles of clothing as a keepsake. Please don't take it amiss."

The wet nurse got down on her knees and kowtowed, saying with tears in her eyes, "I had truly hoped that I would be able to serve you to the end. You have never so much as gotten angry with me, or raised your voice to criticize me. It's just my bad luck that the boy died, and that you have contracted this fatal disorder. Please, whatever happens, do tell the First Lady that my husband is dead, and that as long as I live, I hope to be able to continue serving the master and mistress. If I were to leave, where would I go?"

When she had finished speaking, she accepted the clothes and ornaments, kowtowed, and then got up and stood to one side, while wiping the tears from her eyes.

Li P'ing-erh then called over Ying-ch'un and Hsiu-ch'un, who knelt down before her while she addressed them, saying, "The two of you have also served me since you were children. Now, after I have died, I won't be able to look after you any more. You both have enough in the way of clothing, so there is no need to give you any, but I will give you these two pairs of gold-headed hairpins, and these two floral ornaments of gold as keepsakes. As my senior maidservant, Ying-ch'un, since Father has already had his way with you, there is no call for you to leave the household. I will ask the First Lady to let you serve in her quarters. As my junior maidservant, Hsiu-ch'un, I'll ask the First Lady to look out for another family for you to serve, lest you be looked askance at for remaining in my quarters, and be subject to criticism by others as a slave without a master. After I'm dead, you may let your true colors show; but if you work for anyone else and affect the:

> Coquetry and petulance of a spoiled child,

or endeavor to:

> Do whatever you like for good or for ill,

the way you have been accustomed to do while in my service, no one will tolerate it."

Hsiu-ch'un knelt down on the ground and wept, saying, "Mother, I won't leave here even to save my life."

"Don't be silly," said Li P'ing-erh. "If you remain in these quarters, who will you serve?"

"I will keep vigil over your spirit tablet," said Hsiu-ch'un.

"Even though offerings may be made to my spirit tablet for a while," said Li P'ing-erh, "eventually the day will come when it will be burnt. You'll have no alternative but to leave then."

"I could serve the First Lady along with Ying-ch'un," said Hsiu-ch'un.

"Well, let's leave it at that," said Li P'ing-erh. "I'm afraid Hsiu-ch'un is still somewhat naive in her understanding of things."

After listening to Li P'ing-erh's injunctions, Ying-ch'un took possession of the head ornaments she had been given, while weeping so hard she could not get a word out. Truly:

> Tear-filled eyes gaze into
> > tear-filled eyes;
> The brokenhearted see off
> > the brokenhearted.[24]

That night Li P'ing-erh managed to issue her final injunctions to everyone.

At dawn the next day, Hsi-men Ch'ing came into her room, and Li P'ing-erh asked him, "Have you purchased a coffin for me, or not?"

"The coffin boards were procured yesterday," said Hsi-men Ch'ing. "They're being made up into a coffin in the front compound right now, with a view to shocking you out of your indisposition. If you recover, we can always donate it to someone else."

"How much silver did you spend on it?" Li P'ing-erh went on to ask. "You shouldn't spend money indiscriminately, or you'll end up with not enough to live on."

"It wasn't much," said Hsi-men Ch'ing. "I only paid a hundred some taels of silver."

"That's still too much," said Li P'ing-erh. "See that you get it prepared in advance and lay it out for me."

After talking with her for a while, Hsi-men Ch'ing went back out to the front compound to watch the progress of the coffin construction.

Who should appear at this juncture but Wu Yüeh-niang and Li Chiao-erh, who came into her room and, seeing that her condition was extremely serious, asked, "Sister Li, how are you feeling?"

Li P'ing-erh grasped Yüeh-niang by the hand and wept, saying, "First Lady, I am not going to recover."

Yüeh-niang wept with her, saying, "Sister Li, if you have anything you want to say, the Second Lady is here with me, you can say it to the two of us."

"What have I got to say?" said Li P'ing-erh. "During these several years that we've been sisters, you've never let me down. I had really hoped to remain together with you until our heads of hair turned white, but, contrary to my expectations, my fate has turned out to be bitter. First, I lost my darling boy, and now, I've been so unfortunate as to come down with this awkward ailment, which is going to be the death of me. After I'm dead, these two maidservants of mine will have no one to look after them. Since Father has already had his way with the senior maidservant, I suggest that she be assigned to your quarters, where she can wait on you. As for the junior maidservant, if you wish to employ her, then keep her. Otherwise, see if you can't arrange a monogamous marriage for her with some humble family, so there will be but:

One husband and a single wife.

That way she won't be subject to criticism as a slave without a master, and it would be a fitting reward for the service she has rendered me. In that case, my mouth and eyes will be content to remain closed after my death. In addition, the wet nurse Ju-i has repeatedly expressed her unwillingness to leave the household. If you consent to do me the favor of assenting to her wishes, it will be an appropriate reward for her service in nursing my child. And in the future, when your own ten months of pregnancy are up, if you bear a son, she can take over the job of breast-feeding him."

"Sister Li," said Yüeh-niang, "you can put your mind to rest about these matters. The two of us will take responsibility for taking care of them. We must:

Prepare for the worst and hope for the best.

If you should end up:

High as the hills or deep as the sea,

I will arrange to have Ying-ch'un work for me, and Hsiu-ch'un work for the Second Lady. The maidservant who is assigned to the Second Lady's quarters at present is not a reliable worker and will have to be gotten rid of sooner or later. I'll have Hsiu-ch'un wait on her instead. As for the wet nurse Ju-i, although you say that she has no place to go, there is no room for her in my quarters. No matter whether I have a child or not, in the future I'll arrange a match for her with one of the servants, so that she can remain in the household as a servant's wife. That ought to take care of it."

Li Chiao-erh then spoke up from the side, saying, "Sister Li, you should stop worrying about these matters. The two of us will take responsibility for them. In the future, after your funeral observances are over, I'll take her into my quarters to wait upon me, and see that she receives preferential treatment."

Li P'ing-erh then told the wet nurse and her two maidservants to come over and kowtow to their two benefactors. Yüeh-niang was unable to control her tears.

Before long, Meng Yü-lou, P'an Chin-lien, and Sun Hsüeh-o came in to see how she was, and Li P'ing-erh bestowed a few sisterly words that were both kind and just upon each of them, but there is no need to describe this in detail.

Later on, after Li Chiao-erh, Meng Yü-lou, P'an Chin-lien, and the others had left, leaving Yüeh-niang alone in the room with her, Li P'ing-erh wept quietly and said to her, "Mother, in the future, if you bear a son, be sure to raise him carefully so that he can be the root that perpetuates Father's ancestral line. Don't be as careless as I was and allow yourself to be undone by anyone else."

"Sister," said Yüeh-niang, "I understand what you're saying."

Gentle reader take note: This single sentence had such an effect on Yüeh-niang that, later on, after the death of Hsi-men Ch'ing, when Chin-lien was no longer permitted to remain in the household, it was all due to her memory of this deathbed remark of Li P'ing-erh's. Truly:

> It has always been true that gratitude for kindness
> > and festering resentment;
> Even in a thousand or ten thousand years
> > will never be allowed to gather dust.

As they were speaking, who should appear but Ch'in-t'ung, who told them to straighten up the room and burn some incense because Taoist Master P'an from the Temple of the Five Peaks had arrived. Yüeh-niang supervised the maidservants as they cleaned up the room, prepared some clear tea brewed with purified water, and ignited some genuine "hundred-blend" incense.[25] Yüeh-niang and the other women then concealed themselves in the bedroom next door in order to eavesdrop on the proceedings.

Before long, whom should they see but Hsi-men Ch'ing, who ushered Taoist Master P'an into Li P'ing-erh's room. What did he look like? Behold:

> On his head is a Taoist cap with the Five Peaks
> > wreathed in sunset clouds;
> His body is appareled in a short robe of coarse
> > black cotton cloth.
> His waist is bound by a girdle woven of
> > varicolored silken thread;
> On his back he bears a sword of antique bronze
> > incised with a pine-grain pattern.[26]
> On his two feet he wears a pair of
> > double-looped hemp sandals;

In his hand he holds a five-luminary
    demon-dispelling fan.[27]
His eyebrows are peaked,
His two eyes are almond-shaped;
His mouth is foursquare,
Trailing a set of side whiskers.[28]
His demeanor is awe-inspiring;
His appearance is imposing.
If he is not a roving immortal wandering
    beyond the clouds,
He must hail from the Isles of the Blest
    or the Jade Palace.

Lo and behold, as he came in through the postern gate and made his way around the screen-wall, just as he approached Li P'ing-erh's quarters, beneath the stylobate under the veranda, the Taoist master stepped backwards two paces, seemed to be berating someone, and repeated a few occult formulas, before he stepped inside, as the servants pulled the portiere aside, and approached the sickbed. Once there:

He focused his two eyes upon her,
Exerting the wise discernment of their divine vision,
Brandished his sword in one hand,
Performed calculations on the joints of his fingers
        while pacing the dipper, and
Recited an incantation,[29]
Instantly comprehending the situation.

Going out into the parlor, he proceeded to set up an incense table facing the exterior of the building, and Hsi-men Ch'ing ignited some incense.

After burning some written talismans, Taoist Master P'an cried out in a loud voice, "Divine marshal on duty this day, why have you not yet appeared?"

He then spurted a mouthful of consecrated water out of his mouth, whereupon a strong gust of wind arose, and a yellow-turbaned warrior[30] appeared before him. Behold:

His forehead is enveloped in a yellow silk turban;[31]
His body clad in a purple robe of embroidered silk.
A Lion Barbarian girdle[32] tightly binds
    his wolflike waist;
Leopard-skin trousers securely enclose
    his tigerlike body.
He constantly wanders the highways of the clouds;
He is accustomed to navigating the astral winds.
The grotto heavens and blessed abodes[33]
    he traverses in an instant;

The sacred peaks, rivers, and Feng-tu
>   he visits in a snap of the fingers.
If a malevolent dragon wreaks havoc,
He can apprehend it from the bottom of the sea;
If evil sprites should make trouble,
He can smash their mountain lairs and nab them.
Within the halls of the Jade Emperor,
He is known as a talismanic functionary;
Before the carriage of the Northern Dipper,
He holds the title of celestial warrior.[34]
He is always on duty before the altar
>   to protect the law;
He constantly visits the mundane world
>   to vanquish demons.[35]
On his breast is suspended the bronze plaque
>   of the Board of Thunder;
In his hand he holds a brilliantly decorated
>   gilded battle-axe.[36]

That divine marshal stood respectfully beneath the steps and said in a loud voice, "Having summoned me, what would you command me to do?"

Taoist Master P'an said, "The woman, née Li, of the Hsi-men household is unwell, and he has lodged an appeal on her behalf before my altar. I command you to apprehend the local tutelary god, and the six household spirits, in order to ascertain whether there are any evil spirits at work, and hale them before me. This matter will brook no delay."

When he had finished speaking, the spirit disappeared.

In a little while, Taoist Master P'an closed his eyes and changed countenance, sat upright at his place, and rapped his tablet of authority on the surface of the altar table, just as if he were hearing a case in court. It was some time before he stopped and came outside.

Hsi-men Ch'ing ushered him out to the summerhouse in the front compound and asked him what he had ascertained.

"Unfortunately," said Taoist Master P'an, "this woman is being sued in the court of the underworld by someone who suffered an injustice at her hands in a former existence. It is not a case of evil spirits, so they are not subject to apprehension."

"Ritual Master," said Hsi-men Ch'ing, "is there anything you can do to exorcise the source of the problem?"

"In the case of an:
>   Enemy or creditor,
from a previous existence," said Taoist Master P'an, "it is up to the plaintiff himself. If he is willing to drop the case, it may be dropped; but even the authorities of the underworld cannot force him to do so."

Taoist Master P'an Conjures Up a Yellow-turbaned Warrior

Because he saw that Hsi-men Ch'ing was courteous and sincere, he then went on to ask, "How old is your lady?"

"She was born in the year of the sheep," said Hsi-men Ch'ing, "and is currently in her twenty-seventh year."

"All right then," said Taoist Master P'an, "let me perform a sacrifice at the altar to the star that governs her destiny, and see what happens to the lantern that corresponds to her fate."

"When will you perform the sacrifice?" asked Hsi-men Ch'ing. "And what will you need in the way of incense, paper money, and sacrificial offerings?"

"This evening," said Taoist Master P'an, "during the third watch, at midnight, I will delineate the boundaries of the sacred area with white ash, set up a lantern altar, invest it with yellow damask, place the lantern representing the star that governs her date of birth upon it, and make sacrificial offerings of the five grains, dates, and soup, without need of wine or meat. Then I will merely set out twenty-seven lanterns of destiny, corresponding to the years of her age, and cover them with a canopy. Nothing else will be required. While I am officiating at the sacrifice, chickens and dogs must be excluded from the premises, to prevent them from coming in and interfering with the proceedings. During the ceremony, you sir, having observed the appropriate ritual abstentions, should dress yourself in black, and prostrate yourself below the altar."

Hsi-men Ch'ing saw to it that all the suggested preparations were carried out to the letter and did not presume to enter the consecrated area, but remained in his study, where he performed his ablutions, observed the ritual abstentions, and changed into clean clothing. He also asked Ying Po-chüeh to remain with him rather than going home, in order to share a vegetarian repast with Taoist Master P'an.

During the third watch, when the setting up of the lantern altar had been completed, Taoist Master P'an took a seat in lofty isolation at the upper end of the consecrated area. The lantern altar was arrayed before him, with representations of the Green Dragon of the East, the White Tiger of the West, the Red Bird of the South, and the Dark Warrior of the North presiding over the four directions. Above it was suspended a three-tiered canopy, on which were represented the symbols of the twelve constellations correlated with the twelve earthly branches, arranged in a circle. Beneath this were arrayed the twenty-seven lanterns of destiny.

The celebrant began by declaiming the words of a petition, while Hsi-men Ch'ing, dressed in black, prostrated himself beneath the steps. The servants had all been excluded from the area, so that there was no one else present. The area was:

Ablaze with lamps and candles,

as the twenty-seven lanterns were simultaneously lighted. Taoist Master P'an, seated upon his ritual throne, let down his hair, brandished his sword, and:

Recited an incantation.

After which, he proceeded to:
>Invoke the Dipper,
>Imbibe the primordial breath,
>Pace the void, and
>Perambulate the jasper altar.

Truly:
>When three sticks of incense are burnt
>>the Three Realms unite;
>Each command that is issued results in
>>a clap of thunder.

Behold:
>In the clear sky, the stars and moon
>>shine brightly,
>When all of a sudden,
>The earth turns black and the sky darkens.[37]
>The curtains suspended on all four sides
>>of the summerhouse,
>Are suddenly swept by a gust of eerie wind.

Truly:
>It is not the roaring of tigers,
>Nor is it the droning of dragons.[38]
>It appears to penetrate the doors and
>>permeate the curtains;[39]
>It certainly destroys the flowers and
>>scatters the leaves.
>It drives the clouds out of the hills;
>And sends the rain back to the rivers.
>The wild geese are separated from their mates
>>and cry in distress;
>The gulls and herons in their startled flocks
>>seek the treetops.
>The goddess Ch'ang-o hastens to batten down
>>her palace in the moon;
>The wind-borne Lieh-tzu, high up in space,
>>calls out to be rescued.[40]

In the wake of three powerful gusts of wind, a chill breeze blew in that extinguished every last one of Li P'ing-erh's twenty-seven lanterns of destiny. Only a single flame recovered, by the light of which Taoist Master P'an, seated on his ritual throne, was able to see clearly a figure clothed in white, who came in from outside, accompanied by two black-clad servitors and, holding a document in his hand, proceeded to present it before the altar. When Taoist Master P'an examined it, he saw that it was an arrest warrant issued by the court of the underworld, which bore three official seals.

Startled by this, he descended from his ritual throne and, stepping forward, urged Hsi-men Ch'ing to get to his feet, saying, thus and so, "Sir, please stand up. It seems that, in your lady's case:
>One who has offended Heaven, has nowhere else to pray.[41]

Her lanterns of destiny have been extinguished. How then is she to be saved? I fear that her end is imminent."

When Hsi-men Ch'ing heard this, he lowered his head without a word, and his eyes brimmed over with tears.

Weeping, he besought the exorcist, saying, "My only hope, Ritual Master, is that you can do something to save her."

"One's allotted years are hard to evade."
said Taoist Master P'an. "It will be difficult to save her."

He then expressed a desire to depart.

Hsi-men Ch'ing urged him repeatedly to stay, saying, "Wait until daybreak, and you can get an early start."

"We people who have left home to enter the priesthood," said Taoist Master P'an, "are accustomed to:
>Hiking through the underbrush and sleeping in the dew;[42]
>Camping in the mountains and stopping over at temples.

It is only natural."

Hsi-men Ch'ing did not press him on the subject any further but ordered his attendants to bring out a bolt of fabric and three taels of silver as compensation for his performance of the ritual.

"I am a practitioner of the ultimate way of August Heaven," said Taoist Master P'an, "and have sworn an oath to Heaven itself that I would not presume to covet worldly wealth. Were I to do so, I would:
>Suffer for my culpability."[43]

Only after demurring repeatedly did he direct his acolyte to accept the fabric in order to make a Taoist robe, and then he prepared to take his leave and depart.

Before doing so, he enjoined Hsi-men Ch'ing, saying, "This evening, sir, you should observe the taboo against going into the sickroom, lest you bring a catastrophe upon yourself. Beware! Beware!"

Having finished speaking, he was escorted out to the front gate, where he:
>Shook his sleeves in disdain and departed.[44]

Hsi-men Ch'ing returned to the summerhouse to oversee the clearing away of the lantern altar. When he understood that there was no saving star to be hoped for, he was profoundly saddened, and when he sat down with Ying Po-chüeh, without his realizing it, his eyes overflowed with tears.

"This is merely an instance of the fact that everyone has a predetermined number of years to live," said Ying Po-chüeh. "When things come to such a pass, no amount of effort will avail. Brother, you should try to worry yourself less about it."

Then, upon hearing the sounding of the fourth watch, he said, "Brother, you are tired. You should get yourself some rest. I will go home for the time being, and come back tomorrow."

"I'll have a page boy get a lantern and see you on your way," said Hsi-men Ch'ing.

He then ordered Lai-an to fetch a lantern and accompanied them outside, after which he saw to the closing of the gate and came back inside. Hsi-men Ch'ing sat in the study all by himself, with a candle in his hand, feeling deeply disturbed at heart.

All he could do was give vent to long sighs as he thought to himself, "The ritual master warned me not to go into her sickroom, but how can I bear not to do so? Even if it should cost me my life, what of it? I feel the need to keep vigil, and have a word with her."

Thereupon, he went into her room and saw that Li P'ing-erh was lying with her face to the wall.

When she heard Hsi-men Ch'ing come in, she turned over, and said to him, "My brother, why didn't you come in before?"

She then went on to ask, "What did that Taoist master have to say about the lantern ritual?"

"You can relax on that score," said Hsi-men Ch'ing. "The lanterns did not indicate anything to worry about."

"My brother," said Li P'ing-erh, "you're deceiving me. Just now, that wretch, with two other people in tow, appeared before me once again and troubled me for a while. He said, 'You may have invited a ritual master to come and exorcise me, but my plaint against you has already been approved by the authorities in the underworld. You will not be allowed to escape.' He was angry when he went away and is likely to come back to get me tomorrow."

When Hsi-men Ch'ing heard this:

> Two streams of tears crisscrossed his face,

and he commenced to weep out loud, saying, "My sister, you should just set your mind at rest, and pay no attention to him. I had really hoped to be able to keep company with you throughout the days to come, but who could have anticipated that you would abandon me and go off this way? I, Hsi-men Ch'ing, would rather suffer the closing of my own mouth and eyes in death, rather than this:

> Stomach-turning and gut-wrenching suspense."[45]

Li P'ing-erh put both arms around Hsi-men Ch'ing's neck and gave way to:

> Sobbing and wailing.

After weeping grievously for some time, she became too hoarse to cry audibly any longer and said, "My brother, I had hoped that we could:

> Share our life together like a double-headed flower.

Hsi-men Ch'ing Weeps Painfully on Behalf of Li P'ing-erh

Who could have anticipated that today I would have to leave you in death? Taking advantage of what time is left before my eyes are closed, I'd like to say a few words to you. Your household wealth is extensive, and you are without paternal relatives to rely on, or anyone to assist you in managing it. You must consider carefully whatever you do, and not give way to the impulse of the moment. And you must not do anything to the detriment of the First Lady or the others. She is feeling poorly in her present condition, and, sooner or later, she may give birth to a child that can serve as a foundation for the perpetuation of your ancestral line, and prevent the dissipation of your property. Moreover, you occupy an official post. From now on, you ought not to go out drinking so often and should endeavor to come home earlier when you do. Your household responsibilities are important. The situation will not be the same as when I was here to admonish you. If I die, who will there be to deter you with bitter-tasting but well-meant advice?"

When Hsi-men Ch'ing heard these words, he felt just as though:

A knife were slashing his heart and liver,

and he wept, saying, "My sister, I understand what you're saying. Don't you worry yourself about me. I, Hsi-men Ch'ing, must have been:

Bereft of affinity and short on fortune,

in a former existence, to be:

Unable to remain husband and wife to the end,[46]

with you in this incarnation. It pains me to death! Heaven is destroying me!"

Li P'ing-erh went on to say, "With regard to Ying-ch'un and Hsiu-ch'un, I have already spoken to the First Lady about them. In the future, when I am dead, Ying-ch'un can be reassigned to wait on the First Lady. With regard to the junior maidservant, the Second Lady has already agreed to take responsibility for her. She lacks any satisfactory maidservant in her quarters, so she can be deputed to wait on her."

"My sister," said Hsi-men Ch'ing, "you don't need to instruct me on that score. Once you are dead, who would presume to separate your maidservants? And the wet nurse, also, will not be dismissed. They will all be expected to keep vigil over your spirit tablet."

"What's so important about the spirit tablet?" said Li P'ing-erh. "Once it's been brought home after the funeral, and the fifth of the seven weekly commemorations have been held, it can simply be burned, and that will be the end of it."

"My sister," said Hsi-men Ch'ing, "don't you worry about any such thing. So long as I, Hsi-men Ch'ing, am alive, offerings will continue to be made to your spirit tablet."

As their conclave continued, Li P'ing-erh urged him, saying, "You'd better go get some sleep. It's late."

"I'm not going to sleep," said Hsi-men Ch'ing. "I'll keep you company here in your room."

"I'm not about to die just yet," said Li P'ing-erh. "This room is contaminated with foul odor, and you'll be bothered by the smoke of the incense. Moreover, it won't be convenient for them to look after me with you here."

Hsi-men Ch'ing had no alternative but to issue instructions to the maidservants to look after their mistress with care, after which, he returned to the master suite in the rear compound and told Yüeh-niang in detail about how the lantern ritual had been of no avail.

"Just now, when I went into her room," he said, "I observed that she could still talk clearly enough. If Heaven will only take pity on her, I imagine she may recover yet. Who knows?"

"The sockets of her eyes have contracted," said Yüeh-niang. "Her lips have dried up, and her ears are burning. How can she be expected to recover? It's only a question of time. This ailment of hers is one that allows her to remain clearheaded and to speak distinctly right up until she stops breathing."

"Ever since she became a member of our household," said Hsi-men Ch'ing, "she has never given offense to anyone, high or low. Moreover, she has a most accommodating disposition and never has a bad word to say about anybody. How can I bear to give her up?"

Having said this, he started to weep again, and Yüeh-niang also could not prevent her tears from falling, but we will say no more at present about this colloquy between Hsi-men Ch'ing and Yüeh-niang.

To resume our story, Li P'ing-erh called for Ying-ch'un and the wet nurse and said, "Help me turn over to face the wall, so I can take a nap."

"What time has it gotten to be?" she then went on to ask.

"The cock has not yet crowed," said the wet nurse. "It must be sometime in the fourth watch."

She then said to Ying-ch'un, "Let's replace the absorbent grass paper under her body, help her turn over to face the wall, and cover her with a quilt, so she can get some sleep."

Everybody had been staying up all night without any sleep. Old Mother Feng and Nun Wang finally went to bed behind the latched door in the adjacent room, while Ying-ch'un and Hsiu-ch'un put their bedding down on the floor in front of their mistress and lay down to sleep.

They had not been asleep for more than an hour and were still:

In a state of profound slumber,

when Ying-ch'un dreamed that Li P'ing-erh got down off the k'ang and gave her a shake, saying, "The two of you look after the house. I'm going away."

She suddenly woke up with a start and saw that the lamp on the table had not yet gone out. When she looked at the bed, her mistress was still lying with her face to the wall, but when she felt with her hand, she found that there was no longer any breath coming out of her mouth. She did not know just when it happened, but:

> Alas and alack;
> She had stopped breathing and died.
> What a pity that the life of such a beautiful woman,
> Should turn into only an instance of a spring dream.[47]

Truly:

> When King Yama decrees that you will die
>   during the third watch;
> The hour of your death cannot be delayed
>   until the fifth watch.[48]

Ying-ch'un hastily woke everyone up, and they lit lamps and gathered to see what had happened. Sure enough, they observed that she was no longer breathing, and that her body was lying in a pool of blood. In a state of panic, they ran back to the rear compound to inform Hsi-men Ch'ing of the situation.

When Hsi-men Ch'ing heard that Li P'ing-erh was dead, he and Wu Yüeh-niang hastened to the front compound:

> Covering two steps with every one,

and lifted the quilt off her body. Behold:

> The color of her face was unchanged;
> Her body still retained some warmth;
> She had slipped away unobtrusively.

Her body was clothed in nothing but a bodice of red satin.

Hsi-men Ch'ing, disregarding the fact that her body was stained with coagulated blood, embraced her with both arms and kissed her fragrant cheeks, protesting again and again, "My lost sister! My kind and just sister, with your accommodating disposition! How can you abandon me this way? I would rather that I, Hsi-men Ch'ing, had died in your stead. I also am:

> Not long for this world.

What have I got left to live for?"

There in her bedroom, he leapt three feet off the ground and started to cry out loud in full voice. Wu Yüeh-niang also wiped away her tears while weeping incessantly. Before long, Li Chiao-erh, Meng Yü-lou, P'an Chin-lien, Sun Hsüeh-o, and the members of the entire household, high and low, including the maidservants and waiting women, commenced weeping as though they were endeavoring to raise the roof, so that:

> The sound of their lamentations shook the earth.[49]

Yüeh-niang said to Li Chiao-erh and Meng Yü-lou, "We don't know just when she died during the night. She doesn't even have an article of clothing on her body."

"I felt her body," said Meng Yü-lou, "and it's still warm. It must not be very long since she departed. If we don't seize the opportunity to put some clothes on her while her limbs are still warm, what are we waiting for?"

Yüeh-niang observed that Hsi-men Ch'ing was reclining face-to-face on top of her body, weeping, and crying out, "Heaven is bent on destroying me, Hsi-men Ch'ing! Sister, during the three years you've been a member of my household, you haven't enjoyed a single good day. I've been the ruination of you."

When Yüeh-niang heard these words, she was somewhat perturbed at heart and said, "What ridiculous palaver!

Weep for her a couple of times and forget it.

Have you no compunction about crying that way face-to-face with a corpse? You run the risk of being contaminated by the foul emanations from her mouth. If she hasn't enjoyed a single good day, who is there who has?

A person's death is like the extinction of a lamp.

Even half a day of borrowed time is not to be had.

If you were able to keep her alive, that would be fine, but when a person's allotted years are up, who can avoid going by this path?"

She then went on to instruct Li Chiao-erh and Meng Yü-lou, "The two of you take the keys and look in the other room for the burial garments that she has prepared in advance, so that we can help each other get them onto her."

She also said, "Sister Six, the two of us had better see if we can straighten up her hair."

Hsi-men Ch'ing said to Yüeh-niang, "Try to select two sets of garments that she was particularly fond of to dress her with."

Yüeh-niang accordingly instructed Li Chiao-erh and Meng Yü-lou, saying, "Look for that newly tailored jacket of scarlet satin brocade, with the willow-yellow brocade skirt; that blouse of lilac-colored, cloud-patterned, figured silk, that she wore earlier this year for our visit to kinsman Ch'iao Hung's place, with the wide trailing skirt of kingfisher-blue; and that newly made up white satin jacket, with the skirt of yellow pongee."

Thereupon, with Ying-ch'un holding a lamp, and Meng Yü-lou holding the keys, they proceeded to open the interior door to the adjacent bedroom and take down the second lacquer chest adorned with gold tracery, which was stored on top of the bedstead with retractable steps and contained newly made up clothing. After opening the lid to the chest, Meng Yü-lou and Li Chiao-erh searched through it for some time and came up with the three outfits of clothing they were looking for, as well as a short, close-fitting purple satin camisole, a petticoat of white pongee, a pair of scarlet underdrawers, a pair of white satin woman's stockings, and a pair of figured ankle leggings. Li Chiao-erh carried these things over to the adjacent room and showed them to Yüeh-niang.

Yüeh-niang was engaged, together with Chin-lien, in arranging Li P'ing-erh's chignon by the light of a lamp. They coiled it securely, wrapped it in a raven-black kerchief, and used four gold hairpins to hold it in place.

Li Chiao-erh then asked, "What-colored shoes should we look for to put on her?"

"Sister," said P'an Chin-lien, "the pair of shoes that she fancied the most was that one made of scarlet brocade, embroidered with the motif of 'A Parrot Plucking a Peach,' with white satin high heels. She hardly wore them more than a couple of times. We might as well try to find that pair to put on her."

"That will never do," said Yüeh-niang. "If she wore those when appearing before the court of the nether world, she'd be condemned to jump into the fiery pit. Look instead for that pair that she wore the other day when she went to her sister-in-law's place outside the city gate, the pair made of purple silk brocade, with high heels, that is also embroidered with the motif of 'A Parrot Plucking a Peach.' That would be a more appropriate pair for us to put on her."

When Li Chiao-erh heard this, she went to look in the four small lacquer chests adorned with gold tracery in which Li P'ing-erh kept her hundred or more pairs of shoes, but, though she went through them all, she failed to find them.

"When Mother wore them," said Ying-ch'un, "she always put them back here. Where could they have gone?"

She then went back to the kitchen to ask Hsiu-ch'un about it.

"I saw Mother wrap them up and put them in the commode on top of which the boxes rest," said Hsiu-ch'un.

When they opened the drawers of the commode, they finally located them, inside another large package of new shoes. The group of them then proceeded, hugger-mugger, to get the corpse properly clothed.

Hsi-men Ch'ing then supervised a number of page boys in taking down and rolling up the scrolls of painting and calligraphy in the main reception hall, and creating an enclosed space there with standing screens, to which Li P'ing-erh's body was carried out on the leaf of a door and laid out in state. A brocade mat was placed underneath her body, and it was covered with a paper shroud. A table for her spirit tablet and an incense table were set up, and a vigil lamp was lighted. Two page boys were deputed to serve the spirit of the departed, one of them to strike the chime, and the other to burn paper money. Tai-an was dispatched to fetch Yin-yang Master Hsü as quickly as possible, so he could ascertain the time of her death and interpret his divinatory texts. Once Yüeh-niang had supervised the removal of the articles of clothing needed to dress the corpse, the door to Li P'ing-erh's bedroom was locked. Only the room with the k'ang was left open for the use of the maidservants and waiting women.

When Old Mother Feng saw that her mistress was dead, she wept as though she had:

Three noses from which to drivel,

As well as two eyes to shed tears.

Nun Wang, for her part, murmured monotonously as she recited the *Heart Sutra*,[50] the *Sutra of the Healing Buddha*,[51] the *Scripture on Delivery from*

Enmity,[52] the *Śūrangama Sutra,*[53] and the *Great Compassion Dhāranī,*[54] as she besought the Bodhisattva King Who Escorts the Dead to conduct her on the road to the shades.

Meanwhile, in the front reception hall, Hsi-men Ch'ing beat his breast in sorrow, and couldn't help caressing the corpse, as he wept until his voice became hoarse, protesting again and again, without ceasing, "My kind and just sister, with your accommodating disposition."

While everyone was so preoccupied, the cock crowed, and Tai-an came back with Yin-yang Master Hsü, who saluted Hsi-men Ch'ing with the words, "I can see that Your Honor is distressed. At what time was it that your lady died?"

"The precise time is not known," said Hsi-men Ch'ing. "At the time she went to sleep the fourth watch had already been sounded, and the people in her quarters were so fatigued that they were all fast asleep, so we don't know exactly when it was that she died."

"Which of your ladies was it?" asked Master Hsü.

"It was my sixth insignificant concubine," replied Hsi-men Ch'ing. "She had developed an awkward ailment that dragged on interminably right up to the present time."

"It doesn't matter," said Master Hsü, who then directed the attendants to light the lamps in the reception hall and lifted aside the paper shroud in order to have a look at her.

Calculating the time on his fingers, he said, "Since we are now precisely two-fifths of the way through the fifth watch, she must have expired during the previous watch, which corresponds to the earthly branch *ch'ou,* or the ox."

Hsi-men Ch'ing then ordered that a writing brush and inkstone be provided and asked Master Hsü to interpret his divinatory texts.

Master Hsü, by the light of the lamps, opened his black bag, took out an almanac with its perpetual calendar, and consulted it. Having ascertained her maiden name and the eight characters that determined her horoscope, he proceeded to pronounce as follows:

The deceased wife, née Li, of Hsi-men Ch'ing, an officer of the Embroidered-Uniform Guard, was born at noon on the fifteenth day of the first month in the *hsin-wei* year of the Yüan-yu reign period; and died at 2:00 AM on the seventeenth day of the ninth month of the *ting-yu* year of the Cheng-ho reign period. The fact that this day of her death is a *ping-tzu* day of a *wu-hsü* month indicates a conflict between the celestial stems and earthly branches, which makes it an inauspicious day for any undertaking and portends a double bereavement. The baleful spirit of the departed is ten feet high and is headed in a southwesterly direction. If it encounters the baleful spirit of the Year God,[55] it will portend a fatal situation. The members of her immediate family should abstain from crying until after they have put on their mourning clothes, when it will not matter. On the day of the encoffining ceremony, people born in the year of the dragon, the year of the tiger, the year of the cock, and the year of the snake should stay out of the way, although relatives by marriage need not do so.

At this point, Wu Yüeh-niang sent Tai-an out to instruct Master Hsü to proceed with consulting the *Black Book*[56] about what the future might hold in store for her.

Master Hsü, accordingly, consulted his esoteric yin-yang texts and pronounced:

> Today is a *ping-tzu* day, and her death took place during the *chi-ch'ou* hour, so she is governed by the zodiacal palace Precious Vase[57] above, which corresponds to the area of Shantung below. In her former life, she was the son of a family named Wang in Pin-chou and was guilty of killing a pregnant ewe. Consequently, in this life she was reborn as a female in the year of the sheep, her nature was gentle and compliant, and she was given to artifice from her earliest years. Both her father and her mother died, and she had no relatives on whom she could depend. Initially, she entered someone's household as a concubine but suffered from the hostility of his legitimate wife. Later, upon acquiring a husband of her own, she found that they were incompatible, and her fate was crossed by the "three penalties" and "six banes."[58] Although she acquired a distinguished husband in her years of maturity, she suffered from continual ailments, and the "matched shoulders" in her horoscope. She gave birth to a son, but he died prematurely, and her suppressed anger brought on hemorrhaging from her lower body that resulted in her death. Earlier, on the ninth day of this month, her soul left her to be reborn as the daughter of Commander Yüan in the metropolis of Pien-liang, or K'ai-feng prefecture, in Honan province. The difficulties she encounters there imperil her survival, but she will endure to the age of nineteen, when she will marry a wealthy man of much greater age than herself. She will enjoy prosperity during her mature years, and live to the age of forty-one, when she will succumb to a fit of anger and die.

When he had finished his prognostication from the *Black Book*, the assembled womenfolk all sighed with wonder. Hsi-men Ch'ing then asked Master Hsü to ascertain what would be auspicious days for breaking ground for her tomb, and for the burial ceremony.

"Permit me to ask Your Honor," said Master Hsü, "how long do you intend for her to lie in state?"

Hsi-men Ch'ing wept, saying, "She still looks so vibrantly alive. How can I bear to send her on her way? I'd like to keep her here until after the fifth weekly commemoration."

"There are no appropriate days for burying her in the fifth week," said Master Hsü, "but there are in the fourth week. I would suggest that you break ground for her tomb at noon on the eighth day of the tenth month, which is a *ting-yu* day; and that the burial ceremony should take place at 10:00 AM on the twelfth, which is a *hsin-ch'ou* day. The horoscopes of all six members of the family will not create any conflicts on that day."

"All right then," said Hsi-men Ch'ing, "the funeral procession will set out on the twelfth day of the tenth month, without fail."

Master Hsü, thereupon, wrote out the death certificate and placed it on the body of the deceased, after which, he said to Hsi-men Ch'ing, "The encoffining ceremony should take place at 8:00 AM on the nineteenth. Your household will be responsible for making all the necessary preparations."

By the time Master Hsü had been ushered out the gate, the day had already dawned. Hsi-men Ch'ing sent Ch'in-t'ung, riding on a donkey, outside the city gate to invite the attendance of Hua the Elder, after which, he deputed teams of servants to go to the homes of all the other relatives of the family and inform them of Li P'ing-erh's death. He also sent someone to the yamen to request a leave of absence, so he could remain at home to take charge of the funeral arrangements. He sent Tai-an to the shop on Lion Street to obtain twenty bolts of bleached Hsiang-yang ramie and thirty bolts of porous ramie fabric, and he arranged for Tailor Chao to engage the services of a considerable number of tailors, who were put to work in an anteroom on the western side of the front courtyard. They were hired for the purpose of making the marquees and table-cloths that would be required for the funeral, the burial clothes and waistband for the encoffining ceremony, and the blouses and skirts for the womenfolk in their respective chambers. In addition, white T'ang-style caps and long white robes were supplied for each of the page boys and other servants. He also weighed out a hundred taels of silver and entrusted them to Pen the Fourth with the mission of going to the specialty shops outside the city gate and urging them to provide thirty bolts of lustrous hemp fabric and two hundred lengths of yellow damask suitable for the mourning garments of relatives of different degrees of mourning. He then went on to arrange for carpenters to erect a large, thirty-foot-wide, covered structure in the main courtyard.

As Hsi-men Ch'ing contemplated the habits, conduct, and looks of Li P'ing-erh, it suddenly occurred to him that he had forgotten to have a portrait of her painted.

Calling over Lai-pao, he asked him, "Where is there a good painter to be found, who is skilled at making portraits? I'd like to find one in order to make a posthumous portrait of her. I had completely forgotten about this matter."

"That Master Han who painted some standing screens for us in the past," said Lai-pao, "was formerly a court painter attached to the Hsüan-ho Academy. He has lost his position there and returned home, but he is an excellent portraitist."[59]

"Where does he live?" asked Hsi-men Ch'ing. "Go at once and invite him to come here."

Lai-pao nodded in assent and proceeded to set off on this errand.

Hsi-men Ch'ing had been up all evening without any sleep and had been busy through all five watches of the night, in addition to which, he was suffering from the sorrows of bereavement, so that his spirits were disturbed, and he was out of sorts and resorted to cursing the maidservants and kicking the page boys. As he kept vigil over the dead body of Li P'ing-erh, he couldn't help weeping and howling with grief. Tai-an, who remained at his side, also wept until he could neither weep nor utter a sound. Meanwhile, Wu Yüeh-niang, together with Li Chiao-erh, Meng Yü-lou, and P'an Chin-lien, were behind the curtain, sharing responsibility for directing the maidservants from the various quarters and the servant wives as they went about their tasks.

When she saw the way in which Hsi-men Ch'ing had given himself over to crying until his voice was hoarse, refused the offer of so much as a drink of tea, and was manifestly out of sorts, Wu Yüeh-niang said, "Just look at the ridiculous way he's carrying on! If she's dead, she's dead, and that's that.

You can't cry her back to life again.

Weep for her a couple of times and forget it.

All he seems bent on is stretching out the weeping as long as he can stand it. He hasn't gotten any sleep for two or three nights and hasn't even taken the time to comb his hair or wash his face. He's been busy through all five watches of the night, without so much as a taste of:

Saffron soup or flavored water.[60]

Not even an iron man could take it. If he would only comb his hair and come outside for something to eat, he might be able to keep going; but, slight as he is, if he were to collapse, what would we do?"

"Do you mean to say he hasn't even combed his hair or washed his face?" said Meng Yü-lou.

"It would have been a good start if he had washed his face," said Yüeh-niang, "but, a while ago, when I sent a page boy to ask him to return to the rear compound and wash his face, he kicked him outside. Who would venture to ask him again?"

"Whoever saw the like!" exclaimed Chin-lien, picking up where Yüeh-niang left off. "When I went into the room a while ago to look for some garments, did I not admonish him with the best of intentions, saying, 'Although you may have lost someone, you're only wearing yourself to a frazzle by carrying on this way. If you come and have something to eat in your room before you continue, it won't delay anything.' But he opened his red eyes wide, and cursed me, saying, 'You dog-fucked whore! What business is it of yours?' The fact is that, nowadays, if I'm not to be fucked by the dog, who else is there to fuck me? The unreasonable good-for-nothing! All he does is claim that everyone else is giving him a hard time."

"When she died so suddenly, while still seeming vibrantly alive," said Yüeh-niang, "how could he help being pained? But even if you're pained, you ought to take it easy, rather than letting it all hang out this way. When a person is dead, to caress her lip to lip, without paying any attention to whether or not there are foul emanations from her mouth, and howl with grief that way, is no way to carry on. When I criticized him with a few words, what should he do but come out with the claim that during the last three years she hasn't enjoyed a single good day. As though, every day, she'd been required to:

Carry water and turn the millstone."

"That's not it at all," said Meng Yü-lou. "It's not that Sister Li had anything to complain about. But she has suffered from Father's propensity to sort people differentially into:

Three classes and nine categories."

"If she was able to enjoy her days," said Chin-lien, "it would appear that some people are more privileged than others, when we should all be:

Walking along the same gangplank."

As they were speaking, who should appear but Ch'en Ching-chi, holding nine lengths of watered-silk in his hand, who said, "Father has ordered that you ladies should cut handkerchiefs out of this material for the use of the women in each of your quarters, and that, if anything is left over, it can be used to make skirts for you ladies."

Yüeh-niang took the silk and then said, "Son-in-law, go and invite your father to come in here and have a bite to eat. It's already nearly noon, and he hasn't had so much as a sip of tea."

"I wouldn't dare do that," said Ch'en Ching-chi. "A while ago, when one of the page boys invited him to have something to eat, he kicked him nearly to death. Why should I risk pestering him?"

"If you won't ask him," said Yüeh-niang, "wait until I send someone else to ask him to come and eat."

In a little while, she called over Tai-an and said to him, "Your master hasn't yet had anything to eat but has been crying all day long. You take some food in to him, and take advantage of the presence of Licentiate Wen, to get him to share something with him."

"If you invite Master Ying the Second and Master Hsieh to come over," said Tai-an, "and wait until after they get here to send someone in with the food, I guarantee that it won't take more than a few words on their part to get him to eat."

"You filthy-mouthed jailbird!" exclaimed Yüeh-niang. "You're just like a:

Tapeworm in his belly.

We womenfolk of his are no match for you. How can you be so sure that only if those two come over will he consent to eat anything?"

"You ladies don't understand," said Tai-an. "Those two are Father's closest friends. At drinking parties, large or small, he is never without them. If Father consumes three mace worth of refreshments, they will have three mace worth, and if Father is content with two mace worth, they will settle for two.

No matter how upset Father may be, they have but to say a few words
before:

His eyebrows blossom and his eyes light up."[61]

They continued talking for a while, until Ch'i-t'ung showed up with Ying
Po-chüeh and Hsieh Hsi-ta.

The two of them, upon their arrival, no sooner came in the door than they
prostrated themselves on the ground in front of Li P'ing-erh's spirit tablet
and wept for some time, repeating, over and over again, the words, "My kind
and just sister-in-law."

This provoked both P'an Chin-lien and Meng Yü-lou into cursing them,
saying, "The lousy oily mouthed jailbirds! Do they suggest that none of the
rest of us are kind or just?"

When the two of them had finished their weeping, they got to their feet, and
Hsi-men Ch'ing returned their salutation.

The two of them commenced to weep all over again, saying, "Brother, it is
most distressing, most distressing."

They were then ushered into the anteroom, where they exchanged greetings with Licentiate Wen and sat down.

Ying Po-chüeh was the first to speak, asking, "When did our sister-in-law
die?"

"She stopped breathing at two o'clock in the morning," said Hsi-men
Ch'ing.

"It was already past the fourth watch when I got home," said Ying Po-chüeh.
"When my wife asked how she was, I said, 'All we can do is hope that the good
deeds she has done in secret will avail. Sister-in-law's illness is already in its
final stages.' Who would have thought that I had no sooner fallen asleep than
I had a dream in which Brother sent a servant to invite me to attend a party at
your place in celebration of an official promotion and urged me to come as
quickly as possible. Upon arrival, I saw that you were dressed entirely in scarlet
clothing. You took two jade hairpins out of your sleeve to show me and told
me that one of them was broken. After examining them for some time, I said,
'Brother, it's too bad. This one that is broken is made of jade, while the one
that is intact is made of artificial crystal.' But you insisted that they were both
made of jade. My wife and I were asleep together when I woke up and said to
myself that this dream boded no good. My wife noticed that I was smacking
my lips and asked me who I was talking to, but I said, 'It's something you don't
know about. I'll tell you in the morning.' But when morning came, who should
appear but your servant, dressed in white mourning garments, which led me
to stamp my feet in consternation. And now, sure enough, Brother, I see that
you are wearing mourning clothes."

"I had a dream just like yours last night," responded Hsi-men Ch'ing. "I
dreamed that my kinsman Chai Ch'ien in the Eastern Capital had sent me a
set of six hairpins, one of which was broken. I said it was too bad, and I was

just telling my wife about it in the middle of the night when, unexpectedly, we learned that the lady in the front compound had stopped breathing. Heaven must be blind to leave me so destitute! I would rather that I, Hsi-men Ch'ing, had died in her stead, rather than having to confront this event. In the future, whenever I think of her during any:

Single hour or half a minute,

how can I help but be pained at heart? What have I ever done to anyone that Heaven should now see fit to rob me so egregiously of my beloved![62] First that child of ours died, and now she too has departed:

With her legs stretched out straight.[63]

What have I still got to live for in this world? Though in my home:

The piles of money reach higher than the dipper,

what good will it do me?"

"Brother," said Ying Po-chüeh, "these sentiments of yours are wrong. It is true that my sister-in-law has been a good wife to you, and when she died so suddenly, while still seeming vibrantly alive, how could you help being pained at heart? But the fact is that you are not only the possessor of considerable wealth, but also have an official career before you. You are like the bastion of Mount T'ai, upon which the members of this entire household, both high and low, are dependent. If anything were to happen to you, what would become of them? These other ladies of yours, for example, would be left without a husband to support them. As the saying goes:

So long as one of us lives, all three will live;

Whenever one of us perishes, all three will die.[64]

Brother, you are not only intelligent, but clever. What need is there for your brothers to point these things out to you? It is no wonder that the death of our sister-in-law in the springtime of her youth is something the pain of which is hard to get over, hard to survive. But when you have put on your mourning clothes, arranged for Buddhist monks and Taoist priests to recite scriptures on her behalf, mounted an impressive funeral procession, and seen that she is properly buried in her tomb, your feelings for her will have been given full expression, as is only appropriate in commemoration of your relationship with her. What more can you do? You must set your mind at rest."

At the time, this single conversation with Ying Po-chüeh had such an effect on Hsi-men Ch'ing that:

The ground of his heart was profoundly affected;

The obstruction in his mind was abruptly removed,[65]

and he stopped weeping. Before long, when tea was served, he actually drank it.

He then called for Tai-an and said to him, "Go back to the rear compound, and tell them to prepare some food for me to share with your Second Master Ying, Licentiate Wen, and Master Hsieh."

"Brother," said Ying Po-chüeh, "do you mean to say that you haven't even eaten yet?"

"Ever since you left," said Hsi-men Ch'ing, "I've been busy all night. Up until now, I haven't had so much as a taste of anything to eat."

"Brother," said Ying Po-chüeh, "it is foolish of you not to eat. As the saying goes:

> It is preferable to forfeit your capital,
> Rather than opting to suffer from hunger.[66]

Is it not said in the *Hsiao-ching*, or *Classic of Filial Piety*, 'People should be taught that the dead should not hurt the living,[67] and that disfigurement should not lead to the detriment of life'?[68] The dead are dead, and the survivors must continue to get on with their lives. Brother, you must get ahold of yourself."

Truly:

> A few words serve to disclose the proper path
>   to a gentleman;
> A single speech suffices to awaken the sleeper
>   from his dream.

> If you want to know the outcome of these events,
> Pray consult the story related in the following chapter.

Chapter 63

FRIENDS AND RELATIVES OFFER FUNERAL OBLATIONS AT A MEMORIAL FEAST; HSI-MEN CH'ING IS REMINDED OF LI P'ING-ERH WHILE WATCHING A DRAMA

Even among the twelve jasper terraces[1] and jeweled
   balustrades of paradise,
Once the alabaster blossoms have fallen, they are
   unlikely to bloom again.
Even medications concocted out of dragon's beard[2]
   have not been efficacious;
Though pills were being made up from bear's gall,
   they weren't ready in time.
Behind hibiscus curtains the night brings sorrow,
   the red candles have expired;
Within paper windows, as autumn comes to an end,
   the kingfisher quilt is cold.
One feels empathy with the goose that has lost
   it's fellows and flies alone;
As frost falls and the wind rises, it's image
   appears in forlorn isolation.

THE STORY GOES that on that day, as a result of Ying Po-chüeh's persuasion, Hsi-men Ch'ing wiped away his tears, ceased his weeping, and ordered a page boy to go back to the rear compound and bring them some food.

Before long, Wu K'ai and Wu the Second arrived, performed their obeisances before the spirit tablet of the deceased, saluted Hsi-men Ch'ing, and communicated their distress at his bereavement. They were invited into the anteroom, where they sat down with the others.

Meanwhile, Tai-an went back to the rear compound and said to Yüeh-niang, "How come you ladies did not believe me? Master Ying the Second had no sooner arrived than, with a single conversation, he succeeded in persuading Father to have something to eat."

"You lousy inveterate jailbird!" exclaimed Chin-lien. "Since you spend all day outside the house playing the role of pander for him, it's scarcely surprising that you understand his character."

"I've attended the master since my childhood," said Tai-an. "How could I fail to be familiar with his innermost feelings?"

"Just who are the people sitting in the anteroom who will be sharing a meal with him?" asked Yüeh-niang.

"Your elder brother and your second brother have just showed up," said Tai-an. "Along with Licentiate Wen, Second Master Ying, Master Hsieh, Manager Han, your son-in-law, and Father, there are eight in all."

"Ask our son-in-law to come back here and eat in the rear compound," said Yüeh-niang. "Why should he insist on joining the party?"

"He has already sat down with them," said Tai-an.

"You and the other page boys go to the kitchen and take the food out to them," said Yüeh-niang. "And take an extra bowl of congee for Father to eat. He hasn't had any breakfast this morning."

"What other page boys are there?" said Tai-an. "I'm the only one left at home. All the rest have been deputed to announce the death to friends and relatives, to burn paper money, or to buy things. And Wang Ching has been sent to Kinsman Chang Kuan's place to borrow a cloud-shaped gong for the occasion."

"Why don't you get that slave Shu-t'ung to help you out?" said Yüeh-niang. "Though I suppose he's:

Reluctant to set the fins on his
    silk hat aflutter."[3]

"Shu-t'ung and Hua-t'ung have been assigned to serve before her spirit tablet," said Tai-an, "one of them to strike the chime, and the other to burn paper money. And as for Ch'un-hung, Father has sent him to go with Pen the Fourth to exchange the damask that he bought earlier today. He doesn't think it's good enough and wants to exchange it for a grade of damask that costs six mace per length, in order to make mourning garments for the visitors."

"If you stop to consider it," said Yüeh-niang, "that damask that cost five mace per length would have been good enough, but he would insist on exchanging it."

She then went on to say, "You call that little slave Hua-t'ung off his post and get him to help you take the food out. What are you waiting around for?"

Thereupon, Tai-an, together with Hua-t'ung, proceeded to carry the food out to the front compound, in:

Large platters and large bowls,
and set up an Eight Immortals Table on which to serve it.

While the company were eating their meal, who should appear but P'ing-an, carrying in his hand an accordion-bound calling card, who reported, "His Honor Hsia Yen-ling from the yamen has sent along a professional scribe, and three members of the guard unit, for your benefit and would like a note of acknowledgment."

After reading the card, Hsi-men Ch'ing issued instructions, saying, "Get three mace of silver to reward the messenger, and write out an accordion-bound thank-you note, indicating that the sender is in one-year mourning, in reply to His Honor Hsia Yen-ling."

When the company had finished their meal, the utensils were cleared away.

Who should appear at this juncture but Lai-pao, who brought with him the painter Master Han.

After saluting him, Hsi-men Ch'ing said, "I would trouble you, sir, to paint a portrait of my deceased consort."

"I understand," said Master Han.

"If there is any further delay," said Ying Po-chüeh, "I fear that the appearance of her countenance will have changed."

"It doesn't matter," said Master Han. "I can capture her likeness even after death."

Just as they were finishing their tea, P'ing-an suddenly came in and announced that Hua the Elder from outside the city gate had arrived. Hsi-men Ch'ing accompanied Hua Tzu-yu as he wept in front of the spirit tablet for a while, after which, salutations were exchanged as he joined the rest of the company.

He then went on to ask, "At what time did she die?"

"She stopped breathing at 2:00 AM," said Hsi-men Ch'ing. "She was still speaking:

Clearly and distinctly,

shortly before her death. She had not been asleep for long when her maidservant got up to see how she was and found that she had stopped breathing."

Hua Tzu-yu, upon noticing that the young attendant standing beside Master Han was holding an easel, and that he had pulled a painting brush and some pigments out of his sleeve, said to Hsi-men Ch'ing, "Brother-in-law, are you planning to have her portrait painted?"

"I am so heartsick over her death," said Hsi-men Ch'ing, "that I can't bear not to have an image of her likeness that I can look at from time to time to remind me of her."

He then issued instructions that the womenfolk from the rear compound should stay out of the way and then lifted aside the curtain and led Master Han, along with Hua the Elder and the rest of the company, into the partitioned area in which Li P'ing-erh was lying in state.

Master Han then proceeded to lift the funeral banderole aside with his hand and concentrated the gaze of those vigilant organs of his, with their:

Five concentric rings,
Eight precious attributes, and
Two spots of magic liquid,[4]

upon the sight revealed below. He saw that her hair was done up in a raven-black kerchief, and that, although she had been ill for a long time:

Her coloration was still lifelike,[5] and
Her countenance remained unaltered.

Although she appeared sallower than before, her lips were still adorably red and moist. Hsi-men Ch'ing could not help wiping the tears from his eyes as he wept at the sight.

Thereupon, Lai-pao and Ch'in-t'ung set up the easel at her side and laid out the pigments. Master Han took in her appearance at a glance, and the company crowded around him, urging him to begin to paint.

Ying Po-chüeh ventured to address him, saying, "Sir, you must realize that this is the visage of an invalid. In the past, when she was well:

Her face was fuller than this, and
Her countenance was enchanting."[6]

"There is no need for the venerable gentleman to instruct me," said Master Han. "I understand the situation. May I venture to ask Your Honor, is this, by any chance, the same person that I caught a glimpse of formerly, on the first day of the fifth month, when she was paying a visit to the Temple of the God of the Eastern Peak?"

"She is that very one," said Hsi-men Ch'ing. "She was still herself at the time. If you will endeavor to remember what she looked like, sir, and paint one full-length portrait, as well as a half-length one to be worshipped beside her spirit tablet, I will present you with a bolt of satin, and ten taels of silver to boot."

"With regard to Your Honor's instructions," said Master Han, "I will, of course, do my best."

In hardly any time at all, he succeeded in producing a half-length portrait. Truly:

Her jade face exhibits the rare beauty
of a secluded flower;
Her full flesh is a delicate jade that
exudes its own bouquet.

When he showed it to the assembled company, they saw that it was, indeed, a portrait of a beauty.

When Hsi-men Ch'ing had looked at it, he said to Tai-an, "Take it back to the rear compound and show it to the ladies, to see what they think. If they find anything wrong with it, come tell us, so that it can be corrected."

Tai-an, accordingly, took it back to the rear compound and said to Yüeh-niang, "Father says that you ladies should examine this portrait of the Sixth Lady to see how well it is done. If you find any feature that is not true to life, say what it is, so that Master Han can correct it."

"Why that:

Inveterate mischief-maker!"

exclaimed Yüeh-niang.

"Nobody knows where the dead end up going to.

Master Han Produces a Portrait as a Posthumous Memento

And yet he insists on having her portrait painted. It doesn't even resemble her all that much."

P'an Chin-lien picked up where she left off, saying, "And where are her children, if her likeness is to be perpetuated in the form of a portrait so they can:

> Kowtow and perform obeisances,

before it? In the future, when all six of his womenfolk have died, he'd better have portraits painted of all six of us."

Meng Yü-lou and Li Chiao-erh took the portrait in hand and examined it, saying, "First Lady, come and see. This painting depicts her the way she looked when she was well. She's dolled up very vividly, but her lips look a little flat."

"The left side of her forehead is a bit too low," said Yüeh-niang. "And her eyebrows were more curved than those depicted here. But it's amazing that this gentleman could capture such a likeness from her dead body."

"He caught a glimpse of the Sixth Lady at the Temple of the God of the Eastern Peak," explained Tai-an. "Just now, he was able to produce this likeness from memory."

In a little while, who should appear but Wang Ching, who came in and said, "If you ladies have had a chance to examine it, I've been instructed to have it taken back outside. Your kinsman Ch'iao Hung has arrived and is anxious to have a look at it."

Tai-an, accordingly, took it back to the front compound and said to Master Han, "The ladies in the rear compound say that her lips are a bit flat, the left corner of her forehead is a bit too low, and her eyebrows should be made to curve a little more."

"That's no problem," said Master Han, and he took up his brush forthwith, made the desired corrections, and then presented it to Ch'iao Hung for his approval.

"This portrait of my kinswoman is masterfully done," announced Ch'iao Hung.

> "It lacks only the breath of life."[7]

Hsi-men Ch'ing was delighted by this response and proceeded to toast Master Han with three cups of wine. After he had been wined and dined, he rewarded him with a bolt of silk and ten taels of silver, presented to him upon a red lacquer tray.

He then told him, "Finish the half-length portrait first, as I want to hang it up immediately. As for the full-length portrait, it will be all right as long as it's ready in time for the funeral procession. She must be depicted in bright blue and green style, with pearls and trinkets adorning her chignon, wearing a scarlet full-sleeved variegated brocade robe, over a flower-sprigged skirt. And it should be mounted on patterned damask, with ivory knobs on the ends of the roller."

"There is no need for you to instruct me any further," said Master Han. "I understand what is wanted."

He then accepted the silver, told his young attendant to carry the easel, bowed in farewell, and went out the gate.

Ch'iao Hung and the others spent some time looking over the newly constructed coffin, after which, he said, "I suppose the preliminary laying out ceremony for my kinswoman will be performed today."

"Right now," said Hsi-men Ch'ing, "as soon as the coroner's assistant and his workers arrive, we will carry out the preliminary laying out. The encoffining ceremony will take place on the third day."

After finishing his tea, Ch'iao Hung said his farewells, stood up, and departed.

Before long, the coroner's assistant and his workers arrived to perform their functions. The papier-mâché funerary objects were made up, and the burial clothes laid out. Hsi-men Ch'ing himself performed the ceremony of swabbing the eyes of the deceased with a ball of damp cotton, so she could see her way more clearly in the underworld, and had Ch'en Ching-chi play the role of a filial son by closing her eyelids. Hsi-men Ch'ing then came up with an imported pearl, which he inserted into her mouth. In no time at all, the preliminary laying out was completed satisfactorily, she was left to lie in state as before, the curtains were let down, and the entire household, high and low, wept to mark the occasion.

Lai-hsing had already obtained from a shop that specialized in burial objects for the dead gold-flecked effigies of four maidens to wait on her, bearing a chamber pot, a towel, a washbasin, and a comb, respectively. They wore pearl necklaces and enchased silver pendant earrings that looked just like the real thing, and they were dressed in clothes of variegated satin. Two of them were placed to each side of the body. Before her spirit tablet there were arrayed antique bronze incense burners and vases from the Shang and Chou dynasties, as well as candlesticks and incense cases, made to order by pewterers, that graced the table on which they were placed:

> With a glitter that rivals the sun's.

Ten taels of silver were also weighed out for a silversmith to be made into three sets of silver ceremonial goblets.

Hsi-men Ch'ing was in the anteroom in the front courtyard, deciding, with the help of Ying Po-chüeh, how to handle the record books for the expenses of the funeral proceedings. To begin with, he weighed out five hundred taels of silver and a hundred strings of cash and entrusted them to Han Tao-kuo to keep account of. Pen the Fourth and Lai-hsing were put in charge of making the necessary purchases, both large and small, and were also made responsible for the outside kitchen. Ying Po-chüeh, Hsieh Hsi-ta, Licentiate Wen, and Manager Kan Jun, the four of them, were to take turns keeping company with the guests who came and went to offer condolences. Ts'ui Pen was placed in charge of monitoring the expenses incurred by providing the guests with mourning wear. Lai-pao was put in charge of the outer storeroom. Wang Ching was given responsibility for the wine cellar. Ch'un-hung and Hua-t'ung were deputed to be in attendance before the spirit tablet. P'ing-an was responsible every day, with the help of four orderlies, for striking the cloud-shaped gong, and presenting incense sticks and paper money to the guests whenever they arrived. The professional scribe, along with another four orderlies, were stationed at the main gate to record the names of the visitors, hold the baldachin on the days when scriptures were being recited, be available to carry the heraldic pennants, and, when they had nothing else to do, help guard the gate. Once these duties had all been assigned, they were written down and posted on a screen wall, for the benefit of the parties concerned as they went about their respective tasks.

Lo and behold, at this juncture, Eunuch Director Hsüeh, the supervisor of the local imperial estates, sent people to deliver sixty pine planks, thirty stems of sturdy bamboo, three hundred reed mats, and a hundred lengths of hemp cord, together with his calling card, which they showed to Hsi-men Ch'ing, who rewarded the head messenger with five mace of silver and sent him back with a card indicating that he was in one-year mourning.

He then directed the carpenters to raise the main beam of the temporary covered structure they were erecting in order to enlarge it further, so that it would accommodate two portals, with a screen wall in between. He also told them to erect an eighteen-foot-wide covered structure in front of the kitchen in the front compound, and a forty-two-foot-wide structure outside the main gate for the display of placards detailing the particulars of the funereal arrangements.

Twelve Buddhist monks from the Pao-en Temple, or Temple of Kindness Requited, were engaged to come and recite sutras for the salvation of the deceased. Two waiters were hired to be on duty every day in order to provide a regular supply of tea from a local tea house, and two cooks were engaged to work in the outer kitchen and produce whatever foods might be called for.

That day, Hua Tzu-yu and Wu the Second visited for a while and then got up and left.

Hsi-men Ch'ing asked Licentiate Wen to draft the text of an obituary notice that he intended to have printed and told him to include the words, "My poor wife has unexpectedly died."

When Licentiate Wen surreptitiously showed this to Ying Po-chüeh for his advice, Ying Po-chüeh said, "You cannot logically say such a thing as long as my sister-in-law Wu occupies the position of his legitimate wife. How can he disseminate such a statement without arousing criticism? Even Brother Wu K'ai is certain to be distressed at heart. Let me take the subject up with him at my leisure. You had better not put it that way."

They continued to keep Hsi-men Ch'ing company until evening arrived, at which they separated and returned home.

That evening Hsi-men Ch'ing did not go back to the rear compound but had a summer bedstead set up beside Li P'ing-erh's spirit tablet, surrounded by standing screens and provided with the necessary bedding, so that he could sleep there by himself, with Ch'un-hung and Shu-t'ung close by to wait upon him. At dawn the next morning he went back to the master suite to perform his ablutions and put on the white T'ang-style mourning cap, mourning robe, white velveteen socks, white shoes, and mourning girdle that the tailor had made for him.

On this second day after Li P'ing-erh's death, early in the morning, Judicial Commissioner Hsia Yen-ling came to visit the bereaved, offer his condolences, and urge his host to moderate his grief. When Hsi-men Ch'ing had returned his salutation, Licentiate Wen joined them for a cup of tea, after which Hsia Yen-ling got up to go.

On his way out the gate, he admonished the scribe that he had sent over, saying, "Be sure to do a conscientious job while you're here. If any of the orderlies fail to show up for duty, report it to the yamen so that they can be disciplined."

When he had finished speaking, he mounted his horse and headed back to the yamen.

Hsi-men Ch'ing then directed Licentiate Wen to send out the obituary notices and sent servants to invite the relatives of the family to come early on the third day after Li P'ing-erh's death to attend a service for her benefit and the recitation of sutras on her behalf. That afternoon vergers from the temple arrived, whose job it was to prepare the consecrated space in which the ceremony would be held and hang up Buddhist effigies, but there is no need to describe this in detail.

That same day, Wu Yin-erh in the licensed quarter heard the news of Li P'ing-erh's death and came in a sedan chair to weep in front of her spirit tablet and burn paper money on her behalf. Upon her arrival in the rear compound, Wu Yüeh-niang led her back out front, where she kowtowed to Yüeh-niang and wept, saying, "When the Sixth Lady died I didn't know a thing about it. No one came to say so much as a word to me. It's really distressing."

"You are her adopted daughter, after all," said Meng Yü-lou. "She has been unwell for some time, and you didn't even come to see her."

"My good Third Lady!" protested Wu Yin-erh. "If I had only known, how could I have failed to come? May I die if I'm not telling the truth. The fact is, I didn't know anything about it."

"You may not have come to see your mother," said Yüeh-niang, "but she still bore you in mind and set aside something to give you as a keepsake. I've been keeping it for you."

She then instructed Hsiao-yü, "You go get it and show it to Sister Yin."

Hsiao-yü, accordingly, went into the inside room and brought out a bundle containing a set of satin clothing, two gold-headed hairpins, and a floral ornament of gold. This had the effect of causing Wu Yin-erh to:

Weep so copiously she seemed to be made of tears.

"If I had only known that she was so unwell," she exclaimed, "I would have come and waited on her for a couple of days."

As she spoke, she bowed to Yüeh-niang in gratitude. Yüeh-niang entertained her with tea and asked her to stay until the third day ceremonies were completed before going home.

On the third day after Li P'ing-erh's death, the monks began to strike their chimes, conducted the flag-raising ceremony to invite the presence of the gods, and proceeded to recite their sutras. Paper money was carried outside to be burned, and the members of the entire household, high and low:

Donned hempen garments and put on mourning apparel.[8]

Ch'en Ching-chi, attired in heavy mourning and a hempen headband, prostrated himself before the effigies of the Buddhas. The neighbors in the area, friends and relatives, and senior officials who came to extend their condolences, burn paper money, and offer oblations on behalf of the deceased could not be numbered. Yin-yang Master Hsü put in an early appearance in order to preside over the encoffining ceremony, and when the sacrificial announcements had been completed, the body was carried over to be placed inside the coffin.

Hsi-men Ch'ing had Yüeh-niang search out four outfits of Li P'ing-erh's first-class clothing and fit them into her coffin, in addition to which, he placed four small ingots of silver in the four corners of the coffin.

At this, Hua Tzu-yu remarked, "Brother-in-law, there is no need to put those in there. Gold and silver are sure to reemerge in the world at some time in the future. That is not:

A good long-term plan."[9]

Hsi-men Ch'ing refused this advice and proceeded to put them where he had intended. A "seven star board"[10] had been placed inside the coffin for the corpse to rest on, the purple interior cover was put in place, and the coroner's assistants, standing on all four sides, then simultaneously drove "longevity nails" into the four sides of the lid of the casket. At this point, the members of the entire household, high and low, commenced weeping and wailing out loud.

Hsi-men Ch'ing, for his part, wept himself into a stupor, protesting again and again, without ceasing, "My tender-aged sister! I'll never be able to see you again."

After some time, once the formal wailing was over, he treated Yin-yang Master Hsü to a vegetarian repast and saw him on his way.

When the officiating monks had done with the ceremony of scattering paper flowers and rice on the bier, a placard on which there were pasted four large characters reading "May the votive lamps ensure her peace" was set up before the spirit tablet. The friends and relatives, managers, and others were all dressed in mourning garments for the occasion, so that when the ritual of circumambulation while burning incense was performed, the area in front of the gate was turned into a patch of white.

Licentiate Wen had recommended that Privy Councilor Tu, who resided in the northern quarter of the city, should be invited to inscribe the funeral banner. His given name was Tzu-ch'un,[11] his courtesy name was Yün-yeh, and he had served in the Hsüan-ho[12] Palace Hall during the reign of Emperor Chentsung[13] but was now living in retirement at home. Hsi-men Ch'ing, accordingly, provided him with a gift of gold currency and a box of candied fruit and entertained him in the summerhouse, where he personally toasted him with three cups of wine in the presence of Ying Po-chüeh and Licentiate Wen. The funeral banner of scarlet government-quality linen was laid out for him to inscribe.

Hsi-men Ch'ing wanted him to write the words "Coffin of the Respected Lady of the Imperially Commissioned Commandant Hsi-men Ch'ing of the Embroidered-Uniform Guard," but Ying Po-chüeh repeatedly objected, saying, "Your legitimate wife is alive and well. How can you say such a thing?"

"I understand that the deceased had borne him a son," said Privy Councilor Tu Tzu-ch'un. "Under the circumstances, that way of putting it would not offend against propriety."

They argued about it for some time before substituting the term "consort" for the term "respected lady."

"The term 'respected lady,'" said Licentiate Wen, "is a title bestowed by an imperial patent of nobility, whereas the term 'consort' simply means 'the person who shares the bedroom with you.' It is a term of much wider application."

Thereupon, Tu Tzu-ch'un inscribed the banner, as directed, in white pigment and also applied gold leaf to the words "Imperially Commissioned." The banner was then suspended before Li P'ing-erh's spirit tablet. He was also invited to inscribe the name of the deceased on her spirit tablet. When these tasks were completed, Hsi-men Ch'ing expressed his gratitude with a bow and entertained him with a collation, after which he took his leave and departed.

That day, Ch'iao Hung, Brother-in-law Wu K'ai, Hua the Elder, as well as Mr. Han, the husband of Meng Yü-lou's elder sister, and Mr. Shen, the husband of Wu Yüeh-niang's elder sister from outside the city gate, all contributed offertory tables of the three sacrificial animals and came to burn paper money. Ch'iao Hung's wife, Wu K'ai's wife, Wu the Second's wife, and Hua the Elder's wife all came to offer their condolences, make sacrifices, and weep over the bier. Yüeh-niang and the others, all wearing white hempen covers over their chignons, held in place with hempen headbands, with hempen girdles around their waists and hempen skirts, came out to return their salutations and join in the wailing, after which they ushered them into the rear compound to entertain them with tea and a vegetarian repast. Only Hua the Elder's wife and Hua the Elder himself wore heavy mourning, being dressed in long robes cut like those of a Taoist priest. The rest of the guests all wore light mourning.

That day, Li Kuei-chieh in the licensed quarter learned of Li P'ing-erh's death and came in a sedan chair to burn paper money on her behalf.

When she saw that Wu Yin-erh was already there, she asked, "When did you get here? And why didn't you let me know about it? Some friend you are! All you ever think about is yourself."

"I also hadn't known about Mother's death," said Wu Yin-erh. "Had I known about it, I would have come sooner."

Yüeh-niang entertained them in the rear compound, but there is no need to describe this in detail.

Time passed quickly, and it was not long before the day came for the first of the seven weekly commemorations of Li P'ing-erh's death. For this occasion, Buddhist Superior Lang,[14] the abbot of the Pao-en Temple, or Temple of Kindness Requited, led a contingent of sixteen senior monks in coming to perform a "land and water" mass for the salvation of the deceased. The liturgy included excerpts from the *Lotus Sutra*[15] and the *Litany of the Compassionate Water of Samādhi*.[16] Among the household's relatives, friends, and managers there was not one who did not attend.

On the day in question, Abbot Wu of the Temple of the Jade Emperor also came to burn paper money and offer his condolences, with a view to securing the job of presiding over the services for the second weekly commemoration. Hsi-men Ch'ing invited him into the summerhouse to join the rest of the guests in a vegetarian repast.

At this juncture, a page boy suddenly appeared to announce that Master Han had come to deliver the half-length portrait, and everyone was invited to have a look at it. Behold:

> The chignon on her head was adorned with gold
> > and turquoise ornaments,
> With two phoenixes, from whose beaks dangled
> > bangles on ropes of pearls.[17]
> She was dressed in a gown of figured
> > scarlet material,
> And her countenance was pale and fragrant,
> Looking exactly as it did when she was alive.

When Hsi-men Ch'ing saw it, he was utterly delighted and had it suspended above the head of the coffin. Among those present there were none who did not praise it extravagantly, saying:

"It lacks only the breath of life."[18]

Hsi-men Ch'ing invited Master Han into the summerhouse to share in the vegetarian repast and enjoined him, saying, "With regard to the full-length portrait, you must lavish even greater attention than usual upon it."

"Your humble servant," said Master Han, "will expend his utmost skill with the brush upon it. How could he presume to be inattentive?"

After Hsi-men Ch'ing had rewarded him generously, he made his departure.

At noon, Ch'iao Hung came to present the offerings of his household. These included pigs and sheep and other sacrificial offerings; fancy table settings of a kind intended as much for display as for eating; high-stacked pyramids of cone-shaped fruit; candied effigies of the Five Ancients and ingot shaped cakes; square-shaped confectionery and trees of wheat-gluten candy; soup and rice in gold saucers; ornate bowls containing the flesh of the five sacrificial animals; mountain-shaped stacks of imitation gold and silver ingots; satins, silks, and variegated fabrics; paper money for the use of the dead and offertory incense; more than fifty carrier-loads in all. Local mummers on stilts, performing to the beat of gongs and drums, and musicians playing more refined music on percussion and wind instruments, along with hired mourners carrying tasseled banners, all arrived, filling the air with noise, along with innumerable male and female guests.

Yin-yang Master Hsü was engaged to declaim the funeral eulogy, while Hsi-men Ch'ing and Ch'en Ching-chi, attired in mourning garments, positioned themselves in front of the spirit tablet to return the salutations of the visitors, and Ying Po-chüeh and Hsieh Hsi-ta, together with Licentiate Wen Pi-ku and Manager Kan Jun, devoted themselves to entertaining the guests.

That day, Ch'iao Hung had invited Provincial Graduate Shang, Censor Chu, Wu K'ai, School Official Liu, Battalion Commander Fan, and Kinsman Tuan, the father of Big Sister Tuan, some seven or eight relatives and friends in all, to come with him in order to burn incense in front of Li P'ing-erh's spirit tablet. After the three sacrificial libations had been offered, they knelt down to hear the recitation of his funeral eulogy, which read as follows:

On this, the twenty-second day *hsin-ssu*, of the ninth month, the first day of which was *keng-shen*, in the year *ting-yu*, the seventh year of the Cheng-ho reign period, her kinsman Ch'iao Hung and others respectfully offer a stiff-bristled pig and a soft-haired sheep,[19] along with other offertory foods,[20] in sacrifice before the spirit tablet of our late kinswoman, née Li, the consort of Hsi-men Ch'ing. Alas! The lady was, by nature, magnanimous and kindhearted. In regulating her household she was diligent and thrifty.[21] In governing her inferiors she was compassionate and good-natured. Her total exemplification of the female virtues aroused the admiration of the neighborhood. As the flower of the women's quarters, she exuded the fragrance of orchids. In her marriage with her husband she did her best to simulate the relations of the male and female phoenix. In nurturing her offspring she exhibited judgment and talent. In emulation of the paragons of female conduct she was submissive and virtuous. In setting a moral example for the women of the household she displayed harmony and purity in her relations with her in-laws. The jade was planted in Indigo

Field[22] and the pearl from Ho-p'u had begun to shine.[23] Everyone expected her to live forever in marital harmony with her husband like that between zither and cithara, enjoying an extended longevity without limit. Who could have anticipated that as the result of a single illness the Yellow Millet Dream[24] should have ended? At the death of a good person, who is not grief-stricken? Our infant daughter, while still in her diapers, rejoiced in the love of our kinswoman. Who could have anticipated that before the union between our families could be consummated, Heaven should fail to comply with our wishes,[25] and the phoenix should have lost its mate? We are doomed to endure the separation between the living and the dead, there being nothing that can be done about it. May our ties of friendship remain long-lasting, and find expression in this proffered libation. Should the spirit of the deceased be cognizant of our actions,[26] may it deign to come and enjoy our offering.[27] Pray come and partake thereof.[28]

When the male guests had finished with their offerings and had received a salutation in return, they were ushered into the summerhouse, where a collation had been prepared for them. But no more of this.

Afterwards, Ch'iao Hung's wife, her sister-in-law Mrs. Ts'ui, the wife of Censor Chu, the wife of Provincial Graduate Shang, Big Sister Tuan, and the other female guests and relatives presented their offerings. Meanwhile, local mummers, to the accompaniment of gongs and drums, performed an ensemble dance depicting the Assessor of the underworld, which created quite a din. Wu Yüeh-niang joined her guests in ceremonial wailing before the spirit tablet, after which, she invited them into the rear compound, where they were served tea, and then an ample repast, complete with the usual:

Three soups and five courses,
but there is no need to describe this in detail.

Hsi-men Ch'ing was in the summerhouse entertaining his guests with wine, when they suddenly heard the sound of the cloud-shaped gong in the front compound being struck, and a servant appeared in a state of obvious agitation, to report, "His Honor Prefect Hu Shih-wen has come to burn paper money. He is descending from his sedan chair at the front gate."

This threw Hsi-men Ch'ing into a state of consternation, as he hastened to don his formal mourning garments and await the arrival of his guest in front of the spirit tablet. He also had Licentiate Wen, dressed in the cap and gown of a licentiate, but in mourning white, go out to greet the visitor and assist him in changing out of his outer garments in the front reception hall.

Only after his attendants had entered bearing the offertory incense and paper money did Prefect Hu Shih-wen, dressed in white mourning-clothes with a gold girdle, come in himself, surrounded by a retinue of officials and functionaries who:

Smoothed his garments and adjusted his girdle,
Dancing attendance upon him without cessation.[29]

Thereupon, Ch'un-hung, who was kneeling before the spirit tablet, held the incense up high for him while he prostrated himself twice.

"Venerable sir, please stand up. We have put you to a great deal of trouble," Hsi-men Ch'ing protested, as he hastily came forward to return his salutation.

"I fear I have been remiss in offering my condolences," said Prefect Hu Shih-wen. "When did your honorable spouse die? Your pupil only found out about it yesterday."

"Who could have foreseen," responded Hsi-men Ch'ing, "that my humble spouse should come down with an incurable ailment? I am the undeserving recipient of the concern you have deigned to express."

When Licentiate Wen had saluted him, he and Hsi-men Ch'ing sat down to either side of their visitor to offer him a cup of tea, after which Prefect Hu got up to go, while Licentiate Wen saw him to the gate and into his sedan chair. The guests who had come to offer sacrifices were entertained until the afternoon, before the party broke up and they went their separate ways.

The next day, Cheng Ai-yüeh from the licensed quarter came to burn paper money on behalf of the deceased. When she descended from her sedan chair, she was dressed in a jacket of white cloud-patterned damask that opened down the middle, over a skirt of blue silk, while her chignon was wrapped in a white drawnwork kerchief, held in place with a pearl headband. When she came inside and burnt an offering of paper money before the spirit tablet, Yüeh-niang observed that she had brought with her eight platters of patisserie, meat of the three sacrificial animals, soup and rice, to offer in sacrifice to the deceased, and hastened to provide her with a mourning skirt of plain damask. Wu Yin-erh and Li Kuei-chieh also came and offered three mace apiece as sacrificial gifts.

When Yüeh-niang told Hsi-men Ch'ing about it, he said, "What does it matter? Provide each of them with a plain damask mourning headband and girdle, and invite them into the rear compound, where they can be served with tea and stay overnight."

That evening, the relatives, friends, and employees of the family all gathered to participate in an all-night wake. A troupe of Hai-yen[30] actors was engaged to perform southern-style plays of the genre known as hsi-wen.[31] Li Ming, Wu Hui, Cheng Feng, and Cheng Ch'un were also in attendance.

For this evening, Hsi-men Ch'ing had set up fifteen banquet tables in the large temporary structure in the main courtyard. Among the more prominent guests were Ch'iao Hung, Wu K'ai, Wu the Second, Hua Tzu-yu, Brother-in-law Shen, Brother-in-law Han, Licentiate Ni, Licentiate Wen, Dr. Jen Hou-ch'i, Li Chih, Huang the Fourth, Ying Po-chüeh, Hsieh Hsi-ta, Chu Jih-nien, Sun T'ien-hua, Pai Lai-ch'iang, Ch'ang Shih-chieh, Fu Ming, Han Tao-kuo, Kan Jun, Pen Ti-ch'uan, the two nephews Wu Shun-ch'en and Ts'ui Pen, in addition to which there were seven or eight neighbors. Each of the banquet tables was replete with the customary:

Ten dishes and five appetizers,

and ten or more great candles on raised candlesticks were lighted. In the adjacent reception hall, blinds were let down, and banquet tables were set out for the female guests, surrounded by standing screens, so arranged that they were able to look outside in order to watch the dramatic performance.

On this occasion, after the guests had finished making their sacrificial offerings, and Hsi-men Ch'ing and Ch'en Ching-chi had saluted them in return, they sat down in their designated places, while the actors struck up their gongs and drums before them. The play they performed was *Yü-huan chi*, or *The Story of the Jade Ring*, the tale of the two lives of love between Wei Kao and the courtesan Yü-hsiao.

Hsi-men Ch'ing had deputed four orderlies to be in charge of carrying the platters of food, while Ch'in-t'ung, Ch'i-t'ung, Hua-t'ung, and Lai-an were responsible for serving the individual dishes, and the four boy actors, Li Ming, Wu Hui, Cheng Feng, and Cheng Ch'un, poured the wine at the banquet tables.

Before long, after the prelude to the drama, the *sheng* (young male lead), playing the part of Wei Kao, sang for a while and then went offstage, followed by the *t'ieh-tan* (supporting female role), playing the part of Yü-hsiao, who also sang for a while before exiting the stage. At this point, the chef arrived from the kitchen to supervise the serving of the soup and rice and carve the goose.

Ying Po-chüeh then turned to Hsi-men Ch'ing and said, "I hear that the three singing girls from the quarter are here. Why not have them come out to serve a cup of wine to your venerable kinsman Ch'iao Hung and your elder brother-in-law Wu K'ai? They would then be better situated to watch the play, so you'd actually be doing them a favor."

Hsi-men Ch'ing accordingly told Tai-an to go inside and invite the attendance of the three singing girls.

"That really isn't appropriate," remarked Ch'iao Hung. "They are here to offer their condolences. How can you call on them to serve the wine?"

"Venerable kinsman," said Ying Po-chüeh, "you don't understand the situation. Little whores like this should not be allowed to cool their heels. Have them dragged out for me immediately. Tell them that Master Ying the Second says that since the Sixth Lady has died, they ought to demonstrate their filiality by serving each of us a cup of wine."

Tai-an went inside on this errand and was gone for some time before coming back to report, "When they heard that Master Ying the Second was present, they all refused to come out."

"In that case," said Ying Po-chüeh, "I'll have to go myself."

After taking a few steps, however, he came back and sat down.

"Why have you come back?" Hsi-men Ch'ing laughed at him.

"I really intend to drag those three little whores out here," said Ying Po-chüeh, "but I need to utter a few words of abuse in order to vent my spleen before I'll be prepared to go."

After this, Tai-an was sent inside to summon them once again before the three of them finally came out, as nonchalantly as could be. All of them were dressed in white satin jackets that opened down the middle, over blue silk skirts. After facing the company and:

Neither correctly nor precisely,

bowing in greeting, they stood by to one side with ingratiating smiles.

"Since you knew that we were all here," said Ying Po-chüeh, "how could you bring yourselves to:

Adduce three excuses or four pretexts,[32]

for refusing to appear?"

The three of them did not respond to this sally but stepped up to serve a round of wine and then sat down at a table that had been set up for them.

Below them:

Drums and music began to sound,

as the players came on to perform another scene in which the *sheng*, playing the part of Wei Kao, and the *ching* (comic-villain role), playing the part of Pao Chih-shui, pay a visit together to the bordello in which the singing girl Yü-hsiao is employed.

When the madam came out to receive them, Pao Chih-shui said, "You go and call out that girl for me."

"Master Pao," responded the madam, "you don't know how to treat people properly. My daughter is not accustomed to come out for just anybody. Are you incapable of uttering the word 'please'? How can you speak of simply call-ing her out?"[33]

At this, Li Kuei-chieh turned to the company and laughed, saying, "This character named Pao is just like Beggar Ying, a lame donkey who doesn't know the score."

"If I don't know the score," said Ying Po-chüeh, "how is it that the madam of your establishment likes me so much?"

"What she likes is for you to keep out of the way," responded Li Kuei-chieh.

"Let's watch the play," said Hsi-men Ch'ing. "What are you dithering about anyway? If you say another word, you'll have to drink a large bumper of wine as a forfeit."

Only then did Ying Po-chüeh consent to remain silent, while the players finished the scene they were performing and went offstage.

Meanwhile, Sister-in-law Wu, Wu the Second's wife, Aunt Yang, Old Mrs. P'an, Wu Yüeh-niang's elder sister, Meng Yü-lou's elder sister, Wu Shun-ch'en's wife Third Sister Cheng, Big Sister Tuan, together with Yüeh-niang and her sister-wives from the Hsi-men household, were all watching the play through the suspended blinds on the left side of the reception hall, while Ch'un-mei, Yü-hsiao, Lan-hsiang, and Hsiao-yü were all crowded together watching the play through the suspended blinds on the right side.

The servant Cheng Chi, in charge of serving the tea to the ladies on the other side, happened to pass underneath the blinds where the maidservants were gathered carrying a serving of tea flavored with fruit kernels, when Ch'un-mei called him to a halt, asking, "Who are you serving this tea to?"

"It's for Sister-in-law Wu and the ladies on the other side," responded Cheng Chi.

Ch'un-mei appropriated a cup for herself and was holding it in her hand, when, unexpectedly, Hsiao-yü, on hearing that down below the actor playing the female role was performing the part of a character named Yü-hsiao, grabbed hold of Yü-hsiao, saying, "Whore, your patron has shown up, and the madam is calling for you to receive the customer. Why haven't you gone out?"

As she spoke, she gave her a vigorous shove, which pushed her outside the suspended blinds and splashed the tea in Ch'un-mei's hand all over her person.

Ch'un-mei cursed Yü-hsiao, saying, "You crazy whore! What do you think you're doing? By horsing around this way you've splashed my tea all over. You're lucky you didn't break the teacup."

When Hsi-men Ch'ing overheard this altercation, he sent Lai-an over to inquire who was responsible for the commotion.

Ch'un-mei remained seated on her chair, saying, "Go tell him that Yü-hsiao, the wanton whore, couldn't help responding wantonly on catching sight of her lover."

After Hsi-men Ch'ing had made this inquiry, he was busy seeing to the wine service at the banquet and let the matter drop.

Yüeh-niang came over to the other side of the reception hall and scolded Hsiao-yü, saying, "You've been out here for some time. You ought to go back and see to things in the master suite. When all of you are out here, who is there to look after the place?"

"Your step-daughter Hsi-men Ta-chieh just went back there," said Hsiao-yü. "The two nuns are also sitting in your room."

"Whenever we let you lousy dog-begotten creatures come out here to watch the show," expostulated Yüeh-niang, "you end up:

Provoking an altercation."[34]

When Ch'un-mei saw that Yüeh-niang had come over, she stood up and said, "Mother, you ought to interrogate them. The whole lot of them have been carrying on crazily, with total abandon, guffawing raucously, heedless of whether anyone sees them or not."

After Yüeh-niang had given them a scolding, she returned to the other side of the reception hall.

By this point, Ch'iao Hung and Licentiate Ni had gotten up and departed.

Brother-in-law Shen, Dr. Jen Hou-ch'i, and Brother-in-law Han were also about to go, but Ying Po-chüeh stopped them, appealing to Hsi-men Ch'ing with the words, "Our host. You, too, say something. Some of us are your friends, after all, and ought not to leave you in the lurch, but even your relatives are threatening to leave. Brother-in-law Shen does not reside outside the city gate, and though Brother-in-law Han, Dr. Jen Hou-ch'i, and Hua the Elder live outside the wall, it's only the third watch, and the gates aren't even open yet. What's the hurry? We should all sit down together for a while longer. After all, the performance isn't over yet."

Hsi-men Ch'ing responded by ordering a page boy to bring out four jugs of Ma-ku wine[35] and put them down in front of him, saying, "If you gentlemen will only finish off these four jugs of wine, I won't insist on detaining you any longer."

He then took a large loving cup and put it down in front of Wu K'ai, saying, "Whoever elects to:

Leave the feast and break up the party,

by threatening to get up and go, will have to drink a penalty cup of wine enforced by this gentleman."

Thereupon, the company all sat down again, while Hsi-men Ch'ing ordered Shu-t'ung, "Urge the players to lose no time in putting on another scene, and to choose one that is lively."

In no time at all, the drums and clappers began to sound, and the *mo* (supporting male role) came out and addressed Hsi-men Ch'ing, saying, "May I ask, would the scene entitled 'Bequeathing the Self-Portrait' be appropriate?"

"I don't care," said Hsi-men Ch'ing, "just so it's lively."

The *t'ieh-tan*, playing the part of Yü-hsiao, then proceeded to sing for a while.

When Hsi-men Ch'ing heard the player sing the words:

In this life we are unlikely to meet again.
For this reason, I bequeath this self-portrait to you.[36]

it suddenly brought to mind the image of Li P'ing-erh on her sickbed, and his heart was so moved that he couldn't help starting to shed tears, which he wiped away constantly with a handkerchief.

This was spotted at once by P'an Chin-lien, who was gazing with a sardonic eye through the lowered blinds and pointed it out to Yüeh-niang, saying, "First Lady, just look at that feckless good-for-nothing! Why on earth should he have started to cry while drinking wine and watching the performance of a play?"

"Smart as you are," said Meng Yü-lou, "it's a wonder you don't understand such things.

Music expresses man's sorrows and joys,
partings and reunions.[37]

Hsi-men Ch'ing Is Deeply Stirred While Watching a Drama

I imagine that on seeing this episode of the drama, his heart was moved.

> Upon seeing an object one remembers its owner;[38]
> Upon seeing a saddle one thinks of one's horse.[39]

That is why he started to shed tears."

"I, for one," said Chin-lien, "do not believe that:

> The storyteller, when he lets his tears fall,
> Empathizes with the sorrows of the ancients.

It is all nothing but an act. Only if he could reduce *me* to tears by his singing would I rate him a good actor."

"Sister Six, quiet down," said Yüeh-niang. "We're listening to the performance."

Meng Yü-lou then turned to Wu K'ai's wife and explained, "Our Sister Six here, for some reason or other, is given to shooting off her mouth."

The players continued to perform for a while until, during the fifth watch, everyone got up to go. Though Hsi-men Ch'ing, holding a large goblet of wine in his hand, blocked the door and urged them to have another drink, he was unable to detain them any longer, and finally saw them out to the front gate.

After overseeing the clearing away of the utensils, Hsi-men Ch'ing directed the players to leave their costume trunk behind, saying, "Tomorrow, Eunuch Director Liu and Eunuch Director Hsüeh are coming to offer a sacrifice and spend the day, so I'll expect you to put on another day's performance."

The players assented to this and, after having been treated to food and wine, returned to their lodgings to rest. The four young musicians, Li Ming and company, also returned home. But no more of this.

Hsi-men Ch'ing, seeing that the day was about to dawn, also returned to the rear compound to get some rest. Truly, it is a case of:

> As the red sun illuminates the windows
>   the night chill diminishes;
> As the thin mist envelopes the bamboos
>   the dawn light is exiguous.

> If you want to know the outcome of these events,
> Pray consult the story related in the following chapter.

Chapter 64

YÜ-HSIAO KNEELS IN MAKING AN APPEAL

TO P'AN CHIN-LIEN;

OFFICERS OF THE GUARD SACRIFICE

TO A RICH MAN'S SPOUSE

Infatuated by love, on awakening to find
    the night almost over;
He tentatively examines the handkerchief
    woven of mermaid silk.
Only when dead does the spring silkworm's
    thread come to an end;
Not until burnt to ashes do the tears of
    the wax candle dry up.[1]
The male and female phoenix mates have been
    blown apart by the wind;
Her soft jade and captivating fragrance[2] are
    no longer of this world.
Before he has finished boasting of the two
    words that spell "romance";
The cock has crowed beneath the waning moon
    and the fifth watch is chill.[3]

THE STORY GOES that by the time the company had dispersed, the cocks were already crowing and Hsi-men Ch'ing retired to rest.

Tai-an took a large jug of wine and several saucers of food out to the shop in the front compound, intending to share them with Manager Fu and Ch'en Ching-chi. Manager Fu was getting along in years and had stayed up all night, so he didn't feel like sitting around any longer but proceeded to spread out a mat and lay down on the k'ang to go to sleep.

"You and P'ing-an help yourselves," he said to Tai-an. "I doubt if Son-in-law Ch'en will show up."

Tai-an lit a candle on the counter and invited P'ing-an to come inside where the two of them proceeded to share the wine:

    First a cup for you,
    Then a cup for me,

until it was all gone, after which, they put the utensils away and P'ing-an went back to the gatehouse to sleep. Tai-an then secured the gate to the shop and lay down foot-to-foot on the k'ang next to Manager Fu.

Manager Fu, idly responding to something in the preceding conversation, said to Tai-an, "Now that the Sixth Lady is dead, the quality of the coffin, the sacrifices, the sutra recitations, and the funeral arrangements are certainly more than sufficient, are they not?"

"On the one hand," responded Tai-an, "she was blessed with good fortune, but not with longevity. Although Father has spent all this money on her, he has not had to dip into his own pocket. When the Sixth Lady married Father, there is no disguising the fact, as you well know, that she brought with her a considerable dowry. Others may not know the extent of it, but I do. Without even taking into account the amount of silver specie, the gold and pearl jewelry, objets d'art, jade-ornamented girdles, chatelaines, pendants, silver frets, and valuable gemstones were too numerous to count. Why do you suppose Father was so enamored of her? He was not enamored of her person, but enamored of her money.

"Even though that was the case, if one were to bring up the subject of the late Sixth Lady's disposition, no one in this whole household was her equal. She was self-deprecating and congenial, and greeted everyone with a smile. As far as we servants were concerned, she never once raised her voice in criticism, made the mistake of reviling us as slaves, or threatened us with dire consequences.

"When commissioning us to buy anything for her, she would simply hand us a nugget of silver. And when we suggested, 'Mother, why don't you put it on the scale and weigh it, so we'll know what we're spending,' she would laugh, saying, 'Just take it. What's the point of weighing it? If you don't expect to make a little something out of the transaction, what are you hoping for? Just see that I get my money's worth.'

"Who is there in this entire household who hasn't borrowed silver from her? And though she lent it out, no one ever returned it. She didn't seem to care whether she got it back or not. The First Lady and the Third Lady are also liberal as far as money is concerned, but the Fifth Lady and the Second Lady are a bit tight. When it is their turn to be in charge of the household finances, we feel plague-stricken. They are more than willing to grind our legs down to the bone. At best, they simply will not give full value. Even without any other funny business, for an expense of a mace of silver, they will weigh out only nine and a half candareens worth, or, when you get right down to it, no more than nine candareens, apparently expecting us to make up the difference."

"Well, at least the First Lady is better than that," said Manager Fu.

"Although the First Lady is all right," said Tai-an, "she's got a hair-trigger temper. One minute, she'll be in a good mood, talking away as pleasantly as can be, but the next minute, should anyone offend her, no matter who it might be, she'll let you have it in no uncertain terms. In the final analysis, she's no match for the Sixth Lady, who aroused resentment in nobody and was often willing to put in a good word with Father on our behalf. Even in the weightiest matters of a kind that would not brook appeal, if we appealed to her, she would speak to Father on our behalf, and he would never fail to comply. The Fifth Lady, on the other hand, is quick to make groundless allegations, is forever saying, 'Just you see if I don't tell Father about this,' and constantly threatens people with a beating. And now, this sister of ours, Ch'un-mei, is another star of contention, and, as fate would have it, they are both to be found in the same quarters."

"The Fifth Lady has been here for some years now," averred Manager Fu.

"You know what kind of a person she is," said Tai-an, "and can remember back to the time when she first arrived. She doesn't even show any respect to her own mother. On more than one occasion when the old lady has visited, she has treated her so badly she has gone home in tears. And now that the Sixth Lady has died, she is able to preside over the world of the front compound. She feels free to abuse whoever is in charge of sweeping the flower garden for not getting it clean enough, so that, early in the morning, he ends up looking as though:

His head has been sprayed with dog's blood."

The two of them talked for a while until Manager Fu started to snore stertorously as he fell asleep on his pillow. Tai-an also had had more than enough to drink and no sooner closed his eyes than he became oblivious to:

Heaven above and earth below.

By the time:

The red sun was three rods high in the sky,[4]

they had still not gotten up.

It so happens that Hsi-men Ch'ing often chose to sleep in front of Li P'ing-erh's spirit tablet in the front compound. In the morning, when Yü-hsiao came out to dispose of the bedding, Hsi-men Ch'ing would go back to the rear compound to comb his hair, while Shu-t'ung, with his own hair still undressed, would take advantage of the opportunity for the two of them to:

Engage in badinage and repartee,

joking and contending with each other for some time before she returned to the rear compound.

Who could have anticipated that, on this particular day, when Hsi-men Ch'ing had gone back to the master suite to get some rest, Yü-hsiao availed herself of the fact that people weren't up yet, to surreptitiously come out to the front compound and give Shu-t'ung a wink, upon which the two of them snuck out to the studio in the garden and proceeded to get down to business together.

They could hardly have foreseen that P'an Chin-lien would arise early that morning and abruptly make her way to the reception hall, where she found that the lamp in front of the spirit tablet had gone out, while the tables and chairs in the large temporary structure were lying around:

      Higgledy-piggledy,[5]

with no one in attendance but Hua-t'ung, who was busily engaged in sweeping the grounds.

"You lousy jailbird!" Chin-lien said to him. "Do you mean to say that you are the only one here sweeping the grounds? Where have all the others gone?"

"They haven't gotten up yet," replied Hua-t'ung.

"Drop your broom for the time being," said Chin-lien, "and go up front to ask our son-in-law for a length of white damask for my mother, Old Mrs. P'an, who doesn't have a mourning skirt. You can also pick up a mourning headband and girdle for her. She's going home later today."

"I fear your son-in-law may still be asleep," said Hua-t'ung, "but I'll go ask him for you."

After some time, he returned and reported, "Your son-in-law says that it's not part of his responsibility, since it is Shu-t'ung and Ts'ui Pen who are in charge of monitoring the expenses incurred by providing the guests with mourning wear. The thing for you to do is to ask Shu-t'ung for what you want."

"Who knows where that slave has gone off to?" said Chin-lien. "You go see if you can find him."

Hua-t'ung looked into the studio in the front courtyard and reported back, saying, "He was there a minute ago. He must have gone to the studio in the garden to do his hair."

"You can finish your sweeping," said Chin-lien. "I'll go ask that jailbird for what I need myself."

Thereupon, she:

      Lightly moved her lotus feet,
      Gently lifted her beige skirt,

and headed toward the studio in the garden. Upon chancing to hear the sound of laughter within, she pushed open the door, only to find Shu-t'ung and Yü-hsiao just in the thick of things on the bed inside.

"A dandy jailbird you are!" she exclaimed. "A fine thing the two of you are up to in here!"

The two of them, who were still entwined with each other, were thrown into such consternation by her appearance that they were barely able to extricate themselves in time to kneel down on the ground before her and plead for mercy.

"You lousy jailbird!" said Chin-lien to Shu-t'ung. "Just go fetch me a bolt of mourning damask and a bolt of cotton cloth, so I can send my mother home with them."

Shu-t'ung lost no time in fetching the wanted articles and proffering them to her, whereupon, Chin-lien went straight back to her quarters, with Yü-hsiao following in her wake.

Upon their arrival there, Yü-hsiao knelt down on the floor and groveled around on her knees, appealing to Chin-lien with the plea, "Fifth Lady, whatever happens, don't tell Father about this."

"You lousy little bitch!" Chin-lien demanded. "Tell me the truth. All this while, how many times has that slave made out with you? You'd better not try to deceive me by so much as a single word."

Yü-hsiao then confessed the whole story of how the two of them had been carrying on an affair.

"If you want me to let you off," said Chin-lien, "you'll have to agree to three conditions."

"If you consent to spare me," said Yü-hsiao, "no matter how many conditions you impose, I'll agree to them all."

"The first condition," Chin-lien said, "is that you will tell me everything that happens in your mistress's quarters, no matter how trivial. If you fail to tell me anything, and I hear about it, I will definitely not let you off the hook. The second condition is that if I ask you for anything, you'll find a way to see that I get it. The third condition is that you tell me how it is that your mistress, who has not been pregnant before, should now have managed to conceive."

"I will not deceive you, Fifth Lady," said Yü-hsiao. "The fact of the matter is that my mistress, thus and so, conceived after taking a fertility potion, provided by Nun Hsüeh, containing the afterbirth of a firstborn male child."

Chin-lien made a mental note of everything she had said and only then consented not to report anything to Hsi-men Ch'ing.

When Shu-t'ung saw the sardonic smile on the face of P'an Chin-lien as she led Yü-hsiao off to her quarters, he realized that this was an affair that was not likely to end propitiously for him. He therefore availed himself of the opportunity to help himself to the considerable number of handkerchiefs, scarves, ornamental toothpicks, hairpins, toggles, and other gifts from visitors that were stored in a cabinet in the studio. He had managed to scrounge something over ten taels of silver for himself, and he also went to the counter of the shop out front and finagled Manager Fu into giving him another twenty taels by saying they were needed to buy additional supplies of mourning damask. He then went straightaway outside the city gate and hired a long-distance mount to take him to the nearest embarkation point, where he boarded a boat from his hometown and embarked for his place of origin in Su-chou. Truly:

> Breaking to pieces the jade cage,
>   the phoenix flies away;
> Smashing apart the metal padlock,
>   the dragon breaks free.[6]

It so happened that on that day Li Kuei-chieh, Wu Yin-erh, and Cheng Ai-yüeh all returned to their respective establishments. In the morning, Eunuch Director Hsüeh and Eunuch Director Liu sent men to deliver offertory tables

Yü-hsiao Kneels in Order to Accept the Three Conditions

Shu-t'ung Secretly Decamps Setting Sail before the Wind

of the three sacrificial animals, so that they would be able to offer oblations
and burn paper money on behalf of the deceased. Each of them also donated
a tael of silver as their contributions toward the expenses of an all-night wake
and engaged the services of two professional performers of the genre known as
Tao-ch'ing, or Taoist songs, proposing to come visit with Hsi-men Ch'ing during the day.

Hsi-men Ch'ing was anxious to be able to supply his visitors with mourning
damask and started looking for Shu-t'ung in order to get the necessary key but
couldn't find him anywhere.

"This morning," reported Manager Fu, "he came to the counter in the shop
and asked me for twenty taels of silver to buy mourning damask with. He said
that you had told him the existing supply of mourning damask was inadequate.
No doubt he has gone outside the city gate to purchase some more."

"I didn't tell him any such thing," said Hsi-men Ch'ing. "So why should he
be asking you for silver?"

He then sent someone outside the city gate to the shops that sold mourning
damask to look for him, but he was nowhere to be found.

"I suspect this slave has been up to some funny business," said Yüeh-niang
to Hsi-men Ch'ing. "Who knows what sort of scurvy tricks he's capable of?
And now it looks like he's appropriated several taels of silver and made off with
them. You had better open up those studios of yours and give them a good
going over. It's not a job for a legless crab like myself. I fear he may have absconded with other things as well."

Hsi-men Ch'ing, accordingly, went to inspect his two studios and found that
the keys to the storeroom were still hanging on the wall, but that a considerable number of handkerchiefs, scarves, gifts of books and silver, ornamental
toothpicks, toggles, and the like, were missing from the large cabinet.

Hsi-men Ch'ing was enraged and called in the neighborhood authorities,
telling them to seek out and apprehend the fugitive throughout the:

Three quarters and two alleys,
of the pleasure precincts, but he was nowhere to be found. Truly:

Not only was he impatient to return to
his native place;
But the misty waters of the Five Lakes[7]
were impenetrable.

By this time, at about noon that afternoon, Eunuch Director Hsüeh had
arrived in his sedan chair, and Hsi-men Ch'ing invited Wu K'ai, Ying Po-
chüeh, and Licentiate Wen to help entertain him.

Before doing anything else, Eunuch Director Hsüeh went up to Li P'ing-
erh's spirit tablet to burn incense and perform an obeisance, after which, he
saluted Hsi-men Ch'ing, saying, "How sad! How sad! What ailment was it that
your lady died of?"

"Unfortunately," said Hsi-men Ch'ing, "she suffered from a severe case of hemorrhaging, which was not looked after properly, and resulted in her death. I am grateful to you, venerable sir, for your expression of concern."

"I haven't much to offer," said Eunuch Director Hsüeh. "It is but a paltry expression of my feelings."

Then, catching sight of the portrait of Li P'ing-erh that was hanging nearby, he said, "What a beautiful lady. She looks just as though she were:

Enjoying prosperity in the springtime of her youth.
What a pity that she has departed this world so early."

"That things are unequal is part of their nature,"[8] opined Licentiate Wen, who was standing to one side. "After all:

Failure or success, long life or short,[9]
are things that are predetermined. Even a sage can do nothing to alter them."

Eunuch Director Hsüeh turned his head to look at Licentiate Wen and, noticing that he was dressed in the cap and gown of a licentiate, but in mourning white, asked, "What school is this venerable gentleman enrolled in?"

Licentiate Wen responded with a bow, saying, "Your unworthy pupil is enrolled in the Prefectural School."

Changing the subject, Eunuch Director Hsüeh said, "I'd like to see the lady's coffin, if I may."

Hsi-men Ch'ing then ordered his attendants to lift aside the curtains suspended to either side, so that Eunuch Director Hsüeh could go inside and take a look.

Expressing the most fulsome admiration, Eunuch Director Hsüeh said, "What a fine coffin. May I ask how much you paid for it?"

"I got it through a relative," said Hsi-men Ch'ing, "and compensated him appropriately."

"Venerable sir," said Ying Po-chüeh, "why don't you hazard a guess. Where did the wood come from, and what is it called?"

After carefully examining it, Eunuch Director Hsüeh said, "If it didn't come from Chien-ch'ang,[10] it must have come from Chen-yüan."[11]

"Even if it came from Chen-yüan," said Ying Po-chüeh, "it wouldn't be worth all that much."

"The best coffin wood," said Eunuch Director Hsüeh, "is surely Yang-hsüan Elm."[12]

"Boards cut from the Yang-hsüan Elm are comparatively thin and short," said Ying Po-chüeh. "How could they pass muster? These coffin boards are superior to those made from the Yang-hsüan Elm. They come from a place called Peach Blossom Cavern, located on the Wu-ling River in Hu-kuang province. In former days, during the T'ang dynasty, a fisherman entered this cavern where he encountered the Hairy Woman, a refugee from the Ch'in dynasty, who had sought shelter there from the military conflicts of the time.[13] It is a secluded place where people seldom come. These boards were all more than seven feet long, four inches thick, and two feet five inches wide. As a special favor to a kinsman the owner gave him a substantial discount, so the asking price was only 370 taels of silver. You have never seen the like, sir. When they were sawed open, they exuded a pungent aroma and had flower-like patterns on both sides."

"The lady is fortunate indeed," said Eunuch Director Hsüeh, "to be able to enjoy a coffin of this quality. We eunuchs, when we pass away, cannot expect such elaborate funeral arrangements."

"Venerable sir," said Wu K'ai, "that's a fine way to talk! People like you have direct access to the imperial court and enjoy great rank and emolument. We outer officials can hardly hope to compete with the likes of you, venerable sir, who are daily exposed to the pure radiance of the sovereign and transmit the words of the Lord of Ten Thousand Years. At present, His Honor T'ung Kuan has been promoted to the rank of Commandery Prince,[14] and his sons and grandsons are all entitled to:

Wear python robes and girdles of jade.

What limit is there to your prospects?"[15]

"Might I ask," said Eunuch Director Hsüeh, "what is the name of this glib-tongued gentleman?"

"This is my wife's elder brother, Wu K'ai," said Hsi-men Ch'ing. "At present he holds the position of battalion commander in the local guard."

"Is he the elder brother of this deceased lady?" asked Eunuch Director Hsüeh.

"No," said Hsi-men Ch'ing. "He is the elder brother of my humble spouse."

Eunuch Director Hsüeh then saluted Wu K'ai with a bow, saying, "Pray forgive my unmindfulness."

After he had inspected the coffin for a while, Hsi-men Ch'ing escorted him to the summerhouse, where a folding armchair had been placed in the position of honor, upon which Eunuch Director Hsüeh sat down.

After a servant had served them with tea, Eunuch Director Hsüeh said, "How is it that Eunuch Director Liu is not here yet? I'll have one of my retainers go out to meet him."

At this, a black-clad retainer knelt down and reported, "When Your Honor left home, you sent your humble servant to invite His Honor Liu to start out, and his sedan chair was already in waiting. He should be here any minute."

Eunuch Director Hsüeh then went on to ask, "Have those two performers of Tao-ch'ing arrived, or not?"

"They arrived this morning," reported Hsi-men Ch'ing. "I'll have them called in."

It was not long before they appeared before the company and kowtowed.

"Have you had anything to eat?" asked Eunuch Director Hsüeh.

"We have been given something to eat," they replied.

"Since you've already been fed," said Eunuch Director Hsüeh, "I want you to do the best you can today. I'll see that you are amply rewarded."

"Venerable sir," said Hsi-men Ch'ing, "your pupil also has a troupe of players here, who are prepared to perform for you."

"Where are these players from?" asked Eunuch Director Hsüeh.

"It is a troupe of Hai-yen actors," said Hsi-men Ch'ing.

"What with that barbarous accent of theirs," pronounced Eunuch Director Hsüeh, "who knows what they are singing about? Their plots are only concerned with those poor discontented scholars who endure hardship for three years within their unheated chambers and then wander abroad for nine years, carrying their:

Zithers, swords, and book boxes,[16]

on their backs, making their way to the capital in order to compete in the examinations, in the hope of obtaining an office. They don't even have the consolation of wives or children by their sides. What do the vicissitudes of such people mean to celibate old eunuchs like ourselves? We can do without them."

Licentiate Wen, who was seated beside him, laughed at this diatribe, saying, "Venerable sir, what you have just said is quite unreasonable.

Those who reside in Ch'i speak with a Ch'i accent;
Those who reside in Ch'u speak with a Ch'u accent.

Though you may reside in your:

High halls and spacious structures,[17]

how can your heart fail to be moved by such things?"

At this rejoinder, Eunuch Director Hsüeh clapped his hands and laughed, saying, "I had forgotten that Licentiate Wen was present. You outer officials always come to the defense of each other."

"After all," said Licentiate Wen, "it is from us licentiates that members of the official class are recruited. Venerable sir:

For every branch you chop down,
A hundred trees are threatened.[18]
When the hare dies, the fox is sad;
Creatures grieve for their fellows."[19]

"That is not so," responded Eunuch Director Hsüeh:

"In the space of any particular quarter,
There are both the wise and the foolish."

As they were talking, an attendant suddenly came in and reported that Eunuch Director Liu was getting out of his sedan chair, at which, Wu K'ai and the others went out to greet him. Upon coming inside, Eunuch Director Liu bowed in front of Li P'ing-erh's spirit tablet.

When they had finished with the customary amenities, Eunuch Director Hsüeh addressed his fellow eunuch, saying, "Why is it, venerable sir, that you have not arrived until now?"

"Eunuch Director Hsü from the northern quarter dropped by for a visit," Eunuch Director Liu explained, "and I had to entertain him for a while before sending him off."

The company thereupon sat down in their respective places, while attendants served them with tea.

Eunuch Director Liu then asked one of his servitors, "Have our offertory tables been set up yet, or not?"

"They have all been properly set up," the servant replied.

"We might as well proceed to burn paper money on behalf of the deceased, then," said Eunuch Director Liu.

"Venerable sir," said Hsi-men Ch'ing, "there is no need for any further ritual observances. You have already demonstrated your respect for the deceased."

"Why else did we come?" said Eunuch Director Liu. "We ought to present our offerings in person."

At this juncture, the attendants provided them with incense sticks, and the two eunuchs proceeded to light them before the spirit tablet, offer the customary three libations, and then perform an obeisance.

"Venerable sirs, please get up," said Hsi-men Ch'ing.

Thereupon, after performing two kowtows, they stood up, and Hsi-men Ch'ing kowtowed to them in return.

The company then returned to the summerhouse and sat down, while the preparations for the feast were completed, and wine was served. The two eunuchs were seated in the places of honor to left and right, with Wu K'ai, Licentiate Wen, and Ying Po-chüeh placed below them, while Hsi-men Ch'ing occupied the position of host at the lower end of the seating arrangement. As their:

Drums and gongs began to sound,

the players came on and presented the program of pieces they were prepared to perform. The two eunuch directors examined it for a while and chose a selection from the play entitled *Liu Chih-yüan hung-p'ao chi*, or *Liu Chih-yüan and the Crimson Robe*.[20]

Before many scenes had been played, however, they grew tired of it and called in the performers of Tao-ch'ing, saying, "It would be more fun if they were to sing a Tao-ch'ing for us."

Thereupon, the two of them began to tap their "fisherman's drums,"[21] as they stood shoulder to shoulder, facing their audience, and sang in high-pitched voices the story entitled *Han Wen-kung hsüeh-yung Lan-kuan*, or *Han Yü Is Impeded by Snow at Lan-kuan*.[22]

At this juncture, the chef came out and kowtowed before the company, and the two eunuch directors rewarded him with appropriate gratuities. Hsi-men Ch'ing had also prepared meat and wine to serve to their attendants, but there is no need to describe this in detail.

During the course of the banquet, Eunuch Director Hsüeh began a conversation with Eunuch Director Liu, saying, "Brother Liu, you may not have heard about it yet, but, the other day, on the tenth day of the eighth month, during:

> A great downpour of rain,[23]

the thunder and lightning destroyed the owl-tail-shaped ornaments at the ends of the roof beam of the Ning-shen Hall in the grounds of the Imperial Palace, frightening any number of palace women to death. The Emperor himself was greatly alarmed and ordered that all his officials should engage in self-examination,[24] that daily petitions should be presented to the spirits during propitiatory services in the Temple of Highest Clarity, that the butchering of animals should be prohibited for ten days, that the judicial offices should suspend punishments, and that no officials should be permitted to present memorials to the throne.

"Recently, an envoy from the Jurchen regime of the Great Chin has presented a memorial demanding that we cede them the territory of our three frontier defense commands,[25] and that old villain Ts'ai Ching proposed that we should agree to this, and that the troops and horses under the command of T'ung Kuan should be turned over to Censor-in-Chief T'an Chen,[26] along with Huang Yu[27] and the other ten commissioners in charge of the Three Border Regions, but the troops refused to return, and the matter has been turned over to the court officials for deliberation.

"The other day, at the solar term 'Beginning of Winter,' the Lord of Ten Thousand Years was scheduled to come out to sacrifice at the Imperial Ancestral Temple. That morning, an erudite of the Court of Imperial Sacrifices named Fang Chen,[28] who was supervising the sweeping of the premises, observed that a brick in the wall of the temple was oozing blood,[29] and that there was a declivity in the northeastern corner of the floor of the hall. He reported these observations in a memorial to the throne. In response to this, a supervising secretary in the Office of Scrutiny sent up a memorial stating in the strongest possible terms that T'ung Kuan had been given too much authority, and that eunuchs ought not to be granted the rank of commandery prince. At present, an imperial mandate written in letters of gold has been dispatched by express courier, ordering Commander T'ung Kuan to return to the capital."

"Now that you and I have been sent out to be local officials," responded Eunuch Director Liu, "such affairs at court are no longer any business of ours. As the saying goes:

> Each day you live is merely another day.[30]
> Even if the sky should be about to fall,
> There are the four giants to hold it up.[31]

Sooner or later this realm of the Great Sung dynasty is sure to come to grief at the hands of this bunch of discontented scholars.

     Wang Ten-plus-nine,
     Let's sip our wine!"[32]

He then called for the two performers of Tao-ch'ing to come forward and instructed them, saying, "Sing us the story of *Li Po hao t'an-pei*, or *Li Po's Addiction to the Cup*."[33]

The two performers then began to tap their "fisherman's drums" and sang to them for a while.

The feasting continued until evening, when the two eunuchs ordered their servants to prepare their sedan chairs and got up to go. Hsi-men Ch'ing was unable to detain them any longer and saw them out to the front gate, where they departed, with their escorts shouting to clear the way.

When Hsi-men Ch'ing came back inside, he ordered that candles should be lit and the tables left in place, instructed the caterers to set things back in order, and urged Wu K'ai, Ying Po-chüeh, and Licentiate Wen to keep their seats. In addition, he sent a page boy to invite Manager Fu Ming, Manager Kan Jun, Han Tao-kuo, Pen Ti-ch'uan, Ts'ui Pen, and Ch'en Ching-chi to join them.

When they had all been seated, he called for the players and instructed them, saying, "Continue to perform the *Yü-huan chi* from where you left off yesterday."

He then turned to Ying Po-chüeh and remarked, "These eunuchs have no taste for the flavor of southern-style drama. If I had known they didn't like it, I would not have urged them to stay."

"They failed to appreciate your intentions," said Ying Po-chüeh. "Eunuchs, with their perverted tastes, only go for pieces like *Lan-kuan chi*,[34] and the:
     Suggestive songs and lewd tunes,
performed by their boy actors. What do they know of major works that treat of:
     Sorrows and joys, partings and reunions?"

Thereupon, the drums and clappers began to sound, and the players proceeded to present:
     With lively action and slow singing,
the remaining scenes from *Yü-huan chi* that they had not finished performing the day before. Hsi-men Ch'ing ordered the page boys to serve the company by:
     Promptly pouring the fine wine.[35]

Ying Po-chüeh, who was sitting at the same table with Hsi-men Ch'ing, asked him, "Have the three singing girls gone home yet? If not, why don't you have them come out and serve us a cup of wine?"

"You're still dreaming of them, are you?" said Hsi-men Ch'ing. "They've long since had enough of it and gone home."

"They must have stayed over here for two or three days," said Ying Po-chüeh.

"Wu Yin-erh stayed the longest time of all," said Hsi-men Ch'ing.

That day, the company remained seated at their places until the third watch after the performance of the play was over, before the party finally broke up. Hsi-men Ch'ing asked his brother-in-law, Wu K'ai, to come a little early the next morning in order to help entertain the official visitors who were coming to offer a sacrifice to the deceased, after which, he rewarded the players with four taels of silver and sent them on their way.

The next day, Commandant Chou Hsiu, Military Director-in-Chief Ching Chung, Militia Commander Chang Kuan, Judicial Commissioner Hsia Yen-ling, and a sizable contingent of officials from the local guard all clubbed together to provide a pig and a sheep, and a fancy table setting of a kind intended as much for display as for eating, as their sacrificial offerings. A ritual specialist had been engaged to declaim the funeral eulogy. Hsi-men Ch'ing had prepared a banquet for the occasion, and the three boy actors, Li Ming and company, were also in attendance.

At noon, the sound of drums was heard, indicating that the offertory gifts had arrived. Brother-in-law Wu K'ai, Ying Po-chüeh, and Licentiate Wen went out to the gate to welcome the visitors and looked on as the group of officials, with their attendants:

Crowding behind and clamoring in front,[36]
dismounted and were ushered into the front reception hall to change their clothes.

Before long, the sacrificial offerings were duly displayed, the group of officials gathered in front of Li P'ing-erh's spirit tablet, and Hsi-men Ch'ing and Ch'en Ching-chi returned their salutations. The ritual specialist, whose job it was to act as master of ceremonies, then called out his instructions, presented the three sacrificial libations, knelt down to one side, and proceeded to declaim the funeral eulogy, which read as follows:

> On this, the twenty-fifth day *chia-shen*, of the ninth month, the first day of which was *keng-shen*, in the year *ting-yu*, the seventh year of the Cheng-ho reign period, his devoted colleagues Chou Hsiu, Ching Chung, Hsia Yen-ling, Chang Kuan, along with their fellow officials Fan Hsün, Wu K'ai, Hsü Feng-hsiang, P'an Chi, and others, respectfully offer a stiff-bristled pig and a soft-haired sheep, along with other offertory foods, in sacrifice before the spirit tablet of the late consort, née Li, of Hsi-men Ch'ing, an officer of the Embroidered-Uniform Guard. We address the spirit of the departed. Delicately raised in the women's quarters, she was chaste and adept at female occupations. Her virtue was that of gold or jade, her appearance that of fragrant orchids. In regulating her household she exhibited judgment, in managing her domestic tasks she left nothing to be desired. She showed respect for learning and was on good terms with her in-laws. Revering her husband as her Heaven, she paid him respect by raising the serving tray as high as her eyebrows.[37] Though she hoped to live to a ripe age, Heaven chose to curtail her remaining years. She and her

husband should have enjoyed the harmony of phoenix mates or musical instruments, but, alas, Heaven begrudged her her remaining years and chose to hurry
them to an abrupt end. Alas! The length or brevity of life are predetermined.[38]
Heaven seems to reject persons of worth. Pearls sink below the waves and jade disks
are shattered. Clouds can be threatening and winds bring sorrow in their wake.
Though we knock at the door of the grave, it will not open. We may sigh for the dew
on the shallot, but it will soon evaporate.[39] I, Chou Hsiu, and the others, occupying
the position of colleagues, and mindful of the obligations of friendship, hereby offer
up meat in sacrificial vessels, and decant wine into offertory goblets, in the hope that
the spirit of the departed will deign to enjoy them. Should she be mindful of our
eulogy on this sad occasion, may she come and partake thereof.

When the sacrificial ceremony was finished, and Hsi-men Ch'ing had
thanked the participants, Wu K'ai and company led the group of officials to
the summerhouse, where they divested themselves of their mourning garments and were served with tea. The boy actors started to play their instruments and sing for their entertainment as they sat down at their places to enjoy
the collation that had been prepared for them. Their servants and attendants
were also properly attended to. The chef then came out to supervise the presentation of the:
    Three soups and five courses,
which were even more lavish than those served on the preceding two days,
and kowtowed before the company. Hsi-men Ch'ing, along with Wu K'ai,
Ying Po-chüeh, and Licentiate Wen, occupied the position of hosts, plying
their guests with wine until:
    Drinking vessels and game tallies lay helter-skelter,
while the three boy actors, Li Ming and company, with their:
    Silver psalteries and ivory clappers,
played and sang to entertain the company. Meanwhile, outside, Hsi-men
Ch'ing's managers and storekeepers saw to it that the carriers who had accompanied the official guests all received appropriate gratuities of silver according
to precedent.
    The officials remained in their places until mid-afternoon before getting up
to go, but Hsi-men Ch'ing would not hear of it and, together with Wu K'ai,
Ying Po-chüeh, and company, with large goblets in hand, endeavored to detain them, while telling Li Ming and the other boy actors to strike up their
instruments and sing songs to them. They continued drinking and enjoying
themselves until evening before the party broke up.
    Hsi-men Ch'ing tried to persuade Wu K'ai and Ying Po-chüeh to stay a little
longer, but Wu K'ai said, "We've all been imposing on you for days on end,
and you must be tired out yourself, Brother-in-law. We'd better go our respective ways and get some rest."
    Thereupon, they bade him farewell, and went home. Truly:

The verdant peaches in the celestial realm
    are saturated with dew;
The red apricots that grow beside the sun
    are enveloped in clouds.[40]
If your family possesses immoderate wealth[41]
    people will toady to you;
When you have ample means at your disposal
    price is no consideration.

If you want to know the outcome of these events,
Pray consult the story related in the following chapter.

Chapter 65

ABBOT WU MEETS THE FUNERAL PROCESSION

AND EULOGIZES THE PORTRAIT;

CENSOR SUNG IMPOSES ON A LOCAL MAGNATE

TO ENTERTAIN EUNUCH HUANG

Moved by the respect she always showed him,
   he admired her gentleness;
Not having expected to be parted forever,
   he can sing only sad songs.
The waning moon, hovering beside the clouds,
   suspends its broken mirror;
Time's flowing light flies past as swiftly
   as the shuttle on a loom.
Sorrow, like the color of verdant foliage,
   fades by the end of spring;
Bitterness, suffusing the yearning heart,
   serves to prolong the night.
If you should inquire how many tears have
   fallen, only to evaporate;
They are as numerous as the autumn colors
   in a grove of maple trees.

THE STORY GOES that the twenty-eighth day of the ninth month was the time for the second of the seven weekly commemorations of Li P'ing-erh's death. Abbot Wu of the Temple of the Jade Emperor, who had secured the job of presiding over the services on that day, brought sixteen Taoist priests to come to Hsi-men Ch'ing's home to conduct the flag-raising ceremony inviting the presence of the gods, and erect the ritual altar for the performance of the "Litany Addressed to the Heavenly Savior from Distress Who Dwells in the Blue Heaven of the East"[1] for the second weekly commemoration.

While they were setting up the altar that morning, a messenger came to deliver a letter from Secretary An Ch'en of the Ministry of Works, and Hsi-men Ch'ing saw that he was properly entertained before going on his way.

Abbot Wu had brought with him from the temple vessels for the meat of the three sacrificial animals, offerings of soup and rice, patisserie, vegetarian fare, imitation gold and silver ingots, paper money, and the like, along with a bolt of fabric, to serve as his sacrificial gifts. When the Taoist priests had circumambulated the coffin reciting their spells, Abbot Wu prostrated himself in front of the spirit tablet.

Hsi-men Ch'ing and Ch'en Ching-chi kowtowed to him in return, saying, "Your Reverence has put himself to considerable expense.

What can we do to be worthy of such largess?"

"I am most embarrassed," responded Abbot Wu. "I really should have provided for the recitation of an additional scripture to pray for the salvation of your lady, but my means would not permit me to do so. As for these coarse offerings of tea and rice that I have presented:

They are no more than tokens of my esteem.

I hope that Your Honor will see fit to accept them with a smile."

When the presentation of the sacrificial offerings had been completed, Hsi-men Ch'ing agreed to accept them and saw to the dismissal of the carriers who had brought them.

That day the sacred texts recited at the three morning, noon, and evening audiences included the *Chiu-t'ien sheng-shen chang ching*, or *Scripture of the Stanzas of the Vitalizing Spirits of the Nine Heavens*,[2] a litany designed to destroy the Hells of the Nine Realms of Darkness,[3] a ritual for attracting and summoning the soul of the deceased, a memorial written in red characters addressed to the above-mentioned Heavenly Savior from Distress Who Dwells in the Blue Heaven of the East, and the talismans notifying the various Perfected Beings of the rites that were being celebrated. These rituals were all performed in their entirety, but there is no need to describe this in detail.

The next day, the first person who came to offer a sacrifice to the deceased was Han Ming-ch'uan, the husband of Meng Yü-lou's elder sister, who lived outside the city gate. At the time, Meng Yü-lou's younger brother, Meng Jui, who had been away from home as a traveling merchant for five or six years, had happened to arrive home the day before and, learning from his elder sister that there was to be a funeral observance at Hsi-men Ch'ing's place, chose to accompany his brother-in-law Han Ming-ch'uan in coming to offer a sacrifice to the deceased and acquire the appropriate mourning garment. He also brought with him something considerable in the way of gifts. After exchanging the customary amenities with Hsi-men Ch'ing, he proceeded to Meng Yü-lou's quarters to pay his respects. By this time, there were some ten or more female guests on the premises, and Hsi-men Ch'ing had also provided a collation for their entertainment. But no more of this.

At noon on the same day, the district magistrate of Ch'ing-ho, Li Ta-t'ien, the vice magistrate, Ch'ien Ch'eng, the assistant magistrate, Jen T'ing-kuei, the docket officer, Hsia Kung-chi, and the magistrate of Yang-ku district, Ti

Ssu-pin, five officials in all, who had clubbed together to provide the necessary funds, came, attired in appropriate mourning garb, to burn paper money and offer their condolences. Hsi-men Ch'ing had prepared a collation for them and saw that they were accommodated in the summerhouse. He had asked his brother-in-law, Wu K'ai, along with Licentiate Wen, to help keep them company, and also engaged the services of the three boy actors to play their musical instruments and sing for their entertainment. The grooms that had accompanied them to tend their horses were also provided with platters of assorted snacks, which they carried to the place that had been set aside for them so they could sit down and eat.

Just as the guests at the party were devoting themselves to their cups and having a high time of it, as luck would have it:

Without coincidences there would be no stories.

It was unexpectedly announced that the secretary of the Ministry of Works, Huang Pao-kuang, who was the superintendent of the Imperial Brickyard, had come to offer his condolences. This threw Hsi-men Ch'ing into such consternation that he hastily changed into his mourning clothes and went before Li P'ing-erh's spirit tablet to await his guest. Licentiate Wen, who had gone outside the front gate to welcome him, ushered him into the front reception hall, where he changed his clothes, and then led him inside. The servants who accompanied him, bearing incense sticks and candles, paper money, and bolts of satin brocade, arrayed on red lacquer trays, knelt down, holding up the incense in their hands.

After Huang Pao-kuang had offered up the incense and kowtowed before the spirit tablet, and Hsi-men Ch'ing and Ch'en Ching-chi had stepped forward to return his salutation, Huang Pao-kuang said, "Your pupil did not know of the death of your respected spouse. I have been remiss in offering my condolences. Forgive me. Forgive me."

"Your pupil has hitherto neglected to pay you his respects," said Hsi-men Ch'ing. "And now, venerable sir, you have not only condescended to express your condolences, but have deigned to bestow these lavish gifts upon me.

My gratitude will be impossible to contain."

When they had finished exchanging these amenities, Huang Pao-kuang was conducted to the summerhouse, where he was invited to sit down in the place of honor at the head of the table, while Hsi-men Ch'ing and Licentiate Wen sat down in the position of hosts to keep him company, and the attendants served them with tea.

Upon finishing his tea, Huang Pao-kuang said, "Yesterday Sung Ch'iao-nien asked me to convey his greetings to you. He has also learned of the demise of your respected lady and would like to have been able to offer his condolences in person. Unfortunately, however, he has a plethora of pressing matters on his hands. At present he is stationed in Chi-chou.

"You may not have heard about it yet, sir, but the Emperor is currently en-gaged in constructing the Mount Ken Imperial Park[4] and has issued an edict ordering Chu Mien, the defender-in-chief of the Embroidered Uniform Guard, to proceed to the Hu-Hsiang region of Chiang-nan to take charge of the Flower and Rock Convoys[5] that will transport the rare flowers and rocks required for the embellishment of the park. The boats in these convoys are proceeding, one after the other, along the waterways, and the first contingent is about to arrive in the Huai River region.

"Moreover, the eunuch Huang Ching-ch'en, the defender-in-chief of the Palace Command, has been put in charge of the safe delivery of the rock for-mation known as 'The Fabulous Peak of Auspicious Clouds and a Myriad Shapes.'[6] This object is twenty feet long and several feet thick and has been wrapped in yellow felt. A number of boats are involved in its transport, all fly-ing yellow flags, and the convoy is proceeding through Shantung on the canal. But the water in the canal is low, and corvée laborers from eight prefectures have been requisitioned to tow the boats, with the result that:

The officials are in dire straits, and

The people are reduced to destitution.[7]

"His Excellency Sung Ch'iao-nien has been put in charge of the function-aries from the prefectures and districts and is personally involved in everything that happens.

The quantity of paperwork is mountainous, and

He is obliged to work both day and night,

without any respite whatever. On top of which, Defender-in-chief Huang Ching-ch'en is about to show up from the capital, and His Excellency Sung Ch'iao-nien is expected to lead the officials of the Two Provincial Offices in receiving him.

"Not being on familiar terms with anyone else in the area, he has deputed your pupil to respectfully ask if you would consent to allow your distinguished mansion to be used for his reception, and to host a banquet in honor of De-fender-in-chief Huang. But I don't know if you will assent to this or not."

He then instructed an attendant to summon the servitors of His Honor Sung Ch'iao-nien, whereupon two functionaries, dressed in black livery, knelt down in front of them, reached into a felt bag, and presented two bolts of satin brocade, a stick of aloeswood incense, two sticks of white wax, and a quire of "cotton paper," made from the bark of the paper-mulberry.[8]

"Those are the consolatory contributions offered by His Honor Sung Ch'iao-nien," said Huang Pao-kuang. "These other two packets are the joint donations toward the banquet expenses presented by the officials of the Two Provincial Offices and eight prefectures. The twelve officials from the Two Provincial Offices have donated three taels apiece, and the eight prefectural officials have given five taels apiece, making twenty-two contributions, amounting to 106 taels in all."[9]

He handed these over to Hsi-men Ch'ing, saying, "May I trouble your worthy staff to take care of this, or not?"

Hsi-men Ch'ing hesitated to assent, saying, "Your pupil is currently in mourning. What am I to do? What am I to do?"

He then went on to inquire, "When is this reception to take place?"

"It's early yet," said Huang Pao-kuang. "It will not be until the middle of next month. Eunuch Director Huang Ching-ch'en has not even left the capital yet."

"The funeral procession for my late consort will not take place until the twelfth day of the tenth month," said Hsi-men Ch'ing. But if I am directed to undertake this at the behest of the venerable Sung Ch'iao-nien, how could I refuse? And please extend my thanks for his generous consolatory offerings. With regard to these other contributions, however, you must take them back.

I absolutely refuse to accept them.
You have but to let me know the number of table settings needed. Your pupil will not fail to provide everything that is required."

"Ssu-ch'üan," said Huang Pao-kuang, "this proposal of yours is mistaken. Sung Ch'iao-nien entrusted me with the task of asking you to undertake this burdensome responsibility. These are the joint contributions of the officials from the entire province of Shantung and are not proffered by Sung Ch'iao-nien himself. How can you refuse them? If you should not accept them, your pupil would be constrained to report the fact back to Sung Ch'iao-nien, and he would not presume to trouble you any further."

When Hsi-men Ch'ing heard these words, he said, "In that case, your pupil will accept them for the time being."

He then directed Tai-an and Wang Ching to take possession of the contributions and put them away.

"How many table settings should be prepared?" he then went on to ask.

"For Defender-in-chief Huang Ching-ch'en," replied Huang Pao-kuang, "there should be a large table setting of the kind intended as much for display as for eating. For His Honor Sung Ch'iao-nien and the officials of the Two Provincial Offices, individual table settings of the ordinary sort will do. And for the prefectural officials who rank below them, communal seating will suffice. The musicians required for their entertainment will be provided. There is no need for your household to engage any."

When he had finished speaking, after the tea had been twice replenished, he got up to leave.

Hsi-men Ch'ing endeavored to detain him, but Huang Pao-kuang said, "Your pupil must pay another call on the venerable gentleman Shang Liut'ang, who formerly served as district magistrate in my native place before being promoted to the post of prefectural judge in Ch'eng-tu. His son, Shang Hsiao-t'ang, is also a fellow student of mine, having passed the provincial civil service examinations the same year that I did."

"Your pupil was unaware, venerable sir," said Hsi-men Ch'ing, "that you were on intimate terms with Shang Hsiao-t'ang. Your pupil and he are also acquainted."

When Huang Pao-kuang stood up to go, Hsi-men Ch'ing said, "Venerable sir, pray convey my sentiments to Sung Ch'iao-nien, and assure him that, when the time comes, he will find my humble .abode respectfully at his disposal."

"Shortly beforehand," said Huang Pao-kuang, "Sung Ch'iao-nien will send someone to let you know. There is no need to be overly extravagant."

"Your pupil understands," said Hsi-men Ch'ing, as he escorted him to the front gate, where he mounted his horse and departed.

When the officials from the district yamen learned that the secretary of the Ministry of Works, Huang Pao-kuang, with other high-ranking officers from the regional inspector's office, had visited the premises, they were thrown into such consternation that they secreted themselves in the small summerhouse beneath the artificial hill as they drank their wine and ordered their subordinates to get their sedan chairs and horses out of the way.

On this occasion, when Hsi-men Ch'ing rejoined his guests in the summerhouse, he told the assembled officials all about how the regional investigating censor Sung Ch'iao-nien was planning to lead the officials of the Two Provincial Offices and eight prefectures in welcoming Defender-in-chief Huang Ching-ch'en next month and had asked him to provide a reception in his honor.

On hearing this, the assembled officials, with one voice, said, "This visit will entail insuperable tribulation for the prefectures and districts involved. When such imperial emissaries come, all of the expenses for the attending personnel, provisions, public banquets, utensils, and corvée laborers are borne by the prefectures and districts, which, in turn, must extract them from the people. As a way of bringing about the utter depletion of both public and private resources:

Nothing could surpass this.[10]
We all hope, Ssu-ch'üan, that you will put in a good word with your superiors on our behalf in order to alleviate our plight. That would constitute a signal demonstration of our mutual esteem."

When they had finished speaking, they chose not to remain any longer, but got up, mounted their horses, and departed.

To make a long story short, when the time came for the third weekly commemoration of Li P'ing-erh's death, Abbot Tao-chien of the Temple of Eternal Felicity outside the city wall led sixteen Buddhist monks of high attainments to come and recite scriptures on her behalf. Wearing their cassocks of cloud-patterned brocade and their Vairocana hats, and accompanied by the music of large cymbals and large drums, in the morning they performed the ceremonies of "obtaining sacred water," "paying homage to the five directions," "invoking the Three Treasures," and "bathing the Buddha." At noon, they went on to perform the ceremonies of "soliciting the aid of the Tathāgata," "summoning the soul," "breaking out of Hell," reciting the *Litanies of Emperor Wu of the Liang Dynasty*,[11] and declaiming the dhāranīs of the *Sutra of the Peacock King*.[12] Everything was done with appropriate solemnity.

That evening, Ch'iao Hung's wife, and the wives of Hsi-men Ch'ing's employees, joined Yüeh-niang and company in participating in an all-night wake, during which they were entertained with puppet shows in front of Li P'ing-erh's spirit tablet, while Hsi-men Ch'ing, along with Ying Po-chüeh, Wu K'ai, and Licentiate Wen, drank wine behind a screen at the eastern end of the temporary structure that had been erected in the courtyard.

The eighth day of the tenth month was the date for the fourth of the weekly commemorations of Li P'ing-erh's death. For this occasion, Lama Chao, the head priest of the Pao-ch'ing Lamasery outside the west gate of the city, was engaged to bring sixteen monks and recite their foreign scriptures. They set up an altar, performed a shamanistic dance, scattered paper flowers and rice on the bier, and circumambulated it while burning incense and reciting dhāranīs. The oblations consisted of cow's milk, tea, cheese, and the like. The suspended effigies were in the form of *pien-hsiang*, or transformation tableaux, representing nine horrific aspects of Māra, in which he was depicted wearing a chaplet of glass beads, with a necklace of skulls around his neck, in the act of devouring an infant, while seated astride an evil sprite, with serpents and hornless dragons encircling his waist. He was portrayed with four heads and eight arms, brandishing dagger-axes and halberds in his hands, with red hair and a blue face, presenting an incomparably ugly appearance.[13] Once the noon vegetarian repast was over, the celebrants fell to consuming meat and wine.

Hsi-men Ch'ing was not at home that day. Together with Yin-yang Master Hsü, he had gone to the family graveyard outside the city gate in order to break ground for the excavation of the tomb and did not return until the afternoon. That evening the rites were concluded and the lamas were dismissed.

The next day, he made arrangements for the transportation of the requisite accoutrements, wine, rice, table settings, and other culinary supplies to the grave site. He also deputed his managers and employees to go to his country estate and see to the erection of temporary structures at both the front and rear of the grounds, including four or five rooms to serve as wine depositories and kitchens, and also put up an eighteen-foot-wide covered structure by the graveside. The local residents and the neighbors who had previously been invited were entertained to a feast there with:

Unlimited quantities of meat and wine,

after which, when the party broke up, they returned home with their:

Shoulders and backs loaded with gifts,
but there is no need to describe this in detail.

On the eleventh, during the day, professional boy singers of funeral dirges and actors who performed exorcistic skits to the accompaniment of gongs and drums came to put on a farewell show before the spirit tablet of the deceased. The skits they played were entitled "The Five Devils Plague the Assessor,"[14] "Celestial Master Chang Tao-ling[15] Is Befuddled by Devils," "Chung K'uei[16] Hoodwinks the Little Devils," "Lao-tzu Traverses the Han-ku Pass,"[17] "The Six Traitors Plague Maitreya,"[18] "The Plum Blossom in the Snow,"[19] "Chuang Chou Dreams That He Is a Butterfly,"[20] "The Four Heavenly Kings Subdue Earth, Water, Fire, and Wind,"[21] "Lü Tung-pin Beheads Huang-lung with His Flying Sword,"[22] and "Emperor T'ai-tsu Escorts Ching-niang on a Thousand-Li Journey."[23]

When this medley of vaudeville acts had been performed, the female guests, who had been looking on through a hanging screen, paid their farewell respects to Li P'ing-erh's spirit tablet and then went inside, after which the male relatives came in to bid farewell to the spirit tablet and burn paper money before it. Copious tears were shed.

The next day was the date for the funeral procession. Early in the morning, the funeral banner and all the various banderoles, portable pavilions, and papier-mâché funerary objects were carried outside, and the Buddhist and Taoist monks, drummers, musicians, and carriers all assembled. In preparation for this event, Hsi-men Ch'ing had solicited the services of fifty military patrolmen from Commandant Chou Hsiu of the Regional Military Command, all of whom came with their archery gear and horses, and were:

Attired in full-dress uniforms.[24]

He left ten of them to guard his residence, while directing the remaining forty to divide themselves into two contingents and march in front of the casket on either side of the road. In addition, there were twenty orderlies from his yamen to clear the road ahead of the procession and look after the burial objects, while yet another twenty had been sent ahead to guard the gate to the family graveyard and receive whatever sacrificial offerings might be delivered there.

That day, the officials and gentry, relatives and friends, who came to take part in the funeral procession:

Created a hubbub with their horses and carriages,
Overflowing the streets and blocking the alleys.[25]

The sedan chairs of the members of the Hsi-men family and their male and female relatives and guests alone numbered more than a hundred, in addition to which, there were several tens of smaller sedan chairs for the madams and painted faces from the licensed quarter.

Yin-yang Master Hsü had determined that 8:00 AM would be the right time for the ceremony of raising the coffin. Hsi-men Ch'ing left Sun Hsüeh-o and the two nuns to look after the house and ordered P'ing-an together with two orderlies to guard the front gate. His son-in-law Ch'en Ching-chi performed the role of filial son by kneeling in front of the casket and smashing an earth-enware crock to signal that the procession was about to begin. Sixty-four professional coffin bearers fastened the main carrying poles to the catafalque,[26] while an assistant coroner stood on a platform attached to one end of this structure, from which vantage point he beat a wooden clapper to provide a cadence as they hoisted it onto their shoulders and proceeded along the route of the procession. Hsi-men Ch'ing had arranged beforehand for Buddhist Superior Lang, the abbot of the Temple of Kindness Requited, to preside over the coffin-raising ceremony. The procession had no sooner turned onto Main Street and headed toward the south than:

Mountains and seas of people,[27]

lined up to watch on either side. It happened to be a fine, clear day, and it was truly a spectacular funeral procession. Behold:

A genial breeze livens the handsome streets;
A tenuous drizzle moistens the fragrant dust.
In the eastern quarter the morning sun has just arisen;
In the northern sector the lingering mists clear away.[28]
Tung-tung lung-lung,
The decorated funeral drums maintain
    a constant din;
Ting-ting tang-tang,
The exorcistic players' gongs resound
    night after night.
The funeral banner sways in the breeze,
Inscribed with large characters on
    nine feet of red silk;
High-rising rockets soar into the sky,
Bursting asunder the yellow clouds
    suspended in midair.
Fiercely and ferociously,
The Road-clearing Demon[29] nonchalantly
    holds his golden battle-axe;
Prancing and swaggering,
The Spirit of the Perilous Paths[30] grimly
    grips his silver dagger-axe.
Wandering freely and easily,[31]
The Eight Taoist Immortals appear surrounded
    by tortoises and cranes;
Gracefully and seductively,
The four handmaidens come into sight followed
    by tigers and by deer.
The exorcistic devils,

Flash by to a crashing of gongs;
The rack of fireworks,
Explodes into a myriad crackers.
Creating quite a stir,
A float of a lotus-gathering boat comes by,
Presenting skits of slapstick humor;[32]
Lanky and large-sized,[33]
Local mummers performing on lofty stilts,
Are dressed in armor, wearing helmets.
Clean-cut and good-looking,[34]
A company of sixteen young Taoist acolytes,
Each attired in a roseate robe and Taoist cap,
Sound the bells from the court of Mt. K'un-lun,
And play eight gong-chimes hanging in a frame,[35]
Producing strains of immortal music;
Big-bellied and overweight,[36]
A band of twenty-four aged Buddhist monks,
Each one garbed in a cloud-patterned cassock,
Beat their large cymbals, and
Strike their great drums,
Paying homage to the five directions.
There are twelve large damask portable pavilions,
Each of which is conspicuous for its
    dancing greens and flying reds;[37]
And twenty-four little damask portable pavilions,
Every one of which exhibits clustering
    pearls and kingfisher ornaments.
On the left,
Counterfeit open-air storehouses and underground
    vaults follow one after another;
On the right,
Papier-mâché mountains of gold and mountains of
    silver sweep past in formation.
Portable kitchens display containers of the
    eight culinary delicacies;
Pavilions for incense and candles convey the
    three sacrificial libations.
Six pavilions of artificial flowers,
Parade their thousand spheres of brocade;
The solitary soul-bearing palanquin,
Exhibits a hundred knots of yellow ribbon.
On the one hand,

Artificial lotus blossoms and snowy willows
   vie with each other in brilliance;
On the other hand,
Jeweled canopies and silver-hued banderoles
   march with each other in formation.
Banners inscribed in gold, and
Banners inscribed in silver,
Securely protect the catafalque;
Canopies of white damask, and
Canopies of green damask,
Hover about the attached platform.
Talismanic axes enveloped in clouds,
Three on either perimeter,
Are all depicted in vibrant colors;
Presenting jugs and offering towels,
Maidservants on both sides,
Are made up so as to look lifelike.
As directed by the mourning banner,[38]
The filial relatives set up a wail.
Preceded by five pacesetters and
   six singing boys,
The pyramidal pedestal, shaped like Mt. Sumeru,
   to which the soul banner is affixed,
Sways up and down as it proceeds.
The sixty-four pallbearers,
Wearing black livery and white caps,
Steadfastly support the bier
   and its baldachin,
With its crimson, gold lamé floral designs,
Decorated with images of the Five Ancients
   on their cloud-scaling cranes,
And with tassels dangling from its four corners,
That surmounts the brocaded catafalque,
Majestic and unmoved.[39]
Behold:
To either side, the orderlies who protect
   the procession and clear the road,
All wear mourning caps on their heads,
Black jackets on their bodies,
Mourning girdles about their waists,
Puttees on their legs,
Long-legged boots on their feet,

And hold staves in their hands,
Clamoring in front and crowding behind.
To either side, the equestrian acrobats
    who perform their stunts,
Are attired in sesame-patterned flat-topped caps,[40]
Held in place with hammered gold rings that
    float at the back of their heads,
And two or three layers of satin jackets,
The waists of which are enclosed in purple belts,
While their feet are shod in four-seamed
    dark-tan eagle-talon boots,[41]
Set off by variegated embroidered stockings
    depicting frolicking sea creatures.
The acrobats resemble eagles or falcons,
The horsemen are like gibbons or monkeys.
Some brandish a gleaming spear in one hand,
While flourishing a blue standard mounted on
    a vermilion staff with the other,
Some do headstands or execute somersaults,
Some perform feats of archery under the
    bellies of their mounts,
Some assume the pose of "The Golden Cock
    Standing on a Single Foot,"[42]
Some adopt the posture of "The Immortal
    Crossing the Bridge,"
While some do the trick of "Hiding Their
    Bodies in the Stirrups."[43]
Everyone expresses his admiration,[44]
One and all vying in their approval.
Shoving shoulders and bumping backs,
In their confusion, no distinction is made
    between the wise and the foolish;[45]
Pressing to see and crowding to watch,
Amid the chaos, none discriminate between
    the distinguished and the humble.
Chang the Third, who is clumsy and fat,
Can only pant for breath;
Li the Fourth, who is short of stature,
Repeatedly stamps his feet.
White-haired old gentlemen,
Prop their beards upon their walking sticks;[46]
Black-haired young beauties,[47]
Bring their children to watch the procession.

Truly:

> The thunder of gongs and drums mingles with
>   the dust of the streets;
> Amid clustering blossoms and clinging brocade
>   a myriad people look on.
> The sound of lamentation begins to fade away
>   as the catafalque departs;
> This funeral procession can truly be said to
>   outdo any in the capital.

Wu Yüeh-niang in a large sedan chair, headed up the ten or more chairs of Li Chiao-erh and the other members of the household in following, single file, in the wake of the casket. Hsi-men Ch'ing, attired in a palmetto hat and mourning clothes, led the assembled relatives and friends after them, while Ch'en Ching-chi accompanied the catafalque, keeping one hand upon it, until the procession arrived at the entrance to East Street.

Hsi-men Ch'ing had previously provided an honorarium and invited Abbot Wu Tsung-che of the Temple of the Jade Emperor to preside over the ceremony of displaying and dedicating the full-length portrait of Li P'ing-erh. His body was clothed in a Taoist vestment emblazoned with twenty-four cranes on a crimson background flying amidst variegated sunset clouds. On his head he wore a ninefold-yang thunder cap[48] adorned with a jade ring. His feet were shod in red shoes, he held an ivory tablet in his hands, and he was seated in an open sedan chair, borne by four bearers, as he came to meet the procession. When he held up the full-length portrait of Li P'ing-erh in both hands, Ch'en Ching-chi knelt down in front of it, and the procession came to a halt. The crowd of spectators listened attentively as, from his elevated position, and in a loud voice, he intoned a eulogy to the portrait.

> The hare scampers and the raven flies[49]
>   west and then east;
> The hundred years of a man's life are
>   like a windblown lamp.
> The people of today do not understand[50]
>   the meaning of no-birth;
> Only at this time do they realize that
>   phenomena are ephemeral.

In solemn commemoration of the spirit of the late respected lady of Commandant Hsi-men Ch'ing of the Embroidered Uniform Guard, whose life in this world extended into her twenty-seventh year. She was born at noon on the fifteenth day of the first month in the year *hsin-wei*, and died at 2:00 AM on the seventeenth day of the ninth month in the seventh year of the Cheng-ho reign period. We respectfully submit that: as the genteel daughter of a prominent family, and a winsome occupant

Desire to Share Her Afterlife Inspires a Lavish Funeral

of ornate chambers, she possessed a countenance reminiscent of blossoms and moonlight and was naturally endowed with an orchid-like fragrance. It was her sa-lient virtue to be gentle and compliant, and she was by nature both temperate and mild. In her match with the gentleman Hsi-men Ch'ing, she demonstrated her fit-ness for wedded bliss. As a dweller in the women's quarters she was both worthy and chaste, exhibiting marital harmony like that between zither and cithara. Jade was planted in Indigo Field,[51] only to perish like the orchids of Ch'u.[52] Though she might have looked forward to a lifetime of prosperity, unfortunately the springtime of her life lasted only twenty-seven years. Alas! The bright moon wanes all too soon, the finest objects are difficult to preserve.[53] Persons of worth suffer unexpected ca-lamities, the length or brevity of life are predetermined. At present, the catafalque occupies the highway, and red pennants flutter in the breeze. Her husband stamps his feet in grief before the casket, while her relatives wail in lamentation along the alleys. The feelings engendered by separation are deep and difficult to dispel, but the longer we are deprived of her voice and appearance the easier they become to forget. Unworthy though we be to wear these caps and pins, we are ordained devo-tees of the Taoist religion. Though we unhappily lack the divine arts of a Hsin-yüan P'ing,[54] we faithfully adhere to the tradition bequeathed by Lao-tzu, the founder of the school of the Mysterious Origin. All we can do is display this mirrorlike portrait of Ts'ui Hui,[55] being unable to bring back the butterfly of Chuang Chou's dream. May she be enabled to imbibe sweet dew and bathe in the carnelian nectar of the gods, transcend her position as an immortal, and ascend to the Purple Elysium.[56] May she bedeck herself with a hundred jewels and be presented before the Seven Perfected Ones,[57] that they may enable her purified soul to escape from the road to the shades. Her one mind will then be without impediments, in realizing that the four elements are all illusory.

It is bitter! Bitter! Bitter!
The breath is transformed into a clear breeze,
     the form returns to earth;
The numinous soul's true nature, once lost,
     will never be recovered;
The head is altered and the face replaced
     an infinite number of times.
Harken now to the final words. So:
Nobody knows to what place her vital essences
     may have returned;[58]
Only her portrait remains to be passed on to
     later generations.

When Abbot Wu had finished intoning the eulogy, he sat upright in his sedan chair and it backed out of the way of the procession. Thereupon:
          Drums and music resounded to the heavens, and
          The sounds of lamentation shook the earth,

as the funeral procession started up again and wended its way toward the South Gate of the city. The friends and relatives kept Hsi-men Ch'ing company in walking as far as the gate before they mounted their horses. Ch'en Ching-chi accompanied the casket on foot, keeping one hand upon it, all the way to the family graveyard at Wu-li Yüan.

It so happens that Chang Kuan, the militia commander of Ch'ing-ho, at the head of two hundred troops, along with Eunuch Director Liu and Eunuch Director Hsüeh, had already set up a tent on the high ground in front of the grave site, where wind and percussion instruments started to play, and the bronze gong and bronze drum were beaten, to welcome the funeral procession. As the mourners looked on, the papier-mâché burial objects were set up and burned:

The smoke and flames flaring up to the sky.[59]

Within the graveyard there were arrayed ten or more sacrificial offerings for the wake, which had been provided by the courtesans of the two Music Offices. Marquees had also been put up for the accommodation of the female guests and relatives.

When the catafalque arrived and had been set down by the bearers, Yin-yang Master Hsü, leading several coroner's assistants, consulted his geomancer's compass[60] in order to assure the correct alignment of the casket in the grave. After sacrificing to the Earth God and the tutelary gods of the locality at 10:00 AM, the casket was duly interred, and covered with soil. When Hsi-men Ch'ing had changed his clothes, he presented a gift of two bolts of silk to Commandant Chou Hsiu of the Regional Military Command and asked him to perform the ceremony of dotting the spirit tablet.[61]

After the sacrificial rites were completed, the officials of the Ch'ing-ho Guard and the assembled relatives, friends, and employees competed with one another in offering wine to Hsi-men Ch'ing.

Drums and music resounded to the heavens, and
The remnants of fireworks littered the ground.

The servitors responsible for the disposal of the sacrificial oblations did as they were directed, and the workers did not indulge in disorderly conduct. Refreshments for the mourners were provided in four or five places, the female guests were seated in the rear summerhouse, and each location had a set number of servants assigned to it. Everything was done on a festive and lavish scale, but there is no need to describe this in detail.

When the formal collation was finished, the owners of the adjacent estates had also set up tables at which they invited Hsi-men Ch'ing to partake of wine in celebration of the wake, which involved a considerable expenditure in the way of gratuities.

That afternoon, when it was time for the return of the spirit tablet, Wu Yüeh-niang sat in the sedan chair designated for the conveyance of the soul of the departed, holding the spirit tablet and the soul banner, while Ch'en Ching-chi walked alongside the bier that held the spirit bed, keeping one hand upon it. It was draped with a spirit shroud of jet satin and was invested in a jade-colored, gold lamé, waterproof canopy, with tassels dangling from its four corners. The procession also included the portable pavilion in which the full-length portrait of Li P'ing-erh was suspended, the large damask pavilions, the little damask pavilions, and the pavilions for incense and candles, and was accompanied on either side by sixteen drummers and musicians, and the young Taoist acolytes, all performing on their instruments.

Wu K'ai, Ch'iao Hung, Wu the Second, Hua Tzu-yu, Brother-in-law Shen, Meng the Second, Ying Po-chüeh, Hsieh Hsi-ta, Licentiate Wen, as well as all the managers and employees of the household kept company with Hsi-men Ch'ing as he reentered the city, while the sedan chairs of the female guests brought up the rear. When they arrived at the gate of the residence they observed the custom of leaping over a fire before entering.[62] After the spirit tablet had been set up in Li P'ing-erh's quarters, Yin-yang Master Hsü offered a sacrifice to the gods and performed a ritual purification in the front reception hall and then proceeded to paste pollution-dispelling spells on all the doors. Hsi-men Ch'ing brought out a bolt of silk and five taels of silver to thank Master Hsü for his services and then escorted him to the gate. The hired personnel were then dispatched, and twenty strings of cash were distributed between them, five strings for the military patrolmen from the Regional Military Command, five strings for the orderlies from the yamen of the Provincial Surveillance Commission, and ten strings for the militiamen. Hsi-men Ch'ing also sent cards to express his gratitude to Commandant Chou Hsiu of the Regional Military Command, Militia Commander Chang Kuan, and Judicial Commissioner Hsia Yen-ling. But no more of this.

Hsi-men Ch'ing ordered his attendants to set up tables and urged Ch'iao Hung, Wu K'ai, and the rest of his guests to sit down and stay a little longer, but they all refused, said goodbye, and departed. Lai-pao came in and reported that the carpenters who had set up the temporary structures for the funeral observances were waiting outside and proposed to come back the next day to take down the structures.

"There's no need to take down the structures quite yet," said Hsi-men Ch'ing. "Have them come back to take them down the day after the banquet ordained by His Honor Sung Ch'iao-nien is over."

The carpenters were consequently sent on their way.

Meanwhile, in the rear compound, the wife of Hua the Elder, along with Ch'iao Hung's wife and the other female guests, had waited until after Li P'ing-erh's spirit tablet was set up to engage in a round of wailing, after which they, too, made their departure.

As for Hsi-men Ch'ing:

He could not bear to part with her so precipitously.[63]
That evening he went back to Li P'ing-erh's quarters with the intention of spending the night by her spirit tablet. Once there, he saw that her spirit bed had been set up in the position of honor, with her full-length portrait hanging to one side, and her half-length portrait placed inside it, along with a little brocade quilt, a bed table, some clothing, a dressing case, and the like.

There was nothing that had not been provided.
There was even a pair of her tiny golden lotuses resting below it. On the table in front of it there were:

Incense, flowers, lamps, and candles,[64]
Golden saucers, goblets, and vessels,
replete with every kind of offering.

Hsi-men Ch'ing wept incessantly and directed Ying-ch'un to make up his bed on the k'ang across from it. In the middle of the night, confronted with a lonely lamp and:

The slanting moon in the half-open window,[65]
he tossed and turned, unable to sleep:

Giving vent to long sighs as well as short,
as he yearned for his vanished beauty. There is a poem that testifies to this:

Giving vent to long sighs as well as short,
   he contemplates the window;
The solitary image of the dancing phoenix[66]
   is enough to break his heart.[67]
The orchids have withered like those of Ch'u[68]
   during the rains of autumn;
The maple leaves have fallen on the Wu River,[69]
   succumbing to the night frost.
In our former lives we had already expressed
   the wish to twine our branches;
But in this lifetime it is difficult to find
   a soul-resuscitating incense.
If her pure spirit continues its existence
   beneath the Nine Springs,
In the nether world as in this human realm
   two hearts will be broken.

During the daylight hours, when the offerings of tea and rice were made to Li P'ing-erh's spirit tablet, Hsi-men Ch'ing came into her room to supervise the maidservants as they laid them out and then seated himself at a table facing the tablet and proceeded to eat with her, raising his chopsticks and asking her to partake with him as he did so. Thus he carried out the principle of:

Sacrificing to the spirits as if they were present.[70]

When they saw this, the maidservants and waiting women could not help wiping the tears from their eyes.

The wet nurse, Ju-i, when no one else was about, constantly appeared before him:

> Serving tea or serving water,
> Touching him or bumping him,
> Pinching him or teasing him,

interrupting him or engaging him in repartee. It did not take more than two or three nights of this before Hsi-men Ch'ing, having had too much to drink while entertaining someone one day, returned to Li P'ing-erh's quarters, where Ying-ch'un helped him into bed. During the night, he wanted some tea to drink and called for Ying-ch'un, but she did not respond. Ju-i got up and brought him some tea, after which she noticed that his quilt was falling off the k'ang and, having collected the teacup, reached down with her hand to put it back in place. Hsi-men Ch'ing, seized by a momentary impulse, embraced her by the neck and gave her a kiss, sticking his tongue into her mouth, to which the woman responded by sucking his tongue, without saying so much as a word. Hsi-men Ch'ing told her to take off her clothes and get onto the k'ang with him, where the two of them proceeded to embrace under the quilt, where:

> Unable to contain their pleasure,

they engaged in the sport of clouds and rain together.

"Since you have seen fit to favor me, Father," said Ju-i, "now that my mistress is dead, I am more than willing to remain in your household, and let you do with me as you will."

"My child," responded Hsi-men Ch'ing, "if you are content to cater to my desires with all your heart, you need not worry about my willingness to support you."

At this juncture, as far as the woman was concerned:

> Upon the pillow and the mat,[71]

there was nothing she refused to do in order to please him. The two of them:

> Tumbled and tossed like male and female phoenixes,

as she bent herself to his will, which delighted Hsi-men Ch'ing no end.

The next day, the woman got up early in the morning, fetched Hsi-men Ch'ing's footwear for him, and folded his bedding, so that Ying-ch'un's services were no longer required.

> Catering to him with the utmost assiduity,[72]
> There was no length to which she would not go.

Hsi-men Ch'ing unlocked the door to the inner room and sought out four of Li P'ing-erh's ornamental hairpins with which to reward her, and the woman kowtowed to him in thanks. Ying-ch'un realized that he had been intimate with her, and the two of them decided to ally themselves with each other.

During a Nightly Vigil He Succumbs to the Scent of Rouge

The woman, for her part, relying upon the favor that had been shown her, felt that she was on a firm footing and no longer sought help in any other quarter.

Three days after Li P'ing-erh's burial, when Hsi-men Ch'ing came back from the ceremony of revisiting the grave, to which he had invited a host of officials, female guests, the singing girls Li Kuei-chieh, Wu Yin-erh, and Cheng Ai-yüeh from the licensed quarter, along with the four boy actors Li Ming, Wu Hui, Cheng Feng, and Cheng Ch'un, it was observed that Ju-i had assumed a demeanor:

Different from that of former days.

What with her:

Phony eyebrows and bogus airs,

she made herself conspicuous among her fellow maidservants by the way in which:

She talked, and she laughed;

a fact which immediately caught the attention of P'an Chin-lien.

The next morning, while Hsi-men Ch'ing was sitting with Ying Po-chüeh, it was suddenly announced that His Honor the regional investigating censor Sung Ch'iao-nien had sent someone to deliver a consignment of complimentary gifts for Defender-in-Chief Huang Ching-ch'en. These consisted of a table setting of gold and silver wine vessels, including two gold flagons, a pair of gold goblets on raised stands, ten little silver cups, two silver ewers with hinged lids, four silver loving cups, two crimson variegated python robes, two bolts of satin brocade, ten jugs of wine, and two carcasses of mutton.

The messenger also stated, "The defender-in-chief's boat has already arrived in Tung-ch'ang prefecture, and my master would impose upon Your Honor to make the necessary arrangements for the banquet in good time, so that the welcoming ceremony can definitely take place on the eighteenth."

Hsi-men Ch'ing took careful possession of the gifts, rewarded the messenger with two taels of silver, and sent him back with a written reply. He then proceeded to weigh out the necessary silver to Pen the Fourth and Lai-hsing, so that they could order the table settings, see to the preparation of the sweetmeats, and contract for all the other needed supplies, but there is no need to describe this in detail.

He then turned to Ying Po-chüeh and said, "From the time that she first became ill, right up until the present moment, I haven't been able to relax for even a single day. I have barely been able to finish off the business of the funeral, when this kind of thing comes up, leaving me with:

Groping hands and floundering feet."[73]

"There is no need for you to complain, Brother," said Ying Po-chüeh. "After all, you did not solicit this obligation. He sought you out and imposed it upon you. Even though this banquet stands to cost you a good deal of money, in the future, the fact that you have entertained the presiding officials from the whole

province of Shantung, including the grand coordinator, the regional inspector, and miscellaneous military officers, not to mention the imperially commissioned defender-in-chief of the Palace Command, will only serve to shed
glory on this household of yours, and further enhance your prestige."

"That's not the point," said Hsi-men Ch'ing. "I had hoped that it would be
scheduled for some time after the twentieth, but now, contrary to my expectation, the welcoming event is to be held on the eighteenth. I'm feeling altogether too:

Pressured and pushed.

Moreover, the eighteenth falls within the fifth week after her death, and I've
already paid Abbot Wu Tsung-che to draft the petitions for the observance
scheduled for that day. How can I change it? But if I don't:

The ends of the fire tongs will get
entangled with each other.

How will I ever manage it?"

"That's no problem," said Ying Po-chüeh. "As I calculate it, since Sister-in-
law died on the seventeenth day of the ninth month, the twenty-first day of this
month marks the end of the fifth week after her death. If you hold your banquet on the eighteenth, you can still schedule a scripture recitation on the
twentieth without its being too late."

"You're right," said Hsi-men Ch'ing. "I'll send a page boy to tell Abbot Wu
to reschedule the date."

"Brother," said Ying Po-chüeh, "I've got another suggestion to make. You
should take advantage of the fact that at the present time Perfect Man Huang
Yüan-pai from the Eastern Capital is in temporary residence at his temple.
The Emperor dispatched him to the subprefecture of T'ai-an in order to present a hanging censer decorated with golden bells for the burning of imperial
incense,[74] and officiate at a seven-day rite of cosmic renewal[75] on the sacred
peak of Mount T'ai. This presents you with the opportunity, before he returns
to the capital, to ask Abbot Wu to invite him to preside as the high priest at
your ceremony on the twentieth. Thus you can avail yourself of his name to
add luster to the occasion."

"To be sure," said Hsi-men Ch'ing, "I, too, have heard that this Perfect Man
Huang is a very charismatic prelate. In that case I would have to make arrangements for a plenary service, with an additional twenty-four Taoist priests, in
order to make a day and night ceremony out of it. The only problem is that
Abbot Wu has already presented a sacrificial offering during the second weekly
commemoration, and I also prevailed upon him to preside over the ceremony
of displaying the portrait during the funeral procession, and to supply the Taoist acolytes who accompanied the catafalque. Not having any other way to
compensate him, I engaged his services to officiate at this scripture recitation,
meaning it to be:

No more than a token of my esteem.
Now if I should invite this Perfect Man Huang to act as the chief celebrant, is he not likely to be offended?"

"The responsibility for the ceremony as a whole," said Ying Po-chüeh, "will remain in the hands of Abbot Wu. He will only be inviting Perfect Man Huang to officiate, that's all. It will cost you a few more taels of silver, Brother, but, after all, it is for my sister-in-law that you are doing it, not for anyone else."

Hsi-men Ch'ing forthwith instructed Ch'en Ching-chi to write out a card on his behalf addressed to Abbot Wu, enclosing another five taels of silver for the drafting of the ceremonial petitions, and requesting him to extend the invitation to Perfect Man Huang, reschedule the scripture recitation for the twentieth, supply an additional twenty-four Taoist priests, and expand the ceremony into a Water and Fire sublimation ritual extending over a day and a night. As soon as this was completed, he ordered Tai-an to go on horseback to deliver it.

When Hsi-men Ch'ing had seen off Ying Po-chüeh, he went back to the rear compound where Wu Yüeh-niang greeted him by saying, "Pen the Fourth's wife has purchased two gift boxes for us. She has come to kowtow and inform us that their daughter, Chang-chieh, has become engaged to someone."

"To whom has she become engaged?" asked Hsi-men Ch'ing.

Pen the Fourth's wife, who was wearing a blue damask jacket, a white damask skirt, and a black satin cloak, and her daughter, who was dressed in a jacket of crimson satin over a skirt of yellow damask, and whose hairdo was adorned with trinkets, kowtowed to Hsi-men Ch'ing four times as formally as though inserting a taper in its holder.

"I didn't know about it either," said Yüeh-niang, who was standing to one side. "It turns out that this child is to be elevated to the position of a concubine in the household of His Honor Hsia Yen-ling. The engagement was only formalized yesterday, and she is to be carried across his threshold on the twenty-fourth. They have obtained a mere thirty taels of silver for her. If you stop to consider it, the child has already developed a good figure. She doesn't look like a fourteen-year-old, but more like a girl of fifteen or sixteen. It's been some time since we've seen her, and she's grown up to such an extent in the interim."

"The other day, at a drinking party," said Hsi-men Ch'ing, "he mentioned that he was planning to secure a couple of girls in order to have them trained as musicians, but I didn't know that you had offered your daughter to him."

Thereupon, he suggested to Yüeh-niang that she usher them into her parlor and invite them to stay for a cup of tea. Later on, Li Chiao-erh, Meng Yü-lou, P'an Chin-lien, Sun Hsüeh-o, and Hsi-men Ta-chieh all came in to greet them and help keep them company. As they were about to leave, Hsi-men

Ch'ing and Yüeh-niang gave them a set of heavy silk brocade clothing and a tael of silver, while Li Chiao-erh and the others each gave them trinkets, handkerchiefs, cosmetics and the like.

That evening, Tai-an came back and reported that Abbot Wu had accepted the silver and understood what was wanted, that Perfect Man Huang was still in residence at the temple and would not return to the Eastern Capital until after the twentieth, and that he would come a day early, on the nineteenth, in order to set up the altar.

The next day, Hsi-men Ch'ing remained at home to supervise the chefs in making advance preparations for the banquet, and see that everything was in proper order. Outside the main gate he erected a seven-story-high tower of variegated bunting in the shape of a mountain, and in front of the reception hall another one of five stories.

On the seventeenth, the regional investigating censor Sung Ch'iao-nien sent two district officials to inspect the preparations for the banquet. They found that at the head of the reception hall:

> The screens displayed their peacocks' tails, and
> The floor was covered with woolen carpets;
> The tablecloths were fabricated of brocade, and
> The seat cushions flaunted floral designs.

The place of honor for Defender-in-Chief Huang Ching-ch'en, from which he would be in a position to survey the feast, featured a large portable table with a setting of a kind intended as much for display as for eating, to be supplied with seasonal delicacies and other culinary specialties, cone-shaped piles of fruit and ingot-shaped cakes, as well as high-stacked pyramids of square-shaped confectionery stamped with the images of the Five Ancients and richly decorated with brocade. There were two smaller portable tables beside it so that the grand coordinator and the regional investigating censor could keep him company. Ranged along either side were the tables for the officials of the Two Provincial Offices, while the communal seating for the officials of the eight prefectures was in a temporary structure outside the reception hall. The arrangements for the officials seated on either side of the hall were to be individual table settings of the ordinary kind, provided with five appetizers and five dishes. When the district officials had finished their inspection of the arrangements they were entertained to tea by Hsi-men Ch'ing, after which they got up and returned to report on their findings.

The next day, the grand coordinator Hou Meng and the regional investigating censor Sung Ch'iao-nien, at the head of an entourage of mounted men, proceeded early in the morning to meet the boat of Defender-in-Chief Huang Ching-ch'en. The resulting procession was preceded by a large yellow banner emblazoned with the two words "Imperially Commissioned" in the Emperor's own hand. The local military officials, Commandant Chou Hsiu, Military Director-in-Chief Ching Chung, Militia Commander Chang Kuan, and the seal-holding officers of the left and right battalions of the Ch'ing-ho Guard, all attired in their martial uniforms and armor, at the head of their mounted subordinates, followed in its wake. Accompanied by an honor guard of soldiers bearing blue flags, tasseled spears, and tridents, the procession extended over several li in length.

Defender-in-Chief Huang Ching-ch'en was dressed in a crimson robe emblazoned with the images of two pythons, one on the front and one on the back, done in variegated embroidery. He rode in a curtained sedan chair with a silver finial on top, carried by eight bearers, accompanied by eight outriders, and shielded by a tea-leaf-colored canopy above. The staff officers who followed in his entourage were without number, all of them mounted on mettlesome steeds that neighed as they proceeded. All in all, the procession resembled a glittering tapestry of a myriad figures, as it wended its way along the road, to the music of drums and wind instruments.

> Clouds of yellow dust enveloped the highway;
> Sounds of chickens and dogs were not heard;[76]and
> Woodcutters and gatherers stayed out of sight.

As the cavalcade of men and horses passed through Tung-p'ing prefecture and entered Ch'ing-ho district, the area by the roadside was rendered black by the number of district officials kneeling there to welcome the procession. The attendants of the defender-in-chief ordered them to rise and assist in clearing the streets all the way to the main gate of Hsi-men Ch'ing's residence, where:

> The beat of the Music Office drums,
> Reverberated to the cloudy empyrean,

and the officers and functionaries, attired in black livery, were drawn up in order like the wings of a formation of wild geese.

Hsi-men Ch'ing, in formal black attire, stood there waiting respectfully as he gazed at the approaching dust. It took some time for the escorting cavalcade to pass by, after which, the defender-in-chief finally alighted from his sedan chair and came inside, while the grand coordinator and the regional investigating censor, at the head of the other officials, both high and low:

> Swarmed inside as a single throng,[77]

and entered the reception hall. Within the reception hall, the refined music of psaltery and mandola, metallophone and gong-chimes, dragon flutes and phoenix pipes,[78] was heard to resonate.

The first persons to formally present themselves to the visitor were the grand coordinator of Shantung, Hou Meng, and the regional investigating censor, Sung Ch'iao-nien, and the defender-in-chief responded to them with appropriate protocol.

Next came left provincial administration commissioner of Shantung, Kung Kuai,[79] left administration vice commissioner, Ho Ch'i-kao,[80] right provincial administration commissioner, Ch'en Ssu-chen,[81] right administration vice commissioner, Chi K'an, left assistant administration commissioner, Feng

T'ing-hu, right assistant administration commissioner, Wang Po-yen,[82] investigation commissioner, Chao No,[83] investigation commissioner, Han Wenkuang, surveillance vice-commissioner of education, Ch'en Cheng-hui,[84] assistant commissioner of the Military Defense Circuit, Lei Ch'i-yüan, and so forth. When the personnel of the Two Provincial Offices had finished presenting themselves, the defender-in-chief responded to them with somewhat less elaborate protocol.

When it came to Prefect Hsü Sung of Tung-ch'ang, Prefect Hu Shih-wen of Tung-p'ing, Prefect Ling Yün-i[85] of Yen-chou, Prefect Han Pang-ch'i[86] of Hsüchou, Prefect Chang Shu-yeh[87] of Chi-nan, Prefect Wang Shih-ch'i[88] of Ch'ingchou, Prefect Huang Chia[89] of Teng-chou, and Prefect Yeh Ch'ien[90] of Laichou, the presiding officials of these eight prefectures presented themselves as a group, and the defender-in-chief merely responded to them with a low bow.

When the local military officials, including Commandant Chou Hsiu, Military Director-in-chief Ching Chung, Militia Commander Chang Kuan, and so forth, presented themselves, the defender-in-chief simply remained sitting upright in his place, allowing them to dispose themselves as they would, standing in attendance outside the reception hall.

Finally, Hsi-men Ch'ing and Judicial Commissioner Hsia Yen-ling stepped up to pay their respects and offer their visitor tea, after the consumption of which, the grand coordinator, Hou Meng, and the regional investigating censor, Sung Ch'iao-nien, came forward with cups in hand to offer toasts to the defender-in-chief. At this, the drums struck up beneath the dais, as the defender-in-chief was presented with floral ornaments of gold and toasted in jade goblets. Only after toasts had been exchanged and the wine replenished did the defender-in-chief take his seat in the place of honor, while the grand coordinator and the regional investigating censor sat down in their positions below him to preside over the feast. The rest of the officials, including Hsi-men Ch'ing, then proceeded to sit down in their respective places.

When a director from the Music Office had presented an album listing the program of pieces they were prepared to perform, the music commenced. Every one of the performances, including both instrumental and vocal music, and ensemble dance pieces, was presented in appropriate order, displaying to maximum advantage the beauties of sound and color. During the feast, after a scene from the ch'uan-ch'i drama *P'ei Chin-kung huan-tai chi* (The story of P'ei Tu's return of the belts)[91] had been performed, the chef came out to preside over the carving of the entrées of roast venison and pork, served with a soup of a hundred ingredients, other culinary specialties, and steamed opentopped dumplings. After this, four of the musicians, playing the psaltery, mandola, *p'i-p'a*, and harp, without any percussion instruments, sang a song suite in the Nan-lü mode, beginning with the tune "A Sprig of Flowers":

Holding office as one of the Eight Bulwarks of the state,
Drawing a salary of a thousand bushels,[92] or thereabouts,

His deeds will be remembered for a hundred generations,
His name will be renowned for a myriad years of spring.
His strict propriety ensures his success and honesty.
Governing the realm and stabilizing the country[93]
    are his only considerations;
His mode of presiding over the vessels of state[94]
    is innovative.[95]
In his adherence to protocol and leadership of
    the loyal and true,
His only concern is to requite his ruler and
    display magnanimity.
In relying upon the worthy and upright while
    adhering to justice,
His sole endeavor is to clarify the laws and
    transform the people.[96]

By the time the singing was over, the second soup course had not yet been
served, although three musical performances had been presented.

Meanwhile, the regional investigating censor, Sung Ch'iao-nien, deputed
two district officials to take care of the various servitors and attendants in the
visitor's entourage in Hsi-men Ch'ing's summerhouse, where tables had been
set up for their entertainment. As for Commandant Chou Hsiu, Militia Commander Chang Kuan, and the other local officials, Hsi-men Ch'ing had arranged for them to be entertained in a guest room in the front compound,
where seats had been provided for them.

At this point, Defender-in-Chief Huang Ching-ch'en ordered his attendants
to reward the serving staff with ten taels of silver, after which, he called for his
sedan chair and prepared to make his departure. The various officials present,
after having repeatedly endeavored to detain him without success, proceeded
to see him out to the front gate.

    The music of drums and pipes resounded once more, as
    The clamor of his escort filled the adjacent streets.
    Outriders prepared to clear the way, as
    Men and horses lined up in formation.

The officials mounted their horses and proposed to escort him for some distance, but the defender-in-chief ordered them to desist, raised his hand in salute, got into his sedan chair, and proceeded on his way. Regional Investigating Censor Sung Ch'iao-nien and Grand Coordinator Hou Meng ordered the
guards officers serving under Militia Commander Chang Kuan to escort him
all the way to the imperial vessel in which he had come, and then come back
and report to them. The table settings and utensils that had been prepared for
the visitor, along with the congratulatory offerings of mutton and wine, were
turned over to Prefect Hu Shih-wen of Tung-P'ing and Commandant Chou
Hsiu of the Regional Military Command, together with an accordion-bound

album listing the perquisites involved, for them to deliver to the imperial vessel and hand over in person.

When Regional Investigating Censor Sung Ch'iao-nien returned to the reception hall, together with Grand Coordinator Hou Meng, he thanked Hsi-men Ch'ing, saying, "Today we have imposed egregiously upon your illustrious household. We are profoundly grateful, profoundly grateful. If our contribution to the expenses proves to have been inadequate, we will endeavor to make up the difference."

Hsi-men Ch'ing hastily:

Bent his body to perform an obeisance,

saying, "Your pupil has repeatedly benefited from your instruction and consideration, and has often been the recipient of your lavish presents, not to mention the consolatory gifts you bestowed upon me the other day. As for these:

Paltry and insignificant expenses,

They are:

Hardly worth hanging on the teeth.[97]

My snail-like abode is so inadequate I fear it may not have lived up to your expectations. My only hope is that Your Excellency will excuse my remissness. That would be fortunate indeed."

No sooner had Regional Investigating Censor Sung Ch'iao-nien finished expressing his thanks than he ordered his attendants to call for his sedan chair and departed, along with Grand Coordinator Hou Meng. The officials of the Two Provincial Offices and the eight prefectures, having said their farewells, followed suit, after which the various members of the serving staff that had been hired for the occasion:

Dispersed in a single tumult.

When Hsi-men Ch'ing returned to the reception hall, he arranged for the directors and musicians from the Music Office to be rewarded with food and drink, after which they, too, were allowed to depart. He retained only the services of the four boy actors that were on duty for the occasion. Whatever was left of the table settings that had been provided for the various officials both inside and outside the reception hall was carried off by their servants. But no more of this.

Observing that it was still relatively early in the day, Hsi-men Ch'ing had the utensils cleared away and found that there was enough left over to supply four tables with a sumptuous repast. He then sent servants to invite his brother-in-law Wu K'ai, Ying Po-chüeh, Hsieh Hsi-ta, Licentiate Wen, Fu Ming, Kan Jun, Han Tao-kuo, Pen the Fourth, and his son-in-law Ch'en Ching-chi, who had been up since the fifth watch that morning and was exhausted by all the matters he had been made responsible for, to join him for a drink.

It did not take long for the group of them to arrive. Wu K'ai, Licentiate Wen, Ying Po-chüeh, and Hsieh Hsi-ta were seated at the head table, Hsi-men Ch'ing presided over the proceedings as host, and the various managers were arrayed to either side, while the servants brought out the wine to be served at the party.

"Brother, you've certainly had a busy day of it," opined Ying Po-chüeh. "How long did Defender-in-Chief Huang stay, and was he pleased by the occasion, or not?"

"Today," remarked Han Tao-kuo, "the venerable eunuch Huang, on seeing what a splendid banquet had been provided for him, could not have been anything but pleased. The grand coordinator and the regional investigating censor certainly felt that:

> Their gratitude knew no bounds,

and expressed their gratitude again and again."

"If any other household had attempted to put on a banquet of this kind, they could never have pulled it off," stated Ying Po-chüeh. "They would not have the space available in this household of yours and would lack the number of hands that you have at your disposal. At a conservative estimate, you must have had more than a thousand people on your premises today, and they all had to be provided for. Even though it must have cost you a good deal of silver, Brother, it will have the effect of spreading your fame throughout the entire province of Shantung."

"Even your pupil's mentor," chimed in Licentiate Wen, "the venerable vice-commissioner of education, was present at the feast today."

When Hsi-men Ch'ing asked him to explain, Licentiate Wen said, "His name is Ch'en Cheng-hui. He is the son of the venerable Ch'en Kuan[98] of the Remonstrance Bureau. His native place is Chüan-ch'eng district in Honan province. He began to compete in the examination system at the age of seventeen and became a metropolitan graduate in the year *jen-ch'en*.[99] At present he holds the local office of surveillance vice-commissioner of education and is renowned for his erudition."

"This year then," said Hsi-men Ch'ing, "he is no more than twenty-three years old."

As they were chatting, soup and rice were served. After they had finished eating, Hsi-men Ch'ing called up the four boy actors and asked them their names.

"Your servants are called Chou Ts'ai, Liang To, Ma Chen, and Han Pi," they replied.

"You must be from Han Chin-ch'uan's place, aren't you?" said Ying Po-chüeh.

Han Pi knelt down and replied, "Han Chin-ch'uan and Han Yü-ch'uan are both my younger sisters."

"Have you had anything to eat and drink?" asked Hsi-men Ch'ing.

"Your servants have just finished our food and wine," replied Chou Ts'ai.

Because the memory of Li P'ing-erh had come into his mind, and he had been disappointed at not being able to see her during the banquet that day,

Hsi-men Ch'ing said to the boy actors, "Fetch your instruments and come over here. Can you perform the song that begins with the words:

The flowers of Lo-yang,
The moon of Liang-yüan,[100]

or not? I'd like you to sing it for me."

Han Pi knelt down before him and said, "Your servant and Chou Ts'ai do know it."

Thereupon:

Strumming the psaltery and plucking the mandola,[101]
To the beat of the clappers inlaid with red ivory,

they sang the song to the tune "The Whole Realm Rejoices":

The flowers of Lo-yang,
The moon of Liang-yüan;[102]
Fine flowers must be purchased;
The bright moon is only on loan.
Leaning on the balustrade, we viewed the flowers
    as their blossoms proliferated;
With wine cups in hand, we interrogated the moon
    on the nights we were together.
The moon waxes only to wane;[103]
Flowers blossom only to wilt.
It seems that in this life the hardest thing
    to bear is separation.[104]
The wilting of the flowers means that
    the end of Spring is near;
The waning of the moon indicates that
    Mid-Autumn will soon come;
But once one's loved one has departed
    when will she ever reappear?[105]

When they had finished singing this song, Ying Po-chüeh, who noticed that Hsi-men Ch'ing's eyes were feeling sour and were on the brink of tears, said, "Brother, other people may not understand what is on your mind, but I know a thing or two about it. You asked them to sing this particular song because its words related to something in your heart. It must be because you were think-ing of my late sister-in-law, and how the two of you used to be like intertwined branches, or the fish that swim in pairs, having only one eye apiece. Now that you are separated, how can you help longing for her?"

Observing that saucersful of sweetmeats were being brought out for them from the rear compound, Hsi-men Ch'ing said, "Brother Ying the Second, you may take exception to what I say, but when she was here she would have prepared these things with her own hands. Ever since she died, it's been left to the maidservants to concoct them, with the result that they're hardly worth looking at. There isn't so much as a single tasty morsel for me to enjoy."

"Confronted with such a lavish spread as this," Licentiate Wen objected, "the venerable gentleman can hardly be said to lack a competent domestic staff. It is more than sufficient."

"Brother," said Ying Po-chüeh, "you really oughtn't to talk that way. It may well be only because you can't get over your heartache that you say such things, but they are likely to have a chilling effect on the feelings of my other sisters-in-law."

As they continued to converse over their drinks, they were not aware that P'an Chin-lien was standing behind the hanging screen in order to listen to the singing. When she overheard what Hsi-men Ch'ing said, she went back to the rear compound and repeated it, word for word, to Yüeh-niang.

"You might as well let him say whatever he likes," said Yüeh-niang. "After all, what can you do about it? Remember how, the other day, when she was still alive, I promised her that I would arrange to have Hsiu-ch'un work for the Second Lady. But when I tried to do so, he opened his eyes wide and shouted at me, saying, 'How long has she been dead, after all, that you would presume to separate the maidservants from her quarters?' I was reduced to having nothing further to say about it. And you, too, must have noticed, the last few days, how that wet nurse and her two maids have been carrying on. And if I so much as open my mouth about it, he accuses me of trying to get rid of them."

"Mother," said Chin-lien, "I also have noticed how that woman has altered her demeanor the last few days. I fear that that lousy shameless good-for-nothing of ours, who has been spending all day in her quarters, is making out with that woman. It would hardly surprise me. I've heard that, the other day, he gave her two pairs of ornamental hairpins, and that the woman has had the effrontery to wear them on her head, showing them off, first to this one, and then to that one."

"Bean sprouts don't lend themselves to being bundled,"
said Yüeh-niang.

Thus it was that, behind their backs, everyone:
Conveyed the clear impression that they were not happy.
Truly:
If one's real work had ever found favor in the eyes
of one's contemporaries;
One would not have had to spend money on rouge
in order to paint peonies.[106]
There is a poem that testifies to this:

Beneath the terrace of King Hsiang of Ch'u[107]
the water flows on unhurried;

A single case of heartsickness[108] is able to
 produce sorrow in two places.[109]
The moon itself is completely oblivious of
 the changes in human affairs;
As, late at night, it continues to shine on
 the crest of the plastered wall.[110]

  If you want to know the outcome of these events,
  Pray consult the story related in the following chapter.

Chapter 66

MAJORDOMO CHAI SENDS A LETTER WITH A CONSOLATORY CONTRIBUTION;

PERFECT MAN HUANG CONDUCTS A RITE FOR THE SALVATION OF THE DEAD

The translucent windows on all eight sides
  open one after the other;
Yielding a view of her girdle pendants as she
  descends the jasper terrace.
Outside the boudoir door the Spring colors
  blend with the new willows;
On the mountain ridges the cold plum blossoms
  bedeck the verdant slopes.
The shadows of the plum branches begin to stir
  as the bright moon ascends;
A breeze agitates the bamboos along the path,
  auguring a friend's arrival.
The beauty, having left behind a specimen of
  her mandarin duck brocade;
It is up to the Lord of the East to decide
  what should be done with it.[1]

THE STORY GOES that on that day, as Hsi-men Ch'ing continued drinking with Wu K'ai, Ying Po-chüeh, and company, he asked Han Tao-kuo, "When is the convoy of merchant vessels with its armed escort scheduled to start out, so we can get things packed up in advance?"

"Yesterday someone came to inform me about it," said Han Tao-kuo. "The boats will start out on the twenty-fourth."

"In that case," said Hsi-men Ch'ing, "we can wait until after the scripture service on the twentieth to pack up."

"Which two people are you sending on this expedition?" asked Ying Po-chüeh.

"I'm sending three people in all," said Hsi-men Ch'ing. "I plan to have Ts'ui Pen return first next year with a boatload of merchandise from Hang-chou, while Han Tao-kuo and Lai-pao go on to the five entrepots below Sung-chiang to acquire cotton goods for sale. I have enough in the way of satin and silk fabrics already in stock."

"Brother," said Ying Po-chüeh, "what you propose is right on the mark. As the saying goes:

> You've got to have everything in stock
>   in order to do good business."

By the time this conversation was finished it was already the first watch and Wu K'ai got up to go, saying, "Brother-in-law, you've been wearing yourself out for days on end, and we've already had enough to drink. We had better take our leave so you can get yourself some rest."

Hsi-men Ch'ing objected to this and endeavored to retain them a little longer, ordering the boy actors to serve them with wine and sing a few more songs for their entertainment. Only after each of his guests had downed another three goblets of wine did he allow them to leave the premises.

Hsi-men Ch'ing proposed to reward the four boy actors with six mace of silver, but they repeatedly refused to accept the gratuity, saying, "His Excellency Sung Ch'iao-nien issued summonses mandating our attendance. How could we accept Your Honor's generous reward?"

"Even though you were here on official orders," said Hsi-men Ch'ing, "this is my personal expression of appreciation. What are you afraid of?"

Only then did the four of them kowtow in gratitude, accept the gratuity, and depart. But no more of this.

Hsi-men Ch'ing then proceeded to go back to the rear compound and go to bed.

The next day, he got up early and went off to the yamen.

Early that morning, Abbot Wu Tsung-che of the Temple of the Jade Emperor sent a disciple of his, along with two vergers, to take charge of setting up the altar space in the large reception hall. At the upper end of the altar space were placed images of the Three Pure Ones and the Four August Ones.[2] In the middle was placed an image of the Grand Monad Heavenly Worthy Who Saves from Distress,[3] with images of the Gods of the Eastern Peak and Feng-tu[4] to either side of it. At the lower end of the altar space were placed images of the Ten Kings[5] who rule over the Nine Realms of Darkness that constitute the underworld; the two marshals with their Divine Tiger talismans that guard the altar; the Four Great Celestial Lords Huan,[6] Liu,[7] Wu,[8] and Lu;[9] the Divine Empress of the Moon; the Seven Perfected Jade Maidens who govern the fates of deceased women; and the seventeen divine marshals of the Tribunal for Suspended Lives whose job it is to summon up the souls of the dead.[10]

> Both within and without the altar space,
> Everything is arranged in perfect order;
> The incense, flowers, lamps, and candles,
> Are arrayed in glittering resplendence.

Censers are supplied with the famous
    "hundred-blend" incense;[11]
Hanging lamps are suspended loftily
    around the sacred area.
The scripture lecterns are in place,
Curtained off by drapes of gold lamé;
Ritual drums are situated on high stands,
Surrounded by cranes in variegated clouds.

When Hsi-men Ch'ing returned home and saw the preparations that had been made, he was utterly delighted. After seeing to it that the disciple and the two vergers had been supplied with a vegetarian meal before returning to their temple, he immediately told Licentiate Wen to write out cards inviting Ch'iao Hung, Wu K'ai, Wu the Second, Hua Tzu-yu, Brother-in-law Shen, Meng Jui, Ying Po-chüeh, Hsieh Hsi-ta, Ch'ang Shih-chieh, Wu Shun-ch'en, and all the other relatives and female guests to attend the scripture reading on the following day. He also directed the chefs that had been hired for the occasion to make the advance preparations for the oblations that would be required. But no more of this.

The next day, at the fifth watch, the cohort of Taoist priests that had been engaged for the occasion waited for the opening of the gate in the city wall before being allowed to enter and proceed to Hsi-men Ch'ing's residence. Once there, after calling for the opening of the front door, they went directly to the altar space that had been set up for the scripture reading, where they lit the lamps and candles, washed their hands and ignited the incense, struck up their musical instruments, and began the recitation of the sacred texts, beginning with the *Chiu-t'ien sheng-shen chang ching*.[12]

Meanwhile, outside the main gate, the vergers suspended a long banner announcing the rites to be performed, hung up a placard with an inscription describing the nature and purpose of the ceremony, and pasted parallel statements, written on yellow paper in large characters, to either side of the doorway. The parallel statements read:

    The Sovereign of the East displays benevolence,
    Enabling the souls of the dead to transcend
        the position of immortals and
        ascend to the Purple Elysium.
    The Celestial Lord of the South forgives sins,
    Enabling purified souls, after undergoing
        the refining of sublimation, to
        mount to the Vermilion Height.

The inscription on the placard read as follows:

In order to uphold the Way and save the soul of the departed, her devoted husband, the faithful office holder Hsi-men Ch'ing, resident of such and such a precinct of the Ch'ing-ho district of Tung-p'ing prefecture in Shantung province of the Great Sung Empire, together with his entire household and the assembled relatives and guests, wish on this day to express their sincere devotion, and appeal to your powers of compassionate magnanimity on behalf of the spirit of his consort, née Li, whose life in this world extended into her twenty-seventh year. She was born at noon on the fifteenth day of the first month in the year *hsin-wei* and died at 2:00 AM on the seventeenth day of the ninth month in the seventh year of the Cheng-ho reign period. I respectfully submit that: As our connubial feelings were profound, I cannot but sigh over the untimely parting of the male and female phoenixes; since the moon shines coldly on her boudoir, I deplore the fact that we can no longer harmonize like zither and cithara. Merely grieving over her memory is unbearable, yet I cannot but think longingly of her voice and appearance. Light and darkness alternate all too swiftly,[13] and it is already time for the fifth weekly commemoration of her death. Wishing to rescue her incarcerated soul, I respectfully tender my ardent expectations. On this twentieth day of the present month I have reverently engaged the services of these duly ordained Taoist officiants to come to my house of mourning and erect an altar for the performance of a sublimation ritual of the sworn alliance with the perfected, including the promulgation of the talismanic texts inscribed on jade tablets; and the nine recitations according to hallowed precedent of the *Chiu-t'ien sheng-shen chang ching*, and invocations from the sacred texts contained in the precious storehouse of the Taoist Canon. We solicit the attendance of the deities riding on their lion steeds to bestow the light of their beneficence, so that their golden lamps can dispel the darkness; and the conferment of their talismans in dragon script that abolish guilt, so that its pain may be as surely impeded as by iron pillars. In the deep of night, may the souls of the departed be enabled to cross the variegated bridge to the tinkle of their jade pendants; and may they be able to dine on the evening mist, ascend to the azure empyrean and meet with the Golden Perfected. It is our humble desire that the Supreme Deity may confer his benevolence from the jade steps of his palace, and that the Lord of the East may vouchsafe his attention from the vantage point of his Verdant Abode. May they broadly extend the benevolence of their compassion, and greatly display their powers of salvation, so that the souls of the departed may soon mount to the realm of freedom and ease, and the incarcerated spirits may all be able to ascend to the Celestial Paradise. May the relatives of the household, both living and dead, enjoy propitious auspices, and may their kindred be able to attain the Taoist shore. It is to be hoped that all those who participate in this rite of redemption shall be enabled to achieve salvation. Such is the purpose of this placard.

The placard is dated such and such a day, in such and such a month, of such and such a year of the Cheng-ho reign period.

The officiant is the Savant of the Highest Purity Great Cavern Scriptures and Registers, the Grand Master of the Golden Gates of the Nine Heavens, the Assessor of the Jade Palace of the Divine Empyrean, the Superintendent of the Various Thunder Bureaus, the Prelate of Lofty Attainments Who Elucidates Tenuity, Amplifies the

Way, Embodies the Mystery, Cultivates Simplicity, and Upholds the Doctrine, the
Superintendent of the Temple of the Supreme Unity, the Precentor of the Imperial
Altar, and Director of Taoist Affairs throughout the Empire, the High Priest Huang
Yüan-pai.[14]

Over the altar space that had been set up for the scripture reading in the main
reception hall there was suspended a twenty-character announcement of the
rite to be performed, written in a large script, which read:

> Litany to be addressed to the Heavenly Savior from Distress Who Dwells in the Blue
> Heaven of the East, including the dispatch of talismanic announcements, on the
> occasion of the scripture recitation on the fifth weekly commemoration of the de-
> cease of the departed, on the ritual altar for the performance of a Water and Fire
> sublimation rite of salvation.

That day, Perfect Man Huang. dressed in a crimson robe, riding in an ivory
sedan chair, girt with a golden girdle, surrounded by his attendants, with his
outriders shouting to clear the way, did not arrive until the sun was already
high in the sky. Abbot Wu, at the head of his cohort of Taoist priests, ushered
him up to the altar space and went through the ceremonies of greeting, after
which Hsi-men Ch'ing, dressed in white clothing and a mourning cap, paid
his respects. After tea had been served, a lectern for the scripture reading was
set up beside the altar table, supplied with a crimson gold lamé altar cloth and
a figured seat cushion. Two Taoist acolytes stood in waiting to either side of
him. Perfect Man Huang had a distinguished demeanor, wore a cap of black
satin with a jade ornament in front, and was dressed in a robe of crimson silk
that featured a *tou-niu* design,[15] and a pair of black shoes. Hsi-men Ch'ing had
prepared a bolt of satin brocade to present to him when he was ready to dispatch the documents.

When the documents had been signed and he was ready to ascend the altar,
Perfect Man Huang changed into a ninefold-yang thunder cap, a crimson
Taoist robe embroidered with golden clouds and white cranes, the pattern of
which extended to its flying sleeves,[16] soft white satin socks, and vermilion
cloud-scaling ceremonial slippers. An outward-facing Pavilion of Heaven and
Earth was set up, covered by two gilded flabella, where Golden Lads presented incense, and Jade Maidens scattered flowers, while holding aloft pennants and standards. As for the divine marshals who guard the altar, the talismanic functionaries of the Three Worlds, the four duty officers in charge of
the year, the month, the day, and the hour,[17] the God of Walls and Moats, the
divinity of the soil, the local tutelary god, and his attendants, there were none
whose presence was not invoked. On the high priest's incense table were arrayed five talismanic writs for summoning the celestial sovereigns, a black
pennant for evoking thunder deities, the jade ruler of the celestial general
T'ien-p'eng,[18] a sword incised with a diagram of the seven stars of the Dipper,
and a ritual ewer of purified water.

Only when the lector had finished declaiming the text of the announcement, and Hsi-men Ch'ing, as the ordainer of the rites, had washed his hands
and presented incense, did two thurifers, swinging their hand-held censers
and facing outwards, perform the ceremony of presenting incense three times
in order to invite the presence of the various deities invoked. At this point, the
high priest rapped his tablet of authority on the table and burnt incense in
order to dispel pollution and cleanse the altar space, sent flying talismans in
order to summon the generals, dispatched all the relevant documents and
talismans,[19] petitioned the Three Heavens, and enunciated the covenant to
the Ten Courts of the Underworld. After the three sacrificial libations had
been offered, music was struck up, paper money was burned, and the rite of
circumambulation while burning incense was performed. Hsi-men Ch'ing
and Ch'en Ching-chi, carrying hand-held censers, followed in the wake of the
procession, while orderlies shouted to clear the way. In front and behind there
were four gold lamé flabella, as well as three pairs of tasseled standards.

The relatives of the family were all lined up outside the front gate, where a
temporary structure housing the spirit tablet of the deceased was erected in
the street, and orderlies were deputed to look after the soup, rice, and other
purified offerings that were presented before it. When the circumambulatory
parade returned, and the consecration of the ritual altar was complete, a vegetarian repast was provided in the summerhouse. That day, the relatives and
friends, neighbors, and employees of the household who came to make sacrificial contributions:

> Arrived in an unbroken stream.[20]

Hsi-men Ch'ing had Tai-an and Wang Ching accept these gifts, make a record
of them, and bestow gratuities on the servants who took back the boxes in
which they were contained.

After the morning invocation the Three Treasures were invited to authenti-
cate the covenant, the various talismans and texts were promulgated, and the
ceremonies of "breaking out of Hell" and "summoning the soul" were performed. Music was struck up again, and a ritual for attracting and summoning
the soul of the deceased was performed in front of Li P'ing-erh's spirit tablet.
During the morning audience, the table that held her spirit tablet was placed
at the foot of the altar so that while paying court before the jade steps[21] she
might hear the scriptures and achieve enlightenment. The high priest, seated
on his elevated throne, recited the *Chiu-t'ien sheng-shen chang ching*, and
burnt petitions addressed to the Grand Monad, the Gods of Feng-tu and the
Eastern Peak, and the Ten Kings of the courts of the underworld, dressed in
their caps and capes, and riding in their cloud chariots.

At the noon audience, the high priest, attired in his formal headgear and
vestments, proceeded to:

> Pace the stars and tread the Dipper,[22]

respectfully presented a memorial written in red characters to the Verdant
Abode of the Heavenly Savior from Distress Who Dwells in the Blue Heaven

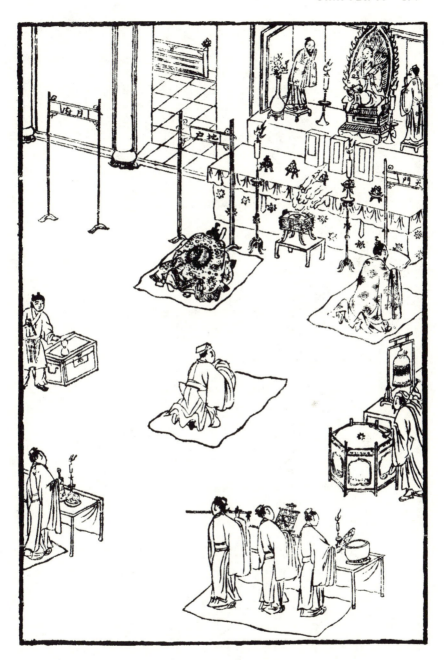

Perfect Man Huang Petitions for the Salvation of the Dead

of the East, requesting him to dispatch the divine marshals to fly down to Mount Lo-feng.[23]

It so happens that Perfect Man Huang was about thirty years old, and:

His demeanor was out of the ordinary.

When he was garbed in his formal regalia in order to preside over the noon audience, he looked just like a living god or immortal. Truly, what did he look like? Behold:

His star-embellished cap is enhanced with leaves of jade;
His crane-decorated robe is embroidered with gold clouds.
His spirit is as pure as the hoary moon
    over the Yangtze River;
His visage is as ancient as a tall pine
    on the summit of Mount Hua.
When treading the stars, his red shoes
    traverse the glowing clouds;
When pacing the void, his sacred texts
    float amid auspicious vapors.
With his long beard and broad cheeks,
He has practiced austerities until attaining
    the Heaven of No Imperfection;
With his white teeth and bright eyes,[24]
He has mastered the registers that give him
    command over the Five Thunders.
The Three Isles and the Ten Continents,[25]
    he visits by conserving his nature;
The grotto heavens and blessed abodes,
    he explores by self-induced trance.
Loftily he dines upon the evening mist;
Quietly he attends upon the Primordial.
When he traverses the moon at the third watch
    the cries of the phoenix are distant;
When he mounts the clouds for ten thousand li
    his seat on the crane's back is high.[26]
It is as if the Grand Master of the Immortals
    has come to visit the mundane realm;
Or just as though the Perfect Man Kuang-hui[27]
    has chosen to visit the world below.[28]

Once the memorials had been presented, Abbot Wu presided over the altar, where he dispatched the *Sheng-t'ien pao-lu*, or *Precious Registers for Rebirth in Heaven*, and the *Shen-hu yü-cha*, or *Jade Talismans of the Divine Tigers*. After the rite of circumambulation while burning incense had been performed at noon, the celebrants returned to the summerhouse where a vegetarian repast had been prepared for them. Perfect Man Huang was placed before a large table setting, replete with ingot-shaped cakes, Abbot Wu and the other Taoist officiants were provided with somewhat smaller-scale table settings, and the rest of the Taoist company had individual table settings of the ordinary kind. Perfect Man Huang and Abbot Wu were each given a bolt of satin, the four officiants who were entitled to wear figured vestments each received a bolt of woven silk, and each of the remaining Taoist priests was rewarded with a bolt of cotton fabric. The table settings were turned over to servants to take back to the temple, and the Taoist priests had their disciples put the bolts of fabric they had received into their trunks, but there is no need to describe this in detail.

After the midday vegetarian repast was over, the Taoist celebrants thanked Hsi-men Ch'ing for his hospitality and then proceeded to wander through the various pavilions, terraces, and grottoes in the garden as they digested their meals. Meanwhile, the utensils were cleared away, and new table settings of greater and lesser elaborateness were provided with vegetarian fare, of which Wu K'ai and the other relatives and friends of the household were invited to partake.

As they were eating, it was suddenly announced that Majordomo Chai Ch'ien in the Eastern Capital had sent a courier to deliver a letter. Hsi-men Ch'ing immediately went out to the reception hall and invited the messenger to come in. It turned out to be one of the factotums on the staff of the grand councilor's establishment, dressed in black livery, with tight-fitting trousers, wearing a flat-topped cap and dark-tan boots, and equipped with a complete set of bow and arrows. After he had come forward and bowed in greeting, and Hsi-men Ch'ing had returned the compliment, he pulled out a letter and presented it to Hsi-men Ch'ing, who found that the outer envelope contained a packet of ten taels of silver as a consolatory contribution.

When Hsi-men Ch'ing asked the courier his name, he replied, "Your humble servant's surname is Wang, and his given name is Yü. I have been commissioned by His Honor Chai Ch'ien to deliver this letter to you. He didn't know about your bereavement. It wasn't until a letter from His Honor An Ch'en arrived in the capital that he learned about it."

"When did His Honor An Ch'en's letter arrive?" asked Hsi-men Ch'ing.

"His Honor An Ch'en's letter did not reach the capital until sometime in the tenth month," replied the courier. "Because his one-year appointment to be in charge of expediting the delivery of imperial lumber has expired, he has been promoted to the position of secretary of the Bureau of Irrigation and Transportation in the Ministry of Works. Right now, he has been imperially commissioned to take charge of the repair work on the Grand Canal and will not return to the capital until that task is completed."

After Hsi-men Ch'ing had questioned him for a while, he told Lai-pao to provide him with a vegetarian meal in one of the side rooms in the front courtyard and directed him to return the next day to pick up his reply.

Majordomo Chai Sends a Letter with a Consolatory Present

"Where does Han Tao-kuo reside?" the courier asked. "I have a letter for him here from his daughter in Chai Ch'ien's household. After seeing him, I have to go on to deliver a letter in Tung-p'ing prefecture."

Hsi-men Ch'ing immediately summoned Han Tao-kuo, and, after keeping the courier company as he ate his vegetarian meal, the two of them went off to Han Tao-kuo's house together.

Hsi-men Ch'ing opened the letter to see what it was about and then happily took it to the summerhouse to show to Licentiate Wen, saying, "You can draft a letter in reply to this one, and I'll also send him ten crepe handkerchiefs, ten satin handkerchiefs, ten low-grade gold toothpicks, and ten black gold wine cups as a return gift. The courier is coming back tomorrow to pick up the reply."

Licentiate Wen took the letter and proceeded to peruse its contents, which read as follows:

Respectfully indited by his devoted servant in the capital, Chai Ch'ien, for the perusal of the newly promoted officer of the Embroidered Uniform Guard, his distinguished kinsman Hsi-men Ssu-ch'üan:

Since the day when we shook hands and bade each other farewell at my residence in the capital, I have not had the opportunity for a leisurely chat with you, which I profoundly regret. As for those matters which you entrusted to me, I have already laid them out before His Honor the grand councilor.

It is only recently, in a letter received from An Ch'en, that I learned that my venerable kinsman was drumming on a basin and sighing[29] over the death of his wife, but the fact that I have not been able to express my condolences in person is an occasion for sorrow. What is one to do? What is one to do? I respectfully hope that the observance of the rites will serve to moderate your grief. In addition, I offer a consolatory contribution, as a paltry expression of my heartfelt feelings, in the hope that you will deign to accept it with a smile.

I have long admired the way in which, in your distinguished post, you have conspicuously devoted yourself to the promotion of virtuous government, with the result that the populace sing of their five pairs of trousers,[30] and you are renowned for their having tried three times to prevent you from relinquishing your position. At this year's merit rating you are certain to receive a promotion. The other day, the officers in charge of the Divine Shipments of the Flower and Rock Convoys reported on their last two missions, and I have already spoken to His Honor the grand councilor about adding my kinsman's name to the list of deserving officials. When the memorial on the completion of the Mount Ken Imperial Park is submitted, you are sure to be the beneficiary of imperial largess. My kinsman will have the pleasure of being promoted to the office of judicial commissioner, while Hsia Yen-ling, on the basis of the annual end-of-year evaluation, will be transferred to the position of commander of the escort for imperial processions in the capital. I respectfully provide advance notice of this in the humble expectation that you will give it your highest attention. I am unable to express myself more fully.[31]

PS. This letter is for your perusal alone. No word of it should be allowed to reach his ears. It is strictly confidential. Strictly confidential.

PPS. His Honor Yang Chien died in prison on the twenty-ninth day of last month. Indited during the first decade of the first month of winter.

To resume our story, when Licentiate Wen had finished reading the letter, he was about to put it in his sleeve when Ying Po-chüeh snatched it away from him, read it over, and then handed it back to him, saying, "Venerable sir, whatever happens, do your very best to compose a well-written reply. In Master Chai Ch'ien's household there are many men of talent, and we wouldn't want to give them any occasion for mirth at our expense."

Licentiate Wen replied:

"When sable-tailed cap ornaments run out,
They can only be supplanted by dog tails.[32]
Your pupil is lacking in talent. How could I:
Show off my skill with an axe before the gate
of Lu Pan, the master carpenter?[33]
All I can do is endeavor to fulfill my responsibilities."

"The venerable gentleman will have his own ideas about how to go about it," said Hsi-men Ch'ing. "What does a dog like you know about such things?"

Before long, when they had finished with the midday vegetarian repast, Hsi-men Ch'ing directed Lai-hsing to see to the delivery of the leftover delicacies to the homes of the various relatives and neighbors. But no more of this.

Tai-an went to deliver return gifts to the six establishments in the licensed quarter that had sent contributions toward the cost of the ceremony, namely, those of Li Kuei-chieh, Wu Yin-erh, Cheng Ai-yüeh, Han Chin-ch'uan, Hung the Fourth, and Ch'i Hsiang-erh. Each of them received a bolt of muslin and a tael of silver.

During the course of the afternoon, the three boy actors, Li Ming, Wu Hui, and Cheng Feng, were called upon to entertain the company.

After some time, the group of Taoist celebrants once again ascended to the altar space, where they proceeded to beat their drums, pay reverence to the celestial court, perform the ritual of penance, conduct the lamp-lighting ritual,[34] take temporary leave of the altar, and then perform the rite of seeing off the celestial worthies.

In the waning light, by the time the preparations for the chiao ritual had been completed, it was already the first watch. Hua Tzu-yu, who resided outside the city gate, was invited to stay overnight by Hsi-men Ch'ing and so did not take his leave. Ch'iao Hung, Brother-in-law Shen, and Meng the Second said farewell and went home before the others. This meant that only Wu K'ai, Wu the Second, Ying Po-chüeh, Hsieh Hsi-ta, Licentiate Wen, Ch'ang Shih-chieh, and the group of employees remained behind to observe the Water and Fire sublimation rite of salvation that was to take place that evening.

In the temporary structure outside the large reception hall, an elevated throne had been set up, a variegated bridge of papier-mâché had been constructed, a basin containing water and a basin containing fire were put in place, and food for the souls of the dead was provided. Offerings were neatly arrayed before the table that held Li P'ing-erh's spirit tablet, under its own marquee. Her soul banner was placed beside it, together with a red banner and a yellow banner, and above it was suspended an inscription that read:

Overcome demons and guarantee the opportunity,[35]
To undergo sublimation in the Southern Palace.

The cohort of Taoist priests and musicians were already arrayed on either side, while four Taoist acolytes stood in waiting to either side of the ritual throne, grasping tallies, and holding a ritual ewer and a sword. Perfect Man Huang, wearing a yellow gold demon-subduing cap and a crimson silk robe embroidered with variegated sunset clouds, ascended to the elevated throne, and:

Recited an incantation.

At this point, the music stopped, and two thurifers, swinging their hand-held censers, declaimed a gatha:

May the benevolent worthy, the Grand Monad,
    order his carriage to descend,
And the somber gates of the valley of night
    to open one after the other;
In order to let the acolytes, pair by pair,
    go in front and lead the way,
That the dead souls may undergo sublimation[36]
    and mount the cloudy stairs.

Perfect Man Huang, having fumigated his vestments, performed his ablutions, and burned incense, went on to chant an invocation, as follows:

We humbly submit that: The Mysterious Sovereign, in founding our religion, opened up a way of salvation from the road to the shades; the sect of Orthodox Unity, in transmitting its rites, has enabled us to refine the bodies of the dead so they may achieve transcendence. These mercies extend to incarcerated souls; these benefits ameliorate the fate of hungry spirits. Diligently dispersing genuine incense, we sincerely invoke the attendance at this sacred rite of the Great Compassionate and Merciful Occupant of the Palace of the Eastern Apogee Who Listens to the Voices of the Distressed and Is Moved to Respond to Their Needs, the Grand Monad Heavenly Worthy Who Saves from Distress, i.e., the Sovereign Deity Who Dwells in the Blue Heaven of the East and Presides over the Nine Yang, his avatars, the Great Perfect Men Who Save from Distress of the Ten Directions, the celestial and terrestrial transcendents, the officers of the Three Worlds, the deities of the Five Peaks, the Ten Kings of the Underworld, and the worthies of the Water Bureau and Mount Lo-feng. We respectfully hope that your lion throne will float through the void,[37] and your dragon pennant sparkle in the sunlight, that you may dispense the malachite elixir that dispels distress, and the sweet dew and ambrosia that generously alleviate the hunger of bereaved souls. Today, we dedicate a provisional offering upon the table holding the spirit tablet of the deceased and transmit the talismans that will abolish the guilt of those incarcerated in the Nine Realms of Darkness, so that their interrogations may be ended and their punishments cease. We humbly observe that the human beings who dwell in this world of dust are daily entangled in mundane affairs. Oblivious of their impending death, they merely seek to covet life. Few are able to plant the roots of goodness; most, consequently, fall into evil ways. Too befuddled to achieve enlightenment, they give free rein to their desires, resorting to covetousness and anger. In the expectation that they will live forever, they do not believe how easily death may come. When the day arrives and they suddenly pass away, everything reverts to nothingness.[38] Karmic encumbrances beset their bodies, as they suffer torments in the court of the underworld. At present, in accordance with the Way, we humbly observe that because the spirit of Hsi-men Ch'ing's deceased consort, née Li, has relinquished its worldly ties and been engulfed for some time in the eternal night, if it is not rescued from the impediment of its sins, it is sure to find it hard to avoid a painful retribution. We respectfully hope that the Heavenly Worthy, whose name has been renowned for untold kalpas, and whose pneuma coordinates the Nine Yang, will exercise his benevolent nurture of life by rescuing those souls that cry out in pain; asperse his sweet dew so as to nourish the diverse species; shed his auspicious light in order to illuminate the paths of darkness; order the Three Officers to relax the protocols of interrogation; command the Kings of the Ten Courts of the Underworld to set aside their adjudicatory brushes; liberate the incarcerated and set free the imprisoned; forgive their transgressions and dispel their enmities; allowing each one of them to follow the talismanic functionaries in escaping completely from the somber gates. May they all experience the purgation of the basins of water and fire in order to bathe the yellow efflorescence of their refined bodies, so that they may all be reborn, and hope to regain the Taoist shore.

The high priest then recited the *Wu-ch'u ching*, or *Scripture of the Five Feasts*,[39] and the sacred spell that transmutes the food offerings, thereby distributing the ritual foodstuff to the hungry spirits. The high priest then continued to declaim, as follows:

As I have heard: the Nine Pneumas float in Heaven, though the Nine Pneumas came into existence before the Great Void;[40] the Nine Realms of Darkness lie clustered beneath the Earth, and the Nine Realms of Darkness are concealed beneath stacks of layered Yin. When the Nine Pneumas are properly arrayed,[41] the myriad beings are all brought to life,[42] which is why they are the root of Heaven and Earth. Each being is conceived in the womb[43] and depends for its nurture on the Three Origins.[44] The reason why human beings suffer from death and decay is that they are unable to cherish their forms, preserve their spirits, value their pneumas, and solidify their roots,[45] thus forsaking their true natures.[46] In order to be reborn, their forms must be bathed in the Great Yin, and their substance refined by the Great Yang, so that the Nine Pneumas may cause them to coalesce, and the Three Origins re-create them in the womb, thereby giving renewed shape to their forms. Were they not able to rely upon the immutable laws of the Most High, and the esoteric commands of Lao-tzu, the founder of the school of the Mysterious Origin, how could they hope to find a way of salvation for their incarcerated souls, or expect the restoration of their original bodies, enabling them to mount the auspicious clouds and attend upon the Primordial,[47] while overcoming demons and being guaranteed redemption? To this end, we shall reverently present the true talisman of the Numinous Treasure for the refinement of the bodies of the dead.

> The Lord of Grand Tenuity summons
>   with his yellow pennant,
> The deity of Florescent Nonbeing
>   directs the soul banners.[48]
> Attracting and summoning the dead
>   from their eternal night,
> They provide a way of salvation for
>   their resurrected souls.[49]

The Taoist celebrants first took Li P'ing-erh's soul banner, immersed it in the basin of water, and burnt a talisman addressed to Chieh-lin, or the Ladies of the Moon, after which they exchanged it for the red banner. They then put this in the basin of fire and burnt a talisman addressed to Yü-i, the Emperors of the Sun, after which they replaced it with the yellow banner.[50] The high priest then declaimed the words:

> The Heavenly number one begets water,
> The Earthly number two begets fire;
> When water and fire are refined together,
> They give birth to the true form.[51]

Once the sublimation ceremony was completed, the soul of the deceased, attired in its formal cap and cape, was invited to cross the golden bridge, pay court before the jade steps, and confess her allegiance to the Three Treasures.[52]

The assembled celebrants then intoned the three refuges and presented the "Five Offerings"[53] before each of them:

HOMAGE TO JADE CLARITY

> In the Taoist school we honor,
> The Lord of Jade Clarity.
> The primordial chaos, devoid of light,
>   harbored the Brahma pneumas;
> The myriad phenomena in their diversity
>   were in a grain-sized pearl.
> When the souls of the dead undergo sublimation,
> They are able to ascend to the immortal realm.

HOMAGE TO UPPER CLARITY

In the Taoist school we honor,
The Lord of Upper Clarity.
In the Ch'ih-ming era the graphs appeared,[54]
    disclosing the end of days;
The primordial net flowed out,[55] penetrating
    the mysterious illimitable.
When the souls of the dead undergo sublimation,
They are able to ascend to the immortal realm.

HOMAGE TO GRAND CLARITY

In the Taoist School we honor,
The Lord of Grand Clarity.
The Way embraced Heaven and Earth from the
    outset of the Mysterious Origin;
For countless kalpas it has provided a way
    of salvation for befuddled souls.
When the souls of the dead undergo sublimation,
They are able to ascend to the immortal realm.

The high priest then said, "Having acknowledged the three refuges, we should proclaim the nine precepts:

1st precept: Be respectful and courteous; filially
    nourish your father and mother.
2nd precept: Be diligent and industrious; exhibit
    loyalty toward your rulers.
3rd precept: Do not kill; compassionately preserve
    all living creatures.
4th precept: Do not engage in venery; be upright in
    your approach to others.
5th precept: Do not steal; promote justice even at
    your own expense.
6th precept: Do not give way to anger; abusing others
    in the heat of wrath.
7th precept: Do not be dishonest; practicing deception
    and harming the good.
8th precept: Do not be arrogant; proudly indifferent to
    the truly virtuous.
9th precept: Do not be duplicitous; obey these precepts
    with a single mind.[56]

You must listen attentively. Take heed! Take heed!"
    When he had finished enunciating the nine precepts, the Taoist priests performed an interlude of music, after which Perfect Man Huang intoned the

appropriate talismanic commands, followed by an incantation addressed to
the ten classes of homeless souls,[57] to the tune "Hanging Chains of Gold":

> May the Great Compassionate and Merciful,
> Imperial Savior of the Blue Heaven of the East,
> Whose lion throne floats through the void,
> Who is able to miraculously transform departed spirits,
> Purify this offering of food for the dead,
> And appear before the scorched demons of Hell,
> So that the homeless souls that crowd the underworld,
> Can come to savor the taste of this sweet dew.
>
> May those who campaign to north and south,
> The soldiers who don armor and wear uniforms,[58]
> Who risk death and forget life,
> In order to repay their debt to their country,
> Who after a single burst of cannon fire,
> Are left to lie upon the battlefield;
> The homeless souls who perish in battle,
> Come to savor the taste of this sweet dew.
>
> May those good boys and good girls,[59]
> Serving others as their slaves or servants,
> Who are cursed at night and beaten in the morning,
> Whose clothes do not cover their bodies,
> Who are driven out of their masters' gates,
> To lie helplessly in the long streets;
> The homeless souls who starve to death,
> Come to savor the taste of this sweet dew.
>
> May sedentary traders and traveling merchants,[60]
> As well as itinerant Buddhist and Taoist priests,
> Who are compelled year in and year out,[61]
> To seek their sustenance away from home,
> Who find themselves afflicted with illness,
> And with no one to rely on in their wayside inns;
> The homeless souls who die upon the road,
> Come to savor the taste of this sweet dew.
>
> May criminals guilty of assault and battery,
> Who must wear the cangue and chains in prison,
> And are beheaded, strangled, or sliced to death,
> Thus forfeiting their lives in the long streets,
> According to the clear articles of the statutes,[62]
> For the crime of violating the law of the land;

The homeless souls who suffer capital punishment,
Come to savor the taste of this sweet dew.

May enemies from a previous incarnation,[63]
Who encounter each other in this life,
And resort to secret schemes or covert plots,
To disrupt each other's bowels with poison,
So that vapors arise from their nine apertures,
With the result that they lose their lives;
The homeless souls who die of poisoning,
Come to savor the taste of this sweet dew.

May those who breast-feed infants for three years,[64]
Demonstrating the illimitable kindness of parents,
Who bear the fetus in their wombs for ten months,[65]
Enduring the rigors of accouchement and parturition,
While their lives are hanging by a thread,
The babies and mothers who return to the shades;
The homeless souls who die in childbirth,
Come to savor the taste of this sweet dew.

May those endangered by grave misfortunes,
The threats of which are difficult to avoid,
Those burdened by private debts and tax arrears,
For which they are dunned day after day,
Who slit their own throats or hang themselves,
Thereby severing their three inches of breath;
The homeless souls who are driven to suicide,
Come to savor the taste of this sweet dew.

May those who suffer from prolonged illness,
Abdominal distension, paralysis, or consumption,
Scabrous suppurations, or flesh wounds,
Whose entire bodies reek of purulent discharges,
With no relatives to proffer them beans or water,
For whom prescribed medications offer no cure;
The homeless souls who perish of disease,
Come to savor the taste of this sweet dew.

May those beset by huge waves, windblown breakers,
Or spreading floods that surge up to the heavens,[66]
Whose hawsers break and whose vessels sink,
So that their bodies are lost in the long river,
Who are homesick for their native places,[67]
But have no one to send them even a letter;

The homeless souls who go to watery graves,
Come to savor the taste of this sweet dew.

May those encountering fire, with wind and smoke,
Who are caught by surprise and unable to escape,
From the fierce conflagration that knows no mercy,
Whose entire bodies are subjected to the flames,
Leaving them with singed scalps and scorched heads,[68]
So that even in death they are smoke-cured ghosts;
The homeless souls who perish in the flames,
Come to savor the taste of this sweet dew.

May the sprites and goblins who inhabit the trees,
As well as other varieties of ungovernable demons,
And the fish, crustaceans, and feathered creatures,
None of whom would not like to be reborn as humans,
Look up to the Most High and compassionate one,
To widely extend the scope of his benevolence;
So that the ten classes of homeless souls,
Can come to savor the taste of this sweet dew.

Once the sublimation ritual was completed, Perfect Man Huang came down from his elevated throne, and the Taoist priests struck up their music as they escorted him outside the front gate where paper money was burnt and a coffer of papier-mâché goods for the dead was incinerated. Once they came back inside, the ceremony was officially over, and the Taoist celebrants changed their clothes while the vergers proceeded to take down the scrolls depicting the Taoist deities.

Meanwhile, Hsi-men Ch'ing had already ordered that:

Painted candles be set alight, and
An array of banquet tables set out,

in the large reception hall, where the three boy actors were on hand to play their musical instruments and sing for the assembled relatives and friends.

Hsi-men Ch'ing started out by offering a toast to Perfect Man Huang, while his attendants proffered him a bolt of ultramarine cloud-crane brocade, a bolt of variegated satin, and ten taels of silver.

After kowtowing to him four times, Hsi-men Ch'ing said, "My deceased consort has this day, as a result of the efficacy of the scripture recitation conducted by my reverend teacher, been enabled to gain salvation and attain reincarnation. For all of which my gratitude is profound. These insignificant gifts are no more than an expression of my heartfelt feelings."

Perfect Man Huang replied, "Unworthy though I am to wear this cap and vestment and claim to be a devotee of the Taoist religion, what virtue could I possess that would enable me to affect mankind or Heaven? It is only owing to the effect of Your Honor's sincere devotion that your revered lady has been enabled to mount the auspicious clouds and attend upon the Primordial. Were I to accept these gifts, it would truly be a cause of embarrassment."

"These gifts are paltry in the extreme," said Hsi-men Ch'ing. "I humbly beseech you to accept them with a smile."[69]

Only then did Perfect Man Huang direct a young acolyte to take charge of them.

After toasting Perfect Man Huang, Hsi-men Ch'ing went on to offer a toast to Abbot Wu and presented him with a bolt of satin brocade and five taels of silver, in addition to the fee of ten taels of silver as payment for arranging the scripture reading.

Abbot Wu would only accept the fee for the scripture reading, and refused the other gifts, saying, "Whatever efforts I may have expended in arranging for the scripture recitation designed for the salvation of your lady, so that she could be reborn in the immortal realm, were no more than the fulfillment of my responsibilities. I ought not even to accept this fee, let alone these other lavish gifts."

"Your Reverence is wrong," said Hsi-men Ch'ing. "Although Perfect Man Huang may have presided over the ceremony, all of the documents and protocols for the ritual were arranged for by you. These gifts are merely intended to compensate you for your efforts. How can it be right for you to refuse them?"

Only then did Abbot Wu feel that he had no alternative but to accept them, and he thanked him profusely.

After Hsi-men Ch'ing had presented a toast to the entire group of Taoist priests, Brother-in-law Wu K'ai, Ying Po-chüeh, and the others came up to assist Hsi-men Ch'ing in enjoying the food and drink that had been offered in sacrifice.

Wu K'ai presented the toast, Ying Po-chüeh held the flagon, Hsieh Hsi-ta proffered some viands, and they all knelt down in front of him, while Ying Po-chüeh said, "Brother, you have held this ceremony today, invited Perfect Man Huang to preside over it, and availed yourself of the efforts of Abbot Wu. Just now, as the paper money was being burnt at the conclusion of the ritual, I saw a vision of my sister-in-law, wearing a phoenix cap on her head, dressed in white clothing, with a feather fan in her hand, mounting into the clouds on the back of a white crane. This is all due to the efficacy of Perfect Man Huang's rites of salvation, your own sincere heart, and my sister-in-law's good fortune, and it is a source of delight to me as well."

Thereupon, he filled a cup of wine and handed it to Hsi-men Ching.

"I am indebted to all of you gentlemen," said Hsi-men Ch'ing, "for all you have done during the last few days. I cannot thank you enough. I am scarcely worthy of your surpassing generosity."

When he had finished speaking, Hsi-men Ch'ing:

    Drained it in one gulp.

Ying Po-chüeh then proceeded to fill another cup of wine, saying, "Brother, in drinking wine, you should make a twosome out of it, rather than confining yourself to a single cup."

Hsieh Hsi-ta hastened to proffer him a chopstick-serving of viands, which he promptly consumed.

When Hsi-men Ch'ing had finished toasting the company, they all sat down at their places, while the boy actors entertained them by playing their musical instruments and singing, and the chef came out to present the first serving. That night, during the course of the banquet, what with:

Playing at guess-fingers or gaming at forfeits, and
Performing on woodwind and string instruments,

the party continued until the second watch and Hsi-men Ch'ing was half inebriated before the company said farewell, got up to go, and went their ways.

Hsi-men Ch'ing then came inside, rewarded the boy actors with three mace of silver, and returned to the rear compound. Truly:

During this life, if wine is on hand,
    you might as well get drunk;
Not a single drop has ever been known
    to reach the Nine Springs.[70]

There is a poem that testifies to this:

One day, you may swear to live your lives together,
But, one night, your oath will vanish like a cloud.
Her flying phoenix golden hairpin will tumble out,
The soaring phoenix precious mirror will fracture.
Your delight in her salvation will prove ephemeral,
While your lasting mortification will not diminish.
Only by frequent resort to the contents of the cup,
Can you gain temporary relief from your affliction.

If you want to know the outcome of these events,
Pray consult the story related in the following chapter.

Chapter 67

HSI-MEN CH'ING APPRECIATES THE SNOW

WHILE IN HIS STUDIO;

LI P'ING-ERH DESCRIBES HER INTIMATE

FEELINGS IN A DREAM

Throughout the livelong day I think of you,
    but I cannot see you;[1]
The sounds of the drum and the cold bugle
    are difficult to bear.
The ruptured mirror in your dressing case only
    reflects the waning moon;
The remaining clothes in your chest are but
    clusters of broken clouds.
The shivering sparrow finds it hard to perch
    upon the sparse branches;
The migrating goose breaks formation and cries
    as it deserts the flock.
The jade hairpin may be smashed to pieces, but
    emotion is hard to shatter;
When I envisage you, it is heartbreaking that
    my recollections are unreal.

THE STORY GOES that when Hsi-men Ch'ing returned to the rear compound he was so exhausted that he slept until the sun was high in the sky
without getting up.

Lai-hsing came in at this point and reported, "The carpenters are waiting
outside and want to know if they are to dismantle the temporary structures that
they put up for the funeral rites."

Hsi-men Ch'ing responded irritably to Lai-hsing, saying, "As for the dismantling, just go ahead and have them do it. What need is there to bother me
about it?"

The carpenters outside then proceeded, hugger-mugger, to take down the
matting, cordage, and pine planks of the structures in question and transport
them to the building across the street for storage. But no more of this.

Yü-hsiao came into the room and reported, "The weather outside is really threatening."

Hsi-men Ch'ing told her to fetch his clothes from on top of the heated k'ang and prepared to get up and put them on.

"You were tired out last night," said Wu Yüeh-niang, "and the weather looks threatening. Why don't you get a good sleep before getting up. Why should you feel compelled to crawl out of bed so soon? You might just as well not go to the yamen today."

"I'm not planning to go to the yamen," said Hsi-men Ch'ing. "I'm afraid that messenger from our kinsman Chai Ch'ien will come by looking for a reply, and I'll need to be here to send him off with it."

"In that case," said Yüeh-niang, "you might as well get up. I'll have a maid-servant heat some congee for you to eat."

Without even performing his morning ablutions, and leaving his hair in dis-array, Hsi-men Ch'ing threw on a woolen robe, donned a felt cap, and headed straight for his studio in the Hidden Spring Grotto in the front garden.

It so happens that, ever since Shu-t'ung had absconded, Hsi-men Ch'ing had arranged for Wang Ching to look after the garden and the keys to the two doors on either side of his studio there, and deputed Ch'un-hung to take care of cleaning up and sweeping his other studio in front of the large reception hall. During the winter months, Hsi-men Ch'ing spent his leisure time in the studio in the Hidden Spring Grotto. On the surface of the bed frame over the k'ang, which was heated by an underground firebox, there was also a brazier of yellow brass. Warmth was retained in the room by a hanging portiere of thin oiled silk, decorated with a motif of the moon amid the plum branches. The outer parlor was embellished with an oleander, a variety of chrysanthemums;

> Cool slender bamboos, and
> Turquoise-hued orchids.

The studio itself was furnished with:

> Brushes, inkstones, and a plum in a vase;
> Zither and books were elegantly displayed.

On the bed frame over the k'ang there were:

> A madder red strip of felt lying on top of,
> A brocade mat figured with silver flowers.
> The pillow was decorated with water birds;
> The hanging curtains were of mermaid silk.

Hsi-men Ch'ing lay down casually on the bed frame, while Wang Ching hastened to retrieve some ambergris incense from an ivory box on the table and ignited it in a small gilded censer.

Hsi-men Ch'ing then said to Wang Ching, "Go find Lai-an, and tell him to go invite Master Ying the Second to come join me."

Wang Ching accordingly went out and sent Lai-an off on this errand.

Whom should Wang Ching run into at this juncture but P'ing-an, who came up to him and said, "Little Chou, the barber, is waiting outside."

Wang Ching went back into the studio and told this to Hsi-men Ch'ing, who had him call Little Chou inside.

When Little Chou had kowtowed to him, Hsi-men Ch'ing said, "You've come at just the right moment to comb my hair and give me a massage."

He then went on to ask, "Why is it that you haven't shown up for such a long time?"

"On hearing that your Sixth Lady had died," said Little Chou, "I imagined that you were probably preoccupied, so I didn't come."

Hsi-men Ch'ing, thereupon, seated himself on a "Drunken Old Gentleman's" lounge chair, let down his hair, and told him to trim and comb it for him.

Who should appear at this juncture but Ying Po-chüeh, who had been summoned by Lai-an. He was wearing a felt hat on his head, a green woolen jacket on his torso, a pair of old black boots on his feet, and a palmetto cloak, as he lifted aside the portiere, came in, and bowed in greeting.

Hsi-men Ch'ing, whose hair was in the process of being combed, said, "There's no need for you to perform an obeisance. Pray sit down."

Ying Po-chüeh pulled a chair over and sat down next to the brazier.

"How come you're dressed that way today?" enquired Hsi-men Ch'ing.

"You may not be aware of it," said Ying Po-chüeh, "but snow is falling outside, and it's extremely cold. Yesterday, it was so late when I went home that the rooster had already crowed. You sent a servant to see us on our way, but we could hardly walk by that point. When I saw how overcast it was, I asked for a lantern and made my way home together with your brother-in-law, Wu K'ai. Today, I could hardly crawl out of bed. If Lai-an hadn't come to call for me, I'd be asleep yet. Brother, you're quite a stout fellow to be able to get up this early. If it were me, I couldn't manage it."

"Luckily, you've been a witness to it all," said Hsi-men Ch'ing. "I haven't had a moment's peace. Ever since the day of her burial, I've been preoccupied with entertaining Defender-in-Chief Huang Ching-ch'en and arranging for the scripture reading ceremonies, so that, from that time to this, my mind has been perturbed. This morning, my wife said, 'You're tired out. Why don't you get a good sleep before getting up?' But I was worried that the messenger from my kinsman, Chai Ch'ien, would come by for a reply to his letter, and I also had to see to the dismantling of the temporary structures that were erected for the funeral rites. On the twenty-fourth, I'm sending off Manager Han Tao-kuo and some other employees on a trip and need to see that everything is packed up, and the statement of account written out. The various funeral arrangements have also put people to a lot of trouble. As far as the relatives and friends are concerned, it might be all right, but when it comes to the gentry and officials, if you fail to pay them a personal visit to thank them for their generosity, it will constitute a breach of propriety."

"That's so," said Ying Po-chüeh. "I, too, have been concerned about your need to pay these personal visits to thank people for their generosity. You'll have to do it, I guess, but you might as well select only the most important households, and let it go at that. As for the rest, since you're on good terms with them, if you run into each other, all you need to do is apologize, that's all. Who doesn't know how busy you've been? You can rely on their mutual understanding."

As they were speaking, what should they see but Wang Ching, who lifted aside the portiere to allow Hua-t'ung to bring in a square box of painted lacquer, with two teacups of carved lacquer inlaid with silver, containing boiled cow's milk flavored with butterfat and crystallized sugar.

Ying Po-chüeh picked up a cup and cradled it in his hand, admiring the way in which the glistening white goose-fat-like butterfat floated on the surface, and said, "What a wonderful treat. It's boiling hot, and if you hold it in your mouth, it's:

Fragrant, sweet, and delectable."

Without any trouble at all, he managed to finish it off with a few swallows. Hsi-men Ch'ing, on the other hand, waited until Little Chou had finished with his hair and then told him to clean the wax out of his ears, setting the milk aside on a table, without drinking any of it.

"Brother," said Ying Po-chüeh, "why don't you drink some of it? It would be a pity to let it get cold. If you drink a cup of this first thing every morning, it's sure to have a restorative effect on your constitution."

"I'm not going to drink it," said Hsi-men Ch'ing. "You can have it. In a little while I'm going to eat some congee."

This was just the signal Ying Po-chüeh had been waiting for, and, picking it up in his hand, he:

Finished it off with a single gulp,[2]
after which Hua-t'ung took the cups away.

When the wax had been cleaned out of Hsi-men Ch'ing's ears, he told Little Chou to take the wooden roller and go over his body with it, employing the art of massage and the therapeutic gymnastic techniques called "guiding and pulling."[3]

"Brother," asked Ying Po-chüeh, "now that your body has been gone over with the roller, do you feel any improvement in your sense of well-being?"

"There is no reason for me to deceive you," said Hsi-men Ch'ing. "The fact is that in the evening my body regularly starts to hurt, and I feel pain in my lower back. If I didn't get this kind of going over, I don't know how I'd stand it."

"For someone with such a corpulent figure as yours," opined Ying Po-chüeh, "and one who eats such rich food every day, it is hardly surprising that you should suffer from phlegm-fire."

"The other day," responded Hsi-men Ch'ing, "Jen Hou-ch'i said to me, 'Venerable sir, although you possess an imposing stature, you suffer from an excess of vacuity.' He gave me a jar of life-prolonging restorative pills and said that they were concocted from a prescription made up for the use of His Majesty the Emperor by Perfect Man Lin Ling-su, and that I should take one every morning, and wash it down with human milk. I've been so distracted the last few days, however, that I haven't taken any of them yet. You all say that I've got a plethora of bedmates at my disposal, and indulge in this business every day, but ever since she died, I haven't been in the mood to consider such matters."

As they were speaking, whom should they see but Han Tao-kuo, who came in, bowed in greeting, and sat down, saying, "Just now, all the parties concerned have come to terms about our expedition. The boats have been chartered and we are all set to embark on the twenty-fourth."

Hsi-men Ch'ing gave instructions that Manager Kan Jun should prepare the accounts and weigh out the silver so that they could wrap things up the next day.

He then went on to ask, "How much silver in the way of profits from the two shops is available?"

"It comes to something over six thousand taels altogether," said Han Tao-kuo.

"I'll weigh out an allotment of two thousand taels," said Hsi-men Ch'ing, "and turn it over to Ts'ui Pen so he can go to Hu-chou to buy silk. As for the other four thousand taels, you and Lai-pao can proceed to Sung-chiang to purchase piece goods. You must try to be on time to join the first fleet of boats that returns north in the new year. Each of you can take an advance of five taels of silver to cover the expenses of packing up for the trip at home."

"I've got another problem," said Han Tao-kuo. "As the holder of a hereditary corvée labor obligation on the staff of the Prince of Yün, I have to report for duty in person at periodic intervals and am not permitted to pay a fee for hiring a substitute. What am I to do about it?"

"Why can't you pay a fee to hire a substitute?" asked Hsi-men Ch'ing. "Lai-pao also holds a nominal appointment on the staff of the Prince of Yün, and he merely pays three mace of silver a month to avoid having to report for duty."

"As for Brother Pao's case," said Han Tao-kuo, "his right to do so was stipulated in the document of appointment from the grand preceptor so no one dares to interfere with him. In my case, it's a hereditary position which mandates the drafting of another able-bodied adult male from my clan if I am unable to serve."

"In that case," said Hsi-men Ch'ing, "you draft a memo about it, and I'll ask Jen Hou-ch'i to speak to Attendant Wang on the prince's staff, and have your name removed from the roster of those whose corvée service is mandated, so that you can commute your obligation to regular payments in money. Every month all you'll have to do is depute a reliable person from your household to go make the necessary payment for you."

Han Tao-kuo bowed to him to express his gratitude.

"Brother," chimed in Ying Po-chüeh, "once you've taken care of this problem for him, he'll have an easier mind while out on the road."

Before long, after Little Chou had finished massaging him with the roller, Hsi-men Ch'ing went back to the rear compound to comb his hair and directed that Little Chou should be given something to eat.

After some time, Hsi-men Ch'ing came back out wearing a white velveteen "loyal and tranquil hat" on his head and a fine woolen robe on his body. He rewarded Little Chou for his services with three mace of silver and then sent Wang Ching to summon Licentiate Wen.

Before long, Licentiate Wen came in, formally attired in the typical garb of a scholar:

> A high hat and a wide girdle.[4]

When they had finished exchanging greetings, the servants set out a table and brought in the congee. This repast included four side dishes, namely, a bowl of slow-boiled ham hocks, a bowl of blanched donkey meat flavored with chives, a bowl of blanched chicken wonton flavored with pickled fish, and a bowl of slow-boiled squab, along with four bowls of congee made from nonglutinous rice. Four pairs of ivory chopsticks were also provided. Ying Po-chüeh together with Licentiate Wen were seated at the head of the table, Hsi-men Ch'ing played the role of host, and Han Tao-kuo was seated to one side.

Hsi-men Ch'ing instructed Lai-an, saying, "Fetch another bowl of congee and a pair of chopsticks, and ask our son-in-law to come have some congee with us."

Before long, Ch'en Ching-chi arrived, wearing a mourning cap on his head, an outer robe of white pongee cut like that of a Taoist priest, over a loose undergown of pale green satin, and rush sandals with velvet socks. After bowing to Ying Po-chüeh and the others, he also sat down to one side. In a little while, when they had finished the congee and the utensils had been cleared away, he departed, and Han Tao-kuo also got up to go, leaving only Ying Po-chüeh and Licentiate Wen sitting in the studio.

Hsi-men Ch'ing then turned to Licentiate Wen and asked, "Have you finished writing the reply, or not?"

"Your pupil has already prepared a draft, which I have brought with me," said Licentiate Wen. "I won't copy out the final version until you have had a chance to peruse it, venerable sir."

He then pulled it out of his sleeve and handed it to Hsi-men Ch'ing to look over. The letter read as follows:

Earnestly indited by his devoted servant in Ch'ing-ho, Hsi-men Ch'ing, in response to His Eminence of surpassing virtue, the pillar of state Chai Ch'ien, his venerable kinsman:

Since I forsook your illustrious countenance after exchanging views during our meeting at your residence in the capital, without my being aware of it, half a year has abruptly elapsed. Your pupil having been so unfortunate as to suffer the loss of his consort, is especially grateful for the receipt of his kinsman's consolatory contribution, conveyed from a distance, as well as his admonitory advice, which suffices to demonstrate the profundity and generosity of his efforts on my behalf. I am both moved and impressed more than words can tell, and shall not forget my debt of gratitude as long as I shall live.[5] My only fear is that if I should ever be remiss in the performance of my official duties, since I depend upon your influence, I should fail to live up to your expectations. The fact that I can rely upon you to protect my interests before the venerable minister is something for which your pupil will remain forever grateful, since it is entirely due to his kinsman's largess. At present, taking advantage of a convenient messenger, I wish to respectfully enquire after your well-being, and to convey my unsurpassable regard. I humbly expect that you will comprehend my sentiments, and am not able to express myself more fully.

In addition, I am sending ten handkerchiefs of Yang-chou crepe, ten handkerchiefs of variegated satin, twenty low-grade gold toothpicks, and ten black gold wine cups, as a paltry expression of my sentiments from afar, in the hope that you will accept them with a smile.

When Hsi-men Ch'ing had finished reading the draft, he told Ch'en Ching-chi to get out the presents there in the studio and assist Licentiate Wen in wrapping them up. The letter was then copied out on brocade notepaper, after which the envelope was securely closed, and a seal affixed to it. A packet containing five taels of silver was also sealed up as a gratuity for the courier, Wang Yü. But no more of this.

After a while, they noticed that the snow was falling more heavily, and Hsi-men Ch'ing kept Licentiate Wen in the studio so they could appreciate the snow together. The table was wiped off, and some appetizers were provided to go with their wine. What should they see at this juncture but someone lifting aside the portiere and peeking inside.

Hsi-men Ch'ing asked who it was, and Wang Ching replied, "Cheng Ch'un is here."

Hsi-men Ch'ing told him to come in. Holding a pair of boxes up high in his hands, Cheng Ch'un came in and knelt down in front of the company. There was also a little square box adorned with gold tracery balanced on top of the other two.

"What's in the boxes?" Hsi-men Ch'ing asked.

"My elder sister, Ai-yüeh," Cheng Ch'un replied, "knowing that Your Honor is tired out from the scripture-reading ceremony for the Sixth Lady yesterday, and having nothing better to offer, has sent these two boxes of tea pastries for Your Honor to give away to someone if you like."

Hsi-men Ch'ing Appreciates the Snow While in His Studio

When he proceeded to open them, one box turned out to contain stuffed cream puff pastries, while the other one turned out to hold butterfat "abalone shell" sweets.

"These were made by my sister Ai-yüeh with her own hands," said Cheng Ch'un. "She knows that Your Honor is fond of these sweets and has sent them as a sign of her filial respect."

"I am already beholden to your establishment for the gifts you provided yesterday," said Hsi-men Ch'ing, "and today your sister Ai-yüeh has taken the trouble to send these things as well."

"Wonderful!" said Ying Po-chüeh. "Bring them over here so I can taste them. Having lost one daughter who was adept at making these things, another daughter who is good at the same task has appeared."

Picking one up and sticking it in his mouth, Ying Po-chüeh also chose another one and handed it to Licentiate Wen, saying, "Venerable sir, have a taste of this. Once you have eaten it:

Your loose teeth will grow again;[6]
You'll feel like a new individual.[7]
Even to gaze upon such an exotic object,
Is superior to gaining ten years of life."[8]

When Licentiate Wen proceeded to savor it, he found that:

It melted on entering the mouth,

and said, "This delicacy must come from the Western Regions. It is not something known to the human world.

It irrigates the lungs and transfuses the heart.

Surely it is a rare specialty from the Realms Above."

Hsi-men Ch'ing went on to ask, "And what's in the little box?"

Cheng Ch'un calmly knelt down in front of Hsi-men Ch'ing and opened the box, saying, "This is a personal gift from my sister Ai-yüeh to Your Honor."

Hsi-men Ch'ing put the box on his knee and was about to take a look at the contents, when Ying Po-chüeh snatched it away with one hand and opened it up himself. Inside there was a tasseled peach-red satin handkerchief with a diapered, double-patterned, border and a meticulously worked motif of overlapping antique cash coins and joined hearts in the shape of interlocking lozenges, containing a package of melon seeds which the donor had cracked with her own teeth. Ying Po-chüeh tossed the handkerchief back to Hsi-men Ch'ing but proceeded to cram the melon seeds into his mouth in two handfuls and gobble them up.

By the time Hsi-men Ch'ing endeavored to grab them back, there were hardly any left, and he expostulated, "You crazy dog! Are you suffering from such:

Acute consumption or avid craving?

If you leave me so much as a glimpse of them, it will show that you have a human heart after all."

"They were a gift from my daughter," said Ying Po-chüeh. "If she didn't intend to show her filial feelings toward me, to whom should she display them? As I see it, you ordinarily have more than enough to eat."

"Since Licentiate Wen is here," responded Hsi-men Ch'ing, "I can hardly give you the cursing you deserve. You dog! That's hardly acceptable conduct."

With that, he tucked the handkerchief into his sleeve and told Wang Ching to take the boxes back to the rear compound. Before long:

> The cups and plates were duly arrayed,[9]

and the wine was served.

They had only finished one round of wine when Tai-an came in and reported, "Li Chih and Huang the Fourth have finally received payment and have come to deliver the silver they owe you."

"How much does it come to?" asked Hsi-men Ch'ing.

"They say they've brought a thousand taels," said Tai-an, "and that they'll deliver the remainder at a later date."

"Just take a gander at those two goddamned characters," said Ying Po-chüeh. "They've been keeping me, too, in the dark, without telling me what they're up to. It's no wonder they never showed up for that scripture-reading ceremony of yours yesterday. They must have gone to Tung-p'ing prefecture to collect their silver. Now that you've received this repayment, you'd better not let them have any more silver in the future. These two "bare sticks" owe money to so many people that I fear, in the future:

> Their reserves will prove to be inadequate.[10]

The other day, Eunuch Director Hsü from the northern quarter was so upset at this prospect that he said he planned to go to Tung-p'ing prefecture himself, and bring back the silver he was due in person. I fear that if that:

> Old ox with his rapacious snout,[11]

makes off with the whole bundle, you may have difficulty recovering the remainder of your investment."

"I'm not afraid of the likes of him," stated Hsi-men Ch'ing. "It doesn't matter to me whether it's Eunuch Director Hsü or Eunuch Director Li. How do you suppose he would like it if I were to have his servant detained in the lockup? There's no reason to fear that he would fail to cough up the silver."

Turning to Ch'en Ching-chi, Hsi-men Ch'ing said, "Take the steelyard out with you, and take care of weighing his silver and putting it away. That should settle the terms of the contract. There's no need for me to go out."

After some time, Ch'en Ching-chi came back and reported, "I've weighed out the silver, which comes to exactly a thousand taels, and taken it back to the rear compound for the First Lady to put away. Huang the Fourth says that he'd like you to go outside and have a few words with him."

"Tell him I'm busy entertaining someone," said Hsi-men Ch'ing. "After all, the only thing he wants to discuss is the renegotiation of the contract. Tell him to come back after the twenty-fourth."

"It's not that," said Ch'en Ching-chi. "There's a different matter that he'd like to solicit your help with. He's asking you to go outside so he can explain it to you in person."

"I wonder what it could be," said Hsi-men Ch'ing. "I'd better go out and see."

When he got to the reception hall, Huang the Fourth kowtowed to him and then stood up and said, "The thousand taels of silver that I brought with me has already been accepted by your son-in-law and I am prepared to write a promissory note for the remainder. But there is another matter that I would like to solicit Your Honor's assistance with today."

As he spoke he knocked his head on the floor and wept.

Hsi-men Ch'ing helped him to his feet and said, "What is it, actually. Tell me about it."

"My father-in-law Sun Ch'ing," said Huang the Fourth, "employs a manager named Feng the Second to handle his cotton business in Tung-ch'ang prefecture. Who could have anticipated that this Feng the Second had a son named Feng Huai who:

Was not the sort to abide by his lot,

but was in the habit of locking the door of the shop at night and going out to patronize prostitutes. One day, two large bales of cotton were found to be missing, and when my father-in-law, Sun Ch'ing, complained about it, Feng the Second punished his son with a few strokes of the cane. His son, consequently, engaged in an affray with my brother-in-law, Sun Ch'ing's son, Sun Wen-hsiang, in which he managed to knock out one of his antagonist's teeth and also suffered a head injury himself, before the other employees were able to break it up. Who could have anticipated that his son would develop a case of tetanus and die in his home half a month later? His father-in-law, who is a notorious local tyrant named Pai the Fifth, nicknamed Moneybags Pai, who operates as a fence for stolen goods in the area west of the Grand Canal, incited Feng the Second into preparing a deposition and lodging a complaint at the yamen of the regional investigating censor, who has muddle-headedly deputed Lei Ch'i-yüan, the assistant commissioner of the military defense circuit, to hear the case. But His Honor Lei Ch'i-yüan is so busy facilitating the Imperial Flower and Rock Convoys that he has assigned the case to Prefectural Judge T'ung. The Pai family has bought off Prefectural Judge T'ung and suborned the neighbors into falsely testifying that my father-in-law, Sun Ch'ing, egged on his son from the sidelines during the affray, so that, at present, a warrant has been issued for my father-in-law's arrest. My only hope is that, whatever happens, Your Honor will deign to take pity on me by writing a letter to Lei Ch'i-yüan requesting him to hold my father-in-law in custody for a few days before submitting a final decision. Only if His Honor Lei Ch'i-yüan has the time to hear the case is there any chance that my father-in-law may escape with his life. The fact that the two of them engaged in an affray had nothing to do with my father-in-law, and moreover, the death of Feng Huai did not take place until after the event, when the period of responsibility for the crime had elapsed. After all, Feng Huai had already been beaten by his father, Feng the Second, so why should Sun Wen-hsiang alone be held responsible for his death?"

Hsi-men Ch'ing glanced over his explanatory note and saw that it said, "Please look with favorable eyes on the two prisoners, Sun Ch'ing and Sun Wen-hsiang, who are currently being detained in Tung-ch'ang prefecture."

He then went on to say, "Although it is true that Assistant Commissioner Lei Ch'i-yüan did attend a banquet here some days ago, I have only met him that once and am not well acquainted with him. Under the circumstances, it would hardly be appropriate for me to address a letter to him."

At this, Huang the Fourth knelt down, weeping and wailing, and appealed to him, saying, "If Your Honor does not take pity on them, my father-in-law and his son will both, most likely, be fated to die. As things now stand, if Sun Wen-hsiang must lose his head, so be it, but if you could only contrive to have my father-in-law removed from the case:

My obligation to you could not be greater.

My father-in-law is fifty-nine years old this year and has no one at home to tend to his needs. If he remains incarcerated during the cold winter months, he will be as good as dead."

Hsi-men Ch'ing pondered this for some time and then said, "All right then, I'll ask His Honor Ch'ien Lung-yeh of the Lin-ch'ing customs house to intervene on his behalf. He and Lei Ch'i-yüan are fellow graduates, both having obtained the *chin-shih* degree in the year *jen-ch'en*."[12]

Huang the Fourth then proceeded to kowtow once again, after which he pulled a promissory note for "one hundred piculs of white rice"[13] out of his sleeve and handed it to Hsi-men Ch'ing, at the same time also extracting two packets of silver from the wallet at his waist.

Hsi-men Ch'ing refused to accept these offerings, saying, "What would I want with these monetary inducements of yours?"

"If Your Honor sets no store by them," said Huang the Fourth, "they may just as well be used to thank Ch'ien Lung-yeh."

"That's not a problem," said Hsi-men Ch'ing. "If the request is successful, I'll buy an appropriate gift to thank him."

As they were speaking, whom should they see but Ying Po-chüeh, who emerged from the postern gate to the garden, saying, "Brother, you ought not to intervene on Huang the Fourth's behalf. This is a case of someone who:

At leisure, doesn't bother to burn incense, but

When in a jam, embraces the legs of the Buddha.[14]

Yesterday, when you were holding the scripture-reading ceremony, he didn't even bother to send a gift, or come to pay a visit. Yet today, he shows up and asks you to do him a favor."

Huang the Fourth responded by bowing to Ying Po-chüeh and said, "My good Uncle Two, you're killing me. I've been running myself ragged over this matter for the last half month. Since when have I had any leisure? Yesterday I had to go to the prefectural yamen to collect this silver due to His Honor. This morning Brother Li the Third got up early to report for duty, and I came straight to His Honor's place here to turn over the silver and solicit his intervention in this affair in the hope of saving my father-in-law. If His Honor persists in his refusal to accept these presents, it will indicate that he no longer intends to patronize me."

When Ying Po-chüeh saw that Hsi-men Ch'ing was being offered a hundred taels of "snowflake" government silver, he went on to ask, "Brother, are you going to speak up on his behalf, or not?"

"I am not on familiar terms with Assistant Commissioner Lei Ch'i-yüan," said Hsi-men Ch'ing, "so, at present, I plan to ask Secretary Ch'ien Lung-yeh of the Lin-ch'ing customs house to say a word on his behalf. In the future, I can buy a gift to thank the venerable Ch'ien Lung-yeh. That ought to suffice. So why should I accept these presents from him?"

"Brother," said Ying Po-chüeh, "what you propose to do is not appropriate. Do you mean to say that when someone comes to solicit a favor from you, you should be put to the expense of having to buy a thank-you gift on his behalf? That doesn't make any sense. If you refuse to accept what he is offering, it looks as though you disdain it as being insufficient, which leaves him in an awkward position. You ought to take my advice and accept these presents of his. Although you may not set much store by them yourself, they may be drawn upon just as well in thanking Ch'ien Lung-yeh."

"And as for you, Brother Huang the Fourth," he went on to say, "listen to what I have to say. The fate of your father-in-law and brother-in-law hangs in the balance, and if it should happen that, as a result of the letter you have solicited, they are fortunate enough to escape unscathed, His Honor here has clearly not been swayed by your money, and it would be only appropriate for you to lay on a feast in the licensed quarter to provide us all with a day's entertainment."

"Uncle Two," said Huang the Fourth, "in view of your efforts, it goes without saying that your humble servant will host a party, and I'll have my father-in-law buy a present and come to kowtow to you in gratitude. There is no reason for me to deceive you, but on account of this affair of the two of them, father and son, I have been running around, day and night, high and low, without being able to find any way out of their predicament. If His Honor will not take pity on them, I will be at my wit's end."

"Don't be silly," said Ying Po-chüeh. "Since you embrace his daughter as your wife, if you were not really concerned about him, who would be?"

"My wife does nothing but cry at home," said Huang the Fourth. "Even if my father-in-law had been able to hide out somewhere, there would have been no one at home to deliver food to him."

At this juncture, Hsi-men Ch'ing, having allowed himself to be persuaded by Ying Po-chüeh, agreed to accept the promissory note for a hundred taels but told Huang the Fourth to take back his additional gifts.

"Venerable sir," said Huang The Fourth, "you don't seem to realize what a momentous matter this is, that you should quibble so about it."

Upon saying which, he started to go outside.

"Come over here," said Ying Po-chüeh. "Let me have a word with you. When do you need this letter by?"

"Life and death are hanging in the balance at this moment," said Huang the Fourth. "If His Honor will deign to produce a letter today, and depute someone to deliver it, I'll send my son to accompany him first thing in the morning."

He then proceeded to implore him again and again, saying, "Which of your honorable servants do you intend to send, so I can have a chance to get together with him?"

"I'll write the letter for you right away," said Hsi-men Ch'ing.

He then called over Tai-an and told him, "You go to deliver it tomorrow, along with Young Master Huang."

When Huang the Fourth saw Tai-an, he said goodbye to Hsi-men Ch'ing and went out the door. When he got to the front gate, he asked Tai-an for the return of the bag in which he had brought the silver. Tai-an went back to the master suite in the rear compound, where he found Yüeh-niang, together with Yü-hsiao and Hsiao-yü, engaged in tailoring some clothes.

When she saw Tai-an standing there waiting for the bag, Yü-hsiao said, "We're busy and don't have the leisure to empty it right now. You might as well have him come back for it tomorrow."

"Huang the Fourth is anxiously waiting for it right now," said Tai-an. "Tomorrow morning he has to get up early and go to Tung-ch'ang prefecture, so he can't come back then. Why don't you just empty it for him?"

"You had better go get it for him," said Yüeh-niang, "rather than keeping him waiting."

"The silver is still lying where we left it on the surface of the bed, isn't it?" said Yü-hsiao.

Going into the inner room she proceeded to dump the silver out of the bag onto the bed, after which, she brought the bag out with her, saying, "You crazy jailbird! Did you think someone had eaten this bag of his, that you should be as persistent as a leech in sucking it out of us?"

"If someone had not wanted it," said Tai-an, "what reason would I have had to come back to the rear compound for it?"

Thereupon, he took it out with him, and, when he got as far as the ceremonial gate between the front and rear compounds, gave it a shake, when what should fall out but a mushroom-shaped lump of silver, worth about three taels. It so happens that the paper packet in which it was wrapped had broken when Yü-hsiao dumped the silver carelessly out in her fit of pique, so that this lump had fallen out and remained in the bottom of the bag.

"What a stroke of luck," said Tai-an to himself. "I've managed to pick up something for nothing."

Thereupon, tucking it into his sleeve, he went out to the front compound, where he turned the bag over to Huang the Fourth and arranged to set out with him first thing in the morning.

To resume our story, Hsi-men Ch'ing returned to his studio, where he proceeded right away to instruct Licentiate Wen to compose the letter and turn it over to Tai-an. But no more of this.

Having noticed that outside the door:
> Fluttering and swirling,

the snow was coming down just like:
> Windblown willow catkins,[15] or
> Wildly dancing pear blossoms,

Hsi-men Ch'ing ordered the opening of a jug of high-quality Ma-ku wine and told Ch'un-hung to strain it through a cheesecloth sieve and serve it. Meanwhile, Cheng Ch'un was standing to one side, strumming his psaltery and singing in a low voice. Hsi-men Ch'ing told him to sing the song suite that begins with the words:

> Beneath the willows the breeze is gentle.[16]

As he was singing, whom should they see but Ch'in-t'ung, who came in and said, "Uncle Han Tao-kuo asked me to show you this note."

When Hsi-men Ch'ing had read it, he said, "You deliver it to the residence of Dr. Jen Hou-ch'i outside the city gate and get him to speak up on his behalf. Ask him to go tomorrow and speak to Attendant Wang on the staff of the Prince of Yün about it, in order to have Han Tao-kuo's name removed from the roster of those whose corvée labor is mandated."

"It's late today," said Ch'in-t'ung. "I'll go early tomorrow morning."

"That will be all right," said Hsi-men Ch'ing.

Not long afterwards, Lai-an came in bearing a square box that contained eight bowls of delicacies. These included one bowl of braised yams with chicken, one bowl of minced pork with leeks, one bowl of yams with pork meatballs, one bowl of slow-boiled sheep's head, one bowl of roast pork, one bowl of soup flavored with tripe and lungs, one bowl of broth flavored with blood and intestines, one bowl of beef tripe, and one bowl of quick-fried pork kidneys, as well as two large plates of steamed pastries with rose-flavored stuffings, made of dough kneaded with hot water, and basted with rendered goose fat. When the four of them, including Ch'en Ching-chi, had eaten their fill, Hsi-men Ch'ing told Wang Ching to take a tray with two bowls of delicacies and a plate of pastry and give them to Cheng Ch'un to eat. He also awarded him two large goblets of wine.

Cheng Ch'un knelt down and said, "I can't drink the wine."

"My good child!" said Ying Po-chüeh, "It's ice-cold outside. How can you refuse it when it's awarded to you by your master? How is it that your elder brother drinks what he is provided?"

"My elder brother may drink wine," said Cheng Ch'un, "but I don't drink it."

"Just drink one goblet," said Ying Po-chüeh, "and I'll get Wang Ching to drink the other one for you."

"Master Two," said Wang Ching, "I can't drink it either."

"My child," insisted Ying Po-chüeh, "just drink some of it in his stead. It's not as though you'd be doing him a big favor, or anything like that. It has always been true that:

When an elder bestows something, a junior
    does not presume to refuse it."[17]

Standing up, he then went on to say, "No matter what happens, I'm going to see to it that you drink this cup."

Wang Ching, while holding his nose with one hand, managed to drink it off in one gulp.

"You crazy dog!" exclaimed Hsi-men Ch'ing. "If the young good-for-nothing doesn't drink, why should you force him to do so? There's still half a cup left over. Let Ch'un-hung drink it for him, after which he can clap his hands to keep time and sing some southern songs for us."

Hsi-men Ch'ing then went on to say, "Let's play a game of forfeits with Licentiate Wen. Whenever, in the course of the game, anyone has to pay a forfeit by drinking a cup of wine, he can sing to accompany it. That should make it more interesting."

Thereupon, he directed Wang Ching to fetch the dicebox and suggested that Licentiate Wen should start the game off.

"How could your pupil be so presumptuous?" said Licentiate Wen. "It would be more appropriate for the venerable Master Ying to do so."

He then went on to say, "May I enquire, venerable sir, what is your courtesy name?"

"My courtesy name is Nan-p'o, or Southern Slope," replied Ying Po-chüeh.

"Venerable sir," said Hsi-men Ch'ing, with tongue in cheek, "let me explain it to you. His wife takes on such a large number of customers that, at night, when it is time to empty the commode, there is so much shit in it that he is embarrassed to empty it anywhere close by and has a maidservant lug it all the way to the southern edge of the city and dump it underneath the wall of the district granary. That is the origin of his courtesy name, Nan-p'o, or Southern Slop."

Licentiate Wen laughed, saying, "That is a different character pronounced p'o, which is composed of the water radical on the left and the character fa, or 'to transmit,' on the right. The *p'o* character he means is composed of the earth radical on the left and the character *p'i*, or 'skin,' on the right."

"Venerable sir," said Hsi-men Ch'ing, "you've deciphered it correctly. His wife is besieged by skinheads all day long."

"How can you bring yourself to say such a thing?" laughed Licentiate Wen.

"You may not be aware of it, sir," said Ying Po-chüeh, "but he has forever been adept at offending other people."

"It has always been true," opined Licentiate Wen, "that:

      Language which is not off-color fails to amuse."

"Venerable sir," said Ying Po-chüeh, "you're interrupting our game of forfeits. What's the point of arguing with him? He's forever given to:

      Hurting other people with his shitty mouth,[18]

so why pay any attention? There's no need to make excuses for him."

"Well then," said Licentiate Wen, "whatever number comes up when you throw the die, you must quote a line, whether it be from a poem, a lyric, a song, or a rhapsody, in which the word 'snow' occurs in the position corresponding to the number you have thrown. If you come up with an appropriate quote, you must drink a small cup of wine. If you fail to come up with one, you must drink a large cup of wine."

Thereupon, Licentiate Wen threw a one-spot and said, "I've got a line:

Snow has melted off the water birds
    for some time now."[19]

He then passed the dicebox to Ying Po-chüeh, who threw a five-spot.

Ying Po-chüeh, after pondering for what seemed like half a day and coming up blank, said, "I can't think of anything for the life of me."

After a further interval, he said, "I've finally managed to dredge something up:

Snow-clad plum blossoms[20] in snow
    are blooming.[21]

How will that do?"

"Venerable sir," said Licentiate Wen, "you've committed an error by introducing the word 'snow' twice. There's a redundant occurrence of the word 'snow' at the head of your line."

"The initial instance refers only to light snow," explained Ying Po-chüeh, "whereas the second instance denotes a heavy snow."

"You dog!" Hsi-men Ch'ing exclaimed. "All you ever do is talk nonsense."

He then told Wang Ching to pour him a large goblet of wine, while Ch'un-hung, clapping his hands to keep time, sang a southern song to the tune "Stopping the Horse to Listen":

On this cold night, needing some tea,
I plod toward the village ahead
   in search of an inn.
This snow lightly sprinkles the monks' quarters,
While densely bespattering the sing-song houses,[22]
And distantly delaying the homebound watercraft.
Along the riverbank people seize the chance
   to admire the plum blossoms;
Within their courtyards they enjoy the scene
   while burning silver candles.
As far as the eye can see,[23]
As far as the eye can see,
Like the willow catkins at the Pa River Bridge,[24]
It fills the sky as it flutters down.[25]

Ying Po-chüeh was about to take up his forfeit of wine to drink when whom should they see but Lai-an, who came in from the rear compound carrying several saucers of snacks for them to eat. These included a saucer of stuffed pastries, a saucer of cream puff pastries, a saucer of baked chestnuts, a saucer of sun-dried dates, a saucer of hazelnut kernels, a saucer of melon seeds, a saucer of snow pears, a saucer of apples, a saucer of dried caltrops, a saucer of water chestnuts, a saucer of butterfat "abalone shell" sweets, and a saucer of black spherical dumplings wrapped in orange leaves. When Ying Po-chüeh picked one of these up and smelled it, he found that it exuded a pungent fragrance, and when he put it in his mouth, it tasted like a mixture of malt sugar and honey, being fine-textured, sweet, and delicious, but he couldn't identify it.

"Why don't you take a guess?" said Hsi-men Ch'ing.

"They must be sugared torreya nuts?" Ying Po-chüeh ventured.

"Sugared torreya nuts don't taste nearly as good as that," declared Hsi-men Ch'ing.

"I would have said they were sugared plum bonbons," said Ying Po-chüeh, "were it not that they have kernels."

"You dog!" said Hsi-men Ch'ing. "Come over here and let me tell you. You wouldn't arrive at the right answer even in your wildest dreams. These were brought to me the other day by one of my employees on the boat from Hang-chou. They are called 'coated plums.' They consist of red bayberries, covered with a paste of distilled medicinal spices and honey, with an outer coating of peppermint, and wrapped in orange leaves. That's why they have such a pleasing flavor. If you let one dissolve in your mouth first thing in the morning every day, it will engender saliva, strengthen the lungs, eliminate bad breath, reduce phlegm, relieve hangovers, and control the appetite. They are much superior to sugared plum bonbons."

"If you hadn't told me," said Ying Po-chüeh, "how could I have known?"

He then turned to Licentiate Wen and said, "Venerable sir, let's each have another one, shall we?"

After which, he said to Wang Ching, "Fetch a sheet of paper, so I can wrap up two of them to take home for my wife."

He also picked up one of the "abalone shell" sweets and said to Cheng Ch'un, "Were these 'abalone shell' sweets really prepared personally by your sister Ai-yüeh?"

Cheng Ch'un knelt down and said, "You don't mean to suggest that I would dare tell a lie do you? I don't know how much care my sister Ai-yüeh devoted to preparing these few samples in order to show her filial respect for His Honor."

"Thanks to her skill," said Ying Po-chüeh, "she's twisted each of their surfaces into the spiral shape of a snail shell, and made two kinds, one pink, and one white."

"When I see these things," said Hsi-men Ch'ing, "I can't help feeling sore at heart. The late Sixth Lady was the only member of my household that could make these sweets, and now that she's dead there's no one left who knows how to make them."

"Did I not say earlier," remarked Ying Po-chüeh, "that I have no cause for regret? Having lost one daughter who was adept at making these 'abalone shell' sweets in order to show her filial respect for me, another daughter who knows how to make them has turned up. You're amazingly gifted at finding such people, and they all turn out to be real stunners, to boot."

This caused Hsi-men Ch'ing to:

Laugh until the slits of his eyes disappeared,

and he went after Ying Po-chüeh and gave him a playful slap, saying, "You Dog! All you ever do is talk nonsense."

"You two venerable gentlemen," remarked Licentiate Wen, "are certainly on as intimate terms as you can get."

"Venerable sir," said Ying Po-chüeh, "you may not know it, but he's just like a member of your humble nephew's family."

"In fact," said Hsi-men Ch'ing, "I've been a regular customer of his establishment for twenty years."

When Ch'en Ching-chi saw that the two of them were getting increasingly indecent with each other, he got up and went away, while Licentiate Wen merely covered his mouth with his hand and laughed.

Before long, Ying Po-chüeh finished off the large goblet of wine, and it was Hsi-men Ch'ing's turn to throw the dice.

Thereupon, when his throw ended up with seven spots, after pondering for what seemed like half a day, he said, "I've come up with a quote from a song to the tune 'A Girdle of Fragrant Silk,'" and proceeded to sing it:

Spring is taking flight;
Pear blossoms are like snow.[26]

"You've committed an error," said Ying Po-chüeh. "The word 'snow' is in the ninth position rather than the seventh. You'll have to drink a large goblet of wine."

Thereupon, he filled a chased silver goblet to overflowing and placed it in front of Hsi-men Ch'ing, telling Ch'un-hung to sing, and challenging him by asking, "My child:

> If you saw that date pit in your stomach to pieces,
> How many pieces can you ever hope to come up with?"[27]

Ch'un-hung responded by clapping his hands to keep time and singing to the same tune:

On all sides dark clouds are hovering,
When I look around me, the rivers and mountains
  stretch to the horizon.
This snow is as light as willow catkins,[28]
As fine as goose down,
And whiter than plum blossoms.
The twisting paths on the hillside
  become even muddier;
The insipid wine in the villages
  becomes more costly.
Heavenly flowers flutter down in profusion,
Heavenly flowers flutter down in profusion.
The moats are leveled, the ditches are full;
It is enough to make one sigh in amazement.[29]

As they were enjoying their drinking bout, evening arrived, and candles were lighted.

When Hsi-men Ch'ing had finished drinking his penalty cup, Ying Po-chüeh said, "Since your son-in-law is no longer here, it is the turn of the venerable gentleman Licentiate Wen to finish the game."

Licentiate Wen, accordingly, took up the dicebox and threw a one-spot. After thinking for a while, he noticed that there was a pair of framed hanging scrolls on the wall of the studio, on which a couplet was inscribed in gold-flecked characters, that read:

> Wind ruffles the flaccid willows beside the
>   level bridge at eventide;
> Snow sprinkles the cold plum blossoms in the
>   small court at springtime.[30]

So he quoted the second line of the couplet.

"That doesn't count. That doesn't count," objected Ying Po-chüeh. "It's not something you came up with out of your own mind. You'll have to drink a large goblet of wine."

Ch'un-hung, accordingly, proceeded to fill the goblet for him. Licentiate Wen:

Could not handle the effects of the drink,

but found himself dozing off on his chair, and asked to be excused. Ying Po-chüeh was unable to persuade him to stay.

"That's enough. That's enough," said Hsi-men Ch'ing. "The venerable gentleman is a man of culture and is not accustomed to carousing."

He then turned to Hua-t'ung and said, "You take good care of Master Wen, and escort him across the street to get some rest."

This was just the signal Licentiate Wen had been waiting for, and he said goodbye and departed.

"It seems that Wen Pi-ku is not up to it today," opined Ying Po-chüeh. "How much wine did he have, after all, before getting drunk like that?"

Thereupon, after drinking together for some time more, Ying Po-chüeh got up to go, saying, "It's dark underfoot, and I've had enough to drink."

He then went on to say, "Brother, be sure to have Tai-an deliver that letter on his behalf first thing tomorrow morning."

"Weren't you aware of it?" said Hsi-men Ch'ing. "I've already given him the letter and told him to deliver it tomorrow morning."

When Ying Po-chüeh lifted aside the portiere and saw that the sky was dark and the ground was slippery, he asked for a lantern and set off together with Cheng Ch'un. Hsi-men Ch'ing gave Cheng Ch'un five mace of silver for himself and also put a canister of "coated plums" in the box that he had brought with him, for him to take back and present to his elder sister Cheng Ai-yüeh.

As they were on their way out the door, Hsi-men Ch'ing joked with Ying Po-chüeh, saying, "See that you two brethren take good care of each other."

"You're wasting your breath," responded Ying Po-chüeh.

"When a father and son hike together,
    It's a case of each man for himself.[31]

I might just as well go now and have a word with that little whore, Cheng Ai-yüeh."

As he finished speaking, Ch'in-t'ung escorted them out the gate.

Hsi-men Ch'ing, having watched while the utensils were cleared away, leaned for support on Lai-an, who held a lantern for him as they went through the postern gate. As they passed by the door of P'an Chin-lien's quarters, he saw that the side gate was closed and silently made his way past it to the gate of Li P'ing-erh's quarters, where he proceeded to rap gently at the door. Hsiu-ch'un opened the door to let him in, and Lai-an then went back out of the garden.

When Hsi-men Ch'ing entered the parlor, he saw Li P'ing-erh's portrait and asked if the daily offering of soup and rice had been presented before it, or not.

Ju-i then came out and replied to his question, saying, "The maidservants and I just finished presenting it."

Hsi-men Ch'ing then went into the bedroom and sat down on a chair, while Ying-ch'un served him with tea, after which, he asked her to help him undress.

Ju-i, realizing that he intended to spend the night there, hastily proceeded to spread out the bedding and heat the quilt by inserting a hot-water bottle until it was good and warm, whereupon, she helped him into bed. Hsiu-ch'un locked the postern gate, and the three of them then laid out their bedding on wooden benches in the parlor and prepared to go to sleep.

When Hsi-men Ch'ing called for another serving of tea, the two maidservants, who understood the state of affairs, encouraged the wet nurse to go inside and sleep with him. The woman, accordingly, took off her clothes and burrowed her way under his quilt. Hsi-men Ch'ing, exhilarated by the wine he had drunk, took a dose of the aphrodisiac and fastened the clasp on his member. The woman then lay faceup on the k'ang, raised her legs, and allowed him to peg away at her for all he was worth. Slamming away at her recklessly, he kept it up until:

> The tip of her tongue became ice-cold, and
> Her vaginal fluids began to overflow,[32]

while she called out "Daddy" incessantly. In the quiet of the night the noise that they made could be heard several houses away.

When Hsi-men Ch'ing saw that the woman's flesh was as soft as cotton wadding, he embraced her with both arms and then directed her to squat down under the quilt and suck his cock. There was nothing the woman would not debase herself to do in ministering to his pleasure.

"My child," said Hsi-men Ch'ing, "it turns out that the flesh of your body is every bit as fair as that of your late mistress. When I embrace you, it feels just the way it did when I slept with her. If you try your best to cater to me, I will look after you."

"It hardly needs saying, Father," the woman replied, "but, how can you compare Heaven to Earth? You'll be the death of me yet. How can I be compared to my mistress in any way? Seeing that your servant's husband is already dead, whenever the spirit moves you, early or late, if you don't reject me for my homeliness, all you have to do is tip me a wink, and I'll be at your service."

"How old are you?" Hsi-men Ch'ing went on to ask.

"Since I was born in the year of the hare," the woman replied, "this year I'm thirty years old."

"It turns out then," said Hsi-men Ch'ing, "that you're a year younger than I am."

He was impressed by the fact that she was both glib with her tongue and fond of the pillow-top game of breeze and moonlight.

The next morning, when it was time to get up, the woman got out of bed first in order to minister to him by fetching his shoes and socks, and helping with his morning ablutions.

> Catering to him with the utmost assiduity,
> she succeeded in putting Ying-ch'un and Hsiu-ch'un in the shade.

She also made a request of Hsi-men Ch'ing, saying, "I'd like to have a piece of pale green pongee to make into a jacket so that I can wear mourning for my mistress."

Hsi-men Ch'ing agreed to everything she asked, sending a servant to get three lengths of pale green pongee from the shop, and saying, "Each of the three of you can make a mourning garment for yourselves."

As a result of this night together, having had two or three encounters with her, Hsi-men Ch'ing's heart was moved, and, behind Yüeh-niang's back, he began to supply her with silver, clothing, and jewelry, in fact, there was nothing he refused her.

The next day, when P'an Chin-lien learned that Hsi-men Ch'ing had spent the night in Li P'ing-erh's quarters sleeping with the wet nurse, Ju-i, she went straight to the rear compound and said to Yüeh-niang, "Elder Sister, you'd better have something to say to that lousy shameless good-for-nothing of ours. Yesterday, he made his way surreptitiously into her quarters next door and spent the night with that woman, the wet nurse. He is just like someone whose:

Hungry eyes have alighted on a melon skin.

What kind of a good-for-nothing is he, to pick up whatever comes his way, no matter whether it be good or bad:

Neither light nor dark?[33]

In the future, if she should produce a child, whose would it be? She'll be just like Lai-wang's wife was:

Assuming privileges above her station.

What kind of a spectacle would that create?"

"All you seem bent on doing," said Yüeh-niang, "is to get me to do the dirty work of accusing him of having an affair with the servant woman of his deceased lady, while you play the role of an innocent bystander behind my back. Do you think you can simply:

Put a water crock over my head?

What sort of a fool do you take me for? If you want to take him to task, go ahead and do it. I'm not going to get myself involved in your idle undertakings."

When Chin-lien heard Yüeh-niang's response, she did not have another word to say, but simply went back to her quarters.

Hsi-men Ch'ing got up early that morning and, seeing that the weather was clear, proceeded to dispatch Tai-an on his errand to deliver the letter to Secretary Ch'ien Lung-yeh's office. After he had gone to the yamen and returned home, P'ing-an came inside and reported that the messenger from Chai Ch'ien's place had come back to pick up his reply.

After giving him the letter, Hsi-men Ch'ing went on to ask, "How come you didn't come back to pick it up yesterday?"

"Your humble servant," the messenger replied, "had to deliver another letter to His Honor Hou Meng, the grand coordinator of Shantung province, and was held up for two days."

When he finished speaking, he took the letter and went out the gate.

After eating a meal, Hsi-men Ch'ing went over to the house across the street to supervise the weighing out of the silver, the packing up, and the writing out of the statement of account, so that on the twenty-fourth he could burn propitiatory paper money and send off the managers, Han Tao-kuo, Ts'ui Pen, and Lai-pao, along with the young men, Jung Hai and Hu Hsiu, the five of them, on their expedition to the South. He also saw to the writing of a letter to be delivered by them to Miao Ch'ing, thanking him for his lavish presents.

By the twenty-fifth or twenty-sixth day of the month, Hsi-men Ch'ing had finished paying the personal visits to relatives and friends to thank them for their condolences during the funerary rites for Li P'ing-erh.

One morning, as he was sitting in the master suite after eating his breakfast, Yüeh-niang said to him, "The first day of the coming month is the birthday of our kinsman Ch'iao Hung's daughter Chang-chieh. We really ought to buy something in the way of a gift and have it sent over there. As the saying goes:

A betrothal, once made, should not be altered.

We ought not to cease extending these courtesies merely because our son in dead."

"Of course we should send something," agreed Hsi-men Ch'ing.

Thereupon, he told Lai-hsing to buy two roast geese, a set of pig's trotters, four fresh chickens, two smoked ducks, a platter of birthday noodles, an outfit of figured satin clothing, two gold lamé handkerchiefs, and a box of costume jewelry. When this had been done, he wrote a note to accompany them and had Wang Ching deliver them.

When he had finished taking care of this, Hsi-men Ch'ing went out to the garden in the front compound and sat down in his studio in the Hidden Spring Grotto. Who should appear at this juncture but Tai-an, who had come back after delivering the letter to report on his errand.

"His Honor Ch'ien Lung-yeh," he said, "on seeing your note, immediately wrote a letter and sent one of his functionaries to accompany me and Huang the Fourth's son to deliver it to Assistant Commissioner Lei Ch'i-yüan at the office of the Shantung Military Defense Circuit in Tung-ch'ang prefecture. His Honor, in turn, dispatched an order requesting Prefectural Judge T'ung to forward to him the documents in the case, along with the defendants, so that he could conduct a new hearing of the case. As a result, Sun Ch'ing, as well as his son Sun Wen-hsiang, have been exonerated. The latter has been assessed the sum of ten taels of silver to pay for the burial expenses of the deceased and has only been charged with the crime of manslaughter, for which the penalty of seventy strokes with the heavy bamboo is redeemable for a cash payment. I then had to return to the customs house in order to report back to His Honor Ch'ien Lung-yeh, and obtain a reply from him, before I could come home."

When Hsi-men Ch'ing saw how competently Tai-an had performed his task, he was delighted. When he opened the reply, he found that Assistant Commissioner Lei Ch'i-yüan's note in reply to Ch'ien Lung-yeh was also included, and read as follows:

> Your behest has already been fully complied with. In view of the fact that Feng the Second had previously beaten his son, and that, moreover, both his son and Sun Wen-hsiang had sustained injuries as a result of their affray, and that the ensuing death of his son took place after the period of responsibility for the crime had already expired, to sentence Sun Wen-hsiang to the death penalty would hardly be equitable. It has therefore been adjudged that the defendant shall be assessed the sum of ten taels of silver to compensate Feng the Second for his burial expenses, and the appropriate measures have already been carried out.
>
> Respectfully indited in reply.
>
> Your devoted fellow graduate Lei Ch'i-yüan humbly salutes you.

When Hsi-men Ch'ing had finished reading this document he was very pleased and went on to ask, "Where is Huang the Fourth's father-in-law now?"

"Upon being released, they have both gone home," replied Tai-an. "Tomorrow, he will come with Huang the Fourth in order to kowtow in gratitude to you. Huang the Fourth's father-in-law also gave me a tael of silver."

"You can keep it to buy shoes for yourself," said Hsi-men Ch'ing.

Upon this, Tai-an kowtowed and went out.

Hsi-men Ch'ing then sprawled out on the k'ang frame and went to sleep, while Wang Ching lit some incense in a small burner on the table and then quietly made his way out of the room.

After some time, Hsi-men Ch'ing suddenly heard the sound of someone lifting aside the portiere, when whom should he see but Li P'ing-erh abruptly entering the room. She was dressed in a violet blouse over a white damask skirt:

> Her raven locks were carelessly coiled,

and her complexion was sallow.

Advancing up to the bed, she cried out, "My Brother, you're asleep here, are you? I've come to pay you a visit. That wretch has lodged a formal complaint against me, as a result of which I have been locked up in prison, where:

> I am dripping with blood,[34]

befouled by my own filth, and have been suffering torments all this time. But the other day, as a result of the appeal you lodged with the court on my behalf, the charges against me have been reduced by three degrees. That wretch, however, adamantly refuses to accept this verdict and is angrily determined to file a complaint against you, and have you taken into custody. I wouldn't have come to tell you about this, but I feared that, sooner or later, you might find yourself the unexpected victim of his venomous skullduggery. Right now, I am going to look for a place of refuge for myself. You had better be on your guard. If you are not obliged to, try to avoid going out drinking at night, and, wherever you do go, come home early. Whatever happens, keep my words firmly in mind, and don't forget them."

When she had finished speaking, the two of them embraced each other and then burst out crying.

"Sister," said Hsi-men Ch'ing, "Tell me where it is that you are going."

But, suddenly, she broke away from him with a jerk, revealing it to be but:

A dream of the Southern Branch.[35]

When Hsi-men Ch'ing awoke from his dream, he found himself to be weeping. Upon seeing the shadows of the blind that pervaded the studio, he realized that it was already noon. When he recollected the dream, he couldn't help feeling sorely distressed at heart. Truly:

When the blossoms fall and are buried in the earth
    their fragrance is not perceptible;
The mirror is void of the image of the phoenix mate[36]
    when he first awakes from his dream.

There is a poem that testifies to this:

The dwindling snow, having just cleared,
    illuminates the paper window;
The embers in the brazier have burnt out,
    and cold penetrates the couch.
The lovers, having chanced to encounter
    each other in a lovelorn dream;
Wind wafts the fragrance of plum blossoms
    inside the drapery of the bed.[37]

Who could have anticipated that, in response to the presents that had been sent to the Ch'iao household that morning, Ch'iao Hung's wife sent Ch'iao T'ung to deliver a card inviting Yüeh-niang and her sister wives to a party? When the page boy told them that Hsi-men Ch'ing was asleep in his studio, no one dared to disturb him, and Yüeh-niang merely decided to entertain Ch'iao T'ung, for the time being, in the rear compound.

"Give me that card," said P'an Chin-lien. "Let me go ask him what to do about it."

Thereupon, she abruptly proceeded out to his studio. She was wearing a blouse of jet satin that opened down the middle, had a diapered border with purfled gold lamé edging, and was adorned with a row of five gold buttons decorated with a three rivers pattern. Underneath this she wore an overskirt of

Li P'ing-erh Describes Her Intimate Feelings in a Dream

light silk, above an underskirt of Lu-chou silk with a gold-spangled border, fastened in front with a girdle of communion,[38] braided out of mermaid silk, and displaying the motif of a pair of amorous water birds. On her feet, the upturned points of her golden lotuses peeked out beneath her red brocade ankle leggings. On her head, her cloudy locks were enclosed in a chignon. Altogether, she was made up as if:

Modeled in plaster, carved of jade,

while from her ears there dangled a pair of pendant onyx earrings.

Pushing open the door of his studio and finding Hsi-men Ch'ing sprawled on the k'ang frame, she proceeded to park her posterior on a chair, saying, "My child, what are you doing here, talking to yourself all by your lonesome? No wonder you were nowhere to be seen. It turns out you've been here all the time, catching up on your sleep."

As she spoke, she cracked melon seeds with her teeth.

She then went on to ask Hsi-men Ch'ing, "How come you've been rubbing your eyes until they're all red?"

"I must have fallen asleep on my face," said Hsi-men Ch'ing.

"Actually," said the woman, "it looks more as if you've been crying."

"You crazy slave!" protested Hsi-men Ch'ing. "Why should I have been crying for no good reason?"

"It seems more likely to me," said Chin-lien, "that you've happened to remember something about someone who is uppermost in your mind."

"Don't talk such nonsense," said Hsi-men Ch'ing. "Who could there be who is either uppermost or undermost in my mind?"

"Li P'ing-erh is uppermost in your mind," said Chin-lien, "and her wet nurse is undermost in your mind, while the rest of us are completely outside your mind, not even worth taking into account."

"You crazy little whore!" protested Hsi-men Ch'ing. "You're indulging once again in your:

Ridiculous blatherskite."

He then went on to inquire, "What I say to you now is serious. On that earlier occasion, when you were dressing your sister Li in her burial clothes, what kind of garments did you put on the lower part of her body?"

"Why do you ask?" responded Chin-lien.

"For no particular reason," said Hsi-men Ch'ing. "I just thought I'd ask."

"There must be a reason behind your asking," said Chin-lien. "On the outside, she was dressed in two outfits of satin brocade, underneath which she wore a white satin jacket and a skirt of yellow pongee, over a purple satin camisole, a petticoat of white pongee, and a pair of scarlet underdrawers."

Hsi-men Ch'ing responded by nodding his head in recognition.

"Do you suppose," Chin-lien remarked, "that:

After practicing veterinary medicine for twenty years,

I would fail to diagnose the stomach ailment of an ass?

If you weren't thinking of her, why should you ask?"

"I had just seen her in a dream," explained Hsi-men Ch'ing.

Chin-lien said:

"Dreams are produced by what is on your mind;[39]

Sneezes are induced by a tickle in your nose.[40]

Even though she's dead, you're still so preoccupied with her, it would seem that the rest of us no longer tickle your fancy. In the future, when we die, I fear, there will be no one to commemorate us. You're so preoccupied with her that your mind is in a daze."

Hsi-men Ch'ing stood up, reached out with one hand, embraced her by the neck, and gave her a kiss, saying as he did so, "You crazy little oily mouth! You've certainly got:

A sharp mouth and a sharp tongue,

don't you?"

"My son," responded Chin-lien, "do you really think this old mother of yours is oblivious to the fact that:

You may be a brown cat, but you've got a black tail?"

As she spoke, she transferred the mouthful of melon seeds she had been cracking from her mouth into his. The two of them then fell to sucking each other's tongues for a while, until he became aware that:

Her sweet spittle transfused his heart,[41]

Her scented lips were imbued with rouge, and

The odor of orchid and musk from her body

assailed his senses.

Thereupon, Hsi-men Ch'ing's:

Lecherous desires were suddenly aroused.

Pulling her onto the bed where he was sitting, he leaned against the comb-back-shaped back rest, exposed his organ, and told the woman to indulge him by "toying with the flute." The woman then actually proceeded to:

Bend low her powdered neck, and

Engulf and release it with her mouth.

As she moved back and forth:

The sound of her sucking was audible.

When Hsi-men Ch'ing noticed that her head was adorned with a gold tiger-shaped tiara, her fragrant tresses were studded all round with plum-blossom-shaped ornaments with kingfisher feather inlays, and the hair behind her temples was embellished with a profusion of pearl headgear, he could hardly contain his excitement.

Just as they were approaching their climax, they suddenly heard Lai-an, from outside the portiere, saying, "Master Ying the Second is here."

"Invite him to come in," said Hsi-men Ch'ing.

This threw the woman into such consternation that she called out inarticulately, "Lai-an, you louse! Don't you let him come in until I've had a chance to get out of the way."

"He's already come in," said Lai-an, "and is waiting in the little courtyard."

"Why don't you go tell him to stay out of the way?" said the woman.

Lai-an, accordingly, went out and said to him, "Master Two, you'd better get out of the way for the time being. There's someone in the room with him."

Ying Po-chüeh then went out beside the juniper hedge, where he could contemplate the sight of the bamboos, embellished as they were with snow. Wang Ching lifted aside the portiere, and all that could be heard was a swish of her skirts as Chin-lien disappeared in a puff of smoke on her way back to the rear compound. Truly:

> Concealed by the snow, the presence of the egrets
>   is not seen until they fly;
> Hidden by the willows, the existence of the parrots
>   is not known until they speak.

Ying Po-chüeh then went inside, greeted Hsi-men Ch'ing with a bow, and sat down.

"How come you haven't been around the last few days?" asked Hsi-men Ch'ing.

"Brother," said Ying Po-chüeh, "I've been stuck at home, where things have been as aggravating as can be."

"What's been aggravating you?" asked Hsi-men Ch'ing. "Tell me about it."

"It's embarrassing to have to explain it," said Ying Po-chüeh. "The fact is, I'm short of money at home right now. Yesterday, that concubine of mine went and produced another child for no good reason. It's possible for a person to cope with such contingencies by daylight, but it happened during the third watch in the middle of the night. My wife is incapacitated, suffering from:

> Seven pains and eight ailments,

so I had to crawl out of bed, collect the necessary absorbent grass paper and bedding, check on how the mother was doing, and then go out to find the midwife. On top of everything else, Ying Pao was not at home, my elder brother having sent him out to his country estate to bring back some fodder. Not having anyone else at hand in this emergency, I had to take a lantern and go off myself to engage Midwife Teng, who lives at the mouth of the alley. By the time she came through the door, the baby was already born."

"What was the sex of the child?" asked Hsi-men Ch'ing.

"She gave birth to a baby boy," replied Ying Po-chüeh.

"You silly dog!" exclaimed Hsi-men Ch'ing. "If she's produced a son for you, isn't that a good thing? What have you got to be annoyed about? Was it that slave of yours, Ch'un-hua, who gave birth to him?"

"It was, indeed, your sister-in-law Ch'un-hua," Ying Po-chüeh responded with a laugh.

"That lousy bitch of a leg-waggling slave!" said Hsi-men Ch'ing. "Whoever recommended that you take her on in the first place? And now you're complaining simply because you had to go looking for the midwife."

"Brother," said Ying Po-chüeh, "you don't understand the situation. During these cold winter months, our situation is not to be compared with that of well-to-do households like yours. You not only have plenty of money, but also hold an official position with prospects of future advancement, so that, if a son is born to you, it is just like:

Adding a flower to a piece of brocade.[42]

No wonder you are happy. Whereas, right now, I've got one shadow too many as it is. And I've got to provide food and clothing for that nestful of people in my household. On top of which, for the last several days, I've been driven out of my mind by matchmaking problems. Ying Pao is tied up every day with his corvée labor obligations, and my elder brother, for his part, doesn't pay any attention to my problems. Although my eldest daughter has been married off, thanks to Heaven above, as well as the assistance you rendered, Brother, as you have seen with your own eyes, my second daughter is growing up and will be twelve years old next year. Yesterday, a matchmaker came and asked for a card giving the year, month, day, and hour of her birth. I said it was early days yet and told her to hold off for the time being. It was really driving me to distraction, and then, all of a sudden, in the middle of the night, this new karmic encumbrance turned up. When one has to:

Grope one's way in the dark of night,[43]

where can one go to convert anything into ready cash? When my wife saw the state of perturbation I was in:

For lack of any alternative option,[44]

she took one of her silver stick-pins and gave it to the midwife in order to settle the matter. Tomorrow is the time for the third day lustration ceremony,[45] so everyone in the neighborhood will find out about it. When it comes time for the full-month celebration,[46] where am I going to find the wherewithal to pay for it. When the day comes, I guess I'll have to vacate the house, make myself:

As free as you please,

and go off to stay at some Buddhist monastery for a few days."

"If you do make yourself scarce," laughed Hsi-men Ch'ing, "you'll only open the way for one of the monks to take your place in the warm bedding. You dog! When you get right down to it, all you ever care about is gaining petty advantages for yourself."

He continued to laugh at his expense, but Ying Po-chüeh only made a deliberate pout with his lips, and remained silent.

"My son," said Hsi-men Ch'ing, "don't be so annoyed. How much silver do you need? If you just tell me, I'll take care of it for you."

"Who knows how much it will take?" said Ying Po-chüeh.

"You'll need enough to take care of things satisfactorily," said Hsi-men Ch'ing. "And if you find yourself short in the midst of things, you can always go pawn some of your clothes, after all."

"Brother," said Ying Po-chüeh, "if you deign to help me out, twenty taels of silver ought to suffice. I'll write a promissory note for you on the spot. I'm putting you to so much trouble and expense that I've found it difficult to broach the subject. I wouldn't presume to quibble over the amount. Whatever you decide, Brother, will be fine by me."

Hsi-men Ch'ing refused to accept his promissory note, saying, "Don't talk such rot! Among friends, who needs a promissory note?"

As they were speaking, whom should they see but Lai-an, who came in with a serving of tea.

"Put down those teacups," said Hsi-men Ch'ing to the servant, "and go tell Wang Ching to come here."

Before long, Wang Ching came in, and Hsi-men Ch'ing said to him, "You go back to the rear compound and tell the First Lady to look on top of the cabinet on the rear wall of the bedstead in the inner room for the two packets of silver that were provided by His Honor the regional investigating censor Sung Ch'iao-nien on the occasion of the banquet we put on for him the other day, and bring one of them back to me."

Wang Ching nodded his assent and was not gone for long before coming back with the silver.

Hsi-men Ch'ing handed it over to Ying Po-chüeh, saying, "This packet contains fifty taels of silver. You can take all of it and use whatever you need, thus sparing me the trouble of opening it, since:

The original seals have not been tampered with.[47]

You can open it and see for yourself, if you want."

"It's too much," said Ying Po-chüeh.

"If it's more than you need at the moment," said Hsi-men Ch'ing, "you can keep the remainder on hand. At present, seeing that your second daughter has reached marriageable age, you can use it to pay for the making of some shoes, footbindings, and clothing for her, so that she'll appear to advantage during the full-month celebration."

"Brother, what you say makes sense," said Ying Po-chüeh.

When he opened the packet of silver and saw that it did, indeed, contain the joint contributions made by the officials of the Two Provincial Offices and the eight prefectures, in ingots of three taels apiece of the highest grade of incised silver stamped with the mark of the Sung-chiang mint, he was utterly delighted.

Hastily bowing in thanks, he said, "Who could match Brother's magnanimous feelings? Are you really unwilling to accept my promissory note?"

"You silly child!" said Hsi-men Ch'ing. "Why should I treat you the way I would anyone else? After all, I'm in the position of your parent. Were that not the case, would you presume to come pester me over every problem that comes up? This child is not even your own child but may be considered the product of our joint efforts. The truth of the matter is that at the time of the full-month ceremony, if you should make that slave Ch'un-hua of yours available to serve me for a while in lieu of interest, it would not be asking too much of you."

"Your sister-in-law Ch'un-hua, these last few days," responded Ying Po-chüeh, "has become just as emaciated by the demands made upon her as your wife."

We will say no more at this point about the banter between the two of them in the studio.

Ying Po-chüeh then went on to ask, "What has happened with regard to that predicament of Huang the Fourth's father-in-law?"

Hsi-men Ch'ing, in giving him a complete account of Tai-an's mission, said, "Upon receiving Ch'ien Lung-yeh's letter, Assistant Commissioner Lei Ch'i-yüan dispatched an order requiring that the defendants in the case be sent back to his jurisdiction so that he could conduct a new hearing of the case, as a result of which he exonerated both Sun Wen-hsiang and his father Sun Ch'ing. Sun Wen-hsiang has been assessed the sum of ten taels of silver to cover the burial expenses of the deceased and has only been charged with the offense of manslaughter, for which the penalty of seventy strokes with the heavy bamboo is redeemable for a cash payment. Thus the matter has been brought to a successful conclusion."

"What a stroke of luck for him!" exclaimed Ying Po-chüeh. "If he had lit a lantern to look for help, where else could he have found anyone capable of doing him such a favor? If you persist in refusing to accept what he is offering you, that's up to you; but though you may not set much store by it yourself, it would be a good idea to keep it in order to compensate Ch'ien Lung-yeh. Don't let him off the hook. Whatever happens, you should get him to lay on a lavish drinking party somewhere in the licensed quarter and invite us to partake thereof. If you don't want to suggest it to him, I'll be happy to do so. You've prevented his brother-in-law from being charged with a capital offense, after all, which is not an inconsequential matter."

To resume our story, while they were talking in the studio, after Yüeh-niang in the master suite had located the silver and given it to Wang Ching to deliver, whom should she see but Meng Yü-lou, who came into the room and said that her younger brother, Meng Jui, was at her brother-in-law Han Ming-ch'uan's place.

"Right now," she went on to say, "he is planning to set out before long on an expedition to buy miscellaneous merchandise in Szechwan and the Hu-Kuang region and has come today to say goodbye to Father. He's sitting in my quarters. Wherever Father happens to be, Sister, could you send a page boy to let him know about it?"

He's in his studio in the garden, visiting with Ying Po-chüeh," said Yüeh-niang.

"As to inviting Father to come inside," she went on to say, "a while ago, Sister P'an the Sixth did a fine job on her mission of inviting him back here.

Ch'iao T'ung had delivered an invitation card and was waiting for a chance to speak to Father in order to get a verbal reply, so that we would know whether or not to prepare to go out tomorrow. I kept him here in the expectation of getting a response and served him with tea, but despite:

> Waiting for long periods as well as short,

Father never showed up, and when Ch'iao T'ung could endure it no longer, he got up and left. After what seemed like half a day, lo and behold, Sister Six came back from the front compound, and when I asked her if she had fulfilled her mission or not, she was at a loss for words, merely saying, 'Oops! I completely forgot to mention it to him, and, in a little while, Ying the Second came in and I had to leave. Who has the patience to:

> Stick around and wait forever,[48]

just for the chance to say a word to him? The card is still in my sleeve.' This caused me to say to her:

> 'When biting the stalk of a crisp vegetable,
> start with the root end.

Luckily it wasn't a matter of critical importance, but you've kept everybody waiting. You're just a good-for-nothing creature who lacks the tail to follow up with.' Who knows what she was up to out there that kept her from coming back inside for half a day, only to report that she hadn't remembered to say what she went for? After I had given her a piece of my mind, she took herself off to the front compound."

A little while later, Lai-an came in, and Yüeh-niang sent him to summon Hsi-men Ch'ing, saying, "Tell him that Brother-in-law Meng the Second is here."

Hsi-men Ch'ing then got up, but told Ying Po-chüeh to stay where he was, saying, "Don't you go anywhere. I'll be right back."

When he arrived in the rear compound, Yüeh-niang first told him that Ch'iao Hung's household had sent them an invitation.

"On the day in question," said Hsi-men Ch'ing, "You ought to go by yourself. While we are still in mourning, it would hardly be appropriate for the whole family to go."

"Brother-in-law Meng the Second has come to say goodbye to you," said Yüeh-niang. "He's planning to set out in the next day or two on an expedition to Szechwan and the Hu-Kuang region. He's sitting in his sister's quarters over there waiting to see you."

She then went on to ask, "A while ago, when you asked for that packet of silver, who did you want to give it to?"

Hsi-men Ch'ing explained the whole situation to her, saying, "Last night Brother Ying the Second's concubine Ch'un-hua gave birth to a son, and he asked me to loan him a few taels of silver. He also said that his second daughter had reached marriageable age and he was feeling as hard up as could be about the situation. So I decided to help out by lending him a few taels of silver."

"He's lucky enough, at his age, to finally beget a son," said Yüeh-niang. "His wife must be very happy about it. Tomorrow, we'll have to send them some rice for making congee."

"That goes without saying," said Hsi-men Ch'ing. "When the time comes for the full-month celebration, I'm not going to let that beggar off the hook, but put him to the trouble, no matter what, of issuing invitations to the lot of you to visit his home, where you can take a look at what sort of a woman Ch'un-hua is."

"In any case," laughed Yüeh-niang, "she's bound to resemble those in your own household in having a nose, and having eyes. How could she be any different?"

She then sent Lai-an to invite Brother-in-law Meng the Second to join them. It was not long before Meng Yü-lou and her younger brother came in to pay their respects. When they had done with the customary amenities, Hsi-men Ch'ing chatted with him for a while and then invited him to accompany him to his studio in the front compound, where he introduced him to Ying Po-chüeh. He also told a servant to fetch something to eat from the rear compound.

Thereupon, a table was set up, and wine and delicacies were laid out so that the three of them could have a drink together.

Hsi-men Ch'ing further instructed the servant, saying, "Fetch another wine goblet and pair of chopsticks, and go invite Master Wen from across the street to come and help keep Brother-in-law Meng the Second company.

Lai-an came back in a little while and reported, "Master Wen is not at home but has gone to visit Master Ni P'eng."

"Ask our son-in-law to join us then," said Hsi-men Ch'ing.

After some time, Ch'en Ching-chi came in, saluted Meng the Second with a bow, and sat down to one side.

Hsi-men Ch'ing questioned Meng Jui, saying, "Brother-in-law, when are you setting out on your expedition, and how long will you be gone?"

"I'm scheduled to set out on the second day of next month," replied Meng Jui, "but how long I'll be gone is impossible to say. I've got to go to Ching-chou to buy paper, and to Szechwan and the Hu-Kuang region to purchase incense and wax. When you get right down to it, it's likely to take no less than a year or two before I'll be able to purchase everything I need and return home. On this expedition I will take the overland route by way of Honan, Shensi, and Han-chou on the way out, and return on the water route by way of the Yangtze Gorges and Ching-chou. The round-trip will amount to seven or eight thousand li."

"How old are you, Mr. Meng?" asked Ying Po-chüeh.

"I'm twenty-five," replied Meng Jui.

"It's remarkable that someone as young as you are should be so familiar with the various routes on the rivers and lakes," said Ying Po-chüeh, "while people like myself have grown old in vain, sitting around at home."

Before long, a new serving of delicacies was brought in, and:

The cups and plates were duly arrayed.

Meng the Second remained drinking with them until the sun began to set in the West before he said goodbye and took his leave. Hsi-men Ch'ing saw him off and then came back to rejoin Ying Po-chüeh and drink a while longer.

Lo and behold, at this point, two coffers for burnt offerings to the dead were brought in, and Hsi-men Ch'ing told Ch'en Ching-chi to take charge of preparing them, and to ask Yüeh-niang for two outfits of Li P'ing-erh's brocade clothing, along with imitation gold and silver paper money, to put into the coffers.

He then said to Ying Po-chüeh, "Today is the date for the sixth weekly commemoration of Li P'ing-erh's death, and, rather than holding a scripture-reading ceremony, we are going to burn these two coffers for her."

"How swiftly time flies," said Ying Po-chüeh. "My sister-in-law has already been dead for a month and a half."

"The fifth day of the coming month," said Hsi-men Ch'ing, "is the time for the final weekly commemoration of her death. We will have to have a sutra reading for her then."

"So, on that occasion," said Ying Po-chüeh, "the recitation of a Buddhist sutra will suffice."

"My wife," said Hsi-men Ch'ing, "has reminded me that, while she was still alive, after the birth of her son, she promised two of the Buddhist nuns that frequent our household that they could preside, together with some other nuns that will be engaged for the purpose, over a recitation of the *Hsüeh-p'en ching*, or *Blood Pool Sutra*, and other litanies of repentance, on her behalf."

When Hsi-men Ch'ing had finished speaking, Ying Po-chüeh, observing that it was getting late, said, "I'd better be off, so that you can proceed with the ceremony of burning paper money for my sister-in-law."

He then made a deep bow and said, "As the unworthy recipient of Brother's profound generosity:

I will find it hard to forget either dead or alive."[49]

"My son," said Hsi-men Ch'ing, "whether you find it hard to forget or not, you'd better not pretend to be:

Still asleep in dreamland.

When it comes time for the full-month ceremony, your whole bevy of mothers will buy presents and show up at your place."

"What need is there for them to purchase gifts," said Ying Po-chüeh. "If I have to kowtow to each one of them, whatever happens, I would like to invite the entire group of my sisters-in-law to condescend to visit my humble household."

"When the day comes," said Hsi-men Ch'ing, "whatever happens, I hope you will get that slave of yours, Ch'un-hua, to doll herself up, and trot her out so I can take a look at her."

"Your sister-in-law Ch'un-hua," responded Ying Po-chüeh, "has remarked that now she has a son, she has no further use for you."

"That's enough of your lies," said Hsi-men Ch'ing. "When I see that slave, I'll know what to say to her."

Ying Po-chüeh, thereupon, nonchalantly took himself off with a laugh, while Hsi-men Ch'ing told the page boys to clear away the utensils and then went over to Li P'ing-erh's quarters.

Ch'en Ching-chi and Tai-an had already completed the task of preparing the coffers. That day, the Temple of the Jade Emperor, the Temple of Eternal Felicity, and the Temple of Kindness Requited had all sent over effigies to be burned at the ceremony. That from the Taoist temple was an effigy of the Perfected Lord of Precious Solemnity and Manifest Accomplishment,[50] while those from the two Buddhist temples were effigies of the Great King of Trans-formation who sits in judgment over the Sixth Court of the Tribunal of the Underworld.[51] The household of Brother-in-law Hua Tzu-yu outside the city gate sent a box of steamed dumplings and ten quires of paper money for the use of the dead, and the household of Wu K'ai did likewise.

Hsi-men Ch'ing looked on as Ying-ch'un put the offerings of soup and rice in place, with the steamed dumplings below them, and lit the incense and candles. He then sent Hsiu-ch'un back to the rear compound to invite Wu Yüeh-niang and the other ladies to join him. After Hsi-men Ch'ing had fin-ished burning the offering of paper money to Li P'ing-erh, he had the coffers carried out and deputed Ch'en Ching-chi to supervise their incineration out-side the front gate. But no more of this. Truly:

> Her fragrant soul has probably not perished
>   along with the dying ashes;
> But has gone to perpetuate its old affinity
>   in the incarnation to come.[52]

> If you want to know the outcome of these events,
> Pray consult the story related in the following chapter.

Chapter 68

CHENG AI-YÜEH FLAUNTS HER BEAUTY

AND DISCLOSES A SECRET;

TAI-AN PERSEVERES ASSIDUOUSLY IN

SEEKING OUT AUNTIE WEN

Snow buries the scattered red blossoms
    that have fallen overnight;
As day dawns, beyond the window blinds,
    it continues to blow about.
The numerous branches of emerald leaves
    vainly confront each other;
The myriad remnants of fragrant souls
    cannot be recalled to life.
Only the dream in the Ch'ang-lo Palace[1]
    relieves his spring sadness;
Once the fisherman of Wu-ling has left[2]
    even the waters are remote.
The sound of a jade flute perpetuates
    his lingering remorsefulness;
As it penetrates the window casement,
    propelled by the east wind.[3]

THE STORY GOES that after Hsi-men Ch'ing had finished the ceremony
of burning paper money on Li P'ing-erh's behalf, he went to P'an Chin-lien's
quarters, where he spent the night.

The next day, first, Ying Po-chüeh's household sent over a box of noodles in
celebration of their birth of a son, and then, Huang the Fourth, along with his
young brother-in-law, Sun Wen-hsiang, came to kowtow to Hsi-men Ch'ing,
bringing with them offerings of a newly slaughtered pig, a jug of wine, two
roast geese, four roast chickens, and two boxes of fruit.

Hsi-men Ch'ing repeatedly refused to accept these things, until Huang the
Fourth knelt down and groveled around on his knees, saying, "Your Honor has
done Sun Wen-hsiang:
    The favor of saving his life.
My entire family:
    Feels profoundly grateful to you.[4]

Now, we have nothing with which to express our filial respects but these few paltry gifts for Your Honor to give away to someone if you like. How can you refuse to accept them?"

After persisting in his refusal to accept the proffered gifts for what seemed like half a day, Hsi-men Ch'ing finally consented to accept only the pig and the wine, saying, "They will serve as well as anything else to send to His Honor Ch'ien Lung-yeh to thank him for his intervention on your behalf."

"In that case," said Huang the Fourth, "I will have no way of fully expressing what I only intended to be:

A token of my gratitude."

After reluctantly agreeing to take back the other proffered comestibles, he went on to ask, "When does Your Honor have any free time available? I have already consulted Uncle Ying the Second and would like to invite you to a party in the licensed quarter."

"You shouldn't pay any attention to his foolery," said Hsi-men Ch'ing. "It is only putting you to further expense. But the best time would be sometime during the New Year's celebrations."

At this juncture, Huang the Fourth and his young brother-in-law took their leave with:

A thousand thanks and ten thousand
expressions of gratitude,

while Hsi-men Ch'ing tipped the bearers that had brought the gifts and sent them on their way.

On the first day of the eleventh month, Hsi-men Ch'ing, after coming home from the office, went to attend a party hosted by the magistrate, Li Ta-t'ien, in the district yamen, while Yüeh-niang:

All by her solitary self,[5]

dressed herself in white mourning, got into a sedan chair, and went to celebrate Chang-chieh's birthday in the home of Ch'iao Hung. As a consequence, neither of them was at home.

That afternoon, Nun Hsüeh from the Lotus Blossom Nunnery, who had learned of Yüeh-niang's plan to arrange for her to engage the services of eight other nuns and come to the house on the fifth in order to preside over the final weekly commemoration of Li P'ing-erh's death, recite scriptures, and perform the litany of the *Blood Pool Sutra*, proceeded, while keeping Nun Wang in the dark, to buy two boxes of presents, and come to pay a call on Yüeh-niang.

Since Yüeh-niang was not at home, Li Chiao-erh and Meng Yü-lou invited her to stay for a cup of tea and said, "The First Lady is not here but has gone to the home of our kinsman Ch'iao Hung in order to celebrate their daughter Chang-chieh's birthday. You'd better stay until she comes home in order to see her. She wants to talk to you, and to pay you for the drafting of the petitions that will be needed for the observance in question."

Nun Hsüeh, consequently, continued to sit and wait.

P'an Chin-lien, meanwhile, happened to remember having been told by Yü-hsiao that Yüeh-niang had only been able to conceive after taking a fertility potion provided by Nun Hsüeh. Moreover, ever since the death of Li P'ing-erh, Hsi-men Ch'ing had continued to frequent her quarters, where he had established a liaison with the wet nurse. She was afraid that if the wet nurse should produce a child, she might succeed in usurping her favored position. As a result, she took the opportunity to invite Nun Hsüeh to accompany her to her quarters in the front compound, where there was no one else about, and surreptitiously appealed to her, offering her the inducement of a tael of silver, to concoct a fertility potion for her that would enable her to conceive, and, with this end in mind, to acquire for her the afterbirth of a firstborn male child. But no more of this.

That evening, when Yüeh-niang returned home, she invited Nun Hsüeh to stay overnight, and the next day she asked Hsi-men Ch'ing for five taels of silver and gave them to her to contract for the drafting of the ceremonial petitions. Nun Hsüeh, for her part, kept Nun Wang and the abbess of the Kuan-yin Nunnery in the dark, without saying a word to them about it.

On the fifth day of the month, together with the eight nuns she had engaged for the occasion, she proceeded to set up an altar in the summerhouse in the garden, post announcements on hanging scrolls at each of the doorways, preside over the recitation of the *Avatamsaka Sutra*,[6] the *Diamond Sutra*, and the litany of the *Blood Pool Sutra*, the scattering of paper flowers and rice, and the recitation of the *Sutra of the Names of the Thirty-five Buddhas*.[7] That evening, the ritual of distributing food in order to save the hungry ghosts with their burning mouths was performed.[8]

On this occasion, Wu K'ai's wife and Hua Tzu-yu's wife, along with the male guests Wu K'ai, Ying Po-chüeh, and Licentiate Wen, were invited to partake of the vegetarian repast. The nuns did not make an elaborate performance out of the rites, choosing merely to accompany themselves by striking the wooden fish and the hand chime as they recited the sutras.

That day, Ying Po-chüeh brought with him a servant from Huang the Fourth's household with an invitation for Hsi-men Ch'ing to attend a party at Cheng Ai-yüeh's establishment in the licensed quarter on the seventh day of the month, but when Hsi-men Ch'ing saw the invitation, he laughed and said, "I'm not free on the seventh since I have an engagement to attend a birthday party at the home of Chang Hsi-ts'un that day. But I am free tomorrow."

He then went on to ask, "Who else will be there?"

"He's not inviting anyone else," said Ying Po-chüeh, "other than myself and Brother Li the Third to keep you company. But he has gone to the trouble of engaging four girls to sing scenes from the *Hsi-hsiang chi*."

Hsi-men Ch'ing saw to it that Huang the Fourth's servant was given some vegetarian fare to eat and then sent him on his way.

Ying Po-chüeh then went on to ask, "That day, when Huang the Fourth came to thank you, what had he purchased in the way of presents?"

Hsi-men Ch'ing replied, thus and so, "I didn't accept all that he brought. He kowtowed to me repeatedly, but I only consented to accept the pig and the wine. After adding to these two bolts of silk decorated with a silver pheasant motif, two bolts of capital brocade, and fifty taels of silver, I sent them off to thank Ch'ien Lung-yeh for his intervention in the case."

"It would have been more than sufficient if you had refused to accept his silver," said Ying Po-chüeh. "After all, you certainly deserved it. Those four bolts of fabric must be worth thirty taels of silver, at the very least. Where could he have hoped to obtain such a favor for a mere twenty taels of silver? You're letting him off easy. After all, you saved his father-in-law's and brother-in-law's lives."

That day, they continued to chat together until evening before breaking up.

"You'll come by again tomorrow, won't you?" Hsi-men Ch'ing said to Ying Po-chüeh.

"I understand," replied Ying Po-chüeh as he took his leave.

The eight Buddhist nuns prolonged the fuss of their ritual performance until the middle of the first watch before concluding the ceremony, burning the coffers, and going on their way.

The next day, Hsi-men Ch'ing went off to the yamen in the morning.

To resume our story, when Nun Wang got wind of these events, she made her way to Hsi-men Ch'ing's house first thing in the morning, complained that Nun Hsüeh had usurped the privilege of putting on the ritual performance, and demanded her share of the fee.

Yüeh-niang took exception to this, saying, "Why didn't you show up yesterday? Nun Hsüeh said that you had gone to the home of that distaff relative of the imperial family, Wang the Second, to celebrate a birthday."

"That was just a trick on the part of that old whore of the Hsüeh family," said Nun Wang. "She told me that your household had changed the date and were not going to hold the scripture reading until the sixth. So she made off with the entire fee, leaving me with nothing at all."

"But, at this late date, you failed to take part in the rite," said Yüeh-niang, "and the fee for the performance and the drafting of the petitions has already been paid to her in full. Luckily, I still have a bolt of fabric on hand to compensate you with."

She then instructed Hsiao-yü, saying, "Quickly, serve up some of the vegetarian fare left over from yesterday for her to eat, and give her that bolt of blue cloth."

Nun Wang muttered to herself as she cursed, saying, "The old whore made off with a tidy amount of the Sixth Lady's silver behind my back while negotiating for the printing of those sutras. And it was originally agreed that the two of us should share the fee for this sutra-reading rite, but you've made off with the whole thing for yourself."

"Nun Hsüeh," remarked Yüeh-niang, "claims that you received five taels of silver from the Sixth Lady as compensation for the recitation of the *Blood Pool Sutra* on her behalf. How is it that you have failed to recite it for her?"

"On the occasion of the fifth weekly commemoration of her death," responded Nun Wang, "I arranged for four nuns to recite it, and they kept at it for half a month."

"If you did recite it," said Yüeh-niang, "why did you keep it to yourself, without mentioning it to me? If you had told me about it, I might have given you something more for your pains."

Nun Wang did not have another word to say but sat there in embarrassed silence for a while, before going off to Nun Hsüeh's place to have it out with her.

Gentle reader take note: black-clad Buddhist nuns of this ilk ought never to be patronized under any circumstances.

> Their faces may be like the faces of nuns,
> But their hearts are the hearts of whores.[9]

It is simply the case that:

> Their six senses are unpurified,
> Their basic natures are unclear,
> Their vows are entirely ignored,
> Their sense of shame is effaced.
> Though falsely boasting of their compassion,
> They are driven entirely by profit and lust.
> Ignoring karma and the wheel of transmigration,
> They think solely of the pleasure of the moment.
> Having inveigled the frustrated young maidens
>   of humbler households,[10]
> They set their sights on the susceptible wives
>   of prominent families.[11]
> At their front doors they welcome
>   benefactors and donors,
> At the back doors they dispose of
>   their unwanted fetuses.[12]
> When not promoting illicit liaisons,
> They are devising adulterous trysts.[13]

There is a poem that testifies to this:

> At Buddhist gatherings, monks and nuns
>   are the members of one family;[14]
> The wheel of the law turns unceasingly[15]
>   at the Dragon Flower Assembly.[16]

Yet creatures of this ilk are either
  preoccupied with procreation;[17]
Or the wrongful use of metal implements
  in order to effect abortions.[18]

To resume our story, when Hsi-men Ch'ing returned from the yamen, before he had even finished his meal, Ying Po-chüeh showed up.

Attired in a newly blocked satin cap, an aloeswood-colored tunic, and white-soled black boots, he bowed in greeting to Hsi-men Ch'ing and said, "It's already approaching noon, so we'd better be off. They have already sent a servant to urge us on our way more than once. We oughtn't to make things difficult for them."

"I think I'll invite Licentiate Wen to go with us," said Hsi-men Ch'ing, and, turning to Wang Ching, he said, "Go across the street and ask Master Wen to join us."

Wang Ching went off on this errand and returned before long, saying, "Master Wen is not at home but has gone out to visit a friend. Hua-t'ung has gone after him to extend the invitation."

"We ought not to wait for him," said Ying Po-chüeh. "These scholarly types carry on:
    As though they don't know any better.
If he's gone out to visit a friend, who knows when he'll show up? We ought not to let him spoil the occasion."

Hsi-men Ch'ing accordingly turned to Ch'in-t'ung and said, "Saddle up that sorrel horse for Master Ying the Second to ride."

"I don't wish to ride a horse," said Ying Po-chüeh. "It would be a good idea to keep a low profile, without:
    Ringing bells and beating drums.
I'll just go a step ahead of you, and you can come along at your leisure in a sedan chair."

"What you say makes sense," said Hsi-men Ch'ing. "You go on ahead of me."

Ying Po-chüeh then proceeded to raise his hand in farewell and set off first, while Hsi-men Ch'ing directed Tai-an, Ch'in-t'ung, and four orderlies to get ready a closed sedan chair and prepare to accompany him.

Just as he was about to go out the door, P'ing-an suddenly came in from outside in a state of obvious agitation, holding in his hand an accordion-bound calling card, and reported, "His Honor An Ch'en of the Ministry of Works is on his way to pay you a visit and has sent a functionary ahead to deliver a calling card. His Honor is right behind him and will be here any minute."

This threw Hsi-men Ch'ing into such a state of consternation that he ordered the servants to have some food prepared and sent Lai-hsing out to purchase platters of ready-made snacks for the occasion. After some time,

Secretary An Ch'en duly arrived, along with a sizable entourage, and Hsi-men Ch'ing, in formal attire, came out to receive him. The secretary was dressed in a figured round-collared robe emblazoned with a mandarin square featuring an egret in the clouds,[19] and a girdle with a decorative plaque that was both embossed and gilded. When he had entered the gate, and the customary exchange of salutations had taken place, they sat down in the positions of guest and host, while attendants served them with tea. Having finished their tea, they proceeded to a discussion of:

What had occurred since their last meeting.[20]

"Venerable Sir," said Hsi-men Ch'ing, "I very much regret to say that I have not yet had the chance to congratulate you on your illustrious promotion. The other day, when I received the elegant epistle and lavish gifts that you bestowed upon me, I was so busy with the funeral arrangements that I was unable to wait upon you in person, for which I can only apologize."

"Your pupil," said An Ch'en, "is guilty of failing to offer his condolences in person. Upon my arrival in the capital, I spoke to Chai Ch'ien about it, but I don't know whether you have received a gift from him, or not."

"It is the case," said Hsi-men Ch'ing, "that I have occasioned my kinsman Chai Ch'ien the trouble of sending a consolatory gift from a great distance."

"Ssu-ch'üan," said An Ch'en, "this year you yourself are sure to have an occasion for congratulation before long."

"Your humble servant," said Hsi-men Ch'ing, "is the possessor of slight ability and an insignificant office. How could I presume to hope for more than I deserve?"

"Venerable Sir," he continued, "this illustrious promotion to an important office that you have just received will provide you with the opportunity to further develop your:

Outstanding talent and bold vision.[21]

The success of your repair work on the Grand Canal is something:

The entire empire looks forward to."[22]

"Ssu-ch'üan," responded An Ch'en, "You do me too much honor. I am nothing but:

An insignificant Confucian scholar,[23]

who has been fortunate enough, by means of the examination system, to qualify for a humble post in the bureaucracy. It is thanks to the support of the venerable gentleman Ts'ai Ching that I occupy a position in the Ministry of Works and have undeservedly been made responsible for the irrigation and transportation system. For the past year I have been so busy traveling back and forth in the Hu-Hsiang region that:

Engaged upon the ruler's business,[24]

I have not had a minute's respite.

At present, I have also been ordered to take charge of the repair work on the Grand Canal, at a time, moreover, when:

The people are impoverished and finances are depleted.[25]
Recently, when the imperial vessels were engaged in the Flower and Rock
Convoys, they:

> Demolished the dikes and destroyed the embankments,
> Leaving nothing but a trail of havoc in their wake,

so that:

> Public and private resources are totally exhausted.[26]

At present, all along its route, in Kua-chou, Nan-wang, Ku-t'ou, Yü-t'ai,
Hsü-p'ei, Lü-liang, An-ling, Chi-ning, Su-ch'ien, and Lin-ch'ing, the Grand
Canal is in a state of disrepair. The southern branch of the Yellow River has
overflowed its banks and moved further south, silting up the canal to such an
extent that its bed is dry in places, leaving the populace of the eight prefectures
in dire straits. Moreover:

> Bandits interfere with the repair work, and
> Fiscal resources are utterly deficient,[27]

so that even if we were able to deploy:

> The power of gods or the art of ghosts,
> It would not avail to execute the task."[28]

"Venerable sir," said Hsi-men Ch'ing, "if you but exert the talent and faculties that you possess, you will have everything in good order before long and
are certain to be rewarded with a substantial promotion."

He then went on to ask, "Venerable sir, does your imperial commission
have a time limit, or not?"

"The imperial commission is for a period of three years," said An Ch'en.
"When the repair work on the Grand Canal is completed, His Majesty will
depute an official to come and offer sacrifices to the God of the River."

While they were speaking, Hsi-men Ch'ing ordered that a table should be
set up, but An Ch'en said, "The truth of the matter is that your pupil still intends to pay a visit to Huang Pao-kuang's place."

"In that case," said Hsi-men Ch'ing, "stay a little longer, and I will arrange
for your attendants to have something to eat."

Before long, a table was set up and provided with a platter of cold hors
d'oeuvres and an assortment of other delicacies to go with the wine, served in
a set of sixteen matched bowls, containing slow-boiled appetizers such as
chicken feet, goose and duck, fresh fish, sheep's head, tripe and lungs, blood
and intestines, soup flavored with pickled fish, and so forth, along with congee
made from pure white, fresh, nonglutinous rice, served in silver-mounted
bowls, and flavored with granulated sugar, hazelnuts, and pine and melon
seeds. These were accompanied by small gold cups of heated vintage wine.
The attendants, for their part, were provided with platters of assorted snacks as
well as meat and wine.

At this repast, Secretary An Ch'en, after downing only three cups of wine,
took his leave and got up to go, saying, "Your pupil will return to seek your
instruction another day."

Hsi-men Ch'ing was unable to detain him any longer and saw him to the gate, where he got into his sedan chair and departed.

On returning to the reception hall, Hsi-men Ch'ing divested himself of his official hat and girdle, replacing them with a cap and headband, dressed himself in a long gown of purple velvet featuring only a mandarin square with an embroidered lion, and sent to ask if Licentiate Wen had come home, or not.

Upon coming back, Tai-an reported, "Master Wen has not yet returned home, but Cheng Ch'un, along with Lai-ting from Huang the Fourth's place, have been here to urge you on your way for half a day already."

Hsi-men Ch'ing, thereupon, went out the gate, got into his sedan chair, and, accompanied by his attendants, set out directly for Cheng Ai-yüeh's establishment in the licensed quarter. When he arrived at the gate of the quarter, the "cribbers" and the "ball clubbers"[29] stayed out of his way, and only the file leaders from the Music Office on duty that day stood to attention on either side, not presuming to kneel down and receive him, while Cheng Ch'un and Lai-ting went ahead to announce his coming.

Ying Po-chüeh was engaged in playing backgammon with Li the Third, and when they heard that Hsi-men Ch'ing had arrived they barely had time to put the game pieces away. Cheng Ai-yüeh and Cheng Ai-hsiang, wearing sealskin toques over their "bag of silk" chignons in the Hang-chou style, held in place by plum-blossom-shaped ornaments with kingfisher feather inlays that enhanced their:

> Glossy hair and powdered faces,[30]

and made up to resemble flower fairies, came out to the door to meet him.

When Hsi-men Ch'ing got out of his sedan chair and came into the parlor he directed them to refrain from the customary welcoming flourish of wind and percussion instruments and suspend any drum music. After Li the Third and Huang the Fourth had saluted him, and the madam of the Cheng Family Establishment had come out to welcome him, Cheng Ai-yüeh and her sister kowtowed to him:

> Just as though inserting a taper in its holder.

Two folding chairs were placed at the upper end of the room, upon which Hsi-men Ch'ing and Ying Po-chüeh took their seats, while Li Chih, Huang the Fourth, and the two Cheng sisters took their places to either side.

Tai-an, who was standing in attendance, asked, "Should we keep the sedan chair here, or send it back home?"

Hsi-men Ch'ing directed that the orderlies and the sedan chair should be sent home and instructed Ch'in-t'ung, saying, "When you get home, see if Master Wen has come back, and, if he has, prepare the sorrel horse for him and escort him here."

Ch'in-t'ung nodded in assent, and departed on his errand.

Ying Po-chüeh then asked, "Brother, how come you delayed half a day before getting here?"

Hsi-men Ch'ing then told him all about how Secretary An Ch'en of the Ministry of Works had showed up for a visit, and he had felt compelled to detain him for a bite to eat.

Before long, Cheng Ch'un came in with some tea, and Cheng Ai-hsiang served a cup to Ying Po-chüeh, while Cheng Ai-yüeh presented one to Hsi-men Ch'ing.

Ying Po-chüeh hastily intervened by reaching out his hand for this cup as well, saying, "Oh, I guess I'm mistaken. I thought you intended it for me."

"I should grant precedence to you?" exclaimed Cheng Ai-yüeh. "You haven't earned the right to it."

"Just look at this little whore," said Ying Po-chüeh. "She only has eyes for her patron and gives no heed to her guests."

"It's not your turn to be a guest today," laughed Cheng Ai-yüeh, "but there may be other guests in the offing."

When they had finished their tea, the cups and their raised saucers were taken away.

Before long, the four singing girls who had been engaged to perform scenes from the *Hsi-hsiang chi* came out and kowtowed to Hsi-men Ch'ing:

Like sprigs of blossoms swaying in the breeze,
Sending the pendants of their embroidered sashes flying,

and he asked each of them her name.

Hsi-men Ch'ing then turned to Huang the Fourth and said, "When they come out to sing for us later on, see that they perform only to the beat of a drum, without any other wind or percussion instruments."

"I understand," replied Huang the Fourth.

Who should appear at this juncture but the madam, who came out and said, "I fear that Your Honor may be cold."

She then told Cheng Ch'un to let down the portiere to keep the heat in. Animal-shaped briquettes were constantly added to the brazier, and the fragrance of orchid and musk pervaded the air.

Just at this juncture, what should they see but several black-clad "ball-clubbers," who, having heard that His Honor Hsi-men Ch'ing had come into the quarter and was drinking at the Cheng Family Establishment, came to loiter at the door:

Sticking out their heads and craning their necks,

but not daring to proceed inside. One of them, who was acquainted with Tai-an, bowed to him and asked him to help them out. Tai-an quietly came inside and asked if they could come in, but Hsi-men Ch'ing merely responded with a shout, which so disconcerted them that they disappeared in a puff of smoke.

It was not long before the fruits and appetizers suitable to accompany a drinking party were served. Two tables were set out at the upper end of the room, one for Hsi-men Ch'ing alone, and the other to be shared by Ying

Po-chüeh and Licentiate Wen, with the empty place reserved for Licentiate Wen on the left end. On that side of the room there was a table for Li the Third and Huang the Fourth, while on the right side there was one for the two sisters. Truly:

> Platters are piled with exotic viands,
> Blossoms are displayed in golden vases.

Cheng Feng and Cheng Ch'un provided musical entertainment on the sidelines.

Just as the wine was being poured and they were about to take their seats, Licentiate Wen appeared, wearing a raised, bridge-shaped scholar's cap,[31] a jacket decorated with a motif of green clouds, a pair of shoes with cloud patterned toes, and velvet socks. As he entered the door, he merely made a ceremonial bow to the company.

"Venerable sir," said Ying Po-chüeh, "why have you arrived so late? A place has been saved for you for some time already."

"Your pupil is at fault," replied Licentiate Wen. "I did not know that the venerable gentleman had called for me. I happened to have gone to my fellow student's place for a literary gathering and am consequently a step too late."

This flustered Huang the Fourth into hastily seeing that he was provided with a cup and chopsticks, and directing him to sit down next to Ying Po-chüeh.

Before long, soup and rice were served, together with steamed open-topped dumplings flavored with hotbed leeks, a soup of eight ingredients, and saucers of ginger and vinegar. The two boy actors entertained them by singing for a while and then retired. Truly:

> Wine is poured, gleaming with glaucous foam,[32]
> Lyrics are sung to the tune "Golden Threads."[33]

Only then did the four singing girls come out and perform the two opening scenes of the *Hsi-hsiang chi*, starting with the aria to the tune "Dabbing the Lips Red" that begins with the words:

I travel for study through the Central Plain.[34]

Who should appear at this point but Tai-an, who came in and reported that Wu Yin-erh from the alley behind theirs had sent Wu Hui and La-mei to deliver a gift of tea. It so happens that Wu Yin-erh's establishment was located on the alley behind the Cheng Family place, and, when she heard that Hsi-men Ch'ing had come for a drinking party there, she made a point of sending a gift of tea.

Hsi-men Ch'ing called them inside, and when Wu Hui and La-mei had kowtowed to him, they said, "Sister Wu Yin-erh sent us over to deliver a gift of tea to Your Honor."

When they opened the gift box and poured out the tea, there was a cup of the fragrant beverage, flavored with melon seeds, shredded chestnuts, marinated bamboo shoots, sesame seeds, and attar of roses, for each member of the company.

"What is Wu Yin-erh doing at her place?" asked Hsi-men Ch'ing.

"She's at home today and hasn't gone out," replied La-mei.

When they had drunk the tea, and Hsi-men Ch'ing had rewarded the two of them with three mace of silver, he turned to Tai-an and Wu Hui and instructed them, saying, "Go and invite Wu Yin-erh to come join us."

Cheng Ai-yüeh, who was quick on the uptake, said to Cheng Ch'un, "You go along with them, and make sure, whatever happens, that you persuade Wu Yin-erh to come. If she refuses to do so, tell her that in the future I won't treat her as a colleague any longer."

"You make me laugh," exclaimed Ying Po-chüeh. "After all, the two of you are only colleagues in the cunt-peddling trade."

"My dear sir," said Licentiate Wen. "How can you be so:
    Out of touch with human nature?³⁵
It has always been true that:
    Notes of the same key resonate with each other;
    Beings of the same nature seek one another out.³⁶
    What is rooted in Heaven inclines to what is above;
    What is rooted in Earth inclines toward that below.³⁷
Their feelings for each other as colleagues are governed by the same principle."

"Beggar Ying," said Cheng Ai-yüeh, "you, also, are a colleague of Cheng Ch'un and the others, in that, like them, you are here in order to provide entertainment."

"Silly child!" exclaimed Ying Po-chüeh. "I'm an old hand in the procuring trade. Back in the days when I was making out with your mother, you were still in her belly."

As they were talking and laughing together, the chef came out to preside over the carving of a set of pig's trotters, which were served together with four bowls of other culinary items, including dock and celery cabbage, minced pork with leeks, soup flavored with tripe and lungs, broth flavored with blood and intestines, and the like.

The singing girls then came out and sang the song suite from the *Hsi-hsiang chi*, starting with the aria to the tune "Powdery Butterflies" that begins with the words:

Five thousand rebellious troops.³⁸

When they were finished, Hsi-men Ch'ing called for the girl surnamed Han who had performed the part of Ts'ui Ying-ying and asked her, "Are you from the Han Family Establishment?"

"Father," responded Cheng Ai-hsiang, "you don't recognize her, but she is a niece of Han Chin-ch'uan, and her given name is Hsiao-ch'ou. This year she is just twelve years old."

"This youngster," opined Hsi-men Ch'ing, "will grow up to be a fine woman. Her demeanor is sprightly, and she sings very well."

He consequently told her to join the company and serve them with wine. Huang the Fourth, for his part, in presiding over the repast:

Catered to his guests with the utmost assiduity.

It was not long before Wu Yin-erh arrived. Her chignon was enclosed in a fret of white crepe, held in place with a pearl headband, ornaments with cloud-shaped kingfisher feather inlays, and an array of little pins all around the edge. From her ears dangled a pair of gold, clove-shaped pendant earrings. On her upper body, she wore a jacket of white satin with purfled edging that opened down the middle; while below, she wore a skirt of sand-green Lu-chou silk, trimmed with purfled gold-spangled edging, and shoes of plain ink-black satin. After coming in the door with an ingratiating smile and kowtowing to Hsi-men Ch'ing, she proceeded to bow in greeting to Licentiate Wen and each of the other members of the company.

"What a laugh!" exclaimed Ying Po-chüeh. "You have only to appear in order to rub me the wrong way. The rest of us are no more than stepchildren I suppose. You recognize only your father with a kowtow, while sparing merely a nod for the rest of us. You denizens of the Verdant Spring Bordello[39] treat your customers too rudely. If I presided over a yamen, I would certainly not spare you the squeezing you deserve."

"Beggar Ying," exclaimed Cheng Ai-yüeh, "you shameless pip-squeak! As I see it, your ball-handling is not that great. All you can do is brag about it."

A place was then arranged for Wu Yin-erh, and she sat down beside Hsi-men Ch'ing's table, while a cup and chopsticks were hastily provided for her.

When Hsi-men Ch'ing noticed that she was wearing a white fret over her chignon, he asked, "who are you wearing mourning for?"

"Father, what a question to ask!" replied Wu Yin-erh. "I've been wearing mourning for Mother ever since she died."

When Hsi-men Ch'ing heard that she was wearing mourning for Li P'ing-erh, his heart was filled with delight, and he moved his seat closer to hers so they could converse more readily.

In a little while, soup and rice were served, and Cheng Ai-yüeh got up from her place to serve the wine.

Wu Yin-erh also stood up, saying, "I haven't yet had a chance to pay my respects to Auntie Cheng," as she went into the madam's room to exchange greetings and then came out again.

"Ai-yüeh," said the madam, "give Sister Yin-erh a seat. I'm afraid she may be cold. And have the maidservant heat a hand warmer so she can warm up her hands."

Immediately afterwards, a new course of hot dishes was served. Wu Yin-erh, in her place at Hsi-men Ch'ing's side, ate only half of one of the delicacies supplied, and drank two mouthfuls of soup, before putting down her chopsticks and engaging Hsi-men Ch'ing in conversation.

Subsequently, she picked up her wine cup and said, "Father, this wine is cold and needs to be replaced with some warmed wine."

Cheng Ch'un then stepped up and served new wine to Ying Po-chüeh and the rest of the company.

After they had drunk one round, Wu Yin-erh asked, "Did you have a sutra reading service on the occasion of the final weekly commemoration of Mother's death?"

"I would like to thank you," said Hsi-men Ch'ing, "for the offering of tea that you sent on the occasion of the fifth weekly commemoration of her death."

"That's a fine way to talk," said Wu Yin-erh. "That coarse tea that we sent induced you to send us a gift in return. We are grateful for your return present, the lavishness of which caused my mother no little perturbation. On the occasion of Mother's final weekly commemoration yesterday, I consulted with Cheng Ai-yüeh and Li Kuei-chieh about sending you another offering of tea, but we didn't know whether you were holding a sutra reading in your home, or not."

"For the final weekly commemoration," said Hsi-men Ch'ing, "we merely engaged the services of several Buddhist nuns to perform a ritual of penance and did not even invite a single relative to attend, lest we put them to further expense."

As they drank wine and chatted together, Wu Yin-erh went on to ask, "Are the First Lady, and the other ladies in your household, doing all right?"

"They're all fine," replied Hsi-men Ch'ing.

"Father," continued Wu Yin-erh, "after having lost Mother unexpectedly this way, when you go into her quarters and find yourself all alone, you must long for her in your heart."

"It goes without saying that I long for her," said Hsi-men Ch'ing. "The other day, while I was in my studio, she appeared to me in a dream in broad daylight, which caused me no end of grief."

"When she died so suddenly, while still seeming vibrantly alive," said Wu Yin-erh, "you could hardly help longing for her."

"The two of you are so wrapped up in your conversation," said Ying Po-chüeh, "that you are completely ignoring the rest of us. If you don't order another round of drinks and provide some songs for our entertainment, we might as well get up and go."

This remark threw Li the Third and Huang the Fourth into such consternation that they hurriedly urged the two Cheng sisters to serve a round of wine and prepare their musical instruments. Wu Yin-erh also got up to join them. The three painted faces, sitting in a row to one side of the company, with their feet propped on the brazier, joining their voices together:

Opened their ruby lips,
Exposed their white teeth,

and sang the song suite in the Chung-lü mode the first number of which, to the tune "Powdery Butterflies," begins with the words:

"Three Variations on the Plum Blossom."[40]

Truly:

> When words emerge from the mouth of a beauty,
> They have a sound that causes rocks to split and
> sets the clouds in motion.

When they had finished singing this song suite, Hsi-men Ch'ing turned to Ying Po-chüeh and said, "You are the one who harassed the three girls into singing for us; so you ought to get up and offer them something in return."

"That's no problem," responded Ying Po-chüeh,

> "It's not going to kill me.

Let me consider how I might disport myself with them. I could do it lying on my back, standing straight up, or reclining on my side. I could take my pleasure by adopting the position of 'The Golden Cock Standing on a Single Foot.'[41] Then again, I might avail myself of the positions known as 'The Wild Stallion Stamping the Turf,' 'The Feral Fox Pulling Threads,'[42] 'The Gibbon Offering Fruit,'[43] 'The Yellow Dog Spraying Urine,' 'The Immortal Pointing the Way,'[44] 'The Culprit with His Back to the Post,' or 'Embracing the Wooden Doll at Night.'[45] Let them choose whatever posture they prefer."

"I'd just be wasting my breath on you," said Cheng Ai-hsiang. "You're delirious, you lousy beggar. You're just:

> Talking nonsense and uttering rubbish."[46]

Ying Po-chüeh arranged three wine cups on a saucer and said, "My children, down two cups of wine at my behest. If you don't do so, I'll splash it all over you."

"I'm not drinking any wine today," pronounced Cheng Ai-hsiang.

"Only if you genuflect to your Auntie Ai-yüeh," said Cheng Ai-yüeh, "and allow me to give you a slap on the face, will I consent to drink any wine."

"Sister Yin-erh," asked Ying Po-chüeh, "what do you say?"

"Master Two," responded Wu Yin-erh, "I'm feeling distressed at heart today. I'll drink half a cup. That's all."

"You beggar," said Cheng Ai-yüeh, "if you don't kneel down for me, I won't drink anything at your behest for a hundred years."

"Master Two," intervened Huang the Fourth, "if you refuse to kneel, it will show that you don't know how to take a joke. Just kneel down, and she may dispense with the slap."

"Nothing doing," declared Cheng Ai-yüeh. "Only if he accepts two slaps on the face from me will I consent to drink this cup of wine."

"I call upon the venerable Licentiate Wen to witness," said Ying Po-chüeh, "the extent to which this crazy little whore is prepared to carry things to extremes."

Thereupon, seeing that he was up against it, he actually got down on his knees, so his torso looked as though it were sticking straight out of the ground like a post, while Cheng Ai-yüeh:

> Lightly rolled up her variegated sleeves,
> Fastidiously exposed her slender fingers,

and took him to task, saying, "You lousy beggar. Will you ever dare to offend your Auntie Ai-yüeh so discourteously again? If not, answer me out loud. If you fail to respond, I will refuse to drink any wine."

Ying Po-chüeh, finding himself:

> At a loss for what to do next,

could only respond by promising, "I will never dare to offend my Auntie Ai-yüeh again."

Cheng Ai-yüeh then proceeded to slap him across the face twice in a row before drinking the cup of wine.

Ying Po-chüeh got back on his feet and said, "What an unkind and unjust little whore you are! You might, at least, have saved a mouthful for me, instead of draining the entire cup yourself."

"If you kneel down again," said Cheng Ai-yüeh, "I'll reward you with a cup of wine."

Thereupon, she filled a cup to the brim and laughed as she proceeded to pour it down Ying Po-chüeh's throat.

"You crazy little whore!" Ying Po-chüeh expostulated. "In the course of your mischievous tricks you've splashed the wine all over me. Old fogy that I am, all I've got is this one outfit of formal clothes, and you've managed to soil it the very first day I've worn it. I'll have to ask that man of yours to replace it for me."

After trifling with each other for a while, they returned to their places.

As the day began to grow dark, candles were lit, and the final complement of dishes was served. Meanwhile, a table was set up in the madam's quarters, on which soup and rice, food and wine, were provided for the entertainment of Tai-an, Ch'in-t'ung, Hua-t'ung, and Ying Pao.

Before long, additional saucers of assorted delicacies were served, and Ying Po-chüeh, while urging Licentiate Wen to try them, proceeded to uninterruptedly stuff them into his own mouth and fill his sleeves with them. Hsi-men Ch'ing then called for a dicebox and suggested that Licentiate Wen initiate the game.

"Whoever heard of such a thing," responded Licentiate Wen. "It is you who ought to begin, venerable sir."

Thereupon, Hsi-men Ch'ing and Wu Yin-erh commenced playing "Competing for the Red"[47] with twelve dice, while the four singing girls below took up their instruments and proceeded to play and sing, calling for the participants to drink a cup of wine at appropriate intervals. After one round had been consumed, Wu Yin-erh changed places in order to play "Competing for the Red" with Licentiate Wen and Ying Po-chüeh, while Cheng Ai-hsiang came over to offer Hsi-men Ch'ing a cup of wine and play guess-fingers with him. Before long, Cheng Ai-yüeh moved over to play "Competing for the Red" with Hsi-men Ch'ing, while Wu Yin-erh left her place in order to offer wine to Li the Third and Huang the Fourth.

It so happens that Cheng Ai-yüeh then withdrew to her room and came out again after dressing herself anew. She was wearing a jacket of iridescent satin that opened down the middle and had a diapered border, over a gosling-yellow skirt of Hang-chou silk, shot with turquoise and embellished with gold thread, as well as figured ankle leggings, and shoes the points of which were adorned with red phoenixes. Under the lamplight, her sealskin toque served to enhance the quality of her thickly powdered snow-white face, rendering her a fit contender for a beauty contest. Behold:

> Her fragrant features and lovely person are
>   more alluring than ever;
> The sparkle of her limpid gaze[48] sets off the
>   beauty of her snowy face.
> The semicircular curves of her phoenix eyes
>   conceal her amber pupils;
> The seamless protuberance of her ruby lips[49]
>   is like a painted cherry.
> When exposed, the jade shoots of her fingers
>   are slender and delicate;
> When walking, the golden lotuses of her feet
>   captivate with every step.
> She is white jade that exudes its own bouquet,
>   a flower that can also speak;
> Even at a thousand taels for one night
>   her like cannot be found.[50]

How could Hsi-men Ch'ing have been anything but captivated? After having drunk several cups of wine, he was half intoxicated. Remembering that Li P'ing-erh had admonished him in a dream not to stay out drinking late at night, he got up and headed toward the rear of the establishment to relieve himself. This flustered the madam into calling for a maidservant to light a lantern and lead him back to perform his ablutions. Cheng Ai-yüeh made haste to follow in their wake and, after he had finished relieving himself, took him by the hand and drew him into her room.

This chamber had been prepared in advance, so that:

> The moon-shaped window was half open,
> Candles in silver sconces burned high,
> The atmosphere was as genial as that of spring,
> Amid the fragrance of orchid and musk;

while at her bedside:

Clouds of vapor hovered athwart the drapery,[51] and
Haze enveloped the curtains of mermaid silk.
Thereupon, Hsi-men Ch'ing took off his outer garments, leaving only his
white satin tunic, cut like the robe of a Taoist priest, and the two of them
cuddled up to each other on the bed, thigh over thigh.

To start off with, Cheng Ai-yüeh asked, "Father, why don't you plan not to
return home tonight?"

"I'll have to go home," responded Hsi-men Ch'ing. "In the first place, Wu
Yin-erh is here, so it could be embarrassing for me to stay. In the second place,
I occupy an official position and am subject to an impending merit evaluation, so I fear it might get me in trouble. I had better only come to visit you by
daylight."

He then went on to say, "I am profoundly grateful for those butterfat 'abalone shell' sweets that you sent me the other day, though your gift caused me
half a day of heartache. Originally, my late Sixth Lady was adept at making
them, but since she died, there has not been anyone in my household who
knows how to do so."

"They're not hard to make," said Cheng Ai-yüeh. "You've just got to get the
knack of it. On that occasion I casually made a few up, not very many of them,
and, knowing that you liked them, sent Cheng Ch'un to deliver them to you.
The melon seeds that I sent with them were all cracked by my own teeth, one
at a time, and the handkerchief that they came in was one that I took the
trouble to add the tassels to in my spare time. With regard to the melon seeds,
I hear that Beggar Ying helped himself to most of them."

"As for that shameless beggar-in-chief you speak of," said Hsi-men Ch'ing,
"I watched him cram the melon seeds into his mouth in two handfuls and
gobble most of them up, without leaving many of them for me."

"So it turns out I was only benefiting that lousy beggar," said Cheng Ai-
yüeh, "as though I meant to show my filial respects to the likes of him."

She then went on to say, "Thank you, Father, for the 'coated plums' you
sent me. When my mother saw them, she ate one and found it very much to
her taste. She often suffers from buildups of phlegm that cause her to cough
in the evenings and keep the rest of us awake half the night. As a result, her
mouth is always dry, but when she lets one of these 'coated plums' dissolve in
her mouth, it produces a good deal of saliva. My elder sister and I had only
eaten a few of them before the old lady took them away and secreted them in
her room, where she helps herself to them early and late, and no one else
dares to disturb them."

"That's no problem," said Hsi-men Ch'ing. "Tomorrow I'll send a page boy
to deliver another canister of them for you to enjoy."

Cheng Ai-yüeh then went on to inquire, "Father, have you seen anything of
Li Kuei-chieh recently?"

"From the time of the funeral until now," said Hsi-men Ch'ing, "I haven't seen anything of her."

"At the time of the fifth weekly commemoration of the Sixth Lady's death," asked Cheng Ai-yüeh, "did she send a gift of tea?"

"Her establishment sent Li Ming to deliver a gift of tea," replied Hsi-men Ch'ing.

"I have something to say to you," said Cheng Ai-yüeh, "but you must keep it to yourself."

"What do you have to say?" asked Hsi-men Ch'ing.

Cheng Ai-yüeh thought to herself for a while and then said, "I'd better not say it. If I do, it will only look as though I'm telling stories about one of my sisters behind her back, which would be embarrassing."

Hsi-men Ch'ing embraced her by the neck, saying as he did so, "You crazy little oily mouth! Whatever you have to say, say it to me. You can rest assured I'll not give you away."

Just as the conversation between the two of them started to warm up, Ying Po-chüeh suddenly strode in and cried out in a loud voice, "A fine couple of people you are; abandoning the rest of us and coming in here to engage in a private conversation."

"Eeyuck!" exclaimed Cheng Ai-yüeh. "What an obnoxious, crazy, shameless beggar you are, to break in on us that way, and give us such a start!"

"You crazy dog!" swore Hsi-men Ch'ing. "Get back to the front of the place immediately, where you've left Licentiate Wen and Wu Yin-erh, or they might choose to follow you back here."

But Ying Po-chüeh proceeded to park his posterior on the bed beside them, saying, "Give me your arm, so I can take a bite out of it before I go, and leave the two of you to screw around together."

Thereupon:

Without permitting any further explanation,

he reached into Cheng Ai-yüeh's sleeve and dragged out her snow-white arm, as smooth as goose fat, adorned with a silver bracelet, and the unblemished jade of her ten slender fingers, ensheathed in gold rings.

"My child!" he exclaimed in admiration. "These two hands of yours are made to order for the task of inducing an ejaculation."

"You crazy chunk of knife-bait!" protested Cheng Ai-yüeh. "I'd only be wasting my breath on you."

But Ying Po-chüeh took up her arm and took a nip at it before consenting to go, causing the woman to revile him in a loud voice, saying, "You crazy beggar, to barge in here for no good reason only to drive people to distraction."

She then called in the maidservant T'ao-hua and said to her, "You escort him back out, and see that the door to the covered passageway is closed."

Ying Po-chüeh Playfully Nibbles at a Jade-white Forearm

When the door was closed, Cheng Ai-yüeh told Hsi-men Ch'ing the whole story of how Li Kuei-chieh had recently resumed her indulgence in "the play of boys and girls"[52] with Wang the Third.

"Once again," she reported, "he is frequenting her place day after day, in the company of the touts Blabbermouth Sun, Pockmarked Chu, and Trifler Chang, the 'cribbers' Stupid Yü and Tiptoe Nieh, and the 'ball-clubbers' Mohammedan Pai and Yokel Sha. He is no longer involved with Ch'i Hsiang-erh but is carrying on with Ch'in Yü-chih. Since he is spending his money at both places, he has run out of funds and has had to pawn his fur coat for thirty taels of silver. He has also turned over a set of his wife's gold bracelets to the Li Family Establishment in lieu of the monthly charge for his liaison with Li Kuei-chieh."

When Hsi-men Ch'ing heard this, he swore, saying, "That little whore! I told her she ought not to carry on with that youngster, but she disregarded my advice and even resorted to:
    Swearing by the gods and uttering oaths,
while choosing to deceive me all the while."

"Father," said Cheng Ai-yüeh, "you needn't get upset about it. I'll tell you a scheme by which you can arrange for Wang the Third to get a slap in the face, and thereby vent your spleen."

Taking Cheng Ai-yüeh onto his lap, Hsi-men Ch'ing wrapped his white satin sleeve around her powdered neck and kissed her fragrant cheek, while she put the opening of her sleeve over a warmer with a cover of brass wire, in which there were smoldering pellets of aromatic incense, in order to fumigate her person.

"Father," she then went on to say, "you must not let a single person know what I am going to tell you. Even Beggar Ying should be kept in the dark, lest any inkling of it should leak out."

"My child," responded Hsi-men Ch'ing, "tell me what you have to say. I am not such a fool as to let anyone else know about it. Really, what is this scheme of yours?"

Cheng Ai-yüeh then proceeded to lay it out in detail, saying, "Wang the Third's mother, Lady Lin, is currently no more than thirty-nine years old and is still a spectacle to behold.
    Painting her brows and making up her eyes,
she dolls herself up in such a way as to:
    Appear the veritable simulacrum of a vixen.
While her son spends his days in the licensed quarter, she is left to her own devices at home and does not scruple to peddle her wares on the side. Pretending to attend services at a nunnery, she actually drops in on the go-between Auntie Wen, who functions as her procuress. She is reputed to be an old hand at the game of breeze and moonlight. I can assure you, Father, that if you should wish to arrange an assignation with her sometime in the future, it

would not be difficult. But there is another fortuitous benefit to this scheme. Wang the Third's wife is now just eighteen years old and is the niece of Defender-in-Chief Huang Ching-ch'en of the Eastern Capital. She is as pretty as a picture, and proficient at backgammon and chess. Since Wang the Third chooses to spend so much of his time out of the house, she might as well be observing her widowhood. As a result, she is:

    So angry she scarcely cares whether she is
        dead or alive,

and has had to be rescued after trying to hang herself two or three times. Father, such an opportunity is not to be missed. If you succeed in initiating an affair with the mother, there is no reason to fear that the daughter-in-law will not fall into your hands."

This single conversation had the immediate effect of arousing:

    Depraved intentions and excited anticipation,

in the mind of Hsi-men Ch'ing, who embraced the painted face, saying, "My darling, let me ask you, how did you ever come by all this inside information?"

Cheng Ai-yüeh withheld the fact that she often performed in the Wang mansion herself but merely said, "An old client of mine, thus and so, once had a rendezvous with Lady Lin at her place, which was arranged for him by Auntie Wen."

"Who was that?" asked Hsi-men Ch'ing. "No doubt it was Chang the Second, the nephew of Mr. Chang, the well-to-do merchant, who lives on Main Street."

"Why that fucking Chang Mao-te!" exclaimed Cheng Ai-yüeh. "His cheeks are all covered with pockmarks, and his two eyes are mere slits. He'd only give me the creeps. No one but the likes of Fan Pai-chia-nu, or Hundred Customers Fan, would take him on. His affair with Tung Chin-erh has been 'a-nail-eighted'[53] for some time now."

"I'm at a loss then," said Hsi-men Ch'ing. "Just who was it?"

"I might as well tell you," replied Cheng Ai-yüeh. "It was that southerner who originally deflowered me. He comes here on business twice a year, and, after spending a night or two in the quarter, he customarily ventures outside and indulges himself in the furtive pleasures of:

    Snitching cats and filching dogs."

When Hsi-men Ch'ing heard this and realized that everything the painted face proposed resonated with his own feelings, he was more pleased than ever and said, "My child, if you are willing to cater to my tastes, I'll undertake to pay your mother thirty taels of silver a month for your keep, and you won't have to take on any other customers. I'll visit you whenever I have the free time."

"Father," said Cheng Ai-yüeh, "if you have taken a liking to me, what difference does the sum of thirty taels or twenty taels make? You can just fork out a

few taels to my mother every month or two. Since I am personally disinclined
to take on any other customers anyway, I'll just put myself at your disposal."

"What a thing to say!" protested Hsi-men Ch'ing. "I'll be sure to come up
with thirty taels of silver."

When they had finished speaking, the two of them:

> Got into bed and engaged each other in amorous sport.

The comforters on the bed were nearly a foot thick.

"Father," Cheng Ai-yüeh asked, "are you going to take off your clothes, or
not?"

"We might as well indulge ourselves with our clothes on," said Hsi-men
Ch'ing. "I fear they're waiting for us to come back, up front."

He then repositioned a pillow, and the painted face unfastened her lower
garments and draped herself face up over its surface. She was wearing underdrawers of red Lu-chou silk and pulled down one of her ankle leggings. Hsi-
men Ch'ing hoisted her two tiny golden lotuses onto his shoulders, opened up
his blue satin drawers, and fastened the clasp around his organ. Behold:

> The flower's heart is lightly exposed, as
> She gently wriggles her willowy waist.[54]

Truly:

> The blossom is too tender to be disturbed,
> But the spring breeze refuses to spare it.[55]
> The flower's heart does not feel satiated,
> Its prodigal feelings are yet unsatisfied.
> In a low voice she intimates to her lover,
> "The spring night's pleasure is not over."[56]

By the time the two of them reached the point at which he was about to
ejaculate,[57] Hsi-men Ch'ing had exerted himself to such an extent that he was:

> Panting and puffing,

while the painted face gave voice to lascivious sounds without end.

As her cloudy locks tumbled over the pillow, all she could manage to say
was, "My own daddy, slow down a bit."

Sometime later, as the saying goes:

> When pleasure reaches its height passions are intense,

and he:

> Ejaculated like a geyser.

After:

> The clouds dispersed and the rain evaporated,[58]

they proceeded to readjust their clothing, and, by the light of the lamp:

> Straighten themselves up before the mirror.

When Hsi-men Ch'ing had washed his hands in the basin in front of the bed,
and put all his clothes on, the two of them held hands as they went back to
rejoin the rest of the company.

Wu Yin-erh was looking after Ying Po-chüeh, and Cheng Ai-hsiang was snuggled up to Licentiate Wen as they engaged in:

> Casting dice and playing at guess-fingers,[59]

while:

> Drinking vessels and game tallies lay helter-skelter.

The merrymaking was at its height. When the company saw Hsi-men Ch'ing come back in, they all stood up and offered him a seat.

"Since you have seen fit," said Ying Po-chüeh, "to abandon the rest of us here, all this time, before deigning to rejoin us, you'd better have a pick-me-up to restore your energy after your recent exertions."

"We were just having a chat together," protested Hsi-men Ch'ing. "What other silly business would we have been up to?"

"That's a fine way of putting it!" responded Ying Po-chüeh. "I suppose you would have us believe that the two of you were merely engaged in a private conversation."

Thereupon, Ying Po-chüeh handed him a large goblet filled with warm wine, and the rest of them kept Hsi-men Ch'ing company as he drank it. Meanwhile, the four singing girls picked up their instruments and played and sang for their entertainment.

At this point, Tai-an, who was standing at his side, covered his mouth with his hand and whispered, "Your sedan chair is here."

In response, Hsi-men Ch'ing made a meaningful moue, and Tai-an, accordingly, hastened out to tell the orderlies to light their lanterns and stand by outside.

When Hsi-men Ch'ing indicated that he would not stay any longer, the company all:

> Stood up to toast him with drinks in hand,

while he turned to the four singing girls and asked, "Can you sing for me the set of songs that starts off with the words:

> On first seeing that bashful beauty?"

"We do know it," responded Han Hsiao-ch'ou.
Thereupon, taking up her *p'i-p'a*, she:

> Gently displayed her coquettish voice,

doing her best to show off her talent, as she sang:

> On first glimpsing that bashful beauty,
> The passions evoked by clouds and rain
>   brought us together.
> I saw that she had a thousand coquetries
>   and a hundred allurements,[60]
> Displaying her seductiveness in a myriad ways;
> A veritable handful of warmth and softness.
> In corresponding with me, she selected

her words carefully;
In revealing her feelings, she secretly
    let her glances flow.
I kept her message in my heart,[61]
In my heart;
But did not know when our desires
    would be fulfilled.

When the first song in the set was finished, Wu Yin-erh served Hsi-men
Ch'ing with wine, Cheng Ai-hsiang served Ying Po-chüeh, and Cheng Ai-
yüeh served Licentiate Wen. Li Chih and Huang the Fourth were also supplied with wine. Han Hsiao-ch'ou then continued by singing the second
song:

I speak to the maidservant, saying,
I wish to build a golden altar, on which to
    appoint my commander.
Before the morrow dawns, tell that young
    scholar to prepare for,
The clouds and rain on Witch's Mountain.[62]
This night my double doors have
    not even been locked;
In my secluded boudoir, I await
    the advent of my lover.
The night is quiet, the watches nearly over,[63]
The watches nearly over.
This time, that master of seduction will be
    hard to resist.

When the song was finished, Hsi-men Ch'ing called for more wine, and
Cheng Ai-hsiang came forward to serve him, while Wu Yin-erh served Licentiate Wen, Cheng Ai-yüeh served Ying Po-chüeh, and Cheng Ch'un stood by to
proffer refreshments. Han Hsiao-ch'ou then continued by singing the third
song:

I dream of that tryst at Kao-t'ang,
Upon my assignation with that romantic
    and enticing maiden.
She and I grasp each other by
    our white hands,[64]
As we enter the silken bed curtains together,[65]
To make a lasting pact between the phoenixes.
The transfusing touch of the magic rhinoceros horn
    penetrates her innermost regions.
Beneath the mermaid silk bed curtains[66] the coverlet
    is disturbed by crimson waves.

Her powdered sweat becomes congealed fragrance,[67]
  Congealed fragrance.
A mere quarter hour of this evening[68]
  is like Heaven on Earth.

When the song was finished, another round of wine was called for. Cheng Ai-yüeh then moved over to wait on Hsi-men Ch'ing, while Wu Yin-erh served Ying Po-chüeh, and Cheng Ai-hsiang served Licentiate Wen, as well as Li the Third and Huang the Fourth. More wine was poured, after which Han Hsiao-ch'ou continued by singing the fourth song:

In the spring warmth under the hibiscus curtains,
My coiffure is in disarray, my hairpins askew,
  and my chignon disheveled.
All on his account, my fragrance is alluring,
  and my jade is soft.
As we emulate billing swallows and cooing orioles,
Our feelings are ardent, our passions are intense.[69]
My waist has become languorous,
  and my eyes are bleary,
But in the depths of our passion
  my eyebrows are wanton.
The two of us share an affinity,
An affinity;
Desirous of enjoying a lifetime of love,[70]
  in harmony like phoenix mates.

When the song was finished, and they had all enjoyed another round of drinks, Hsi-men Ch'ing stood up and ordered Tai-an to take eleven packets of gratuities, of differing quantities, out of his letter case. There were three mace of silver for each of the four singing girls, five mace of silver for the chef, who was called out to receive them, three mace of silver each for Wu Hui, Cheng Feng, and Cheng Ch'un, two mace of silver each for the servant and the boy who served the tea, as well as three mace of silver for the maidservant T'ao-hua. All of them kowtowed to him in gratitude.

Huang the Fourth did his best to prevent him from leaving, saying, "Uncle Ying the Second, won't you say a word to dissuade him? It's early yet, and if His Honor will consent to stay a little longer, it will enable me to convey the full extent of my feelings. Why should he insist upon leaving right away? Auntie Ai-yüeh, won't you also endeavor to detain him?"

"I have tried to detain him," said Cheng Ai-yüeh, "but he simply won't stay."

"You don't know about it," explained Hsi-men Ch'ing, "but there are things I have to do tomorrow."

Then, bowing to Huang the Fourth and Li the Third, he said, "Thank you for all the trouble you have taken on my behalf."

"I fear," responded Huang the Fourth, "that since we have only invited Your Honor to partake of meager fare, and you are unwilling to stay any longer, you will conclude that we have been lacking in respect."

As they spoke, the four singing girls kowtowed together, saying, "When Father gets home, please convey our regards to your First Lady, and the other ladies. When we have some free time, we'll get together with Wu Yin-erh and come to your place to visit the First Lady."

"When you have the time," responded Hsi-men Ch'ing, "do come and spend the day with us."

By this time, the lanterns had been lit, and, when Hsi-men Ch'ing descended the stairs, he was met by the madam of the Cheng Family Establishment, who bowed to him, saying, "Won't Your Honor consent to stay a while longer? The fact that you are so anxious to leave must show that you do not find our fare to your taste. There is another course remaining that has not yet been served."

"I've eaten my fill," said Hsi-men Ch'ing, "and would stay a little longer, were it not that I have a lot of business to take care of. I have to get up early tomorrow morning in order to deal with matters pending at the yamen. Since Brother Ying the Second has no such responsibilities, I'm sure that he can be persuaded to stay a while longer."

Ying Po-chüeh was going to get up and follow him out, but he was forcefully detained by Huang the Fourth, who said, "Master Two, if you insist on leaving, it will certainly spoil the fun."

"That's not the case," responded Ying Po-chüeh, "and there's no need for you to try to retain me. But if you have the prowess to detain the venerable Licentiate Wen, I'll consider you a stout fellow."

Licentiate Wen actually did try to bolt out the gate but was prevented from doing so by Huang the Fourth's page boy, Lai-ting, who held him back by embracing him around the waist.

When Hsi-men Ch'ing arrived at the main gate, he asked Ch'in-t'ung, "Does Master Wen have a mount here, or not?"

"His donkey is here ready for him," replied Ch'in-t'ung. "Hua-t'ung is looking after it."

"Since you have a mount here, venerable sir," Hsi-men Ch'ing said to Licentiate Wen, "you might as well keep Brother Ying the Second company and stay a while longer. I am compelled to leave before you."

Thereupon, they all escorted him outside the gate to see him off.

Cheng Ai-yüeh took Hsi-men Ch'ing's hand and surreptitiously gave it a pinch, while simultaneously turning to face him and saying in a loud voice, "Father, make sure you keep what I told you just now to yourself. As you know:

The dharma must not be divulged to six ears."

"I understand," responded Hsi-men Ch'ing.

She then turned to Cheng Ch'un and said, "You escort His Honor on his way home, and give our regards to his ladies when you get there."

Wu Yin-erh also chimed in, saying, "Give my regards to the First Lady."

"I really oughtn't to mention it," said Ying Po-chüeh, "but these lousy little whores are all attempting to:

Monopolize the trade and compete for business,

in conveying their regards, while I'm left without anyone to convey my regards to."

"You beggar!" retorted Cheng Ai-yüeh. "Get out of the way."

Wu Yin-erh then said goodbye to the group of guests, and the two Cheng sisters, and set out for home, accompanied by Wu Hui, who held a lantern to light her on her way.

"Sister Yin-erh," Cheng Ai-yüeh called after her, "if you run into that wastrel, whatever you do, don't mention this occasion to him."

"I understand," replied Wu Yin-erh.

The remaining company then returned to the scene of their party, where:

Animal-shaped briquettes were replenished, and

New servings of "sunset clouds" were decanted;

as amid:

Song and dance and wind and string instruments,

They enjoyed the pleasure of drinking together.

The party continued until the third watch before breaking up. Huang the Fourth, who hosted this drinking party, paid out ten taels of silver for it, and Hsi-men Ch'ing also contributed three or four taels. But no more of this.

That day, Hsi-men Ch'ing sat in his sedan chair as the two orderlies, holding lanterns, escorted him out through the gate of the licensed quarter, after which he sent Cheng Ch'un back home.

Of the events of that evening there is no more to tell.

The next day, Judicial Commissioner Hsia Yen-ling sent someone to summon him, and Hsi-men Ch'ing went to the yamen early in order to participate in the adjudication of some criminal cases and related matters. The hearings continued until noon, after which he came home and ate his midday meal.

Before this, Brother-in-law Shen had sent his servant Shen Ting with a calling card to recommend a young man named Liu Pao to serve as a cook in the silk goods store, and Hsi-men Ch'ing agreed to employ him. He was in his studio, in the process of providing Shen Ting with a reply to take home with him, when he noticed that Tai-an was standing at his side.

Hsi-men Ch'ing turned to him and asked, "What time did Master Wen come home last night?"

"I had been asleep in the shop for quite a while," replied Tai-an, "when I heard Hua-t'ung knocking on the gate across the street. It was sometime in the third watch before he got home. When I asked about it this morning, I learned that although Master Wen was not in his cups, Master Ying the Second was so drunk he spit up all over the street. Auntie Ai-yüeh was concerned that it was so late at night and sent Cheng Ch'un to escort him home."

When Hsi-men Ch'ing heard this, he guffawed with laughter.

He then called Tai-an over to him and said, "Do you know the address of that Auntie Wen who acted as go-between at the time of our son-in-law's marriage some time ago? If you can locate her, I'd like to have a word with her in the house across the street."

"I don't know Auntie Wen's address," replied Tai-an. "I'll go ask your son-in-law about it."

"As soon as you've finished eating," said Hsi-men Ch'ing, "go ask about it, and then set out immediately."

Tai-an, accordingly, went back to the rear compound for his noonday meal and then went out to the shop to ask Ch'en Ching-chi about it.

"What are you looking for her for?" asked Ch'en Ching-chi.

"Who knows what he wants with her?" said Tai-an. "Without any warning, he just asked me to go find her."

"After emerging on East Main Street," said Ch'en Ching-chi, "head straight south until you get to the memorial arch on the other side of the T'ung-jen Bridge, at which point you turn east on Wang Family Lane, halfway down which there is an administrative police station, across from a stone bridge. On the other side of the bridge there is a Buddhist nunnery, next to which there is a small alley. If you head west on the small alley, the third house you come to will be a bean curd shop, right next to which, on the upper side, you will see the double leaves of a red outer door with latticework on the top to let in the light. That is her place. If you just call, 'Auntie Wen,' she will come outside in response."

When Tai-an had heard him out, he exclaimed, "Enough already!

When an itinerant tinker follows behind a parade
     of incense-burning pilgrims:
The tinkling of his implements seems interminable.

You'll have to go over all that again for me. It's more than I can remember."

Ch'en Ching-chi, accordingly, ran over the directions for him a second time.

"It's not exactly a short jaunt," remarked Tai-an. "I'd better ride a horse."

Thereupon, he led out a large white horse, equipped it with a saddlecloth, fitted on a bit, stood up on the mounting platform, vaulted into the saddle, and gave it a stroke with his riding crop. The horse responded by neighing and prancing as it took off on its way.

Having emerged on East Main Street, Tai-an headed due south to the memorial arch on the other side of the T'ung-jen Bridge and entered Wang Family Lane, halfway down which, sure enough, he found a police station across the street from a dilapidated stone bridge, on the other side of which was a segment of red wall belonging to the Ta-pei An, or Nunnery of Great Compassion.

Tai-an Surreptitiously Sets Out to Find a Bee Go-between

There he found the small alley leading to the west, on the northern, or upper, side of which there was suspended a signboard advertising bean curd. In front of the door of this shop there was an old woman engaged in spreading horse dung out to dry.

While still mounted on his horse, Tai-an asked her, "Old mother, is there a go-between named Auntie Wen around here?"

"The house with the latticed outer door right next door is her place," the old woman replied.

Tai-an proceeded in front of it and, sure enough, found the double leaves of a red outer door, just as he had been told.

Hastily leaping off his horse, he knocked on the door with his riding crop and called out, "Is Auntie Wen at home, or not?"

Lo and behold, it was her son, Wen T'ang, who opened the door and inquired, "Where have you come from?"

"I've come with an invitation for your mother from His Honor Judicial Commissioner Hsi-men Ch'ing who resides in front of the district yamen," replied Tai-an. "Ask Auntie Wen to come out immediately."

When Wen T'ang heard that it was someone from the home of the influential official, Judicial Commissioner Hsi-men Ch'ing, he invited him to come inside and take a seat. Tai-an, accordingly, tethered his horse and went into the parlor inside, where he saw that a paper print of the auspicious God of the Marketplace[71] was displayed. In the inner part of the house, a number of persons had just finished holding a conclave and were still engaged in burning incense and settling accounts.

After what seemed like half a day, Wen T'ang came back out and offered him a cup of tea, saying, "My mother is not at home. When she returns, I'll tell her about it, and she can go to your place tomorrow morning."

"Her donkey is still here," objected Tai-an. "How can you pretend that she's not at home?"

So saying, he slipped past his interlocutor and headed toward the back of the house. Who could have known that Auntie Wen and her daughter-in-law were engaged in entertaining a number of devout Taoist women to tea and were unable to avoid being seen by him?

Whereupon, he said, "Is this not Auntie Wen? You told me just now that she was not at home. If I were to go back and tell such a story to my master, how could he avoid being annoyed with me?"

Auntie Wen laughed out loud at this, bowed in greeting to Tai-an, and said, "May I trouble you, Brother, to go home and tell your master that I am engaged in presiding over a tea meeting today. I don't know what His Honor wants to see me about, but I'll pay a visit to his residence tomorrow morning."

"He only told me to come looking for you," said Tai-an. "Who knows what he wants you for? Not knowing that you lived in this out-of-the-way corner, finding you has really put me out."

"For these last few years," said Auntie Wen, "the venerable gentleman has depended on Old Mother Feng and Auntie Hsüeh to buy maidservants, act as go-betweens, and supply artificial flowers for his household. What use has he had for me? But today, all of a sudden, it would seem:

The beans are popping in this cold pot.[72]

My guess is that since his Sixth Lady has passed away, he must want me to seek another match for him in order to take her place."

"I don't know about that," said Tai-an. "But when you get there and see my master, of course, he'll explain things to you."

"Brother," said Auntie Wen, "just sit down for a bit while I see off the guests at my tea meeting, and then I'll go with you."

"While I wait till you're finished with your tea meeting," said Tai-an, "there's nobody to look after my horse outside. My master is at home, meanwhile, burning with anxiety, like:

A fire within a fire.

He instructed me over and over again to have you come as quickly as possible, so he could have a word with you. Right now he also has another engagement to attend a party with Lo Wan-hsiang,[73] the vice prefect of Tung-p'ing prefecture."

"All right," said Auntie Wen, "wait until I get you a snack to eat, and I'll go with you."

"Don't bother," said Tai-an.

She then went on to ask, "Has Hsi-men Ta-chieh given birth to a child, or not?"

"Not as far as I can tell," responded Tai-an.

Auntie Wen proceeded to provide Tai-an with a snack while she changed her clothes and then said, "You go ahead on your horse, and I'll follow behind you more slowly on foot."

"Old mother," said Tai-an, "since you've got a donkey at your disposal, why don't you saddle it up for yourself?"

"Where would I get a donkey from?" said Auntie Wen. "That donkey belongs to the bean curd shop next door. I have merely loaned them the use of my courtyard to graze it in, and you have mistaken it for my donkey."

"I remember seeing you riding a donkey here and there in the past," said Tai-an. "What has become of it?"

"It so happens," said Auntie Wen, "that one year, some time ago, one of the maidservants whose sale I had negotiated hanged herself, and the resulting lawsuit forced me to dispose of my old house, not to mention my donkey."

"The loss of your house doesn't amount to much," said Tai-an, "but you ought to have held on to that donkey in order to keep you company early and late. Aside from anything else, I noticed that he always had quite a whip of an organ dangling beneath him."

Auntie Wen laughed out loud at this, saying, "You crazy monkey of a short-life! I thought you were saying something serious, so I made the mistake of bending my ear to listen to you. A fine creature you've turned out to be! In the few years since I saw you last, you've developed quite an:

> Oily mouth and a slippery tongue;[74]

and in the future you'll still expect me to find a match for you."

"My horse goes at a good clip," said Tai-an, "and if you walk, who knows how long it will take you to get there, which will only have the effect of irritating Father. You get on the horse, and the two of us can ride tandem."

"You crazy little short-life!" exclaimed Auntie Wen. "I'm not the one you're after. The people on the street are bound to look askance at us when they see what we're doing."

"If not that," said Tai-an, "saddle up the donkey from the bean curd shop and ride it instead. When we get there, I'll see that they're properly compensated."

"That's more like it," said Auntie Wen.

She then told Wen T'ang to prepare the donkey, put on her eye shades, and proceeded to mount it, after which, she set out with Tai-an for Hsi-men Ch'ing's residence. Truly:

> If you want to seek an alluring beauty
>> from a secluded boudoir,
> You must rely entirely upon a red leaf
>> to be a good go-between.[75]

There is a poem that testifies to this:

> Who believes that there is a road leading
>> to the Peach Blossom Spring?
> Yet the peach blossoms, drenched with dew,
>> smile in the spring breeze.[76]
> The Peach Blossom Spring is to be found
>> among the hills and streams;
> Even today, the young fisherman is still
>> trying to find his way there.

> If you want to know the outcome of these events,
> Pray consult the story related in the following chapter.

Chapter 69

AUNTIE WEN COMMUNICATES HSI-MEN
CH'ING'S WISHES TO LADY LIN;
WANG TS'AI FALLS FOR A TRICK AND
INVITES HIS OWN HUMILIATION

Casually he cooks a fish in the hope of finding
    a message on a square of silk;[1]
If a road exists to the realm of the immortals,
    he is ready to embark upon it.
While sweeping the steps he happens upon a leaf
    inscribed with amorous desires;[2]
In strumming a tune beneath the moon he deploys
    the zither of Ssu-ma Hsiang-ju.[3]
Seeking an assignation beneath the mulberry trees,
    Ch'iu Hu has lascivious intent;[4]
Though finding the opportunity sitting in his lap,
    Liu-hsia Hui is not so inclined.[5]
Having strayed inside the gold lamé bed curtains
    in the darkening twilight;
He seems only desirous of pouring the vintage wine
    for his solitary amusement.[6]

THE STORY GOES that when Auntie Wen arrived at the Hsi-men residence, P'ing-an told her, "Father is in the house across the street."

Tai-an went inside to announce her arrival and found Hsi-men Ch'ing sitting in the study with Licentiate Wen. Upon seeing Tai-an, he immediately came out and sat down in a small reception room, while Tai-an told him all about his vicissitudes in locating Auntie Wen.

"I've succeeded in bringing her here," he said, "and she's waiting outside."

Hsi-men Ch'ing, thereupon, told him to call her inside; and Auntie Wen proceeded to cautiously lift aside the portiere that was hanging over the door to keep in the heat and come into the room, where she kowtowed to Hsi-men Ch'ing.

"Auntie Wen," said Hsi-men Ch'ing, "it's been a long time since I saw you last."

"Well, here I am," responded Auntie Wen.

"Where are you living now, since you moved?" asked Hsi-men Ch'ing.

"Because I was so unfortunate as to be involved in a lawsuit," said Auntie Wen, "I was forced to get rid of my old house. At present, I have moved to the southern edge of the city and am living on Wang Family Lane."

"You can get up in order to talk to me," said Hsi-men Ch'ing.

Auntie Wen, thereupon, got to her feet and stood beside him, while Hsi-men Ch'ing ordered his attendants out of their presence. P'ing-an and Hua-t'ung waited for him on the other side of the postern gate, but Tai-an concealed himself outside the portiere so he could eavesdrop on what they had to say.

Hsi-men Ch'ing then proceeded to ask, "What households of prominent families do you frequent?"

"Well," replied Auntie Wen, "I am on familiar terms with the household of Wang the Second, the distaff relative of the imperial family, who resides on Main Street; the household of Commandant Chou Hsiu of the Regional Military Command; the household of the distaff relative of the imperial family named Ch'iao; that of His Honor Chang the Second; and that of His Honor Hsia Yen-ling."

"Are you familiar with the household of Imperial Commissioner Wang I-hsüan, or not?" asked Hsi-men Ch'ing.

"They are old patrons of mine," replied Auntie Wen. "Lady Lin and her daughter-in-law, the wife of Wang the Third, frequently buy costume jewelry from me."

"If you are on familiar terms with them," said Hsi-men Ch'ing, "there is a mission I would like to entrust to you. You mustn't refuse me."

Reaching into his sleeve, he proceeded to pull out a five-tael ingot of silver and hand it to her, saying, thus and so, "See if you can find some way or other of inveigling Lady Lin into visiting your place, so I can have a meeting with her. If you succeed in doing so, I will see that you are further rewarded."

On hearing this, Auntie Wen laughed out loud, saying, "Whoever told you about her? Venerable sir, how did you happen to find out about this?"

"As the saying goes," said Hsi-men Ch'ing:

"Just as a man has his reputation,
A tree has its shadow.

How could I help hearing about it?"

"Well, if you want me to describe this lady," said Auntie Wen, "she was born in the year of the pig, so, this year, she would be thirty-four years old. She is really a first-class lady, is as clever as can be, and could pass for being no more than twenty-nine. Although she does engage in this sort of business, she does so with the greatest discretion. When she goes out, she rides in a large sedan chair, accompanied by attendants who shout to clear the way, and proceeds directly to her destination before coming straight home. Since her son, the venerable Wang the Third, has a position in society to maintain, she would scarcely agree to an assignation at someone else's place. Whoever suggested to you that she might was mistaken. It is only within the:

Vast courtyards and secluded mansions,

of her own place that, occasionally, when the venerable Wang the Third is not at home, she may surreptitiously consent to secrete a lover:

Unbeknownst to humans,
Unperceived by ghosts.

But this must be arranged in advance. As for the narrow confines of a place like mine, I would scarcely take the risk of attempting to get her to come there. This silver that you have offered me, I cannot agree to accept. I had better simply tell the lady what you have proposed, and leave it at that."

"If you refuse to accept it, and continue to make excuses," said Hsi-men Ch'ing, "I will be annoyed. If the affair should be successful, I will reward you with some additional pieces of silk fabric for you to wear. If you persist in refusing what I have offered, you will be standing in my way."

"I am scarcely worried about your lack of largess," responded Auntie Wen. "As they say:

When a superior deigns to patronize you,
It spells the advent of your lucky star."[7]

Kowtowing to him, and accepting the proffered silver, she went on to say, "If you wait until I have had a chance to speak to the lady, venerable sir, I will get back in touch with you."

"You must treat this as a serious undertaking," said Hsi-men Ch'ing. "I will be waiting to hear from you here. When you return, be sure to come to this location. I won't send a page boy to summon you."

"I understand," responded Auntie Wen. "If not tomorrow, then the next day, early or late, as soon as I get the word from her, I'll come back to see you."

As she made her way out, Tai-an said to her, "Auntie Wen, it's up to you, but I would like to have at least a tael of silver for my pains in taking the trouble to find you. You oughtn't to keep everything for yourself."

"You monkey!" exclaimed Auntie Wen.

"If you throw a winnowing sieve over the wall,
Who knows whether it will land right side up
    or upside down?"

Thereupon, she proceeded out the gate, mounted the donkey, and went straight off, with her son holding the bridle, while Hsi-men Ch'ing continued to visit for a while longer with Licentiate Wen.

Sometime later, Judicial Commissioner Hsia Yen-ling showed up, and Hsi-men Ch'ing went back to the house in order to offer him some tea and change into more formal attire, after which they set out together for the prefectural office in order to attend a party for Vice Prefect Lo Wan-hsiang. It was not until after the lamps had been lighted that he returned home.

To resume our story, when Auntie Wen arrived home with Hsi-men Ch'ing's five taels of silver in hand:

Her delight knew no bounds.

After the people attending her tea meeting had departed, late in the day, she went over to Imperial Commissioner Wang I-hsüan's mansion, where she greeted Lady Lin with a bow.

"How is it," asked Lady Lin, "that you haven't come by to visit me the last few days?"

Auntie Wen then proceeded to explain to Lady Lin how she had been busy presiding over a conclave and tea meeting at her place in order to plan for a pilgrimage to offer incense at the temple on the summit of Mount T'ai during the twelfth month.

"Why don't you let your son take care of it?" said Lady Lin. "There's no need for you to go."

"I'm not able to go myself," replied Auntie Wen. "I plan to let Wen T'ang take charge of the incense offering pilgrimage."

"When the time comes," said Lady Lin, "I'll donate something toward the traveling expenses."

"Many thanks for your generosity," responded Auntie Wen.

When they had finished this preliminary exchange, Lady Lin urged her to move closer in order to warm herself at the brazier, and a maidservant served them with tea.

While Auntie Wen was drinking her tea, she inquired, "Is the Third Master not at home?"

"He hasn't come home for two nights in a row," said Lady Lin. "He spends his nights in the licensed quarter. He goes there every day with that crowd of sharpers:

Sleeping among the flowers and lolling
    beneath the willows,

and leaving his blossoming young wife to vegetate in her room, without paying her the slightest attention. What is one to do? What is one to do?"

"Why is the Third Master's wife not to be seen?" Auntie Wen went on to ask.

"She's still in her room," explained Lady Lin, "and hasn't even come out yet."

When Auntie Wen saw that there was no one else about, she said, "That needn't be a problem, Madame, you can relax about it. I have a scheme by means of which you can be sure of dispersing that crowd of hangers-on, and bringing about a change of heart on the part of the Third Master, so that he will not venture into the licensed quarter again. If madame will permit me to explicate it, I will do so; but, should you object, I will not presume to do so."

"When have I ever refused to go along with anything you have to say?" protested Lady Lin. "If you have anything to suggest, go right ahead and say it. I won't object."

Only then did Auntie Wen go on to say, "His Honor, Hsi-men Ch'ing, whose residence is located in front of the district yamen, currently occupies the post of assistant judicial commissioner of the local office of the Provincial Surveillance Commission. His household not only engages in money lending to both officials and functionaries, but also operates four or five businesses, including a satin piece goods store, a pharmaceutical shop, a silk goods store, and a knitting and sewing supplies store. In addition, he operates fleets of merchant vessels with armed escorts on the rivers and lakes, trades salt vouchers in Yang-chou, and purveys incense and wax in Tung-p'ing prefecture for use by the imperial household. He has several tens of assistants and managers in his employ. Grand Preceptor Ts'ai Ching in the Eastern Capital is his adoptive father. Defender-in-Chief Chu Mien of the Embroidered Uniform Guard is his superior. And Majordomo Chai Ch'ien of the grand preceptor's household is his relative by marriage. The grand coordinator and the regional inspector of Shantung are on familiar terms with him, not to mention the local prefects and district magistrates. The wealth of his household is such that:

> The paths run crisscross between the fields;[8]
> The stores of rotting rice suggest a granary.
> What glitters is gold,
> What is white is silver,
> What are round are pearls,
> What sparkle are jewels.

"In addition to his First Lady, who is the daughter of Battalion Commander Wu of the Ch'ing-ho Left Guard, and is his legitimate wife by a second marriage, he has five or six other ladies who preside over quarters of their own and are entitled to wear formal gowns. And, below these, there are several tens of:

> Singing boys and dancing girls,[9]

as well as favored maidservants, at his disposal. Truly, for him:

> Every day is a Cold Food Festival;
> Every night is a Lantern Festival.[10]

"At the present time, His Honor is no more than thirty-three or thirty-four years old; truly, a man in the prime of life, who has an imposing physique and is good-looking. He also resorts to aphrodisiacs to nurture his 'turtle'[11] and is an old hand at initiating romantic affairs. When it comes to backgammon and elephant chess, there is:

> Nothing he has not mastered;

and as for playing at kickball or suchlike sports, there is:

> Little he is not proficient at.

With regard to the works of the hundred schools, and the various word games played by breaking characters down into their component parts, he has but to be exposed to them in order to demonstrate his mastery. Truly, his voice is like:

> Tinkling jade or plangent bronze,[12]

and he is as clever as can be.

"Upon hearing that this family of yours has:

    Worn the regalia of officials for generations,[13]

and that your:

    Financial foundation is anything but shallow,

as well as the fact that the Third Master is enrolled in the Military School, he has expressed a desire to become acquainted with you. The only problem is that, since he has never met you, he is uncertain how to proceed.

"The other day, upon hearing that your birthday is near at hand, and that you are accustomed to accepting worthy gentlemen from anywhere within the four seas, he is single-mindedly desirous of the chance to come and offer you his birthday congratulations. I told him that it would be awkward for him to seek an audience with you precipitously, and that he should wait until I had a chance to approach you on the subject, and obtain your consent. If you should now invite him to come make your acquaintance, not only could you establish a meaningful relationship, but you could also ask his aid in getting rid of this band of rascals that are preying on your son. Such a request would surely do nothing to injure the reputation of your household."

Gentle reader take note: To seek the lower depths, like water, is the nature of women.

On that day, as Lady Lin listened to the encomium on Hsi-men Ch'ing delivered by Auntie Wen, her heart was:

    Thrown into a state of confusion,[14] and

    Her lustful feelings were aroused.

In the course of considering what to do, she turned to Auntie Wen with a smile and said, "Since he and I:

    Are newly acquainted and hardly know each other,

how can we suddenly arrange to meet?"

"That's no problem," responded Auntie Wen. "In speaking to His Honor, I'll just say that you initiated matters by asking me to approach him with a request that he file a complaint on your behalf in the office of the Provincial Surveillance Commission against that gang of hangers-on that are inveigling the Third Master into the licensed quarter; and that you also hope that he will favor you with a private visit beforehand. There is nothing unfeasible about such a scheme."

This suggestion produced a feeling of delight in Lady Lin's heart, and she agreed to await his visit on the evening of the day after next. Having obtained the consent of Lady Lin, Auntie Wen went home.

The next day, around dinnertime, Auntie Wen returned to Hsi-men Ch'ing's residence. That day, after coming home from the yamen, Hsi-men Ch'ing had nothing to do and was sitting in the studio in the house across the street when Tai-an suddenly came in and announced that Auntie Wen had arrived. Upon hearing this, Hsi-men Ch'ing immediately went into the small reception room and told his attendants to let down the blinds. In due course, Auntie Wen came in and kowtowed to him. Tai-an, who understood the situation, tactfully withdrew, so that the two of them could speak freely to each other.

Auntie Wen then explained how she had exercised her powers of persuasion on Lady Lin, telling him, "I gave an extravagant account of your personal character and wealth, your fashionable standing, and your familiarity with the members of the local bureaucracy; how you are:

Chivalrous by nature and open-handed with your wealth;
as well as being:

Romantic and dashing as can be;
with the result that she expressed herself to be:

Willing a thousand times if not ten thousand times.[15]
She agreed that tomorrow evening, while the Third Master is not there, she will prepare a repast in her home and await your visit, so that, on the pretext of asking you for a favor, the two of you can indulge in a secret rendezvous."

When Hsi-men Ch'ing heard this he was utterly delighted and ordered Tai-an to reward her with two pieces of silk fabric.

"If Your Honor plans to go tomorrow," said Auntie Wen, "don't go early, but wait until after the lamps are lit and there are fewer people in the streets. Make your way to the rear gate of her residence by way of Dumpling Alley. There is a certain Old Mother Tuan in her employ, who lives right next door to the rear gate of her residence. I'll wait for Your Honor there. Just have your servant tap on the door and I'll come out and conduct you into the inner sanctum, without letting any of the neighbors know about it."

"I understand," said Hsi-men Ch'ing. "Be sure to get there before me tomorrow, and don't budge by so much as an inch. I'll be there right on time."

When they had finished speaking, Auntie Wen respectfully bade him farewell and returned to report to Lady Lin, while Hsi-men Ch'ing went back to Li Chiao-erh's quarters to spend the night. Concerning that evening there is nothing more to relate.

Hardly able to wait for the day to come, that night Hsi-men Ch'ing chose to conserve his energy. At noontime, he put on a white "loyal and tranquil hat" and joined Ying Po-chüeh in riding on horseback to Hsieh Hsi-ta's place to attend a birthday party in his honor. Two singing girls had been hired for the occasion.

After drinking no more than a few cups of wine, around lamp-lighting time, Hsi-men Ch'ing left the party and mounted his horse, with the two page boys, Tai-an and Ch'in-t'ung, to accompany him. It was the ninth day of the month, and:

The light of the moon was dusky.
Putting on his eye shades, after traversing Main Street, he made his way along Dumpling Alley, until he arrived at the rear gate of the late Imperial Commissioner Wang I-hsüan's residence. The lamps had already been lighted, and the

streets were relatively deserted. When Hsi-men Ch'ing was half a house away
from the rear gate, he reined in his horse and told Tai-an to tap on Old Mother
Tuan's door.

It so happens that this Old Mother Tuan occupied quarters in the rear of
Imperial Commissioner Wang's residence and had been recommended for
her position by Auntie Wen. It was her job to look after the rear entrance, early
and late, in order to:

> Open the gates and close the doors,

and to act as a lookout, enabling anyone bent on an assignation to penetrate
the inner sanctum.

When Auntie Wen, who was inside her quarters, heard the tap on the door,
she promptly opened it and saw that Hsi-men Ch'ing had arrived. She waited
inside the rear gate until Hsi-men Ch'ing had dismounted and then led him
inside, still wearing his eye shades, while telling Ch'in-t'ung to take the horse
and wait with it under the eaves of the house on the west side across the
street. Tai-an, for his part, concealed himself in Old Mother Tuan's
quarters.

Auntie Wen then invited Hsi-men Ch'ing inside, closed the rear gate, and
secured it with the crossbar, after which she led him into the interior through
an enclosed passageway that skirted a tier of auxiliary rooms, before arriving at
the main suite of five compartments in which Lady Lin resided. There was a
closed postern gate to one side, on which Auntie Wen lightly tapped with the
door knocker. It so happens that this was a prearranged signal, so that, in no
time, a maidservant came out to open the double-leaved door, and Auntie
Wen led Hsi-men Ch'ing into the rear reception room.

As they lifted aside the portiere over the latticework of the door and went in,
Hsi-men Ch'ing saw that the interior was:

> Ablaze with lamps and candles.

In the place of honor at the head of the room there hung a full-length portrait
of the military commissioner of T'ai-yüan and Commandery Prince of Pin-
yang, Wang Ching-ch'ung,[16] the founding ancestor of the house of Wang I-
hsüan. He was wearing a crimson python robe decorated with roundels of
entwined dragons, and a jade-ornamented girdle, and was seated on a folding
armchair, covered with a tiger skin, reading a book on military strategy. He
resembled Kuan Yü, the God of War, except that his beard was a little shorter,
and his spear, sword, and bow and arrows were arrayed by his side. The cinnabar-red plaque over the door was inscribed with three characters meaning Hall
of Integrity and Righteousness. The two sidewalls of the room were adorned
with works of calligraphy and painting, and:

> Zither and books were elegantly displayed.

To the left and right of the portrait there hung a pair of scrolls, on which a
couplet was inscribed in gold-flecked characters that were written in the ar-
chaic clerkly script of the Han dynasty and read:

The integrity he bequeathed to the family endures
    like pine trees and bamboos;
His services to the country are as conspicuous as
    the Dipper or a mountain peak.

As Hsi-men Ch'ing was engaged in surveying this scene, he heard the tinkling of a bell on the portiere, and Auntie Wen came in from the interior to
serve him with a cup of tea.

"Invite the venerable Lady to come out so that I can pay my respects," said
Hsi-men Ch'ing.

"She will appear by the time Your Honor finishes your tea," said Auntie
Wen. "I have just informed the Lady of your arrival."

Who could have anticipated that Lady Lin was surreptitiously engaged in
scrutinizing Hsi-men Ch'ing from the other side of the portiere? She saw
that:

His physique was awe-inspiring,
His speech out of the ordinary;
He displayed a splendid figure,
Both dignified and outstanding.

On his head, he wore a white satin "loyal and tranquil hat," with sable earmuffs. On his body, he wore a crane-decorated robe of purple cashmere. On
his feet, he wore white-soled black boots. On his upper torso, he wore a riding
jacket, emblazoned with a green cut-velvet mandarin square that featured an
embroidered lion and was fastened with a row of five gold buttons. Manifestly,
he was:

A wealthy but untrustworthy, crafty
    and treacherous person;
An abuser of the innocent and good,
    addicted to wine and sex.

Upon seeing him, Lady Lin was utterly delighted and quietly called over
Auntie Wen to ask her who he was wearing mourning for.

"He is wearing mourning for his Sixth Lady," explained Auntie Wen, "who
passed away not long ago in the ninth month. At the very least, he still has at
his disposal as many more ladies as the fingers on your hand. You may not be
able to tell by looking at him, but he is like:

A fighting quail, just released from his cage:
Ever ready to engage."

When the woman heard this:

Her delight knew no bounds,

and Auntie Wen urged her to go out and meet Hsi-men Ch'ing.

"I'd be too embarrassed,"[17] the woman said. "How can I put myself forward
like that? Just ask him to come inside."

Auntie Wen, accordingly, went out and said to Hsi-men Ch'ing, "The Lady
invites Your Honor to come into her room in order to meet her."

Thereupon, she hastened to lift aside the portiere, and Hsi-men Ch'ing proceeded into the inner room, where he observed that:

> The drapery consisted of hanging red curtains,[18]
> The floor was completely covered with carpets.
> Amid the fragrance of orchid and musk,
> The atmosphere was as genial as that of spring.
> The embroidered bed was enhanced by clouds of vapor
>   hovering athwart the curtains;
> The brocaded screen showed the radiance of the moon
>   invading the asterism Hsüan-yüan.[19]

On the woman's head, she wore a headdress of gold filigree enhanced with emerald leaves. On her body, she wore a wide-sleeved jacket of white satin, over a brocaded, aloeswood-colored, crane-decorated robe of figured satin, and a wide-bordered skirt of palace-style crimson brocade. On her feet, she wore shoes of raven-hued fabric with embroidered patterns, and high white satin heels. Manifestly, she was:

> An alluring and lascivious female inhabitant
>   of ostentatious chambers;
> A veritable bodhisattva of coition, dwelling
>   in her sequestered bower.

There is a poem that testifies to this:

> Her face is glossy, her locks are thick,
>   and her brows curvaceous;
> When her lotus feet are lightly animated,[20]
>   she is remarkable indeed.
> When intoxicated, her lusts are aroused
>   within the bed curtains;
> Only then does one come to see just how
>   extraordinary the lady is.

Upon seeing her, Hsi-men Ch'ing:

> Bent his body to perform an obeisance,

saying, "Will Your Ladyship please assume the position of honor so that your pupil may pay his respects to you."

"Your Honor," said Lady Lin, "you can skip the obeisance."

But Hsi-men Ch'ing was unwilling to do so and, bending his body, proceeded to kowtow to her twice. The woman, for her part, responded in kind. When they had finished with these amenities, Hsi-men Ch'ing took his seat on a chair in the position of honor, while Lady Lin kept him company by sitting at an angle on the edge of the k'ang next to him, and leaning against a comb-back-shaped back rest. Auntie Wen had long since secured the ceremonial gate leading into the front courtyard, so that there was not a single male servant left in the rear compound. The postern gate leading into the Third

Master's quarters had also been locked. A young maidservant, named Fu-jung, brought in a serving of tea on a red lacquer tray, and Lady Lin kept Hsi-men Ch'ing company while he drank it, after which the maidservant took the tea cups and their raised saucers away.

Auntie Wen then initiated the conversation, saying, "The Lady has long known that Your Honor holds a judicial appointment in the yamen of the Provincial Surveillance Commission and has presumed to send me to invite you here in order to ask a favor of you. But she doesn't know whether Your Honor will agree to her request, or not."

"I don't know what it is that her venerable Ladyship would have me do for her," said Hsi-men Ch'ing.

"I would not deceive you, sir," said Lady Lin, "but the fact is that, although my husband's family has held the hereditary post of Imperial Commissioner for generations, it is some years now since he passed away, and he had not accumulated much in the way of savings. My son is still young, and has been delicately nurtured, but has not yet qualified to succeed to his father's position. Although he is currently enrolled in the Military School, he is still immature and uneducated and is given to entertaining a number of crafty and uncouth[21] characters who daily entice him into going out whoring and drinking with them, to the complete neglect of his family responsibilities. On several occasions I have been on the verge of reporting them to the authorities, but since I am unaccustomed to venturing outside my private quarters, I am afraid that by:

Exposing my face to the public gaze,[22]

I might damage the reputation of my late husband. That is why, today, I have ventured to invite Your Honor to my humble abode in order to confide my innermost thoughts to you, which will serve as an equivalent of my lodging a formal complaint against them. It is my earnest hope that Your Honor will consent to sympathize with my feelings, and find a way of preventing this bunch of characters from continuing to prey on my son, so that he will be able to:

Correct his faults and renew himself,[23]

devoting himself to mastering the requirements for public office, so that he can perpetuate the inheritance of his ancestors. If Your Honor is able to do this, you will have given him:

The favor of a new lease on life,[24]

and I will not only:

Feel profoundly grateful to you,

but will see that you are handsomely rewarded."

"How can your venerable Ladyship bring yourself to utter the word 're-ward'?" protested Hsi-men Ch'ing. "The members of your distinguished family have:

Worn the regalia of officials for generations,

serving the court as generals and ministers. Your household is no ordinary one. Since your noble son has twice been enrolled in the Military School, he certainly ought to strive to achieve success, in order to follow in the footsteps of his ancestors, rather than succumbing to the wiles of such parasites, and allowing himself to become besotted with women and wine as so many young men do. At Your Ladyship's behest, as soon as your pupil returns to the yamen, he will see to it that this bunch of characters is appropriately disciplined. Your son will not be implicated in any way, but this may serve as a warning to him not to continue walking in the same rut and may, I hope, prevent him from doing so in the future."

When the woman heard this, she hastily got to her feet and bowed to Hsi-men Ch'ing, saying, "On a future occasion, I will express my gratitude to Your Honor."

"You and I are like members of the same family," responded Hsi-men Ch'ing.

"How can you say such a thing?"

As the two of them were:

Talking back and forth,

they exchanged meaningful glances with each other. Before long, Auntie Wen set up a table and brought in a serving of wine.

Hsi-men Ch'ing intentionally refused, saying, "Your pupil has come for the first time, with a view to making your acquaintance, but has not brought a gift with him. How can he consent to accept your venerable Ladyship's magnanimous hospitality?"

"I did not anticipate that Your Honor would deign to pay me a visit," said Lady Lin, "so I was unable to make the appropriate preparations. The weather is cold, and I have supplied a meager cup of watery wine.

It is no more than a token of my esteem."

The maidservant then proceeded to pour the wine. Truly:

Golden flagons decant the rarest vintage;

Jade goblets overflow with Yang-kao wine.

Lady Lin stood up and proffered him a cup of wine, but Hsi-men Ch'ing, for his part, also got up from his seat and said, "I ought to first offer Your Ladyship a cup."

Auntie Wen, who was standing to one side, interrupted him, saying, "There is no need for Your Honor to offer Her Ladyship any wine today. The fifteenth day of the eleventh month is the Lady's birthday. Why don't you plan to deliver a present to her on that day, and wish her a happy birthday?"

"Ai-ya," exclaimed Hsi-men Ch'ing. "It's a good thing you mentioned it. Today is the ninth, so it is only six days away. I will be sure to ascend her hall and wish her a happy birthday when the time comes."

"How could I be so presumptuous," responded Lady Lin with a smile, "as to put Your Honor's generosity to such a test?"

Before long, in:

    Large platters and large bowls,

an assortment of delicacies was put before them in a set of sixteen matched bowls. These dishes, with their:

    Enticing flavors and rare ingredients,[25]

were steaming hot, and cooked to perfection. They included sautéed chicken and fish, fried and roasted goose and duck, fastidiously prepared vegetable dishes, and rare fruits in season. Beside them:

    Crimson candles blazed on high,[26]

at their feet:

    Fuel was replenished in golden braziers.
    Exchanging cups as they drank,
    Gaming at forfeits and playing at guess-fingers,[27]
    They joked suggestively about clouds and rain,
    As the wine enhanced their lustful daring.

They continued drinking until the time when:

    The lotus-shaped clepsydra dripped its last, and
    The moonbeams in the window reached their height.
    They both felt the effects of the Bamboo Leaf wine,[28]
    And their amorous feelings were already stimulated.

Auntie Wen had disappeared, and when they called for more wine, no one responded. Hsi-men Ch'ing, upon seeing that:

    There was nobody about,

gradually:

    Moved his seat closer to her,

and:

    Their conversation became rather risqué.

It was not long before they reached the stage of:

    Holding hands and squeezing wrists,[29]
    Rubbing shoulders and nudging elbows.

Initially, when he:

    Playfully embraced her powdered neck,

the woman merely:

    Smiled but did not choose to respond.[30]

Eventually, however, the woman:

    Gently parted her scarlet lips,

and Hsi-men Ch'ing:

    Shot his tongue into her mouth, so that
    The sound of their sucking was audible,
    And their pleasantries became intimate.

Thereupon, the woman got up and closed the door to the room, after which, she:

    Removed her clothes, undid her girdle, and

Slightly parted the brocade bed curtains.
Across the bed there lay:
    An embroidered quilt and mandarin duck pillow.[31]
    The bedding was fumigated with phoenix incense.
    Their jade bodies in intimate contact,
    He began to fondle her creamy breasts.
    It so happens that, because Hsi-men Ch'ing knew that the woman was fond of the game of breeze and moonlight, before leaving home he had picked up his bag of sexual implements and taken a dose of the Indian monk's medication. The woman discovered, by both visual and tactile means, that his male organ was extremely large, and Hsi-men Ch'ing, also, proceeded to manually stimulate her clitoris.
    Devoting themselves to each other's pleasure,
    Their lascivious excitement burned like fire.[32]
The woman placed an absorbent mermaid silk handkerchief within reach beside the bed, while Hsi-men Ch'ing, underneath the quilt, rendered his chowrie handle rampant. Thereupon:
    As he extended his apelike arms,
    The butterflies were driven to madness
        and the bees to wantonness;
    As she raised up her jade legs,
    She was scarcely bashful at the clouds
        or embarrassed by the rain.
Truly:
    Back and forth, they are both practiced hands
        at amorous engagement;
    What matter if her jade hairpin should happen
        to fall by the bedside?[33]
There is a poem that testifies to this:

The tunes performed in the nuptial chamber
    are low-pitched and secretive;
As incense burns in the duck-shaped censer[34]
    the lucent vapor spirals upward.
Their dreams are rehearsed amid the pale
    liquescence of the moonlit night;
As they toss and turn on the ivory bedstead
    the spring colors are marvelous.
Unexpectedly, on this occasion, she has found
    herself with a young lothario;
When she is accustomed only to playing games
    with the wealthiest merchants.
Overcome with desire, she yearns for union,

In Wang I-hsüan's Mansion He Enjoys a Tryst with Lady Lin

but is so languid and enervated;
She has to urge her Sung Yü to embark upon
    his own expedition to Kao-t'ang.[35]
As he pushes his way through the double gates
    that have never been locked;
Dew comes to inundate the blossoming branch of
    crimson herbaceous peonies.[36]

Hsi-men Ch'ing, on this occasion, exerted to the full the skills he had acquired during a lifetime as he dallied with the woman, and a watch and a half
elapsed before he ejaculated. As for the woman:
    Her hair is in disarray, her hairpins askew,
    Her blossoms withered, and her willows tired.
    The oriole's cries and swallow's twittering,
    Still continue to resonate within their ears.
After lying together:
    Head to head and thigh over thigh,
    And embracing one another a while,
they got up and put their clothes back on. Upon getting down from the bed,
the woman:
    Deftly trimmed the silver lamp's wick,
opened the door of the room, and:
    Gazing at the mirror, made herself up.
After calling for the maidservant to bring in some water so they could wash
their hands, they:
    Resumed drinking the fragrant wine,
    Trading toasts in the fine vintage.
After they had exchanged three cups with each other, Hsi-men Ch'ing got up
to go, and the woman was unable to detain him any longer, though
she urged him repeatedly to return. Hsi-men Ch'ing bowed in consent and
apologized politely for the trouble he had put her to, after which he took his
leave and departed, while the woman saw him out as far as the postern gate.
Auntie Wen had already opened the rear gate and called Tai-an and Ch'in-
t'ung to bring the horse over for him to mount for the return journey. Out on
the street, the night watchman was already:
    Shouting the hour and ringing his bell;
    The time was late, the night was still.[37]
Behold:
    The atmosphere was pervaded with frost;
    The myriad pipes of Heaven were silent.[38]
Hsi-men Ch'ing proceeded on his way home. Concerning that evening there
is nothing more to relate.

The next day, after Hsi-men Ch'ing had disposed of his routine business at the yamen, he retired to the rear chamber and summoned the adjutant and detectives assigned to the area in question and ordered them:

Thus and thus, and

So and so,

saying, "Go and find out who it is that is inveigling the third son of Imperial Commissioner Wang into the licensed quarter, and what establishments he is frequenting. Ascertain their names, and come back to report to me."

He then turned to Judicial Commissioner Hsia Yen-ling and said, "Master Wang the Third is allowing himself to be led astray. The other day, his mother importuned someone to come and tell me about it. It's not really her son's fault, but he is being led into temptation's way by this bunch of 'bare sticks.' If steps are not taken now to see that they are severely disciplined, in days to come, they are likely to end up leading the heir of this family badly astray."

"What my colleague says is true enough," responded Hsia Yen-ling. "They ought, certainly, to be apprehended."

The adjutant and detectives, upon receiving Hsi-men Ch'ing's instructions, set to work that very day and actually succeeded in ascertaining the names of the persons in question. Having made out a report on the matter, they came to Hsi-men Ch'ing's residence that afternoon and presented their findings. Hsi-men Ch'ing saw that the names in the document were those of Blabbermouth Sun, Sticky Chu, Trifler Chang, Tiptoe Nieh, Yokel Sha, Stupid Yü, and Mohammedan Pai; and that the singing girls in question were Li Kuei-chieh and Ch'in Yü-chih. Picking up his writing brush, he crossed out the names of Li Kuei-chieh and Ch'in Yü-chih, as well as those of Blabbermouth Sun and Sticky Chu.

He then instructed the officers, saying, "You need only take action against Trifler Chang and the rest of those five 'bare sticks.' Arrest them for me, and deliver them to the yamen first thing in the morning."

The functionaries assented and set off on their mission. That evening, having learned that Wang the Third and the others were all drinking and playing kickball at Li Kuei-chieh's place, they concealed themselves behind the rear gate. Late at night, when the party dispersed, they arrested Trifler Chang, Tiptoe Nieh, Stupid Yü, Mohammedan Pai, and Yokel Sha, all five of them. While Blabbermouth Sun and Sticky Chu managed to hide out in one of the back rooms of the establishment, Wang the Third concealed himself under the frame of Li Kuei-chieh's bed and dared not come out. The personnel of the Li Family Establishment were thrown into such consternation that they broke into a sweat. Not knowing who was behind the proceedings, all they could do was to seek information from anyone who could learn the truth of the matter. Wang the Third spent the whole night under the bed, not daring to come out. The madam of the Li Family Establishment feared that the officers involved had been sent all the way from the Eastern Capital to make the arrests. When the fifth watch came around, she persuaded Li Ming to change into different clothes and escort Wang the Third home. The adjutant and detectives involved took Trifler Chang and the rest of them to their orderly room where they hung them up for the night.

Early the next morning, Hsi-men Ch'ing went to the yamen and took his place on the bench together with Hsia Yen-ling. The instruments of punishment were arrayed to either side. When the prisoners were led in, each of them was subjected to a squeezing and given twenty strokes with the heavy bamboo. They were beaten until:

The skin was broken, the flesh was split, and
Fresh blood spurted out.
The sound of their cries shook the heavens;
Their howls of distress disturbed the earth.

Hsi-men Ch'ing exhorted them, saying, "As for the bunch of you 'bare sticks,' who devote yourselves to inveigling young men into:

Toying with the breeze in the licensed quarter,
Instead of being content to abide by their lots,

you deserve to be punished severely; but, today, I am letting you off lightly with no more than these few strokes of the bamboo. If you should happen to fall into my hands again, however, you can count on being sentenced to public exposure in the cangue outside the gate of the yamen."

He then shouted an order that the attendants should drive them out of the courtroom. As they were forced outside, they felt as though:

Whether their fates were governed by metal or by water,
There was no place for them to hide.

After having disposed of this case, the two officials retired from the bench and were enjoying a cup of tea in their private quarters, when Hsia Yen-ling said to Hsi-men Ch'ing, "The other day, I received a letter from my relative, Privy Councilor Ts'ui Shou-yü, saying that the report on the merit evaluation for the members of the Embroidered Uniform Guard has been submitted, but that the results have not yet been promulgated. Having met with my colleague here today, I propose that we should send a messenger to our colleague Lin Ch'eng-hsün, the judicial commissioner in the Huai-ch'ing office of the Provincial Surveillance Commission, since that is closer to the capital, to find out if there is any further news on this head."

"My colleague's proposal is most perspicacious," said Hsi-men Ch'ing.

They then summoned one of the couriers on duty, who knelt down before them, and instructed him, saying, "We will provide you with five mace of silver for your traveling expenses. You are to set out immediately, with calling cards from each of the two of us, travel by way of the southern branch of the Yellow River to Huai-ch'ing prefecture, and present them to Battalion Commander Lin Ch'eng-hsün of the Provincial Surveillance Commission there. We want you to find out for us whether the results of the recent merit

In Verdant Spring Bordello Wang Ts'ai Is Frightened Away

evaluations for the members of the Embroidered Uniform Guard have come
down from the capital yet. That is to say, whether the formal notification from
the Registry Office has been promulgated or not. It is essential that you ascertain the true facts of the matter, and return to report them to us."

The courier in question took possession of the silver and the calling cards,
returned to his office, put on his broad-brimmed hat of Fan-yang felt, accoutered himself for the trip, procured a horse from the stable, and set out on his
long journey, while the two officials got up and went home.

To resume our story, when Trifler Chang and the rest of them were expelled
from the yamen of the Surveillance Commission and found themselves wandering along the street, they were in a state of trepidation. Completely in the
dark as to what had ignited the fuse that resulted in their predicament, they
resorted to mutual recriminations.

"No doubt," ventured Trifler Chang, "it must, once again, be something
instigated by Defender-in-Chief Huang Ching-ch'en in the Eastern Capital."

"That's not likely," pronounced Mohammedan Pai. "If that were the case,
how would he be willing to:
	Let anyone lightly out of his clutches?
As the saying goes:
	No one is more perverse than a singing girl;
	No one is more dishonest than a silversmith;
	No one is more accomplished than a 'cribber.'"

Tiptoe Nieh then chimed in, saying, "None of you seem to get it. I'm the
only one who has guessed the truth. This must surely be the result of Hsi-men
Ch'ing's harboring a grudge against Wang the Third for patronizing his mistress, and choosing to vent his spleen at our expense. Truly:
	When the dragon battles the tiger,
	The one hurt is the innocent fawn."[39]

"Gentlemen, that may well be the case," opined Trifler Chang, "it is certainly we who are enduring the pain. Blabbermouth Sun and Pockmarked
Chu were just as involved as we were, but it is we alone who are being made
to take the blame."

"How can you talk so naively?" said Stupid Yü. "The two of them are friends
of his. How could he bring himself to hale them into court to kneel down
before him and sentence them to punishment from on high?"

"I wonder why he didn't arrest the women involved?" ventured Trifler
Chang.

"The two women are both sweethearts of his," explained Tiptoe Nieh, "and
Li Kuei-chieh is his mistress. He could hardly have consented to have her arrested. There's no point in trying to blame anybody. It's just our bad luck to
have stumbled into this dragnet. Why do you suppose His Honor Hsia Yen-
ling had nothing to say just now? It was only Hsi-men Ch'ing who did the
talking. That in itself makes it clear that the fix was in. Right now, we ought to

go to Li Kuei-chieh's place and try to get hold of Wang the Third. After all, it's only thanks to him that our buttocks are covered with welts and our thighs beaten to a pulp. If we can get a few taels of silver out of him as compensation, we can avoid being laughed at by our wives."

Thereupon:

> Coming this way and going that way,
> Rounding bends and turning corners,[40]

they made their way straight to Li Kuei-chieh's establishment in the licensed quarter, where they found that the gate was:

> Locked tight as an iron bucket, so that
> Not even Fan K'uai himself could get through.[41]

They shouted out loud for what seemed like half a day before a maidservant finally responded from the other side of the door, asking who was there.

"It's us," said Trifler Chang. "We're looking to have a word with Master Wang the Third."

"He went home in the middle of the night that day," responded the maidservant. "He's not here, and there's no one else at home either, so I don't dare open the gate."

The bunch of them could think of no alternative but to go back to the residence of Imperial Commissioner Wang I-hsüan, where they barged right into the reception room and sat down. When Wang the Third heard that they had come looking for him, he was so perturbed that he hid out in his own quarters, not daring to emerge.

After what seemed like half a day, he sent his page boy, Yung-ting, out to say to them, "My master is not at home."

They responded by saying, "He's certainly bent on having an easy time of it. If he's not at home, just where has he gone to that he can't be called back from?"

"Let me remind you of the facts of the case," said Stupid Yü. "There's no use pretending that you're:

> Still asleep in dreamland.

We've just been beaten in the yamen of the Provincial Surveillance Commission and then thrown out into the street. Right now, they're demanding that the Third Master make a personal appearance before the bench."

They then pulled up their clothes, exposing their thighs for Yung-ting to see, and told him to go back inside and report on the situation.

"After all," they went on to say, "the fact that we've been subjected to a beating on his account is no trivial matter."

Each and every one of them then proceeded to recline on the benches and give vent to moans and cries of pain.

As a result, Wang the Third became even more fearful of coming out and pleaded with his mother, saying, "Can't you, somehow or other, find a way of rescuing me from this situation?"

"I'm only a woman," responded Lady Lin. "How should I know how to go about persuading anyone to pull strings on your behalf?"

After he had pleaded with her for what seemed like half a day, they learned that the gang out in the reception room were getting restive and were demanding to speak with the venerable lady of the house.

Lady Lin did not go out but spoke to them from the other side of the standing screen, saying, "You will have to be patient. The fact of the matter is that he is out on our country estate and is not at home; but I will send a servant to go and summon him."

"Venerable Lady," said Trifler Chang, "you'd do well to send someone after him as soon as possible. If this boil is not lanced it will ooze pus, and letting it fester is not the thing to do. It is on his account that we have suffered this beating. When His Honor dismissed us just now, he insisted that he be turned over to the court. If he does not appear:

There can be no hope of peace,[42]

for anyone involved, and matters can only go from bad to worse."

Upon hearing this, Lady Lin lost no time in sending a page boy out to serve them with tea. Wang the Third, for his part, was as scared as the devil and pressed his mother, once again, to find someone to pull strings on his behalf.

Only after he became frantic did Lady Lin say to him, "Auntie Wen just happens to be acquainted with the household of Judicial Commissioner Hsi-men Ch'ing. Years ago, she was the go-between who proposed the betrothal of his daughter, so she is familiar with their household."

"If she is acquainted with the judicial commissioner," said Wang the Third, "send a page boy to invite her here as quickly as possible."

"Ever since you criticized her on a former occasion," said Lady Lin, "she's been miffed and has stopped coming over here. Under the circumstances, how can we invite her? She's unlikely to come."

"My good mother," said Wang the Third, "things have reached the crisis stage. Invite her here, and I will humble myself so far as to beg her pardon."

Lady Lin then agreed to send Yung-ting on this errand, saying, "Go out the rear gate as quietly as possible, and invite Auntie Wen to come over here."

Wang the Third implored her, again and again, saying, "Auntie Wen, if you are acquainted with the judicial commissioner, His Honor Hsi-men Ch'ing, pray use whatever influence you can to rescue me from this predicament."

Auntie Wen deliberately made a specious show of emphasizing the difficulties involved, saying, "Although it is true that, in the past, it was I who proposed the betrothal of his daughter, it has been some years now since I have had any occasion to cross his threshold. When it comes to such prominent families, with their:

Vast courtyards and secluded mansions,

I don't venture to trouble them."

Wang the Third hastily knelt down in front of her and said, "Auntie Wen:

> You shall have an ample reward;[43]
> I will never dare to forget it.

That bunch of people up front are insisting that I appear in court. How can I afford to do that?"

Auntie Wen kept her eyes fixed on his mother, who eventually said, "You might as well see if you can intervene on his behalf."

"There's no point in my going by myself," said Auntie Wen. "Third Master, you must put on formal attire and let me take you to visit His Honor Hsi-men Ch'ing's house in person. If you will pay your respects to him and plead with him, while I speak up from the sidelines on your behalf, I guarantee that this problem, great as it is, can be brought to a successful conclusion."

"Right now," said Wang the Third, "that bunch of characters up front are pressing their demands most vociferously. If they should happen to catch sight of me, what would I do?"

"As for that problem," said Auntie Wen:

> "What's the difficulty there?[44]

Let me go out and see what I can do to placate them. If you will provide wine and meat, refreshments and tea, they can be beguiled into partaking of them, while I surreptitiously sneak you out by the rear gate, fulfill our mission, and return, without their having so much as an inkling of what we are about."

Auntie Wen, thereupon, went out to the front reception room, bowed twice to the assembled group, and said, "The lady of the house has asked me to come out and respectfully explain to you gentlemen that the Third Master has really gone to their country estate and is not at home. She has sent someone to ask him to come back, and he should be here sometime soon if you will only consent to remain sitting here a little while longer. It's a pity that your implication in this affair has resulted in your suffering such punishment and vituperation; and your feelings are just as understandable as the fact that:

> We are all dependent on salt and rice.

When the Third Master returns, he will surely treat you with the consideration you deserve.

> No matter how egregiously wrong a verdict may be,
> The men deputed to carry it out are not to blame.[45]

After all, the only thing everybody wants is to settle the matter amicably.

> Since you are here under official orders,
> You have no choice but to do as directed.[46]

Once the Third Master appears, this problem, great as it is, can be brought to a successful conclusion."

At this, the group of them responded as with a single voice, saying, "It is Auntie Wen who truly understands the situation. If you had only come out earlier and spoken to us in such a reasonable way, we would not have become as agitated as all this. Instead, we were told, in the most obdurate terms, that he was not at home, as though they believed that this was merely a pickle that we had gotten ourselves into, when, in fact, it was he who was actually responsible for the fact that we were subjected to a judicial beating. Do you really think that when the authorities demand your appearance, you can merely pretend not to be at home, and continue:

Drinking wine or eating meat,

while getting others to suffer in your stead? Auntie Wen, you are amenable to reason. Since you've come out to speak to us, we can suggest a way of coping with the situation. All they need to do is spend some money to purchase a little favorable influence, and the matter can be settled to everyone's satisfaction. If you had not come out to parley with us, the matter would certainly have had to be adjudicated. A yamen charged with penal investigations is not likely to drop the case for nothing."

"What you gentlemen say makes sense," responded Auntie Wen. "If you will remain sitting here a while longer, I'll speak to the lady, and also have her provide some wine and refreshments for you. You've already been here for half a day and must be hungry."

"It is only our Auntie Wen," they said with one voice, "who really:

Understands man's vicissitudes.[47]

The truth of the matter is that ever since we were driven out of the yamen, we haven't had so much as a taste of yellow soup."

Auntie Wen then returned to the rear of the compound and saw to the purchase of two mace of silver's worth of wine, and a mace of silver's worth of other refreshments, including pork, lamb, and beef, which were duly chopped up to fill several large platters, and taken out to serve to them. Thus she succeeded in inveigling them into turning their attention to feasting upon these:

Unlimited quantities of meat and wine,

in the front reception room.

Meanwhile, Wang the Third put on his scholar's cap and robe, wrote out a message on a calling card, and, with Auntie Wen leading the way, donned his eye-shades, sneaked inconspicuously out the rear gate, and set out to walk to Hsi-men Ch'ing's residence.

When they arrived at the front gate, P'ing-an, who recognized Auntie Wen, said, "Father has been in the front reception hall, but has just gone inside. What does Auntie Wen wish to speak to him about?"

Auntie Wen handed him Wang the Third's calling card and said, "Brother, may I trouble you to report this gentleman's arrival."

Hastily turning to Wang the Third, she asked him for two mace of silver and handed it to P'ing-an. Only then did he consent to go inside and report the situation to Hsi-men Ch'ing.

When Hsi-men Ch'ing looked at the accordion-bound calling card, he saw that it read, "Your humble pupil Wang Ts'ai:

Presents his compliments with a hundred salutations."[48]

He first called in Auntie Wen to interrogate her about the situation and then opened the latticed door to the great reception hall and sent a page boy to invite Wang the Third to come in. When the attendants in the great reception hall hastily lifted aside the portiere that was hanging over the door to keep in the heat, they revealed that Hsi-men Ch'ing, with a "loyal and tranquil hat" on his head, and dressed in informal garb, was coming out to receive him.

Upon seeing that Wang the Third was formally attired, Hsi-men Ch'ing made a point of saying, "Auntie Wen, why didn't you tell me beforehand? I'm here in my informal clothes."

He then turned to his attendants, saying, "Bring me my formal clothing."

This threw Wang the Third into such consternation that he stepped forward to stop him, exclaiming, "Distinguished elder, make yourself easy. Your humble junior has made bold to come and impose upon you. How could I presume to put you to any inconvenience?"

Upon entering the reception hall, Wang the Third made a point of asking Hsi-men Ch'ing to assume the position of honor so that he could kowtow to him, but Hsi-men Ch'ing repeatedly demurred, saying with a smile, "This is my humble abode, after all."

Hsi-men Ch'ing then seized the initiative by paying the first reverence to his visitor.

"Your humble junior," said Wang the Third, "is guilty of a transgression. I have long been an admirer of yours but have failed to pay you my respects."

"Let us both dispense with further formalities," said Hsi-men Ch'ing.

Wang the Third, however, persisted in begging Hsi-men Ch'ing to accept his obeisance, saying, "As your humble junior, it is only appropriate that my venerable elder should accept my obeisance in order to atone for my failure to pay you my respects any earlier."

After an exchange of polite demurrals, Hsi-men Ch'ing finally permitted him to kowtow to him twice, after which he was offered a seat and sat down respectfully on the edge of his chair.

After a little while, tea was served, and Wang the Third saw that in Hsi-men Ch'ing's reception hall:

Brocaded standing screens were arrayed;

on the four walls were suspended scrolls depicting landscapes in golds and greens; the chairs were adorned with inlaid patterns and draped with green brocaded silk; while their seats were provided with sable cushions; and beneath them:

The entire floor was covered with rugs.[49]

In the middle of the room there stood a four-cornered brazier of yellow brass, polished:

With a glitter that rivaled the sun's.

Under the plaque over the door was an inscription reading "Bestowed by Imperial Favor" in the distinctive calligraphy of Mi Fu.[50]

Upon surveying these surroundings, Wang the Third appeared somewhat more composed, as he addressed Hsi-men Ch'ing, saying, "Your humble junior has a matter that he is reluctant to trouble Your Eminence with."

So saying, he reached into his sleeve to extract his written statement of the case and handed it to Hsi-men Ch'ing, getting up from his seat in order to do so, and kneeling down in front of him.

Hsi-men Ch'ing reached out a hand to help him up, saying, "My worthy acquaintance, if you have something to say to me, there is no reason not to say it."

Wang the Third then said, "Your humble junior is devoid of talent and is genuinely guilty of an offense. It is my earnest hope that my venerable elder, out of consideration for the position of my late father as a high-ranking military official, will consent to be lenient toward your humble junior's ignorant offense. If you will but allow him to preserve his sense of shame by relieving him of the necessity to appear in court, you will spare your humble junior from imminent death and confer upon him the good fortune of a return to life. He will:

Carry rings and knot grass in order to repay you,[51]
And awaits your decision in fear and trepidation."[52]

When Hsi-men Ch'ing opened the document and observed that it contained the names of the five "cribbers," Trifler Chang and the rest, he said, "As for this bunch of 'bare sticks,' I have already dealt with them in the yamen today by punishing them severely and then letting them go. What business do they have trying to put the bite on you?"

"They are demanding that I do thus and so," said Wang the Third. "They claim that my venerable elder, after presiding over their punishment in the yamen, drove them out with the promise that your humble junior would also be required to appear in court. They have chosen to camp out in my home, where they are swearing oaths and raising a ruckus, and demanding monetary compensation, so that:

Peaceful existence is utterly impossible.[53]

Having no other recourse, I have come to my venerable elder's home to acknowledge my guilt."

So saying, he also handed over his list of proposed gifts.

When Hsi-men Ch'ing saw it, he said, "Whoever heard of such a thing?"

He then went on to say, "This bunch of 'bare sticks' are truly detestable. I actually let them off, so what business do they have going anywhere else to make trouble?"

Giving the list of proposed gifts back to Wang the Third, he continued, "My worthy acquaintance, please return home. I won't keep you any longer. Right now, I will dispatch people forthwith to arrest this bunch of 'bare sticks,' and, in days to come, I am prepared to put myself at your disposal."

"How could I presume upon such a thing?" responded Wang the Third. "Since my venerable elder has seen fit not to reject my request, I will be sure to return to your door in the future in order to express my humble thanks."

So saying, with:

A thousand thanks and ten thousand
     expressions of gratitude,

he started out the door.

Hsi-men Ch'ing saw him off as far as the second gate before saying, "Since I am wearing my informal clothes, it would not be appropriate for me to escort you any further."

Wang the Third continued out through the main gate, put his eye-shades back on, and went his way, accompanied by a page boy, while Auntie Wen requested a further word with Hsi-men Ch'ing.

"Don't do anything to alarm them," Hsi-men Ch'ing instructed her. "I will dispatch people to arrest them right away."

Auntie Wen caught up with Wang the Third, and the two of them made their way surreptitiously back into the house.

Unbeknownst to them, Hsi-men Ch'ing promptly dispatched an adjutant and four orderlies, who marched straight into Imperial Commissioner Wang's residence, where they found the bunch of 'bare sticks' drinking wine and raising a ruckus as before. When these functionaries barged in and:

Without permitting any further explanation,

proceeded to arrest them, and put them in handcuffs, they were so frightened:

Their complexions turned the color of dirt.[54]

"Wang the Third has played a nice trick on us," they objected. "He induced us to stay put in his house, while reversing the angle of the hoe and turning us over like the clods that we are."

The orderlies and the adjutant took them to task, saying, "You characters had better stop talking such nonsense. What good will it do you? Each of you should be preparing to plead for his life in front of His Honor. That would be more like it."

"What you gentlemen suggest is correct," responded Trifler Chang.

Before long, they were all escorted under guard to Hsi-men Ch'ing's residence, where the orderlies at the gate, and P'ing-an as well, all stuck out their hands and demanded a bribe before they would go inside and announce their arrival. The bunch of them had no recourse but to divest themselves of their jackets, or take the hairnet rings off their heads, to comply with these demands, before they were directed to proceed inside. After what seemed like half a day, Hsi-men Ch'ing came out and seated himself in the reception hall as though he were presiding over a court of law, while the adjutant ushered the culprits in and directed them to kneel at the foot of the hall.

Hsi-men Ch'ing upbraided them, saying, "What am I to do with you bunch of 'bare sticks'? I treated you leniently, after all, so what business did you have claiming to speak for my yamen, and going to his home in the attempt to extort money from him? Tell me the truth. Just how much money did you manage to extort? If you don't tell me, I'll order my attendants to put the squeezers on you and give you a real squeezing."

He had no sooner uttered these words than the orderlies in attendance promptly brought out five or six sets of brand new squeezers and stood ready to apply them.

Trifler Chang and the rest of them had no recourse but to kowtow to him in their abased position and plead with him, saying, "Your humble servants did not extort so much as a candareen in the way of compensation from anybody. All we did was to relate the fact that we had been driven out of the yamen, and request the opportunity to explain the situation to him. His household even provided wine and food for our entertainment. We never attempted to extort anything from him."

"You never should have gone to his home in the first place," pronounced Hsi-men Ch'ing. "You bunch of 'bare sticks' make it your business to take advantage of young men of good family and always have your hands out for whatever you can get out of them. Such conduct is truly reprehensible. As long as you won't confess the truth, I'll have you taken to the yamen and incarcerated there. Tomorrow, I'll subject you to a severe interrogation, obtain your confessions, and sentence you to public exposure in the cangue."

The group of them, as one man, pled for mercy as they wept, saying, "Your Heavenly Honor, save our lives, we pray. Your humble servants will never presume to approach his door again in order to make trouble for him. Not to mention public exposure, to imprison us in these cold winter months is tantamount to a death sentence."

"What am I to do with you 'bare sticks'?" said Hsi-men Ch'ing. "I tell you that if I let you go, I expect you to:
    Cleanse your hearts and correct your faults,
devoting yourselves to making an honest living. You must cease:
    Colluding with the bordellos in the quarter,
to lead young men astray and cheat them out of their possessions. If you are ever haled before my yamen again, I will have you all beaten to death."

He then shouted, "Get out of here," and the bunch of them, feeling lucky to have escaped with their lives, flew outside as fast as they could go. Truly:
    Breaking to pieces the jade cage,
        the phoenix flies away;
    Smashing apart the metal padlock,
        the dragon breaks free.

Hsi-men Ch'ing, having thus disposed of the bunch of them, returned to the rear compound, where Yüeh-niang asked him, "Was this something to do with Wang the Third?"

"It does indeed have to do with the third son of Imperial Commissioner Wang," responded Hsi-men Ch'ing, "the same one who was responsible for that fix that Li Kuei-chieh got herself into some time ago. And today, that

lousy little whore has not changed her ways but has taken up with him again.
He has been maintaining her as his mistress for a fee of thirty taels of silver a
month. No wonder she has been hoodwinking me all this time. But what she
did not anticipate was that there was an insider involved who explained the
situation to me, so that, yesterday, I dispatched some minions to apprehend
this bunch of scamps and bring them before me in the yamen, where I had
them put in the squeezers and subjected to a beating. But who could have
anticipated that this bunch of scamps would go to his home and kick up a fuss
in the hope of shaking him down for a few taels of silver? Fearing that his presence would be demanded in the yamen, and never having appeared in court
before, he was thrown into such consternation that he importuned Auntie
Wen into coming with a written offer of fifty taels of silver if I would intervene
on his behalf. Just now, I had these characters brought back before me here
and bombarded them with enough in the way of empty threats to keep them
from bothering him anymore.

"His family is unfortunate to have spawned such an unworthy young man.
Your ancestors established a firm foundation for the household, serving as imperial commissioners, and you are currently enrolled in the Military School,
but you have chosen not to pursue the opportunities for success that are yours
for the asking. You deliberately neglect the wife you have at home, though she
is as pretty as a sprig of blossoms, the niece of Defender-in-Chief Huang Ching-
ch'en in the Eastern Capital, paying her no heed, while, day and night, you
choose instead to tag along after this bunch of 'bare sticks,' giving yourself over
to debauchery in the licensed quarter. He has even gone so far as to pawn his
wife's jewelry when in need of spending money. This year, he is no more than
twenty years old, still only a youngster, but he will never amount to anything."

Yüeh-niang responded, "Why don't you:
        Piddle a bladderful of piss, and
        Take a look at your own reflection?
You're like:
        A raven scoffing at the blackness of a pig.[55]
Truly:
        The lampstand casts no light upon itself.[56]
You may well think you have the capacity to amount to something yourself,
but:
        You too have drunk water from that well.
        There's nothing you won't do.
What's so pure about your own conduct that you should have the right to criti-
cize the conduct of others?"

With these few words she managed to reduce Hsi-men Ch'ing to silence.

Just as their meal was being served to them, the page boy Lai-an came in
and reported, "Master Ying the Second is here."

"Ask him to have a seat in the studio," said Hsi-men Ch'ing. "I'll be right there."

Wang Ching promptly proceeded to open the door to the studio by the front reception hall, and Ying Po-chüeh went inside and sat down on a chair beside the heated k'ang. Sometime later, Hsi-men Ch'ing came outside, exchanged salutations with him, and then sat down on the k'ang so the two of them could have a chat together.

"Brother," said Ying Po-chüeh, "how is it that, the day before yesterday, when we were at Hsieh Hsi-ta's place, you got up to go so early?"

"I had to get an early start the following day," said Hsi-men Ch'ing. "I've been busy at the yamen for days on end. Moreover, since I am subject to an impending merit evaluation, I have had to send someone to the Eastern Capital to see if he could pick up any news of the outcome. I am scarcely to be compared with the likes of you who have nothing else to do."

"Brother," continued Ying Po-chüeh, "have you really been tied up at the yamen for days on end?"

"Not a day goes by without something to keep me busy," said Hsi-men Ch'ing.

"Wang the Third tells me," went on Ying Po-chüeh, "that you dispatched people from the yamen on the evening of the tenth and arrested Trifler Chang and company, all five of them, at Li Kuei-chieh's place, allowing only Blab-bermouth Sun and Pockmarked Chu to escape. This morning, moreover, you had them brought before you at the yamen and subjected them to a beating before throwing them out. The bunch of them have all subsequently gone to the residence of Imperial Commissioner Wang. Why have you kept me in the dark and failed to tell me about it?"

"You silly dog!" expostulated Hsi-men Ch'ing. "Whoever told you such a thing? You must have heard incorrectly. It wasn't my yamen, but it may have been the office of Chou Hsiu, the commandant of the Regional Military Command."

"The office of the Regional Military Command," opined Ying Po-chüeh, "would hardly concern itself with such trivial matters."

"I fear then," said Hsi-men Ch'ing, "it must have been someone from the district yamen who arrested them."

"That's not the case," said Ying Po-chüeh. "This morning, Li Ming told me that the members of their whole establishment were scared out of their wits, and that Li Kuei-chieh was so frightened that she took to her bed and hasn't gotten up and about for the last two days, simply keeping to her k'ang. They feared that, once again, it was men who had been sent down from the Eastern Capital to make the arrests. Only this morning, upon making inquiries, did they discover that it was the office of the Provincial Surveillance Commission that had ordered the arrests."

"I haven't really been to the yamen the last few days," said Hsi-men Ch'ing, "and don't know anything about it. I've sworn an oath not to have anything further to do with Li Kuei-chieh, so what do I care if she has chosen to get herself into a predicament that scares her into taking to her bed?"

Ying Po-chüeh saw that Hsi-men Ch'ing's face was puffed out as though he were trying to contain a laugh and said, "Brother, what sort of a person are you, that you should even try to pull the wool over my eyes, and keep me in the dark? Since Li Ming told me about things today, I understand what you're up to in letting Pockmarked Chu and Blabbermouth Sun off the hook. After all, a judicial yamen like yours is unlikely to let people escape so easily. This is a case of your contriving things so that:

When the sheep is beaten, the colt and donkey tremble.

You just wanted to put the fear of God into Li Kuei-chieh's outfit so they would be reminded of what you're capable of. If you had dragged everyone involved into the yamen, you would have ruptured your relationships with them and created a lot of bad feelings.

Although you have taken the first step,
You are not obliged to take the second,

and, as a result, right now, when Blabbermouth Sun and Pockmarked Chu run into you, they are bound to feel somewhat discomfited. This scheme of yours is an instance of:

Conspicuously repairing the cliffside roadways,
While surreptitiously emerging at Ch'en-ts'ang.[57]

I trust you will not take offense, Brother, if I say that this is a brilliant ploy on your part. As the saying goes:

A Perfected Being does not reveal himself as such;
Were he to do so, he would not be a Perfected Being.[58]

If you were openly to play a trick of this kind, you would reveal your true colors and not be the clever character that you are. Brother, you are truly a master strategist and a man of capacious vision."

On hearing these few words, Hsi-men Ch'ing broke out laughing and said, "Since when am I any master strategist?"

"My guess would be," said Ying Po-chüeh, "that there certainly must have been some insider who told you the whole story. If not, how could you ever have ascertained the facts so accurately, or been able to employ such:

Devices beyond the ken of ghosts or spirits?"[59]

"You silly dog!" responded Hsi-men Ch'ing.

"The best way to avoid being found out,
Is not to do it in the first place."

"Brother," said Ying Po-chüeh, "at present, you would be well advised not to demand Wang the Third's appearance in court, that's all."

"Who is demanding that he do any such thing?" said Hsi-men Ch'ing. "Originally, when the functionaries presented the bill of particulars about the case, I personally struck out the names of Wang the Third, Pockmarked Chu, and Blabbermouth Sun, as well as those of Li Kuei-chieh and Ch'in Yü-chih, ordering them only to arrest that bunch of 'bare sticks.'"

"So why are they still bothering him right now?" asked Ying Po-chüeh.

"The truth of the matter is," said Hsi-men Ch'ing, "that they expected to be able to extort a few taels of silver out of him. How could they have anticipated that, just now, he would personally come to pay me a visit, kowtow to me, and offer an apology for his misbehavior? I consequently sent people to round up those 'bare sticks' and threatened to sentence them to public exposure in the cangue, whereupon they all pled for mercy and repeatedly promised that they would never dare make demands upon him again. Wang the Third, for his part, addressing me again and again as his venerable elder, presented me with a gift card offering me fifty taels of silver. I refused to accept anything from him, but he promised that he would invite me to his place sometime soon in order to express his gratitude."

"Really, he actually came to your place to apologize for his misbehavior?" asked Ying Po-chüeh in astonishment.

"Surely you don't suggest that I would deceive you," responded Hsi-men Ch'ing, who then called for Wang Ching and told him, "Go fetch that calling card from Wang the Third and show it to Master Ying the Second."

Wang Ching went back to the master suite and brought out the calling card, which read, "Your humble pupil Wang Ts'ai:
        Presents his compliments with a hundred salutations."

When Ying Po-chüeh saw this, all he could do was to exclaim:
        Expressing the most fulsome admiration,
"Brother, your schemes are:
        Both marvelous and inscrutable."

"If you run into any of them," Hsi-men Ch'ing admonished Ying Po-chüeh, "don't reveal the fact that I had any prior knowledge of the situation."

"I understand," said Ying Po-chüeh:
        "The secret must not be disclosed.
How could I presume to say anything about it?"

After they had visited together for a while, and consumed a serving of tea, Ying Po-chüeh said, "Brother, I'd better be on my way. If, by any chance, Blabbermouth Sun and Pockmarked Chu should find their way here, don't tell them that I've been to see you."

"If they should come here," said Hsi-men Ch'ing, "I won't even receive them, but have the servants report that I'm not at home."

He then called in the people responsible for the front gate and told them, "If either of those persons should show up, simply report that I am not at home."

From this time on, Hsi-men Ch'ing refused to have anything more to do with Li Kuei-chieh and, when entertaining at home, no longer engaged Li

Ming to sing for the company, so his relations with the Li Family Establishment became cool. Truly:

> After last night's rainfall along the
>   Flower-washing Stream;[60]
> The green willows and fragrant verdure[61]
>   remain for whom to see?[62]

There is a poem that testifies to this:

> Who is able to visit the T'ien-t'ai Mountains
>   in pursuit of immortal maidens?[63]
> The Three Isles of the Blest remain invisible,
>   hidden amid the waves of the sea.[64]
> To vanish inside a nobleman's gates is to be
>   as unreachable as the ocean depths;
> From this point on, one's lover might as well
>   be a stranger along the highway.[65]

> If you want to know the outcome of these events,
> Pray consult the story related in the following chapter.

Chapter 70

HSI-MEN CH'ING'S SUCCESSFUL EFFORTS

PROCURE HIM A PROMOTION;

ASSEMBLED OFFICIALS REPORT BEFORE

DEFENDER-IN-CHIEF CHU MIEN

Last night, carried by the west wind,
    drums and bugles resounded;
At daybreak, in the bitter chill, one
    shivers under the cold felt.
Wrapped in impenetrable mist, the ground
    appears entirely invisible;
Spreading vastly in all four directions,
    all one can see is the sky.
Fancy accommodations, under such desolate
    conditions, are not available;
Even the hero Li Kuang was forced to tarry
    at the Pa-ling relay station.[1]
My patron, a virtual embodiment of Spring,[2]
    dispenses oceanlike favors;
May he set aside some of his residual warmth
    to bestow upon this sojourner.

THE STORY GOES that, from this time on, Hsi-men Ch'ing broke off relations with Li Kuei-chieh. But no more of this.

To resume our story, when the courier arrived at Judicial Commissioner Lin Ch'eng-hsün's place in Huai-ch'ing prefecture to inquire about the news, the commissioner gave him a sealed copy of the announcement of official promotions in the government gazette and rewarded him with five taels of silver. The courier set out on his return journey that very night and, upon arriving home, turned over the sealed material to the two judicial commissioners.

In the reception hall of the yamen, Hsia Yen-ling opened the envelope and, together with Hsi-men Ch'ing, perused the formal notification of the results of the merit evaluation for the members of the Embroidered Uniform Guard, the relevant parts of which read as follows:

Memorial from the Ministry of War

In re: The Strict Merit Evaluation of the Members of the Embroidered Uniform Guard, as Ordained by Explicit Imperial Command, in Order to Clarify the Grounds of Motivation and Discipline, and Glorify Your Majesty's Sage Administration

Submitted by Chu Mien, Defender-in-Chief in Charge of all the Officers and Staff of the Embroidered Uniform Guard Unit of the Imperial Insignia Guard, and Concurrently Grand Guardian, and Grand Guardian of the Heir Apparent

With regard to the above-mentioned evaluation of the officers of the Imperial Guard, this senior official will submit a report on his own conduct. As for the remainder, including the two divisions of detectives attached to the Imperial Prison under the jurisdiction of the Embroidered Uniform Guard, and the investigators, inspectors, and surveillance commissioners attached thereto, the director of the horse pasturages of the imperial domain and the inner and outer Capital Surveillance Commissions, as well as the battalion and company commanders serving under them, and the judges of the military guards, etc., they have all been classified on the basis of the dossiers that indicate whether their posts are hereditary, due to routine promotion, promotion for merit, privilege, or purchase. On the basis of their seniority and qualifications, they have all been fairly evaluated as to their worthiness, or lack thereof, and the results are hereby reported to Your Majesty with the request that they be sent to the appropriate board for further discussion as to the appropriate promotions, demotions, transfers, or dismissals.

This memorial elicited an imperial rescript that read as follows:

Upon being returned to the Ministry of War, let this memorial be:

Respectfully received and respectfully acted upon.

A copy of this edict was duly received by the Office of Scrutiny, and transmitted to the above ministry. Upon its perusal by the Defender-in-Chief Chu Mien, in accordance with established precedent, the said official proceeded to do everything in his power to demonstrate his loyalty by conducting an impartial evaluation. It is his responsibility to determine the worthiness, or lack thereof, of all the military officials subordinate to him, whether serving in or outside the capital, on the basis of their dossiers and public opinion, while ensuring that the reports he has received on them are both honest and without prejudice. By so doing, the said official exhibits his awareness of his proximity to the imperial presence, on the one hand, and his loyal concern for the welfare of the state, on the other. It goes without saying that differentiating into categories those who deserve encouragement, while distinguishing between the worthy and the unworthy in an orderly manner,[3] provides motivation for human ambition and accords with the public's sense of justice. But magnanimity and severity, rewards and punishments, are the prerogative of Your Majesty and, upon receipt of Your mandate, will be meted out in accordance with precedent. It is to be hoped that, if the evaluations are cogent, they will command general assent, and if redundant posts are eliminated, bureaucratic discipline will be enhanced.

The imperial rescript elicited by this memorial read:

> Let this memorial be respectfully received and the recommendations therein be enacted as proposed.

The relevant parts of the evaluation read as follows:

> As for the judicial commissioner of the Shantung Provincial Surveillance Commission, and concurrently battalion commander of the Embroidered Uniform Guard, Hsia Yen-ling, his qualifications and reputation are long-standing, and his talent and experience are well established. In the past, when in charge of herds in the horse pasturages of the imperial domain, the area of his jurisdiction was tranquil; and now that he presides over judicial matters in Shantung, his reputation for effective government is outstanding. It is appropriate that his ambitions should be encouraged by promotion to the post of commander of the escort for imperial processions.
>
> As for the assistant judicial commissioner, and concurrently battalion vice-commander, Hsi-men Ch'ing, his abilities and initiative have long been acknowledged to be exceptional. Since his family is affluent, he has not been acquisitive in office. He is diligent and industrious in his support of the national interest, and his censorial work has been meritorious. In facilitating the Divine Shipments of the Flower and Rock Convoys he has scrupulously avoided any peculation. For his administration of the laws he is universally admired by the people of Shantung. It is appropriate that he be promoted to the post of full commissioner in order to preside over the judicial system.
>
> As for the commissioner of the Huai-ch'ing office of the Provincial Surveillance Commission, and battalion commander of the Embroidered Uniform Guard, Lin Ch'eng-hsün, having been an assiduous student in his youth, he has won a place in the military recruitment examinations, entitling him to succeed to a hereditary office. He is a man of no ordinary ambition, who is meticulous in performing his judicial functions. It is appropriate that he be encouraged by selection for a higher position.
>
> As for the assistant judicial commissioner and battalion vice commander Hsieh En, he exhibits the effects of old age and is inconsistent in the way he dispenses lenience and severity. Previously, when he served in the ranks, his performance was respectable enough, but since he has occupied a judicial office, his incapacity for the position has become increasingly evident. It is appropriate that he be cashiered and dismissed from office.

When Hsi-men Ch'ing saw that he was to be promoted to the post of full judicial commissioner:

His heart was filled with great joy;[4]

but when Hsia Yen-ling saw that he was to be promoted to the post of commander of the escort for imperial processions, he had nothing to say for what seemed like half a day, and:

The color drained out of his visage.[5]

They then opened and read the enclosed copy of a memorial from the Ministry of Works, submitted upon the completion of the Divine Shipments of the Flower and Rock Convoys, that read as follows:

Memorial from the Ministry of Works

In re: The Arrival in the Capital of the Divine Shipments of the Flower and Rock Convoys Is an Occasion for Celestial and Human Celebration. We Urgently Request a Demonstration of Your Majesty's Benevolence in Deigning to Bestow the Appropriate Rewards, in Order to Relieve the Distress of the Masses,[6] While Broadening the Scope of Your Sage Magnanimity

The imperial rescript elicited by this memorial read:

These Divine Shipments of the Flower and Rock Convoys, which are intended to supply the needs of the Forbidden City, and facilitate the completion of the Mount Ken Imperial Park, have been carried out at Our behest, and enhanced Our gratification. You have exerted your efforts to assist Us in Our pursuit of the ultimate goal of serving the school of the Mysterious Origin.

In the localities through which the Flower and Rock Convoys passed, it is acknowledged that the common people have been made to suffer privation. It is hereby ordered that the offices of the grand coordinators and regional investigating censors should clearly investigate the facts[7] and remit one-half of the annual land taxes due this year from the affected regions. As for the embankments and dikes that have been destroyed, your ministry must send officials to join with the grand coordinators and censors in having them repaired forthwith. When this work is completed, we will depute the palace attendant Meng Ch'ang-ling[8] to go to the areas in question and offer a sacrifice on Our behalf.

Ts'ai Ching, Li Pang-yen, Wang Wei,[9] Cheng Chü-chung,[10] and Kao Ch'iu, who lend their support to Our Person by serving in the Inner Court, have all been distinguished for their meritorious efforts in facilitating this undertaking. Let Ts'ai Ching be granted the title of grand preceptor, Li Pang-yen be granted the titles of pillar of state and grand preceptor of the heir apparent, Wang Wei be granted the title of grand mentor, and Cheng Chü-chung and Kao Ch'iu be granted the title of grand guardian; and let each of them be rewarded with fifty taels of silver and enough fabric to supply both exterior and lining for four sets of clothing. Let Ts'ai Yu also be granted the privilege of having his son, Ts'ai Hsing,[11] appointed as director of the Palace Administration.

The preceptor of state, Lin Ling-su,[12] clearly understands what We are hoping to accomplish by protecting the realm, proclaiming the means of transformation, conveying the Divine Shipments from a distance, and launching a northern expedition against the barbarian invaders, all of which things are truly undertaken with divine sanction. Let him be awarded the additional rank of Earl of Loyalty and Filiality, with an annual stipend of a thousand piculs of grain, be presented with a dragon robe featuring a roundel with the motif of a full-face coiled dragon,[13] be granted the privilege of riding into the palace in a sedan chair, and be rewarded further with the titles the Supreme Patriarch of the Jade Perfected,[14] the Perfect Man of Profound Lucidity, Mysterious Subtlety, and Broad Virtue, the Feathered Sojourner from the Golden Portal,[15] and the Master of Penetrating Perfection, Realized Numinousness, and Mysterious Subtlety.[16]

Chu Mien and Huang Ching-ch'en have shown commendable loyalty and diligence in supervising the Divine Shipments of the Flower and Rock Convoys. Let Chu Mien be granted the additional titles of grand mentor and grand mentor of the heir apparent, and Huang Ching-ch'en be granted the title of defender-in-chief of the Palace Command and put in charge of the Supervisorate of Palace Transport. Let each of them also be granted the privilege of having one son appointed battalion commander in the Imperial Insignia Guard.

Let the palace attendants Li Yen, Meng Ch'ang-ling, Chia Hsiang, Ho Hsin, and Lan Ts'ung-hsi[17] be granted the title of the Five Court Attendants of the Yen-fu Palace.[18] Let them each be presented with a python robe and a jade girdle, and be granted the privilege of having one younger brother or nephew appointed to the substantive post of battalion vice commander in the Imperial Insignia Guard.

Let the minister of rites Chang Pang-ch'ang,[19] the left vice minister of rites and academician Ts'ai Yu, the right vice minister of rites Pai Shih-chung,[20] the minister of war Yü Shen, and the minister of works Lin Shu[21] all be granted the title of grand guardian of the heir apparent, and let each of them be further rewarded with forty taels of silver and enough variegated satin to supply both exterior and lining for two sets of clothing.

Let the grand coordinator of Liang-Che, and concurrently assistant censor-in-chief, Chang Ko,[22] be promoted to the post of right vice minister of the Ministry of Works. Let the grand coordinator of Shantung, and concurrently censor-in-chief, Hou Meng be promoted to the post of chief minister of the Court of Imperial Sacrifices. Let the regional investigating censors of Liang-Che and Shantung, Yin Ta-liang[23] and Sung Ch'iao-nien, as well as the secretaries of the Bureau of Irrigation and Transportation in the Ministry of Works, An Ch'en and Wu Hsün, each be promoted one class in rank, and be rewarded with twenty taels of silver.

Let the battalion commanders who facilitated the Divine Shipments of the Flower and Rock Convoys Wei Ch'eng-hsün, Hsü Hsiang, Yang T'ing-p'ei, Ssu Feng-i, Chao Yu-lan, Fu T'ien-tse, Hsi-men Ch'ing, T'ien Chiu-kao, etc., each be promoted one class in rank.

Let the palace attendants Sung T'ui, etc., and the commanders of training divisions Wang Yu, etc., be rewarded with ten taels of silver; the battalion officers Hsüeh Hsien-chung, etc., be rewarded with five taels of silver; and the commandants Ch'ang Yü, etc., be rewarded with two lengths of silk.

Let these orders be directed to the attention of the appropriate offices.

When Hsia Yen-ling and Hsi-men Ch'ing had finished reading these documents, they left the yamen and returned home.

That afternoon, Wang the Third sent Yung-ting and Auntie Wen to deliver a letter box containing a gold-flecked accordion-bound invitation to Hsi-men Ch'ing, inviting him to a dinner party in his mansion on the eleventh day of the month as a meager expression of gratitude for the favor he had shown him. Upon receiving this missive, Hsi-men Ch'ing was:

Unable to contain his delight,

and assumed that it would not be long before Wang the Third's wife fell into his hands.

Who could have anticipated, however, that on the evening of the tenth a formal notification arrived from the Registry Office of the Embroidered Uniform Guard in the Eastern Capital, that read:

For the information of the judicial officers of all the provinces.

You must proceed to the capital as quickly as possible in order to arrive in time to present your memorials of gratitude to the throne at an audience on the Winter Solstice.

This order is not to be disobeyed, or

You will suffer for your culpability.[24]

After having read this, the next day, Hsi-men Ch'ing went to the yamen and, together with Hsia Yen-ling, wrote acknowledgments in accordion-bound albums and sent them off with the courier. But no more of this.

Each of them then returned to their homes, got together their luggage, prepared the customary presentation gifts, and arranged with each other to set out without delay.

Hsi-men Ch'ing sent Tai-an to summon Auntie Wen and told her to inform Wang the Third that he would be unable to make it to the dinner party to which he had been invited on the eleventh, because, thus and so, he had to go to the capital to attend an audience and express his gratitude to the throne.

Upon hearing this, Wang the Third said, "If my venerable elder has business to attend to, I will be happy to wait until his return before extending another invitation with the utmost sincerity."

Hsi-men Ch'ing then summoned Pen the Fourth, told him that he wanted him to accompany him on the trip, and gave him five taels of silver to cover his household expenses while he was away. He left Ch'un-hung behind to look after the household but took Tai-an and Wang Ching with him to attend to his needs on the road. He also borrowed four police officers and four ponies from Commandant Chou Hsiu, saw that the luggage was properly packed up, and arranged for a closed sedan chair, a horse, and orderlies to carry the sedan chair. Hsia Yen-ling, for his part, was accompanied by his servant Hsia Shou. The two officials, between them, had an entourage of more than twenty persons.

They set out from Ch'ing-ho district on the twelfth day of the month.

It was winter when the days are short, and

They traveled both by day and by night.

When they reached Huai-ch'ing prefecture in Huai-hsi and called upon Battalion Commander Lin Ch'eng-hsün, they found that he had already departed for the Eastern Capital. Along the way:

When cold, they sat in their sedan chairs;
When warm, they made their way on horseback.
Each morning they tramped the purple road and red dust;[25]
Every evening they stayed in relay stations or in inns.

Truly:

When thoughts are pressing one wants to wave
  the blue-felt banner;
When the mind is eager one beats to tatters
  the purple-cord whip.

To make a long story short, when they arrived in the Eastern Capital and entered by way of the Myriad Years Gate, Hsi-men Ch'ing wanted to separate, intending to go stay at the Hsiang-kuo Temple, or Temple of the Protector of the State,[26] but Hsia Yen-ling would not agree, insisting that he come and stay with his relative, Privy Councilor Ts'ui Shou-yü. Hsi-men Ch'ing thus felt constrained to prepare a calling card and send it ahead for presentation to his prospective host.

When they arrived, Privy Councilor Ts'ui was at home and came out to greet them. After they had entered the reception hall and exchanged the customary amenities of introduction, commented on the weather, and expressed:

The sentiments they had felt while apart,

they dusted themselves off and sat down for a serving of tea, whereupon their host saluted Hsi-men Ch'ing with clasped hands and asked him for his distinguished courtesy name.

"My courtesy name is Ssu-ch'üan," responded Hsi-men Ch'ing.

He then went on to inquire, "May I ask your distinguished courtesy name, venerable sir?"

Privy Councilor Ts'ui replied, "Your pupil is unsophisticated by nature and lives in idle seclusion. My humble name is Shou-yü, and my courtesy name is Hsün-chai, or Unassuming Studio."

He then went on to say, "My relative, Hsia Yen-ling, has long sung the praises of your surpassing virtue and acknowledged his dependence on your support. Your single-minded cooperation could not have been more generous."

"I am hardly deserving of such praise," said Hsi-men Ch'ing. "I have constantly benefitted from his instruction. And now that he has been elevated to a senior position in the capital, his opportunities for further advancement can only be enhanced. He is to be congratulated! He is to be congratulated!"

"How can you say such a thing?" exclaimed Hsia Yen-ling.

"Though one may possess the tools for the task,
It is better to wait for the times to be right."[27]

"What Ssu-ch'üan says is quite right," opined Privy Councilor Ts'ui. "Your status being what it is, it cannot be otherwise."

At the conclusion of this conversational exchange they all laughed. It was not long before their luggage was stored away, and as evening fell, Privy Councilor Ts'ui ordered his servants to set up a table and provide them with something to eat. Needless to say, the fare consisted of fruits, wine, seasonal delicacies, and the like, but there is no need to describe this in detail. That night, the two of them slept in Privy Councilor Ts'ui's home. But no more of this.

Early the next morning, they each got ready their gifts and calling cards and set off, accompanied by their attendants, to pay their respects at the mansion of Grand Preceptor Ts'ai Ching. That day the grand preceptor had not yet returned from the Secretariat. The officials and functionaries who had assembled in front of the mansion were like:

Swarming bees and gathering ants,[28]
Jammed together into an indivisible mass.
Hsi-men Ch'ing and Hsia Yen-ling persuaded the functionaries in charge of the gate to take their calling cards inside by presenting them with two packets of silver.

When Majordomo Chai Ch'ien saw their cards, he came out to greet them and invited them into his private residence at the front of the mansion. Hsia Yen-ling began by introducing himself, after which, Hsi-men Ch'ing and Chai Ch'ien exchanged the customary amenities and alluded to the correspondence between them that had occurred since their last meeting. Only then did they sit down in the positions appropriate for host and guests.

Hsia Yen-ling was the first to present his list of gifts, which consisted of two bolts of cloud-crane brocade and two bolts of variegated satin for the grand preceptor, along with ten taels of silver for Chai Ch'ien. Hsi-men Ch'ing's list of presents for the grand preceptor consisted of a crimson variegated python robe, a jet, figured, round-collared robe emblazoned with a mandarin square that featured a *tou-niu*[29] design, and two bolts of capital brocade. His personal gifts to Chai Ch'ien consisted of a bolt of black velvet decorated with a cloud pattern in green thread, and thirty taels of silver. Chai Ch'ien ordered his attendants to take the gifts for the grand preceptor into the mansion and see that they were properly registered. The only item that he agreed to accept for himself was the bolt of cloud-patterned velvet presented by Hsi-men Ch'ing.

He refused to accept the thirty taels of silver from Hsi-men Ch'ing and the ten taels of silver from Hsia Yen-ling, saying, "Whoever heard of such a thing? Were I to do so, it would violate the feeling of intimacy between us."

He then ordered his attendants to set up a table and serve them a meal, saying, "Today His Majesty is dedicating the plaques to be installed in the newly completed Mount Ken Imperial Park, and His Honor has gone out to the Precious Tablet Temple of Highest Clarity[30] in order to preside over the sacrifices. The ceremony will not be over until this afternoon, and, when he gets home, he plans to go with His Honor Li Pang-yen to attend a party at the home of the

distaff relative of the imperial family, Cheng Chü-chung. I fear that if my kinsman and Judicial Commissioner Hsia wait for him, it will only interfere with
your other activities. Whenever His Honor happens to be free, I will undertake to inform him of your presence. It's all the same, one way or the other."

"We are grateful for my kinsman's efforts on our behalf," said Hsi-men
Ch'ing. "If you do that, it will be fine by us."

Chai Ch'ien went on to ask, "Where is my kinsman staying?"

Hsi-men Ch'ing then explained that they were staying in the home of Hsia
Yen-ling's relative, Ts'ui Shou-yü.

It was not long before a table was formally set up, and soup, rice, and assorted delicacies were simultaneously served up in:

> Large platters and large bowls.

These were all delicious fried and roasted specialties prepared by the Court
of Imperial Entertainments:

> Than which there were no finer.

After they had each consumed three cups of wine, served in golden goblets,
they were prepared to say their farewells and get up to go, but Chai Ch'ien
endeavored to retain them a little longer and ordered his attendants to pour
another serving of wine.

Hsi-men Ch'ing then inquired, "Kinsman, when are we scheduled to appear at the imperial audience?"

"Kinsman," replied Chai Ch'ien, "your case differs from that of His Honor
Hsia. His Honor is now a senior official serving in the capital, and his case falls
into a different category. You will appear at the audience together with the
newly appointed assistant battalion commander of the Embroidered Uniform
Guard, the nephew of Eunuch Director Ho Hsin, Ho Yung-shou. He will take
your place as assistant judicial commissioner, since you are now the chief
commissioner, so the two of you will be colleagues. He has already presented
his memorial of gratitude, so, as soon as you have appeared at an audience and
presented your memorial, the two of you can go together to receive your orders of appointment. You might as well arrange to do everything in concert
with him."

When Hsia Yen-ling heard this, he did not have a single word to say.

Hsi-men Ch'ing said, "Kinsman, let me ask you, since you are knowledge-
able about such things, how would it be if I were to wait until after the Emperor has returned from performing the Suburban Sacrifice to Heaven on the
day of the winter solstice to attend an audience?"

"Kinsman," responded Chai Ch'ien, "you ought not to wait that long. On
the day of the winter solstice, when His Majesty has returned from performing
the Suburban Sacrifice to Heaven, and the officials from the entire empire
have offered their congratulatory memorials, a banquet will be held to celebrate the completion of the ceremony. Are you willing to wait until after that?
The best thing for you to do is to go and report your name to the Court of State
Ceremonial today, and then submit your individual memorial of gratitude to

the throne at the early audience tomorrow morning. Then, on the day of the winter solstice, after Chu Mien, the senior official of the Embroidered Uniform Guard, has led the officials under his jurisdiction in submitting a joint memorial of gratitude to the throne, you can collect your orders of appointment and set out for home."

Hsi-men Ch'ing expressed his gratitude, saying, "I thank my kinsman for his advice.

What can I do to be worthy of such largess?"

When they were on the verge of departure, Chai Ch'ien took Hsi-men Ch'ing aside to have a word with him in private and reproached him severely, saying, "In the letter that I sent you a while ago, I insisted that the matter of your impending promotion should be kept strictly confidential and not be divulged to any of your colleagues. How is it then that my kinsman spoke of it to His Honor Hsia Yen-ling, with the result that he solicited a note from Perfect Man Lin Ling-su, bringing pressure to bear on Defender-in-Chief Chu Mien? The defender-in-chief then took the matter up with His Honor the grand preceptor, telling him that Hsia Yen-ling did not wish to be transferred to the capital as commander of the escort for imperial processions and preferred to remain in his current post as judicial commissioner for another three years. Eunuch Director Ho Hsin, who also serves in the Inner Court, in his turn, sought the aid of Consort An, née Liu,[31] the favorite of the Emperor, in seeing that an order was issued appointing his nephew, Ho Yung-shou, to replace you as assistant judicial commissioner in Shantung, and personally spoke to the grand preceptor and Defender-in-Chief Chu Mien about it. Thus, the favors sought on the two sides were in direct conflict with each other, and His Honor was put in an extremely difficult position. If I had not been able to insistently maintain your interest before His Honor, so that he ended by turning down Perfect Man Lin Ling-su's request, my kinsman might well have been pushed aside."

This speech had the effect of throwing Hsi-men Ch'ing into such consternation that he hastily performed an obeisance to Chai Ch'ien, saying, "I am profoundly indebted to my kinsman for his magnanimity. But I didn't speak to anyone about this matter. As for the gentleman in question, how could he ever have learned of it?"

Chai Ch'ien responded, "It has always been true that:

If critical matters are not kept secret
    harm will result.[32]

In the future, I trust that my kinsman will be more discreet about things. That's all."

At this point, Hsi-men Ch'ing, with:

A thousand thanks and ten thousand
    expressions of gratitude,

rejoined Hsia Yen-ling, and, after saying farewell, they made their departure. Upon arriving back at the home of Privy Councilor Ts'ui Shou-yü, Hsi-men

Ch'ing sent Pen the Fourth to report his name to the Court of State Ceremonial.

The next day, he and Hsia Yen-ling both went into the palace to attend the audience, dressed in their black gowns and official caps and girdles. Who could have anticipated that as they were coming out through the main gate to the palace after submitting their memorials of gratitude to the throne and were walking past the gate tower on the west, what should they see but a black-clad lictor who came forward and asked, "Which of you is His Honor Hsi-men Ch'ing, the judicial commissioner of Shantung?"

Pen the Fourth asked him, "Who have you come from?"

"I come from Eunuch Director Ho Hsin of the Directorate for Buildings in the Palace Treasury," he replied, "who would like to have a word with His Honor."

Before he had even finished speaking, what should they see but a eunuch director, dressed in a crimson python robe, with a "three mountain hat"[33] on his head, and white-soled black boots on his feet, who approached them from the imperial roadway, and called out in an assertive voice, saying, "I would like to issue an invitation to His Honor Hsi-men Ch'ing."

Hsi-men Ch'ing, thereupon, parted company with Hsia Yen-ling and allowed himself to be conducted into an orderly room for the use of officers on duty that was located nearby. It was fitted with clear windows and translucent latticework, the fire in the brazier inside made it comfortably warm, and the table was laden with partitioned boxes for the serving of assorted delicacies. When they confronted each other inside, the eunuch saluted him with a bow, and Hsi-men Ch'ing hastened to bend his back and return the compliment.

The eunuch then said, "Your Honor doesn't know me, but I am Eunuch Director Ho Hsin of the Directorate for Buildings in the Palace Treasury and serve as an attendant in the fourth building of the Yen-ning Palace, the residence of Consort Tuan, née Feng.[34] The other day, when the palace construction was completed, the Lord of Ten Thousand Years rewarded me by appointing my nephew, Ho Yung-shou, to the position of battalion vice-commander in the Left Guard of the Embroidered Uniform Guard unit of the Imperial Insignia Guard, so he will serve as assistant judicial commissioner in your jurisdiction and will be a colleague of yours."

"So you are the venerable Eunuch Director Ho Hsin," said Hsi-men Ch'ing. "I did not recognize you. Forgive me. Forgive me."

He then bowed to him again and said, "In these precincts of the Forbidden City I cannot presume to make a proper obeisance to you. Permit me to call upon you in your private residence someday soon and pay my respects."

Thereupon, the customary amenities having been performed, his host offered him a seat, and a servant presented them with tea, served with raised saucers on a platter of cinnabar-red lacquer decorated with gold tracery. When they had finished their tea, the lids were removed from the partitioned boxes

The Eunuch Ho Hsin Treats a Guest in a Palace Building

on the table, exposing a rich supply of soup and rice and other delicacies, and they were provided with cups and chopsticks.

"There is no need for small cups," said Eunuch Director Ho Hsin. "I am aware that Your Honor has just come from an audience, and the weather is cold. Were I to entertain you with small cups, while offering you no more than this meager fare, it would be an affront to Your Honor. What you need is a pick-me-up."[35]

"I ought not to impose upon you to such an extent," said Hsi-men Ch'ing.

Eunuch Director Ho thereupon filled a large cup to the brim and handed it to Hsi-men Ch'ing.

"I am much obliged to you, venerable sir," responded Hsi-men Ch'ing, "and your pupil will be happy to accept what you proffer. The only thing is that, upon leaving your presence, I must meet with other officials and pay my respects at the ministry. If my face is flushed from drinking:

It would hardly be appropriate."[36]

"Drink two cups to ward off the cold," said Eunuch Director Ho. "What harm can it do?"

He then went on to say, "My nephew is young, and unfamiliar with judicial matters. I hope that, for my sake, Your Honor will agree to afford him guidance in all things when he takes his place among your colleagues."

"How could I be so presumptuous?" said Hsi-men Ch'ing. "There is no need for such modesty on your part, venerable sir. My new colleague, your distinguished nephew, may be young, but:

Status affects character as nurture affects health.[37]
It is only natural that:
Good fortune serves to stimulate the intelligence."[38]

"That's a fine way to talk!" said Eunuch Director Ho. "As the sayings go:
Even if one studies for a lifetime, areas
    of ignorance will remain.[39]
The affairs of this world are as profuse
    as the hairs of an ox;
Even Confucius himself could not master
    more than a leg's worth.
I fear there are things he didn't know.
At all events, Your Honor must try to explain matters to him."

"Your pupil will endeavor to obey your instructions," said Hsi-men Ch'ing.

He then went on to ask, "Venerable sir, where is your private residence located? Your pupil would like to come there to pay his respects."

Eunuch Director Ho replied, "My humble abode is located in the Wen-hua fang, or Cultural Florescence precinct, to the east of the Heavenly River Bridge. It can be identified by the two stone lions that serve as a mounting platform outside the gate."

He then went on to ask, "Where is Your Honor staying? I would like to send the new official in my household over to pay you his respects."

"Your pupil," Hsi-men Ch'ing replied, "is lodging temporarily in the home of Privy Councilor Ts'ui Shou-yü."

After they had exchanged addresses, Hsi-men Ch'ing consumed a large cup of the proffered pick-me-up and then got up to go.

Eunuch Director Ho Hsin saw him to the door and saluted him with clasped hands, saying, "With regard to what I spoke of to you just now, I hope that Your Honor will consent to look out for my nephew in all things. He is waiting to accompany you when you submit your memorial of gratitude and go to proffer the customary gifts to Chu Mien, the senior official of the Embroidered Uniform Guard, after which you can go together to collect your orders of appointment."

"Venerable sir," responded Hsi-men Ch'ing, "there is no need for you to instruct me any further. Your pupil understands the situation."

Thereupon, he exited the gate of the Forbidden City and went to report to the Ministry of War, where he ran into Hsia Yen-ling and joined him in going to pay his respects to the appropriate officials. By the time he had gone to formally present himself to Defender-in-Chief Chu Mien, handed in his curriculum vitae, applied for his order of appointment, and reported to the Registry Office and the other appropriate officials, it was already late in the afternoon. Judicial Commissioner Hsia Yen-ling, for his part, had changed into the uniform of his new position as commander of the escort for imperial processions, prepared his own curriculum vitae, formally presented himself to Defender-in-Chief Chu Mien, where he was excused from having to kowtow, and selected a date for his assumption of office in the Southern Yamen, the headquarters of the Embroidered Uniform Guard.

When Hsia Yen-ling came out the door of the ministry, he found that Hsi-men Ch'ing was there waiting for him, though he hesitated to ride alongside him, and suggested that he be the first to mount. Hsia Yen-ling protested at this and insisted that they ride side by side.

Hsi-men Ch'ing addressed him as his superior in rank, but Hsia Yen-ling objected, saying, "Ssu-ch'üan, the two of us are former colleagues, after all. How can you start addressing me that way?"

"Our differences in status have been determined," said Hsi-men Ch'ing.

"It is only natural.
There is no need for such modesty on your part."

He then went on to ask, "Since Your Honor has been raised to such an exalted position and will not be returning to Shantung, when are you going to send for your esteemed dependents?"

"I would like to move them here as soon as possible," said Hsia Yen-ling, "but were I to do so, there would be no one to look after my property there. Right now, I plan to stay temporarily at my relative's place until after the New

Year's celebrations, and send someone to fetch the members of my household then. Meanwhile, I hope that my colleague will consent to look after them, early and late. If anyone is interested in purchasing my property, I hope that my colleague will take care of it on my behalf. I should be very grateful were you to do so."

"Your pupil will endeavor to obey your instructions," said Hsi-men Ch'ing. "May I ask what your property is worth?"

"That house of mine," replied Hsia Yen-ling, "was originally purchased from Eunuch Director Hsü for 1,200 taels. I subsequently had an extra story built in the rear, and the cost of the improvements came to 200 taels. Right now, I would be willing to let it go for the original purchase price."

"Since my distinguished colleague has confided in me," said Hsi-men Ch'ing, "if anyone should ask me about it, I will be able to answer without letting you down."

"The only thing is, I fear I am putting my colleague to a lot of trouble," responded Hsia Yen-ling.

When the two of them arrived back at the home of Ts'ui Shou-yü, Wang Ching approached them and reported, "His Honor, the newly appointed official Ho Yung-shou, came to pay you a visit. When he had dismounted and come into the reception hall, I told him that you had not yet returned from the Ministry of War. His Honor Ho said to give you his best regards. He also left calling cards for His Honor Hsia, and His Honor Ts'ui, and, at noon, he sent someone to deliver two pieces of satin brocade together with a calling card of safflower red paper."

He then showed these to Hsi-men Ch'ing, who saw that the card read, "The enclosed two satin kerchiefs are deferentially presented as a token of his respect by your humble colleague and student, Ho Yung-shou."

When Hsi-men Ch'ing had read this message, he promptly told Wang Ching to wrap up and seal two round-collared robes made in Nanking, featuring mandarin squares with variegated embroidered lions. After writing out a gift card, and having something to eat, he set off immediately for Eunuch Director Ho's home in order to pay a return visit.

Upon Hsi-men Ch'ing's arrival at the reception hall, Ho Yung-shou hurriedly straightened his clothing and came out to welcome him. He was wearing a variegated, figured, round-collared robe of jet cloud-patterned velvet, featuring a mandarin square with an embroidered lion; black shoes with black silk uppers; and a girdle with a decorative plaque of gilded tortoiseshell around his waist. He was not more than nineteen years old.

> His face looked as though it were powdered;
> He was bright-eyed and clean-cut; and
> His lips looked as though they were rouged.[40]

Hastening down the steps to greet his visitor, he proceeded to bow and scrape in the most deferential manner, exhibiting the utmost in the way of modesty and respect. As Hsi-men Ch'ing ascended the steps, the household servants hurried to lift aside the portiere, giving a welcoming shout as they waited upon him, fore and aft.

When the two of them had entered the reception hall and exchanged formal greetings, Hsi-men Ch'ing ordered Tai-an to open the box containing the robes he had prepared; proceeded to proffer:

The customary presentation gifts;

and kowtowed, saying, "When you deigned to pay me a visit a while ago and bestowed such lavish gifts upon me, I fear I was not there to welcome you. And, this morning, the venerable gentleman, your uncle, treated me to a repast in his orderly room, for which consideration I could not be more grateful."

Ho Yung-shou hastened to kowtow in return, saying, "Having received this trifling appointment, which entitles me to become a colleague of yours, I look forward to being the beneficiary of your instruction.

Such good fortune would suffice for three lives.

I went to pay you my respects a while ago but failed to see you, and now you have deigned to demonstrate your good will by:

Shedding glory on my humble abode."

He then ordered his attendants to put away the gifts. In the meantime, he pulled up some formal seats, upholstered in deerskin, and the two of them sat down in the positions of host and guest. His attendants served them with tea, and Ho Yung-shou bowed deeply as he presented a cup to Hsi-men Ch'ing, who got up from his seat and returned his salutation. As they were drinking their tea, they asked after each other's courtesy names.

"Your pupil's courtesy name is Ssu-ch'üan," replied Hsi-men Ch'ing.

To which Ho Yung-shou responded, "Your pupil's courtesy name is T'ien-ch'üan, or Heavenly Spring."

He then went on to ask, "Has my colleague already paid his respects to the officials at the Ministry of War today?"

"Upon coming out of the Forbidden City after being entertained by your venerable uncle," said Hsi-men Ch'ing, "I reported to the Ministry of War, paid my formal respects to the commander of the Embroidered Uniform Guard, applied for my order of appointment, and reported to the other appropriate officials. When I returned, I saw your calling card and learned that you had condescended to pay me a visit. The fact that I was not there to welcome you has left me feeling:

Scarcely able to conquer my fear and trepidation."[41]

"Not knowing that my colleague had arrived," said Ho Yung-shou, "your pupil was tardy in paying his respects."

He then went on to ask, "Did my colleague and His Honor Hsia Yen-ling attend the audience this morning?"

"Hsia Yen-ling has now been promoted to the post of commander of the escort for imperial processions," said Hsi-men Ch'ing. "He and I attended the audience together this morning and expressed our gratitude for our new appointments. But when we reported to the Ministry of War to pay our respects to our superiors, he handed in his own documents and was interviewed separately."

When he had finished questioning him, Ho Yung-shou went on to say, "Since we have had a chance to consult together today, when do you think we should go to present our customary gifts to His Honor the defender-in-chief of the Embroidered Uniform Guard, preparatory to receiving our orders of appointment?"

"According to my kinsman Chai Ch'ien," said Hsi-men Ch'ing, "we should go first to the home of the defender-in-chief to present our gifts, before presenting our memorials of gratitude at the great audience. After that, we should proceed to report to the office of the Embroidered Uniform Guard, where we will receive our orders of appointment together with the rest."

"Since that is what my colleague suggests," said Ho Yung-shou, "let us prepare our gifts and go to present them early tomorrow morning."

Thereupon, the two of them went over their respective gifts together. Ho Yung-shou's consisted of two python robes and a jade girdle. Hsi-men Ch'ing's consisted of a length of scarlet satin brocade, emblazoned with a mandarin square that featured an embroidered *ch'i-lin*,[42] a python robe of blue silk, as well as a chatelaine of gold-embossed jade. Each of them also agreed to present four jugs of Chin-hua wine, and they arranged to go together to assemble in front of Defender-in-Chief Chu Mien's residence the following morning. Once these arrangements had been agreed upon, and they had consumed two servings of tea, Hsi-men Ch'ing took his leave and returned to Ts'ui Shou-yü's dwelling. He did not confide anything about these plans to Hsia Yen-ling. Of the events of that evening there is no more to tell.

Early the next morning, Hsi-men Ch'ing returned to Ho Yung-shou's place, where he found that his host had already prepared a small repast, along with a pick-me-up, which was duly served in:

Large platters and large bowls,

as neatly as could be. Even their servants were enabled to eat their fill. After finishing their meal, they went together to assemble before the front gate of Defender-in-Chief Chu Mien's residence, where they found that Pen the Fourth and a servant from the Ho household, who had gone ahead with the gifts, had already been waiting for them for some time.

At this time, Defender-in-Chief Chu Mien had recently been promoted to the rank of grand guardian, and Emperor Hui-tsung had deputed him to go to the Southern Altar, the site of the Suburban Sacrifice to Heaven, in order to preside over the inspection of the sacrificial animals, preparatory to the ceremony on the day of the winter solstice. He had not yet returned from this mission, and the area outside the gate of his residence was rendered black by the number of officials and functionaries who were gathered there in order to present him with congratulatory gifts, who were so closely packed together that it felt as though they were:

> Locked tight in an iron bucket.

Ho Yung-shou, together with Hsi-men Ch'ing, dismounted and sat down to wait in the home of an acquaintance of his that was located nearby, while sending a servant to listen for the sound of the criers that would precede the entourage of the defender-in-chief, so that he could come back and report on his impending arrival.

Their wait extended until the early afternoon, at which time they suddenly saw a man flying along on horseback, who announced, "His Honor is on his way back from inspecting the sacrificial animals. He has already entered the city through the Southern Breeze Gate[43] and has ordered that casual onlookers should be cleared out of the way."

Not long afterwards, another mounted courier appeared and reported, "His Honor has already crossed the Heavenly River Bridge."

At this juncture, the first contingent of chefs, together with their tea boxes and partitioned food boxes, passed by. It was only after what seemed like another half day had elapsed that a squad of cavalry, with their identifying insignia, appeared in the distance.

> These officers all wore iron helmets on their heads,
> Decorated with chain patterns and emblazoned with
>   the character for courage;
> Their torsos were clad in hauberks of nankeen,
>   stiffened with carved lacquer;
> Over which they wore jackets of blue satin with
>   narrow sleeves and flowered roundels,
> Held in place with red chiffon cummerbunds,
> On top of battle skirts of green deerskin adorned
>   with drawnwork aquatic creatures;
> While their feet were shod with four-seamed
>   tight-fitting black boots.
> Their bows were adorned with painted magpies;
> Their arrows were fitted with eagle feathers;[44]
> And in brocade bags across their shoulders they bore
>   blue command standards in gilt lettering.

Truly:

> The men look like fierce tigers;
> The horses rival flying dragons.[45]

Before long, a squad of soldiers bearing blue flags passed by, enclosing between them a squad of adjutants, dressed in black. Each and every one of them was:

> Lanky and large-sized,
> Ruthless and menacing.

On their heads they sported jet-black caps,
On their bodies they wore long black gowns,
Their feet were clad in dark brown
    leather-soled boots,
At their waists there were hanging
    tiger-head tallies.[46]
Mounted on their horses, truly:
Their air was awe-inspiring,[47]
Their appearance was imposing.

Before long, when these three squads of cavalry, with their identifying insignia, had passed by, what should they hear but the approaching sound of shouting to clear the way. The outriders who were creating this din were all:

Officers of the Imperial Insignia Guard,
Orderlies on assignment for the occasion,
More than six feet in stature, and
Broad-shouldered as they come.
Each of them wore a tall black cylindrical hat,
All were togged out in puttees and black boots.
In their left hands they wielded rattan canes,
While their right hands hiked up their clothes.

As these outriders advanced, continuously shouting to clear the way, the people in the roadway ahead of them were:

Truly frightened out of their wits;
Suddenly the streets were deserted.

After the squad of outriders had passed, they were followed by two additional contingents of guardsmen, who were succeeded in turn by a squad of twenty detectives in black livery, spread out on either side of the street like the wings of a formation of wild geese, all of whom were tall and sturdy in stature. They were uniformly:

Stout-waisted thick-stomached types;
Golden-eyed brown-bearded specimens.
Each of them was as rapacious and cruel as a tiger;
None of them was capable of showing the least pity.

In the wake of these ten pairs of black-liveried guardsmen appeared an open sedan chair, carried by eight bearers, accompanied by eight outriders, in which Defender-in-Chief Chu Mien was seated.

Wearing on his head the black silk hat of an official,
His body was clad in a robe of crimson velvet
    with a *tou-niu* mandarin square;
His waist was enclosed in a four-finger-wide girdle
    with an openwork plaque of white jade
    from the Ch'u Mountains,[48]
His feet were shod in black boots;

At his midriff there hung the ivory insignia
     of a grand guardian and a fish-shaped
     key of yellow gold,
Affixed to his hat were a dangling sable tail
     and a golden cicada;[49]
His feet were firmly planted on a footrest
     draped in tiger skin.
The bearers bore his sedan chair so high that
     it was three feet off the ground.
It was preceded by two household servants, one on
     either side, clad in blue satin, and
     girdles with rhinoceros horn plaques,
And was followed by yet another squad of cavalry,
     carrying six identifying insignia,
     and six more blue command standards,
Who kept close at hand in order to receive orders.
Behind these there came several tens of others,
     riding fine steeds with jeweled saddles,
     jade bridles, and golden stirrups,
All of whom were majordomos, factotums, file clerks,
     clerical subofficials, or scribes;
One and all of whom were gilded and pampered youths
     from influential households,
Who were motivated only by lust and avarice,
Utterly indifferent to regulations and laws.

In rapid succession, one squad after another arrived in front of the defender-in-chief's residence, where they arrayed themselves in a straight line. The on-lookers fell silent and stayed out of the way, not one of them daring to cough. The assembled officials and functionaries who had come to offer their gifts rendered the area black as they knelt down by the side of the road.

After some time, when the sedan chair of the defender-in-chief arrived before them, his attendants shouted, "Stand up, and remain at attention!" To which the assembled crowd assented with a single shout. Truly:

The sound shook the cloudy empyrean.

To the east, all that could be heard was a steady beat as:

Drums and music began to sound.

It so happens that the six senior officers in his yamen, on learning that the defender-in-chief had been elevated to the rank of grand master of the imperial household, and grand guardian, and been granted the privilege of having a son appointed battalion commander in the Imperial Insignia Guard, had all prepared lavish gifts, including wine and ingredients for a feast, and assembled in order to proffer their congratulations. For this reason, there were quite a few officials from the Music Office in attendance, who had begun to strike up their music. No sooner did the defender-in-chief descend from his sedan chair than the music came to a halt, and the various officials and functionaries made ready to present themselves.

All of a sudden, shouting to clear the way was heard, and a servitor in black livery, holding two red calling cards in his hand, came flying up on horseback and handed them to the guards at the gate, saying, "The minister of rites Chang Pang-ch'ang, and His Honor the academician Ts'ai Yu, are coming to pay their respects."

This information was promptly conveyed inside. Before long, their sedan chairs showed up at the gate, and the minister Chang Pang-ch'ang and vice minister Ts'ai Yu, wearing scarlet ceremonial robes with mandarin squares featuring embroidered peacocks, one of them sporting a girdle with a plaque of rhinoceros horn, and the other a girdle with a plaque of gold, went inside to pay their respects.

After they had been entertained with tea and seen on their way, the minister of personnel Wang Tsu-tao,[50] the left vice minister Han Lü, and the right vice minister Yin Ching[51] also came to pay their respects to Defender-in-Chief Chu Mien.

After they had been entertained with tea and seen on their way, the imperial relative and Duke of Chia, Chao I, the military affairs commissioner Cheng Chü-chung, and the commandant-escort and director of the Court of the Imperial Clan, Wang Shen, clad in nankeen robes with jade girdles, also came to pay their respects. Of the three, Cheng Chü-chung alone rode in a sedan chair, the other two being mounted on horseback.

After they had been seen off, the six senior officers in the defender-in-chief's yamen arrived, surrounded by criers proclaiming the protocol, and drawn up in appropriate order. The first of these was the superintendent of justice for the two townships of the Eastern Capital, Sun Jung;[52] the second was the chief inspector, Liang Ying-lung; the third was the director of the Office of Herds in the Inner and Outer Demesnes of the Court of the Imperial Stud, the nephew of Defender-in-Chief T'ung Kuan, T'ung T'ien-yin; the fourth was the surveillance commissioner of the thirteen gates of the capital city, Huang Ching-ch'en; the fifth was the commander of the Capital Training Divisions and capital security commissioner, Tou Chien;[53] and the sixth was the ward-inspecting commandant of the inner and outer precincts of the Eastern Capital, Ch'en Tsung-shan. All of them were garbed in crimson robes and wore hats adorned with dangling sable tails and golden cicadas. Only Sun Jung, who held the rank of grand guardian of the heir apparent, wore a jade girdle, while the rest of them wore girdles of gold. When they dismounted and went inside, each of them took with him gifts of gold currency and bolts of fabric.

After a little while, the sound of music was heard, as the group of senior officers, wearing floral ornaments of gold, and jade girdles, exchanged toasts with Defender-in-Chief Chu Mien. Beneath the steps:

Strains of classic melodies saturate the ears;
Tones of woodwinds and strings are harmonious.
Truly:
The tables, ten-foot square, are laden with food;
Served amid clustering flowers upon brocade mats.
What did this conspicuous display of the defender-in-chief's wealth and distinction look like? Behold:
He holds a position of the first rank;[54]
His office is one of the three highest.[55]
In his majestic reception hall,
The days are long and the bell-cords are silent;
In the vast minister's mansion,[56]
The clepsydras are mute and the halberds arrayed.
The forest flowers of colored paper
    rival those of spring;
The pearls hanging from the drapery
    light the evening hours.[57]
Fragrant and aromatic,
Otter's marrow has been newly compounded
    with "hundred-blend" incense;[58]
In serried profusion,
Tripods with dragon motifs and seal script
    are worth thousands in gold.
The bedclothes are half embroidered
    with kingfisher feathers;
The pillows are emblazoned with the
    "eight treasures" in coral.
From time to time, one hears the tinkling
    of jade girdle pendants;
One's vision is focused on the glittering
    of the moving lanterns.
With their tiger-head tallies and jade insignia,
The armored ranks in the forecourt are formidable;
With their ivory clappers and silver psalteries,[59]
The production of the puppet show is entertaining.[60]
All day long, those who come to pay their regards,
Consist only of noble scions or royal princelings;
Year after year, those who cultivate his company,
Are noblemen or relatives of the imperial family.
When singing girls perform their songs,[61]
One is amazed at the repertory of three thousand pieces;
When the mica screens are pulled aside,[62]

There suddenly appear twelve girls with gold hairpins.[63]
Where the lotus blossoms are in bloom,
The frolicking fish in the pond do not
　　startle the beholder;
Where birdcages are suspended on high,
The coquettish fowl beneath the eaves
　　engage in conversation.
What do such persons know of the arts of
　　compromise or reconciliation?
All they are familiar with are the ways
　　of toadying and sycophancy.

Truly:

In humorous conversation they initiate hostilities;
With idle boasts they disturb the national safety.
When they issue spurious decrees,
The eight chief officials in the realm
　　bow in acquiescence;
When they employ clever arguments,
The Emperor in his nine-gated palace[64]
　　nods his head in consent.
By initiating the Flower and Rock Convoys,
He has inflicted calamity upon the Chiang-nan
　　and the Huai-pei regions;
By seizing boxwood to offer to the throne,
He has exhausted both the national treasury
　　and the people's resources.
Among those who serve at court there are none
　　whose hearts have not been chilled;
Among the ranks of men of integrity there are
　　none who are not holding their breath.

Truly:

In the capital precincts he ranks first among
　　the wielders of power;
Among the wealthy and prominent of this world[65]
　　he is without an equal.[66]

In a little while, when the toasting was over, they all sat down in their places,
and a troupe of five actors came forward. To the accompaniment of psaltery,
mandola, *p'i-p'a*, metallophone, harp, and clappers inlaid with red ivory, they
proceeded to perform the song suite in the Cheng-kung mode that begins
with the tune "Decorous and Pretty." Truly:

The enduring tones linger around the rafters;
To a surge of pure melody and lovely harmony.

Enjoying wealth and distinction,
The recipient of imperial favor;[67]
Having risen from bleak poverty,
You occupy an exalted position.
Wielding the scales of power, your authority
    dominates the capital;
Relying on imperial favor, you endeavor to
    deceive our sovereign,
In total disregard of benevolence or righteousness.

To the tune "Playing with a Brocade Ball"

You employ corvée labor to construct ponds,
You buy landed estates for your descendants.
In your every endeavor, you explore only the
    means of insuring your own benefit;
In your treacherous greed, what do you care
    if Yüeh suffers while Ch'in prospers?[68]
Those who curry favor with you reach instant distinction;
Those who offend you find that their lives are endangered.
Envious of the worthy and talented,
You prefer the intimacy of the petty minded.
Motivated only by personal grudges, you show total
    disregard for the public interest.
You keep the Emperor in his nine-gated palace
    entirely in the dark,
While allowing the people within the four seas
    to descend into chaos.
But, as the saying goes, Heaven's net
    only seems to be loose.[69]

To the tune "The Lucky Graduate"

With your clever words, you seek to elicit the
    transient amusement of the ruler;
But do not exert loyal effort toward achieving
    harmony among the myriad states.
You only try to subvert the work of real heroes
    in order to deceive the world.
Vainly scratching an itch through the hide of your boot;[70]
Exhibiting the same symptoms that you pretend to cure;[71]
You show no concern whatever for Heavenly principle.

To the tune "Playing with a Brocade Ball"

You have the intent of Chao Kao of the Ch'in
    dynasty in pointing to a deer,[72]

And the design of T'u-an Ku in loosing his dog.[73]
You would emulate Wang Mang of the Han dynasty
    in your disloyal objectives,[74]
And deserve the same fate as the traitor Tung Cho
    whose navel was set on fire.[75]
Wherever you move, you are accompanied by pipes and strings;
When you go out the gate, you are protected by armed guards.
When you enter the court, the hundred officials
    are rigid with apprehension;
Relying on the ruler, you usurp the tiger's might
    in flaunting your authority.[76]
There are no few clients who abase themselves to
    cater to your perfidious cabal;
But who is there willing to wield his sword to
    execute the toadying villains,
Rather than letting them do as they please?

CODA

Your designation as a minister is not found
    beneath the golden goblet;[77]
But in the works of historians your faults
    will be duly enumerated.
What do you know of reconciling yin and yang[78]
    or nurturing the vital energy?
All you can do is betray the country and make
    pacts with foreign barbarians.
You have no right to the jade girdle and gold fish[79]
    suspended from your python robe;
Accepting emolument without achievement, you should
    be ashamed to sleep and to eat.
As long as power remains in your hands,
    people will be afraid of you;
But when catastrophe descends upon you,
    it will be too late to repent.[80]
All the bamboo on the southern hills would not suffice
    on which to enumerate your crimes;
When the waves on the eastern ocean are completely dry
    your stench of infamy will remain.[81]
It will be perpetuated for a myriad years,[82]
Forevermore inducing people to revile you.[83]

On this occasion, after:
      Three rounds of wine had been offered, and
      One suite of songs had been performed,

the six senior officers got up to go, and Defender-in-Chief Chu Mien escorted them on their way out.

When he returned to the reception hall, the sound of music was temporarily suspended, and the majordomo prepared to announce the names of the officials from their various jurisdictions as they came in to pay their respects to him. Defender-in-Chief Chu Mien ordered his attendants to bring in his desk and then took his seat on a folding chair upholstered in tiger skin.

He first ordered that the contingent of meritorious imperial relatives, prominent eunuchs, and high officials, together with their servitors and clerks, who had come to present their gifts, should be admitted.

It was not long before they were sent on their way and were succeeded by the contingent of secretaries attached to the headquarters of the Embroidered Uniform Guard, the officers from the Southern and Northern Yamens of that organization, the two detective bureaus with their five offices and seven departments, the investigators, inspectors, surveillance commissioners, and supervisors, the director of the horse pasturages of the imperial domain, the commander of the escort for imperial processions, the prison warden, the battalion and company commanders, and so forth. The leaders at the head of each of these categories were supplied with accordion-bound albums containing the credentials of their subordinates, which they duly handed up before being dismissed.

Only then were the judicial commissioners of the Two-Huai regions, the Two-Che regions, Shantung, Shansi, Kuan-tung, Kuan-hsi, Ho-tung, Hopei, Fukien, Kuang-nan, Szechwan, all thirteen provinces, ordered to present themselves in turn.[84] Hsi-men Ch'ing and Ho Yung-shou were in the fifth group, and when their presents were carried in, the majordomo saw to it that Eunuch Director Ho Hsin's calling card was placed conspicuously on the defender-in-chief's desk.

As the two of them stood beneath the steps, waiting for their names to be called, Hsi-men Ch'ing lifted up his head to look around and saw that in front of him was a spacious thirty-foot-wide structure, with a double-eaved, sloping, gable and hip roof, and exposed supporting beams beneath the corners.[85] Its beaded blinds were rolled high,[86] and it was surrounded on all sides by a green balustrade.[87] A vermilion plaque was suspended over the lintel that had been presented by Emperor Hui-tsung himself and was inscribed in the imperial hand with four gold characters as large as dippers, which read "Hall of the Commander of the Imperial Insignia Guard." This was the home of the Emperor's eyes and ears, teeth and claws; the headquarters of his secret police. Any commoner who found himself there could expect to be executed. Six anterooms were arrayed on either side of the interior.

The steps were wide and spacious, and
The courtyard was secluded and imposing.

Defender-in-Chief Chu Mien, attired in his crimson robe, was seated at the head of the steps, and, before long, he summoned them before him. The two of them obediently ascended the steps until they stood under the eaves, where they bent their bodies to pay their respects, kneeling down and kowtowing four times, as they awaited their instructions.

Defender-in-Chief Chu Mien remarked, "As for you two battalion commanders, what need was there for you to have your kinsman Eunuch Director Ho Hsin present me with these gifts?"

After ordering his attendants to put them away, he went on to say, "As long as you conscientiously carry out your official duties in the area of your jurisdiction, I, for my part, will see that you are treated fairly. After you have attended the great audience and submitted your memorials of gratitude, you can come back to the office to receive your orders of appointment, and proceed to your posts."

The two of them assented with one voice, after which the attendants called out, "You are dismissed," and they made their way out through the postern gate on the left.

As they exited the main gate and waited for Pen the Fourth and the others to come out with the empty gift boxes so they could be on their way, they suddenly noticed a messenger, who flew up on horseback, carrying a calling card of safflower red paper, and reported, "His Honor Wang and His Honor Kao are about to arrive."

Hsi-men Ch'ing and Ho Yung-shou then ducked inside someone's gateway so they could observe what took place. It was not long before the soldiers preceding them shouted to clear the way, and the two dignitaries appeared:

> Accompanied by a contingent of mounted horsemen,
> Overflowing the streets and blocking the alleys.

Whom should they see, garbed in crimson robes with jade girdles, and riding in sedan chairs, but Wang Wei, the supreme commander of the 800,000 imperial guards in the Capital Training Divisions and Duke of Lung-hsi, and Kao Ch'iu, the defender-in-chief of the Inspired Strategy Corps of the Imperial Bodyguard. Upon their arrival, the officials from the various provinces who had come to pay their respects all surged outside, and the newcomers were lost to sight.

Hsi-men Ch'ing and Ho Yung-shou waited for some time until Pen the Fourth came out with the empty gift boxes. Only then did the two of them withdraw to a secluded spot, order their attendants to bring up their horses, mount their steeds, and go back to their lodgings.

Truly:

> Solely because the wicked and sycophantic
>   occupied positions of power,
> It was only appropriate that the Central Plain
>   should become soaked in blood.[88]

The Two Judicial Commissioners Report before Chu Mien

Gentle reader take note:

> Just as womenfolk may ruin a household,
> Petty men may reduce the realm to chaos;
> It is only natural.

The perspicacious already foresaw that this bunch of traitors were bound to overturn the empire, and, sure enough, at the expiration of the Hsüan-ho reign period, Emperor Hui-tsung and Emperor Ch'in-tsung were taken north in captivity, Emperor Kao-tsung fled south, and the empire fell into the hands of the barbarians. Surely, this outcome is to be profoundly lamented. The reflections that arise in the mind of the historian cannot be exhausted. There is a poem that testifies to this:

> Calamitous are the deeds of those who abuse their
>   power and betray the national interest;[89]
> When founding a dynasty or inheriting a household,
>   one must strive to keep petty men at bay.
> Though the "six traitors" may all have been executed,
>   that is hardly worthy of consideration;[90]
> It did not mitigate the plight of the two emperors
>   as they suffered exile and confinement.[91]

> If you want to know the outcome of these events,
> Pray consult the story related in the following chapter.

Chapter 71

LI P'ING-ERH APPEARS IN A DREAM IN BATTALION COMMANDER HO'S HOUSE;

THE JUDICIAL COMMISSIONERS PRESENT THEIR MEMORIALS AT THE AUDIENCE

Let me temporarily cease strumming the zither
    that rests upon my knee;
In order to idly rehearse the past events that
    are recorded in history.
One cannot but admire the worthy rulers who are
    both diligent and thrifty;
While deeply sorrowing at the mediocre monarchs
    who indulge in debauchery.
Those who maintain peace and stability seek out
    men of worth and wisdom;
While those who only engender chaos fraternize
    with sycophantic ministers.
If one exposes the many factors that result in
    either success or failure;
As with "lofty mountains and flowing waters,"[1]
    the attuned will understand.[2]

THE STORY GOES that when Hsi-men Ch'ing and Ho Yung-shou arrived back on the main thoroughfare, Ho Yung-shou first sent someone to report to Eunuch Director Ho Hsin and then invited Hsi-men Ch'ing to come back to their home for a meal. Hsi-men Ch'ing repeatedly demurred, but Ho Yung-shou had one of his attendants take hold of his horse's bit with his hand, while he said to him, "Your pupil has another matter which he needs to discuss with you."

Thereupon, they proceeded to ride side by side until they dismounted in front of Ho Hsin's house, while Pen the Fourth and the carriers of the empty gift boxes went straight back to the home of Privy Councilor Ts'ui Shou-yü.

It so happens that Ho Yung-shou had made prior arrangements for a lavish feast that was awaiting them at his home. When they entered the reception hall, behold:

    Screens display their peacock's tails,

Cushions conceal their hibiscus blossoms.
Animal-shaped briquettes are smoldering,
Amid the fragrance from a golden brazier.

In the middle of the hall, at the upper end of the room, there was a single table setting, with another one facing it below, and yet another set up on the eastern side.

Platters are piled with exotic fruits,
Blossoms are displayed in golden vases.
The tables and chairs are spic-and-span,[3]
The standing screens are neatly arrayed.

Hsi-men Ch'ing inquired, "Who is my colleague entertaining today?"

"My uncle, the eunuch director, has taken the day off," Ho Yung-shou replied, "and would like to entertain my colleague with a meal."

"For you to put yourself to such trouble on my behalf," said Hsi-men Ch'ing, "is scarcely fitting among colleagues."

Ho Yung-shou laughed, saying, "It was my uncle's idea to prepare this meager repast, in the hope that you would condescend to offer me the benefit of your instruction."

After they had consumed a serving of tea, Hsi-men Ch'ing asked when he could pay his respects to the old gentleman.

"My uncle will be here any minute now," replied Ho Yung-shou.

It was not long before Eunuch Director Ho Hsin came out from the rear of the residence. He was wearing a python robe of green velvet, an official hat, black boots, and a jeweled chatelaine.

Hsi-men Ch'ing prostrated himself preparatory to kowtowing four times as a sign of respect, saying as he did so, "Pray accept my obeisance," but Eunuch Director Ho Hsin demurred, saying, "That will never do."

"Your pupil and your nephew Ho Yung-shou are colleagues of a younger generation," explained Hsi-men Ch'ing. "Whereas you, venerable sir:

Are exalted in both age and virtue,

and serve as a prominent eunuch. It is only appropriate that you should accept my obeisance."

They dickered politely for a while before Ho Hsin agreed to accept a half kowtow from him, after which, he ushered Hsi-men Ch'ing to the seat of honor, while he prepared to take the position of host, and indicated to Ho Yung-shou that he should occupy the place on the side.

"Venerable sir," said Hsi-men Ch'ing, "that will never do. Since your nephew and I are colleagues, how can he be relegated to the side? If it were just a case of you and your nephew, it might be all right, but for your pupil to occupy such a preferential position would never do."

Ho Hsin was greatly pleased by this and said, "Your Honor is well-versed in etiquette. In that case, I'll presume to take the grand secretary's position adjacent to the throne and allow my nephew, the new official, to play the role of host vis-à-vis Your Honor."

"Such an arrangement," responded Hsi-men Ch'ing, "would be more comfortable for your pupil."

Thereupon, they all exchanged the customary amenities and sat down.

Ho Hsin ordered, "Attendants, add some new charcoal to the brazier. The weather's rather cold today."

Before long, the servants brought in a package of finely polished charcoal for interior heating purposes and dumped it into the four-cornered brazier of yellow brass that stood in the center of the room. They also let down the translucent, oilpaper, heat-holding drapes at the door of the room, which let in the flickering sunlight so that everything was brightly illuminated.

"Your Honor," said Ho Hsin, "pray divest yourself of your formal outer garments."

"Your pupil doesn't have anything appropriate on underneath," said Hsi-men Ch'ing. "I'll send a servant to fetch something from my lodgings."

"There's no need for you to send for anything," said Ho Hsin.

Then, turning to his attendants, he told them to take Hsi-men Ch'ing's outer garments and said, "Fetch that green velvet flying fish python robe[4] that I've been wearing for His Honor to put on."

Hsi-men Ch'ing laughed, saying, "That is part of your official regalia, venerable sir. How could your pupil presume to wear it?"

"Go ahead and put it on, Your Honor," said Ho Hsin. "What is there to be afraid of? The other day the Lord of Ten Thousand Years bestowed a regular python robe on me, so I will no longer be wearing it. In fact, I will donate it to Your Honor to wear over your other clothes."

It was not long before the attendants came out with it. Hsi-men Ch'ing unfastened his girdle and took off his round-collared gown, handing it over to Tai-an. He then put on the flying fish python robe and bowed to Ho Hsin in order to express his thanks. He went on to ask Ho Yung-shou to take off his outer clothing in order to keep him company. At this point, another serving of tea was brought out, and they drank it together.

Ho Hsin then said, "Have the household musicians come out."

It so happens that he maintained a troupe of twelve household musicians who had been taught to perform on musical instruments. Led by their two instructors, they duly came out and kowtowed to the company. Ho Hsin ordered that the bronze gong and bronze drum be brought out and set up at the lower end of the hall, and the musical performance began. Truly:

> The sound shakes the cloudy empyrean;
> The tones startle both fish and birds.

After this prelude, the attendants served the feast and they were invited to take their places.

Eunuch Director Ho Hsin prepared to offer a drink to Hsi-men Ch'ing, but he hastily protested, saying, "Venerable sir, please make yourself easy. My colleague can do the honors on your behalf. It will suffice merely to provide the goblet and chopsticks at my place."

"I insist on offering Your Honor a drink," said Ho Hsin. "This newly appointed official from my household:

Upon first entering the bulrushes,
Has no way of gauging their depth.[5]

It is my fervent hope that, in all things, Your Honor will do what you can to
uphold his interests. That would be most gratifying."

"Venerable sir," said Hsi-men Ch'ing, "how can you talk that way? As the
saying goes:

The fellow feeling between colleagues endures
for three generations.

Your pupil is also much indebted to your diffracted radiance. How could we
not:

Do our best to help each other out?"[6]

"Well said! Well said!" responded Ho Hsin. "It is, indeed, our duty to:

Cooperate in the ruler's service,
By coming to each other's support."

Hsi-men Ch'ing did not wait for Ho Hsin to hand him the cup but went
forward to accept it and put it down at his place. He then responded by offering two cups in return, which he put down at the places of Ho Yung-shou and
Ho Hsin. After they had all bowed to each other, they sat down.

When the musical prelude was completed, three of the household musicians, together with their two instructors, came forward with their:

Silver psaltery, ivory clappers,
Three-string guitar, and p'i-p'a,

and performed the song suite in the Cheng-kung mode that begins with the
tune "Decorous and Pretty."[7]

The Crystal Palace,
Mermaid silk drapes;
Moonlight illumines the Crystal Palace,
Cold penetrates the mermaid silk drapes.
It is late at night, and We are unable to sleep
upon Our dragon couch.
Leaving the palace gate, We venture out onto the
streets of the capital,
Upon which windblown snow is falling.

TO THE TUNE "PLAYING WITH A BROCADE BALL"

It is like the flitter of fluttering butterfly wings;
It resembles the tumbling of carefree willow catkins.
Frozen flakes dance, as the swirling wind
blows them about;
Treading fragments of alabaster, Our steps
are impulsive.
Snow covers the sleeves of Our white scholar's gown;

The wind rumples Our commoner's black silk skullcap.
Suddenly looking back, We gaze fixedly on the phoenix
    towers of the palace;
Utterly unable to discern the mandarin ducks of azure
    vitreous tile on the eaves.
In no time at all, the nine-gated palace halls appear
    to be paved with silver;
In half an instant, the infinite expanse of the world[8]
    seems mantled in jade;
It looks just as though the entire realm is completely
    enveloped in powder.

TO THE TUNE "THE LUCKY GRADUATE"

We see that the double doors of the minister's mansion
    are locked tight as an iron bucket.
And proceed to give a resounding blow to the rings of
    the two animal-head-shaped knockers.
The person knocking at your gate is Chao the Elder, who
    resides in front of the Myriad Years Mount.[9]
Is your master entertaining anyone in his chamber?
So, he's reading works of literature by lamplight.
We have come expressly to hear him explicate them.

TO THE TUNE "LAZYBONES"

Braving the cold wind and enduring the frozen snow,
    We have come to pay him a visit.
There are some confidential matters that We urgently
    feel the need to discuss with him.
What are you so flustered about, being as you are
    a sophisticated public servant?
You can skip the obeisance, Our grand councilor, who
    has attracted so many worthies.
This is the residence of one of the Three Dukes, who
    presides over the vessels of state;
Not the abode of one who has taken the tonsure, such
    as Tripitaka[10] of the T'ang dynasty.
We will take this proffered seat in order to listen
    to your expounding of the classics.
But, as for your servant, We don't wish to have him
    about our ears offering more tea.

TO THE TUNE "THE LUCKY GRADUATE"

We will not emulate Emperor Kao-tsu of the Han dynasty
    who resided in the Wei-yang Palace;[11]

Nor the T'ang dynasty Son of Heaven who spent the night
   sleeping in the Chin-yang Palace,[12]
Merely anxious to share the gilded phoenix pillow, when
   the kingfisher-hued quilt felt chilly.[13]
We are only interested in learning about Fu Yüeh;[14]
Rather than dreaming of the meeting at Kao-t'ang.
This is the proper business of anyone who aspires to
   the position of a ruler.

TO THE TUNE "PLAYING WITH A BROCADE BALL"

Since We occupy the unique position of the ruler
   over all within the Four Seas,
We must devote Ourself to upholding the Three Bonds
   and observing the Five Constants.[15]
In the years of Our youth, We dedicated Ourself to
   mastering the spear and quarterstaff;
But Our only regret is that We failed to penetrate
   the gates of the school of Confucius.
How many chapters are there in the *Book of Documents*?
How many poems in all are there in the *Book of Songs*?
Through the explication of the *Book of Rites*, one
   can learn modesty and accommodation;
By discussion of the *Spring and Autumn Annals*, one
   can discern the lessons of the past.
We would learn from the examples of the rulers Yü, T'ang,
   Wen, and Wu;[16] in emulating Yao and Shun;[17]
You live up to Fang Hsüan-ling, Tu Ju-hui, Hsiao Ho, and
   Ts'ao Shen,[18] who helped found the Han and T'ang.
We depend upon you to undertake responsibility for the
   ministerial task of reconciling yin and yang.

TO THE TUNE "THE LUCKY GRADUATE"

You maintain that by relying on *The Analects of Confucius*
   one may establish one's authority at court;
And that even half of that text may suffice to gain control
   over the mountains and rivers of the realm.[19]
The way of the Sage is comparable to that of Heaven itself,
   in that it is immeasurable in extent.
To listen to your explication of the classics
   in front of the crimson curtain,[20]
Is certainly superior to a banquet at which the
   host provides singing girls in red.[21]
By the time your discourse is over, Our spirit is
   purified and Our energy enhanced.[22]

To the tune "Playing with a Brocade Ball"

On silver candlesticks the painted candles are bright;
From golden censers waft calligraphic fumes of incense.
We ought not to put Our elder brother to the trouble
    of pouring the vintage wine himself;
And it is hardly necessary for Our sister-in-law to
    offer Us a goblet of "sunset clouds."
You say that "A wife who has shared one's poverty-
    stricken fare must never be abandoned";
We too remember that "The friends one makes while
    poor and mean must never be forgotten."[23]
As the sayings go, "Outer strength is no match for
    inner strength";[24]
"If a wife is worthy, her husband will be able to
    avoid calamity."[25]
Our relationship with you resembles that between
    T'ai-chia and I Yin;[26]
Your union with your wife is like that of Liang
    Hung and Meng Kuang.[27]
We only hope that your good fortune and longevity
    will be prolonged.[28]

To the tune "The Lucky Graduate"

Whenever We try to sleep, We cannot avoid thinking of
    early rulers and later rulers;
No sooner do Our eyes close than we are obsessed with
    why states rise and states fall.
For this reason, by day and by night We cannot sleep,[29]
    pondering a myriad courses of action.
It is not a case of "When happy one dislikes
    the shortness of the night";
Nor an instance of "When lonely one hates it
    that the watches are so long."[30]
There are so many things to feel worried about.

To the tune "Playing with a Brocade Ball"

We worry about soldiers at their posts who
    lack adequate clothing;
We worry about families that lack sufficient
    grain for the next day;[31]
We worry about the poor who sleep by day in
    their secluded alleys;
We worry about the students who doze at night
    before unheated windows;

We worry about resentful wives and husbands
    complaining of the cold;
We worry about the carters forced to drive
    a myriad li in search of trade;
We worry about the boatmen on the rivers,
    threatened by wind and waves;
We worry about the starving children who
    cry out for their mothers;
We worry about the worthy commoners who
    lack a means of livelihood;
We worry about those who hasten to the
    battle in their coats of mail.
The mention of these things cannot but
    cause Us to sigh with sorrow.

To the tune "The Lucky Graduate"?

Worry about the hardships of the people disrupts
    Our rest and racks Our brains;[32]
Concern for the size of the empire occupies Our
    thoughts in sleep and in dreams.
At present, T'ai-yüan prefecture to the north is
    still ruled by the House of Liu.[33]
We intend to temporarily abandon the vermilion
    phoenix gates of Our palace;
Personally take Our place within the blue-green
    oiled curtains of Our carriage;
And initiate Our campaign by taking the city of
    Shang-tang in Ho-tung province.

To the tune "Playing with a Brocade Ball"

You speak of the rulers Ch'ien Ch'u of Wu-Yüeh[34]
    and Li Yü of the Southern T'ang;[35]
As well as Liu Ch'ang of the Southern Han[36]
    and Meng Ch'ang of the Later Shu.[37]
None of them exercises benevolent rule, causing
    their citizenry to lose hope;[38]
When they practice tyranny, they bring calamity
    down upon their populations.
Whom should We depute to pacify Szechwan
    in the West;
Whom should we direct to restore order to
    the Two-Kuang?
The conquest of the kingdom of Wu-yüeh will
    require a general of renown;

The subjugation of Chiang-nan will call for
  someone who is loyal and true.
Extending the borders of the realm will require someone
  like a pillar of white jade holding up the sky;[39]
Setting the universe to rights will demand an individual
  like a bridge of yellow gold spanning the sea.[40]
Pray give it your most careful consideration.

To THE TUNE "TAKING OFF THE COTTON GOWN"[41]

In order to take Chin-ling you must speedily
  cross the Yangtze River.[42]
When you get to Ch'ien-t'ang you must pacify
  that area of the country.[43]
In Szechwan to the west you must not be daunted by
  the state of the cliffside roadways;[44]
In the territories of the southern barbarians you
  must confront the poisonous miasmas.[45]

To THE TUNE "EXHILARATED BY PEACE"

In battle you must disperse the tiger-and-wolf-like foe;
Personally experiencing the hardships of wind and frost.
You must use *The Six Tactics* and *The Three Strategies*[46]
  in order to stabilize the frontiers,
While holding the seals of supreme military commanders.
We hope that when you don your coats of mail, thus
  enhancing your prowess;
Your horses, flaunting their jade bridles, will be
  impossible to obstruct;
And the drumbeat of whips on your golden stirrups[47]
  will proclaim victory,
As you lead your armies in triumph back to Pien-liang.

PARACODA[48]

Anyone who complies with Heaven's will; understands
  Heaven's principles; and is prepared to
  forsake evil and return to the true,[49]
  should be spared.
Anyone who imposes a tyrannical regime; opposes the
  imperial forces; and tries to show off
  his prowess and demonstrate his might,[50]
  must be destroyed.
Do not rob the people of their wealth;[51]
Do not exterminate the people's lives;[52]
Do not debauch the people's womenfolk;

Do not set fire to the people's homes.

Treat your men and horses with consideration,
    combining mercy and justice;

See that they are properly paid and fed, with
    clear rewards and punishments.

Protect the city walls and moats, pursue the
    rebels, and grant them amnesty.

Along the highways, put up posters in order
    to help pacify the populace;

Initiate welfare programs where needed, and
    open up the public granaries.

Coda

We await the day when, in formal attire and with respectful
    mien, We may proceed to the Ling-yen Pavilion[53]
    and have the portraits of you meritorious
    officials publicly displayed.

You must not fail to be worthy of having your names engraved
    on metal and stone, and inscribed on bells and
    tripods, so that the fragrance of your fame
    may be perpetuated in history.

Your use of your forces displays good generalship;

You possess strategic ability and possess courage.

By gazing upward to contemplate astronomical phenomena[54]
    you may predict events from the stars;

By gazing downward to examine the mountains and rivers
    you may evaluate the lay of the land.

In proceeding to battle you must first ascertain
    which of the nine terrains is relevant;[55]

In determining the outcome of a conflict you must
    rely on the five types of secret agents.[56]

In daylight battles you must employ
    flags and pennants;

In nighttime battles you must deploy
    fires and drums.[57]

In infantry battles you must use smoke screens
    to disguise your deployments;

In naval conflicts you must adjust to the wind
    in using your sails and oars.

When irregular and regular tactics abet each other,[58]
    your military strength is enhanced;

When benevolence and wisdom are practiced together,
    no amount of valor can resist them.

We delegate Our authority to you generals, so that
    you may pacify the four quarters;
To second-guess our supreme commanders while seated
    on the throne would invite chaos.
We hope you will send urgent memorials announcing
    your achievements on the frontier;
So we may all rejoice at the attainment of peace
    as you head back for the capital.
Before We begin to allot land and bestow fiefdoms[59]
    in granting you titles of nobility,
We will first see to it that the troops under your
    various commands are amply rewarded.[60]

When the household musicians had finished performing the song suite, they withdrew. After:

    Several rounds of wine had been consumed, and
    Two main courses had been served,

it gradually grew toward evening, and the lamps were lighted.

Hsi-men Ch'ing summoned Tai-an and instructed him to offer gratuities to the chef and the various musicians who had performed for them and then got up to go, saying, "Your pupil has imposed upon your hospitality all day long. It is time for me to take my leave."

But the venerable eunuch was unwilling to let him go, saying, "The reason I took the day off, today, was that I wanted to benefit from Your Honor's instruction. I haven't provided anything special in the way of entertainment, but only an opportunity for us to talk together. I fear Your Honor may still be hungry."

"Having just enjoyed the luxurious repast that you provided, venerable sir," protested Hsi-men Ch'ing, "how can you possibly suggest that I should still be hungry? Your pupil merely needs to return to his lodgings to get some rest. Tomorrow morning, I must join your nephew in reporting to the Ministry of War in order to receive our orders of appointment and register our names."

"In that case," responded Eunuch Director Ho Hsin, "there is no need for Your Honor to return to your lodgings. You can spend the night here at my place, which will make it more convenient for you and the newly appointed official from my household to go take care of your business in the morning. May I venture to ask, where are you staying at present?"

"Your pupil," replied Hsi-men Ch'ing, "is lodging for the time being in the home of my colleague Hsia Yen-ling's relative Privy Councilor Ts'ui Shou-yü, and all of my luggage is there."

"That's no problem," said Ho Hsin. "You Honor might just as well send someone to go fetch your luggage and bring it here, where I can put you up for a few days. How would that be? In my back garden there are several small rooms that are pleasantly secluded. If you agree to this proposal, it will make it more convenient for you and my nephew to conduct your business. That would be a better arrangement than if you stay somewhere else, since you'll both be in the same place."

"To stay here would be fine by me," said Hsi-men Ch'ing. "My only fear is that Hsia Yen-ling might take it amiss and think that your pupil is slighting him."

"In this day and age," responded Ho Hsin, "as the saying goes:

If one's colleague forfeits his office in the morning,
One is no longer obliged to bow to him in the evening.[61]

The yamen is just like a puppet theater. Though you were initially a colleague of his, now that the previous official has left, his replacement is ready to:

Assume his position and carry out his duties.[62]

He no longer has anything to do with it. If he were to interpret it that way, it would only show how little he understands the way of the world. Today, I am determined to spend the evening with Your Honor and simply won't let you go."

He then called for his attendants and ordered them, "Have some tables set up forthwith in the room below, and see to it that the servants of His Honor Hsi-men are provided with food and wine. Afterwards, send some people from our household to accompany them in going to bring his luggage back here. Also, issue instructions to have the chamber in the west courtyard in the back garden swept clean and provided with bedding. And light some charcoal under the k'ang."

From in the hall a single call;
Below the steps a hundred yeps.

The attendants assented obsequiously and set out about their tasks.

"That is extremely kind of you, venerable sir," said Hsi-men Ch'ing, "but your pupil is still concerned lest he offend Hsia Yen-ling."

"Don't talk such rot!" said Ho Hsin. "He no longer serves in your yamen.

He who occupies no post in an office,
Has no right to discuss its policies.[63]

He is now responsible for the depot in which the imperial equipage is stored and no longer has any say with regard to the provincial judicial commissions. He is in no position to feel offended by you."

Thereupon:

Without permitting any further explanation,

he ordered that, after Tai-an and the grooms tending the horses had been provided with food and wine, several soldiers should also be dispatched, equipped with ropes and carrying poles, to proceed to the home of Privy Councilor Ts'ui Shou-yü and bring back Hsi-men Ch'ing's luggage.

Ho Hsin then went on to say, "There is another favor I would like to ask of Your Honor. When my nephew, the newly appointed official, arrives at his place of office, I hope that Your Honor will consent to help him find a house to live in, so that it will be convenient for him to send for his dependents later on. I'll have him accompany Your Honor on your way back, and then, after he has found a home, I'll arrange to send his dependents off to join him. There are not a lot of them, but, including several families of servants, there will be twenty or thirty persons, in all."

"When your nephew is gone," said Hsi-men Ch'ing, "who will there be to look after this house of yours, venerable sir?"

"There are two adopted nephews in my household," said Ho Hsin. "The second one, whose name is Ho Yung-fu, is currently residing on my country estate. I'll ask him to come and reside here."

"Venerable sir," asked Hsi-men Ch'ing, "how much silver are you willing to spend on a place for your nephew?"

"It will probably require a place costing more than a thousand taels of silver to accommodate them all," responded Ho Hsin.

"My colleague Hsia Yen-ling," said Hsi-men Ch'ing, "now that he has a capital appointment, will not be going back to Ch'ing-ho and will have to dispose of the house he owns there. Venerable sir, why don't you purchase that place of his in order to provide a house for your nephew? That would be a good move, since it would:

Accomplish two objectives with a single act.

His house has a fifty-four-foot-wide frontage and five interior courtyards, receding along a vertical axis. Inside the ceremonial gate there is a large reception hall with vaulted stag's head roofs over the galleries connecting it to the anterooms on either side of the courtyard. In the rear there are located residential quarters, ornamental pavilions, and a host of other rooms on all sides, with passageways leading between them. It is more than spacious enough to accommodate your nephew."

"What price does he expect to get for it?" asked Ho Hsin.

"He has told me," said Hsi-men Ch'ing, "that he originally paid twelve hundred taels for it, and that he has since added two flat-roofed rooms to the rear, and erected an ornamental pavilion. However, if you would like to acquire it, venerable sir, he would probably let you have it for whatever you are prepared to offer."

"I'm putting the matter in Your Honor's hands," said Ho Hsin. "Whatever Your Honor proposes will be all right with me. Since I am at home today, why don't you send someone to speak to him and ask for the loan of the original deed of sale, so that I can take a look at it? It would be a rare stroke of luck to succeed in locating a house so that my nephew will have a place to stay when he assumes his new office."

Before long, whom should they see but Tai-an and the other servants who came back to report that they had fetched the luggage.

Hsi-men Ch'ing asked, "Did Pen the Fourth and Wang Ching come back with you or not?"

"Wang Ching is already here, having overseen the transport of the trunks of clothing and other luggage," reported Tai-an. "The sedan chair is still there, and Pen the Fourth remained to look after it."

Hsi-men Ch'ing thereupon:

> Whispered into his ear in a low voice,
> Thus and thus, and
> So and so,

saying, "Take my calling card and request that His Honor Hsia Yen-ling loan me the original deed of sale for that place of his, so that Eunuch Director Ho Hsin can examine it; and bring Pen the Fourth back with you."

Tai-an assented and set off on this errand.

It was not long before Pen the Fourth, wearing black livery and a commoner's informal skullcap, came back with Tai-an, who handed the deed of sale to Hsi-men Ch'ing and reported, "His Honor Hsia Yen-ling responded to your request by saying, 'Since it is the venerable eunuch Ho Hsin who is interested in my place, how can I put a price on it?' This is the original deed of sale that I have brought back with me. He also said that he had spent a good deal of money on making improvements to the property, but that he would go along with whatever Your Honor proposes."

Hsi-men Ch'ing handed the original deed of sale to Ho Hsin, who read it over and saw that the purchase price was stated to be twelve hundred taels.

"I imagine he must have resided in this house for some years by now," he said, "so the interior can hardly help showing some signs of wear and tear, which would offset whatever he may have spent on improvements. Out of respect for Your Honor, however, I am willing to invest in the property on my nephew's behalf and am prepared to pay the original purchase price."

On hearing this, Pen the Fourth hastily knelt down in front of him and said, "What Your Honor proposes is appropriate. It has always been true that:

> You must be ready to spend lavishly,
> In order to acquire a good property.
> In a thousand years a dwelling may have
>   a hundred owners;[64]
> But each time it is refurbished it will
>   be as good as new."[65]

When Eunuch Director Ho Hsin heard these words, he was utterly captivated and exclaimed, "Where do you come from? This character certainly has a way with words. As the saying goes:

> Those who would accomplish great things,
>   do not balk at petty outlays.[66]

What he says is right enough. What is his name?"

"He is one of my managers," said Hsi-men Ch'ing, "and he is called Pen the Fourth."

"Well then," Ho Hsin said to him, "since we don't yet have an intermediary, you can serve as our middleman, and go request a deed of sale on my behalf. Since today is a propitious day for such a transaction, I might as well proceed to weigh out the silver for him forthwith."

"It's already late right now," said Hsi-men Ch'ing. "You might as well wait until tomorrow."

"At the fifth watch I have to report for early duty in the palace," explained Eunuch Director Ho Hsin, "and tomorrow is the day of the great audience. I might as well wrap the matter up by turning the silver over to him today and thereby conclude the matter."

"At what time will the imperial equipage leave the palace tomorrow?" asked Hsi-men Ch'ing.

"The imperial equipage will leave the palace in order to proceed to the Altar of Heaven at 11:00 tonight," said Ho Hsin. "The Suburban Sacrifice should be over by 1:00 AM at the end of the third watch. By 4:30 AM the imperial equipage will have returned to the palace for the serving of a morning meal, after which the Emperor will emerge to preside over the audience in the main hall of the palace, and receive the congratulations of the assembled officials. The various bureaucratic offices of the entire empire will all submit memorials in celebration of the winter solstice. On the following day, a banquet will be held for the principal civil and military officials of the capital to celebrate the completion of the ceremony. Since the two of you are outer officials, serving in the provinces, once you have submitted your memorials at the great audience, there will be nothing more for you to do."

When he had finished speaking, Ho Hsin instructed his nephew Ho Yung-shou, the newly appointed battalion commander, to go back to the interior of the residence and bring out twenty-four large silver ingots weighing fifty taels apiece, and put them in food boxes for carrying. He then deputed two household servants to accompany Pen the Fourth and Tai-an in escorting them to Privy Councilor Ts'ui Shou-yü's house and delivering them to Hsia Yen-ling.

When Hsia Yen-ling saw that they had brought the silver for him, he was utterly delighted and immediately wrote out a deed of sale in his own hand and turned it over to Pen the Fourth and his companions. When they took this back and delivered it to Eunuch Director Ho Hsin, he was:

Unable to contain his delight,
and rewarded Pen the Fourth with ten taels of silver, and Tai-an and Wang Ching with three taels each.

"They're only youngsters," protested Hsi-men Ch'ing. "You ought not to reward them so lavishly."

"I'm just offhandedly giving them enough with which to buy something to eat," responded Ho Hsin.

The three recipients kowtowed to him in gratitude, and Ho Hsin ordered that they also be provided with food and wine.

He then turned to Hsi-men Ch'ing and bowed twice, saying, "This outcome is entirely due to Your Honor's diffracted radiance."

"Whoever heard of such a thing?" protested Hsi-men Ch'ing. "It is really owing to your golden reputation."

Ho Hsin went on to say, "I hope that Your Honor will speak to Hsia Yen-ling and urge him to vacate that place of his as soon as convenient, so that my nephew's dependents can prepare for their departure."

"Your pupil will certainly speak to him," said Hsi-men Ch'ing, "and urge him to vacate the premises as soon as possible. My new colleague, your nephew, when he first arrives, can stay temporarily in the residential quarters of the yamen for a few days, until Hsia Yen-ling's dependents have moved to the capital, and the place has been put in order. It will not be too late if my colleague's dependents delay their departure until then."

"It should be possible to carry out whatever renovations are necessary by the end of the New Year's celebrations," said Ho Hsin. "It would be best for my nephew's dependents to make their move at that time. It will not be convenient if they have to stay in the yamen for too long."

As their conversation continued, it was already the second watch of the night, and Hsi-men Ch'ing said, "Venerable sir, let us say good night. Your pupil:
Cannot handle the effects of the drink."

Only then did Eunuch Director Ho Hsin consent to call it a night and retreat to his heated chamber in the rear of the house.

Meanwhile, Ho Yung-shou called for the household musicians to perform for them again and proceeded to play a game of pitch-pot with Hsi-men Ch'ing. Only after they had continued drinking for a while longer did they get up and go back to the rear garden.

The accommodation provided for Hsi-men Ch'ing consisted of a three-room studio ranged along the northern end of the garden, which was surrounded on all four sides by a whitewashed wall, and enhanced with terraces and kiosks, ornamental rock formations, potted miniature plants, flowers and trees. Inside the studio:
Crimson candles blazed on high;
Drapes enclosed layered quilts.
Brocaded curtains set off Japanese screens
decorated with gold tracery;
Zithers, books, tables, and mats enhanced
the air of elegant seclusion.
The kingfisher blinds hung low;
The furnishings were faultless.
On the stove, tea was steeping in a precious pot;
Within the censer, cakes of musk were smoldering.

Ho Yung-shou continued to make small talk with Hsi-men Ch'ing, and, sometime later, a servant lad served them with tea. Only then did Ho

Yung-shou say good night and go back to his own quarters in the rear of the house. Hsi-men Ch'ing warmed himself at the stove for a while before he finally disposed of his headgear:

Took off his clothes and went to bed.[67]

Wang Ching and Tai-an helped him off with his boots and stockings, put out the lamps and candles, and prepared to sleep after laying out their bedding on a heated k'ang at the lower end of the room.

Hsi-men Ch'ing was somewhat inebriated. As he lay on the pillow, he observed that his quilts and mattresses were of satin and brocade, his bed curtains were of embroidered sable, and the bed itself was like a heated alcove decorated with gold tracery. As he lay under his quilt, he saw that:

The window was illuminated by moonlight,

and:

He tossed first this way and then that,

unable to get to sleep. After a while, as he listened to the steady dripping of the clepsydra and watched the quiet movements of the flower shadows, he became aware that the cold wind was rattling the papered window panes. His feeling of loneliness was exacerbated by the fact that he had been away from home for some time, and he was on the verge of inviting Wang Ching to come sleep with him.

All of a sudden, he heard the faint sound of a woman's voice outside the window and, hastily donning a robe and getting out of bed, slipped on his shoes and stockings and cautiously opened the door to see who it was. Lo and behold, it was Li P'ing-erh:

With misty locks and cloudy tresses,
Faintly made up, lovely and elegant.
A well-worn plain white gown veiled
　　her snow-white body;
Soft light-yellow stockings set off
　　her upturned shoe-tips.[68]
Lightly moving her lotus feet,
She appeared beneath the moon.

As soon as Hsi-men Ch'ing saw her, he:

Took her into the room,[69]
Embraced her, and wept,[70]

saying, "Darling, what are you doing here?"

"I've come looking for you," said Li P'ing-erh, "in order to tell you that I've found a new home. I especially wanted to see you tonight because I'll be moving in before long."

"Where is this home of yours located?" Hsi-men Ch'ing inquired anxiously.

"It's not far away at all," replied Li P'ing-erh. "If you go out from here, it's located on Potter's Alley, off the east side of the main thoroughfare."

When they had finished speaking, she and Hsi-men Ch'ing:

> Enfolded each other in a mutual embrace,[71]
> Got into bed to play at clouds and rain,[72]

and experienced scarcely endurable transports of delight. Once it was over, she:

> Adjusted her attire, redid her chignon, but
> Hesitated reluctantly to part from him.[73]

Li P'ing-erh repeatedly enjoined Hsi-men Ch'ing, saying, "My Brother, be sure you remember to abstain from late night drinking parties, and return home as early as possible. That wretch of mine is forever on the lookout for a means of bringing you to grief. Whatever you do, don't forget these words of mine. You must keep them constantly in mind."

When she had finished speaking, she took Hsi-men Ch'ing by the hand and urged him to see her on her way home. When they arrived out on the main thoroughfare, he saw that:

> The moonlight was as bright as day.[74]

Sure enough, when they headed east past the memorial arch, they arrived at a small alley and, almost immediately thereafter, came to a double-leaved gate of white planks.

Li P'ing-erh pointed it out, saying, "This is my home."

No sooner had she finished speaking, than she:

> Shook herself loose and went inside.

Hsi-men Ch'ing hastily stepped forward to stop her but suddenly awoke with a start to find that it was but:

> A dream of the Southern Branch.

All he could see was:

> The moonbeams slanting across the window, and
> The rising shadows of the flowering branches.

Feeling the bedding beneath him, Hsi-men Ching found that:

> His flow of semen covered the mat,
> Her fragrance saturated the quilt,
> The taste of her saliva was sweet.
> Grieving over her was of no avail,
> His anguish could not be overcome.[75]

Truly:

> The good things of this world are
>   none too enduring;
> Colored clouds are prone to scatter
>   and glass is brittle.

There is a poem that testifies to this:

> The jade firmament is somewhat nebulous,
>   pervaded as it is by frost;

Li P'ing-erh Appears in a Dream in Ho Yung-shou's House

Faint moonlight penetrates the casement,
    as his dreaming soul awakes.
In desolation, he tries to go to sleep
    until he can try no longer;
How he hates it that the torpid rooster
    refuses to announce the dawn.[76]

Hsi-men Ch'ing:
        Tossed first this way and then that,
waiting for the rooster to crow, and longing for the break of day. But, when the
day finally broke, he had dozed off.

Early in the morning, the page boys in Ho Yung-shou's house got up and
waited on Hsi-men Ch'ing with hot water and towels so he could wash his
face. After Wang Ching and Tai-an had helped Hsi-men Ch'ing to comb his
hair and perform his ablutions, Ho Yung-shou came out to keep him company. When they had drunk a serving of ginger-flavored tea, he had a table set
up and invited Hsi-men Ch'ing to have some congee.

"Why has the old gentleman not appeared?" Hsi-men Ch'ing asked.

"My venerable uncle had to report for duty in the palace at the fifth watch,"
Ho Yung-shou replied.

In no time at all, the congee was served as they sat around the brazier, accompanied by four saucers of tastefully presented appetizers, and four large
bowls of stewed meats. When they had finished eating the congee, a wine-
laced pick-me-up containing pork meatballs, eggs, and wonton was served,
with gold spoons and carved lacquer cups enchased with silver. As they ate,
they ordered their servants to go outside and prepare their horses.

Ho Yung-shou and Hsi-men Ch'ing then proceeded, dressed in formal attire and attended by their servitors, to go into the Forbidden City and report to
the Ministry of War. When they came out, they separated, as Ho Yung-shou
headed for home, while Hsi-men Ch'ing went to the Hsiang-kuo Temple to
pay a call on Abbot Chih-yün. The abbot retained him for a vegetarian repast,
but Hsi-men Ch'ing ate only a single delicacy himself, conferring the remainder on his attendants.

When they left the temple, Tai-an was carrying some satins and brocades in
a felt bag as they went along East Street, intending to go to Privy Councilor
Ts'ui Shou-yü's residence in order to pay a congratulatory visit to Hsia Yen-
ling. On their way there, halfway through Potter's Alley, Hsi-men Ch'ing actually saw a double-leaved gate of white planks, exactly like the one he had seen
in his dream.

Hsi-men Ch'ing unobtrusively sent Tai-an to ask the old woman who sold
bean curd next-door who the house belonged to, and the old woman replied,
"It is the home of Commander Yüan."

On hearing this, Hsi-men Ch'ing:
        Could not suppress a sigh of astonishment.

When they arrived at the residence of Privy Councilor Ts'ui Shou-yü, Hsia Yen-ling was in the process of leading out his horse in order to go pay a social call. When he saw that Hsi-men Ch'ing had arrived, he told his attendants to take the horse aside and invited him into the reception hall, where they bowed to each other and exchanged the customary amenities. Hsi-men Ch'ing told Tai-an to bring out his congratulatory gifts, consisting of a length of brocaded damask on a blue ground and a length of variegated satin.

"Your pupil has not yet had the chance to congratulate his colleague," said Hsia Yen-ling, "but has allowed you to anticipate me. And yesterday, you also went to a good deal of trouble on my behalf with regard to the disposition of my humble abode.

My gratitude knows no bounds."

"Eunuch Director Ho Hsin asked your pupil to assist him in finding a house for his nephew," explained Hsi-men Ch'ing, "and since Your Honor had asked me to help with the disposition of your property, I mentioned it's availability to him. Ho Hsin having expressed an interest in purchasing it, your pupil could scarcely have refrained from helping to complete the transaction, and when I sent for the original deed of sale, and he had perused it, he readily consented to pay the original purchase price. It is the nature of eunuchs to be impulsive, expecting:

Bridges to be built while they wait on horseback,

that accounts for this successful conclusion. It is a stroke of good luck for Your Honor."

When he had finished speaking, they had a laugh together.

"I haven't yet had a chance to repay Ho Yung-shou's visit," said Hsia Yen-ling.

He then went on to ask, "Is he going to accompany my colleague on his return trip?"

"He has already agreed to travel with your pupil," replied Hsi-men Ch'ing. "He will send for his dependents later. Last night the venerable eunuch made a point of asking me to urge Your Honor to vacate the premises as soon as possible, so that his nephew can arrange for his dependents to join him. At present, he is planning to stay temporarily in the yamen for a few days."

"Your pupil will not procrastinate about it," Hsia Yen-ling assured him. "As soon as I succeed in finding a place here, I will send someone to fetch my dependents. I should be able to manage it by early next month."

When they had finished speaking, Hsi-men Ch'ing got up to go and left a calling card for Privy Councilor Ts'ui Shou-yü.

"I would like to retain my colleague for a longer visit," said Hsia Yen-ling, "but we are both only sojourners here. You know how it is."

He then escorted Hsi-men Ch'ing outside, where he mounted his horse and returned to the home of Ho Yung-shou.

Ho Yung-shou had already seen to the preparation of a noon repast and was waiting for him there.

Hsi-men Ch'ing told him everything that Hsia Yen-ling had said, explaining that he would undertake to have his property in Ch'ing-ho vacated by early next month, so that Ho Yung-shou could arrange to have his dependents move in at that time.

Ho Yung-shou was delighted to hear this and thanked him, saying, "This is but a further demonstration of my colleague's concern for my welfare."

After their meal, the two of them were in the reception hall playing a board game together, when an attendant suddenly came in and announced, "His Honor Chai Ch'ien from the grand preceptor's mansion has sent people to deliver a gift for the road to you. They went looking for you at the home of Privy Councilor Ts'ui Shou-yü, but he sent them on here to find you."

Thereupon, he handed over a calling card of safflower red paper, with a list of presents that read, "The enclosed one length of satin brocade, one length of cloud-patterned linen, one freshly slaughtered pig, one northern sheep, two jars of wine from the imperial palace, and two boxes of sweetmeats are deferentially presented as a token of his respect by your kinsman Chai Ch'ien."

Upon speaking to the messenger, Hsi-men Ch'ing said, "I am once again the recipient of His Honor Chai Ch'ien's generosity."

He then accepted the presents, wrote a card in reply, rewarded the messenger with two taels of silver, and the bearers of the gift boxes with five mace of silver each; saying to the messenger as he did so, "I am inconvenienced by being away from home and fear that this paltry compensation may be regarded as a slight."

The messenger promptly took the gratuity, though protesting the while, "Your servant dares not presume to accept it."

"Inadequate as it is," said Hsi-men Ch'ing, "it should suffice to buy you a cup of wine."

Only then did the messenger kowtow in gratitude and formally accept it.

At this point, Wang Ching, who was standing beside Hsi-men Ch'ing, interjected in a low voice, "My elder sister enjoined me to go to the grand preceptor's residence in order to visit Ai-chieh and entrusted me with some things for her."

"What things are those?" asked Hsi-men Ch'ing.

"They are two pairs of shoes and foot bindings made for her by my sister at home," replied Wang Ching.

"If that's all, it will hardly be adequate," said Hsi-men Ch'ing.

Then, turning to Tai-an, he said, "In my leather trunk, there are some rose hip–flavored pastries that I brought with me. Take two containers of them and put them into a small gift box decorated with gold tracery."

He then wrote out a card to go with them and handed it to Wang Ching, who had put on his black livery, telling him to go back to Chai Ch'ien's residence with the messenger and pay a visit to Ai-chieh. But no more of this.

Hsi-men Ch'ing then proceeded to write out a card and sent the sheep and one of the jars of wine to Privy Councilor Ts'ui Shou-yü to thank him for his hospitality, while arranging to have the pig, the other jar of wine, and the two boxes of sweetmeats taken back to the rear of the residence for the delectation of the venerable Eunuch Director Ho Hsin; saying as he did so, "I have put you here to quite a lot of trouble."

This threw Ho Yung-shou into such consternation that he hastily bowed in thanks, saying, "My colleague, you and I are like members of the same family. What need is there for you to do all this?"

To resume our story, when Wang Ching arrived at the grand preceptor's mansion, he invited Han Ai-chieh to come out and paid his respects to her in the outer reception hall. She was adorned as resplendently as:

A tree of jade in a forest of alabaster,[77]

quite unlike the appearance she had presented in her old home, and had also increased considerably in stature. She arranged for him to be entertained with food and wine and, having noticed that he seemed to be rather thinly clad, presented him with a sable cloak lined with ultramarine satin, and five taels of silver. When he returned to report on his trip, he showed these gifts to Hsi-men Ch'ing, who expressed his gratification.

As Hsi-men Ch'ing and Ho Yung-shou continued playing their board game, they suddenly heard the sound of outriders clearing the road, and a gatekeeper came in to report that His Honor Hsia Yen-ling had come to pay his respects and presented two calling cards from him. The two of them hastily adjusted their attire and welcomed him into the reception hall, where they exchanged the customary amenities, and Ho Yung-shou thanked him for his agreement to sell his property the day before. Hsia Yen-ling had brought with him a pair of satin kerchiefs to present to the two of them as congratulatory gifts, and Hsi-men Ch'ing and Ho Yung-shou thanked him repeatedly and turned them over to their servants to put away. He also presented Pen the Fourth, Tai-an, and Wang Ching with a gratuity of ten taels of silver. As they sat down in the positions appropriate for guests and host, and tea was served, they chatted about the weather.

Hsia Yen-ling then asked, "Might I invite the venerable eunuch to come out so that I can pay him my respects?"

"My uncle is on duty in the palace at present," responded Ho Yung-shou.

Hsia Yen-ling left behind a red accordion-bound calling card, saying, "Please convey my regards to the venerable eunuch. I have been tardy in paying my respects. Pray forgive me."

When he had finished speaking, he said goodbye, got up, and departed.

Ho Yung-shou, for his part, promptly prepared a bolt of satin brocade as a congratulatory gift for Hsia Yen-ling and dispatched someone to deliver it. But no more of this.

That evening, Ho Yung-shou also entertained Hsi-men Ch'ing to a late-night drinking party in his heated chamber in the rear garden. The household musicians sang for them until the second watch before they went to bed.

Concerned about the wet dream he had had the night before, Hsi-men Ch'ing ordered Wang Ching to bring his bedding inside that evening and sleep on the floor of the studio. When the night was half over, he called him onto his own bed and proceeded to embrace his naked body under the bedclothes:

> Stuck out his clove-shaped tongue, and
> Mingled his sweet spittle with his.

Truly:

> Failing to consummate his assignation
>   with Ts'ui Ying-ying;
> He settled for a tryst with Hung-niang
>   to relieve his lust.[78]

Of the events of that evening there is no more to tell.

The next morning, he arose at the fifth watch and set out with Ho Yung-shou, accompanied by their servants, to attend the audience in the palace. They first proceeded to the Tai-lou Yüan, or Clepsydra Waiting-Hall, where they waited until the Tung-hua Men, or Eastern Floriate Gate, of the Forbidden City opened, when they proceeded to enter the imperial precincts. Behold:

> The stars are still visible in the sky, as
>   the palace clepsydra runs out;[79]
> The jade girdle ornaments of the courtiers
>   sound a tinkling *shan-shan*.
> Blossoms brush against swords and halberds
>   as the stars begin to sink;
> Pennants sweep away the willows, on which
>   the dew is not yet dry.[80]
> Amid the glow of an auspicious nimbus, they
>   gaze upon the Emperor;
> An exhalation of propitious vapor envelops
>   the thousand officials.
> If you wish to foresee the sentiments of the
>   Son of Heaven this day;
> Gaze afar at the purple vapor emanating from
>   the Isles of the Blest.

In a little while, behold:

> The portals of the Forbidden City are opened,
> To the harmonious clanging of phoenix
>   girdle pendants;
> The doors of the celestial palace are parted,

Making visible the majestic regalia of
    the dragon robe.
On this day of prolonged prosperity
    and extended peace,[81]
We celebrate the dawning of an era
    of auspicious joy.[82]

At that time, the Son of Heaven had already returned from presiding over the Southern Suburban Sacrifice to Heaven, and the civil and military officials had all assembled at court to await his appearance at the great audience.[83] Before long, after the tolling of a bell, the equipage of the Son of Heaven emerged from the palace, and he ascended to the Great Hall for Veneration of Governance to accept the congratulations of the hundred officials. Shortly thereafter:

The incense burners commenced their revolution;
The drapes were raised and the flabella parted.[84]

What did the imposing ceremonial of the imperial audience that day look like? Behold:

The imperial aura is clear and peaceful,
Genial and agreeable, like an
    enveloping mist;
The resplendent sun dominates the void,
Voluminous and rising, clouds
    of vapor linger.
Nebulous and indistinct,
The dragon towers and phoenix pavilions,[85]
Are enveloped with a fragrant haze;
Pervading and spreading,[86]
The pearly palaces and jeweled halls,[87]
Reflect the glow of morning clouds.
The Ta-ch'ing Hall,
The Ch'ung-ch'ing Hall,
The Wen-te Hall, and
The Chi-hsien Hall,
Sparkle and glisten;[88]
Their golds and greens blending their hues.
The Ch'ien-ming Palace,
The K'un-ning Palace,
The Chao-yang Palace,
The Ho-pi Palace, and
The Ch'ing-ning Palace,
Shimmer and shine;
Their reds and greens glowing brilliantly.
Bleakly and coldly,[89]

The sun illumines the jade flagstones
    and carved balustrades;[90]
Drifting and floating,
The mist enshrouds the gilded rafters
    and the painted beams.
Within purple portals and yellow chambers,
In precious tripods, billowing and streaming,
Aloeswood incense smolders;
Along crimson steps and maroon stairways,
On jade terraces, brightly and resplendently,[91]
Painted candles burn high.
Lung-lung tung-tung,
The Heaven-shaking drums beat out
    a triple paradiddle;
K'eng-k'eng hung-hung,
The Ch'ang-lo Palace bell tolls
    a hundred eight times.
Entangled and confused,[92]
Sword-bearing guardsmen bump
    into each other;
Thronging and swarming,
Dragon and tiger flags swirl
    about in disorder.
Soldiers with brocade robes and floriate caps,[93]
Bearing round baldachins and square baldachins,
Array themselves both in front and behind;
Officers with jade tallies and dragon banners,
Driving in gilded carriages and jade carriages,
Deploy themselves both to left and to right.
Also to be seen are:
    Vertically held maces, and
    Horizontally held maces,
    By threes and by twos;[94]
    Paired dragon flabella, and
    Single dragon flabella,
    Doubled and redoubled.[95]
    Squad by squad and troop by troop,[96]
    Horses with gold saddles, and
    Horses with jade bridles,
    Display their discipline;
    Brace by brace and pair by pair,[97]
    Cabin-bearing elephants, and
    Cart-pulling elephants,

Show their prodigiousness.
The elite guardsmen protecting the hall,[98]
Each and every one of them lanky and large-sized,
    comparable to celestial deities,
Are clothed in plates of gilded armor;
The palace wardens securing the audience,
Every single one of them rigorously disciplined,
    resembling terrestrial spirits,
Are armed with florally incised swords.
Rigid and ordered,[99]
Within the gate of the hall are arrayed
    the ceremonial supervisors,
Each of them wearing a high judicial cap,
Holding his tablet in front of his chest;[100]
Straight and proper,
Beside the inclined stairway are standing
    the assembled officials,
Each of them in a brightly brocaded robe,
Ready to receive announcements and edicts.
Within the golden hall, in plenteous profusion,[101]
Ornamented flabella open simultaneously;
Before the decorated rafters, deftly and gently,[102]
The beaded blinds have been rolled high.[103]
Atop the bell tower, chiao-chiao yüeh-yüeh,
Heralds proclaim the dawn three times;
In front of the jade stairs, la-la kua-kua,
Silence-commanding whips crack thrice.
Rigorously disciplined,
Beside the sculpted dragons,
Arrayed in official regalia,
There stand holders of the five noble ranks;
Majestic and inspiring,[104]
Seated on his dragon throne,
Resting on a brocade cushion,
They look upon the Lord of a Myriad Chariots.[105]
Gazing at him from a distance:[106]
On his head he wears the flat-topped crown
    with twelve tassels,[107]
His body is clad in a yellow ocher imperial
    dragon robe,
His waist is bound by a girdle adorned with
    Indigo Field jade,[108]

On his feet he wears thick-soled, polished,
    black leather boots,
In his hands he grasps a tablet of white jade
    inlaid with gold,
At his back stands a nine thunder cloud, dragon
    and phoenix screen.

Truly:

On a clear day the green latticed doors
    of the palace open wide;
A celestial breeze broadcasts the aroma
    of the imperial incense.[109]
A thousand strands of auspicious vapor[110]
    float by the golden gates;
While a solitary crimson-colored cloud[111]
    envelops the Jade Emperor.[112]

This emperor was born with:
    The eyebrows of Yao and the eyes of Shun,
    The back of Yü and the shoulders of T'ang.[113]
    If one were to describe this emperor:
    His talents were superior to those of other men,
    He was skilled at extemporaneous poetic rhyming,
    He was able to tally herds of sheep at a glance.[114]
    He was as good as Wen T'ung at painting
        inkwash bamboos,[115]
    And as skillful as Hsüeh Chi at dashing
        off calligraphy.[116]
    He was versed in the books of the three religions,
    And acquainted with the texts of the Nine Schools.
    Indulgent in pleasure, by day and by night,
    He was just like the ruler of Chien-ko, Meng Ch'ang of
        the Later Shu dynasty;[117]
    In love of beauty and addiction to the cup,
    He was much like the ruler of Chin-ling, Ch'en Shu-pao
        of the Ch'en dynasty.[118]

During the twenty-six years after he ascended the throne at the age of seventeen, he changed the titles of his reign periods six times, starting with Chien-chung ching-kuo, and continuing with Ch'ung-ning, Ta-kuan, Cheng-ho, Ch'ung-ho, and Hsüan-ho.[119]

That day, when the Emperor had ascended the throne, and the silence-commanding whips had cracked, the civil and military officials in the wake of the nine ministers and four directors,[120] holding their tablets in front of their chests, mounted the red steps leading up to the dais, performed the ceremony of five obeisances and three kowtows,[121] and presented their memorials.

When they had finished doing so, the eunuch who held the post of palace foreman, with his body clad in a close-fitting purple gown, and his waist encircled with a gold-embossed girdle, strode out to the head of the golden stairs and orally proclaimed an imperial edict,[122] saying, "It is now twenty years since We acceded to the throne.[123] The Mount Ken Imperial Park has been completed, and Heaven has vouchsafed propitious omens. This day inaugurates the dawn of an auspicious era, the benefits of which We intend to share with all of you gentlemen."

Before he had even finished speaking, a great minister at the head of the gathered ranks stepped forward:

His court boots resound upon the ground,
The sleeves of his robe stir the breeze.
If you do not know his official rank,
His jade girdle proclaims his status.

When the assembled officials looked at him, it turned out to be the left grand councilor, grand academician of the Hall for Veneration of Governance, minister of personnel, grand preceptor, and Duke of Lu, Ts'ai Ching.

Wearing his official headgear and holding his ivory tablet,[124] he prostrated himself upon the golden stairs[125] and kowtowed, saying, "May Your Majesty live ten thousand years, ten thousand years, ten thousand times ten thousand years![126] Your minister and his cohorts, in sincere fear and trepidation, kowtow and render their obeisance.[127] We respectfully observe that during the twenty years since Your Majesty acceded to the throne:

The sea-girt realm has been at peace,[128]
The whole empire has been prosperous.
Exalted Heaven, having observed this,[129]
Has produced untold auspicious omens:
The sun has radiated double coronas,
The stars have shone notably bright,
The seas have expanded their extent.
Your Sage Majesty holds the celestial mandate,
Ensuring You of a reign of ten thousand years.
Heaven will be stable,
Earth will be pacific,
People will be serene.
The size of the realm and solidity of the dynasty,
Only enhance the probability of a perpetual reign.
The Three Border Regions have benefited
   from a cessation of warfare;
The myriad states have come to pay court[130]
   before the celestial portals.

Mount Ken towers athwart the empyrean,[131]
The Jade Capital flaunts its elegance.
The Precious Registers conferring the mandate are
    exhibited before the palace gates;
The Scarlet Empyrean Tower soars loftily into the
    sky above the celestial structures.[132]
How fortunate Your minister and his cohorts are,
To have the joy of living in this exalted reign,
And associating with such brilliant compatriots.
May Your Majesty profit eternally from the three
    wishes of the border guard at Hua;[133]
And reap the constant benefits of the light shed
    upon You by the sun and the moon.
Unable to overcome our extreme trepidation
    on gazing upward at the celestial
    and sage presence of Your Majesty,[134]
We humbly submit this eulogy for Your attention."

After some time, an imperial rescript was proclaimed, saying, "The eulogy submitted by Our worthy minister only accentuates his loyalty and sincerity, while serving to enhance Our gratification. We hereby decree that the coming year will be the first year of the Ch'ung-ho reign period. On the first day of the first month, We shall formally accept the newly created seal of state known as the Mandate Determining Seal,[135] declare a general amnesty, and issue rewards to Our ministers in accordance with their ranks."

When Grand Preceptor Ts'ai Ching had descended the steps after receiving the rescript in response to his eulogy, the eunuch who held the post of palace foreman proclaimed the Emperor's command, saying:

"If you have a report to make, proceed forthwith;
If not, roll up the blinds and depart the court."[136]

Before he had finished speaking, what should they see but a man who:

Stepped forward out of the ranks,
His tablet lowered and body bent,[137]
Garbed in red, with an ivory tablet,
Wearing a jade girdle and gold fish,

and proceeded to prostrate himself on the golden stairs, stating, "Your minister, Grand Master of the Imperial Household, Defender-in-Chief of the Embroidered Uniform Guard, Grand Guardian, and Grand Guardian of the Heir Apparent, Chu Mien, hereby presents before Your Majesty the twenty-six judicial commissioners kneeling behind me, Chang Lung and company, from the thirteen provinces of the empire, the Two-Huai regions, the Two-Che regions, Shantung, Shansi, Honan, Hopei, Kuan-tung, Kuan-hsi, Fukien, Kuang-nan, and Szechwan. They have been evaluated according to precedent, and recommended for either promotion or reassignment, and are here

waiting to receive their credentials. Since it is mandated that these recom-
mendations be presented before Your Majesty, and I lack the presumption to
act on my own,[138] I request the issuance of a rescript to decide the matter."[139]

In response to this request, an imperial rescript approving the recommenda-
tions according to precedent was duly proclaimed. After Defender-in-Chief
Chu Mien had descended the steps upon receiving the rescript, the Son of
Heaven, with one flip of his sleeves, dismissed the assembled ministers, got
into his carriage, and returned to the palace, while the officials, divided into
their civil and military ranks, exited the Forbidden City through the Tuan-li
Gate, or Gate of Correct Protocol. The twelve trained elephants from the
imperial entourage preceded them without the help of their attendants, and
the elite guardsmen followed in their wake as they went their separate ways.

> All that can be heard is the clinking of armor,
> As the sword-bearing guardsmen,
> And the red-clad palace guards,
> Emerge simultaneously.
> All that can be seen is the glint of poleaxes,
> Where outside of the palace gate,
> Carriages and horses are arrayed,
> And guardsmen lined up.
> The shouting of men resembles,
> The turmoil of oceans and crashing of breakers;
> The neighing of horses is like,
> The collapse of mountains and cracking of earth.[140]

The crowd of judicial commissioners all emerged from the palace grounds,
mounted their horses, and proceeded to the headquarters of the Embroidered
Uniform Guard, where they congregated as closely as though they were:

> Locked tight in an iron bucket.

Before long, whom should they see but a seal-keeper, who came out with
his badge of office in hand and announced, "His Honor the defender-in-chief
will not return to the yamen today. His sedan chair is already waiting for him
just inside the Hsi-hua Men, or Western Floriate Gate, and he is about to set
out for the mansions of His Honor Ts'ai Ching and His Honor Li Pang-yen in
order to join them in celebrating the winter solstice."

As a result, the assembled officials all scattered, and Hsi-men Ch'ing and
Ho Yung-shou returned to the residence of Eunuch Director Ho Hsin, where
they spent the night.

The next day, Hsi-men Ch'ing reported back to the Ministry of War to receive his orders of appointment and register his name with the appropriate
offices, along with the other expectant officials, after which, he collected what
was left of his belongings, packed his luggage, and prepared to set out together
with Ho Yung-shou.

Defender-in-Chief Chu Presents a Memorial to the Throne

That evening, Eunuch Director Ho Hsin put on a farewell party for them, during which he said to Ho Yung-shou, "See that you seek the advice of His Honor Hsi-men Ch'ing in everything, lest, by acting on your own, you should fail in your social obligations."

On the twenty-first day of the eleventh month, they started off from the Eastern Capital, with some twenty attendants between them in their entourage, and set out on the high road to Shantung.

They had already embarked upon:

> The ninety coldest days of the winter season,
> A time when drops of water turn into icicles.

Along the way, they encountered nothing but:

> Empty suburbs and deserted roads,
> Desiccated trees and cold ravens.[141]
> In the sparse woods the pale sun
>   sheds a slanting glow;
> The evening snow and cold clouds
>   obscure the dusky ford.
> Before one mountain is surmounted
>   another comes in view;[142]
> By the time one village is passed
>   another comes in sight.

When they had crossed the Yellow River and reached the customs station at Pa-chiao Chen, all of a sudden, they were confronted with a violent windstorm. Behold:

> It is not the roaring of tigers,
> Nor is it the droning of dragons.
> With a sudden rush, a frigid blast
>   strikes the face;
> With a violent sough, a cold wind
>   beleaguers them.
> Still too weak to strip the willows
>   or bring blossoms out;
> Concealed within it are water sprites
>   and mountain goblins.[143]
> At the outset, it is utterly devoid of
>   either trace or shadow;[144]
> But afterwards, it rolls away the mists
>   and effaces the clouds.
> It is so alarming that:
> Along willow-lined embankments, the seagulls
>   fly away in pairs;
> On banks of red smartweed, the mandarin ducks
>   take off together.

Just see the way it:

Penetrates gauze windows,
Extinguishes silver lamps,
Permeates painted bowers,
Pervades silken garments.
In its frenzied dancing, it blows down the
   blossoms and bends the willows;
In its somber ferocity, it sets stones in
   motion and raises clouds of sand.[145]
In its boundless obscurity,
It blows the great trees into sounding
   with repeated blasts;
In its whistling cacophony,
It startles a solitary wild goose into
   sheltering in a ditch.
In no time at all:
The sand and the rocks strike the ground,
And clouds of dirt obscure the heavens;[146]
When the sand and rocks strike the ground,
It is just like the unexpected arrival of
   a skyful of opportune rain;
When clouds of dirt obscure the heavens,
It is like the dust raised by the approach
   of a million fierce troops.[147]
It has the effect of:
Driving the old village fisherman into
   ceasing his angling,
Packing up his gear, and racing toward home;
And causing the mountain woodcutter to
   lose his composure,
Put away his tools, and head for his cottage.
It is so frightening that:
The tigers and leopards in the hills,
Pull in their heads,
Conceal their tracks,
And hide themselves in the ravines.
It blows so hard that:
The horned dragons deep in the oceans,
Clench their claws,
Curl up their tails,
And fail to flaunt their ferocity.
After blowing for some time,
One notices that the rooftop tiles
   fly off like sparrows;
After blustering for a while,

It appears that the hillside stones
    have taken to flight.
The rooftop tiles fly off like sparrows,
Assaulting the traveling merchants into missing
    the track and losing their way;[148]
The hillside stones have taken to flight,
Scaring the merchant ships into securing their
    hawsers and trimming their sails.
Tall trees are blown down and uprooted;[149]
Short trees are divested of branch tips.
Just how strong is this wind? Truly:
    It overturns the trees that protect
        the gates of Hell;
    It raises the dust on the summit of
        Feng-tu Mountain.[150]
    Ch'ang-o hastily shuts the gates of
        the moon palace;
    Airborne Lieh-tzu, high in the void,
        appeals for help.
    It imperils the Jade Emperor's residence
        on the peak of Mount K'un-lun;
    It blows both the world and the universe[151]
        into violent motion up and down.

Hsi-men Ch'ing and Ho Yung-shou, riding in two closed sedan chairs with
felt curtains, were so buffeted by the wind that they found it:

    Difficult to proceed a step further.[152]

They also observed that in the waning light they were in danger of being as-
saulted by criminal elements hiding in the woods. Ho Yung-shou, therefore,
suggested to Hsi-men Ch'ing that they head for the next village to seek lodging
for the night and proceed the next day when the wind had abated. After searching for what seemed like half a day, they saw in the distance an old monastery
by the side of the road, located in a grove of bare willow trees, behind what
remained of a crumbling wall. Behold:

By the stone steps the steles have toppled
    over and are covered by creepers;
The zigzag galleries and the ancient halls
    have half fallen into decrepitude.
Late at night the sojourners are devoid of
    either lamplight or braziers;
As the moon sets they can only sigh at the
    monks engaged in meditation.

When Hsi-men Ch'ing and Ho Yung-shou went into the monastery to seek lodging for the night, they noticed a placard indicating that it was named the Yellow Dragon Monastery. On looking into the abbot's quarters, they saw that several monks were sitting there, engaged in meditation. There were no lamps or braziers to be seen, and the living quarters were in a state of dilapidation, some of the gaps in which were patched with woven bamboo. The abbot came out and greeted them with a Buddhist salutation, after which, he lighted a fire to heat some tea and cut some stalks of hay with which to feed their horses. In his luggage, Hsi-men Ching had brought some dried chicken, cured pork, biscuits, hardtack, and the like, which he and Ho Yung-shou managed to make a meal out of that night, while the abbot supplemented it by cooking up a potful of lentil-flavored congee for them, after which, they went to bed for the night.

The next day, when the wind had stopped and the weather had cleared, they rewarded the old monk with a tael of silver for his hospitality, took their leave, and continued on their journey to Shantung. Truly:

Galloping abroad upon the ruler's business,
  they are undeterred by the effort;[153]
Mountains and passes prolong the distance,[154]
  as they travel toward the capital.
Spending the night in an ancient monastery,
  they lack fire for heat or meals;
It is quite enough to cause the wayfarers
  to be acutely perturbed at heart.

  If you want to know the outcome of these events,
  Pray consult the story related in the following chapter.

Chapter 72

WANG THE THIRD KOWTOWS TO HSI-MEN
CH'ING AS HIS ADOPTED FATHER;
YING PO-CHÜEH INTERCEDES TO ALLEVIATE
THE GRIEVANCE OF LI MING

The cold and the heat impel each other forward[1]
    as spring gives place to autumn;
Both for those abroad, and those remaining home,[2]
    their feelings remain persistent.
In the cold season, the traveler is plagued by
    the hardships of wind and frost;
Beset by obstacles, the ruler's loyal servant[3]
    allows his teardrops to overflow.
Endangered by the wind and the waves, he knows
    not whether he will float or sink;
But meeting with a beauty or enjoying a drink[4]
    may serve to alleviate his sorrow.
A snail's-horn of fame, a fly's-head of profit,[5]
    have never ceased to be alluring;
How often have they led the black-haired youth
    to scoff at the white-haired elder.[6]

THE STORY GOES that Hsi-men Ch'ing and Ho Yung-shou continued on their journey. But no more of this.

We return instead to the story of Wu Yüeh-niang back at home. It happened that during Hsi-men Ch'ing's former trip to the Eastern Capital, Ch'en Ching-chi was spotted by the wet nurse Ju-i having a drink with P'an Chin-lien in her room, and when Hsi-men Ch'ing came home, Yüeh-niang had borne the brunt of his anger, and they had had a falling out about it.[7] For that reason, on this occasion when Hsi-men Ch'ing was away from home, Yüeh-niang refrained from doing any entertaining. Even when her brother and sister-in-law came to visit, she would not allow them to stay but sent them abruptly on their way. She instructed P'ing-an to keep the main gate closed unless there were some reason to open it, and she had the ceremonial gate that led into the second courtyard locked up every night. The members of her sorority of wives and concubines did not venture outside but remained in their quarters doing needlework. If Ch'en Ching-chi needed to fetch pawned garments from the storage loft in the rear compound, Yüeh-niang saw to it that either Ch'un-hung or Lai-an accompanied him both on his way in and on his way out. She constantly checked to see if the doors were properly secured and in everything presided over the household more strictly than had been her wont. For this reason, P'an Chin-lien was unable to carry on with Ch'en Ching-chi and, because it had been the wet nurse Ju-i who had reported her former indiscretion to Yüeh-niang, she was constantly on bad terms with her.

One day, Yüeh-niang got out a considerable number of Hsi-men Ch'ing's undershirts and underpants and handed them over to Ju-i, suggesting that she get Auntie Han to help her in seeing that they were properly washed and starched, and then hung outside to dry in Li P'ing-erh's quarters. Who could have anticipated that in Chin-lien's quarters next door Ch'un-mei was also engaged in laundering her mistress's clothing and was about to begin the process of beating her skirts in order to get them clean, so she sent Ch'iu-chü over to ask if she could borrow a laundry bat for the purpose.

Since Ju-i, along with Ying-ch'un, was engaged in beating Hsi-men Ch'ing's underwear at the time, she refused to give it to her, saying, "You borrowed a laundry bat for your own use just the other day, and here you are asking for it again. Auntie Han, here, is using it right now to beat Father's underpants and undershirts."

Ch'iu-chü, in a fit of temper, angrily marched next door and said to Ch'un-mei, "You insisted on sending me over to borrow it for no good reason, and now they won't let me have it. Ying-ch'un actually said, 'Take it then,' but Ju-i stopped her and refused to let me have it."

"Ai-ya! Ai-ya!" Ch'un-mei exclaimed. "How can she be so uncooperative? It seems as though:

> Even in broad daylight, one can't borrow
>   an empty oil lamp from her.

Who knows but what Mother may also expect me to launder her foot bindings after I get through starching this yellow damask skirt of hers. If I ask that woman to lend us a laundry bat but she refuses to let me have it, when I've done washing Mother's things, what am I going to beat them with?"

She then said to Ch'iu-chü, "You'd better go back to the rear compound and see if they have a laundry bat we could use."

When P'an Chin-lien, who was sitting on the k'ang in her room, engaged in putting on her foot bindings, happened to overhear this, she asked, "What's going on?"

Ch'un-mei then told her the whole story of how she had tried to borrow a laundry bat, but Ju-i had refused to give it to her.

Because Chin-lien harbored a long-standing grudge against her, this was just the pretext she had been looking for, and she reviled her, saying, "That lousy whore! How could she refuse to give it to you? You'd better go yourself to demand it of her. And if she refuses, it will be all right to give that whore a piece of your mind."

Ch'un-mei, who was in the prime of youth and needed no urging, set off in a fit of rage for Li P'ing-erh's quarters, where she arrived like a gust of wind, saying, "Just who do you take to be an outsider in this household, anyway, that you should refuse to let her have a laundry bat when she asks for it? It would seem that yet another mistress has emerged out of nowhere in these quarters."

"Ai-ya! Ai-ya!" exclaimed Ju-i. "The laundry bat is right here. Go ahead and take it if you need to. Who do you think is monopolizing it here, anyway, that you should feel justified in getting so angry about it? The First Lady has instructed me that when Auntie Han, here, has finished starching these undershirts and cotton briefs of Father's they should be taken out and beaten with the laundry bat. When Ch'iu-chü came and asked for it, I said to her, 'Wait until I've finished giving these clothes of Father's a couple of strokes with the bat, after which you can take it for your own use.' She has grossly misrepresented the case in claiming that I refused to give it to her. Fortunately, Sister Ying-ch'un is here and can be my witness."

Who could have anticipated that Chin-lien had followed right behind Ch'un-mei and started to curse Ju-i, saying, "That's enough of your lip, woman! Since your mistress died, you act as though you have taken over her place in these quarters, and that Father won't be satisfied to have anyone but you take care of his intimate clothing for him. The rest of us wives might just as well be dead, since only you are fit to launder and starch his clothes for him. You think that by adopting this strategy you can lord it over the rest of us, do you? Well, I'm:

Quite inured to such alarms."

"Fifth Lady, how can you say such a thing?" protested Ju-i. "If the First Lady had not instructed us to do so, do you really think we would have had the nerve to insist on being the only ones to take care of Father's things for him?"

"Why you lousy splay-legged, man-hunting whore!" exclaimed Chin-lien. "You still insist on defending yourself, do you? Who is it that served Father with tea and adjusted his bedding for him in the middle of the night? And who talked him into having a jacket made for her? You think the things you're up to behind our backs are unknown to me, do you? Even if your furtive shenanigans should result in a pregnancy, I won't be intimidated by you."

"His legitimate consort and her son both came to grief," said Ju-i.

"Where can I hope to get to?"

If Chin-lien had not heard these words nothing might have happened, but having heard them:

A fire blazed up in her heart, and
Her powdered face became suffused with red.

Striding forward, she grabbed hold of the woman's hair with one hand and proceeded to thump her in the belly with the other until Auntie Han intervened and succeeded in separating them.

"You shameless whore! You man-baiting whore!" Chin-lien cursed. "Here we all are, bored enough to scream as it is, and you come along trying to seduce our husband. What role do you think you play in these quarters anyway? You're simply a reincarnation of Lai-wang's wife; but I'm not afraid of you."

Ju-i, weeping on the one hand, and trying to straighten her hair on the other, responded by saying, "I'm a latecomer here and know nothing of any Lai-wang's wife. All I know is that I serve as a wet nurse in Father's household."

"If you're a wet nurse," said Chin-lien, "you ought to confine yourself to being a wet nurse, instead of preening yourself on your ability to play the preternatural role of:

The fox who flaunted the tiger's might,[8]

in these quarters.

As an old hand at snaring wild geese,[9]
I'll hardly let you get away with any
of your devilish tricks."

As she continued to curse away, who should appear but Meng Yü-lou, who came strolling out from the rear compound and intervened, saying, "Sister Six, I invited you to come back to my place for a board game. Why haven't you come, instead of getting into a brawl over something here?"

She then grabbed hold of Chin-lien with one hand, dragged her back to her quarters, and sat her down, saying, "Tell me, what's it all about?"

Chin-lien allowed her anger to gradually subside, and Ch'un-mei served them with tea, while drinking which she said, "Just look. That lousy whore has made me so angry my hands are cold, and I can hardly lift my tea cup."

She then went on to say, "I was in my quarters, engaged in sketching a design to be embroidered on a pair of shoes, when you sent Hsiao-luan to invite me over. I told her I'd come after lying down for a while, and I was reclining on the bed without having yet fallen asleep, when I became aware that this little piece of mine was anxious to beat the skirts she had been laundering for me. I told her, 'Why don't you beat these foot bindings of mine while you're at it?' After what seemed like half a day, I heard the sound of a dispute. She had sent Ch'iu-chü next door to borrow a laundry bat for this purpose, and Ju-i had refused to give it to her, grabbing it back out of her hands and saying, 'You borrowed a laundry bat for your own use just the other day, and now that you can't find it, you're here asking for it again. We're just about to use it to beat some clothes of Father's.' Upon hearing this, I became annoyed, and said to Ch'un-mei, 'You go there yourself and give that lousy whore a piece of your mind.' Since when has she found the nerve to lord it over other people this way? As though we would ever let her get away with it. Who does she think she

P'an Chin-lien Thumps Chang Ju-i's Stomach with Her Fists

is, putting on such airs in those quarters of hers? Just as though she had been weighty enough to risk breaking the carrying poles of the bridal palanquin on being brought into the household. Why you're not even a match for that wife of Lai-wang's. I chose to follow right behind Ch'un-mei, and when we got there, Ju-i was still spouting off, yakkety-yak, with that mouth of hers. I gave her a severe tongue-lashing, and if it hadn't been for Auntie Han, who stepped between us and obstinately insisted[10] on dragging me away, I'd have hooked the guts of that lousy, shameless, man-baiting whore right out through her mouth. Does she really think she can pull the wool over our eyes in those quarters of hers by selling scallions for leeks and suchlike mischief? Have you ever seen the likes of our elder sister's irresponsibility? It's reminiscent of the way she indulged that lousy slave of a whore, Lai-wang's wife, to the point where she lost all sense of decorum, with the result that the two of us ended up:

    Feeling resentment and harboring hostility,

toward each other. And after that, she had the nerve to besmirch me with the gross allegation that I was responsible for driving that slave out of the household. Now, once again, she's indulging this woman to the point that:

    All the rules of propriety are turned upside down.[11]

If you're a wet nurse, you ought to confine yourself to being a wet nurse, rather than being allowed to flaunt your:

    Showy glamour and gaudy airs.

I'm really:

    Not the sort of person to let dust
      be thrown in her eyes.

And as for that shameless good-for-nothing:

    Nobody knows where the dead end up going to,

but he persists in frequenting her quarters. No matter where he's been, on coming home, he makes a point of going in there, bowing before her portrait, and muttering some mumbo jumbo of who knows what significance. During the night, if he happens to want some tea to drink, that whore gets up and bestirs herself to serve the tea to him, and even goes so far as to adjust his bedding for him. And, the next thing you know, the two of them are going at it together. She's nothing but an inveterate whore. When he calls for the maidservant to bring him some tea, who authorized you to insist upon:

    Sticking your neck out and horning in,[12]

that way, in your craving for a man? And how is it that, when she asked him for a jacket, that shameless good-for-nothing lost no time in going out to the shop, getting some silk fabric, and having it made into a jacket for her? And there's something else you don't know about. On the day of the final weekly commemoration of Li P'ing-erh's death, Father was persuaded to go into her quarters to burn some paper money and caught the maidservant and that woman sitting on the k'ang engaged in playing a game of jacks, which they hadn't had time to clear away before he came in. But, rather than raising any objection, he said, 'Go on playing if you like, and you needn't bother to send the offerings of dumplings and wine back to the rear compound. You can enjoy them yourselves.' For him to indulge her to such an extent was in recompense for what do you suppose? That whore responded by saying, 'Father, you can come and join us or not, as you see fit. We won't wait up for you.' What she could not have anticipated was that I chose to:

> Take two or three strides,

and walk right in on her, which startled her to such an extent that she was rendered:

> Wide-eyed and speechless,

whereupon she had nothing more to say. In the eyes of that good-for-nothing of ours, what kind of a decent woman is she, anyway? She's nothing but a lousy whore, and with a living husband to boot. And yet, you respond to her just like someone whose:

> Hungry eyes have alighted on a melon skin;

and insist on sheltering her:

> Regardless of the outcome for good or ill.[13]

The fact of the matter is, she's a good-for-nothing overripe peach with too much fire in her eyes. How could she be expected to pay any attention to the proprieties? That whore may allege that her husband is dead, but the other day, was that not her husband, with a baby boy in his arms, inquiring after her at the front gate? She's utterly:

> Open-eyed and brazen-faced,[14]

in the way she tries to deceive people with her tricks. Just look at the way she persists in putting on the gaudy airs that she's so good at right in front of people's eyes, constantly altering her demeanor to suit the circumstances. You can tell from the way she carries on that she regards herself as a reincarnation of Li P'ing-erh. And meanwhile, our elder sister keeps to the rear compound:

> Pretending to be both deaf and dumb,

and criticizing anyone who opens her mouth about it."

When Meng Yü-lou had heard her out, she merely smiled.

Chin-lien said:

> "Just as Nanking has its Shen Wan-san,[15]
> Peking has its withered willows;
> Just as a man has his reputation,
> A tree has its shadow.

How can she fail to be aware that:

> If one buries a body in the snow,
> It will be exposed when it melts."[16]

"It was originally claimed that this woman had no husband," said Meng Yü-lou. "Where did this husband of hers appear from?"

Chin-lien responded, saying:

"If the day lacks wind, it will not be clear;

If people don't lie, they will never succeed.

If she had not resorted to deception, how could she have hoped to find employment? Remember what she looked like when she first came here. She had a ravenous-looking face, her yellow skin was sallow and withered, and she appeared to be:

Both impoverished and emaciated;[17]

but after two years of eating her fill, the lousy whore is robust enough to resort to her man-baiting tricks. If you don't attempt to restrain her, before you know it, she'll start:

Assuming privileges above her station;

and if, in due course, she should happen to produce a child, whose would it be?"

Meng Yü-lou laughed at this, saying, "Slavey Six, you surely don't lack the cunning to deal with it."

After sitting a while longer, the two of them went back to the rear compound to play a board game together. Truly:

The three luminaries cast shadows, but

who can catch them;

The ten thousand things have no roots, they

just arise of themselves.

There is a poem that testifies to this:

A mere handful of spring warmth suffices

to stir nature into glory,

Bright crimsons and light greens[18] begin

to be engendered everywhere.

Even the wild plum blossom provides ample

stimulation for enjoyment,

What need is there to insist upon having

a tree of purple magnolias?[19]

To make a long story short, one day, in the afternoon, Hsi-men Ch'ing arrived back in Ch'ing-ho district and told Pen the Fourth and Wang Ching to take the luggage and go to the house before him, while he accompanied Ho Yung-shou to the yamen. After seeing that the residential quarters there were properly prepared and swept out in order to provide him with a place to stay, he mounted his horse and returned home.

Wu Yüeh-niang received him in the rear reception hall and proceeded to dust the dirt from the journey off his clothes and ladle out some water so he could wash his face. No sooner was he done with his ablutions than he ordered a maidservant to set up a table in the courtyard, where he:

Lit a full burner of incense,

and proceeded to make a vow before the tablets representing Heaven and Earth.

"Why are you making such a vow?" Yüeh-niang asked.

"Not to mention anything else," replied Hsi-men Ch'ing, "I'm lucky to be alive."

He then proceeded to tell her about the events on the road during their return trip, saying, "Just yesterday, on the twenty-second day of the eleventh month, we had barely crossed the Yellow River and arrived at Pa-chiao Chen in I-shui district when we ran into a violent windstorm, so nasty that we were blinded by the blowing sand and quite unable to proceed any further. It was late in the day already, and we hadn't seen a soul for the last hundred li of our journey, which threw us all into consternation. On top of which, we had numerous saddlebags and trunks full of valuables and didn't know what to do if we were confronted by robbers. As we proceeded, we came upon an old monastery. Though it was already night, the monks there were so impoverished they didn't even have a lamp lighted. Each of us had some dry rations and hardtack with us, and the abbot not only lent us a light and cooked up a pot of lentil-flavored congee, which we shared between us, but also cut some fodder with which to feed our horses. I then spent the night, foot to foot, on a meditation platform with Ho Yung-shou. The next day, it was only after the wind had died down that we were able to set out again. These hardships were ten times more severe than those I encountered on my last trip to the capital. That time, although the weather was hot, it was not too bad; but this time, not only was the weather bitterly cold, but we had to put up with some fearful conditions. Fortunately, we were on level ground at the time. If we had encountered such a tempest on the Yellow River, who knows what we would have done. While I was still on the road, I made a vow that on the first day of the twelfth month I would sacrifice a pig and a sheep to Heaven and Earth."

"Why didn't you come straight home, just now," asked Yüeh-niang, "instead of going first to the yamen?"

"Hsia Yen-ling," explained Hsi-men Ch'ing, "has recently been promoted to the position of commander of the escort for imperial processions and will consequently no longer be returning here. Ho Yung-shou, the nephew of Eunuch Director Ho Hsin of the Directorate for Buildings in the Palace Treasury, has just been promoted to my former post as assistant judicial commissioner in the Ch'ing-ho office of the Provincial Surveillance Commission. He is not more than nineteen years old, just a little squirt of a youngster, and quite ignorant of the bureaucratic world. His uncle, the eunuch director, repeatedly urged me to look after him in all things and offer him the benefit of my experience. If I had not accompanied him to the yamen and arranged a place for him to stay, he wouldn't have known what to do. I have also made a deal for him to buy that house of Hsia Yen-ling's for twelve hundred taels of silver, but, for the time being, he will have to put up in the yamen until Hsia

Yen-ling has vacated the premises, so he can arrange for his own dependents to move in.

"The other day, before we even left town, Hsia Yen-ling was unhappy about the prospect of being transferred to a position in the capital. Some unknown person must have leaked the news of our impending appointments to him. When we arrived in the capital, it turned out that he had previously spent who knows how much silver to solicit the intervention of Perfect Man Lin Ling-su at court, who informed Defender-in-Chief Chu Mien that Hsia Yen-ling wished to retain his rank of battalion commander and preferred to remain in his current post as judicial commissioner for another three years. Defender-in-Chief Chu Mien, accordingly, took the matter up with His Honor the grand preceptor, which put him in an extremely awkward position. If Kinsman Chai Ch'ien had not done everything in his power to maintain my interest, I would have been shunted aside. When I arrived there, Kinsman Chai Ch'ien was extremely annoyed with me and reproached me for not being able to keep a secret. I don't know who it could have been that leaked the information to him."

"You don't believe what I say," responded Yüeh-niang, "but you're altogether too impulsive in the way you carry on, just as if your legs were on fire. You can't keep anything to yourself but are always telling specious stories, first to this one, and then to that, giving people the impression that you're only:
    Peddling your influence and parading your wealth.
Truly:
    When the mindful plot against the unmindful,
    How can the unprepared cope with the prepared?
Having already seen the way you carry on, people think they know what you're up to and can't be bothered to take you seriously. They are able to pursue their own interests on the quiet:
    Just as easy as you please,
without your knowing anything about it."

Hsi-men Ch'ing went on to say, "When I was about to depart from the capital, Hsia Yen-ling repeatedly requested that I look after the welfare of his family, early and late. Someday soon, you ought to buy an appropriate gift and go pay a call on them."

"Since his wife's birthday is on the second day of the coming month," said Yüeh-niang, "I can accomplish both purposes by paying a call on her then. As I was saying, in the future, you ought to amend the reckless way you go about your business. As the sayings go:
    On first meeting one should express no more than
        three-tenths of one's thoughts;
    Never under any circumstances should one disclose
        the whole content of one's heart.
    Even one's wife may harbor duplicitous intent,
    Not to mention people in the world at large."

As they were talking, whom should they see but Tai-an, who came in and reported, "Pen the Fourth would like to know whether Father is ready to have him go to the home of His Honor Hsia in order to let them know what has happened, or not?"

"Tell him to go after he has had something to eat," said Hsi-men Ch'ing.

"He says he doesn't need to eat anything," replied Tai-an.

At this point, Li Chiao-erh, Meng Yü-lou, P'an Chin-lien, Sun Hsüeh-o, and Hsi-men Ta-chieh all trooped in to pay their respects, ask about his trip, and keep him company. Hsi-men Ch'ing happened to remember that when he had returned from his former trip to the Eastern Capital, Li P'ing-erh had also been among them, but today she was no longer there. Without more ado, he went out to her quarters in the front compound, bowed before her spirit tablet, and shed a few tears, after which Ju-i, Ying-ch'un, and Hsiu-ch'un all came forward and kowtowed to him.

Yüeh-niang lost no time in sending Hsiao-yü out to invite him back to the rear compound for a meal. When he had finished eating, he ordered that four taels of silver should be provided to reward the officers who had looked after the ponies on his trip, and he also wrote a calling card thanking Commandant Chou Hsiu for their loan. In addition, he told Lai-hsing to procure a half-carcass of pork, a half-carcass of mutton, forty catties of white flour, a package of white rice, a jar of wine, two legs of smoked pork, two geese, ten chickens, kindling and charcoal, and appropriate amounts of cooking oil, salt, vinegar, and the like, to be delivered to Ho Yung-shou as a welcome gift to provide for his needs. He also engaged the services of a chef to cater to him there.

Just as these provisions were being collected in the reception hall, preparatory to Tai-an's delivering them, Ch'in-t'ung suddenly came in and said, "Master Wen and Ying the Second have come to pay you a visit."

"Invite them to come in," Hsi-men Ch'ing promptly responded.

Licentiate Wen, wearing a gown of green satin, cut like the robe of a Taoist priest, and Ying Po-chüeh, in a jacket of purple velvet, came in from the front compound to pay their respects to Hsi-men Ch'ing. Bowing repeatedly in greeting, they asked him about the hardships of wind and frost he had been exposed to on his journey.

Hsi-men Ch'ing, for his part, said, "I am grateful to you two gentlemen for keeping an eye on my home, early and late."

"Not only did I keep an eye on your home," said Ying Po-chüeh, "but this morning, when I was about to get up, I suddenly heard the chattering of auspicious magpies on the roof of the house. My wife anticipated me by saying, 'I imagine it's an indication that His Honor has returned home. Why don't you go take a look?' To which I replied, 'Brother departed on the twelfth, and it's only been half a month or so since then. How could he get back so quickly? Every third day I go by there to ask after him, but I haven't heard any news as yet.' 'No matter whether he's come back or not,' said my wife, 'why don't you go take a look?' And she urged me to get dressed. When I arrived at your place, I was surprised to hear that Brother had actually returned, and when I ventured across the street to call on the venerable Master Wen, I found that he, too, was just putting on his clothes. 'Why don't I go over there with you, venerable sir?' he said."

Ying Po-chüeh then went on to ask whom he had encountered on the road to the Eastern Capital. He also noticed that there were quantities of foodstuffs, wine, rice, and so forth, packed up and resting on the stylobate outside the reception hall, and asked, "Who are these for?"

"They are for my new colleague, His Honor Ho Yung-shou," said Hsi-men Ch'ing. "He accompanied me on my return trip, but his dependents have not arrived yet, so he is staying temporarily in the yamen. I am sending these things to him as a gift to provide for his needs while he is there. I am also sending him a card inviting him to come over tomorrow for a welcoming party after the hardships of the road. I'm not planning to invite anyone else, but I hope that you two gentlemen and my brother-in-law Wu K'ai will be able to come and keep him company."

"There is one problem," said Ying Po-chüeh. "Your brother-in-law Wu K'ai, like you, Brother, are both officials, and Master Wen, here, wears a square-cut scholar's cap, while I am only entitled to wear a commoner's skullcap. How can I be comfortable socializing with him? Who knows what he will make of me? Will I not be merely an object of amusement in his eyes?"

Hsi-men Ch'ing laughed, saying, "In that case, I'll lend you my newly purchased silk 'loyal and tranquil hat' to wear, and if he should ask you about it, you can say that you are my eldest son. How would that be?"

They all had a laugh at this.

"To get serious about it," continued Ying Po-chüeh, "my head size is eight and three-tenths inches, so I couldn't wear any hat of yours."

Licentiate Wen chimed in, saying, "Your pupil's head size is also eight and three-tenths inches; so how would it be if I lent you my square-cut scholar's cap to wear?"

"Venerable sir," said Hsi-men Ch'ing, "you mustn't lend it to him. If he gets used to borrowing it, he might violate protocol by forgetfully showing up with it when reporting for duty at the local office of the Board of Rites, and you would be implicated."

"What a thing to say, venerable sir!" laughed Licentiate Wen. "What a thing to say! No doubt I'd end up being dragged into the soup with him."

At this point, a servant served them with tea, and after they had drunk it, Licentiate Wen inquired, "So His Honor Hsia Yen-ling has received a capital appointment and will not be coming back here anymore?"

"He has been elevated to the position of a senior official," said Hsi-men Ch'ing. "As the commander of the escort for imperial processions, he is entitled to wear a mandarin square featuring a *ch'i-lin*,[20] and wield a rattan cane. As the holder of such an illustrious position in the capital, why should he return here?"

Before long, after the invitation had been written, the gifts had been carried outside, and Hsi-men Ch'ing had deputed Tai-an to take charge of their delivery, he conducted Licentiate Wen and Ying Po-chüeh into an anteroom where they could sit down on a heated k'ang, and warm themselves at a brazier. He also dispatched Ch'in-t'ung to the licensed quarter to engage the services of the four boy actors, Wu Hui, Cheng Ch'un, Cheng Feng, and Tso Shun, who were to report for duty early the next day. He then arranged to have a table set up so he could keep his two guests company for a drink of wine.

When Lai-an had brought the table in and set it up, Hsi-men Ch'ing said to him, "Bring another place setting of goblet and chopsticks, and invite my son-in-law to join us."

In due course, Ch'en Ching-chi came in, bowed to the company, and took a seat to one side. The four of them sat down together around the brazier and proceeded to pour the wine, after which, they fell to talking about Hsi-men Ch'ing's adventures on the road.

"Brother," opined Ying Po-chüeh, "you must have a good heart. Since:

One case of good fortune can override
a hundred calamities,[21]

even if there had been highwaymen about at the time, the threat they posed would naturally have been dissipated."

Licentiate Wen chimed in, saying:

"If good men were to rule a state for a hundred years,
they could put an end to violence and killing.[22]

Quite aside from the fact, venerable sir, that you are forever galloping abroad upon the ruler's business, High Heaven will not permit good people to suffer injury."

Hsi-men Ch'ing then asked, "Did anything of importance happen at home during my absence?"

"After Father's departure," replied Ch'en Ching-chi, "nothing particular happened at home. The only thing is that His Honor An Ch'en of the Ministry of Works sent people to ask after you twice. Yesterday they came again to ask me, and I told them that you had not returned yet."

As they were talking, whom should they see but Lai-an, who came in carrying a large platter of stuffed, chive-flavored, pork dumplings. Hsi-men Ch'ing kept them company as they ate but had only had time to eat one dumpling for himself, when P'ing-an came in and announced that two clerks from the yamen office and a group of adjutants had come to report on something. Hsi-men Ch'ing went out to the reception hall, where he remained standing, and ordered them to come in.

The two clerks knelt down in front of him and asked, "If it please Your Honor, on what day do you intend to assume your new office? And how much in the way of public funds should be drawn upon for the occasion?"

"Just do as you have been accustomed to do in the past," said Hsi-men Ch'ing.

"Last year," said the clerks, "Your Honor was the only one to assume office. But now, not only has Your Honor been promoted to the post of judicial commissioner, but His Honor Ho Yung-shou is also assuming office as assistant judicial commissioner. Since these two events are occurring together, the normal precedents do not apply."

"In that case," said Hsi-men Ch'ing, "you can spend another ten taels of silver for the occasion, making a total of thirty taels in all."

The two clerks assented and were on their way out when Hsi-men Ch'ing called them back and said, "As for the day on which to schedule our formal assumption of office, you can ask His Honor Ho Yung-shou when he would like it to be."

"His Honor Ho Yung-shou has already determined that he would like it to be on the twenty-fifth,"[23] the two clerks reported.

"In that case," responded Hsi-men Ch'ing, "you can go ahead and prepare for it then."

The two of them then proceeded to draw the specified amount of silver and expend it on arranging the necessary table settings, and purchasing provisions for the occasion.

Sometime later, Ch'iao Hung also came by to pay his respects and proffer his congratulations. Hsi-men Ch'ing invited him to stay for a visit, but he declined and, after drinking a serving of tea, got up and departed. Hsi-men Ch'ing continued to keep his two guests company until lamplighting time before the party broke up, after which, he went back to Yüeh-niang's quarters, where he spent the night. Of the events of that evening there is no more to tell.

The next day, preparations were set in order for the party to welcome Ho Yung-shou after the hardships of his trip.

Auntie Wen had also learned of Hsi-men Ch'ing's homecoming by this time and mentioned it to Wang the Third, who immediately prepared a calling card inviting him to come over for a visit. Hsi-men Ch'ing responded by arranging for the purchase of two sets of pig's trotters, two fresh fish, two roast ducks, and a jar of southern wine, and sending Tai-an to deliver them as a belated birthday present for Lady Lin. Tai-an was rewarded for his efforts with a gratuity of three mace of silver. But no more of this.

In the main reception hall the preparations for the party were complete.

> The brocade screens dazzled the eyes,
> The tables and chairs were spic-and-span,
> The floor was covered with brocade carpets,
> Landscapes by famous artists adorned the walls.

Brother-in-law Wu K'ai, Ying Po-chüeh, and Licentiate Wen all came ahead of time. Hsi-men Ch'ing joined them while tea was served and sent someone to remind Ho Yung-shou of his invitation. In a little while, the boy actors appeared and kowtowed to the company.

"Brother," inquired Ying Po-chüeh, "why did you not engage the services of Li Ming for this occasion?"

"He no longer frequents my household," replied Hsi-men Ch'ing, "so I no longer employ him."

"I guess you're still angry with them," said Ying Po-chüeh, but he did not pursue the matter further.

As they were talking, whom should they see but P'ing-an, who hastily came in with a calling card and reported, "His Honor Chou Hsiu of the Regional Military Command has come to pay his respects and has already dismounted."

At this, Brother-in-law Wu K'ai, Licentiate Wen, and Ying Po-chüeh all retired to an anteroom on the west side of the courtyard, while Hsi-men Ch'ing donned his official cap and girdle and went out to welcome his guest into the reception hall. After exchanging the customary amenities, Chou Hsiu spoke of Hsi-men Ch'ing's recent promotion and extended his congratulations, and Hsi-men Ch'ing thanked him for the loan of the officers and horses for his trip. Thereupon, the two of them sat down in the positions of guest and host, while Chou Hsiu asked him to describe his experience of the imperial audience in the capital. Hsi-men Ch'ing responded by telling him about it in some detail.

"Since Hsia Yen-ling is not coming back," said Chou Hsiu, "he surely must be planning to send someone to conduct his dependents to the capital."

"He is not going to send for them until sometime next month," said Hsi-men Ch'ing. "In the interim, my colleague Ho Yung-shou is staying at the yamen. In response to my advocacy, Hsia Yen-ling has also agreed to sell his house to him."

"That sounds like an ideal solution," said Chou Hsiu.

Upon noticing the preparations for a party in the reception hall, he then went on to ask, "Who are you entertaining today?"

"I'm merely providing a libation to welcome His Honor Ho Yung-shou after the hardships of his journey," explained Hsi-men Ch'ing. "Since we are now colleagues, it's the least I can do for him."

When the two of them had finished their tea, Chou Hsiu got up to go, saying, "Someday soon, the officers of the guard will get together to offer their congratulations to you two gentlemen."

"How could I presume to put you to such trouble?" said Hsi-men Ch'ing. "I am grateful for your offer."

After bowing to his host, Chou Hsiu went out the gate, mounted his horse, and departed.

Hsi-men Ch'ing then came back inside, divested himself of his formal attire, and rejoined his three visitors, after which, a meal was served for them in the studio.

It was already afternoon by the time Ho Yung-shou arrived. Wu K'ai and the others were all introduced to him, and, when they had finished with the customary amenities, they proceeded to chat about the weather. When the first serving of tea had been replaced, they all relaxed by loosening their clothing.

Ho Yung-shou perceived that Hsi-men Ch'ing's household was appropriately prosperous, and that the preparations for the party were lavishly complete. The four boy musicians, with their:

> Silver psalteries, ivory clappers,
> Jade mandolas, and balloon guitars,

joined the company to serve the wine. Within the hall:

> Animal-shaped briquettes burn in golden braziers;
> Jade goblets are overflowing with Yang-kao wine.

The blinds are all suspended, so that:

> The whole area is suffused with spring warmth;
> The entire hall is filled with genial feeling.[24]

Truly, it is a case of:

> Golden goblets are brimming with vintage wine;
> Jade candles are trimmed amid sounds of spring.

The party continued until the first watch, when Ho Yung-shou got up and returned to the yamen, while Wu K'ai, Ying Po-chüeh, and Licentiate Wen also took their leave and returned home. After Hsi-men Ch'ing had seen the boy actors off, he ordered the utensils to be cleared away and made his way to P'an Chin-lien's quarters in the front compound.

The woman, for her part, was waiting in her room, where she had proceeded to:

> Apply generous coats of rouge and powder,
> Deck herself out in a new set of apparel,
> Light incense and wash her private parts,

in the hope that Hsi-men Ch'ing would visit her quarters.

> Her face was wreathed in smiles,[25]

as she went forward to help him off with his clothes and promptly ordered Ch'un-mei to pour out a serving of tea for him. After he had drunk the tea, the two of them went to bed for the night. Truly:

> Under heated bedding and heated quilts,
> Brocade curtains hold an air of spring,
> And the fragrance of musk is luxuriant.
> Beneath the quilt, their white bodies
>   are in intimate contact;
> Upon the pillow, their smooth breasts
>   press against each other.

> Above, they project their clove-shaped tongues;
> Below, the pearl is imbedded inside the oyster.

As for the woman:

> Throughout the game of clouds and rain,[26]
> Her hundred allurements are on display;[27]

As for Hsi-men Ch'ing:

> When through thrusting and retracting,
> His "magic rhinoceros horn" is erect.[28]

Unable to go to sleep, they spent some time discussing events during their period of separation. Even after intercourse, their lascivious feelings were still unsatisfied, and Hsi-men Ch'ing obliged her to get down and play his phoenix flute. As for the woman, her sole desire was to strengthen her hold upon Hsi-men Ch'ing's heart. Moreover, having been neglected for half a month:

> Her innermost feelings were starved;[29]
> Her libidinous desires were on fire.

Now that his body was again at her disposal, her only regret was that she couldn't:

> Bore her way into his belly,

and she was prepared to toy with his organ all night without its ever leaving her mouth.

Hsi-men Ch'ing needed to get out of bed in order to urinate, but the woman wouldn't let him go, saying, "My darling, no matter how much urine you may have, go ahead and piss it into my mouth, and I'll swallow it for you. It's ice-cold, and it would be better not to have to expose your warm body to the frigid temperature."

When Hsi-men Ch'ing heard these words, he was more gratified than ever and exclaimed, "My precious child, no one else cares for me as much as you do."

Thereupon, he actually pissed into the woman's mouth, while she allowed the urine to collect there, and then slowly swallowed it in one mouthful.

"How do you like the taste?" Hsi-men Ch'ing asked.

"It has a somewhat salty flavor," responded Chin-lien. "If you have any breath-sweetening lozenges handy, give me some of them to suppress the odor."

"The breath-sweetening lozenges are in my white satin jacket," said Hsi-men Ch'ing. "You can help yourself to them."

The woman put an end to the episode by tugging at the sleeve of his jacket, which was lying over the headboard, groping out a few lozenges, and popping them into her mouth. Truly:

> The minister in waiting is not as thirsty
>   as the diabetic Ssu-ma Hsiang-ju;[30]
> But is willing to accept the gift of a cup
>   of dew from atop a brazen pillar.[31]

Gentle reader take note: It is all too often the way of wives or concubines to set out deliberately to bewitch their husbands:

There is no length to which they will not go,
Humbling themselves to the most shameful acts,
Without showing even a trace of embarrassment.

Legitimate wives, on the other hand, are:

Straightforward and honorable,[32]

and could never bring themselves to resort to such practices.

That night, Hsi-men Ch'ing and the woman continued to dally with each other without restraint.

The next day, Hsi-men Ch'ing reported to the yamen early in order to participate, together with Ho Yung-shou, in the ceremony marking their formal assumption of office, and to attend the public banquet arranged to celebrate the occasion. Musicians from the two Music Offices were enlisted to provide for their entertainment. It was already afternoon by the time he returned home, and orderlies from the yamen also delivered to his residence what remained from his table setting at the banquet.

Wang the Third also sent someone to extend an invitation to him. Hsi-men Ch'ing responded by sending Tai-an to the silk goods store to pick up an outfit of clothing as a gift, and arrange to have it wrapped up in a felt bag.

Just as he was completing his preparations for departure, an attendant came in and announced that His Honor An Ch'en had come to pay him a visit, which threw Hsi-men Ch'ing into such consternation that he hardly had time to straighten his clothing before going out to welcome him.

An Ch'en, who was benefiting from his newly enhanced rank as secretary of the Bureau of Irrigation and Transportation in the Ministry of Works, was wearing a girdle with a decorative plaque enchased with gold, and a mandarin square emblazoned with a silver pheasant, and was followed by a retinue of lesser officials.

His face was wreathed in smiles,

as he was conducted into the reception hall, where they exchanged the customary amenities and congratulated each other on their recent promotions.

When they had seated themselves in the positions of guest and host, Secretary An Ch'en said, "Your pupil has sent people to ask after you several times, but they were told that you had not yet returned."

"That was the case," responded Hsi-men Ch'ing. "I had to remain in the capital until I could attend the great audience at the time of the winter solstice, and submit my congratulatory memorial, before I was able to set out for home."

In a little while, after they had consumed a serving of tea, An Ch'en said, "Your pupil has respectfully come to ask a favor that it is probably inappropriate to trouble you with. At present, the prefect of Chiu-chiang, Ts'ai Hsiu, who is the ninth son of the venerable Grand Preceptor Ts'ai Ching,[33] is en route to the capital for his triennial audience with the Emperor. The other day, I received a letter from him, stating that he would be arriving here very soon. Your pupil, along with Sung Ch'iao-nien, Ch'ien Lung-yeh, and Huang Pao-kuang, the four of us in all, intend to play host to him and would like to borrow the use of your mansion for the purpose, and invite him to a feast. But we don't know whether you will consent to this or not."

"If that is your esteemed behest, venerable sir," said Hsi-men Ch'ing:

"I could hardly presume to disobey it.[34]
Just let me know when it will be needed."

"It will be on the twenty-seventh," responded An Ch'en. "Your pupil will send over our joint contributions toward the cost of the event tomorrow. If your exemplary staff is able to manage it for us, it would be an ample demonstration of your consideration."

Having finished speaking, and having consumed another serving of tea, he took his leave, mounted his horse, and went his way, accompanied by outriders shouting to clear the way.

Immediately thereafter, Hsi-men Ch'ing proceeded to go out the gate and make his way to the mansion of Imperial Commissioner Wang I-hsüan in order to attend the party to which he had been invited. Upon arriving at the gate, he sent in his calling card, and when Wang the Third heard that Hsi-men Ch'ing had arrived, he hastened out to welcome him and escorted him into the reception hall, where they exchanged the customary amenities.

It so happens that this hall was a spacious thirty-foot-wide structure, with a rounded goalpost-shaped main door; topped with a double-eaved, five-ridged, gable and hip roof, decorated with animal figures; and enhanced with doors and windows of caltrop-patterned latticework. Over the lintel a plaque was suspended that had been presented by the Emperor and was inscribed in the imperial hand with three gold characters that read "Hall of Ancestral Loyalty." To either side of the door were suspended tablets inscribed with the parallel statements:

Mansion of a pillar of the state;
Home of a protector of the realm.[35]
In the place of honor in the middle of the hall was positioned a formal chair, upholstered in tiger skin, with a closely clipped woolen rug on the floor in front of it.

After Wang the Third had greeted Hsi-men Ch'ing with the appropriate amenities, he ushered him to the seat of honor, while he drew up a chair for himself and sat down to one side. Before long, a serving of tea was brought out on a red lacquer tray. When they had politely offered cups to each other and consumed the tea, the attendants took the utensils away, and they fell into casual conversation. It was only after this that the drinking vessels were laid out and the wine poured. It so happens that Wang the Third had engaged the services of two boy actors to entertain them by singing and playing their musical instruments.

Hsi-men Ch'ing interrupted the proceedings by saying, "Why don't you invite the venerable lady of the house to come out so that I can pay her my respects?"

This elicited such consternation on the part of Wang the Third that he promptly told an attendant to go back to the interior of the residence and convey the request.

In a little while, the attendant came out again and said, "Her Ladyship invites His Honor to come visit her inside."

Wang the Third, accordingly, prepared to usher him inside, and Hsi-men Ch'ing said, "My worthy acquaintance, pray precede me."

Thereupon, they went straight back to the main room in the interior of the residence.

Lady Lin was already fully decked out for the occasion.

Her head was adorned with pearls and trinkets;[36] her torso was garbed in a scarlet full-sleeved robe; her waist was encircled with a girdle featuring a plaque of green jade inlaid with gold, beneath which she wore a flower-sprigged skirt of jet brocade; her face was so heavily daubed with makeup that she resembled a silver figurine; her hair was done up in a raised coiffure; her lips were red with rouge; her earlobes were adorned with a pair of pearl earrings; and from the upper border of her skirt were suspended two strings of:

Jade pendants that tinkled when she moved.[37]

Hsi-men Ch'ing:

Bent his body to perform an obeisance,

saying, "Will Your Ladyship please assume the position of honor."

"Your Honor is our guest," responded Lady Lin. "Will you please assume the position of honor."

After dickering for what seemed like half a day, the two of them ended up kowtowing to each other.

"I fear," said Lady Lin, "that my young son, who is as yet:

Unconscious of right and wrong,

imposed upon Your Honor the other day but was fortunate enough to receive your forgiveness. And you also undertook to settle matters with that bunch of characters on his behalf, for which:

My gratitude knows no bounds.

Today I have prepared a meager cup of watery wine and invited you here, with the intention of kowtowing to you in order to express my gratitude. How is it that, instead, I have been the recipient of Your Honor's gifts, putting me in a position in which it would be:

Discourteous to refuse, and

Embarrassing to accept?"

"How could I be so presumptuous?" said Hsi-men Ch'ing. "It was only because your pupil had to go to the Eastern Capital on business and was therefore unable to proffer my congratulations on the occasion of Your Ladyship's birthday that I have offered this:

Insignificant lot of paltry gifts,[38]

to Your Ladyship to give away to someone if you like."

Upon noticing that Auntie Wen was also present, Hsi-men Ch'ing turned to her, saying, "Auntie Wen, would you fetch me a set of goblets on raised stands so I can proffer a drink of birthday wine to Her Ladyship."

He also hastily called for Tai-an to come forward. It so happens that Hsi-men Ch'ing had prepared an outfit of fashionable brocaded clothing as a birthday present for Lady Lin, which Tai-an was carrying in his felt bag. It consisted of a lilac-colored, wide-sleeved, satin jacket, and a kingfisher-blue, long trailing skirt, and was presented to her upon a tray. When Lady Lin saw it, with its:

Golden tints that caught the eye,

she was more than a little delighted.

Auntie Wen forthwith presented a set of:

Golden goblets on silver stands,[39]

and Wang the Third also ordered the two boy actors to bring their musical instruments and come in to help celebrate the occasion.

But Lady Lin protested, saying, "See here, what's the point of calling them in here? Let them wait outside for now."

Accordingly, they were sent outside again.

Hsi-men Ch'ing then toasted her with a goblet of wine, and Lady Lin expressed her gratitude by returning the compliment.

After this, Wang the Third proffered Hsi-men Ch'ing a goblet of wine, and Hsi-men Ch'ing was about to kowtow to him in return, but Lady Lin intervened, saying, "Your Honor, please get up, and permit him to kowtow to you."

"How could I do that?" said Hsi-men Ch'ing. "Whoever heard of such a thing?"

"My good sir," said Lady Lin, "how can you talk that way? Do you mean to suggest that someone with such a high-ranking office as yours is not fit to be his adopted father? My son has been undereducated since his childhood and has not had the opportunity to associate with the right sort of people. If Your Honor will only deign to demonstrate your good will by teaching him how to become a better person in all respects, I will have him, today, in my presence, kowtow to Your Honor as his adopted father. If you should detect any faults in his conduct, Your Honor should feel free to admonish him. I will certainly not endeavor to defend his shortcomings."

"Although there is something to what Your Ladyship suggests," responded Hsi-men Ch'ing, "your noble son, my worthy acquaintance, is naturally endowed with intelligence. At present, he is young and is still feeling his way with regard to the rules of proper conduct. In the future:

When the scope of his perceptions has become broader,
He will correct his faults and change for the better.[40]
Your Ladyship need not be concerned about it."

Thereupon, Lady Lin had Hsi-men Ch'ing assume the position of honor, while Wang the Third poured out three goblets of wine and performed the ceremony of kowtowing to him four times. When these acts of homage had been performed, Hsi-men Ch'ing moved to a lesser position and bowed to Lady Lin to express his gratification, in response to which, she smiled broadly and made him a deep obeisance in return. From this time on, whenever Wang the Third encountered Hsi-men Ch'ing, he addressed him as Father. Can such things be? As for Hsi-men Ch'ing, truly:

He was ever prepared to enjoy the pleasure of
    "abusing the innocent and good";
As a makeshift substitute for the delight of
    "addiction to clouds and rain."

The poet, on observing this conduct, must have felt a sense of outrage, which inspired him to compose a poem lamenting it.

Since men and women are forbidden to exchange
    drinks with each other;
Flaunting one's beauty and inviting seduction[41]
    are really shameful acts.
But Wang the Third, who was in the dark about
    the significance of it all;
Not only contributed to his mother's adultery
    but kowtowed to her lover.

There is also another poem inspired by this event:

The women's quarters of great households
    should be strictly guarded;
For the hen to announce the break of dawn[42]
    is extremely inauspicious.
Not only does it forebode the destruction
    of the family's reputation;
But it desecrates the name of the Hall of
    Integrity and Righteousness.

After they had consumed the wine, Lady Lin directed Wang the Third to invite Hsi-men Ch'ing back to the reception hall in the front of the residence, where the two of them sat down and loosened their clothing. Tai-an brought out Hsi-men Ch'ing's "loyal and tranquil hat," and he changed into it.

It was not long before the table settings were arranged and they sat down in their places, while the boy actors struck up their musical instruments and prepared to sing for their entertainment. The chef came out and carved the

Wang Ts'ai Kowtows to Hsi-men Ch'ing as an Adopted Father

entrée, while Tai-an stood by to offer him an appropriate gratuity. Standing in front of the company, the boy actors then proceeded to sing the song suite that begins with the tune "Fresh Water Song":

Kingfisher blinds closely enclose
    the small chamber;
The jade hook of the moon dangles
    low in the heavens.
Within the suspended felt drapery,
And tortoiseshell brocade screens,
An amorous atmosphere is suffused.
Branches of plum blossoms exude a subtle fragrance.

To the tune "A Tricky Play"

Their slender shadows cross the window lattices;[43]
Green parakeets are hanging on them upside down.
Snow, like a cloud of pear blossoms, re-creates
    the dream on Mount Lo-fu.[44]
It is deep at night and the dripping of the cold
    clepsydra seems endless.

To the tune "Sweet Water Song"

The alabaster trees have borne blossoms;
The jade dragons have lost their scales;
Bits of hail cascade from the Milky Way;
Auspicious snow dances in the swirling wind.
The azure empyrean is immaculate;
Pale moonlight browses the eaves;
Dark clouds invade the ridgepole;
The iridescent gates and pearly palaces[45]
    present a blinding whiteness.

To the tune "Plucking the Cassia"

The brocade setting enhances his delight
    in the creative work of spring,
The pubescent maidservants,
And teenaged singing boys.
He plays "Hiding the Tally" under the flowers,[46]
Gaming at forfeits during a drinking bout,
Or throwing the dice at the banquet table.
Alluringly, she contends in beauty
    and competes for favor;
Jubilantly, he hugs the turquoise
    and cuddles the red.

She serves cups and offers goblets;[47]
Alters the pitch or switches modes;[48]
Dances seductively and sings songs;[49]
Gently strums or lightly melodizes.[50]

To the tune "The Water Nymphs"

The fragrant fumes of musk-scented charcoal
    form ornate lotus blossoms;
The wavery light of phoenix-painted candles[51]
    engenders aureate rainbows;
Ivory bedsteads provide a springtime warmth
    in the lanes of the quarter.
The rouge and powder exude fragrance where
    pearls and trinkets cluster;
Like strata of colored clouds, the layers
    of silken fabrics are thick.
The scent of ambergris in jeweled censers
    is diaphanous;
Animal-shaped briquettes in gold braziers
    glow fire-red;
A warm aura creates the genial atmosphere
    of the spring breeze.

To the binary tunes "Wild Geese Alight" and "Victory Song"

On the silver psaltery the bridges are
    ranged like wild geese;
The sound of the jade flute is like the
    warble of a baby oriole;
The flowers are as brightly colored as
    a kingfisher's wings;
A plenitude of wine fills to the brim
    the vitreous decanter.
Variegated sleeves proffer golden goblets;
Slender fingers handle silk handkerchiefs;
The frosty rinds of fresh oranges are peeled;
Melted snow is used to boil the fragrant tea.
Pleasure abounds,
Inebriated feelings are profoundly stimulated;
The feast is over,
The night is late but desire is not yet sated.

To the tune "Procuring Good Wine"

By means of only a single glance and a smile,

Their mutual feelings are fully communicated.
Under the lamplight, he scrutinizes
    the object of his desire;
She is like Ch'ang-o emerging from
    her palace in the moon;
Or the Goddess of Witches' Mountain
    descending from her peak.

To the tune "Song of Great Peace"

From the sloping hair at her temples the flying
    phoenix hairpin has fallen;
The kingfisher-hued motif of a coiled dragon on
    her dancing skirt is loose;
Her powdered sweat moistens the white cosmetics
    on her bewitching features;
Sticking out its tip, she tentatively lets her
    clove-shaped tongue protrude.
Her arm is encircled with a bracelet, and the
    red mark of a chastity charm.[52]
Truly, they make a pair of fledgling male and
    captivating female phoenixes.[53]

To the tune "River-bobbed Oars"

It is a happy reunion,
A reunion with the object of his desire.
Her willows are fatigued, her blossoms languid;[54]
Her jadelike body is warm, her breast melting;
As they savor to the full the romance
    of their rendezvous.
Quiveringly, her chignon becomes disheveled;
Lazily, the autumn ripples of her eyes stir;
Archly, the mascara of her eyebrows gathers.

To the tune "Seven Brothers"

Intoxication ignites,
Her jade countenance,
Into a delicate red glow.
Addicted to flowers and lusting for jade,
    they indulge their desires.
He actually believes he is participating,
    while in a somnolent trance,
In a dream visit to the goddess who lives
    in the Floriate Pearl Palace.[55]

To the tune "Plum Blossom Wine"

As they reach the climax of their game
    of clouds and rain,
They are in a dither, though the event
    is ordinary enough.[56]
The watch drums sound incessantly,
The chimes under the eaves tinkle;
The neighboring cock crows,
The trumpet plays reveille;
The jade clepsydra drips,
Resounding reiteratively;
The silver lamp burns out,
Casting its golden sparks;
Beyond the silken windows,
The light of dawn impends;
At the azure Heaven's rim,
The sun begins to radiate.

To the tune "Conquering the Southland"

Ah! What does he hear but the sound of the well-pulley
    beyond the whitewashed wall;[57]
And the early cawing of the ravens in the phoenix trees
    beside the gilded wellhead?
Spring beauty still fills his eyes, but
    he is not yet fully awake.
Alas, this vision of surreptitious joy
    and secret infatuation,[58]
Has been idly interrupted for no good
    reason, which is a pity.[59]

Before long, after:

    Five main courses had been served, and
    Two suites of songs had been performed,

the candles were lit, and Hsi-men Ch'ing got up to change his clothes and take his leave. Wang the Third, however, insisted upon retaining him a little longer and invited him into his private studio, which was located at the side of the courtyard. It was a small, freestanding structure, only eighteen feet wide, but inside:

    Flowers and trees cast intersecting shadows, and
    The cultural artifacts were elegantly displayed.

A plaque emblazoned with four powdered-gold characters read "San-ch'üan's Poetic Skiff." On the four walls there hung antique paintings depicting the following subjects:

The Yellow Emperor Asks about the Way,[60]
Fu Sheng Conceals the Forbidden Books,[61]
Ping Chi Makes Inquiries about the Ox,[62]
Sung Ching Examines the History Books.[63]

Upon seeing the plaque, Hsi-men Ch'ing asked, "Who might San-ch'üan, or Three Springs, be?"

Wang the Third endeavored to avoid the question and did not wish to reply, but finally, after what seemed like half a day, he said, "It is your son's insignificant courtesy name."

Hsi-men Ch'ing, upon hearing this, did not have another word to say on the subject.

At this point, a tall narrow-necked vessel was brought in, and they proceeded to play pitch-pot and drink wine together, while the two boy actors stood to one side, struck up their instruments, and sang for their entertainment. Meanwhile, Lady Lin, in the rear of the residence, supervised her maidservants and waiting women in replenishing their refreshments, and supplying them with saucers of seasonal delicacies. They continued drinking until the second watch, when Hsi-men Ch'ing, who was already half inebriated, took his leave and got up to go. He gave each of the boy actors a tip of three mace of silver, and Wang the Third escorted him to the front gate and saw him into his sedan chair. The two orderlies who had accompanied him lit their lanterns, while Hsi-men Ch'ing put on his earmuffs, donned his sable cloak, said goodbye to his host, and set out for home.

When he arrived there, he remembered something Chin-lien had said to him earlier in the day and made his way straight into her quarters. It so happens that the woman had not yet gone to bed but had just taken off her headdress and was engaged in doing up her cloud-shaped chignon. Still:

Delicately made up and heavily powdered,[64]

she was in her room, leaning on the base of her makeup stand, with her feet propped on the rim of the brazier, cracking melon seeds in her mouth as she waited for him. Beside the brazier:

A kettle of hydrangea-flavored tea was brewing;[65]

upon the table:

Incense curled from a golden lion-shaped censer.[66]

As soon as she saw Hsi-men Ch'ing come in, she:

Lightly moved her lotus feet,
Gently lifted her beige skirt,

and hastened forward to take his outer garments and put them away. Hsi-men Ch'ing sat down on her bed, while Ch'un-mei brought out a clean cup for him, and the woman, after brushing away a few drops of water from the rim of the cup with her slender fingers, poured out a cupful of dense and full-bodied tender-leaved Sparrow Tongue Liu-an tea,[67] steeped with sesame seeds, marinated bamboo shoots, shredded chestnuts, melon seeds, a blend of walnut

kernels and potherb mustard greens called "The Sea Eagle Attacks the Swan,"
osmanthus, and attar of roses. Upon swallowing no more than a mouthful and
savoring its delectable fragrance and sweetness, Hsi-men Ch'ing was utterly
delighted. He then had Ch'un-mei:

Take off his boots, unfasten his girdle,[68]

and help him into bed. Meanwhile the woman, under the lamplight, removed
her head ornaments and changed into her sleeping shoes, after which the two
of them lay down:

Head to head and thigh over thigh, while
The coverlet was disturbed by crimson waves,
And they reposed upon their phoenix pillows.

Ch'un-mei extinguished the silver lamp on the table, closed the two leaves of
the door, and went into the adjacent room.

Hsi-men Ch'ing proceeded to pillow the woman's head on his arm and
embrace her naked body, which was just like:

Soft jade and warm incense.

The two of them fell to it, with their:

Creamy breasts squeezed together,
Their jadelike legs intertwined;
Their two faces nuzzling each other,[69]
Audibly sucking each other's tongues.

The woman picked up a handful of melon seed kernels that were in a saucer
beside her pillow, popped them into her mouth, and transmitted them into
Hsi-men Ch'ing's mouth with the tip of her tongue. It was not long before:

Her sweet spittle transfused his heart, and
His magic rhinoceros horn was awakened.

The woman reached down and manipulated his organ persistently with one
hand, while she opened the bag of sexual implements with the other and proceeded to fasten the silver clasp in place.

Hsi-men Ch'ing then asked, "My child, while I was away from home, did
you think of me, or not?"

"During the half-month or so that you were away," the woman said, "I
couldn't get you out of my mind for so much as a quarter of an hour. When
evening came, the nights were long, and, all by myself, I was unable to sleep.
No matter what lengths I went to in order to:

Warm the bed and warm the bedding,

I continued to feel cold. When I extended my legs and encountered a cold
spot, I had to retract them, and my hands became so cracked that they hurt. I
would count the days till your return, but you failed to appear. There is no
telling how many tears I shed upon my pillow. After a while, that little piece
Ch'un-mei noticed the extent to which I was giving vent to:

Long sighs as well as short,

and persuaded me to kill time by playing board games with her in the evening. After sitting together till the first watch, the two of us would lie down foot-to-foot on the same k'ang and go to sleep together. My brother, that's what my feelings were for you. But I don't know what your feelings were for me."

"You crazy oily mouth!" protested Hsi-men Ch'ing. "Although there are those others in the household, who is not aware that I prefer to spend my time with you?"

"That's enough of that," the woman responded. "Who do you think you're kidding? You tend to:

> Wolf down the rice in your bowl,
> While keeping an eye on the pot.

It's the same way you carried on with that wife of Lai-wang's:

> Mixing oil in with the honey,

while ignoring me completely. And afterwards, when Li P'ing-erh produced a son, you treated me just like an angry fighting cock. Now that the two of them have gone to their fates, whatever they may be, I'm the only one left at your disposal. You're just like:

> A willow catkin in the wind,[70]
> Bobbing up and bobbing down.[71]

And now you've started to bestow your favor on Ju-i, that lousy splay-legged creature. No matter how you look at it, she's only a wet nurse, and since she manifestly already has a husband of her own, she's the wife of a flesh-and-blood person. If you insist on taking her for yourself, in the future, her husband is likely to:

> Come grazing his sheep in front of your gate,
> The better to befoul it with their droppings.

Since you are:

> An incumbent, office-holding official,

if word of this should get out, it will hardly redound to your credit. Just look at the way that lousy whore carried on the other day while you were away. In the course of a dispute with Ch'un-mei over a laundry bat, the two of them got into:

> A vituperative altercation,

and she wouldn't allow me to get a word in edgewise."

"My child," admonished Hsi-men Ch'ing. "No matter how you look at it, she's only a servant. How could she have the:

> Seven heads and eight galls,

to challenge you?

> If you raise your hand,
> She will be able to get by;
> If you lower your hand,
> She'll be unable to get by."

"Ai-ya!" the woman exclaimed. "You may say that I have the power to either
raise my hand or prevent her from getting by, but after the death of Li P'ing-
erh, she took over her place in the nest. I've heard tell that you said to her, 'If
you do your best to cater to me, I'll turn over your mistress's property to you.'
Did you ever really say that to her?"

"Don't be so foolishly suspicious," responded Hsi-men Ch'ing. "Since when
did I say any such thing? If you are so magnanimous as to forgive her, I'll tell
her to come kowtow to you and apologize tomorrow."

"There's no need for her to come and apologize to me," the woman said,
"but I won't permit you to go on sleeping in her room."

"The only reason I sleep in her place," responded Hsi-men Ch'ing, "is that
I can't get over my feelings for Li P'ing-erh if I have to spend so much as a
night or two away from her quarters. As for Ju-i, she's only there to keep vigil
over her spirit tablet. Since when have I been indulging in any:

      Illicit salt or illicit vinegar,

with her."

"I don't believe those excuses of yours," declared the woman. "She's already
been dead for more than a hundred days, so what need is there for anyone to
keep vigil over her spirit tablet? She's not there to keep vigil over any spirit
tablet. She's more like:

      The watchman at a rice warehouse, who spends
      The first half of the night ringing his bell,
      And the second half, like a voyeuristic maid,
      Listening to the sound of the pounding inside.

With these few words she managed to get under Hsi-men Ch'ing's skin,
with the result that he embraced her by the neck and gave her a kiss, saying,
"You crazy little whore! You're up to your usual tricks."

Thereupon, he had her turn over so he could:

      Poke up the fire on the other side of the mountains,

inserted his organ into her vagina, embraced her legs under the quilt, and
proceeded to slam away at her with all his might until:

      The reiterated sounds reverberated loudly,

causing the woman to cry out, "What an enormous thing!"

"Do you fear me, or not?" he demanded. "Will you dare to keep on trying
to manage me in the future?"

"You crazy knave!" the woman exclaimed. "If there were no one to manage
you, you would fly straight up to Heaven, I suppose. I'm well aware that you
can't bring yourself to shake off that whore. In the future, however, you'd better get my permission before going over to her place. And if she asks you for
anything, you'd better tell me about it, rather than giving it to her surreptitiously. If you violate this compact, and I find out about it, just see whether I
kick up a real rumpus about it, or not. I'll put my life up against that whore's
any day; what's it to me? It's just like the situation when Li P'ing-erh first en-

He promptly arranged for them to be put away, wrote a card in reply, rewarded the messenger with five mace of silver, and asked him, "At what time will the gentlemen be arriving tomorrow, and will they expect actors to be engaged for the occasion, or not?"

"They will probably be arriving early," replied the messenger. "As for the actors, you should engage those from Hai-yen, rather than local ones."

The messenger was then sent on his way.

Hsi-men Ch'ing ordered his attendants to take the miniature flowering plants and put them in his studio in the Hidden Spring Grotto. He also engaged a mason to erect two heated k'angs there, with a firebox outside the retaining wall, so that the fumes from the burning charcoal would not affect the plants, and assigned Ch'un-hung and Lai-an the task of seeing that they were regularly watered, without fail. Hsi-men Ch'ing then sent Tai-an off to engage the services of the actors and weighed out an appropriate amount of silver for Lai-an so that he could purchase the necessary provisions. That day was also the eve of Meng Yü-lou's birthday, so arrangements were made to hire some boy musicians from the licensed quarter to play and sing in celebration of the occasion that evening. Let us put this strand of our narrative aside for a moment.

To resume our story, while still at home, Ying Po-chüeh took five blank calling cards, had Ying Pao put them in a box, and set out for the house across the street from Hsi-men Ch'ing's place, in order to ask Licentiate Wen to inscribe them with invitations to the five ladies of Hsi-men Ch'ing's household, asking them to come to his home for the full-month celebration of the birth of his son on the twenty-eighth.

He had just gone out the door and turned onto the main street when someone behind him called out in a loud voice, "Master Two, please come back here for a minute."

Ying Po-chüeh turned around to look back and, seeing that it was Li Ming, came to a standstill.

Li Ming walked up to him and asked, "Master Two, where are you going?"

"I'm on my way to Licentiate Wen's place," responded Ying Po-chüeh. "I've got something to ask of him."

"If you'll just return home for a minute," said Li Ming, "I've got something to say to you."

Noticing that he had an idler following closely behind him who was carrying a gift box, Ying Po-chüeh determined that he might do well to invite him back into the parlor of his residence. Upon arriving there, Li Ming promptly kowtowed to him and, getting up, directed that the gift box be brought inside and put down. When it was opened, it turned out to contain two roast ducks and two jars of vintage wine.

"Having nothing better to offer," said Li Ming, "these paltry gifts are merely an expression of my filial regard, for you to give away to someone if you like. I have made bold to come here, Master Two, in order to make a request of you."

So saying, he knelt down on the floor and refused to get up.

Ying Po-chüeh pulled him to his feet with one hand, saying, "You silly child! If you have something to say, just say it to me. What need was there for you to purchase any gifts for me?"

"Ever since I was a youngster," said Li Ming, "I have served in Father's household for lo these many years. But now, Father is patronizing others and is no longer calling upon me. No doubt, it is on account of that affair of Li Kuei-chieh's. But the two of us:

> Maintain independent establishments,

and the members of my household do not even know what she is up to. Since Father is upset with her, he is giving me a hard time, and as a result, I have:

> Suffered injustice and harbor resentment,

but I have no place to seek redress. That is why I have sought you out, Master Two. If you happen to visit his residence and run into Father, perhaps you could put in a good word on my behalf and explain the situation to him. Kuei-chieh may well be guilty of:

> Some kind of misdeed or indiscretion,

but that has nothing to do with me. The mere fact that Father has chosen to be irritated with me is neither here nor there, but my colleagues have also taken to treating me disdainfully."

"Do you mean to say that you actually haven't been performing in his household for all this time?" said Ying Po-chüeh.

"I haven't been called upon to do so," replied Li Ming.

"No wonder, then," said Ying Po-chüeh, "that the other day, after your Father returned from the Eastern Capital, on the occasion when he hosted a welcoming party for Ho Yung-shou, to which I, along with his brother-in-law Wu K'ai and Licentiate Wen, were invited, he only engaged the services of Wu Hui, Cheng Ch'un, Cheng Feng, and Tso Shun. When I wondered why I didn't see you there and asked him about it, he said, 'If he doesn't show up, do you expect me to send for him?' You silly child! You would do well to bestir yourself. Who have you got to blame but yourself?"

"If someone from Father's household doesn't send for me," said Li Ming, "how can I simply go there on my own? The other day, he called on those four to perform for him, and since today is the eve of the Third Lady's birthday, early this morning, he sent Tai-an into the quarter to engage the services of another two musicians for the occasion. Tomorrow, Father is putting on another party, for which he has once again engaged the services of those four. But I am being left out in the cold. How could I not be upset about it? My only hope, Master Two, is that you will put in a word on my behalf, and if you are successful, I will come and kowtow to you tomorrow."

"I will not fail to speak up for you," said Ying Po-chüeh. "All this while, I don't know how many times I've intervened to help people out with their problems. How could I fail to speak up on your behalf about such a paltry matter as that you're asking me about? Do as I say, and take these gifts of yours back. What would I want with that hard-earned money of yours, anyway? Just come along with me now, and I'll find a way of gently approaching your Father on the subject."

"Master Two," objected Li Ming, "if you refuse to accept these gifts, I won't presume to accompany you. Though they may not mean much to you, they are merely intended to be:

A token of my gratitude."

So saying, with:

A thousand thanks and ten thousand
 expressions of gratitude,

he implored his assistance again and again.

Ying Po-chüeh finally agreed to accept the gifts and came up with a gratuity of thirty candareens for the man who had carried the box before sending him on his way.

"Permit me to leave the box here at your place for the time being," said Li Ming. "I'll come back and get it after visiting the mansion."

Thereupon, he accompanied Ying Po-chüeh out the gate as they wended their way:

Rounding bends and turning corners,

to the house across the street from Hsi-men Ch'ing's residence.

Upon reaching the gate to the studio therein, and rapping the door knocker, Ying Po-chüeh inquired, "Is the venerable gentleman Wen Pi-ku at home?"

Licentiate Wen, who was engaged at the time in writing a note under the studio window, promptly responded, "Please come in and have a seat."

Hua-t'ung opened the door for them, and Ying Po-chüeh took a seat in the well-lighted parlor within. At the upper end of the room four Tung-p'o chairs[73] were formally arrayed to either side of a hanging scroll depicting the philosopher Chuang-tzu regretting the evanescence of time. On the two side walls were displayed ink rubbings of the parallel statements:

The aroma of the plum blossoms in the vase
 invades the brush and inkstone;
The coldness of the snow outside the window
 permeates the zither and books.

The door of the room was protected by a cloth portiere.

When Licentiate Wen saw that they had arrived, he came out from inside to greet them and, after exchanging the customary amenities and asking them to be seated, said, "Venerable sir, you are up early today. What are you about?"

"I make so bold," said Ying Po-chüeh, "as to avail myself of your great literary talent to compose a few invitations for me. It so happens that the full-
month celebration of the birth of my son falls on the twenty-eighth of the
month, and I would like to invite the ladies of the Hsi-men household to come
visit for the event."

"Where are the cards?" said Licentiate Wen. "Give them to me and your
pupil will write them out for you."

Ying Po-chüeh told Ying Pao to take out the five cards and hand them over,
after which, Licentiate Wen took them into his inner room and ground some
new ink for the purpose.

He had only finished writing two of them when whom should they see but
Ch'i-t'ung, who came inside in a state of obvious agitation and said, "Master
Wen, write out another two cards in the First Lady's name. She also wants to
invite Kinswoman Ch'iao from the eastern quarter, and Sister-in-law Wu.
Have the two cards that Ch'in-t'ung came for a while ago, addressed to Mrs.
Han, the Third Lady's elder sister from outside the city gate, and her second
brother's wife Mrs. Meng, been sent off yet, or not?"

"Your brother-in-law, Ch'en Ching-chi, took care of sending them off some
time ago," responded Licentiate Wen.

"Master Wen," said Ch'i-t'ung, "after you have done writing out these two
invitations, you are requested to compose four more, for the wife of Pen the
Fourth, the wife of Fu Ming, the wife of Han Tao-kuo, and the wife of Kan
Jun. I'll have Lai-an come to pick them up."

After he had gone, when Lai-an came by to pick up the four additional invitations, Ying Po-chüeh asked him, "Is your Father at home, or has he gone
to the yamen?"

"Father has not gone to the yamen today," said Lai-an. "He is in the reception hall, overseeing the reception of some presents sent by the household of
his kinsman Ch'iao Hung. Master Two, you might as well go over there for a
visit."

"As soon as these invitation cards have been written out I'll come over," responded Ying Po-chüeh.

"Last night," Licentiate Wen said, "the venerable gentleman arrived home
rather late after attending a party at the Wang residence."

"Which Wang residence was that?" asked Ying Po-chüeh.

"It was the residence of the late Imperial Commissioner Wang," said Licentiate Wen.

The implications of this fact were not lost on Ying Po-chüeh.

It was sometime later, after Lai-an had waited for his cards and gone his way,
before the remaining invitations for Ying Po-chüeh were completed, and he
took Li Ming with him across the street. He found Hsi-men Ch'ing, with his
hair still in disarray, supervising the reception of presents in the reception hall,
and preparing the replies for them. The table settings he had ordered were

arrayed to one side. When he saw Ying Po-chüeh come in, he greeted him with a bow and offered him a seat. A brazier was burning to heat the room.

Ying Po-chüeh thanked him for his hospitality the other day and then went on to ask, "Brother, who are these table settings provided for?"

Hsi-men Ch'ing explained that Secretary An Ch'en had shown up and asked him to host a party the following day for Ts'ai Hsiu, the prefect of Chiu-chiang.

"Will you be engaging the services of an acting troupe or boy musicians on that occasion?" asked Ying Po-chüeh.

"I have already hired a troupe of Hai-yen actors," said Hsi-men Ch'ing, "and have also engaged the services of four boy musicians to entertain the company."

"Which four boy musicians might they be, Brother?" asked Ying Po-chüeh.

"Wu Hui, Cheng Feng, Cheng Ch'un, and Tso Shun," said Hsi-men Ch'ing.

"Brother," said Ying Po-chüeh, "why don't you employ Li Ming?"

"He's already flown to a higher branch," said Hsi-men Ch'ing. "What interest would he have in a place like mine?"

"Brother, how can you say such a thing?" expostulated Ying Po-chüeh. "Only if you summon him would he presume to come. I also was unaware that you have been annoyed with him all this while. The two of them operate independently of each other, and the cause of your displeasure has nothing to do with him. He is hardly privy to the doings of Auntie Li the Third and her establishment. You ought not to do him the injustice of presuming such a thing. Early this morning, he showed up at my place, weeping and wailing, and said to me, 'Quite aside from the fact that my elder sister is one of the ladies in Father's household, I, too, have been accustomed to serve there for lo these many years. But now, he is employing others, and there is no longer any place there for me.'

Swearing by the gods and uttering oaths,

he assured me again and again that he didn't know a word about the goings on of Auntie Li the Third and her establishment. The fact that you have made him a target of your annoyance has made life very difficult for him. After all, for a person of such inferior status, what sort of standing does he possess? If you take it into your head to turn against him, how could he hope to withstand you?"

He then proceeded to summon Li Ming, saying, "Come over here and explain things to your Father in person. What are you keeping out of sight for? You're acting like the proverbial:

Ugly daughter-in-law who is fearful of
    seeing her parents-in-law."[74]

Li Ming had moved closer and was standing by the latticework partition:

With lowered head and dragging feet,
Like a ghost trying to abide unseen,

as he observed the two of them discussing his case, without daring to utter a word.

Upon hearing Ying Po-chüeh call for him, he went inside, knelt stiff-leggedly down on the floor, and kowtowed, saying, "Father, you really ought to look more closely into what they've been up to over there. If I knew so much as a single word about it, I would deserve to be run over by a chariot, trampled by horses, subjected to judicial punishment, and put to death by dismemberment. The kindness you have shown me and my entire family all this while is:

As high as Heaven and as thick as Earth.[75]

Though:

My body should be pulverized and my bones shattered,

I could hardly hope to repay you. But now that you have chosen to show your displeasure toward me, I have been subjected to ridicule by the colleagues in my profession, and taken advantage of by them. Under the circumstances, where am I to turn in order to discover a patron?"

When he had finished speaking, he gave vent to loud sobs and cried out in pain as he knelt on the ground and refused to get up.

"That's enough! That's enough!" interjected Ying Po-chüeh from the side-lines. "Brother, you really ought to give him another chance. After all:

A great person does not deign to notice
the faults of petty persons.

Quite aside from the fact that he is not at fault, even if he had actually done something to offend you, his willingness to appeal to you in this way should lead you to make amends by forgiving him."

"As for you," he continued, addressing himself to Li Ming, "come over here. It has always been the case that:

If you don the black livery of a servant,
You must cling to even the blackest post.

Now that I have explained the situation to your Father, he should no longer hold anything against you."

"What you say is true, Master Two," responded Li Ming.

"If one is aware of a fault one must correct it.[76]

I will act accordingly in the future."

Ying Po-chüeh said:

"You've only endured a slap with a flour sack,
but you've done a complete about-face."

Hsi-men Ch'ing thought to himself in silence for some time before saying, "Since Master Two has repeatedly interceded on your behalf, I will no longer harbor any resentment toward you. You can get up now, and remain in attendance."

"You had better kowtow, and be quick about it," chimed in Ying Po-chüeh.

Li Ming hastily performed a kowtow and then proceeded to stand in attendance to one side.

Only after this did Ying Po-chüeh tell Ying Pao to take out the five invitation cards and give them to Hsi-men Ch'ing, saying as he did so, "The twenty-eighth is the day for the full-month celebration of the birth of my baby son. I am inviting the entire group of my sisters-in-law to be so good as to pay a visit to my humble household in honor of the occasion."

Hsi-men Ch'ing opened one of the invitations and saw that the text read as follows:

> The twenty-eighth is the date for the full-month ceremony to celebrate the birth of our baby son. Our humble household has prepared a meager potation as a deferential compensation for your generous largess. It is our ardent wish that you will deign to mount your elegant equipages and condescend to attend. Our gratitude for your favor will know no bounds.
>
> Respectfully indited with straightened skirts by the lady, née Tu, of the Ying family.

When Hsi-men Ch'ing had finished perusing the text, he ordered Lai-an to take the invitations, together with the box that they came in, to show to the First Lady and then said to Ying Po-chüeh, "You can be certain that they won't be able to go to your place the day after tomorrow. The truth of the matter is that tomorrow is the Third Lady's birthday, and moreover, I will also be hosting a party for Secretary An Ch'en at my place. And on the twenty-eighth the First Lady is planning to pay a call on the wife of His Honor Hsia Yen-ling. So they will hardly be able to go to your place."

"Brother," said Ying Po-chüeh, "you're killing me. If they refuse to go:

Though one's orchard may contain
   a variety of fruits:
On which can one rely?

I guess I'll just have to go back to their quarters and invite them myself."

In a little while, whom should they see but Lai-an, who came out carrying the empty box and reported, "The First Lady says to thank you for the invitation, which is gratefully accepted."

Ying Po-chüeh turned the box over to Ying Pao and laughed, saying, "Brother, you were kidding me just now. If my sisters-in-law had refused the invitation I would have kowtowed to them until my head was bloody in order to induce them to attend, no matter what."

To this Hsi-men Ch'ing responded by saying, "Don't you go off now, but have a seat in the studio while I go inside to comb my hair, after which we can have something to eat together."

When he had finished speaking, he headed back into the rear compound.

Ying Po-chüeh then turned to Li Ming and said, "How do you like that? If I hadn't spoken to him the way I did just now, he would have continued to harbor his resentment against you. It's the nature of those possessed of money to insist on having their say, and you just have to put up with it. As the saying goes:

> An angry fist does not strike a smiling face.[77]

In this day and age, if you wish to play the role of a sycophant, whatever capital you may have for your undertaking, you must be prepared to sacrifice 30 percent of it in order to maintain goodwill. If you insist on propelling your craft against the current, who will pay any attention to you? Quite aside from the fact that you must be ready to:

> Adjust yourself to circumstances as they arise,[78]

only if you are prepared to move in any direction, as the flow of the current allows, will you be capable of making any money. If you insist on butting your head against the wall, others will be able to eat their fill while you suffer from starvation. You have been dancing attendance on him for all these years, but you still don't seem to understand his temperament. Tomorrow, if you get that Kuei-chieh of yours to follow hot on your heels in coming to celebrate the Third Lady's birthday, you can kill two birds with one stone. If she will only consent to make him a propitiatory obeisance, this problem, great as it is, can be brought to a successful conclusion."

"Master Two," responded Li Ming, "what you say makes sense. As soon as I get home, I'll go over and speak to Auntie Li the Third about it."

Whom should they see at this point but Lai-an, who came in to set the table and said, "Master Ying the Second, please have a seat. Father will be out in a minute."

Before long, Hsi-men Ch'ing, having performed his ablutions, came out and sat down to keep Ying Po-chüeh company, asking him as he did so, "Have you seen anything of Sun T'ien-hua or Chu Jih-nien recently?"

"I have run into them," replied Ying Po-chüeh, "but they are apprehensive lest you are still ill-disposed toward them. I said to them, 'Brother is a man of magnanimous feelings, who:

> Looks up to those above and regards those below.[79]

It is true that on that occasion:

> The locust and the grasshopper,
> Were swatted in the same breath,

but what are you prepared to do about it?' They swore an oath that in the future they would not run around with that young rascal Wang the Third any more. I have heard that yesterday you attended a party at his place, but they didn't know anything about it."

"Yesterday," said Hsi-men Ch'ing, "thus and so, he laid on quite a spread on my behalf and acknowledged me as his adopted father. I didn't get home afterwards until the second watch. As for their not associating with him any longer, so long as their actions don't interfere with mine, let them do as they please. What do I care? After all, I am not Wang the Third's real father, so I am not in a position to control his conduct."

"Brother," said Ying Po-chüeh, "if that is the position you have decided to take, the two of them will seek you out in a day or two and offer you a propitiatory gift in order to ameliorate the rift between you."

"You can simply tell them to come by," said Hsi-men Ch'ing. "What need is there for any propitiatory gift?"

At this juncture, Lai-an brought in a repast, consisting of various tasty delicacies, both roasted and boiled, which Hsi-men Ch'ing partook of with his congee, while Ying Po-chüeh ate rice.

When they had finished eating, Hsi-men Ch'ing inquired, "Have those two boy actors shown up, or not?"

"They've already been here for some time," said Lai-an.

Hsi-men Ch'ing directed that they should be given something to eat, along with Li Ming. The two of them, whose names were Han Tso and Shao Ch'ien, came forward and kowtowed to Hsi-men Ch'ing, after which they withdrew in order to eat.

After a while, Ying Po-chüeh stood up, and said, "I've got to go. The members of my household are, no doubt, anxiously awaiting me. People of humble status such as myself find it very hard to keep up appearances. Whenever we entertain, everything has to be newly purchased, from the base underneath the frame of the brazier to the door of the parlor."

"You go and take care of things," said Hsi-men Ch'ing, "and when you're done, come back for a visit this evening in order to offer your birthday greetings and kowtow to the Third Lady on the eve of her birthday, thereby demonstrating your filial respect."

"I'll be certain to come," responded Ying Po-chüeh, "and I'll have my wife send her a birthday present to boot."

When he had finished speaking, he took himself off without more ado. Truly:

> When a favored friend arrives, one's feelings
>   can never be satiated;
> When a real confidant shows up, conversation
>   is mutually agreeable.

There is a poem that testifies to this:

> If you wish to get along, say what people want to hear;
> If you try to be honest, you'll only arouse antagonism.
> In the affairs of this world, it is best to be lukewarm;
> People's true sentiments become apparent only with time.

> If you want to know the outcome of these events,
> Pray consult the story related in the following chapter.

Chapter 73

P'AN CHIN-LIEN IS IRKED BY THE SONG

"I REMEMBER HER FLUTE-PLAYING";

BIG SISTER YÜ SINGS "GETTING THROUGH

THE FIVE WATCHES OF THE NIGHT"

> If you're clever, you'll be considered labored,
>   if you're awkward, idle;
> If you're good, you'll be disdained as weak,
>   if you're bad, callous.
> If you're rich, you'll meet with envy,
>   if you're poor, disgrace;
> If you're diligent, you'll be thought grasping,
>   if you're economical, stingy.
> If you deal with things consistently,
>   you'll be scorned as simple;
> If you adapt yourself to circumstances,
>   you'll be suspected of deceit.
> If you think about it, it is hardly possible
>   to satisfy anyone;
> The role of human being is an arduous one,
>   to be a man is hard.[1]

THE STORY GOES that, after Ying Po-chüeh went home, Hsi-men Ch'ing went to the Hidden Spring Grotto in his garden and sat down to watch the mason working on the two heated k'angs, with a firebox outside the retaining wall, so that the floor of the interior would be as warm as spring, and the fumes from the burning charcoal would not affect the plants that had been placed there.

Who should suddenly appear at this point but P'ing-an, who brought in a calling card and reported, "His Honor Chou Hsiu of the Regional Military Command has sent a courier to deliver some joint contributions."

The box they came in contained five packets, enclosing five mace of silver and two ordinary handkerchiefs each, from Commandant Chou Hsiu, Director-in-Chief Ching Chung, Militia Commander Chang Kuan, and the two eunuch directors Liu and Hsüeh, and were said to be deferentially presented as tokens of their respect. Hsi-men Ch'ing told his attendants to take them back to the rear compound and sent the courier off with a calling card in reply.

To resume our story, that day Aunt Yang, along with Sister-in-law Wu and old Mrs. P'an, arrived early in their sedan chairs and were followed by Nun Hsüeh, the abbess of the Kuan-yin Nunnery, Nun Wang, Nun Hsüeh's two young disciples Miao-ch'ü and Miao-feng, and Big Sister Yü, all of whom had purchased gift boxes and had come to celebrate the eve of Meng Yü-lou's birthday. Wu Yüeh-niang served them with tea in the master suite, and the whole sorority of wives and concubines were also there to keep them company. Before long, they finished their tea and then proceeded to visit together at leisure.

Before anyone knew it, P'an Chin-lien, who remembered that she had promised to make a band of white satin in order to enhance Hsi-men Ch'ing's sexual performance, took herself off to her room, got out her sewing box, selected a strip of white satin, and employed backstitching in order to crimp it. She then reached into the porcelain container in her cabinet with her slender fingers, poured out some of the aphrodisiac powder called "The Quavery Voices of Amorous Beauties,"[2] and backstitched it securely inside the band with her deft technique, so that it would be ready that evening when she indulged with Hsi-men Ch'ing in:

The pleasures of clouds and rain.[3]

Who could have anticipated that at this juncture Nun Hsüeh suddenly came into the room in order to bring her the fertility potion containing the afterbirth of a firstborn male child that would enable her to conceive. The woman hurriedly put aside what she was doing and sat down to consult with her.

Nun Hsüeh, upon seeing that:

There was nobody about,

furtively handed the potion to her, saying, "It's all been properly prepared. If you select a *jen-tzu* day and imbibe it on an empty stomach before sleeping with your husband that night, you will be sure to conceive. For corroboration, you can look to the case of the First Bodhisattva in the rear compound. It was I who enabled her to conceive, and she's already got half a bulge in her belly to show for it. I've also got another trick to share with you. If you make a brocade scent bag, I'll slip you a charm inscribed with cinnabar and realgar. If you put it inside the scent bag and wear it next to your body, you are sure to give birth to a male child. It's guaranteed to be effective."

Upon hearing this, the woman was utterly delighted. On the one hand, she took the fertility potion and concealed it in a trunk, while on the other, she consulted a calendar and saw that the twenty-ninth was a *jen-tzu* day.

Thereupon, she weighed out three mace of silver and gave it to Nun Hsüeh, saying, "This doesn't amount to anything. Just take it home and use it to buy yourself a vegetable to eat. But should I really conceive, and you bring me the

charm inscribed in cinnabar, I'll give you a bolt of silk to make a garment
out of."

"Bodhisattva," said Nun Hsüeh, "there's no need for you to engage in such
calculations. I'm not avaricious in the way that Nun Wang is. In the past,
when I undertook to recite scriptures on behalf of that deceased Bodhisattva,
she claimed that I was trying to do her out of a piece of patronage. The two of
us had quite a quarrel over it, and she has been slandering me wherever she
goes. My God! Let her suffer the consequences of her evil karma. I'm not
going to waste my time contending with her, but devote myself instead to
doing good deeds for others, and rescuing people from their calamities."

"Mistress Hsüeh," the woman said, "you can do as you like. It's just a case
of:

Different people having different intentions.
But you mustn't mention a word of this business of mine to her."

Nun Hsüeh responded:

"The dharma must not be divulged to six ears.
How could I ever mention it to her? Last year, in connection with the pregnancy of the First Bodhisattva in the rear compound, she accused me of making a considerable profit behind her back, and I had to split the proceeds with
her before she was willing to call it quits. Though she may be a member of the
Buddhist sangha, she ignores her vows, and her avariciousness is notorious.
Though she accepts alms from:

The patrons in the ten directions,[4]
she does not perform meritorious works on their behalf. When she dies in the
future, she won't even deserve to be reborn:

With hair on her body and horns on her head."[5]

After they had talked for a while, the woman ordered Ch'un-mei to provide
a serving of tea for Nun Hsüeh. When she had finished the tea, the two of
them went over to Li P'ing-erh's quarters and paid their respects to her spirit
tablet, after which they went back to join the others in the rear compound.

That afternoon, Wu Yüeh-niang had two tables put up in the room with the
k'ang in her quarters and invited her guests to be seated there. She also saw to
the setting up of:

Brocaded curtains and standing screens,[6]
in the parlor, along with an Eight Immortals table, replete with appetizers to
go with the drinks.

That evening, when the time came for Meng Yü-lou to offer Hsi-men
Ch'ing a drink, he wore the variegated flying fish python robe that Eunuch
Director Ho Hsin had bestowed upon him, over a tunic of white satin, and
occupied the position of honor together with Yüeh-niang, while the four other
ladies of the household were arranged to either side of them. Before long,
within the chamber:

Painted candles burned high,[7]

while in the flagons:

Yang-kao wine brimmed over.

The two boy actors, Shao Ch'ien and Han Tso, with their:

Silver psaltery, ivory clappers,

And moon-shaped balloon guitar,

proceeded to accompany themselves as they sang the birthday song suite that begins with the tune "A Sprig of Flowers," the opening lines of which are:

Swirling around, the auspicious vapors blow;
One by one, the propitious clouds come down.[8]

Meng Yü-lou was made up so that she looked to be:

Modeled in plaster, carved of jade; and

Her lotus face evoked an air of spring,[9]

as she offered a drink to Hsi-men Ch'ing and kowtowed to him four times:

Like a sprig of blossoms swaying in the breeze;

Sending the pendants of her embroidered sash flying.

Only after this did she pay obeisance to Yüeh-niang and her fellow ladies and take her place at the table. Who should appear at this juncture but Ch'en Ching-chi, accompanied by Hsi-men Ta-chieh, who held the flagon as he offered drinks to Hsi-men Ch'ing and Yüeh-niang, before wishing Meng Yü-lou a happy birthday. When they had finished their obeisances, they sat down to one side. Meanwhile, birthday noodles and dessert treats were brought in together from the kitchen.

Who should appear at this point but Lai-an, who came in with a gift box, saying, "Ying Pao has come to deliver some presents."

Hsi-men Ch'ing told Yüeh-niang to accept them and then said to Lai-an, "Take a card in reply to Brother Ying's wife, and invite Ying the Second, along with Brother-in-law Wu K'ai, to come visit with us. I know that his wife will probably not consent to join us tomorrow, but ask Brother Ying the Second to come see us today. We'll take care of sending return gifts to them another day."

Lai-an, accordingly, took the return card and went off along with Ying Pao.

As Hsi-men Ch'ing sat at the head of the table, it occurred to him unconsciously that, on the occasion of Meng Yü-lou's birthday the previous year, Li P'ing-erh had been there with them; but that today, among the sorority of five ladies, only she was absent. As a result, he couldn't help being pained at heart, and tears began to drop from his eyes.

Sometime later, after the musicians had consumed their soup and rice below, Li Ming poured a round of drinks for the company, and the two boy actors came before them.

Wu Yüeh-niang asked them, "Do you know the song suite that begins with the tune 'Four Pieces of Jade,' the opening lines of which are:

Like lovebirds, flying wing to wing;
Or trees with intertwining branches?"[10]

"Yes we do," replied Han Tso.

They were just about to pick up their instruments and start to sing, when
Hsi-men Ch'ing called them before him and ordered, "You perform the song
suite that begins with the words:

I remember her flute-playing."

The two boy actors hastily switched modes and proceeded to perform the
song suite in question, beginning with the tune "A Gathering of Worthy
Guests":

I remember her flute-playing, but where is
    the jade damsel now?[11]
Tonight, my lovesickness grows more intense.
The white dew is cold, and the scent of the
    autumn lotus blossoms is fading;
Beneath the whitewashed wall the bright moon
    insists on sinking out of sight.
Though merely a case of temporary separation, the mirror
    is fractured and the hairpin divided;[12]
Which is much better than a period of ten years in which
    news is interrupted and word cut off.
Facing the west wind, all I can do is lean against the
    belvedere and sigh to myself in vain.
The tiers upon tiers of trees upon the mountain ridge
    stretch as far as the eye can see.
What I fear is that time flows away like
    a galloping steed,
Or like a long snakelike formation of
    migrating geese.

TO THE TUNE "FREE AND EASY WANDERING"

The pleasure we shared on that previous evening,
Was presaged by the popping of the lantern-wick.
A fragrance wafted from the clasp of her girdle.
But no sooner had we discovered our mutual affinity,
Than, unexpectedly, we were obliged to be separated.
I constantly remember the way we laughed and joked
    as we snuggled up against each other.
Within the decorated hall everything that day was
    done with extravagant pretentiousness.
We enjoyed the wine, gleaming with glaucous foam,

The music of red ivory clappers under dancing fans,[13]
And the frolicking of butterflies upon the pillow.

TO THE TUNE "GOURD OF VINEGAR"

On the day that she and I first met, my visage
    revealed my embarrassment.
When we first engaged in amorous sport together
    I was apprehensive at heart;
Half feigning to be drunk, half feigning to be
    sober, half feigning to be silly.
Our feelings for each other were so intense
    that I have yet to get over them.
No sooner were we warm inside the brocade curtains,
    beneath the mandarin duck bedding,
Than her phoenix hairpin ended up getting broken
    into some two or three pieces.

TO THE SAME TUNE

On her account, I struggled to compose good lines
    of poetry by lamplight,
The better to express my heartfelt feelings behind
    other people's backs,
Until the shadow of the phoenix tree outside the
    window began to sink.
Loving flowers as I do, I fear to reveal the ardor
    of my spring feelings.
Treading the green moss, I step lightly
    on the tips of my shoes;
The pearls of dew constantly wetting my
    meadow-tripping boots.

TO THE SAME TUNE

On her account, I went so far as to tell lies
    even among my friends;
On my account, she engaged in deceptive conduct
    even before her mother.
On her account, I exhausted my artful tongue in
    order to deceive the family;
On my account, she doffed her skirt and accepted
    the bloodstains on the azalea.[14]

It so happens that when P'an Chin-lien heard the performance of this song suite, she was fully aware that Hsi-men Ch'ing had called for it because he was thinking of Li P'ing-erh.

Upon the singing of the last line, she deliberately began to stroke her cheek with her finger, first this way and then that, in order to embarrass Hsi-men Ch'ing in front of the company, saying, "My child, you're just like:

Chu Pa-chieh, sitting in a homeless shelter:[15]

How much more ugly can you get?

For someone who had been previously married and was certainly no virgin, how could she have come up with any 'bloodstains on the azalea'? What a shameless good-for-nothing you are."

"You crazy slave!" protested Hsi-men Ch'ing. "I understand the situation, but what do you know about it?"

The two boy actors continued to sing:

On her account, my ears were forever burning;
On my account, she hid her blushes with a fan.

TO THE TUNE "THE LEAVES OF THE PHOENIX TREE"

One of us was an amorous maiden from
    a minister's mansion,
One of us was a sword-strumming client
    from before his gate,[16]
Who happened to encounter each other
    in the course of our lives.
After only a few nights worth a
    thousand pieces of gold,
We were, all of a sudden, forced to
    abandon each other.
How could I ever consent to be
    so depraved as to,
Go and pick another flower from
    atop a garden wall?

TO THE TUNE "THE FLOWER IN THE REAR COURTYARD"

Upon my pillow, fluttering airily,
    I dream of a butterfly;
As I hear the ding-donging of the
    chimes under the eaves.
No sooner did I have the temerity to tender
    Wen Ch'iao's mirror stand,[17]
Than the vehicle of Cho Wen-chün's intended
    elopement was intercepted,[18]
Leaving me here, unable to do anything
    but sigh in distress.
The phoenix bed curtains are cold, the fragrance
    of orchid and musk has dissipated.[19]

Chin-lien Is Irked over "I Remember Her Flute-playing"

Beset by fatigue, I have just fallen asleep,
But the road to the Radiant Terrace is long.
How can I ever overcome this sorrow of mine?
I am doomed to suffer from this lovesickness.
Gazing at the Milky Way, it seems straight and then bent;
Facing the lonely lamp, it lights up and then fades away.

To the tune "The Greenhorn"

Ah! The wind wildly scatters the yellow leaves
     on the stairways, on the stairways;
The clouds half conceal the waning moon amid the
     willow branches, the willow branches.
This sorrow at separation has become even harder
     to endure than it seemed last spring.
I am so affected that things are all a blur;[20]
I am so emaciated that I can hardly bear it.[21]
Even when the mulberry fields are resubmerged
     and the sea has once again dried up,
This karmic debt of love can never be fully repaid.[22]

To the tune "Borne on the Waves"

No sooner had this sorrow ceased to hover
     about the corners of my eyes,
Than it came back to haunt me above the eyebrows,
Wishing to engrave itself upon the spirits of the
     Three Corpses in my innermost heart.
If the day comes when, within the brocade curtains,
     our jade bodies should touch again,
I will take the tips of her fingers in my hand
     and gently squeeze them,
As I talk to her until the handle of the Northern
     Dipper sets above our abode.[23]

When they had finished singing, P'an Chin-lien was still upset at the fact
that he had called for them to perform this particular song suite, and the two
of them continued to bandy words about it in front of the company.

When Yüeh-niang could abide it no longer, she said, "Sister Six, show a
little patience. What are the two of you squabbling about, anyway? Aunt Yang
and Sister-in-law Wu have been left to themselves in the other room, without
anyone to keep them company. Two of you ought to go there to visit with
them, and I'll join you in a minute."

Thereupon, P'an Chin-lien and Li Chiao-erh proceeded to go into the other
room to keep Aunt Yang, Old Mrs. P'an, and Sister-in-law Wu company.

Before long, who should appear but Lai-an, who came in and reported, "The card for Ying the Second's wife has been delivered, and Master Ying the Second himself has arrived. Brother-in-law Wu K'ai will be here shortly."

Hsi-men Ch'ing responded by saying, "Go across the street and invite Master Wen to come join us."

Turning to Yüeh-niang, he said, "Tell the kitchen to send the refreshments out to us. I'm going to the front compound to keep them company."

He then called up Li Ming and said, "You go up to the front compound too, in order to sing for us."

Li Ming, accordingly, accompanied Hsi-men Ch'ing out to the front compound, where they joined Ying Po-chüeh in the studio on the west side of the courtyard.

Hsi-men Ch'ing thanked Ying Po-chüeh for his gifts and said, "Whatever happens, be sure to invite your wife to come visit us tomorrow."

"I'm afraid she won't be able to come," said Ying Po-chüeh. "There isn't anyone to be relied on at home."

After some time, Licentiate Wen arrived, bowed to the company, and sat down.

Ying Po-chüeh raised his hand in greeting and said, "I really put you to a lot of trouble this morning, venerable sir."

"It was nothing worth mentioning," responded Licentiate Wen.

Brother-in-law Wu also arrived, and after he had exchanged greetings with the company and been offered a seat, Ch'in-t'ung came in with some candles, and the four of them sat down together around the brazier, while Lai-an brought in a platter of appetizers to go with the wine and placed it on the table.

Under the lamplight, Ying Po-chüeh observed that, over his white satin tunic, Hsi-men Ch'ing was wearing a green velvet variegated flying fish python robe, the coiled image on which was:

> Showing its claws and brandishing its fangs,[24]
> The horns on its head projecting formidably;[25]
> Flaunting its whiskers and shaking its mane,
> Its golds and greens setting each other off.

It gave him quite a start, and he asked, "Brother, where did that garment of yours come from?"

Hsi-men Ch'ing responded by standing up and saying, "Take a good look at it, all of you, and then guess where it came from."

"How could we hope to guess correctly?" said Ying Po-chüeh.

"It was given to me by Eunuch Director Ho Hsin in the Eastern Capital," said Hsi-men Ch'ing. "I was having a drink at his place and was feeling cold, so he brought out this garment and gave it to me to put on. This is the flying fish version of the python robe. Since the Emperor had recently bestowed a regular python robe and a jade girdle upon him, he no longer planned to wear this one, so he gave it to me, which was a considerable favor."

Ying Po-chüeh, expressing himself in exaggerated terms, said, "Such an ornately decorated garment must, at the very least, be worth a good deal of money. This is a propitious omen for you, Brother. In the future, when you are promoted to the position of commander-in-chief, you need not worry about wearing a regular python robe and a jade girdle yourself, not to mention a flying fish robe, for your rank will entitle you to more than that."

As they talked together, Ch'in-t'ung set out the goblets and chopsticks, soup and rice, appetizers and wine, while Li Ming prepared to sing for their entertainment.

"I really ought to go inside and offer a cup of wine to my third sister-in-law," said Ying Po-chüeh, "before commencing to drink out here."

"My son," responded Hsi-men Ch'ing, "if you really have such filial intentions, you might as well go back to the rear compound and kowtow to her. What need is there to ask?"

"It doesn't matter," said Ying Po-chüeh. "I'll go and kowtow to her. And, if there's any problem with that, and I don't succeed in kowtowing to her, I'll simply come back out after giving her a taste of my prowess on the edge of the k'ang."

At this, Hsi-men Ch'ing gave him a sharp rap on the top of his head and cursed, saying, "You dog! As ever, you choose to ignore distinctions of status."

"Even if we children of yours wished to," responded Ying Po-chüeh, "which of us would feel it right to assume the superior position?"

The two of them continued to bandy words with each other for a while.

Before long, the birthday noodles were served, and Hsi-men Ch'ing offered portions of them to Brother-in-law Wu, Licentiate Wen, and Ying Po-chüeh. Because he had already eaten in the rear compound, he gave his own portion to Li Ming. When Li Ming had finished eating his noodles, he came before them once again to sing for their entertainment. Ying Po-chüeh urged Brother-in-law Wu to select a song suite for him to sing, but he demurred, saying, "I don't want to put him to any trouble. Just let him sing one that he's familiar with."

Hsi-men Ch'ing said, "My brother-in-law is fond of the suite that begins with the tune "The Earthenware Crock.""

He then told Ch'in-t'ung to pour another round of wine, while Li Ming, with:

> The bridges on his psaltery ranged like wild geese,
> Gently adjusted the icy strings,

and proceeded to sing the song suite in question, the opening lines of which were:

> It's enough to cause one to stare at
>   the scenery in silence;

As one's fragrant countenance grows
more emaciated by the day.[26]

When he had finished singing, he retired.

Who should appear at this juncture but Lai-an, who came in and reported, "The chef is about to go home and wants to know how many people you will need for tomorrow."

Hsi-men Ch'ing said, "Tell him that I will need six cooks and two waiters for the banquet tomorrow. There will be five table settings, and I want them all to be properly prepared."

Lai-an assented and went out.

At this point, Wu K'ai asked, "Brother-in-law, who are you entertaining tomorrow?"

Hsi-men Ch'ing explained about how Secretary An Ch'en of the Ministry of Works was hosting a party for Ts'ai Hsiu, the prefect of Chiu-chiang.

"If the secretary is going to be at the party tomorrow," said Wu K'ai, "that's very fortunate."

"Why so?" asked Hsi-men Ch'ing.

"It's on account of my part in supervising the repair of the local Charity Granary," said Wu K'ai. "Since it is the secretary's responsibility to submit a report on the project, I hope that you will speak to him about it tomorrow, and urge him to look upon my efforts favorably, in the hope that when his term of office expires at the end of the year he may be willing to put in a good word on my behalf. It would be a great favor to me, Brother-in-law, if you were to do so."

"That's no problem," said Hsi-men Ch'ing. "If you will write out a card with your curriculum vitae and get it to me by tomorrow, I'll speak to him about it when a convenient opportunity arises."

Wu K'ai promptly got up and bowed to him in gratitude.

"Venerable Brother-in-law," interjected Ying Po-chüeh, "you can relax about that. After all, you are a mainstay of the family. If he were unwilling to speak up on your behalf, on whose behalf would he consent to do so? You can rest assured that it will take but little in the way of a recommendation from him to insure that he will:

Hit the bull's-eye with the first arrow."

They continued drinking in the front compound until the second watch before the party broke up.

When Hsi-men Ch'ing was seeing Li Ming and the boy actors out the gate, he said, "See to it that you all report early tomorrow."

When Li Ming and the others had left, the servants cleared up the utensils and took them back to the rear compound.

The master suite was still crowded with people, but when they heard that the party in the front compound had broken up, they went back to their various quarters.

To resume our story, P'an Chin-lien was expecting that Hsi-men Ch'ing would go straight to her own quarters, so she hastily headed out in that direction, but, contrary to her expectations, he made his way past the ceremonial gate into the rear compound. Chin-lien concealed herself in the black shadow behind the spirit screen to keep track of him, and when she saw that he went into the master suite, she surreptitiously crept under the window to eavesdrop on him.

Whom should she see at this juncture but Yü-hsiao, who was standing in the doorway of the parlor and said, "Fifth Lady, why don't you go inside? Father is there, keeping company with the Third Lady, is he not?"

She also went on to ask, "And where is Old Mrs. P'an?"

"The old good-for-nothing," responded Chin-lien, "is suffering from some bodily discomfort, so she has gone back to her room to sleep."

Before long, she overheard Yüeh-niang saying, "Why ever did you engage the services of those two little bastards today? They hardly know how to sing. All they can sing is that song suite the first number of which, to the tune "Powdery Butterflies," begins with the words:

Three Variations on the Plum Blossom."[27]

"It was only toward the end," said Meng Yü-lou, "when you asked them to sing that song suite the first number of which, to the tune "Drunk in the Flowers' Shade," begins with the words:

By the Phoenix Bank, the lotus blooms,[28]

that they acceded to your request and sang the suite in question. What slippery little bastards they are. We don't even know their names. All they did for the whole day they were here was to enjoy themselves."

"One of them is called Han Tso," said Hsi-men Ch'ing, "and the other one is called Shao Ch'ien."

"Who cares whether they are called this or that?" said Yüeh-niang.

Before they knew it, P'an Chin-lien, who had slowly proceeded with:
  Skulking step and lurking gait,
to lift aside the portiere, sneak in, and position herself behind the heated k'ang, spoke up, saying, "What you should be asking him is why he didn't let them sing the song suite that his legitimate wife had called for, but instead, for no good reason, proceeded to:
  Fool with the branches and tug at the leaves,
telling them to sing:

I remember her flute-playing,

that is to say, Li P'ing-erh's flute-playing; thereby throwing the two little bastards into such consternation that they didn't know who they were supposed to take their orders from?"

When Meng Yü-lou turned her head around and saw that it was Chin-lien who had spoken, she said, "So it's Slavey Six, is it? Where did you appear from? When you suddenly intervened with that speech of yours, you gave me quite a start. You're always up to mischief of some kind. How long have you been standing behind me there? How is it that I didn't see you come in, or hear the sound of your footsteps?"

"The Fifth Lady has been there behind the Third Lady for some time already," said Hsiao-yü.

Chin-lien nodded her head and then said to Hsi-men Ch'ing, "Brother, you'd do well to slack off a bit. Do you really think that no one else is onto those little tricks of yours? What kind of an 'amorous maiden from a minister's mansion' was she, anyway? She was like me in that we had both been previously married. How can you pretend that on your account 'she doffed her skirt and accepted the bloodstains on the azalea?' It's like:

Three officials, only two of whom bother
   to bow to each other:
Whoever saw such a thing?[29]

My response is the one received by that oaf, Squire Sun, when he questioned his clever servant, Chu Chi,[30] that is to say, 'I may be willing to overlook everything else; but this I will never accept.' You actually went so far as to complain to someone, 'Ever since she died, I haven't been served so much as a single saucer of food that appeals to my taste.' As the saying goes:

Since Butcher Wang is dead and gone,
One must eat pork with the bristles.[31]

The implication is that your bevy of womenfolk merely stand by with their eyes open as you are constrained to stuff yourself with shit every day. You may retain some respect for our elder sister as your legitimate wife, but the rest of us don't count for anything, since none of us appeals to your taste. And even though our elder sister may be able to take charge of the household, she doesn't seem to be able to satisfy your needs. Since only the Sixth Lady was good enough for you, it would seem, why didn't you hold on to her and prevent her from dying? Originally, before she entered the household, you managed to get on all right, but now, no matter what the rest of us do, it fails to meet with your approval. Whenever the thought of her comes up, it causes your heart to start thumping away. But now that you've found someone else as a stand-in for her, it's like:

Trying a new sauce with your noodles,

and you're as pleased as can be. Can it be that only the water from her quarters appeals to your taste?"

"Good Sister Six," interjected Yüeh-niang, "as the saying puts it all too well:

Good people do not live for long,[32]
The wicked live a thousand years.

It has always been true that:

> What you can't round on the lathe,
> You can round with an axe.

You and I are only pieces of inferior merchandise, incapable of appealing to his taste. Let him say what he likes, and let it go at that."

"It's not that," said Chin-lien. "It's just that if I don't call him to account, the things he says are too depressing. I'm merely pointing out that people can't get over their resentment at the things he says."

Hsi-men Ch'ing merely laughed at this and chided her, saying, "You crazy little whore! You're talking nonsense. When did I ever say anything like that?"

"It was on that day when you were entertaining Eunuch Director Huang Ching-ch'en," said Chin-lien. "While you were talking with Ying the Second and that southerner Licentiate Wen, did you not say to them, 'Ever since she died, I haven't been provided with so much as a single saucer's worth of decent food'? It's no wonder you feel that way, since you act as though the rest of your womenfolk have all died off. Even when she was still alive, you didn't pay much attention to the rest of us. No doubt, in the future, you'll raise up some-one else to be a match for her, won't you? You lousy, shameless, profligate good-for-nothing!"

This speech of hers got under Hsi-men Ch'ing's skin to such an extent that he jumped up and chased after her in the endeavor to give her a kick with his booted foot, but the woman had already made it out the door and disappeared in a puff of smoke. Hsi-men Ch'ing chased outside after her, but she was no-where to be seen. The only thing he saw was Ch'un-mei, who was standing outside the door of the master suite, so he proceeded to grab her with one hand and set out for the front compound, supporting himself on the back of her shoulder.

Yüeh-niang, who had observed that he was drunk, had only been waiting for an opportunity to bundle him off to the front compound to sleep it off, because she wanted to spend the evening listening to the three nuns recite a precious scroll. Thereupon, she told Hsiao-yü to take a lantern and escort him to the front compound. Chin-lien and Yü-hsiao were standing concealed in the black shadow underneath the veranda, so Hsi-men Ch'ing did not see them.

Yü-hsiao said to Chin-lien, "My guess would be that Father is surely headed for your quarters."

"He's drunk enough to start acting up," responded Chin-lien. "Let him go to sleep first, and I'll join him a little later."

"If you'll wait for me," said Yü-hsiao, "I'll get you some fruit for your mother to eat."

Thereupon, she went into the bedroom, hid two tangerines, two apples, a package of candied sweetmeats, and three pomegranates in her sleeve and brought them out to give to the woman, who put them in her own sleeve, and then headed straight back toward the front compound.

Whom should she run into at this point but Hsiao-yü, who was on her way back after escorting Hsi-men Ch'ing and said, "Fifth Lady, where have you been? Father has been looking all over for you."

When Chin-lien arrived at the door of her quarters, she didn't go inside but peeked through an aperture in the window lattice and saw that Hsi-men Ch'ing was sitting on the bed, embracing Ch'un-mei and amusing himself with her.

Not wishing to disturb them, she hastily slipped into the other room, turned the fruit over to Ch'iu-chü, and asked her, "Has my mother gone to sleep yet, or not?"

"She's been asleep for some time already," replied Ch'iu-chü.

After enjoining her to be sure to put the fruit safely away in the cabinet, Chin-lien went back to the rear compound.

What should she find upon her arrival in the master suite but a whole roomful of people sitting together, including Yüeh-niang, Li Chiao-erh, Meng Yü-lou, Hsi-men Ta-chieh, Sister-in-law Wu, Aunt Yang, and the three nuns, along with their two teenage disciples Miao-ch'ü and Miao-feng. The nuns were seated on Yüeh-niang's k'ang, with their legs folded in the lotus position, and Nun Hsüeh in the center. A bed table had been placed in front of her, on which incense was burning, and the rest of the company were crowded around them, waiting to hear the exposition of the Buddhist dharma.

Whom should they see at this point but Chin-lien, who lifted the portiere aside with a smile and came in, causing Yüeh-niang to say, "You've brought a calamity down on your own head. He's gone to your quarters looking for you. If you haven't been able to get him to bed, what have you come back here for? Did he beat you when he got to your place?"

Chin-lien laughed at this, saying, "Just ask him whether he dares to beat me, or not."

"If he doesn't beat you," said Yüeh-niang, "it must be because he's afraid of the stink it would cause. It seems to me that you took him to task somewhat too severely just now. As the saying goes:

> The male of the species has dog's hair
>   growing on his face;[33]
> The woman of the species has the fleece
>   of a female phoenix.

He was drunk, after all. My fear is that if you irritate him to the point where he loses his temper:

> If he doesn't beat you,
> Should he beat the dog instead?

I actually broke into a sweat on your behalf, but it turns out you're enough of a minx to tough it out."

"Even if he loses his temper with me," said Chin-lien, "I'm not afraid of him. But I can't put up with his sorting people differentially into:

Three classes and nine categories.
He didn't let them sing the song suite that his legitimate wife had called for
but instead cast about:

Plowing the eastern ditch, and
Harrowing the western ditch;[34]

thereby throwing the two little bastards into such confusion that they didn't
know who they were supposed to take their orders from. Since this is our third
sister Meng Yü-lou's birthday, it was inappropriate to sing a song suite like the
one beginning with the words:

I remember her flute-playing,

which deals with the sorrows of separation. After all:

Nobody knows where the dead end up going to,

but he insists on exhibiting this counterfeit compassion and fake filiality. I
can't stomach it."

"You sisters have been quarreling with each other all this time," interjected
Sister-in-law Wu, "and I don't even know what it's about. My brother-in-law
came in and sat down politely, so why was he driven out again?"

"Sister-in-law," said Yüeh-niang, "you don't understand what happened.
That husband of mine recalled the fact that Sister Li was still with us on the
occasion of Sister Meng Yü-lou's birthday last year, but that she is no longer
with us this year, which caused him to shed a few tears. So he told the boy
actors to sing the song suite that begins with the words:

I remember her flute-playing, but where is
the jade damsel now?

This sister here was angry at the fact that he called for this song suite and told
him off so effectively that she got under his skin and caused him to chase after
her with the intent of giving her a drubbing. That's why the rascal ran out on
us."

"Sister," said Aunt Yang, "you ought to let your husband call for whatever
song suite he likes. What's the point of taking him to task over it. I imagine
that he's accustomed to seeing all you sisters together but noticed that Li P'ing-
erh was not here today. How could his heart not be stricken under the
circumstances?"

"My good lady," said Meng Yü-lou, "they've been singing what they were
asked to sing for what seems like half a day already, and who among the rest of
us objected to what they sang? But Sister Six here has always had a better understanding of the significance of the songs than the rest of us. This song suite
suggests that Li P'ing-erh was superior to any of the female paragons of old,
extols the closeness of their relationship, and how they swore to be as faithful
as the hills and seas, you to me, and I to you, as though she were utterly incom-
parable. So this inveterate nitpicker of ours couldn't help taking him verbally
to task for it and has been giving him a hard time ever since."

"So this sister of ours is as sharp as all that," remarked Aunt Yang.

"What songs are there that she doesn't know?" said Yüeh-niang.

> "If you quote the first line,
> She'll come up with the last.[35]

As for the likes of me, if we engage the services of professional female singers or boy actors, all we can do is let them sing and leave it at that. She is the only one among us who can say, 'That segment wasn't performed correctly; that line wasn't sung right; or that section was left out.' Whenever our husband proposes a song, she starts to carry on with him, giving him tit for tat, until he really becomes annoyed, before laying off, while the rest of us merely let them go at it."

"Aunt Yang," Meng Yü-lou interjected humorously, "you may not be aware of it, but I've had three or four children, of whom this slavey is the only one who survived. She has always been clever but unmannerly, and now that she has grown up and become a woman, she no longer allows herself to be governed by me."

Chin-lien responded by giving her a playful slap and laughed, saying, "So you're playing the role of my mother again, are you?"

"You see," said Meng Yü-lou, "she's been spoiled to the point that she's so:

> Discourteous and ill-bred,

as to strike a member of the older generation."

"Sister," said Aunt Yang, "you'd do well in the future to let that husband of yours have his say. As the sayings go:

> One night as man and wife gives rise to
>   a hundred nights of love.
> To walk a hundred steps with one another,
> Is enough to develop a lingering affinity.

She still seems vibrantly alive to him. You womenfolk of his are like his fingers. If he should lose one of them, how could he fail to think of it, to yearn for it, and to commemorate it?"

"Whether he thinks of her or not," responded Chin-lien, "there ought to be an appropriate time for it. We are all spouses of his after all. What does he mean by:

> Raising one person up, and
> Putting another down?

Are we all nothing but:

> The ghosts of Liu Chan's daughters,
> Who don't amount to anything?[36]

Our elder sister resides in the rear compound and may not be aware of it, or have seen what he's up to. Every day, when he comes home after drinking somewhere, he makes his way first to her quarters, where he bows deeply before her portrait, mutters some mumbo jumbo on her behalf, makes her an offering of soup and rice, and proffers her something with his chopsticks just as though she were alive. Who knows what all he's up to? And he criticizes the rest of us for not wearing mourning on her behalf. As we have pointed out to him, none of us stands to her in the position of a mother. We all wore mourning for her through the final weekly commemoration of her death. How much longer are we supposed to do so? But he continues to quarrel with us about it."

"Sisters," responded Aunt Yang, "you ought to:

Take notice of half of what he does,
And take no notice of the other half."

"How time flies," said Sister-in-law Wu. "The seventh weekly commemoration occurred some time ago, and now the hundredth-day anniversary of her death is about to come up."

"When will the hundredth-day anniversary occur?" asked Aunt Yang.

"It's early yet," said Yüeh-niang. "It will not be until the twenty-sixth day of the twelfth month."

"You'll have to have a scripture-reading ceremony to mark the occasion," said Nun Wang.

"It will fall too close to the New Year's celebrations," said Yüeh-niang, "for us to have any scripture-reading then. Father will probably put the scripture-reading off until after the New Year's festival."

As they were speaking, whom should they see but Hsiao-yü, who brought in a serving of tea flavored with taro, a cup of which was provided for each of them.

Shortly thereafter, when they had drunk their tea, Yüeh-niang washed her hands, lit some incense in the burner, and prepared to listen to Nun Hsüeh expound the Buddhist dharma.[37]

Nun Hsüeh began by reciting a gatha, which went as follows:

The Ch'an school of the Buddhist teaching
　is really quite extraordinary;
It has been transmitted by the Buddhas and
　patriarchs to the human world.
It is easy enough for a wind-blown leaf to
　fall tumbling to the ground;
But for it ever to be reattached to its
　original branch is difficult.[38]

These four lines of verse refer to the fact that for monks to adhere faithfully to their vows is difficult. It points out that man's life is like a leaf on an iron tree, which may fall off easily, but will find it hard to ever be reattached to its original branch. It is easy enough to suffer the consequences of one's evil karma, but difficult to become a Buddha or a patriarch.[39]

To resume our story, originally, during the Chih-p'ing reign period (1064–67), in the ancient Ching-tz'u Hsiao-kuang Monastery on the Southern Mountain outside the Ch'ien-t'ang Gate of Ning-hai military prefecture in Chekiang province, there were two dedicated monks who had attained to an understanding of the Way. One of them was called Ch'an Master Wu-chieh (Five Precepts), and the other Ch'an Master Ming-wu (Clear Enlightenment). To what does the term Five Precepts refer? The first is to abstain from killing; the second is to abstain from stealing; the third is to abstain from lascivious music and alluring beauty;[40] the fourth is to abstain from drinking wine or eating meat;[41] and the fifth is to abstain from uttering untrue or misleading statements.[42] To what does the term Clear Enlightenment refer? It means to illuminate one's mind and perceive one's nature,[43] thereby achieving an understanding of one's true self. Now this Ch'an Master Wu-chieh was just thirty years old in terms of lay reckoning, was not quite three feet tall, and presented an altogether most extraordinary aspect. He had been intelligent ever since his youth but was blind in one eye. His lay surname was Chin, and he was thoroughly versed in the Ch'an School and Buddhist doctrine. He and Ming-wu were like elder and younger brothers in the dharma. One day they visited the monastery together to call on the Ch'an Master Ta-hsing, and when the Master realized that Wu-chieh was so well versed in Buddhist doctrine, he retained him in the monastery in the post of rector. Some years later, when Ta-hsing passed away, the monks of the monastery made him the abbot, and henceforth he spent his days in meditation. The other one, Ming-wu, was twenty-eight years old and was born with a round head and large ears,[44] a broad face and a square mouth.[45] He was tall of stature,[46] and his appearance resembled that of an arhat. His lay surname was Wang, and the two of them were as close as though they were born of the same mother. When the time came to explicate the dharma, the two of them would mount the rostrum together.

One day, at the end of winter and the onset of spring, the weather was extremely cold. Snow had been falling for two days but had finally ended, and the sky was clear. Ch'an Master Wu-chieh was sitting on his meditation chair early that morning when his ears caught the sound of an infant crying in the distance. Turning to the trusted lay worker at his side, whose name was Ch'ing-i, he said to him, "Go out in front of the monastery gate to see what is going on, and report back to me." The lay worker opened the gate of the monastery and saw a baby lying on a tattered mat on the snowy ground under a pine tree. "I wonder who could have left the child here?" he thought to himself. When he went closer to take a look, he found that it was a five- or six-month-old baby girl, wrapped in ragged clothing, who had a strip of paper on her breast inscribed with the eight characters indicating the year, month, date, and hour of her birth. Ch'ing-i thought to himself, "To save a single human life is better than building a seven-story pagoda."[47]

Hastening back to the abbot's quarters, he told him what he had found. "Good!" said the abbot. "Someone with a heart as good as yours is hard to find. Take her back to your quarters and see that she is properly nourished. To have saved her life is a good deed." When she had lived through her first year, the abbot gave her the name Hung-lien, or Red Lotus.

As the days went and the months came,[48] the lay worker Ch'ing-i raised her in his quarters in the monastery, without anyone being the wiser,[49] and in a while the abbot himself forgot all about it.

Before anyone knew it, Hung-lien grew to the age of fifteen. The lay worker Ch'ing-i kept her secluded in his own quarters, locking the door every day, each time he went out or came in, just as though she were his own daughter. The girl's clothing, shoes, and socks were all those of a male novice, and she was favored with a naturally clear-cut appearance. When she had nothing else to do, she devoted herself to needlework in her room. The only hope of Ch'ing-i was that he might find her a husband so that the two of them could support him in his old age and arrange for his funeral.[50]

One day, during the hot weather of the sixth month, Ch'an Master Wu-chieh happened to remember the events that had occurred more than ten years before and went directly back to the lay worker Ch'ing-i's quarters behind the Hall of a Thousand Buddhas. "You seldom venture here," said Ch'ing-i. "What brings you here today?" "Where is that girl Hung-lien?" asked Ch'an Master Wu-chieh. Ch'ing-i did not dare to conceal the truth of the matter[51] and led the abbot into his quarters.

No sooner did he catch sight of Hung-lien than his thoughts were led astray,[52] and lustful desires were suddenly aroused. "Tonight you must bring her to my quarters," he instructed Ch'ing-i. "You must do so without fail.[53] If you consent to do as I say, I will see to it that your lot is improved in the future, but you must not let anyone else into the secret." Ch'ing-i did not dare not to comply, but thought to himself, "Tonight this girl of mine is sure to lose her virginity." When the abbot saw that his response was somewhat reluctant, he called him into his own quarters and gave him ten taels of silver, along with an ordination certificate that would entitle him to become a monk himself. Ch'ing-i felt that he had no alternative but to accept the silver.

That evening, he took Hung-lien to the abbot's quarters, and the abbot accordingly deflowered her. After this, the abbot kept her hidden out of sight in a paper-curtained cabinet behind his bed and personally provided her with enough food to eat.

To resume our story, that very night, when the abbot's brother-monk Ch'an Master Ming-wu emerged from a trance while sitting on his meditation couch, he was already aware that Wu-chieh had allowed his thoughts to stray and had broken his vow to abstain from sexual activity by violating the girl Hung-lien, thereby allowing his virtuous conduct of many years to be cast aside on a single day. "I had better go and admonish him to mend his ways," he thought to himself.

The next day, the lotus flowers were in bloom in front of the monastery gate. Ming-wu ordered an acolyte to pluck a white lotus for him, put it in a gallbladder-shaped vase, and then invite Wu-chieh to come join him in enjoying the lotus blossoms, and composing verses, while chatting and laughing together. Before long, Wu-chieh arrived, and the two Ch'an Masters sat down beside each other. "My Brother," said Ming-wu, "I noticed today that these flowers were in full bloom and invited you to come enjoy them with me, and each compose a verse on the subject."

When the acolyte had served them with tea, and they had finished drinking it, they were provided with the four treasures of the writer's studio.[54]

"Let's choose the lotus root as our topic," said Wu-chieh, but Ming-wu said, "No, let's choose the lotus flowers as our topic instead." Wu-chieh took up his brush and composed a quatrain, as follows:

The petals of the stalk of lotus flowers
   are in full bloom;
Accompanied by the hollyhocks, exuding
   their rich fragrance.
The fiery red pomegranates are ablaze
   like rolls of brocade;
But their scent is no match for that of
   the green-coated caltrops.

"Since my elder brother has composed a poem," said Ming-wu, "how could I fail to do so?" Whereupon, he also picked up his brush and composed a quatrain, as follows:

In spring, the peach trees, apricots, and
   willows begin to flourish;
Their thousand blossoms and myriad blooms
   contending in fragrance.
In summer, one enjoys the caltrop and the
   lotus, in all their glory;
But the red lotus is no match for the white
   lotus in its fragrance.[55]

When he had finished writing it out, he laughed out loud.
   Upon hearing the words of this poem, Wu-chieh realized their significance, and his embarrassment showed in his face.[56] Turning around and excusing himself, he returned to the abbot's quarters, where he told an acolyte to heat some bath water. After bathing himself, and changing into a new set of clothing, he took paper and brush and hastily wrote a farewell elegy of eight lines, as follows:

Now I have existed forty-seven years,
The myriad phenomena revert to unity.
Only because my thoughts went astray,
I must now suddenly depart this life.
My message to my fellow monk Ming-wu,
Is, "There is no need to pressure me."
My ephemeral body is like lightning,
That leaves the sky azure as before.

When he had finished writing it, he placed it in front of an image of the Buddha, returned to his meditation couch, and passed away in the lotus position.
   An acolyte hastened to report this event to Ming-wu, who was greatly surprised to hear it. Upon going in front of the Buddha's image and reading the farewell elegy,

he said, "You were not a bad monk, after all, but it's too bad that you made this one false move. And now, although you may be reborn as a man, you will grow up not believing in the Three Jewels, the Buddha, the Dharma, and the Sangha; and are sure to disparage the Buddha and slander the clergy, bringing bitter consequences on yourself in future lives, and preventing yourself from reverting to the true path.[57] It is greatly to be regretted. Do you really think that you have gotten away, and that I will not be able to catch up with you?"

Thereupon, he returned to his quarters, told an acolyte to heat bath water for him, bathed, and sat down on his meditation couch. Turning to the acolyte, he said, "I am going to pursue my fellow monk Wu-chieh. You can place our bodies in two caskets, and see that they are properly cremated together, after lying in state for three days." When he had finished speaking, he also passed away while sitting in the lotus position.

His fellow monks were all astonished at this extraordinary event, and word that two monks at the monastery had passed away sitting in the lotus position on successive days quickly spread to the four quarters. As a result, when their caskets were carried out in front of the monastery and cremated, mountains and seas of people came to burn incense, pay their respects, and offer donations. The lay worker Ch'ing-i subsequently married Hung-lien to a commoner so that they could support him in his old age. But no more of this.

In later days, Wu-chieh was reborn as the son of the layman Su Hsün of Mei prefecture in western Szechwan, who was given the name Su Shih,[58] and is also known by the courtesy name Tzu-chan, and the cognomen Tung-p'o. Ming-wu was reborn as the son of one Hsieh Tao-ch'ing from the same prefecture, who was given the name Tuan-ch'ing, and later left home to become a monk,[59] who took the name Fo-yin. The two of them continued to confront each other in their new incarnations, and their relationship remained extremely close. Truly:

> Since he arrived in Szechwan several
>   decades have gone by;
> During which he has devoted himself
>   to the Buddha Vairocana.[60]
> Although he apprehended the crux of
>   Chao-chou's[61] sayings;
> His good affinity has turned out to
>   be a bad affinity.
> The red peach blossoms and the green
>   willows remain the same;
> The water flowing over the boulders
>   makes a gurgling sound.
> Today, the road to enlightenment has
>   been pointed out to you;
> Never again allow your thoughts to
>   stray for love of Hung-lien.[62]

When Nun Hsüeh finished her recitation, whom should they see but Lan-hsiang, from Meng Yü-lou's quarters, who brought in two square boxes of fastidiously prepared vegetarian fare, saucers of fruit, tea pastries, and sweetmeats, which were placed on the table after the incense burner had been removed. A kettle of tea was also provided, and the audience joined the three nuns in enjoying the repast. After this, some meat dishes were served, a jug of Ma-ku wine was opened, and the company gathered around the brazier to enjoy the wine.

Yüeh-niang and Sister-in-law Wu began to throw dice as they played "Competing for the Red," while Chin-lien and Li Chiao-erh played guess-fingers with each other. Yü-hsiao stood beside them to pour the wine and at the same time passed information to Chin-lien underneath the table, which enabled her to win round after round, forcing Li Chiao-erh to down several cups of wine.

"Let me play with you," said Meng Yü-lou. "You seem bent only on beating her."

She then went on to say, "Chin-lien, expose your hands. You mustn't conceal them in your sleeves that way. And Yü-hsiao must not be allowed to stay so close to you."

As a result, that evening, she succeeded in overcoming Chin-lien, who was forced to down several cups of wine.

They also asked Big Sister Yü to play and sing for them, Yüeh-niang telling her, "Sing a version of 'Getting through the Five Watches of the Night' for us."

Big Sister Yü, thereupon, tuned the strings of her instrument and sang in a loud voice the song suite that begins with the tune "Interlaced Jade Branches":

Amid dense masses of dark clouds,
Like bits of goose down, the snowflakes
    are dancing wildly.
The north wind is piercingly cold,[63] as it
    penetrates the windows.
Your heart is hard, and I have been
    the victim of it.
The abuse I have suffered at the hands of
    my parents is too cruel.
The promises you made me have been
    utterly ignored.
All I can do is count the watches
    of the night.

To the tune "Sutra in Letters of Gold":

The night is long, and I have been
    left all alone.

It is desolate in the quiet of
   the early watches.
You have not sent me a single sheet
   of news about yourself.
My cheeks are streaked with pearly tears.
Our good times together are nothing to you.
During the first watch, my suffering
   is unbounded.

To the tune "Interlaced Jade Branches":

The first watch is finally over;
But I have been left all alone here
   amid the bed curtains.
I toss first this way and then that,
   but how am I to sleep?
During the second watch my
   pearly tears fall.

To the same tune:

The second watch is hard to endure.
In trying to go to sleep, I do
   periodically nod off,
Hoping that this night, this night, he will
   appear to me in my dreams.
I long for him; he longs for me.
When he first left, the flowering crab apple
   had just begun to bloom;
But by this time, the leaves of the tree
   have all fallen;
Leaving me with no recourse but to
   foolishly wait in vain.

To the tune "Sutra in Letters of Gold":

I have been foolishly waiting
   for you all day long;
When will you ever consent to come?
We spend less time together than apart;[64]
   it's just my bad luck, bad luck.
I have been left all alone, but
   what can I do about it?
It makes it really hard to keep going.
During the third watch, my dreams
   are recurrent.

To the tune "Interlaced Jade Branches":

By the third watch the moon has risen.
How hard it is to bear this
    interminable night.
The candle in its silver stand
    is sputtering out.
My pearly tears fall in two
    or three streaks.
Under my red satin comforter, half
    the bed is empty.
Where has he bestowed the handkerchief that
    I recently stitched for him?
My waist has become emaciated, as emaciated
    as that of Shen Yüeh.[65]

To the tune "Sutra in Letters of Gold":

My waist has become as emaciated
    as that of Shen Yüeh.
Every day I am more brokenhearted
    than ever with sorrow.
Yearning for my lover,[66] I shed tears
    in two streams, two streams.
Facing the caltrop-patterned mirror, I am
    reluctant to make myself up.
My alluring figure has become emaciated.[67]
During the fourth watch, the night seems
    longer than ever.

To the tune "Interlaced Jade Branches":

The fourth watch is as long as the day.
As I think of him on my pillow, before I
    know it, my tears begin to flow.
In the numinous god's temple, we swore
    fealty to each other.
We exchanged snippets of black hair
    as tokens of our love.
But the promises he made to me
    have not been kept.
By now, he has abandoned me just like
    that "willow" in the quarter;[68]
And I am left foolishly waiting
    for him in vain.

To the tune "Sutra in Letters of Gold":

I have been foolishly waiting
    for you all day long;
When will this ever cease?
Longing for my lover, in vain do I lean on the
    belvedere, lean on the belvedere.
I fear my lover has wiped the slate clean
    with a single stroke.
I can't help knitting my brows.
During the fifth watch my
    pearly tears flow.

To the tune "Interlaced Jade Branches":

At the fifth watch the cock crows.[69]
Gradually I perceive that the day
    is beginning to dawn.
Breaking into tears, I am about to
    break into tears,
But I fear that other people will
    only laugh at me.
For a time my heart is on fire;
Burning incense, I seek my fortune
    before the gods.
The intentions of my fickle lover
    are known only to Heaven;
And I am left foolishly waiting
    for him in vain.

To the tune "Sutra in Letters of Gold":

I have been foolishly waiting
    for you all day long;
When will this ever end?
Beyond the eaves, ding-dong the wind chimes
    sound, the wind chimes sound;
Making it impossible for me to sleep.
While, at the same time, the
    cold ravens caw;
Desolately and disconsolately,[70]
    right up till dawn.

To the tune "Interlaced Jade Branches":

At dawn I do my hair and wash my face;
But, confronting my dressing mirror, I am
    reluctant to paint my eyebrows.

Then, on the eaves of my room, auspicious
    magpies begin to chatter;
And my maidservant comes to report the good news,
Saying, "Your lover has actually
    chosen to return."
As the two of us enter the silken
    bed curtains together,
I tell him, "You come closer. "I've
    got something to ask you."

To the tune "The Flower in the Rear Courtyard":

"I've got something to ask you, you
    unfaithful scoundrel.
As you well know, you've been away
    for half a year now;
So why didn't you send me so much
    as a single letter?
I believed that you had gone to take the examinations
    in order to become an official;
How could I know you were bewitched by 'misty willows'
    and addicted to the wine cup?
On your account, I had no choice but
    to endure loneliness;
While you were there, cuddling the red
    and hugging the turquoise.
On your account, I am sick with depression
    and unable to eat,
So that my jade body has become
    utterly emaciated.
I can endure the clear mornings, but
    fear the evenings.
During the first watch, I heard the cry of the
    solitary wild goose at the sky's edge;
During the second watch, I suffered my dreaming
    soul to yearn after my absent lover;
But, during the fifth watch, upon my awakening,
    I was unable to see any trace of you."

To the tune "The Leaves of the Willow Tree":

"Ah! I found myself all alone beneath my
    mandarin duck brocade quilt;
Deserted for my swallows' tryst, swallows'
    tryst or orioles' assignation.

In the Temple of the God of the Sea[71] may
    be found an analogous case.[72]
I could hardly help being angry at heart.
As you well know, the intentions of my fickle
    lover are known only to Heaven."

CODA:

Within the tasseled brocade curtains,[73]
    the lovers are entwined;
Beneath the brocade quilt, the mandarin
    ducks proceed to pair.
They will remain forever reunited,[74] till
    the end of their lives.[75]

By this time, Chin-lien had lost a series of rounds as she played at guess-
fingers with Meng Yü-lou and had been forced to down ten or twenty cups of
wine. No longer able to sit at her place, she set off for her quarters in the front
compound, where she had to call out for what seemed like half a day before
the postern gate was opened for her by Ch'iu-chü, who was still rubbing the
sleep out of her eyes.

"So, you lousy slave, you've been asleep have you?" the woman said to her
accusingly.

"I haven't been to sleep," protested Ch'iu-chü.

"It's obvious that you've just gotten up," the woman said. "You're just trying
to deceive me. You've been taking it easy, rather than thinking of coming back
to the rear compound to get me."

She then went on to ask, "Has Father gone to bed yet?"

"Father's been asleep for some time already," responded Ch'iu-chü.

The woman then went into the room that was furnished with a k'ang, where
she pulled up her skirt and sat down on the k'ang to warm herself, while calling for some tea.

Ch'iu-chü hastily poured out a cup of tea for her, but the woman said, "You
lousy slave! You'd pour tea for me to drink with those dirty hands of yours,
would you? I won't drink any of that stale tea that has been steeped for so long
it smells of the pot. Go call Ch'un-mei, and tell her to fill a little kettle with
sweet water, put in an abundance of tea leaves, and boil it until it is good and
strong, for me to drink."

"She's asleep in the other room with the bed in it," said Ch'iu-chü. "Wait
till I call her to bring it for you."

"Don't call her, but let her sleep," the woman said.

Ch'iu-chü did not obey her but went into the other room, where she found
Ch'un-mei lying fast asleep at Hsi-men Ch'ing's feet.

Shaking her awake, she said, "Mother has come back and wants some tea to drink. Haven't you even gotten up yet?"

Ch'un-mei spat at her, and cursed, saying, "You slave! You've been seeing things! So Mother has come back. So what? Why should you be in such a frightful stew over it, for no good reason?"

She then proceeded to get up:

> Just as slow and easy as you please,

stretched her waist, pulled on her trousers, and came to see the woman, still rubbing her eyes as she approached the k'ang.

The woman, for her part, chose to criticize Ch'iu-chü, saying, "That slave! You were fast asleep, and she woke you up."

"The kerchief on your head has jumped out of place," she then remarked to Ch'un-mei. "Why don't you pull it back down where it belongs?"

She went on to ask, "How is it that you're only wearing one pendant ear-ring? Where did the other one go?"

When Ch'un-mei felt her ears, she found that she was, indeed, wearing only one gold openwork pendant earring. Lighting a lamp, she went to take a look at the bed in the other room but failed to find the missing object. After some time, unexpectedly, she found that it had fallen onto the footboard of the bed and picked it up.

"Where did you find it?" the woman asked her.

"It was all her fault," said Ch'un-mei, "when she insisted on:

> Making such an unnecessary fuss,[76]

over waking me up. It got caught on a curtain hook and fell onto the foot-board, where I was able to recover it."

"I told her not to disturb you," the woman explained, "but she insisted on waking you up anyway."

"She said that you wanted some tea to drink," said Ch'un-mei.

"I do want a drink of tea," the woman said, "but I fear that her hands are not clean."

Ch'un-mei then dipped up a little kettleful of water, placed it on the bra-zier, and raked some charcoal around it. Before long it was hot enough to brew tea, and after rinsing out a cup, she poured out a strong serving of tea and handed it to the woman.

The woman then asked Ch'un-mei, "How long has Father been asleep?"

"I helped him to bed some time ago," responded Ch'un-mei. "He asked where you were, and I told him that you had not yet returned from the rear compound."

When the woman had finished her tea, she said to Ch'un-mei, "A while ago, I brought back some fruit and candied sweetmeats in my sleeve, that had been given to me by Yü-hsiao for my mother to eat. I turned them over to this slave here to take inside for you to put away."

"I haven't seen anything of them," said Ch'un-mei. "Who knows where she put them?"

The woman then called in Ch'iu-chü and asked her, "Where did you put that fruit?"

"It's here," responded Ch'iu-chü. "I put it in the cabinet."

So saying, she went and brought the things over to her.

The woman counted them over and, finding that a tangerine was missing, asked her what had happened to it.

"When Mother gave them to me," said Ch'iu-chü, "I brought them inside and put them in the cabinet. Surely you don't imagine I was suffering from such an avid craving as to blight my own mouth with it, do you?"

"You lousy slave!" the woman responded. "You still insist on talking back, do you? If you didn't snitch it, where did it go? I counted them with my own hand before turning them over to you. You lousy slave! You've simply been picking them up and secreting them for yourself, until only these measly:

  Odds and ends,[77]

are left. You've already consumed more than half of them. Under the circumstances, I'll have to teach you a lesson."

Then, turning to Ch'un-mei, she said, "You give that slave ten slaps on each side of her face."

"Those dirty cheeks of hers," responded Ch'un-mei. "I'd only be dirtying this hand of mine."

"You drag her over to me, then," the woman said.

Ch'un-mei pushed her over in front of the woman with both hands, and the woman pinched her cheeks, while taking her to task, saying, "You lousy slave! It was you who snitched this tangerine to eat, wasn't it? If you tell me the truth, I won't beat you. But if you don't, I'll get the riding crop, strip you naked, and whip you until I lose track of the strokes. No doubt, you thought I was drunk enough so that you could snitch it for yourself, while pulling the wool over my eyes, didn't you?"

She then turned to Ch'un-mei and asked her, "Am I drunk, or not?"

"Mother is perfectly sober," replied Ch'un-mei. "What does wine have to do with it? If you believe her, then she didn't eat it. But if you don't believe her, try groping inside her sleeve. I wouldn't be surprised if there were still tangerine peels in her sleeve."

The woman, then, pulled the sleeve over and started to grope inside it, but Ch'iu-chü tried to brush her aside with one hand, in order to prevent her from doing so. Ch'un-mei, then, intervened by pulling her hand away and, sure enough, was able to grope out some remnants of tangerine peel.

The woman responded by pinching her cheeks twice, as hard as she could, and giving her two full-handed slaps on the face, as she reviled her, saying, "You lousy slave! You hopeless scamp of a slave! You're hardly good at anything else, but it seems you're proficient at telling tales and snitching food to eat. These tangerine peels in your sleeve constitute:

Irrefutable proof of your guilt,[78]

so you can hardly try to blame anyone else. I would give you a whipping right now, but Father is asleep here, and it's not an appropriate time to whip you while;

Anticipating tea or recovering from wine.

Tomorrow, when I'm completely myself, I'll settle accounts with you."

"Mother," said Ch'un-mei, "you ought not to be perfunctory about it tomorrow, but have her stripped completely naked, and get someone to give her a real shellacking, administering several tens of strokes with the bamboo. If she is made to suffer some real pain, it might throw some fear into her. If you merely touch her up with a few strokes of the rod, as if you were playing with a monkey, she won't take it to heart."

Ch'iu-chü's face was swollen from the pinches she had received at the woman's hands, and she took herself off to the kitchen with a pout on her lips.

The woman divided the other tangerine in two and also took an apple, and a pomegranate, and offered them to Ch'un-mei, saying, "I'm giving you these things to eat, while the rest should be kept for my mother."

Ch'un-mei did not evince any interest in these offerings but accepted them as indifferently as though she were:

Uncertain whether they were there or not,

and tossed them into a drawer.

The woman was also about to divide up the candied sweetmeats, but Ch'un-mei said, "There is no need for you to divide them. I am disinclined to eat such sweet things. Save them for your mother."

For this reason, the woman did not divide them and set them aside for her mother. But no more of this.

The woman sat down on the commode and urinated, after which she told Ch'un-mei to bring in the portable bidet and washed her private parts.

She then went on to ask Ch'un-mei, "What time is it by now?"

"The moon is sinking in the West," said Ch'un-mei, "so it must be sometime in the third watch."

The woman took off her jewelry and went into the bedroom, where she saw that the silver lamp on the table was guttering out, and proceeded to trim the wick. When she looked at the bed, she saw that Hsi-men Ch'ing was lying there fast asleep and snoring loudly. Unfastening her silken girdle and doffing her skirt, she sat down to change into her sleeping shoes, took off her drawers, climbed into bed, and bored her way under the covers, where she:

Lay down head to head on the same pillow,[79]

with Hsi-men Ch'ing.

After lying there for a little while, she reached between his loins and felt for his organ. Although she manipulated it for a while, it refused to stand up. It so happens that Hsi-men Ch'ing had engaged in sexual intercourse with Ch'un-mei not long before, so that his organ was as flaccid as cotton and could not be made to rise immediately. The woman, who had a bellyful of wine, and whose:

Lecherous desires were on fire,[80]

squatted down underneath the bedding and began to suck his organ. Titillating the mouth of his urethra with her tongue, she engulfed his turtle head with her mouth and proceeded to move it:

Back and forth without ceasing.[81]

Hsi-men Ch'ing abruptly woke up and, seeing what she was up to under the covers, said, "You crazy little whore! Why did you not come back until now?"

"We have been drinking wine in the rear compound," explained the woman, "where Meng the Third had provided two square boxes of delicacies to go with the wine, and Big Sister Yü was singing to entertain us. We were keeping company with Sister-in-law Wu and Aunt Yang and have been enjoying ourselves all this time playing at guess-fingers and throwing dice. I defeated Li Chiao-erh and made her drunk in the process, but afterwards, Meng the Third outplayed me at guess-fingers, and I had to drink several goblets of wine. You're lucky to have had some sleep, but if you think you can hold out on me, just see if I put up with it, or not."

"Have you got that band you were going to make?" asked Hsi-men Ch'ing.

"It's right here under the mattress," the woman said, pulling it out and showing it to Hsi-men Ch'ing.

She then proceeded to fasten it around the root of his chowrie handle, and then tie the two ribbons attached to it securely behind his back.

"Have you taken anything?" she went on to ask; to which Hsi-men Ch'ing replied, "Yes I have."

Before long, thanks to the woman's manipulation of his organ, behold:

Its protuberances swelled, its head sprang up, and
Its body swelled itself erect,

until it reached the exceptional length of more than seven inches. The woman crawled on top of him and, finding that his turtle head was proud and large, stretched her labia apart with both hands and abruptly inserted it into her vagina. The woman embraced Hsi-men Ch'ing around the neck with both hands and told him to clasp her waist, while she continued to knead away at him in her superior position until his organ finally penetrated her to the root.

"Daddy," the woman cried out to Hsi-men Ch'ing, "take my bodice and put it under your waist to prop it up."

Hsi-men Ch'ing picked up her bodice of crimson satin from the head of the bed, folded it over itself four times, and used it to prop up his waist, while the

Hsi-men Ch'ing First Tries Out the Band of White Satin

woman straddled his body on all fours. After no more than a few thrusts, his organ penetrated her to the hilt.

"Daddy," the woman said, "you can feel it with your own hand. It's gone all the way in and has stretched me to capacity on the inside. In case you're not satisfied yet, you can try to thrust it in further."

Hsi-men Ch'ing investigated with his hand and found that it had penetrated all the way to the root:

Without leaving a gap of even a hairsbreadth,[82] while only his two testicles remained outside,[83] and inside he felt a melting sensation the pleasure of which was indescribable.

"You certainly were in a hurry," the woman said. "The problem is that it's so cold we can't light a lamp and enjoy the sight of what we're doing. It's not as nice as it is in the summer. During these winter months, it's altogether too cold."

She then went on to ask Hsi-men Ch'ing, "How do you find this band compares with that silver clasp? It certainly seems superior to me, in that it doesn't hurt when it rubs against my labia. This band makes your organ grow even larger and increases its length significantly. If you don't believe me, try feeling my lower abdomen. It has penetrated almost as far as my heart."

She then went on to say, "You hold me. Today, I'd like to go to sleep on top of you."

"My child," said Hsi-men Ch'ing, "go ahead and sleep. Daddy will hold you."

The woman stuck her tongue into his mouth and had him hold it there, while her starry eyes grew dim, as he embraced her fragrant shoulders.

After sleeping for a brief period, she could not prevent the flames of desire from enveloping her body, as her fragrant heart became disturbed.

Thereupon, supporting herself with her hands on his shoulders, she alternately raised and lowered herself, while he retracted his organ as far as the knob of the glans, and then plunged it in all the way up to the root, as she called out, "My own darling! That's enough. Your Fivey is dying."

But he continued coming and going, thrusting and retracting another three hundred times, until she finally came.

"My own daddy!" the woman cried out. "Squeeze me tightly around the waist."

At the same time, she offered Hsi-men Ch'ing a nipple to suck, and then, before she knew it:

She swooned completely away, and
Her vaginal fluids overflowed.

Before long, as the two of them lay in a mutual embrace, the woman became aware that:

Her heart was hopping like a little fawn.[84]

In no time at all:

  Her four limbs had become limp, and
  Her cloudy locks were in disarray.
But, when Hsi-men Ch'ing's organ was withdrawn, it was still as stiff and hard
as ever.

  The woman wiped it off with a handkerchief, saying, "My own daddy! How
is it that you haven't ejaculated?"

  "Wait until we've had some sleep," said Hsi-men Ch'ing, "after which, we
can start to play again."

  "I'm not sure I'll be up to it," the woman said, "my body's feeling so flaccid
and feverish."

  Afterwards, once:
    The clouds dispersed and the rain evaporated,
the two of them:
    Shoulder to shoulder and thigh over thigh,
went to sleep on the bed:
    Unaware that the sun had already
      risen in the East.[85]
Truly:
    If one were to casually shine the light of
      a silver lamp upon them;
    They would appear to be a natural-born pair
      of interlocking branches.

    If you want to know the outcome of these events,
    Pray consult the story related in the following chapter.

Chapter 74

CENSOR SUNG CH'IAO-NIEN SOLICITS

THE EIGHT IMMORTALS TRIPOD;

WU YÜEH-NIANG LISTENS TO THE *PRECIOUS*

SCROLL ON WOMAN HUANG

Years ago, when I was traveling in the South,
    you entertained me as a guest;
Provided with cups of Tun-hsün wine,[1] together
    we enjoyed the verdant spring.
Foaming over from its sparrow-shaped vessels,
    the barbarian wine was smooth;
As you remind me with the jeweled words of your
    message on new Szechwan paper.
The flowers were allured by our passing steeds,
    their reds following the bridles;
The grass was attracted by our moving vehicles,
    its green surrounding the wheels.
Since we parted amid the flourishing foliage
    on the road south of Cheng-chou,
Who knows who has been heir to those beauties
    of the breeze and the moonlight?[2]

THE STORY GOES that Hsi-men Ch'ing embraced P'an Chin-lien and slept until the dawn of the following day.

When the woman saw that his organ was still standing straight up as though it were a stick, she said, "Daddy, you'd better make the best of it by letting me off for now. I can't handle any more. Let me suck you off instead."

"You crazy little whore!" responded Hsi-men Ch'ing. "You might as well give it a suck. If you succeed in sucking it off, it will be your good fortune."

The woman actually squatted down between his loins and, pillowing her head on one of his thighs, proceeded to manipulate his organ with her mouth, sucking away at it for a good hour, without getting it to ejaculate. Hsi-men Ch'ing held onto her powdered neck with one hand while alternately submerging and exposing the knob of his glans, and wobbling his organ back and forth. She pumped it in and out of her mouth unceasingly, until white saliva overflowed from her lips, and rouge stains appeared on the stem of his organ.

Just as he was about to ejaculate, the woman questioned Hsi-men Ch'ing, saying, "Ying the Second has sent invitations inviting us to his place on the twenty-eighth. Are we going to go, or not?"

"Why shouldn't you go?" said Hsi-men Ch'ing. "You should all get your-selves ready and go."

"There is something I'd like to ask of you," the woman said. "Will you agree to it, or not?"

"You crazy little whore!" responded Hsi-men Ch'ing. "What have you got to ask? Why not just come out with it?"

"I'd like you to get out that fur coat of Sister Li's and let me wear it," the woman said. "Tomorrow, when we come back from the party, the others will all be wearing their fur coats, but I alone will be without one to wear."

"There is that fur coat that was pawned with us last year by the household of Imperial Commissioner Wang," said Hsi-men Ch'ing. "You might as well wear that."

"I don't want to wear something that's been pawned," the woman said. "Be-sides, you've already turned it over to Li Chiao-erh to wear, and given Li Chiao-erh's fur coat to Sun Hsüeh-o. I'd like to wear that fur coat of Sister Li's. If you get it out and give it to me today, I'll attach two crimson brocaded sleeve linings and wear it with my white satin jacket. If you let me have it, rather than giving it to anyone else, it will be an acknowledgment that I've been a good wife to you all this time."

"You lousy little whore!" responded Hsi-men Ch'ing. "All you care about is gaining petty advantages for yourself. That fur coat of hers is worth sixty taels of silver, with its glossy, jet black fur trimming. If you wear it, you will only make an ostentatious show of yourself."

"You crazy slave!" the woman retorted. "It's not as though you were giving it away to the wife of some nobody. After all, it's your own spouse you're giving it to, and it will only serve to enhance your prestige. What's the point of mak-ing such a fuss about it? How would you like it if I refused to comply with your wishes in the future?"

"You're:

  Asking a favor on the one hand, and
  Being hard-boiled on the other,"

said Hsi-men Ch'ing.

"You crazy indecent good-for-nothing!" the woman said. "Am I no more than a maidservant in your room, who must give in to your every demand?"

As she spoke, she laid his organ against her powdered cheek and brushed it back and forth for some time before, once again, inserting it into her mouth,[3] and titillating the orifice of his urethra with her tongue. After a while, she fell to licking his frenum with the tip of her tongue and toying with the knob of his glans and then, engulfing it with her ruby lips, devoted herself to moving it back and forth.

P'an Chin-lien Uses Her Fragrant Cheek to Caress the Jade

The extremity of Hsi-men Ch'ing's magic rhinoceros horn felt anointed, his brain was flooded with a range of lustful feelings,[4] and in a little while, as his semen began to rise, he called out repeatedly, "You little whore! Squeeze it tightly. I'm about to come."

Before he had finished speaking, his semen ejaculated all over the woman's mouth and face, and she dutifully swallowed it down, mouthful after mouthful. Truly:

> Past mistress of the intimate arts,
>> she caters to his every whim;
> How quick she is, and diligent,
>> to "play the purple flute."

That day was the one on which Secretary An Ch'en had arranged to host a party on his premises, so Hsi-men Ch'ing got up to comb his hair and wash his face and had started to go outside when the woman, who was still lying under the covers, said, "You'd better take this opportunity to find that fur coat for me. If you put it off, you won't have any time to spare."

Hsi-men Ch'ing, thereupon, made his way over to Li P'ing-erh's quarters, where the wet nurse and maidservant had already arisen, straightened things up, and prepared a kettle of tea water in anticipation of his arrival.

When Hsi-men Ch'ing came in and sat down, he asked, "Have you presented an offering to your mistress, or not?"

"By now," said Ju-i, "it is already quite a while since the offering was presented."

Hsi-men Ch'ing observed that Ju-i was wearing a jade-colored jacket that opened down the middle, over a white cotton skirt, and pale green satin shoes with high sand-green heels. Her face was lightly daubed with rouge and powder,[5] her mothlike eyebrows were painted long, her lips were tinted bright red with shiny rouge, from her ears were suspended two gold clove-shaped ear pendants, and on her hands she sported four black gold rings that had been bestowed upon her by Li P'ing-erh. With an ingratiating smile, she presented him with tea and then sat down to one side in order to chat with him.

Hsi-men Ch'ing sent Ying-ch'un back to the rear compound to get the keys to the bedroom, and Ju-i asked him, "Father, what are you getting them for?"

"I am looking for her fur coat," responded Hsi-men Ch'ing, "in order to let the Fifth Lady wear it."

"Do you mean that sable coat of Mother's?" asked Ju-i.

"Yes," said Hsi-men Ch'ing. "She would like to wear it, so I am going to give it to her now."

When Ying-ch'un had departed on her errand, Hsi-men Ch'ing took the woman onto his lap, cupped her breasts with his two hands in order to stimulate her nipples, and remarked, "My child, though you have borne a child, your nipples are still tight."

The two of them then fell to kissing each other face to face, and sucking each other's tongues.

"I have noticed, Father," said Ju-i, "that you are constantly choosing to spend your time with the Fifth Lady. I haven't seen you frequenting the quarters of any of the other ladies. Whatever her other characteristics may be, she is altogether too touchy and unable to make allowances for others. Some time ago, while you were still away from home, she got into a big row with me over the laundry bat, but fortunately Auntie Han and the Third Lady were able to intervene and separate us. Later on, when you returned home, I did not venture to mention it to you; but some talkative person, I don't know who, not only mentioned it to you, but also told her that you had been making out with me. Did she also tell you about our quarrel?"

"Yes, she did tell me about it." said Hsi-men Ch'ing. "In the future, you would do well to offer her an apology. If she manages to pick up so much as a sweet date from someone, she's as pleased as can be. Although she may be sharp-tongued, she doesn't really mean what she says."

"When you came home, the day after we had our quarrel," said Ju-i, "she made a point of speaking nicely to me, saying that since you chose to spend much of your time with her, the other ladies of the household were prone to cut her some slack. 'But if you are careful not to keep me in the dark about anything,' she went on to say:
'There's water enough in the channel
         for all the boats,
why should I go out of my way to make trouble for you?'"

"In that case," said Hsi-men Ch'ing, "the two of you ought to be reconciled to each other."

He then went on to promise the woman, "If you wait up for me, I'll come to this room to sleep tonight."

"Are you really going to come?" asked Ju-i. "Don't try to deceive me."

"Who's trying to deceive you?" Hsi-men Ch'ing protested.

As they were speaking, whom should they see but Ying-ch'un, who came back with the keys. Hsi-men Ch'ing told her to unlock the bedroom door and then open the cabinet and get out the fur coat. After giving it a good shaking and wrapping it up in a package, he told Ying-ch'un to take it over to the adjacent room.

Ju-i then said to Hsi-men Ch'ing in a low voice, "I don't have a good fur coat myself. How about taking advantage of the occasion to find another one for me? And if any of Mother's undergarments are available, you might also provide me with a set of them."

Hsi-men Ch'ing promptly told her to open the trunk and came up with a set of clothes consisting of a kingfisher-blue satin jacket, a yellow cotton skirt, a pair of blue Lu-chou silk drawers, and a pair of figured ankle leggings. He turned them over to her, and the woman kowtowed to him in thanks, after which Hsi-men Ch'ing locked the bedroom door and went out, telling her to take the fur coat and deliver it to Chin-lien's quarters next door.

Chin-lien had just gotten up, and was still sitting on her bed engaged in putting on her foot bindings, when Ch'un-mei announced, "Ju-i has come to deliver the fur coat."

The woman, who understood the significance of the fact that she had been sent on this errand, said, "Tell her to come in," and, when she had done so, asked her, "Was it Father that sent you?"

"It was Father who told me to bring it for you to wear," Ju-i replied.

"And did he also present you with anything, or not?" Chin-lien inquired.

"Father did provide me with two items of silk clothing to wear during the New Year's celebrations," said Ju-i. "And he also told me to come and kowtow to you."

So saying, she came forward and kowtowed to her four times.

"That is not appropriate among sisters," the woman said. "If your master has taken a fancy to you, as the saying goes:

A multitude of boats need not clog the channel,
A multitude of carts need not block the road.

Why should I go out of my way to make trouble for you? So long as you do nothing to offend me, I'll have no reason to interfere with you. I've got one shadow too many around here as it is."

"Ever since my mistress died," said Ju-i, "although the First Lady in the rear compound has taken her place, you are still the presiding mistress of the front compound, and the one I look to for support, early and late. If I presumed to take any liberties with you, where would I be when:

The fallen leaves return to the root?"[6]

"As for those items of clothing that you have received," the woman said, "you had better mention the matter to the First Lady, hadn't you?"

"I asked the First Lady for them a while ago," said Ju-i, "and she said, 'Wait until Father opens her bedroom someday, and he'll give you an item or two.'"

"So long as you have spoken to her about it, it should be all right," the woman said.

Ju-i thereupon took her leave and returned to Li P'ing-erh's quarters next door, where she found that Hsi-men Ch'ing had already gone out to the front reception hall.

Ju-i then asked Ying-ch'un, "When you went to get the keys, just now, did the First Lady have anything to say about it?"

"The First Lady asked me, 'What does Father want the keys for?'" replied Ying-ch'un. "But I didn't tell her that he wanted to give her fur coat to the Fifth Lady, but merely said, 'I don't know.' The First Lady didn't have anything further to say."

To resume our story, when Hsi-men Ch'ing went out to the reception hall, he saw that the preparations for the banquet were under way. The troupe of

Hai-yen actors, including Chang Mei, Hsü Shun, and Kou Tzu-hsiao, performers of the leading male and female roles, arrived, bearing their costume
trunk, and, along with the four boy musicians, Li Ming and company, who had
come earlier, they all proceeded to kowtow to him. Hsi-men Ch'ing directed
that food should be provided for all of them and then ordered that Li Ming
and two of the other boy musicians should perform in the front reception hall,
while Tso Shun should entertain the female guests in the rear compound.

That day, Han Tao-kuo's wife Wang Liu-erh did not attend but sent Second
Sister Shen in a sedan chair, with two boxes of gifts, accompanied by their
servant Chin-ts'ai, in order to help celebrate Meng Yü-lou's birthday. Wang
Ching escorted them back to the rear compound and sent the sedan chair on
its way. That day, Meng Yü-lou's elder sister, the wife of Han Ming-ch'uan,
and her sister-in-law, Meng the Elder's wife, from outside the city gate, also
came, as well as the wives of Fu Ming and Kan Jun, Big Sister Tuan, the wife
of Ts'ui Pen, and Pen the Fourth's wife.

Hsi-men Ch'ing was in the reception hall when he saw Tai-an escorting a
woman through the enclosed passageway who was petite in stature and was
attired in a green satin jacket over a red skirt and a blue gold lamé headband,
whose face was devoid of rouge and powder,[7] and whose two eyes were mere
slits, reminding him of the appearance of Cheng Ai-yüeh. When Hsi-men
Ch'ing asked who it was, Tai-an replied that it was the wife of Pen the Fourth.
On hearing this, Hsi-men Ch'ing had nothing further to say but went back to
the rear compound to see Yüeh-niang.

Yüeh-niang was serving tea to her guests when Hsi-men Ch'ing came in to
eat some congee and handed the keys back to her.

"What did you open her bedroom door for?" asked Yüeh-niang.

Hsi-men Ch'ing explained, "P'an the Sixth said that when you all go to attend the party at Ying the Second's place tomorrow she will be the only one
without a fur coat and would like to have Li P'ing-erh's fur coat to wear."

Yüeh-niang gave him a look and said, "You don't seem able to control your
own mouth. When she died, you were angry that anyone would even suggest
reassigning the maidservants in her quarters, but in the present case, you
haven't a word to say about disposing of her property. There is a fur coat available for her, but she refuses to wear it and adamantly insists on having this
particular coat to wear. It's lucky for you that Li P'ing-erh is dead, so you can
hanker after this fur coat of hers. If she weren't dead, you wouldn't be entitled
to do anything more than take a look at it."

With these few words, she succeeded in reducing Hsi-men Ch'ing to
silence.

Suddenly, it was reported that School Official Liu had come to return the
silver he had borrowed, and Hsi-men Ch'ing went out to the reception hall to
receive him.

Who should appear at this point but Tai-an, who came in with a calling card and said, "The household of Imperial Commissioner Wang has delivered some presents."

"What sort of presents are they?" asked Hsi-men Ch'ing.

"They are congratulatory gifts," said Tai-an, "consisting of a bolt of fabric, a jar of southern wine, and four delicacies to go with the wine."

Hsi-men Ch'ing saw that the calling card read, "Deferentially presented as a token of his respect by your kinsman and pupil Wang Ts'ai."

Hsi-men Ch'ing promptly summoned Wang Ching and told him to prepare a thank-you note in reply, award the messenger with five mace of silver, and send him on his way.

Who should appear at this point but Li Kuei-chieh, who got out of her sedan chair at the front gate, accompanied by a male servant from her establishment bearing four square boxes of gifts.

This threw Tai-an into such consternation that he offered to carry her felt bag for her, saying, "Kuei-chieh, let me escort you inside through the enclosed passageway. School Official Liu is being entertained in the reception hall."

Li Kuei-chieh, accordingly, made her way back into the rear compound through the enclosed passageway, while Lai-an carried the gift boxes into Yüeh-niang's room.

"Has Father seen these gifts, or not?" asked Yüeh-niang.

"Father is entertaining a guest and hasn't seen them yet," explained Tai-an.

"Leave the gifts in their boxes and put them in the parlor for the time being," directed Yüeh-niang.

After a while, when School Official Liu had left, Hsi-men Ch'ing came back to the master suite to have something to eat, and Yüeh-niang told him, "Li Kuei-chieh has brought some gifts for us here."

"I didn't know anything about it," said Hsi-men Ch'ing.

When Yüeh-niang told Hsiao-yü to open up the boxes, they saw that one contained molded cakes of glutinous rice flour, with a sweet stuffing, and the character for long life embossed on their surfaces; one contained molded cakes embossed with the images of the Eight Immortals and flavored with attar of roses; one contained two roast ducks; and one contained a pair of pig's trotters.

Whom should they see at this point but Li Kuei-chieh, who came out from one of the inner rooms.

Her head was adorned with pearls and trinkets,
further enhanced with a white drawnwork kerchief, and she wore a crimson jacket that opened down the middle, over a blue satin skirt. Facing Hsi-men Ch'ing, she proceeded to kowtow to him four times.

"That's enough of that," said Hsi-men Ch'ing. "What did you go to the trouble of buying these presents for?"

"Just now," said Yüeh-niang, "Kuei-chieh told me that she was afraid you were annoyed with her, but that she was not responsible for what happened. If you consider the matter, it was all her mother's fault. On the day in question, Kuei-chieh was suffering from a headache, when Wang the Third, with a bunch of followers, who was on his way to Ch'in Yü-chih's place to engage her services, happened to pass by the door of her establishment and dropped in for a cup of tea. That was when the authorities stormed in and broke up the party, but Kuei-chieh never even came out to see him."

"On that occasion you never came out to see him," said Hsi-men Ch'ing, "and on this occasion you never came out to see him. Your story simply doesn't hold water. But, on due consideration, I'm hardly in a position to control you. It's not as though the door of your Verdant Spring Bordello were piled high with baked wheat cakes, or anything like that.

> The hole in the cash has much the same shape
>> wherever you find it.

I'm really not annoyed with you."

Li Kuei-chieh remained kneeling on the floor and refused to get up, saying, "Father is right to be annoyed. But if he ever laid a hand on me, may my body rot completely away, and develop an abscess in every hair follicle. It was all the fault of my senile old dotard of a mother, who doesn't know what she's doing. She indiscriminately welcomes both the good and the bad into our place and only ends up annoying Father for no good reason."

"Well, since you're here," interjected Yüeh-niang, "you might as well make it up between you. What's the point of continuing to be annoyed?"

"You can get up," said Hsi-men Ch'ing. "I'm no longer annoyed with you, that's all."

Li Kuei-chieh, putting on a deliberate act, said, "Father, you'll have to give me a smile before I'll get up. If you refuse to give me a smile, I'll remain kneeling here for a year without getting up."

Without any warning, P'an Chin-lien interrupted from the sidelines, saying, "Kuei-chieh, you should stand up for yourself. As long as you continue to kneel there, beseeching the favor of that pip-squeak, you're only encouraging him to put on airs. At present, you may be kneeling to him here, but in the future, when he visits your establishment, he will have to kneel to you. When that happens, you should pay no attention to him."

This speech caused both Hsi-men Ch'ing and Yüeh-niang to laugh, and it was only then that Li Kuei-chieh stood up.

Who should appear at this juncture but Tai-an, who came inside in a state of obvious agitation and announced that His Honor Sung Ch'iao-nien and His Honor An Ch'en had arrived. Hsi-men Ch'ing sent for his formal clothes, put them on, and went out to welcome them.

Li Kuei-chieh then said to Yüeh-niang, "Ai-ya-ya! From now on, I'll have nothing to do with Father but will continue to be a daughter to you, Mother."

"As for those empty oaths of yours," said Yüeh-niang, "I've already heard enough of them. On two earlier occasions when he went into the quarter to visit you, you were nowhere to be found."

"My Heavens!" exclaimed Li Kuei-chieh. "You're killing me. Father never came to my place. If he ever paid a visit to my place and I allowed him to lay a hand on me, may I die an early death, and my whole body break out in abscesses. Mother, you've been taken in by a false report. It wasn't my place he visited on those two occasions but was probably that of Cheng Ai-yüeh, where he's been patronizing that young powdered face. This accusation must have been fabricated by her and been motivated by jealousy. Why else should Father be annoyed with me?"

"Each of us has her own life to live," interjected Chin-lien. "Why should she make such an accusation against you?"

"Fifth Lady," said Kuei-chieh, "you don't understand the nature of people in our profession, who are given to taking out their anger on one another."

Yüeh-niang picked up where she left off, saying, "What is the difference between you denizens of the quarter and the rest of us? We are all alike in that when we get angry with each other, the one with the most favor will trample the other underfoot."

Yüeh-niang then proceeded to provide her with a serving of tea. But no more of this.

To resume our story, when Hsi-men Ch'ing had welcomed Censor Sung Ch'iao-nien and Secretary An Ch'en into the reception hall, they exchanged greetings, and each of them affirmed his esteem by presenting him with the customary gifts of a piece of fabric and a book. Upon seeing the meticulous preparations that had been made for the banquet, they:

Expressed their gratitude without end.[8]

After the three had taken their seats in the positions appropriate for guests and host, the actors were summoned into their presence and instructed that when His Honor Ts'ai Hsiu arrived they should do their utmost to put on a good performance.

Before long, after they had consumed a serving of tea, Censor Sung Ch'iao-nien said, "Your pupil has a request that he would like to trouble you with, Ssu-ch'üan. At present, the Grand Coordinator of Shantung, Hou Meng, has just been promoted to the post of chief minister of the Court of Imperial Sacrifices. Your pupil, along with the officials of the Two Provincial Offices, would like to host a party in his honor on the thirtieth, if we could borrow your distinguished premises in order to proffer him a farewell cup of wine, since he is scheduled to leave for the capital on the second day of the coming month. But we don't know if you are willing to consent to this, or not."

"Whatever you propose, venerable sir," replied Hsi-men Ch'ing, "I will not fail to comply with your command. But I do not know how many table settings will be required."

"Your pupil has some joint contributions here," said Censor Sung Ch'iao-nien."

He then summoned an attendant and took out of his felt bag contributions from the officers of the Provincial Administration Commission and Provincial Surveillance Commission, including one from himself, making a total of twelve in all. Each person having contributed one tael, this amounted to a sum of twelve taels of silver.

"We will need," he went on to say, "one table setting of the kind intended as much for display as for eating, while, for the rest, communal seating will suffice. And you will also need to engage a troupe of actors for the occasion."

Hsi-men Ch'ing consented to the proposal and accepted the contributions, whereupon Censor Sung Ch'iao-nien got up from his place and bowed in gratitude.

In a little while, they were invited to take their seats in the great summer-house in the garden, the Hall of Assembled Vistas, where they were joined before long by the secretary of the Ministry of Revenue in charge of the Lin-ch'ing customs station, Ch'ien Lung-yeh. After greeting each other, and con-suming another serving of tea, the three officials proceeded to set out the pieces and play a board game with each other.

Censor Sung Ch'iao-nien observed that in Hsi-men Ch'ing's residence:

The buildings were spacious,
The courtyards were secluded, and
The books, paintings, and other cultural objects,
Were among the finest of the day.

He noticed that suspended in the chamber there was an antique horizontal scroll depicting four male figures holding aloft the character for long life. At the upper end of the room there was also a standing screen inlaid with mother-of-pearl, in front of which there stood an incense burner in the shape of a gilded tripod depicting the Eight Immortals bearing birthday gifts, which was several feet high and of exquisite craftsmanship. On seeing that the smoke of aloeswood incense was emerging from the mouths of the auspicious tortoise, crane, and deer depicted thereon, he went up to examine it, praising it unceasingly.

"This incense burning tripod is beautifully made, is it not?" he remarked to Hsi-men Ch'ing.

Then, turning to the other two officials, he said, "Your pupil has written to his fellow graduate Mr. Liu in Huai-an, asking him to send such a vessel to me for presentation to the venerable Ts'ai Hsiu, but it has not yet arrived. Where did you ever get such a piece, Ssu-ch'üan?"

"It was also presented to your pupil by someone from the Huai region," responded Hsi-men Ch'ing.

When this conversation ended, they continued to play at their board game. Hsi-men Ch'ing then ordered his servants to bring in two partitioned tabletop boxes of assorted delicacies and stuffed pastries, and he also called for the actors who played the male and female leads to entertain them with some southern-style songs.

"The guest of honor has not yet arrived," said Censor Sung Ch'iao-nien. "It would hardly do for him to find the faces of his hosts already flushed from drinking."

"In this cold weather," opined Secretary An Ch'en, "it will do no harm to have a cup."

It so happens that Censor Sung Ch'iao-nien had already deputed a functionary to go and extend their invitation to Prefect Ts'ai Hsiu aboard the boat he was traveling on. Around noontime, this messenger reported back that he had conveyed the invitation, and that Ts'ai Hsiu was currently playing a game of chess at the home of Minister Huang Pao-kuang of the Imperial Brickyard but would arrive shortly. Censor Sung Ch'iao-nien accordingly dismissed him but told him to remain in waiting.

As they continued to play at their board game and drink wine, Secretary An Ch'en called for the players and said to them, "Sing that song suite that begins with the tune 'A Song of Spring' to go with our wine."

Thereupon, the actor who played the *t'ieh-tan* (supporting female role) began to sing to the tune "A Song of Spring":[9]

T'ieh-tan (playing the part of Hung-niang):
    First, in order to allay your anxiety,
    Second, to thank you for your efforts,
    She has slain a sheep and provided refreshments.
    By the time you show up, everything
       will have been prepared.
    Uninvolved persons have not been invited;
    It is no party for kinfolk and neighbors;
    It is to celebrate your betrothal with Ying-ying.
    I can see that nothing in Heaven or Earth
       could make him happier,
    As he says, "I respectfully accept the invitation."[10]

To the tune "Five Offerings":

    Back and forth, he regards his image in the mirror.
    What a pedantic scholar he seems to be;
       what a foppish fellow!
    He devotes all this attention to
       slicking his hair;

Sooner or later, a fly will lose
 his footing on it.
It is so shiny that it bids fair
 to blind one's eyes.
His affectedness is enough to set
 one's teeth on edge.
What a born young gallant;
What a congenital prodigy!

TO THE TUNE "AN ORIOLE AS ALLURING AS JADE":

During your happy engagement tonight,
Remember that Ying-ying has scarcely
 had any experience.[11]
You must do everything you can to be
 tender and gentle.[12]
When entwining your necks like mandarin
 ducks under the lamplight,
Give your inamorata a real looking over.
Whether or not you are equally devoted,
The two of you can demonstrate to
 each other tonight.
Sheng (male lead):
Thank you sweetheart.
I am touched, Hung-niang, by your misplaced affection,
And your help in consummating this match.

TO THE TUNE "RELIEVING THREE HANGOVERS":

T'ieh-tan:
Tortoiseshell mats are spread; incense
 smolders in precious tripods;
Beyond the brocade curtains, the breeze
 sweeps the deserted courtyard.
Fallen red petals cover the ground,
 their rouge now cold;
On the green jade balustrade,[13] flowers
 cast their shadows.
Awaiting you are gold lamé bed curtains depicting
 mandarin ducks in the moonlight;
And folding jade screens adorned with kingfishers
 enjoying the breezes of spring.
The music of wedding bells,
Will be accompanied with phoenix flutes
 and ivory clappers,[14]
Patterned cithara and phoenix pipes.

To the same tune:

Sheng:

    Alas, I am a wayfarer with only my books and sword,[15]
      and can offer little as a betrothal gift.
    If this match should actually be consummated,
      I cannot thank you enough.
    If preparations have really been made for me to
      enjoy a wedding celebration,[16]
    I cannot but respond by plucking the cassia[17]
      in order to ensure our future.
    If we are fortunate enough to ride off together
      astride a pair of phoenixes,[18]
    Tonight you can recline while contemplating
      the Herd Boy and the Weaving Maid.[19]
    It is not mere luck that I may revel amid clustering
      pearls and kingfisher ornaments;
    And thus conclude my former routine of devotion to
      yellow scrolls under a blue lamp.[20]

Coda:

T'ieh-tan:

    My venerable mistress is anxiously awaiting you.

Sheng:

    As the saying goes, a respectful demeanor is not
      as good as obedient compliance.[21]

T'ieh-tan:

    Don't make Hung-niang come to summon you again.[22]

When they had finished singing, a docket officer suddenly came in and announced that His Honor Ts'ai Hsiu and His Honor Huang Pao-kuang had arrived. Censor Sung Ch'iao-nien promptly ordered that the table should be cleared, and, after adjusting their attire, they went out to receive their guests.

Prefect Ts'ai Hsiu was wearing a plain gown and a girdle with a plaque of gold and was accompanied by a considerable number of functionaries. He presented his calling card, which read, "Your devoted servant Ts'ai Hsiu," to Hsi-men Ch'ing, and then proceeded into the reception hall.

"This is our host, His Honor Hsi-men Ch'ing," Secretary An Ch'en said by way of introduction. "He is currently serving as a battalion commander here and is also a protégé of your venerable father in the capital."

Prefect Ts'ai Hsiu bowed to him once again, saying politely, "I have long been an admirer of yours."

"I shall owe you a return visit," responded Hsi-men Ch'ing.

When they had finished with the customary amenities, they all loosened their clothing before sitting down, while the attendants served them with tea. After chatting for some time, they took their places at the table, and Hsi-men Ch'ing directed the boy actors to stand by in order to play and sing for them. Prefect Ts'ai Hsiu occupied the seat of honor, while the other four took their places as hosts. The chef came out and carved the entrée, which was accompanied by soup and rice, and the Hai-yen actors presented the list of pieces they were prepared to perform, from which Prefect Ts'ai Hsiu selected the drama *Shuang-chung chi*, or *The Loyal Pair*.[23]

After two scenes had been performed, and:

Several rounds of wine had been consumed,

Censor Sung Ch'iao-nien called for the players of the leading male and female roles to serve them with drinks and then perform the song suite that begins with the tune "Fresh Water Song," the first line of which is:

On my proud piebald steed I depart
    the imperial capital.[24]

Prefect Ts'ai Hsiu laughed, saying, "What an appropriate choice of a piece for performance, sir. You can be said to be:

The censor on a new piebald steed;

while these three gentlemen are like:

The purple-bearded adjutant of old."[25]

"Today," said Secretary An Ch'en, "one can hardly say:

The marshall of Chiang-chou's blue gown
    is wet with tears."[26]

When he finished speaking, they all broke out laughing.

Hsi-men Ch'ing then ordered Ch'un-hung to sing the song suite the first line of which is:

At the palace gate he has presented a memorial
    about pacifying the barbarians,[27]

which made Censor Sung Ch'iao-nien as pleased as could be.

He then turned to Hsi-men Ch'ing and said, "This lad is quite adorable."

"He is one of my servants," said Hsi-men Ch'ing, "and is a native of Yang-chou."

Censor Sung Ch'iao-nien took him by the hand, asked him to pour a cup of wine for him, and rewarded him with three mace of silver, for which Ch'un-hung kowtowed to him in thanks. Truly:

The sunlight outside the window goes its way
    in a snap of the fingers;
The flower shadows in the banquet hall move
    among the revelers' seats.

No cup is drained but to the accompaniment of
    the music of pipes and song;
As, from below the steps, one hears the news
    that it is already 4:00P.M.[28]

Before anyone knew it:
        The sun began to sink in the West.[29]
When Prefect Ts'ai Hsiu became aware that it was getting late, he ordered his
attendants to fetch his outer garments, put them on, and announced his departure. The other members of the company were unable to detain him any
longer and escorted him to the front gate to see him off. Two docket officers
were immediately dispatched to deliver his table setting of mutton and wine
and a complimentary bolt of fabric to the port on the New Canal where he
was staying overnight. But no more of this.

Censor Sung Ch'iao-nien also bade Hsi-men Ch'ing farewell, saying, "I will
not bother to express my gratitude today, since we will be troubling you again
in a few days."

He and his fellow officials then got into their sedan chairs and departed.

When Hsi-men Ch'ing came back inside after seeing them off, he dismissed
the actors and enjoined them, saying, "You are engaged to come back and
perform again two days from tomorrow. Be sure to bring some of your best
singers with you. His Honor Sung Ch'iao-nien is entertaining Grand Coordinator Hou Meng that day."

"We understand," the actors replied.

Hsi-men Ch'ing then ordered that another table for a drinking party be set
up and sent Tai-an to invite Licentiate Wen to join him, and Lai-an to go and
invite Ying Po-chüeh. It was not long before they arrived, one after the other,
bowed in greeting, and took their seats, while three boy musicians stood by to
entertain them and pour the wine.

Hsi-men Ch'ing then turned to Ying Po-chüeh and said, "When your sisters-in-law attend your celebration tomorrow, have you engaged singing girls,
or vaudeville performers, for the occasion?"

"Brother," said Ying Po-chüeh, "you have a nice way of putting it. How
could a poor household like mine accommodate such numbers? I've merely
engaged two singing girls, that's all. I hope that my sisters-in-law will deign to
come by early tomorrow."

To resume our story, the two boy musicians, Cheng Ch'un and Tso Shun,
had been singing all day to entertain the ladies in the rear compound, when
Meng Yü-lou's elder sister, and her sister-in-law, Meng the Elder's wife, were
the first to get up and go.

Later on, Aunt Yang also prepared to leave, but Yüeh-niang said, "Auntie,
why don't you stay another day before going home? Nun Hsüeh has instructed
her disciples to bring a precious scroll with them, and they are going to recite
it for us tonight."

"To tell you the truth," said Aunt Yang, "I would prefer to stay, were it not for the fact that my second nephew, Yang Tsung-pao, from outside the city gate, has sent someone to invite me to his betrothal party, which is taking place tomorrow, and I would like to attend."

Thereupon, she said her farewells and departed.

Yüeh-niang kept the wives of Fu Ming and Kan Jun, along with Pen the Fourth's wife, and Big Sister Tuan, in the master suite to keep company with Sister-in-law Wu, Old Mrs. P'an, and Li Kuei-chieh, while Second Sister Shen and Big Sister Yü took turns singing song suites to entertain them, the two boy musicians having been sent off to the reception hall in the front compound. The party continued until after the lamps had been lighted, when the wives of Hsi-men Ch'ing's three employees said goodbye and left. Only Big Sister Tuan remained, and she went off to spend the night in Sun Hsüeh-o's quarters in the rear compound, while Old Mrs. P'an made her way to P'an Chin-lien's quarters. The only people left sitting in Yüeh-niang's room were Sister-in-law Wu, Li Kuei-chieh, Second Sister Shen, and the three nuns, along with Big Sister Yü, and Li Chiao-erh, Meng Yü-lou, and P'an Chin-lien.

Suddenly, they learned that Hsi-men Ch'ing's drinking party had broken up, and the page boys began to bring back the utensils, at which Chin-lien hastily withdrew and set out toward the front compound. When she arrived there, she stood silently in the dark shadows beside the postern gate, where she saw Hsi-men Ch'ing, being supported by Lai-an, as he staggered in the direction of Li P'ing-erh's quarters. When he caught sight of Chin-lien standing by the gate, he took her by the hand and accompanied her into her quarters, while Lai-an proceeded back to the master suite to turn over the goblets and chopsticks he was carrying.

Yüeh-niang, assuming that Hsi-men Ch'ing was on his way back, sent Second Sister Shen, Li Kuei-chieh, and Big Sister Yü off to Li Chiao-erh's quarters and asked Lai-an, "Has Father come with you? What's he doing in the front compound?"

"Father has retired to the Fifth Lady's quarters," replied Lai-an. "He's had enough of it for this evening."

When Yüeh-niang heard this, she became annoyed at heart and said to Meng Yü-lou, "Just look at that feckless good-for-nothing! I assumed that to-night, of all nights, when he came back inside, he would plan to go into your quarters, but instead, without anyone's knowing it, he has groped his way into that place of hers. These last few days, he has been so driven by his lecherous desires that all he wants to do is fool around with her in the front compound."

"Sister," said Meng Yü-lou, "let him fool around if he likes. If we object, it makes it look as though we give this one thing priority over everything else and are merely competing with each other for his favors. It reminds me of the punchline in that joke of Nun Wang's. After all, he has the run of all six chambers, does he not?[30] What Father lusts after in his heart is not something that you or I can control."

"It must surely have been prearranged," remarked Yüeh-niang. "Just now, upon hearing that the party up front had broken up, she took off for the front compound as though her life depended on it."

She then turned to Hsiao-yü and said, "If there is no longer anyone working in the kitchen, you can lock the ceremonial gate between the front and rear compounds for me, and then invite the three nuns to come back here, so we can listen to them recite a precious scroll for us."

She also invited Li Kuei-chieh, Second Sister Shen, Big Sister Tuan, and Big Sister Yü to rejoin them, after which, she turned to Sister-in-law Wu and explained, "I have already asked the nuns to send one of their disciples to fetch a copy of *Huang-shih nü chüan*, or *The Precious Scroll on Woman Huang*, to recite for us. It's too bad that Aunt Yang has already left today."

She then ordered Yü-hsiao to brew some good tea, but Meng Yü-lou addressed Li Chiao-erh, saying, "Let the two of us take turns providing the tea. It's not appropriate to impose a further burden on Elder Sister's staff."

Thereupon, they each went back to their own quarters and told their maid-servants to take care of the tea.

Before long, when the three nuns had come in, and a bed table had been placed on the k'ang, they seated themselves behind it, in the lotus position, while the rest of the company crowded into the room and took their seats in order to hear the recitation of the precious scroll. Yüeh-niang washed her hands and lit some incense, while Nun Hsüeh opened *The Precious Scroll on Woman Huang* and proceeded to declaim it in a loud voice as follows.[31]

I have heard tell that, although the Dharma is not subject to annihilation, it is through extinction that we achieve nirvana; although the Way is not created, it is through creation that it is negated. The dharmakāya gave rise to the eight phases of the Buddha's life; the eight phases were manifestations of the dharmakāya. The lamp of wisdom is burning brightly,[32] the better to open the doorways of this world; the mirror of the Buddha is shining clearly, in order to illuminate the paths of darkness.[33] The events of our hundred years of life elapse in an instant; the four elements that form our bodies[34] are as ephemeral as bubbles or shadows. Every day we exhaust ourselves in mundane labor; all day long we are obsessed by karmic consciousness. How can we comprehend perfect enlightenment[35] when our six senses are devoted to greed and lust? World-famous achievements[36] are merely grandiose dreams;[37] the most amazing wealth and distinction will not enable us to evade the word impermanence.[38] When we expire like wind or fire, neither the old nor the young are spared;[39] when the hills and streams are eroded away, what heroes will there be?[40] What I propose to do is: broadcast a gatha to the ten directions, summoning all eight classes of supernatural beings to the altar;[41] to save them from incineration in the burning house,[42] and give them a key to nirvana.

Nun Hsüeh Recites a Precious Scroll in the Buddhist Style

Gatha:

> Wealth and distinction, poverty and want,[43]
>   each have their causes;
> Since they are predetermined, there is no
>   reason to question them.
> If you have neglected to plant your seeds
>   during the springtime;
> It is vain to expect your barren fields to
>   produce an autumn harvest.[44]

If you assembled bodhisattvas will listen to my exposition of the Buddhist dharma, this gatha of four lines that I have just recited was bequeathed to us by a patriarch of old. How should we explain the line:

> Wealth and distinction, poverty and want,
>   each have their causes?

In the case of you bodhisattvas, you are married to a husband who is possessed of high office and ample emolument,[45] and you reside in vast courtyards and secluded mansions. You have slaves and maidservants at your beck and call and are studded with gold and decked with silver. You grew up amid nests of satin and brocade and were born amid piles of silk and gauze.[46] When you desire clothing, you have a thousand trunks of satin and brocade; when you want food, you have delicacies of every variety.[47] You are fated to bask in glory and luxury, and enjoy wealth and distinction. These are all the results of the karma accumulated in your prior lives, which has bequeathed you a solid foundation, to which you are entitled without having to ask for it. For the same reason, I am fortunate to be here promulgating the scriptures and reciting Buddha's name, as well as enjoying such delicious refreshments, thanks to your benevolent hospitality. That I am fated to fare so well is no inconsequential matter.[48] We are all predestined to be present at the Dragon Flower Assembly,[49] thanks to the good karma that we have earned during our previous lives. Had we failed to do so, it would be like neglecting to plant seeds in the springtime, only to face barren fields at the time of the autumn harvest. In such a case, where would the ripened seed-bearing fruit come from? Truly:

> Sweep clear the spirit tower of your mind,
>   the better to begin to work;
> However happy and gratified you may become,
>   do not relax your efforts.
> Struggle to wash clean the five impurities
>   along with the six senses;
> Only then will you apprehend the mysterious
>   doctrine[50] and find the truth.

The hundred years of one's human existence[51]
    vanish in the blink of an eye;
This body of ours is fated to be transformed
    into nothing but flying ashes.
Who is able during this present incarnation
    to attain true enlightenment;
To arrive at total comprehension of the need
    to revert to the noncreated?[52]

Human existence is absolutely impermanent,[53]
    gone in the space of a breath;
It resembles the sight of the red sun as it
    sinks behind the western hills.
Just like returning empty-handed after one
    traverses a hill of treasures;
Once your human life is lost,[54] it may be hard
    to recover in a myriad kalpas.[55]

When one comes to think about it, wealth and honor, glory and luxury,[56] are like snow when sprinkled with scalding water.[57] Upon careful consideration, not one of them amounts to anything; but will prove to be as evanescent as an interrupted dream. Though you may, at present, have achieved incarnation as a human being, in your heart you are distressed[58] and troubled lest, upon your death, the four elements of which you are constituted may be transformed to dust,[59] and you do not even know where what is left of your soul will be sent to suffer. If you are fearful of the revolving wheel of life and death,[60] you must resolve to take a step in order to move forward.[61]

To THE TUNE "A SINGLE MISSIVE":

Confronted with the alternatives
    of life and death,
One's days are spent sighing over
    this floating life.
Though one may have rooms full of
    boys and girls,
When death comes, one is forced to
    face it oneself.
One's life is like a spring dream,[62]
    certain to be short;
One's fate is but a wind-blown lamp[63]
    that cannot last long.[64]
When one thinks about it,
One can only be saddened;
To bring it up is enough to cause
    one's heart to break.[65]

The prolegomenon of the precious scroll says: The Buddha who reveals himself in response to cries of distress, who neither comes nor goes,[66] the supreme patriarch Amitābha, whose great vows are so vast and profound, has sworn his forty-eight vows[67] to work for the salvation of all living beings, until each and every one of them is enabled to achieve the realization of his true nature. The mind of Amitābha is ever pure, enabling him to ferry all living beings across the sea of bitterness, the great waves of the sea of bitterness, so they may attain the wonderful fruits of enlightenment. The recitation of this text will serve to alleviate sins as numerous as the sands of the Ganges; the invocation of this text will serve to augment good fortune without limit. Those who copy this text or recite it will be reborn in the Heaven of the Lotus Treasury;[68] those who either read it or hear it, upon their deaths will proceed to the Pure Land of the Western Paradise. All those who recite Buddha's name will achieve unlimited merit. Relying on his compassion, his compassion, his great compassion, commit yourselves to the Buddha, the Dharma, and the Sangha in all ten directions, sincerely paying homage to the eternal nature of the Three Jewels, for the wheel of the law turns unceasingly, to save all living beings.[69]

Gatha:

The subtle and mysterious dharma
    of utmost profundity,
Is difficult to encounter even
    in myriads of kalpas.
Now that we have heard it, and
    are able to keep it,
We wish to understand the true
    meaning of the Tathāgata.[70]

The Precious Scroll on Woman Huang
    has just been opened;
May all the Buddhas and Bodhisattvas[71]
    come down to hear it.[72]
The incense in the burner permeates
    the world of vacuity;
The sound of Buddha's names shakes
    the nine directions.

In former days, when the Han emperor governed the world, the rains were seasonable, the winds were favorable,[73] the country prospered, and the people were content,[74] which elicited the birth of a good-hearted woman, the daughter of a householder named Huang, who resided in Nan-hua district of Ts'ao-chou prefecture. She possessed well-proportioned and good-looking features and was only six years old when she determined to restrict herself to vegetarian fare,[75] and recite the Diamond Sutra, in order to repay the profound kindness of her father and mother.[76] She did this every day without fail, which moved the Bodhisattva Kuan-yin to manifest herself to her in midair. When her parents saw that she devoted herself all day long to the recitation of the sutra, they did their best to dissuade her, but she refused to comply. One day, they sought out a go-between, selected a propitious day and hour,[77] and married her off to a son-in-law, whose name was Chao Ling-fang, and who was a butcher by vocation. They remained married for twelve years, during which they gave birth to one son and two daughters. One day, Woman Huang said to her husband, "You and I have been married for twelve years and have given birth to these attractive children, but to devote ourselves solely to our mutual affection is to be eternally immersed in samsara.[78] I happen to know a little lyric, which I would persuade you to listen to, my husband. It goes as follows:

> Our fates determined that we should become
>   a couple as husband and wife.
> Although we have a son and daughters,
> Who can enable us to stave off death?
> I humbly hope that you as my husband,
> Will reach a determination like mine,
> To practice religious cultivation,
> For the rest of our natural lives.
> Our fondness for wealth and honor,
> Should be given a diminished role.
> Ceasing to long for fame and fortune,
> We should live out our allotted days.

When Chao Ling-fang had assimilated the content of the lyric, he did not feel that he could accept it. One day, he said farewell and set out for Shantung in order to purchase some pigs. Woman Huang, seeing that her husband was not at home, took her rest in a purified chamber every day, faithfully performed her ablutions, lit incense, and devoted herself to the reverent recitation of the *Diamond Sutra*.

> Chao Ling-fang, at the time, had already
>   departed for Shantung;
> While their three boys and girls were to
>   be found in the parlor.

Gatha in decasyllabic verse:

> The Woman Huang, in her western chamber,
>   bathed in perfumed water;[79]
> Changed her clothes, removed her earrings,
>   and made herself up lightly.
> Every single day, she faced toward the west,
>   burnt incense, and worshipped;
> Confronted her rosary, and precious scroll,
>   and recited the *Diamond Sutra*.

While perusing the text, before she had done,
    the incense smoke dispersed;
Reciting Buddha's name, her voice resounded,
    pervading the empty firmament.
At the gates of Hell, and the halls of Heaven,
    rays of light became manifest;
When King Yama himself, became aware of this,
    his face was suffused with joy.
"It must be that, in the realm of the living,
    a Buddhist patriarch has appeared."
Hastily calling his two underworld Assessors,
    he bade them ascertain the details.
The Assessors reported back, "Your Majesty,
    the testimony heard affirms that,
In Nan-hua district, of Ts'ao-chou prefecture,
    there is a virtuous believer;
The Woman Huang, who studies the sacred texts,
    and eats only vegetarian fare;
Whose good deeds, and meritorious austerities,
    have startled the halls of Heaven."

TO THE TUNE "SUTRA IN LETTERS OF GOLD":

On hearing these words, King Yama's heart
    was moved to respond,
And he hastily called before him a pair of
    messengers of death.
The pair of messengers speedily hastened to
    the Chao family's home.
The Woman Huang was at the time engaged in
    reading the sacred texts,
When she suddenly observed that there were
    two immortal lads before her.

RECITATION IN HEPTASYLLABIC VERSE:

Virtuous persons are summoned to the shades
    by immortal lads;
Whereas evil persons must have yakshas sent
    to summon them.
Woman Huang, while perusing her sacred text,
    quickly enquired,
"Whose young lads are you that have chosen
    to come visit me?"

The immortal lads responded to Woman Huang
    with the words,
"Good-hearted woman that you are, you need
    not be concerned.
We do not belong among the mortal denizens
    of the mundane world,
But are, rather, immortal lads who come from
    the world of shades.
At present, because you so assiduously study
    the sacred texts,
King Yama himself has sent you an invitation,
    good-hearted lady."
Upon hearing these words, Woman Huang became
    disturbed at heart,
Proceeding, one point at a time, to plead with
    the immortal lads,
"You must be looking for someone of the same
    name and surname.
Why should you be so insistent on summoning me
    before King Yama?
I am not unwilling to suffer a thousand or ten
    thousand deaths,[80]
But how can I abandon my precious boy and my
    two daughters?
My eldest daughter, Chiao-ku, is only eight
    years of age.
Pan-chiao is only five. How could she manage
    without her mother?
My precious son, Ch'ang-shou, is merely two
    years of age.
I constantly cradle him in my arms and could
    never forget him.
If you can, somehow, find a way to spare this
    soul of mine,
I undertake to perform more meritorious deeds
    on your behalf."
The immortal lads only replied to Woman Huang
    by reiterating,
"Who is there as assiduous as you in reciting
    the Diamond Sutra?"

PROSE:

The two lads responsible for recording good and evil deeds[81] were piteously pleaded
with by Woman Huang, who repeatedly expressed her reluctance[82] to proceed to the

Underworld because of her love for her three children, whom she could bear neither to leave nor to abandon. The immortal lads urged her, saying, "Good-hearted woman:

If the Underworld decides to summon you
    during the third watch;
The hour of your death cannot be delayed
    until the fourth watch.[83]

The situation is not like that in the world of the living, where deadlines can be evaded. When you are summoned by the Underworld, if the deadline is not met, we are held strictly accountable, with no room for allowances."

RECITATION IN HEPTASYLLABIC VERSE:

Woman Huang, after considering the situation
    in her heart,
Proceeded to order a maidservant to heat hot
    water for her.
No sooner did she finish bathing herself in
    perfumed water,
Than she proceeded to make her way into the
    Buddhist chapel,
Where she sat down in the lotus position and
    remained silent,
While her numinous soul's true being appeared
    before King Yama.[84]

TO THE TUNE "AUTUMN ON THE CH'U RIVER":

During the dream of mankind's life,[85]
One's allotted time is not enduring.
When faced with danger, each of us is
    but a wind-blown lamp;
In no time at all, we must return once
    more to face King Yama.
One must hastily prepare for the journey,
And gaze upon one's home from the Terrace
    of Homeward Gazing Spirits.[86]
As one's sons cry and one's daughters weep,[87]
    it is a scene of desolation.
To the tune of clanging cymbals and beating
    drums, the funeral is held;
Donning hempen garments and mourning apparel,
    one's family lays one to rest.

Rather than speaking of Chao Ling-fang's
    sense of desolation,
Let us tell of the trip of Woman Huang's
    soul to the underworld.
As she gradually approached the bank of
    the River of No Recourse,
She came to a Golden Bridge that enabled
    her to cross unharmed.
Should you enquire what the function of
    this bridge might be,
It is only for those who read sutras and
    recite Buddha's name.[88]
By the banks of the River of No Recourse
    flow waves of blood,
In which are seen the numerous drowning
    souls of sinful beings.
The sorrowful sound of their weeping and
    wailing is ever present,
As, on all sides, poisonous serpents bite
    into their exposed sinews.
As she continued, she came to the Mountain
    of Damaged Paper Money.
Woman Huang then stepped forward and asked
    to have it explained to her.
"When you inhabitants of the world of the
    living burn paper money,
And neglectfully discard it before it has
    been completely incinerated,
The remains of it are blown about, reduced
    to tattered fragments,
And are collected here to form the Mountain
    of Damaged Paper Money."
Her route then took her by the base of the
    City of the Unjustly Dead,[89]
Where there were innumerable homeless souls
    who had not yet been reborn.
When Woman Huang learned of this, her heart
    was filled with compassion,
And, lifting up her voice, she proceeded to
    recite the *Diamond Sutra*.
At this, the sinful beings in the River of No
    Recourse opened their eyes;

Lunar woods became perceptible to the corpses
    of the burned and flayed;
Lotus blossoms appeared to those in boiling
    cauldrons and lakes of fire;
And auspicious clouds, forthwith, descended
    to envelop the Avici Hell.
Thereupon, the immortal lads could not help
    feeling the pressing need,
To hasten as quickly as possible in order to
    make a report to King Yama.

To the tune "Sheep on the Mountain Slope":

When Woman Huang found herself in the
    Sen-lo Palace of King Yama,
A lad reported that they had brought the
    scripture-reading person.
King Yama decreed that she be invited
    into his presence,
And Woman Huang kowtowed to him beneath
    the golden steps,
Unable to do anything other than to
    genuflect before him.
King Yama asked, "How many years ago did you
    start to recite the *Diamond Sutra*?
And on what day, month, and year did you move
    Kuan-yin to appear before you?"
Woman Huang folded her hands in front of her
    and related the preceding events.
"Ever since I was six, I have eaten vegetarian
    fare and worshipped Her Holiness.
I hope that Your Highness will consent to
    believe me when I state that,
Since becoming married, my zeal for reciting
    the sutra has not diminished."

Recitation in heptasyllabic verse:

King Yama, upon hearing this, hastened to
    transmit an injunction,
Saying, "Good-hearted woman, pay heed to
    what I have to ask you.
How many characters are contained in the
    text of the *Diamond Sutra*?

And how many strokes are required to render
    its esoteric profundities?
With what character does it begin, and with
    what character does it end?
And what two characters are found to be
    situated at its midpoint?
If you prove capable of reciting the sutra
    without making any errors,
Your soul will be released in order to return
    to the world of the living."
Woman Huang, at this juncture, stood beneath
    the steps and replied, saying,
"I hope that Your Majesty will listen to my
    report on the *Diamond Sutra*.
The text consists of exactly five thousand
    and forty-nine characters,
Which are written with eighty-four thousand
    dots and strokes of the brush.
It commences with the character *ju*, and it
    ends with the character *hsing*.
The two characters *ho-tan* are found to be
    situated at its midpoint."
Before Woman Huang had even finished her
    explication of the sutra,
In his palace, King Yama emitted rays of
    light between his eyebrows.
Raising his hand, and evincing pleasure
    on his dragon countenance,
He stated, "Your soul is hereby released
    to return to the human world."
Upon taking in these words, Woman Huang
    hastened to respond, saying,
"I hope that Your Majesty will condescend
    to pay heed to my requests.
Firstly, I do not wish to be reincarnated
    in the home of a butcher.
Secondly, I do not wish to be reincarnated
    in the household of a dyer.
My only desire is to be reincarnated into
    the home of a good family,
Where I can spend my time reading sutras
    and reciting Buddha's name."
King Yama thereupon took up his brush and
    promptly issued a decision,

"You will be reborn as a male child in the
　　Chang family of Ts'ao-chou.
That household has accumulated a fortune
　　of considerable proportions,
But lacks a filial son to offer sacrifices
　　at the family burial ground.
The householder and his spouse are equally
　　devoted to cultivating virtue,
And their reputation for so doing is widely
　　known within the four seas."
No sooner did Woman Huang swallow a cup of
　　a soul-disorienting drug,[90]
Than the wife of householder Chang conceived
　　a male child in her belly.
Once the ten months of her pregnancy were
　　fulfilled, she bore a son,
On whose left rib cage were inscribed two
　　lines of characters in red,
Reading, "This is a reincarnation of Woman
　　Huang who recited the sutras,
And was formerly married to Chao Ling-fang,
　　who is a native of Kuan-shui.
This reincarnation is the karmic result of
　　her dedication to the sutras,
Which has enabled her to become a man who
　　is fated to live a long life."
When householder Chang had finished reading
　　this text with his own eyes,
He cherished his child as a precious jewel,[91]
　　showing his joy on his face.

TO THE TUNE "BLACK SILK ROBE":

Woman Huang was reincarnated in the home
　　of householder Chang,
Her transformation into a male having
　　occurred without a hitch.
When householder Chang beheld his son,
　　his pleasure was enhanced.
After his first three years, it became
　　clear he would grow up.
By the time he was six years old, his
　　intelligence was obvious.
He assiduously studied his lessons and
　　practiced his characters,

And took the name Chün-ta, or "Clever One."
At the age of seventeen, he earned first
    place in the examinations.

PROSE:

To resume our story, when Chang Chün-ta was in his seventeenth year, he was successful in passing the examinations and was appointed magistrate of Nan-hua district
in Ts'ao-chou prefecture. Suddenly, he recalled that this had been his native place
during his former incarnation. After going to the district to take up his office, he first
saw to the payment of the taxes owed to the government and then took his place in
the courtroom in order to preside over his jurisdiction. As his first order of business,
he dispatched two runners to summon Chao Ling-fang on the grounds that he had
something to say to him. The two runners did not dare to be remiss but went immediately to the home of Chao Ling-fang in order to summon him to court.

RECITATION IN DECASYLLABIC VERSE:

Chao Ling-fang, in his home, was reading
    sutras and reciting Buddha's name.
The two runners, greeting him with a bow,
    hastened to explain their mission.
In no time at all, he adjusted his attire,
    and accompanied them to the yamen.
Once in the courtroom, he performed a bow,
    and proceeded to identify himself.
Magistrate Chang rose and returned his bow,
    directing him to take a seat.
Exchanging amenities, they sat down as guest
    and host, while tea was served.
"You really are," he declared, "my husband,
    whose name is Chao Ling-fang;
While I am none other than your former wife,
    known by the name Woman Huang.
If you doubt me, in a quiet room, I'll undress
    so you can see for yourself.
On my left rib cage, in cinnabar characters,
    is an explanatory inscription.
Our eldest daughter, whose name is Chiao-ku,
    has already found a married home.
Our second daughter, whose name is Pan-chiao,
    is wed to a man called Ts'ao Chen.
Our son Ch'ang-shou was so concerned for me,
    that he kept vigil by my grave.
Let the two of us ride our horses together,
    to visit our ancestral tombs."

PROSE:

Magistrate Chang, together with Chao Ling-fang and their children, five persons in all, proceeded to the grave of Woman Huang, where, upon opening her coffin and examining her corpse, they found that her countenance remained unaltered. After going home, they conducted a religious service for seven days, and Chao Ling-fang declaimed the *Diamond Sutra*, whereupon, in a flutter of propitious snow,[92] all five of them, men and women, ascended to Heaven on an auspicious cloud. There is a lyric to the tune "Immortal at the River" that testifies to this:

> Woman Huang read the *Diamond Sutra* and
>   reaped the true fruit.
> That same day, mounting to paradise,
> All five of them ascended to Heaven.
> Good people, pray to Kuan-yin,
> "Bodhisattva come and save us."

PROSE:

Now that the recitation of the precious scroll is finished, the Buddhas and holy saints are aware of it. Since the dharma realm is responsive,[93] may it enable us all to ascend to the celestial assembly. Homage to the infinite significance of the Mahāyāna school of the One Vehicle, as embodied in the truly empty yet marvelously existing truth of the *Diamond Sutra*.[94] May the Buddhas in their vast assembly heed our invocation from afar, that they may enable all of us, in our multitudes as numerous as the sands of the Ganges, to proceed to the Pure Land of the Western Paradise. It is our humble wish that the sound of the recitation of the sutra and the names of the Buddhas should penetrate the halls of Heaven above and the courts of the Underworld below, with the result that those who recite the Buddha's name may be delivered from the Sea of Bitterness;[95] those who commit evil deeds may be eternally immersed in samsara; those who achieve enlightenment may be conducted on the way toward salvation by the host of Buddhas, whose rays of glory illuminate the ten directions,[96] so that, to both east and west, the fading light may return to illuminate their path,[97] to both north and south, they may be able to find their way to their true home, and attain nirvana, as their drifting boats reach the shore.[98] Like little children, they may be reunited with their mother. Upon reentering their mother's womb, they will no longer have to fear the three calamities.[99] For a myriad kalpas, they may attain eternal peace.[100]

Gatha:

> The karmic encumbrances that have been
>   produced by living beings,
> From their very nonbeginning, on down
>   until the present time,
> Have isolated them from the Sacred Peak,[101]
>   obscuring their true natures,[102]

But, a single ray of numinous light[103] can
    deliver all forms of life.

Firstly, we must repay the kindness of Heaven
    and Earth for supporting us;
Secondly, we must repay the kindness of the
    sun and moon for shining on us;
Thirdly, we must repay the kindness of our
    ruler for governing our land;
Fourthly, we must repay the kindness of our
    parents for nurturing us;
Fifthly, we must repay the kindness of our
    mentors for teaching the dharma;
Sixthly, we must pray that the ten classes of
    homeless souls may all be reborn,
And attain the perfection of wisdom, enabling
    them to reach the other shore.[104]

By the time Nun Hsüeh finished reciting the precious scroll, it was already the second watch. Even before she was done, Yüan-hsiao from Li Chiao-erh's quarters had brought out some tea and served it to the company. After it was over, Lan-hsiang from Meng Yü-lou's quarters brought out a selection of exquisitely prepared appetizers, a jug of wine, and a large container of fine tea and served them to Sister-in-law Wu, Big Sister Tuan, Li Kuei-chieh, and the rest of the company. Yüeh-niang also directed Yü-hsiao to bring out four boxes of fine pastries and sweets to go with the tea for the three nuns.

Li Kuei-chieh ventured to say, "Since our three preceptors have entertained us by reciting a precious scroll, I ought to show my gratitude by singing a song for you."

"Kuei-chieh," said Yüeh-niang, "it would be an imposition to ask you to sing once again."

Big Sister Yü said, "Let me sing something for you first."

"All right," said Yüeh-niang, "let Big Sister Yü be the first to sing."

Second Sister Shen said, "After my elder sister has sung her piece, I will also sing a song for you."

Li Kuei-chieh, however, insisted on being the first to sing and asked Yüeh-niang, "What would you like to hear?"

Yüeh-niang responded, "Sing us that set of songs that begins with the words:

Late at night, all is silent."

Thereupon, Li Kuei-chieh, after serving the company with wine, took up her balloon guitar:

    Deftly extended her slender fingers,
    Gently strummed the silken strings,

>　　　Opened her ruby lips,
>　　　Exposed her white teeth,
> and proceeded to sing to the tune "Flowers in the Moonlight":

Late at night, all is silent.
I have fumigated my bedclothes,
And waited until the moon has risen above
　　　the flowering branches.
It is as quiet as can be, and I have not
　　　heard any news at all.
Only after the watch-drums have finished
　　　beating does he appear.
Upon seeing this face of mine, he pays it
　　　no attention whatever,
But kneels down at my side to make his plea.
I deliberately pretend to be angry;
He surreptitiously gives me a look;
But before I can even clench my teeth,
I simply can't help starting to smile.

To THE SAME TUNE:

That profligate is hard at work,
Like a moth darting into the flame.
He does his best to keep me in the dark
　　　about his intentions,
But, for my part, it costs me no effort
　　　to figure them out.
Recently, however, I've had some trouble
　　　holding onto the rudder.
He's gone to such pains to manipulate me
　　　that my heart is touched,
Turning it into a honey-filled pastry.
Whoever it might be,
To say nothing of me,
Though I were made out of iron,
I might find it hard to resist.

To THE SAME TUNE:

He is altogether too untrustworthy,
My fickle lover leaves me helpless.
For two or three nights, he has failed
　　　to come back to me;
Yet, when questioned, he makes excuses
　　　and pays no attention.

I can't help thinking that, maybe, I should
   simply put up with it.
With an ingratiating smile, he proceeds to
   turn down the bedclothes,
Waiting for me, half-exposed under the covers.
I pretend to be sewing a shoe, and ignore him.
That he is so exasperated with me,
Only causes me to be angry at him.

To THE SAME TUNE:

He visits the flower lanes and willow markets,[105]
The bee go-betweens and butterfly ambassadors.[106]
While I remain here, as pure as jade and
   immaculate as ice,[107]
He is there, enjoying the sweet melons
   and honeyed apricots.
Upon returning, though sober, he pretends
   to be under the influence,
And devotes himself to beating the bushes
   to scare off the snakes.[108]
He engages in such egregious nitpicking,
That I am tempted to scratch his cheeks,
But I fear it might destroy our intimacy.
Though I may want to let him have his way,
I'm too angry to let him get away with it.[109]

When Li Kuei-chieh had finished singing, Big Sister Yü was about to take over the balloon guitar, but Second Sister Shen grabbed it away from her, hung it over her arm, and said, "I'll entertain Sister-in-law Wu and the rest of you by singing a song from a sequence on the twelve monthly festivals, to the tune "The Hanging Portrait." She then proceeded to sing the song suite that begins with the lines:

On the fifteenth day of the first month we
   celebrate the Lantern Festival,[110]
Burning so much incense that both Heaven
   and Earth seem to be on fire.

When she had finished singing, Yüeh-niang smiled and said, "We can continue to chat at our leisure. After all, the night is long enough for us to go on as long as we like."

At the time, Sister-in-law Wu was feeling fatigued by the lateness of the hour and retired without waiting to hear Big Sister Yü's performance. At this, after drinking a round of tea, the party broke up, and they all went back to their rooms to sleep. Li Kuei-chieh went back to Li Chiao-erh's quarters, Big Sister

Tuan went to Meng Yü-lou's quarters, and the three nuns went to Sun Hsüeh-o's quarters in the rear compound to spend the night. Big Sister Yü and Second Sister Shen went to bed with Yü-hsiao and Hsiao-yü in the room with the k'ang, while Yüeh-niang and Sister-in-law Wu spent the night in the bedroom of the master suite. But no more of this. Truly:

Orion is sinking, the Dipper is turning,[111]
    it is after the third watch;
The solitary hook of the waning moon[112]
    appears in the gauze window.

If you want to know the outcome of these events,
Pray consult the story related in the following chapter.

Chapter 75

CH'UN-MEI VILELY ABUSES SECOND
SISTER SHEN;
YÜ-HSIAO SPILLS THE BEANS TO
P'AN CHIN-LIEN

The newly dug graves throughout the realm
    are all those of the young;
One should start to cultivate one's virtue
    before one's hair turns gray.
The fact that death and life are important
    matters[1] must be understood;
The length of time one may suffer in Hell
    is no trivial consideration.
If one's good karma has not been built up,
    on what can one hope to rely?
Once one loses the status of a human being,[2]
    when can it ever be recovered?
The path ahead of one is cloaked in darkness,
    the thoroughfare is dangerous;
Throughout the twenty-four hours of the day
    one should bear this in mind.[3]

T HESE EIGHT LINES of verse merely reiterate the message that:
    Good will be rewarded with good,
    Evil will be rewarded with evil;[4]
    Just as shadow follows shape,[5]
    Or as valleys return an echo.
You may think that only those who:
    Assume the lotus position to practice meditation,[6]
    Will all be successful in reaping the true fruit.[7]
But even:
    Simple men and simple women,[8]
    Who cultivate piety at home,
are not precluded from achieving the Way.
    Those who worship the Buddha,
    Will benefit from his virtue;

Those who recite Buddha's name,
Will benefit from his kindness;
Those who consider the sutras,
Will grasp the Buddha's truth;
Those who practice meditation,
Will tread the Buddha's realm;
Those who achieve enlightenment,
Will exhibit the Buddha's truth.[9]

But:

There is nothing easy about it.[10]

There are many who:

Commit sin first and practice austerity later,
Or practice austerity first only to sin again.[11]

To take the case of Wu Yüeh-niang, although she received her just reward
for daily:

Honoring goodness and reciting scriptures,
Worshipping Buddha and dispensing charity,

she ought not, on the present occasion, while:

She was pregnant with a child in her womb,[12]

to have listened to the recitation of such a piece of religious literature. Although whether one is fated to be rich or poor, to enjoy a long life or a short,
or to be wise or foolish, may all be determined by the endowment one receives
from one's parents at the time of conception; nevertheless, these things may
also be affected by the environmental influences to which one is exposed during pregnancy.

In olden times, when mothers were pregnant, they did not sit in awkward
positions, or lie upon their sides, and did not listen to lascivious sounds, or
gaze upon suggestive sights.[13] They would amuse themselves with the practice
of poetry and calligraphy, or the appreciation of exotic objects of gold or jade,
and would engage blind musicians to entertain them with ancient lyrics. As a
result, when they subsequently gave birth to children of either sex, they would
be well-formed and attractive and would grow up to be clever and intelligent.
This is the mode of prenatal education prescribed by King Wen of the Chou
dynasty.[14]

On this occasion, when Wu Yüeh-niang was pregnant, she ought not to
have ordered Buddhist nuns to recite precious scrolls that dealt with the revolving wheel of life and death. Later on, this inspired an ancient Buddha to
manifest himself by:

Entering her womb and taking an abode,

only to subsequently vanish into thin air, so that she was left without an heir to
carry on the family line, which was very much to be regretted. Truly:

The path ahead of one is clothed in darkness,
    the thoroughfare is dangerous;

Throughout the twenty-four hours of the day
    one should bear this in mind.

But this is a subsequent event; having mentioned it, we will say no more about
it.

At this point, in the rear compound, once the recitation of the *Precious
Scroll on Woman Huang* was finished, everyone went back to their rooms for
the night.

Let us now return to the story of P'an Chin-lien, who had been standing for
some time beside the postern gate when she saw Hsi-men Ch'ing coming by
and, taking him by the hand, conducted him into her quarters.

When she saw that Hsi-men Ch'ing simply sat down on her bed, she asked
him, "Why aren't you taking your clothes off?"

Hsi-men Ch'ing embraced the woman and proceeded to say with an ingratiating smile, "I came expressly to tell you that I would like to spend the night
next door, and to ask you to get out the bag of sexual implements for me."

"You lousy jailbird!" the woman swore at him. "You think you can fool me
with your tricks by putting such a good face on things, do you? If I hadn't been
standing by the postern gate just now, you'd have been over there already and
would hardly have had the patience to come ask me for anything. This is
something that you and that splay-legged creature must have agreed on between you this morning, so that the two of you could go at it together. You're
merely trying to fool me with a trumped up excuse for coming over here. It's
not surprising that, a while ago, rather than sending a maidservant, you sent
her to deliver that fur coat to me, and kowtow to me into the bargain. That
lousy little splay-legged creature! Who do you take me for, that you should try
to play such tricks on me? Back when Li P'ing-erh was still alive, you may have
thought you could bury me alive, but:

    The sparrow is no longer in that nest.
I'm not jealous of the likes of her."

Hsi-men Ch'ing laughed at this, saying, "Nothing of the kind ever happened. If she had not kowtowed to you, you would have been just as critical of
her."

The woman thought to herself in silence for some time before saying, "I'll
let you go then, but I won't let you take that bag of sexual implements with
you. If you go at it with that splay-legged creature they'll get:

    Polluted and unclean,
and are likely to remain contaminated when you come to sleep with me in the
future."

"If you won't give them to me," responded Hsi-men Ch'ing, "I've come to
depend on them. What am I to do?"

After they had disputed about it for what seemed like half a day, the woman
tossed the silver clasp to him, saying, "If you insist, you can take this gadget
with you."

"I guess that will have to do," said Hsi-men Ch'ing as he tucked it into his sleeve and started to stagger outside.

"Come back here," the woman said. "I've got something to ask you. No doubt you intend to:

Sleep together all night long,

staying on the same bed the whole time, which would cause even the two maidservants to feel embarrassed. It would be better if you were to sleep together for a while, and then get her to go sleep somewhere else."

"Who intends to sleep with her all that long?" responded Hsi-men Ch'ing as he started outside.

The woman called him back again, saying, "Come over here. I've got something else to say to you. What are you in such a hurry about?"

"What else have you got to say?" asked Hsi-men Ch'ing.

"Since I'm permitting you to sleep with her," the woman said, "go ahead and sleep with her. But I won't permit you to exchange any idle gossip with her:

Emboldening her to take liberties with me.

If I ever hear anything of that kind, you had better stay away from my place, or I'll bite your balls off."

"You crazy little whore!" protested Hsi-men Ch'ing. "You're nit-picking me to death."

So saying, he headed straight for Li P'ing-erh's quarters next door.

Ch'un-mei admonished the woman, saying, "Let him go. What's the point of trying to control him that way?

The more loquacious a mother-in-law gets,

The less her daughter-in-law will listen.

After all, you don't want to end up:

Feeling resentment and harboring hostility,

toward each other. And besides, it gets in the way of our enjoying a board game together."

On the one hand, she then proceeded to tell Ch'iu-chü to lock the postern gate, while on the other, she set up a table and laid out the pieces for a board game.

"Is my mother asleep yet?" the woman asked.

"No sooner did the party break up in the rear compound," said Ch'un-mei, "than she came back to her room and went to sleep."

There in their room Ch'un-mei and her mistress sat down to their board game. But no more of this.

To resume our story, when Hsi-men Ch'ing arrived in Li P'ing-erh's quarters and lifted aside the portiere, he found that Ju-i, together with Ying-ch'un and Hsiu-ch'un, were sitting on the k'ang eating their supper. On seeing Hsi-men Ch'ing come in, they jumped to their feet in consternation.

"Go ahead and finish your supper," said Hsi-men Ch'ing.

Thereupon, he went into the parlor and sat down on a folding chair in front of Li P'ing-erh's portrait.

Before long, whom should he see but Ju-i, who came into the parlor with an ingratiating smile and said, "Father, it's cold in here. Why don't you go into the bedroom?"

Hsi-men Ch'ing pulled her onto his lap with one hand, embraced her, and gave her a kiss; after which, he went into the bedroom and sat down on the front of the bed. A pot of tea was brewing on the brazier, and Ying-ch'un promptly poured out a cup for him.

Ju-i stood beside the k'ang warming herself at the brazier, as she said, "Father, you don't seem to have had much wine today. The party in the front compound must have broken up early."

"Tomorrow," said Hsi-men Ch'ing, "I have to get an early start in order to go and pay my respects to Prefect Ts'ai Hsiu on his boat. Were that not the case, I might well have stayed a little longer."

"Father," said Ju-i, "if you'd like some more wine, I can pour some for you. The table of dishes sent out from the rear compound as an offering for my mistress, together with a flask of Chin-hua wine, are still here. We have eaten the soup and rice but did not presume to touch the wine and the other dishes, leaving them for you to enjoy."

"What you've eaten is no problem," said Hsi-men Ch'ing. "As far as something to eat for me is concerned, I don't need anything else. Just a few saucers of delicacies will do. But I don't want any of the Chin-hua wine."

He then turned to Hsiu-ch'un and said, "You take a lantern and go into the garden, to my studio in the Hidden Spring Grotto. There is a jug of grape wine there. Ask Wang Ching to get it out for you. That's the wine I'd like to drink."

Hsiu-ch'un assented, took the lantern, and set out on her errand, while Ying-ch'un hastily set up a table and got out the delicacies he had requested.

"Sister," said Ju-i, "open up the containers and let me select a delicacy or two for Father to consume with his wine."

Thereupon, under the lamplight, she chose a saucer of duck meat, a saucer of squab, a saucer of pickled herring, a saucer of lotus root and bean sprouts, a saucer of jellyfish flavored with chives, a saucer of roast chitterlings and fermented sausage, a saucer of sautéed whitebait, and a saucer of sautéed bamboo shoots flavored with potherb mustard greens. The two square containers, each holding four boxes of delicacies, were laid out on the table, and a goblet and pair of chopsticks that had been wiped clean were placed before Hsi-men Ch'ing. Before long, Hsiu-ch'un came back with the wine. After it had been opened up and heated, Ju-i poured some into a goblet and handed it to Hsi-men Ch'ing to taste. It turned out to be an incomparably fine wine of a dark red color.

Ju-i moved closer and remained standing next to the table in order to pour wine for Hsi-men Ch'ing and also personally peeled roasted chestnuts for him, to go with the wine. Ying-ch'un, who understood the situation, tactfully withdrew and went back to the kitchen, where she sat down with Hsiu-ch'un.

As soon as Hsi-men Ch'ing saw that they were alone, he had the woman sit on his knee and embraced her, as the two of them drank wine together, passing the same goblet back and forth between them.

The woman continued to peel chestnuts and put them into his mouth, while Hsi-men Ch'ing unfastened her jade-colored silk jacket that opened down the middle by undoing the buttons, removed her bodice, revealing the creamy texture of her pale and fragrant breasts, and proceeded to fondle her nipples with his hand, as he exclaimed, "My child, the one thing your daddy loves more than anything else about you is the pure whiteness of your flesh, which is just like your mistress's. When I embrace you, it feels just as though I were embracing her."

"Needless to say," Ju-i responded with a laugh, "my mistress's body was whiter than mine. It seems to me that although the Fifth Lady looks good enough, her appearance is only mediocre, her flesh displaying tints of both red and white. The color of her flesh is not as white as that of the First Lady or the Third Lady in the rear compound, though the Third Lady's skin is marred by a few pockmarks. Sun Hsüeh-o, on the other hand, is not only naturally attractive but has pure white skin and is petite in stature."

She then went on to say, "There's something else I want to bring up with you. Sister Ying-ch'un has a pin for the front of the coiffure in the shape of a Taoist goddess that she is prepared to give to me, but she would like to ask you for the gold tiger-shaped tiara that our mistress used to wear, so that she can wear it during the New Year's celebrations next month. Are you willing to let her have it?"

"If you don't have anything for the front of your coiffure," responded Hsi-men Ch'ing, "I'll have a silversmith make something out of gold for you. Your mistress's jewelry box has been taken back to the master suite by the First Lady, and I would hardly feel comfortable asking for it."

"All right," the woman said, "have another tiger-shaped tiara made for me then."

So saying, she moved in front of him and kowtowed in thanks.

After the two of them had been drinking for what seemed like half a day, Ju-i said, "Father, why not ask my sister to come share a cup of wine with us, lest she feel resentful at being left out."

Hsi-men Ch'ing then called for Ying-ch'un, but there was no response.

The woman then went back to the kitchen herself and said, "Sister, Father is calling for you."

Ying-ch'un, accordingly, went back into his presence, and Hsi-men Ch'ing told Ju-i, "Pour her a cup of wine, and pick out a few chopsticks' worth of delicacies and put them on a tray for her."

Ying-ch'un stood beside them while she consumed what had been offered to her.

"Why don't you call Sister Hsiu-ch'un to come in and have something as well," the woman said.

Ying-ch'un went off on this errand but came back and said, "She doesn't want anything to eat."

After some time, she picked up her bedding from the k'ang and headed to the kitchen to sleep, saying, "If I don't go back there, but try to sleep on the bench in the parlor, I'll freeze to death. I'm going to the kitchen to sleep on the k'ang with Hsiu-ch'un. Father's tea is on the brazier. You can pour it for him yourself."

"Sister," said Ju-i, "close the back door on your way out, so I can put the latch on it."

Ying-ch'un, carrying her bundle of bedding, then went straight back to the rear.

Meanwhile, the woman, after continuing to drink wine with Hsi-men Ch'ing for a while, put the utensils away, poured out some tea for Hsi-men Ch'ing, and put the latch on the back door.

It so happens that she had prepared a separate set of bedding for Hsi-men Ch'ing to sleep on, replete with satin and chiffon, and a pillow with an embroidered pattern, all of which had been heating on the k'ang until it was nice and warm.

The woman then asked him, "Father, do you want to sleep on the k'ang, or on the bed?"

"I'd prefer to sleep on the bed," said Hsi-men Ch'ing.

Ju-i then proceeded to bundle up the bedding and take it over to put in place on the bed. Telling Hsi-men Ch'ing that he should get into bed and take off his clothes, she helped him off with his boots. She then fetched some water, took it into the parlor, and washed her private parts, closed the door to the bedroom, and put the lampstand on a small table beside the bed, after which she took off her drawers, climbed onto the bed, and bored her way under the covers, where she and Hsi-men Ch'ing proceeded to hug and embrace each other, as they:

Lay down head to head on the same pillow.

When the woman manipulated his organ with her hand, she found that the clasp was already in place:

It was aroused and its head sprang up;
So that she was both happy and fearful.

The two of them:

Stuck out their clove-shaped tongues,

and proceeded to engage each other. When Hsi-men Ch'ing saw that she was reclining face-up on the bedding:

> Without a stitch of clothing on her,[15]

he was afraid that she would be cold and, reaching for her bodice, placed it over her chest, after which, he took her pair of feet in his two hands and started thrusting and retracting for all he was worth.

The woman was reduced to:

> Panting and puffing,

as he plunged away at her until:

> Her face was fiery red.

"This bodice was given to me by my mistress while she was still alive," she explained.

"My own darling!" exclaimed Hsi-men Ch'ing. "That's not a problem. To-morrow, I'll get half a bolt of red chiffon from the shop, which you can use to make underwear for yourself. You can also make a pair of red chiffon sleeping shoes to wear on your feet when you're indulging me."

"That would be fine," the woman said. "After you've given it to me, I'll make them up as soon as I have the time to do so."

"I happen to have forgotten," said Hsi-men Ch'ing, " how old you are this year, as well as your maiden name, and your position among your siblings. All I can remember is that your husband is surnamed Hsiung."

"His surname is Hsiung, and his full name is Hsiung Wang," the woman said. "My maiden name is Chang, and I am the fourth sibling in my genera-tion. This year I am thirty-one years old."

"It turns out then that I am one year older than you," said Hsi-men Ch'ing.

On the one hand, he continued to couple with her, while on the other, he called out to her, "Chang the Fourth, my child, if you will devote yourself wholeheartedly to serving me, when the First Lady gives birth to her child, you can be responsible for breast-feeding it. And if you are fortunate enough yourself to come up with so much as:

> A single boy or half a girl,

I'll raise your status to that of one of my concubines, so you can take over your mistress's place in the nest. What do you think of that?"

"My husband is already dead," the woman said, "and I have no relatives left on my side of the family. I will be more than happy to devote myself single-mindedly to you, Father. I am not of two minds about it, having no wish to leave your home before I die. If you deign to take pity on me, that would be wonderful."

When Hsi-men Ch'ing saw that her response was just what he fancied, he was more delighted than ever. Grasping her two snow-white legs, which were adorned with a pair of green silk shoes with an embroidered pattern, he con-tinued to alternately submerge and expose the knob of his glans. The two of them rammed away at each other, thrusting and retracting, to such effect that the woman, in her abject position, left nothing unsaid as she gave vent to her feelings:

> Groaning in a quavery voice,
> As her starry eyes grew dim.

After some time, he told her to get down on all fours and stick her two feet straight back, while he put the red satin bedspread over him and proceeded to straddle her body, as he stuck his organ into her orifice.

Under the lamplight, he took hold of her snow-white bottom and began banging away at it, as he called out, "Chang the Fourth, if you keep on crying, 'My own daddy,' without stopping, I'll come for you."

The woman, in her abject position, proceeded to raise her haunches in response to him, while:

> In a trembling voice and faint tones,
> She called out, "Daddy!" unceasingly.

They continued to play with each other for a full two-hour period before Hsi-men Ch'ing finally ejaculated. Sometime later, he pulled out his chowrie handle, and the woman took a handkerchief and wiped it off for him, after which they fell asleep in each other's arms and did not wake up until the cock crowed during the fifth watch.

The woman then began to suck him off, and Hsi-men Ch'ing said to her, "The Fifth Lady once sucked away at me for half the night, and, fearing lest I get cold, wouldn't even let me get out of bed to urinate, but swallowed it for me."

"That's no problem," the woman said. "I'll swallow it for you too, if you like."

Hsi-men Ch'ing then actually pissed a whole bladderful of his urine into the woman's mouth. The two of them continued their:

> Impassioned love-making,
> In all its myriad forms,

as they went at it together all night long.

The next day, the woman got up first, opened the door, and fetched a basin and towel for him, as Hsi-men Ch'ing put on his clothes and performed his ablutions. Upon leaving, he headed for the front compound, where he told Tai-an to dispatch two orderlies to take the gilded Eight Immortals tripod from its place of honor in the summerhouse, have a note written to accompany it, and carry it to Sung Ch'iao-nien at the office of the regional investigating censor of Shantung, where, after it had been duly delivered, he was to solicit a written reply. He also told Ch'en Ching-chi to seal up a bolt of satin brocade, and a bolt of variegated satin, and have Ch'in-t'ung stow them in a felt bag and saddle his horse for him, so he could make an early departure to go pay his respects to Prefect Ts'ai Hsiu at the port on the New Canal.

He was engaged in eating his breakfast congee in Yüeh-niang's room, when she asked him, "Are all of us expected to go to Brother Ying the Second's place today? We had better leave someone behind to look after the place. One of us sisters should remain at home to keep company with Sister-in-law Wu."

"I've already prepared five sets of presents for the occasion," said Hsi-men Ch'ing. "Yours includes a waistband, a gold pendant, and five mace of silver; while those for the other four of you consist of two mace of silver and a handkerchief apiece. All of you ought to go together. After all, my daughter Ta-chieh will be here to keep Sister-in-law Wu company. That will do just as well. I have already promised Ying the Second that all of you would come to his place for the occasion."

Yüeh-niang, upon hearing this, did not have another word to say on the subject.

Li Kuei-chieh, then, proposed to take her leave, saying, "Mother, I'm going to go home today."

"What's your hurry?" responded Yüeh-niang. "Why don't you stay over another day?"

"I have no reason to deceive you, Mother," said Li Kuei-chieh, "but my mother is not feeling well, and my elder sister is not at home, so there's no one to look after the place. Someday soon, during the first month of the coming year, I'll come and stay for a couple of days."

She then said her farewells to Hsi-men Ch'ing, while Yüeh-niang filled two food boxes with delicacies for her and presented her with a tael of silver, after which, having drunk a serving of tea, she was sent on her way.

Only then did Hsi-men Ch'ing put on his formal clothes and go out to the front compound.

Unexpectedly, P'ing-an came in and reported, "His Honor, Military Director-in-Chief Ching Chung, has come to pay you his respects."

Hsi-men Ch'ing immediately went out to welcome him into the reception hall, where they exchanged the customary amenities.

Military Director-in-Chief Ching Chung, who was attired in a round-collared robe with a mandarin square, a pair of earmuffs, and a girdle with a plaque of gold around his waist, after making his obeisance in the reception hall, said, "Not having seen you for a long time, I have been negligent in paying my respects. I have failed, thus far, to congratulate you on your lofty promotion."

"I am much obliged for your magnanimity," said Hsi-men Ch'ing. "I, too, have not yet been able to offer you my congratulations."

When they had finished expressing:

>The sentiments they had felt while apart,

they sat down in the positions of guest and host, and an attendant provided a serving of tea.

Military Director-in-Chief Ching Chung then said, "I see your fine steed is waiting for you. Where are you going?"

Hsi-men Ch'ing explained, "The prefect of Chiu-chiang, Ts'ai Hsiu, who is the ninth son of His Honor Grand Preceptor Ts'ai Ching in the capital, is passing by on his way to court. Yesterday, the regional investigating censor of Shantung, Sung Ch'iao-nien, along with Secretary An Ch'en of the Ministry of Works, Secretary Ch'ien Lung-yeh of the Ministry of Revenue, and Huang Pao-kuang from the Imperial Brickyard, borrowed my place in order to host a banquet in his honor. Since he took the trouble to present me with a calling card upon his arrival yesterday, I could hardly fail to return the courtesy by paying a call upon him. I am concerned lest he depart before I am able to do so."

"There is a request that I have come to trouble you with," said Ching Chung. "Censor Sung Ch'iao-nien's term of office will expire at the end of the year next month, and he will submit a report evaluating the performance of the local officials in his jurisdiction. I hope that I can prevail upon you to put in a good word with him on my behalf. Upon learning that he was entertained at your place yesterday, I have screwed up the courage to presume on your goodwill in this matter.

> Should I advance but an inch in my career,
> I will never dare to forget it."

"This is a good deed," responded Hsi-men Ch'ing. "Since you and I are on the best of terms, how could I fail to comply with your command? You should write out an explanatory note for me. Fortunately, he will be attending another banquet at my place the day after tomorrow, so I can speak to him in person. That would be even better."

Military Director-in-Chief Ching Chung promptly got up from his place and bowed to Hsi-men Ch'ing, saying, "I am deeply moved by your lavish generosity, I will:

> Carry rings and knot grass,[16] and never forget it."

He then went on to say, "I have already prepared a copy of my curriculum vitae for you."

So saying, he called in his clerk to get it out and presented it for Hsi-men Ch'ing's perusal with his own hands. It read as follows:

> The military director-in-chief from Shantung, and assistant commander of the left battalion of the Ch'ing-ho Guard, Ching Chung, who is thirty-one years of age, is a native of the ultramontane prefecture of T'an-chou. Owing to the military accomplishments of his ancestors, he was promoted to the post of commander of the left battalion of the said guard. Having passed the military examinations in such-and such a year, he was successively promoted to his present post as military director-in-chief of Chi-chou.

The years in which these successive promotions took place were duly enumerated.

When Hsi-men Ch'ing had finished reading this document, Ching Chung also pulled out of his sleeve a card describing the gift he proposed to give him and presented it to him, saying, "This meager gift is offered in the hope that you will consent to accept it with a smile."

When Hsi-men Ch'ing saw that the words "Two hundred piculs of white rice"[17] were written on it, he said, "Whoever heard of such a thing? This is something that I absolutely cannot accept. To do so would make a mockery of the relationship between friends."

"That is not so," responded Ching Chung. "If you refuse to accept it, Ssu-ch'üan, you can pass it on to Sung Ch'iao-nien if you like. It amounts to the same thing. How can you be so adamant in refusing to take it? If you won't accept it, I will not presume to trouble you any further."

After objecting repeatedly, Hsi-men Ch'ing finally consented to take it, saying as he did so, "I will accept it provisionally. When I have spoken to him day after tomorrow, I'll send someone to report back to you."

After the tea had been twice replenished, Military Director-in-Chief Ching Chung expressed his gratitude with a bow, got up, and departed.

When Hsi-men Ch'ing had seen him off, he instructed P'ing-an, saying, "If anyone comes to see me, simply accept their calling cards, and if you have to vacate your post at the gate for any reason, depute four orderlies to guard the gate on your behalf."

When he had finished speaking, he mounted his horse and, accompanied by Ch'in-t'ung, set off to pay his respects to Prefect Ts'ai Hsiu.

To resume our story, after Yü-hsiao had seen Hsi-men Ch'ing on his way that morning, she went over to P'an Chin-lien's quarters and said, "Fifth Lady, why did you not remain in the rear compound yesterday? Last night, the ladies all gathered there to hear Nun Hsüeh recite the *Precious Scroll on Woman Huang*, which went on until late in the evening. After it was over, the Second Lady provided the company with tea, and a maidservant from the Third Lady's quarters also served wine and appetizers, after which they listened to Li Kuei-chieh and Second Sister Shen compete in singing songs for them. It was the third watch before we were able to go to sleep.

"My mistress was really critical of you, Fifth Lady. She said that when you heard that Father's party in the front compound had broken up, you couldn't wait to head off to your own quarters; that yesterday was the eve of the Third Lady's birthday, but that you wouldn't even let him visit her quarters, you were so anxious to monopolize his favors. The Third Lady responded by saying, 'How embarrassing can you get? Who has the patience to contend for him? After all, since he has all these quarters to choose from, let him go wherever he chooses.'"

"I can hardly respond to that without resorting to obscenity!" exclaimed Chin-lien. "Has she been fucked so blind she doesn't have an aperture left to see out of? Does she really suppose that it was my quarters he slept in last night?"

"He generally does choose to frequent your quarters in the front compound," said Yü-hsiao. "Since the death of the Sixth Lady, who else's quarters should Father prefer to frequent?"

Chin-lien said:

> "Though chickens may not piddle,
> People all have to go somewhere.

When somebody dies, there's always someone to take their place."

Yü-hsiao went on to say, "My mistress is really annoyed at you for asking Father for that fur coat without consulting her. Later on, when Father went back to the master suite in order to return the keys, my mistress really gave him a hard time about it. She said, 'When Li P'ing-erh died, you were angry that anyone would even consider reassigning the maidservants in her quarters, but now, you're taking the fur coat she was so fond of, and giving it away to someone else to wear, without saying so much as a word about it.' Father protested, 'But she doesn't have a fur coat of her own to wear right now.' To which my mistress responded, 'How can you say she doesn't have a fur coat to wear? There is a fur coat available for her, but she refuses to wear it and adamantly insists on having this particular fur coat to wear. It's lucky for her that Li P'ing-erh is dead, so she can hanker after her things. If she were not dead, she could hardly presume to covet them.'"

"She should stop talking through her cunt!" exclaimed Chin-lien. "A husband has the right to do as he sees fit. Are you my mother-in-law, seeking to exert control over me? I'm monopolizing him, am I? No doubt I've managed to tie him up by the legs with a length of rope, the better to monopolize him for a while. You're just shooting off your cunt as usual."

"What I'm here to tell you," said Yü-hsiao, "you must keep to yourself. Don't let anyone else know I told you about it. Today, Li Kuei-chieh has already left for home, and my mistress is putting on her jewelry. She wanted to leave Sun Hsüeh-o at home today, to keep Sister-in-law Wu company, but Father wouldn't agree to it. He has already prepared gifts to present for the occasion and wants all five of you to go together. You ought to start getting ready to go yourself."

When she had finished speaking, Yü-hsiao headed back to the rear compound.

Chin-lien, accordingly, sat down before the mirror:

> Putting on makeup and applying powder,[18]
> Sticking flowery trinkets in her hair,

while sending Ch'un-mei to ask Meng Yü-lou, "What color of clothing are you planning to wear today?"

"Father will be annoyed if we change out of mourning garb," said Meng Yü-lou. "He wants us all to wear pale-colored clothing."

The five ladies agreed that they would wear white frets over their chignons, with pearl headbands, covered with kingfisher-blue kerchiefs of gold lamé damask. On their heads:

> Pearls and trinkets rose in piles,

while below, they wore pink silk brocade jackets that opened down the middle, over blue silk skirts. Wu Yüeh-niang alone donned a white crepe gilt-ridged cap under a sealskin toque, with a pearl headband and pearl earrings, while below, she wore an aloeswood-colored jacket of figured silk brocade emblazoned with a mandarin square, over a sand-green brocade skirt. When they were ready to set out in one large sedan chair and four small sedan chairs, which had been furnished with brass foot-warmers, accompanied by Wang Ching, Ch'i-t'ung, and Lai-an, and with orderlies shouting to clear the way, they said goodbye to Sister-in-law Wu, the three nuns, and Old Mrs. P'an and headed for Ying Po-chüeh's house to attend the full-month celebration for the birth of his son. But no more of this.

To resume our story, in Li P'ing-erh's quarters in the front compound, Ju-i and Ying-ch'un refurbished the table of delicacies that had been left over from Hsi-men Ch'ing's wine drinking the night before. They had the flask of Chin-hua wine and poured out a flask of the grape wine as well. That noon, they invited Old Mrs. P'an and Ch'un-mei to join them, as well as Big Sister Yü in order to play and sing for their entertainment. The four or five of them had forgathered there and were in the midst of enjoying their repast, but this was one of those occasions on which:

Something was bound to happen.

Ch'un-mei happened to remark, "Second Sister Shen is said to be adept at singing songs to the tune 'The Hanging Portrait.' Why don't we send someone to the rear compound and get her to come here so we can induce her to sing a song to that tune for us?"

Ying-ch'un was about to send Hsiu-ch'un on this errand, when who should appear but Ch'un-hung, who came in and started to warm himself at the brazier.

"You lousy little jailbird of a southerner!" Ch'un-mei said to him. "How come you didn't go to accompany the sedan chairs today?"

"Father deputed Wang Ching to accompany them," said Ch'un-hung, "and told me to stay home and look after the house."

"You lousy little jailbird of a southerner!" resumed Ch'un-mei. "You must be frozen, or you wouldn't have barged in here to warm yourself at the fire."

She then said to Ying-ch'un, "Pour out half a cup of wine for him to drink."

Turning back to Ch'un-hung, she went on, "When you've finished drinking it, go back to the rear compound on my behalf, and ask Second Sister Shen to come here. Tell her that I want her to sing a song for Old Mrs. P'an."

Ch'un-hung promptly finished off the wine and headed back to the rear compound. Who could have anticipated that Second Sister Shen was sitting in the master suite, together with Sister-in-law Wu, Hsi-men Ta-chieh, the three nuns, and Yü-hsiao, engaged in drinking a serving of tea flavored with coriander and sesame seeds?

Unexpectedly, they saw Ch'un-hung lift aside the portiere and come in, saying, "Second Sister Shen, the young lady in the front compound wants you to come sing a song for their entertainment."

"The young lady of the household is right here," responded Second Sister Shen. "Do you mean to say that another young lady has appeared?"

"It is Ch'un-mei from the front compound who is calling for you," said Ch'un-hung.

"What's so special about Ch'un-mei," responded Second Sister Shen, "that gives her the right to order me about? Big Sister Yü is there, who can do just as well as I can. I am singing here in order to entertain Sister-in-law Wu."

"That's all right," said Sister-in-law Wu. "Second Sister Shen, you might as well go ahead, and come back later."

Second Sister Shen simply remained sitting where she was, without making a move.

Ch'un-hung went straight back to the front compound and said to Ch'un-mei, "I summoned her, but she wouldn't come. They are all sitting there together in the master suite."

"Tell her that I'm the one calling for her," said Ch'un-mei, "then she'll come."

"I told her that it was you," said Ch'un-hung. "I said, 'It is the young lady in the front compound who is calling for you.' But she was not affected by that, saying, 'The young lady of the household is right here. Do you mean to say that another young lady has emerged out of nowhere?' I said, 'It is Ch'un-mei,' and she said, 'Since when has Ch'un-mei had the status to order me around? I'm too busy right now, singing for Sister-in-law Wu.' Sister-in-law Wu actually said, 'You might as well go ahead, and come back later,' but she refused to come."

If Ch'un-mei had not heard these words nothing might have happened, but having heard them:

The spirits of her Three Corpses became agitated;
The breaths of her Five Viscera ascended to Heaven.[19]
A spot of red appeared beside each ear, and
In an instant her cheeks turned purple.

Before anyone could stop her, like a whirlwind, she swept into the master suite, pointed her finger at Second Sister Shen, and began a tirade against her, saying, "How dare you say of me to a page boy that 'another young lady has emerged out of nowhere,' or express amazement that I should have the nerve to order you around? Are you the wife of some regional commander, that I would not dare send for? Whose cunt do you suppose I was squeezed out of, only to be sized up by the likes of you, who pronounce that I've emerged out of nowhere? As for you, you're nothing but a lousy dog-fucked blind whore, who frequents:

The doors of a thousand households,
The gates of ten thousand families.

How long have you been coming to this household, that you have the audacity to evaluate its members? And what kind of presentable song suites are you able to perform? You merely cast about with your:

> Oily mouth and canine tongue,
> Plowing the eastern ditch, and
> Harrowing the western ditch,

in search of:

> Suggestive songs and lewd tunes,
> Not worth committing to writing,

and then start:

> Assuming attitudes and putting on airs.

I don't know how many professional singing girls from the licensed quarter have performed here. What makes you so special? That whore, the wife of Han Tao-kuo, may hold you in high regard, but we here do nothing of the kind. You can repeat what I say to that whore if you like. I'm not afraid of you. You would do well to get out of here as quick as you can. Or else, like a dishonest nanny, I'll have you:

> Driven away from this door for good."

Sister-in-law Wu tried to intervene, saying, "You should stop bandying words that way immediately."

Second Sister Shen was reduced by this tirade to staring with wide-open eyes, but:

> Though she dared to be angry,
> She dared not speak.

"Ai-ya-ya!" she exclaimed in due course. "How can this young lady be so crude? I didn't say anything wrong to the servant just now that would justify such a spate of uninhibited abuse.

> If there is no room for me here,
> There are other places I can go."[20]

This only made Ch'un-mei angrier than ever, and she continued to curse her, saying, "You lousy blind whore! You're ready to be:

> Laid by every man in the street, and
> Fucked by every guy in the alley.

Since your family has been blessed with such a fine young lady as yourself, who is possessed of such a temperament, you ought hardly to spend your time begging for food and clothing in other peoples' homes, and singing for their amusement. You'd better get out of here immediately, and never come back again."

"I'm no dependent of your household," protested Second Sister Shen.

"If you were a dependent of this household," responded Ch'un-mei, "I'd have the page boys pluck the hair off your head."

Sister-in-law Wu intervened, saying, "My child. Why are you acting up this way today? You had better go back to the front compound."

Ch'un-mei simply remained where she was, without making a move.

Second Sister Shen then got down off the k'ang, weeping and wailing, said goodbye to Sister-in-law Wu, and collected her bag of clothing. She was unwilling to wait for a sedan chair, but asked Sister-in-law Wu to send P'ing-an across the street to summon Hua-t'ung, so he could escort her back to the home of Han Tao-kuo.

Ch'un-mei, having vented her spleen, then made her way back to the front compound.

After she had left, Sister-in-law Wu turned to Hsi-men Ta-chieh and Yü-hsiao and said, "She must have been drinking wine up front before coming back here. Otherwise, how could she have resorted to such offensive language? It was an embarrassment to me the way she carried on. She could just as well have allowed her to take her time in getting her things together, rather than driving her out so precipitously, and without even arranging for a page boy to escort her.

If the water is too deep, no one can cross it.

What did she expect her to do? It is really upsetting."

"They probably had been drinking up front," agreed Yü-hsiao.

To resume our story, when Ch'un-mei returned to the front compound, she was still in a fit of high dudgeon and, turning to the company assembled there, said, "I gave that lousy blind whore a piece of my mind and saw to it that she was driven out of the house forthwith. If it hadn't been for the intervention of Sister-in-law Wu, I would have given that lousy blind whore a couple of good slaps in the face. She still doesn't seem to know who I am. When I called for her, she had the nerve to put on quite a scene:

Assuming attitudes and putting on airs."

Ying-ch'un admonished her, saying:

"For every branch you chop down,
A hundred trees are threatened.

You ought to be a little more tactful. Big Sister Yü is here, and you keep ranting about blind whores."

"That's not it at all," said Ch'un-mei. "Big Sister Yü has been performing in this household for lo these many years, and all that time she has never spoken ill of anyone of whatever status, high or low. When called upon to sing, she has sung. Since when has she exhibited the nerve of this lousy blind whore, who can only perform such a limited selection of tunes? What presentable song suites does that whore know? And yet she continues to put on such outlandish airs.

Trying first this and then that,

all she can come up with are the vulgar suggestive words of tunes such as 'Sheep on the Mountain Slope' and 'Shrouding the Southern Branch,' that are scarcely fit to be performed in the best company. I no sooner heard her propose to sing such songs here than I sensed that she was trying to push Big Sister Yü aside so she could take her place."

"Something like that did happen," said Big Sister Yü. "Last night, the First Lady asked me to sing some songs, but she promptly grabbed the balloon

guitar away from me and said that she would sing first. After which, the First
Lady said, 'Big Sister Yü, let her sing first, and you can sing afterwards.'"

Big Sister Yü then went on to say, "Young lady, you ought not to hold it
against her. After all, she was not familiar with the relative standings of the
people in this household and didn't know how it was appropriate to respond to
you. Such things are not easy to understand."

"I pointed that out to her just now," said Ch'un-mei. "I told her she could
report back to that lousy whore, the wife of Han Tao-kuo. 'You can repeat my
words to her if you like,' I said. 'I'm not afraid of her.'"

"My child," protested Old Mrs. P'an, "you have no reason to get so worked
up about it."

"Let me pour out a cup of wine for my elder sister, in order to assuage her
anger," said Ju-i.

"This daughter of mine," joshed Ying-ch'un, "is prone to vent her anger
whenever she is annoyed."

She then went on to say, "Big Sister Yü, why don't you choose a set of good
songs and perform them in order to propitiate her?"

Big Sister Yü, accordingly, picked up the balloon guitar and said, "Let me
sing a set of songs for Old Mrs. P'an and the young lady to the tune 'Sheep on
the Mountain Slope' on the topic 'Ts'ui Ying-ying Makes a Fuss in Her
Boudoir.'"[21]

"You concentrate on your singing," said Ju-i, "while I pour out some
wine."

Ying-ch'un then picked up the cup of wine and offered it to Ch'un-mei,
saying, "Enough! Enough! My elder sister, although you've been angered and
annoyed, be good enough to down this cup of wine offered you by your
mother."

Ch'un-mei couldn't help laughing, as she chided Ying-ch'un, saying, "You
crazy little whore! You're playing the role of my mother again, are you?"

"Big Sister Yü," she went on to say, "don't sing those songs to the tune
'Sheep on the Mountain Slope.' Sing that set of songs to the tune 'River Water,
with Two Variations' for us."

Big Sister Yü stood up beside them and strummed her balloon guitar, as she
sang:

My flowerlike countenance and moonlike allure
    have faded completely away.
The double gates are always closed.
It is just the time when the east wind is chilly,
Fine rain sprinkles continuously, and
Fallen red petals by the thousands dot the ground.
I am too indolent to burn another coil of incense,
And reluctant to pick up my needle.

My emaciated body is cadaverous,
Beset as it is by spectral visitations.
When I reexamine the old feelings that
    we had for each other,
Sorrow weighs down the turquoise peaks
    of my painted eyebrows;
Which only serves to arouse the distaste
    of my young lover,
So that, for some time, despite the orioles and the flowers,
    I have not bothered to roll up my curtain.[22]

To THE SAME TUNE:

The courtyard, shaded by its locust trees,[23]
    is as tranquil as can be.
The plantain flowers have just opened.
I can see the orioles flying in pairs,
And the fluttering of the butterflies,
But my lover is as distant as the heavens.
Atop the tall willows cicadas are murmuring,[24]
In the limpid waves the mandarin ducks play.
As I pass before the railing,
And sit down by the poolside,
All I can hear is someone singing a
    lotus-gathering song,
Which so affects me that a myriad
    sorrows invade my breast.[25]
I pick up the handle of my delicate fan
    fashioned of fragrant silk,
On which is written half a lyric to the
    tune "The Lover's Return."

To THE SAME TUNE:

As for the steaming hot weather of the summer,
    I have managed to endure it.
A new coolness has invaded my brocade curtains.
Though lighted by flaring lantern-wicks,
And followed by the glimmer of the moon,
My shadow is all alone, with no one to address.
The migrating geese are flying toward the South;
The geese return, but my lover has not returned.[26]
Envisioning the girth of his waist, I have
    made up his winter clothing;
But I don't know where he is dallying, and
    have no reliable news of him.

I've entrusted his garments to a traveler
    to deliver to him;
But the distance is great, and the clothes
    may arrive too late.

TO THE SAME TUNE:

More than once, I have ventured to ask
    the plum blossoms,
"How emaciated have I recently become?"
They say my face has lost its fragrance,
And my emotions their jadelike quality.
I have withered before the flowering branches.
Reluctantly, I heat the kingfisher-hued quilt,
And light the incense burner night after night,
In the expectation of finding loving comfort;[27]
But my dreams are broken and my spirits upset.[28]
All night long, I am unable to sleep,
    and can find no rest;
My pillow is cold, and on top of that,
    my lamp sputters out.
All by myself, there is no one with whom
    to discuss my plight;
No matter how I try, I can't ever forget
    the love of my heart.[29]

The singing continued for the entertainment of the company. But no more of this.

When Hsi-men Ch'ing had paid his respects to Prefect Ts'ai Hsiu at the port on the New Canal, he returned home.

No sooner did he dismount at the gate than P'ing-an reported, "Today, His Honor Ho Yung-shou from the yamen sent a retainer to ask you to come there first thing in the morning. Some robbers have been arrested, and the case is scheduled for trial. Also, His Honor Hu Shih-wen, the prefect of Tung-p'ing, has sent you the gift of a hundred copies of the calendar for the coming year, and His Honor, Military Director-in-Chief Ching Chung, has sent you the gift of a freshly slaughtered pig, a jug of mung bean wine, and four packets of silver. Your son-in-law has taken charge of these things but has not ventured to write a thank-you note for them, since he is waiting for a decision from you. The messenger who brought the latter gifts is going to return this evening in order to speak to you. A return note was written for His Honor Hu Shih-wen, however, and the messenger was rewarded with a mace of silver. In addition, your kinsman Ch'iao Hung has sent you a card inviting you for a drink at his place tomorrow."

Tai-an also brought him the reply he had received from Censor Sung Ch'iao-nien, saying, "I delivered the tripod to the office of the regional investigating censor, and His Honor Sung Ch'iao-nien said that he would come to repay you for it tomorrow. He rewarded me and the two orderlies who carried it with five mace of silver and also sent you a hundred copies of the new calendar."

Hsi-men Ch'ing summoned Ch'en Ching-chi to ask what had been done with the four packets of silver and was told that they had already been delivered to the master suite.

Hsi-men Ch'ing then proceeded into the reception hall, and Ch'un-hung promptly reported his return to Ch'un-mei and company, saying, "Father has arrived home. Are you going to continue your drinking here?"

"You crazy little jailbird of a southerner!" responded Ch'un-mei. "So Father has come home. Let him do as he pleases. What's it got to do with us? Since the ladies of the household are not at home, there's no reason for him to come here."

The group of them, consequently, continued drinking and joking with each other, without venturing to make a move.

When Hsi-men Ch'ing arrived in the master suite, Sister-in-law Wu and the three nuns all got out of the way and went to sit down in another room. Yü-hsiao came forward to relieve him of his outer garments and, after he had taken a seat, set up a table in order to feed him.

Hsi-men Ch'ing then summoned Lai-hsing and told him to order table settings, saying, "On the thirtieth, Censor Sung Ch'iao-nien is going to host a party here to see off Grand Coordinator Hou Meng. On the first, we will need to sacrifice a pig and a sheep here at home in order to fulfill the vow I made after encountering the storm on my way back from the capital. And on the third, I have invited the two eunuch directors Liu and Hsüeh, along with Chou Hsiu and the others from the Regional Military Command, to attend a party in celebration of my official promotion."

When he had finished issuing these instructions, Yü-hsiao, who was standing beside him, asked, "Father, when I have set up the table for you, what kind of wine should I pour for you to drink?"

"You can serve whatever dishes you have at hand," said Hsi-men Ch'ing. "There is that mung bean wine that Military Director-in-Chief Ching Chung sent me just now. Why don't you bring it here and open it so I can see what it tastes like."

Who should appear at this juncture but Lai-an, who had come back from escorting the ladies to Ying Po-chüeh's place.

Yü-hsiao promptly brought in the wine, broke open the clay stopper, poured some of it into a goblet, and handed it to Hsi-men Ch'ing to taste. After swallowing a mouthful, he found that it was pure green in color and possessed a:

Robust and lingering flavor.[30]

"Pour some more of it for me to drink," said Hsi-men Ch'ing.

In no time at all, a repast was set out for him, and Hsi-men Ch'ing proceeded to consume it there in the master suite.

To resume our story, Lai-an, together with an orderly, took two lanterns with them and set out that evening to escort Yüeh-niang and the other ladies back home. Yüeh-niang was wearing a fur coat of white ermine over a lavender silk jacket and a kingfisher-blue skirt. Li Chiao-erh and the others wore sable coats over white satin jackets and lilac-colored brocaded skirts. It happens that when Yüeh-niang saw that Chin-lien was wearing Li P'ing-erh's fur coat, she had given Chin-lien's old coat to Sun Hsüeh-o to wear.

Upon arriving in the master suite, they all bowed to Hsi-men Ch'ing. Sun Hsüeh-o, alone, kowtowed to Hsi-men Ch'ing and, after getting to her feet, also kowtowed to Yüeh-niang. They then went into the adjacent room and paid their respects to Sister-in-law Wu and the three nuns.

Yüeh-niang then went back and sat down to chat with Hsi-men Ch'ing, saying, "When Ying the Second's wife saw that all of us had come for the occasion, she was as happy as can be. Their next-door neighbor Mrs. Ma was there, together with Ying the Elder's wife, his cousin Tu the Third's wife, and ten or so other female guests. They had engaged two singing girls for our entertainment. The baby whose birth was being celebrated has a flat head and a chubby face. The mother of the child, his concubine Ch'un-hua, looks somewhat darker and thinner than she did before. She wore a long face, like a donkey's, indicating that she is not very happy. The tension between his wife and concubine has disturbed the household, and there are not enough people to take care of it. When we were on the point of leaving, Ying the Second kowtowed to us and expressed his gratitude again and again, asking us to convey his thanks to you for your lavish gifts."

"Ch'un-hua, that preternatural slave!" scoffed Hsi-men Ch'ing. "So she actually got dressed up and came out to meet the company, did she?"

"She's got a nose and eyes like everyone else," responded Yüeh-niang. "She's not a ghost. Why shouldn't she come out to meet people?"

"As for that slave," said Hsi-men Ch'ing, "she's just like a handful of black beans, fit only to feed to a pig."

"I've had enough of that bad-mouthing of yours," said Yüeh-niang. "You act as though only concubines of yours are presentable enough to be seen in public."

Wang Ching, who was standing to one side, said, "When Master Ying the Second saw that the ladies from our household had arrived, he did not initially venture to come out and meet them but hid himself in an adjacent room and spied on them through an aperture in the window. I happened to catch him in the act and taunted him, saying, 'How shameless can you get? What are you spying at, for no good reason?' At which he chased me out, threatening me with his fist."

This induced Hsi-men Ch'ing to:

> Laugh until the slits of his eyes disappeared,

saying, "That lousy beggar! The next time he shows up, I'll really powder his face white for him."[31]

"I'll be looking out for it," laughed Wang Ching.

Yüeh-niang reprimanded him, saying, "This page boy is talking nonsense. Since when did he ever spy on us? This servant is just indulging his penchant for being:

> Bad-mouthed and evil-tongued,

for no good reason. Throughout the day, none of us saw so much as his shadow. It was only when we were about to leave that he came out and kowtowed to us."

After having stood around for a while, Wang Ching finally took himself off. Yüeh-niang then went over to the adjacent room in order to pay her respects to Sister-in-law Wu and the three nuns, and Hsi-men Ta-chieh, along with Yü-hsiao and the other maids and servants' wives, proceeded to kowtow to her.

Yüeh-niang then asked, "How is it that I don't see Second Sister Shen?"

The company remained silent until Yü-hsiao spoke up, saying, "Second Sister Shen has gone home."

"Why is it," asked Yüeh-niang, "that she failed to wait for my return, but went home before I arrived?"

Seeing that concealment was no longer possible, Sister-in-law Wu told her about the episode in which Ch'un-mei had so abused her that she felt compelled to leave.

Yüeh-niang was annoyed at this and said, "What did it matter that she refused to sing? That maidservant has been indulged to the point that:

> All the rules of propriety are turned upside down.

Why did she feel justified in abusing her, for no good reason? No wonder that in this household of ours:

> When the master is not a proper master,
> The slaves ignore the rules of conduct.

What kind of sense does that make?"

Turning to Chin-lien, she went on to say, "You really ought to exercise some control over her. You've indulged her to the point that she's lost all sense of decorum."

Chin-lien, who was standing by her side, laughed at this and said, "Whoever saw such a blind millstone-turning donkey?

> If the wind does not blow,
> The tree will not tremble.[32]

Since you frequent:

> The doors of a thousand households,
> The gates of ten thousand families,

the only reason you are privileged to be there is to sing. For someone to ask you to sing is no breach of etiquette. Who entitled her to start:

       Assuming attitudes and putting on airs?

Not to have taken her to task would only have enhanced the stink of her pretensions."

"You certainly can talk a good line," said Yüeh-niang. "But, according to your logic, she should be allowed to abuse both the good and the bad at will, and drive them out of the household, since you choose not to exercise any control over her."

"No doubt you would have me give her a few strokes of the cane on behalf of that blind whore," retorted Chin-lien.

When Yüeh-niang heard these words, her face turned bright red with anger, and she said, "If you continue to indulge her this way, in the future she'll end up alienating every one of our neighbors and relatives."

Thereupon, she got up and went to join Hsi-men Ch'ing in the other room.

"What's going on?" Hsi-men Ch'ing asked.

"You know perfectly well who it's about," replied Yüeh-niang, "since you insist on retaining such an unmannerly young lady in your household."

And she went on, thus and so, to tell Hsi-men Ch'ing all about how Ch'un-mei had abused Second Sister Shen and driven her out of the house.

Hsi-men Ch'ing merely laughed at this, saying, "Whoever told her not to sing for her? It doesn't matter though. Tomorrow, I'll just send a page boy to give her two taels of silver. That ought to placate her."

"Second Sister Shen's box is still here," said Yü-hsiao. "She didn't take it with her."

When Yüeh-niang saw that Hsi-men Ch'ing only laughed at the matter, she said, "So, you're not even going to call her on the carpet and give her a talking to, are you? It's just like you to moon around with your mouth open that way. I don't know what you find so funny about it."

When Meng Yü-lou and Li Chiao-erh saw how angry Yüeh-niang had become, they took themselves off to their own quarters, but Hsi-men Ch'ing merely continued to drink his wine.

After some time, when Yüeh-niang had gone into the inner room to change her clothes and take down her hair, she asked Yü-hsiao, "Where did these four packets of silver on top of the trunk come from?"

Hsi-men Ch'ing responded, saying, "They are the two hundred taels of silver that Military Director-in-Chief Ching Chung gave me to conduct some business for him. He wants me to employ them in approaching Censor Sung Ch'iao-nien day after tomorrow, in the hope of securing a promotion for him."

"Your son-in-law brought them in a while ago," explained Yü-hsiao, "and I put them on top of the trunk but forgot to tell you about them."

"Since they belong to someone else," said Yüeh-niang, "they should have been put away in the cabinet immediately."

Yü-hsiao, accordingly, proceeded to put them safely away in the cabinet. But no more of this.

Meanwhile, Chin-lien remained sitting in the other room, in the expectation that Hsi-men Ch'ing would rejoin her so they could go back to the front compound together. That evening, she intended to take the fertility potion that Nun Hsüeh had provided her with, and engage in intercourse with Hsi-men Ch'ing, since it was a *jen-tzu* day, which would be conducive to the conception of a male child.

When she saw that Hsi-men Ch'ing showed no sign of moving, she lifted aside the portiere and called to him, saying, "Aren't you going out to the front compound? I can't wait for you any longer, so I'll go back before you."

"My child," responded Hsi-men Ch'ing, "you can go a step ahead of me. I'll come as soon as I've finished this wine."

Chin-lien then went straight back to the front compound.

"I really don't want you to go there," said Yüeh-niang. "I've got something to say to you on the subject. The two of you seem to be as close as though you were:

> Both wearing the same pair of pants.[33]

She must think she's entitled to:

> Lord it over the world,[34]

the way she insisted on barging into my room and calling for you, the shameless good-for-nothing. As though you were his only wife, and the rest of us were not wives of his."

She then went on to rebuke Hsi-men Ch'ing, saying, "You lousy thick-skinned good-for-nothing! No wonder people find fault with you. You ought to:

> Treat everyone with the same regard.[35]

We are all your wives, after all. You ought not to favor any one of us over the others. Yet you have allowed her to monopolize you there in the front compound. Ever since you returned from the Eastern Capital, not even your shadow has chosen to spend the night with anyone in the rear compound. How can any of us help being annoyed with you? It's always wise to:

> Add a stick of fuel to the cold stove,
> As well as a stick of fuel to the hot;

but you've allowed her to completely monopolize you. As far as I'm concerned, I can make allowances for you; but it's doubtful if the others are ready to let you off the hook. Though they may not give voice to their feelings, no matter how well disposed they may seem to be, they will harbor resentment in their hearts. Today, while we were at Sister-in-law Ying the Second's place, Sister Meng the Third was unable to eat anything at all. I don't know whether she has caught a chill of some kind, or what, but she is suffering from depression and nausea. When we were about to come home, Sister-in-law Ying the Second offered her two cups of wine, but they only caused her to vomit. You really ought to go pay a visit to her quarters and see how she is."

When Hsi-men Ch'ing heard this, he remarked, "Can she really be so unhappy at heart?"

He then ordered that the utensils be cleared away and said, "I won't drink any more wine."

Thereupon, he went to Meng Yü-lou's quarters, where he found that she had already shed her outer garments and taken off her head ornaments and was lying with her clothes on sprawled over the side of the k'ang, in the process of vomiting, while Lan-hsiang was lighting the charcoal brazier on the floor.

When Hsi-men Ch'ing saw that she was groaning incessantly, he said, "My child, how are you feeling inside? Tell me all about it, and, tomorrow, I'll send for someone to examine you."

The woman said not a word in response but merely continued to vomit; at which, Hsi-men Ch'ing helped her into an upright position and sat down beside her.

Upon seeing that she was massaging her breast with both hands, he said, "My own darling, what's going on in your heart? Tell me about it."

"I'm as depressed as can be," said the woman. "Why do you bother to ask? You might as well go on about your business."

"I didn't know anything about it," said Hsi-men Ch'ing. "The First Lady told me about it just now, which was the first I knew of it."

"No wonder you didn't know about it," the woman said. "You hardly treat me as a wife of yours, after all. Why don't you go make love to the one you care about?"

Hsi-men Ch'ing, thereupon, putting an arm around her powdered neck, gave her a kiss, saying, "You crazy oily mouth! You're just making fun of me."

He then called to Lan-hsiang, saying, "Quickly, boil up some extra strong tea for your mistress to drink."

"I've already prepared tea for her," responded Lan-hsiang, and she proceeded to bring it in.

Hsi-men Ch'ing personally held a cup of it up to her mouth for her to drink, but she responded, "Let me drink it myself. There's no need for you to put yourself out that way:
Reheating your cakes and selling them hot.
There's no one competing for your services here.
The sun must have risen in the West today,
it's such a rare event for you to visit these quarters of mine. The First Lady must have put you up to it, for no good reason, and you've forced yourself to comply, no matter how bilious it makes you feel."

"You don't know," protested Hsi-men Ch'ing, "how busy I've been the last few days. What with:

Seven of this and eight of that,
I haven't had a moment of free time."

"No wonder you haven't had a moment of free time," the woman responded.
"It's obvious that the one you care about has got such a hold on you that such
outmoded goods as the rest of us have all been:
Relegated to the realm of the superfluous,
merely waiting to be called up. Perhaps ten years from now you may recollect
something about us."

Upon becoming aware that Hsi-men Ch'ing had started to nuzzle her fragrant cheek, she protested, "You're simply reeking of stale wine. Keep your
distance from me. For someone who hasn't been able to keep down so much
as a taste of:
Saffron soup or flavored water,
all day long, you can hardly expect me to be in the mood to fool around with
you."

"If you haven't had anything to eat," said Hsi-men Ch'ing, "why don't you
get your maidservant to bring us something to eat. I haven't had anything to
eat either."

"Needless to say," the woman responded, "while I'm here in such pain that
I can hardly stand it, you propose that we have something to eat. If you want
something to eat, you can go eat it somewhere else."

"Since you don't want to eat," said Hsi-men Ch'ing, "I won't venture to eat
anything either. The two of us might as well get ready to go to bed together.
Early tomorrow morning, I'll send a page boy to ask Dr. Jen to come and examine you."

"You can forget about summoning any Dr. Jen, or Dr. Li," the woman said.
"If I send for Dame Liu and take whatever medicine she prescribes, I'll be all
right."

"If you lie down," said Hsi-men Ch'ing, "and let me massage your chest for
you, I'm sure you'll feel better. You may not know it, but I'm rather good at
diagnosing ailments by feel and can:
Dispel an illness with a touch of the hand."[36]

"I'd just be wasting my breath on you!" exclaimed the woman. "Since when
could you diagnose anything?"

Hsi-men Ch'ing suddenly remembered something and explained, "Yesterday, School Official Liu gave me a gift of ten wax-encased bovine bezoar
heart-clearing pills from Kuang-tung. If you take one of them, and wash it
down with some medicinal wine, you should feel better."

He then said to Lan-hsiang, "Go ask the First Lady for some of them.
They're in a porcelain jar in the master suite. And bring a flagon of wine as
well."

"There's no need to bring any wine," said Meng Yü-lou. "I have wine here
in my quarters."

Before long, Lan-hsiang came back from the master suite with two of the pills. Hsi-men Ch'ing saw to the heating of the wine, broke off the wax coating, revealing the gold leaf on the pills inside, and looked on as Meng Yü-lou swallowed them.

He then said to Lan-hsiang, "Pour out a goblet of wine for me, and I'll take some medicine of my own."

Meng Yü-lou gave him a look, saying, "Don't be so delirious! If you want to use that medicine of yours, go to someone else's quarters to take it. What do you think you're doing here, acting up that way? No doubt, on observing that I'm not dead yet, you're bent on helping me onto the road to that destination. Despite the fact that I'm in enough pain to drive me out of my mind, you want to pester me that way. It's just like you to see fit to do so, but who has the patience to carry on with you that way?"

Hsi-men Ch'ing laughed at this, saying, "Enough! Enough! My child, I won't take any medicine then. But let the two of us go to bed together."

The woman, on the one hand, finished taking her medicine and then took off her clothes and got into bed in order to sleep with Hsi-men Ch'ing. Hsi-men Ch'ing, for his part, once underneath the quilt, proceeded to massage her creamy breasts with his hand and fondle her fragrant nipples.

Putting an arm around her powdered neck, he said, "My darling, are you feeling any better inside since taking the medicine?"

"The pain has stopped," said the woman, "but my stomach is still somewhat unsettled."

"That doesn't matter," said Hsi-men Ch'ing. "If you give it a little while to digest, it should get better."

He then went on to say, "While you were not at home today, I weighed out fifty taels of silver and gave them to Lai-hsing. Day after tomorrow, Censor Sung Ch'iao-nien is hosting a banquet here. On the first, we will need to burn paper money in order to fulfill the vow I made after encountering the storm on my way back from the capital. And on the third, we must dedicate a couple of days to entertaining people. We have received an abundance of good wishes and presents, and it would not do were we to fail to reciprocate."

"Whether you invite people or not," the woman said, "is not up to me. Day after tomorrow, on the thirtieth, I'll reckon up the accounts and have a page boy present them to you. You can then turn them over to Sister Six to take care of, if you like. It's high time for her to take a turn being responsible for them. As she herself said just the other day, 'What's the big deal? If I had to:

    Carve the eyes of a Buddhist idol,

that would be difficult. Just leave it to me.'"

"Do you actually take that little whore seriously?" said Hsi-men Ch'ing. "She may assume that she can handle it, but when she gets right down to it, she's likely to become flustered. It would be better if you waited until after these events are over, before turning the accounts over to her."

"Brother," responded Meng Yü-lou, "whoever taught you to be so disin-
genuous? And you claim not to be favoring her. This proposal of yours merely
shows where your heart really lies. Waiting until these coming affairs are finished with before turning things over to her would be the death of me. I'd
hardly have time to comb my hair first thing in the morning before the page
boys would begin:

Coming and going, one after the other,[37]

requiring me to weigh out silver and make change for them, wearing me out
completely in the process. And no matter how much trouble I took, who
would even bother to commend me for it?"

Hsi-men Ch'ing embraced her, saying, "As the saying goes:

If you manage a household for three years,
    even the dog will resent you."

As he spoke, he lifted up one of her legs and hung it over his arm, cuddling
her against his breast, while he grasped the calf of her fresh, white leg, which
was enhanced with an embroidered shoe of scarlet damask.

"My child," he said, "your daddy doesn't love anything else about you as
much as your white legs. There isn't another woman in the entire world with
such a soft, lovable pair of legs."

"What a glib-tongued good-for-nothing you are!" exclaimed the woman.
"Who can take seriously that cottony mouth of yours? You claim that there
isn't another woman in the entire world with legs like mine, do you? I don't
doubt that there are thousands, if not ten thousands, of them. Rather than
complaining that my flesh is coarse, you resort to:

Misstating wrong as right."

"My darling," said Hsi-men Ch'ing, "if I have said anything untrue, may I
die for it."

"You crazy good-for-nothing!" responded the woman. "Why swear oaths
over such a trivial matter?"

As Hsi-men Ch'ing talked with her, he proceeded to fasten the silver clasp
on his organ and insert it into her vagina.

"Just as I thought!" remarked the woman. "Your every move is directed toward this unseemly end."

She then went on to say, "Hold on a minute. I don't know if that lousy little
piece of mine took care of things, or not."

So saying, she reached under the mattress with one hand and groped out a
handkerchief with which to wipe herself.

In the process of doing so, she felt the silver clasp and said, "Whenever did
you fasten on this thing of yours, without anyone being aware of it? Take it off
immediately."

Hsi-men Ch'ing not only refused to comply but, embracing her leg, proceeded to alternately submerge and expose the knob of his glans, as he gave
himself over to a series of shallow retractions and deep thrusts. It was not long

Feeling Indisposed Meng Yü-lou Harbors Jealous Sentiments

before her vaginal secretions began to flow,[38] and his movements back and forth produced a sound like that of a dog slurping up slops.

The woman, for her part, wiped herself with the handkerchief, though her secretions flowed again after every wipe, while in her mouth she gave vent to incessant mutterings in a trembling voice, saying, "Daddy, don't try to penetrate any further. These last few days, the lumbar region of my lower back has been aching, and I've been producing a white discharge below."

"Tomorrow," said Hsi-men Ch'ing, "I'll ask Dr. Jen Hou-ch'i to prescribe a dose of a warming medication for you. You should feel better after taking it."

We will say no more for the moment about how the two of them indulged in amorous sport together, but return to the story of Wu Yüeh-niang, who continued to chat with Sister-in-law Wu and the three nuns in the master suite that evening.

The subject of how Ch'un-mei had abused Second Sister Shen came up, and Yüeh-niang was told how she had been reduced to tears, how Ch'un-mei had refused to let her wait for a sedan chair, and how she had been forced to ask Sister-in-law Wu to summon Hua-t'ung from the house across the street in order to escort her back to Han Tao-kuo's place.

"The fact is," reported Sister-in-law Wu, "that the language Ch'un-mei came out with was coarse. No matter what I said to deter her, she insisted on continuing to revile her in the most abusive language. Under the circumstances, how could she help being upset? I had not previously known that Ch'un-mei was capable of resorting to such uninhibited abuse. As I said at the time, she must have been drinking."

"The five of them had been drinking wine together in the front compound," reported Hsiao-yü.

"What an unreasonable good-for-nothing!" exclaimed Yüeh-niang. "She has clearly indulged that maidservant of hers until she is:
     Oblivious to distinctions of status,
     Assuming privileges above her station.
And yet she objects if anyone criticizes her for it. In the days to come:
     Regardless of the outcome for good or ill,
she'll end up driving everyone out of our household. What will anyone want to do with the likes of us in that case? That female singer frequents:
     The doors of a thousand households,
     The gates of ten thousand families.
The stories she has to tell about us will hardly redound to our credit. People will say that the legitimate wife in that household of Hsi-men Ch'ing's presides over a chaotic world, in which no one knows who is a master, and who is a slave. They won't assume that it's our servants who have been indulged till they lack all sense of decorum, but that it is we ourselves who are hopelessly at sea. What sort of sense does that make?"

"Let it go," suggested Sister-in-law Wu. "If my brother-in-law has nothing to say about it, what's the point of stirring up any further trouble?"

Of the events of that night there is no more to tell, as they all proceeded to return to their quarters.

The next day, Hsi-men Ch'ing got up early in the morning and went to the yamen.

P'an Chin-lien, on seeing that Yüeh-niang had prevented Hsi-men Ch'ing from spending the night with her, and that she had been unable to have intercourse with him on a *jen-tzu* day, was extremely unhappy about it. Early the next day, she had Lai-an go summon a sedan chair for her and sent Old Mrs. P'an home in it.

When Wu Yüeh-niang got up the next morning, the three nuns expressed a wish to go home, and Yüeh-niang presented each of them with a box of delicacies and five mace of silver. In addition, she promised Nun Hsüeh that she would commission her to preside over a service at her nunnery during the first month of the coming year and gave her a tael of silver in advance, asking her to purchase incense, candles, and paper money for the occasion. She also said that during the twelfth month she would send her sesame oil, white flour, polished rice, and vegetarian fare with which to feed the nuns and make offerings to Buddha.

She then served tea to them in the master suite, together with Sister-in-law Wu, and Li Chiao-erh, Meng Yü-lou, and Hsi-men Ta-chieh, whom she had previously invited.

When they were all seated, she asked Meng Yü-lou, "After you took those wax-encased pills, did your heartburn get any better?"

"This morning," replied Meng Yü-lou, "it was only after I spit up a few mouthfuls of sour-tasting fluid that I felt better."

Yüeh-niang then called for Hsiao-yü, saying that she would send her to the front compound to invite Old Mrs. P'an and the Fifth Lady to come share some pastries with them.

"Hsiao-yü is back in the kitchen, seeing to the steaming of the pastries," reported Yü-hsiao. "I'll go and invite them."

Thereupon, she went straight to Chin-lien's quarters in the front compound, where she inquired, "Why do I not see Old Mrs. P'an? The two of you are invited back to the rear compound for tea."

"I sent her home early this morning," replied Chin-lien.

"Why didn't you say anything," asked Yü-hsiao, "rather than sending her off that way without anyone being aware of it?"

"She has overstayed her welcome," said Chin-lien. "Why should she have remained any longer? She has already been here for some days, leaving that adopted niece of hers at home, without anyone to look after her. It was my idea to send her home."

"I brought a chunk of cured pork and some eggplant julienne in a sweet sauce to give her," said Yü-hsiao, "not knowing that she had already left. Fifth Lady, you can keep them for her."

So saying, she handed them over to Ch'iu-chü, who put them away in a drawer.

Yü-hsiao then went on to say to Chin-lien, "Yesterday evening, after you came back to your quarters, my mistress spoke to Father, accusing you, thus and so, of trying to:

Lord it over the world,

and saying that you and he were as close as though you were:

Both wearing the same pair of pants;

and that the way in which you monopolized Father by keeping him in the front compound, and not letting him spend any time in the rear compound, was utterly shameless. Afterwards, she sent Father to the Third Lady's quarters to spend the night. On top of that, she accused you to Sister-in-law Wu and the three nuns, of indulging Ch'un-mei to the point where she was unmannerly enough to vilely abuse Second Sister Shen. Father said that tomorrow he would send a tael of silver to Second Sister Shen to compensate her for her embarrassment."

Word for word, she recounted the entire episode to Chin-lien, and, when Chin-lien heard it, she took it to heart.

Yü-hsiao then went back to report to Yüeh-niang, saying, "Old Mrs. P'an got up early this morning and went home, but the Fifth Lady will be here shortly."

Yüeh-niang then said to Sister-in-law Wu, "You see, yesterday I directed a few words of criticism to her, and today, in a fit of temper, without saying a word to me, she has responded by sending her mother packing. My guess would be that this sister of mine is surely harboring the intention of stirring up some kind of waves over it."

At the time, Yüeh-niang thought that she was speaking in the privacy of her room, not realizing that Chin-lien had silently made her way up to the portiere leading into the parlor and had been eavesdropping there for some time.

All of a sudden, she opened her mouth and spoke, saying, "First Lady, are you saying that I sent my mother packing, and that I have been monopolizing our husband?"

"That's right," replied Yüeh-niang. "I have said that. Now, what are you going to do about it? The fact is that ever since our husband returned from the Eastern Capital, you've been monopolizing him all day long up there in the front compound, so that here in the rear compound we haven't been given so much as a glimpse of his shadow. As though you were his only wife, and the rest of us were not wives of his. When anything he does comes up for discussion, you claim that nobody else knows about it, but that you do. When Li

Kuei-chieh went home yesterday, for example, Sister-in-law Wu asked, 'Why has Li Kuei-chieh left for home after staying here for only one day? Why is my brother-in-law upset with her?' To which I responded, 'Who knows what he's upset with her about?' You then stuck your neck out and insisted on saying, 'Nobody else knows about it. I'm the only one who does.' Since you attach yourself to him all day long, how could you help being better informed than the rest of us?"

"If he didn't come to my quarters of his own volition," said Chin-lien, "are you suggesting that I keep him tied up there all day long with a length of hog-bristle rope? As though I were as wanton as all that."

"If you're not as wanton as all that," said Yüeh-niang, "how is it that yester-day, when he was sitting quietly in my room, you had the nerve to lift aside the portiere and barge into the room, telling him to accompany you to your place in the front compound, just as though you had the right to:

Lord it over the world?

How can you justify that? Our husband is the sort of man who:

Stands erect between Heaven and Earth,
Bearing hardship and enduring travail.[39]

What crime has he committed that entitles you to tie him up with a length of hog-bristle rope? You don't know your place, you lousy baggage, but at least I keep quiet about it; while you don't seem to know that:

In pressing people you should not press them too far.[40]

You surreptitiously asked our husband for Li P'ing-erh's fur coat to wear but kept it to yourself, without even coming back to the rear compound and men-tioning it to me. If everyone were to treat me that way, I might as well be rais-ing ducks in this position of mine. After all:

Even in an old-folks' home,
There is someone in charge.

But you are so close to that maidservant of yours that it is like:

A cat and a mouse sleeping together.[41]

You've indulged her to the point where she has lost all sense of decorum and continues to abuse people:

Regardless of the outcome for good or ill;

while you insist on shooting your mouth off:

Refusing to acknowledge any responsibility."[42]

"So she is a maidservant of mine," said Chin-lien. "What of it? You can beat her if you like. I've got one shadow too many around here as it is. I did ask him for that fur coat; but it wasn't because I wanted the fur coat that he unlocked the door and took a number of articles of clothing to give to someone else. Why are you not criticizing her? So you would accuse me of indulging a maidservant and being wanton, would you? But, since you have gone to such lengths to please our husband, which of us is the more wanton?"

These few words struck Yüeh-niang where it hurt, and her two cheeks turned purple, as she retorted, "So I am the one who is wanton, am I? But, no matter how you put it, I was originally a virgin when I was formally married to him and was not just some woman that he had picked up. It is the shameless man-hunter who is wanton. I am the genuine article, and not the wanton one."

Sister-in-law Wu attempted to intervene, saying, "Sister-in law, what's going on with you? There's no need for you to bandy words that way."

But no matter how hard she tried to dissuade her, the words continued to pour out of Yüeh-niang's mouth, as she said, "You've already done away with one of us, and I guess I'm next."

"Ai-ya! Ai-ya!" exclaimed Meng Yü-lou. "First Lady, how is it that you're getting so carried away with your annoyance today? You're implicating the rest of us in what you say:

Hitting a number of us with one swipe of the stick.
And whoever saw the likes of you, Sister Six? You really ought to show a little deference to the First Lady, rather than bandying words with her that way."

"As the saying goes," said Sister-in-law Wu:

"No good blows are struck when people fight;
No good words are spoken when people quarrel.[43]
When you sisters engage in these altercations, we relatives who stay with you are embarrassed. Sister-in-law, if you don't agree to desist, I will leave. If my presence means so little to you, I'll call for my sedan chair and go home."

At this, Li Chiao-erh took hold of Sister-in-law Wu in order to prevent her from leaving.

When P'an Chin-lien heard the words with which Yüeh-niang berated her, she sat down on the floor and started to roll around, giving herself a series of slaps on the face, and knocking off the fret on her head, which fell to one side.

Commencing to weep out loud, she cried, "I'm as good as dead. What good is this life of mine? Our husband may have legally:

Named articles and cited clauses,
in marrying you; but if, as you claim, I was just some woman he picked up, it would have been an easy enough matter to settle at the time. If you had waited until your husband came home and persuaded him to give me a writ of divorce, I would have had to leave, and that would have been the end of it.

In pressing people you should not press them too far."

"Just look at this trashy creature," exclaimed Yüeh-niang. "Before anyone else can even get a word out:

Her mouth is like the Huai River in spate.
And she rolls around on the floor, trying to shift the blame onto someone else. No doubt you'll wait until our husband comes home, good wife that you are, and get him to give me a hard time. You've got just such a knack for knavery, but who's afraid of you?"

In Defense of Her Shortcomings Chin-lien Throws a Tantrum

"Since you claim to be the genuine article," retorted Chin-lien, "who would dare give you a hard time?"

Yüeh-niang became even more enraged at this and said, "If you would have it that I'm not the genuine article, are you suggesting that I've been harboring a lover in this room of mine?"

"If you haven't been harboring a lover," Chin-lien retorted, "who has been harboring a lover? You'd better produce him for me."

When Meng Yü-lou saw that the altercation between them was going from bad to worse, she endeavored to pull Chin-lien to her feet, saying, "You'd better get back to the front compound."

She then continued, "Things have gotten out of hand. The two of you had better both curtail your tongues. When you wrangle with each other this way, engaging in such mutual vituperation, you make yourselves a laughingstock in the eyes of these three nuns here."

Turning to Chin-lien, she went on to say, "You get up, and I'll escort you back to the front compound."

Chin-lien, however, refused to get up until Meng Yü-lou and Yü-hsiao joined forces in dragging her to her feet and escorting her to the front compound.

Sister-in-law Wu then admonished Yüeh-niang, saying, "Sister-in-law, while you're feeling poorly in your present condition, you ought not to let yourself get so upset over things like this that are clearly of no importance. When you and your sister wives are getting along with each other:

> Happily and cheerfully,[44]

those of us who are staying over with you are able to share in your pleasure. But when you get into altercations like this and ignore our admonishments, what are we to do?"

The three nuns, seeing that things were getting out of hand, told their young disciples to finish what they were eating, wrapped up their boxes, and took their leave of Yüeh-niang, placing their palms together and saluting the company in the Buddhist fashion.

"I hope," said Yüeh-niang, "that you three reverends will not laugh at us."

"Bodhisattva," responded Nun Hsüeh, "needless to say:

> Who is there without smoke in his stove?[45]
> The fire of ignorance that resides
>   in one's heart,[46]
> Has only to be touched in order to
>   give off smoke.

It would be better if everyone were a little more accommodating. As the Buddhist Dharma expresses it:

> You must strive to maintain a cool heart,
>   like a solitary boat;
> Sweep clear the spirit tower of your mind,
>   and control yourself.

If you allow the ropes to slacken and the
  knots to grow loose;
Even a myriad guardian deities could not
  reduce you to order.[47]
If you can only:
Keep the monkey of your mind and the horse
  of your will under control,[48]
it is possible to become a Buddha or a patriarch. In taking leave of you, Bodhisattva, I would like to thank you for all the trouble I have put you to. It is
time for me to return home."

So saying, she put her palms together and saluted her twice in the Buddhist
fashion.

Yüeh-niang hurriedly bowed in return, saying, "I fear you have fared none
too well. I have been rather remiss in entertaining you. On another day, I will
send someone to deliver the supplies for the religious observances I have
commissioned."

She then turned to Hsi-men Ta-chieh and said, "Would you and the Second Lady escort our three preceptors to the gate, and look out for the dog?"

Thereupon, the three nuns were sent on their way.

Yüeh-niang then sat down to keep Sister-in-law Wu and the rest company,
saying, "This has gotten me so angry that my two arms have gone soft on me,
and my hands have turned ice-cold. All I've had to drink this morning is a
mouthful of plain tea, but it's still troubling my stomach."

"Sister-in-law," said Sister-in-law Wu, "I tried to dissuade you from letting
yourself get so worked up, but you rejected my advice. For someone in the
final month of her pregnancy, what's the point of getting so upset over a trivial
matter?"

"Sister-in-law," responded Yüeh-niang, "fortunately you have been staying
here and have seen for yourself what's been going on. Since when have I
picked a quarrel with her? This is a case of:
The curfew violator arresting the watchman.[49]
I have been all too willing to accommodate her, but she has refused to accom-
modate me. There is only one husband for all of us, but she has attempted to
completely monopolize him for herself, while:
Colluding in chicanery,[50]
with that maidservant of hers. As for her doings up front there:
There's nothing she won't do.
Things no one else would do,
She can bring herself to do.
Her conduct as a wife is utterly shameless. Though:
Her lampstand casts no light upon herself,
she's always opening her mouth to accuse others of wantonness. It seems that
whatever rival may be in her way, she will pick quarrels with all day long,

accusing her to me of being at fault, thousands of times, if not more, while acting as though she herself is:

An immaculate nun.
She is a double-dealing:
Crooked-hearted false-bellied,[51]
person, with a:
Human face but a bestial heart,[52]
who refuses to accept responsibility for what she says and does. The oaths that she takes are truly frightful. I'm going to keep my eyes peeled where she's concerned. Who knows what sort of a bad end she'll come to in the future? Fortunately, all of you here saw what she did just now with your own eyes. I had prepared to serve tea and was waiting with the best of intentions for her mother to come share it with us, when she sent her packing, without anybody being aware of it, and then, with quarrelsome intent, snuck in here to eavesdrop on me. What did she need to eavesdrop for? Does she think I'm afraid of her, or what? No doubt she'll just wait until she sees that husband of ours and then engage in:

Telling tales and embroidering on the facts,
in order to persuade him to divorce me."

"We were all in your room together," said Hsiao-yü, "standing around the brazier. "Who knows when the Fifth Lady came into the parlor and sat down to eavesdrop on us? None of us even heard the sound of her footsteps."

"She's always up to mischief of some kind," said Sun Hsüeh-o. "She wears shoes with felt soles, in order to make sure that the sound of her footsteps will not be heard. I remember, when she first entered the household, how frequently she picked quarrels with me, and bad-mouthed me to others behind my back, inciting Father to beat me those two times. And you even criticized me at the time, Mother, for being too disputatious."

"She's a past master at burying people alive," said Yüeh-niang, "and today she's doing her best to bury me alive. Didn't you see, just now, how she threw a tantrum:

Banging her head on the floor and rolling around?
Her one hope is that when Father comes back and hears about it, he'll debase me beneath her."

Li Chiao-erh laughed at this, saying, "First Lady, needless to say, that would be to turn the world upside down."

"You don't understand," said Yüeh-niang. "She is an avatar of the nine-tailed fox fairy,[53] who has already done innocent people to death. Why should she balk at doing the same to me? Do I have the physical stamina to withstand her? You have been a member of this household for all these years, but despite the fact that you were once a denizen of the licensed quarter, you have never conducted yourself like the hardened offender that she is. Just look at the way she insisted on barging into my room yesterday and calling for our husband, saying, 'Aren't you going out to the front compound? I can't wait for you any longer, so I'll go back before you.' She acted just as though our husband belonged to her alone, and that she had the right to monopolize him. I wouldn't be so upset were it not for the fact that ever since he returned from the Eastern Capital she wouldn't let him spend even a single night in the rear compound. And even when it was someone's birthday, she didn't want to let him visit her quarters. She wants to put all ten fingers into her own mouth, that's all."

"Sister-in-law," admonished Sister-in-law Wu, "try to be more patient. Since you are so frequently indisposed or in pain, this matter is not so important for you. Let him do as he pleases. It would be better for all of us if you would refrain from:

Feeling resentment and harboring hostility."

She continued admonishing her for a while, and Yü-hsiao set out some food for her, but Yüeh-niang refused to eat, saying, "I've had a headache for some time, and my stomach is feeling queasy."

She then said to Yü-hsiao, "Put out a pillow on the k'ang over there, and let me lie down for a bit."

Addressing herself to Li Chiao-erh, she went on to say, "The rest of you can keep Sister-in-law Wu company in having something to eat."

That day, Big Sister Yü also expressed a desire to go home, and Yüeh-niang directed that a gift box be filled with delicacies for her, and that she be given five mace of silver, and sent on her way.

To resume our story, Hsi-men Ch'ing had gone to the yamen that morning to preside over the trial of a criminal case, and it was not until noon that he returned home. His arrival coincided with that of the retainer from Military Director-in-Chief Ching Chung, who had come to solicit a reply for the gifts he had sent.

"Tell your master that I appreciate his lavish gifts," said Hsi-men Ch'ing, "but there is no need for him to trouble himself about it. I would like you to carry the gifts back to him until after I have succeeded in doing what he asks of me tomorrow, after which you can deliver them again."

"As long as my master has not directed me to do so," said the retainer, "I can hardly presume to take them back. If they are left here at Your Honor's place until then, it will do just as well."

"In that case," said Hsi-men Ch'ing, "express my thanks to him, and tell him that I understand the situation."

He then provided him with a reply and proposed to reward the retainer with a tael of silver.

When Hsi-men Ch'ing, subsequently, made his way back to the master suite, he found Yüeh-niang lying on the k'ang, and though he called to her for what seemed like half a day, she did not respond. When he asked the maidservants what was going on, they did not dare to tell him. He then went to Chin-lien's quarters in the front compound, where he found the woman, with her hairdo in disarray, lying down and hugging a pillow. When he asked her what was the matter, she also refused to reply.

Hsi-men Ch'ing sealed up the silver he had promised to the retainer from Military Director-in-Chief Ching Chung's place and sent him on his way, after which he went to Meng Yü-lou's quarters and asked her what had happened.

Seeing that concealment was no longer possible, Meng Yü-lou told him all about the angry altercation between Yüeh-niang and Chin-lien that had occurred earlier that morning.

This threw Hsi-men Ch'ing into such consternation that he went straight back to the master suite, pulled Yüeh-niang up from her reclining position with one hand, and said to her, "At a time like this, while you're feeling poorly in your present condition, why should you pay any attention to that little whore? What's the idea of quarreling with her for no good reason?"

"Whose words have you been listening to?" demanded Yüeh-niang. "Do you believe that it was I who picked a quarrel with her, or that I am the one who is disputatious and sought her out to pick a fight with? It was she who chose to pick a fight with me. You can ask the others if you don't believe me. This morning, with the best of intentions, I had prepared tea, and invited her mother to come share it with us; only to have her send her mother packing in a fit of temper and come barging in here, sticking her neck out in order to quarrel with me:

Rolling around and banging her head on the floor,
knocking the fret on her head to one side, and screaming like the crowd at an emperor's coronation ceremony. She did everything short of striking me in the face. If the others present had not intervened to restrain her, we might well have ended up:

Beating each other into an undifferentiated lump.[54]
She is so accustomed to taking advantage of other people for no good reason, that she expects to be able to force me to submit to her. She constantly says, 'Since you claim that your husband legally:

Named articles and cited clauses,
in marrying you, while I am just some woman he picked up, you might as well just get rid of me, so I won't be in your way any longer.' For every sentence I get out, she comes back with ten. There's no way of stopping her.

Her mouth is like the Huai River in spate.
I hardly have the physical stamina to bandy words with her. In no time at all, that:

Rascally double-crossing creature,[55]
made me so angry that my body became flaccid and feverish. As for the fetus I am carrying, whether it be a child, or a plum, or even a crown prince, it will never survive. At present, it's been so affected that it's:

Neither dead nor alive.[56]

My abdomen feels distended, and the downward pressure in my stomach is painful. My head aches, and my two arms have turned numb. I sat down on the commode for quite a while just now, but the fetus did not come out. If it had, it would have been a good thing, as I might have avoided dying with a spectral fetus in me. Tonight, I'll take a length of rope and hang myself, so you can carry on with her as you like. That way, in the future, I'll avoid the fate of Li P'ing-erh, who was done to death by her. I'm well aware that if you don't lose a wife every three years, you consider it a great misfortune."

If Hsi-men Ch'ing had not heard these words nothing might have happened, but having heard them, the more he listened the more perturbed he became.

Cuddling Yüeh-niang against his breast, he said to her, "My good sister! You've got to make allowances for that little whore. She doesn't even know the rudiments about keeping to her place. Allowing yourself to become so incensed about her isn't worth the risk. I'll go out to the front compound and give the lousy little whore a piece of my mind."

"You wouldn't dare give her a hard time," retorted Yüeh-niang, "or she'll tie you up with a length of hog-bristle rope."

"You can tell her from me," responded Hsi-men Ch'ing, "that if she provokes me, I'll give her a good kicking."

He then went on to ask Yüeh-niang, "How are you feeling inside right now? Have you had anything to eat, or not?"

"Who's had anything to eat?" replied Yüeh-niang. "Early this morning, I had just prepared tea and was waiting for her mother to come share it with us, when she barged in here and started a fight with me. Right now, my abdomen feels distended, I'm suffering from downward pressure in my stomach, my head aches, and my two arms are numb. If you don't believe me, just feel my hands. I haven't even been able to flex them for what seems like half a day."

When Hsi-men Ch'ing heard this, all he could do was stamp his feet in consternation, saying, "What are we to do? I'd better send a page boy immediately to summon Dr. Jen Hou-ch'i and have him examine you and prescribe the necessary medication. But it's late, and he won't be able to get inside the city gate before it's closed for the night."

"What's the point of summoning the likes of Dr. Jen for no good reason?" said Yüeh-niang. "Let matters take their course. If the fetus is fated to live, so be it. If it is not fated to live, let it die, which will satisfy her wishes. What good is a wife after all? She's no more than:

A layer of plaster on a wall:[57]
If you peel off one layer, there will be
another beneath it.

Once I am dead, you can raise her to the status of your legitimate wife. She's certainly intelligent enough to manage the household."

"You must be more forbearing," said Hsi-men Ch'ing. "That little whore is as expendable as a piece of stinking shit.[58] What can she do to you? Right now, if we don't invite Dr. Jen Hou-ch'i to examine you, your anger will continue to envelop the fetus, without being able to escape, either above or below. What then?"

"In that case," said Yüeh-niang, "I'll call in Dame Liu, have her examine me, and take whatever medication she prescribes. Or else, I'll get her to probe my head with two acupuncture needles, and see if that will take care of things."

"That's ridiculous," said Hsi-men Ch'ing. "What does that old whore Dame Liu know about obstetrics? I'll send a servant right away to go on horseback and invite Dr. Jen to come examine you."

"You may insist on inviting him," said Yüeh-niang. "But, even if you get him to come, I won't allow him to examine me."

Hsi-men Ch'ing chose to disregard this statement and went out to the front compound, where he summoned Ch'in-t'ung and told him, "Take a horse and proceed immediately to the home of His Honor Dr. Jen Hou-ch'i outside the city gate; and wait for him, if necessary, so that you can accompany him on the way back."

Ch'in-t'ung assented to this and, mounting a horse, took off on his errand like a cloud scudding before the wind.

Hsi-men Ch'ing returned to her room in order to look after Yüeh-niang and directed the maidservants to quickly heat some congee and serve it to her, but, though he urged her to eat the congee, she refused to eat it.

He waited there until the afternoon, when Ch'in-t'ung finally came back empty-handed and said, "His Honor Dr. Jen is currently on duty in the prefectural yamen and has not come home yet. His household is informed that we have called for him, so there is no need for us to send anyone after him tomorrow. His Honor Dr. Jen will come on his own in the morning."

Yüeh-niang, on observing that Ch'iao Hung had sent someone again and again to remind Hsi-men Ch'ing of his invitation, said to him, "Since the doctor is coming tomorrow, you might as well go ahead over to our kinsman Ch'iao Hung's place. It's late in the day already, and if you refuse to go, you can't help annoying our kinsman."

"If I go," said Hsi-men Ch'ing, "who will look after you?"

Yüeh-niang laughed at this, saying, "Just look at the state you're in! If you go, I'll be all right. In a little while, I'll pull myself together and sit down to a meal with Sister-in-law Wu. What are you so concerned about?"

Hsi-men Ch'ing instructed Yü-hsiao, "Quickly, go and invite Sister-in-law Wu to come and sit down with your mistress."

He then went on to ask, "Where is Big Sister Yü? You can get her to sing something for your mistress."

"Big Sister Yü has gone home," responded Yü-hsiao. "She ran out of patience some time ago."

"Who told her to go home?" demanded Hsi-men Ch'ing. "It would have been better for her to stick around for another day or two."

So saying, he chased after Yü-hsiao and gave her a couple of kicks.

"When she saw the way you have managed to:

Turn the whole household upside down,"

pronounced Yüeh-niang, "she wanted to go. What's that got to do with her?"

"The one who actually abused Second Sister Shen," complained Yü-hsiao, "is not the one you've chosen to kick."

Hsi-men Ch'ing pretended not to hear this and proceeded to get dressed and set out to attend the drinking party he had been invited to at Ch'iao Hung's place.

Before the first watch had begun, he returned home and went into the master suite, where he found Yüeh-niang, together with Sister-in-law Wu, Meng Yü-lou, and Li Chiao-erh, the four of them, sitting together. When Sister-in-law Wu saw Hsi-men Ch'ing come in, she promptly took herself elsewhere in the rear compound.

Hsi-men Ch'ing then asked Yüeh-niang, "Are you feeling any better by now?"

"Sister-in-law Wu," said Yüeh-niang, "joined me for a couple of mouthfuls of congee, and my abdomen is not feeling as distended as it was before. But I still have a lingering headache, and the lumbar region of my lower back is still aching."

"It doesn't matter," said Hsi-men Ch'ing. "Tomorrow, Dr. Jen Hou-ch'i will come to examine you, and if you take a couple of doses of the medication he prescribes, it should dissipate your pent-up anger and tranquilize the fetus in your womb. Then you'll be all right."

"I told you in no uncertain terms not to send for him," said Yüeh-niang, "but you went ahead and sent for him anyway. How can you be so:

Bare-faced and red-eyed,

as to invite a male physician to examine me? Just wait and see whether I'll come out to be examined tomorrow, or not."

She then went on to ask, "What did our kinsman Ch'iao Hung invite you over for anyway?"

"He indicated," said Hsi-men Ch'ing, "that ever since I came back from the Eastern Capital, he has wanted to have a chance to sit down with me; and today he went out of his way to prepare a variety of delicacies and engaged two singing girls as well. He didn't ask me over to discuss anything in particular. Later on, he also invited Censor Chu from next door to come over and help keep me company. But I was so concerned about you that I was uneasy at heart, so, after downing a few goblets of wine, I came home early."

"What a glib-tongued good-for-nothing you are!" exclaimed Yüeh-niang. "I've had enough of your:

Clever words and deceptive phrases.

You would have it that you were concerned for me, would you? Even if I
were:

A manifestation of a living Buddha,[59]

I would hardly occupy a place in your heart. I can foresee that once I am dead,
I will mean no more to you than a shard of broken crockery."

She then went on to ask, "Did our kinsman Ch'iao Hung really have nothing more to say to you?"

Only then did Hsi-men Ch'ing acknowledge the truth, saying, "At present,
our kinsman Ch'iao Hung wishes to take advantage of the new regulations to
purchase a position as an honorary official, for which he is prepared to pay
thirty taels of silver. The money is already sealed up, and he wants me to speak
to Prefect Hu Shih-wen about it. I said to him, 'That's not a problem. Yesterday, Prefect Hu Shih-wen sent me a hundred copies of the calendar for the
coming year, and I have not yet sent him a return gift. When I send the gift,
I'll send a card with it, requesting an order of appointment as an honorary official, and then turn it over to you.' He objected to this, saying that payment in
silver was the standard procedure, and that if I consented to intervene on his
behalf, it would spare him the need to spend additional money high and low,
and thus save him ten taels of silver or more."

"Since he has requested you to do so," said Yüeh-niang, "you might as well
intervene on his behalf. Have you already accepted his silver?"

"He is going to send the silver over tomorrow," said Hsi-men Ch'ing. "He
wanted to buy an additional gift for me, but I told him to forget about it. Tomorrow, I'll prepare the carcass of a pig, and a jug of wine, and send them to
Prefect Hu Shih-wen. That ought to take care of it."

Once this conversation was concluded, Hsi-men Ch'ing chose to spend the
night in the master suite.

The next day was the date on which Censor Sung Ch'iao-nien had arranged
to host a party to see off Grand Coordinator Hou Meng at Hsi-men Ch'ing's
residence. The provision of appropriate wines and comestibles for the banquet
had already been completed in the rear reception hall. The prefectural yamen
had issued summonses for thirty musicians from the two Music Offices, together with two directors and four file leaders, to report for duty at Hsi-men
Ch'ing's house early that morning. Hsi-men Ch'ing told them to stand by in
an anteroom on the eastern side of the courtyard inside the ceremonial gate
leading to the front reception hall. The troupe of Hai-yen actors were directed
to use an anteroom on the western side of the courtyard as their green room.

Who should appear at this juncture but Dr. Jen Hou-ch'i, who had gotten
up early that morning and come on horseback. Hsi-men Ch'ing promptly invited him into the reception hall and sat down with him, exchanging remarks
on the events that had occurred since they last met.

"Yesterday," said Dr. Jen, "when your esteemed servant came for me, I was
on duty at the prefectural yamen. It was only when I arrived home last evening

that I was able to read your respected summons. Today, I have made haste to come, without waiting for my carriage. May I presume to ask who it is that is not well?"

"It is my humble principal wife who is unexpectedly feeling somewhat indisposed," said Hsi-men Ch'ing. "I hope that you will be able to diagnose the problem."

In a little while, after tea had been served and they were in the process of drinking it, Dr. Jen said, "The other day, I heard about your promotion from Han Ming-ch'uan. Permit me to proffer my congratulations."

"With my meager talent, I merely occupy the position," said Hsi-men Ch'ing. "What is there to congratulate me for?"

When they had done with their tea, and Ch'in-t'ung had cleared away the cups with their raised saucers, Hsi-men Ch'ing instructed him, "Go back to the rear compound and tell the First Lady that His Honor Dr. Jen is here, and that she should prepare to receive him in the parlor."

Ch'in-t'ung assented and headed back to the rear compound, where he found Sister-in-law Wu, Li Chiao-erh, and Meng Yü-lou in the room with Yüeh-niang.

"Dr. Jen is about to come in," reported Ch'in-t'ung, "and Father has instructed me to tell you to prepare to receive him in the parlor."

Yüeh-niang sat where she was, without making a move, and said, "I told him not to summon the doctor, but he has insisted on asking this male figure to open wide his fervid eyes, and proceed to:

Holding hands and squeezing wrists,

with me, for no good reason. Who knows what else he will do. If he had invited Dame Liu instead, and I had taken a dose or two of her medicine, I would have been fine. But by insisting on:

Ringing bells and beating drums,

to expose me in this way, he's merely giving someone else's husband an opportunity to feast his eyes on me."

"First Lady," said Meng Yü-lou, "the doctor he engaged is here already. If you don't go out and see him, what do you propose to do? You can hardly just send him away."

Sister-in-law Wu also admonished her from the side, saying, "Sister-in-law, if you let him take your pulse, he may be able to ascertain the cause of your indisposition, whence it arose, and which conduits may have been affected by your anger. And if you take the medication he prescribes, it may serve to rectify the flow of your vital energy and blood, and tranquilize the fetus in your womb. If you won't let him examine you, and your husband allows you to call in Dame Liu instead, what does she know of pathology or the principles of pulse taking? And who knows what such a delay might portend?"

Only then did Yüeh-niang consent to begin combing her hair and putting on her headgear. Yü-hsiao brought over her mirror, Meng Yü-lou jumped onto the k'ang and proceeded to use a small brush to smooth the hair behind her temples, Li Chiao-erh helped attach her hair ornaments, and Sun Hsüeh-o stood by to fetch her garments. Yüeh-niang's head was adorned with six gold-headed pins and a toque. Without formally making up her face, she:

Scantily applied rouge and powder, and
Lightly painted her moth eyebrows.

From her ears were suspended two gold clove-shaped ear pendants; in front of her coiffure she wore a gold tiara representing the toad in the moon; her body was clad in a white satin jacket that opened down the middle, over a willow-yellow wide-cut drawnwork skirt that served to set off her wave-tripping silk stockings, and the upturned points of her pair of golden lotuses; while beside her skirt there hung a cachet of purple brocade, a yellow brass key, and a pair of embroidered sashes. Truly:

The immortal of Mount Lo-fu has appeared
in the mundane world;[60]
The beauty of the moon palace has emerged
from her painted hall.

If you want to know the outcome of these events,
Pray consult the story related in the following chapter.

Chapter 76

MENG YÜ-LOU ASSUAGES YÜEH-NIANG'S WRATH;

HSI-MEN CH'ING REPUDIATES LICENTIATE WEN

> Before deciding upon appropriate action,
>   one must think thrice;
> So as to avoid being the author of one's
>   own dissatisfactions.
> For humans residing in this world the wind
>   and waves are dangerous;
> Wind and waves arise throughout the twenty-
>   four hours of the day.[1]

THE STORY GOES that when Hsi-men Ch'ing saw that Yüeh-niang had not come out for what seemed like half a day, he went into her bedroom himself and urged her to do so. Upon seeing that she was in the process of getting dressed, he went back out and invited Dr. Jen Hou-ch'i to come in and take a seat in the parlor of the master suite. Once there, Dr. Jen observed that the upper end of the room was concealed by a gold-flecked hanging screen, beside which there were arrayed wide benches provided with cushions, while the floor was covered with carpets, and there was a brazier in place.

Before long, Yüeh-niang emerged from her bedroom. Behold:

> She is petite in stature,
> With a round visage, and
> A clear off-white complexion.
> Her figure is neither plump nor thin,
> Her stature is neither short nor tall.
> Her eyebrows are like crescent moons;
> Her phoenix eyes are slender and long.
> Her graceful fingers reveal the jade of
>   Consort Chen of the Wei;[2]
> Her ruby lips display the cloves of the
>   Han dynasty Secretariat.[3]

When she approached him and bowed in greeting, Dr. Jen was thrown into such consternation that he stepped deferentially aside and bent low in response to her salutation. Yüeh-niang then sat down facing him, while Ch'int'ung placed a table with a brocade cushion in front of her, and she:

> Stretched out her jade wrist,
> Revealed her slender fingers,

and directed Dr. Jen to take her pulse. After an appropriate time, Yüeh-niang withdrew and returned to her room, from which she sent a page boy out with a serving of tea.

When he had finished his tea, Dr. Jen said, "Your venerable lady's symptoms reveal that her vital energy and blood circulation are weak, and the pulse at her wrist is floating and rough. Though she possesses fetal energy, its constructive and defensive elements are imbalanced, which is conducive to anger, and has stirred up the fire in her liver. At present, her head and eyes are unclear, and her abdominal duct is somewhat obstructed, resulting in a state of depression. In her four limbs, there is a deficiency of blood and an excess of energy."

Yüeh-niang sent Ch'in-t'ung out to report, "Right now, Mother is suffering from headache and heart distention. Her arms feel numb, the downward pressure in her abdomen is painful, the lumbar region of her lower back is aching, and:

She cannot taste what she eats and drinks."[4]

"I am already aware of these symptoms," said Dr. Jen, "and have clearly described them."

"I will not conceal from you, Hou-ch'i," said Hsi-men Ch'ing, "that my wife is currently in the last month of her pregnancy, but because she has gotten so upset, her vital energy has difficulty circulating, being trapped below her diaphragm. I beseech you, venerable sir, to take care in determining whether to increase or decrease the dosage of the medications you prescribe. To do so would be a manifestation of your magnanimity."

"There is no need for you to instruct me," responded Dr. Jen. "I will, of course, do my best. Once I get home, I will prepare medications for her that should protect her fetus, repair her vital energy, settle her stomach, improve her resilience, and alleviate her pain. Once your venerable lady has taken them, she would do well to avoid occasions for anger, and reduce her consumption of rich foods."

"I beseech you, venerable sir," said Hsi-men Ch'ing, "to do whatever you can to tranquilize her fetus."

"Of course," responded Dr. Jen, "I will endeavor as best I can to tranquilize her fetus, repair her vital energy, and nourish the constructive and defensive elements in her constitution. There is no need for you to enjoin me any further. I will give it my most careful consideration."

"My Third Lady," Hsi-men Ch'ing went on to say, "is suffering from a chill in the stomach. I hope that you will be able to come up with some womb-warming pills to alleviate her condition."

"Your pupil will respectfully comply with your command," said Dr. Jen. "I will seal them up for you immediately."

So saying, he got up and went out to the front reception hall, where he noticed that there were a considerable number of musicians from the Music Office waiting in the courtyard.

"Venerable sir," he asked, "what sort of event are you putting on in your residence today?"

Hsi-men Ch'ing responded by explaining, "His Honor Regional Investigating Censor Sung Ch'iao-nien, together with the officials of the Two Provincial Offices, have invited the grand coordinator of Shantung, Hou Meng, to a banquet to be held here today."

Upon hearing this, Dr. Jen was astonished at heart and felt more respect than ever for Hsi-men Ch'ing. He bowed and scraped before mounting his horse outside the front gate, showing greater deference than ever before, and double his previous regard. When Hsi-men Ch'ing came back from seeing him off, he immediately sealed up a tael of silver and two handkerchiefs and sent Ch'in-t'ung off with them in a gift box, to go on horseback in order to pick up the medicines.

Meanwhile, Li Chiao-erh, Meng Yü-lou, and the rest were all in Yüeh-niang's room, engaged in preparing boxes of candied fruit, and polishing the silver utensils.

"First Lady," they asked, "how is it that, though you hadn't originally wanted to go out and be seen, no sooner did the doctor examine you than he was able to tell, thus and so, exactly what you were suffering from?"

"What sort of a wife does he take me for?" said Yüeh-niang. "Let me die if I must, for all he cares. Who knows what that whore is up to? She constantly tries to exert control over me, while claiming that I treat her as though I were her mother-in-law. The only difference between us is one of relative age, and I happen to be eight months older than she is. She maintains that since our husband loves her, it is only appropriate that he should treat us as equals. If she had not made sure of his backing, how would she have dared engage me in such:

A vituperative altercation?

If the rest of you had not urged me so strongly to go out and see the doctor, I wouldn't have gone out for ten years. Let me die if I must. As the saying goes:

If one cock dies, another will crow in its stead.[5]

Is not the crowing of the new cock great to hear?

Once I'm dead, he can raise her to my position, and thus eliminate all this quarreling and wrangling.

When you weed out the turnips, there is
    room for other things."

"Ai-ya! Ai-ya!" exclaimed Meng Yü-lou. "First Lady, how can you say such things? I am prepared to swear an oath on her behalf. This Sister Six, and I don't say this judgmentally, is indeed prone to act as though she:

Didn't know any better,

and is given to throwing her weight around, engaging in backbiting, and acting officiously. She's just a baggage, for whom, all too often:

The words are mouthed but the heart isn't in it.

First Lady, to allow yourself to get so worked up over her is a mistake."

"Do you really think that she is more thoughtless than you?" responded Yüeh-niang. "On the contrary, she knows exactly what she's doing. How is it that she is so prone to surreptitiously eavesdropping on people, and then using their words to reflect satirically on them?"

"First Lady," said Meng Yü-lou:

> "The head of a household is a receptacle
> > for catching dirty water.

If you lack the capacity to take it, what are you to do? As the saying goes:

> A single gentleman can accommodate
> > ten petty persons.
> If you raise your hand,
> She will venture to get by,

but if you refuse to make allowances for her,

> She'll be unable to get by."

"The fact is," said Yüeh-niang, "that, as long as our husband stands up for her this way, his legitimate wife will be relegated to the rear."

"Who are you fooling?" said Meng Yü-lou. "Right now, while you are in the unhealthy condition that you are, would Father have the gall to visit her quarters?"

"Why wouldn't he?" said Yüeh-niang. "Didn't she suggest that she could keep him tied up there with a length of hog-bristle rope? A man's heart is just like a horse without a bridle. Whomever he chooses to favor, he will favor. And anyone who presumes to try and restrain him, she will accuse of being wanton."

"That's enough, First Lady," objected Meng Yü-lou. "You've already had your say. Try to restrain your anger somewhat. Let me go get her to come and kowtow to you, and offer an apology for her misconduct. If we avail ourselves of the presence of Sister-in-law Wu, maybe the two of you can be induced to make it up somehow. If not, Father will be left in a very awkward position:

> Damned if he does, and damned if he doesn't,

so that his every move will be problematical. If he wants to go to her quarters, he'll be afraid of your anger; and if he fails to do so, she won't venture to come out. Today, a banquet is being held in the front compound, and we are here, busy as can be, preparing boxes of candied fruit. If she is allowed to skulk by herself in her own quarters, the rest of us will find it hard to forgive her. Sister-in-law Wu, is what I say right, or isn't it?"

"Sister-in-law," responded Sister-in-law Wu, "what the Third Lady says is right. If the two of you continue to be at odds, and persist in refusing to see each other, it will make things hard for my brother-in-law, who will find it awkward to approach either of you."

Yüeh-niang did not say so much as a word in response to this, and Meng Yü-lou started to leave, and go toward the front compound.

"Meng the Third," objected Yüeh-niang, "don't you go after her. Let her come, or not, as she pleases."

"She won't dare not to come," said Meng Yü-lou. "If she won't come, I'll simply tie her up with a length of hog-bristle rope and drag her here."

With that, she made her way straight to Chin-lien's quarters, where she found her, with disheveled hair and a sallow complexion, sitting on the k'ang.

"Sister Six," said Meng Yü-lou, "why are you playing the fool? Do up your hair. Today, a banquet is being held up front, and we are as busy as can be preparing for it in the rear compound. You ought to come back and join us. What's the point of merely venting your spleen this way? Just now, thus and so, I've been arguing with the First Lady, urging her to relent, for quite a while. You ought to come back to the rear compound, keep your bad temper to yourself, while displaying your good temper, and see if you can't bring yourself to kowtow to her, and offer her an apology for your misconduct. Both you and I are in a position in which:

> When confronted with low eaves,
> How can we not lower our heads?[6]

As the saying goes:

> Honeyed words and plausible speeches
>   can make the twelfth month warm;
> Cruel words that are hurtful to others
>   can turn the sixth month cold.

The two of you have already had your exchange of words. How long are you going to persist in venting your spleen?

> Men are as fond of expressing their anger,
> As Buddhas are of receiving burnt incense.

If you will only go and offer her an apology for your misconduct, this problem, great as it is, can be brought to an end. If you refuse, however, you will put Father in an awkward position with regard to both of you, and if he wants to come to your place, she is certain to be annoyed."

"Ai-ya! Ai-ya!" exclaimed Chin-lien. "There's no comparison between us. As she has declared, she is the genuine article, the legitimate wife, while you and I are merely women he has picked up after cohabiting with us amid the dewdrops.[7] What sort of standing do we possess? We're not to be compared to the toes on her feet."

"Let her say what she likes," responded Meng Yü-lou. "As I said to her yesterday, 'You're:

> Hitting three or four of us with one swipe of the stick.

When I married your husband, I was not just someone he picked up along the way but was duly married, with the help of the standard:

> Three matchmakers and six witnesses,[8]

before consenting to enter your household.

For every branch you chop down,
A hundred trees are threatened.
When the hare dies, the fox is sad;
Creatures grieve for their fellows.
Even if Sister Six has exasperated you, there are others of us who have not.
Though one may possess the authority, one
should not use it completely;
Though one may have something to say, one
should not say it completely.[9]
In all things, it is best to:
Look up to those above and regard those below,
in order to provide against future developments. How can you ignore the fact
that:
The locust and the grasshopper,
Are maligned in the same breath,
here in the presence of the three nuns and Big Sister Yü?
Every person has a face;
Every tree has its bark,[10]
but our faces are being drained of blood, and our intercourse will come to an
end.'
"Now, if you refuse to go see her, what do you propose to do? There is no
avoiding the fact that, day after day, the two of you will be in close proximity
to each other:
As inseparable as the lip and the cheek.
You ought to fix your hair right away, so the two of us can go back to the rear
compound together."
When P'an Chin-lien heard what she had to say, she could only ponder it
for what seemed like half a day;
Swallow her anger and keep her own counsel,
before picking up the dressing mirror in front of her mirror stand, brushing
her hair, putting on her fret, getting into appropriate clothes, and accompanying Meng Yü-lou back to the master suite in the rear compound.
Meng Yü-lou lifted aside the portiere and went inside before her, saying,
"First Lady, I went there as I said I would do and have managed to drag her
back with me. She dared not refuse to come."
Then, turning to Chin-lien, she said, "My child, why haven't you come
over and kowtowed to your mother?"
Standing to one side, she continued, "Kinswoman, my child is young, and
is still so:
Unconscious of right and wrong,
that she has offended you. If you will only:
Lift high your gracious hand,

make allowances for her, and forgive her this once; should she ever be rude to you again in the future, you may punish her as you see fit. I will not have a word to say about it."

Then P'an Chin-lien:

Just as if inserting a taper in its holder,

proceeded to kowtow four times to Yüeh-niang.

After which, she jumped up and hit Meng Yü-lou a blow, saying, "You're delirious, you insensate whore! You're playing the role of my mother again, are you?"

Everyone laughed at this, and even Yüeh-niang herself couldn't help laughing.

Meng Yü-lou carried on, saying, "You lousy slave! On seeing your mistress show you a favorable countenance, you ruffle up your feathers and strike your own mother."

"It is such a relief to see you sisters making it up with each other so light-heartedly," said Sister-in-law Wu. "Even though this sister-in-law of mine may sometimes be guilty of saying:

A word or half a word,[11]

that grates on your ears, if you will only agree to:

Support and respect each other,[12]

and be sparing in your responses, all will be well. As the saying goes:

Although the peony blossom may be lovely,
It requires verdant leaves to set it off."[13]

"If she had not said what she did," responded Yüeh-niang, "who would have chosen to criticize her?"

"You are Heaven, while we are the Earth," said Chin-lien. "If you see fit to grant us your accommodation, we will venerate it as though it were engraved in our minds."

At this, Meng Yü-lou gave her a smack on the shoulder, saying, "My child:

You've only endured a slap with a flour sack."[14]

She then continued, "Don't you say anything more. We've been working away here all day long. It's high time for you to lend us a hand."

Chin-lien, thereupon, proceeded to:

Wash her hands and trim her nails,

before getting onto the k'ang and joining Meng Yü-lou in preparing boxes of candied fruit. But no more of this.

Sun Hsüeh-o was engaged in directing the group of servants' wives in preparing dishes at the stove in the kitchen. The hired chefs were also working in the large kitchen in the front compound, frying and roasting, steaming and boiling, as they roasted brocade-wrapped mutton and carved flowered pork.

When Ch'in-t'ung returned with the medicines he had been sent to fetch, Hsi-men Ch'ing read the labels and had the pills sent to Meng Yü-lou's quarters, and the ingredients for a decoction turned over to Yüeh-niang.

Yüeh-niang then said to Meng Yü-lou, "So you've sent for a prescription too, have you?"

"It's for that problem I had the other day," said Meng Yü-lou. "I was feeling considerable pain in my lower regions, and I asked Father to tell Dr. Jen about it, and get him to prescribe a couple of doses of pills for me."

"It was because you hadn't been able to eat anything that day that you caught a chill," said Yüeh-niang. "It's only right that you should take a chill in the abdomen seriously."

But let us put aside the events in the rear compound for the moment.

To resume our story, in the front reception hall Censor Sung Ch'iao-nien was the first to arrive, in order to look over the arrangements for the banquet. Hsi-men Ch'ing invited him into the summerhouse, where they sat down together.

Sung Ch'iao-nien thanked him profoundly for his gift of the incense-burning tripod, saying, "Your pupil really ought to repay you for it."

"The fact is," said Hsi-men Ch'ing, "that, from the beginning, I would have liked to present it to Your Excellency but feared that you might not accept it. How can you speak of repayment?"

"In that case," said Sung Ch'iao-nien:

"What can I do to be worthy of such largess?"

So saying, he made a bow in order to express his gratitude.

When they had finished their tea, he started to interrogate Hsi-men Ch'ing about his assessment of the condition of the people and public morality in the district, and Hsi-men Ch'ing responded to his questions with perfunctory affirmatives and negatives.

He then went on to ask his opinion of the local officials, and Hsi-men Ch'ing said, "Your humble subordinate is only aware that, as for Prefect Hu Shih-wen of Tung-p'ing prefecture:

His repute among the people is long established;[15]
and the magistrate of Ch'ing-ho district, Li Ta-t'ien, is:

Conscientious in performing his official duties.
As for the rest:

I am not familiar with all the relevant details;[16]
and would not presume to speak irresponsibly."

Sung Ch'iao-nien went on to ask, "Commandant Chou Hsiu is an associate of yours. How would you assess his character?"

"Although Commandant Chou is:

Both experienced and reliable,"[17]
replied Hsi-men Ch'ing. "He is not a match for Military Director-in-Chief Ching of Chi-chou, who passed the military examinations in his youth and is:

Both talented and courageous.
Your Excellency ought to take him into consideration."

"You must be referring to Military Director-in-Chief Ching Chung," said Sung Ch'iao-nien. "How do you happen to be familiar with him?"

"He and I have a nodding acquaintance with each other," said Hsi-men Ch'ing. "The other day he presented me with a copy of his curriculum vitae and asked me to show it to you, in the hope that you might be induced to:
        Look favorably upon it."

"I have also heard long since that he is an excellent military officer," said Sung Ch'iao-nien. "Is there anyone else whom you would recommend?"

"There is one Wu K'ai," responded Hsi-men Ch'ing, "who is the elder brother of your humble subordinate's wife. He currently holds the position of battalion commander of the Ch'ing-ho Left Guard and has recently been deputed to repair the local Charity Granary. According to precedent, he is eligible to be promoted to the rank of a commander of the Ch'ing-ho Guard. If Your Excellency should see fit to put in a good word on his behalf, your humble subordinate would feel much indebted to your kindness."

"Since he is a relative of yours," said Sung Ch'iao-nien, "in the future, when I submit my report, I will not only recommend him for promotion, but also guarantee that he will continue to hold his current substantive position."

Hsi-men Ch'ing promptly bowed to him as an expression of his gratitude and presented him with the curricula vitae of Ching Chung and Wu K'ai.

After Censor Sung Ch'iao-nien had finished perusing them, he turned them over to his clerical docket officer, saying, "When the time comes for me to draft my report, show them to me again."

The docket officer, accordingly, took charge of them, and Hsi-men Ch'ing arranged for one of his attendants to surreptitiously present him with three taels of silver, in return for which the docket officer assured him that the charge would be engraved upon his heart. But no more of this.

As they were speaking, they heard the sound of drum music from the front reception hall, and an attendant came in to announce that the officials from the Two Provincial Offices had arrived. This threw Hsi-men Ch'ing into such consternation that he immediately went out to the reception hall to receive them and exchange formal greetings, while Censor Sung Ch'iao-nien took his time as he slowly made his way out the postern gate from the garden.

When the crowd of officials had finished with the customary exchange of greetings and observed that in the center of the room there stood a large portable table, on which were displayed candied effigies of the Five Ancients, ingot-shaped cakes, square-shaped confectionery, a high-stacked pyramid of fruits, the flesh of the five sacrificial animals, and an array of other comestibles fit for a major banquet, all of which were neatly arranged and surrounded by a cluster of lavishly furnished table settings:

Their hearts were filled with great joy,

and they all thanked Hsi-men Ch'ing, saying, "We have put you to a lot of trouble. Allow us to supplement our prior contributions to the expenses."

"It is true that our contributions have been inadequate," said Censor Sung Ch'iao-nien, "but, if you will do so for my sake, Ssu-ch'üan, let us spare these gentlemen the need to make any further contributions."

"Whoever heard of such a thing," responded Hsi-men Ch'ing.

They all then proceeded to sit down in order of precedence, while the attendants served them with tea.

The group of officials then explained, "As for the venerable gentleman Hou Meng, all of us have sent subordinates to remind him of the invitation, but he is still at the yamen of the Regional Military Command and has not set out yet."

The file leaders and musicians lined up to either side inside the second gate, as closely as though they were:

Locked tight in an iron bucket,

with their drums, flutes, pipes, and metallophones, in expectation of his arrival. They remained on the lookout for him until the early afternoon, when a messenger on horseback arrived and reported that His Honor Hou Meng was on his way. The musicians to either side began to play their instruments, and the crowd of officials all went outside the main gate to receive him, while Censor Sung Ch'iao-nien stood in waiting inside the second gate.

Before long, after a squad of soldiers bearing blue flags had preceded him to clear the way, Grand Coordinator Hou Meng, wearing a gown emblazoned with a scarlet peacock, sable earmuffs, and a gold-buckled girdle, and riding in a large sedan chair borne by four bearers, arrived at the gate and descended from his sedan chair. The crowd of officials welcomed him inside, and Censor Sung Ch'iao-nien, who had changed into a round-collared scarlet robe, emblazoned with a motif of golden clouds and a white *hsieh-chih*, a mythical one-horned goat that was said to gore wrongdoers, and a girdle with a plaque of rhinoceros horn, ushered him deferentially into the great reception hall. Only after the two of them had exchanged the customary greetings, and the various officials had individually paid their respects, did the time come for him to be presented to Hsi-men Ch'ing.

"This is our host, Battalion Commander Hsi-men Ch'ing," said Censor Sung Ch'iao-nien. "He is currently serving as judicial commissioner in the local office of the Provincial Surveillance Commission and is also a protégé of the venerable Grand Preceptor Ts'ai Ching."

Grand Coordinator Hou Meng, thereupon, directed one of his clerical attendants to present Hsi-men Ch'ing with a red accordion-bound calling card, which read, "Your devoted friend Hou Meng pays his respects."

Hsi-men Ch'ing respectfully received it with both hands and turned it over to a servant for safekeeping.

When they had finished paying their mutual respects, they all loosened their clothing and assumed their seats. The various officials were seated to either side, while Censor Sung Ch'iao-nien occupied the position of host. After tea had been served, the musicians struck up their music beneath the steps, and Censor Sung Ch'iao-nien took up a cup and proffered wine to Grand Coordinator Hou Meng, stuck flower ornaments in his cap, and presented him with a bolt of fabric. Immediately afterwards, the guest of honor's table setting was carried downstairs, the comestibles displayed thereon were packed in boxes, and personnel were dispatched to deliver them to his official residence. After this, they resumed their seats, a repast with soup and rice was duly presented, and the chef came out to carve the entrée of flowered pork, but there is no need to describe this in detail.

By this time, the musicians from the Music Offices had put on a number of ensemble dance pieces in which the performers were all clad in officially supplied brand new embroidered costumes, and a medley of vaudeville acts had been performed, all of which were superbly presented. Only after that did the troupe of Hai-yen actors come forward, kowtow to the company, and present the program of pieces they were prepared to perform. His Honor Hou Meng told them to perform something from the ch'uan-ch'i drama *P'ei Chin-kung huan-tai chi*.[18] When they had finished performing one scene, they withdrew, and the chef proceeded to carve the entrée of brocade-wrapped mutton. Truly:

> Amid clustering blossoms and clinging brocade,
> Wind and string instruments, song, and dance,
> Classical melodies saturate the ears, and
> Gold and sable finery fill the banquet chamber.

There is a poem that testifies to this:

> The auspicious aura filling the ornate hall
>   is neither fog, nor is it mist;
> The singing diverts the moving clouds, and
>   the tables are laden with wine.
> Not only are the beauties, like red moths,
>   dangling their jade pendants;
> But the black locks at their temples are
>   studded with golden cicadas.

Grand Coordinator Hou Meng remained in his place only until the sun began to sink in the West. After:

> Several rounds of wine had been consumed, and
> Two dramatic episodes had been performed,

he got up to go and directed his attendants to take five taels of silver and distribute it among the cooks, waiters, musicians, and servants. He then put on his outdoor clothes and took his leave, while the assembled officials escorted him to the front gate and looked on as he got into his sedan chair and departed. When they came back inside, Censor Sung Ch'iao-nien and the other officials also thanked Hsi-men Ch'ing, took their leave, and departed.

After Hsi-men Ch'ing had seen them off and come back inside, he dismissed the musicians and, seeing that it was still rather early, directed that the tables should be left in place, and that the caterers should set what remained of the various dishes and delicacies in order. He then sent page boys to go and invite Wu K'ai, Licentiate Wen, Ying Po-chüeh, his managers, Fu Ming and Kan Jun, Pen Ti-ch'uan, and Ch'en Ching-chi to come join him and enjoy a dramatic performance. He also had two table settings of wine and savories provided for the troupe of Hai-yen actors to eat while he waited for the guests to arrive, after which, he told them to be ready to perform the winter scene entitled *Han Hsi-tsai yeh-yen* (Han Hsi-tsai's nocturnal banquet), from the ch'uan-ch'i drama *Ssu-chieh chi* (The four seasons).[19] In addition, he had pots of plum blossoms brought out and displayed on the tables to either side, so they could enjoy the plum blossoms while consuming their wine.

It so happens that, on that day, Pen the Fourth and Lai-hsing had been in charge of the kitchen, Ch'en Ching-chi had been in charge of the wine, and the managers Fu Ming and Kan Jun had been in charge of the utensils for the banquet. When they learned that Hsi-men Ch'ing had invited them to join him, they all came and sat down in his presence. Before long, Licentiate Wen came from across the street, made a bow, and sat down, after which Wu K'ai, Wu the Second, and Ying Po-chüeh also arrived.

Ying Po-chüeh greeted Hsi-men Ch'ing with a bow, saying, "I fear I provided but scant entertainment for my sisters-in-law the other day, and I am grateful for your lavish gifts."

Hsi-men Ch'ing laughed and upbraided him, saying, "Why you lousy goddamned dog! You got a real eyeful spying on your mothers through an aperture in the window, didn't you?"

"You shouldn't believe the nonsense people talk," protested Ying Po-chüeh. "Whoever heard of such a thing. It can't be anyone else, now I think about it."

Pointing at Wang Ching, he then accused him, saying, "So it was you, you lousy dog-bone! You actually came home and told him such a tale, did you? When I get the chance, I'll take a bite out of your flesh, you little dog-bone!"

After this exchange of words was over, and they had consumed their tea, Wu K'ai expressed a wish to go back to the rear compound, and Hsi-men Ch'ing agreed to accompany him.

As they went along, Hsi-men Ch'ing explained to his brother-in-law, thus and so, "I spoke to Censor Sung Ch'iao-nien about that matter of yours, and he looked over your curriculum vitae and then entrusted it to a clerk, to whom I also gave three taels of silver. He accepted it along with the curriculum vitae of His Honor Ching Chung and promised that when the time came for him to draft his report, he would give it his special attention."

Upon hearing this, Wu K'ai was utterly delighted and bowed to Hsi-men Ch'ing, saying, "I am much beholden to you, Brother-in-law, for your efforts on my behalf."

"I just told him that you were my wife's elder brother," said Hsi-men Ch'ing, "and he replied, saying, 'Since he is a relative of yours, I will be sure to take care of it for your sake.'"

Thereupon, they went into the master suite together in order to see Yüeh-niang.

After Yüeh-niang had greeted her elder brother with a bow, Wu K'ai turned to his wife and said, "Hadn't you better go home? There's no one there to look after the house. Why are you so reluctant to leave?"

"My sister-in-law wanted me to stay," said Sister-in-law Wu. "She has invited me to remain through the third day of the coming month, and return home on the fourth."

"Since it is my sister who is keeping you," said Wu K'ai, "you might just as well come home on the fourth, then,"

When they had finished speaking, Yüeh-niang suggested that he stay for a visit, but he chose not to sit down and went back to the front compound, where the wine had already been provided, and he could have a drink.

At this juncture, Wu K'ai, together with Wu the Second, Ying Po-chüeh, and Licentiate Wen, took their places as guests, while Hsi-men Ch'ing sat down in the host's position, and managers Fu Ming, Kan Jun, Pen Ti-ch'uan, and Ch'en Ching-chi took their places to either side, making a total of five tables in all; while below, the troupe of actors began to play their gongs and drums and then proceeded to perform the scene from the *Ssu-chieh chi* entitled *Han Hsi-tsai yeh-yen yu-t'ing chia-yü* (Han Hsi-tsai's nocturnal banquet exposes the tryst in the relay station).

Just as the merrymaking was at its height, Tai-an suddenly came in and said, "Your kinsman Ch'iao Hung's household has sent Ch'iao T'ung here, and he is waiting down below to have a word with Father."

Hsi-men Ch'ing immediately got up from his place and went to the postern gate on the east to see Ch'iao T'ung, who had been sent by his kinsman Ch'iao Hung.

"Father says to apologize to you for the scant entertainment he provided the other day," said Ch'iao T'ung. "He has sent me today to deliver the customary fee of thirty taels of silver for the purchase of a position as an honorary official, which he has sealed up here, together with an additional sum of five taels, to be distributed to the staff of the personnel office."

"I will turn it over to Prefect Hu Shih-wen tomorrow," said Hsi-men Ch'ing, "and he will supply the order of appointment in return. "What need is there to spend any silver on the staff of the personnel office? You can take it back with you."

He then directed Tai-an to tell the kitchen to take care of providing wine and something to eat for Ch'iao T'ung in the studio in the summerhouse, and then send him on his way.

To make a long story short, that day, by the time the actors had performed two scenes from the play about the tryst in the relay station, it was already the first watch, and the party for Hsi-men Ch'ing and his guests in the front compound broke up.

Once the utensils had been cleared away, Hsi-men Ch'ing went back to Yüeh-niang's room, where she was sitting on the k'ang with Sister-in-law Wu. When Sister-in-law Wu saw Hsi-men Ch'ing come in, she promptly got up and moved into an adjacent room.

Hsi-men Ch'ing then said to Yüeh-niang, "Today, I spoke, thus and so, on behalf of your elder brother, to Regional Investigating Censor Sung Ch'iao-nien, and he promised not only to see that he is promoted one class in rank, but also that he will continue to hold his current substantive position, so he will become the assistant commander of the Ch'ing-ho Guard. I told your elder brother about it just now, and he is as pleased as can be. After the censor's report is submitted at the end of the year, the imperial rescript confirming his appointment will come down."

"Needless to say," responded Yüeh-niang, "as a poor officer of the guard, he can hardly come up with the two or three hundred taels of silver he will need to expend."

"Who is asking him for even so much as a hundred cash?" said Hsi-men Ch'ing. "I simply said to Censor Sung Ch'iao-nien that he was my wife's elder brother, and he personally promised that he would not fail to take care of it as a favor to me."

"You can do as you like in dealing with him," said Yüeh-niang. "I won't interfere with you."

Hsi-men Ch'ing then asked Yü-hsiao, "Have you decocted that medicine for your mistress? Bring it here so I can see that your mistress takes it."

"You can go about your business," said Yüeh-niang. "Don't worry about it. I'll take it when I'm ready to go to bed."

Hsi-men Ch'ing was about to go outside, but Yüeh-niang called him back, saying, "Just where are you headed? If you are headed for the front compound, you'd better not go there. She came back here and apologized to me for her misconduct a while ago. All that she needs is for you to go and apologize to her."

"I'm not going to her quarters," said Hsi-men Ch'ing.

"If you're not going to her quarters," responded Yüeh-niang, "whose quarters are you going to? You ought not to have anything to do with that wet nurse in the front compound either. The other day, in front of Sister-in-law Wu, the Fifth Lady belittled me by saying that I allowed you to carry on with her in order to curry favor with you. But you continue to be as shameless as ever."

"Why do you pay any attention to that little whore?" said Hsi-men Ch'ing.

"Just do as I say," responded Yüeh-niang. "I don't want you to go to the front compound today. And I don't want you to stay here either. Why don't you go and spend the night in Li Chiao-erh's quarters? You can go wherever you want tomorrow, and I won't interfere with you."

On hearing this, Hsi-men Ch'ing, finding himself:

At a loss for what to do next,

felt compelled to go spend the night in Li Chiao-erh's quarters.

The next day was the first day of the twelfth month. Hsi-men Ch'ing went to the yamen early in the morning and joined Ho Yung-shou in issuing directives; after which, he took his place on the bench, held roll call, and dealt with the accumulated paperwork. The morning was over by the time he returned home.

He then took care of preparing gifts of a newly slaughtered pig and a jug of wine, along with the thirty taels of silver, and sent Tai-an to deliver them to Hu Shih-wen, the prefect of Tung-p'ing prefecture. Prefect Hu Shih-wen accepted the gifts and immediately proceeded to seal up the order of appointment for Ch'iao Hung.

Meanwhile, at home, Hsi-men Ch'ing invited Yin-yang Master Hsü to set up an altar in the reception hall and make an offering of a pig and a sheep, wine and fruit, and burn paper money, in order to fulfill the vow he had made after encountering the storm on his way back from the capital. When the ceremony was finished, he sent Yin-yang Master Hsü on his way.

Thereupon, seeing that Tai-an had returned, he examined the reply from Prefect Hu Shih-wen and saw that he had provided the order of appointment, that it was duly stamped with numerous seals, and that it read: "Ch'iao Hung is hereby appointed as an honorary official of this prefecture." He then sent Tai-an to deliver two boxes of the meat from the foregoing sacrificial offering to the household of Ch'iao Hung, and invite him to come over for a drink, so he could show him the order of appointment. He also had boxes of the sacrificial meat delivered to Wu K'ai, Licentiate Wen, Ying Po-chüeh, Hsieh Hsi-ta, and his managers, Fu Ming, Kan Jun, Han Tao-kuo, Pen Ti-ch'uan, and Ts'ui Pen, one box for each of them. But no more of this.

In addition, he sent invitations for a party on the third day of the month to Commandant Chou Hsiu, Military Director-in-Chief Ching Chung, Militia Commander Chang Kuan, Eunuch Directors Liu and Hsüeh, Battalion Commander Ho Yung-shou, Battalion Commander Fan Hsün, Wu K'ai, Ch'iao Hung, and Wang the Third, ten persons in all. He also engaged troupes of vaudeville performers and musicians, as well as four singing girls, for the occasion.

On that day, Meng Yü-lou went to Yüeh-niang's room to hand over the household accounts, which she had finished reckoning, to Hsi-men Ch'ing, in the expectation that he would turn them over to Chin-lien, so that she would no longer be responsible for handling the household expenses.

While there, she enquired of Yüeh-niang, "First Lady, after taking that medicine yesterday, are you feeling any better?"

"No wonder people say that all a wanton woman needs is to have a man fondle her wrist," remarked Yüeh-niang. "Today I'm feeling fine. I no longer have a headache, and my abdomen no longer feels distended."

Meng Yü-lou laughed at this, saying, "First Lady, it would seem that all you needed was that touch."

Sister-in-law Wu also laughed at this.

Hsi-men Ch'ing came in at this juncture to ask Yüeh-niang's opinion on the managing of the accounts, and Yüeh-niang said, "Hand them over to whoever's turn it is, that's all. Why are you asking me about it? Who cares who they are turned over to?"

Only then did Hsi-men Ch'ing weigh out thirty taels of silver and thirty strings of cash and turn them over to Chin-lien to manage. But no more of this.

After some time, Ch'iao Hung arrived, and Hsi-men Ch'ing sat down with him in the reception hall and explained, thus and so, what had happened, showing him the order of appointment he had obtained from Prefect Hu Shih-wen, which confirmed that he had been appointed as an honorary prefectural official, in return for the customary donation of "thirty piculs of white rice," to be used for the logistic needs of border defense.

He was utterly delighted by this and promptly bowed in thanks to Hsi-men Ch'ing, saying, "I am much beholden to you, Kinsman, for your efforts on my behalf.

Permit me to offer you an obeisance in gratitude."[20]

He then called in Ch'iao T'ung and told him to take the order of appointment home for him, after which, he turned to Hsi-men Ch'ing and said, "In the future, should you invite me to a formal engagement, I will be entitled to wear the cap and girdle of an official and can thus presume to keep your other guests company."

"On the third, Kinsman," said Hsi-men Ch'ing, "I hope that, whatever you do, you will deign to come by early."

When they had finished their tea, Hsi-men Ch'ing told Ch'in-t'ung to set up a table in his studio in the anteroom on the west side of the courtyard and invited Ch'iao Hung to accompany him there, where it was somewhat warmer, and they could also take advantage of a recessed brazier.

Once Hsi-men Ch'ing and Ch'iao Hung were seated there, face to face, Hsi-men Ch'ing told him, "Yesterday, Regional Investigating Censor Sung Ch'iao-nien, and the officials of the Two Provincial Offices, hosted a banquet here, to which they invited His Honor Grand Coordinator Hou Meng, who turned out to be highly gratified. Tomorrow, he is leaving for the capital, and my colleagues and I will have to go out to the suburbs to see him off before returning home."

The table had just been wiped off, and an assortment of dishes was about to be served, when who should appear but Ying Po-chüeh, who had collected some contributions and had Ying Pao bring them in a box to present to Hsi-men Ch'ing.

"These are the congratulatory contributions from the gentlemen concerned," he explained.

Hsi-men Ch'ing opened the box to have a look and saw that the first name was that of the Taoist Abbot Wu Tsung-che, followed by the names of Ying Po-chüeh, Hsieh Hsi-ta, Chu Jih-nien, Sun T'ien-hua, Ch'ang Shih-chieh, Pai Lai-ch'iang, Li Chih, Huang the Fourth, and Tu the Third, ten contributors in all.

"For my part," said Hsi-men Ch'ing, "I am also inviting my kinsmen Wu the Second, and Brother-in-law Shen, as well as Dr. Jen Hou-ch'i and Hua Tzu-yu, who live outside the city gate, my three managers, and Licentiate Wen. There will be twenty or more of us altogether, and you are all invited to come here on the fourth."

He then directed an attendant to take the contributions back to the rear compound and sent Ch'in-t'ung to take a horse and go invite Wu K'ai to join them in order to keep Ch'iao Hung company.

He went on to ask, "Is Master Wen Pi-ku at home or not?"

"Master Wen is not at home," responded Lai-an. "Early this morning, he went out to visit a friend."

Before long, Wu K'ai arrived, and they were joined by Ch'en Ching-chi, so there were five of them sitting down together to have a drink. A variety of hot dishes to go with the wine, and bowls of soup, were arrayed upon the table, including, as might be expected, pig's feet and sheep's head; roasted, stewed, boiled, and sautéed chicken, fish, goose, and duck; and other supplementary dishes.

While they were enjoying their drinks, Hsi-men Ch'ing told Wu K'ai about Ch'iao Hung's occasion for congratulation, saying, "Today, he has received his order of appointment as an honorary prefectural official. Someday soon, we should prepare gifts, and inscribe a scroll, in order to express our felicitations over his ascension to the prefectural bureaucracy."

"You embarrass me," protested Ch'iao Hung. "What sort of appointment is this, that I should presume to put you gentlemen to so much trouble?"

At this juncture, there suddenly arrived a messenger from the district yamen, who had been deputed to deliver copies of the new calendar for the coming year, a total of 250 copies in all. Hsi-men Ch'ing sent a note in reply, tipped the messenger, and sent him on his way.

"We haven't yet seen the new calendar," said Ying Po-chüeh.

Hsi-men Ch'ing broke open a package of fifty calendars and divided them up between Wu K'ai, Ying Po-chüeh, and Ch'iao Hung. Ying Po-chüeh, on taking a look at one of them, saw that the new year had been designated as the first year of the Ch'ung-ho reign period, and that the first month was to be an intercalary month. But we will say no more about how they enjoyed themselves at the party that day:

Playing at guess-fingers or gaming at forfeits.

They continued drinking until the evening, when Ch'iao Hung was the first to get up and go home. Hsi-men Ch'ing kept Wu K'ai company until the first watch before the party broke up.

Hsi-men Ch'ing issued orders to his attendants, saying, "Stand by with my horse early in the morning, and go and invite His Honor Ho Yung-shou to join me here, so we can proceed together to the suburbs to see off His Excellency Hou Meng. Also, designate four orderlies, along with Lai-an and Ch'un Hung, to accompany the sedan chair of the First Lady on her visit to the Hsia household."

When he had finished speaking, he went to the quarters of P'an Chin-lien. Before he entered her room, the woman had:

Removed her headdress,
Carelessly coiled her raven locks,
Left her flowery countenance in disarray,
And neglected to apply rouge and powder.

She was lying with her clothes on, sprawled on the surface of the bed, and had not lit any lamps in the room, so everything was very still. When Hsi-men Ch'ing came into the room, he first called for Ch'un-mei, but there was no response. Upon seeing the woman lying on the bed, he called to her, but she did not make a sound.

Hsi-men Ch'ing sat down on the bed and said, "You crazy oily mouth! Why are you carrying on this way, refusing to answer?"

Hsi-men Ch'ing pulled her up from her reclining position with one hand and said, "What are you so resentful about?"

The woman, putting on a succession of deliberate acts, twisted her face into a grimace and allowed an endless cascade of tears to roll down her fragrant cheeks.

Hsi-men Ch'ing, even though he had been forged out of iron or stone, could not help feeling his heart soften.

Embracing her by the neck with one hand, he enquired of her, saying, "You crazy oily mouth! You're perfectly fine. Why did the two of you get into such an altercation for no good reason?"

The woman refused to reply for what seemed like half a day before saying, "Who began any altercation with her? It was she who came up with an excuse for finding fault with me, accusing me, in front of other people, of being an inveterate husband-monopolizer and man-hunter, whom you had picked up somewhere; whereas she is the genuine article, and your legitimate wife. Who told you to come to my room, and for what purpose? You should stick to her, that's all. That way, I won't be able to monopolize you. She claims that whenever you come home, you insist on coming to pester me in this room of mine. Luckily, I heard her say that with my own ears. Have you really been spending the last few nights in this room of mine? How can anyone be so:

Barefaced and red-eyed,
as to engage in such backbiting? And as for that fur coat, she is critical of me for
asking you for it on my own initiative, without mentioning it to her beforehand.
Am I a slave or a maidservant of yours, that I should have to go to your room
and kowtow to you when I want something? And as for that little piece of mine,
who abused that lousy blind whore, she criticizes me for not disciplining her.
Why should she insist on making such a fuss about it? If you were a real man,
and wanted to do so, you could settle the matter with a single blow of your fist,
and thereby dispense with all this:

Idle chatter and superfluous talk.[21]

No doubt I ought to be:

Content to abide by my humble lot.

As the saying goes:

What is cheaply purchased
    is cheap when sold;
What is easily acquired is
    easily relinquished.

Since I was taken into your household merely to be your concubine, my status
is unpropitious. It has always been true that:

Good people are subject to being gulled;[22]
Good horses are subject to being ridden.[23]

That's just the way it is. If you take a look at the facts of the situation, who was
it who, for fear of offending her, spent the night in someone else's quarters?
Who was it who, on her behalf, sent for Dr. Jen Hou-ch'i? Who was it who
allowed himself to be persuaded to do everything she asked? Meanwhile, it
was I who was left to suffer in my room here:

On the far side of the mountains of Hell,

where I might just as well have died, for all anyone else cared. All this simply
reveals what kind of a heart she possesses. On top of which, I was forced to
hold back my tears, go back to the rear compound, and offer her an apology
for my misconduct."

As she spoke, an incessant flow of pearly tears rolled down her peach-flower
cheeks, and she fell into Hsi-men Ch'ing's arms:

Sobbing and wailing,

as she wiped the mucus from her nose and tried to dry her tears.

Hsi-men Ch'ing embraced her on the one hand, and admonished her on
the other, saying, "That's enough, my child. I've had too many things on my
mind the last few days. The two of you ought to be more circumspect in what
you say to each other. You can hardly expect me to say which of you is in the
right. Last night I wanted to come see you, but she said I was going to apologize
to you and wouldn't let me come, so I spent the night in Li Chiao-erh's place.
Although I was sleeping with somebody else, I was only thinking of you."

"That's enough," the woman said. "I can see into that heart of yours. You
consistently lavish your:

False affection and phony consideration,[24]
on me; while, all the time, it is really that legitimate wife of yours whom you
love. And right now, she is bearing your child. I'm nothing but a stalk of straw.
There's no comparison between us."

Hsi-men Ch'ing embraced her by the neck and gave her a kiss, saying, "You
crazy oily mouth! Don't talk such nonsense."

Who should appear at this juncture but Ch'iu-chü, who brought in a serving of tea.

"That lousy slave!" protested Hsi-men Ch'ing. "She's hardly sanitary. How
come you have her serving the tea?"

He then went on to ask, "Why is Ch'un-mei nowhere to be seen?"

"You still want to ask after Ch'un-mei, do you?" the woman replied. "She's
so starved she hardly has a breath of life left in her. She's lying prostrate in the
other room. Including today, she's gone three or four days without so much as
a sip of soup or water. All she wants to do in there is to die. She says that the way
the First Lady abused her as a slave in front of other people has made her:

So angry she scarcely cares whether she is
      dead or alive.

She has done nothing but cry for the last three or four days."

When Hsi-men Ch'ing heard this, he asked, "Is that true?"

"Do you think I'm trying to fool you?" the woman said. "Why don't you go
see for yourself?"

Hsi-men Ch'ing, in a state of consternation, went into the adjacent room,
where he found Ch'un-mei lying on the k'ang with:

Her fair countenance in disarray, and
Her cloud-shaped chignon all awry.

"You crazy little oily mouth!" Hsi-men Ch'ing called to her. "Why don't
you get up?"

Though he called out to her, she did not make a sound and pretended to be
asleep. Hsi-men Ch'ing then embraced her with both arms and lifted her up;
but Ch'un-mei, stretching her torso while still in a seeming stupor, like:

A carp flexing its tail,

nearly swept Hsi-men Ch'ing off his feet. Fortunately, he had embraced her
firmly and was able to prevent himself from falling by leaning against the
bedrail.

"Daddy, take your hands off me," responded Ch'un-mei. "What do you
think you're doing coming here to bother with a slave like myself? You'll only
soil those two hands of yours."

"You little oily mouth!" said Hsi-men Ch'ing. "So what if the First Lady told
you off with a word or two. It's hardly worth your getting so worked up about.
I'm told that you haven't had a thing to eat for the last few days."

"What's it to you whether I eat or not?" retorted Ch'un-mei. "After all, I'm
no more than a good-for-nothing slave, whom you might as well let die if she

Ch'un-mei Manages Coquettishly to Resist Hsi-men Ch'ing

chooses to. Ever since I've been a slave in your household, what business of yours have I ever ruined? I've never given my mistress any reason to rebuke me with so much as a word, or to give me so much as a slap. Merely on behalf of that lousy blind whore, who has been:

Laid by every man in the street, and

Fucked by every guy in the alley,

why should I deserve to be so reviled by the First Lady? She is critical of my mistress for failing to discipline me. No doubt she would have me dragged down and given five strokes with the bamboo on behalf of that blind whore. In the future, if that wife of Han Tao-kuo's fails to come here, so be it. But if she should come, just see what sort of a talking to I'll give her. It was she who sent that blind whore here, so she is the root of the problem."

"Even if it was she who sent her here," said Hsi-men Ch'ing, "it was with the best of intentions. Who could have known that she would be the cause of such a quarrel?"

"If she had only been a little more accommodating," said Ch'un-mei. "I rebuked her with the best of intentions, but she was too narrow-minded to take it."

"When I came in, just now," said Hsi-men Ch'ing, "why didn't you pour out a cup of tea for me? That slave's hands are unclean. I wouldn't drink any tea that she poured."

Ch'un-mei responded by saying:

"Since Butcher Wang is dead and gone,

One must eat pork with the bristles.

Right now, while I am in here, so weak I can hardly walk, you would have me pour your tea, would you?"

"You crazy little oily mouth!" responded Hsi-men Ch'ing. "Who told you not to eat anything anyway?"

He then went on to say, "Let's move into the other room. I haven't had anything to eat yet either. I'll have Ch'iu-chü go back to the kitchen in the rear compound and bring us some food. They can pour us some wine, bake some stuffed pastries, and heat some soup flavored with pickled fish for us to eat." Thereupon:

Without permitting any further argument,[25]

he took hold of Ch'un-mei's hand and dragged her into Chin-lien's room next door, where he ordered Ch'iu-chü to take a box back to the rear compound and bring them some dishes of food to go with their rice.

Before long, she came back with a square box of delicacies, containing a bowl of braised pig's head, a bowl of slow-boiled mutton, a bowl of blanched chicken, and a bowl of sautéed fresh fish, along with a supply of white rice. There were also four bowls of side dishes to go with the wine, consisting of jellyfish, bean sprouts, potted pork, dried shrimp, and the like. Hsi-men Ch'ing told Ch'un-mei to sprinkle some euryale seeds[26] over the potted pork, add some marinated bamboo shoots and leeks, and mix these ingredients into a large bowl of savory wonton soup. A table was set up, the dishes were placed upon it, the bowls were filled with rice, and a box of baked stuffed pastries was provided.

Hsi-men Ch'ing and Chin-lien:

Sat down shoulder to shoulder,

while Ch'un-mei placed herself to one side and proceeded to share their repast. The three of them fell to drinking together:

First a cup for you,

Then a cup for me,

until the first watch, before the party broke up and they went to bed.

The next day, Hsi-men Ch'ing got up early. As prearranged, Battalion Commander Ho Yung-shou came to join him, and they enjoyed a pick-me-up, before setting out for the suburbs together in order to see off Grand Coordinator Hou Meng.

Back at home, Wu Yüeh-niang first sent a present ahead and then dressed herself up, seated herself in a large sedan chair, and set out, with orderlies shouting to clear the way, and accompanied by Lai-an and Ch'un-hung, for the home of Hsia Yen-ling, in order to attend a party, and pay a visit to his wife. But no more of this.

Tai-an and Wang Ching were left at home to look after the place. Whom should they see that afternoon but Dame Wang, the proprietress of the teahouse in front of the district yamen, who brought with her Ho the Ninth.

When they arrived at the front gate, she asked Tai-an, "Is His Honor at home or not?"

"Dame Wang and the venerable Ho the Ninth, what a surprise!" exclaimed Tai-an. "What wind has blown you this way today?"

"Without a reason for doing so," responded Dame Wang, "we would scarcely have ventured to:

Dawdle at your door or loiter at your gate.

I would not have come today were it not for a problem that has arisen for Ho the Ninth's younger brother, for whose sake I have ventured to seek a favor from His Honor."

"His Honor has gone to see off His Excellency Hou Meng today," explained Tai-an, "and the First Lady is also not at home. If you will wait here a minute, I will go inside and speak to the Fifth Lady about it."

It was not long after he went inside before he came out again and said, "The Fifth Lady invites you to come in."

"How would I dare go in by myself?" said Dame Wang. "You had better escort me. I am afraid of the dog."

Tai-an escorted her into the garden and right up to the door of Chin-lien's quarters, where he lifted aside the portiere for her. When Dame Wang went inside, she found the woman wearing her usual toque on her head, and dressed in clothing of brocaded silk. She was made up so that she looked to be:

Modeled in plaster, carved of jade,

and was in her room, sitting on the k'ang, with her feet propped on the rim of the brazier, cracking melon seeds in her mouth. Within the room:

> The drapes are made of embroidered brocade,
> The bed is incised with gold ornamentation,
> Rare antiques vie with each other in beauty,
> Vanity cases gleam brightly in the sunlight.

Upon entering the room, Dame Wang felt obliged to make an obeisance to her, which threw the woman into such consternation that she returned the salutation, saying, "My venerable friend, there is no need for that."

When Dame Wang had performed her obeisance, she sat down on the edge of the k'ang, and the woman asked, "How is it that it has been such a long time since I saw you last?"

"I have thought about you, my lady," responded Dame Wang, "but I have not presumed to intrude upon you."

She then went on to ask, "Have you borne a son, or not?"

"It would have been great if I had," the woman said. "I have had two miscarriages, but neither of them survived."

She then went on to ask, "Has your son gotten married?"

"I haven't started looking for a wife for him yet," said Dame Wang. "He was working for a merchant from the Huai River region but has been home now for more than a year. He has, somehow or other, accumulated enough capital for a small business and has bought a donkey, which he uses to grind flour, the sale of which gives him enough to get by on. I'll find a wife for him sooner or later."

She then went on to ask, "Is His Honor not at home?"

"Father has gone outside the city gate today," the woman said, "in order to join his fellow officials in seeing someone off. The First Lady is also not at home. What did you want to talk to him about?"

"The venerable Ho the Ninth has a matter that he asked me to come and speak to His Honor about," said Dame Wang. "His younger brother, Ho the Tenth, has been implicated in a case of thievery and is currently under arrest in the local office of the Provincial Surveillance Commission, where his case is due to be tried by the commissioner. He is accused of acting as a fence for stolen goods, but he has nothing to do with the matter. He hopes that His Honor will let him off the hook when the matter comes before the bench. If the thieves try to implicate him again, and His Honor rejects the accusation, that will take care of it. If Ho the Tenth is set free, he will purchase gifts and see that His Honor is handsomely rewarded. I have his explanatory note here."

When the woman had read the explanatory note, she said, "Leave it with me. When Father comes home, I'll show it to him."

"The venerable Ho the Ninth is waiting out front," said Dame Wang. "To-morrow, I'll have him come to seek an answer."

The woman told Ch'iu-chü to bring some tea, and before long she brought
in a cup of tea and gave it to Dame Wang to drink.

As Dame Wang sat there, she said, "My lady, you're certainly enjoying an
ample degree of prosperity."

"What's so ample about it?" the woman responded. "It would be all right if
it weren't for all the resentment; but the squabbling goes on all day around
here, without ever coming to an end."

"My lady," objected Dame Wang, "you have only to:
>Open your mouth when the food is served,[27] and
>Rinse your hands when the water arrives.
Since you:
>Are studded with gold and decked with silver,
and have:
>Slaves and maidservants at your beck and call,
what reason do you have to be resentful?"

"As the sayings aptly put it," the woman said, "if there are:
>Three nests where there's only room for two,
and they contain:
>Both legitimate wives and lowly concubines,[28]
>A pair of serving spoons in the same crock,
>Will either bump or rub against each other.
How can there fail to be some friction?"

"My good lady," said Dame Wang, "no one else is as smart as you are. So
long as His Honor continues to enjoy such prosperous times, where your personal consumption is concerned, you need only:
>Deal with matters as they occur."

She then went on to say, "Tomorrow, I'll have him come to seek an
answer."

Thereupon, she said farewell and got up to go.

"My venerable friend," said the woman, "why don't you stay a little longer
before you go?"

"That would be an imposition on Ho the Ninth, who is waiting for me,"
said Dame Wang. "I won't stay any longer but will come and see you another
day."

The woman did not endeavor to detain her any further, but let her go.

When she got to the gate, she also reminded Tai-an why she had come, and
he reassured her, saying, "You can go on home, venerable dame. When Father
comes home, I'll speak to him about it."

"Brother Tai-an," said Ho the Ninth, "I'll come early tomorrow morning to
seek an answer."

Thereupon, he went off together with Dame Wang.

That evening, when Hsi-men Ch'ing arrived home, Tai-an told him about
the matter.

Upon going to Chin-lien's quarters, he read the explanatory note and turned it over to an attendant, saying, "Remind me about this when I get to the yamen tomorrow."

He then instructed Ch'en Ching-chi to take care of sending out the invitations for the following day, the third of the month; and also, without informing Ch'un-mei, sent Ch'in-t'ung to deliver a tael of silver and a box of delicacies to the home of Han Tao-kuo, and explain that they were intended to mollify Second Sister Shen's resentment.

Wang Liu-erh received them with an ingratiating smile and said, "She would not dare to harbor resentment. Tell your master and mistress that she is sorry to have offended the young lady, Ch'un-mei."

But no more of this.

That evening, when Yüeh-niang arrived home, she was wearing a fur coat of white ermine, over a brocaded jacket, and a skirt of blue brocade; and riding in a large sedan chair, accompanied by four orderlies bearing lanterns. Upon arriving home, she first greeted Sister-in-law Wu and the others and then went to salute Hsi-men Ch'ing, who was in the master suite drinking wine.

"When Hsia Yen-ling's wife saw that I had come," she reported, "she was as pleased as could be and expressed her thanks for our lavish gifts. There were many female guests, both relatives and neighbors, there today. It so happens that she has received a letter from Hsia Yen-ling, along with a letter for you, which she will have delivered to you tomorrow. They are scheduled to depart on the sixth or seventh of the month and have already hired carts in which to transport the entire household to the capital. She repeatedly requested that we allow Pen the Fourth to escort them to the capital, from which he would return immediately. Pen the Fourth's daughter, Chang-chieh, kowtowed to me today. She has grown up, and developed quite an attractive figure. It was no wonder that she kept stealing glances at me as she stood to my side to serve the tea. I did not recognize her. It was only when Hsia Yen-ling's wife, who has renamed her as Jui-yün, said to her, 'Come over and kowtow to the wife of Hsi-men Ch'ing,' that she put down the tea tray and proceeded to kowtow to me four times. I presented her with two floral ornaments of gold. By this time Hsia Yen-ling's wife has developed a real fondness for her and has raised her status above that of a mere concubine, treating her as though she were her own daughter."

"That child is certainly lucky," Hsi-men Ch'ing remarked sardonically. "She could scarcely have expected to be treated so indulgently at anyone else's hands. Who else would not only have refrained from cursing her as a slave, and peppering her with abuse, but also have been willing to elevate her status?"

Yüeh-niang gave him a look and said, "Why you filthy-mouthed good-for-nothing! No doubt you refer to the fact that I have been known to castigate your favorite concubine."

Hsi-men Ch'ing laughed at this and then went on to ask, "If she borrows Pen the Fourth to escort the family to the capital, who will take charge of my silk goods store?"

"You might as well close the shop for a few days," said Yüeh-niang.

"Closing the shop for a few days would be bad for business," responded Hsi-men Ch'ing. "As we approach the New Year's festival, silk goods and sewing supplies are selling fast. How can we afford to close the shop? I'll have to decide about it another day."

When they had finished their conversation, Yüeh-niang went into her boudoir, where she doffed her outer clothes and removed her headgear. She then entered the parlor next door and sat down to visit with Sister-in-law Wu and the others, while the members of the household, high and low, all came in to pay their respects and kowtow to her. That evening, Hsi-men Ch'ing spent the night in Sun Hsüeh-o's quarters in the rear compound.

Early the next morning, he went off to the yamen. Who should appear at this juncture but Ho the Ninth, who came to ask Tai-an about the answer to his request and presented him with a tael of silver.

Tai-an explained the situation to him, thus and so, saying, "Yesterday, when Father came home, I told him about your request; and today he has gone to the yamen, where he will exonerate your brother and set him free. You can go to the gate of the yamen and wait for him there."

Upon hearing this, Ho the Ninth was as pleased as could be and set off immediately for the yamen.

When Hsi-men Ch'ing arrived at the yamen, he took his place on the bench, ordered the thieves in the case to be haled before him, and had each of them put in the ankle-squeezers and given twenty strokes of the bamboo, so severely that:

Fresh blood flowed down their legs.

After dismissing the accusation against Ho the Tenth and setting him free, he proceeded to arrest a monk from the Hung-hua Temple to take his place, on the trumped up charge that he had sheltered the thieves in his temple overnight. Can there actually be such cases of injustice in this world? Truly:

Mr. Chang drinks wine, but Mr. Li
    gets drunk;
The mulberry branch is cut with a knife,
    but the willow bark is scarred.[29]

There is a poem that testifies to this:

The destiny of the Sung dynasty was
    coming to an end;
The holders of judicial appointments
    were so dishonest.

Since the scrutiny of the cosmos can
   not to be evaded;
It will ultimately dispel the turbid
   and exalt the pure.

For the party that day, Hsi-men Ch'ing engaged the services of four singing
girls, Wu Yin-erh, Cheng Ai-yüeh, Hung the Fourth, and Ch'i Hsiang-erh.
They arrived before noon, with their costume bags in hand, and trooped into
the master suite, where they kowtowed to Yüeh-niang, Sister-in-law Wu, and
the others. Yüeh-niang saw that they were provided with a serving of tea, after
which, they began to play their instruments and sing for the entertainment of
Sister-in-law Wu, Yüeh-niang, and the others. Whom should they see at this
juncture but Hsi-men Ch'ing, who suddenly came into the room after returning from the yamen. The four singing girls all put down their instruments, came forward with ingratiating smiles, and kowtowed to Hsi-men
Ch'ing:

Just as though inserting a taper in its holder.

After he had sat down, Yüeh-niang asked, "Why is it that you have only now
returned from the yamen?"

"I had to preside over quite a few cases today," explained Hsi-men Ch'ing.

He then turned to Chin-lien and said, "With regard to that matter of the
younger brother of Ho the Ninth that Dame Wang came to intercede for yesterday; I have already exonerated him and set him free today. Those two
thieves continued to implicate him, but I had them each given twenty strokes
with the bamboo and subjected to the squeezers, and then arrested a monk
from a temple outside the city walls to take his place. Tomorrow, I'll fill out the
documents in the case, and have them sent to Tung-p'ing prefecture.

"I also had to deal with a case of illicit fornication between a mother-in-law
and her son-in-law. The son-in-law is still young, not more than thirty-odd
years of age, and is named Sung Te. He married into his wife's family in order
to care for her parents and will not return to his own. Subsequently, his mother-in-law died, and his father-in-law remarried a Ms. Chou, who so exhausted
him that he died less than a year later. This Ms. Chou is still young and, finding it difficult to maintain her chastity, resorted to constantly carrying on with
her son-in-law so outrageously that the members of the household became
aware of it, and she found herself in an untenable position.

"One day, while Sung Te was escorting his mother-in-law into the country
to pay a visit to her natal family, Ms. Chou said to him, 'Although you and I
are not guilty of any transgression:

We have an unearned repute for doing so.[30]
Since we are passing through these deserted hills, why don't the two of us take
advantage of the opportunity to:

Consummate a conjugal relationship?'[31]

Sung Te thereupon proceeded to fornicate with her. After returning from this visit to her natal family, the two of them continued to commit fornication with each other on a regular basis. Later on, after she had punished one of her maidservants, the maid told her neighbors what was going on, and they lodged an accusation against them. Today, after obtaining their depositions, I have had them remanded to Tung-p'ing prefecture. Once they get there, since they are guilty of the crime of fornication between a son-in-law and mother-in-law, thus falling within the fifth degree of mourning relationships,[32] the penalty for both parties is strangulation."

"If it were up to me," said P'an Chin-lien, "I would not think it excessive to have that tale-bearing maidservant beaten to a pulp and sentenced to death.

If you don the black livery of a servant,
You must cling to even the blackest post.

With a single sentence, she brought ruin upon her employers."

"I did submit that slave to some severe treatment with the squeezers," said Hsi-men Ch'ing. "Merely on account of a temporary peccadillo on their part, that slave will be responsible for the death of the two of them."

Yüeh-niang responded to this by saying:

"If superiors act improperly, their subordinates
    will fail to respect them.[33]
If the bitch does not wag her tail,
Dogs will not attempt to mount her.[34]

Generally speaking, it is the depravity of the woman that is at fault. If they are chaste, who would dare to molest them?"

The four singing girls all laughed at this, saying, "What Mother says is right enough. Even we singing girls inside the quarter must avoid taking on the friends of our patrons. How much the more should this be true for women on the outside."

After this conversational exchange was completed, a meal was provided for Hsi-men Ch'ing to eat.

Suddenly, they heard the sound of drums and music coming from the reception hall in the front compound, indicating that Military Director-in-Chief Ching Chung had arrived. Hsi-men Ch'ing promptly donned his official cap and girdle and went out to welcome him into the reception hall. After exchanging the conventional amenities, he thanked his visitor for his lavish gifts, and they sat down in the positions of guest and host.

After tea had been served, Hsi-men Ch'ing told him, thus and so, "Censor Sung Ch'iao-nien received your explanatory note and immediately agreed to your request. You are to be congratulated, and your promotion should occur in the near future."

Upon hearing this, Ching Chung turned around, got up from his seat, and bowed to express his thanks, saying, "I have put you to a lot of trouble venerable sir. Your efforts on my behalf will be:

Imprinted in my heart, never to be forgotten."

Hsi-men Ch'ing went on to say, "I also put in a word or two on behalf of Commandant Chou Hsiu, and Censor Sung Ch'iao-nien is sure to take appropriate action."

As they were talking, it was suddenly announced that Eunuch Director Liu and Eunuch Director Hsüeh had arrived, and they were conducted inside to the accompaniment of drums and music. Hsi-men Ch'ing descended the steps to welcome them into the reception hall, where they exchanged the customary amenities. The two eunuchs were both dressed in python robes of blue silk with a raised pattern, wore jeweled chatelaines, and proceeded to take their places at the center of the seating arrangement.

After this, Commandant Chou Hsiu arrived and sat down to join in the conversation.

Military Director-in-Chief Ching Chung addressed Commandant Chou Hsiu, saying, "Ssu-ch'üan is really magnanimous. The other day, when Censor Sung Ch'iao-nien hosted a farewell banquet for His Excellency Hou Meng at his place here, he took advantage of the occasion to sing your praises to Censor Sung, and he promised to keep you in mind. A lofty promotion for you is imminent."

Commandant Chou also bowed to Hsi-men Ch'ing and expressed no end of gratitude.

Later on, Militia Commander Chang Kuan, Battalion Commander Ho Yung-shou, Wang the Third, Battalion Commander Fan Hsün, Wu K'ai, and Ch'iao Hung all arrived, one after the other.

On coming in the gate, Ch'iao Hung wore his newly acquired official cap and girdle and was accompanied by four attendants in black livery. After greeting the assembled company, he proceeded to bow four times to Hsi-men Ch'ing, who was sitting in an oversize chair.

The assembled guests asked about the occasion for celebration, and Hsi-men Ch'ing said, "In return for the customary donation, my kinsman has just received the gracious distinction of appointment as an honorary prefectural official."

"Since he is a relative of Ssu-ch'üan's," said Commandant Chou Hsiu, "the rest of us should all tender our congratulations."

"I appreciate the good will of you venerable gentlemen," said Ch'iao Hung, "but I can hardly presume to put you to any trouble."

When this exchange was completed, they all took their seats in order of precedence, while a round of tea was served, after which, they prepared to take their places at the banquet table.

Before the brocade screens, tortoiseshell
    mats are spread;
In the painted chamber, valuable antiques
    vie in splendor.

> Beneath the steps, the tones of pipes and
>> voices resound;
> Upon the table, platters of exotic fruits
>> are displayed.

In a while, when the wine was served and everyone had been assigned a seat, the servants of the various households came forward to take charge of the outer garments of their masters, and the guests sat down in their places.

Wang the Third repeatedly expressed his diffidence over taking a seat among them, but Hsi-men Ch'ing said, "It's just an informal get-together here in my humble abode. It is appropriate for you to keep the other gentlemen company on this occasion."

Wang the Third felt that he had no alternative but to hang his head and sit down to one side.

Before long, after soup and rice had been served, the chef came out to carve the entrée of roast goose and offer a selection of side dishes. Meanwhile, below the steps, the musicians from the Music Offices presented a number of ensemble dance pieces, followed by tumbling performances, vaudeville acts, and a comic farce, after which the four singing girls sedately appeared and proceeded to pay their respects to the company.

> Every one of them is made up to present
>> a flowery countenance;
> Each one sports an immortal's raiment,
>> pearls, and trinkets.
> With silver psalteries and jade mandolas,
>> they sing voluptuously;
> In their hugging turquoise and clinging red,
>> they laugh incessantly.

Truly:

> Amid dancers' skirts and singers' clappers
>> one is forever seeking novelty;
> But when all one's yellow gold is spent
>> nothing but one's body remains.
> A word of advice to wealthy young men:
>> "Don't spend it all too fast;
> The practice of economy is like good medicine,
>> for it can cure poverty."[35]

We will say no more about how, that day, Eunuch Director Liu occupied the seat of honor and distributed extravagant amounts of silver. They continued drinking wine and enjoying themselves until the first watch before the party broke up. Hsi-men Ch'ing provided gratuities for the musicians and sent them on their way, while the four singing girls went back to the master suite to play and sing for Yüeh-niang and her female companions. Yüeh-niang invited

Wu Yin-erh to stay overnight and sent the other three singing girls home. On their way out, they ran into Hsi-men Ch'ing, who was still in the reception hall, and paid their respects to him.

Hsi-men Ch'ing said to Cheng Ai-yüeh, "Tomorrow, bring Li Kuei-chieh with you, so the two of you can sing for us."

Cheng Ai-yüeh realized that because Wang the Third had been there that day, Li Kuei-chieh had not been invited to sing, and laughed, saying, "Father, it's rather late in the game:

The wall of the Warden's Office[36] having collapsed:

the miscreant has escaped."[37]

She then went on to ask, "Who have you invited to your party tomorrow?"

"They're all relatives and friends," said Hsi-men Ch'ing.

"If that beggar Ying the Second is here," said Cheng Ai-yüeh, "I won't come. I have no wish to set eyes on that ugly monstrosity of an adversary."

"He won't be here tomorrow," responded Hsi-men Ch'ing.

"As long as he isn't here, it will be all right," said Cheng Ai-yüeh. "But if that crazy chunk of knife-bait is here, I won't come."

Having spoken, she kowtowed to him and went nonchalantly off without more ado.

After Hsi-men Ch'ing had seen to the clearing away of the utensils, he went to Li P'ing-erh's quarters and went to bed with Ju-i. Of the events of that evening there is no more to tell.

Early the next day, Hsi-men Ch'ing went to the yamen and had the culprits in the two criminal cases he had dealt with the day before remanded to Tung-p'ing prefecture to stand trial. He then went home to host his party.

Those who were invited included Abbot Wu Tsung-che, Brother-in-law Wu the Second, Hua Tzu-yu, Brother-in-law Shen, Brother-in-law Han Ming-ch'uan, Dr. Jen Hou-ch'i, Licentiate Wen, Ying Po-chüeh and the other members of the brotherhood of ten, Li Chih, Huang the Fourth, Tu the Third, and Hsi-men Ch'ing's three business managers. Twelve tables were set up for the guests, while the three powdered-faces, Li Kuei-chieh, Wu Yin-erh, and Cheng Ai-yüeh, served the wine, and the three boy actors, Li Ming, Wu Hui, and Cheng Feng, played and sang for their entertainment.

Just as the wine was being poured, P'ing-an suddenly came in and reported, "Uncle Yün the Second has just succeeded to his elder brother's official position and has come to pay his respects to Father and deliver some gifts."

Upon hearing this news, Hsi-men Ch'ing promptly said, "Invite him to come in."

When Yün Li-shou appeared, he was formally attired in a round-collared robe of black satin with a mandarin square, and a girdle with a plaque of gold around his waist. He was followed by his attendants, bearing the gifts. The first thing he did was to give Hsi-men Ch'ing a card to read, on which was written:

Your protégé Yün Li-shou, who has just succeeded to the post of vice commander of
the Left Guard in Ch'ing-ho district of Shantung province, presents his compliments with a hundred salutations, while deferentially proffering the local products,
ten sable skins, one saltwater fish, one packet of dried shrimp, four preserved geese,
ten preserved ducks, and two sets of oil-paper drapes, as a meager expression of his
respect.

Hsi-men Ch'ing ordered his attendants to accept the gifts and hastened to
express his thanks.

"I only arrived home yesterday," said Yün Li-shou, "and today, I have come
especially to pay my respects to Your Honor."

Thereupon, he proceeded to perform:

> Four brace makes eight kowtows,

saying:

> "My obligation to you could not be greater.

As for these paltry local products:

> They are no more than tokens of my esteem."

After this, he proceeded to exchange the customary amenities and pay his
respects to the rest of the company. When Hsi-men Ch'ing realized that he
now held office as an official, he treated him differently from before, seating
him at the same table with Brother-in-law Wu the Second, promptly seeing to
it that he was provided with a wine goblet, chopsticks, and servings of soup
and rice, and that his attendants were also provided with platters of assorted
snacks as well as meat and wine. He then went on to ask him about the funeral
arrangements for his elder brother, and his inheritance of his official post.

Yün Li-shou then explained in detail how the minister of war, Yü Shen, had
been so affected by the fact that his elder brother had died of illness at his post
on the frontier that he had mandated not only that his right to succeed to his
elder brother's hereditary post should be honored, but that he also be appointed to the position of vice commander of the local guard.

Hsi-men Ch'ing was pleased at this, saying, "Congratulations! Congratulations! On a day to come, I will be sure to come and offer my felicitations."

That day, each member of the company toasted him with a cup of wine,
and the three singing girls kept refilling his goblet, so that it was not long before Yün Li-shou was drunk. Ying Po-chüeh too, at his place at the table, appeared just like a puppet on its strings, constantly jumping up and sitting
down, while teasing Li Kuei-chieh and Cheng Ai-yüeh so that their mutual
badinage seemed as though it would never come to an end.

One of them ridiculed him, saying, "Your affectation is about as incongru-
ous as a left-hand Gate God masquerading with a white face,[38] you profligate
good-for-nothing."

While the other one taunted him as an ugly monstrosity of an adversary, as
unsightly as:

Chu Pa-chieh, sitting in a homeless shelter.[39]

To which Ying Po-chüeh retorted in kind, saying, "As for you two sl/imy kn/aves,[40] your grimy features are utterly repulsive."[41]

We will say no more about the fun and laughter at the party that day as they enjoyed themselves:

> Amid clustering blossoms and clinging brocade, until
> Drinking vessels and game tallies lay helter-skelter.

It was the second watch that night before the party broke up, the three singing girls went their way, and Hsi-men Ch'ing returned to the master suite to spend the night.

The next day, he got up late, ate some congee in the master suite, got dressed, and prepared to go pay a visit to Yün Li-shou.

Who should appear at this juncture but Tai-an, who came in and said, "Pen the Fourth is in the front compound and would like to discuss something with you."

Hsi-men Ch'ing realized that it must be about escorting Hsia Yen-ling's dependents to the capital and went out to meet him in the reception hall.

Pen the Fourth pulled a letter from Commander Hsia Yen-ling out of his sleeve and presented it to Hsi-men Ch'ing, saying, "His Honor Hsia Yen-ling would like to have me escort his dependents to the capital, after which, I could return without delay. I have come to ask Your Honor whether I should go or not."

When Hsi-men Ch'ing had glanced at the language in the letter and saw that it merely expressed regret over their separation, thanked him for looking after his dependents, early and late, and asked if he could avail himself of Pen the Fourth's services to escort them to the capital, he said, "Since he has asked you to do so, there is no reason for you not to go."

He then went on to ask, "When do they plan to start out?"

"This morning," responded Pen the Fourth, "a servant from His Honor's household summoned me, and I was told that they had made definite plans to get into their vehicles and start out on the sixth, which means that I should be able to return by mid-month."

When he had finished speaking, he turned over the keys to the shop on Lion Street to Hsi-men Ch'ing.

"While you are gone," said Hsi-men Ch'ing, "I'll have Brother-in-law Wu the Second take your place in the shop for a couple of days."

Only then did Pen the Fourth bid him farewell, walk out the gate, and go home to pack his luggage.

Hsi-men Ch'ing then donned his formal attire, went out the gate, and set out to call on Commander Yün Li-shou, with a retinue of servants following his horse.

That day it was time for Sister-in-law Wu to return home, and a sedan chair had been engaged to wait for her outside the gate, but this was one of those occasions when:

Something was bound to happen.

Yüeh-niang had filled two gift boxes with a variety of delicacies and was in the master suite preparing to see off Sister-in-law Wu. When she escorted her out the gate to get into her sedan chair, whom should they see but the page boy Hua-t'ung, who was lurking in the saddle room beside the gate, crying his head off. P'ing-an was doing his best to restrain him, but the harder he pulled at the youngster, the louder he cried, and the disturbance was overheard by Yüeh-niang and the others.

After seeing Sister-in-law Wu into her sedan chair and sending her off, Yüeh-niang turned to P'ing-an and demanded, "You lousy jailbird! Why are you pulling at him that way for no good reason? It's only causing him to cry more dementedly than ever."

"Licentiate Wen from across the street has called for him," said P'ing-an, "but he simply refuses to go and is reviling me instead."

"Tell him he must resign himself to going," said Yüeh-niang.

Then, turning to Hua-t'ung, she said, "My child, when Master Wen summons you over there, you simply ought to go. What are you crying about?"

Hua-t'ung continued to protest to P'ing-an, saying, "It's none of your business. I won't go, that's all. What are you tugging me about for?"

"Why won't you go?" asked Yüeh-niang, but the page boy refused to answer.

"This little jailbird," declared Chin-lien, "is nothing but a stiff-necked, sycophantic rascal. When Mother asks you a question, how can you refuse to answer?"

P'ing-an stepped forward at this point and gave him a slap on the face, but the page boy only cried the louder.

"You crazy jailbird!" interjected Yüeh-niang. "Why did you slap him for no good reason? Give him a chance to explain himself. Why do you refuse to go?"

Just as they were interrogating him, who should appear but Tai-an, who came in the gate on horseback.

"Has Father come home?" Yüeh-niang asked him.

"Uncle Yün Li-shou has kept him there for a drink," replied Tai-an. "He sent me home with his formal clothes and wants me to take his felt cap back to him."

When he saw the way that Hua-t'ung was crying, he asked him, "Little gentleman, how can you carry on so frantically, as though your tears would suffice to tear down a wall or fill in a pit?"

"Licentiate Wen from across the street has called for him," explained P'ing-an, "but he refuses to go and has chosen to cry and rail at me instead."

"Brother," said Tai-an, "if Master Wen is calling for you, you'd better be on your guard. His name puns with the words 'warm buttocks,' and he can hardly last a day without enjoying a pair of warm buttocks. But since you've put up with his attentions so far, why are you trying to avoid him today?"

"You crazy jailbird!" protested Yüeh-niang. "What do you mean by all this about warm buttocks?"

"You'd better ask him, Mother," responded Tai-an.

As for P'an Chin-lien:

Before she even got wind of anything,
She was ready for the rain.

Calling Hua-t'ung over to her, she said to him, "Little slave, tell us the truth about it. What does he want with you? If you refuse to tell us, I'll have Mother give you a beating."

She pressed the page boy so hard that he became agitated and said, "All he ever wants from me is to insert that thing of his into my asshole. It's gotten so swollen that it hurts. When I ask him to pull it out as quickly as possible, he refuses to retract it and insists on moving it back and forth. I finally pulled it out myself and ran over here to escape him, but he insists on calling me back."

When Yüeh-niang heard this, she shouted at him, "You crazy little louse of a slave! You'd better get out of here. And as for you, Sister Six, your insistence on interrogating him has solicited this unspeakably obscene talk. Not knowing what was coming, and assuming that it would be in acceptable language, I bent my ear to listen to it. This gentleman is really a good-for-nothing, unfit for decent company. When we lend him the services of a page boy, he has the gall to commit such offenses behind our backs."

"First Lady," said Chin-lien, "not only do persons fit for decent company commit such deeds; even beggars in their homeless shelters are known to do such things."

"That southerner has a wife," remarked Meng Yü-lou. "How can he conduct himself so shamelessly?"

"The whole time he's been here," said Chin-lien, "we haven't caught so much as a glimpse of his wife. How can that be?"

"How can that be?" responded Tai-an. "You ladies are unlikely to see her at best. Whenever he goes out, he locks the door behind him. In the last half year, the only time I've seen her is the one time she took a sedan chair to go pay a visit to her mother; and on that occasion, she came back before evening. She practically never ventures outside the gate. At night, she goes out to the gate to empty the commode, that's all."

"That wife of his must be a hopeless wretch," said Chin-lien. "Having married a man like that, I doubt if she ever sees the light of day. I venture to say that, confined to her room that way, it must feel as though she's serving a sentence in the penitentiary."

After discussing it for a while, Yüeh-niang and the rest of them went back to the rear compound.

Upon arriving home around sunset, Hsi-men Ch'ing went into the master suite and sat down.

Hua-t'ung Is Reduced to Tears in Escaping Licentiate Wen

"Did manager Yün Li-shou keep you for a visit?" asked Yüeh-niang.

"When he saw that I had come to call on him," said Hsi-men Ch'ing, "he was so pleased that:

There was nothing he was not prepared to do.[42]

He set up a table, opened a jug of wine, and invited me to sit down and join him for a drink. At present, since Commander Ching Chung of the local guard has been promoted, he is in line to succeed him as the seal-holding officer. Tomorrow, I am planning to prepare congratulatory gifts for him and Kinsman Ch'iao Hung, and our colleagues have agreed to present them with commemorative scrolls. I'll have to prevail upon Licentiate Wen to draft two appropriate inscriptions and purchase scrolls right away, so he can inscribe them for us."

"How can you bring yourself to employ any such Licentiate Wen or Licentiate Wu?" exclaimed Yüeh-niang. "If you make use of that kind of shameless good-for-nothing, and the word gets out, it will have the effect of showing us in the ugliest possible light."

When Hsi-men Ch'ing heard this, it gave him quite a start, and he asked, "What do you mean?"

"There's no need for you to ask me," said Yüeh-niang. "Ask your page boy."

"Which page boy is that?" asked Hsi-men Ch'ing.

"You know perfectly well who it is," said Chin-lien. "It's Hua-t'ung, that lousy little slave. When we went out to see off Sister-in-law Wu, he was crying by the gate and complained, thus and so, about how that southerner, Wen Pi-ku, was abusing him."

On hearing this, Hsi-men Ch'ing remained somewhat incredulous and said, "Call that little slave here so I can interrogate him."

He then sent Tai-an to the front compound to summon Hua-t'ung, who came back to the master suite and knelt down before him.

Hsi-men Ch'ing threatened to subject him to the squeezers and said, "You lousy slave! Tell me the truth. What does he do when he calls for you?"

"He calls for me," said Hua-t'ung, "in order to get me drunk, so he can get down to his dirty business with me. Today, he hurt me so badly that I got away and refused to go back, but he kept sending P'ing-an after me, and P'ing-an was hitting me when Mother came out and saw what was going on. He constantly questions me about the intimate details of what goes on in the private quarters of the ladies of the household, but I refuse to say anything. And yesterday, while Father was hosting a party here, he even tried to induce me to snitch a few silver utensils and give them to him. On another occasion, he went to visit Master Ni P'eng and showed him the text of a letter he had drafted for Father; and Master Ni also showed it to His Honor Hsia Yen-ling."

If Hsi-men Ch'ing had not heard these words nothing might have happened, but having heard them, he exclaimed:

"In painting a tiger, you can paint the skin,
      but you can't paint the bones;
   In knowing people, you can know their faces,
      but you can't know their hearts.[43]
I took him to be a decent human being. Who could have known that he was
nothing but:
      The skeleton of a dog wrapped in human skin.[44]
What further use do I have for the likes of him?"

He then ordered Hua-t'ung to get up and go, saying, "You don't need to go
over there anymore."

Hua-t'ung, accordingly, kowtowed to him and went out to the front
compound.

Hsi-men Ch'ing turned to Yüeh-niang and said, "It's no wonder that, the
other day, our kinsman Chai Ch'ien chided me, saying:

      If critical matters are not kept secret
         harm will result.
I couldn't think who could have done it at the time, but now it turns out that
he was the person guilty of leaking my information to an outsider. How could
I have known? What point is there in continuing to keep such a worthless dog-
bone of a creature around for no good reason?"

"Who do you think you're telling about it?" said Yüeh-niang. "We don't
have any child who requires schooling, so what need is there to maintain
someone in the household merely to handle our social correspondence? After
all, how much do we have in the way of social correspondence to justify maintaining such a person, only to have him carry on so egregiously, while peddling our secrets to others?"

"Needless to say," responded Hsi-men Ch'ing, "tomorrow I'll simply send
him packing, that's all."

He then summoned P'ing-an and told him, "Tell the gentleman across the
street that your master needs the space he is living in for the storage of merchandise, and that he will have to look for accommodations elsewhere. And if
he should come over to see me, stop him at the gate and tell him that I am not
at home."

P'ing-an nodded in assent and went back to his post.

Hsi-men Ch'ing then said to Yüeh-niang, "Today, Pen the Fourth came to
say goodbye. He is going to leave on the sixth, in order to escort Hsia Yen-
ling's dependents on their way to the Eastern Capital. It occurs to me that,
since there won't be anyone in charge of the silk goods store, I might as well
ask Brother-in-law Wu the Second to take charge of the store for a few days.
One way or the other, he and Lai-chao can take turns, three days at a time,
spending the night at the shop, and they can eat together. What do you
think?"

"I won't express an opinion," said Yüeh-niang. "It's up to you. You can call on him if you like. I won't interfere, but people may say that I've intervened in favor of my brother."

Hsi-men Ch'ing paid no attention to this but immediately dispatched Ch'i-t'ung, telling him, "Go and invite Brother-in-law Wu the Second to come here."

It was not long before Brother-in-law Wu the Second showed up. Hsi-men Ch'ing sat down with him to share a drink in the front reception hall and turned the keys to the shop over to him. The next day, he and Lai-chao proceeded to Lion Street together to open the shop. But no more of this.

To resume our story, when Licentiate Wen saw that Hua-t'ung refused all night long to come back and sleep with him, he became apprehensive about the situation.

The next day, P'ing-an came over and said to him, "My master sends his regards to you, but sooner or later he is going to need the space you are occupying to store merchandise and would like you to find accommodations elsewhere."

When Licentiate Wen heard this, he:
        Turned pale with consternation,
and realized that Hua-t'ung must have let the cat out of the bag.

Putting on his formal attire, he expressed a desire to speak to Hsi-men Ch'ing, but P'ing-an said, "Father is at the yamen and hasn't come home yet."

When the time he normally came home arrived, Licentiate Wen, garbed in formal attire, came across the street to wait for him and handed a long letter that he had prepared to Ch'in-t'ung, but Ch'in-t'ung refused to accept it, saying, "Father has just returned from the yamen and is tired out. He has gone back to the rear compound to rest, and I would not presume to disturb him."

Only then did Licentiate Wen fully realize that he was being deliberately kept at a distance, and he went to Licentiate Ni P'eng's place to consult about it, after which, he moved his dependents back to his original dwelling place. Truly:
        Even if one could draw off all the water
            of the West River,
        It would hardly suffice to wash away
            this day's shame.

No one lacks a beginning, but few
    come to a good end;[45]
Friendship as insipid as water is
    most likely to last.[46]

From of old, humans do not have a
   thousand good days;
Just as flowers do not remain red
   after being plucked.[47]

     If you want to know the outcome of these events,
     Pray consult the story related in the following chapter.

Chapter 77

HSI-MEN CH'ING SLOGS THROUGH
THE SNOW TO VISIT CHENG AI-YÜEH;
PEN THE FOURTH'S WIFE SITS BY
THE WINDOW WAITING FOR A TRYST

Flying oars in their commotion disturb
    the early plum blossoms;
Which defy the frigid weather as they
    undulate back and forth.
The wind savors their fragile charm,
    wafting their fragrance;
The moon enjoys their subtle allure,
    enhancing their beauty.
At the Liang court they were portentous
    omens for Emperor Hsiao;[1]
In the Ch'i palace they were matchmakers
    for Consort P'an Yü-nu.[2]
Unaware of the gut-wrenching heartache
    caused by separation;
They only augment one's grief as they
    hover above the water.[3]

THE STORY GOES that when Licentiate Wen realized that Hsi-men
Ch'ing would not grant him an interview, he felt ashamed at his own guilt and
proceeded forthwith to move his dependents back to his old dwelling place.
Hsi-men Ch'ing subsequently arranged to have the studio that he had occupied cleaned up and made into a guest room. But no more of this.

One day, Provincial Graduate Shang Hsiao-t'ang came to take his leave
before setting out for the capital in order to compete in the *chin-shih* examinations and asked Hsi-men Ch'ing if he could borrow a leather trunk and a felt
jacket for the trip. Hsi-men Ch'ing sat down with him while they shared a
serving of tea and also presented him with a farewell gift.

He then went on to say, "My kinsman Ch'iao Hung has recently received
an appointment as an honorary official, and my associate Yün Li-shou has succeeded to a hereditary post while continuing to hold his current substantive

position, and I would like to present them with a pair of commemorative scrolls in celebration of these events. I wonder, venerable sir, if you have any acquaintances whom you might prevail upon to lend a hand for this purpose. Your pupil would see to it that they were appropriately compensated for their efforts."

Shang Hsiao-t'ang laughed, saying, "Venerable sir, what need is there for any compensation? Your pupil's former schoolmate Nieh Liang-hu, who is a degree candidate in the local Military School, is currently living in my humble abode, where he is acting as tutor to my son. He has a knack for literary composition in a variety of modes. Your pupil will speak to him about your request. All you have to do, venerable sir, is to send your esteemed servant to my place with the scrolls."

Hsi-men Ch'ing hastened to express his gratitude, and after drinking his tea, Shang Hsiao-t'ang took his leave. Hsi-men Ch'ing forthwith sealed up two handkerchiefs and five mace of silver and sent Ch'in-t'ung to deliver them, along with the scrolls, the felt jacket, and the leather trunk, to Shang Hsiao-t'ang's place, where they were duly accepted.

In less than two days, the scrolls were inscribed, and when they were delivered, Hsi-men Ch'ing hung them up on the wall of the reception hall. Behold, they were:

Brocade scrolls of green velvet,
With characters of blazing gold,

which had been dashed off:

Without altering a single stroke.

Hsi-men Ch'ing was utterly delighted by them.

Who should appear at this juncture but Ying Po-chüeh, who came in and asked, "When are you planning to hold the celebrations in honor of Ch'iao Hung and Yün Li-shou; have the inscriptions on the scrolls been completed or not; and why is it that the venerable Licentiate Wen has been nowhere to be seen the last few days?"

"Why refer to the venerable Licentiate Wen?" responded Hsi-men Ch'ing. "He is nothing but a canine excuse for a human being."

He then proceeded, thus and so, to tell Ying Po-chüeh what had happened.

"Brother," responded Ying Po-chüeh, "I have always said of that person that:

His words overstate the facts,

and:

He is as superficial as can be.

It's a good thing you had the foresight to get rid of him, or he might well have corrupted the other page boys in the household."

He then went on to ask, "As for the commemorative scrolls for the two gentlemen, who did you get to inscribe them?"

"Yesterday, Shang Hsiao-t'ang came to call on me," said Hsi-men Ch'ing, "and mentioned that his friend Nieh Liang-hu was good at literary composition. So I urged him to get Nieh Liang-hu to inscribe them, and the completed scrolls are already here. Let me show them to you."

Thereupon, he led Ying Po-chüeh into the reception hall to take a look at them, and he expressed no end of admiration, saying, "Brother, you have fulfilled our social obligations. You ought to send them off to their recipients as soon as possible, so they can make the necessary preparations."

"Tomorrow is an auspicious day," said Hsi-men Ch'ing. "I've already prepared the congratulatory gifts of mutton and wine, red banners, and boxes of candied fruit and will have them delivered as early as possible."

As they were speaking, a servant suddenly reported, "His Honor Hsia Yen-ling's son has come to bid you farewell. Early tomorrow morning, the eighth, he is planning to set out for the capital. When I told him that you were not at home, he said that you ought to let His Honor Ho Yung-shou know, so that he can send someone over to look after the place first thing tomorrow morning."

Hsi-men Ch'ing looked at the accordion-bound six-leaved card and saw that the message on it read, "The junior member of your colleague's family, Hsia Ch'eng-en, presents his compliments in order to thank you for your assistance and bid you farewell."

He then remarked, "The departures of Shang Hsiao-t'ang and the dependents of the Hsia household will require the presentation of two lengths of fragrant silk fabric as parting gifts."

Turning to Ch'in-t'ung, he instructed him, "Go quickly to buy these gifts, and then get my son-in-law to seal them up and write cards to deliver with them."

Just as he was settling down in his studio together with Ying Po-chüeh, whom he had invited to share a meal with him, P'ing-an suddenly appeared, in a state of obvious agitation, and presented three calling cards, reporting, "Administration Commissioner Wang, Assistant Commissioner Lei, and Secretary An have come to pay their respects."

Hsi-men Ch'ing, upon looking at the cards and seeing that they were from Wang Po-yen, Lei Ch'i-yüan, and An Ch'en, hurriedly proceeded to don his formal garb and buckle his girdle.

"Brother," said Ying Po-chüeh, "I can see that you are busy. As soon as I have finished eating, I'd better go."

"I'll get together with you again tomorrow," said Hsi-men Ch'ing, as he straightened his clothes and went out to greet his visitors.

The three officials politely deferred to each other as they came in. They wore mandarin squares, one of which was emblazoned with a silver pheasant, one of them with an egret in the clouds, and one of them with a *hsieh-chih*, the mythical one-horned goat that was said to gore wrongdoers, and they were attended by a host of subordinate officials. Upon entering the large reception hall, they exchanged the customary amenities and referred gratefully to the trouble they had put him to in the past.

In a little while, after they had consumed a serving of tea and were sitting together in conversation, An Ch'en said, "Lei Ch'i-yüan, Wang Po-yen, and I have come to impose upon you once again. Chao T'ing, the prefect of Hang-chou in Chekiang, has recently been promoted to the post of minister of the Court of Judicial Review, and the three of us would like to borrow the use of your distinguished premises in order to invite him to a party in his honor. We have already sent him an invitation to attend the party on the ninth. Including you as our host, five tables will be required, and your pupil will take care of providing actors for the occasion, but I don't know whether you will consent to this or not."

"In response to your command, venerable sir," said Hsi-men Ch'ing, "your pupil cannot but:

Sweep the doorway in respectful anticipation."[4]

Secretary An Ch'en ordered one of his clerks to hand over a joint contribution of three taels of silver, and Hsi-men Ch'ing had one of his attendants put it away.

As he was escorting them to the gate, Lei Ch'i-yüan said to Hsi-men Ch'ing, "The other day, in response to a letter from Ch'ien Lung-yeh stating that Sun Wen-hsiang was one of your employees, your pupil saw to it that both he and his father were released. Have they come to tell you about it or not?"

"Yes they have," said Hsi-men Ch'ing, "and I am much obliged to you for your efforts on my behalf.

Permit me to offer you an obeisance in return."

"You and I are good friends," responded Lei Ch'i-yüan. "There is no need to concern yourself further about it."

When they had finished speaking and bowing in farewell to each other, his guests got into their sedan chairs and departed.

It so happens that, from the time that P'an Chin-lien took over responsibility for the household expenses, she had supplied herself with a new set of scales. Every day, when the page boys came home with the groceries they had bought, she insisted that they bring in their purchases for her to evaluate before she would pay out the money to reimburse them. She had Ch'un-mei pay out the money and take charge of the scales. The page boys were frequently cursed by Ch'un-mei till they looked as though:

Their heads had been sprayed with dog's blood,

and they felt as though they were:

Braving the danger of extinction.[5]

On the slightest pretext, she would tell them off and threaten to have Hsi-men Ch'ing beat them.

For this reason, the page boys all harbored resentment against her and said to each other, "It was much better when the Third Lady was handling the money. As for the Fifth Lady, whatever we do, she:

Rarely says a word without threatening a beating."[6]

To resume our story, that day Hsi-men Ch'ing went to the yamen early, and when the session was over, he said to Ho Yung-shou, "Hsia Yen-ling's dependents have left by now. Have you delegated someone to go look after the place, and see that the doors are locked or not?"

"Yes I have," responded Ho Yung-shou. "Yesterday, they sent someone over to speak to me about it, and your pupil has already sent a servant to take care of it."

"Today," said Hsi-men Ch'ing, "I would like to accompany my colleague over there to take a look at the place."

Thereupon, the two of them left the yamen and rode their horses, side by side, to Hsia Yen-ling's former residence. His dependents had already vacated the premises, and Ho Yung-shou's servant was standing by at the gate. The two officials dismounted and went inside to the reception hall, after which, Hsi-men Ch'ing led Ho Yung-shou on a tour of inspection, both front and rear. When they came back to the ornamental pavilion in the front garden, they saw that it was surrounded by a stretch of vacant ground, without anything in the way of grass or vegetation growing on it.

"When my colleague moves in," said Hsi-men Ch'ing, "you ought to make a pleasure ground out of this area. You can plant it with ornamental flowers, and make some repairs to this pavilion."

"I will do that for sure," said Ho Yung-shou. "This coming spring, I plan to refurbish the place, procure bricks and tiles, lumber and stone, with which to construct three summerhouses, and invite my colleague over to:

Alleviate his ennui and dispel his melancholy."

Hsi-men Ch'ing then went on to ask, "How many dependents from your household will come to reside here?"

"There are only a few members of your pupil's own household," said Ho Yung-shou, "but there will also be several families of servants and other attendants, something over ten persons in all."

"In that case," said Hsi-men Ch'ing, "you will hardly fill the place. The front and rear compounds of this residence contain more than fifty rooms."

After they had finished inspecting the place, Ho Yung-shou told his servants to clean it up, sweep it out, and take care of locking the doors.

He then went on to say, "In a few days, I will write to my venerable uncle in the Eastern Capital, and arrange to have my dependents transported here by the year's end."

That day, after Hsi-men Ch'ing had said farewell and returned home, Ho Yung-shou took another look around and then went back to his quarters in the yamen. It was not until the next day that he collected his luggage and moved into his new residence. But no more of this.

Hsi-men Ch'ing had no sooner arrived home and dismounted from his horse than he found that Ho the Ninth had purchased a bolt of fabric, a selection of four delicacies, a chicken and a goose, and a jar of wine and brought them to thank him for his intervention on behalf of his younger brother. In addition, Eunuch Director Liu had sent a servant to deliver a box of delicacies, a selection of large and small pure-red candles decorated with yellow tracery, twenty tablecloths, eighty sticks of government-grade incense, a box of aloeswood incense, a jar of wine he had brewed himself according to a palace recipe, and a freshly slaughtered pig.

As Hsi-men Ch'ing came in the gate, Eunuch Director Liu's servant kowtowed to him and said, "My master wishes to convey his compliments, along with these paltry gifts, for Your Honor to give away to someone if you like."

"I provided your venerable master with but scant entertainment the other day," said Hsi-men Ch'ing, "yet still he sends me these lavish presents."

He then ordered an attendant to take charge of the gifts and invited the messenger to wait a minute. Before long, Hua-t'ung came in with a cup of tea for him, while Hsi-men Ch'ing sealed up five mace of silver as a gratuity and sent him off with a written reply.

When Ho the Ninth was invited to come in, he found Hsi-men Ch'ing standing in the reception hall, having removed his official cap and exchanged it for a "loyal and tranquil hat" of white felt. Upon seeing Ho the Ninth, he took him by the hand and led him into the reception hall.

Ho the Ninth hastened to bend his back and kowtow to him, saying, "In the past, thanks to the way in which Your Honor's:

Celestial grace permitted him to be reborn,
my younger brother's:
Gratitude for your kindness is not shallow."

He begged Hsi-men Ch'ing to accept his obeisance, but Hsi-men Ch'ing would not allow him to kowtow and dragged him to his feet, saying, "Old Ninth, you and I are long-standing friends. There is no need for that sort of thing."

"Your Honor," responded Ho the Ninth:

"The present cannot be compared to the past.[7]
Insignificant as I am, I could hardly presume to sit down in your presence."

He insisted on standing to one side while Hsi-men Ch'ing kept him company for a serving of tea.

"Old Ninth," Hsi-men Ch'ing went on to say, "what need was there for you to go to the trouble of presenting these gifts to me? I absolutely refuse to accept them. If anyone should try to take advantage of you, just come tell me about it, and I will see to it that your indignation is assuaged. If the district yamen should assign some onerous task to you, I can intervene on your behalf by sending a card to His Honor Li Ta-t'ien."

"I am cognizant of Your Honor's consideration," said Ho the Ninth, "but I am old now, and have already arranged for my son, Ho Ch'in, to take over my duties."

"That's all right then," said Hsi-men Ch'ing. "You should be able to enjoy your greater leisure."

He then went on to say, "Since you refuse to take them back, I will agree to accept your gifts of food and drink, but you must consent to take that bolt of fabric home with you. I won't retain you any longer."

Ho the Ninth then proceeded to bid him farewell with:

A thousand thanks and ten thousand
    expressions of gratitude.

Hsi-men Ch'ing remained sitting in the reception hall, where he supervised the packing of the congratulatory gifts: the boxes of candied fruit, red banners, mutton and wine, inscribed scrolls, and so forth, including the individual contributions of his colleagues. When this was completed, he dispatched Tai-an to deliver the first consignment to the home of Ch'iao Hung and then sent Wang Ching to take the other consignment to the home of Yün Li-shou.

Upon Tai-an's return, he reported that he had been given a gratuity of five mace of silver by the Ch'iao household. When Wang Ching arrived at the home of Yün Li-shou, he was served food and wine and rewarded with a length of pure-black muslin and a pair of loafers. He returned with an accordion-bound thank-you note that read, "Your protégé presents his compliments, and will extend an invitation on another day." Hsi-men Ch'ing was utterly delighted by this and went back to Yüeh-niang's room in the rear compound to have something to eat.

While there, he said to Yüeh-niang, "Since the departure of Pen the Fourth, Brother-in-law Wu the Second has been handling the business at the store on Lion Street. Since I have some free time today, I propose to go there and see how things are going."

"You might as well go ahead," said Yüeh-niang. "If any food and wine is required, send a page boy back here for it."

"I understand," said Hsi-men Ch'ing.

Having issued orders that his horse be prepared, he donned his felt "loyal and tranquil cap," his sable earmuffs, a green woolen tunic emblazoned with a mandarin square, and a pair of white-soled black boots and set out for Lion Street, accompanied by Ch'in-t'ung and Tai-an.

When he arrived at the store he found that Brother-in-law Wu the Second and Lai-chao had hung out the flowery braided basket that served as a shop sign and were busily engaged in selling the stock of piece goods, sewing supplies, and silk floss. The store was so crowded with customers that they could hardly handle them all. Hsi-men Ch'ing dismounted, took a look at the situation, and then went back to a heated inner room and sat down.

Brother-in-law Wu the Second came in, bowed to him, and said, "We are currently making a profit of twenty taels of silver a day."

Hsi-men Ch'ing instructed Lai-chao's wife, "The Beanpole," saying, "Make sure that Brother-in-law Wu the Second is supplied with tea and food every day, as usual. Don't be remiss about it."

"I personally prepare wine and food for him every day," said Lai-chao's wife.

Hsi-men Ch'ing observed that the sky was overcast. Behold:

Amid dense masses of dark clouds,
Gusts of cold wind beleaguer one.

It looked as though it were going to snow. Hsi-men Ch'ing suddenly thought that he would like to visit Cheng Ai-yüeh's establishment in the licensed quarter.

Thereupon, he ordered Ch'in-t'ung, "Ride my horse back to the house and bring me my fur coat. And tell the First Lady that if she has a serving of wine and food available, to send it in a box for Brother-in-law Wu the Second to consume."

Ch'in-t'ung assented, set off on his errand, and returned before long with Hsi-men Ch'ing's full-length sable coat, followed by an orderly bearing a box of wine and food, which contained four saucers of marinated chicken appetizers and sautéed pigeon, four saucers of seafood to go with the wine, a plate of leek stalks, and a pewter flagon of wine.

Hsi-men Ch'ing remained in the room with Brother-in-law Wu the Second and drank three cups of wine, after which he said to him, "Since you are going to remain here overnight, you can enjoy these things at your leisure. I am going to go home."

Thereupon, he put on his eye shades, mounted his horse, and, with Tai-an and Ch'in-t'ung attending him, headed straight for Cheng Ai-yüeh's establishment in the licensed quarter. As he passed the corner of East Street, lo and behold:

Fluttering and swirling from on high,
A skyful of auspicious snow came flying down.

Truly:

Large snowflakes, the size of a fist,
    danced in the void;
The pedestrians on the road could do
    nothing but complain.[8]

Behold:

Silently, a severe cold envelops the ground;
The snowfall creating a truly awesome scene.
Just like tattered floss or shredded cotton,[9]

Each flake seems as large as a flower basket.
In the woods, bamboo huts and thatched sheds,
Are faced with the risk of imminent collapse.
Members of rich houses and powerful families,
Claim that snow purges pestilence, and
    say there is not enough.
Huddled beside red braziers with their
    animal-shaped briquettes;[10]
Accoutered in their sable cloaks and
    their embroidered gowns;
While fingering plum blossoms in their hands,[11]
They proclaim it to be an auspicious
    portent for the nation;[12]
Without caring for the destitution it
    inflicts upon the poor.
There are even men, living in lofty seclusion,
Who produce a plethora of poems in its praise.[13]

Hsi-men Ch'ing made his way along the street:

Trampling the scattered fragments of alabaster and jade;
His sable coat infested with powdery butterflies;
His horses hoofs disturbing the silvery blossoms;

until he entered the licensed quarter and dismounted at the gate of Cheng Ai-yüeh's establishment.

Upon seeing him, a maidservant flew inside and announced, "His Honor has arrived."

Auntie Cheng came outside to receive him, conducted him into the reception hall, and greeted him, saying, "We are most grateful for the lavish gifts you bestowed upon us the other day. Not only did Ai-chieh impose upon your hospitality, but the First Lady and the Third Lady also rewarded her with a gift of costume jewelry and a handkerchief."

"I fear she received but scant entertainment that day," said Hsi-men Ch'ing, as he proceeded to take a seat.

He then instructed Tai-an, saying, "Bring my horse inside. They have a courtyard in which it can be accommodated."

"Would Your Honor please come back into the parlor and take a seat there?" said Auntie Cheng. "Ai-yüeh has just gotten up and is still combing her hair. She thought that Your Honor was going to pay her a visit yesterday and waited for you all day long. As a result, she is somewhat out of sorts today and got up later than usual."

Hsi-men Ch'ing, consequently, went back to the parlor of her living quarters in the rear of the establishment, where he saw that:

The green gauze window was half open,[14] and
The felt curtains were suspended low,

while in the middle of the floor there stood a brazier of yellow brass, filled with burning charcoal.

Hsi-men Ch'ing sat down in the place of honor, and Cheng Ai-hsiang came out first to greet him, and offer him a serving of tea. Only after that did Cheng Ai-yüeh appear. She wore a "bag of silk" chignon in the Hang-chou style, held in place by a plum-blossom-shaped ornament, and studded with combs and hairpins of incised gold, under a sealskin toque. She was made up so that her cloudy locks resembled swirling mist, enhanced with fragrant powder and incised blossoms. Her torso was clad in a white satin jacket and green brocaded vest, beneath which she wore a six-pleated beige skirt, under which there peeked out the high pointed tips of her tiny golden lotuses:

> Resembling crescent moons,
> Shaped like moth eyebrows.

Truly:

> The immortal of Mount Lo-fu has appeared
>   in the mundane world;[15]
> The Goddess of Witches' Mountain has come
>   into the human realm.[16]

The painted face came out with an ingratiating smile, bowed to Hsi-men Ch'ing, and said, "Father, I didn't get home until late the other day. Not only did the party in the front compound break up late, but when we returned to the rear compound, the First Lady refused to let us go until we had had something to eat. It was the third watch by the time I got home."

Hsi-men Ch'ing laughed, and said, "Little oily mouth! You and Li Kuei-chieh, between you, really managed to land a few resounding hits on Beggar Ying."

"Who was it," responded Cheng Ai-yüeh, "who allowed that ugly monstrosity to join the party, only to attack us with his shitty mouth? On that day, Pockmarked Chu also got drunk and speciously offered to escort us home, but I said to him, 'Isn't Father going to send us home with a lantern escort?'

> When Fatty Chiang falls into the sewer,
> The muck may splash on you."

"That day," said Hsi-men Ch'ing, "I heard Hung the Fourth say that Pockmarked Chu has once again conspired with Wang the Third to patronize Jung Chiao-erh on Main Street."

"He only spent one night at Jung Chiao-erh's place," said Cheng Ai-yüeh. "He burnt moxa on her that once[17] but never went back. At present, he's still patronizing Ch'in Yü-chih."

After they had talked for a while, she said, "Father, I fear you may be cold. Why don't you come into my room and sit there."

Hsi-men Ch'ing then proceeded to move into her room, where he took off his sable cloak and sat down by the painted face next to the brazier. In the room:

> A fragrant aroma assailed the senses.[18]

What should he see but a maidservant who came in to set up a table, on which she placed four saucers of assorted delicacies, and three dishes of ginger sauce; shortly after which, she came in with three bowls of steamed pork dumplings flavored with celery cabbage and chives, and inch-long boiled dumplings. The two sisters kept Hsi-men Ch'ing company as they each consumed one of the bowls.

Cheng Ai-yüeh even offered to give half the contents of her bowl to Hsi-men Ch'ing, but he said, "I've had enough. Just now, in that silk goods store of mine, I was sharing a bite to eat with my brother-in-law Wu the Second when it occurred to me that I would like to come pay you a visit. Unexpectedly, it started to snow, and I sent a page boy home to fetch my fur coat and then proceeded to come over here."

"The other day," said Cheng Ai-yüeh, "didn't you agree to come see me yesterday? I waited for you all day, but you never showed up. How could I have known that you would show up today?"

"Yesterday," said Hsi-men Ch'ing, "a couple of gentlemen came to see me, and I was too busy to come."

"I'd like to ask you, Father," said Cheng Ai-yüeh, "if you happen to have a sable skin you could give to me, so I can make a muffler out of it to wear?"

"That's no problem," said Hsi-men Ch'ing. "The other day, one of my managers came back from Liao-tung and presented me with ten fine sable skins. None of the ladies of my household have mufflers for themselves, so when I have them made up, I'll have one made for you as well."

"Father," said Cheng Ai-hsiang, "you only care for my sister, without bothering to give me one too."

"I'll provide one for each of you sisters," responded Hsi-men Ch'ing.

Thereupon, Cheng Ai-hsiang and Cheng Ai-yüeh hastily got to their feet and bowed to him in gratitude.

"If you see Li Kuei-chieh or Wu Yin-erh," said Hsi-men Ch'ing, "don't tell them about it."

"I understand," responded Cheng Ai-yüeh.

"The other day," she went on to say, "when Li Kuei-chieh saw that Wu Yin-erh had been invited to stay overnight, she asked me how long she had been there, and I did not deceive her but said, 'Yesterday, when His Honor Chou Hsiu was here, the four of us were all present and sang for their entertainment all day. Father said that because Wang the Third was present, he had not invited you. But since today's party was for his relatives and friends and the members of his brotherhood of ten, he had invited you to come and sing for them.' She had nothing further to say about it."

"Your response to her was quite correct," said Hsi-men Ch'ing. "Previously, I had also ceased to engage the services of Li Ming, but he repeatedly asked Ying the Second to intervene on his behalf; and later, on the occasion of the

Hsi-men Ch'ing Tramples the Snow to Visit Cheng Ai-yüeh

Third Lady's birthday, Li Kuei-chieh herself bought presents and came to apologize to me for her misconduct. The ladies of my household spoke up on her behalf, but I did not pay any attention. The other day, I arranged to invite Wu Yin-erh to stay overnight just to show her where things stood."

"I didn't know about the Third Lady's birthday," said Cheng Ai-yüeh, "so I failed to help celebrate it."

"Tomorrow," said Hsi-men Ch'ing, "His Honor Yün Li-shou is giving a party, and I told him, the other day, that you and Wu Yin-erh might be willing to sing for us on that occasion."

"If that is Father's wish, I will do so," responded Cheng Ai-yüeh.

Before long, a maidservant came in and took away the dinner table; after which, the painted face fetched a catalpa-wood box, from which she dumped out a set of thirty-two ivory dominoes and proceeded to play a game of dominoes with Hsi-men Ch'ing upon a felt strip laid over the k'ang, while Cheng Ai-hsiang sat beside them and looked on.

Meanwhile, within the courtyard, the snow continued to come fluttering and swirling down:

Like wind-blown pear blossoms.

Behold:

Dimly it obscures the ornate well curbs;
At every other moment,
One must brush away the bee's whiskers.
Jade dragon's-scales appear to
pervade the firmament;
White crane's-feathers seem to
settle gently to earth.
It reminds one of crabs moving
across the sand;
It is like shattered alabaster
piled on the pavement.

Truly:

Though everyone calls it an omen of a good harvest,
As an omen of a good harvest, what are its effects?
There are indigent people in the city of Ch'ang-an,
Who think it is propitious, but only in moderation.[19]

The three of them continued playing dominoes for some time, without anyone being established as the winner. In a little while, wine was served, and they proceeded to drink it. On the tabletop:

Platters are piled with exotic fruits;
Only the rarest delicacies are arrayed.
Tea is brewed from dragon tablets;

Wine is poured of amber coloration.[20]
Lyrics are sung to the tune "Golden Threads,"
As, with a smile, they part their ruby lips.

Cheng Ai-hsiang and Cheng Ai-yüeh proffered wine to their guest as they stood to either side. Then, with:

The bridges on their psalteries ranged like wild geese,
As they gently strummed the silken strings,

the two sisters entertained him with the song suite that begins with the tune "Green Jacket":

I think of that captivating beauty, with her
   striking personality;
I think of that captivating beauty, who was
   so indulgent with me.
I recall how we walked together hand in hand,[21]
   laughing as we went;
Saluting the breeze and apostrophizing the moon,[22]
   in lines of poetry.
She was warm and soft; I was handsome and clever;
Both in the springtime of our youth.
Who could have anticipated that these fish who
   swim as a pair should be separated?
The vase has fallen, the hairpin is broken;[23]
And at this time, the fish are submerged,
   the geese are distant.[24]

To the tune "Cursing One's Lover":

Once that captivating beauty was gone,
I have had no further news of her.
In thinking of her, my feelings are like lacquer,
   my sentiments like glue.
I constantly remember how we enjoyed each other
   on the same pillow.
I think of her flowery loveliness, and
   her willowy sinuosity;
A face that could topple kingdoms and cities.[25]

To the tune "Beating the Festival Drum":

She exhibits a thousand graceful charms;[26]
Romantic and quick-witted;
Her demeanor is alluring,
Her every move marvelous.
Strumming the psaltery, plucking the mandola,

Singing and dancing, or playing on the flute,
Even an expert painter would find
   her hard to depict.

To the tune "Moved by Imperial Favor":

Ah! It is more than enough to make me
   both bored and depressed,[27]
It racks my brains and disrupts my rest;[28]
Leaving me too languid to review
   Tu Fu's poetry,
Construe Han Yü's compositions,
Or study Liu Tsung-yüan's prose.[29]
In this state, my sorrowful heart is
   only more agitated;
As time goes on, my countenance is
   ever more emaciated.
Unable to share our pleasures,
   or to become mates,
All we are fated to do is to
   suffer in torment.

To the tune "Wen-chou Song":

As prematurely gray as P'an Yüeh,
As sorely emaciated as Shen Yüeh,[30]
I regret that, though we met, we did
   not follow through.
My heart is distressed, my feelings
   are lacerated.
Roaring flames consume the Zoroastrian Temple;[31]
Turbulent waves have engulfed the Blue Bridge.[32]
How will I ever escape my lovesickness?

To the tune "Tea-picking Song":

How will I ever escape my lovesickness?
The sorrow of separation is as difficult to
   overcome as a battle formation.
Even someone forged out of iron or stone
   would find his spirit disturbed.
His sorrow would rise, layer upon layer, like
   the hills of the Southern Mountain;
His despair would swell, wave upon wave, like
   the waters of the Eastern Ocean.

To the tune "Transition":

Who could have anticipated this day?
From of old, students are destined
   to be unfortunate.
My feelings are lacerated.
My foolish heart merely evokes the
   laughter of others.[33]
To whom can I complain?

To the tune "Crows Cry at Night":

I remember the times when I enjoyed cuddling
   the red and hugging the turquoise,
Tripping the grass and comparing botanical specimens.[34]
Upon meeting each other and gazing at the scenery,
   we enjoyed it together.
In the springtime, twittering swallows
   sought out their nests;
In summertime, the fragrance of lotus
   blossoms filled the ponds;
In the autumn, chrysanthemum blossoms
   pervaded the empty suburbs;
And in the winter, the auspicious snow
   fluttered everywhere.[35]
I recall those painted chambers, replete with
   song and dance, and rare repasts;
But now, I am at loose ends, sleeping upon
   a lonely pillow in a wayside inn.
I am beset by spectral visitations,
That are not susceptible to remedy;
Which causes my feelings to be agitated
   and my thoughts disturbed.[36]
The pain of heartache is difficult to dispel.[37]

To the tune "Higher Ever Higher":

I am too depressed to sleep.
I think of that captivating beauty,
Who is conversant with the laws of music
   and its various modes.
Everything about her is superb;
Her countenance outshines the moon,
Her face puts the flowers to shame.
Her words are captivating, and
   her mind is sharp.

She is like an immortal maiden
    come down to earth.
Her golden lotuses traipse gently[38]
    with high phoenix toes;
Her ruby lips and her white teeth
    smile enigmatically.

TO THE TUNE "THE QUAILS":

Just look at the daintiness of
    her demeanor;[39]
Enhanced by an outfit of plain
    white silk.
Her cosmetics are evenly applied;
Her moth eyebrows lightly painted.[40]
The myriad ways in which she displays
    her seductiveness,
Are hard to depict, hard to depict.
The finest Yang-kao vintage is decanted;
Incense burns in the duck-shaped censer;
Candles in silver sconces burn brightly.
Now that we may finally become a loving
    husband and wife;
Surely, our hearts will be one till the
    end of our lives.[41]

CODA:

There is a pathway to the azure clouds
    that ensures one's arrival.[42]
If it is not one's fate to succeed, it
    will be difficult to do so.
I admonish you, never fail to recall the
    date of this happy event.[43]

When they had finished singing the song suite, the two sisters brought out
a dicebox and proceeded to amuse themselves by playing "Competing for the
Red" with Hsi-men Ch'ing. As they:

    Passed their wine cups back and forth,
    Their faces took on the glint of spring.

Hsi-men Ch'ing noticed that beside the bed in Cheng Ai-yüeh's room there
was a brocaded screen, on which there hung a scroll entitled "Picture of a
Moon-loving Beauty," on which there was inscribed a poem that read:

There is a lovely woman,[44] who stands
    out above the crowd.

A gentle breeze obliquely flutters her
    pomegranate skirt.
Blossoms open in Golden Valley in the
    third month of spring;
The moon moves the flower shadows in
    the depth of the night.
Her jade or snowlike spirit reminds
    one of Ts'ai Yen;[45]
Her alabaster features surpass those
    of Cho Wen-chün.[46]
One's youthful dreams are inevitably
    attracted to her;
Hoping she will not be as indifferent
    as a white cloud.[47]

The signature at the end of the poem read, "Drunkenly inscribed by The Master of the Three Springs."

When Hsi-men Ch'ing saw this, he asked, "Isn't The Master of the Three Springs the courtesy name of Wang the Third?"

This threw Cheng Ai-yüeh into such consternation that she hastened to cover up by saying, "This is something that he wrote some time ago. At present, he no longer uses the courtesy name Three Springs but is using the name Hsiao-hsüan, or Little Studio, instead. He says that ever since you told him your courtesy name was Four Springs, he felt he could no longer use the name Three Springs without offending you. That's why he has changed to using the name Little Studio."

So saying, she stepped forward, picked up a brush, and crossed out the character for "Three."

Hsi-men Ch'ing was utterly delighted by this and said, "I didn't know he had changed his courtesy name."

"I overheard him explaining it to someone else," responded the painted face, "or I wouldn't have known about it either. It seems that his deceased father used the name I-hsüan, or Leisure Studio, so he deferentially switched to using the courtesy name Hsiao-hsüan, or Little Studio, for himself."

When this exchange was over, Cheng Ai-hsiang went outside, leaving Cheng Ai-yüeh alone to entertain Hsi-men Ch'ing in her room. The two of them continued "Competing for the Red" and drinking wine, while sitting:
    Shoulder to shoulder and thigh over thigh.

Hsi-men Ch'ing then brought up the subject of Lady Lin, about whom he said, "She has a great capacity for wine and is devoted to love-making. That day, when I was being entertained by Wang the Third, I was invited into the interior of the residence to pay my respects to her, and she took the initiative in telling Wang the Third to kowtow to me as his adoptive father, and telling me to accept his obeisance, and undertake the task of teaching him how to become a better person."

Upon hearing this, the painted face clapped her hands and laughed, saying, "You have me to thank for suggesting this scheme to you in the first place. In the future, I have no doubt, even Wang the Third's wife will fall into your hands."

"I'll start out by burning some moxa on Lady Lin," said Hsi-men Ch'ing. "Then, I'll invite her to come to my place, and bring Wang the Third's wife with her, for a lantern-viewing party at New Year's, and see if she'll consent to come or not."

"Father," said the painted face, "you don't even comprehend yet what a beauty Wang the Third's wife is. Not even a figure on a decorative lantern is as romantic and bewitching as she is. She is just eighteen years old this year, but she might as well be observing her widowhood since Wang the Third spends so little time at home. If you are willing to make a play for her, there is no reason to doubt that she will end up in your hands."

As they were talking, they moved closer to each other. Who should appear at this juncture but a maidservant who brought in several saucers of delicacies, including baked nut kernels, dried caltrops, fresh tangerines, betel nuts, snow pears, apples, "abalone shell" sweets, candied orange pieces frosted with crystallized sugar, and so forth. The painted face, with her own hand, fed the delicacies to Hsi-men Ch'ing to go with his wine and also employed her tongue to transfer a phoenix-embossed breath-sweetening lozenge from her mouth to his. At the same time, she used her slender hand to lift aside Hsi-men Ch'ing's lavender silk tunic and expose his white satin trousers. Hsi-men Ch'ing responded by undoing his belt and exposing his organ for her to manipulate. The painted face saw that the silver clasp was already fastened around its root.

> It was aroused and its head sprang up,
> Becoming both empurpled and shiny.

Hsi-men Ch'ing told her to suck it off for him, and the painted face actually:

> Bent low her powdered neck,
> Gently parted her ruby lips,
> Half swallowing, half disgorging it,[48]
> So it moved alternately in and out.
> The sound of her sucking was audible.

When she had toyed with it a while:

> His "magic rhinoceros horn" was erect,
> His libidinous fantasies were on fire,[49]

and he was ready to engage in intercourse. The painted face then went back to the interior, while Hsi-men Ch'ing also left the room to go to the bathroom, where he noticed that the snow was falling thicker than ever.

When he returned to the room, a maidservant was engaged in:

> Suspending the brocaded curtains,
> Placing the mandarin duck pillow,
> Spreading the mermaid silk covers,
> Lighting the oval incense burners,

and arranging a thick layer of comforters on the bed. After she had helped him to:

> Take off his boots and unfasten his girdle,

he got into the ivory bedstead. When the painted face returned after washing her private parts, she closed the double-leaved door and joined him inside the mandarin duck bed curtains. Truly, it is a case of:

> The spring beauty arouses the beholder,
>   complaisantly alluring;
> The fragrant corolla attracts the butterfly,
>   in redolent surrender.

There is a poem that testifies to this:

Meetings and partings are undependable
    when they occur in dreams;
When one gets up, the sputtering candle
    turns the window gauze red.
Real infatuation, from of old, produces
    a communion between spirits;
Who says that the road to the Radiant
    Terrace is not approachable?[50]

The two of them enjoyed:

> The raptures of clouds and rain,

until the first watch before getting up, upon which a maidservant brought a lamp into the room, enabling them to straighten their clothes and tidy up their hair. They then:

> Resumed decanting vintage wine,
> Reordered the sumptuous repast,

and shared a few more drinks. Hsi-men Ch'ing then asked Tai-an if he had brought a lantern and an umbrella.

"Ch'in-t'ung went home," replied Tai-an, "and brought back a lantern and an umbrella."

Only then did Hsi-men Ch'ing prepare to leave. The procuress and the painted face accompanied him out the gate and looked on as he mounted his horse.

Cheng Ai-yüeh raised her voice, saying, "Father, whenever you want me, let me know in good time."

"I understand," replied Hsi-men Ch'ing.

Having mounted his horse, with his umbrella in hand, he rode out the gate of the licensed quarter and slogged through the snow as he made his way home. When he got there, he merely told Yüeh-niang that he had been drinking at the store on Lion Street with Brother-in-law Wu the Second. But no more of this. Of the events of that evening there is no more to tell.

The next day, the eighth, knowing that Ho Yung-shou had moved his belongings into the former home of Hsia Yen-ling, Hsi-men Ch'ing sent him four boxes of fancy tea and assorted delicacies, along with five mace of silver in lieu of the customary kerchief, as a housewarming gift.

Who should appear at this juncture but Ying Po-chüeh, who came in unexpectedly. Hsi-men Ch'ing, seeing that the snow had cleared, but that there was a cold wind blowing, invited him into his studio in the front compound to warm himself at the brazier and directed a page boy to set up a table, and fetch some viands, so he could share a serving of congee with him.

He then went on to say, "Yesterday, I took care of sending the appropriate congratulatory presents to my kinsman Ch'iao Hung, and Brother Yün the Second. As for the gifts from the rest of you, I have already provided two mace of silver for each of you, so there is no need to give them anything. All you need to do is wait until they issue their invitations."

Ying Po-chüeh raised his hand in acknowledgment and thanked him.

Hsi-men Ch'ing went on to say, "His Honor Ho Yung-shou has already moved into Hsia Yen-ling's place. Today, I have sent him a present of tea and a housewarming gift. Shouldn't you also send him a gift of tea?"

"Only if he invites me over," said Ying Po-chüeh.

He then went on to ask, "Yesterday, what did His Honor An Ch'en and the other two come to visit you for? And who were those two who came with him?"

"One of them was Lei Ch'i-yüan, the assistant commissioner of the Shantung Military Defense Circuit," said Hsi-men Ch'ing, "and the other one was Administration Commissioner Wang Po-yen. Both of them are natives of Chekiang province. They plan to host a party here tomorrow in honor of Chao T'ing, the prefect of Hang-chou, who has recently been promoted to a position in the capital as minister of the Court of Judicial Review and has been the presiding officer of their native prefecture. There is no reason I should refuse to honor him with a table setting on their behalf, along with communal seating for the rest of us. They have undertaken to provide actors for the occasion, and I also feel obliged to engage the services of two boy actors to entertain the company. They saw fit to give me a joint contribution of a mere three taels of silver."

"Generally speaking," opined Ying Po-chüeh, "civil officials tend to be closefisted with their money. What is three taels of silver good for, after all. You will be obliged to supplement it, Brother."

"This Assistant Commissioner Lei Ch'i-yüan," responded Hsi-men Ch'ing, "is the one who presided over the trial of Sun Wen-hsiang, the son of Huang the Fourth's brother-in-law. Yesterday, he chose to remind me that it was he who had undertaken to exonerate him."

"You may say he is not closefisted," said Ying Po-chüeh, "but he reminded you of this as a means of settling accounts with you. He will not feel adequately repaid unless you take on the costs of putting on the party."

In the course of their conversation, Ying Po-chüeh summoned Ying Pao and said to him, "Call in that person to meet His Honor."

"Who might that be?" asked Hsi-men Ch'ing.

"There is a young man who resides in my neighborhood," replied Ying Po-chüeh, "who comes from an established family, but whose father and mother are both deceased. From his youth he has worked for Wang the Second, the distaff relative of the imperial family, for quite a few years by now, and has already taken a wife. But, because he did not get along with the other servants on the estate, he has left that position and is currently out of work, not having the wherewithal to go into business on his own. He is a friend of Ying Pao's and has requested him to help him find employment as a servant somewhere. This morning, Ying Pao said to me, 'Father, you're in a good position to recommend him for a job in His Honor's household. I imagine that His Honor could use some additional help.' To which I replied that I didn't know whether you could use him or not."

He then said to Ying Pao, "What name does he go by? Have him come in."

"His name is Lai-yu," said Ying Pao.

Who should appear at this juncture but Lai-yu, who wore an outfit of blue cloth, a four-piece tile-shaped hat,[51] cotton socks, and sandals and proceeded to prostrate himself on the floor and kowtow, after which he stood up outside the screen.

"If you consider this creature's physique," remarked Ying Po-chüeh, "he is more than strong enough to:

Sustain the light and bear the heavy."

He then went on to ask him, "How old are you?"

"I am nineteen," the young man responded.

"Has your wife borne any sons or daughters?" he continued.

"There are only the two of us," he replied.

"Your Honor," said Ying Pao, "the truth of the matter is that his wife is only eighteen. She is adept at cooking and needlework and can create articles of clothing, both large and small."

Hsi-men Ch'ing saw the way the young man stood deferentially with his head lowered and his feet together, exhibiting an artless nature, and said, "Since Ying the Second has seen fit to recommend you, I will give you the opportunity to render me your faithful service. If you will select an auspicious day for the event and produce a written contract, the two of you can move in."

The young man kowtowed in response, and Hsi-men Ch'ing told Ch'in-t'ung to take him back to the rear compound in order to kowtow to Yüeh-niang and the others, and explain his decision to them. Yüeh-niang decided to let him reside in the quarters that had previously been occupied by Lai-wang.

After Ying Po-chüeh had remained sitting there a while longer, he went home, and Ying Pao helped Lai-yu to draft a contract of indenture and turn it over to Hsi-men Ch'ing, who changed his name to Lai-chüeh. But no more of this.

To resume our story, ever since Pen the Fourth's wife, Yeh the Fifth, had given her daughter Pen Chang-chieh to Hsia Yen-ling as a concubine, she had fallen into the daily habit of:

> Buying this and buying that,

and inviting P'ing-an, Lai-an, Hua-t'ung, or Han Hsiao-yü, the son of her next-door neighbor Auntie Han, all of them young servants in Hsi-men Ch'ing's household, to come and share drinks together at her place on a dutch treat basis. Pen the Fourth's wife was of an accommodating nature and would promptly come up with whatever they requested in the way of snacks or tea. Even when Pen the Fourth happened to come home from the shop and run into them, he did not object. For this reason, when he was not at home, and she needed something done, none of them was averse to acting on her behalf. Tai-an and P'ing-an were the two who frequented her place most often.

The ninth of the month was the day on which Hsi-men Ch'ing had agreed to put on a party in honor of Prefect Chao T'ing, on behalf of Secretary An Ch'en, Administration Commissioner Wang Po-yen, and Assistant Commissioner Lei Ch'i-yüan. On the morning of that day, Lai-chüeh and his spouse moved in, and his wife went back to the rear compound to kowtow to Yüeh-niang and the rest. Yüeh-niang saw that she was wearing a purple damask jacket, a cape of blue cotton, and a green cotton skirt.

> She was petite in stature, with
> A face shaped like a melon seed,
> Decorated with rouge and powder,
> That embellished her ruby lips,

and her two bound feet displayed their upturned tips. When asked, she responded that she was adept at all forms of needlework. She was given the new name of Hui-yüan and was assigned, together with Hui-hsiu and Hui-hsiang, to take turns working in the kitchen every third day. But no more of this.

One day, Aunt Yang, who lived outside the city gate. died, and her page boy came to report her demise. Hsi-men Ch'ing's household prepared a portable table, along with meat of the three sacrificial animals, soup, and rice; and also sealed up five taels of silver as a contribution toward the cost of the obsequies. Wu Yüeh-niang, Li Chiao-erh, Meng Yü-lou, and P'an Chin-lien, riding in four sedan chairs, set out for the northern quarter to burn paper money and offer their condolences. Ch'in-t'ung, Ch'i-t'ung, Lai-chüeh, and Lai-an also left home to accompany the sedan chairs.

During their absence, Hsi-men Ch'ing went to the studio in the silk goods store across the street and looked on while a furrier prepared to make a sable muffler for Yüeh-niang. Before he did so, he had him make another muffler out of the same sable skin and gave it to Tai-an to take to Cheng Ai-yüeh in the licensed quarter, as he had promised. In addition, he sealed up ten taels of silver, to present to her as a New Year's gift. The Cheng Establishment treated Tai-an to food and drink and gave him three mace of silver with which to buy melon seeds for himself.

When Tai-an returned to report to Hsi-men Ch'ing, he said, "Cheng Ai-yüeh presents her compliments and thanks. She said that she had offered you but scant entertainment the other day, and she also rewarded me with three mace of silver."

"Keep it for yourself," responded Hsi-men Ch'ing.

He then went on to say, "Pen the Fourth is not at home, so what were you doing when I saw you come out of his place a while ago?"

"Pen the Fourth's wife," responded Tai-an, "ever since her daughter was married off, has had no one to run errands for her, so she often calls on us servants to purchase things on her behalf."

"As long as she has no one to run errands for her," said Hsi-men Ch'ing, "you might as well do your best to help out."

He then whispered to Tai-an, saying, "I'd like you to feel her out, thus and so, saying, 'Father would like to come to your place for a visit. What would you think of that?' Then see how she responds. If she reacts favorably, ask her for a handkerchief to give to me as a token."

"I understand," replied Tai-an, who accepted Hsi-men Ch'ing's directive, nodded in assent, and set out on his mission.

Hsi-men Ch'ing arranged for Ch'en Ching-chi to supervise the furrier's tailoring of the sable in his stead and then prepared to go back to the house.

Who should appear at this juncture but Wang Ching, who came back from Silversmith Ku's shop with the gold tiger-shaped tiara he had ordered, along with four pairs of gold-headed silver pins, and turned them over to Hsi-men Ch'ing, who stashed two pairs of pins in the studio before hiding the other articles in his sleeve and proceeding to Li P'ing-erh's quarters and sitting down. He gave the tiger-shaped tiara and one pair of pins to Ju-i, and the other pair of pins to Ying-ch'un. The two of them accepted these gifts and immediately:

Just as if inserting a taper in its holder,
kowtowed to Hsi-men Ch'ing.

Hsi-men Ch'ing then ordered Ying-ch'un to bring him something to eat, and she returned with it in no time at all. After he had eaten, he went to his studio and sat down. Who should appear at this juncture but Tai-an, who approached him hesitantly but, on seeing that Wang Ching was present, did not say anything.

Only after Hsi-men Ch'ing had sent Wang Ching back to the rear compound to fetch some tea did Tai-an say, "I communicated your message to her, and she responded with a smile. She agreed, later this evening, to expect a visit from you and told me to bring you this handkerchief."

When Hsi-men Ch'ing saw that the packet of red "cotton paper," made from the bark of the paper-mulberry, contained a handkerchief of red satin brocade with a diapered border, and that when smelled it exuded a pungent fragrance, he was absolutely delighted and promptly secreted it in his sleeve. When Wang Ching returned with the tea, he drank it and then went back across the street to watch the furrier at his work.

Suddenly it was reported that Hua Tzu-yu had come to pay him a visit, and Hsi-men Ch'ing said, "Ask him to join me over here."

Hua Tzu-yu made his way to the heated chamber in the studio across the street, where he saluted Hsi-men Ch'ing with a bow and sat down, thanking him for the trouble he had put him to the other day. While they were conversing, Hua-t'ung brought over a serving of tea from across the street.

While he was drinking it, Hua Tzu-yu explained, "There is a merchant outside the city gate who has five hundred bags of Wu-hsi rice on his hands, which he is anxious to dispose of because the river is frozen, and he would like to return home. It occurred to me that you might be interested in buying it, and waiting for the price to go up."

"What would I want with that?" responded Hsi-men Ch'ing. "No one wants it while the river is frozen, and when the ice breaks up and the boats can come through, the price will drop even further. And besides, at the present time, I don't have any silver on hand."

He then instructed Tai-an, "See to the setting up of a table, and then go back to the house to order some food."

He also told Hua-t'ung, "Go invite Ying the Second to come and provide company for Hua Tzu-yu."

When they had sat there for a while, Ying Po-chüeh showed up, and the three of them arranged themselves around the brazier and fell to enjoying the wine. The table was set with four platters and four saucers of viands, including sautéed chicken and fish, and roasted and stewed dishes to go with the wine. Sun Hsüeh-o had also been ordered to bake two batches of pastries, and to provide four bowls of soup flavored with tripe, lungs, and curds.

Sometime later, who should appear but Abbot Wu's disciple Ying-ch'un, who came to deliver New Year's gifts, and the customary memorials and writs for the occasion. Hsi-men Ch'ing invited him to sit down with them to have some wine and also engaged him to take care of the scripture recitation on the "hundredth day" after Li P'ing-erh's death, and paid him the silver for it in advance. They continued drinking until sunset, at which time Ying-ch'un and Hua Tzu-yu left.

Afterwards, Manager Kan Jun closed the shop and was invited to join them, whereupon he fell to throwing dice and playing at guess-fingers with Ying Po-chüeh. As they talked together, before they knew it, it was already past lamp-lighting time, and Wu Yüeh-niang and the other ladies arrived home in their sedan chairs.

When Lai-an came in to report their return, Ying Po-chüeh asked, "Where did my sisters-in-law go today?"

"Aunt Yang from the northern quarter of the city has died," explained Hsi-men Ch'ing. "Today, they are holding the "third day" scripture recitation in her honor. We have prepared a portable table, and appropriate sacrificial offerings for the occasion, and have also sent a contribution toward the cost of the obsequies. They went to offer their condolences."

"The venerable lady must have reached an advanced age," opined Ying Po-chüeh.

"She was probably seventy-four or seventy-five," said Hsi-men Ch'ing. "She didn't have any children of either sex and depended on her nephew who resides outside the city gate for support. It is also some years now since I undertook to provide a coffin for her."

"She was a lucky old lady," remarked Ying Po-chüeh. "To have a coffin at hand prepares one for the day when your:
　　Yellow gold is stored in the coffer.[52]
That was really a good deed on your part, Brother."

When this conversational exchange was finished, and:
　　Several rounds of wine had been consumed,
Ying Po-chüeh and Kan Jun said farewell and departed.

Hsi-men Ch'ing then said, "It's the eleventh, so it's the turn of my son-in-law to spend the night here."

"In the shop over there," said Tai-an, "Uncle Fu the Second has also gone home, so I will be spending the night in the shop by myself."

Hsi-men Ch'ing then got up and went across the street, where he told his young servant Wang Hsien, "Be careful with the braziers and candles."

"I understand," responded Wang Hsien.

Hsi-men Ch'ing looked on while he locked the gate and then, observing that there was no one around, proceeded to step nimbly into Pen the Fourth's quarters, where, whom should he see but Pen the Fourth's wife, who had been standing there all by herself for some time.

When she heard the sound made by the locking of the gate and saw Hsi-men Ch'ing approaching her in the dark, she promptly opened the outer door for him and then closed it, saying, "Father, come inside the sliding paper door and sit down."

It so happens that the inner room was divided by a papered latticework partition, behind which there was a small k'ang with a smoldering brazier, a table with a lighted lamp, and two bedrails. The room had been newly plastered so that it looked as white as snow and was decorated with four framed hanging scrolls. On her head she wore a kingfisher-blue gold lamé headband, her fret was adorned with four gold pins, and a pair of clove-shaped earrings dangled from her ears. Her body was clad in a purple damask jacket and a black chiffon cape, over a jade-colored silk chiffon skirt. She stepped forward and greeted Hsi-men Ch'ing with a bow, after which, she promptly served him a cup of tea to drink.

Speaking in a whisper, she said, "I'm afraid that Auntie Han next door may become aware of us."

"Never fear," said Hsi-men Ch'ing. "I kept in the dark, so she couldn't have seen me."

Thereupon:

Without permitting any further explanation,

he proceeded to embrace the woman and give her a kiss. Pulling over a pillow, he undressed her, laid her down on the edge of the k'ang, lifted up her legs, and started to thrust away. The clasp was already fastened on his organ. No sooner had he inserted it into her vagina and withdrawn it several times than, down below:

Her vaginal fluids began to overflow,

leaving her blue cotton drawers soaking wet. Hsi-men Ch'ing then withdrew his organ, groped a packet of the aphrodisiac powder known as "The Quavery Voices of Amorous Beauties" out of his wallet, rubbed some of it on his turtle head, and thrust it back inside. Only then did he stem the flow of her vaginal fluids. While he gave himself over to thrusting and retracting, the woman clasped Hsi-men Ch'ing around the shoulders with both hands. As they responded to each other, the woman from underneath him raised her quavery voice and gave vent to unending groans of satisfaction. Hsi-men Ch'ing, exhilarated by the wine, lifted her two legs over his shoulders and proceeded to alternately submerge and expose the knob of his glans:

Advancing with alacrity and galloping forward,

as he slammed away at her no less than two or three hundred times. In no time at all:

Her cloud-shaped chignon became disheveled,[53]
The tip of her tongue became ice-cold, and
Her voice became completely inarticulate;[54]

while Hsi-men Ch'ing was:

Reduced to panting and puffing,

as the melting sensation in his "divine turtle" was such that he:

Ejaculated like a geyser.

After some time, he retracted his organ, releasing her vaginal secretions, which she proceeded to wipe up with a handkerchief.

Pen the Fourth's Wife Braves the Cold to Engage Her Lover

After the two of them had readjusted their clothing, fastened their girdles, and put themselves to rights, Hsi-men Ch'ing groped five or six taels worth of loose silver out of his sleeve, together with two pairs of gold-headed hairpins, and presented them to the woman with which to buy costume jewelry for the New Year's season. The woman bowed to him in gratitude and surreptitiously let him out the door. Tai-an was waiting in the shop, listening intently for the sound of the door knocker, and promptly opened the main gate to let Hsi-men Ch'ing in. He was confident that no one was aware of his actions, and afterwards, as the mornings and evenings succeeded one another, he made out with her several times.

Truly:

> The best way to avoid being found out,
> Is not to do it in the first place.

Who could have known that Auntie Han would perceive the situation with her sardonic eye and pass the information on to Chin-lien in the rear compound, who opted not to expose the state of affairs for the time being.

One day, on the fifteenth of the twelfth month, the household of Ch'iao Hung hosted a party, and Hsi-men Ch'ing, along with Ying Po-chüeh and Brother-in-law Wu K'ai, set out to attend it together. There were many relatives and friends there that day, and they enjoyed the performance of theatrical selections and drinking wine until the second watch before the party broke up. The next day, each of them also received the gift of a table setting of food, but there is no need to describe this in detail.

Let us return to the story of Ts'ui Pen, who had purchased two thousand taels worth of silk piece goods in Hu-chou, hired a boat to transport them, and set out for home early in the twelfth month. Upon arriving at the dock in Lin-ch'ing, he left the young employee Jung Hai to look after the goods, hired a donkey on which to ride, and headed for home in order to get the silver for the cartage fee.

When he arrived at the gate of the shop and dismounted, Ch'in-t'ung said, "So Brother Ts'ui has come home. Take a seat in the reception hall. Father is in the house across the street. I'll go fetch him."

Upon going across the street, he did not see Hsi-men Ch'ing and asked P'ing-an where he was.

"Father has probably gone back to the rear compound," said P'ing-an.

Ch'in-t'ung, accordingly, went back to the master suite and asked Yüeh-niang where he was.

"You lousy jailbird. You've been seeing things," said Yüeh-niang. "Father went out early this morning and hasn't been back inside since."

Ch'in-t'ung proceeded to look for him in the quarters of all the residents, as well as the garden and the studio, but failed to find him.

On coming back to the main gate, he raised his voice, saying, "How utterly frustrating! Who knows where Father has gotten to that he is nowhere to be found? Even in broad daylight, he is nowhere to be seen. Brother Ts'ui Pen has been here all this time and has been forced to wait in vain."

Tai-an was well aware of the situation but did not utter a word. Unexpectedly, Hsi-men Ch'ing emerged from the front compound to the utter befuddlement of the page boys. It so happens that he had been in Pen the Fourth's quarters making out with his wife and had only just come out. P'ing-an directed Hsi-men Ch'ing to the shop across the street and then stuck out the tip of his tongue at Ch'in-t'ung.

They all broke into a sweat on his behalf, saying, "No doubt, once Brother Ts'ui Pen has gone, you'll be in for a few strokes of the cane."

Who could have anticipated the fact that when Hsi-men Ch'ing made his way into the reception hall, Ts'ui Pen kowtowed to him and turned over his account books, saying, "When the boat arrived at the dock I found that I lacked sufficient silver for the cartage fee. We set out together on the first day of the twelfth month, but on arriving in Yang-chou I separated from the other two while they went on to Hang-chou. We all stayed for two days at the home of your kinsman Miao Ch'ing."

He then went on to say, "Miao Ch'ing has expended ten taels of silver to purchase the daughter of a battalion commander of the Yang-chou Guard as a present for you. She is only fifteen years old and is named Ch'u-yün. Words are inadequate to describe her.

> Her face is like a flower,
> Her flesh is like jade,
> Her eyes are like stars,
> Her eyebrows are like crescent moons,
> Her waist is like a willow,
> Her stockings are like hooks, and
> Her two feet are barely three inches long.

Truly:

> She has a face that induces fish to
>   dive and geese to plunge;
> Her visage outshines the moon while
>   putting flowers to shame.[55]

She has a repertory of three thousand short songs and eight hundred long songs. Truly:

> If one were to describe her glamour:
> It is like a shining pearl
>   rolling on a crystal plate.
> If one were to speak of her demeanor:
> It is like a red apricot on a branch tip
>   caught in the morning sun.

Miao Ch'ing is maintaining her in his home for the time being, so he can have a vanity case made for her and provide her with an appropriate wardrobe.

This coming spring, Han Tao-kuo and Lai-pao will bring her on their boat so she can wait upon Your Honor and serve to:
> Dissipate your melancholy and dispel your gloom."[56]

When he heard this, Hsi-men Ch'ing was utterly delighted and remarked, "You could just as well have brought her on your boat. What need is there for him to provide her with a wardrobe, or to have a dressing case made for her? As though my household were unable to supply such things."

Thereupon, his only regret was that he could not:
> Mount the clouds and spread his wings,

in order to fly to Yang-chou, take possession of this voluptuous beauty, and enjoy the happy event to his heart's content. Truly:

> The case of the deer was one that the minister
> of Cheng was unable to solve;[57]
> Whether the butterfly was Chuang Chou, or vice
> versa, cannot be determined.[58]

There is a poem that testifies to this:

> He has heard tell that in Yang-chou
>   there is one Ch'u-yün;
> But the word of such an obscure bird
>   may not be reliable.
> He does not realize that good things
>   are often evanescent;
> Just ask their owner about the fate
>   of his plum blossoms.[59]

Hsi-men Ch'ing kept Ts'ui Pen company while he had something to eat and then weighed out fifty taels of silver to cover the cartage fee. He also wrote a letter to Secretary Ch'ien Lung-yeh of the Lin-ch'ing customs house, requesting that he be granted favorable treatment. When they had finished talking together, Ts'ui Pen took his leave and went to Ch'iao Hung's household to report his return.

When P'ing-an saw that Hsi-men Ch'ing did not bother to find fault with Ch'in-t'ung, he remarked, "You don't know how lucky you are. Were it not so, when Father came inside, at the very least, you would have been in for several strokes of the cane."

Ch'in-t'ung laughed at this, saying, "I guess you're the only one who truly understands Father's nature."

By the time the cargo of silk piece goods had been transported from Lin-ch'ing and unloaded at the shop on Lion Street, it was the last decade of the month. Hsi-men Ch'ing was at home at the time, supervising the delivery of New Year's gifts, when a messenger from Director-in-Chief Ching Chung arrived unexpectedly with a calling card that read: "Censor Sung Ch'iao-nien's report should have arrived in the capital some days ago, but I don't know whether the imperial rescript in response to it has come down yet or not. I humbly submit, venerable sir, that if you could send someone to the censor's yamen to inquire about it, it would be most gratifying."

Hsi-men Ch'ing forthwith sent an adjutant with five mace of silver to inquire about it from a clerical subofficial in the provincial censor's yamen, and, sure enough, the government gazette had come down the previous day, and the clerk agreed to make a copy of the relevant material for Hsi-men Ch'ing's perusal. It read as follows:

Memorial submitted by Sung Ch'iao-nien, Regional Investigating Censor of Shantung

In re: The Evaluation, According to Precedent, of the Local Civil and Military Officials, with a View toward Inspiring the Feelings of the Populace, and Enhancing Your Majesty's Sage Administration

I venture to observe that civil officials exist to nurture the people, and military officials exist to prevent disorder, so as to protect the territory,[60] and ensure the people's livelihood. Should the wrong men hold office,[61] their actions will be illegitimate, the people will suffer, and the state will have no one on whom to rely. No institution is more important than the censorial evaluations for the inspiration and motivation of the civil and military officials, and they cannot but be undertaken with due diligence. Your servant has been delegated to survey the situation in the territory of Shantung, and to personally monitor the state of public morality. With regard to the effectiveness of the administration, the hardships of the people, and the qualifications of the civil and military officials, he has scrupulously looked into all of them, has sought the assessments of the highest authorities regarding the worthiness, or lack thereof, of all the relevant officials, and is confident that he has succeeded in ascertaining the truth about them. Now that the end of my assignment is imminent, it is incumbent upon me to present in detail the results of my investigation.

The provincial administration commissioner of Shantung, Ch'en Ssu-chen, is loyal and honest in his personal conduct, and proficient at nurturing the people.

The investigation commissioner for Shantung, Chao No, upholds the legal standards with clarity, so that both gentry and commoners submit to them.

The vice-commissioner of education, Ch'en Cheng-hui, exemplifies motivational conduct and adheres strictly to the principles of leadership.

I have also ascertained that the assistant commissioner of the Military Defense Circuit, Lei Ch'i-yüan, has earned the respect of both soldiers and civilians for his judicious exercise of mercy and severity, and won the praise of both colleagues and subordinates for his experienced direction.

The prefect of Chi-nan, Chang Shu-yeh, is respected for his thrifty administration and has demonstrated a talent for governing.

The prefect of Tung-p'ing, Hu Shih-wen, is honest and scrupulous in the exercise of his office and is as solicitous of the populace as though they were invalids.[62]

The prefect of Hsü-chou, Han Pang-ch'i, is sedulous in his devotion to his duties, and worthy of a position in the imperial court.

The prefect of Lai-chou, Yeh Ch'ien, has repulsed the maritime pirates and governed so effectively that people do not pick up articles dropped by the wayside.[63] He has also served the agricultural needs of the populace by preventing their land from becoming too saline.

These several officials are all worthy of being rewarded with promotion to higher positions.

I have also learned that the left assistant administration commissioner, Feng T'ing-hu, has a humpbacked physique and is in the sunset of his life.[64] Though he has no more vitality than a wooden puppet, he remains as rapacious as ever.

The prefect of Tung-ch'ang, Hsü Sung, allows the father of his concubine to engage in bribery, so that the court is swamped with accusations. He is so extortionate in assessing taxes that censure is rampant in his jurisdiction.

These two officials deserve to be promptly removed from office.

In addition, I have ascertained that the commandant of the Left Army and notary of the Bureau of Military Affairs, Chou Hsiu, is imposing in stature, and skilled at maintaining discipline, having mastered the qualifications of a military commander. He has won the allegiance of the troops in his command, and quelled the banditry in his jurisdiction.

The military director-in-chief of Chi-chou, Ching Chung, is both young and energetic, and his talent and faculties are fully developed. He won first place in the military examinations and is renowned as an erudite officer whose masterful tactics enhance his ability to engage in combat. His commands are uniform and strictly enforced, and his strategies enable him to resist aggression.

The military director-in-chief of Yen-chou, Wen Hsi, is proficient at military strategy, and practiced at archery and horsemanship. He maintains a contingent of cavalry in order to prepare for the unexpected[65] and labors to erect fortifications as a defense against the unforeseen.[66]

These three officials deserve to be promptly promoted to higher office.

The battalion commander of the Ch'ing-ho Guard, Wu K'ai, possesses fully developed talent and understands the responsibilities of a guard commander. In commanding his forces to attack the most hardened opponents, he never fails to win every engagement. By stocking provisions with which to feed his men, not one of them is forced to go unfed. His ability to express empathy for others[67] inspires his troops to put their lives at risk. He is truly a bastion in defense of the region and a bulwark ensuring the safety of the state. He ought to be specially promoted in order to motivate his fellow officials.

If Your Majesty sincerely believes that your servant's suggestions are worthy of consideration and chooses to implement them, it is to be hoped that the ranks of officialdom may be cleansed of superfluity, the resolution of the people may be inspired,[68] the right men may be appointed to office, and Your sage administration will have a foundation on which to rely.

The rescript elicited by this memorial read:

> These proposals have met with imperial approval and should be directed to the attention of the appropriate boards.

There followed a response from the Ministry of Personnel and the Ministry of War which read as follows:

> Having perused the contents of the memorial submitted by Censor Sung Ch'iao-nien, we find that his evaluation of the civil and military officials in his jurisdiction is an expression of his loyalty to the state. It incorporates public opinion and is based on honest investigation, with the intent of bolstering Your Majesty's sage administration. We humbly submit that if Your Majesty's sage wisdom sees fit to enact these proposals, the empire would then be fortunate indeed, and the people would then be fortunate indeed.[69]

The rescript elicited by this memorial read:

> These recommendations are imperially approved. Let them be enacted as proposed.

When Hsi-men Ch'ing had finished reading this material he was utterly delighted and, taking the government gazette with him, made his way back to the rear compound, where he said to Yüeh-niang, "The response to Censor Sung Ch'iao-nien's evaluation has already come down. Your elder brother has been promoted to the position of assistant commander of the Ch'ing-ho Guard, with the substantive position of supervisor of the State Farm Battalion. Commandant Chou Hsiu and His Honor Ching Chung have also been promoted to the rank of assistant commander-generals. Right now, we ought to promptly send a page boy to invite your elder brother over so we can tell him about it."

"You go ahead and send someone to invite him," responded Yüeh-niang. "I'll get a maidservant to fetch wine and refreshments for him. My only worry is that he will be short of silver to spend on the ceremony of assuming office."

"That doesn't matter," said Hsi-men Ch'ing. "I'm prepared to lend him a few taels of silver to take care of it."

It was not long before Brother-in-law Wu K'ai arrived, and Hsi-men Ch'ing showed him the texts of the relevant memorials and rescripts.

Wu K'ai promptly bowed in gratitude to Hsi-men Ch'ing and Yüeh-niang, saying, "I am greatly indebted to the support of my brother-in-law and my sister.

> Your kindness will be amply rewarded,
> I will never dare to forget it."

"Brother-in-law," said Hsi-men Ch'ing, "if you are short of money with which to put on a party to celebrate your assumption of office, I am willing to weigh out a thousand taels of silver for you to use for the purpose."

Wu K'ai, once again, bowed in gratitude, after which, wine was served in Yüeh-niang's room, and Yüeh-niang herself sat down to keep them company. Hsi-men Ch'ing then directed Ch'en Ching-chi to make a copy of the relevant data from the government gazette and give it to Wu K'ai, and he also sent Tai-an to deliver copies of the gazette to the homes of Military Director-in-Chief Ching Chung and Commandant Chou Hsiu in order to convey the good news. Truly:

You are urged not to waste your means on
    engraving adamantine rock;
The mouths of the pedestrians on the road
    are like memorial tablets.[70]

If you want to know the outcome of these events,
Pray consult the story related in the following chapter.

Chapter 78

HSI-MEN CH'ING VENTURES UPON A SECOND
ENGAGEMENT WITH LADY LIN;
WU YÜEH-NIANG INVITES HO YUNG-SHOU'S WIFE
TO VIEW THE LANTERNS

The pitch changes in the lowest pitch-pipe
    as a propitious breath blows;
When the yin retreats and the yang ascends
    the temperate ether returns.[1]
The sunflower's shadow begins to shift on
    the day of the winter solstice;
The plum blossom begins to bloom at the time
    of the solar term Little Cold.
The day of the sacrifice to the Eight Spirits[2]
    portends an auspicious year;
As the ether blows into the pitch-pipes, the
    ash of the pith is disturbed.
The willows on the riverbanks are all ready
    for the change of season;
In their profusion, they are more than happy
    to usher in the Spring.[3]

THE STORY GOES that on that day Hsi-men Ch'ing kept Brother-in-law
Wu K'ai company as they drank together until he went home that evening.

Early the next morning, Military Director-in-Chief Ching Chung came on
horseback to thank him, saying, "When I read the rescript that you sent me
yesterday, I was:

    Unable to contain my satisfaction.

It is more than sufficient to show the extent of your generous regard. I will
certainly:

    Carry rings and knot grass, and never forget it.

Battalion Commander Fan Hsün is getting old, and Militia Commander
Chang Kuan had hoped for a promotion, but they have been left where they
were and may feel somewhat disappointed."

After they had finished speaking, and the tea had been twice replenished, Ching Chung got up to go and asked, "When is His Honor Yün Li-shou going to invite us over for a drink to celebrate his promotion?"

"He won't be able to invite us during these few days before New Year's," said Hsi-men Ch'ing. "It will have to wait until sometime next month."

He then escorted him to the gate, where he mounted his horse and departed.

Hsi-men Ch'ing then supervised the preparation of a freshly slaughtered pig, two jars of Chekiang wine, a round-collared scarlet robe of velvet embroidered with gold thread and emblazoned with a *hsieh-chih*, the mythical one-horned goat who was said to gore wrongdoers, a round-collared robe of black figured satin, and a hundred stuffed gold-colored pastries, as an expression of his gratitude to Censor Sung Ch'iao-nien, and sent Ch'un-hung, with a calling card, to deliver them to the provincial censor's yamen. The gatekeeper went inside to report his arrival, and Censor Sung Ch'iao-nien called him into a heated chamber in the rear reception hall, where he was provided with tea while he waited for him to write an answer. When he had done so, he put it into an envelope, sealed it, and rewarded Ch'un-hung with three mace of silver.

When Ch'un-hung arrived home and presented it to Hsi-men Ch'ing, he tore it open and saw that it read as follows:

> Having twice imposed upon your illustrious household, I am profoundly embarrassed. And now, I am once again the undeserving recipient of your magnanimity. What can I do to be worthy of such largess? I have already memorialized on behalf of your kinsman, Wu K'ai, and your colleague, Ching Chung, as I expect you know. For days on end I have longed for a glimpse of your radiant countenance, so that we may discuss things in person, and I may have an opportunity to express my gratitude.

The signature at the end read: "Respectfully indited by his devoted servant, Sung Ch'iao-nien, for the perusal of the distinguished officer of the Embroidered Uniform Guard, His Honor the gentleman Hsi-men Ch'ing."

Censor Sung Ch'iao-nien, soon thereafter, sent someone to deliver a hundred copies of the official calendar for the coming year, four hundred sheets of stationery, and a pig as a return gift to Hsi-men Ch'ing.

One day, a document came down from the higher authorities confirming that Brother-in-law Wu K'ai should report to the yamen of the local guard and assume the duties of his new office. Hsi-men Ch'ing visited him in order to offer his congratulations and gave him thirty taels of silver, and four bolts of capital brocade, to expend, both high and low.

On the twenty-fourth, Hsi-men Ch'ing, who was entitled to a recess for the holiday season, put away his seal of office and came home, where he had prepared mutton and wine, red banners, and an inscribed scroll, and invited his relatives and friends for a party to celebrate Wu K'ai's accession to office. Upon returning from the guard yamen after assuming office, Wu K'ai was welcomed to the home of Hsi-men Ch'ing, where a sumptuous feast was provided in his honor.

Around the same time, the dependents of Battalion Commander Ho Yung-shou arrived from the Eastern Capital, and Hsi-men Ch'ing sent a welcoming gift of tea to them in Wu Yüeh-niang's name.

On the twenty-sixth, Abbot Wu Tsung-che of the Taoist Temple of the Jade Emperor, along with twelve of his acolytes, came to the Hsi-men Ch'ing residence to perform the scripture recitation on the "hundredth day" after Li P'ing-erh's death. The appropriate texts for the salvation of the departed were recited ten times over, the ritual was performed with due solemnity, and there was:

Loud playing on wind and percussion instruments,[4]

to further enhance the incense-burning procession. A large number of relatives and friends came to offer gifts of tea and were duly invited to partake of the sacrificial oblations. The party did not break up until the evening. But no more of this.

On the twenty-seventh, Hsi-men Ch'ing supervised the sending out of New Year's gifts. The households of Ying Po-chüeh, Hsieh Hsi-ta, Ch'ang Shih-chieh, Manager Fu Ming, Manager Kan Jun, Han Tao-kuo, Pen Ti-ch'uan, and Ts'ui Pen were each given half a pig, half a sheep, a jar of wine, a sack of rice, and a tael of silver. Li Kuei-chieh, Wu Yin-erh, and Cheng Ai-yüeh from the licensed quarter were each given an outfit of Hang-chou silk clothing and three taels of silver. Wu Yüeh-niang had also commissioned Nun Hsüeh to preside over a service at her nunnery and ordered Lai-an to deliver incense, lamp-oil, rice, flour, and silver for the occasion. But no more of this.

Before long, it was the last day of the year.

The moon shines on the plum trees in the window;
The wind disturbs the snow lying upon the eaves.[5]
Firecrackers explode before a thousand doors;
Lanterns burn in front of ten thousand gates.[6]
Every home displays lucky interlocking lozenges;
Everywhere hang couplets inscribed on peachwood.

Hsi-men Ch'ing burned paper money and then went to Li P'ing-erh's quarters to make a sacrificial offering before her spirit tablet, after which wine was served in the rear reception hall. When the whole household, high and low, including Yüeh-niang, Li Chiao-erh, Meng Yü-lou, P'an Chin-lien, Sun Hsüeh-o, Hsi-men Ta-chieh, and his son-in-law Ch'en Ching-chi, had saluted him with a drink, they sat down arrayed to either side. Then Ch'un-mei, Ying-ch'un, Yü-hsiao, Lan-hsiang, and Ju-i, the five of them, kowtowed to him, followed by Hsiao-yü, Hsiu-ch'un, Hsiao-luan, Yüan-hsiao, Chung-ch'iu, and Ch'iu-chü. After this, Lai-chao's wife, "The Beanpole," Hui-ch'ing, Lai-pao's wife Hui-hsiang, Lai-hsing's wife Hui-hsiu, and Lai-chüeh's wife

Hui-yüan, the spouses of the four principal servants, kowtowed. Only after this did Wang Ching, Ch'un-hung, Tai-an, P'ing-an, Lai-an, Ch'i-t'ung, Ch'in-t'ung, Hua-t'ung, Lai-chao's son Little Iron Rod, Lai-pao's son Seng-pao, and Lai-hsing's daughter Nien-erh kowtow to him in turn. Hsi-men Ch'ing and Yüeh-niang presented each of them with handkerchiefs, kerchiefs, and silver.

The next day was New Year's Day, the first day of the first month of the first year of the Ch'ung-ho reign period.[7] Hsi-men Ch'ing got up early, donned his formal cap and crimson robe, lit incense dedicated to Heaven and Earth, burned paper money, had something to eat, called for his horse, and set out to proffer his New Year's greetings to Regional Investigating Censor Sung Ch'iao-nien.

Yüeh-niang and the other ladies of the household also got up early:

> Daubed on makeup and applied powder,
> Stuck floral trinkets in their hair;
> Donned brocade skirts, embroidered jackets,[8]
> Silken hose, and shoes with upturned tips;
> Dressed themselves up to look captivating,
> Decorated themselves to appear enchanting;

and forgathered in Yüeh-niang's room to exchange greetings.

P'ing-an and the orderly on duty that day stationed themselves at the front gate to accept the calling cards and record the names of the officials and gentlemen who came to call.

Tai-an and Wang Ching, wearing new clothes, new boots, and new caps, went outside the gate, where they played at shuttlecock, let off firecrackers, cracked melon seeds with their teeth, concealed sachets of pomander in their sleeves, and sported quivering paper cutouts of spring moths on their heads.

The vast number of Hsi-men Ch'ing's employees, managers, and protégés who gathered to extend their New Year's greetings was so great they could hardly be counted. Ch'en Ching-chi was assigned the task of single-handedly entertaining them in the front guest room.

The furnishings for an elaborate feast were laid out in the large reception hall in the rear compound for the entertainment of the friends and relatives of the family.

In the summerhouse in the garden, felt curtains and heat-holding drapes were suspended, brocade carpets and embroidered rugs were arrayed, along with braziers burning animal-shaped briquettes, and ten tables replete with gold lamé tablecloths and figured seat cushions.

> Platters were piled high with rare fruits,
> Vases were embellished with gold blossoms,
> The feast was spread on tortoiseshell mats,[9]

all reserved for the entertainment of the visiting gentlemen and officials.

Around noontime, Hsi-men Ch'ing came home after making his formal calls at the prefectural and district yamens. He had just dismounted from his horse when Wang the Third from the household of Imperial Commissioner Wang, garbed in formal attire and followed by four or five attendants, showed up to proffer his greetings. On arriving in the reception hall, he proceeded to perform:

Four brace makes eight kowtows,

after which he asked if Wu Yüeh-niang could come out so he could meet her. Hsi-men Ch'ing, accordingly, invited him into the rear compound to meet Yüeh-niang and then ushered him back to the front reception hall and offered him a seat. They had just saluted each other with a cup of wine when Battalion Commander Ho Yung-shou came by to proffer his greetings. Hsi-men Ch'ing directed Ch'en Ching-chi to entertain Wang the Third, while he went to the summerhouse to receive Ho Yung-shou. Upon drinking a little while longer, Wang the Third said goodbye, and Ch'en Ching-chi escorted him to the front gate, where he mounted his horse and departed. After this, Military Director-in-Chief Ching Chung, Commander Yün Li-shou, and Ch'iao Hung also showed up one after the other.

By this time, as a consequence of entertaining visitors all day long, Hsi-men Ch'ing was:

Half inebriated with wine.

That evening, after seeing everyone off, he returned to the master suite and went to sleep for the night.

The next morning, Hsi-men Ch'ing went out again to make New Year's calls and did not return until evening. In his absence, Han Ming-ch'uan, Ying Po-chüeh, Hsieh Hsi-ta, Ch'ang Shih-chieh, and Hua Tzu-yu had all come to call, and Ch'en Ching-chi had the task of entertaining them in the reception hall, where they had been waiting for some time. When Hsi-men Ch'ing arrived, a new serving of wine and accompanying delicacies was provided, and they fell to drinking again. Since Han Ming-ch'uan and Hua Tzu-yu lived outside the city wall, they were the first to get up and go, but Ying Po-chüeh, Hsieh Hsi-ta, and Ch'ang Shih-chieh continued to sit there until they were so drunk they bobbed about like the float valve in an oil jar, without venturing to leave. Brother-in-law Wu the Second also showed up. After expressing his greetings, he went back to the rear compound to pay a visit to Yüeh-niang and then came out again to join them. They continued drinking until after the lamps were lit before the party broke up. Hsi-men Ch'ing was already stinking drunk by the time he saw off Ying Po-chüeh and the others at the front gate.

When Hsi-men Ch'ing saw that Tai-an was standing beside him, he squeezed his hand, and Tai-an, who understood what this meant, said, "No one else is in her place."

Hsi-men Ch'ing, thereupon, made his way toward Pen Ti-ch'uan's quarters. The woman, who was already standing inside the outer door, welcomed him inside, and the two of them, without wasting any words, went into the inner room, where the woman:

> Took off her clothes, undid her girdle, and
> Lay down on the k'ang with her legs spread.

Hsi-men Ch'ing let down his trousers and lifted up her legs. The silver clasp was already fastened on his organ, and he proceeded to set to work with it. It so happens that the woman liked to keep her thighs together during intercourse, but she used her two hands to separate them so that Hsi-men Ch'ing could better stimulate her clitoris. In consequence, her vaginal secretions flowed out in a warm flood, soaking the mattress. Hsi-men Ch'ing had applied an aphrodisiac to his turtle head, and he plunged it inside her, clasping her around the waist with both hands, while the two of them proceeded to knead away at each other until his chowrie handle penetrated her to the root:

> Without leaving a hairsbreadth outside.[10]

The woman opened her eyes wide, while calling out, "My own daddy!"

Hsi-men Ch'ing asked her, "What is your given name? Tell me."

"My maiden name is Yeh," she responded, "and I am the fifth sibling in my family."

Hsi-men Ch'ing muttered to himself, saying, "Yeh the Fifth, I don't know whether you are familiar with oral intercourse, or not."

This woman had originally been employed as a wet nurse and had engaged in an affair with Pen the Fourth, who absconded with her and took her as his wife. She was petite in stature, with a sultry, treacle-sweet gaze, and was born in the year of the hare, so that she was just thirty-one years old, and there wasn't much she didn't know about anything.

Repetitions of the words "My own daddy" poured out of her mouth in an endless stream until Hsi-men Ch'ing's feelings came to a climax, and he:

> Ejaculated like a geyser.

When Hsi-men Ch'ing retracted his chowrie handle and wanted to wipe it off, the woman prevented him from doing so, saying, "Don't wipe it off. Let this whore of yours get down and suck it clean for you."

Hsi-men Ch'ing was utterly delighted by this proposal.

The woman then actually squatted down on her haunches, took hold of his organ with both hands, and sucked it completely clean, before allowing him to refasten his trousers.

She then went on to ask Hsi-men Ch'ing, "Why is it that my husband has been gone all this time without coming home?"

"I've also been expecting him," responded Hsi-men Ch'ing. "I fear that His Honor Hsia Yen-ling in the capital may be keeping him there for some reason."

He then proceeded to reward the woman with two or three taels of silver as pin money, saying, "I would give you an outfit of clothes, but I fear that if Pen the Fourth were to find out about it, it would prove embarrassing. It's better to give you this silver, so you can buy what you want for yourself."

The woman then opened the door and let him out. Tai-an was alone in the shop, where he waited behind the closed door for Hsi-men Ch'ing to come in, before securing it for the night, while Hsi-men Ch'ing made his way back to the rear compound.

Gentle reader take note: It has always been true that:

If the ridgepole is not straight,
The rafters will be crooked.
This is a natural principle.[11]

If the head of a household commits morally questionable acts, the servants in his home will follow his example. It so happens that this wife of Pen the Fourth was not the sort to abide by her lot. She had already been carrying on an affair with Tai-an, and now she had succeeded in enticing Hsi-men Ch'ing as well.

No sooner had Tai-an seen Hsi-men Ch'ing into the house than he took advantage of the fact that Manager Fu Ming was not spending the night in the shop to join P'ing-an in filling two large vessels of wine and visiting Pen the Fourth's wife in her quarters, where they drank together until the second watch. When P'ing-an returned to the shop to sleep, Tai-an proceeded to spend the night with Pen the Fourth's wife. Can such things be? Truly:

There is no need for the people of today to
practice threading needles;
How could the Weaving Maid have the leisure
to confer such dexterity?[12]

There is a poem that testifies to this:

Romantic feelings bedazzle the eyes, causing
one's vision to blur;
Why is it that the scattered blossoms end up
trampled into the mud?
Laying aside his zither, he ceases to perform
Shang-ling's sad lament;[13]
Which is making the mountain fowl chatter as
they fly among the trees.[14]

To resume our story, that evening Pen the Fourth's wife said to Tai-an, "The only thing I'm afraid of is that Auntie Han next door may leak information about what's going on to the ladies in the rear compound. As in the case of Manager Han Tao-kuo's wife, if they have anything to say about it, I'll be utterly mortified[15] to be seen by them."

"Aside from the First Lady and the Fifth Lady," said Tai-an, "the others don't matter. The First Lady is all right, but the Fifth Lady is prone to be officious. If you take my advice, buy something as a New Year's gift and go inside to offer it to the First Lady as a demonstration of your filial respect. She may not care that much about anything else, but she has always had a liking for steamed shortcake. You ought to buy a mace worth of stuffed steamed-short-cake pastries and a box of large melon seeds to present to her. The ninth day of the month is the Fifth Lady's birthday. You ought to give her a gift as well, and go in person to present her with a box of melon seeds. If you go inside and kowtow to them tomorrow, I guarantee it will have the effect of stopping their mouths."

Pen the Fourth's wife chose to act on Tai-an's advice, and the next day, while Hsi-men Ch'ing was not at home, Tai-an bought the gift boxes for her and took them back to Yüeh-niang's room in the rear compound.

"Where do these come from?" Yüeh-niang asked.

"Pen the Fourth's wife is presenting these boxes of delicacies and melon seeds for Mother to eat," responded Tai-an.

"When her husband is not even at home," remarked Yüeh-niang, "how did she come up with the money to go to such trouble on my behalf?"

She promptly accepted them and sent her a box of steamed dumplings and a box of fruit in return, saying, "Present her with my respects, and thank her for me."

That day, when Hsi-men Ch'ing returned home from paying New Year's visits, Abbot Wu Tsung-che of the Taoist Temple of the Jade Emperor came to extend his compliments. Hsi-men Ch'ing entertained him for a drink in the reception hall before seeing him off.

Hsi-men Ch'ing then took off his formal clothes and said to Tai-an, "You take the horse and go pay a visit to Auntie Wen. Say to her, 'Father would like to come pay his respects to Lady Lin today,' and see what she says."

"There is no need for me to go, Father," responded Tai-an. A while ago, I ran into Auntie Wen, who was riding her donkey past the front gate. Tomor-row, on the fourth, Wang the Third is going to depart for the Eastern Capital to pay his respects to his wife's uncle, the eunuch Huang Ching-ch'en. Lady Lin says she would like Father to pay her a New Year's visit on the sixth. She will be expecting you then."

"Did she really say that?" asked Hsi-men Ch'ing.

"You don't mean to suggest that I would dare tell a lie, do you?" protested Tai-an.

Hsi-men Ch'ing then proceeded to go back to the rear compound. He had hardly arrived in the master suite and sat down before Lai-an suddenly ap-peared and reported that Brother-in-law Wu had come.

Wu K'ai, accordingly, came into the rear parlor, dressed in formal attire, including a girdle with a gold plaque, and bowed to Hsi-men Ch'ing, saying:

"It's a long story,
but I, Wu K'ai, am greatly indebted to you, Brother-in-law, for promoting my interests and looking after me the way you have. It has cost you something to do so, and I am extremely grateful for your lavish gifts. The other day when you condescended to pay me a visit, I was not at home. The fact that I was not

there to welcome you has left me feeling as though I let you down. Today, I have come to respectfully kowtow to you in the hope that you will forgive my remissness."

So saying, he offered him a kowtow.

Hsi-men Ch'ing promptly kowtowed to him in return, saying, "Brother-in-law, congratulations on your promotion.

It is only a natural development;
as a close relative of mine:

What need is there to discuss it?"

When Wu K'ai had finished paying obeisance to Hsi-men Ch'ing, Yüeh-niang came out and kowtowed to her elder brother. She was decked out in a gilt-ridged cap of pale lavender crepe under a sealskin toque, a white satin jacket that opened down the middle, an aloeswood-colored brocaded vest, and a wide-cut skirt of jade-colored satin. On her ears she wore a pair of earrings adorned with two pearls apiece, her chignon was studded with combs and hairpins in the shape of gold phoenixes, and on her breast there hung a gold chatelaine with its three pendant charms that served as a clasp for her collar. Beside her skirt was suspended a purple brocaded purse with eight tassels, and a key chain of variegated cord. On her feet she wore a pair of high-heeled shoes of white satin brocade with an embroidered pattern. In short, she was dolled up very vividly. Coming forward:

Like a sprig of blossoms swaying in the breeze:
Sending the pendants of her embroidered sash flying;
Just as if inserting a taper in its holder;

she kowtowed to her brother four times.

This threw Wu K'ai into such consternation that he promptly performed a half kowtow in return, saying, "Sister, two kowtows are enough."

He then continued, "Your elder brother and his wife are so:
Unconscious of right and wrong,

that we are constantly coming and imposing on the two of you. Your elder brother is aging, and we are increasingly dependent on you."

"If we ever let you down," responded Yüeh-niang, "I hope that you will forgive us."

"Sister," said Wu K'ai, "it goes without saying that we have put the two of you to no small trouble on our behalf."

When this exchange of courtesies was over, Hsi-men Ch'ing invited Wu K'ai to sit down, saying, "By this time of day, I assume that my brother-in-law will not be visiting anyone else to extend his New Year's greetings. Why don't you loosen your clothes and sit down in the room here for a visit."

Who could have anticipated that Meng Yü-lou and P'an Chin-lien, who were both in an adjacent room, upon hearing the stir that Brother-in-law Wu's arrival had created, would promptly proceed to come in and kowtow to him. They both wore sealskin toques, white satin jackets, and jade-colored drawnwork skirts. One of them wore a green brocaded vest, and the other a purple brocaded vest. On their heads, they both sported frets, but Meng Yü-lou's was set off with pearl circlets, while P'an Chin-lien's was enhanced by pendant onyx earrings, and below they revealed the upturned points of their golden lotuses. After kowtowing to Brother-in-law Wu K'ai, they retreated to their own quarters.

After Hsi-men Ch'ing had ushered his brother-in-law to a seat in the room, a table was placed over the brazier, and platters of appetizers, boxes of candied fruit, assorted bowls of hot viands, large steamed dumplings, and a soup of eight ingredients were brought in and placed upon it. Hsiao-yü and Yü-hsiao also came in and kowtowed to Brother-in-law Wu. In a little while, after they had finished with the soup and rice, Yüeh-niang took up a small gold goblet, inlaid with tortoiseshell, filled it with wine, and offered it to Wu K'ai, while Hsi-men Ch'ing continued to play the role of host.

Brother-in-law Wu demurred, saying, "Sister, why don't you come and sit down with us?"

"I'll be there in a moment," responded Yüeh-niang, as she went into the inner room and came out with an assortment of delicacies to go with the wine, consisting of bamboo shoots, whitebait, ground squirrel, minced sturgeon, jel-lyfish, edible fungus, apples, betel nuts, fresh tangerines, pomegranates, dried caltrops, snow pears, and the like.

Hsi-men Ch'ing then asked, "Has my brother-in-law's recent promotion gone through satisfactorily?"

"Thanks to my brother-in-law's support," responded Wu K'ai, "my new ap-pointment came through at New Year's. I have already distributed 70 or 80 percent of the customary gratuities, both above and below, but have not yet visited the site of the State Farm Battalion. Tomorrow is an auspicious day for me to go and assume my new office. The Ch'ing-ho Guard has already issued my official seal of office. When I return home, I will have to prepare some gift boxes and have them carried to the yamen of the State Farm Battalion in time for my assumption of office, and also dispatch an order for the heads of the State Farms to assemble so I can issue their instructions. My predecessor, Di-rector Ting, having mismanaged affairs, has already been impeached by Grand Coordinator Hou Meng, and been removed from office. Now that I have been appointed to:

Assume his position and carry out his duties,

I will have to examine closely the lists of registered tenants, and motivate the heads of the State Farms to go over them with a fine-tooth comb and clearly report any additions or subtractions, in order to facilitate the collection of the autumn and summer tax assessments."

"How extensive, altogether, are the State Farms that will be under your ju-risdiction?" asked Hsi-men Ch'ing.

"As for these State Farms," replied Wu K'ai, "I will be candid with you, Brother-in-law. According to the precedent promulgated by Emperor T'ai-tsu,[16] units of the Military Guard were assigned to work on State Farms, which were established in order to save the transportation costs of logistical support. Later on, the grand councilor Wang An-shih introduced the Green Sprouts system,[17] which involved the additional assessment of this summer tax. Prior to that time, the State Farms were only required to submit the autumn tax assessment, and this summer tax was not applied to land owned by the civilian population. At present, within the jurisdiction of Chi-chou, leaving aside uncultivated land, the Imperial Reed Beds, harbors, and narrows, the total area of the State Farms is twenty-seven thousand mou. The total value of the produce collected by the autumn and summer tax assessments is one tael and eight mace per ch'ing of land, which amounts to no more than five hundred taels of silver. At the end of the year, when the taxed produce has been collected, it is turned over to the authorities in Tung-p'ing prefecture, who in turn engage merchants to transport it, in order to provide logistical support and fodder for the army."

"Is there anything left over to profit from?" asked Hsi-men Ch'ing.

"Although there are always some unregistered tenants," replied Wu K'ai, "these rural villagers are a wily lot. If you try too hard to extort anything out of them by using weighted scales or oversize containers, you run the risk of arousing adverse public opinion."

"As long as there is something left over," opined Hsi-men Ch'ing, "it should be all right. The government can hardly be expected to extract everything. If something can be retained through the manipulation of containers and scales, it should be sufficient to take care of your necessary expenditures, both high and low."

"To be candid with you, Brother-in-law," said Wu K'ai, "if I am adroit in managing these State Farms, in the space of no more than a year, I should be able to realize as much as a hundred or more taels of silver. In addition to which, at the end of the year, there will be tenants who choose to present me in person with chickens, geese, pigs, or rice. These gifts are not demanded of them and fall outside what can be expected in the way of income. I am greatly indebted to you, Brother-in-law, for the strength of your support."

"As long as it suffices for your needs," responded Hsi-men Ch'ing, "I will do what little I can on your behalf."

As they were talking, Yüeh-niang came in and sat down at their side. The three of them continued drinking together until after the lamps were lit before Brother-in-law Wu K'ai got up and took his leave. That day, Hsi-men Ch'ing went to Chin-lien's quarters in the front compound to spend the night.

The next day, Hsi-men Ch'ing reported to the yamen, where he resumed the use of his seal of office, taking his place on the bench, calling the roll, and dispatching official business.

Before this, the household of Yün Li-shou had sent out cards inviting Hsi-men Ch'ing and the officers of the Guard to attend a party on the fifth in celebration of his official appointment, and Ho Yung-shou's wife, née Lan, had sent a card inviting Yüeh-niang and her sister wives for a get-together on the sixth.

On the fifth, Hsi-men Ch'ing, Ying Po-chüeh, and Brother-in-law Wu, the three of them, set out together to attend the party at Yün Li-shou's place. It so happens that Yün Li-shou had rented the house next door for the occasion and used the eighteen-foot-wide parlor there to entertain his guests. He had engaged musicians playing wind and percussion instruments to welcome his visitors, each of whom was provided with an individual table setting. They enjoyed themselves there until the evening before returning home.

Hsi-men Ch'ing could hardly wait until Yüeh-niang had departed to attend the party at the home of Ho Yung-shou the next day. He then proceeded to dress himself up to befit the occasion, stuffed packets of gratuities into his sleeve, mounted his horse, put on his eye shades, and, attended by Tai-an and Ch'in-t'ung, set out in the early afternoon for the mansion of Imperial Commissioner Wang in order to extend his New Year's greetings. Wang the Third was away from home at the time, but he left a calling card for him. Auntie Wen was already there and, taking possession of his calling card, promptly went inside to report his arrival to Lady Lin.

Upon coming out, she said, "Your Honor is invited to come back to the rear of the residence and take a seat."

Making his way past the large reception hall, he headed toward the rear of the establishment, passed through the ceremonial gate, lifted aside the translucent portiere, and entered the thirty-foot-wide parlor in the residential quarter. In the place of honor at the head of the room there was suspended a full-length portrait of the family patriarch Wang Ching-ch'ung, before which there stood two tables with sacrificial offerings of food and wine. He was depicted seated on a crimson dais in a folding armchair, covered with a tiger skin. Before the portrait:

> The entire floor was covered with rugs, and
> The drapery consisted of hanging red curtains.

Before long, Lady Lin appeared, wearing a full-sleeved jacket of scarlet material:

> Her head was covered with pearls and trinkets, and
> Her face was glossy with powder and cosmetics.

After exchanging the customary courtesies with Hsi-men Ch'ing, she invited him to sit down and share a serving of tea, and ordered a servant to lead his horse back to the stables in the rear and take care of feeding it. When they had finished drinking their tea, she suggested that Hsi-men Ch'ing should loosen his outer clothing and sit down with her in her own room.

"My son set out for the Eastern Capital on the fourth," she explained, "in order to kowtow to his wife's uncle, Defender-in-Chief Huang Ching-ch'en. He will not come back until after the Lantern Festival."

Hsi-men Ch'ing, accordingly, took off his outer garments, under which he wore a white satin jacket, an ultramarine flying fish python robe, and white-soled black boots, presenting a really natty appearance. In the woman's room a table was set up beside a square brazier of yellow brass with animal heads protruding from its four sides, filled with smoldering charcoal. The chamber was facing the sun, which shone through the windows, so that it was brightly illuminated.

In a little while, maidservants brought in the wine.

> The cups and plates were duly arranged,
> Filled to the brim with rare delicacies.
> The wine overflowed with golden ripples, and
> A kettle of hydrangea-flavored tea was brewing.

The woman, garbed in:

> A brocade skirt and embroidered jacket,
> With her white teeth and bright eyes,
> Passed the cup with her jadelike hands,
> Conveying ardent feelings in her glance.

The two of them engaged in:

> Playing at guess-fingers and throwing dice,
> As their laughing banter became suggestive.
> Chatting for some time,
> Their thoughts were genial and their feelings warm;
> Drinking quite a while,
> Their gazing became risqué and their hearts stirred.
> By degrees,
> The sun set and dusk descended,
> Before long,
> Silver candles burned brightly.[18]

Tai-an and Ch'in-t'ung were provided with wine and food at a table set up in a side chamber under the supervision of Auntie Wen. Wang the Third's wife resided in a room on the other side of the postern gate and was waited on by her own maidservants and waiting women, so that she did not ordinarily intrude on Lady Lin's living quarters. The woman had also seen to it that the postern gate was locked from the inside, so that none of the male servants would venture to barge in upon her.

When the two of them began to feel the effects of the wine, they went into the woman's boudoir together, where they:

> Raised the brocade curtains, and
> Closed the window casements.
> A maidservant deftly trimmed the silver lamp;
> The beauty hastily closed the vermilion door.
> The gentleman took off his clothes and went to bed;

The lady washed her feet and climbed in beside him.
The pillows were decorated with peonies;
The coverlet disturbed by crimson waves.

It so happens that before leaving home Hsi-men Ch'ing, had:
Made ready his arsenal of weapons,[19]
and brought his bag of sexual implements with him, intending to engage the woman in a furious battle. He had already taken a dose of the Indian monk's medicine, washing it down with wine, and had attached a pair of clasps to his organ. Under the coverlet, he lifted up the woman's two legs, inserted his chowrie handle into her vagina, arched his back and set vigorously to work. In the ensuing bout, as he lifted her body into the air and pegged away at it, the sound resembled that made by a throng of coolies plunging through the mud.[20]

The reiterated sounds reverberated loudly.
The woman, in her abject position, called out "Daddy!" unceasingly. Truly:
Amid autumn colors, the battle flags and banners
     are reflected in the sea;
By the light of the moon, the Heaven-smiting beat
     of military drums resounds.
There is a long set-piece of parallel prose that describes this engagement. Behold:
Before the brocade screen,
A soul-disorienting formation[21] is arrayed;
Under embroidered curtains,
A spirit-conjuring banderole is unfurled.
From the soul-disorienting formation,
There emerges a guardian deity of wine,
     a demon king of sex.
On his head is a flesh-colored helmet,
     with a brocade visor;
On his body is a suit of glossy armor,
     and a vermilion gown,
With protuberant bands, a fish skin belt,
     and seamless boots.
He flaunts a black-tasseled spear,
A tiger-eyed whip,
A shooting star double-balled mace,
And featherless arrows.
Astride his curly-haired sunken-eyed roan,
He waves a rain-flipping cloud-flapping[22]
     commander's flag.
Beneath the spirit-conjuring banderole,

Lady Lin Has a Second Engagement within the Bed Curtains

There appears a powdered skeleton,[23]
    a flamboyant vixen.
On her head is a two-phoenix ornament,
    with hanging ropes of pearls;
On her body is a blouse of white silk,
    a kingfisher skirt waist,
A crotch of white treated silk, with
    wave-tripping stockings,
A waistband of mermaid silk, replete
    with phoenix-toed shoes.
She wields dismissive lashes,
A garrulous tongue,
Invisible arrows,
A blubbering bludgeon,
An emaciated mace,
And silk-curtained scutcheon.
Astride her coquettish jade-surfaced cunt,
She sports a tossing and tumbling mating
    phoenixes[24] parasol.
Before long, on one side, with a *p'u tung-tung*,
    drums resound like spring thunder;
While on the other side, in wild profusion, the
    scent of orchid and musk disperses.
On one side, amid a warm aura, the coverlet
    is disturbed by crimson waves;
On the other side, with a rustle, curtains
    are suspended on silver hooks.
As the coverlet is disturbed by crimson waves,
    his passions are demanding;
Beneath the curtains suspended on silver hooks,
    her sentiments are bizarre.
One of them, urgently, tries to run the gamut
    of all twenty-four positions;[25]
The other, abruptly, finds it hard to manage
    eighteen rolling responses.
One of them is used to wielding a red floss
    noose[26] and tying a lovers' knot;
The other is adept at using the kidnapper's
    shooting star date-shaped mace.
One of them, wielding his flaring
    cylindrical spear,
Looks forward to jabbing her three
    thousand times;

The other, deploying her quivering
   labia bucklers,
Expects to be surmounted at least
   fifty times.
This one is accustomed to don his armor and
   wear a uniform when he fights;
That one is deft at purloining the semen and
   sucking the marrow of her foe.
One of them, riding his fighting steed,
   with a *p'a t'a-t'a,*
Tramples the realm of song and dance;
The other, like a cunning foot soldier,
   surreptitiously,
Hides in the densely wooded gorge.
One of them presents an ugly, belligerent,
   and unbending physique;
The other reveals a seductive apricot face
   and peach-colored cheeks.
One of them flaunts his ability to maintain
   even a prolonged conflict;
The other her skill at giving forth oriole's
   notes and swallow's cries.[27]
One of them, after undergoing a
   protracted engagement,
Drips with sweat, her hairpins askew, her
   coiffure in disarray;[28]
The other, after maintaining a
   relentless assault,
Pants and puffs, his pillow dislodged, his
   mattress displaced.
Before long, behold, the ballista attacks have
   reduced Crotch County to rubble,
Leaving each of them with bulging brows
   and swollen eyes;
In no time, one perceives, the sparsely wooded
   field is so gored with the spear,
That they are each left with split flesh
   and broken skin.[29]

Truly:

The thundering clouds rise up as high as
   the nine-layered heavens,
While down below the defeated combatants
   lie tumbled on the field.[30]

> Although he had often engaged lascivious
>   women in furious battles,
> None of them had ever risen to the level
>   of this one's intensity.[31]

On this occasion, Hsi-men Ch'ing burned two pellets of moxa on the middle of the woman's chest and her mons veneris and promised that he would put on a party at his residence in the near future, and invite her and Wang the Third's wife to come and enjoy viewing the lanterns. The woman's body and mind had already been so tightly entrammeled by Hsi-men Ch'ing that she:

> Effusively voiced her acceptance,[32]

promising that they would both go. Hsi-men Ch'ing was utterly delighted to hear this. On getting up, they resumed drinking heartily and enjoying each other's company until the second watch, when the horse was led out to the back gate, and Hsi-men Ch'ing took his leave and returned home. Truly:

> Do not fear lest the bright moon should set,
>   It will be succeeded by a subtle fragrance.

There is a poem that testifies to this:

> All day long I yearn for you, within
>   my painted boudoir;
> Having met, I cannot give you up, but
>   press you to remain.
> Master Liu[33] is undeterred by the age
>   of the peach blossoms;
> Wantonly scattering the pink petals
>   into the flowing stream.[34]

To resume our story, when Hsi-men Ch'ing arrived home, he was met at the gate by P'ing-an, who reported, "Today, Eunuch Director Hsüeh sent someone to deliver a written invitation for you to pay a visit to the imperial estates outside the city wall tomorrow morning, in order to enjoy the advent of spring. In addition, Yün Li-shou has sent someone to deliver five calling cards inviting the ladies of your household to a New Year's party. I have already sent the cards inside."

When Hsi-men Ch'ing heard this, he had nothing to say, but proceeded to make his way back to Yüeh-niang's room in the rear compound. Meng Yü-lou and P'an Chin-lien were already sitting there. Yüeh-niang, who had just returned from the party at Ho Yung-shou's place, had already removed her head ornaments and was only wearing a fret, held in place with six gold pins, and a pearl headband. Attired above in a blue satin jacket, and below a skirt of soft yellow cotton material, she had sat down to chat with them. When Hsi-men Ch'ing came in, she hastily stood up and greeted him with a bow.

After Hsi-men Ch'ing had taken a seat at the head of the room, she asked him, "Where have you been today that you have come home so late?"

Hsi-men Ch'ing hesitated before replying, "I was at Brother Ying the Second's place, where he retained me until now."

Yüeh-niang then told him about the party at Ho Yung-shou's place that day, saying, "It so happens that Battalion Commander Ho's wife is still young, being only seventeen-years-old this year. She is as pretty as a figure on a decorative lantern, possesses an impressive demeanor:

Is well-informed about the present and the past,[35]

and is as vivacious as can be. She treated me as intimately as though we had already met more than once and showed herself to be extremely congenial. She has been married to Ho Yung-shou for only two years or so, but she already has four maidservants, two waiting women, and two servants' wives at her disposal."

Hsi-men Ch'ing said, "She is the niece of Eunuch Director Lan Ts'ung-hsi, who is in charge of the Daily Provisions Office of the Imperial Household Department and provided her with a substantial dowry when she was married."

Yüeh-niang went on to say, "As the page boy has probably told you, the household of Yün Li-shou has also invited us womenfolk to a New Year's party, sending five individual invitations, which are lying there on top of the cabinet, along with the invitation from Eunuch Director Hsüeh."

She then turned to Yü-hsiao and said, "Bring them over for Father to take a look at."

Hsi-men Ch'ing looked over the invitation from Eunuch Director Hsüeh and those from Yün Li-shou's household and noticed that the latter were signed below by his wife with the words, "Respectfully indited with straightened skirts by the lady, née Su, of the Yün family."

"Tomorrow, all of you might as well get your things together and go," said Hsi-men Ch'ing.

"We should leave Sister Sun Hsüeh-o at home," said Yüeh-niang. "I fear that during this major festival season, if someone were to pay us a call, there would be no one to cope with the situation."

"All right, then," responded Hsi-men Ch'ing, "you can leave Sun Hsüeh-o at home while the other four of you go. I won't be going anywhere tomorrow either. Eunuch Director Hsüeh has invited me to come to his place outside the city wall to enjoy the advent of spring with him, but I'm reluctant to go. The last few days, I don't know whether it is due to the advent of spring, or what, but I've developed a pain on one side of my waist and my thigh."

"If you are feeling pain in your waist and thigh," opined Yüeh-niang, "I fear it must be an outbreak of phlegm-fire. You ought to get Doctor Jen Hou-ch'i to prescribe a couple of doses of medicine to treat it. What's the point of merely putting up with it?"

"It doesn't matter," responded Hsi-men Ch'ing. "If I wait a few days before seeking any medication, things will calm down."

He then went on to discuss his plans with Yüeh-niang, saying, "On the occasion of the Lantern Festival a few days from now, we'll have to throw a party and invite Ho Yung-shou's wife, Commandant Chou Hsiu's wife, Ching Chung's wife, Chang Kuan's wife, Ch'iao Hung's wife, Yün Li-shou's wife, Wang the Third's mother, Sister-in-law Wu, and Ts'ui Pen's mother for a get-together. On the twelfth or thirteenth, we'll have to hang up the lanterns, and engage the services of the troupe of actors maintained by Wang the Second, the distaff relative of the imperial family, to entertain us for the day. Unfortunately, however, last year Pen the Fourth was here and took care of the erection of stands for the fireworks display, but this year he has gone off to the Eastern Capital and hasn't come back yet, so who are we to get to take care of the fireworks?"

Chin-lien interrupted him from the sidelines, saying, "Since Pen the Fourth is not here, his wife is equally adept at dealing with erections."

At this, Hsi-men Ch'ing gave Chin-lien a look, saying, "Why you little whore! You can't utter three sentences without getting vulgar."

Yüeh-niang and Meng Yü-lou chose to ignore this exchange, and Yüeh-niang went on to say, "As for the mother of Wang the Third, none of us has formally met her.

We are newly acquainted and hardly know each other.
What's the point of inviting her? I fear she is unlikely to come."

"Since she has acknowledged me as a kinsman," said Hsi-men Ch'ing, "we might as well send her an invitation. Whether she chooses to come or not is up to her."

Yüeh-niang then went on to say, "I don't think I'll go to Yün Li-shou's place tomorrow. I'm in the last month of my pregnancy, and if I continue to run around this way it will only cause tongues to wag."

"Sister," remarked Meng Yü-lou, "there's really nothing to be afraid of. The fact that you are pregnant is not conspicuous, and I doubt if your child will actually be born within the month. It doesn't matter. You might as well relax and enjoy yourself during such a major festival."

When they had done discussing it, Hsi-men Ch'ing finished his tea and headed for Sun Hsüeh-o's quarters in the rear compound. When P'an Chin-lien saw that he had chosen to go to Sun Hsüeh-o's quarters, she spoke to Hsi-men Ta-chieh and accompanied her out to the front compound. Upon arriving in Sun Hsüeh-o's quarters that evening, Hsi-men Ch'ing had her pummel his legs and massage his body for half the night. Of the events of that evening there is no more to tell.

The next morning, who should appear but Ying Po-chüeh, who came to borrow some clothes and head ornaments, saying to Hsi-men Ch'ing, "Yesterday, the wife of Yün Li-shou sent a card inviting my wife to join my sisters-in-law at her party. Although she has some old clothes at home, they are all in bad shape. During the first month of the new year:

Venturing out and returning home,[36]

without decent clothes to wear can only give rise to ridicule. For this reason, I have made bold to come pay my respects to my sister-in-law, in the hope that if she has any sets of clothing and head ornaments, hairpins, or bracelets to spare, I might borrow a few of them so she can be appropriately garbed for the occasion."

Hsi-men Ch'ing accordingly turned to Wang Ching and said, "Go inside and convey the message to the First Lady."

Ying Po-chüeh also addressed Wang Ching, saying, "Ying Pao is waiting outside with a felt bag and a box. May I impose on you to take them inside and bring them back out when the borrowed things have been packed in them?"

Wang Ching, thereupon, collected the felt bag and went back to the rear compound.

After some time, he came back out with the parcel and handed it to Ying Pao, saying, "There are two outfits of first-class satin brocaded garments, five head ornaments, large and small, and a pair of earrings adorned with two pearls apiece inside."

Ying Pao took the package and set out for home, while Hsi-men Ch'ing drank tea with Ying Po-chüeh, saying, "Yesterday, my wife attended a party at Ho Yung-shou's place and did not return home until late. And today, unexpectedly, Yün Li-shou's wife has sent five cards inviting my spouses to a get-together. My First Lady is in the last month of her pregnancy and was reluctant to go, but I said to her, 'Since they have taken the trouble to invite you on the occasion of a major festival like this, all of you might as well go.' I also haven't had any free time the last few days. It was only yesterday that I finished paying my New Year's courtesy calls. The other day, we all went to that party at Yün Li-shou's place, and yesterday, I had to go out again to fulfill a minor obligation and didn't arrive home until late. On top of which, today, Eunuch Director Hsüeh has invited me to visit his place outside the city wall in order to enjoy the advent of spring. How can I find the time to go? Abbot Wu Tsung-che of the Temple of the Jade Emperor has also sent a card reminding me that he is going to perform the annual *chiao* rites of cosmic renewal on the ninth. I won't be able to go myself but will send my son-in-law instead. The last few days, I don't know whether it's because I've had too much to drink, or what, but I've been suffering from pain in my lower back and haven't felt like doing anything."

"Brother," responded Ying Po-chüeh, "it probably is a case of excessive drinking causing damp phlegm to accumulate in the lower body."

"During this festival season," remarked Hsi-men Ch'ing, "who is going to let you off lightly? One can scarcely avoid drinking."

"How many of my sisters-in-law are going to attend the party today?" asked Ying Po-chüeh.

"The First Lady, the Second and Third Ladies, and the Fifth Lady, the four of them, are going," replied Hsi-men Ch'ing. "As for me, I'm going to stay home and rest for a few days."

As they were speaking, who should appear but Tai-an, carrying a card box in his hand, who announced, "His Honor Ho Yung-shou's household has sent someone to deliver an invitation to a New Year's party on the ninth."

"You see what I mean," Hsi-men Ch'ing remarked to Ying Po-chüeh. "When people take the trouble to invite you, one can hardly refuse."

Thereupon, he looked in the card box and saw that it contained three invitations. One of them, inscribed on safflower red paper, was addressed, "To My Superior the Venerable Gentleman Ssu-ch'üan," one of them, "To the Assistant Commander of the Guard the Venerable Gentleman Wu K'ai," and another, "To the Respected Member of the Community the Venerable Gentleman Ying Po-chüeh." All of them were signed, "Respectfully indited with his compliments by your devoted servant, Ho Yung-shou."

Tai-an explained, "The sender said that since he was not yet acquainted with the other two gentlemen, he hoped that we would forward their invitations on his behalf."

On taking this in, Ying Po-chüeh said, "What am I to do about this? Before I have sent anything to him, he has seen fit to send an invitation to me. How can I go under the circumstances?"

"I can seal up the customary gift of a handkerchief on your behalf," said Hsi-men Ch'ing, "and you can have Ying Pao deliver it to him. That ought to take care of it."

So saying, he said to Wang Ching, "Go seal up two mace of silver and a handkerchief, write Ying Po-chüeh's name on the package, and give it to him."

He then turned to Ying Po-chüeh, and said, "If you put this invitation of yours in your sleeve you can save me the trouble of having it forwarded to you. I'll have Lai-an deliver Wu K'ai's invitation to him."

Before long, Wang Ching sealed up the gift of the handkerchief and handed it to Ying Po-chüeh, who thanked Hsi-men Ch'ing, saying, "Brother, you've made it a lot easier for me. I'll come over early the day after tomorrow, and we can set off together."

When he had finished speaking, he took his leave and departed.

To resume our story, that noon, Wu Yüeh-niang and the others, having dressed themselves appropriately, set out in one large sedan chair and three smaller sedan chairs, followed by Hui-yüan, the wife of Lai Chüeh, who accompanied them in a small sedan chair in order to look after their clothes. With four orderlies preceding them to clear the way, and attended by Ch'in-t'ung, Ch'un-hung, Ch'i-t'ung, and Lai-an, they proceeded to the residence of Yün Li-shou to attend the party. Truly:

With blackened eyebrows and cloudy locks,
    they are pretty as pictures;
Displaying slender and lithesome waists,
    they are out of this world.

Veritable models of the Goddess of the
    Moon, up in the heavens;
In their seductive beauty they generate
    fervent spring feelings.[37]

We will say no more about how Wu Yüeh-niang, together with Li Chiao-erh, Meng Yü-lou, and P'an Chin-lien, set out to attend the party at Yün Li-shou's residence.

Hsi-men Ch'ing gave orders to P'ing-an, the keeper of the main gate, saying, "No matter who may come, simply tell them that I am not at home. If they have cards to leave, just accept them, that's all."

P'ing-an, having already suffered the consequences of failing to strictly obey such orders in the past, did not dare to stray from his post but remained seated at the gate. No matter who showed up, he simply told them that the master was not at home.

As for Hsi-men Ch'ing, that day he went into Li P'ing-erh's quarters and sat down to warm himself at the stove.

Ever since Li P'ing-erh had died, Yüeh-niang had instructed Ju-i not to bind up her breasts in order to prevent lactation, but to breast-feed Lai-hsing's baby daughter Ch'eng-erh every day. For several days in a row, Hsi-men Ch'ing had been suffering from pain in his legs. Suddenly he recalled that Dr. Jen Hou-ch'i had given him a prescription for life-prolonging pills that were to be taken with human milk. For this reason, on coming into Li P'ing-erh's quarters, he asked Ju-i to squeeze out some of her milk for him.

Ju-i, in celebration of the New Year's festival, had studded her chignon with frosty gold-colored pins and rings, so that:
        Her head was covered with costume jewelry,
set-off with a kingfisher-blue gold lamé headband. She wore a jacket of blue pongee, and a cloak of jade-white cloud-patterned satin, over a yellow cotton skirt, and a pair of sand-green Lu-chou silk shoes with high white-satin heels. She was dressed up quite differently from the way she had been in the past and was also wearing four silver-coated pewter rings on her hands.

She sat down beside Hsi-men Ch'ing in order to assist him in taking his medication and then proceeded to pour wine for him and urge him to have something to eat. After Ying-ch'un had seen to providing a meal for him, she withdrew into the next room, where she sat down to play at a board game with Ch'un-mei. If tea or water were required, Hsiu-ch'un was available to fetch them from the kitchen.

When Hsi-men Ch'ing saw that the maidservants had vacated the room, he leaned nonchalantly against the back of the k'ang, undid the white satin cord of his woolen trousers, exposed his organ, which was already fitted with a silver clasp, and told her to suck it for him. As she did so, he was able to help himself to the wine and delicacies that were conveniently arrayed at his side.

Chang Ju-i Savors the Taste of the Dew on the Jade Stalk

Calling out, "Chang the Fourth, my child," he went on to say, "if you do your best to suck it off for me, tomorrow, I'll find a patterned satin vest for you to wear for the Lantern Festival that begins on the twelfth."

"I appreciate your concern," the woman responded.

After she had played with his organ for the time it would take to eat a meal, Hsi-men Ch'ing said, "My child, I'd like to burn some moxa on your body."

"Do as you please," the woman replied. "You can burn moxa on me wherever you like."

Hsi-men Ch'ing told her to close the door to the room, take off her skirt, climb onto the k'ang, and recline face-up on the pillow. On her lower body, she was wearing a pair of newly made scarlet drawers of Lu-chou silk, one leg of which she proceeded to pull down. In his sleeve, Hsi-men Ch'ing still retained three pellets of the moxa steeped in distilled spirits that he had burnt on Lady Lin. Removing her bodice, he placed one of them on the middle of her chest, one on her lower abdomen, and one on her mons veneris. Igniting them with a stick of benzoin incense, he thrust his organ into her vagina and lowered his head in order to observe its movements. Alternately submerging and exposing the knob of his glans, he proceeded to move it in and out without ceasing. He also moved a mirror stand over beside him so he could better observe the action. In a little while, as the moxa burnt its way down to the skin, the woman:

> Knit her brows and clenched her teeth,[38]

in order to endure the pain.

> In a trembling voice and faint tones,
> While groaning for all she was worth,

she cried out inarticulately, "Daddy! Father! You'll be the end of me yet. It's really hard to take."

"Chang the Fourth, whore that you are," said Hsi-men Ch'ing, "whose wife are you?"

"I'm Father's wife," the woman responded.

Hsi-men Ch'ing instructed her, "Say to me, 'I was once Hsiung Wang's wife, but today I belong to my own daddy.'"

The woman did as she was told, saying, "Whore that I am, I was originally Hsiung Wang's wife, but today I belong to my own daddy."

Hsi-men Ch'ing went on to ask, "Do I know how to fuck or not?"

"Daddy really knows how to fuck a cunt," the woman replied.

What with their:

> Obscene noises and lascivious words,

there was nothing the two of them left unsaid. Hsi-men Ch'ing's organ was thick and large, stretching the woman's vagina to the limits. As it went back and forth and in and out, it agitated her clitoris:

> As red as a parrot's tongue,
> And as dark as a bat's wing,

in a pleasurable way. Hsi-men Ch'ing thereupon placed her two legs around his waist, so that their four limbs were intertwined as they responded to each other. His organ penetrated her all the way to the root:

> Without leaving a hairsbreadth outside.

The woman opened her eyes wide and cried out involuntarily as her vaginal fluids flowed out below. When Hsi-men Ch'ing's passion became intense and his pleasure reached its height, his semen spurted out like a gushing spring. Truly:

> Not yet apprised that the tidings of spring
>   had already arrived;
> They knew only that their bodies and joints
>   were melting away.[39]

There is a poem that testifies to this:

> Letting him have his way in proffering his
>   cups of "sunset clouds,"[40]
> Her brain is flooded with lustful feelings,
>   vast and without limit.
> Her whole body is at the disposal of The
>   Lord of the East's whim;
> What does she care if her jeweled hairpin
>   should fall by the bedside?[41]

On that day, after Hsi-men Ch'ing had finished burning three pellets of moxa on the woman's body, he opened the door, searched out a patterned vest of jet-colored satin, and presented it to her.

That evening, when Yüeh-niang and the others returned home, she said to Hsi-men Ch'ing, "It turns out that Yün Li-shou's wife is also in a late state of pregnancy. At the party today, the two of us toasted each other and agreed that when the time comes for us to give birth, if one of the babies is a boy and the other a girl, our two households will betroth them to each other, and thus become related. If they are both boys, we will arrange for them to study together, and if they are both girls, we will have them treat each other as sisters, do their needlework together, and play with each other as if they were related. Ying Po-chüeh's wife undertook to act as a witness to the agreement."

When Hsi-men Ch'ing heard this, he merely smiled.

To make a long story short, the next day was the eve of P'an Chin-lien's birthday. Hsi-men Ch'ing got up early that morning to go to the yamen. Before doing so, he ordered the page boys to get out the lanterns, clean them up, take care of suspending them in the large reception hall, the summerhouse, and elsewhere, and set out brocade hangings and standing screens for the occasion. He also told Lai-hsing to buy fresh fruits and so forth, and engage the services of boy musicians, for the celebration that evening.

That morning, P'an Chin-lien dressed herself up and came out:

> Richly adorned and daubed with powder,
> In turquoise sleeves with rouged lips,

and ventured into the large reception hall, where she saw Tai-an and Ch'in-t'ung, standing on high stools, in order to suspend the three beaded hanging lanterns with their large bowls.

With an ingratiating smile, she said, "I wondered who I would find here, and it turns out to be the two of you, hanging up the lanterns."

"Today is the eve of your birthday," said Ch'in-t'ung, "and Father ordered us to hang up the lanterns so they will be in place for your birthday party tomorrow. This evening, we will all come and kowtow to you, and expect to be rewarded appropriately."

"If it's a beating you want, I will be happy to oblige," the woman responded. "But as for rewards, there won't be any."

"Ai-ya!" exclaimed Ch'in-t'ung. "You:

> Rarely say a word without threatening a beating.

Whatever we do, you respond by proposing to beat us. We are all like your children, after all. It would be better if you were to care for us instead of constantly threatening us with punishment."

"You lousy jailbird!" the woman responded. "You had better stop shooting off your mouth and get back to the task of carefully hanging up the lanterns. If you don't watch what you're doing, you're likely to lose your grip, and let one of them fall to the ground. The other day, before New Year's, when Ts'ui Pen arrived home, you were heard to say, 'Even in broad daylight, Father is nowhere to be seen.' On that occasion, despite the risk you ran, you were lucky enough to escape a beating. But, on this occasion, you may be in for one."

"Mother," protested Ch'in-t'ung, "how can you persist in using such disparaging language? My existence is precarious enough as it is without your continuing to frighten me."

"Mother was not there to hear that remark of his," interjected Tai-an. "How did you know about it?"

The woman responded:

> "Outside the palace is a pine tree,
> Inside the palace there is a bell;
> Just as a bell has its sound,
> A tree has its shadow.

How could I not know about it? The other day, Father said to the First Lady, 'Last year Pen the Fourth was here and took care of the erection of stands for the fireworks display, but this year he is not here, so there is no one to take care of the fireworks.' This prompted me to remark, 'Although he is not here, his wife is equally adept at handling erections. You might as well let her take care of it.'"

"Mother," protested Tai-an, "how can you bring yourself to utter such an allegation? You're talking about the household of his own manager. How could there be any such thing?"

The woman responded:

> "What kind of talk is that?
> It's got a sandalwood haft.

Such things do indeed occur. Though you may draw a line against such conduct, people will be tempted to violate the boundary."

"Mother," said Ch'in-t'ung, "you ought not to believe what people accuse her of. I fear that when Pen the Fourth arrives home, he will find out about it."

"You may succeed in deceiving a thousand gullible cuckolds," the woman responded, "but I pronounce this cuckold to be an open cuckold. It is not surprising that he should be willing to go off to the Eastern Capital while leaving his wife behind, knowing full well that she would be unwilling to let her cunt lie idle. You lousy jailbirds should keep your mouths shut. You band together to act as procurers for your master and make it possible for him to have his way, while hoping to be able to follow in his footsteps. Am I right, or am I not? And yet you dare to suggest that I don't know what I'm talking about. No wonder that lousy whore bought me a birthday gift, made a present of steamed shortcake to the First Lady, and even had a large box of melon seeds delivered to me in order to buy my silence. She's an old hand at taking on lovers, and my guess is that one of them is none other than Tai-an. It's that lousy jailbird that has:

> Laid plans and hatched a scheme,

on her behalf."

"Mother," protested Tai-an, "you do me a mortal injustice. Why should I concern myself with her doings, for no good reason? I don't ordinarily frequent her quarters. You really ought not to listen to what that wife of Mohammedan Han has to say. The two of them have been quarreling vociferously over their children. As the sayings go:

> It is hard to keep on good terms,
> But it is easy to pick a quarrel.
> The collapse of a house may not be deadly,
> But an evil tongue can lead to your death.
> If you believe something, it will be true,
> If you disbelieve in it, it will be false.

If you stop to consider it, Pen the Fourth's wife possesses an accommodating nature. Dwelling as she does by the gate of the residence, she has not antagonized even a single member of the household, great or small. Who is there who has not procured a serving of tea from her? Do you mean to suggest that she has taken them all on as lovers? There would hardly be room for them all."

"I know that watery-eyed whore for what she is," responded Chin-lien. "What with her short stature, she's no bigger than half a brick, and when she squeezes those eyes of hers, you could almost scoop the liquid out of them with a spoon. She's nothing but a crazy whore, just like that overgrown pumpkin head of a whore, the wife of Han Tao-kuo. I don't know but what I'd rather scratch my eyes out than have to contemplate the likes of her."

As they were speaking, who should appear but Hsiao-yü, who came in and said, "My mistress is calling for you, Fifth Lady. Your mother, Old Mrs. P'an, has arrived and needs you to pay the cost of her sedan chair."

"I've been standing here all this time," responded Chin-lien. "When did she come in?"

"The old lady entered through the enclosed passageway," said Ch'in-t'ung, "and I escorted her inside. The bearers who brought her want six candareens of silver."

"Where would I get the silver from?" said Chin-lien. "Whoever heard of anyone coming by sedan chair without bringing the money to pay the fare?"

She then went back to the rear compound to see her mother but did not give her the money for the fare, saying, "I don't have it."

"You can give your mother a mace of silver," said Yüeh-niang, "and enter it in your account book for the household expenses."

"I can't touch that money," said Chin-lien. "It is provided by our husband in definite amounts to purchase provisions for the household. He wouldn't want me to spend it on sedan chair fares."

They sat there for a while, merely staring at each other with wide-open eyes, while the sedan chair bearers outside pressed for the fare so they could leave. Finally, Meng Yü-lou, seeing that they had reached an impasse, groped a mace of silver out of her sleeve and took care of sending the sedan chair on its way.

Before long, Sister-in-law Wu, Wu the Second's wife, and the abbess of the Kuan-yin Nunnery arrived, and Yüeh-niang provided them with a serving of tea.

Old Mrs. P'an then set out for her daughter's quarters in the front compound, and Chin-lien proceeded to upbraid her severely, saying, "Who asked you to come if you didn't even have enough money to pay for the sedan chair? If you make such a shameful spectacle of yourself, you will only cause people to look down on you."

"My daughter," protested Old Mrs. P'an, "if you refuse me the money to pay for a visit, where am I to get it? It was hard enough for me to come up with the cost of a gift for you."

"You may have expected to get the money from me," said Chin-lien, "but where am I to get it from? If you will only open your eyes, you will see that for every seven outlays, there are eight people waiting to be paid. In the future, if you have the money to pay for a sedan chair, come here to visit; but if you don't have enough money to pay for a sedan chair, don't bother to come. I doubt if his household will feel diminished by the lack of such poor relatives as yourself. Don't risk the retribution of having your face slapped. You've got to be tough like:

> Kuan Yü, the God of War, peddling
>   his bean curd:
> The man is hard, even though his
>   goods are not.[42]

I'm sick and tired of having to listen to people shooting off their cunts about me behind my back. The other day, merely because you went home earlier than she expected, I ended up getting into:

> A vituperative altercation,

with the First Lady. If you knew how it is for me, you'd shut up.

> The droppings of a donkey may be shiny
>   enough on the outside;[43]
> But you are quite unaware of how messy
>   they are on the inside."

With these few remarks she managed to reduce Old Mrs. P'an to a state of:

> Sobbing and wailing,

as she broke out in tears.

"Mother," Ch'un-mei protested, "whatever has induced you to find fault with your old lady this way today?"

So saying, she helped the old woman onto the k'ang in the inner room and hastened to pour her a serving of tea. Old Mrs. P'an was so exasperated that all she could do was lie down on the k'ang and go to sleep. Only when someone from the rear compound came to invite her to join Sister-in-law Wu for a meal did she get up and go back to the rear compound.

Hsi-men Ch'ing had returned home from the yamen and was about to sit down for a meal in the master suite, when Tai-an suddenly came in with a calling card and said, "His Honor Ching Chung has been promoted to the post of commander-general of the Southeast and has come to pay his respects."

When Hsi-men Ch'ing looked at the card he saw that it read, "Respectfully indited with his compliments by the newly promoted commander-general of the Southeast, and concurrently grain transport commander, Regional Commander Ching Chung."

This threw Hsi-men Ch'ing into such consternation that he ordered the dining table to be removed, hastened to don his formal garments, including his official cap and girdle, and went out to welcome his guest. What should he see but Commander-General Ching Chung, wearing a crimson robe emblazoned with a mandarin square featuring a ch'i-lin, and a gold-buckled girdle, followed by a retinue of subordinates and soldiers. Hsi-men Ch'ing ushered

him into the large reception hall, where they exchanged the customary amenities and then sat down in the positions of guest and host.

Tea was served, and after it was finished, Ching Chung said, "The rescript
confirming my promotion only arrived the other day, and before even formally
assuming office, I have come to express my gratitude to you, venerable sir."

"Venerable commander," responded Hsi-men Ch'ing, "you are to be congratulated on your illustrious promotion. Talents as great as yours are sure to
be put to significant use.

It is only natural,

and redounds to the credit of the rest of us. It is appropriate that we should
offer our congratulations."

Going on to say, "Please loosen your respected garments, and sit down for
something to eat," he ordered his attendants to set up a table.

Ching Chung repeatedly expressed his thanks, saying, "Your pupil must
inform you, venerable sir, that I have not yet gone to pay my respects anywhere else and have a great many insignificant tasks to attend to. Allow me to
come seek your instruction another day."

So saying, he got up to go, but Hsi-men Ch'ing would not have it and proceeded to order his attendants to come forward and take his outer garments,
wipe off the table, and provide it with wine and food.

> Animal-shaped briquettes smolder,
> Heat-holding drapes are suspended.
> Golden flagons decant jade hued liquids,
> Turquoise goblets contain Yang-kao wine.

Just as the wine was being poured, who should appear but Cheng Ch'un
and Wang Hsiang, the two boy actors, who came in, knelt down before them,
and kowtowed.

"Why are the two of you so late?" inquired Hsi-men Ch'ing.

"And what is the name of this other fellow?" he asked Cheng Ch'un.

"His name is Wang Hsiang," said Cheng Ch'un, "and he is the younger
brother of Wang Chu."

Hsi-men Ch'ing then told them, "Get out your instruments and come play
and sing for the entertainment of His Honor Ching Chung."

In no time at all, when the two boy actors had readied their instruments,
they proceeded to perform the song suite the first number of which, to the
tune "Flowers in Brocade," begins with the words:

The fair weather is balmy.[44]

As they did so, the attendants brought out two partitioned food boxes filled
with pastries and refreshments, and two bottles of wine, for the people that had
come with Ching Chung.

"This will never do," said Ching Chung. "Your pupil is the recipient of your
magnanimity, and my servants are also to enjoy the bestowal of refreshments.

What can I do to be worthy of such largess?"

So saying, he ordered his servants to come forward and kowtow.

"In a few days," said Hsi-men Ch'ing, "my wife plans, with the utmost sincerity, to invite your honorable spouse to attend a party in order to enjoy the lanterns. It is our humble hope that she will condescend to come. Those she plans to invite include your venerable lady, my kinsman Chang Kuan's wife, my colleague Ho Yung-shou's wife, and two other female relatives of ours. No one else has been invited."

"Upon receipt of your venerable lady's invitation," said Ching Chung, "my humble spouse will be sure to attend."

Hsi-men Ch'ing then inquired, "How is it that the venerable Commandant Chou Hsiu has not yet received a promotion?"

"I have heard," replied Ching Chung, "that in the third month Chou Hsiu will be promoted to a position in the Capital Training Divisions."

"That seems appropriate," remarked Hsi-men Ch'ing.

After sitting for a while, Ching Chung said goodbye and got up to go. Hsi-men Ch'ing escorted him to the gate and looked on as he mounted his horse and departed, with his attendants shouting to clear the way.

That evening, they celebrated the eve of P'an Chin-lien's birthday. The boy actors played their instruments and sang to entertain the company in the rear reception hall. When everyone had been provided with wine, Hsi-men Ch'ing got up and went out to Chin-lien's quarters, while Yüeh-niang, along with Sister-in-law Wu, Old Mrs. P'an, the professional singer Big Sister Yü, and the two nuns sat down in the master suite to enjoy their wine.

P'an Chin-lien accompanied Hsi-men Ch'ing to her quarters, where she set out more wine and personally proffered him a drink and kowtowed to him. After a while, Old Mrs. P'an came in, and Chin-lien packed her off to Li P'ing-erh's quarters to spend the night, while she kept Hsi-men Ch'ing company, drinking wine and enjoying themselves, as they went on to play with each other.

To resume our story, when Old Mrs. P'an arrived in Li P'ing-erh's quarters next door, Ju-i and Ying-ch'un invited her to sit down on the heated k'ang. On her way in, Old Mrs. P'an noticed that before Li P'ing-erh's spirit tablet in the parlor there were arrayed candied effigies of Buddhist lions, immortals, and the Five Ancients; tree-borne fresh fruits such as tangerines, pomegranates, apples, and snow pears; steamed-shortcake pastries, crullers, and fried dough twists. A brazier was burning powdered incense, and a candle was lit in the long-lasting vigil lamp. The table was shrouded in a gold lamé tablecloth, and beside it there hung her half-length portrait, dressed in a crimson brocaded gown, a brocade skirt and embroidered jacket, and a chignon decorated with two phoenixes, from whose beaks dangled bangles on ropes of pearls.

Stepping forward, she saluted the portrait in the Buddhist fashion, saying, "Sister, you are blessed in having ascended to Heaven."

Then, after sitting down on the k'ang, she said to Ju-i and Ying-ch'un, "Your mistress is lucky to have a husband who has gone to such lengths to insure her salvation, and in being the recipient of such lavish offerings. It is more than ample. She is fortunate indeed."

"Recently," said Ju-i, "on the occasion of the 'hundredth-day' ceremony after our mistress's death, though you were invited to attend, you failed to come. Hua Tzu-yu's wife from outside the city wall and Sister-in-law Wu were both here. Twelve Taoist acolytes came to perform the scripture recitation, and there was:

Loud playing on wind and percussion instruments.

What with the flag-raising ceremony to invite the presence of the gods, and the Water and Fire sublimation ritual, night had fallen before they left."

"With the New Year's festivities so close at hand," explained Old Mrs. P'an, "and the child I am taking care of at home, if I had come, there would have been no one to look after the place. So I chose not to come. Why have I not seen Aunt Yang here today?"

"You must not have heard about it yet," said Ju-i, "but Aunt Yang finally died of sickness and old age so she also was unable to come for our mistress's 'hundredth-day' scripture-reading ceremony. The ladies of our household all went to the northern quarter of the city to offer their sacrifices to the deceased."

"How sad," exclaimed Old Mrs. P'an. "She was older than I am, but I didn't know that she had died. No wonder I didn't see her today."

After they had talked about Aunt Yang for a while, Ju-i said, "We have some sweet wine on hand. Why don't you try some of it?"

She then turned to Ying-ch'un and said, "Sister, set up a bed table on the k'ang, and pour out some sweet wine so Old Mrs. P'an can have a cup of it."

In no time at all, the wine was provided, and as they were drinking it, Old Mrs. P'an brought up the subject of Li P'ing-erh again, saying, "Your mistress was a good person. She was both kind and just, and she had a warm disposition. Whenever I came here, she never treated me as a stranger, but always provided me with hot tea and hot water, and only objected if I didn't drink them. At night she would sit up and talk to me, and when I was ready to go home, she would always wrap something up to take with me. I swear, she never let me depart empty-handed. Not to deceive the two of you, this cape I am wearing right now is something your mistress gave me. This perverse daughter of mine, on the other hand, has never come up with so much as half a broken needle for me.[45] I am not lying when I state before Amitābha Buddha himself that even if:

I had neither water nor rice to eat,[46]

if she were willing to cough up so much as a mace of silver for me, my eyeballs would drop onto the ground. When your mistress gave me anything, she would accuse me of being:

Mean-spirited and covetous,

hankering after other people's possessions. Today, for example, with regard to the fare for the sedan chair I came in, though you have a large amount of silver at your disposal, were you willing to cough up a few candareens on my behalf, or what? Instead, you just clenched your teeth and denied that you had any money to spare, so that, in the end, the Lady from the west side of the rear compound had to come up with a mace of silver to take care of the bearers of the sedan chair, and send them on their way. And when we returned to her quarters, she upbraided me severely, saying, 'In the future, if you have the money to pay for a sedan chair, go ahead and come; but if you don't have enough money to pay for a sedan chair, you had better not cross my doorstep.' When I leave this time, I won't come back. Who wants to come here only to become a target for her anger? Let her do as she pleases. No doubt there are many hard-hearted people in this world, but none of them is a match for this death-bound short-life of a daughter of mine. You two pay heed to what I say. Should I die, in the future, what with her refusal to take anyone's advice, who knows what sort of a harvest she will reap for herself. You ought to remember how, after your father died when you were only six years old, I have continued to care for you right up to the present. How I taught you to do needlework while you were still a child. How I sent you to a girls' school in the home of Licentiate Yü. How I made sure that you had:

Compressed hands and bound feet.[47]

You have always been just as smart as can be, which has made it possible for you to arrive at your present state. But now, she orders her mother around, this way and that, without giving her so much as a glance."

"So the Fifth Lady went to school as a child, did she?" said Ju-i. "No wonder, now that you mention it, she is as literate as she is."

"She started to a girls' school when she was six years old," said Old Mrs. P'an, "and attended it for three years. While there, she learned to trace characters from books of sample calligraphy, so there are hardly any characters in the printed copies of poetry, lyrics, songs, or rhapsodies that she doesn't know."

As they were speaking, they heard the sound of knocking at the postern gate, and Ju-i said, "I wonder who it could be knocking at the gate?"

She then turned to Hsiu-ch'un and said, "Second Sister, go see who it is."

Hsiu-ch'un came back and reported, "It's Sister Ch'un-mei who has come."

At this, Ju-i hastily squeezed the hand of Old Mrs. P'an and said, "You'd better watch what you say. Ch'un-mei is here."

"I understand," said Old Mrs. P'an. "She could be said to share a leg with that perverse daughter of mine."

What should they see at this juncture but Ch'un-mei, who came in sporting a cloud-shaped chignon with turquoise ornaments on her head, a gold-spangled pearl headband, a blue satin jacket that opened down the middle, over a yellow cotton skirt, gold lantern earrings, and a sable muffler.

Upon coming in and seeing that they were drinking wine with Old Mrs. P'an, she said, "I see that Granny hasn't gone to bed yet. I've come to visit with her."

Ju-i offered her a seat, and Ch'un-mei hoisted up her skirt and proceeded to park her posterior on the k'ang. Ying-ch'un sat down next to her on one side, while Ju-i sat to her right by the head of the k'ang, and Old Mrs. P'an sat in the middle.

"Have your master and mistress gone to bed yet, or not?" asked Old Mrs. P'an.

"They finished drinking just now," said Ch'un-mei, "and I have sent the two of them off to bed. I have come over here to visit with you, Granny, and have several delicacies and a flagon of wine to share with you."

She then asked Hsiu-ch'un, "Would you go next door and tell Ch'iu-chü to bring them over here? I have already prepared them."

Hsiu-ch'un, accordingly, went next door to fetch them and came back in no time at all, with Ch'iu-chü carrying a square box containing the delicacies, while she brought a pewter pitcher of Chin-hua wine.

Ch'un-mei then ordered Ch'iu-chü, "You go back to our place and keep your ears open. If they should call for me, come back here and let me know."

Ch'iu-chü went back as she was told, but with a pout on her lips.

The repast was duly laid out on the bed table that had been placed on the k'ang. It consisted of roast duck, ham, smoked goose, marinated fish in a fine mash, nut kernels, savory preserved fruits, seafood, and so forth, covering the entire table surface. Hsiu-ch'un closed the postern gate and then came in and sat down beside them. Thereupon, when the wine had been poured, Ch'un-mei first offered a cup to Old Mrs. P'an, and then a cup to Ju-i, and a cup to Ying-ch'un. Hsiu-ch'un sat down on the edge of the k'ang, and the five of them proceeded to enjoy their drinks.

Ch'un-mei, protecting her clothes with a napkin, selected morsels from each of the dishes and offered them to Old Mrs. P'an and the rest, saying, "Granny, these are all special delicacies. Feel free to sample them."

"Sister," the old woman responded, "I'll help myself."

She then went on to say, "Even your mistress has never gone to the trouble to entertain me in the way you are doing. Sister, you possess a heart that is:
    Concerned for the bereft and kind to the aged.
In the future, you will surely be able:
    Step by step,[48]
to better your condition. That perverse daughter of mine, on the other hand, is utterly lacking in humanity and righteousness. On more than one occasion, when she has been acting outrageously, and I have attempted to remonstrate

with her, she has turned her wrath against me and caused me to lose face. This morning, as you saw for yourself, Sister, I came to visit in the hope of picking up a few morsels of cold food, and she once again treated me as badly as she did."

"Granny," said Ch'un-mei:

"You only see one side of it,
Without perceiving the other.[49]

It is the disposition of my mistress to:

Contend for supremacy without conceding defeat.[50]

She cannot be compared to the Sixth Lady, who had a fortune at her disposal, while she has no money of her own. You allege that she refuses to give you anything. Others may not know the true story, but I do. Although Father has entrusted her with the silver for household expenses, which is stored in her quarters, my mistress does not presume to regard it as her own. When she needs to buy costume jewelry or things like that for herself, she is meticulous about asking him for them up front, rather than:

Surreptitiously acquiring things on the sly,[51]

thereby causing people to look down on her, and making it hard for her to open her mouth and accuse anyone else of anything. Since she really has no money of her own, for you to hold it against her, Granny, is unjust. You may accuse me of endeavoring to excuse her conduct, but one must be just about it."

"You are wrong to hold it against the Fifth Lady," said Ju-i. "It has always been true that:

Relatives are one's own flesh and blood.

If the Fifth Lady had any money of her own, were she not to show her filiality by sharing it with you, Granny, whom should she lavish it upon? As the sayings have it:

Before beating a child one should regard
    it's mother's face.
Even a thousand peach blossoms may stem
    from a single tree.[52]

In the future, when the day comes when your:

Yellow gold is stored in the coffer,

the Fifth Lady will be bereft of any close relatives, like the rest of us whose mothers have died."

The old woman responded, "As for me:

I've lived to this year, but not the next.

Who knows whether:

I'll succumb today, or succumb tomorrow?

I won't hold it against her any longer."

Ch'un-mei, upon seeing that the old woman, after consuming two goblets of wine, was becoming more loquacious, said to Ying-ch'un, "Go get the dice-box. Let's throw the dice and amuse ourselves by playing at 'Competing for the Red.'"

In no time at all, a dicebox with forty dice in it was brought out, and Ch'un-mei proceeded to play a game with Ju-i. After they had played for a while, she went on to play with Ying-ch'un. The losers of each round had to down large goblets of wine.

What with:

> First a cup for you,
> Then a goblet for me,

it was not long before they:

> Felt the effects of the Bamboo Leaf wine, and
> Peach blossoms bloomed upon their cheeks,[53]

as they polished off the entire pewter pitcher of wine. Ying-ch'un then produced half a jar of Ma-ku wine, and they managed to finish it as well. As the time approached the second watch, Old Mrs. P'an could not hold out any longer and took to:

> Swaying forwards and backwards,

as she started to doze off. Only then did the party break up.

Ch'un-mei headed back next door and gave the postern gate a push. When it opened, she proceeded through the courtyard and found that Ch'iu-chü was situated on a wide bench in the parlor, next to a crack in the wooden partition, eavesdropping on Hsi-men Ch'ing and Chin-lien as they engaged in sexual intercourse in the bedroom in order to hear what noises they produced and what exclamations they uttered.

She was so preoccupied that she failed to prevent Ch'un-mei from coming right up to her and giving her a slap on the cheek with all her strength, saying as she did so, "You lousy dead duck of a slave! Just what are you listening to, for no good reason?"

She hit Ch'iu-chü so hard that she opened her eyes wide and protested, "I was only dozing here. What was I listening to that would justify your slapping me that way?"

Who could have anticipated that this exchange was overheard by the woman in the bedroom, who asked Ch'un-mei who she was talking to.

"There's nobody here," replied Ch'un-mei. "I told Ch'iu-chü to close the door, and she failed to respond. That's all."

In this way she covered up for Ch'iu-chü, who rubbed her eyes and went to close the door of the room. Ch'un-mei then got onto the k'ang, removed her headdress, and went to sleep. But no more of this. Truly:

> Though the oriole wishes to retain
>   the evanescent day;
> The unfeeling cuckoo relishes the
>   luster of the night.[54]

Of the events of that evening there is no more to tell.

The next day was P'an Chin-lien's birthday, and those who were present to celebrate it included the wife of Manager Fu Ming, the wife of Manager Kan

Jun, Pen the Fourth's wife, Ts'ui Pen's wife Big Sister Tuan, Wu Shun-ch'en's wife Third Sister Cheng, and Wu the Second's wife.

Hsi-men Ch'ing, along with Wu K'ai and Ying Po-chüeh:

> Straightened his robe and cap;
> Assumed a dignified demeanor,[55]

and set out on horseback, with attendants shouting to clear the way, to attend the party at the home of Battalion Commander Ho Yung-shou. There were many other officials there that day, and they were entertained by four singing girls and a vaudeville troupe. Commandant Chou Hsiu was also among those present. They continued drinking until evening, when Hsi-men Ch'ing returned home and spent the night with Ju-i in the front compound.

On the tenth, invitations were sent out inviting the wives of the various officials to a party, and Yüeh-niang said to Hsi-men Ch'ing, "For this lantern-viewing party on the twelfth, I suggest that we also invite Meng Yü-lou's elder sister from outside the city gate and my elder sister to attend, lest they find out about it and resent the fact that they were not invited."

"It's a good thing you mentioned it," said Hsi-men Ch'ing, and he told Ch'en Ching-chi to write out two additional invitations and send Ch'in-t'ung to deliver them.

P'an Chin-lien, who was standing nearby, overheard this and was disturbed by it. Going back to her quarters, she pressed Old Mrs. P'an to depart immediately.

When Yüeh-niang learned of this, she said, "Granny, what are you in such a hurry to leave for? Why not stay over another day?"

"Sister," said Chin-lien, "it's the New Year's season, and she has left a child at home with no one to look after her. You had better let her go."

This threw Yüeh-niang into such consternation that she hastily prepared two boxes of delicacies for her, provided her with a mace of silver with which to pay her sedan chair fare, and sent her on her way.

Chin-lien subsequently explained this to Li Chiao-erh, saying, "She's invited her well-to-do elder sister to come to the lantern-viewing party, and that old baggage of mine is only likely to be looked askance at. If I hadn't sent her away, what would be the point of keeping her around here? If she were taken to be a guest, she would not be appropriately dressed. If she were taken to be a charwoman, she doesn't really look the part. It could only have the effect of driving me to my wit's end."

Hsi-men Ch'ing sent Tai-an to deliver another two invitations to Imperial Commissioner Wang's residence, one to invite Lady Lin, and one to invite Wang the Third's wife, née Huang. He also sent to the licensed quarter to engage the services of the four singing girls, Li Kuei-chieh, Wu Yin-erh, Cheng Ai-yüeh, and Hung the Fourth, as well as the three young actors, Li Ming, Wu Hui, and Cheng Feng.

Who could have anticipated that Pen the Fourth should arrive back from the Eastern Capital that day. After washing his face and combing his hair, he dressed himself appropriately and came to kowtow to Hsi-men Ch'ing, presenting him with a letter of reply from Hsia Yen-ling.

"How come you stayed as long as this before returning?" Hsi-men Ch'ing demanded to know.

Pen the Fourth explained that he had been stricken with a severe cold in the capital, saying, "It was not until the second day of the first month that I was able to get my things together and set out for home. His Honor Hsia Yen-ling sends you his compliments and wishes to thank you for all you have done on his behalf."

Hsi-men Ch'ing gave him the keys as before and put him back in charge of his knitting and sewing supplies store. He also opened an adjacent shop in which Wu the Second could continue to sell silk goods. In the future, when the boatload of goods from Sung-chiang arrived, he planned to have it all stored in the house on Lion Street, where Lai-pao could cooperate with the others in selling it. He also told Pen the Fourth to hire a fireworks specialist to come and prepare two racks of fireworks, ready to be set off on the twelfth for the entertainment of their female guests. He had already invited Ying Po-chüeh, Hsieh Hsi-ta, Wu K'ai, and Ch'ang Shih-chieh to convene with him in an anteroom during the daylight hours on that occasion.

That evening, who should appear but Ying Po-chüeh, bringing Li the Third with him to see Hsi-men Ch'ing. After first thanking him for the help he had received the other day, and then sitting down to drink his tea, he initiated the conversation by saying, "Brother Li the Third is here because there is a piece of business he would like to propose to you, if you are willing to participate in it."

"Really?" said Hsi-men Ch'ing. "What piece of business is that? Tell me about it."

"At present," responded Li the Third, "a document has come down from the court in the Eastern Capital requiring each of the thirteen provinces in the realm to submit to it several tens of thousands of taels worth of antiquarian relics. This Tung-p'ing prefecture of ours has been allotted a quota of ten thousand taels worth of these antique artifacts. The rescript authorizing this behest is still in the hands of the grand coordinator and has not yet come down to the lower levels of the bureaucracy. At present, Chang the Second of Main Street has put up two hundred taels of silver in a bid to secure this contract, but it will require a total of ten thousand taels in all. I have come, together with Uncle Ying the Second, to broach the subject with Your Honor. If Your Honor is willing to participate, Chang the Second will put up five thousand taels, Your Honor will put up the other five thousand taels, and the two of you can close the deal between you. No one else will be involved but Uncle Ying the Second, myself, and Huang the Fourth on your side, and two of Chang the Second's managers on the other, and the profits will be shared on a ratio of eight to two between the principals and their backers. But I don't know what Your Honor thinks about it."

"What sort of antiquarian relics are involved?" inquired Hsi-men Ch'ing.

"Your Honor may not know about it yet," said Li the Third, "but at present the Emperor has changed the name of the recently completed Mount Ken Imperial Park in the Forbidden City to the Mount Longevity Imperial Park. Within it he has erected numerous pavilions, terraces, halls, and chambers, including the Precious Tablet Temple of Highest Clarity,[56] the Chamber of the Assembled Perfected, the Hall of Meditative Concentration,[57] and even the dressing chamber of his favorite, Consort An, née Liu.[58] He has stocked them with:

> Rare birds and unusual animals,[59]
> Chou vessels and Shang tripods,[60]
> Han censers and Ch'in burners,
> The stone drums of King Hsüan,[61]
> Bronze ladles of various eras,
> Immortals' palms,
> Dew-catching pans,[62]

and rare antiques and relics of all kinds.[63] He has initiated lavish building projects and expended no insignificant amount in the way of resources."

When Hsi-men Ch'ing heard this, he said, "Rather than going into partnership with anyone else, why shouldn't I undertake to do it on my own? No doubt you assume that I would be unable to come up with ten or twenty thousand taels of silver."

"If Your Honor wants to take it all on yourself, that would be fine," said Li the Third. "We can keep the other side in the dark about it, and on our side, no one will be involved other than Uncle Ying the Second, Huang the Fourth, and myself."

"Brother," said Ying Po-chüeh, "do you plan to bring in anyone from your household, or not?"

"When he shows up, I'll have Pen the Fourth participate," said Hsi-men Ch'ing. "He can do some of the legwork for us."

Hsi-men Ch'ing then went on to ask, "Where is the document authorizing this transaction at present?"

"It is still in the hands of the grand coordinator," said Li the Third, "and has not yet come down to the lower levels of the bureaucracy."

"That shouldn't be a problem," said Hsi-men Ch'ing. "I'll send someone with a letter, and an appropriate gift, to ask Sung Ch'iao-nien to obtain it for us."

"If Your Honor is going to try to get hold of it," said Li the Third, "the matter will brook no delay. It has always been the case that:

In warfare, speediness of execution is fundamental.[64]
The first one to cook the rice is the first to eat.
I fear that by the time you get to the prefectural yamen, someone else may have gotten hold of it before you."

Hsi-men Ch'ing laughed at this, saying, "I'm not afraid of that. Even if someone should get to the prefectural yamen before me, I would still be able to induce Sung Ch'iao-nien to recover it. The prefect of Tung-p'ing, Hu Shih-wen, is also an acquaintance of mine."

Thereupon, he invited Li the Third and Ying Po-chüeh to share a meal with him and promised them, saying, "I will have a letter written now and will send off a servant with it tomorrow."

"There is another problem," said Li the Third. "His Honor Sung Ch'iao-nien is making his investigative rounds and is not in Tung-p'ing at present. The day before yesterday, he set out for Yen-chou prefecture to conduct his investigations there."

"You could make the trip to Yen-chou prefecture tomorrow, together with my servant," suggested Hsi-men Ch'ing.

"That would not be a problem," responded Li the Third. "I'll go then. The round trip won't take more than five or six days. Which of your servants does Your Honor intend to send? When we have concluded our plans, and the letter is written, send him over to my place to spend the night, so we can set out early tomorrow morning."

"His Honor Sung Ch'iao-nien is not familiar with any of my other servants," said Hsi-men Ch'ing, "but he has always been fond of Ch'un-hung. I'll have Ch'un-hung and Lai-chüeh, the two of them, go together."

Thereupon, he called the two servants into his presence to meet with Li the Third and instructed them to go spend the night at his place.

"That's the way to do it," remarked Ying Po-chüeh. "This is something that needs to be acted upon as quickly as possible.
        Only he with the most talent and swiftest
                feet can accomplish it."[65]

Thereupon, when he and Li the Third had finished their meal, they took their leave and departed.

Hsi-men Ch'ing, after getting Ch'en Ching-chi to write the letter, also sealed up ten ounces of gold leaf in the packet and entrusted it to Ch'un-hung and Lai-chüeh, saying, "Be careful on the road, and if you succeed in obtaining the document, return immediately. When you get to Yen-chou prefecture, ask His Honor Sung Ch'iao-nien for a note entitling you to pick it up in Tung-p'ing."

"Father, you need not instruct us any further," said Lai-chüeh. "I once worked for Assistant Administration Commissioner Hsü of Yen-chou and will know what to do."

Thereupon, he took the packet containing the letter, secreted it upon his person, and set out with his companion for the house of Li the Third. We will say no more at present about how Lai-chüeh, Ch'un-hung, and Li the Third hired long-distance mounts early on the morning of the eleventh and set out for Yen-chou prefecture.

To resume our story, on the twelfth, Hsi-men Ch'ing's family had invited the wives of the various officials to a party, and he chose to remain at home without going out. He had already invited Wu K'ai, Ying Po-chüeh, Hsieh Hsi-ta, and Ch'ang Shih-chieh, the four of them, to join him in the summer-house that evening to enjoy the lanterns and drink wine together. The troupe of actors that he had arranged to engage from Wang the Second, the distaff relative of the imperial family, showed up that morning, carrying their box of costumes, and set up an anteroom in the front compound as their green room. When the female guests arrived, they beat on bronze gongs and bronze drums to welcome them.

Commandant Chou Hsiu's wife was suffering from an eye ailment and was thus unable to come, though she sent someone to explain the situation. The wife of Commander-General Ching Chung, the wife of Militia Commander Chang Kuan, the wife of Commander Yün Li-shou, along with Ch'iao Hung's wife, Ts'ui Pen's mother, Wu Yüeh-niang's elder sister, and Meng Yü-lou's elder sister, were the first to arrive. Only Ho Yung-shou's wife, Wang the Third's mother Lady Lin, and Wang the Third's wife had not yet come, and Hsi-men Ch'ing sent an orderly, along with Tai-an and Ch'in-t'ung, back and forth two or three times, urging them to come. He also sent Auntie Wen to the household of Imperial Commissioner Wang for the same end.

At noontime, Lady Lin arrived in a large sedan chair, followed by a smaller one, and asked to pay her respects to Hsi-men Ch'ing, who inquired, "Why has Wang the Third's wife not come?"

"My son is not at home," replied Lady Lin, "so there is no one to look after the place."

After paying her respects, she withdrew to the rear compound.

It was well after noon before Ho Yung-shou's wife finally arrived, riding in a large sedan chair borne by four bearers, with a servant's wife riding in a smaller sedan chair behind her, and accompanied by orderlies carrying her dressing case, as well as two servants in black livery, trotting close beside the carrying poles. Only after being borne past the second gate did she deign to get out of her sedan chair, to the welcoming music of drums, and wind and percussion instruments, as Wu Yüeh-niang and her sister wives came out to the ceremonial gate to receive her.

Hsi-men Ch'ing had concealed himself in the anteroom on the western side of the courtyard and let down the blinds, so that he could gaze at her surreptitiously. Ho Yung-shou's wife, née Lan, was no more than nineteen years old. She was:

> Tall and slender in stature,

and was made up so that she looked to be:

Modeled in plaster, carved of jade.
On her head:
>Pearls and trinkets rose in piles,
>Phoenix feathers emerged in pairs.

She was wearing a full-sleeved crimson jacket, adorned with a variegated motif of the four animals representing the cardinal directions paying homage to the *ch'i-lin*, her waist was encircled with a girdle featuring a plaque of green jade inlaid with gold, beneath which she wore a skirt of blue brocade, hanging from which decorative pendants tinkled, exuding the scent of musk and orchid. Behold:

>Her image is captivating;[66]
>Her demeanor is delicate.[67]
>By nature, she is as clever
>>as can be;
>Her height is neither short
>>nor tall.
>Delicately curved, her two
>>moth eyebrows,[68]
>Extend to her temples;
>With a flutter, her pair of
>>phoenix eyes,
>Glance back and forth.
>Her captivating voice is like that of an
>>oriole singing in the sun;
>Her lissome waist reminds one of willow
>>fronds tossed in the wind.

Truly:

>Although born amid quantities of silk and gauze,
>She opts to avoid the trappings of luxury;
>Though raised amid piles of pearls and trinkets,
>She adorns herself with elegant simplicity.
>The flowering crab apples are in full bloom,
>But she does not ask how many blossomed overnight;
>The willow catkins are scattered everywhere,
>But she is unaware of the spring season's advance.
>The only one who knows anything of her true feelings,
>Is the bright moon that penetrates her gauze windows;
>The only thing that affects the content of her heart,
>Is the clear breeze that flutters her brocade drapes.[69]
>Lightly moving her lotus feet,
>She is alluring as an immortal from the
>>Palace of Clustered Pearls;
>Gently lifting her beige skirt,

She has the bearing of the Bodhisattva
Kuan-yin of the Water Moon.[70]
Truly:
She is like a bloom that can converse;
She is like jade that emits fragrance.[71]
If Hsi-men Ch'ing had not seen her, that would have been that; but having
seen her:
His ethereal souls flew beyond the sky, and
His material souls fled to the Nine Heavens.
Even without any physical contact,
He had already forfeited his soul.
It did not take long for Yüeh-niang and the others to usher her into the par-
lor in the rear compound where, after they had exchanged the customary
amenities, she asked to be introduced to Hsi-men Ch'ing. This was just the
signal he had been waiting for, and he hastily adjusted his formal attire and
came in to present himself to her. It seemed to him just as though:
A tree of jade in a forest of alabaster had
descended into the world;
The Goddess of Witches' Mountain had emerged
in the subcelestial realm.
Hsi-men Ch'ing:
Bent his body to perform an obeisance.
His heart was agitated and his eyes disturbed,
to such an extent that:
He was unable to control himself.
When they had finished paying their respects to each other, Yüeh-niang
invited her guests into the summerhouse where tables had been set up for tea,
and an assortment of exotic viands had been provided; after which they took
their places in the large reception hall, where:
Rare delicacies from land and sea,
were already arrayed.
Behold:
At the head of the room,
There stand Shih Ch'ung's brocade windbreak[72]
and folding screens;
On all four sides,
There are tortoiseshell mats and capacious
table settings.
Decorated lanterns are raised on high;
Colorful ropes are suspended in midair.
From the carved rafters brocaded
bands droop low;

Painted candles throw light upon
    jeweled canopies.
Lanterns depicting fish and dragons
    sporting in the mountains,
Scintillate like a cluster of pearls;
Others depicting halls and chambers,
    towers and terraces,
Gather like a thousand balls of jade.
On the left,
The nine older and ten younger sisters,
Are depicted as portraits of beauties[73]
    in red and green;
On the right,
The nine stars and eight grotto heavens,
Are seen with their gods and immortals
    in gold and azure.
The food provided consists of,
Dragons' livers and phoenix marrow,
Bears' paws and dromedaries' humps;
The music performed is that of,
Patterned cithara, silver psaltery,
Phoenix flute, and ivory clarinet.
The resounding beat of alligator drums
    startles the flying birds;
The melodious sound of singing voices
    diverts the moving clouds.
The alluring beauties at the feast,
Are like clustering pearls and kingfisher ornaments;
The entertainers beneath the steps,
Enact life's partings and reunions, sorrows and joys.[74]
Truly, it is the case that:
    The maidservants proffering wine are duplicates of
        the Goddess of the Lo River;[75]
    The serving girls presenting soup are replicas of
        Ch'ang-o, the Goddess of the Moon.[76]
On this occasion, when Lady Lin had taken her seat at the feast, the hsi-wen drama *Hsiao T'ien-hsiang pan-yeh ch'ao-yüan*, or *Little Heavenly Fragrance Ascends to Paradise at Midnight*,[77] was performed. After the first two scenes had been acted, the players withdrew, and the four singing girls, Li Kuei-chieh, Wu Yin-erh, Cheng Ai-yüeh, and Hung the Fourth, came out to play their musical instruments and sing for the entertainment of the company. Because Meng Yü-lou's elder sister resided outside the city gate, she was the

first to get up to go, and in order to see her off they sang the song suite in celebration of the Lantern Festival that begins with the tune "Drunk in the Flowers' Shade," the first line of which is:

Decorative embroidered lanterns are
  suspended in midair.[78]

Meanwhile, Hsi-men Ch'ing was drinking in the summerhouse with Wu
K'ai, Ying Po-chüeh, Hsieh Hsi-ta, and Ch'ang Shih-chieh, while the three
boy actors, Li Ming, Wu Hui, and Cheng Feng, played their instruments and
sang for their entertainment. From time to time, he left the others and peered
into the large reception hall through the latticework. The servants and attendants who had accompanied the sedan chairs of the female guests were supplied with food and wine in the front reception hall, but there is no need to
describe this in detail.
    Gentle reader take note:
        Only at intervals is the bright moon full;
        The variegated clouds are easily dispersed.
        When joy reaches its zenith, it gives birth to sorrow;
        The nadir will be followed by the zenith.
        This is a self-evident principle.
Hsi-men Ch'ing was only bent on:
        Competing for prestige and usurping profit;[79]
        Indulging his desires and slaking his lust.
He was utterly oblivious to the fact that, since:
        The Way of Heaven is inimical to excess;[80]
        The recorders of Hell were on his heels,
        And the hour of his death was impending.[81]
    That evening, as the lanterns in the chamber were lit, and the boy actors
sang songs in celebration of the Lantern Festival, even before the first watch
began, Hsi-men Ch'ing, while sitting in the presence of his guests, began to
snore loudly as he dozed off.
    Ying Po-chüeh continued:
        Gaming at forfeits and playing at guess-fingers,
and pestered him, saying, "Brother, you don't seem to be in high spirits today.
How is it that you keep dozing off this way?"
    "I didn't get enough sleep yesterday," said Hsi-men Ch'ing. "I don't know
why, but today I don't seem to have any energy, and keep dozing off."
    When the four singing girls came in from entertaining the ladies, Ying Po-
chüeh told two of them to sing Lantern Festival songs, and the other two to
serve the wine. Thereupon, Hung the Fourth and Cheng Ai-yüeh accompanied themselves on the psaltery and the balloon guitar as they sang for them,
while Wu Yin-erh and Li Kuei-chieh served the wine.
    Just as they were enjoying themselves to the full, Tai-an suddenly came in
and announced that Lady Lin and Ho Yung-shou's wife were preparing to

leave. Hsi-men Ch'ing promptly withdrew from the gathering and, concealing himself in the dark shadows, made his way to the second gate in order to catch a surreptitious view of them as they got into their sedan chairs.

Yüeh-niang and the others escorted them as far as the front courtyard to watch the setting off of the fireworks. Ho Yung-shou's wife, née Lan, had on a jacket of crimson brocade, a sable cloak, and a skirt of kingfisher-blue brocade. Lady Lin wore a white satin jacket, a sable cloak, and a crimson skirt, with gold bracelets and jade bangles. Their attendants, carrying lanterns, clustered around them as they got into their sedan chairs and made their departure.

As for Hsi-men Ch'ing, truly:

> Though his hungry eyes were about to burst,[82]
> He could only swallow his thirsting saliva,[83]

and could hardly wait to begin an affair with her. Having watched Ho Yung-shou's wife, née Lan, depart, he was quietly making his way inside through the enclosed passageway when:

> Without coincidences there would be no stories;
> Predestined unions have a way of happening;
> Strange as it may seem,

he could not have anticipated that Lai-chüeh's wife, Hui-yüan, on seeing that the female guests had left, was coming back up front in order to open the door to her quarters, when she happened to run right into Hsi-men Ch'ing and had no way of avoiding him.

It so happens that Hsi-men Ch'ing had already observed the natural seductiveness of Lai-chüeh's wife and had long since set his sights on her. Although she was not quite as attractive as Lai-wang's wife, Sung Hui-lien, she was more than adequate as a substitute. Thereupon, exhilarated by the wine he had consumed, he embraced her with both arms, stepped into her quarters with her, and proceeded to kiss her. Originally, this woman had worked for Wang the Second, the distaff relative of the imperial family, but she had engaged in hanky-panky with her master, which caused such an uproar in his household that she was driven out. On this day, confronted with an opportunity to pursue the same path, she saw no reason to refuse. There and then, she responded by sticking her tongue into Hsi-men Ch'ing's mouth, and the two of them proceeded to unfasten their clothing and let down their pants. Lying down on the edge of the k'ang and raising her legs, she allowed Hsi-men Ch'ing to thrust away at her until he might well have ejaculated:

> Is it not delightful?

Truly:

> Failing to consummate his assignation
>   with Ts'ui Ying-ying;
> He settled for a tryst with Hung-niang
>   to relieve his lust.

There is a poem that testifies to this:

> The competing lusters of lanterns and moon[84]
>   bathe the jade flagon;
> Their clear rays of light serve separately
>   to illuminate Lü-chu.[85]
> Protest not that the gentleman already has
>   a wife of his own;
> He is tempted, beneath the mulberry trees,
>   to seek out Lo-fu.[86]

> If you want to know the outcome of these events,
> Pray consult the story related in the following chapter.

Chapter 79

HSI-MEN CH'ING IN HIS SEXUAL INDULGENCE

INCURS AN ILLNESS;

WU YÜEH-NIANG BEARS A CHILD UPON

THE DEATH OF HER HUSBAND

Even the kindest of men are seldom able to
    maintain consistency;
Be careful, whatever you do, never to say,
    "It doesn't matter."
Those who always strive for precedence
    resort to evil devices;
Words that are uttered in due turn
    have a more enduring savor.
A surfeit of tasty foodstuffs will end up
    making you sick;
Pleasurable events, once over, are sure to
    result in disaster.
Rather than having to seek for medicine
    after you are sick;
It would be better to take preventive steps
    before falling ill.[1]

THESE EIGHT LINES of poetry are by Shao Yung. Their message is that:
    The Way of Heaven ensures fortune for the good;[2]
    Both ghosts and spirits are inimical to excess.
    Those whose conduct is good will be rewarded
      with a hundred blessings;
    Those whose conduct is evil will be rewarded
      with a hundred disasters.[3]
Hsi-men Ch'ing only knew how to:
    Defile the wife and children of another,[4]
but remained:
    Unaware that his own death was imminent.
    That day, after encountering Lai-chüeh's wife in the enclosed passageway
and committing adultery with her, he went back to the summerhouse and

continued drinking with Wu K'ai, Ying Po-chüeh, Hsieh Hsi-ta, and Ch'ang
Shih-chieh.

The wife of Commander-General Ching Chung, the wife of Militia Commander Chang Kuan, Ch'iao Hung's wife, Ts'ui Pen's mother, Wu Yüeh-
niang's elder sister, Wu K'ai's wife, and Big Sister Tuan remained for some
time. It was only after the Lantern Festival dumplings had been served that
they prepared to go, said their farewells, got into their sedan chairs, and departed. Wu K'ai's wife and Wu Shun-ch'en's wife, Third Sister Cheng, accompanied each other on the way home. Ch'en Ching-chi sent off the troupe of
actors from the household of Wang the Second, the distaff relative of the imperial family, with two taels of silver as remuneration for their performance,
after seeing that they were provided with food and wine. The four singing
girls, and the boy actors, were still in the summerhouse meanwhile, where
they continued to play their musical instruments, sing, and pour wine for the
company.

Ying Po-chüeh said to Hsi-men Ch'ing, "Brother, tomorrow is Hua Tzu-yu's
birthday. Have you sent a present to him, or not?"

"I sent something to him this morning," responded Hsi-men Ch'ing.

Tai-an said, "Hua Tzu-yu's household has already sent Lai-ting to us with an
invitation for the occasion."

"Brother," asked Ying Po-chüeh, "are you going to go tomorrow, or not? I
can come over and go with you."

"I'll have to see how I feel tomorrow," said Hsi-men Ch'ing. "Actually, you'd
better go ahead on your own, and I'll follow when I feel up to it."

After serving a round of wine, the four singing girls went back to the rear
compound, and Li Ming and the other boy actors came forward to play their
instruments and sing for the company. Hsi-men Ch'ing, meanwhile, was constantly dozing off on his chair.

Observing this, Wu K'ai said, "Brother-in-law, you have been wearing yourself out for days on end. Enough is enough. We had better bid you farewell."

Thereupon, they got up to go, but Hsi-men Ch'ing held them back and
insisted on their resuming their seats. It was not until the second watch that
the party broke up. Hsi-men Ch'ing saw off the four singing girls in their
sedan chairs and then rewarded Li Ming and the other two boy actors with
two large goblets of wine apiece and gave them six mace of silver for their
performance.

As they were about to go out the gate, he called Li Ming back and said to
him, "On the fifteenth, I'm going to invite His Honor Chou Hsiu, His Honor
Ching Chung, and His Honor Ho Yung-shou to a party. Would you, as soon
as possible, engage the services of four singing girls for the occasion on my
behalf? It is important that you not be remiss about it."

Li Ming knelt down before him and inquired, "Father, which four do you
want?"

Hsi-men Ch'ing said, "Fan Pai-chia-nu, Ch'in Yü-chih, that Feng Chin-pao who sang the other day at His Honor Ho Yung-shou's place, and Lü Sai-erh. Do your best to engage them for me."

Li Ming assented, saying, "I understand," and then kowtowed and departed.

When Hsi-men Ch'ing went back to Yüeh-niang's room in the rear compound, she said to him, "Today, at the party, Lady Lin and Ching Chung's wife really enjoyed each others' company and stayed quite late before going home. Ching Chung's wife also expressed to me her thanks for the support you have rendered her husband, saying:

'Whatever benefit he may obtain,
He will never dare to forget it.'

Next month he is going to report to the Huai River region to take charge of speeding up the grain transport system."

She then went on to say, "His Honor Ho Yung-shou's wife also had a lot to drink today. She took a liking to Sister Six, who took her into the garden to see the artificial hill. All of the guests today gave generous gifts to the singing girls."

When they had finished talking, Hsi-men Ch'ing chose to spend the night there in the master suite.

In the middle of the night, Yüeh-niang had a dream which she described to Hsi-men Ch'ing the next morning, saying, "No doubt it was because I had noticed the robe of crimson velvet that Lady Lin was wearing at the party, but during the night I dreamed that you had taken a robe of crimson velvet out of Li P'ing-erh's trunk and given it to me to wear, when Sister P'an the Sixth grabbed it away from me and put it on herself. This really annoyed me, and I said to her, 'You have already demanded her fur coat for yourself, and now you are taking this robe as well.' At which, in a fit of temper, she tore a large hole in the robe, which caused me to get into a shouting match with her that woke me up. To my surprise, it turned out to be nothing but:

A dream of the Southern Branch."

"When you woke up," said Hsi-men Ch'ing, "you were cursing angrily. It's not important. I'll find one like it for you to wear in the future, that's all. It has always been true that:

Dreams are produced by what is on your mind."

When Hsi-men Ch'ing got up the next day, his head felt heavy, and he did not feel well enough to go to the yamen. After combing his hair and washing his face, he put on his clothes and went out to his studio in the front compound, where he sat down and warmed himself at the brazier. Who should appear at this juncture but Yü-hsiao, who had gone over to Ju-i's room that morning and had her squeeze out half a cup of milk, which she brought to the studio for Hsi-men Ch'ing to take with his medicine. She found Hsi-men Ch'ing reclining on the bed while Wang Ching pummeled his thighs for him. On seeing Yü-hsiao come in, Wang Ching withdrew. After she had helped him to take his medicine, Hsi-men Ch'ing gave her a pair of gold-plated hairpins and four silver-coated pewter rings and told her to deliver them to the quarters of Lai-chüeh's wife. When Yü-hsiao heard her master send her on this mission, it reminded her of the affair of Lai-wang's wife, and being quick to:

> Stick her head into any cranny,

she tucked them into her sleeve and went off on her errand.

Having delivered the objects, she came back to report to Hsi-men Ch'ing, saying, "She accepted them and said that she would kowtow to you on another day."

Taking the empty cup with her, she went back to the master suite, where Yüeh-niang asked her, "If Father has already taken his medicine, what is he doing in his studio?"

"He didn't say," responded Yü-hsiao.

"You should heat up some congee for him," Yüeh-niang told her, but when breakfast time had come and gone, he had not yet returned.

It so happens that Wang Ching had delivered a package of gifts from his sister Wang Liu-erh, which he handed to Hsi-men Ch'ing to look at, and extended her invitation for him to visit her at home. When Hsi-men Ch'ing opened the paper wrapping, he found a lock of her dark-black glossy hair, bound into a circlet with variegated satin displaying the motif of "joined hearts," and with two brocade straps attached to it, so that it could be fastened around the root of his chowrie handle. It was a work of exquisite craftsmanship. In addition, there was a wallet with two pockets, decorated with a pair of mandarin ducks, with a diapered border of close-stitched embroidered brocade, and filled with melon seeds. Hsi-men Ch'ing admired them for some time and was utterly delighted. Eventually, he put the wallet in the bookcase and tucked the brocade circlet into his sleeve.

Just as he was lost in thought, Wu Yüeh-niang suddenly came in. Lifting aside the portiere, she saw that he was lying on the bed, while Wang Ching knelt beside him, pummeling his thighs.

"Why do you insist on staying here in the front compound," she said, "instead of coming back to our quarters, where your congee is waiting for you? Tell me what's going on. How are you feeling, that you seem to be so lethargic?"

"I don't know why," said Hsi-men Ch'ing, "but I'm feeling out of sorts, and I'm suffering from pain in the thighs."

"I imagine it must be due to the advent of spring," said Yüeh-niang. "Take your medicine, and go easy on your way back."

Having induced him to return to the master suite, and fed him his congee, she said, "During a major festival like this, you had better pluck up your spirits. Today is the birthday of Hua Tzu-yu, who resides outside the city wall, and he has invited you to pay him a visit. You can summon Ying the Second to go with you."

"He's not at home," said Hsi-men Ch'ing. "He's already left to attend Hua Tzu-yu's birthday party. If you would have some wine and food prepared for me, I could go pay a visit to the house by the Lantern Market and share a drink with Brother-in-law Wu the Second."

"You might as well saddle up your horse and go," said Yüeh-niang. "I'll have the maidservants prepare the food and wine for you."

Hsi-men Ch'ing, thereupon, told Tai-an to prepare his horse, asked Wang Ching to accompany him, put on his clothes, and headed straight for the Lantern Market on Lion Street. What did the Lantern Market look like? Behold:

> Carriages and horses rumble like thunder;
> The round lanterns are ablaze with color.
> The revelers swarm like ants;
> The merrymaking is at its height.

In this era of great peace,[5] beneficent
    breezes enhance the scene;
Beauties in gauze and silk return after
    showing off their finery.
Hills of lanterns soar into the heights[6]
    above the azure clouds;
From whence do revelers not congregate
    to take in the sights?[7]

After pausing to admire the lanterns, Hsi-men Ch'ing proceeded to the door of the house on Lion Street, where he dismounted, went inside, and sat down. This threw Brother-in-law Wu the Second and Pen the Fourth into such consternation that they both hastened to come forward and welcome him with a bow, reporting that the shop was doing a thriving business. Lai-chao's wife, "The Beanpole," quickly lit a brazier in the studio and provided a serving of tea. It was not long before Wu Yüeh-niang sent Ch'in-t'ung and Lai-an to deliver two square boxes of appetizers and other dishes to go with the drinks. There was a supply of mung bean wine in the shop that had been brought back from the South, a jug of which was opened and taken upstairs to be heated on the brazier in the studio. Hsi-men Ch'ing invited Brother-in-law Wu the Second and Pen the Fourth to join him in toasting each other as they drank, and they enjoyed the spectacle of the Lantern Market right outside the window, where crowds of people moved back and forth incessantly, and the goods purveyed by the various guilds were piled up like mountains.

When they had indulged themselves until after the normal lunch hour, Hsi-men Ch'ing sent Wang Ching to inform Wang Liu-erh of his visit. Upon hearing that Hsi-men Ch'ing was coming, Wang Liu-erh prepared a table replete with boxes of candied fruit, wine, and other delicacies and awaited his arrival. Hsi-men Ch'ing told Lai-chao to keep what was left of the table setting of food and wine for Wu the Second and Pen the Fourth to enjoy that evening while on night duty, rather than sending it home. He also directed Ch'in-t'ung to deliver a jug of wine to Wang Liu-erh's place, after which he mounted his horse and made his way directly to her home.

The woman had dressed herself up to welcome him and conducted him into the parlor, where she kowtowed to him four times:

Just as if inserting a taper in its holder.

Hsi-men Ch'ing responded by saying, "I am grateful for your lavish gifts on more than one occasion, but why is it that the last two times we invited you to our home you failed to come?"

"Father, that's a fine way to talk," she said. "Who else is there to look after the place? I don't know why it is, but the last few days I've been feeling out of sorts, and haven't even felt like eating or drinking. I've hardly been able to get started on anything."

"No doubt," said Hsi-men Ch'ing, "it's because you've been longing for your old man."

"Since when have I been longing for him?" the woman responded. "It's rather because you have neglected me for such a long time. I don't know how I have been remiss toward you that you should put me in the position of:

The rings that hold your hairnet in place, always
        at the back of your head.

I fear you must have found someone else who is uppermost in your mind."

Hsi-men Ch'ing laughed, saying, "Where did you get any such idea? It's simply because during this festival season I've been busy entertaining people at our place the last few days."

"I have heard that yesterday you entertained a bunch of female guests," said the woman.

"That is true," said Hsi-men Ch'ing. "The First Lady had been entertained at two New Year's parties and felt obliged to put on a party in return."

"What female guests were invited?" the woman asked.

"So-and-so and so-and-so," Hsi-men Ch'ing responded, and went on to run through the list from beginning to end.

"So," the woman responded, "for your lantern-viewing party you only invited important guests, but not the likes of me."

"Don't make such a thing out of it," said Hsi-men Ch'ing. "In days to come, on the sixteenth of the first month, we're going to have a party for the wives of my managers and employees, to which you had better come, and not make any excuses for not doing so."

"If Mother deigns to send me an invitation," the woman said, "how would I dare not to come? However, the other day, that young lady from your household reviled Second Sister Shen so severely that she was filled with resentment and took it out on me. That day, she had not wanted to go, and it was I who persuaded her to do so. Afterwards, when she came back after suffering such abuse, she broke down and cried like anything, to my extreme mortification; and it was only after you and Mother sent a box of delicacies and a tael of silver to mollify her, that she stopped complaining. I was unaware that the young lady in question had such an explosive temper. After all:

Before beating a dog, you ought to consider
the face of its owner."[8]

"You don't know that little oily mouth," said Hsi-men Ch'ing. "She's got an extremely gutsy personality and has even been known to brazen it out with me. But if she asked Second Sister Shen to sing a song for her, why should she have refused to do so? Whoever told her not only to refuse to sing, but to criticize her into the bargain?"

"Ai-ya! Ai-ya!" the woman protested. "She assured me that she had never criticized the young lady, but that she came barging in, pointed a finger at her, and began to abuse her, telling her to get out. By the time she got back here, she was in terrible shape and broke out crying:

Sniveling three ribbons of snot, and
Dribbling two rivulets of tears.

I kept her here overnight before sending her home the next day."

After they had talked for a while, a maidservant brought in a serving of tea. The page boy Chin-ts'ai had gone out to purchase appetizers, fresh fish, and other viands, which Old Mother Feng was preparing in the kitchen. She also came out and kowtowed to Hsi-men Ch'ing.

Hsi-men Ch'ing gave her a lump of silver worth three or four mace and said, "Since your mistress died, you have not visited my place very often."

Wang Liu-erh said, "Since her mistress died, what reason would she have to do that? Instead, she frequently comes here to keep me company."

In a little while, when her room had been straightened up, the woman invited Hsi-men Ch'ing to come inside and sit down, asking him, "Father, have you eaten lunch, or not?"

"I had a little congee at home this morning," replied Hsi-men Ch'ing, "and just now I shared a snack with Brother-in-law Wu the Second, but I haven't had a real meal."

A table was, accordingly, set up and a spread laid out to go with the wine, consisting of festival foods, and fine delicacies of all kinds. The woman told Wang Ching to open the jug of mung bean wine, and fill their cups so she could have a drink with Hsi-men Ch'ing.

The woman then said, "Father, I assume that you have looked over the gift that I sent you. I coiled up and cut off a lock of hair from the crown of my head and fashioned it with my own hands. I'm sure that it must have tickled your fancy."

"I'm grateful for your consideration," said Hsi-men Ch'ing.

After they had:

Drunk until they were half inebriated,[9]

observing that they were alone in the room, Hsi-men Ch'ing pulled it out of his sleeve, placed it around the base of his organ, and tied the two brocaded straps around his waist. He also attached a "Yunnanese tickler"[10] to his turtle head and washed down a dose of the Indian monk's medicine with his wine. The woman started to manipulate his organ with her hand, and in no time at all:

> Its protuberances swelled, its head sprang up,
> Its distended blood vessels were all exposed,

and it was the color of purple liver. The device proved to be more than a match for the silver clasp or the white satin band. Hsi-men Ch'ing pulled the woman onto his lap and inserted his organ into her vagina, while up above, the two of them passed the same goblet back and forth between them as they drank wine and sucked each other's tongues. The woman also used the tip of her tongue to pass nut kernels into Hsi-men Ch'ing's mouth.

They continued to play with each other as they ate and drank until lamp-lighting time, when Old Mother Feng came in from the kitchen with some pork and leek pastries that she had made. The woman and Hsi-men Ch'ing ate two of them apiece, after which a maidservant took the leftovers away. The two of them then made their way to the heated k'ang in the inner room where they:

> Lifted aside the brocade curtains,
> Took off their clothes, and went to bed.

The woman knew that Hsi-men Ch'ing liked to engage in intercourse by lamplight, so she moved a lampstand from the parlor and placed it on a table beside the k'ang. She then proceeded to close the sliding paper door, wash her private parts, and put on a pair of slippers made of crimson Lu-chou silk with flat white satin soles; after which, she took off her drawers, burrowed her way under the bedclothes, and snuggled up to Hsi-men Ch'ing. As they hugged and embraced each other, they dozed off for a while.

It so happens that Hsi-men Ch'ing's mind was totally obsessed with Ho Yung-shou's wife, née Lan; and, as a result, his

> Lecherous desires were on fire,

and his organ became stiff and hard. He started out by telling the woman to get down on all fours in front of him and then inserted his organ into the flower in her rear courtyard and proceeded to slam away at her as hard as he could two or three hundred times; slamming into her bottom so hard that:

> The reiterated sounds reverberated loudly,

while the woman beneath him stimulated her clitoris with her hand and called out "Daddy" unceasingly.

Thereupon, still not completely satisfied, he got up and put on a short jacket of white satin, sat down on a pillow, and had the woman recline face up, while he sought out two of her foot bindings and used them to suspend her feet from the bed posts on either side so that she appeared like "A Golden Dragon Extending Its Claws." Upon inserting his organ into her vagina, he began alternately submerging and exposing the knob of his glans, as he gave himself over to a series of shallow retractions and deep thrusts. As his organ continued to be half exposed and half submerged, he finally started:

Advancing with alacrity and galloping forward.

Fearing that the woman might be cold, he also covered her body with a short jacket of red satin. Exhilarated by the wine he had consumed, Hsi-men Ch'ing moved the lampstand closer and:

Bent his head in order the better to savor,
The marvelous sight as it went in and out,

while he retracted his organ as far as the knob of the glans, and then plunged it in all the way up to the root another several hundred times. Meanwhile the woman gave vent to her feelings in a hundred ways:

In a faint voice and trembling tones.

Hsi-men Ch'ing also took some of the pink ointment the Indian monk had given him and daubed it on his turtle head before plunging it back in. The woman's vagina was so intensely stimulated that she could hardly bear it, and she begged him to penetrate more deeply as they responded to each other. But Hsi-men Ch'ing deliberately lingered, playfully dallying around the mouth of her vagina and titillating her clitoris, while refusing to penetrate more deeply, which aroused the woman to the point that her vaginal fluids began to flow, like a snail secreting its slime. As he moved back and forth, it agitated her clitoris in a pleasurable way. By the light of the lamp, Hsi-men Ch'ing contemplated her two fresh white legs, clad in crimson shoes, as they were suspended high on either side. As they moved back and forth, lunging and butting at each other, he could hardly contain his excitement.

Thereupon, he called out, "Whore that you are, do you care for me, or not?"

"How could I not care for my daddy?" the woman responded. "So long as you remain constant like:

The pine and the cypress that are evergreen
    through both winter and summer,

everything will be fine; but you must not:

Grow distant and aloof as the days go by,[11]

and choose to ignore me once you've had your fill of fun. Though I should long to death for you, who could I tell about it, and who would care? When that cuckold of mine comes home, there would be no point in my telling him about it. I hardly think that while he is away from home on business and has money in hand, he chooses to remain chaste for love of me."

"My child," said Hsi-men Ch'ing, "if you can dedicate yourself exclusively to me, when he comes home I'll simply find another wife for him, and you can devote yourself to me on a long-term basis."

"My own daddy," the woman responded, "when he comes home, go ahead, whatever happens, and find him another wife. You can either maintain me outside, or take me into your household, whichever you like. This whore of yours will simply abandon her worthless body to you, that's all. There is no wish of yours that I will refuse to comply with."

"I understand," responded Hsi-men Ch'ing.

While they talked together, they had been going at it for the time it would take to eat two meals before Hsi-men Ch'ing finally ejaculated. He then unfastened the woman's foot bindings and proceeded to embrace her under the bedclothes. The two of them:

> Head to head and thigh over thigh,
> As their drunken eyes grew bleary,[12]

slept until the third watch before waking up.

Hsi-men Ch'ing got out of bed, put on his clothes, and washed his hands, while the woman opened the door of the room and called in a maidservant. Thereupon, they:

> Replenished the special delicacies,
> Resumed drinking the fragrant wine,
> Decanting the warmed-over beverage,

and drank another ten cups or more together. Only after they began to feel intoxicated did they proceed to pour some tea and rinse out their mouths with it.

Hsi-men Ch'ing then groped a card out of his sleeve and handed it to the woman, saying, "Show this to Kan Jun, the manager of my silk goods store, and have him give you an outfit of clothes to wear, of any pattern you choose."

The woman thanked Hsi-men Ch'ing with a bow and saw him to the door. Wang Ching was there to hold the lantern for him, and Tai-an and Ch'int'ung stood by with his horse. Only after she had seen him into the saddle did the woman return inside and shut the door.

Hsi-men Ch'ing sat on his horse wearing a purple sheep's wool coat and a scarf wrapped around his neck. It was already the third watch of the night and dark clouds in the sky:

> Darkened and obscured,[13]

the light of the moon. Silence had descended over the marketplace, the nine thoroughfares were empty, and the only sound to be heard in the streets was the rattle of the night watchman:

> Shouting the hour and ringing his bell.

Hsi-men Ch'ing gave his horse a touch with the whip and started on his way. Just as he arrived in front of the stone bridge at the western end of the street, a dark shadow swirled up from under the bridge and lunged at him. At the sight of the shadow his horse shied and Hsi-men Ch'ing felt a cold shiver go up his spine.[14] Drunkenly he struck his horse with his whip and it shook its mane. Tai-an and Ch'in-t'ung pulled on the bridle with all their might but were unable to hold the beast in check. Like a cloud scudding before the wind, the horse bolted for home and only slowed to a halt when it reached the front gate. Wang Ching, who had charge of the lantern, was unable to catch up with them.

When Hsi-men Ch'ing dismounted, he was unsteady on his legs and had to be helped inside by the servants, whereupon he went straight to P'an Chin-lien's quarters in the front garden. Nothing might have happened if he had not gone there, but since he did go, truly, it was a case of:

A sleepy slugabed encountering the General
    of the Five Ways;
A cold and hungry demon running into
    Chung K'uei.[15]

It so happens that P'an Chin-lien had returned to her quarters from the rear compound but had not yet gone to sleep. Without bothering to undress she had stretched out on the k'ang to wait for Hsi-men Ch'ing. When she heard him come in, she hastily crawled to her feet and came forward to take his clothes from him. He was obviously stinking drunk, and she didn't dare ask him where he had been.

Hsi-men Ch'ing embraced her as best he could with one hand resting on her shoulder and mumbled, "You little whore! Your Daddy's drunk tonight. Get the bed ready so I can go to sleep."

The woman helped him onto the k'ang and got him bedded down for the night. No sooner did Hsi-men Ch'ing's head hit the pillow than he began:

Snoring thunderously,

and could not be shaken awake. The woman then removed her own clothes, burrowed her way under the bedclothes, and began lazily to grope around his loins for his organ. It was as soft as cotton and as lifeless as could be.

"Wherever has he come from?" she wondered as she:

Tossed first this way and then that,

unable to withstand:

The flames of desire that consumed her body;
The lustful visions that disturbed her mind.

For some time she devoted herself to manipulating his organ with her hand. Then she crouched down under the covers and teased it with her lips a hundred ways, but it refused to rise.

Frustrated beyond endurance, she asked Hsi-men Ch'ing, "Where have you put the monk's medicine?"

She had to shake him for what seemed like half a day before he woke up.

"You crazy little whore!" Hsi-men Ch'ing protested. "What makes you so demanding? You want your daddy to take care of you, but today your daddy's just not up to it. The medicine's in the cylindrical gold pillbox in the sleeve of my jacket. Go ahead and take some. If you can suck the thing till it stands up, more power to you."

The woman groped in the sleeve of his jacket until she found the pillbox. When she opened it she saw that there were only three or four pills left.[16] She

picked up a flask of distilled spirits, poured some into a cup, and took one of
the pills. She feared that the normal dosage would not be enough to do the
trick so although:

She never, ever, should have done it,

she put all three pills into his mouth and washed them down with a draught
of distilled spirits. Too drunk to know what he was doing, Hsi-men Ch'ing
closed his eyes and swallowed the whole dose.

In less time than it takes to drink a cup of hot tea, the medicine began to
take effect. The moment the woman tied the white satin band around the root
of his organ:

It sprang lustily to life.[17]

Behold:

In the bursting melon-head the sunken eye
    grows round;
Trailing its side whiskers the body swells
    itself erect.

Although she realized full well that all her partner wanted to do was go back
to sleep, the woman sat astride his body,[18] put a glob of aphrodisiac ointment
in the mouth of his urethra, and plunged the object into her vagina. Thus
impaled, she gave herself over to wriggling until the tip of his organ penetrated
all the way to her cervix. She felt a melting sensation as though her whole
body were turning numb,[19] the pleasure of which was indescribable. Then,
supporting herself on the pillow with both hands, she raised and lowered her
hips, alternately submerging and exposing the knob of his glans one or two
hundred times. At first it felt uncomfortably tight, but once her vaginal secretions began to flow it grew more slippery.

Hsi-men Ch'ing let her disport herself as she pleased without paying any
attention.[20] The woman could control herself no longer. Sticking her tongue
into Hsi-men Ch'ing's mouth, she put her arms around his neck and wriggled
for all she was worth, rubbing up against him this way and that. His chowrie
handle was totally submerged inside her, all the way up to the root, while only
his two testicles remained outside. Meanwhile she stimulated herself with her
hand until she began to feel inexpressible delight.[21] She wiped away her vaginal secretions but they continued to flow. By the time the third watch was over
she had used up five napkins for this purpose[22] and had two orgasms in rapid
succession.[23]

But Hsi-men Ch'ing did not ejaculate. His turtle head had swollen larger
than ever and turned the color of purple liver.[24]

Its distended blood vessels were all exposed,

and it was as hot as fire to the touch. It was gorged with blood, and though he
told the woman to remove the band that was tied around its root, it continued
to swell without ceasing. He told her to suck it, and so she crouched over his
body, engulfed his turtle head with her ruby lips, and proceeded to move it:

Back and forth without stopping.

She continued for as much time as it would take to eat a meal, until the semen in his urethra spurted out en masse like mercury pouring into a bucket. She tried to catch it in her mouth and swallow it but she wasn't quick enough.

The emission went on and on. At first it was semen but it soon changed to blood. There was no stopping it. Hsi-men Ch'ing had fainted and his four limbs lay inert. In a state of panic the woman put a red date into his mouth and he swallowed it.[25] When the flow of semen ceased, it was followed by blood;[26] when the flow of blood stopped, nothing came out but a discharge of cold air. It was some time before this came to an end.

The woman was beside herself. Embracing Hsi-men Ch'ing, she asked, "My darling, what do you feel like inside?"

When Hsi-men Ch'ing finally came to, he said:

"My head feels so dizzy,
I hardly know where I am."[27]

"Why did you have such a big discharge today?" she asked, but said nothing of the overdose of aphrodisiac she had given him.

Gentle reader take note:

The vitality of the individual is finite, but
The prurience in this world is unlimited.

It has also been said that:

Where desires and cravings are deep,
The Heavenly impulse is shallow.[28]

Hsi-men Ch'ing sought only his own sexual gratification but did not realize that:

When its oil is used up the lamp goes out;
When his marrow is drained a man will die.

It so happens that the allure of feminine beauty ensnares men in such a way that:

Where there is initial success,
There will be ultimate disaster.[29]

A poet of yore has left us some words of admonition that put this very well:

A flower-faced guardian god,
A jade-fleshed demon king,[30]
She is a ravenous beast attired
    in silk and satin.
Her bed is an execution ground,
Her ivory couch a penitentiary.
Her willowy brows are blades,
Her starry eyes are swords,
Her ruby lips are spears.
Her sweet mouth and her fragrant tongue,
Mask the designs of a snake or scorpion;[31]

No one who succumbs to her is able
   to avoid disaster.
They are but fine dust in fluid,
Or snowflakes in scalding water.
Thè states of Ch'in and Ch'u were hardy,
The states of Wu and Yüeh were powerful,
But they perished on her account.
You may be warned that beauty is
   a deadly sword,
That slays us all; but few defend
   themselves.[32]

The beauty of sixteen[33] has a body
   as smooth as cream,
Her loins are a sword[34] with which
   to slay the unwary.
Though no one may see your head
   fall from your neck,
Before you know it, the marrow
   of your bones is sapped.[35]

Of the events of that evening there is no more to tell.

Early the next morning Hsi-men Ch'ing got up and started to comb his hair when he was suddenly overcome by a spell of dizziness, which caused him to pitch forward in his chair. Fortunately Ch'un-mei caught him in her arms and prevented him from falling to the floor and hurting his head or face. She sat him back in his chair, and it was some time before he recovered.

Chin-lien was alarmed and blurted out, "You must be feeling debilitated from lack of food. You had better just sit where you are and have something to eat before going anywhere."

She told Ch'iu-chü, "Go back to the kitchen and fetch some congee for Father to eat."

Ch'iu-chü went back to the kitchen in the rear compound and said to Sun Hsüeh-o, "Is the congee ready yet? This morning, thus and so, when Father got up he had a spell of vertigo that nearly caused him to collapse. He needs some congee to eat right away."

Wu Yüeh-niang happened to overhear what Ch'iu-chü said and called her into her presence to ask what had happened. Ch'iu-chü told her the whole story of how Hsi-men Ch'ing had felt so light-headed that morning that he had nearly fallen over while combing his hair.

If Yüeh-niang had not heard this, nothing might have happened; but having heard it:

Her ethereal souls flew beyond the sky, and
Her material souls fled to the Nine Heavens.

After telling Sun Hsüeh-o to prepare the congee right away, she headed straight for Chin-lien's quarters to see for herself what condition her husband was in.

She found Hsi-men Ch'ing sitting in a chair and asked him, "What brought about this attack of giddiness today?"

"I don't know what's the matter with me," responded Hsi-men Ch'ing. "A little while ago I just started feeling woozy."

"It's lucky Ch'un-mei and I were here to catch him," said Chin-lien. "Otherwise, light-headed as he was, he might have had a really nasty fall."

"You must have stayed out late last night," said Yüeh-niang, "and had more to drink than was good for you. It's still affecting your head."

"Whose place were you drinking at anyway," demanded Chin-lien, "that you didn't get back until such an hour?"

"He was drinking with my second brother in the shop on Lion Street," said Yüeh-niang.

Before long, Sun Hsüeh-o finished boiling the congee and told Ch'iu-chü to take it to Hsi-men Ch'ing to eat. Hsi-men Ch'ing took up the congee but lost interest after eating only half a bowl and put it down again.

"What are you feeling inside?" Yüeh-niang asked.

"Nothing in particular," said Hsi-men Ch'ing, "just empty and queasy, and not much like doing anything."

"You really shouldn't go to the yamen today," said Yüeh-niang.

"I'm not going to," Hsi-men Ch'ing replied. "In a while I'll go out to the front compound and get Ch'en Ching-chi to write out the invitations and send them off. I'm inviting Chou Hsiu, Ching Chung, Ho Yung-shou, and some other officials to come over for a drink on the fifteenth."

"You haven't taken your medicine yet today," said Yüeh-niang. "Get your milk and take another dose with it. You've been overextending yourself for days on end and have let yourself get run down."

She had Ch'un-mei ask Ju-i to squeeze a little of her milk into a cup for him and watched Hsi-men Ch'ing take his medicine before getting up and going to the front compound. Ch'un-mei helped him along, but before he had gotten as far as the postern gate into the garden he started to black out. Unable to stand on his tottering legs, he would have fallen down if Ch'un-mei had not been there to help him back inside.

"If I were you," said Yüeh-niang, "I'd take it easy for a couple of days and forget about inviting all those people. Who cares about things like that at a time like this? Stay at home and rest for a few days, and forget about going out."

"And if there's anything you'd specially like to eat," she added. "I'll go back to the kitchen and get the maidservants to prepare it for you."

"I don't feel like eating anything," Hsi-men Ch'ing replied.

When Yüeh-niang returned to the rear compound, she questioned Chin-lien again, saying, "If he wasn't already drunk when he came home last night,

and he didn't have anything more to drink, what sort of shenanigans was he up
to with you?"

When Chin-lien heard this, she:

Wished she had more mouths than nature had provided,

so that she could issue a thousand denials.

"Sister," she protested, "needless to say, by the time he got home he was so
drunk he didn't even bother to greet me. On top of which, he demanded that
I bring him distilled spirits so he could continue drinking. I gave him tea instead, telling him I didn't have any spirits, and then put him right to bed. Ever
since you spoke to me about it, who would have dared to have anything to do
with him in that way? How embarrassing can you get? It may well be that he
had been up to something outside. Of course, I wouldn't know about that. But
I can assure you that absolutely nothing of the kind occurred after he got
home."

Yüeh-niang, who was sitting there along with Meng Yü-lou, called Tai-an
and Ch'in-t'ung before her and interrogated them, saying, "Where was Father out drinking yesterday? If you tell the truth, I'll let it go at that. But if you
engage in:

The slightest deceit or prevarication,

you two jailbirds will be held to account.

Tai-an clenched his teeth and insisted, "He was drinking with Brother-in-
law Wu the Second and Pen the Fourth in the shop on Lion Street and didn't
venture anywhere else."

Later, she called Brother-in-law Wu in to ask him about it, and he said,
"Brother-in-law drank with us for only a short time, and then got up and went
somewhere else."

When Yüeh-niang heard this she became enraged. As soon as Brother-in-
law Wu the Second left, she gave Tai-an and Ch'in-t'ung a real dressing down
and threatened them with a beating. The two of them panicked and finally
admitted, "Yesterday he went to have a drink with Han Tao-kuo's wife."

This was just the signal that P'an Chin-lien had been waiting for, and she
came forward, saying, "Sister, when you showed your resentment against me
just now, it was a case of:

Taking things out on an innocent bystander,

while giving the culprit a laugh.

After all:

Every person has a face;

Every tree has its bark.

When you talk about me that way, it makes it look as though, all day long, I
give this one thing priority over everything else."

She then went on to say, "Sister, you ought to further ask those two jailbirds
why it was that he arrived home so late the other day when you went to the
party at Ho Yung-shou's place. Who knows where he had been? It's hardly

likely that anyone would stay out that late making a New Year's courtesy call."

Tai-an, who was afraid that Ch'in-t'ung would spill the beans, decided not to conceal the truth any longer and told her all about Hsi-men Ch'ing's surreptitious affair with Lady Lin.

Only then did Yüeh-niang believe him and remark, "No wonder he had me send an invitation to her. I said to him:

'We are newly acquainted and hardly know each other.
I fear she is unlikely to come.' Who could have known that he was having an affair with her? It seems to me that, for someone of her age to:

Paint her eyebrows and dye her hair,
powdering her face till it looks as though it's been plastered with putty, only shows her to be nothing but an aging strumpet."

"Sister," remarked Meng Yü-lou, "who ever heard of anyone with a grown-up son, who has already taken a wife, still carrying on that way? If she can't bear her widowhood, she should take another husband."

"That old whore," pronounced Chin-lien, "shameless as she is, could not accept the disgrace that would entail."

"I said that I feared she would refuse to come," said Yüeh-niang. "Who could have anticipated that she would be wanton enough to exhibit herself that way?"

"As far as she is concerned, Sister," said Chin-lien, "you have finally perceived the difference between black and white. But with regard to that whore of Han Tao-kuo's, you have been critical of me for condemning her. The fact is that their whole household collaborates in affairs like this. Her mate is an open cuckold, and yet our husband continues to support that beggar of a cuckold. In the future he may well prove to be as fatal as a ghost-snatching demon."

"You call Wang the Third's mother an old whore," said Yüeh-niang. "But she says that when you were young you were employed as a servant in their household."

If Chin-lien had not heard this, nothing might have happened, but having heard it, her face turned crimson from her ears to her neck and she started to swear, saying, "That lousy old whore is delirious. What would I be doing in her household for no good reason? The fact is that my maternal aunt lived next door to her. They had a garden, and when I was staying with my aunt as a child, I used to go over to their place to play with their maidservants. She may claim that I worked for her family, but I don't acknowledge anything of the sort. She's nothing but an:

Open-eyed and brazen-faced,
old whore."

"You'd better watch that mouth of yours," said Yüeh-niang. "I merely told you what she said, and you start cursing her."

Chin-lien did not have another word to say on the subject.

Yüeh-niang then told Sun Hsüeh-o to make some boiled dumplings for Hsi-men Ch'ing, and she set out for the front compound in order to feed them to him.

Just as she got to the ceremonial gate, she saw P'ing-an going into the garden and called him to a halt, saying, "What are you up to?"

"Li Ming has engaged the services of four singing girls to entertain the company at the party on the fifteenth," P'ing-an explained. "He has come to report this and wants to know whether it will take place as planned, or not. I told him the invitations had not yet been sent out, but he didn't believe me and asked me to come in and tell Father about it."

"You crazy louse of a slave!" Yüeh-niang exclaimed. "How can we have a party under the circumstances? What need is there for you to ask about it? Why didn't you simply send that cuckold away, instead of coming to report anything to your master or mistress?"

She railed at P'ing-an until he fled, as though:

Whether his fate were governed by metal or by water,
There was no place for him to hide.

Yüeh-niang proceeded on her way to Chin-lien's quarters, where she looked on as Hsi-men Ch'ing ate three or four boiled dumplings before stopping and refusing to eat any more.

She then reported to him, "Li Ming came to report that he had engaged the singing girls, but I sent him away, telling him to cancel the engagement, because the party would have to be called off and rescheduled for another day."

Hsi-men Ch'ing nodded in agreement, assuming that he would probably feel somewhat better in a few days.

Who could have anticipated that, after getting through the night, the next day his depleted organ swelled up, his genitalia became inflamed, and his testicles became so swollen they looked like shiny eggplants. When he urinated, his urethra felt as though it were being scraped with a knife; and every time he did so, it hurt the same way.

His orderlies and attendants had saddled his horse and were waiting outside for Hsi-men Ch'ing, in order to escort him to the yamen to preside over the general disposition of impending cases scheduled for the fifteenth of the month. Who could have foreseen that he would be afflicted with these symptoms?

Yüeh-niang said to him, "If you will do as I suggest, send a note to His Honor Ho Yung-shou, telling him that you are staying at home undergoing treatment for the next few days and can't go to the yamen. If you are feeling so debilitated, you ought to send a page boy, as soon as possible, to ask Dr. Jen Hou-ch'i to come and examine you, and then take whatever medications he prescribes. You ought not to delay this way. That's no solution. For someone of your constitution not to eat anything to speak of for two days is hardly sustainable."

But Hsi-men Ch'ing would not give his consent to summoning the doctor, saying, "It doesn't matter. I'll be all right in a couple of days and should be able to go out by then."

He thereupon sent someone off to the yamen with an explanatory note and a tally entitling him to a leave of absence and then lay down on the bed, but he felt restless and out of sorts.

When Ying Po-chüeh heard about his condition, he came to see him, and Hsi-men Ch'ing invited him into Chin-lien's quarters and offered him a seat.

Ying Po-chüeh bowed to him in greeting and said, "I imposed on your hospitality the other day Brother, but I did not know that you were feeling unwell. It is not surprising that you did not go to Hua Tzu-yu's birthday party."

"If I had felt any better, I would have gone," said Hsi-men Ch'ing. "I don't know why, but I just didn't feel up to doing anything."

"Brother," asked Ying Po-chüeh, "how are you feeling right now?"

"It doesn't amount to much," said Hsi-men Ch'ing, "but I've had spells of vertigo, and when I stand up, I'm unsteady on my feet and find it difficult to walk."

"I notice that your face is red," said Ying Po-chüeh. "You must be running a fever. Have you sent for someone to examine you, or not?"

"My wife said I ought to invite Dr. Jen Hou-ch'i to come and examine me," said Hsi-men Ch'ing, "but I told her that I wasn't suffering from any ailment serious enough to justify calling for him."

"Brother, you are mistaken there," pronounced Ying Po-chüeh. "You ought to invite him to come examine you, and see what he has to say. If you take several doses of whatever he prescribes, it should dissipate your fever, and facilitate your recovery. With the advent of spring, people often suffer this way from outbreaks of phlegm-fire. Yesterday, I ran into Li Ming, who told me that you had asked him to engage the services of some singing girls for a party you were going to hold today, but that you were not feeling well and had postponed the date. This news gave me quite a start, and he suggested that I should come to see you first thing today."

"I wasn't even able to go to the yamen today to preside over the ceremony of bowing before the imperial tablet," said Hsi-men Ch'ing, "but had to send in the tally that entitles me to a leave of absence."

"It's obvious that you couldn't go," said Ying Po-chüeh. "If you undergo the appropriate medical treatment for a few days, you should be able to go out again."

When he had finished drinking his tea, he said, "I'll go now, and come back to see you later. I should also let you know that Li Kuei-chieh has arranged with Wu Yin-erh to come see how you are."

"Why don't you stay for a meal before you go?" said Hsi-men Ch'ing.

"I don't want anything to eat," said Ying Po-chüeh, as he went nonchalantly off without more ado.

Hsi-men Ch'ing then sent Ch'in-t'ung outside the city gate to invite Dr. Jen Hou-ch'i to come examine him.

When he came into the room and took his pulse, he said, "This ailment of yours, venerable sir, is a case of vacuity fire flaming upward, and the depletion of semen in your testicles. This lack of equilibrium in your system is symptomatic of a loss of yang energy. Your yin vacuity must be replenished before you can recover."

When he had finished pronouncing his diagnosis, he took his leave, got up, and left.

Hsi-men Ch'ing sealed up five mace of silver in order to pay for the medication he prescribed and took it; but although it put a stop to his bouts of vertigo, his body remained as weak as ever, and he could not stand up. Down below, his scrotum continued to swell painfully, and he found it extremely difficult to urinate.

That afternoon, Li Kuei-chieh and Wu Yin-erh came to see him in their sedan chairs, bringing with them two gift boxes apiece, containing stuffed pastries, rose-flavored gold-colored tarts, a set of pig's feet, and two roast ducks.

Upon entering the room, and kowtowing to Hsi-men Ch'ing, they said, "Father, what is it that's troubling you?"

"It is enough that you two sisters should come to see me," said Hsi-men Ch'ing. "What need was there for you to take the trouble to purchase gifts for me?"

He then went on to say, "I don't know why, but this year I am afflicted with unusually severe phlegm-fire."

"Father," said Li Kuei-chieh, "you must have been drinking too heavily during this festival season. If you will only abstain for a few days, you should recover."

After sitting with him for a while, they went over to Li P'ing-erh's quarters, to convey their holiday greetings to Yüeh-niang and the others. They were invited back to the rear compound and served tea, after which, they returned to the front compound, intending to sit down and visit with Hsi-men Ch'ing.

In the interim, Ying Po-chüeh, accompanied by Hsieh Hsi-ta and Ch'ang Shih-chieh, had come to see him. Hsi-men Ch'ing asked Yü-hsiao to help him up to a sitting position and retained his three visitors, calling for a table to be set up, so they could drink together.

"Has Brother had any congee to eat, or not?" inquired Hsieh Hsi-ta.

Yü-hsiao turned her head away and did not respond, but Hsi-men Ch'ing said, "I haven't had any congee. I don't seem to be able to swallow it."

"Go get some congee," suggested Hsieh Hsi-ta. "We'll keep Brother company as he eats it. That ought to help."

Before long, she came back with some congee and stood by him with a cup of it in hand, while his guests kept him company by eating snacks and other refreshments. Hsi-men Ch'ing took up the congee but only managed to scoop down half a cup of it before he stopped eating. Meanwhile, Yüeh-niang was entertaining Li Kuei-chieh and Wu Yin-erh in Li P'ing-erh's quarters next door.

Ying Po-chüeh asked, "Why are Li Kuei-chieh and Wu Yin-erh not to be seen?"

"They are sitting right next door," responded Hsi-men Ch'ing.

Ying Po-chüeh then turned to Lai-an and said, "You go over there and invite them to come here and sing a song suite for your master's entertainment."

Wu Yüeh-niang was afraid that Hsi-men Ch'ing was in no shape to be thus entertained and refused to let them go on the grounds that they were having a drink together.

After his guests had drunk together for a time, they said, "Brother, we fear that if you continue to sit up with us, you may wear yourself out. We'd better go, so you can lie back down for a while."

"I appreciate your concern for me," responded Hsi-men Ch'ing.

The three of them then said goodbye and proceeded to leave.

When Ying Po-chüeh had gone through the little gate to the courtyard, he called Tai-an over and said to him, "Tell the First Lady that Ying the Second reported that your Father's face has changed color, a sign of stagnant circulation, and that she ought to have someone come and examine him as soon as possible. Dr. Hu, who resides on Main Street, is especially proficient at treating phlegm-fire. Why don't you have someone go and invite him to come and examine him? There is no time to be wasted."

Tai-an did not dare to be remiss and promptly went to report this to Yüeh-niang.

Yüeh-niang hastily went into the room he was in and said to Hsi-men Ch'ing, "Ying the Second, just now, told Tai-an that Dr. Hu, who resides on Main Street, is good at treating phlegm-fire. Why don't you invite him to come examine you?"

"That Dr. Hu," replied Hsi-men Ch'ing, "formerly came to treat Li P'ing-erh, but to no effect. Why should I invite him?"

Yüeh-niang responded:

"Medicine cures only those diseases
      which are not fatal;
The Buddha saves only those destined
      to be saved.[36]

Though he may not have treated her effectively, it could be your destiny to recover after taking his medication."

"All right," responded Hsi-men Ch'ing. "Go ahead and invite him."

Before long, Ch'i-t'ung was sent on this errand and brought Dr. Hu back with him. He arrived just as Brother-in-law Wu K'ai came by to see Hsi-men Ch'ing, and they entered his room together.

After taking his pulse, he said to Wu K'ai and Ch'en Ching-chi, "His Honor is suffering from accumulated toxicity in his genitalia. Unless this is treated in a timely manner, it will produce a leakage of blood in his urine. This condition is the result of engaging in sexual intercourse while suppressing the urge to urinate."

Once again, five mace of silver was sealed up to pay for the medication he prescribed, but when Hsi-men Ch'ing took it, it was no more efficacious than:

> A stone sunk in the vast sea,

and he found himself unable to urinate at all.

Yüeh-niang was so alarmed by this that she sent Li Kuei-chieh and Wu Yin-erh away and then invited Dr. Ho Ch'un-ch'üan, the son of Old Man Ho, to come and examine him.

He said, "This is a urinary blockage due to the inflammatory swelling of the lymph nodes in the groin, caused by the descent of pathogenic fire from the bladder. The accumulation of damp phlegm in the circulatory channels of the four limbs has interrupted the communication between the heart and the kidneys."

Once again, five mace of silver was sealed up to pay for the medication he prescribed, but when Hsi-men Ch'ing took it, his depleted organ rose up until his chowrie handle was as hard as iron and would not relax by day or by night. That night, P'an Chin-lien, as though she:

> Didn't know any better,

sat astride Hsi-men Ch'ing's body and amused herself by "dipping the candle upside down" until he:

> Passed out and then came to again,[37]

a number of times in succession.

The next day, Ho Yung-shou came to see him and sent someone ahead to announce his coming.

On hearing this, Yüeh-niang said to Hsi-men Ch'ing, "His Honor Ho Yung-shou is about to come visit you. Let me help you move back to the rear compound. This out-of-the-way location is not a fit place to receive guests."

Hsi-men Ch'ing nodded in assent, and Yüeh-niang, thereupon, helped him into some warm clothes; after which, she and Chin-lien supported him on either side as he made his way out of Chin-lien's quarters and back to the master suite in the rear compound. Once there, they put down a mattress and bedding, propped him up on a high pillow on the k'ang in the master bedroom, straightened up the room, and lit some incense.

Before long, Ho Yung-shou arrived, and Ch'en Ching-chi invited him into the bedroom in the rear compound, where he found Hsi-men Ch'ing sitting up in his sickbed, and said, "My colleague, I will not bother with a formal obeisance."

Hsi-men Ch'ing in His Sexual Indulgence Forfeits His Life

He then went on to ask, "Do you feel that your ailment is getting any better?"

"The fever in my upper body has receded somewhat," said Hsi-men Ch'ing, "but the toxicity in my swollen scrotum down below is more than I can take."

"That sounds like a case of swollen lymph nodes in the groin," said Ho Yung-shou. "Your pupil has an acquaintance who has been visiting his relatives in Tung-ch'ang prefecture but just arrived back yesterday. I have a note to that effect at home. He is a native of Fen-chou in Shansi province, and his name is Liu Chü-chai. He is some fifty years old and is extremely proficient at treating infectious disorders. I could send someone to invite him to come and diagnose my colleague's disorder."

"I deeply appreciate my colleague's concern," responded Hsi-men Ch'ing. "I will send someone myself to invite him."

When Ho Yung-shou had finished his tea, he said, "You must take it easy and look after yourself, my colleague. With regard to business at the yamen, I will send someone to inform you of what is going on every day. There is no need for you to worry about it."

Hsi-men Ch'ing raised his hand in a gesture of gratitude and said, "I fear I am putting my colleague to a lot of trouble."

When Ho Yung-shou had taken his leave and gone out the door, Hsi-men Ch'ing dispatched Tai-an with a note, accompanied by one of Ho's servants, to go and invite Liu Chü-chai to come examine him.

After taking his pulse and scrutinizing his genitalia, Liu Chü-chai applied a medication to the area and also sealed up a decoction for him to take orally. Hsi-men Ch'ing rewarded him with a bolt of Hang-chou silk, and a tael of silver; but when he took the first cup of the decoction, it produced no visible effect.

That same day, unexpectedly, Cheng Ai-yüeh came to see Hsi-men Ch'ing in her sedan chair, bringing a box of squabs, and a box of stuffed pastries and cream puff pastries for him.

Upon coming in the door:

　　Like a sprig of blossoms swaying in the breeze;
　　Sending the pendants of her embroidered sash flying;

she kowtowed to Hsi-men Ch'ing, saying, "I didn't know that you had fallen ill. Li Kuei-chieh and Wu Yin-erh, fine pair that they are, didn't tell me about it and came ahead of me, so that I have been remiss in coming to see you. Please don't hold it against me."

"You're not remiss," responded Hsi-men Ch'ing, "and your mother has also gone to the trouble of purchasing gifts for me."

Cheng Ai-yüeh laughed, saying, "What do these paltry gifts amount to? You embarrass me no end."

She then went on to say, "Father, since you have lost weight to such an extent, you can supplement your daily diet with these things."

"It would be a good thing if he eats them," said Yüeh-niang. "He hasn't been eating much of anything. This morning, he only consumed a little congee and hasn't had anything else to eat. The doctor was just here to examine him."

"Mother," said Cheng Ai-yüeh, "get a maidservant to boil one of these squabs until it is tender, and I will urge Father to eat some more congee with it. Venerable sir, it won't do for someone of your hefty build not to eat. The whole household depends on you for their support like a mountain of gold. What would they do without you?"

"He's suffering from a feeling of abdominal obstruction," said Yüeh-niang, "and can't get anything down."

"Father," said Cheng Ai-yüeh, "you should do as I say. Though you may not feel like eating or drinking anything from day to day, you've got to force yourself to consume something. What are you afraid of?

　　Human beings have no roots to nourish them;
　　It is food and water that sustain our lives.
The fact is you've got to eat enough to maintain your stamina, or else your vitality will become even more exhausted."

Before long, the squab was boiled until it was tender, and Hsiao-yü brought it in together with some congee. The congee was made with polished nonglutinous rice flavored with sweet squash and eggplant julienne and marinated with ten spices. Cheng Ai-yüeh then jumped onto the k'ang holding the bowl of congee in her hand and knelt down beside Hsi-men Ch'ing, feeding him one mouthful at a time. Although he did the best he could, he was only able to get down half a bowl of congee and two chopstick's worth of squab, before he shook his head and refused to eat any more.

Cheng Ai-yüeh said, "On the one hand, because he knows it's therapeutic, and on the other hand, because I urged him to do so, he has had a little something to eat."

"Father has not been eating that much," said Yü-hsiao, "but today, thanks to your urging, he has eaten more than usual."

Yüeh-niang treated Cheng Ai-yüeh to a serving of tea. That evening she also entertained her with food and wine and rewarded her with five mace of silver before sending her home.

As she was about to leave, Cheng Ai-yüeh kowtowed to Hsi-men Ch'ing once again, saying, "Father, be patient and do your best to recuperate for a few days. I will come back to see you again."

That night, Hsi-men Ch'ing took a second dose of the medicine prescribed by Liu Chü-chai, but his whole body started to ache and he could not help groaning with pain all night long. During the fifth watch, his swollen scrotum burst open, releasing a pool of fresh blood, and chancres appeared on his turtle head that exuded a yellow fluid incessantly. Before he knew it, Hsi-men Ch'ing fell into a faint and blacked out.

Yüeh-niang and the other members of the household were thrown into a panic and came to keep vigil over him. When they saw that the medication was not having the desired effect, they decided to send for Dame Liu to come to the summerhouse in the front compound to light candles in the shape of human figurines, and perform a shamanistic dance on Hsi-men Ch'ing's behalf. They also intended to send a page boy to the home of Commandant Chou Hsiu to inquire if Immortal Wu was there, and to invite him to come and assess Hsi-men Ch'ing's situation, since he had predicted, when he told his fortune, that during this year he would suffer from:

The calamity of spitting blood, and discharging pus, and
The affliction of desiccated bones and emaciated frame.[38]

Pen the Fourth said, "There is no need to ask after him at the home of His Honor Chou Hsiu. At present, he has set up a fortune-telling shop in front of the Temple of the Tutelary God outside the city gate, where he dispenses medical advice and sells fortunes. When people come to him for help, he is not out to make a profit but goes forthwith to diagnose their troubles."

Upon hearing this, Yüeh-niang immediately sent Ch'in-t'ung to summon Immortal Wu.

When he came into the room and looked at Hsi-men Ch'ing, he saw that:

He no longer resembled his former self.
His frame was cadaverous and emaciated;
His diseased body was utterly enervated;[39]

and a kerchief was tied around his head as he lay there on his sickbed.

After first taking his pulse, he said, "Sir, you are suffering from the results of:

Excessive indulgence in drunkenness and lust;[40]
Your reserve of semen is completely depleted.
The pathogenic fire of your generative organ,
Is choking the conduit leading to your heart.
The disease has penetrated your vital organs,[41]
And is no longer possible to treat medically.

There is a poem of eight lines that is relevant to your case, which I will recite for you.

When you engage in sex while drunk and sated,[42]
    lusting after female beauty,
Your vital energy and your blood vessels will
    imperceptibly be worn away.
Your semen will leak, your urine contain blood,
    and you will emit milky muck;
Just as a lamp goes out when its oil is spent,
    your store of semen will dry up.
In the past your only regret was that occasions
    for gratification were too few;

But now, on the contrary, it has come to pass
    that your maladies are too many.
The jade pinnacle will collapse all by itself,[43]
    without anyone else's help;
Even the famous physician, Pien Ch'üeh of Lu,[44]
    would be unable to save you.

When Yüeh-niang realized that Immortal Wu would not be able to cure
him, she said, "Since you cannot prescribe any medication to improve his
condition, would you be willing to predict his fate?"

Immortal Wu then:

    Calculated on the joints of his fingers,

in order to ascertain the eight characters that determined Hsi-men Ch'ing's
horoscope, and said, "He was born in the year of the tiger, in a *ping-yin* year,
during a *wu-shen* month, on a *jen-wu* day, during the *ping-ch'en* time period.
In this *wu-hsü* year of his horoscope he should be thirty-two years old. He is
currently in the third of his 'decennial periods of fate' that is designated by the
combination *kuei-hai*. The elements fire and earth in his horoscope constitute
his 'injurer of the official,' and the element earth that corresponds to the stem
wu in the combination for the current year will overcome the element water
that corresponds to the stem *jen*, so that the combination for the current year
will be in conflict with that for the day of his birth. The first month of this year
is also a *wu-yin* month. Thus the three occurrences of the stem *wu* in the combinations for the month of his birth, the current year, and the current month,
will conflict with the branch *ch'en* in the combination for the time period of
his birth. How can he hope to withstand this? Though he has enjoyed both
wealth and good fortune thus far, his longevity cannot be preserved. I will
render a judgment in four lines of verse, though it may be hard to take.

    When one's fate is crossed by an unlucky star
        it is sure to be unpropitious;
    The body is feeble, the baleful spirit strong,
        and sure to portend catastrophe.
    If the time and day indicate an encounter with
        the genuine ill-boding Year God;
    Even should one be a god or an immortal, one
        would have to knit one's brows."[45]

Yüeh-niang said, "If the prospects for him do not look good, could you calculate the correlations between the five phases, the twenty-eight lunar mansions, and their corresponding animals that govern his fate to see what they
portend?

Immortal Wu proceeded to chart the implications of the animals associated
with the stem-branch combinations in his horoscope and said:

The heart-moon-fox mansion and the
    horn-wood-flood dragon,
Deep under the crimson bed-curtains[46]
    cannot be reconciled.
One constantly sends jade dew flying
    from the moon palace;
The other, beneath the moon, tries to
    seize the golden trophy.
When excited, he is transformed into
    a real fighting cock;
Even on the brink of death, he longs
    for an overripe peach.
Neither celestial deities nor earthly
    spirits can save him;
The Master of the Demon Gorge[47] himself
    would labor in vain."

Yüeh-niang said, "If the prognostication from his horoscopic animals is not propitious, would you interpret a dream for me?"

"Describe it to me," said Immortal Wu, "and I will interpret it for you."

Yüeh-niang said, "I dreamt of a spacious structure on the verge of collapse, of a body covered with a red garment, of the breaking of a green jade hairpin, and the smashing of a caltrop-patterned mirror."

"Pray do not take offense at what I have to say," responded Immortal Wu, "but the spacious structure on the verge of collapse portends a calamity for your husband. The body covered with a red garment portends that you will be wearing mourning clothes. The breaking of the green jade hairpin portends a splitting up of you and your sister wives. The smashing of the caltrop-patterned mirror portends the immanent separation of you and your husband. This dream is also not propitious, not propitious."

"Is there anything you can do to alleviate the situation, sir?" asked Yüeh-niang.

Immortal Wu responded:

"The White Tiger is blocking the road ahead,
Death Knell and Condoler are wreaking havoc,[48]
Gods and immortals are not able to cure him,
The ill-boding Year God cannot be withstood.
The Creator has determined the outcome;
Neither gods nor spirits can modify it."[49]

When Yüeh-niang realized that there was no saving star in his horoscope, she presented Immortal Wu with a bolt of fabric to thank him for his services and sent him on his way. But no more of this. Truly:

In consulting the yin and yang forces
    in the hexagrams,
One should neglect mere trivialities,
    paying them no heed.
If you devote your life to good works,
    Heaven will reward you;
If you refrain from deceiving Heaven,
    mishaps will not occur.[50]

When Yüeh-niang saw that though:

    The gods were besought and diviners consulted,
the results of these prognostications were all:

    Ominous and inauspicious,
her heart was filled with consternation. That evening, she burnt incense in the
courtyard and swore an oath before Heaven that if her husband should recover, she would make three annual pilgrimages to the peak of Mount T'ai in
T'ai-an subprefecture, in order to burn incense and present a robe to Pi-hsia
Yüan-chün, the Goddess of Iridescent Clouds.[51] Meng Yü-lou also promised
that she would pay obeisance to the dipper on the seventh, seventeenth, and
twenty-seventh of each month. Only P'an Chin-lien and Li Chiao-erh failed
to make any vows on his behalf.

Meanwhile, Hsi-men Ch'ing felt that his body was becoming more and
more torpid, and he intermittently lost consciousness. During these episodes,
he saw Hua Tzu-hsü and Wu the Elder standing in front of him, demanding
retribution for the harm he had done them. He was reluctant to tell anyone
about this but merely saw to it that he was not left alone.

On one occasion, observing that Yüeh-niang was not present, he took hold
of P'an Chin-lien with one hand, feeling that he could not bear to relinquish
her, and, letting his eyes brim over with tears, said to her, "My darling, after I
die, I hope that you and your sister wives will keep vigil over my spirit tablet,
and not go your separate ways."

Chin-lien also, feeling that:

    Her anguish could not be overcome,
said, "Brother, my only fear is that I will not be tolerated."

"Wait until the First Lady comes in," said Hsi-men Ch'ing. "I will speak to
her about it."

Before long, Wu Yüeh-niang came in, and seeing that the eyes of the two of
them were red with weeping, said, "Brother, if you have something to say, tell
me about it, as befits the fact that you and I have shared the experience of:

    Being husband and wife all this time."[52]

When Hsi-men Ch'ing heard this, he became so choked up he had difficulty uttering a sound, but finally said, "I realize that I am unlikely to recover,

but there are a few words that I would like to bequeath to you. After I die, if
you give birth to:

A single boy or half a girl,

you and your sister wives ought to devote yourselves to raising it, and continue
to live together, rather than going your separate ways and thereby incurring
the contempt of the community."

Pointing to Chin-lien, he went on to say, "As for Sister Six here, you should
make allowances for what she did in the past."

When he had finished speaking, the pearly tears rolled down Yüeh-niang's
peach-colored face, as she commenced to cry out loud, giving herself over to
boundless sorrow.

"Don't cry," said Hsi-men Ch'ing. "Listen to my injunction."

There is a song to the tune "Stopping the Horse to Listen" that expresses
what he had to say:

"My worthy wife,
I have a heartfelt wish to
    impart to you:
Wife,
Whether the child you are carrying
    is male or female,
After it is born, raise it
    to adulthood,
So it can take charge of my estate.
Follow the example of the former martyrs
    by remaining chaste,
One wife and four concubines looking out
    for each other;
Thus being able to maintain each others'
    reputations.
Though I am dead beneath the Nine Springs,[53]
I will be able to close my mouth and eyes."

When Yüeh-niang heard this, she replied to the same tune:

"Thank you my husband,
For sharing your dying wishes
    with me.
Husband,
Though I fall into the category
    of womenfolk,
I adhere to the four virtues and
    three obediences,[54]
Appropriate to husband and wife.

Throughout my life I have chosen not
    to act ambiguously.[55]
I will remain chaste, and refuse to
    sully my husband's name.
We will tread the same road in life
    and in death.[56]
Only a single saddle for a single horse;[57]
There is no need for you to admonish me."[58]

When he had finished exhorting Wu Yüeh-niang, Hsi-men Ch'ing also summoned Ch'en Ching-chi into his presence and said, "Son-in-law, as the saying goes:

    If you have raised a son, rely on your son;
    If you lack a son, rely on your son-in-law.

As my son-in-law you are the equivalent of a son to me. If I should end up:

    High as the hills or deep as the sea,

after escorting me to my grave, whatever you do, endeavor to:

    Keep the whole household of one mind,[59]

and support your mother-in-law and her sister wives as they live out their lives, without doing anything to arouse the derision of others."

He then went on to instruct him, saying, "The satin piece goods store has a capital worth 50,000 taels of silver, but part of the capital and interest belongs to our kinsman Ch'iao Hung and should be returned to him. Have Manager Fu Ming sell off the stock, one batch at a time, and then close the shop. The knitting and sewing supplies store being managed by Pen the Fourth has a capital worth 6,500 taels of silver, and the silk goods store being managed by Brother-in-law Wu the Second a capital worth 5,000 taels. After selling off the stock, the proceeds should be brought home. As for that contract to supply antiquarian relics to the court that Li the Third has been pursuing, there is no need for us to participate any further. Have Ying the Second find someone else to invest in the scheme. Li the Third and Huang the Fourth still owe us the 500 taels of capital that they borrowed, not to mention the 150 taels of interest that they owe us. If you succeed in collecting these debts, you can use the money to pay for my funeral expenses. You and Manager Fu Ming can continue to operate the two shops in the front of our property. The pawnshop has an operating capital of 20,000 taels, and the pharmaceutical shop one of 5,000 taels. Han Tao-kuo and Lai-pao have 4,000 taels worth of merchandise on their boat in Sung-chiang. As soon as the waterways are open to navigation again, you should go down to meet their boat and bring the cargo back home to be sold. The silver realized by the sale can be used to provide the living expenses for your mother-in-law and the rest of the family. School Official Liu still owes me 340 taels; Assistant Magistrate Hua Ho-lu owes me 50 taels; and Hsü the Fourth's shop outside the city gate still owes me 340 taels of capital

and interest. The contracts for these debts are all in my possession, and someone should be sent as soon as possible to press for their collection. In the
future, you might as well sell the property across the street and the house on
Lion Street as well, since I fear that your mother-in-law and company will be
unable to manage them."

When Hsi-men Ch'ing had finished speaking, he broke into tears, accompanied by loud weeping and wailing.

"Father," said Ch'en Ching-chi, "I understand all of your injunctions."

In a little while, Manager Fu Ming, Manager Kan Jun, Brother-in-law Wu
the Second, Pen the Fourth, and Ts'ui Pen all came in together to see him,
and to ask after his health.

Hsi-men Ch'ing gave each of them his instructions, and they said to him,
"Venerable sir, you should relax. Everything will be all right."

Many other people came to ask after his health that day, and upon seeing
how serious his condition was, they all departed with a sigh.

Two days passed by, during which Yüeh-niang naively hoped that Hsi-men
Ch'ing would recover. Who could have known that:

His fate had already been determined,

and he was destined to die in the thirty-third year of his life. On the twenty-first
day of the first month, during the fifth watch:

His ministerial fire inflamed his body;[60]
Transforming itself into interior wind.

After panting like an ox for some time, during the period from 9:00 to 11:00
that morning:

Alas and alack,
He stopped breathing and died.

Truly:

So long as one has three inches of breath,
one uses it a thousand ways;
But when the messenger of death shows up,
everything comes to an end.[61]

A poet of yore has left us some words of admonition that put this very well:

Humans should try to accumulate good deeds,
Rather than striving to accumulate wealth.
Accumulating good makes one a better person,
Accumulating money only invites catastrophe.
Though Shih Ch'ung was wealthy in his time,
It did not save him from being put to death.
Teng T'ung died suffering from starvation,
What good did the Copper Mountains do him?[62]
Today is not to be compared to the past,
Peoples' minds are completely befuddled.
They say that accumulating wealth is right,

And deride the idiocy of accumulating good.
How many of those who possess great wealth,
Confront death without so much as a coffin?

It so happens that when Hsi-men Ch'ing died a coffin had not yet been prepared for him. This threw Wu Yüeh-niang into such consternation that she called her brother Wu the Second and Pen the Fourth into her presence, opened a trunk from which she extracted four silver ingots weighing fifty taels apiece, and directed the two of them to see to purchasing a set of coffin boards.

She had hardly sent them on their way when Yüeh-niang was suddenly beset with a pain in her belly, staggered into her room, fell down on the bed, and lost consciousness, becoming:

> Oblivious to human affairs.

Meng Yü-lou, P'an Chin-lien, and Sun Hsüeh-o were all in the next room engaged, hugger-mugger, in putting a T'ang-style cap on Hsi-men Ch'ing's head, and getting him properly dressed in his burial clothes.

All of a sudden, they heard Hsiao-yü come in, and say, "Mother has fallen down onto her bed."

This threw them into such consternation that Meng Yü-lou and Li Chiao-erh went over immediately to see what was happening. They found Yüeh-niang holding her hand on the pain in her belly and realized that she was about to give birth.

Meng Yü-lou told Li Chiao-erh to tend to Yüeh-niang while she went out and dispatched a page boy to go as quickly as possible to summon Midwife Ts'ai. Li Chiao-erh also sent Yü-hsiao to the front compound to summon Ju-i. By the time Meng Yü-lou returned to Yüeh-niang's room, Li Chiao-erh had disappeared. It so happens that Li Chiao-erh, taking advantage of Yüeh-niang's unconscious state, had noticed that the trunk was open and had surreptitiously taken out five silver ingots worth fifty taels apiece and carried them off to her quarters.

Returning with a bunch of absorbent grass paper in her hand, she ran into Meng Yü-lou and said, "I didn't find any grass paper in her room, so I went to my quarters to fetch some."

Meng Yü-lou did not pay much attention to this but devoted herself to tending to Yüeh-niang, and preparing the commode for her. She saw that Yüeh-niang's pain was gradually becoming more intense. No sooner did Midwife Ts'ai arrive than Yüeh-niang gave birth to a child, while in the other room, it was only after they had finished dressing Hsi-men Ch'ing in his burial clothes that he breathed his last breath. At this, the members of the entire household, high and low, started to cry out loud in full voice.

Meanwhile Midwife Ts'ai wrapped the baby in swaddling clothes, cut the umbilical cord, decocted a "heart stabilizing potion," fed it to Yüeh-niang, and then helped her into a sitting position on the heated k'ang.

Wu Yüeh-niang Loses Her Husband but Gives Birth to a Son

Yüeh-niang gave Midwife Ts'ai three taels of silver, but she complained that it was too little, saying, "When that other boy was born I received more than this. You could, at the very least, give me the same amount as before, especially since this boy was born to you as the First Lady of the household."

"The situations are not comparable," said Yüeh-niang. "At that time, Father was still here presiding over the household, but now Father has passed away. You had better make the best of it, and take what you are offered. If you come back for the third-day lustration ceremony, I will give you another tael of silver then."

"I would rather have an outfit of clothing," said Midwife Ts'ai, before expressing her thanks and taking her leave.

When Yüeh-niang became more aware of her surroundings, she noticed that the trunk was wide open and took Yü-hsiao to task, saying, "You lousy little stinker! I may have been unconscious, but you seem to have been unconscious too. The trunk has been lying wide open with all these people about. Why didn't you remind me to lock it?"

"I thought that you had locked the trunk," said Yü-hsiao, "so I didn't bother to check it."

So saying, she got the lock and proceeded to snap it in place.

When Meng Yü-lou saw how suspicious Yüeh-niang seemed to be, she chose not to stay in the room but went outside and remarked to Chin-lien, "What a character our elder sister turns out to be. On the very day of her husband's death, she starts acting defensively toward the rest of us."

She did not realize that Li Chiao-erh had already stolen five silver ingots worth fifty taels apiece and carted them off to her quarters.

That day, Brother-in-law Wu the Second and Pen the Fourth went to the home of Prefectural Judge Shang Liu-t'ang, from whom they purchased a set of coffin boards, and hired carpenters to fit them together to form a coffin. The page boys carried Hsi-men Ch'ing's body out to the large reception hall and proceeded to lay him out appropriately. Yin-yang Master Hsü was also invited to come and interpret his divinatory texts.

Before long, Brother-in-law Wu K'ai also came. Wu the Second and the other managers were all in the front reception hall, where they were busy taking down the lanterns, rolling up the picture scrolls, covering the body with a paper shroud, and putting votive incense lamps, tables, and mats in place, while Lai-an was deputed to strike the chime.

After calculating the time on his fingers, Yin-yang Master Hsü said, "He expired at 8:00 in the morning, and no member of the household will be adversely affected by his baleful spirit."

He then consulted with Yüeh-niang and said, "The encoffining ceremony should take place on the third day after his death, the ground breaking for his tomb should take place on the sixteenth of the second month, and the burial ceremony on the twentieth, a day or so after the fourth weekly commemoration."

After Yin-yang Master Hsü had been entertained and seen on his way, servants were dispatched to various places to inform people of Hsi-men Ch'ing's death, and to hand over his seal of office to Ho Yung-shou, while the members of the household devoted themselves to preparing mourning garments for visitors and putting up temporary structures for the funeral observances, but there is no need to describe this in detail.

On the third day, Buddhist monks were engaged to recite sutras for the salvation of the deceased and carry paper money outside to be burned, while the members of the entire household, high and low:

Donned hempen garments and put on mourning apparel.

Hsi-men Ch'ing's son-in-law Ch'en Ching-chi, garbed in untrimmed sackcloth and leaning on a mourning staff, as prescribed for the son of the deceased, bowed to the guests in front of the spirit tablet. Yüeh-niang was not yet able to emerge from her lying-in room, but Li Chiao-erh and Meng Yü-lou entertained the female visitors, while P'an Chin-lien took charge of the storeroom and accepted the offertory tables that people presented. Sun Hsüeh-o superintended the servants' wives in the kitchen as they prepared tea and refreshments for the visitors; Manager Fu Ming together with Brother-in-law Wu the Second took charge of the accounts; Ts'ui Pen was placed in charge of monitoring the expenses incurred by providing the guests with mourning wear; Lai-hsing was made responsible for supplying the kitchen; and Brother-in-law Wu K'ai and Manager Kan Jun entertained the male guests.

Midwife Ts'ai came back to conduct the third-day lustration ceremony, and Yüeh-niang presented her with an outfit of silk clothing before sending her on her way. She decided to name her newborn child Hsiao-ko, or Filial Son, and, as custom demanded, sent celebratory noodles to their relatives and neighbors in honor of the occasion.

The neighbors who lived in the vicinity all remarked, "His Honor Hsi-men Ch'ing's principal wife has borne him a posthumous son, and this son was delivered on the same day and at the same time that he breathed his last. Such a thing is:

Rarely to be seen in this world.[63]

It is as weird and strange as can be."

We will say no more at this juncture about how bewildered they all were by this event.

To resume our story, when Ying Po-chüeh heard that Hsi-men Ch'ing had died, he came to offer his condolences and wept tears over it for some time.

The brothers-in-law Wu K'ai and Wu the Second were in the summerhouse, looking on as an artist painted a portrait of Hsi-men Ch'ing, when Ying Po-chüeh came in, greeted them with a bow, and said, "How regrettable! I never dreamed that Brother would pass away this way."

He then asked if Yüeh-niang could come out so that he could pay her his respects, but Wu K'ai replied, "My younger sister is unable to leave her lying-in room for the present. It so happens, thus and so, that she has given birth to a boy on the very day of her husband's death."

Ying Po-chüeh expressed astonishment, saying:

    "Can such things be?
Oh well. Oh well. At least Brother will have a male heir, so there will be someone to take charge of the property."

Later on, Ch'en Ching-chi came in, attired in heavy mourning, and kowtowed to Ying Po-chüeh.

Ying Po-chüeh said to him, "Son-in-law! Son-in-law! You are certainly being put to the test. Your father-in-law has died, and your mothers-in-law will be like stagnant water, without any source of livelihood. You must be careful how you deal with the affairs of the household. If problems arise, you must not act on your own, but seek the advice of the two brothers-in-law here. Though it may be impolitic for me to say so, you are still quite young, and not too experienced in handling affairs."

"Brother Ying the Second," said Wu K'ai, "you shouldn't say such things. I have public responsibilities to attend to and have little free time. After all, his mother-in-law is here."

"Brother-in-law," responded Ying Po-chüeh, "though my sister-in-law is here, how can she be expected to take care of external affairs? It would be better if you could lend him your advice. It has always been the case that:

    Without distaff relatives one cannot survive;
    Without distaff relatives one cannot flourish.
One's mother's brothers are not to be compared with other people. You are a mainstay of the family, venerable sir. Who is there more important than you?"

He then went on to ask, "Has a date been set for the funeral procession?"

"The ground breaking for his tomb," said Brother-in-law Wu K'ai, "will take place on the sixteenth day of the second month, and the burial ceremony on the twentieth, shortly after the fourth weekly commemoration."

Not long afterwards, Yin-yang Master Hsü arrived to perform the sacrificial announcements and preside over the encoffining ceremony. Hsi-men Ch'ing's body was then laid inside the coffin, the "longevity nails" were driven into the lid, and it was placed in position, with an inscribed funeral banner that read: Casket of Master Hsi-men, Imperially Commissioned Commandant for Military Strategy.

That day, Battalion Commander Ho Yung-shou came to convey his condolences. After he had finished bowing before Hsi-men Ch'ing's spirit tablet, Wu K'ai and Ying Po-chüeh kept him company as he drank a serving of tea. Ho Yung-shou asked what date had been set for the funeral procession and then gave orders that the entire contingent of orderlies and attendants that had been assigned to Hsi-men Ch'ing should remain on duty there, without exception. Only after the date of the funeral procession were they to return to their service at the yamen. He even appointed two underlings to take charge of them and promised that should any instances of disobedience be reported to him, he would see that the culprits were severely punished.

He also said to Wu K'ai, "Venerable brother-in-law, if any outsiders should delay paying their debts to the Hsi-men household, simply report it to me, and your pupil will see that the sums in question are recovered."

After paying his condolences, he went to the yamen, prepared a report on the vacancy created by Hsi-men Ch'ing's death, and submitted it to the headquarters of the Embroidered Uniform Guard in the Eastern Capital.

At this point the story divides into two. To resume our story, one day, Lai-chüeh, Ch'un-hung, and Li the Third arrived at the provincial censor's yamen in Yen-chou prefecture and delivered the letter and the accompanying gift they had been entrusted with.

When Censor Sung Ch'iao-nien read Hsi-men Ch'ing's letter and realized that he was seeking to obtain the document authorizing the procurement of antiquarian relics, he said, "If you had only come a step earlier everything would have been all right, but yesterday I sent the authorization for this procurement down to the various prefectures."

As he thought about it, and noticed that Hsi-men Ch'ing had sealed up ten ounces of gold leaf in the packet, he decided that it would be a pity to refuse and arranged to put up Ch'un-hung, Lai-chüeh, and Li the Third in the yamen, while he dispatched a courier with a validating tally to make haste to Tung-p'ing prefecture and bring back the authorization. When it arrived, he sealed it inside a letter which he entrusted to Ch'un-hung, together with a tael of silver to cover their traveling expenses, and they then set out to return to Ch'ing-ho district. The round trip took them ten days.

As they made their way into the city, they overheard people talking in the street and learned that His Honor Hsi-men Ch'ing had died, that this was the third day after his death, and that a sutra recitation and commemorative rites were being conducted in his household.

When Li the Third heard this:

A crafty scheme arose in his mind,[64]

and as they walked along the street, he suggested to Lai-chüeh and Ch'un-hung, "Let's hold back this authorization, saying that Sung Ch'iao-nien refused to give it to us, and go instead to offer it to Chang the Second on Main Street. If you refuse to go along with me, I'll give you ten taels of silver apiece as long as you promise to keep quiet about it when you get home, and not reveal anything."

Lai-chüeh was tempted by the prospect of this windfall and agreed to the proposition, but Ch'un-hung was reluctant to go along with it and gave only an ambiguous answer.

When they arrived at the gate, they saw that paper money had been brought out to be burnt, that Buddhist monks were performing a ceremony, and that the number of relatives and friends who had come to express their condolences was so great they could hardly be counted. At this prospect, Li the Third parted company with the other two and went to his own home, while Lai-chüeh and Ch'un-hung sought out Wu K'ai and Ch'en Ching-chi and kowtowed to them.

When they were asked if they had succeeded in obtaining the authorization, and why Li the Third was not with them, Lai-chüeh said nothing, but Ch'un-hung took out Censor Sung Ch'iao-nien's letter and the enclosed authorization and handed them to Wu K'ai.

He then proceeded to explain how Li the Third had given each of them ten taels of silver on the road and proposed, thus and so, that they should conceal this fact, hold back the authorization, and join him in going to offer it to Chang the Second.

"How could I be so ungrateful as to:
    Forget favor and break faith?"[65]
exclaimed Ch'un-hung. "So I have respectfully made my way home."

Wu K'ai went back to the rear compound and told Yüeh-niang what had happened, saying, "This youngster really possesses a sense of obligation. How could that rascal of a short-life Li the Third harbor such evil ideas immediately upon learning that my brother-in-law had died a few days ago?"

He then went on to explain the situation to Ying Po-chüeh, saying, "Li Chih and Huang the Fourth signed a loan contract with Hsi-men Ch'ing on which they are obligated to pay back 650 taels of silver in the way of principal and interest. We have been instructed by His Honor Ho Yung-shou to submit this loan contract to the yamen so he can proceed to recover the sum that is owed, and it can be used to cover my brother-in-law's funeral expenses. As a colleague of the deceased, he feels obliged to do him this favor."

Ying Po-chüeh was thrown into consternation by this and said, "Li the Third certainly ought never to have done such a thing, but before you decide on anything, venerable brother-in-law, let me go and speak to him about it."

Thereupon, he went straight to Li the Third's place and sent for Huang the Fourth so they could confer about it together.

"You should never have proffered silver to that page boy," he said. "By so doing you have given him a handle to use against you.
    Having failed to snare the fox,
    You have only defiled yourself.
They now propose, thus and so, to submit your loan contract to the local office of the Provincial Surveillance Commission and sue you for the return of the money that you owe. As the saying goes:
    Officials shield one another.[66]

On top of which, as colleagues in the same office, they will have no reason not to pursue the matter. What likelihood is there that you could resist them? If you will take my advice, you should:

Thus and thus, and

So and so,

surreptitiously present twenty taels of silver to Wu K'ai. You can write it off as something you might have had to expend in Yen-chou prefecture. I have heard that their household is not interested any longer in pursuing this venture. If you can manage somehow to get them to relinquish this authorization, we can go and negotiate a deal with Chang the Second. The two of you should scrape up the sum of two hundred taels, less than that will not do, and also prepare an offertory table. On the one hand, you can present the latter as a sacrificial offering in memory of His Honor Hsi-men Ch'ing, and on the other hand, you can offer the money to them as a partial payment of your debt, and negotiate a new contract for the remainder, allowing you to repay it in installments out of whatever profits you accrue in the future. That way you can:

Kill two birds with one stone,

and smooth things over without rupturing your relationship."

"What you say makes sense," said Huang the Fourth. "Brother Li the Third, you acted too precipitously."

Sure enough, that evening, Huang the Fourth and Ying Po-chüeh took twenty taels of silver and went to Wu K'ai's home, where they proceeded, thus and so, to negotiate for the authorization, saying, "Venerable brother-in-law, we rely on your support."

Wu K'ai had already heard his younger sister say that she was no longer interested in pursuing this venture. Moreover, when his black eyes caught sight of the shiny white silver, how could he bring himself to refuse? Therewith, he agreed to their proposition and accepted the silver.

The next day, Li Chih and Huang the Fourth prepared a portable table, replete with a pig's head and the three sacrificial animals, and two hundred taels of silver, and went to offer a sacrifice in Hsi-men Ch'ing's honor. Brother-in-law Wu K'ai had spoken to Yüeh-niang, who agreed to return the original loan contract and make out a new one for the sum of four hundred taels, forgiving them fifty taels of the original amount they owed, and allowing them to return the remainder in installments out of the proceeds of their business transactions. The document authorizing the local procurement of antiquarian relics for the court was also handed over to Ying Po-chüeh, who went with them to collaborate with Chang the Second in bidding for the contract. But no more of this. Truly:

Only when gold is subjected to smelting
    is its quality assessed;
Only when humans are tempted by riches
    are their hearts exposed.[67]

There is a poem that testifies to this:

> The Creator does not demand too much
>   from human beings;
> Only urging them, in all things, to
>   rein in their hearts.
> Though you may wish to appropriate
>   the property of another,
> There will be someone in your wake
>   to do the same to you.[68]

If you want to know the outcome of these events,
Pray consult the story related in the following chapter.

Chapter 80

CH'EN CHING-CHI RESORTS TO PILFERING

JADE AND PURLOINING PERFUME;[1]

LI CHIAO-ERH MAKES OFF WITH THE SILVER

AND RETURNS TO THE BROTHEL

THERE IS A POEM that reads:

When temples collapse the resident monks are few;
When bridges fall down the crossers are not many.
When households are poor their servants are lazy;
When officials retire their inferiors scorn them.
When waters are shallow the fish will not remain;
When forests are scanty the birds will not roost.
The way of the world responds to cold and warmth;
Human prestige is thereby enhanced or diminished.[2]

These eight lines of verse refer to the fact that:

Warmth and coldness convey the way of the world;[3]
Human sentiments respond to failure and success.

This phenomenon is much to be regretted.

On the first of the seven weekly commemorations of Hsi-men Ch'ing's death, Buddhist Superior Lang, the abbot of the Pao-en Temple, or Temple of Kindness Requited, led a contingent of sixteen monks to come and perform a "land and water" mass for the salvation of the deceased. Abbot Wu Tsung-che of the Taoist Temple of the Jade Emperor came to attend the ceremony and secured the job of presiding over the services for the second weekly commemoration. The household of Ch'iao Hung also made a sacrificial contribution for the occasion. But no more of this.

To resume our story, Ying Po-chüeh got together with several friends who were present for the ceremony. The first of these was Ying Po-chüeh himself; the second was Hsieh Hsi-ta; the third was Hua Tzu-yu; the fourth was Chu Jih-nien; the fifth was Sun T'ien-hua; the sixth was Ch'ang Shih-chieh; and the seventh was Pai Lai-ch'iang.

When the seven of them had sat down together, Ying Po-chüeh addressed them, saying, "His Honor Hsi-men Ch'ing is dead, and the second of the seven weekly commemorations of his death is at hand. In the course of our relationship with him, we have eaten off of him, made use of him, spent money of his, borrowed things from him, and sponged off him. Now that he is dead, we can hardly pretend not to acknowledge all this, or get away with:

Scattering sand in order to blind the eyes
of those behind us.

When he comes before King Yama in the fifth court of the underworld he is unlikely to exonerate us. The best thing to do is for each of us to come up with one mace of silver, making seven mace in all. We can spend one mace and six candareens to purchase a portable table replete with flowers, five bowls of viands, and five saucers of fruits; one mace to purchase a portion of the three sacrificial animals; one mace and five candareens to purchase a flagon of wine; five candareens to purchase paper money for the use of the dead, incense, and candles; two mace to purchase a commemorative scroll and engage Licentiate Shui to compose a funeral eulogy; and one mace and two candareens to hire bearers to convey these purchases before His Honor's spirit tablet where we can present them as a sacrificial offering. We will actually come out ahead, since they will provide each of us with a length of mourning damask worth seven candareens, which we can take home and use to make skirt waists out of. Moreover, they are hardly likely to let us go home without feeding us a meal, and on the day of the burial ceremony we can not only eat our fill at the graveyard but also take home half a table's worth of food from the graveside tables to feed to our wives and children, thus saving them two or three day's worth of money for snacks. What do you think of this proposal?"

They responded with one voice, saying, "Brother, what you say makes sense."

Thereupon, they each contributed the proposed amount of silver and turned it over to Ying Po-chüeh to take care of procuring the sacrificial offerings, purchasing the commemorative scroll, and engaging Licentiate Shui, who resided outside the city wall, to compose a funeral eulogy for the occasion.

Licentiate Shui was well aware that Ying Po-chüeh and his cronies had chosen to ingratiate themselves with Hsi-men Ch'ing, with whom they had formed:

A cabal of petty men.[4]

He therefore chose to refer suggestively to this fact in the eulogy that he composed. This was duly inscribed on the commemorative scroll, which was taken by the seven of them, together with their sacrificial offerings, and displayed before Hsi-men Ch'ing's spirit tablet. Ch'en Ching-chi, clad in his mourning garments, returned their salutations. With Ying Po-chüeh taking the lead, each of them proceeded to show their respects with an offering of incense. They were all too unsophisticated to grasp the hidden significance of the eulogy. After a libation of wine had been poured, the text of the eulogy was intoned out loud, and read as follows:

> On this, the third day *keng-yin*, of the second month, the first day of which was *wu-tzu*, in the year *wu-hsü*, the first year of the Ch'ung-ho reign period, his devoted servants Ying Po-chüeh, Hsieh Hsi-ta, Hua Tzu-yu, Chu Jih-nien, Sun T'ien-hua, Ch'ang Shih-chieh, and Pai Lai-ch'iang respectfully offer a pure libation along with other offertory foods in sacrifice before the spirit tablet of His Honor the late officer of the Embroidered Uniform Guard Hsi-men Ch'ing. During his life, the deceased was upright and unbending, possessed of a rigid and ramrodlike nature. He neither feared the weak nor succumbed to the hard. He was ever ready to share his water with those in need, or moisten them with his dew. In succoring those who were stripped bare, his purse was plentifully supplied. His bearing was manly, ever prepared to respond to stimulation, or succumb to temptation. He lived in the company of brocade trousers, and hid himself amid encircling waistbands. Though his body had eight bulges, he did not bother to scratch them; but when assailed by lice, it itched unbearably. We recipients of his largess have been content to hang around between his legs, joining him to sleep amid the "willows" in the quarter,[5] and keeping him company during sprees in the bordellos. Ever engaged in sticking his neck out and horning in, he took pride in his ability to maintain even a prolonged conflict. Who could have foreseen that he would come down with an ailment from which he would never rise again?[6] Now he has died with his legs stretched out straight, leaving behind a son like a turtledove dropping its egg. On whom are we to rely? We can no longer visit the camps of mist and flowers, or sponge off the bordellos with their peaked red walls.[7] We can no longer feast with him while embracing soft jade, or ride with him to enjoy warm fragrance. We are left with nothing to do but hang our heads and stamp our feet, abandoned to dangle around lackadaisically. Now we present an oblation of milky muck, followed by a meager libation. Should the spirit of the deceased not be incognizant of our actions,[8] may it deign to come and enjoy our offering. Pray come and partake thereof.[9]

When they had finished offering their sacrifice, Ch'en Ching-chi expressed his gratitude with an obeisance and invited them into the summerhouse for an ample repast, complete with the usual:

Three soups and five courses,
after which, he saw them to the door.

That day, Auntie Li the Third, the madam of the Verdant Spring Bordello, upon hearing that Hsi-men Ch'ing had died:

Laid plans and hatched a scheme,
according to which she prepared an offertory table and dispatched Li Kuei-ch'ing and Li Kuei-chieh in their sedan chairs to offer paper money and express their condolences. Yüeh-niang did not come out to welcome them, but Li Chiao-erh and Meng Yü-lou entertained them in the master suite.

Li Kuei-ch'ing and Li Kuei-chieh took the opportunity to speak to Li Chiao-erh surreptitiously, saying, "Our mother says that the man is dead, and we denizens of the licensed quarter are not able to maintain our chastity. It has always been the case that:

> Though you erect a thousand li marquee,
> There is no party that does not come to an end.[10]

If you have any valuables in your hands, you should let Li Ming surreptitiously smuggle them back home for your future use. You mustn't be foolish. As the saying goes:

> Though Yang-chou may be wonderful,
> It's not a place you would choose to make your home.[11]

No matter how long it may be, sooner or later you will have to leave this place."

Li Chiao-erh made a mental note of everything they said.

Who could have anticipated that on that day Han Tao-kuo's wife, Wang Liu-erh, also prepared an offertory table, dressed up in attractive mourning garments, took a sedan chair, and came to burn paper money to Hsi-men Ch'ing. After presenting her offerings before his spirit tablet, she stood there for what seemed like half a day, but nobody came out to welcome her. It so happens that during the first week after Hsi-men Ch'ing's death, Wang Ching had been dismissed and sent back home. When the page boys saw that Wang Liu-erh had arrived, none of them dared to go inside and report it.

Lai-an, however:

> Not understanding the true state of affairs,

went back to Yüeh-niang's room and said to her, "Han Tao-kuo's wife Auntie Han has come to offer paper money in Father's honor, and she has been left standing there in the front compound for a long time. Your elder brother Wu K'ai sent me to tell you about it."

Wu Yüeh-niang, who still couldn't get over her resentment at what had happened, railed at him, saying, "You crazy louse of a slave! Get out of here. So that Auntie Han, or Auntie Cunt, has shown up, has she? That lousy dog-fucked man-baiting whore! Her shenanigans end up:

> Destroying families and killing people;[12]
> Impelling fathers south and sons north;[13]
> Making husbands abscond and wives flee.[14]

How can she have the nerve to come offer her cunt's-worth of paper money?"

This tirade left Lai-an feeling that:

> He hardly knew what to do.[15]

When he went back before the spirit tablet, and Brother-in-law Wu asked him if he had reported the situation in the rear compound or not, Lai-an merely pouted, without saying anything.

Only after being interrogated for what seemed like half a day did he respond, "Mother really cursed me out."[16]

Brother-in-law Wu promptly went back to the rear compound and said to Yüeh-niang, "Sister, how can you act that way? You should stop bandying words that way immediately. It has always been the case that:
People may be bad but civility is not bad.[17]
Her husband has a considerable amount of our capital in hand. How can you treat her that way?
A good reputation is not easily obtained.
You must stop carrying on this way. Even if you choose not to go out yourself, you could send the Second Lady or the Third Lady out to greet her, and see her off. That would do just as well. Why should you open yourself to criticism by acting this way?"

It was only when Yüeh-niang realized how censorious her brother was that she had nothing further to say on the subject.

Shortly thereafter, Meng Yü-lou went to welcome Wang Liu-erh with a bow and sat down with her in front of the spirit tablet. After drinking only one cup of tea, the woman felt uncomfortable about remaining any longer, said good-bye, got up, and departed. Truly:
Even if one could draw off all the water
    of the West River,
It would hardly suffice to wash away
    this day's shame.

Li Kuei-ch'ing, Li Kuei-chieh, and Wu Yin-erh were all sitting in the master suite at the time. Upon hearing Yüeh-niang abuse Han Tao-kuo's wife as every kind of whore, they couldn't help feeling implicated, since:
For every branch you chop down,
A hundred trees are threatened.
The two sisters did not feel comfortable remaining any longer and expressed a wish to go home before the sun set.

Yüeh-niang repeatedly urged the two of them to stay, saying, "This evening, our managers can keep you company while watching the puppet show. You can go home tomorrow."

She continued to urge them to stay for what seemed like half a day, but only Li Kuei-chieh and Wu Yin-erh agreed to remain after seeing off Li Kuei-ch'ing on her way home.

That evening, after the monks had left, sure enough, a good many neighbors, servants, and managers, including Ch'iao Hung, Brother-in-law Wu K'ai, Brother-in-law Wu the Second, Brother-in-law Shen, Hua Tzu-yu, Ying Po-chüeh, Hsieh Hsi-ta, and Ch'ang Shih-chieh, some twenty people or more, were assembled. A troupe of puppeteers had been hired for the occasion, and they put on their performance in the large temporary structure, where a feast had been prepared for the overnight wake. The piece they performed was the hsi-wen drama about the brothers Sun Jung and Sun Hua, entitled Sha-kou ch'üan-fu (The stratagem of killing a dog to admonish a husband).[18]

The female guests were gathered behind standing screens in the reception hall where Hsi-men Ch'ing's spirit tablet was located, in front of which a see-through blind had been suspended, and tables had been set up so they could enjoy the show. Li Ming and Wu Hui were engaged to wait upon them and stayed overnight in order to do so. Before long, after everybody had arrived, and the sacrifices had been completed, the candles in the temporary structure were lit, the guests took their seats, the overture of drum music began, and the performance of the hsi-wen drama commenced. It was the third watch before the performance was finished.

It so happens that since the death of Hsi-men Ch'ing not a day passed during which Ch'en Ching-chi failed to flirt with P'an Chin-lien. They either made eyes at each other in front of his spirit tablet, or joked with each other behind the screens.

At this point, taking advantage of the disorder as the guests were leaving, the women were returning to the rear compound, and the servants were clearing away the utensils, Chin-lien gave Ch'en Ching-chi's hand a squeeze while nobody was looking and said, "My son, today your mother will give you what you want. While Hsi-men Ta-chieh is in the rear compound, we can make use of your quarters for the purpose."

This was just what Ch'en Ching-chi had been waiting for, and he promptly went ahead of her to open the door to his quarters. The woman, concealing herself in the shadows, slipped inside behind him, and:

Without saying another word,[19]
unfastened her skirt, reclined face up on the k'ang, let:

Her pair of wild ducks fly to his shoulders,
and invited Ch'en Ching-chi to commit adultery with her. Truly:

With lustful daring as big as the sky,
    what is there to fear?
Amid mandarin duck curtains the clouds and rain:
    a lifetime of passion.
Having been acquainted for two years,
They have succeeded in becoming mates.
After having been infatuated so long,
This fine day they have come together.
One of them gently wriggles her willowy waist;
The other makes haste to extend his jade stalk.
Into each other's ears they pour the passions
    evoked by clouds and rain;
On their pillows they swear to be as faithful
    as the hills and seas.
What with the oriole's abandon and the
    butterfly's pursuit,
Their turbulent love-making takes a myriad forms;

P'an Chin-lien Peddles Her Charms in Her Son-in-law's Bed

What with the tempestuous rainfall and
    the skittish clouds,
Her captivating maneuvers are infinite in number.
One of them, in a lowered voice,
Calls out "darling" incessantly;
The other, locked in an embrace,
Cannot help calling out "daddy."

Truly, it is the case that:

The hue of the willow has abruptly turned
    a bright new green;
The complexion of the blossom has not lost
    its previous red.[20]

Before long, as soon as their bout of clouds and rain was over, the woman, fearing that someone might come in, hastily left the room and went back to the rear compound.

The next day, the young scamp, still savoring the sweet taste of his conquest, went to Chin-lien's quarters early in the morning and found that she was still in bed, not having gotten up yet.

Peeking through the latticework he saw the woman lying there with:

Her rosy countenance wrapped in the quilt;
Her powdered cheeks like fluted jadestone;

and said to her, "What a fine keeper of the storeroom you are, not to be up yet at this hour. Today, Kinsman Ch'iao Hung has come to make a sacrificial offering, and the First Lady has directed that the offertory tables presented yesterday by Li the Third and Huang the Fourth should be taken inside. You should get up immediately, and get the key for me."

The woman promptly told Ch'un-mei to fetch the key for him, and Ch'en Ching-chi sent Ch'un-mei to precede him upstairs and open the door. Meanwhile, the woman stuck her tongue out through the latticework, and the two of them sucked away at each other for a while. Truly, it is the case that:

The aroma of rouge pervades his mouth,
    as he swallows her saliva;
Her sweet spittle transfuses his heart,
    drenching lungs and liver.

There is a song to the tune "Plucking the Cassia" that testifies to this:

It was annoying that the cries of the cuckoo
    penetrated the beaded blind.
Our hearts seemed stitched together;
Our mutual feelings were like glue.
But all I saw was her smiling face on which,
The hollow cheeks were sad,
The powdered eyebrows thin.

Her fingers were emaciated.
Her chignon was disheveled, hanging loose
   from its turquoise pins;
Her sleepy face was flushed, its jadelike
   pallor daubed with red.
Having tasted her sandalwood mouth,
The aroma still lingers on my lips.
I cannot help recalling the sweet taste.[21]

In a little while, after Ch'un-mei had opened the door to the storeroom on the second floor, Ch'en Ching-chi went back to the front compound to take care of moving the offertory tables.

Before long, the sacrificial offering presented by the Ch'iao Hung household was duly put in place. After Ch'iao Hung's wife, and Ch'iao Hung himself, along with a number of their relations, had finished presenting their sacrificial offering in front of Hsi-men Ch'ing's spirit tablet, Brother-in-law Wu K'ai, Brother-in-law Wu the Second, and Manager Kan Jun invited them into the temporary structure, where Li Ming and Wu Hui stood ready to play and sing for their entertainment.

That day, Cheng Ai-yüeh from the licensed quarter also came to offer paper money and express her condolences, and Yüeh-niang told Meng Yü-lou to provide her with a mourning skirt and girdle, and invite her to join the other female guests who were gathered in the rear compound.

When Cheng Ai-yüeh saw that Wu Yin-erh and Li Kuei-chieh were already there, she was annoyed at the two of them for not keeping her informed and said, "If I had known about Father's death, I would hardly have failed to come before this. A fine pair you are, not to have gotten together with me about it."

When she found that Yüeh-niang had given birth to a son, she said, "Mother, you have:
      One cause for joy and one cause for sorrow.[22]
It is too bad that Father passed away before his time, but now that you have an heir, you need not worry about the future."

Yüeh-niang saw that everyone was provided with mourning garb and kept them there until the evening, when the party broke up.

The third day of the second month was the time for Hsi-men Ch'ing's second weekly commemoration, and on that occasion Abbot Wu Tsung-che of the Taoist Temple of the Jade Emperor led a contingent of sixteen Taoist priests to recite scriptures and perform rites at his residence. On that day, Ho Yung-shou took the initiative in inviting Eunuch Director Liu, Eunuch Director Hsüeh, Commandant Chou Hsiu, Commander-General Ching Chung, Militia Commander Chang Kuan, and Commander Yün Li-shou, his fellow military officers, to join with him in offering a sacrifice in Hsi-men Ch'ing's honor. Yüeh-niang invited Ch'iao Hung, her elder brother Wu K'ai, and Ying

Po-chüeh to keep them company and arranged for Li Ming and Wu Hui, the two boy musicians, to play and sing for them in the temporary structure, but there is no need to describe this in detail.

That evening, after the scripture recitations were concluded, and the spirit of the deceased had been bidden farewell, Yüeh-niang gave orders that Li P'ing-erh's spirit tablet and portrait should be taken outside and burned, and that her trunks of possessions should be carried into the master suite and stored there. She also decided that the wet nurse Ju-i and Ying-ch'un should be kept in the rear compound to work there, gave Hsiu-ch'un to Li Chiao-erh to serve in her quarters, and locked the door of Li P'ing-erh's former quarters. Alas! Truly:

> The painted beams and carved rafters
>   are not yet dry;
> But the doting occupant is no longer
>   to be seen inside.

There is a poem that testifies to this:

> Beneath the terrace of King Hsiang of Ch'u
>   the water flows on unhurried;
> A single case of heartsickness is able to
>   produce sorrow in two places.
> The moon itself is completely oblivious of
>   the changes in human affairs;
> As, late at night, it continues to shine on
>   the crest of the plastered wall.[23]

At this time, every day, Li Ming, on the pretext of helping out in the coffin chamber, surreptitiously urged Li Chiao-erh to secretly hand over her valuables to him so he could smuggle them out and take them back to the brothel. After each trip, he would return in order to continue helping out, staying away from home for two or three nights. He succeeded thereby in pulling the wool over Yüeh-niang's eyes, and no one dared to put a stop to it because her brother, Wu the Second, had been engaging in hanky-panky with Li Chiao-erh.

On the ninth day of the second month, the scripture recitation for the third weekly commemoration of Hsi-men Ch'ing's death was performed, and Yüeh-niang emerged from her lying-in room. No monks came to recite scriptures for the fourth weekly commemoration, and on the twenty-sixth day of the month, Ch'en Ching-chi went to take care of the ground breaking for the tomb and then returned home. The funeral procession took place on the twentieth day of the month and involved a considerable number of burial objects and papier-mâché funerary fabrications, as well as people who came to escort the casket, but the crowd was not nearly as large as it had been for Li P'ing-erh's funeral procession.

When the coffin was ready to be carried outside, Ch'en Ching-chi prepared to perform the role of filial son by smashing an earthenware crock to signal that the procession was about to begin, and accompanying the casket on foot, keeping one hand upon it. Buddhist Superior Lang, the abbot of the Pao-en Temple, was invited to preside over the ceremony of raising the coffin. Sitting in his sedan chair, in an elevated position, he recited a few lines of eulogy about Hsi-men Ch'ing's life that put it very well.

In solemn commemoration of the spirit of the late Commandant for Military Strategy in the Embroidered Uniform Guard, His Honor Hsi-men Ch'ing. For humans living in this world,

> The flash of lightning is quickly extinguished;
> The spark from a flint is difficult to sustain.
> Fallen blossoms are not fated to
>   return to the tree;
> Flowing water is not destined to
>   return to its source.
> Though living in painted hall and brocade room,
> When your life is over, it is like
>   a windblown lamp;
> Though you enjoy supreme rank and lofty office,
> When your time is up, they resemble
>   nothing but dreams.
> Yellow gold and white jade,
> Are merely prerequisites for disaster;
> Red powder and light furs,
> Are but the expenses of mundane labor.
> Wives and children cannot ensure
>   a lifetime of happiness;
> The darkness of the grave entails
>   a myriad forms of grief.
> One fine day, while sleeping on your pillow,
> You'll end up underneath the Yellow Springs.
> An empty epitaph will proclaim
>   your specious fame;
> The yellow earth will entomb
>   your fragile bones.
> Your hundred acres of fields and gardens,
> Will only create dissension among your
>   sons and daughters;
> Your thousand trunks of satin and brocade,
> Will not furnish you an inch of thread
>   after your death.[24]
> When we expire like wind or fire, neither
>   the old nor the young are spared;

When the hills and streams are eroded away,
    what heroes will there be?[25]
It is bitter! Bitter! Bitter!
The breath is transformed into a clear breeze,
    the dust returns to earth;
Once your three inches of breath are finished,[26]
    they will go and not return;
The head is altered and the face replaced
    an infinite number of times.

As the poem says:

In this life the hardest thing to bear
    is the coming of death;
Every one of us, on approaching the end,
    is frantically disturbed.
The elements earth, water, fire, and wind[27]
    mutually assail us;
Our spirits and our ethereal and material
    souls all fly away.
While still alive, we do not know how to
    seek the road to life;
After our death, who knows what will be
    our final destination?
Every last thing that we possess, we are
    unable to take with us;
Without so much as a stitch of clothing[28]
    we must face King Yama.

When Buddhist Superior Lang had finished reciting the eulogy, Ch'en Ching-chi smashed the earthenware crock in which the paper money had been burned, and the casket was raised and carried on its way. The members of the household, both high and low, as well as the relatives, dressed in mourning garb, all wept until:

Their cries shook the heavens.

Wu Yüeh-niang sat in the sedan chair designated for the conveyance of the soul of the departed right behind the casket, while the female guests followed in the wake of the procession as it made its way to the family graveyard five li outside the South Gate for the interment. Ch'en Ching-chi had prepared a gift of a bolt of silk for Commander Yün Li-shou and asked him to perform the ceremony of dotting the spirit tablet. Yin-yang Master Hsü presided over the interment, and the relatives in their mourning garb participated by each throwing a spadeful of earth into the tomb. Unfortunately, the offertory tables produced at the graveside were not many in number, consisting only of those presented by Brother-in-law Wu K'ai, Ch'iao Hung, Ho Yung-shou, Brother-in-law Shen,

Brother-in-law Han, and the five or six managers of Hsi-men Ch'ing's business enterprises. Abbot Wu Tsung-che also left twelve Taoist acolytes behind to preside over the return of the spirit tablet, which was placed in a position of honor in the parlor of the master suite. After the tablet had been set in place, and Yin-yang Master Hsü had performed a ritual purification, the crowd of relatives departed, and Wu Yüeh-niang and her fellow wives kept vigil beside his spirit tablet as an expression of their filiality.

A day or so later, after they had returned from the ceremony of revisiting the grave, Wu Yüeh-niang sent all the orderlies and adjutants who had been assigned to serve Hsi-men Ch'ing back to the yamen.

On the occasion of the fifth weekly commemoration of Hsi-men Ch'ing's death, Yüeh-niang invited Nun Hsüeh, Nun Wang, and the abbess of the Kuan-yin Nunnery, along with twelve nuns, to recite sutras, and perform a litany of repentance, in order to release Hsi-men Ch'ing's soul from purgatory and allow it to be reborn in Heaven. Sister-in-law Wu and Wu Shun-ch'en's wife, Third sister Cheng, both came to keep her company.

It so happens that on the day of the burial ceremony, Li Kuei-ch'ing and Li Kuei-chieh, while at the graveside, had secretively spoken to Li Chiao-erh, thus and so, saying, "Mother says that you ought to consider the fact that since you no longer have anything of value in your hands, there is no reason for you to remain any longer in his household. You have no sons or daughters, so what is there to keep you there? She suggests that you initiate a quarrel that will give you an excuse for breaking clear of the place. The other day, Brother Ying the Second came and reported that His Honor Chang the Second who lives on Main Street is willing to spend five hundred taels of silver to acquire you as his Second Lady and let you take charge of his household. If you go there, you can get a new start in life, whereas if you remain faithful to his memory until you grow old and die, what will you gain by that? After all, as denizens of the licensed quarter we are accustomed to:

Abandoning the old to welcome the new,
and seeking advantage by:
Playing up to the rich and successful.[29]
We can hardly afford to waste our time."

Li Chiao-erh made a mental note of everything they said and resolved that after the fifth weekly commemoration of Hsi-men Ch'ing's death, she would:

Let the wind fan the flames,
And take the easiest course.[30]

Who could have anticipated that P'an Chin-lien would tell Sun Hsüeh-o, "On the day of the burial ceremony, while we were at the graveside, I saw Li Chiao-erh engaged in private conversation with Brother-in-law Wu the Second in one of the small chambers in the garden. And Ch'un-mei, with her own eyes, also saw Li Chiao-erh, behind the screen in the coffin chamber, hand over a package of goods to Li Ming, who stuffed it into his waist and took it home with him.""

When Yüeh-niang got word of this, she called her brother, Wu the Second, onto the carpet and told him off, sending him back to the shop to take care of the business, and refusing him permission to enter the rear compound in the future. She also ordered P'ing-an, who was in charge of the gate, not to let Li Ming in anymore. At this, the former prostitute, Li Chiao-erh:

Her discomfiture turning into anger,

felt that she had found just the pretext she was looking for. One day, because Yüeh-niang was drinking tea with Sister-in-law Wu in the master suite and had invited Meng Yü-lou but not invited her, she got into:

A vituperative altercation,

with Yüeh-niang, pounding on the base of Hsi-men Ch'ing's spirit tablet, weeping and wailing, and yelling and screaming. While in her quarters, at the third watch in the middle of the night, she threatened to hang herself, and when her maidservant reported this to Yüeh-niang, she panicked. After consulting with Sister-in-law Wu, Yüeh-niang summoned Auntie Li the Third, the madam of the Li Family Establishment, to negotiate about sending her back to the bordello.

Auntie Li the Third, who was apprehensive that she might be forced to leave all her clothes and jewelry behind, interjected a few words, saying, "This kinswoman of mine, while here, has been forced to:

Humble herself and experience humiliation,[31]

Taking the blame for the faults of others.

If you insist on severing the relationship, hard as it may be for her, you ought to offer her the sum of several tens of taels of silver to compensate her for her embarrassment."

Wu K'ai, as the occupant of an official post, was reluctant to express an opinion on the matter, one way or the other, but after negotiating for what seemed like half a day, he suggested that Yüeh-niang should let her keep all the clothing, jewelry, luggage, bedding, and other accessories from her quarters, and send her on her way, but not permit her to take the maidservants Yüan-hsiao and Hsiu-ch'un with her.

Li Chiao-erh really wanted to retain the two maidservants, but Yüeh-niang adamantly refused to allow this, saying, "You must only want to procure them in order to make prostitutes out of them."

This accusation threw the procuress into such consternation that she did not dare utter another word on the subject, but put on an ingratiating smile and said farewell to Yüeh-niang, while Li Chiao-erh got into a sedan chair and was borne off to the bordello.

Gentle reader take note: The singing girls in the licensed quarter make their living by flaunting their beauty, and depend for their livelihood on rouge and powder. In the morning, they take on Dashing Chang, and in the evening

Li Chiao-erh Steals the Silver and Returns to the Brothel

they engage Wastrel Li. They let fathers in the front door, while opening the rear door for their sons.

> Abandoning the old to welcome the new,
> Their eyes open at the sight of money.[32]
> This is a self-evident principle.

Before they are taken into your home, they pester you incessantly, allowing you to burn incense upon them and cutting off locks of hair, threatening to commit suicide and pleading for wedlock. But once they are taken into your home and allowed to marry out of their profession, no matter what efforts you may make to:

> Play up to them a thousand ways, or
> Ensnare them with a myriad wiles,
> You cannot control the monkeys of their minds
>   or the horses of their wills.

If they do not choose to fatten themselves at your expense while you are still alive, they will find a pretext for deserting your household once you are dead. Sooner or later, they will revert to:

> Eating congee out of their old pot.[33]

Truly:

> If a serpent is confined in a tube,
>   its sinuosity will remain;[34]
> If a bird is released from its cage,
>   it will resume its flight.

There is a poem that testifies to this:

> It is regrettable that the "misty willows"
>   are so very inconstant;
> In their nuptial chambers they entertain
>   new grooms every night.
> Their jadelike wrists pillow the heads
>   of thousands of patrons;
> Their single daubs of ruby lips are tasted
>   by a myriad customers.
> Though they are given to assuming a host of
>   voluptuous attitudes;
> Their congenital hearts and feelings are
>   utterly untrustworthy.
> No matter how adept you may think yourself
>   to be at controlling them;
> There is no way of guaranteeing they won't
>   long for their former ways.[35]

After sending Li Chiao-erh on her way, Yüeh-niang couldn't help weeping, and the others present did their best to comfort her.

"Sister," said P'an Chin-lien, "forget it. Don't let it disturb you so. As the saying goes:

> When a man marries a whore it is like
> keeping a sea eagle:
> Without access to the water, it longs
> for the Eastern Sea.

She is merely returning to her former profession. There is no reason for you to be so disturbed by it today."

Just as the household was in a state of perturbation, P'ing-an suddenly came in and announced, "His Honor the salt-control censor Ts'ai Yün is here, sitting in the reception hall. I told him that Father had died, and he asked how long ago it happened. I told him that he had died of an illness on the twenty-first day of the first month, and that the seventh weekly commemoration of his death had already taken place. He asked whether there was a spirit tablet, or not, and I told him there was one, and that it was set up in the rear compound. He asked if he could pay his respects to it, and I have come to tell you about it."

"Get our son-in-law to go out and welcome him," directed Yüeh-niang.

Before long, Ch'en Ching-chi, attired in his mourning clothes, went out to welcome Censor Ts'ai Yün, and sometime later, after the appropriate preparations had been made, invited him back to the rear compound where he paid his respects to Hsi-men Ch'ing's spirit tablet.

Yüeh-niang, attired in heavy mourning, came out to bow to him in return, but without exchanging so much as a word with her, he merely said, "Lady, pray return to your chamber."

He then went on to say to Ch'en Ching-chi, "In the past I have often put your household to the trouble of entertaining me, and now that my tour of duty has expired and I am about to return to the capital, I have come to express my gratitude to him. Who could have anticipated that he would already have passed away?"

He then went on to ask, "What illness did he die of?"

"It was an ailment produced by phlegm-fire," replied Ch'en Ching-chi.

"How regrettable! How regrettable!" said Censor Ts'ai Yün.

He then summoned his attendants to bring out two bolts of Hang-chou silk, a pair of velvet socks, four preserved whitefish, and four jars of candied sweetmeats, saying, "May these paltry gifts serve, for lack of anything better, as sacrificial offerings for the dead."

He also brought out a packet containing fifty taels of silver, saying, "This is a sum that His Honor was generous enough to lend me in the past. Now that I have been able to draw upon my official salary, I am returning it as a mark of our abiding friendship. Tell your servant to take it inside."

"Your Honor is being overly conscientious," responded Ch'en Ching-chi, and Yüeh-niang said, "Will Your Honor please take a seat in the front reception hall?"

"There is no need for me to stay any longer," replied Censor Ts'ai Yün. "But if you will offer me some tea, I will drink a cup, that's all."

The attendants promptly brought in a serving of tea, and after drinking it, Censor Ts'ai Yün nonchalantly stood up, got into his sedan chair, and went his way.

Upon receiving these fifty taels of silver, Yüeh-niang felt happy at heart on the one hand, but somewhat stricken on the other. She remembered how, on former occasions, when high officials of this kind visited they would never have been allowed to leave after such scanty entertainment but would have been invited to stay and drink for who knows how long. But now that Hsi-men Ch'ing had died:

> With his legs stretched out straight,

though she still possessed his property, it was obvious that there was no one left to properly entertain visitors. Truly:

> When men form friendships, it is like enjoying
>> the breeze and the moonlight;
> When Heaven unfurls a landscape,[36] it exposes one
>> to its rivers and mountains.[37]

There is a poem that testifies to this:

> Behind gently closed double doors, the
>> spring days seem long;
> For whom does she toss and turn as she
>> resents time's passing?
> How winsome are her incomparable glances
>> like autumn ripples;
> As she yearns in silence for her lover,
>> shedding lines of tears.[38]

The story goes that as soon as Ying Po-chüeh learned that Li Chiao-erh had returned to the bordello, he reported the fact to Chang the Second, who went and spent five taels of silver to spend the night with her. It so happens that Chang the Second was one year younger than Hsi-men Ch'ing, was born in the year of the hare, and was thirty-one years old. Li Chiao-erh was thirty-three years old, but Auntie Li the Third, the madam of the bordello, reduced her age by six years, claiming that she was only twenty-seven, and induced Ying Po-chüeh to conceal the truth about it. Chang the Second consequently paid three hundred taels of silver to acquire her and took her home to be his Second Lady. Meanwhile, Sticky Chu and Blabbermouth Sun continued, as before, to inveigle Wang the Third into patronizing the Li Family Establishment and carrying on with Li Kuei-chieh. But no more of this.

Ying Po-chüeh, along with Li the Third and Huang the Fourth, borrowed five thousand taels of silver from Eunuch Director Hsü, while Chang the Second put up another five thousand taels, which enabled them to secure the contract from Tung-p'ing prefecture for the procurement of antiquarian relics. Every day, on their:

Large horses with jeweled saddles,

they paraded through the licensed quarter. Upon the death of Hsi-men Ch'ing, Chang the Second spent another thousand taels of silver to bribe the imperial relative, Military Affairs Commissioner Cheng Chü-chung, in the Eastern Capital to intervene with Chu Mien, the defender-in-chief of the Embroidered Uniform Guard, and have him appointed to the position of judicial commissioner left vacant by the death of Hsi-men Ch'ing. He also improved his property by purchasing a garden and putting up some new structures. Ying Po-chüeh did not let a day go by without frequenting his place and toadying up to him, and told him every last thing he knew about the affairs of the Hsi-men household, both great and small.

He said to him, "In his household there is the Fifth Lady, P'an Chin-lien, the sixth child in her generation, who is extremely attractive and as pretty as a picture. When it comes to poetry, lyrics, songs or rhapsodies; the works of the hundred schools; the various word games played by breaking characters down into their component parts; or backgammon and elephant chess; there is little she has not mastered. Moreover, she knows how to read, writes a good hand, and is adept at playing the balloon guitar. This year she is not more than twenty-nine years old and is cleverer than any singing girl."

His speech had the effect of lighting a fire in Chang the Second's heart, and he could hardly wait to get his hands on her.

"Was she not the wife of that Wu the Elder who made his living peddling steamed wheat cakes?" he asked.

"That's the one," replied Ying Po-chüeh. "It has been five or six years by now since Hsi-men Ch'ing took her into his household, but I don't know whether she is thinking of remarrying, or not."

"Could I trouble you to inquire on my behalf?" said Chang the Second. "If she is willing to remarry, come tell me about it, and I will arrange to marry her."

"There is someone beholden to me who is working as a servant in that household," said Ying Po-chüeh. "His name is Lai-chüeh, and I will speak to him about it. If there is any indication that she is thinking of remarrying, I will let you know. If you are lucky enough to succeed in marrying her and taking her into your household, she would be superior to any singing girl. Originally, while Hsi-men Ch'ing was still alive, he went to great lengths in order to acquire her. As a general rule:

Everything has its rightful owner,[39]

so there is no telling how it will turn out, but it would be a most propitious union. Now that you are possessed of such influence and prestige, if you should fail to obtain this beautiful mate, to:

Share in your glory and luxury,[40]

all your wealth and distinction would be in vain. I will get Lai-chüeh to surreptitiously inquire on your behalf. If there should be the slightest indication of her willingness to remarry, I will employ my:

Honeyed words and plausible speeches,
To awaken her libidinal propensities.

If you are willing to spend several hundred taels of silver, you can bring her into your household and enjoy her to your heart's content."

Gentle reader take note: Such profligate hangers-on are nothing but:

Petty people seeking personal advantage.[41]

On seeing other persons to be influential and wealthy, in order to secure food and clothing for themselves they will do everything in their power to play up to them, praising their merit and eulogizing their virtue. If they should be spendthrifts, they will extol them for being:

Open-handed with their wealth and chivalrous by nature,[42]
Heroic exemplars of magnanimity.[43]
Shrugging their shoulders and smiling ingratiatingly,[44]
Offering their children and surrendering their wives,[45]
There is no length to which they will not go.

But, no sooner do they see that:

Their forecourts have become deserted,[46]

than they start to:

Belittle them both openly and covertly,
Accusing them of dealing irresponsibly;

saying that they are unwilling to:

Found families and establish livelihoods;[47]
That their ancestors must have been evil,
To have produced such unworthy offspring.

Despite the profound kindness they have received in the past, they treat them as though they were strangers on the road. Originally, Hsi-men Ch'ing had been so close to Ying Po-chüeh that they were:

Like glue and like lacquer,

more intimate with each other than brothers. Hardly a day passed during which he failed to sponge off him, wear something of his, or benefit from his largess; but soon after his death, while his body was still warm, he committed a series of unrightful acts. Truly:

In painting a tiger, you can paint the skin,
    but you can't paint the bones;
In knowing people, you can know their faces,
    but you can't know their hearts.

There is a poem that testifies to this:

In former years their friendship for each other
    was like gold or orchids;

He did everything he could to toady up to him,
   leaving no stone unturned.
But today, no sooner is Hsi-men Ch'ing's body
   safely buried in the grave,
Than he does his best to induce his concubines
   to sleep with someone else.

     If you want to know the outcome of these events,
     Pray consult the story related in the following chapter.

NOTES

CHAPTER 61

1. This poem is by the poetess Chu Shu-chen (fl. 1078–1138). See *Ch'üan Sung shih* (Complete poetry of the Sung), comp. Fu Hsüan-ts'ung et al., 72 vols. (Peking: Pei-ching ta-hsüeh ch'u-pan she, 1991–98), 28:17967, ll. 4–5.

2. According to some schools of traditional hemerology, the fifth, the fourteenth, and the twenty-third days of the month were unlucky days, which should be avoided for any significant undertaking. See *Ch'i-tung yeh-yü* (Rustic words of a man from eastern Ch'i), by Chou Mi (1232–98), pref. dated 1291 (Peking: Chung-hua shu-chü, 1983), *chüan* 20, p. 373, l. 9.

3. On this type of headgear, see *The Plum in the Golden Vase or, Chin P'ing Mei*, vol. 2: *The Rivals*, trans. David Tod Roy (Princeton: Princeton University Press, 2001), chap. 37, n. 5.

4. A synonymous variant of this four-character expression occurs in *Kuan-shih-yin p'u-sa pen-hsing ching* (Sutra on the deeds of the bodhisattva Avalokiteśvara), also known as *Hsiang-shan pao-chüan* (Precious scroll on Hsiang-shan), attributed to P'u-ming (fl. early 12th century), n.p., n.d. (probably 19th century), p. 101a, l. 2. It occurs in the same form as in the novel in *Shui-hu ch'üan-chuan* (Variorum edition of the *Outlaws of the Marsh*), ed. Cheng Chen-to et al., 4 vols. (Hong Kong: Chung-hua shu-chü, 1958), vol. 1, ch. 19, p. 279, l. 9; the Ming dynasty ch'uan-ch'i drama *Yü-huan chi* (The story of the jade ring), *Liu-shih chung ch'ü* ed. (Taipei: K'ai-ming shu-tien, 1970), scene 14, p. 47, l. 12; *T'ang-shu chih-chuan t'ung-su yen-i* (The romance of the chronicles of the T'ang dynasty), by Hsiung Ta-mu (mid-16th century), 8 *chüan* (Chien-yang: Ch'ing-chiang t'ang, 1553), fac. repr. in *Ku-pen hsiao-shuo ts'ung-k'an, ti-ssu chi* (Collectanea of rare editions of traditional fiction, fourth series) (Peking: Chung-hua shu-chü, 1990), vol. 1, *chüan* 4, p. 45a, ll. 10–11; *Pai-chia kung-an* (A hundred court cases), 1594 ed., fac. repr. in *Ku-pen hsiao-shuo ts'ung-k'an, ti-erh chi* (Collectanea of rare editions of traditional fiction, second series) (Peking: Chung-hua shu-chü, 1990), vol. 4, *chüan* 2, ch. 12, p. 14b, l. 1; and *Ta-T'ang Ch'in-wang tz'u-hua* (Prosimetric story of the Prince of Ch'in of the Great T'ang), 2 vols., fac. repr. of early 17th century edition (Peking: Wen-hsüeh ku-chi k'an-hsing she, 1956), vol. 1, *chüan* 3, ch. 22, p. 58a, l. 9. It also recurs in the *Chin P'ing Mei tz'u-hua* (Story of the plum in the golden vase), pref. dated 1618, 5 vols., fac. repr. (Tokyo: Daian, 1963), vol. 4, ch. 77, p. 4a, l. 8.

5. The term *shu-lo* refers to a type of vocal performance in which words are recited at a fast tempo to the accompaniment of a regular beat rather than a melody. The fact that this type of performance was popular in the late Ming period is attested to in *K'o-tso chui-yü* (Superfluous words of a sojourner), by Ku Ch'i-yüan (1565–1628), author's colophon dated 1618 (Peking: Chung-hua shu-chü, 1987), *chüan* 9, p. 302, l. 10; *Wan-li yeh-huo pien* (Private gleanings of the Wan-li reign period [1573–1620]), by Shen Te-fu (1578–1642), author's preface dated 1619, 3 vols. (Peking: Chung-hua shu-chü, 1980), vol. 2, *chüan* 25, p. 647, l. 10; and *Ti-ching ching-wu lüeh* (A brief account of

the sights of the imperial capital), comp. Liu T'ung (cs 1634) and Yü I-cheng (d. c. 1635), pref. dated 1635 (Peking: Ku-chi ch'u-pan she, 1980), *chüan* 2, p. 58, l. 5.

6. This four-character expression is from the first line of a famous quatrain by Liu Yü-hsi (772–842). See *Ch'üan T'ang shih* (Complete poetry of the T'ang), 12 vols. (Peking: Chung-hua shu-chü, 1960), vol. 6, *chüan* 365, p. 4121, l. 7. It occurs frequently in later Chinese literature. See, e.g., a lyric by Yüan Hao-wen (1190–1257), *Ch'üan Chin Yüan tz'u* (Complete lyrics of the Chin and Yüan dynasties), comp. T'ang Kuei-chang, 2 vols. (Peking: Chung-hua shu-chü, 1979), 1:122, upper register, ll. 3–4; a song by Yao Sui (1238–1313), *Ch'üan Yüan san-ch'ü* (Complete nondramatic song lyrics of the Yüan), comp. Sui Shu-sen, 2 vols. (Peking: Chung-hua shu-chü, 1964), 1:211, l. 9; *Yüan-ch'ü hsüan* (An anthology of Yüan tsa-chü drama), comp. Tsang Mao-hsün (1550–1620), 4 vols. (Peking: Chung-hua shu-chü, 1979), 4:1421, l. 18; a song suite by Yang Wen-k'uei (14th century), *Ch'üan Ming san-ch'ü* (Complete nondramatic song lyrics of the Ming), comp. Hsieh Po-yang, 5 vols. (Chi-nan: Ch'i-Lu shu-she, 1994), 1:214, l. 13; *Chien-teng yü-hua* (More wick-trimming tales), by Li Ch'ang-ch'i (1376–1452), author's pref. dated 1420, in *Chien-teng hsin-hua [wai erh-chung]* (New wick-trimming tales [plus two other works]), ed. and annot. Chou I (Shanghai: Ku-tien wen-hsüeh ch'u-pan she, 1957), *chüan* 1, p. 154, l. 6; a song suite by Chu Ying-ch'en (fl. early 16th century), *Ch'üan Ming san-ch'ü*, 2:1266, l. 1; an anonymous song suite in *Yung-hsi yüeh-fu* (Songs of a harmonious era), pref. dated 1566, 20 *ts'e*, fac. repr. (Shanghai: Shang-wu yin-shu kuan, 1934), *ts'e* 9, p. 57b, l. 9; the ch'uan-ch'i drama *Ssu-hsi chi* (The four occasions for delight), by Hsieh Tang (1512–69), *Liu-shih chung ch'ü* ed., scene 28, p. 71, l. 3; a song suite by Liang Ch'en-yü (1519–91), *Ch'üan Ming san-ch'ü*, 2:2235, l. 3; a song suite by Wang Tao-k'un (1525–93), ibid., 2:2389, l. 9; and the ch'uan-ch'i drama *Shuang-lieh chi* (The heroic couple), by Chang Ssu-wei (late 16th century), *Liu-shih chung ch'ü* ed., scene 11, p. 28, l. 12.

7. This is the first line of the song suite from scene 3 of the lost Yüan dynasty tsa-chü drama *Han Ts'ui-p'in yü-shui liu hung-yeh* (Han Ts'ui-p'in sets a red leaf afloat in the palace moat), by Pai P'u (b. 1226). Versions of this suite are preserved in *Sheng-shih hsin-sheng* (New songs of a surpassing age), pref. dated 1517, fac. repr. (Peking: Wen-hsüeh ku-chi k'an-hsing she, 1955), pp. 55–59; *Tz'u-lin chai-yen* (Select flowers from the forest of song), comp. Chang Lu, pref. dated 1525, 2 vols., fac. repr. (Peking: Wen-hsüeh ku-chi k'an-hsing she, 1955), 2:825–32; *Yung-hsi yüeh-fu*, *ts'e* 2, pp. 32a–34b; and *Ch'ün-yin lei-hsüan* (An anthology of songs categorized by musical type), comp. Hu Wen-huan (fl. 1592–1617), 4 vols., fac. repr. (Peking: Chung-hua shu-chü, 1980), 3:1922–27.

8. This is the first line of the song suite from play no. 2, scene 3, of the *Hsi-hsiang chi*. See *[Chi-p'ing chiao-chu] Hsi-hsiang chi* (The romance of the western chamber [with collected commentary and critical annotation]), ed. and annot. Wang Chi-ssu (Shanghai: Shang-hai ku-chi ch'u-pan she, 1987), play no. 2, scene 3, p. 70, l. 9.

9. This idiomatic expression occurs in *Huang-ch'ao pien-nien kang-mu pei-yao* (Chronological outline of the significant events of the imperial [Sung] dynasty), comp. Ch'en Chün (c. 1165–c. 1236), pref. dated 1229, 2 vols., fac. repr. (Taipei: Ch'eng-wen ch'u-pan she, 1966), vol. 2, *chüan* 25, p. 20a, l. 4; and *Shui-hu chih-chuan p'ing-lin* (The chronicle of the *Outlaws of the Marsh* with a forest of commentary), ed. Yü Hsiang-tou (c. 1550–1637), 25 *chüan* (Chien-yang: Shuang-feng t'ang, 1594), fac.

repr. in *Ku-pen hsiao-shuo ts'ung-k'an, ti shih-erh chi* (Collectanea of rare editions of traditional fiction, twelfth series) (Peking: Chung-hua shu-chü, 1991), vol. 3, *chüan* 22, p. 14a, l. 14.

10. See *The Plum in the Golden Vase or, Chin P'ing Mei*, vol. 1: *The Gathering*, trans. David Tod Roy (Princeton: Princeton University Press, 1993), chap. 13, n. 10.

11. This was the site of the love affair between Chang Chün-jui and Ts'ui Ying-ying that is celebrated in the *Hsi-hsiang chi*.

12. This four-character expression occurs in the twelfth-century chantefable *Tung Chieh-yüan Hsi-hsiang chi* (Master Tung's Western chamber romance), ed. and annot. Ling Ching-yen (Peking: Jen-min wen-hsüeh ch'u-pan she, 1962), *chüan* 7, p. 139, l. 10.

13. This four-character expression occurs in a song by Hsü Tsai-ssu (14th century), *Ch'üan Yüan san-ch'ü*, 2:1046, l. 4.

14. This four-character expression occurs in the first line of a quatrain by Chang Hu (c. 792–c. 854), *Ch'üan T'ang shih*, vol. 8, *chüan* 511, p. 5845, l. 12; a lyric by Chi I (1193–1268), *Ch'üan Chin Yüan tz'u*, 2:1203, lower register, l. 14; a quatrain by Chao Meng-fu (1254–1322), *Yüan shih hsüan, ch'u-chi* (An anthology of Yüan poetry, first collection), comp. Ku Ssu-li (1665–1722), 3 vols. (Peking: Chung-hua shu-chü, 1987), 1:589, l. 3; *[Chi-p'ing chiao-chu] Hsi-hsiang chi*, play no. 4, scene 1, p. 142, l. 1; the early vernacular story *Yü Chung-chü t'i-shih yü shang-huang* (Yü Chung-chü composes a poem and meets the retired emperor, Sung Kao-tsung [r. 1127–62]), in *Ching-shih t'ung-yen* (Common words to warn the world), ed. Feng Meng-lung (1574–1646), first published 1624 (Peking: Tso-chia ch'u-pan she, 1957), *chüan* 6, p. 64, l. 10; a lyric by Chang Hsü (15th century), *Ch'üan Ming tz'u* (Complete *tz'u* lyrics of the Ming), comp. Jao Tsung-i and Chang Chang, 6 vols. (Peking: Chung-hua shu-chü, 2004), 2:384, lower register, l. 9; the ch'uan-ch'i drama *Huan-tai chi* (The return of the belts), by Shen Ts'ai (15th century), in *Ku-pen hsi-ch'ü ts'ung-k'an, ch'u-chi* (Collectanea of rare editions of traditional drama, first series) (Shanghai: Shang-wu yin-shu kuan, 1954), item 32, *chüan* 1, scene 16, p. 44a, l. 6; *Ssu-hsi chi*, scene 36, p. 88, l. 9; and a song suite by Mei Ting-tso (1549–1615), *Ch'üan Ming san-ch'ü*, 3:3198, l. 3.

15. This formulaic four-character expression occurs ubiquitously in Chinese vernacular literature. See, e.g., *Tung Chieh-yüan Hsi-hsiang chi*, *chüan* 1, p. 18, l. 3; a song by Hsü Yen (d. 1301), *Ch'üan Yüan san-ch'ü*, 1:79, l. 12; an anonymous Yüan dynasty song suite, ibid., 2:1802, l. 9; *Yüan-ch'ü hsüan*, 4:1384, l. 11; the early vernacular story *Ts'ui Ya-nei pai-yao chao-yao* (The white falcon of Minister Ts'ui's son embroils him with demons), in *Ching-shih t'ung-yen*, *chüan* 19, p. 267, l. 15; the early vernacular story *Hsiao fu-jen chin-ch'ien tseng nien-shao* (The merchant's wife offers money to a young clerk), in ibid., *chüan* 16, p. 225, l. 5; the early vernacular story *Ch'ien-t'ang meng* (The dream in Ch'ien-t'ang), included as part of the front matter in the 1498 edition of the *Hsi-hsiang chi* (The romance of the western chamber), fac. repr. (Taipei: Shih-chieh shu-chü, 1963), p. 4a, l. 8; the early vernacular story *Pai Niang-tzu yung-chen Lei-feng T'a* (The White Maiden is eternally imprisoned under Thunder Peak Pagoda), in *Ching-shih t'ung-yen*, *chüan* 28, p. 422, l. 9; a song by Ch'ü Yu (1341–1427), *Ch'üan Ming san-ch'ü*, 5:6106, l. 4; the middle-period vernacular story *Chieh-chih-erh chi* (The story of the ring), in *Ch'ing-p'ing shan-t'ang hua-pen* (Stories printed by the Ch'ing-p'ing Shan-t'ang), ed. T'an Cheng-pi (Shanghai: Ku-tien wen-hsüeh ch'u-pan she, 1957), p. 247, l. 6; the middle-period vernacular story

Tu Li-niang mu-se huan-hun (Tu Li-niang yearns for love and returns to life), in Hu Shih-ying, *Hua-pen hsiao-shuo kai-lun* (A comprehensive study of promptbook fiction), 2 vols. (Peking: Chung-hua shu-chü, 1980), 2:535, l. 24; a set of songs by Wang Chiu-ssu (1468–1551), *Ch'üan Ming san-ch'ü*, 1:878, l. 10; and an abundance of other occurrences, too numerous to list. It also recurs in the *Chin P'ing Mei tz'u-hua*, vol. 4, ch. 80, p. 9b, l. 1.

16. This formulaic four-character expression occurs ubiquitously in Chinese vernacular literature. See, e.g., *Yüan-ch'ü hsüan*, 2:805, l. 20; *Yüan-ch'ü hsüan wai-pien* (A supplementary anthology of Yüan tsa-chü drama), comp. Sui Shu-sen (Shanghai: Chung-hua shu-chü, 1961), 2:426, l. 8; the anonymous Yüan-Ming ch'uan-ch'i drama *Sha-kou chi* (The stratagem of killing a dog), *Liu-shih chung ch'ü* ed., scene 17, p. 63, l. 4; the Yüan-Ming ch'uan-ch'i drama *Yu-kuei chi* (Tale of the secluded chambers), *Liu-shih chung ch'ü* ed., scene 8, p. 23, l. 3; a song suite by Liu T'ing-hsin (14th century), *Ch'üan Yüan san-ch'ü*, 2:1435, l. 8; a song suite by T'ang Shih (14th–15th centuries), ibid., 2:1516, l. 3; the Yüan-Ming tsa-chü drama *Lü-weng san-hua Han-tan tien* (Lü Tung-pin's three efforts to convert [student Lu] at the Han-tan inn), in *Ku-pen Yüan Ming tsa-chü* (Unique editions of Yüan and Ming tsa-chü drama), ed. Wang Chi-lieh, 4 vols. (Peking: Chung-kuo hsi-chü ch'u-pan she, 1958), vol. 4, scene 2, p. 6a, l. 7; a song suite by Chu Yu-tun (1379–1439), *Ch'üan Ming san-ch'ü*, 1:378, l. 3; the Ming dynasty ch'uan-ch'i drama *Wang Chao-chün ch'u-sai ho-jung chi* (Wang Chao-chün is sent abroad to make a marriage alliance with the Huns), in *Ku-pen hsi-ch'ü ts'ung-k'an, erh-chi* (Collectanea of rare editions of traditional drama, second series) (Shanghai: Shang-wu yin-shu kuan, 1955), item 7, *chüan* 1, scene 5, p. 9a, l. 6; and a song suite by Wang T'ien (16th century), *Ch'üan Ming san-ch'ü*, 1:1012, l. 4.

17. This formulaic four-character expression occurs ubiquitously in Chinese vernacular literature. See, e.g., the ch'uan-ch'i drama *Lien-huan chi* (A stratagem of interlocking rings), by Wang Chi (1474–1540) (Peking: Chung-hua shu-chü, 1988), scene 28, p. 74, l. 3; the sixteenth-century literary tale *Chin-lan ssu-yu chuan* (The story of the four ardent friends), in *Kuo-se t'ien-hsiang* (Celestial fragrance of national beauties), comp. Wu Ching-so (fl. late 16th century), pref. dated 1587, 3 vols., fac. repr. in *Ming-Ch'ing shan-pen hsiao-shuo ts'ung-k'an, ti-erh chi* (Collectanea of rare editions of Ming-Ch'ing fiction, second series) (Taipei: T'ien-i ch'u-pan she, 1985), vol. 3, *chüan* 9, upper register, p. 21b, l. 6; a song suite by Wu Kuo-pao (cs 1550), *Ch'üan Ming san-ch'ü*, 2:2278, l. 9; an anonymous Ming dynasty song published in 1573, ibid., 4:4594, l. 5; a song by Liu Hsiao-tsu (1522–89), ibid., 2:2323, l. 2; a set of songs by Hsüeh Lun-tao (c. 1531–c. 1600), ibid., 3:2791, l. 5; *Ts'an-T'ang Wu-tai shih yen-i chuan* (Romance of the late T'ang and Five Dynasties) (Peking: Pao-wen t'ang shu-tien, 1983), ch. 11, p. 36, l. 25; *Ch'ün-yin lei-hsüan*, 4:2499, l. 2; and *[Hsin-k'o] Shih-shang hua-yen ch'ü-lo t'an-hsiao chiu-ling* ([Newly printed] Currently fashionable jokes and drinking games to be enjoyed at formal banquets), 4 *chüan*, Ming edition published by the Wen-te T'ang, *chüan* 2, p. 19a, upper register l. 9.

18. This formulaic four-character expression occurs ubiquitously in Chinese vernacular literature. See, e.g., *Yü-huan chi*, scene 25, p. 90, l. 11; the ch'uan-ch'i drama *Huai-hsiang chi* (The stolen perfume), by Lu Ts'ai (1497–1537), *Liu-shih chung ch'ü* ed., scene 19, p. 58, ll. 8–9; a set of songs by Wang Chiu-ssu (1468–1551), *Ch'üan Ming san-ch'ü*, 1:895, l. 13; *Hai-fu shan-t'ang tz'u-kao* (Draft lyrics from Hai-fu shan-t'ang), by Feng Wei-min (1511–80), pref. dated 1566 (Shanghai: Shang-hai ku-chi

ch'u-pan she, 1981), *chüan* 4, p. 186, l. 6; an anonymous Ming dynasty song published in 1573, *Ch'üan Ming san-ch'ü*, 4:4597, l. 9; *Hsi-yu chi* (The journey to the west), 2 vols. (Peking: Tso-chia ch'u-pan she, 1954), vol. 1, ch. 27, p. 305, l. 16; the anonymous ch'uan-ch'i drama *Ts'ao-lu chi* (The story of the thatched hut), in *Ku-pen hsi-ch'ü ts'ung-k'an, ch'u-chi*, item 26, *chüan* 4, scene 48, p. 18a, l. 1; a song suite by Mao Chen (c. 1543–c. 1604), *Ch'üan Ming san-ch'ü*, 3:3427, l. 9; and the ch'uan-ch'i drama *Ch'un-wu chi* (The story of the scented handkerchief), by Wang Ling (fl. early 17th century), *Liu-shih chung ch'ü* ed., scene 11, p. 27, l. 3.

19. This formulaic four-character expression occurs in an anecdote describing the fondness of Li Yü (937–78), the last emperor of the Southern T'ang dynasty, for paying visits to houses of prostitution incognito. It is part of an inscription he wrote on a wall while in his cups describing the behavior of the Buddhist monk who has been his temporary host and drinking companion and whose conduct is as dissolute as his own. See *Ch'ing-i lu* (Records of the unusual), attributed to T'ao Ku (903–70), in *Shuo-fu* (The frontiers of apocrypha), comp. T'ao Tsung-i (c. 1360–c. 1403), 2 vols. (Taipei: Hsin-hsing shu-chü, 1963), vol. 2, *chüan* 61, p. 12b, l. 4. It occurs ubiquitously in later Chinese literature. See, e.g., a lyric by Liu Yung (cs 1034), *Ch'üan Sung tz'u* (Complete tz'u lyrics of the Sung), comp. T'ang Kuei-chang, 5 vols. (Hong Kong: Chung-hua shu-chü, 1977), 1:52, upper register, l. 2; a poem by Shao Yung (1011–77), *Ch'üan Sung shih*, 7:4534, l. 4; a famous anecdote about T'ao Ku (903–70) quoted in the Southern Sung anthology of literary tales *Lü-ch'uang hsin-hua* (New tales of the green gauze windows), comp. Huang-tu Feng-yüeh Chu-jen (13th century), ed. Chou I (Shanghai: Ku-tien wen-hsüeh ch'u-pan she, 1957), *chüan* 2, p. 140, l. 1; *Tu-ch'eng chi-sheng* (A record of the splendors of the capital city), by Kuan-yüan Nai-te Weng (13th century), author's pref. dated 1235, in *Tung-ching meng-hua lu [wai ssu-chung]* (A dream of past splendors in the Eastern Capital [plus four other works]), comp. Meng Yüan-lao (12th century) et al. (Shanghai: Shang-hai ku-chi wen-hsüeh ch'u-pan she, 1956), p. 96, l. 15; a song suite by Ching Kan-ch'en (c. 1220–1281), *Ch'üan Yüan san-ch'ü*, 1:140, ll. 6–7; a set of songs by Ma Chih-yüan (c. 1250–c. 1325), ibid., 1:252, l. 10; the early hsi-wen drama *Hsiao Sun-t'u* (Little Butcher Sun), in *Yung-lo ta-tien hsi-wen san-chung chiao-chu* (An annotated recension of the three hsi-wen preserved in the *Yung-lo ta-tien*), ed. and annot. Ch'ien Nan-yang (Peking: Chung-hua shu-chü, 1979), scene 10, p. 297, l. 6; *Yüan-ch'ü hsüan*, 2:480, ll. 7–8; *Sha-kou chi*, scene 11, p. 33, l. 5; the Yüan-Ming ch'uan-ch'i drama *Chin-yin chi* (The golden seal), by Su Fu-chih (14th century), in *Ku-pen hsi-ch'ü ts'ung-k'an, ch'u-chi*, item 27, *chüan* 4, scene 39, p. 14a, l. 1; the anonymous ch'uan-ch'i drama *Chin-ch'ai chi* (The gold hairpin), manuscript dated 1431, modern ed. ed. Liu Nien-tzu (Canton: Kuang-tung jen-min ch'u-pan she, 1985), scene 40, p. 66, l. 10; the ch'uan-ch'i drama *Wu Lun-ch'üan Pei* (Wu Lun-ch'üan and Wu Lun-pei, or the five cardinal human relationships completely exemplified), by Ch'iu Chün (1421–95), in *Ku-pen hsi-ch'ü ts'ung-k'an, ch'u-chi*, item 37, *chüan* 4, scene 28, p. 32b, l. 1; *Lien-huan chi*, scene 23, p. 59, l. 14; a set of songs by Chu Yün-ming (1460–1526), *Ch'üan Ming san-ch'ü*, 1:775, l. 12; a set of songs by Chang Lien (cs 1544), ibid., 2:1684, l. 14; the ch'uan-ch'i drama *Huan-sha chi* (The girl washing silk), by Liang Ch'en-yü (1519–91), *Liu-shih chung ch'ü* ed., scene 14, p. 49, l. 6; *Mu-lien chiu-mu ch'üan-shan hsi-wen* (An exhortatory drama on how Maudgalyāyana rescued his mother from the underworld), by Cheng Chih-chen (1518–95), author's pref. dated 1582, in *Ku-pen hsi-ch'ü ts'ung-k'an, ch'u-chi*, item 67,

chüan 1, p. 62b, l. 8; *San-pao t'ai-chien Hsi-yang chi t'ung-su yen-i* (The romance of Eunuch Cheng Ho's expedition to the Western Ocean), by Lo Mao-teng, author's pref. dated 1597, 2 vols. (Shanghai: Shang-hai ku-chi ch'u-pan she, 1985), vol. 1, ch. 47, p. 604, l. 2; *Ta-T'ang Ch'in-wang tz'u-hua*, vol. 2, *chüan* 8, ch. 60, p. 32a, l. 3; and an abundance of other occurrences, too numerous to list.

20. An orthographic variant of this reduplicative expression occurs in *Yüan-ch'ü hsüan wai-pien*, 3:714, l. 13. It occurs in the same form as in the novel in *Yao-shih pen-yüan kung-te pao-chüan* (Precious volume on the original vows and merit of the Healing Buddha), published in 1544, in *Pao-chüan ch'u-chi* (Precious volumes, first collection), comp. Chang Hsi-shun et al., 40 vols. (T'ai-yüan: Shan-hsi jen-min ch'u-pan she, 1994), 14:320, l. 2. It also recurs in the *Chin P'ing Mei tz'u-hua*, vol. 4, ch. 63, p. 2a, l. 11.

21. The locus classicus for this four-character expression is the *Li-chi* (The book of rites), in *Shih-san ching ching-wen* (The texts of the thirteen classics) (Taipei: K'ai-ming shu-tien, 1955), ch. 17, p. 73, l. 11. It occurs frequently in later Chinese literature. See, e.g., the author's commentary on a long poem by Emperor T'ai-tsung of the Sung dynasty (r. 976–97), *Ch'üan Sung shih*, 1:330, l. 11; a poem by Shen Liao (1032–85), ibid., 12:8313, l. 13; *Shen-hsiang ch'üan-pien* (Complete compendium on effective physiognomy), comp. Yüan Chung-ch'e (1376–1458), in *Ku-chin t'u-shu chi-ch'eng* (A comprehensive corpus of books and illustrations ancient and modern), presented to the emperor in 1725, fac. repr. (Taipei: Wen-hsing shu-tien, 1964), section 17, *i-shu tien, chüan* 631, p. 18a, l. 9; the collection of literary tales entitled *Hua-ying chi* (Flower shadows collection), by T'ao Fu (1441–c. 1523), author's pref. dated 1523, in *Ming-Ch'ing hsi-chien hsiao-shuo ts'ung-k'an* (Collectanea of rare works of fiction from the Ming-Ch'ing period) (Chi-nan: Ch'i-Lu shu-she, 1996), p. 861, ll. 21–22; the ch'uan-ch'i drama *Hsiu-ju chi* (The embroidered jacket), by Hsü Lin (1462–1538), *Liu-shih chung ch'ü* ed., scene 11, p. 29, l. 7; *Huang-Ming k'ai-yün ying-wu chuan* (Chronicle of the heroic military exploits that initiated the reign of the imperial Ming dynasty) (Nanking: Yang Ming-feng, 1591), fac. repr. in *Ku-pen hsiao-shuo ts'ung-k'an, ti san-shih liu chi* (Collectanea of rare editions of traditional fiction, thirty-sixth series) (Peking: Chung-hua shu-chü, 1991), vol. 1, *chüan* 7, p. 7b, l. 13; and *San-pao t'ai-chien Hsi-yang chi t'ung-su yen-i*, vol. 2, ch. 97, p. 1255, l. 4.

22. This four-character expression occurs in a song suite by Ch'in Shih-yung (16th century), *Ch'üan Ming san-ch'ü*, 5:6129, l. 3; and a fragment of the lost drama *Hai-shen chi* (The God of the Sea), as quoted in *Ch'ün-yin lei-hsüan*, 4:2488, l. 7. It also recurs in the *Chin P'ing Mei tz'u-hua*, vol. 4, ch. 78, p. 16a, l. 3; and vol. 5, ch. 93, p. 10b, l. 9.

23. On this practice, see Roy, *The Plum in the Golden Vase*, vol. 1, chap. 8, n. 41.

24. This idiomatic four-character expression recurs in the *Chin P'ing Mei tz'u-hua*, vol. 4, ch. 68, p. 19b, l. 8.

25. This line occurs in *[Chi-p'ing chiao-chu] Hsi-hsiang chi*, play no. 1, scene 3, p. 33, l. 11.

26. This four-character expression recurs in the *Chin P'ing Mei tz'u-hua*, vol. 4, ch. 65, p. 10a, l. 11.

27. This line occurs in *Yüan-ch'ü hsüan*, 1:242, l. 1.

28. A synonymous variant of these two lines recurs twice in the *Chin P'ing Mei tz'u-hua*, vol. 4, ch. 75, p. 11b, l. 2; and ch. 76, p. 14a, l. 6.

29. See Roy, *The Plum in the Golden Vase*, vol. 2, chap. 37, n. 16.

30. This formulaic four-character expression occurs ubiquitously in Chinese vernacular literature. See, e.g., *Hsiao fu-jen chin-ch'ien tseng nien-shao*, p. 228, l. 3; the early vernacular story *Chang Yü-hu su nü-chen kuan chi* (Chang Yü-hu spends the night in a Taoist nunnery), in *Yen-chü pi-chi* (A miscellany for leisured hours), ed. Lin Chin-yang (fl. early 17th century), 3 vols., fac. repr. of Ming edition, in *Ming-Ch'ing shan-pen hsiao-shuo ts'ung-k'an, ch'u-pien* (Collectanea of rare editions of Ming-Ch'ing fiction, first series) (Taipei: T'ien-i ch'u-pan she, 1985), vol. 2, *chüan* 6, lower register, p. 20b, l. 10; the early vernacular story *Fo-yin shih ssu t'iao Ch'in-niang* (The priest Fo-yin teases Ch'in-niang four times), in *Hsing-shih heng-yen* (Constant words to awaken the world), ed. Feng Meng-lung (1574–1646), first published in 1627, 2 vols. (Hong Kong: Chung-hua shu-chü, 1958), vol. 1, *chüan*, 12, p. 238, l. 1; *Shui-hu ch'üan-chuan*, vol. 3, ch. 64, p. 1093, ll. 3–4; the Ming novel *San Sui p'ing-yao chuan* (The three Sui quash the demons' revolt), fac. repr. (Tokyo: Tenri daigaku shuppan-bu, 1981), *chüan* 2, ch. 6, p. 5a, l. 5; *Ch'üan-Han chih-chuan* (Chronicle of the entire Han dynasty), 12 *chüan* (Chien-yang: K'o-ch'in chai, 1588), fac. repr. in *Ku-pen hsiao-shuo ts'ung-k'an, ti-wu chi* (Collectanea of rare editions of traditional fiction, fifth series) (Peking: Chung-hua shu-chü, 1990), vol. 2, *chüan* 3, p. 14a, l. 14; and *Hsi-yu chi*, vol. 2, ch. 78, p. 892, l. 13.

31. This formulaic four-character expression occurs ubiquitously in Chinese vernacular literature. See, e.g., *Yüan-ch'ü hsüan*, 1:368, l. 5; the early vernacular story *San hsien-shen Pao Lung-t'u tuan-yüan* (After three ghostly manifestations Academician Pao rights an injustice), in *Ching-shih t'ung-yen*, *chüan* 13, p. 171, l. 12; the early vernacular story *K'an p'i-hsüeh tan-cheng Erh-lang Shen* (Investigation of a leather boot convicts Erh-lang Shen), in *Hsing-shih heng-yen*, vol. 1, *chüan* 13, p. 253, l. 5; *Sha-kou chi*, scene 25, p. 93, l. 4; the Yüan-Ming ch'uan-ch'i drama *Ching-ch'ai chi* (The thorn hairpin), *Liu-shih chung ch'ü* ed., scene 23, p. 72, l. 1; *Yu-kuei chi*, scene 11, p. 33, l. 10; the ch'uan-ch'i drama *P'i-p'a chi* (The lute), by Kao Ming (d. 1359), ed. Ch'ien Nan-yang (Peking: Chung-hua shu-chü, 1961), scene 30, p. 170, l. 2; the ch'uan-ch'i drama *Ch'ien-chin chi* (The thousand pieces of gold), by Shen Ts'ai (15th century), *Liu-shih chung ch'ü* ed., scene 33, p. 108, l. 11; *Huai-hsiang chi*, scene 37, p. 122, l. 3; *Lien-huan chi*, scene 18, p. 41, l. 12; *Shui-hu ch'üan-chuan*, vol. 2, ch. 49, p. 817, l. 5; *San Sui p'ing-yao chuan*, *chüan* 3, ch. 11, p. 8a, l. 9; the middle-period vernacular story *Jen hsiao-tzu lieh-hsing wei shen* (The apotheosis of Jen the filial son), in *Ku-chin hsiao-shuo* (Stories old and new), ed. Feng Meng-lung (1574–1646), 2 vols. (Peking: Jen-min wen-hsüeh ch'u-pan she, 1958), vol. 2, *chüan* 38, p. 571, l. 11; *Ts'an-T'ang Wu-tai shih yen-i chuan*, ch. 26, p. 100, l. 20; *Pai-chia kung-an*, *chüan* 1, p. 7b, l. 2; *San-pao t'ai-chien Hsi-yang chi t'ung-su yen-i*, vol. 1, ch. 3, p. 30, l. 14; and an abundance of other occurrences, too numerous to list. It also recurs in the *Chin P'ing Mei tz'u-hua*, vol. 5, ch. 95, p. 5b, l. 2.

32. This four-character expression occurs in a lyric by Ou-yang Hsiu (1007–72), *Ch'üan Sung tz'u*, 1:149, upper register, l. 7; a lyric by Li Mi-hsün (1089–1153), ibid., 2:1052, upper register, l. 15; a lyric by Yang Wu-chiu (1097–1171), ibid., 2:1177, lower register, l. 9; a lyric by Ma Yü (1123–83), *Ch'üan Chin Yüan tz'u*, 1:394, lower register, l. 4; a quatrain by the same author, *Ch'üan Chin shih* (Complete poetry of the Chin dynasty [1115–1234]), comp. Hsüeh Jui-chao and Kuo Ming-chih, 4 vols. (Tientsin: Nan-k'ai ta-hsüeh ch'u-pan she, 1995), 1:320, l. 3; and *Chin-yin chi*, *chüan* 3, scene 27, p. 20a, l. 11.

33. This reduplicative expression occurs in the thirteenth-century hsi-wen drama *Chang Hsieh chuang-yüan* (Top graduate Chang Hsieh), in *Yung-lo ta-tien hsi-wen san-chung chiao-chu*, scene 1, p. 3, l. 5; a song suite by Wang T'ing-hsiu (13th century), *Ch'üan Yüan san-ch'ü*, 1:318, l. 5; two anonymous Yüan dynasty song suites, ibid., 2:1878, l. 3; and 2:1879, l. 14; *Yüan-ch'ü hsüan*, 4:1652, l. 11; an anonymous song suite in *Sheng-shih hsin-sheng*, p. 549, l. 1; an anonymous song suite in *Yung-hsi yüeh-fu*, ts'e 9, p. 71b, l. 8; the ch'uan-ch'i drama *Shih-i chi* (The story of ten righteous persons), in *Ku-pen hsi-ch'ü ts'ung-k'an*, ch'u-chi, item 42, *chüan* 1, scene 6, p. 10a, l. 9; the ch'uan-ch'i drama *Yen-chih chi* (The story of the rouge), by T'ung Yang-chung (16th century), in *Ku-pen hsi-ch'ü ts'ung-k'an*, ch'u-chi, item 49, *chüan* 2, scene 37, p. 27a, l. 6; and an abundance of other occurrences, too numerous to list.

34. This four-character expression occurs in a set of songs by Ching Yüan-ch'i (14th century), *Ch'üan Yüan san-ch'ü*, 2:1150, l. 8; an anonymous Yüan dynasty song suite, ibid., 2:1816, l. 14; the tsa-chü drama *Ssu-shih hua-yüeh sai chiao-jung* (The flowers and moonlight of the four seasons compete in loveliness), by Chu Yu-tun (1379–1439), in *Ku-pen Yüan Ming tsa-chü*, vol. 2, scene 2, p. 4a, l. 3; a lyric by Li T'ang (b. 1463, cs 1487), *Ch'üan Ming tz'u*, 2:429, upper register, l. 2; *Hsiu-ju chi*, scene 31, p. 85, l. 5; an anonymous song suite in *Sheng-shih hsin-sheng*, p. 558, l. 8; an anonymous set of songs in *Yung-hsi yüeh-fu*, ts'e 15b, p. 16b, l. 3; the anonymous ch'uan-ch'i drama *Shang Lu san-yüan chi* (Shang Lu [1414–86] wins first place in three examinations), in *Ku-pen hsi-ch'ü ts'ung-k'an*, ch'u-chi, item 28, *chüan* 1, scene 9, p. 12b, l. 5; *Wang Chao-chün ch'u-sai ho-jung chi*, *chüan* 1, scene 3, p. 5a, l. 6; a set of songs by Yang Shen (1488–1559), *Ch'üan Ming san-ch'ü*, 2:1409, l. 8; a set of songs by Chang Shou-chung (cs 1562), ibid., 5:6143, l. 12; and the long sixteenth-century literary tale *Hua-shen san-miao chuan* (The flower god and the three beauties), in *Kuo-se t'ien-hsiang*, vol. 2., *chüan* 6, lower register, p. 35a, l. 10.

35. This anonymous song circulated independently and may have been interpolated at some point into this song suite. See *Chiu-pien nan chiu-kung p'u* (Formulary for the old repertory of the nine southern musical modes), comp. Chiang Hsiao (16th century), pref. dated 1549, fac. repr. in *Shan-pen hsi-ch'ü ts'ung-k'an* (Collectanea of rare editions of works on dramatic prosody) (Taipei: Hsüeh-sheng shu-chü, 1984–87), 26:151, ll. 10–12; and *Tseng-ting nan chiu-kung ch'ü-p'u* (An augmented and corrected edition of the formulary for songs composed in the nine southern musical modes), comp. Shen Ching (1553–1610), originally published in 1606, fac. repr. of late Ming edition, in *Shan-pen hsi-ch'ü ts'ung-k'an*, vol. 28, *chüan* 12, p. 38a, ll. 1–4.

36. This reduplicative expression occurs in an anonymous set of Ming dynasty songs, *Tz'u-lin chai-yen*, 1:53, l. 10; *Shui-hu ch'üan-chuan*, vol. 1, ch. 21, p. 317, l. 13; and *Huan-sha chi*, scene 22, p. 76, l. 2.

37. An orthographic variant of this four-character expression occurs in a lyric by Li Tseng-po (b. 1198) written in 1251, *Ch'üan Sung tz'u*, 4:2808, upper register, l. 13.

38. This anonymous song circulated independently and may have been interpolated at some point into this song suite. See *Chiu-pien nan chiu-kung p'u*, 26:194, l. 10–195, l. 1; and *Tseng-ting nan chiu-kung ch'ü-p'u*, vol. 28, *chüan* 17, p. 16a, l. 6–p. 16b, l. 3.

39. This four-character expression occurs in a song suite by Yü T'ien-hsi (13th century), *Ch'üan Yüan san-ch'ü*, 1:227, l. 13; a song suite by Sung Fang-hu (14th century), ibid., 2:1306, l. 10; a set of songs by K'ang Hai (1475–1541), *Ch'üan Ming san-ch'ü*,

1:1166, l. 4; an anonymous song suite in *Yung-hsi yüeh-fu, ts'e* 5, p. 17a, l. 9; a lyric by
Yang Shen (1488–1559), *Ch'üan Ming tz'u*, 2:824, lower register, l. 1; the ch'uan-ch'i
drama *Pao-chien chi* (The story of the precious sword), by Li K'ai-hsien (1502–1568),
in *Shui-hu hsi-ch'ü chi, ti-erh chi* (Corpus of drama dealing with the *Shui-hu* cycle,
second series), ed. Fu Hsi-hua (Shanghai: Ku-tien wen-hsüeh ch'u-pan she, 1958),
scene 33, p. 61, l. 21; the Ming ch'uan-ch'i drama *T'ou-pi chi* (Throwing down the
brush), in *Ku-pen hsi-ch'ü ts'ung-k'an, ch'u-chi*, item 38, *chüan* 1, scene 5, p. 15b, l. 1;
and *Pai-chia kung-an, chüan* 4, ch. 37, p. 13b, l. 11.

40. This reduplicative expression occurs ubiquitously in Chinese vernacular literature. See, e.g., a song suite by Chao Ming-tao (14th century), *Ch'üan Yüan san-ch'ü*,
1:334, l. 1; a song by Wu Lin-yin (14th century), ibid., 2:1174, l. 8; a song suite by Liu
T'ing-hsin (14th century), ibid., 2:1438, l. 10; *Yüan-ch'ü hsüan*, 2:856, l. 7; *Yüan-ch'ü
hsüan wai-pien*, 3:967, l. 18; the anonymous Ming tsa-chü drama *Ch'ang-an ch'eng
ssu-ma t'ou-T'ang* (In Ch'ang-an city four horsemen surrender to the T'ang), in *Ku-pen
Yüan Ming tsa-chü*, vol. 3, scene 3, p. 15a, l. 8; the ch'uan-ch'i drama *Chiang Shih
yüeh-li chi* (The story of Chiang Shih and the leaping carp), by Ch'en P'i-chai (fl. early
16th century), in *Ku-pen hsi-ch'ü ts'ung-k'an, ch'u-chi*, item 36, *chüan* 3, scene 28,
p. 11a, l. 10; an anonymous Ming dynasty set of songs published in 1553, *Ch'üan Ming
san-ch'ü*, 4:4607, l. 9; *Hsi-yu chi*, vol. 1, ch. 11, p. 119, l. 9; *Pai-chia kung-an, chüan* 5,
ch. 46, p. 10b, l. 3; and an abundance of other occurrences, too numerous to list.

41. Orthographic variants of this onomatopoetic reduplicative expression occur in
an anonymous Yüan dynasty song suite, *Ch'üan Yüan san-ch'ü*, 2:1880, l. 4; *Hsiu-ju
chi*, scene 11, p. 30, l. 6; *Chiang Shih yüeh-li chi, chüan* 1, scene 10, p. 15a, l. 8; the
tsa-chü drama *Pu-fu lao* (Refusal to submit to old age), by Feng Wei-min (1511–80), in
Ming-jen tsa-chü hsüan, scene 1, p. 299, l. 4; *Hsi-yu chi*, vol. 2, ch. 84, p. 956, l. 4; the
ch'uan-ch'i drama *Shih-hou chi* (The lion's roar), by Wang T'ing-no (fl. 1593–1611),
Liu-shih chung ch'ü ed., scene 11, p. 35, l. 6; and an abundance of other occurrences,
too numerous to list.

42. This formulaic four-character expression occurs ubiquitously in Chinese vernacular literature. See, e.g., *Chang Hsieh chuang-yüan*, scene 32, p. 151, l. 11; *Hsiao
Sun-t'u*, scene 9, p. 286, l. 9; an anonymous Yüan dynasty song suite, *Ch'üan Yüan
san-ch'ü*, 2:1852, l. 12; the early vernacular story *Ts'ui Tai-chao sheng-ssu yüan-chia*
(Artisan Ts'ui and his ghost wife), in *Ching-shih t'ung-yen, chüan* 8, p. 101, l. 6; the
early vernacular story *Wang K'uei* (The story of Wang K'uei), in *Tsui yü-ch'ing* (Superlative delights), pref. dated 1647, fac. repr. in *Ku-pen hsiao-shuo ts'ung-k'an, ti erh-shih
liu chi* (Collectanea of rare editions of traditional fiction, twenty-sixth series) (Peking:
Chung-hua shu-chü, 1991), 4:1512, upper register, ll. 11–12; *Chiang Shih yüeh-li chi,
chüan* 2, scene 23, p. 16b, l. 10; *Nan Hsi-hsiang chi* (A southern version of the *Romance of the western chamber*), usually attributed to Li Jih-hua (fl. early 16th century),
Liu-shih chung ch'ü ed., scene 13, p. 32, l. 8; a set of songs by Wang Ch'ung (1494–
1533), *Ch'üan Ming san-ch'ü*, 2:1566, l. 8; the middle-period vernacular story *P'ei
Hsiu-niang yeh-yu Hsi-hu chi* (P'ei Hsiu-niang's night outing on the West Lake), in Hu
Shih-ying, *Hua-pen hsiao-shuo kai-lun*, vol. 1, p. 346, l. 20; the middle-period vernacular story *Shen Hsiao-kuan i-niao hai ch'i-ming* (Master Shen's bird destroys seven lives),
in *Ku-chin hsiao-shuo*, vol. 2, *chüan* 26, p. 392, l. 2; *Jen hsiao-tzu lieh-hsing wei shen*,
p. 580, l. 10; *Ssu-hsi chi*, scene 21, p. 55, l. 8; a song suite by Ku Ta-tien (1540–96),
Ch'üan Ming san-ch'ü, 3:3038, l. 5; an anonymous set of songs in *Ch'ün-yin lei-hsüan*,

4:2368, l. 2; the early seventeenth-century tale *Hai-ling i-shih* (The debauches of Emperor Hai-ling of the Chin dynasty [r. 1149–61]), in *Ssu wu-hsieh hui-pao* (No depraved thoughts collectanea), comp. Ch'en Ch'ing-hao and Wang Ch'iu-kuei, 45 vols. (Taipei: Encyclopedia Britannica, 1995–97), 1:107, l. 7; and an abundance of other occurrences, too numerous to list.

43. Versions of this song suite are preserved in *Sheng-shih hsin-sheng*, pp. 517–19; *Tz'u-lin chai-yen*, 1:247–51; *Yung-hsi yüeh-fu, ts'e* 16, pp. 11a–12a; and *Ch'ün-yin lei-hsüan*, 4:2079–81; but the differences in the tune titles and the wording are such as to make it unlikely that the author of the novel relied on any of them.

44. On Hsi-shih, see Roy, *The Plum in the Golden Vase*, vol. 1, chap. 4, n. 2.

45. On Yang Kuei-fei, see ibid., vol. 2, chap. 21, n. 57.

46. All ten of the above names for particular varieties of chrysanthemums, together with descriptions of their distinguishing characteristics, may be found in the imperially commissioned work, presented to the throne in 1708, entitled *Kuang Ch'ün-fang p'u* (An enlarged version of the Monograph on fragrant plants), comp. Wang Hao (cs 1703) et al., 4 vols. (Shanghai: Shang-hai shu-tien, 1985), vol. 2, *chüan* 48, pp. 1147–57.

47. For the fact that there was an imperial brickyard that made bricks for palace construction located in Su-chou during the Ming dynasty, see *Ming shih* (History of the Ming dynasty), comp. Chang T'ing-yü (1672–1755) et al., 28 vols. (Peking: Chung-hua shu-chü, 1974), vol. 7, *chüan* 82, p. 1999, l. 5; and *T'ien-kung k'ai-wu* (The exploitation of the works of nature), by Sung Ying-hsing (1587–c. 1666) (Hong Kong: Chung-hua shu-chü, 1978), *chüan* 7, p. 188, l. 4.

48. See Roy, *The Plum in the Golden Vase*, vol. 1, chap. 4, n. 6.

49. See ibid., vol. 2, chap. 39, n. 24.

50. This four-character expression occurs in a song suite by Chu Yu-tun (1379–1439), *Ch'üan Ming san-ch'ü*, 1:370, l. 11; and the tsa-chü drama entitled *Ko tai hsiao* (A song in place of a shriek), attributed to Hsü Wei (1521–93), in *Ssu-sheng yüan* (Four cries of a gibbon), by Hsü Wei, originally published in 1588, ed. and annot. Chou Chung-ming (Shanghai: Shang-hai ku-chi ch'u-pan she, 1984), scene 4, p. 156, l. 3.

51. This four-character expression occurs in an anonymous Yüan dynasty song suite, *Ch'üan Yüan san-ch'ü*, 2:1847, l. 12; a lyric by Hsieh Ying-fang (1296–1392), *Ch'üan Ming tz'u*, 1:12, lower register, l. 11; the tsa-chü drama *Nan-chi hsing tu-t'o Hai-t'ang hsien* (The Southern Pole Star delivers the Flowering Crab Apple Immortal), by Chu Yu-tun (1379–1439), originally completed in 1439, in *Ku-pen Yüan Ming tsa-chü*, vol. 2., scene 3, p. 4b, l. 12; *P'u-tung Ts'ui Chang Hai-weng shih-chi* (Hai-weng's set of poems about [the affair of] Ts'ui [Ying-ying] and Chang [Chün-jui] in P'u-tung), included as part of the front matter in the 1498 edition of *Hsi-hsiang chi*, p. 23a, l. 2; a song suite by T'ang Yin (1470–1524), *Ch'üan Ming san-ch'ü*, 1:1081, l. 7; a song suite by Liang Ch'en-yü (1519–91), ibid., 2:2244, l. 1; and an anonymous song in *Ch'ün-yin lei-hsüan*, 4:2443, l. 4.

52. On the Dream of the Southern Branch, see *The Plum in the Golden Vase or, Chin P'ing Mei*, vol. 3: *The Aphrodisiac*, trans. David Tod Roy (Princeton: Princeton University Press, 2006), chap. 59, n. 81.

53. On the Dream of Witch's Mountain, see ibid., vol. 1, chap. 2, n. 47.

54. On the Dream of a Butterfly, see ibid., vol. 3, chap. 56, n. 2.

55. This four-character expression occurs in the Ming ch'uan-ch'i drama *Ching-chung chi* (A tale of perfect loyalty), *Liu-shih chung ch'ü* ed., scene 21, p. 57, l. 7.

56. This four-character expression occurs in a poem by Kao Shih (716–65), *Ch'üan T'ang shih pu-pien* (A supplement to the Complete poetry of the T'ang), comp. Ch'en Shang-chün, 3 vols. (Peking: Chung-hua shu-chü, 1992), 1:34, l. 6; and *Chiang Shih yüeh-li chi, chüan* 3, scene 29, p. 15b, l. 6.

57. On the Dream of the Radiant Terrace, see Roy, *The Plum in the Golden Vase,* vol. 2, chap. 38, n. 37. A version of the first of these four songs occurs in the anonymous early hsi-wen drama *Lin Chao-te* (The story of Lin Chao-te), see *Sung-Yüan hsi-wen chi-i* (Collected fragments of Sung and Yüan hsi-wen drama), comp. Ch'ien Nan-yang (Shanghai: Shang-hai ku-tien wen-hsüeh ch'u-pan she, 1956), p. 87, ll. 14–16. Versions of all four songs are preserved in *Chin-ch'ai chi,* scene 60, p. 101, ll. 10–22; *Tz'u-lin chai-yen,* 1:45–46; *Yung-hsi yüeh-fu,* ts'e 15b, pp. 9a–9b; *Nan-kung tz'u-chi* (Anthology of southern-style song lyrics), comp. Ch'en So-wen (d. c. 1604), in *Nan-pei kung tz'u-chi* (Anthology of southern- and northern-style song lyrics), comp. Ch'en So-wen (d. c. 1604), ed. Chao Ching-shen, 4 vols. (Peking: Chung-hua shu-chü, 1959), vol. 2, *chüan* 4, pp. 216–17; *T'ai-hsia hsin-tsou* (New songs from the empyreal clouds), comp. Feng Meng-lung (1574–1646), originally published in 1627, fac. repr. (Fu-chou: Hai-hsia wen-i ch'u-pan she, 1986), *chüan* 7, pp. 31a–32a; and *Wu-sao ho-pien* (Combined anthology of the songs of Wu), comp. Chang Ch'i (fl. early 17th century) and Chang Hsü-ch'u (fl. early 17th century), pref. dated 1637, 4 ts'e, fac. repr. (Shanghai: Shang-wu yin-shu kuan, 1934), ts'e 2, pp. 89a–91a. The version in the novel is closest to that in *Tz'u-lin chai-yen,* which also bears the title "The Four Dreams and Eight Nothings."

58. This four-character expression occurs in a quatrain by Ou-yang Chan (c.757–c. 802), *Ch'üan T'ang shih,* vol. 6, *chüan* 349, p. 3913, l. 6; a poem by Yüan Chen (775–831), ibid., vol. 6, *chüan* 419, p. 4614, l. 9; a poem by Tsou Hao (1060–1111), *Ch'üan Sung shih,* 21:13956, l. 7; and *Shui-hu ch'üan-chuan,* vol. 2, chap. 27, p. 428, l. 10.

59. This four-character expression occurs in the literary tale entitled *P'eng-lai hsien-sheng chuan* (The story of Mr. P'eng-lai), in the collection of literary tales entitled *Hsiao-p'in chi* (Emulative frowns collection), by Chao Pi, author's postface dated 1428 (Shanghai: Ku-tien wen-hsüeh ch'u-pan she, 1957), p. 71, l. 5. This tale is known to have been drawn upon by the author of the novel in his characterization of Li P'ing-erh. See Roy, *The Plum in the Golden Vase,* vol. 1, chap. 17, n. 37.

60. This four-character expression occurs in *Huan-tai chi, chüan* 2, scene 28, p. 19b, ll. 6–7; and the anonymous ch'uan-ch'i drama *Han Hsiang-tzu chiu-tu Wen-kung sheng-hsien chi* (Han Hsiang-tzu nine times endeavors to induce Han Yü to ascend to the realm of the immortals), in *Ku-pen hsi-ch'ü ts'ung-k'an, ch'u-chi,* item no. 47, *chüan* 2, scene 31, p. 30a, l. 5.

61. This four-character expression occurs in the ch'uan-ch'i drama entitled *Yü-chüeh chi* (The jade thumb-ring), by Cheng Jo-yung (16th century), *Liu-shih chung ch'ü* ed., scene 26, p. 82, l. 3.

62. The text reads Tai-an here, but I have emended it to Ch'in-t'ung on the basis of the information in the *Chin P'ing Mei tz'u-hua,* vol. 4, ch. 61, p. 21b, l. 8.

63. A variant of this line occurs in *Yüan-ch'ü hsüan,* 2:633, l. 14. It occurs in the same form as in the novel in *Ts'an-T'ang Wu-tai shih yen-i chuan,* ch. 3, p. 5, l. 1.

64. A variant of this line occurs in *P'eng-lai hsien-sheng chuan,* p. 71, l. 5.

65. These two baleful stars are mentioned together in *Ch'i-kuo ch'un-ch'iu p'ing-hua* (The p'ing-hua on the events of the seven states), originally published in 1321–23 (Shanghai: Ku-tien wen-hsüeh ch'u-pan she, 1955), p. 55, l. 3; the Yüan-Ming hsi-wen

drama *Su Wu mu-yang chi* (Su Wu herds sheep), in *Ku-pen hsi-ch'ü ts'ung-k'an, ch'u-chi*, item 20, *chüan* 2, scene 16, p. 1b, l. 3; the ch'uan-ch'i drama *Pai-p'ao chi* (Story of the white robe), in *Ku-pen hs'i-ch'ü ts'ung-k'an, ch'u-chi*, item 46, *chüan* 1, scene 12, p. 18b, l. 3; the sixteenth-century ch'uan-ch'i drama *Su Ying huang-hou ying-wu chi* (The story of Empress Su Ying's parrot), in *Ku-pen hsi-ch'ü ts'ung-k'an, ch'u-chi*, item 45, *chüan* 1, scene 18, p. 38b, l. 10; and *Hsi-yu chi*, vol. 2, ch. 76, p. 876, l. 14.

66. See Roy, *The Plum in the Golden Vase*, vol. 1, chap. 17, n. 14. This four-character expression occurs in a lyric by Chao Pi-hsiang (1245–94), *Ch'üan Sung tz'u*, 5:3385, lower register, ll. 6–7.

67. The proximate source of this set piece of descriptive parallel prose, with considerable textual variation, is *Shui-hu ch'üan-chuan*, vol. 2, ch. 52, p. 858, ll. 3–5. A very similar passage occurs in the middle-period vernacular story *K'ung Shu-fang shuang-yü shan-chui chuan* (The story of K'ung Shu-fang and the pair of fish-shaped fan pendants), in *Hsiung Lung-feng ssu-chung hsiao-shuo* (Four vernacular stories published by Hsiung Lung-feng [fl. c. 1590]), ed. Wang Ku-lu (Shanghai: Ku-tien wen-hsüeh ch'u-pan she, 1958), p. 66, ll. 3–5; and p. 68, l. 8.

68. This address is an example of the type of wordplay in which ascending or descending sequences of numbers occur in successive lines. It is significant, however, that all four of these place names existed in sixteenth-century Peking. See Ting Lang, *Chin P'ing Mei yü Pei-ching* (*Chin P'ing Mei* and Peking) (Peking: Chung-kuo she-hui ch'u-pan she, 1996), p. 64, ll. 5–11.

69. The Prince of Ju is Chu Yu-p'eng (d. 1558), the eleventh son of the Ch'eng-hua emperor (r. 1464–87), a younger brother of the Hung-chih emperor (r. 1487–1505), and an uncle of the Cheng-te emperor (r. 1505–21) and the Chia-ching emperor (r. 1521–66). Upon his death without issue in 1558 his princedom was abolished, but a mansion for his surviving dependents was established in Peking in the winter of the same year. This inconspicuous piece of evidence indicates that the novel must have been written after 1558. See ibid., pp. 94–95.

70. Wang Shu-ho (210–85) is the author of the *Mai-ching* (Pulse classic), the earliest Chinese treatise on pulse diagnosis.

71. Li Kao (1180–1251) is the author of numerous medical works and is considered to be one of the four most distinguished physicians of the Chin-Yüan period (1115–1369).

72. Wu-t'ing-tzu (The Skeptic) is the self-chosen cognomen of Hsiung Tsung-li (15th century), a prolific author of medical texts.

73. There are a number of works of this title, all of which deal with the properties of drugs and are composed in verse or parallel prose so as to facilitate memorization.

74. This important medical classic is a composite work, thought to have been composed between 400 B.C. and 260 A.D. For a detailed critical study of this text, see Paul U. Unschuld, *Huang Di nei jing su wen: Nature, Knowledge, Imagery in an Ancient Chinese Medical Text* (Berkeley: University of California Press, 2003).

75. This important medical classic is thought to date from the first or early second century A.D. For an annotated translation of this text, see *Nan-ching the Classic of Difficult Issues*, trans. and annot. Paul U. Unschuld (Berkeley: University of California Press, 1986).

76. This is the abbreviated title of an important medical work by Chu Kung (cs 1088), published in 1118.

77. This is the title of a selection of the most important medical writings of Chu Chen-heng (1281–1385), compiled by Lu Ho (15th century) and published in 1484.

78. This is the title of a work on the medical theories of Chu Chen-heng (1281–1358) compiled by his disciples. It was reedited in its current form by Ch'eng Ch'ung (15th century) and published in 1481.

79. This is the title of a commentary attributed to the famous physician Chang Yüan-su (12th century) on a popular work of uncertain authorship, written in simple verse, that deals with the secrets of pulse diagnosis ascribed to Wang Shu-ho (210–85).

80. This is the title of a work by the physician Chu Jih-hui (16th century). It is mentioned again in the *Chin P'ing Mei tz'u-hua*, vol. 5, ch. 85, p. 2a, l. 4.

81. See Roy, *The Plum in the Golden Vase*, vol. 3, chap. 53, n. 11.

82. This is the title of a work originally begun by Tung Su (15th century), later completed in its present form by Fang Hsien (15th century), and published in 1470.

83. This is the title of a work by Chu Ch'üan (1378–1448). It is mentioned again in the *Chin P'ing Mei tz'u-hua*, vol. 5, ch. 85, p. 2a, l. 4.

84. This is the title of a popular work in heptasyllabic verse, traditionally attributed to Sun Ssu-miao (581–682), but more probably dating from the Sung dynasty or later. It is mentioned again in the *Chin P'ing Mei tz'u-hua*, vol. 5, ch. 85, p. 2a, l. 4.

85. This four-character expression occurs in *Yüan-ch'ü hsüan*, 4:1535, l. 11; *Yüan-ch'ü hsüan wai-pien*, 3:1001, l. 14; *[Hsin-pien] Wu-tai shih p'ing-hua* ([Newly compiled] p'ing-hua on the history of the Five Dynasties), originally published in the 14th century (Shanghai: Chung-kuo ku-tien wen-hsüeh ch'u-pan she, 1954), p. 10, l. 12; *Ch'ien-t'ang hu-yin Chi-tien Ch'an-shih yü-lu* (The recorded sayings of the lakeside recluse of Ch'ien-t'ang, the Ch'an master Crazy Chi [Tao-chi (1148–1209)]), fac. repr. of 1569 edition, in *Ku-pen hsiao-shuo ts'ung-k'an, ti-pa chi* (Collectanea of rare editions of traditional fiction, eighth series) (Peking: Chung-hua shu-chü, 1990), vol. 1, p. 4b, l. 10; *T'ou-pi chi, chüan* 1, scene 12, p. 31b, l. 5; *Pai-chia kung-an, chüan* 3, ch. 23, p. 6b, l. 8; and the ch'uan-ch'i drama *Chin-chien chi* (The brocade note), by Chou Lü-ching (1549–1640), *Liu-shih chung ch'ü* ed., scene 5, p. 13, l. 10.

86. This four-character expression occurs in *San-kuo chih t'ung-su yen-i* (The romance of the Three Kingdoms), attributed to Lo Kuan-chung (14th century), pref. dated 1522, 2 vols. (Shanghai: Shang-hai ku-chi ch'u-pan she, 1980), vol. 1, *chüan* 12, p. 571, l. 23.

87. A close variant of this four-character expression occurs in *Yüan-ch'ü hsüan wai-pien*, 2:418, l. 19; and *Hsi-yu chi*, vol. 1, ch. 43, p. 495, l. 6.

88. This four-character expression occurs in a song on the subject of quack doctors by Ch'en To (fl. early 16th century), *Ch'üan Ming san-ch'ü*, 1:525, l. 7. It also recurs in the *Chin P'ing Mei tz'u-hua*, vol. 4, ch. 61, p. 24b, l. 6; and vol. 5, ch. 88, p. 9a, l. 2.

89. This four-character expression occurs in *Hai-fu shan-t'ang tz'u-kao, chüan* 1, p. 3, l. 3; a song by Wang K'o-tu (c. 1526–c. 1594), *Ch'üan Ming san-ch'ü*, 2:2453, l. 5; and *San-pao t'ai-chien Hsi-yang chi t'ung-su yen-i*, vol. 2, ch. 54, p. 695, l. 10. It also recurs in the *Chin P'ing Mei tz'u-hua*, vol. 4, ch. 75, p. 23b, l. 1; p. 24a, l. 6; ch. 76, p. 4a, l. 4; and p. 12b, l. 4.

90. This four-character expression occurs in *Yüan-ch'ü hsüan*, 3:1074, l. 18; a lyric by Wang Ta (14th century), *Ch'üan Ming tz'u*, 1:219, lower register, l. 2; *Shen-hsiang ch'üan-pien, chüan* 639, p. 16a, l. 4; and *Hsi-yu chi*, vol. 1, ch. 50, p. 575, l. 13.

91. These two lines occur in reverse order in the ch'uan-ch'i drama *Chin-tiao chi* (The golden sable), in *Ku-pen hsi-ch'ü ts'ung-k'an, ch'u-chi*, item 41, *chüan* 4, scene 33, p. 1b, ll. 8–9. The proximate source of the above self-deprecatory verse, with minor textual variation, is *Pao-chien chi*, scene 28, p. 51, ll. 16–20.

92. This sentence is derived from a famous passage in the *Nan-ching*. See Roy, *The Plum in the Golden Vase*, vol. 3, ch. 54, n. 38. The last four characters also occur in *Hsi-yu chi*, vol. 2, ch. 68, p. 781, l. 11.

93. See Roy, *The Plum in the Golden Vase*, vol. 1, chap. 12, n. 49.

94. The proximate source of the preceding eight paragraphs, with considerable textual variation, is *Pao-chien chi*, scene 28, p. 51, l. 21–p. 52, l. 4.

95. The proximate source of this song, with considerable textual variation, is ibid., scene 28, p. 52, ll. 9–10.

96. A variant of this proverbial saying is attributed to Confucius (551–479 B.C.) in *Shuo-yüan* (Garden of persuasions), comp. Liu Hsiang (79–8 B.C.). See *Shuo-yüan chu-tzu so-yin* (A concordance to the *Shuo-yüan*) (Taipei: T'ai-wan Shang-wu yin-shu kuan, 1992), ch. 9, section 25, p. 76, l. 6. Close variants also occur in *Shih-chi* (Records of the historian), by Ssu-ma Ch'ien (145–c. 90 B.C.), 10 vols. (Peking: Chung-hua shu-chü, 1972), vol. 10, *chüan* 118, p. 3088, ll. 5–6; *Hou-Han shu* (History of the Later Han dynasty), comp. Fan Yeh (398–445), 12 vols. (Peking: Chung-hua shu-chü, 1965), vol. 8, *chüan* 74b, p. 2414, l. 6; *Yüan shih* (History of the Yüan dynasty), comp. Sung Lien (1310–81) et al., 15 vols. (Peking: Chung-hua shu-chü, 1976), vol. 13, *chüan* 168, p. 3963, l. 3; the fourteenth-century anthology of moral aphorisms entitled *Ming-hsin pao-chien* (A precious mirror to illuminate the mind), pref. dated 1393 (Microfilm copy of a Ming edition in the East Asian Library, University of Chicago), *chüan* 1, p. 7b, l. 7; *P'i-p'a chi*, scene 32, p. 179, l. 3; the anonymous early Ming ch'uan-ch'i drama *P'o-yao chi* (The dilapidated kiln), in *Ku-pen hsi-ch'ü ts'ung-k'an, ch'u-chi*, item 19, *chüan* 1, scene 14, p. 41b, l. 9; the anonymous Ming tsa-chü drama *Feng-yüeh Nan-lao chi* (Romance in the South Prison), in *Ku-pen Yüan Ming tsa-chü*, vol. 4, scene 1, p. 3a, l. 3; and the anonymous Ming ch'uan-ch'i drama *Hsün-ch'in chi* (The quest for the father), *Liu-shih chung ch'ü* ed., scene 11, p. 32, l. 10. It occurs in the same form as in the novel in *Shih-chi*, vol. 6, *chüan* 55, p. 2037, l. 14.

97. This formulaic couplet is ubiquitous in Chinese vernacular literature. See, e.g., the early hsi-wen drama *Huan-men tzu-ti ts'o li-shen* (The scion of an official's family opts for the wrong career), in *Yung-lo ta-tien hsi-wen san-chung chiao-chu*, scene 5, p. 233, l. 7; *Yüan-ch'ü hsüan*, 2:843, ll. 7–8; *Yu-kuei chi*, scene 11, p. 35, l. 11; *P'i-p'a chi*, scene 16, p. 98, l. 4; *Chin-ch'ai chi*, scene 9, p. 20, ll. 11–12; *Yü-huan chi*, scene 25, p. 92, l. 1; *Hsün-ch'in chi*, scene 8, p. 26, l. 6; the ch'uan-ch'i drama *Hsiang-nang chi* (The scent bag), by Shao Ts'an (15th century), *Liu-shih chung ch'ü* ed., scene 19, p. 53, l. 6; the ch'uan-ch'i drama *Shuang-chung chi* (The loyal pair), by Yao Mao-liang (15th century), in *Ku-pen hsi-ch'ü ts'ung-k'an, ch'u-chi*, item 33, *chüan* 1, scene 5, p. 13b, l. 1; *Huan-tai chi*, *chüan* 2, scene 27, p. 17a, ll. 7–8; the ch'uan-ch'i drama *San-yüan chi* (Feng Ching [1021–94] wins first place in three examinations), by Shen Shou-hsien (15th century), *Liu-shih chung ch'ü* ed., scene 34, p. 90, l. 2; *Hsiu-ju chi*, scene 19, p. 53, l. 11; *Nan Hsi-hsiang chi* (Li Jih-hua), scene 12, p. 32, l. 1; the ch'uan-ch'i drama *Ming-chu chi* (The luminous pearl), by Lu Ts'ai (1497–1537), *Liu-shih chung ch'ü* ed., scene 34, p. 111, l. 2; *Chieh-chih-erh chi*, p. 248, l. 16; the ch'uan-ch'i drama *Tuan-fa chi* (The severed tresses), by Li K'ai-hsien (1502–68), in *Ku-pen hsi-ch'ü*

ts'ung-k'an, wu-chi (Collectanea of rare editions of traditional drama, fifth series) (Shanghai: Shang-hai ku-chi ch'u-pan she, 1986), item 2, *chüan* 1, scene 21, p. 51a, l. 5; *Huan-sha chi*, scene 32, p. 113, l. 11; *Hsi-yu chi*, vol. 1, ch. 28, p. 321, l. 16; and an abundance of other occurrences, too numerous to list. The first line also occurs independently in the ch'uan-ch'i drama *Chu-fa chi* (Taking the tonsure), by Chang Feng-i (1527–1613), completed in 1586, in *Ku-pen hsi-ch'ü ts'ung-k'an, ch'u-chi*, item 61, *chüan* 2, scene 27, p. 27b, l. 2; and the ch'uan-ch'i drama *Pa-i chi* (The story of the eight righteous heroes), *Liu-shih chung ch'ü* ed., scene 39, p. 82, ll. 9–10. The second line also occurs independently in *Yüan-ch'ü hsüan wai-pien*, 2:488, l. 16; and *San-pao t'ai-chien Hsi-yang chi t'ung-su yen-i*, vol. 2, ch. 79, p. 1015, l. 5.

98. For an explanation of these categories, see Chao Wei-pang, "The Chinese Science of Fate-Calculation," *Folklore Studies* 5 (1946), pp. 304–7.

99. For definitive studies of the importance of Mount Wu-tang in Hupei province as a Taoist pilgrimage site during the Ming and Ch'ing dynasties, see John Lagerwey, "The Pilgrimage to Wu-tang Shan," in *Pilgrims and Sacred Sites in China*, ed. Susan Naquin and Chün-fang Yü (Berkeley: University of California Press, 1992), pp. 293–332; and Pierre-Henry de Bruyn, "Wudang Shan: The Origins of a Major Center of Modern Taoism," in *Religion and Chinese Society*, ed. John Lagerwey, 2 vols. (Hong Kong: The Chinese University Press and École française d'Extrême-Orient, 2004), 2:553–90.

100. For an explanation of the horoscopic category "seal ribbon," see Chao Wei-pang, "The Chinese Science of Fate-Calculation," pp. 311–12. This six-character expression recurs verbatim in the *Chin P'ing Mei tz'u-hua*, vol. 5, ch. 91, p. 7a, l. 3.

101. See Roy, *The Plum in the Golden Vase*, vol. 3, chap. 46, n. 68.

102. This four-character expression occurs in the anonymous Ming tsa-chü drama *Shih Chen-jen ssu-sheng so pai-yüan* (Perfected Man Shih and the four generals subdue the white gibbon), in *Ku-pen Yüan-Ming tsa-chü*, vol. 4, hsieh-tzu (wedge), p. 1b, l. 4.

103. This four-character expression occurs in *Shen-hsiang ch'üan-pien*, *chüan* 631, p. 52a, l. 5.

104. This four-character expression occurs in a couplet attributed to the Buddhist monk Shan-chao (947–1024) in *Wu-teng hui-yüan* (The essentials of the five lamps), comp. P'u-chi (1179–1253), 3 vols. (Peking: Chung-hua shu-chü, 1984), vol. 2, *chüan* 11, p. 687, l. 1.

105. This four-character expression occurs in *Yüan-ch'ü hsüan wai-pien*, 2:431, l. 2; the early vernacular story *Sung Ssu-kung ta-nao Chin-hun Chang* (Sung the Fourth raises hell with Tightwad Chang), in *Ku-chin hsiao-shuo*, vol. 2, *chüan* 36, p.538, l. 9; *San-yüan chi*, scene 24, p. 66, l. 3; the ch'uan-ch'i drama *Nan Hsi-hsiang chi* (A southern version of the *Romance of the western chamber*), by Lu Ts'ai (1497–1537), in *Hsi-hsiang hui-pien* (Collected versions of the *Romance of the western chamber*), comp. Huo Sung-lin (Chi-nan: Shan-tung wen-i ch'u-pan she, 1987), *chüan* 2, scene 34, p. 407, l. 7; and *Hsi-yu chi*, vol. 2, ch. 55, p. 634, l. 14. It also recurs in the *Chin P'ing Mei tz'u-hua*, vol. 5, ch. 85, p. 2a, l. 5.

106. In these two lines, the dragon refers to P'an Chin-lien, who was born in the year of the dragon; the sheep refers to Li P'ing-erh, who was born in the year of the sheep; and the tiger refers to Hsi-men Ch'ing, who was born in the year of the tiger.

107. The year of the cock is the current year in the time scheme of the novel, which corresponds roughly to the year 1117 in the Western calendar.

108. This formulaic four-character expression occurs ubiquitously in Chinese vernacular literature. See, e.g., *Yüan-ch'ü hsüan*, 1:75, l. 5; *Yüan-ch'ü hsüan wai-pien*, 3:939, l. 19; *Shen-hsiang ch'üan-pien*, *chüan* 641, p. 29b, ll. 1–2; *Hua Kuan So pien Yün-nan chuan* (The story of how Hua Kuan So was exiled to Yün-nan), originally published in 1478, fac. repr. in *Ming Ch'eng-hua shuo-ch'ang tz'u-hua ts'ung-k'an* (Corpus of prosimetric tz'u-hua narratives published in the Ch'eng-hua reign period [1465–87] of the Ming dynasty), 12 *ts'e* (Shanghai: Shanghai Museum, 1973), *ts'e* 1, p. 5b, l. 10; *San-kuo chih t'ung-su yen-i*, vol. 1, *chüan* 11, p. 520, l. 5; *Lieh-kuo chih-chuan* (Chronicle of the feudal states), by Yü Shao-yü (fl. mid-16th century), 8 *chüan* (Chien-yang: San-t'ai kuan, 1606), fac. repr. in *Ku-pen hsiao-shuo ts'ung-k'an, ti-liu chi* (Collectanea of rare editions of traditional fiction, sixth series) (Peking: Chung-hua shu-chü, 1990), vol. 2, *chüan*, 6, p. 48b, l. 10; *San-pao t'ai-chien Hsi-yang chi t'ung-su yen-i*, vol. 2, ch. 61, p. 785, l. 5; and *Ta-T'ang Ch'in-wang tz'u-hua*, vol. 1, *chüan* 1, ch. 3, p. 36a, l. 4.

109. Variants of this proverbial couplet occur in *K'an p'i-hsüeh tan-cheng Erh-lang Shen*, p. 253, l. 3; *Shui-hu ch'üan-chuan*, vol. 1, ch. 17, p. 249, l. 15; and *San-pao t'ai-chien Hsi-yang chi t'ung-su yen-i*, vol. 1, ch. 19, p. 249, ll. 14–15.

CHAPTER 62

1. This line, together with the following couplet, recurs in the *Chin P'ing Mei tz'u-hua*, vol. 5, ch. 87, p. 5a, ll. 6–7.

2.. This couplet has become proverbial and is ubiquitous in Chinese vernacular literature. Variants occur in *Ying-hsüeh ts'ung-shuo* (Collected observations compiled by the light shed by fireflies and reflected from the snow), by Yü Ch'eng (12th century), author's pref. dated 1200, in *Pai-ch'uan hsüeh-hai* (A sea of knowledge fed by a hundred streams), comp. Tso Kuei (13th century), pref. dated 1273, fac. repr. of original edition (Peking: Chung-kuo shu-tien, 1990), *ting-chi* (fourth collection), p. 341, *chüan* 2, p. 8b, ll. 10–11; *Chang Hsieh chuang-yüan*, scene 12, p. 69, ll. 11–12; *Wu-wang fa Chou p'ing-hua* (The p'ing-hua on King Wu's conquest of King Chou), originally published in 1321–23 (Shanghai: Chung-kuo ku-tien wen-hsüeh ch'u-pan she, 1955), p. 85, l. 3; the anonymous Yüan-Ming ch'uan-ch'i drama *Chao-shih ku-erh chi* (The story of the orphan of Chao), in *Ku-pen hsi-ch'ü ts'ung-k'an, ch'u-chi*, item 16, *chüan* 2, scene 33, p. 23a, l. 5; *P'i-p'a chi*, scene 26, p. 152, l. 7; the Ming tsa-chü drama *Jen chin shu ku-erh hsün-mu* (Identifying the gold [hairpins] and the [jade] comb an orphan seeks his mother), in *Ku-pen Yüan-Ming tsa-chü*, vol. 3, scene 1, p. 3b, ll. 3–4; the earliest extant printed edition of the Yüan-Ming ch'uan-ch'i drama *Pai-t'u chi* (The white rabbit), *[Hsin-pien] Liu Chih-yüan huan-hsiang Pai-t'u chi* ([Newly compiled] Liu Chih-yüan's return home: The white rabbit), in *Ming Ch'eng-hua shuo-ch'ang tz'u-hua ts'ung-k'an*, *ts'e* 12, p. 46a, l. 2; and *[Hsin-k'an ch'üan-hsiang] Ying-ko hsiao-i chuan* ([Newly printed fully illustrated] Story of the filial and righteous parrot), in ibid., *ts'e* 10, p. 9b, ll. 7–8. It occurs in the same form as in the novel in *Yüan-ch'ü hsüan*, 1:299, ll. 9–10; the early vernacular story *Chi Ya-fan chin-man ch'an-huo* (Duty Group Leader Chi's golden eel engenders catastrophe), in *Ching-shih t'ung-yen, chüan* 20, p. 285, l. 14; *Sha-kou chi*, scene 35, p. 126, l. 1; *Yu-kuei chi*, scene 7, p. 16, ll. 3–4; *Ch'ien-chin chi*, scene 31, p. 104, l. 12; the ch'uan-ch'i drama *Shuang-chu chi* (The pair of pearls), by Shen Ch'ing (15th century), *Liu-shih chung ch'ü* ed., scene 44, p. 157, l. 7; the title page of *[Hsin-pien shuo-ch'ang ch'üan-hsiang] Shih-lang fu-ma chuan* ([Newly compiled prosimetric fully illustrated] Story of the imperial son-in-law Shih Ching-t'ang [892–942]), originally published in 1471, in *Ming Ch'eng-hua shuo-ch'ang tz'u-hua ts'ung-k'an*, ts'e 2; *Jen-tsung jen-mu chuan* (The story of how Emperor Jen-tsung [r. 1022–63] reclaimed his mother), in ibid., ts'e 4, p. 19b, l. 6; the ch'uan-ch'i drama *Yüeh Fei p'o-lu tung-ch'uang chi* (Yüeh Fei defeats the barbarians: the plot at the eastern window), by Chou Li (15th century), in *Ku-pen hsi-ch'ü ts'ung-k'an, ch'u-chi*, item no. 21, *chüan* 2, scene 35, p. 26a, l. 6; *Shui-hu ch'üan-chuan*, vol. 4, ch. 119, p. 1799, l. 12; the novel *Pei Sung chih-chuan* (Chronicle of the Sung conquest of the North), attributed to Hsiung Ta-mu (mid-16th century), 10 *chüan* (Nanking: Shih-te t'ang, 1593), fac. repr. in *Ku-pen hsiao-shuo ts'ung-k'an, ti san-shih ssu chi* (Collectanea of rare editions of traditional fiction, thirty-fourth series) (Peking: Chung-hua shu-chü, 1991), vol. 3, *chüan* 9, p. 13b, l. 9; *Pao-chien chi*, scene 24, p. 45, l. 3; *Hsün-ch'in chi*, scene 11, p. 34, l. 11; *Huan-sha chi*, scene 42, p. 149, ll. 9–10; the sixteenth-century ch'uan-ch'i drama *Ming-feng chi* (The singing phoenix), *Liu-shih chung ch'ü* ed., scene 33, p. 139, l. 5; *Mu-lien chiu-mu ch'üan-shan hsi-wen*, *chüan* 2, p. 20a, l. 2; *P'u-ching ju-lai yao-shih pao-chüan* (Precious volume of the Tathagatha P'u-ching: the Buddha of the Key [to salvation]), by P'u-ching (d. 1586), in *Pao-chüan ch'u-chi*, 5:185, l. 9; the ch'uan-ch'i drama *Kuan-yüan chi* (The story of the gardener), by Chang Feng-i (1527–1613), *Liu-shih chung ch'ü* ed., scene 9, p. 17, l. 10; *Hsi-yu chi*, vol. 1, ch. 11, p. 119, l. 13; and *San-pao t'ai-chien Hsi-yang chi t'ung-su yen-i*, vol. 2, ch. 87, p. 1126, l. 12. It also recurs, together with the preceding line, in the *Chin P'ing Mei tz'u-hua*, vol. 5, ch. 87, p. 5a, ll. 6–7.

3. A variant of this line occurs in a lyric by Yüan Hao-wen (1190–1257), *Ch'üan Chin Yüan tz'u*, 1:87, lower register, ll. 4–5.

4. A variant of this couplet occurs in *Hsiao Sun-t'u*, scene 10, p. 296, l. 14.

5. This poem is attributed to the Buddhist monk Ling-ch'ao (d. 890). See *Ch'üan T'ang shih pu-pien*, 2:1203, ll. 7–8. It is also included without attribution in *Ming-hsin pao-chien*, *chüan* 1, p. 1, ll. 8–10.

6. This four-character expression occurs in the fifteenth-century literary language love tale *Chung-ch'ing li-chi* (A pleasing tale of passion), in *Yen-chü pi-chi*, vol. 2, *chüan* 6, upper register, p. 4b, l. 1; the middle-period vernacular story *Feng-yüeh hsiang-ssu* (A tale of romantic longing), in *Ch'ing-p'ing shan-t'ang hua-pen*, p. 83, l. 13; and the scurrilous mid-sixteenth-century novelette *Ju-i chün chuan* (The tale of Lord As You Like It), Japanese movable type edition, colophon dated 1880, p. 20a, l. 7. For a critical study and an annotated translation of this last work, see Charles R. Stone, *The Fountainhead of Chinese Erotica: The Lord of Perfect Satisfaction (Ruyijun zhuan)* (Honolulu: University of Hawai'i Press, 2003). The expression in question is translated on p. 157, ll. 2–3.

7. This four-character expression occurs in *Shuang-chu chi*, scene 10, p. 27, l. 8.

8. This idiomatic expression occurs in an anonymous song in *Yung-hsi yüeh-fu*, ts'e 18, p. 12b, l. 2; and recurs in the *Chin P'ing Mei tz'u-hua*, vol. 4, ch. 62, p. 20a, l. 1.

9. This sect and these rites first became prominent in the final years of the Northern Sung dynasty, the very period in which the story of the *Chin P'ing Mei* is set. For recent studies of these developments, see Edward L. Davis, *Society and the Supernatural in Song China* (Honolulu: University of Hawai'i Press, 2001), 21–44, and passim; and

Robert Hymes, *Way and Byway: Taoism, Local Religion, and Models of Divinity in Sung and Modern China* (Berkeley: University of California Press, 2002), pp. 26–46, 147–52, and passim. For a description of the practice of thunder magic in Taiwan today, see Michael Saso, *The Teachings of Taoist Master Chuang* (New Haven: Yale University Press, 1978), pp. 234–66. This variety of Taoist ritual is frequently referred to in Chinese vernacular literature. See, e.g., *Hsüan-ho i-shih* (Forgotten events of the Hsüan-ho reign period [1119–25]) (Shanghai: Shang-hai ku-tien wen-hsüeh ch'u-pan she, 1955), p. 22, l. 12; *Yüan-ch'ü hsüan*, 4:1694, l. 12; *Pai Niang-tzu yung-chen Lei-feng T'a*, p. 431, l. 11; *Tsao-chiao Lin Ta-wang chia-hsing* (A feat of impersonation by the King of Tsao-chiao Wood), in *Ching-shih t'ung-yen*, *chüan* 36, p. 546, l. 11; *K'an p'i-hsüeh tan-cheng Erh-lang Shen*, p. 251, l. 2; *Shui-hu ch'üan-chuan*, vol. 2, ch. 54, p. 900, l. 5; vol. 3, ch. 60, p. 1005, l. 2; vol. 4, p. 1525, ll. 11–12; and p. 1527, l. 6; *San Sui p'ing-yao chuan*, *chüan* 4, ch. 19, p. 28b, l. 8; and *Hsi-yu chi*, vol. 1, ch. 46, p. 534, l. 13. The character Taoist Master P'an from the Temple of the Five Peaks is derived from *K'an p'i-hsüeh tan-cheng Erh-lang Shen*, pp. 251–52.

10. See Roy, *The Plum in the Golden Vase*, vol. 2, chap. 28, n. 26.

11. There are two texts of this title included in the Taoist canon, which are thought to date from the twelfth and fourteenth centuries, respectively. See *Cheng-t'ung Tao-tsang* (The Cheng-t'ung [1436–49] Taoist canon) (Shanghai: Shang-wu yin-shu kuan, 1926), *ts'e* 167, and *ts'e* 343. Both of these texts are translated and discussed in Hou Ching-lang, *Monnaies d'offrande et la notion de tresorerie dans la religion chinoise* (Paris: College de France, Institut des Hautes Etudes Chinoises, 1975), pp. 35–49.

12. This four-character expression recurs in the *Chin P'ing Mei tz'u-hua*, vol. 4, ch. 79, p. 17b, l. 1. It occurs in a scene, very similar to this one, in which Hsi-men Ch'ing is being urged to eat on his deathbed.

13. This four-character expression occurs in *Yüan-ch'ü hsüan wai-pien*, 2:374, ll. 2–3; and *Shui-hu ch'üan-chuan*, vol. 1, ch. 8, p. 125, l. 9. It also recurs in the *Chin P'ing Mei tz'u-hua*, vol. 5, ch. 89, p. 11b, l. 11.

14. This couplet, meaning "Let the facts speak for themselves," is derived from one in *Hsün-tzu*. See *Hsün-tzu yin-te* (A concordance to *Hsün-tzu*) (Taipei: Chinese Materials and Research Aids Service Center, 1966), ch. 3, p. 7, ll. 15–16; and *Xunzi: A Translation and Study of the Complete Works*, trans. John Knoblock, 3 vols. (Stanford: Stanford University Press, 1988–94), 1:178, ll. 6–7.

15. This is a short apocryphal Buddhist text, the recitation or promulgation of which is designed to save women from the fate of being forced to drink from a pool of menstrual blood after death, in order to atone for the contamination they have caused by their menstrual discharges and the hemorrhaging attendant on childbirth. It is included in *[Shinzan] Dai Nihon zokuzōkyō* ([Newly compiled] great Japanese continuation of the Buddhist canon), 100 vols. (Tokyo: Kokusho kankōkai, 1977), 1:414; and is translated and analyzed in Alan Cole, *Mothers and Sons in Chinese Buddhism* (Stanford: Stanford University Press, 1998), pp. 197–214. This text is referred to in *Shui-hu ch'üan-chuan*, vol. 2, ch. 45, p. 736, l. 13; and *Nan-k'o meng chi* (The dream of the southern branch), by T'ang Hsien-tsu (1550–1616), completed in 1600, ed. and annot. Ch'ien Nan-yang (Peking: Jen-min wen-hsüeh ch'u-pan she, 1981), *chüan* 2, scene 1, pp. 81–82. For a discussion of the significance of this reference, see David T. Roy, "The Case for T'ang Hsien-tsu's Authorship of the *Jin Ping Mei*," *Chinese Literature: Essays, Articles, Reviews*, 8, 1 & 2 (July 1986), pp. 48–49.

16. This plant, the root of which is used for medicinal purposes, is called *san-ch'i* (three and seven) because it typically has three palmae and seven leaflets. See Shiu-ying Hu, *Food Plants of China* (Hong Kong: The Chinese University Press, 2005), p. 588, l. 16.

17. These three names are borrowed from a piece of anticlerical burlesque in *Pao-chien chi*, scene 51, p. 90, l. 15.

18. This four-character expression is derived from a passage in *Chuang-tzu*, which Burton Watson translates: "Thoroughbreds like Ch'i-chi and Hua-liu could gallop a thousand li in one day, but when it came to catching rats they were no match for the wildcat or the weasel." See *Chuang-tzu yin-te* (A concordance to *Chuang-tzu*) (Cambridge: Harvard University Press, 1956), ch. 17, p. 43, l. 16; and *The Complete Works of Chuang Tzu*, trans. Burton Watson (New York: Columbia University Press, 1968), ch. 17, p. 180, ll. 21–23. It is cited as a current expression in *Ya-su chi-yen* (A study of expressions both cultivated and vulgar), comp. Chang Ts'un-shen (17th century), pref. dated 1623, in *Ming-Ch'ing su-yü tz'u-shu chi-ch'eng* (A corpus of Ming and Ch'ing glossaries to common expressions), comp. Nagasawa Kikuya, 3 vols. (Shanghai: Shang-hai ku-chi ch'u-pan she, 1989), 2:2040, lower register, *chüan* 35, p. 21b, l. 10.

19. This was the name of a place, some distance south of Ch'eng-tu, that was famous during the Ming dynasty for its production of high-quality coffin boards. See *Tsang-tu* (Funeral considerations), by Wang Wen-lu (b. 1503), in *Shuo-fu hsü* (*The frontiers of apocrypha* continued), comp. T'ao T'ing (cs 1610), fac. repr. of Ming edition, in *Shuo-fu san-chung* (*The frontiers of apocrypha*: Three recensions), 10 vols. (Shanghai: Shang-hai ku-chi ch'u-pan she, 1988), 10:1435, lower register, p. 1b, ll. 1–2.

20. For a detailed description of the making of Chinese coffins, see J. J. M. De Groot, *The Religious System of China*, 6 vols. (Taipei: Ch'eng Wen Publishing Company, 1972), 1:319–24.

21. This reduplicative expression occurs in a quatrain by the Buddhist monk Chih-pen (1035–1107), *Ch'üan Sung shih*, 13:9031, l. 5; and a poem by the Buddhist monk Cheng-chüeh (1091–1157), ibid., 31:19865, l. 10. It also recurs in the *Chin P'ing Mei tz'u-hua*, vol. 4, ch. 75, p. 2a, l. 9.

22. This formulaic four-character expression occurs ubiquitously in Chinese vernacular literature. See, e.g., *Yüan-ch'ü hsüan*, 1:231, l. 4; *Yüan-ch'ü hsüan wai-pien*, 3:755, l. 5; the tsa-chü drama *Chin-t'ung Yü-nü Chiao Hung chi* (The Golden Lad and the Jade Maiden: The story of Chiao-niang and Fei-hung), attributed to Liu Tui (fl. early 15th century), in *Ming-jen tsa-chü hsüan*, p. 52, ll. 10–11; the anonymous Ming tsa-chü drama *Shih-pa kuo Lin-t'ung tou-pao* (Eighteen states compete to present the most outstanding treasure), in ibid., scene 1, p. 670, l. 9; the anonymous Ming tsa-chü drama *Yüeh-i t'u Ch'i* (Yüeh-i attacks Ch'i), in *Ku-pen Yüan Ming tsa-chü*, vol. 2, scene 1, p. 2b, l. 6; the anonymous Ming tsa-chü drama *Sung ta-chiang Yüeh Fei ching-chung* (The perfect loyalty of the Sung general-in-chief Yüeh Fei), in ibid., vol. 3, scene 1, p. 4b, l. 5; *Shui-hu ch'üan-chuan*, vol. 2, ch. 51, p. 843, l. 4; and *Shuang-lieh chi*, scene 12, p. 33, l. 2. It also recurs in the *Chin P'ing Mei tz'u-hua*, vol. 5, ch. 86, p. 7a, l. 10.

23. There is an illustration of this type of cap ornament in *San-ts'ai t'u-hui* (Assembled illustrations from the three realms), comp. Wang Ch'i (c. 1535–c. 1614), pref. dated 1609, 6 vols., fac. repr. (Taipei: Ch'eng-wen ch'u-pan she, 1970), vol. 4, *i-fu* (clothing), *chüan* 3, p. 7b.

24. Variants of this couplet occur in *P'i-p'a chi*, scene 28, p. 161, ll. 8–9; *[Hsin-pien] Liu Chih-yüan huan-hsiang Pai-t'u chi*, p. 28a, l. 6; *Nan Hsi-hsiang chi* (Li Jih-hua), scene 34, p. 99, l. 4; *Han Hsiang-tzu chiu-tu Wen-kung sheng-hsien chi*, *chüan* 1, scene 12, p. 21b, ll. 1–2; and *Hsi-yu chi*, vol. 2, ch. 73, p. 837, l. 14. It occurs in the same form as in the novel in *P'i-p'a chi*, scene 28, p. 162, l. 3; *Ching-ch'ai chi*, scene 15, p. 46, l. 9; the anonymous Yüan-Ming ch'uan-ch'i drama *Pai-t'u chi* (The white rabbit), *Liu-shih chung ch'ü* ed., scene 13, p. 45, l. 3; a fragment of the lost early Ming ch'uan-ch'i drama *Hsi-kua chi* (The watermelon story), in *Feng-yüeh chin-nang [chien-chiao]* (Brocade pouch of romantic verse [annotated and collated]), annot. and collated by Sun Ch'ung-t'ao and Huang Shih-chung, originally published in 1553 (Peking: Chung-hua shu-chü, 2000), scene 14, p. 631, l. 10; *Hsiang-nang chi*, scene 21, p. 59, l. 3; *San-yüan chi*, scene 9, p. 23, l. 10; *Pao-chien chi*, scene 19, p. 38, l. 13; *Wang Chao-chün ch'u-sai ho-jung chi*, *chüan* 2, scene 28, p. 21b, ll. 4–5; *Chin-tiao chi*, *chüan* 4, scene 34, p. 8a, l. 9; *Mu-lien chiu-mu ch'üan-shan hsi-wen*, *chüan* 2, p. 79a, l. 5; *Su Ying huang-hou ying-wu chi*, *chüan* 1, scene 17, p. 37a, l. 3; *Hsi-yu chi*, vol. 2, ch. 85, p. 975, ll. 9–10; the ch'uan-ch'i drama *I-hsia chi* (The righteous knight-errant), by Shen Ching (1553–1610), *Liu-shih chung ch'ü* ed., scene 10, p. 25, l. 5; and *Shih-hou chi*, scene 26, p. 92, l. 4. The second line also occurs independently in *Yüan-ch'ü hsüan wai-pien*, 2:642, l. 18.

25. For a description of this variety of incense, see Edward H. Schafer, *The Golden Peaches of Samarkand: A Study of T'ang Exotics* (Berkeley: University of California Press, 1963), p. 159.

26. These two lines occur in *Shui-hu ch'üan-chuan*, vol. 1, ch. 15, p. 220, l. 10; and recur, with some textual variation, in ibid., vol. 4, ch. 96, p. 1524, ll. 6–7.

27. The *wu-ming shan* (five-luminary fan) is alleged to have been invented by the legendary Emperor Shun (3rd millennium B.C.). See *Ku-chin chu* (Notes on things ancient and modern), by Ts'ui Pao (fl. late 3rd century) (Shanghai: Shang-wu yin-shu kuan, 1956), *chüan* 1, p. 8, ll. 7–8.

28. These two lines occur in *Shui-hu ch'üan-chuan*, vol. 1, ch. 15, p. 220, l. 11.

29. This formulaic four-character expression occurs ubiquitously in Chinese vernacular literature. See, e.g., the early vernacular story *Lo-yang san-kuai chi* (The three monsters of Lo-yang), in *Ch'ing-p'ing shan-t'ang hua-pen*, p. 75, l. 3; the early vernacular story *I-k'u kuei lai tao-jen ch'u-kuai* (A mangy Taoist exorcises a lair of demons), in *Ching-shih t'ung-yen*, *chüan* 14, p. 194, l. 16; the early vernacular story *Chin-ming ch'ih Wu Ch'ing feng Ai-ai* (Wu Ch'ing meets Ai-ai at Chin-ming Pond), in *Ching-shih t'ung-yen*, *chüan* 30, p. 466, ll. 8–9; the early vernacular story *Hsi-hu san-t'a chi* (The three pagodas at West Lake), in *Ch'ing-p'ing shan-t'ang hua-pen*, p. 31, l. 6; the early vernacular story *Fu Lu Shou san-hsing tu-shih* (The three stellar deities of Fortune, Emolument, and Longevity visit the mundane world), in *Ching-shih t'ung-yen*, *chüan* 39, p. 590, l. 1; the early vernacular story *Lü Tung-pin fei-chien chan Huang-lung* (Lü Tung-pin beheads Huang-lung with his flying sword), in *Hsing-shih heng-yen*, vol. 2, *chüan* 21, p. 462, l. 6; *Shui-hu ch'üan-chuan*, vol. 2, ch. 52, p. 865, l. 5; *San Sui p'ing-yao chuan*, *chüan* 1, ch. 3, p. 28a, l. 3; *Hsi-yu chi*, vol. 1, ch. 28, p. 318, l. 2; *San-pao t'ai-chien Hsi-yang chi t'ung-su yen-i*, vol. 2, ch. 55, p. 708, l. 7; and *Ta-T'ang Ch'in-wang tz'u-hua*, vol. 1, *chüan* 3, ch. 20, p. 42b, ll. 2–3. It also recurs in the *Chin P'ing Mei tz'u-hua*, vol. 4, ch. 62, p. 15b, l. 11; and ch. 66, p. 6b, l. 8.

30. This four-character expression for a genielike Taoist deity that takes human form and serves its summoner occurs in *I-chien chih* (Records of I-chien), comp. Hung Mai (1123–1202), 4 vols. (Peking: Chung-hua shu-chü, 1981), vol. 4, *san-chih, jen* (third record, section nine), *chüan* 3, p. 1490, l. 9; the early vernacular story *Cheng Chieh-shih li-kung shen-pi kung* (Commissioner Cheng wins merit with his magic bow), in *Hsing-shih heng-yen*, vol. 2, *chüan* 31, p. 659, l. 3; *Yüan-ch'ü hsüan wai-pien*, 3:961, l. 18; *Shui-hu ch'üan-chuan*, vol. 2, ch. 53, p. 885, l. 17; *Pei Sung chih-chuan*, vol. 2, *chüan* 3, p. 3b, l. 2; and *San-pao t'ai-chien Hsi-yang chi t'ung-su yen-i*, vol. 1, ch. 26, p. 344, l. 4.

31. This line occurs in *Lo-yang san-kuai chi*, p. 76, l. 14; *I-k'u kuei lai tao-jen ch'u-kuai*, p. 194, l. 17; and *Shui-hu ch'üan-chuan*, vol. 4, ch. 88, p. 1444, l. 8.

32. See Roy, *The Plum in the Golden Vase*, vol. 3, chap. 55, n. 37.

33. The Taoists believed that there were thirty-six grotto heavens and seventy-two blessed abodes on the earth, which were inhabited by immortals. This four-character expression occurs ubiquitously in Chinese literature. See, e.g., the title of a preface to a work on this subject written by Tu Kuang-t'ing (850–933) in 901, *Ch'üan T'ang wen* (Complete prose of the T'ang), 20 vols. (Kyoto: Chūbun shuppan-sha, 1976), vol. 19, *chüan* 932, p. 4b, l. 7; the title to *chüan* 27 of *Yün-chi ch'i ch'ien* (Seven lots from the bookbag of the clouds), comp. Chang Chün-fang (c. 965–c. 1045), ed. and annot. Chiang Li-sheng et al. (Peking: Hua-hsia ch'u-pan she, 1996), p. 153, l. 1; a poem by P'eng Ju-li (1042–95), *Ch'üan Sung shih*, 16:10449, l. 17; a poem by Fan T'ang (cs 1073), ibid., 16:11139, l. 1; a poem by Huang T'ing-chien (1045–1105), ibid., 17:11740, l. 4; a prose essay by Ch'en Liang (1143–94), in *Ch'en Liang chi [tseng-ting pen]* (Collected works of Ch'en Liang [augmented and revised edition]), ed. Teng Kuang-ming, 2 vols. (Peking: Chung-hua shu-chü, 1987), vol. 2. *chüan* 25, p. 280, l. 9; the title of a set of poems by Ch'iu Ch'u-chi (1148–1227), *Ch'üan Chin shih*, 2:164, l. 8; an essay by Yeh Shao-weng (c. 1175–c. 1230), in *Ssu-ch'ao wen-chien lu* (A record of things heard and seen during four reigns), by Yeh Shao-weng (Peking: Chung-hua shu-chü, 1997), *wu-chi* (fifth collection), p. 185, l. 8; a song suite by Teng Yü-pin (13th century), *Ch'üan Yüan san-ch'ü*, 1:305, l. 10; an anonymous Yüan dynasty lyric, *Ch'üan Chin Yüan tz'u*, 2:1281, lower register, l. 15; *Yüan-ch'ü hsüan*, 3:1101, l. 5; *Yüan-ch'ü hsüan wai-pien*, 2:699, l. 11; the tsa-chü drama *Ch'ung-mo-tzu tu-pu Ta-lo T'ien* (Ch'ung-mo tzu ascends to the Grand Veil Heaven), by Chu Ch'üan (1378–1448), in *Ku-pen Yüan Ming tsa-chü*, vol. 2, scene 1, p. 1a, l. 4; the anonymous Ming tsa-chü drama *Li Yün-ch'ing te-wu sheng-chen* (Li Yün-ch'ing attains enlightenment and achieves transcendence), in *Ku-pen Yüan Ming tsa-chü*, vol. 4, scene 4, p. 15a, l. 14; *P'o-yao chi, chüan* 2, scene 29, p. 44a, l. 8; *Pai-t'u chi*, scene 21, p. 59, l. 6; *Yü-huan chi*, scene 15, p. 55, l. 1; a lyric by Ku Hsün (1418–1505), *Ch'üan Ming tz'u*, 1:292, lower register, l. 2; a song suite by Wang Ao (1450–1524), *Ch'üan Ming san-ch'ü*, 1:433, l. 1; a song suite by Chu Ying-teng (1477–1526), ibid., 2:1238, l. 6; a song suite by Hsing I-feng (1509–c. 1572), ibid., 2:1887, l. 6; *Hai-fu shan-t'ang tz'u-kao, chüan* 2a, p. 96, l. 2; the tsa-chü drama *Seng-ni kung-fan* (A monk and a nun violate their vows), by Feng Wei-min (1511–80), in *Ming-jen tsa-chü hsüan*, scene 1, p. 337, l. 7; *Hsi-yu chi*, vol. 1, ch. 30, p. 347, l. 8; *San-pao t'ai-chien Hsi-yang chi t'ung-su yen-i*, vol. 1, ch. 1, p. 10, l. 5; a song suite by Wang Chih-teng (1535–1612), *Ch'üan Ming san-ch'ü*, 3:2914, l. 5; *Ta-T'ang Ch'in-wang tz'u-hua*, vol. 1, *chüan* 4, p. 2b, l. 3; and an abundance of other occurrences, too numerous to list.

34. These eight lines are derived, with some textual variation, from passages in *Lo-yang san-kuai chi*, p. 76, ll. 15–16; and *I-k'u kuei lai tao-jen ch'u-kuai*, p. 195, ll. 1–2.

35. This couplet occurs in *Shui-hu ch'üan-chuan*, vol. 2, ch. 53, p. 887, l. 13.

36. This line occurs in ibid., vol. 2, ch. 53, p. 887, l. 14.

37. This four-character expression occurs in *Huan-sha chi*, scene 41, p. 145, l. 2; and the anonymous ch'uan-ch'i drama *Chü-ting chi* (Lifting the tripod), in *Ku-pen hsi-ch'ü ts'ung-k'an, ch'u-chi*, item 39, scene 8, p. 18a, l. 10.

38. Versions of this formulaic couplet, with only an insignificant variant in the second line, occur in *I-k'u kuei lai tao-jen ch'u-kuai*, p. 194, l. 5; and *Ta-t'ang Ch'in-wang tz'u-hua*, vol. 1, *chüan* 1, ch. 6, p. 65a, ll. 8–9. It also recurs in the same form as it does here in the *Chin P'ing Mei tz'u-hua*, vol. 4, ch. 71, p. 16b, l. 4.

39. This four-character expression occurs in a song suite by Ku Cheng-i (fl. 1575–96), *Ch'üan Ming san-ch'ü*, 3:3158, l. 7.

40. A variant of this couplet occurs in *Hsi-hu san-t'a chi*, p. 31, l. 8. It recurs in the same form as it does here in the *Chin P'ing Mei tz'u-hua*, vol. 4, ch. 71, p. 17a, ll. 5–6.

41. This is a verbatim quotation from the *Lun-yü* (The analects of Confucius). See *Lun-yü yin-te* (A concordance to the *Analects*) (Taipei: Chinese Materials and Research Aids Service Center, 1966), p. 4, book 3, paragraph 13. It also occurs in *Ming-hsin pao-chien*, *chüan* 1, p. 3b, l. 2; *San-kuo chih t'ung-su yen-i*, vol. 2, *chüan* 16, p. 753, l. 17; the tsa-chü drama *Tung-t'ien hsüan-chi* (Mysterious record of the grotto heaven), attributed to Yang Shen (1488–1559), in *Ku-pen Yüan Ming tsa-chü*, vol. 2, scene 2, p. 7a, l. 14; and *Hsi-yu chi*, vol. 1, ch. 8, p. 85, ll. 13–14. The four-character expression that forms the first half of this line also occurs independently in *San-kuo chih t'ung-su yen-i*, vol. 1, *chüan* 2, p. 98, ll. 18–19; *Mu-lien chiu-mu ch'üan-shan hsi-wen*, *chüan* 1, p. 74a, l. 2; and the Ming novel *Yang chia fu shih-tai chung-yung yen-i chih-chuan* (Popular chronicle of the generations of loyal and brave exploits of the Yang household), pref. dated 1606, 2 vols., fac. repr. (Taipei: Kuo-li chung-yang t'u-shu kuan, 1971), vol. 1, *chüan* 1, p. 18b, l. 3.

42. This four-character expression occurs in the biography of Hsieh Hsüan (343–88) in *Chin shu* (History of the Chin dynasty [265–420]), comp. Fang Hsüan-ling (578–648) et al., 10 vols. (Peking: Chung-hua shu-chü, 1974), vol. 7, *chüan* 79, p. 2082, l. 12; *Ch'ing-so kao-i* (Lofty sentiments from the green latticed windows), comp. Liu Fu (fl. 1040–1113) (Shanghai: Ku-tien wen-hsüeh ch'u-pan she, 1958), *pieh-chi* (supplementary collection), *chüan* 3, p. 200, l. 14; *I-chien chih*, vol. 1, *i-chih* (second collection), *chüan* 10, p. 269, l. 2; a postface, dated 1276, to his autobiographical *Chih-nan lu* (Record of my flight to the south), by Wen T'ien-hsiang (1236–83), *Wen T'ien-hsiang ch'üan-chi* (The complete works of Wen T'ien-hsiang), ed. and annot. Hsiung Fei, Ch'i Shen-ch'i, and Huang Shun-ch'iang (Nan-ch'ang: Chiang-hsi jen-min ch'u-pan she, 1987), *chüan* 13, p. 479, l. 9; and *Chien-teng hsin-hua* (New wick-trimming tales), by Ch'ü Yu (1341–1427), in *Chien-teng hsin-hua [wai erh-chung]*, *chüan* 3, p. 79, l. 11.

43. This four-character expression recurs in the *Chin P'ing Mei tz'u-hua*, vol. 4, ch. 70, p. 4a, l. 1.

44. This four-character expression occurs in an anecdote about Ts'ui Hsüan (cs 827) in the lost work *Nan-ch'u hsin-wen* (News about Southern Ch'u), by Yü-ch'ih Shu (9th century), as quoted in *T'ai-p'ing kuang-chi* (Extensive gleanings from the reign of Great

Tranquility), comp. Li Fang (925–96) et al., first printed in 981, 10 vols. (Peking: Chung-hua shu-chü, 1961), vol. 4, *chüan* 175, p. 1303, l. 13; and *I-chien chih*, vol. 1, *i-chih* (second collection), *chüan* 19, p. 352, l. 2.

45. This four-character expression occurs in *[Chi-p'ing chiao-chu] Hsi-hsiang chi*, play no. 4, scene 4, p. 167, l. 13; a song by Kao K'o-li (14th century), *Ch'üan Yüan san-ch'ü*, 2:1082, l. 11; *San-kuo chih t'ung-su yen-i*, vol. 2, *chüan* 18, p. 845, l. 5; a set of songs by Ch'en To (fl. early 16th century), *Ch'üan Ming san-ch'ü*, 1:475, l. 8; a song suite by Yang Shen (1488–1559), ibid., 2:1454, l. 4; and *I-hsia chi*, scene 24, p. 63, l. 6.

46. This idiomatic expression occurs in *Yüan-ch'ü hsüan*, 3:1138, l. 17.

47. A variant of these two lines occurs in *Pai-chia kung-an*, *chüan* 8, ch. 66, p. 6a, l. 7. The entire second line occurs verbatim in *Pei Sung chih-chuan*, vol. 2, *chüan* 2, p. 17a, l. 12. The formulaic four-character expression at the end of the second line occurs ubiquitously in Chinese literature. See, e.g., a poem by Lu Yen-jang (cs 900), *Ch'üan T'ang shih*, vol. 11, *chüan* 715, p. 8213, l. 8; a poem by Chang Pi (10th century), ibid., vol. 11, *chüan* 742, p. 8450, l. 8; a poem by Lu To-hsün (934–85), *Ch'üan Sung shih*, 1:259, l. 13; a lyric by Yen Shu (991–1055), *Ch'üan Sung tz'u*, 1:90, upper register, ll. 13–14; a set of poems by Shao Yung (1011–77) written in 1068, *Ch'üan Sung shih*, 7:4502, l. 10; an anecdote about Su Shih (1037–1101) set in 1099, *Hou-cheng lu* (A patrician potpourri), by Chao Ling-chih (1051–1134), in *Pi-chi hsiao-shuo ta-kuan* (Great collectanea of note-form literature), 17 vols. (Yang-chou: Chiang-su Kuang-ling ku-chi k'o-yin she, 1984), vol. 4, *ts'e* 8, *chüan* 7, p. 5a, ll. 9–10; an anecdote in *Tung-ku so chien* (Observations of Tung-ku), by Li Chih-yen (13th century), author's pref. dated 1268, in *Shuo-fu san-chung*, 6:3428, p. 19a, ll. 8–9; a song by Tseng Jui (c. 1260–c. 1330), *Ch'üan Yüan san-ch'ü*, 1:493, ll. 4–5; a lyric by Kuan Yün-shih (1286–1324), *Ch'üan Chin Yüan tz'u*, 2:950, lower register, l. 9; *Yüan-ch'ü hsüan*, 2:828, l. 3; *Yüan-ch'ü hsüan wai-pien*, 3:744, l. 1; *Cheng Chieh-shih li-kung shen-pi kung*, p. 667, l. 1; the early vernacular story *Su Ch'ang-kung Chang-t'ai Liu chuan* (The story of Su Shih [1037–1101] and the courtesan Chang-t'ai Liu), in *Hsiung Lung-feng ssu-chung hsiao-shuo*, p. 27, ll. 10–11; *Chien-teng yü-hua*, *chüan* 2, p. 192, l. 7; *Wu Lun-ch'üan Pei*, *chüan* 3, scene 18, p. 17a, l. 5; a set of songs by P'eng Tse (cs 1490), *Ch'üan Ming san-ch'ü*, 1:837, l. 13; *Hsiu-ju chi*, scene 17, p. 46, l. 12; *Shui-hu ch'üan-chuan*, vol. 4, ch. 105, p. 1601, l. 3; *Chiang Shih yüeh-li chi*, *chüan* 3, scene 32, p. 20b, l. 3; a lyric by Chou Yung (1476–1547), *Ch'üan Ming tz'u*, 2:596, lower register, l. 6; a lyric by Hsia Yen (1483–1548), ibid., 2:692, lower register, l. 10; *Pao-chien chi*, scene 8, p. 19, l. 4; *Huan-sha chi*, scene 2, p. 3, l. 2; *Mu-lien chiu-mu ch'üan-shan hsi-wen*, *chüan* 2, p. 32a, l. 6; and an abundance of other occurrences, too numerous to list. It also recurs in the *Chin P'ing Mei tz'u-hua*, vol. 5, ch. 91, p. 1a, l. 7.

48. Variants of this proverbial couplet occur in *Chang Hsieh chuang-yüan*, scene 9, p. 50, ll. 14–15; *Yüan-ch'ü hsüan*, 3:1024, ll. 17–18; *Sha-kou chi*, scene 24, p. 93, l. 1; *Pai Niang-tzu yung-chen Lei-feng T'a*, p. 444, l. 2; *[Hsin-pien] Liu Chih-yüan huan-hsiang Pai-t'u chi*, p. 25b, l. 5; the ch'uan-ch'i drama *Pai-she chi* (The story of the white snake), by Cheng Kuo-hsüan (14th century), in *Ku-pen hsi-ch'ü ts'ung-k'an*, ch'u-chi, item 43, *chüan* 2, scene 31, p. 33a, l. 10; *Shih Chen-jen ssu-sheng so pai-yüan*, scene 3, p. 9b, ll. 4–5; *Chin-ch'ai chi*, scene 25, p. 48, ll. 10–11; *Yüeh Fei p'o-lu tung-ch'uang chi*, *chüan* 2, scene 23, p. 5b, l. 4; *Ch'ien-chin chi*, scene 29, p. 99, l. 7; *Huan-tai chi*, *chüan* 2, scene 27, p. 16a, l. 6; *Hsün-ch'in chi*, scene 15, p. 51, ll. 10–11; *Tuan-fa chi*, *chüan* 1, scene 6, p. 14a, l. 3; *Pa-i chi*, scene 36, p. 76, ll. 5–6; *Mu-lien chiu-mu ch'üan-shan*

hsi-wen, chüan 2, p. 20b, l. 3; *Hsi-yu chi*, vol. 2, ch. 76, p. 872, ll. 11–12; *San-pao t'ai-chien Hsi-yang chi t'ung-su yen-i*, vol. 1, ch. 25, p. 332, l. 14; and the *Chin P'ing Mei tz'u-hua*, vol. 4, ch. 74, p. 14b, ll. 5–6.

49. A synonymous variant of this four-character expression occurs in *Tung Chieh-yüan Hsi-hsiang chi, chüan* 8, p. 163, l. 8. It recurs in the same form as it does here in the *Chin P'ing Mei tz'u-hua*, vol. 4, ch. 65, p. 8a, ll. 2–3.

50. The *Heart Sutra*, which is less than a page in length, is a radically succinct epitome of Mahayana Buddhist prajñāpāramitā, or "Perfection of Wisdom," literature that was introduced into China during the Six Dynasties period (222–589) and has been described as the single most commonly recited and studied scripture in East Asian Buddhism. It was translated into Chinese many times, but the best-known rendition is that by the famous Buddhist pilgrim Hsüan-tsang (602–64). For a study of this text, see Donald S. Lopez, Jr., *Elaborations on Emptiness: Uses of the Heart Sutra* (Princeton: Princeton University Press, 1996).

51. This is a Buddhist work introduced into China during the Six Dynasties period (222–589) that was translated into Chinese at least three times between 617 and 707, one of these translations, completed in 650, being by Hsüan-tsang (602–64). For a study of this work, which includes English translations of two of the Chinese versions, including the one by Hsüan-tsang, see Raoul Birnbaum, *The Healing Buddha* (Boston: Shambhala, 1989).

52. This is the abbreviated title of a Taoist work, probably dating from the T'ang dynasty (618–907), included in *Cheng-t'ung Tao-tsang, ts'e* 181. See the description by John Lagerwey, in Kristofer Schipper and Franciscus Verellen, eds., *The Taoist Canon: A Historical Companion to the Daozang*, 3 vols. (Chicago: University of Chicago Press, 2004), 1:561. There are two other Taoist works with titles that contain these three characters. See ibid., 2:961; and 2:1226.

53. See Roy, *The Plum in the Golden Vase*, vol. 3, chap. 59, n. 100.

54. This text was put into its current form by the Sung dynasty T'ien-t'ai master Chih-li (960–1028) and continues to be performed until the present day. For a discussion of this work, see Chün-fang Yü, *Kuan-yin: The Chinese Transformation of Avalokiteśvara* (New York: Columbia University Press, 2001), chap. 7, pp. 263–91, and passim.

55. See Roy, *The Plum in the Golden Vase*, vol. 3, chap. 59, n. 98.

56. See ibid., chap. 59, n. 96.

57. See ibid., n. 97.

58. See ibid., chap. 46, n. 62.

59. There was a court painter named Han Jo-cho (fl. 1111–25), who was highly esteemed at the time for his meticulous paintings of birds and was also regarded as an excellent portraitist. See *Chung-kuo mei-shu chia jen-ming tz'u-tien* (Biographical dictionary of Chinese artists), comp. Yü Chien-hua (Shanghai: Jen-min mei-shu ch'u-pan she, 1981), p. 1482.

60. This idiomatic four-character expression recurs in the *Chin P'ing Mei tz'u-hua*, vol. 4, ch. 75, p. 18a, l. 11.

61. A garbled version of this four-character expression, in which the last two characters appear in reverse order, occurs in *Chieh-chih-erh chi*, p. 251, l. 9. It occurs in the same form as in the novel in *Hsi-yu chi*, vol. 1, ch. 2, p. 13, l. 9.

62. For an interpretation of the significance of this speech of Hsi-men Ch'ing's, see Roy, *The Plum in the Golden Vase*, vol. 1, appendix 1, p. 432, ll. 16–25.

63. This idiomatic expression for death recurs in the *Chin P'ing Mei tz'u-hua*, vol. 4, ch. 80, p. 2b, ll. 7–8; and, in a truncated form, in ibid., ch. 80, p. 10b, l. 2.

64. This couplet occurs in *Yüan-ch'ü hsüan wai-pien*, 3:725, l. 19. It is from an anonymous Yüan-Ming tsa-chü drama and alludes to the famous "Oath in the Peach Orchard" among Liu Pei (161–223), Kuan Yü (160–219), and Chang Fei (d. 221). See Roy, *The Plum in the Golden Vase*, vol. 1, chap. 16, n. 18; and vol. 2, chap. 33, n. 18.

65. This four-character expression occurs in *Hsi-yu chi*, vol. 2, ch. 64, p. 737, ll. 4–5.

66. A synonymous version of this proverbial couplet occurs in *San-pao t'ai-chien Hsi-yang chi t'ung-su yen-i*, vol. 1, ch. 39, p. 507, l. 11.

67. This four-character expression occurs in *Wu Lun-ch'üan Pei*, *chüan* 1, scene 8, p. 38b, l. 1; *Hua-ying chi*, p. 921, l. 12; and the ch'uan-ch'i drama *Mu-tan t'ing* (The peony pavilion), by T'ang Hsien-tsu (1550–1616), ed. and annot. Hsü Shuo-fang and Yang Hsiao-mei (Peking: Chung-hua shu-chü, 1959), scene 25, p. 137, l. 4.

68. See the text of the *Hsiao-ching*, in *Shih-san ching ching-wen*, p. 4, ll. 13–14; and *The Hsiao Ching*, trans. Mary Lelia Makra (New York: St. John's University Press, 1971), p. 39, ll. 9–11.

CHAPTER 63

1. It is alleged that there are twelve jasper terraces clustered on the summit of Mount K'un-lun, the mythological mountain that connects Heaven and Earth. See *Shih-i chi* (Salvaged records of the marvelous), comp. Wang Chia (4th century), ed. and annot. Ch'i Chih-p'ing (Peking: Chung-hua shu-chü, 1981), *chüan* 10, p. 221, l. 12. This four-character expression occurs ubiquitously in later Chinese literature. See, e.g., a poem by Ch'en Hsiang (1017–80), *Ch'üan Sung shih*, 8:5096, l. 13; a quatrain by Hua Chen (b. 1051, cs 1079), ibid., 18:12370, l. 4; a lyric by Ch'en Te-wu (13th century), *Ch'üan Sung tz'u*, 5:3453, lower register, l. 10; the thirteenth-century prosimetric narrative *T'ien-pao i-shih chu-kung-tiao* (Medley in various modes on the forgotten events of the T'ien-pao [742–56] reign period), by Wang Po-ch'eng (fl. late 13th century), in *Chu-kung-tiao liang-chung* (Two exemplars of the medley in various modes), ed. and annot. Ling Ching-yen and Hsieh Po-yang (N.p.: Ch'i-Lu shu-she, 1988), p. 231, l. 13; a lyric by Ku A-ying (1310–69), written in 1350, *Ch'üan Chin Yüan tz'u*, 2:1124, lower register, l. 1; *Yüan-ch'ü hsüan*, 3:1086, ll. 2–3; *Yüan-ch'ü hsüan wai-pien*, 2:553, l. 6; *Li Yün-ch'ing te-wu sheng-chen*, scene 3, p. 11a, l. 8; and an anonymous song suite in *Yung-hsi yüeh-fu*, ts'e 9, p. 47b, ll. 4–5.

2. According to a note by Po Chü-i (772–846), appended to a ballad composed in 809, when Li Chi (594–669) was sick, a doctor told him that only the ashes of a dragon's beard could cure him, whereupon Emperor T'ai-tsung (r. 626–49) cut off his own beard to make a medicine that did, in fact, restore him to health. See *Ch'üan T'ang shih*, vol. 7, *chüan* 426, p. 4690, l. 4. This allusion is but one of the many that suggest that Hsi-men Ch'ing should be viewed as a surrogate for a sovereign.

3. See Roy, *The Plum in the Golden Vase*, vol. 3, chap. 46, n. 50.

4. See ibid., vol. 1, chap. 6, n. 4.

5. This four-character expression occurs in *Ta-Sung chung-hsing yen-i* (The romance of the restoration of the great Sung dynasty), by Hsiung Ta-mu (mid-16th century), 8 *chüan* (Chien-yang: Ch'ing-pai t'ang, 1552), fac. repr. in *Ku-pen hsiao-shuo ts'ung-k'an, ti san-shih ch'i chi* (Collectanea of rare editions of traditional fiction, thirty-seventh series) (Peking: Chung-hua shu-chü, 1991), vol. 1, *chüan* 1, p. 22a, l. 3; and *Hua-shen san-miao chuan*, p. 51a, l. 5.

6. This four-character expression occurs in *Feng-yüeh hsiang-ssu*, p. 80, l. 15; and the novel *Nan Sung chih-chuan* (Chronicle of the Sung conquest of the south), attributed to Hsiung Ta-mu (mid-16th century), 10 *chüan* (Nanking: Shih-te t'ang, 1593), fac. repr. in *Ku-pen hsiao-shuo ts'ung-k'an, ti san-shih ssu chi*, vol. 1, *chüan* 3, p. 14b, l. 10.

7. Variants of this idiomatic expression for a lifelike portrayal occur in *K'an p'i-hsüeh tan-cheng Erh-lang Shen*, p. 245, l. 13; *San-pao t'ai-chien Hsi-yang chi t'ung-su yen-i*, vol. 1, ch. 2, p. 25, l. 14; *Mu-tan t'ing*, scene 26, p. 139, l. 6; and the *Chin P'ing Mei tz'u-hua*, vol. 4, ch. 63, p. 7b, l. 6.

8. This four-character expression occurs in *Yüan-ch'ü hsüan*, 3:1138, l. 5; *Huai-hsiang chi*, scene 38, p. 126, l. 7; and *San-pao t'ai-chien Hsi-yang chi t'ung-su yen-i*, vol. 1, ch. 14, p. 174, l. 9. It also recurs in the *Chin P'ing Mei tz'u-hua*, vol. 4, ch. 74, p. 15a, l. 1; ch. 79, p. 23b, l. 2; and vol. 5, ch. 100, p. 6a, l. 10.

9. This four-character expression occurs in a memorial by Chu Hsi (1130–1200), in *Hui-an hsien-sheng Chu Wen-kung wen-chi* (The collected literary works of Chu Hsi [1130–1200]), *Ssu-pu pei-yao* ed. (Shanghai: Chung-hua shu-chü, 1936), *chüan* 11, p. 11a, l. 9; *Ch'üan-Han chih-chuan*, vol. 2, *chüan* 6, p. 12a, l. 13; and *Pai-chia kung-an*, *chüan* 4, ch. 39, p. 16b, l. 11.

10. This was a plank with seven holes, presumably for drainage, arranged in the pattern of the stars of the Big Dipper. Its use is attested as early as the sixth century. See *Yen-shih chia-hsün [chi-chieh]* (Family Instructions for the Yen clan [with collected commentaries]), by Yen Chih-t'ui (531–91), ed. Wang Li-ch'i (Shanghai: Shang-hai ku-chi ch'u-pan she, 1980), *chüan* 7, ch. 20, p. 536, l. 9; and *Family Instructions for the Yen Clan*, by Yen Chih-t'ui (531–91), trans. Teng Ssu-yü (Leiden: E. J. Brill, 1968), p. 210, ll. 20–21. For further details, see De Groot, *The Religious System of China*, 1:90–91 and 317–18.

11. Tu Tzu-ch'un is the eponymous protagonist of a famous T'ang dynasty literary tale entitled *Tu Tzu-ch'un*, which is attributed to Niu Seng-ju (779–847). See *T'ai-p'ing kuang-chi*, vol. 1, *chüan* 16, pp. 109–112; and James R. Hightower, trans. "Tu Tzu-ch'un," in *Traditional Chinese Stories: Themes and Variations*, ed. Y. W. Ma and Joseph S. M. Lau (New York: Columbia University Press, 1978), pp. 416–19. The introduction of this well-known fictional character into the story is probably intended to reflect ironically on Hsi-men Ch'ing. In the literary tale, Tu Tzu-ch'un is a wastrel who is finally induced to repent and seek immortality by a mysterious stranger. After stoically undergoing a series of harrowing tests, he fails to achieve his goal in the end because he is unable to suppress his agony at seeing a vision of the cruel murder of his son. Hsi-men Ch'ing, on the other hand, is an unrepentant wastrel whose gross favoritism is the indirect cause of his son's death.

12. The text actually reads Ning-ho rather than Hsüan-ho, but I have emended it because the two characters can be easily confused orthographically, and no palace hall of that name is known, but there was a Hsüan-ho Palace Hall in the imperial precincts

during the Northern Sung dynasty. See map no. 4 in the front matter of *Sung-tai Tung-ching yen-chiu* (A study of the Eastern Capital during the Sung dynasty), by Chou Pao-chu (K'ai-feng: Ho-nan ta-hsüeh ch'u-pan she, 1992).

13. Emperor Chen-tsung of the Sung dynasty reigned from 997 to 1022, which would make Tu Tzu-ch'un a very old man indeed in 1117, when this event takes place in the story. It is possible that this is a mistake for Emperor Shen-tsung (r. 1067–85), which would be much more plausible.

14. The text actually reads Buddhist Superior Huang rather than Lang, but I have emended it because this figure appears later as the abbot of the Pao-en Temple. See the *Chin P'ing Mei tz'u-hua*, vol. 4, ch. 65, p. 5a, l. 11; and ch. 80, pp. 1a–7b. It has also been emended in the B edition of the novel. See *[Hsin-k'o hsiu-hsiang p'i-p'ing] Chin P'ing Mei* ([Newly cut illustrated commentarial edition] of the *Chin P'ing Mei*), 2 vols. (Chi-nan: Ch'i-Lu shu-she, 1989), vol. 2, ch. 63, p. 857, l. 10.

15. See Roy, *The Plum in the Golden Vase*, vol. 1, chap. 8, n. 31.

16. This text, the standard form of the title of which is *Tz'u-pei shui-ch'an fa*, is traditionally attributed to the eminent T'ang monk Chih-hsüan (811–83). It is included in *Taishō shinshū daizōkyō* (The newly edited great Buddhist canon compiled in the Taishō reign period [1912–26]), 85 vols. (Tokyo: Taishō issaikyō kankōkai, 1922–32), vol. 45, no. 1910, pp. 967–78.

17. For illustrations of this type of headgear, worn by women of rank during the Ming dynasty, see Chou Hsi-pao, *Chung-kuo ku-tai fu-shih shih* (History of traditional Chinese costume) (Peking: Chung-kuo hsi-chü ch'u-pan she, 1984), pp. 418, 419, and 423.

18. This idiomatic expression occurs verbatim in *Mu-tan t'ing*, scene 26, p. 139, l. 6.

19. According to the traditional rules for sacrifices in the ancestral temple, the pig was referred to as "stiff-bristles" and the sheep as "soft-hair." See *Li-chi*, ch. 2, p. 8, l. 6; and *Li Chi: Book of Rites*, trans. James Legge, 2 vols. (New Hyde Park, N.Y.: University Books, 1967), vol. 1, p. 117, ll. 4–8. This four-character expression recurs in the *Chin P'ing Mei tz'u-hua*, vol. 4, ch. 64, p. 9a, l. 8.

20. This formulaic four-character expression occurs in funeral eulogies addressed to the spirits of the dead at all levels of Chinese society. See, e.g., *Han Ch'ang-li wen-chi chiao-chu* (The prose works of Han Yü with critical annotation), ed. Ma T'ung-po (Shanghai: Ku-tien wen-hsüeh ch'u-pan she, 1957), *chüan* 5, p. 186, l. 9; and *Meng Chiang nü pien-wen* (The story of Meng Chiang), in *Tun-huang pien-wen chi* (Collection of pien-wen from Tun-huang), ed. Wang Chung-min et al., 2 vols. (Peking: Jen-min wen-hsüeh ch'u-pan she, 1984), 1:34, ll. 12–13. A variant of this expression occurs in the *Chin P'ing Mei tz'u-hua*, vol. 4, ch. 64, p. 9a. l. 8; and it also recurs in the same form as it does here in ibid., vol. 4, ch. 80, p. 2b, l. 1.

21. This four-character expression occurs in *Pai-chia kung-an*, *chüan* 7, ch. 59, p. 8a, l. 2; and *Yang-chia fu shih-tai chung-yung yen-i chih-chuan*, *chüan* 1, p. 2b, l. 3.

22. See Roy, *The Plum in the Golden Vase*, vol. 2, chap. 36, n. 22.

23. See ibid., vol. 1, chap. 10, n. 15.

24. This is an allusion to the famous literary tale *Chen-chung chi* (The world inside a pillow), by Shen Chi-chi (d. c. 786), in which the protagonist lives through an entire career in a dream and dies in the end, only to discover upon awakening that the yellow millet, which the landlord of the inn at which he was staying had put on the stove to cook when he fell asleep, was not yet ready to eat. See *T'ang Sung ch'uan-ch'i chi* (An

anthology of literary tales from the T'ang and Sung dynasties), ed. Lu Hsün (Peking: Wen-hsüeh ku-chi k'an-hsing she, 1958), pp. 29–33; and William H. Nienhauser, Jr., trans., "The World Inside a Pillow," in *Traditional Chinese Stories: Themes and Variations*, pp. 435–38.

25. Variants of this expression occur in *Chang Hsieh chuang-yüan*, scene 29, p. 145, l. 17; *Yüan-ch'ü hsüan*, 2:422, ll. 17–18; *Chin-t'ung Yü-nü Chiao Hung chi*, p. 43, l. 10; and the *Chin P'ing Mei tz'u-hua*, vol. 5, ch. 99, p. 11b, l. 3.

26. This formulaic four-character expression occurs in the long sixteenth-century literary tale *T'ien-yüan ch'i-yü* (Celestial destinies remarkably fulfilled), in *Kuo-se t'ien-hsiang*, vol. 3, *chüan* 7, p. 4b, lower register, ll. 1–2.

27. This formulaic four-character expression recurs in the *Chin P'ing Mei tz'u-hua*, vol. 4, ch. 80, p. 11b, l. 11, at the end of a funeral eulogy for Hsi-men Ch'ing.

28. These two sentences occur verbatim in *Shui-hu chih-chuan p'ing-lin*, vol. 2, *chüan* 20, p. 3b, l. 3.

29. This four-character expression occurs in an essay by Wang Yü-ch'eng (954–1001), written in 999, in *Ch'üan Sung wen* (Complete prose of the Sung), comp. Tseng Tsao-chuang et al., 50 vols. (Ch'eng-tu: Pa-Shu shu-she, 1988–94), vol. 4, *chüan* 153, p. 475, l. 8.

30. See Roy, *The Plum in the Golden Vase*, vol. 3, chap. 49, n. 13.

31. See ibid., vol. 1, chap. 17, n. 3.

32. This formulaic four-character expression occurs in *Yüan-ch'ü hsüan*, 1:57, l. 6; *Ching-ch'ai chi*, scene 9, p. 27, l. 1; *Yu-kuei chi*, scene 22, p. 62, l. 9; *Shuang-chu chi*, scene 24, p. 77, l. 4; and an anonymous set of songs in *Ch'ün-yin lei-hsüan*, 4:2367, ll. 6–7.

33. The proximate source of these two paragraphs is the anonymous Ming drama *Wei Feng-hsiang ku Yü-huan chi* (The old version of Wei Kao [746–806] and the story of the jade ring), in *Ku-pen hsi-ch'ü ts'ung-k'an, ch'u-chi*, item 22, *chüan* 1, scene 6, p. 9b, ll. 6–7. Although the same episode also occurs in *Yü-huan chi*, scene 6, p. 15, ll. 5–6, the wording has been altered and is not as close to that quoted in the novel.

34. An orthographic variant of this four-character expression occurs in *Yüan-ch'ü hsüan wai-pien*, 3:988, l. 8; and the anonymous Yüan-Ming tsa-chü drama *Wang Ai-hu ta-nao Tung-p'ing fu* (Short-legged Tiger Wang creates a ruckus in Tung-p'ing prefecture), in *Ku-pen Yüan Ming tsa-chü*, vol. 3, scene 1, p. 2b, ll. 10–11. It occurs in the same form as in the novel in *Hsiao fu-jen chin-ch'ien tseng nien-shao*, p. 227, l. 8; a set of songs by P'eng Tse (cs 1490), *Ch'üan Ming san-ch'ü*, 1:838, l. 4; and *Shui-hu ch'üan-chuan*, vol. 4, ch. 103, p. 1586, l. 17. It also recurs in the *Chin P'ing Mei tz'u-hua*, vol. 5, ch. 96, p. 11a, l. 9.

35. See Roy, *The Plum in the Golden Vase*, vol. 3, chap. 55, n. 12.

36. The proximate source of these two lines is *Wei Feng-hsiang ku Yü-huan chi*, *chüan* 1, scene 10, p. 23b, l. 4. The same two lines also occur verbatim in *Yü-huan chi*, scene 11, p. 39, ll. 1–2.

37. This formulaic four-character expression occurs in a lyric written in 1076 by Su Shih (1037–1101), *Ch'üan Sung tz'u*, 1:280, upper register, l. 6. It occurs ubiquitously in later Chinese literature. See, e.g., a lyric by Hsiang Tzu-yin (1085–1152), ibid., 2:961, upper register, l. 16; *Tung Chieh-yüan Hsi-hsiang chi*, *chüan* 6, p. 126, l. 2; a lyric by Wang Yün (1228–1304), *Ch'üan Chin Yüan tz'u*, 2:649, upper register, l. 10; a document written by Lu Chü-jen (14th century), as quoted in *Ch'o-keng lu* (Notes

recorded during respites from the plough), by T'ao Tsung-i (c. 1316–c. 1403), pref. dated 1366 (Peking: Chung-hua shu-chü, 1980), *chüan* 12, p. 147, ll. 9–10; *Sha-kou chi*, scene 21, p. 78, l. 3; the title of a set of songs published in 1471, *Ch'üan Ming san-ch'ü*, 4:4528, l. 1; *Chung-ch'ing li-chi*, *chüan* 7, p. 24b, l. 15; *Shuang-chu chi*, scene 46, p. 171, l. 2; *Yüeh Fei p'o-lu tung-ch'uang chi*, *chüan* 1, scene 17, p. 27b, l. 3; a lyric by Shih Chien (1434–96), *Ch'üan Ming tz'u*, 1:341, upper register, l. 12; *Chiang Shih yüeh-li chi*, *chüan* 4, scene 40, p. 20b, l. 10; *Feng-yüeh hsiang-ssu*, p. 90, l. 8; the middle-period vernacular story *Ch'en Hsün-chien Mei-ling shih-ch'i chi* (Police chief Ch'en loses his wife in crossing the Mei-ling Range), in *Ch'ing-p'ing shan-t'ang hua-pen*, p. 132, l. 6; *Hsiu-ju chi*, scene 18, p. 49, l. 8; a song suite by Wu Kuo-pao (cs 1550), *Ch'üan Ming san-ch'ü*, 2:2287, l. 4; *Yen-chih chi*, *chüan* 1, scene 1, p. 1a, l. 6; *Su Ying huang-hou ying-wu chi*, *chüan* 1, scene 1, p. 1a, l. 4; and an abundance of other occurrences, too numerous to list.

38. A synonymous variant of this four-character expression occurs in a literary tale entitled *Tseng Chi-heng*, by P'ei Hsing (825–80), in *P'ei Hsing Ch'uan-ch'i* (P'ei Hsing's [825–80] Tales of the marvelous), ed. and annot. Chou Leng-ch'ieh (Shanghai: Shanghai ku-chi ch'u-pan she, 1980), p. 78, l. 23; *Yüan-ch'ü hsüan*, 2:516, ll. 3–4; and *Chien-teng yü-hua*, *chüan* 2, p. 200, l. 8.

39. This four-character expression occurs in a song suite by Yang Li-chai (14th century), *Ch'üan Yüan san-ch'ü*, 2:1273, l. 4; *Ching-ch'ai chi*, scene 39, p. 116, l. 10; *Shuang-chu chi*, scene 19, p. 61, l. 1; and the ch'uan-ch'i drama *Tzu-ch'ai chi* (The story of the purple hairpin), by T'ang Hsien-tsu (1550–1616), ed. and annot. Hu Shih-ying (Peking: Jen-min wen-hsüeh ch'u-pan she, 1982), scene 46, p. 174, l. 15. These two lines occur together, but in reversed order, in *Chang Hsieh chuang-yüan*, scene 25, p. 128, l. 16; *Ching-ch'ai chi*, scene 45, p. 131, l. 5; and *Chieh-chih-erh chi*, p. 253, l. 9.

CHAPTER 64

1. This couplet is derived, with some textual variation, from one in a famous untitled poem by Li Shang-yin (c. 813–58). See *Ch'üan T'ang shih*, vol. 8, *chüan* 539, p. 6168, l. 16; and *The Poetry of Li Shang-yin*, trans. James J. Y. Liu (Chicago: University of Chicago Press, 1969), p. 66, ll. 5–6.

2. This four-character expression occurs in *Chin-ch'ai chi*, scene 14, p. 29, l. 12; a song suite by Chu Yu-tun (1379–1439), *Ch'üan Ming san-ch'ü*, 1:377, l. 10; a song by Wang Chiu-ssu (1468–1551), ibid., 1:913, l. 10; an anonymous song suite in *Yung-hsi yüeh-fu*, ts'e 14, p. 37b, l. 1; and a song suite in *Ch'ün-yin lei-hsüan*, 4:2235, l. 6.

3. The proximate source of this poem, with some textual variation in the third couplet, is the long mid-Ming literary tale *Huai-ch'un ya-chi* (Elegant vignettes of spring yearning), in *Yen-chü pi-chi* (Lin Chin-yang), vol. 3, *chüan* 10, p. 35a, upper register, ll. 9–12.

4. This formulaic four-character expression occurs ubiquitously in Chinese vernacular literature. See, e.g., a lyric by Chou Pang-yen (1056–1121), *Ch'üan Sung tz'u*, 2:604, upper register, l. 16; a quatrain by the Buddhist monk Huai-shen (1077–1132), *Ch'üan Sung shih*, 24:16153, l. 19; a lyric by Chang Yüan-kan (b. 1091), *Ch'üan Sung tz'u*, 2:1081, upper register, l. 4; a lyric by Chu Shu-chen (fl. 1078–1138), ibid., 2:1407, upper register, l. 12; a song by Chang Yang-hao (1270–1329), *Ch'üan Yüan san-ch'ü*,

1:415, l. 10; a song suite by Lü Chih-an (14th century), ibid., 2:1130, l. 12; *Yüan-ch'ü hsüan*, 3:1247, l. 5; *Yüan-ch'ü hsüan wai-pien*, 2:453, l. 19; a lyric by Hsieh Ying-fang (1296–1392), *Ch'üan Ming tz'u*, 1:2, lower register, l. 4; a song suite by Chu Yu-tun (1379–1439), *Ch'üan Ming san-ch'ü*, 1:366, l. 9; *Shen-hsiang ch'üan-pien*, chüan 640, p. 12a, l. 9; a lyric by Ku Hsün (1418–1505), *Ch'üan Ming tz'u*, 1:295, upper register, l. 11; a song suite by Ch'ang Lun (1493–1526), *Ch'üan Ming san-ch'ü*, 2:1556, l. 13; *Hsiu-ju chi*, scene 8, p. 18, l. 5; *Chiang Shih yüeh-li chi*, chüan 4, scene 39, p. 16b, l. 9; *Pao-chien chi*, scene 35, p. 64, l. 14; a set of songs by Hsia Yen (1482–1548), *Ch'üan Ming san-ch'ü*, 2:1299, l. 12; a song suite by Chang Huan (1486–1561), ibid., 2:1341, l. 10; a song suite by Wang K'o-tu (c. 1526–c. 1594), ibid., 2:2475, l. 7; and an abundance of other occurrences, too numerous to list.

5. This four-character expression occurs in a speech attributed to the Buddhist monk K'o-wen (1025–1102), *Wu-teng hui-yüan*, vol. 3, chüan 17, p. 1114, l. 6; a speech attributed to the Buddhist monk Chih-yü (1185–1269), *Hsü-t'ang Ho-shang yü-lu* (Recorded sayings of the Monk Hsü-t'ang), in *Taishō shinshū daizōkyō*, vol. 47, no. 2000, chüan 2, p. 994, lower register, l. 15; and a set of songs by Hsüeh Lun-tao (c. 1531–c. 1600), *Ch'üan Ming san-ch'ü*, 3:2766, l. 2. It also recurs in the *Chin P'ing Mei tz'u-hua*, vol. 5, ch. 88, p. 1a, l. 10; and ch. 100, p. 9b, l. 3.

6. Variants of this formulaic couplet occur in *Yüan-ch'ü hsüan*, 4:1313, l. 4; *Yüan-ch'ü hsüan wai-pien*, 3:963, ll. 12–13; *Yu-kuei chi*, scene 7, p. 14, l. 6; *Chin-ch'ai chi*, scene 47, p. 86, ll. 21–22; *Ch'ien-chin chi*, scene 13, p. 43, l. 11; the anonymous Ming ch'uan-ch'i drama *Ku-ch'eng chi* (The reunion at Ku-ch'eng), in *Ku-pen hsi-ch'ü ts'ung-k'an, ch'u-chi*, item 25, chüan 2, scene 20, p. 11a, l. 6; *Nan Sung chih-chuan*, vol. 1, chüan 3, p. 29a, l. 3; *Lieh-kuo chih-chuan*, vol. 3, chüan 8, p. 54a, l. 9; *Ch'üan-Han chih-chuan*, vol. 2, chüan 1, p. 7a, l. 8; *Hsi-yu chi*, vol. 2, ch. 92, p. 1049, l. 13; *Shuang-lieh chi*, scene 34, p. 95, l. 7; *Ch'eng-yün chuan* (The story of the assumption of the mandate [by the Yung-lo emperor]), in *Ku-pen hsiao-shuo ts'ung-k'an, ti-pa chi*, vol. 3, chüan 2, p. 2b, l. 4; *San-pao t'ai-chien Hsi-yang chi t'ung-su yen-i*, vol. 1, ch. 40, p. 517, l. 5; *I-hsia chi*, scene 32, p. 84, ll. 10–11; *Ta-T'ang Ch'in-wang tz'u-hua*, vol. 1, chüan 4, ch. 27, p. 27a, ll. 6–7; and the *Chin P'ing Mei tz'u-hua*, vol. 4, ch. 69, p. 16b, ll. 3–4; and vol. 5, ch. 81, p. 5b, l. 8. Variants in which the two lines occur in reverse order occur in *Yüan-ch'ü hsüan*, 4:1474, l. 3; and *Pao-chien chi*, scene 46, p. 84, l. 19. The second line, as given here, occurs by itself in *Yüan-ch'ü hsüan*, 4:1632, l. 11; and *Yüan-ch'ü hsüan wai-pien*, 2:602, l. 15; and 3:746, l. 14. The couplet, as given here, also recurs in the *Chin P'ing Mei tz'u-hua*, vol. 5, ch. 84, p. 10a, l. 8.

7. This four-character expression alludes to the story of Fan Li (5th century B.C.), the principal advisor of King Kou-chien of the state of Yüeh (r. 497–465 B.C.), who is said to have retired from office after enabling the king to defeat the rival state of Wu and sailed off onto the misty waters of the Five Lakes. See *Wu Yüeh ch'un-ch'iu chu-tzu so-yin* (A concordance to the *Wu Yüeh ch'un-ch'iu*) (Hong Kong: Shang-wu yin-shu kuan, 1993), ch. 10, p. 48, l. 23. It occurs ubiquitously in Chinese literature. See, e.g., a quatrain by Liu Ch'ang-ch'ing (cs 733), *Ch'üan T'ang shih*, vol. 3, chüan 150, p. 1557, l. 14; a poem by Hsüeh Feng (cs 841), ibid., vol. 8, chüan 548, p. 6327, l. 1; a quatrain by Chao Ku (cs 844), ibid., vol. 9, chüan 550, p. 6366, l. 10; a poem by Wen T'ing-yün (c. 812–c. 870), ibid., vol. 9, chüan 578, p. 6717, l. 12; a poem by P'i Jih-hsiu (cs 867), ibid., vol. 9, chüan 613, p. 7077, l. 8; a quatrain by Wang An-shih (1021–86), *Ch'üan Sung shih*, 10:6690, l. 15; a lyric by Tseng Hsieh (d. 1173), *Ch'üan Sung tz'u*, 2:1356,

lower register, l. 16; a lyric by Hsü Yu-jen (1287–1364), *Ch'üan Chin Yüan tz'u*, 2:981, upper register, l. 3; a lyric by Ni Tsan (1301–74), *Ch'üan Ming tz'u*, 1:27, lower register, l. 14; a lyric by Wu Hung (1448–1525), ibid., 2:392, lower register, l. 12; and an abundance of other occurrences, too numerous to list.

8. This is a quotation from *Mencius*. See *Meng-tzu yin-te* (A Concordance to Meng-tzu) (Taipei: Chinese Materials and Research Aids Service Center, 1966), Book 3A, ch. 4, p. 21, l. 12; and *Mencius*, trans. D. C. Lau (Baltimore: Penguin Books, 1970), p. 104, l. 18. The same quotation also occurs without attribution in *Shuang-chu chi*, scene 39, p. 137, l. 7.

9. This four-character expression occurs in *Wu-wang fa Chou p'ing-hua*, p. 14, l. 14; *Hsi-kua chi*, scene 7, p. 622, l. 7; and *[Hsin-k'o] Shih-shang hua-yen ch'ü-lo t'an-hsiao chiu-ling, chüan* 1, p. 2b, upper register, l. 12.

10. Chien-ch'ang, located some distance south of Ch'eng-tu in Szechwan province, was famous during the Ming dynasty for the quality of its coffin boards. See *Tsang-tu*, 10:1435, p. 1b, l. 1.

11. Chen-yüan was located on an important river transportation system in Kweichow province, through which timber from southwest China was shipped to the east.

12. This was the name of another highly prized wood for the making of coffin boards during the Ming dynasty. See *Tsang-tu*, 10:1435, p. 1b, l. 2.

13. This sentence is surely intended to expose the ignorance of Ying Po-chüeh, for it hopelessly confuses the famous literary tale by T'ao Ch'ien (365–427) entitled "The Peach Blossom Spring," which is set in the Chin dynasty (265–420) rather than the T'ang, with the story of Mao-nü, or Hairy Woman, from the *Lieh-hsien chuan* (Biographies of immortals), attributed to Liu Hsiang (79–8 B.C.). See *The Poetry of T'ao Ch'ien*, trans. James Robert Hightower (London: Oxford University Press, 1970), pp. 254–58; and *A Gallery of Chinese Immortals*, trans. Lionel Giles (London: John Murray, 1948), p. 35.

14. This is an anachronism since this event actually took place in 1125, whereas in the chronology of the novel we are still in 1117. See *Huang-ch'ao pien-nien kang-mu pei-yao*, vol. 2, *chüan* 29, p. 23a, ll. 1–2; *Sung shih* (History of the Sung dynasty), comp. T'o-t'o (1313–55) et al., 40 vols. (Peking: Chung-hua shu-chü, 1977), vol. 2, *chüan* 22, p. 416, l. 5; and *Hsüan-ho i-shih*, p. 80, l. 9.

15. This four-character expression occurs in a speech attributed to Yang K'uan (d. 561), in *Pei shih* (History of the Northern dynasties [386–618]), comp. Li Yen-shou (7th century), 10 vols. (Peking: Chung-hua shu-chü, 1974), vol. 6, *chüan* 49, p. 1787, l. 2; a memorial submitted to the throne by Su Shih (1037–1101) in 1071, *Su Shih wen-chi* (Collected prose of Su Shih), by Su Shih (1037–1101), 6 vols. (Peking: Chung-hua shu-chü, 1986), vol. 2, *chüan* 25, p. 739, l. 7; *Tung-ku so chien*, 6:3424, p. 11a, ll. 2–3; *Yüan-ch'ü hsüan*, 3:863, l. 14; *Chien-teng hsin-hua, chüan* 4, p. 103, l. 7; *Ta-Sung chung-hsing yen-i*, vol. 2, *chüan* 6, p. 16a, l. 8; *T'ang-shu chih-chuan t'ung-su yen-i*, vol. 1, *chüan* 5, p. 28b, l. 11; *Ts'an-T'ang Wu-tai shih yen-i chuan*, ch. 28, p. 111, l. 6; *Sui-T'ang liang-ch'ao shih-chuan* (Historical chronicle of the Sui and T'ang dynasties), 12 *chüan*, (Su-chou: Kung Shao-shan, 1619), microfilm of unique copy in Sonkeikaku Bunko, Tokyo, *chüan* 8, p. 25b, l. 2; and *Ta-T'ang Ch'in-wang tz'u-hua*, vol. 2, *chüan* 8, ch. 63, p. 60b, l. 8.

16. This formulaic four-character expression occurs ubiquitously in Chinese vernacular literature. See, e.g., *Yüan-ch'ü hsüan*, 2:437, l. 6; *Yüan-ch'ü hsüan wai-pien*,

1:92, l. 10; *San-kuo chih p'ing-hua* (The p'ing-hua on the history of the Three King-doms), originally published in 1321–23 (Shanghai: Ku-tien wen-hsüeh ch'u-pan she, 1955), p. 1, l. 10; *Chin-ming ch'ih Wu Ch'ing feng Ai-ai*, p. 459, l. 4; *Ch'ien-t'ang meng*, p. 1a, l. 15; the early vernacular story *Chao Po-sheng ch'a-ssu yü Jen-tsung* (Chao Po-sheng encounters Emperor Jen-tsung in a tea shop), in *Ku-chin hsiao-shuo*, vol. 1, *chüan* 11, p. 165, l. 8; *Yü Chung-chü t'i-shih yü shang-huang*, p. 67, l. 13; the middle-period vernacular story *Liu Ch'i-ch'ing shih-chiu Wan-chiang Lou chi* (Liu Ch'i-ch'ing indulges in poetry and wine in the Riverside Pavilion), in *Ch'ing-p'ing shan-t'ang hua-pen*, p. 2, l. 13; *Ch'en Hsün-chien Mei-ling shih-ch'i chi*, p. 123, l. 13; the middle-period vernacular story *K'uei-kuan Yao Pien tiao Chu-ko* (At K'uei-kuan Yao Pien commemo-rates Chu-ko Liang), in *Ch'ing-p'ing shan-t'ang hua-pen*, p. 306, l. 1; the middle-period vernacular story *Cha-ch'uan Hsiao Ch'en pien Pa-wang* (In Cha-ch'uan Hsiao Ch'en rebukes the Hegemon-King), in *Ch'ing-p'ing shan-t'ang hua-pen*, p. 320, l. 3; the mid-dle-period vernacular story *Li Yüan Wu-chiang chiu chu-she* (Li Yüan saves a red snake on the Wu River), in *Ch'ing-p'ing shan-t'ang hua-pen*, p. 325, ll. 5–6; the middle-pe-riod vernacular story *Chang Sheng ts'ai-luan teng chuan* (The story of Chang Sheng and the painted phoenix lanterns), in *Hsiung Lung-feng ssu-chung hsiao-shuo*, p. 11, l. 9; *Pai-she chi, chüan* 1, scene 4, p. 8a, l. 3; the anonymous Ming tsa-chü drama *Ch'ing feng-nien Wu-kuei nao Chung K'uei* (Celebrating a prosperous year, the Five Devils plague Chung K'uei), in *Ku-pen Yüan Ming tsa-chü*, vol. 4, hsieh-tzu (wedge), p. 1b, l. 8; an anonymous set of songs published in 1471, *Ch'üan Ming san-ch'ü*, 4:4509, l. 2; *P'o-yao chi, chüan* 2, scene 16, p. 1b, l. 6; *Huai-hsiang chi*, scene 2, p. 3, l. 1; *Shui-hu ch'üan-chuan*, vol. 4, ch. 114, p. 1709, l. 13; *Hsiu-ju chi*, scene 2, p. 4, l. 4; *Yen-chih chi, chüan* 1, scene 2, p. 4a, l. 8; *Ts'an-T'ang Wu-tai shih yen-i chuan*, ch. 3, p. 6, l. 2; and an abundance of other occurrences, too numerous to list.

17. This four-character expression occurs in *Huan-sha chi*, scene 29, p. 102, l. 10.

18. Variants of this proverbial couplet recur in the *Chin P'ing Mei tz'u-hua*, vol. 4, ch. 75, p. 12a, l. 6; ch. 76, p. 4a, l. 8; and ch. 80, p. 4a, l. 6.

19. A variant of this proverbial couplet occurs in *Yen-tzu fu* (Rhapsody on the swal-low), in *Tun-huang pien-wen chi*, 1:251, l. 7. It occurs in the same form that it does here in *Huang hsiao-tzu* (The filial son Huang [Chüeh-ching]), in *Ku-pen hsi-ch'ü ts'ung-k'an, ch'u-chi*, item 23, *chüan* 2, scene 20, p. 18a, l. 10; *San-kuo chih t'ung-su yen-i*, vol. 2, *chüan* 18, p. 862, l. 21; *Shui-hu ch'üan-chuan*, vol. 2, ch. 28, p. 437, l. 17; *Lien-huan chi*, scene 27, p. 72, l. 8; *T'ang-shu chih-chuan t'ung-su yen-i*, vol. 2, *chüan* 7, p. 9a, l. 1; *P'u-ching ju-lai yao-shih pao-chüan*, 5:163, l. 5; *Hsi-yu chi*, vol. 2, ch. 62, p. 710, ll. 6–7; *San-pao t'ai-chien Hsi-yang chi t'ung-su yen-i*, vol. 1, ch. 38, p. 496, l. 13; and re-curs in the *Chin P'ing Mei tz'u-hua*, vol. 4, ch. 76, p. 4a, l. 8; and vol. 5, ch. 85, p. 10b, ll. 4–5. The first line also occurs by itself in a lyric by Ma Yü (1123–83), *Ch'üan Chin Yüan tz'u*, 1:336, upper register, l. 15; *Yüan-ch'ü hsüan*, 1:81, l. 11; *T'ien-pao i-shih chu-kung-tiao*, p. 199, l. 12; a set of songs by Wang Yüan-heng (14th century), *Ch'üan Yüan san-ch'ü*, 2:1387, l. 13; *Ku-ch'eng chi, chüan* 1, scene 10, p. 11b, l. 7; *Pao-chien chi*, scene 48, p. 87, l. 5; and *Hai-fu shan-t'ang tz'u-kao, chüan* 2b, p. 110, l. 6. The second line occurs independently in *T'ien-pao i-shih chu-kung-tiao*, p. 219, l. 8, al-though the first line occurs earlier in the same song, so the two are clearly associated.

20. This play is no longer extant, but a similar title occurs in a fifteenth-century list of plays. It was probably another version of the drama *Pai-t'u chi*, scenes 17 and 18 of

which deal with the bestowal upon Liu Chih-yüan (895–948) of a crimson robe by the daughter of the military commander under whom he was serving early in his career. For an analysis of the way in which the allusion to this play functions ironically in the novel, see Katherine Carlitz, *The Rhetoric of Chin p'ing mei* (Bloomington: Indiana University Press, 1986), pp. 99–100.

21. This was a musical instrument made from a three- or four-foot length of hollow bamboo, with a piece of pig's hide stretched over one end, upon which the musician kept time by tapping the hide with his fingers. It was commonly used by itinerant performers of Tao-ch'ing.

22. This is an apocryphal story relating how Han Yü (768–824) was allegedly converted to Taoism by his nephew, Han Hsiang-tzu, when impeded by snow at Lan-kuan on his way into exile in 819. It was inspired by a famous poem by Han Yü: see *Ch'üan T'ang shih*, vol. 5, *chüan* 344, p. 3860, ll. 1–2; and the translation in Stephen Owen, *The Poetry of Meng Chiao and Han Yü* (New Haven: Yale University Press, 1975), p. 282.

23. This formulaic four-character expression occurs in *San-kuo chih t'ung-su yen-i*, vol. 1, *chüan* 3, p. 112, l. 3; the vernacular story *Kuei-chien chiao-ch'ing* (An intimate bond between the exalted and the humble), in *Tsui yü-ch'ing*, 4:1528, upper register, l. 7; *Ts'an-T'ang Wu-tai shih yen-i chuan*, ch. 27, p. 108, ll. 6–7; and *Pai-chia kung-an*, *chüan* 1, ch. 1, p. 13a, l. 10.

24. Similar events, in which the roof ornaments of palace halls were destroyed by thunderstorms and the emperor responded by ordering his officials to engage in self-examination, are said to have taken place in 1537 and 1539 in the Ming dynasty. See *Ming t'ung-chien* (Comprehensive mirror of government under the Ming dynasty), comp. Hsia Hsieh (1799–1875), 4 vols. (Peking: Chung-hua shu-chü, 1959), vol. 3, *chüan* 57, p. 2141, ll. 11–33; and p. 2159, ll. 10–11.

25. This event occurred in 1126. See *Huang-ch'ao pien-nien kang-mu pei-yao*, vol. 2, *chüan* 30, p. 4b, l. 5; *Sung shih*, vol. 2, *chüan* 23, p. 423, l. 10; and *Hsüan-ho i-shih*, p. 88, l. 6.

26. This event took place in 1123. See *Huang-ch'ao pien-nien kang-mu pei-yao*, vol. 2, *chüan* 29, p. 14b, l. 7; and *Sung shih*, vol. 2, *chüan* 22, p. 412, ll. 11–12.

27. The text here actually reads Huang An, but there is no one of this name mentioned in the historical sources for the Sung period. I believe this is an orthographic error for Huang Yu (1080–1126), a historical figure that fits the context, and have emended the text accordingly. For the biography of Huang Yu, see *Sung shih*, vol. 38, *chüan* 452, pp. 13296–97.

28. Fang Chen (fl. early 12th century) is a historical figure who was attached to the Court of Imperial Sacrifices and submitted a scathing memorial to the throne calling for the execution of Ts'ai Ching, although this event took place in 1107. See *Huang-ch'ao pien-nien kang-mu pei-yao*, vol. 2, *chüan* 27, pp. 15a–15b; and Liu Chung-kuang, "Chin P'ing Mei jen-wu k'ao-lun" (A study of the historical figures in the *Chin P'ing Mei*), in Yeh Kuei-t'ung et al., eds., *Chin P'ing Mei tso-che chih mi* (The riddle of the authorship of the *Chin P'ing Mei*) (N.p.: Ning-hsia jen-min ch'u-pan she, 1988), pp. 202–4. This event is also mentioned in *Pao-chien chi*, scene 6, p. 16, l. 9.

29. Such an event, in which a brick in the wall of the Imperial Ancestral Temple was reported to be oozing blood, is said to have occurred in 1119. See *Hsüan-ho i-shih*, p. 28, l. 14.

30. A variant of this proverbial saying occurs in the first line of a quatrain by Lu Yu (1125–1210) written in 1196, *Ch'üan Sung shih*, 40:24953, l. 1.

31. The "four giants" probably refer to the Four Heavenly Kings of Chinese popular Buddhism. Variants of this proverbial couplet occur in *Hsi-yu chi*, vol. 2, ch. 67, p. 761, l. 7; and the *Chin P'ing Mei tz'u-hua*, vol. 5, ch. 83, p. 6a, l. 3; and ch. 85, p. 6b, l. 6.

32. A variant of this catch phrase occurs in ibid., vol. 5, ch. 86, p. 5b, l. 6.

33. Li Po (701–62) is a famous T'ang poet who was notorious for his heavy drinking. This title is the first line of an anonymous set of songs on the four vices, the punch lines of which are, respectively:

> Wine does not delude people, they
>   delude themselves;
> Beauty does not delude people, they
>   delude themselves;
> Wealth does not delude people, they
>   delude themselves; and
> Anger does not delude people, they
>   delude themselves.

This set of songs is preserved in *Yung-hsi yüeh-fu, ts'e* 18, pp. 71a–72a; and *Ch'ün-yin lei-hsüan*, 4:2614–16. For an analysis of the way in which the message of these four lines resonates with one of the major themes of the novel, see Roy, *The Plum in the Golden Vase*, vol. 1, appendix 1, p. 429.

34. See note 22 above.

35. This four-character expression occurs in *Wang Chao-chün ch'u-sai ho-jung chi*, *chüan* 1, scene 2, p. 3a, l. 3.

36. An orthographic variant of this four-character expression occurs in a lyric by Wang Yün (1228–1304), *Ch'üan Chin Yüan tz'u*, 2:657, lower register, l. 8. It occurs in the same form as in the novel in *Yüan-ch'ü hsüan*, 1:321, ll. 14–15; *Chin-yin chi, chüan* 4, scene 38, p. 13a, l. 2; and *San-pao t'ai-chien Hsi-yang chi t'ung-su yen-i*, vol. 2, ch. 87, p. 1126, l. 4.

37. This four-character expression is from the biography of Liang Hung (1st century), whose wife, Meng Kuang, is said to have showed her respect for her husband in this manner. See *Hou-Han shu*, vol. 10, *chüan* 83, p. 2768, ll. 1–2. It occurs ubiquitously in later Chinese literature. See, e.g., a poem by Hu Su (995–1067), *Ch'üan Sung shih*, 4:2081, l. 12; a quatrain by Hsü Ching-heng (1072–1128), ibid., 23:15575, l. 1; a lyric by Hung K'uo (1117–84), *Ch'üan Sung tz'u*, 2:1387, upper register, l. 10; a lyric by Chang Hsiao-hsiang (1132–69), ibid., 3:1696, upper register, l. 10; [*Chi-p'ing chiao-chu*] *Hsi-hsiang chi*, play no. 4, scene 3, p. 159, l. 13; *Yüan-ch'ü hsüan*, 1:262, l. 11; *Yüan-ch'ü hsüan wai-pien*, 1:194, l. 13; *P'o-yao chi, chüan* 1, scene 11, p. 32b, l. 5; *Chung-ch'ing li-chi, chüan* 7, p. 16a, l. 3; *Chiang Shih yüeh-li chi, chüan* 1, scene 3, p. 4b, l. 3; *Ssu-hsi chi*, scene 2, p. 4, ll. 3–4; *Ming-feng chi*, scene 18, p. 76, l. 7; *Shih-hou chi*, scene 25, p. 87, l. 10; *Ta-T'ang Ch'in-wang tz'u-hua*, vol. 1, *chüan* 3, ch. 21, p. 54a, l. 2; and an abundance of other occurrences, too numerous to list.

38. This four-character expression recurs in the *Chin P'ing Mei tz'u-hua*, vol. 4, ch. 65, p. 7b, ll. 4–5.

39. This sentence is derived from the first line of an anonymous funeral lament, said to date from the third century B.C. See *Yüeh-fu shih-chi* (Collection of Music Bureau

ballads), comp. Kuo Mao-ch'ien (12th century), 4 vols. (Peking: Chung-hua shu-chü, 1979), vol. 2, *chüan* 27, p. 396, l. 10; and *Chinese Poems*, trans. Arthur Waley (London: Allen and Unwin, 1956), pp. 55–56.

40. This couplet is from a quatrain by Kao Ch'an (cs 876), *Ch'üan T'ang shih*, vol. 10, *chüan* 668, p. 7649, l. 10. It is also quoted without attribution in *P'o-yao chi, chüan* 2, scene 24, l. 5; and *Ming-feng chi*, scene 24, p. 103, l. 8. The first four characters in each of these two lines occur in conjunction with each other in a lyric by Hsieh Ying-fang (1296–1392), *Ch'üan Ming tz'u*, 1:2, lower register, ll. 12–13; and the ch'uan-ch'i drama *Hung-fu chi* (The story of Red Duster), by Chang Feng-i (1527–1613), *Liu-shih chung ch'ü* ed., scene 8, p. 14, l. 7. The first four characters of the second line also occur independently in a lyric by Ch'eng Wen-hai (1249–1318), *Ch'üan Chin Yüan tz'u*, 2:787, upper register, l. 15; and the ch'uan-ch'i drama *Han-tan meng chi* (The dream at Han-tan), by T'ang Hsien-tsu (1550–1616), author's pref. dated 1601, in *T'ang Hsien-tsu chi* (Collected works of T'ang Hsien-tsu [1550–1616]), ed. Hsü Shuo-fang and Ch'ien Nan-yang, 4 vols. (Peking: Chung-hua shu-chü, 1962), scene 8, p. 2316, ll. 10–11.

41. This four-character expression occurs in an anonymous T'ang dynasty literary tale dealing with the excesses of Emperor Yang of the Sui dynasty (r. 604–18) entitled *K'ai-ho chi* (The opening of the canal), *T'ang Sung ch'uan-ch'i chi*, p. 237, l. 13; *San Sui p'ing-yao chuan, chüan* 1, ch. 1, p. 1b, l. 5; and *Pai-chia kung-an, chüan* 1, ch. 2, p. 14a, l. 1.

CHAPTER 65

1. The first two characters of the title of this litany have been orthographically corrupted. I have emended the text on the basis of a parallel passage that occurs in the *Chin P'ing Mei tz'u-hua*, vol. 4, ch. 66, p. 3a, l. 6. For a succinct description of this litany, see Schipper and Verellen, *The Taoist Canon: A Historical Companion to the Daozang*, 2:993, item 539.

2. See Roy, *The Plum in the Golden Vase*, vol. 3, chap. 59, n. 112. For a description of the contents of this text, see Schipper and Verellen, *The Taoist Canon: A Historical Companion to the Daozang*, 1:220, item 318.

3. There are numerous ritual texts designed for this purpose in the Taoist Canon. See, e.g., those described in Schipper and Verellen, *The Taoist Canon: A Historical Companion to the Daozang*, 1:566–68. For a detailed analysis of such a ritual as performed in Taiwan today, see John Lagerwey, *Taoist Ritual in Chinese Society and History* (New York: Macmillan, 1987), chap. 13.

4. For a definitive study of this grandiose project, see James M. Hargett, "Huizong's Magic Marchmount: The Genyue Pleasure Park of Kaifeng," *Monumenta Serica* 38 (1988–89), pp. 1–48.

5. For a convenient chronological summary of the sources relevant to this notorious, socially disruptive, undertaking, see *Sung-shih chi-shih pen-mo* (Sung historical materials topically arranged), comp. Ch'en Pang-chan (cs 1598, d. 1623), originally published in 1605, 4 vols. (Peking: Chung-hua shu-chü, 1955), vol. 2, *chüan* 50, pp. 400–404.

6. The fanciful name of this rock formation is mentioned in *Huang-ch'ao pien-nien kang-mu pei-yao*, vol. 2, *chüan* 28, p. 17b, l. 8; and the same passage also occurs in *Hsüan-ho i-shih*, p. 26, l. 7.

7. The locus classicus for this four-character expression is a speech recorded in the biography of Chang Erh (d. 202 B.C.) and Ch'en Yü (d. 204 B.C.) in *Shih-chi*, vol. 8, *chüan* 89, p. 2573, l. 14. It occurs ubiquitously in later Chinese literature. See, e.g., a speech attributed to Wei Cheng (580–643) under the year 637, in *Tzu-chih t'ung-chien* (Comprehensive mirror for aid in government), comp. Ssu-ma Kuang (1019–86), 4 vols. (Peking: Ku-chi ch'u-pan she, 1957), vol. 3, *chüan* 194, p. 6127, l. 5; *Chien-chieh lu* (A register of object lessons), comp. Ho Kuang-yüan (10th century), in *Shuo-k'u* (A treasury of literary tales), comp. Wang Wen-ju (fl. early 20th century), originally published in 1915, fac. repr., 2 vols. (Taipei: Hsin-hsing shu-chü, 1963), vol. 1, *chüan* 2, p. 3a, l. 10; a memorial to the throne written in 1071 by Su Shih (1037–1101), *Su Shih wen-chi*, vol. 2, *chüan* 25, p. 732, l. 9; a memorial by Chu Hsi (1130–1200), *Hui-an hsien-sheng Chu Wen-kung wen-chi*, *chüan* 22, p. 16b, l. 6; *Tung-ku so chien*, 6:3425, p. 14a, l. 5; *Wu-wang fa Chou p'ing-hua*, p. 13, l. 3; *San-kuo chih p'ing-hua*, p. 68, l. 10; *[Hsin-pien] Wu-tai shih p'ing-hua*, p. 91, l. 11; *Hsüan-ho i-shih*, p. 65, l. 13; *San-kuo chih t'ung-su yen-i*, vol. 1, *chüan* 2, p. 53, l. 14; *Shui-hu ch'üan-chuan*, vol. 1, ch. 1, p. 2, l. 4; the middle-period vernacular story *Yen P'ing-chung erh-t'ao sha san-shih* (Yen P'ing-chung kills three stalwarts with two peaches), in *Ku-chin hsiao-shuo*, vol. 2, *chüan* 25, p. 384, l. 3; *T'ang-shu chih-chuan t'ung-su yen-i*, vol. 2, *chüan* 7, p. 15b, l. 9; *Nan Sung chih-chuan*, vol. 1, *chüan* 6, p. 8b, l. 8; *Ch'üan-Han chih-chuan*, vol. 2, *chüan* 6, p. 28a, l. 1; and *Sui-T'ang liang-ch'ao shih-chuan*, *chüan* 11, p. 21b, ll. 4–5.

8. For the manufacture and characteristics of this variety of paper, see *T'ien-kung k'ai-wu*, *chüan* 13, p. 331; and *T'ien-kung k'ai-wu: Chinese Technology in the Seventeenth Century*, trans. E-tu Zen Sun and Shiou-chuan Sun (University Park: Pennsylvania State University Press, 1966), p. 230.

9. These figures do not add up, but I do not know how to emend the text in order to make them do so.

10. This formulaic four-character expression occurs in a document coauthored by Han Tzu-hsi (d. 541) as quoted in *Wei-shu* (History of the Northern Wei dynasty [338–534]), comp. Wei Shou (506–72), 8 vols. (Peking: Chung-hua shu-chü, 1974), vol. 4, *chüan* 60, p. 1335, l. 14; a letter by Su Shih (1037–1101), *Su Shih wen-chi*, vol. 4, *chüan* 48, p. 1405, l. 4; *Jung-chai sui-pi* (Miscellaneous notes from the Tolerant Study), by Hung Mai (1123–1202), 2 vols. (Shanghai: Shang-hai ku-chi ch'u-pan she, 1978), vol. 2, collection no. 3, p. 456, l. 12; *Sung-ch'ao yen-i i-mou lu* (Secret writings on the politics of Sung monarchs), comp. Wang Yung (fl. early 13th century), originally published in 1227, in *Pai-ch'uan hsüeh-hai, ting-chi* (fourth collection), *chüan* 3, p. 7a, l. 10; and *Yü-chüeh chi*, scene 34, p. 105, l. 6.

11. See Roy, *The Plum in the Golden Vase*, vol. 1, chap. 8, n. 32.

12. This text, the Chinese title of which is *Fo-mu ta k'ung-ch'üeh ming-wang ching* (Sutra of the Peacock King), was translated into Chinese by Amoghavajra (705–74) and is included in *Taishō shinshū daizōkyō*, vol. 19, no. 982, pp. 415–39.

13. For colored reproductions of the iconographic images of the wrathful deities that play such an important role in Tibetan lamaism, see Rob Linrothe and Jeff Watt, *Demonic Divine: Himalayan Art and Beyond* (Chicago: Serindia Publications, 2004), passim.

14. See Roy, *The Plum in the Golden Vase*, vol. 3, chap. 42, n. 33.

15. Chang Tao-ling (d. 156) is traditionally believed to have been the founder of the Celestial Master School of Taoism.

16. See Roy, *The Plum in the Golden Vase*, vol. 1, chap. 15, n. 8.

17. The myth that at the end of his career Lao-tzu headed west through a pass in the mountains where he transmitted the text of the *Tao-te ching* to Yin Hsi, the keeper of the pass, is already adumbrated in his biography in the *Shih-chi*, vol. 7, *chüan* 63, p. 2141, ll. 6–8. It was greatly elaborated upon in later Taoist hagiography, for critical studies of which, see Robert Ford Campany, *To Live as Long as Heaven and Earth: A Translation and Study of Ge Hong's Traditions of Divine Transcendents* (Berkeley: University of California Press, 2002), pp. 194–211; and Livia Kohn, *God of the Dao: Lord Lao in History and Myth* (Ann Arbor: Center for Chinese Studies, University of Michigan, 1998), pp. 255–73.

18. The Six Traitors is a Buddhist term for the six senses. On Maitreya, see Roy, *The Plum in the Golden Vase*, vol. 3, chap. 49, n. 82.

19. There was a late Ming ch'uan-ch'i drama of this title, the plot of which was set in 1565. It is no longer extant, but the outline of the story is preserved in *Ch'ing-shih* (Histories of love), comp. Feng Meng-lung (1574–1646), originally published between 1628 and 1632, 2 vols. (Shen-yang: Ch'un-feng wen-i ch'u-pan she, 1986), *chüan* 2, p. 45, ll. 2–10.

20. See Roy, *The Plum in the Golden Vase*, vol. 3, chap. 56, n. 2.

21. For the Four Heavenly Kings, see ibid., vol. 1, chap. 2, n. 35. Earth, water, fire, and wind are the four elements of which, according to Buddhism, all things are made. They are mentioned together in the same order in numerous works of Chinese literature. See, e.g., *Ming pao-ying lun* (A treatise on karmic retribution), by Hui-yüan (334–416), written in 402, in *Ch'üan Shang-ku San-tai Ch'in Han San-kuo Liu-ch'ao wen* (Complete Prose from High Antiquity, the Three Dynasties, Ch'in, Han, the Three Kingdoms, and the Six Dynasties), comp. Yen K'o-chün (1762–1843), 5 vols. (Peking: Chung-hua shu-chü, 1965), vol. 3, *Ch'üan Chin wen* (Complete prose of the Chin dynasty), *chüan* 162, p. 3a, l. 3; a poem by the Buddhist monk Tao-fu (868–937), in *Tsu-t'ang chi* (Patriarchal hall collection), ed. Wu Fu-hsiang and Ku Chih-ch'uan, originally published in 952 (Ch'ang-sha: Yüeh-lu shu-she, 1996), *chüan* 10, p. 228, l. 4; the tenth-century vernacular narrative *Lu-shan Yüan-kung hua* (Story of Hui-yüan [334–416] of Mount Lu), in *Tun-huang pien-wen chi*, 1:184, l. 5; *T'ai-tzu ch'eng-tao ching* (Sutra on how the crown prince [Śākyamuni] attained the Way), in ibid., 1:292, l. 10; *Pa-hsiang pien* (Pien-wen on the eight aspects [of Śākyamuni Buddha's life], in ibid., 1:336, l. 15; a poem by Ma Yü (1123–83), *Ch'üan Chin shih*, 1:314, l. 11; a lyric by Hou Shan-yüan (12th century), *Ch'üan Chin Yüan tz'u*, 1:509, upper register, l. 14; a lyric by Wang Chi-ch'ang (12th century), ibid., 1:556, lower register, l. 4; a lyric by the Buddhist monk Fan-ch'i (1296–1369), *Ch'üan Ming tz'u*, 1:14, upper register, l. 3; *K'u-kung wu-tao chüan* (Precious volume on awakening to the Way through bitter toil), by Lo Ch'ing (1442–1527), originally published in 1509, in *Pao-chüan ch'u-chi*, 1:133, l. 2; *T'an-shih wu-wei pao-chüan*, ibid., 1:326, l. 3; *P'o-hsieh hsien-cheng yao-shih chüan*, ibid., 2:473, l. 1; *Cheng-hsin ch'u-i wu hsiu cheng tzu-tsai pao-chüan*, ibid., 3:115, l. 4; *Wei-wei pu-tung T'ai-shan shen-ken chieh-kuo pao-chüan*, ibid., 3:440, ll. 1–2; *Yao-shih pen-yüan kung-te pao-chüan*, ibid., 14:266, l. 1; *[Hsiao-shih] Chen-k'ung pao-chüan*, ibid., 19:267, l. 4; and an abundance of other occurrences, too numerous to list. This four-character expression also recurs in the *Chin P'ing Mei tz'u-hua*, vol. 4, ch. 80, p. 7b, l. 1.

22. The plot of this piece probably drew upon the same stuff material as the early vernacular story *Lü Tung-pin fei-chien chan Huang-lung*, the title of which is nearly identical.

23. Emperor T'ai-tsu is Chao K'uang-yin (927–76), the founding emperor of the Sung dynasty (r. 960–76), about whom many legends accumulated. A late vernacular story, with a nearly identical title, that probably draws upon the same stuff material is *Chao T'ai-tsu ch'ien-li sung Ching-niang* (Chao T'ai-tsu escorts Ching-niang on a thousand-li journey), in *Ching-shih t'ung-yen, chüan* 21, pp. 289–306. For further information on the probable or possible sources of the stories behind these ten skits, see Ts'ai Tun-yung, *Chin P'ing Mei chü-ch'ü p'in-t'an* (A critical evaluation of the drama and song quoted in the *Chin P'ing Mei*) (Nanking: Chiang-su wen-i ch'u-pan she, 1989), ch. 4, pp. 74–94.

24. This four-character expression occurs in *Nan Sung chih-chuan*, vol. 1, *chüan* 5, p. 9b, l. 7; and *Ta-T'ang Ch'in-wang tz'u-hua*, vol. 1, *chüan* 2, ch. 15, p. 67b, l. 6.

25. This four-character expression occurs in *Ch'o-keng lu, chüan* 30, p. 378, l. 14; *San-kuo chih t'ung-su yen-i*, vol. 2, *chüan* 16, p. 733, ll. 12–13; *Han-tan meng chi*, scene 20, p. 2371, l. 8; and recurs in the *Chin P'ing Mei tz'u-hua*, vol. 4, ch. 70, p. 14b, l. 10.

26. For descriptions and illustrations of these elaborate devices for transporting coffins, see *Chu Hsi's Family Rituals: A Twelfth-Century Chinese Manual for the Performance of Cappings, Weddings, Funerals, and Ancestral Rites*, trans. and annot. Patricia Buckley Ebrey (Princeton: Princeton University Press, 1991), pp. 110–12; and De Groot, *The Religious System of China*, 1:179–85.

27. This four-character expression occurs in the thirteenth-century work *Hsi-hu Lao-jen Fan-sheng lu* (The Old Man of West Lake's Record of luxuriant splendor), in *Tung-ching meng-hua lu [wai ssu-chung]*, p. 126, ll. 6–7; *Sung Ssu-kung ta-nao Chin-hun Chang*, p. 544, l. 14; the early vernacular story *Wu-chieh Ch'an-shih ssu Hung-lien chi* (The Ch'an Master Wu-chieh defiles Hung-lien), in *Ch'ing-p'ing shan-t'ang hua-pen*, p. 143, l. 4; *Jen hsiao-tzu lieh-hsing wei shen*, p. 584, l. 6; *Nan Hsi-hsiang chi* (Lu Ts'ai), scene 24, p. 383, l. 10; *Shui-hu ch'üan-chuan*, vol. 2, ch. 51, p. 839, ll. 15–16; *San Sui p'ing-yao chuan, chüan* 3, ch. 13, p. 33a, l. 2; and *Mu-tan t'ing*, scene 52, p. 256, l. 9. It also recurs in the *Chin P'ing Mei tz'u-hua*, vol. 4, ch. 73, p. 14a, l. 8; and vol. 5, ch. 90, p. 1b, l. 2.

28. The proximate source of these four lines, with some textual variation, is *Shui-hu ch'üan-chuan*, vol. 3, ch. 82, p. 1356, l. 8.

29. The Road-clearing Demon is a formidable apotropaic demon whose effigy is carried at the head of Chinese funeral processions.

30. See Roy, *The Plum in the Golden Vase*, vol. 1, chap. 4, n. 22.

31. This four-character reduplicative expression occurs in *Hsi-yu chi*, vol. 2, ch. 80, p. 912, l. 1.

32. This four-character expression occurs in *Yüan-ch'ü hsüan*, 2:1703, l. 18.

33. This four-character reduplicative expression occurs in *Wu Lun-ch'üan Pei, chüan* 2, scene 10, p. 6b, l. 1; *Shui-hu ch'üan-chuan*, vol. 3, ch. 82, p. 1358, l. 6; *Lieh-kuo chih-chuan*, vol. 3, *chüan* 8, p. 4b, l. 1; *Ko tai hsiao*, scene 1, p. 119, l. 1; *San-pao t'ai-chien Hsi-yang chi t'ung-su yen-i*, vol. 1, ch. 15, p. 196, l. 6; and recurs in the *Chin P'ing Mei tz'u-hua*, vol. 4, ch. 70, p. 10b, l. 8; and ch. 71, p. 14a, l. 6.

34. This four-character reduplicative expression occurs in *San-pao t'ai-chien Hsi-yang chi t'ung-su yen-i*, vol. 1, ch. 23, p. 304, l. 2.

35. These two lines occur in close proximity in *Han Wu-ti nei-chuan* (Esoteric traditions regarding Emperor Wu of the Han dynasty), traditionally attributed to Pan Ku

(32–92), but more probably dating from the fifth or sixth century, in *Ts'ung-shu chi-ch'eng* (A corpus of works from collectanea), 1st series (Shanghai: Shang-wu yin-shu kuan, 1935–37), vol. 3436. The first line occurs on p. 3, l. 7; and the second on the preceding line. They describe musical instruments played by fairy handmaidens of the Queen Mother of the West on the occasion of her fabled visit to Emperor Wu of the Han dynasty (r. 141–87 B.C.).

36. This four-character reduplicative expression occurs in *Shang Lu san-yüan chi*, *chüan* 1, scene 10, p. 14a, l. 7; and a song by Hsüeh Lun-tao (c. 1531–c. 1600), *Ch'üan Ming san-ch'ü*, 3:2810, l. 1.

37. This four-character expression occurs in *Shui-hu ch'üan-chuan*, vol. 4, ch. 118, p. 1776, l. 9; an anonymous song suite in *Yung-hsi yüeh-fu*, ts'e 9, p. 51a, l. 9; and *Ts'an-T'ang Wu-tai shih yen-i chuan*, ch. 18, p. 69, l. 16.

38. For a description and picture of a mourning banner, see De Groot, *The Religious System of China*, 1:178.

39. This four-character expression occurs in *Wu Lun-ch'üan Pei*, *chüan* 3, scene 18, p. 19a, l. 2; *Huang-chi chin-tan chiu-lien cheng-hsin kuei-chen huan-hsiang pao-chüan* (Precious volume of the golden elixir and nine-petaled lotus of the Imperial Ultimate period that leads to rectifying belief, reverting to the real, and returning to our true home), originally published in 1498, in *Pao-chüan ch'u-chi*, 8:89, l. 5; the title of *Wei-wei pu-tung T'ai-shan shen-ken chieh-kuo pao-chüan*, 3:350, l. 1; *Yao-shih pen-yüan kung-te pao-chüan*, 14:220, l. 3; *P'u-ming ju-lai wu-wei liao-i pao-chüan* (Precious volume of the Tathāgatha P'u-ming who thoroughly comprehends the meaning of Nonactivism), by P'u-ming (d. 1562), completed in 1558, in *Pao-chüan ch'u-chi*, 4:395, l. 1; *[Hsiao-shih] Chen-k'ung sao-hsin pao-chüan* ([Clearly presented] Precious volume on [the Patriarch] Chen-k'ung's [instructions for] sweeping clear the mind), published in 1584, in ibid., 19:177, ll. 3–4; and *[Hsiao-shih] Chen-k'ung pao-chüan*, 19:272, l. 10.

40. The term for this type of headgear is *wan-tzu t'ou-chin*, literally "headgear like the character *wan* (ten thousand)." This expression is derived from the fact that the abbreviated form of the character *wan* has a flat horizontal line at the top. The proximate source of this line is probably *Shui-hu ch'üan-chuan*, vol. 1, ch. 3, p. 46, l. 2. This type of cap is also mentioned in *Cheng Chieh-shih li-kung shen-pi kung*, p. 658, l. 4; the early vernacular story *Shih-wu kuan hsi-yen ch'eng ch'iao-huo* (Fifteen strings of cash: A casual jest leads to uncanny disaster), in *Hsing-shih heng-yen*, vol. 2, *chüan* 33, p. 697, l. 13; and the middle-period vernacular story *Ts'o-jen shih* (The wrongly identified corpse), in *Ch'ing-p'ing shan-t'ang hua-pen*, p. 223, l. 4.

41. The proximate source of this line is probably *Shui-hu ch'üan-chuan*, vol. 1, ch. 3, p. 46, l. 3.

42. See Roy, *The Plum in the Golden Vase*, vol. 2, chap. 37, n. 29.

43. This four-character expression occurs in *Tung-ching meng-hua lu* (A dream of past splendors in the Eastern Capital), comp. Meng Yüan-lao (12th century), pref. dated 1147, in *Tung-ching meng-hua lu [wai ssu-chung]*, *chüan* 7, p. 44, l. 9; the anonymous Yüan dynasty vernacular narrative *Hsüeh Jen-kuei cheng-Liao shih-lüeh* (A brief account of Hsüeh Jen-kuei's campaign in Liao-tung) (Shanghai: Ku-tien wen-hsüeh ch'u-pan she, 1957), p. 59, l. 9; *Shui-hu ch'üan-chuan*, vol. 1, ch. 13, p. 188, l. 15; *San-pao t'ai-chien Hsi-yang chi t'ung-su yen-i*, vol. 1, ch. 47, p. 603, l. 11; and *Ta-T'ang Ch'in-wang tz'u-hua*, vol. 1, *chüan* 1, ch. 3, p. 28b, l. 1.

44. This four-character expression occurs in *Pai Niang-tzu yung-chen Lei-feng T'a*, p. 432, l. 10; and *Sui-T'ang liang-ch'ao shih-chuan*, *chüan* 7, chap. 69, p. 49b, l. 9.

45. This formulaic four-character expression occurs ubiquitously in Chinese vernacular literature. See, e.g., *[Chi-p'ing chiao-chu] Hsi-hsiang chi*, play no. 5, scene 4, p. 199, l. 3; *Yüan-ch'ü hsüan*, 2:536, l. 20; *Yüan-ch'ü hsüan wai-pien*, 1:143, l. 7; a song by Hsüeh Ang-fu (14th century), *Ch'üan Yüan san-ch'ü*, 1:714, ll. 5–6; a song suite attributed to a fourteenth-century singing girl, ibid., 2:1276, l. 3; *Shih Chen-jen ssu-sheng so pai-yüan*, scene 3, p. 10a, l. 4; *Shui-hu ch'üan-chuan*, vol. 1, ch. 3, p. 53, l. 15; a song suite by Liu Liang-ch'en (1482–1551), *Ch'üan Ming san-ch'ü*, 2:1331, l. 2; *T'ang-shu chih-chuan t'ung-su yen-i*, vol. 1, *chüan* 2, p. 5b, l. 11; *Huan-sha chi*, scene 42, p. 147, l. 4; *Hsi-yu chi*, vol. 1, ch. 28, p. 318, l. 10; and *Ch'eng-yün chuan*, *chüan* 2, p. 15a, l. 7. It also recurs in the *Chin P'ing Mei tz'u-hua*, vol. 5, ch. 100, p. 4b, l. 6.

46. The proximate source of these ten lines, with some textual variation, is *Shui-hu ch'üan-chuan*, vol. 1, ch. 3, p. 53, ll. 15–16.

47. This four-character expression occurs in a poem by Wang Che (1112–70), *Ch'üan Chin shih*, 1:204, ll. 11–12; and an anonymous song suite in *Yung-hsi yüeh-fu*, *ts'e* 10, p. 8b, l. 10.

48. See Roy, *The Plum in the Golden Vase*, vol. 2, chap. 39, n. 45.

49. For the hare and the raven, see ibid., vol. 1, chap. 13, n. 9. This four-character expression occurs ubiquitously in Chinese literature. See, e.g., a poem by Chuang Nan-chieh (fl. early 9th century), *Ch'üan T'ang shih*, vol. 7, *chüan* 470, p. 5345, l. 8; a poem by Wei Chuang (836–910), ibid., vol. 10, *chüan* 695, p. 7997, l. 11; a quatrain by the same author, ibid., vol. 10, *chüan* 695, p. 7999, l. 8; a poem attributed to Lü Tung-pin (9th century), ibid, vol. 12, *chüan* 856, p. 9680, l. 8; a poem by the Buddhist monk Chih-yüan (976–1022), *Ch'üan Sung shih*, 3:1569, l. 12; a lyric by Yen Shu (991–1055), *Ch'üan Sung tz'u*, 1:92, upper register, ll. 4–5; a poem by Ma Yü (1123–83), *Ch'üan Chin shih*, 1:327, l. 11; a lyric by Shih Hsiao-yu (cs 1166), *Ch'üan Sung tz'u*, 3:2034, upper register, l. 4; a lyric by Ch'iu Ch'u-chi (1148–1227), *Ch'üan Chin Yüan tz'u*, 1:455, lower register, l. 4; a lyric by Wang Tan-kuei (12th century), ibid., 1:491, lower register, l. 1; a lyric by Liu K'o-chuang (1187–1269), *Ch'üan Sung tz'u*, 4:2630, lower register, l. 12; a song by Lu Chih (cs 1268), *Ch'üan Yüan san-ch'ü*, 1:114, l. 9; a set of songs by Wang Yüan-heng (14th century), ibid., 2:1390, l. 8; *Yüan-ch'ü hsüan*, 2:728, l. 10; *Yüan-ch'ü hsüan wai-pien*, 2:384, l. 21; *Ching-ch'ai chi*, scene 2, p. 4, l. 11; *Chien-teng yü-hua*, *chüan* 5, p. 302, l. 7; *Hsiao-p'in chi*, p. 80, l. 3; the tsa-chü drama *Pao-tzu Ho-shang tzu huan-su* (The Leopard Monk returns to the laity), by Chu Yu-tun (1379–1439), completed in 1433, in *Shui-hu hsi-ch'ü chi*, *ti-i chi* (Corpus of drama dealing with the *Shui-hu* cycle, first series), ed. Fu Hsi-hua and Tu Ying-t'ao (Shanghai: Ku-tien wen-hsüeh ch'u-pan she, 1957), p. 122, l. 24; *Ch'ung-mo-tzu tu-pu Ta-lo T'ien*, scene 2, p. 3b, l. 4; *San-yüan chi*, scene 2, p. 4, l. 5; a lyric by T'ang Yin (1470–1524), *Ch'üan Ming tz'u*, 2:493, lower register, l. 12; the middle-period vernacular story *Chang Tzu-fang mu-tao chi* (The story of Chang Liang's pursuit of the Way), in *Ch'ing-p'ing shan-t'ang hua-pen*, p. 108, l. 13; a set of songs by Wang Chiu-ssu (1468–1551), *Ch'üan Ming san-ch'ü*, 1:890, l. 8; a song suite by Chang Lien (cs 1544), ibid., 2:1698, l. 11; *Yü-chüeh chi*, scene 8, p. 23, l. 7; a song suite by Yin Shih-tan (1522–82), *Ch'üan Ming san-ch'ü*, 2:2346, ll. 6–7; *Hsi-yu chi*, vol. 1, ch. 44, p. 505, l. 3; a set of songs by Hsüeh Lun-tao (c. 1531–c. 1600), *Ch'üan Ming san-ch'ü*, 3:2720, l. 7; *Yang chia fu shih-tai chung-yung yen-i chih-chuan*, vol. 2, *chüan* 8, p. 54b, l. 1; *Ta-T'ang*

Ch'in-wang tz'u-hua, vol. 1, *chüan* 1, ch. 5, p. 50a, l. 1; and an abundance of other occurrences, too numerous to list.

50. This four-character expression occurs in a lyric by Chang Chi-hsien (1092–1126), *Ch'üan Sung tz'u*, 2:759, upper register, l. 2.

51. See Roy, *The Plum in the Golden Vase*, vol. 2, chap. 36, n. 22.

52. This is an allusion to a famous passage in the *Li sao* (On encountering trouble), a long poem by Ch'ü Yüan (c. 340–278 B.C.) in which he laments his ruler's failure to appreciate him at his true worth, and uses a great deal of floral imagery in describing his plight. The relevant lines, as translated by David Hawkes, read:

I had tended many an acre of orchids, . . .
But I grieve that all my blossoms should waste in rank weeds.

See *The Songs of the South*, trans. David Hawkes (New York: Penguin Books, 1985), p. 69, ll. 25 and 32.

53. This four-character expression recurs in the *Chin P'ing Mei tz'u-hua*, vol. 5, ch. 89, p. 8b, l. 7.

54. Hsin-yüan P'ing (d. 163 B.C.) was a necromancer who came to prominence during the reign of Emperor Wen of the Han dynasty (r. 180–157 B.C.). See *Shih-chi*, vol. 4, *chüan* 28, pp. 1382–83; and *Records of the Grand Historian of China*, trans. Burton Watson, 2 vols. (New York: Columbia University Press, 1961), 2:35–36. This detail is, perhaps, intended to be ironic, since Hsin-yüan P'ing was eventually exposed as a charlatan and executed together with his entire family.

55. Ts'ui Hui (9th century) was a singing girl who fell in love with an official who was transferred to another post after several months. Distraught over her inability to accompany him, she later prevailed upon an artist to paint her portrait and had it delivered to her lover with a message saying, "When the day comes that I no longer live up to the likeness in my portrait, I will die on your account." Subsequently she went mad with grief and suffered the fate that she had predicted. This story was commemorated in a poem by Yüan Chen (775–831), *Ch'üan T'ang shih*, vol. 6, *chüan* 423, p. 4652, ll. 3–7; and was subsequently celebrated in a poem by Su Shih (1037–1101), *Su Shih shih-chi* (Collected poetry of Su Shih), 8 vols. (Peking: Chung-hua shu-chü, 1982), vol. 3, *chüan* 16, pp. 798–99; and verses by Ch'in Kuan (1049–1100), *Ch'üan Sung tz'u*, 1:465, upper register, ll. 6–13; and Mao P'ang (1067–c. 1125), ibid., 2:689, upper register, ll. 9–15.

56. See Roy, *The Plum in the Golden Vase*, vol. 2, chap. 39, n. 35.

57. See ibid., vol. 1, chap. 15, n. 11.

58. This line is probably derived, with some textual variation, from the third line in a quatrain by Li Ch'ün-yü (c. 813–c. 861), *Ch'üan T'ang shih*, vol. 9, *chüan* 570, p. 6608, l. 13.

59. Orthographic variants of this four-character expression occur in *Sung shu* (History of the Liu-Sung dynasty [420–79]), comp. Shen Yüeh (441–513), 8 vols. (Peking: Chung-hua shu-chü, 1974), vol. 1, *chüan* 1, p. 9, l. 2; *San-kuo chih p'ing-hua*, p. 85, l. 11; *Ming-feng chi*, scene 18, p. 78, l. 9; *Ch'üan-Han chih-chuan*, vol. 2, *chüan* 5, p. 16a, l. 8; and *Huang-Ming k'ai-yün ying-wu chuan*, *chüan* 5, p. 9a, l. 5.

60. For a picture of this instrument and a detailed description of its use, see De Groot, *The Religious System of China*, 3:959–82, and plate 26.

61. For a detailed description of this ceremony, see ibid., 1:213–19.

62. This apotropaic postfuneral practice is described as a local custom in Peking in *Wan-shu tsa-chi* (Miscellaneous records concerning the magistracy of Wan-p'ing), by Shen Pang, pref. dated 1592 (Peking: Pei-ching ku-chi ch'u-pan she, 1980), *chüan* 17, p. 193, l. 3.

63. This four-character expression occurs in *Chien-teng yü-hua*, *chüan* 5, p. 289, l. 4; and *Ch'üan-Han chih-chuan*, vol. 2, *chüan* 2, p. 34b, l. 10.

64. This formulaic four-character expression occurs ubiquitously in Chinese vernacular literature. See, e.g., *Pai Niang-tzu yung-chen Lei-feng T'a*, p. 440, l. 12; *Chiang Shih yüeh-li chi*, *chüan* 4, scene 42, p. 23b, l. 1; *Shui-hu ch'üan-chuan*, vol. 1, ch. 1, p. 3, l. 2; *T'ang-shu chih-chuan t'ung-su yen-i*, vol. 1, *chüan* 1, p. 32b, l. 6; *Pei Sung chih-chuan*, vol. 2, *chüan* 3, p. 4a, l. 9; *Ch'ien-t'ang hu-yin Chi-tien Ch'an-shih yü-lu*, p. 26b, l. 6; *Mu-lien chiu-mu ch'üan-shan hsi-wen*, *chüan* 1, p. 28b, l. 3; *Ch'üan-Han chih-chuan*, vol. 3, *chüan* 2, p. 12b, l. 8; and *Sui-T'ang liang-ch'ao shih-chuan*, *chüan* 4, p. 34a, l. 3. It also recurs in the *Chin P'ing Mei tz'u-hua*, vol. 4, ch. 66, p. 2a, ll. 1–2.

65. This four-character expression occurs in a quatrain by Cheng Ku (cs 887), *Ch'üan T'ang shih*, vol. 10, *chüan* 677, p. 7761, l. 5; a lyric by Ho Chu (1052–1125), *Ch'üan Sung tz'u*, 1:534, lower register, l. 10; a lyric by Ts'ai Shen (1088–1156), ibid., 2:1029, lower register, l. 4; and a lyric by Chao Ch'ang-ch'ing (12th century), ibid., 3:1815, lower register, l. 3.

66. This four-character expression occurs in a lyric by Liu Chi (1311–75), *Ch'üan Ming tz'u*, 1:77, upper register, ll. 8–9.

67. According to the preface to a poem by Fan T'ai (355–428), the king of Kashmir once caught a phoenix which he kept in a golden cage, hoping to hear it sing; but, though he kept it for three years, it did not do so. His wife then told him that she had heard that the phoenix would sing only upon seeing another bird of its kind and suggested that he hang up a mirror so that the phoenix could see itself in it. When the captive phoenix saw its own solitary image, it cried out in grief, attempted to take flight, and died. See *Hsien-Ch'in Han Wei Chin Nan-pei ch'ao shih* (Complete poetry of the Pre-Ch'in, Han, Wei, Chin, and Northern and Southern dynasties), comp. Lu Ch'in-li, 3 vols. (Peking: Chung-hua shu-chü, 1983), 2:1144, ll. 3–5.

68. See above, note 52.

69. The locus classicus of this four-character expression, which has become proverbial for an outstanding turn of phrase that outlives the rest of a poet's work, is a line from a lost poem by Ts'ui Hsin-ming (fl. early 7th century), *Ch'üan T'ang shih*, vol. 1, *chüan* 38, p. 490, l. 4. For the anecdote responsible for the perpetuation of this expression, see *Chiu T'ang shu* (Old history of the T'ang dynasty), comp. Liu Hsü (887–946) et al., 16 vols. (Peking: Chung-hua shu-chü, 1975), vol. 15, *chüan* 190a, p. 4988, ll. 9–11; and the translation in Hans H. Frankel, "T'ang Literati: A Composite Biography," in *Confucian Personalities*, ed. Arthur F. Wright and Denis Twitchett (Stanford: Stanford University Press, 1962), p. 73, ll. 37–43. This expression also occurs in a lyric by Hsin Ch'i-chi (1140–1207), *Chia-hsüan tz'u pien-nien chien-chu* (The lyrics of Hsin Ch'i-chi arranged chronologically and annotated), ed. Teng Kuang-ming (Shanghai: Shang-hai ku-chi ch'u-pan she, 1978), *chüan* 5, p. 481, ll. 12–13; and a poem written in 1185 by Lu Yu (1125–1210), *Ch'üan Sung shih*, 39:24630, l. 15.

70. See *Lun-yü yin-te*, Book 3, p. 4, paragraph 12.

71. This four-character expression occurs in the early vernacular story *Nao Fan-lou to-ch'ing Chou Sheng-hsien* (The disturbance in the Fan Tavern and the passionate Chou Sheng-hsien), in *Hsing-shih heng-yen*, vol. 1, *chüan* 14, p. 275, l. 13.

72. This four-character expression recurs in the *Chin P'ing Mei tz'u-hua*, vol. 4, ch. 67, p. 14b, l. 10; and ch. 68, p. 8a, l. 7.

73. This four-character expression occurs ubiquitously in Chinese literature. See, e.g., a speech attributed to the Buddhist monk Shou-ch'u (910–90), in *Ku tsun-su yü-lu* (The recorded sayings of eminent monks of old), comp. Tse Tsang-chu (13th century), in *Hsü Tsang-ching* (Continuation of the Buddhist canon), 150 vols., fac. repr. (Hong Kong: Hsiang-kang ying-yin *Hsü Tsang-ching* wei-yüan hui, 1967), vol. 118, *chüan* 38, p. 325a, lower register, l. 15; a poem by Tsou Hao (1060–1111), *Ch'üan Sung shih*, 21:13969, l. 10; a commentary on the *Vajracchedikā prajñāpāramitā sutra* by Li Wen-hui (cs 1128, d. 1158), as quoted in *Chin-kang ching chi-chu* (The *Vajracchedikā prajñāpāramitā sutra* with collected commentaries), comp. by the Yung-lo emperor of the Ming dynasty (r. 1402–24), pref. dated 1424, fac. repr. of original edition (Shanghai: Shang-hai ku-chi ch'u-pan she, 1984), p. 84a, column 3; a letter from Ch'en Liang (1143–94) to Chu Hsi (1130–1200) written in 1182, *Ch'en Liang chi [tseng-ting pen]*, vol. 2, *chüan* 28, p. 335, l. 2; a letter from Chu Hsi to Lü Tsu-chien (d. 1196), *Hui-an hsien-sheng Chu Wen-kung wen-chi*, *chüan* 47, p. 8b, l. 7; a quatrain by Yang Wan-li (1127–1206), *Ch'üan Sung shih*, 42:26506, l. 18; *Yüan-ch'ü hsüan*, 2:636, l. 14; *Yüan-ch'ü hsüan wai-pien*, 3:712, l. 9; *Ch'ung-mo-tzu tu-pu Ta-lo T'ien*, scene 2, p. 4a, l. 2; the middle-period vernacular story *Tung Yung yü-hsien chuan* (The story of Tung Yung's encounter with an immortal), in *Ch'ing-p'ing shan-t'ang hua-pen*, p. 243, l. 11; *Lien-huan chi*, scene 17, p. 40, ll. 12–13; the tsa-chü drama *Chung-shan lang* (The wolf of Chung-shan), by K'ang Hai (1475–1541), in *Ming-jen tsa-chü hsüan*, scene 3, p. 251, l. 6; and *Shui-hu ch'üan-chuan*, vol. 1, ch. 9, p. 137, l. 7.

74. For an elaborate description of such an ornate device, see *Shui-hu ch'üan-chuan*, vol. 3, ch. 59, p. 990, ll. 3–9. For an illustration to the above text that may give some idea of what it looked like, see *Jung-yü T'ang pen Shui-hu chuan* (The Jung-yü T'ang edition of the *Shui-hu chuan*), originally published in 1610, 2 vols. (Shanghai: Shang-hai ku-chi ch'u-pan she, 1988), vol. 2, p. 869.

75. This type of elaborate Taoist ritual is mentioned as early as 1016 in a work by Wang Ch'in-jo (962–1025). See Schipper and Verellen, *The Taoist Canon: A Historical Companion to the Daozang*, 2:996, ll. 29–35. It is also mentioned in *Shui-hu ch'üan-chuan*, vol. 1, ch. 1, p. 2, l. 9; *Pao-chien chi*, scene 51, p. 93, l. 19; *Hsi-yu chi*, vol. 1, ch. 45, p. 518, l. 6; and *Shih-hou chi*, scene 7, p. 17, l. 10.

76. This four-character expression occurs in a poem by the Buddhist monk Te-hung (1071–1128), *Ch'üan Sung shih*, 23:15162, l. 5; a poem by Ch'iu Ch'u-chi (1148–1227), *Ch'üan Chin shih*, 2:198, l. 4; and twice in *Shui-hu ch'üan-chuan*, vol. 4, ch. 100, p. 1560, l. 5; and ch. 109, p. 1644, ll. 1–2.

77. This four-character expression occurs ubiquitously in Chinese vernacular literature. See, e.g., *Shui-hu ch'üan-chuan*, vol. 4, ch. 91, p. 1483, l. 14; *T'ang-shu chih-chuan t'ung-su yen-i*, vol. 1, *chüan* 1, p. 12a, l. 1; *Ch'üan-Han chih-chuan*, vol. 2, *chüan* 6, p. 12b, l. 3; *Ts'an-T'ang Wu-tai shih yen-i chuan*, ch. 43, p. 174, l. 18; *San-pao t'ai-chien Hsi-yang chi t'ung-su yen-i*, vol. 2, ch. 90, p. 1166, l. 4; *Yang-chia fu shih-tai*

chung-yung yen-i chih-chuan, vol. 2, *chüan* 6, p. 14a, l. 8; and *Sui-T'ang liang-ch'ao shih-chuan*, *chüan* 1, p. 22b, l. 4.

78. This four-character expression occurs in *T'ien-pao i-shih chu-kung-tiao*, p. 167, l. 6; and *Huang-Ming k'ai-yün ying-wu chuan*, *chüan* 1, p. 5a, l. 7.

79. Kung Kuai (1057–1111) is a historical figure, although this is an anachronism since he had already been dead for six years at this point in the time scheme of the novel. For his biography, see *Sung shih*, vol. 31, *chüan* 346, pp. 10982–84.

80. There is a sixteenth-century figure of this name who passed the *chin-shih* examinations in 1532. See Liu Chung-kuang, "*Chin P'ing Mei* jen-wu k'ao-lun," pp. 173–74.

81. This probably fictitious name, the literal meaning of which is "to expound the four admonitions," may be a punning allusion to Lo Yü-jen's (cs 1583) scathing memorial of 1590 in which he admonished the Wan-li emperor (r. 1572–1620) for his addiction to the four vices of drunkenness, lust, avarice, and anger. See Roy, *The Plum in the Golden Vase*, 1:464, n. 4.

82. Wang Po-yen (1069–1141) is a historical figure. For his biography, see *Sung shih*, vol. 39, *chüan* 473, pp. 13745–46.

83. There is a sixteenth-century figure of this name who passed the *chin-shih* examinations in 1559. See Liu Chung-kuang, "*Chin P'ing Mei* jen-wu k'ao-lun," pp. 164–65.

84. Ch'en Cheng-hui (fl. early 12th century), the son of Ch'en Kuan (1057–1122), is a historical figure. See ibid., pp. 129–30, and 208–12.

85. There is a sixteenth-century figure of this name who passed the *chin-shih* examinations in 1547 and died sometime after 1587. See his biography in *Ming shih*, vol. 19, *chüan* 222, pp. 5861–62; and Lu Ko and Ma Cheng, *Chin P'ing Mei jen-wu ta-ch'üan* (Great compendium of the characters in the *Chin P'ing Mei*) (Ch'ang-ch'un: Chi-lin wen-shih ch'u-pan she, 1991), pp. 414–16.

86. Han Pang-ch'i (1479–1556) is a prominent historical figure from the sixteenth century who is known to have held office twice in Shantung. See his biography in L. Carrington Goodrich and Chaoying Fang, eds., *Dictionary of Ming Biography*, 2 vols. (New York: Columbia University Press, 1976), 1:488–91.

87. Chang Shu-yeh (1065–1127) is a historical figure who is known to have served as the prefect of Chi-nan. For his biography, see *Sung shih*, vol. 32, *chüan* 353, pp. 11140–42.

88. There is a sixteenth-century figure named Wang Shih-ch'i (1551–1618) who is known to have served as an official in Shantung, and whose name is identical except for the addition of a jade radical to the final syllable. See *Ming shih*, vol. 19, *chüan* 223, p. 5878, ll. 6–9; and Goodrich and Fang, *Dictionary of Ming Biography*, 2:1441.

89. There is a sixteenth-century figure of this name who passed the *chin-shih* examinations in 1550. See Liu Chung-kuang, "*Chin P'ing Mei* jen-wu k'ao-lun," pp. 162–64.

90. This figure is mentioned only twice in the novel, and on the second mention, in the *Chin P'ing Mei tz'u-hua*, vol. 4, ch. 77, p. 19b, l. 1, his given name appears as *Chao* instead of *Ch'ien*. There is no way to be sure which character is correct, but there is a sixteenth-century figure named Yeh Chao who passed the *chin-shih* examinations in 1523 and is known to have served as an official in Shantung from 1543 to 1546. See *Kuo-ch'ao hsien-cheng lu* (A corpus of primary biographical sources for the Ming

dynasty), comp. Chiao Hung (1541–1620), originally published in 1616, 8 vols., fac. repr. (Taipei: Hsüeh-sheng shu-chü, 1965), vol. 4, *chüan* 62, pp. 36a-38a. Out of the above list of names, those that can be identified as historical figures include seven from the twelfth century and seven from the sixteenth. This is unmistakable evidence of the author's rhetorical strategy of deliberately mixing material from the Sung and Ming periods in order to subtly suggest to the reader that although his story is ostensibly set in the twelfth century, his real focus is on the society of his own day.

91. This is a longer alternative title for *Huan-tai chi* (The return of the belts), by Shen Ts'ai (15th century), in *Ku-pen hsi-ch'ü ts'ung-k'an, ch'u-chi*, item 32. For an illuminating discussion of the plot of this play and the ironic function performed by its introduction at this point in the narrative, see Carlitz, *The Rhetoric of Chin p'ing mei*, p. 110.

92. This formulaic four-character expression occurs ubiquitously in Chinese vernacular literature. See, e.g., a song by Sun Chou-ch'ing (14th century), *Ch'üan Yüan san-ch'ü*, 2:1064, l. 2; *Yüan-ch'ü hsüan*, 2:812, l. 13; *Yüan-ch'ü hsüan wai-pien*, 1:258, l. 11; *Wu Lun-ch'üan Pei*, *chüan* 3, scene 18, p. 19a, ll. 4–5; *P'o-yao chi*, *chüan* 2, scene 23, p. 19b, l. 3; *Sung ta-chiang Yüeh Fei ching-chung*, scene 1, p. 4b, l. 5; *Hsiu-ju chi*, scene 21, p. 62, l. 7; *Pao-chien chi*, scene 49, p. 87, l. 22; a song by Wang Chiu-ssu (1468–1551), *Ch'üan Ming san-ch'ü*, 1:867, l. 2; a song by K'ang Hai (1475–1541), ibid., 1:1160, l. 13; *San-pao t'ai-chien Hsi-yang chi t'ung-su yen-i*, vol. 1, ch. 16, p. 206, l. 11; and *[Hsin-k'o] Shih-shang hua-yen ch'ü-lo t'an-hsiao chiu-ling*, *chüan* 1, p. 2b, upper register, l. 6.

93. This formulaic four-character expression occurs in *Yüan-ch'ü hsüan*, 1:10, l. 2; *Yüan-ch'ü hsüan wai-pien*, 2:440, l. 18; and a set of songs by Hsüeh Lun-tao (c. 1531–c. 1600), *Ch'üan Ming san-ch'ü*, 3:2880, l. 1.

94. This four-character expression occurs ubiquitously in Chinese literature. See, e.g., a letter by Ou-yang Hsiu (1007–72) written in 1063, in *Ou-yang Yung-shu chi* (The collected works of Ou-yang Hsiu), 3 vols. (Shanghai: Shang-wu yin-shu kuan, 1958), vol. 2, *ts'e* 11, *chüan* 7, p. 73, l. 6; a lyric by Chang Yeh (13th–14th centuries), *Ch'üan Chin Yüan tz'u*, 2:900, upper register, l. 4; the prose preface to a song suite by Wang Yüan-ting (14th century), *Ch'üan Yüan san-ch'ü*, 1:690, l. 5; *Yüan-ch'ü hsüan*, 1:6, l. 2; *Yüan-ch'ü hsüan wai-pien*, 1:91, l. 7; the Ming tsa-chü drama *Huang T'ing-tao yeh-tsou Liu-hsing ma* (Huang T'ing-tao steals the horse Shooting Star by night), by Huang Yüan-chi (14th century), in *Ming-jen tsa-chü hsüan*, scene 4, p. 110, l. 10; the anonymous Yüan-Ming tsa-chü drama *Sung Kung-ming p'ai chiu-kung pa-kua chen* (Sung Chiang deploys the nine-palace eight-trigram battle formation), in *Ku-pen Yüan Ming tsa-chü*, vol. 3, scene 1, p. 2a, l. 5; the anonymous Yüan-Ming tsa-chü drama *Nü ku-ku shuo-fa sheng-t'ang chi* (The nun who took the pulpit to expound the dharma), in ibid., vol. 3, *hsieh-tzu* (wedge), p. 1a, ll. 3–4; *P'o-yao chi*, *chüan* 2, scene 25, p. 27a, l. 4; *Wu Lun-ch'üan Pei*, *chüan* 4, scene 27, p. 23a, l. 5; *Yüeh Fei p'o-lu tung-ch'uang chi*, *chüan* 1, scene 10, p. 13a, l. 3; a lyric by Ku Hsün (1418–1505), *Ch'üan Ming tz'u*, 1:288, upper register, l. 4; a lyric by T'ang Yin (1470–1524), ibid., 2:495, upper register, l. 12; *Huang-Ming k'ai-yün ying-wu chuan*, *chüan* 1, p. 9b, l. 10; *Pa-i chi*, scene 6, p. 10, l. 9; a song by Hsüeh Lun-tao (c. 1531–c. 1600), *Ch'üan Ming san-ch'ü*, 3:2807, l. 8; *[Hsin-k'o] Shih-shang hua-yen ch'ü-lo t'an-hsiao chiu-ling*, *chüan* 1, p. 16b, upper register, l. 5; and an abundance of other occurrences, too numerous to list.

95. This five-character line is taken from a poem by Tu Fu (712–70), written in 756. See *Ch'üan T'ang shih*, vol. 4, *chüan* 224, p. 2388, l. 16.

96. The song suite, of which this is the first song, is attributed to Chu Yu-tun (1379–1439). See *Ch'üan Ming san-ch'ü*, 1:378–79. This song is also preserved in *Sheng-shih hsin-sheng*, p. 277, ll. 6–8; *Tz'u-lin chai-yen*, 2:1023, ll. 7–9, and *Yung-hsi yüeh-fu*, ts'e 8, p. 4a, ll. 2–4. The versions in *Sheng-shih hsin-sheng* and *Tz'u-lin chai-yen* are closer to the version in the novel than is that in *Yung-hsi yüeh-fu*. The fulsome praise expressed in this song suite is surely intended to be ironic since it is performed in honor not of a paragon of bureaucratic rectitude but of a corrupt eunuch.

97. This idiomatic four-character expression meaning "scarcely worth mentioning" occurs ubiquitously in Chinese literature. See, e.g., a letter by Su Shih (1037–1101), *Su Shih wen-chi*, vol. 4, *chüan* 59, p. 1790, l. 14; *Yüan-ch'ü hsüan*, 3:1207, ll. 11–12; *Yüan-ch'ü hsüan wai-pien*, 1:22, l. 20; *Pai Niang-tzu yung-chen Lei-feng T'a*, p. 425, l. 15; *San-kuo chih t'ung-su yen-i*, vol. 1, *chüan* 5, p. 207, l. 12; *Ming-chu chi*, scene 9, p. 25, ll. 6–7; *Shui-hu ch'üan-chuan*, vol. 1, ch. 4, p. 60, l. 10; *T'ang-shu chih-chuan t'ung-su yen-i*, vol. 2, *chüan* 8, p. 41b, l. 6; *Nan Sung chih-chuan*, vol. 1, *chüan* 7, p. 24b, l. 2; *Pei Sung chih-chuan*, vol. 2, *chüan* 1, p. 13a, l. 9; *Ming-feng chi*, scene 37, p. 156, l. 8; the ch'uan-ch'i drama *Chieh-hsia chi* (The steadfast knight errant), by Hsü San-chieh (fl. late 16th century), *Liu-shih chung ch'ü* ed., scene 15, p. 37, l. 9; *San-pao t'ai-chien Hsi-yang chi t'ung-su yen-i*, vol. 2, ch. 54, p. 699, l. 13; and *I-hsia chi*, scene 25, p. 68, l. 4.

98. Ch'en Kuan (1057–1122) is a prominent historical figure. For his biography, see *Sung shih*, vol. 31, *chüan* 345, pp. 10961–64.

99. This date corresponds to the year 1112 in the Western calendar.

100. Liang-yüan is the name of a park near K'ai-feng, established by an imperial prince of the Former Han dynasty, and frequented by many of the most famous writers of the day.

101. This four-character expression occurs in *Yüan-ch'ü hsüan*, 3:1260, l. 17; *Yüan-ch'ü hsüan wai-pien*, 2:674, l. 15; and recurs in the *Chin P'ing Mei tz'u-hua*, vol. 4, ch. 77, p. 8b, ll. 6–7.

102. These two lines occur together in a lyric by Wang Yün (1228–1304), *Ch'üan Chin Yüan tz'u*, 2:649, lower register, l. 10.

103. This line occurs in a song suite by Chang K'o-chiu (1270–1348), where it is preceded by a variant of the following line. See *Ch'üan Yüan san-ch'ü*, 1:997, l. 2.

104. This line occurs in *[Chi-p'ing chiao-chu] Hsi-hsiang chi*, play no. 4, scene 4, p. 167, l. 13; *Yüan-ch'ü hsüan*, 2:713, l. 7; a song suite by Sun Chi-ch'ang (14th century), *Ch'üan Yüan san-ch'ü*, 2:1243, l. 14; a song by Sheng Ts'ung-chou (14th century), *Ch'üan Ming san-ch'ü*, 1:250, l. 8; and the tsa-chü drama *Wang Lan-ch'ing chen-lieh chuan* (The story of Wang Lan-ch'ing's heroic refusal to remarry), by K'ang Hai (1475–1541), in *Ku-pen Yüan Ming tsa-chü*, vol. 2, scene 2, p. 3b, l. 11.

105. This song is attributed to Chang Ming-shan (14th century). See *Ch'üan Yüan san-ch'ü*, 2:1280, ll. 1–3. It is also included in the sixteenth-century anthology of short songs entitled *Yüeh-fu ch'ün-chu* (A string of lyric pearls), modern edition edited by Lu Ch'ien (Shanghai: Shang-wu yin-shu kuan, 1957), p. 273, ll. 8–9; *Sheng-shih hsin-sheng*, p. 578, ll. 6–8; and *Tz'u-lin chai-yen*, 1:73, ll. 1–4. The version in the novel is identical to those in the last two anthologies but varies slightly from that in *Yüeh-fu ch'ün-chu*.

106. This couplet has already occurred in the *Chin P'ing Mei*. See Roy, *The Plum in the Golden Vase*, vol. 1, chap. 8, n. 45.

107. This four-character expression occurs in a poem by Lo Yin (833–909), *Ch'üan T'ang shih*, vol. 10, *chüan* 658, p. 7558, l. 6.

108. This four-character expression occurs in a lyric by the poetess Li Ch'ing-chao (1084–c. 1151), *Ch'üan Sung tz'u*, 2:928, lower register, l. 8.

109. Synonymous variants of this line occur in a poem by a Sung dynasty poet named Hsia Chih-chung, *Ch'üan Sung shih*, 72:45517, l. 11; and the long sixteenth-century literary tale *Liu sheng mi Lien chi* (The story of Liu I-ch'un's quest of Sun Pi-lien), in *Kuo-se t'ien-hsiang*, *chüan* 3, p. 31, l. 6. It occurs in the same form as in the novel in a fragment of an anonymous lyric by a Sung dynasty author. See *Ch'üan Sung tz'u*, 5:3745, upper register, l. 9.

110. This poem is taken from *Huai-ch'un ya-chi*, vol. 3, *chüan* 10, p. 21a, ll. 7–8.

CHAPTER 66

1. This poem, with some textual variation, is taken from *Huai-ch'un ya-chi*, *chüan* 10, p. 33a, l. 15–p. 33b, l. 2.

2. See Roy, *The Plum in the Golden Vase*, vol. 2, chap. 39, n. 71. For a comprehensive and meticulously documented study of the Taoist rituals and religious iconography described in this chapter, see Wang Kang, *Lang-man ch'ing-kan yü tsung-chiao ching-shen: wan-Ming wen-hsüeh yü wen-hua ssu-ch'ao* (Romantic feeling and religious consciousness: Trends in late Ming literature and culture) (Hong Kong: T'ien-ti t'u-shu yu-hsien kung-ssu, 1999), pp. 217–42.

3. The name of this Taoist deity occurs in *I-chien chih*, vol. 2, *ping-chih* (third record), *chüan* 10, p. 449, l. 8; and *Hsi-yu chi*, vol. 2, ch. 90, p. 1024, l. 2.

4. Both the Eastern Peak and Feng-tu are alleged in Taoist texts to be the sites of the courts of the underworld.

5. See Roy, *The Plum in the Golden Vase*, vol. 3, chap. 57, n. 66.

6. This name probably refers to Huan K'ai (d. 502). For a study of the development of the legends about this Taoist figure, see Michel Strickmann, "Saintly Fools and Chinese Masters (Holy Fools)," *Asia Major*, Third Series, 7, 1 (1994): 35–57.

7. This name probably refers to Liu Hou (4th century). See *San-chiao yüan-liu sou-shen ta-ch'üan* (Complete compendium on the pantheons of the three religions), pref. dated 1593, fac. repr. (Taipei: Lien-ching ch'u-pan shih-yeh kung-ssu, 1980), p. 195.

8. This name probably refers to Wu T'ao (979–1036). For a study of the legends about this figure and his apotheosis, see Kenneth Dean, *Taoist Ritual and the Popular Cults of Southeast China* (Princeton: Princeton University Press, 1993), pp. 61–97.

9. This name probably refers to a legendary Taoist figure named Lu Feng, about whom an anecdote may be found in *San-tung ch'ün-hsien lu* (Records of the immortals of the three caverns), comp. Ch'en Pao-kuang (12th century), pref. dated 1154, *Cheng-t'ung Tao-tsang*, *ts'e* 994, *chüan* 15, pp. 6a-6b. This anecdote is said to be quoted from a lost work entitled *Hsien-chuan shih-i* (Salvaged biographies of immortals), comp. Tu Kuang-t'ing (850–933).

10. This sentence is garbled in all versions of the text and is unintelligible as it stands. I have adopted the emendation suggested in Mei Chieh, *Chin P'ing Mei tz'u-hua chiao-tu chi* (Collation notes on the text of the *Chin P'ing Mei tz'u-hua*) (Peking: Pei-ching t'u-shu kuan ch'u-pan she, 2004), p. 306, ll. 14–17.

11. This line is taken from *Shui-hu ch'üan-chuan*, vol. 2, ch. 51, p. 845, l. 10.

12. See chap. 65, n. 2.

13. This four-character expression occurs in *Chien-teng yü-hua*, chüan 5, p. 288, l. 16.

14. There is a sixteenth-century figure of this name who passed the *chin-shih* examinations in 1547 and served as an official until 1556, though he was not a Taoist priest. See *Ming-jen chuan-chi tzu-liao so-yin* (Index to biographical materials on Ming figures) (Taipei: Kuo-li chung-yang t'u-shu kuan, 1978), p. 650.

15. See Roy, *The Plum in the Golden Vase*, vol. 2, chap. 35, n. 12.

16. For a photograph of such a robe, with its extended embroidered sleeves, see Lagerwey, *Taoist Ritual in Chinese Society and History*, p. 314.

17. This four-character expression occurs in *Hsi-yu chi*, vol. 1, ch. 5, p. 54, l. 12.

18. On this formidable deity, see Davis, *Society and the Supernatural in Song China*, p. 75. His name occurs frequently in Chinese vernacular literature. See, e.g., *Yüan-ch'ü hsüan*, 1:179, l. 1; *Yüan-ch'ü hsüan wai-pien*, 3:961, l. 18; *San-kuo chih t'ung-su yen-i*, vol. 2, chüan 21, p. 977, l. 8; *Shui-hu ch'üan-chuan*, vol. 1, ch. 13, p. 192, l. 7; and *Hsi-yu chi*, vol. 1, ch. 7, p. 74, l. 13; and passim.

19. This clause occurs verbatim in *Shui-hu ch'üan-chuan*, vol. 3, ch. 71, p. 1194, l. 6.

20. Orthographic variants of this four-character expression occur three times in *Hou-Han shu*, vol. 4, chüan 31, p. 1092, l. 5; vol. 5, chüan 42, p. 1424, l. 7; and vol. 10, chüan 89, p. 2957, l. 3. Each of these occurrences refers to events that date to the first century A.D. It appears in the same form as in the novel in *Sui shu* (History of the Sui dynasty [581–618]), comp. Wei Cheng (580–643) et al., 6 vols. (Peking: Chung-hua shu-chü, 1973), vol. 4, chüan 41, p. 1181, l. 15; *Su-shui chi-wen* (Things heard by a man from Su-shui), comp. Ssu-ma Kuang (1019–86) (Peking: Chung-hua shu-chü, 1989), chüan 8, p. 151, l. 6; *Chien-teng yü-hua*, chüan 4, p. 244, l. 10; *Hsi-yu chi*, vol. 2, ch. 99, p. 1121, l. 8; and *San-pao t'ai-chien Hsi-yang chi t'ung-su yen-i*, vol. 2, ch. 71, p. 921, l. 11.

21. This four-character expression recurs in the *Chin P'ing Mei tz'u-hua*, vol. 4, ch. 66, p. 8a, l. 5.

22. This four-character expression occurs in *San-kuo chih t'ung-su yen-i*, vol. 2, chüan 21, p. 1005, l. 24.

23. See Roy, *The Plum in the Golden Vase*, vol. 2, chap. 39, n. 72.

24. This four-character expression occurs in a lyric by Hsü Fu (1075–1141), *Ch'üan Sung tz'u*, 2:743, lower register, l. 15; a lyric by Ts'ai Shen (1088–1156), ibid., 2:1010, upper register, l. 12; a song by Ao-tun Chou-ch'ing (13th century), *Ch'üan Yüan san-ch'ü*, 1:152, l. 7; a song suite by Ma Chih-yüan (c. 1250–c. 1325), ibid., 1:258, l. 9; a song suite by Kao An-tao (14th century), ibid., 2:1110, l. 3; a song by Chung Ssu-ch'eng (c. 1279–c. 1360), ibid., 2:1355, ll. 7–8; *Yüan-ch'ü hsüan*, 1:89, l. 14; a lyric by Li T'ang (b. 1463, cs 1487), *Ch'üan Ming tz'u*, 2:432, upper register, l. 1; a song suite by Chang Po-ch'un (fl. early 16th century), *Ch'üan Ming san-ch'ü*, 2:1339, l. 6; a song suite by Chang Lien (cs 1544), ibid., 2:1699, l. 13; *Shui-hu ch'üan-chuan*, vol. 2, ch. 42, p. 677, l. 7; and *Ch'ien-t'ang hu-yin Chi-tien Ch'an-shih yü-lu*, p. 15b, l. 7. It also recurs in the *Chin P'ing Mei tz'u-hua*, vol. 4, ch. 78, p. 9a, l. 9.

25. This four-character expression designating the legendary abodes of the immortals occurs ubiquitously in Chinese vernacular literature. See, e.g., a lyric by Lu Yin

(1098–1176), *Ch'üan Sung tz'u pu-chi* (Supplement to Complete *tz'u* lyrics of the Sung), comp. K'ung Fan-li (Peking: Chung-hua shu-chü, 1981), p. 30, lower register, l. 9; a lyric by Shih Hao (1106–94), *Ch'üan Sung tz'u*, 2:1272, upper register, l. 1; a lyric by Wang Che (1112–70), *Ch'üan Chin Yüan tz'u*, 1:211, upper register, l. 13; a lyric by Ma Yü (1123–83), ibid., 1:319, upper register, l. 6; a lyric by Ch'en Liang (1143–94), *Ch'üan Sung tz'u*, 3:2110, upper register, l. 5; a lyric by Ko Ch'ang-keng (1134–1229), ibid., 4:2567, upper register, l. 14; a lyric by Liu Ch'u-hsüan (1147–1203), *Ch'üan Chin Yüan tz'u*, 1:428, upper register, l. 16; a song suite by Pu-hu-mu (d. 1300), *Ch'üan Yüan san-ch'ü*, 1:77, l. 7; the anonymous early hsi-wen drama *Liu Wen-lung ling-hua ching* (Liu Wen-lung's caltrop-patterned mirror), in *Sung-Yüan hsi-wen chi-i*, p. 216, ll. 2–3; *Yüan-ch'ü hsüan*, 3:1048, l. 20; *Yüan-ch'ü hsüan wai-pien*, 3:883, l. 5; *Hai-fu shan-t'ang tz'u-kao*, chüan 1, p. 27, l. 3; a song suite by Yin Shih-tan (1522–82), *Ch'üan Ming san-ch'ü*, 2:2346, ll. 8–9; *Hsi-yu chi*, vol. 1, ch. 26, p. 294, l. 2; *San-pao t'ai-chien Hsi-yang chi t'ung-su yen-i*, vol. 2, ch. 67, p. 865, l. 5; a set of songs by Hsüeh Lun-tao (c. 1531–c. 1600), *Ch'üan Ming san-ch'ü*, 3:2784, l. 10; and an abundance of other occurrences too numerous to list.

26. Variants of this couplet occur in some early versions of the fourteenth-century tsa-chü drama *Liang-shih yin-yüan* (Two lives of love), by Ch'iao Chi (d. 1345), *Ch'iao Chi chi* (The collected works of Ch'iao Chi), ed. and annot. Li Hsiu-sheng et al. (T'ai-yüan: Shan-hsi jen-min ch'u-pan she, 1988), p. 143, l. 13; *Yüan-ch'ü hsüan*, 2:777, l. 3; and 3:1093, ll. 3–4; and *Yüan-ch'ü hsüan wai-pien*, 2:380, l. 5; and 3:809, ll. 2–3. Variants of the second line also occur independently in a song suite from the lost thirteenth-century tsa-chü drama *Ku-p'en ko Chuang-tzu t'an k'u-lou* (Singing while drumming on a basin, Chuang-tzu sighs over a skull), by Li Shou-ch'ing (13th century), in *Yüan-jen tsa-chü kou-ch'en* (Rescued fragments from tsa-chü drama by Yüan authors), comp. Chao Ching-shen (Shanghai: Shang-hai ku-tien wen-hsüeh ch'u-pan she, 1956), p. 35, l. 8; and *Yüan-ch'ü hsüan wai-pien*, 1:33, l. 8.

27. This may refer to Chang Che (1261–1314), the founder of a Taoist sect, whose religious name was Kuang-hui. See *Chung-hua tao-chiao ta tz'u-tien* (Encyclopedia of the Chinese Taoist religion), comp. Hu Fu-ch'en et al. (Peking: Chung-kuo she-hui k'o-hsüeh ch'u-pan she, 1995), p. 68.

28. The proximate source of this passage of parallel prose is *Shui-hu ch'üan-chuan*, vol. 2, ch. 53, p. 882, l. 16–p. 883, l. 2.

29. This four-character expression occurs in *Ju-ju chü-shih yü-lu* (The recorded sayings of layman Ju-ju), by Yen Ping (d. 1212), pref. dated 1194, photocopy of manuscript in the Kyoto University Library, *i-chi* (second collection), chüan 4, p. 5b, l. 4. It is based on a passage in *Chuang-tzu*. See *Chuang-tzu yin-te*, ch, 18, p. 46, l. 15; and Watson, *The Complete Works of Chuang Tzu*, ch. 18, pp. 191–92.

30. According to the biography of Lien Fan (1st century A.D.), his administration was so beneficial to the local populace that they sang a song about him that ended with the line, "All our lives we have not even had a shirt for our backs, but now we have five pairs of trousers." See *Hou-Han shu*, vol. 4, chüan 31, p. 1103, l. 15.

31. A synonymous variant of the preceding six characters occurs in *Tung-t'ien hsüan-chi*, scene 4, p. 13b, l. 7. They occur verbatim as in the novel in *Yüan-ch'ü hsüan wai-pien*, 3:836, l. 5.

32. These two lines describing the substitution of inferior goods for the genuine article are proverbial. They occur in the biography of the usurper Ssu-ma Lun (d. 301)

in *Chin shu*, vol. 5, *chüan* 59, p. 1602, l. 5; and *Ch'ao-yeh ch'ien-tsai* (Comprehensive record of affairs within and without the court), comp. Chang Cho (cs 675) (Peking: Chung-hua shu-chü, 1979), *chüan* 1, p. 7, l. 9.

33. Lu Pan, or Kung-shu Pan of Lu, is a legendary master carpenter who is said to have lived in the state of Lu during the Spring and Autumn period (722–481 B.C.). Variants of this idiomatic expression occur in a prose preface written in 795 by Liu Tsung-yüan (773–819), in *Liu Ho-tung chi* (The collected works of Liu Tsung-yüan), 2 vols. (Peking: Chung-hua shu-chü, 1961), vol. 1, *chüan* 21, p. 375, l. 3; the recorded sayings of the Buddhist monk Wen-yen (864–949), *Ku tsun-su yü-lu*, *chüan* 18, p. 193a, lower register, l. 14; a letter from Ou-yang Hsiu (1007–72) to Mei Yao-ch'en (1002–60) written in 1044, *Ou-yang Yung-shu chi*, vol. 3, *ts'e* 17, *chüan* 6, p. 39, l. 9; *Yüan-ch'ü hsüan*, 3:1252, l. 3; the anonymous early Ming tsa-chü drama *Chang Yü-hu wu-su nü-chen kuan* (Chang Yü-hu mistakenly spends the night in a Taoist nunnery), in *Ming-jen tsa-chü hsüan*, scene 2, p. 607, l. 8; *Shih Chen-jen ssu-sheng so pai-yüan*, scene 3, p. 10b, l. 8; *Yü-huan chi*, scene 6, p. 18, l. 10; *Ch'ien-chin chi*, scene 32, p. 106, l. 12; *San-kuo chih t'ung-su yen-i*, vol. 2, *chüan* 23, p. 1100, ll. 15–16; *Chiang Shih yüeh-li chi*, *chüan* 1, scene 6, p. 10b, ll. 2–3; *Shui-hu ch'üan-chuan*, vol. 1, ch. 21, p. 311, l. 8; *Ssu-hsi chi*, scene 20, p. 51, l. 7; the ch'uan-ch'i drama *Yü-tsan chi* (The story of the jade hairpin), by Kao Lien (1527–c. 1603), probably written in 1570, ed. and annot. Huang Shang (Shanghai: Shang-hai ku-tien wen-hsüeh ch'u-pan she, 1956), scene 16, p. 58, l. 10; *Ssu-sheng yüan*, play no. 4, scene 4, p. 83, l. 15; and *Hsi-yu chi*, vol. 2, ch. 64, p. 735, l. 16.

34. On Taoist lamp rituals, see Schipper and Verellen, *The Taoist Canon: A Historical Companion to the Daozang*, vol. 2, pp. 962–71.

35. This four-character expression occurs in the *Tu-jen ching* (Scripture of salvation), an important Taoist text believed to date from ca. 400. See *Ling-pao wu-liang tu-jen shang-p'in miao-ching* (Most excellent and mysterious scripture of the numinous treasure that saves innumerable human beings), in *Cheng-t'ung Tao-tsang*, ts'e 1, *chüan* 1, p. 7b, ll. 5–6. This text is translated in Stephen R. Bokenkamp, *Early Daoist Scriptures* (Berkeley: University of California Press, 1997), pp. 373–438.

36. This four-character expression occurs in *Ling-pao wu-liang tu-jen shang-p'in miao-ching*, ts'e 1, *chüan* 1, p. 7b, l. 6.

37. This four-character expression recurs in the *Chin P'ing Mei tz'u-hua*, vol. 4, ch. 66, p. 8b, l. 10.

38. This four-character expression occurs in a commentary on the *Vajracchedikā prajñāpāramitā sutra* by Li Wen-hui (d. 1158), as quoted in *Chin-kang ching chi-chu*, p. 66a, column 2; a lyric by Chu Tun-ju (1081–1159), *Ch'üan Sung tz'u*, 2:856, upper register, l. 12; a lyric by Hsin Ch'i-chi (1140–1207), ibid., 3:1919, lower register, l. 8; and a lyric by Ch'en Chu (1214–97), ibid., 4:3050, upper register, l. 2.

39. On this short text, see Schipper and Verellen, *The Taoist Canon: A Historical Companion to the Daozang*, 1:351–52.

40. This line occurs verbatim in *Chiu-t'ien sheng-shen chang ching* (Scripture of the stanzas of the vitalizing spirits of the Nine Heavens), in *Yün-chi ch'i-ch'ien*, *chüan* 16, p. 90, left column, ll. 17–18.

41. This four-character expression occurs in ibid., l. 21.

42. This four-character expression occurs in ibid., l. 22.

43. This five-character expression occurs in ibid., ll. 24–25.

44. For this four-character expression, see ibid., l. 25.

45. These four successive three-character expressions occur in ibid., right column, ll. 3–4.

46. This five-character expression occurs in ibid., l. 7.

47. This four-character expression recurs in the *Chin P'ing Mei tz'u-hua*, vol. 4, ch. 66, p. 10a, ll. 7–8.

48. *T'ai-wei* and *Wu-ying*, the deities named in these two lines, are gods of the body who preside over its various functions while alive and have the power to assist in reconstituting it after death. See Isabelle Robinet, *Taoist Meditation: The Mao-shan Tradition of Great Purity*, trans. Julian F. Pas and Norman J. Girardot (Albany: State University of New York Press, 1993), pp. 100–101, 128–29, and 146–48.

49. These four lines of verse occur verbatim in the fifth of the nine stanzas of penta-syllabic verse appended to *Chiu-t'ien sheng-shen chang ching*, in *Yün-chi ch'i-ch'ien*, *chüan* 16, p. 92, right column, ll. 5–6. They also occur independently in the *Cheng-t'ung tsao-tsang*, see, e.g., *Ling-pao ling-chiao chi-tu chin-shu* (The golden book of salvation according to the Ling-pao tradition), comp. Lin Ling-chen (1239–1302), in *Cheng-t'ung tao-tsang*, *ts'e* 211, *chüan* 11, p. 12a, ll. 3–4.

50. For Chieh-lin and Yü-i, see Schipper and Verellen, *The Taoist Canon: A Historical Companion to the Daozang*, 1:145.

51. These four lines, with an insignificant textual variation in the last line, occur in *Ling-pao yü-chien* (Jade mirror of the Numinous Treasure), probably compiled in the twelfth century, in *Cheng-t'ung Tao-tsang*, *ts'e* 311, *chüan* 40, p. 14b, ll. 3–4.

52. See Roy, *The Plum in the Golden Vase*, vol. 2, chap. 39, n. 12.

53. The "Five Offerings" were ritual presentations of incense, flowers, votive candles, water, and fruits.

54. This four-character expression occurs in *Ling-pao wu-liang tu-jen shang-p'in miao-ching*, *ts'e* 1, *chüan* 1, p. 10b, l. 9.

55. This four-character expression occurs in ibid., *ts'e* 1, *chüan* 1, p. 11a, l. 1.

56. These nine precepts occur in a text at least as old as the T'ang dynasty (618–907). See *T'ai-shang chiu-chen miao-chieh chin-lu tu-ming pa-tsui miao-ching* (Scripture of the golden register for the redemption of sins and for salvation [including] the marvel-ous precepts of the nine perfected), in *Cheng-t'ung Tao-tsang*, *ts'e* 77, p. 5b, l. 9–p. 6a, l. 3. In this version the order of the first two precepts has been reversed. They occur in exactly the same form as in the novel elsewhere in the Taoist Canon. See, e.g., *Ling-pao wu-liang tu-jen shang-ching ta-fa* (Great rites of the preeminent scripture of the numinous treasure that saves innumerable human beings), comp. ca. 1200, in *Cheng-t'ung Tao-tsang*, *ts'e* 85, *chüan* 2, p. 3b, ll. 5–9; and *Shang-ch'ing ling-pao ta-fa* (Great rites of the upper clarity numinous treasure), comp. Chin Yün-chung (13th century), in ibid., *ts'e* 971, *chüan* 37, p. 37b, l. 9–p. 38a, l. 7.

57. This four-character expression occurs in *Huang-chi chin-tan chiu-lien cheng-hsin kuei-chen huan-hsiang pao-chüan*, 8:480, l. 5; *K'u-kung wu-tao chüan*, 1:205, l. 4; and *T'an-shih wu-wei pao-chüan*, 1:535, l. 3. It also recurs in the *Chin P'ing Mei tz'u-hua*, vol. 4, ch. 66, p. 9b. l. 11; and ch. 74, p. 17b, l. 7.

58. This four-character expression occurs in the anonymous early Ming tsa-chü drama *Huang-hua Yü tieh-ta Ts'ai Ko-ta* (Ts'ai the Blister gets his comeuppance in Chrysanthemum Valley), in *Ch'ün-yin lei-hsüan*, 3:1836, l. 9; and *Hung-fu chi*, scene 31, p. 65, l. 5.

59. This four-character expression occurs in a quatrain attributed to Hsü Shou-hsin (1033–1108), *Ch'üan Sung shih*, 12:8381, l. 9; *Yüan-ch'ü hsüan*, 2:773, l. 15; and *Ta-Sung chung-hsing yen-i*, vol. 1, *chüan* 2, p. 23a, l. 9.

60. This four-character expression occurs in a quatrain by Fan Ch'eng-ta (1126–93), *Ch'üan Sung shih*, 41:25783, l. 7.

61. This four-character expression occurs in a song suite by Ch'en To (fl. early 16th century), *Ch'üan Ming san-ch'ü*, 1:588, l. 5; a set of songs by Ch'ang Lun (1493–1526), ibid., 2:1532, l. 3; an anonymous song suite, in *Yung-hsi yüeh-fu*, *ts'e* 6, p. 31a, ll. 7–8; and an anonymous song, in *Nan-kung tz'u-chi*, vol. 2, *chüan* 4, p. 218, l. 4.

62. This four-character expression occurs in the early vernacular story *Shih Hung-chao lung-hu chün-ch'en hui* (Shih Hung-chao: The meeting of dragon and tiger, ruler and minister), in *Ku-chin hsiao-shuo*, vol. 1, *chüan* 15, p. 231, l. 1; *Sha-kou chi*, scene 24, p. 92, l. 1; *Yu-kuei chi*, scene 22, p. 64, l. 5; *Yüeh Fei p'o-lu tung-ch'uang chi*, *chüan* 2, scene 39, p. 32a, l. 9; a song suite by Ch'en To (fl. early 16th century), *Ch'üan Ming san-ch'ü*, 1:621, l. 8; *Huai-hsiang chi*, scene 40, p. 133, l. 12; *Hsiu-ju chi*, scene 35, p. 99, l. 12; *Nan Hsi-hsiang chi* (Li Jih-hua), scene 36, p. 107, l. 8; and *San-pao t'ai-chien Hsi-yang chi t'ung-su yen-i*, vol. 2, ch. 84, p. 1089, l. 6.

63. This four-character expression occurs in a short text dating from the T'ang dynasty (618–907) entitled *T'ai-shang Tao-chün shuo chieh-yüan pa-tu miao-ching* (Marvelous scripture for delivery from enmity and salvation enunciated by the Most High Lord of the Tao), in *Cheng-t'ung Tao-tsang*, *ts'e* 181, p. 1b, l. 9.

64. This four-character expression occurs in the fragmentary tenth-century Tun-huang manuscript *Fu-mu en chung ching chiang-ching wen* (Sutra lecture on the Sutra on the importance of parental kindness), in *Tun-huang pien-wen chi*, 2:700, l. 3; *Kuan-shih-yin p'u-sa pen-hsing ching*, p. 26b, l. 10; *Ju-ju chü-shih yü-lu*, *chia-chi* (first collection), *chüan* 1, p. 5a, l. 14; *Yüan-ch'ü hsüan*, 2:643, l. 8; *Yüan-ch'ü hsüan wai-pien*, 1:107, l. 7; *T'an-shih wu-wei pao-chüan*, 1:449, l. 2; *Wei-wei pu-tung T'ai-shan shen-ken chieh-kuo pao-chüan*, 3:614, l. 4; *Mu-lien chiu-mu ch'üan-shan hsi-wen*, *chüan* 2, p. 38b, l. 7; and *Hsi-yu chi*, vol. 2, ch. 78, p. 892, l. 9.

65. This four-character expression occurs in a poem by Huan-yang-tzu (9th century), *Ch'üan T'ang shih pu-pien*, 2:1183, l. 11; *Fu-mu en chung ching chiang-ching wen* (Sutra lecture on the Sutra on the importance of parental kindness), dated 927, in *Tun-huang pien-wen chi*, 2:675, l. 4; *Yüan-ch'ü hsüan*, 3:1127, l. 21; *Ching-ch'ai chi*, scene 10, p. 29, l. 1; Chüeh-lien's commentary to the *Chin-kang k'o-i*, *[Hsiao-shih] Chin-kang k'o-i [hui-yao chu-chieh]* ([Clearly presented] liturgical exposition of the Diamond Sutra [with critical commentary]), ed. and annot. Chüeh-lien, pref. dated 1551, in *[Shinzan] Dai Nihon zoku zōkyō*, 24:743, middle register, l. 11; and *Ta-T'ang Ch'in-wang tz'u-hua*, vol. 1, *chüan* 1, ch. 5, p. 53a, l. 3.

66. This four-character expression occurs in a speech attributed to the Buddhist monk Ch'ing-chu (807–88), in *Tsu-t'ang chi*, *chüan* 6, p. 149, l. 4; and *Yen P'ing-chung erh-t'ao sha san-shih*, p. 384, l. 3.

67. This four-character expression occurs in *Yu-kuei chi*, scene 19, p. 47, l. 7.

68. This four-character expression occurs in a prose postface to a rhapsody by Lu Chao (cs 843), *Ch'üan T'ang wen*, vol. 16, *chüan* 768, p. 19a, l. 8; a poem by T'ien Hsi (940–1004), *Ch'üan Sung shih*, 1:496, l. 5; a song suite by Ch'ien Lin (14th century), *Ch'üan Yüan san-ch'ü*, 2:1031, l. 5; and a literary tale in *Yüan-chu chih-yü: hsüeh-ch'uang t'an-i* (Supplementary guide to Mandarin Duck Island: tales of the unusual from the snowy window), (Peking: Chung-hua shu-chü, 1997), *chüan* 1, p. 28, l. 8.

69. This four-character expression occurs in *Lieh-kuo chih-chuan*, vol. 3, *chüan* 8, p. 45b, l. 8.

70. This couplet is from a poem by Kao Chu (1170–1241), *Ch'üan Sung shih*, 55:34135, l. 11. The first line occurs independently in a set of songs by Yang Shen (1488–1559), *Ch'üan Ming san-ch'ü*, 2:1415, l. 8; *Yen-chih chi*, *chüan* 2, scene 21, p. 2a, l. 11; and *Mu-lien chiu-mu ch'üan-shan hsi-wen*, *chüan* 1, p. 57a, l. 3. The second line occurs independently in *Yü-huan chi*, scene 3, p. 5, ll. 8–9; *Pao-chien chi*, scene 42, p. 76, l. 9; and *Mu-lien chiu-mu ch'üan-shan hsi-wen*, *chüan* 3, p. 19a, l. 9. The couplet in full is quoted in *Pai-she chi*, *chüan* 2, scene 20, p. 17b, l. 6; *Ming-feng chi*, scene 10, p. 43, ll. 4–5; and *Mu-lien chiu-mu ch'üan-shan hsi-wen*, *chüan* 3, p. 20b, l. 4.

CHAPTER 67

1. A heptasyllabic line identical to this one in structure and meaning but with a different word for "you" occurs in a song by Yang Shen (1488–1559), *Ch'üan Ming san-ch'ü*, 2:1444, l. 3.

2. This four-character expression occurs in *I-chien chih*, vol. 2, *ting-chih* (fourth record), *chüan* 19, p. 698, l. 12; *Chien-teng yü-hua*, *chüan* 5, p. 280, l. 6; and a literary tale in *Yüan-chu chih-yü: hsüeh-ch'uang t'an-i*, *chüan* 2, p. 77, l. 1.

3. See Roy, *The Plum in the Golden Vase*, vol. 3, chap. 52, n. 8.

4. A synonymous variant of this four-character expression occurs in *Mo-tzu yin-te* (A concordance to *Mo-tzu*) (Peking: Yenching University Press, 1948), ch. 48, p. 85, ll. 6–7; and in a literary tale attributed to Niu Seng-ju (779–847), in *Hsüan-kuai lu* (Accounts of mysteries and anomalies), in *Hsüan-kuai lu; Hsü Hsüan-kuai lu* (Accounts of mysteries and anomalies; Continuation of Accounts of mysteries and anomalies), by Niu Seng-ju (779–847) and Li Fu-yen (9th century) (Peking: Chung-hua shu-chü, 1982), *chüan* 2, p. 23, l. 11. It occurs ubiquitously in the same form as in the novel. See, e.g., *Yüan-ch'ü hsüan*, 1:144, l. 4; a lyric by Shen Hsi (14th century), *Ch'üan Chin Yüan tz'u*, 2:1038, lower register, l. 10; a song by Chia Chung-ming (1343–c. 1422), *Ch'üan Ming san-ch'ü*, 1:173, l. 8; the anonymous Yüan-Ming tsa-chü drama *T'ao Yüan-ming tung-li shang-chü* (T'ao Yüan-ming enjoys the chrysanthemums by the eastern hedge), in *Ku-pen Yüan Ming tsa-chü*, vol. 3, scene 2, p. 8a, l. 3; *Hsiao-p'in chi*, p. 101, l. 10; a song suite by Ch'en To (fl. early 16th century), *Ch'üan Ming san-ch'ü*, 1:634, l. 11; *San-kuo chih t'ung-su yen-i*, vol. 1, *chüan* 8, p. 358, l. 7; *Shui-hu ch'üan-chuan*, vol. 4, ch. 90, p. 1473, l. 4; *T'ang-shu chih-chuan t'ung-su yen-i*, vol. 1, *chüan* 1, p. 14b, l. 1; *Nan Sung chih-chuan*, vol. 1, *chüan* 3, p. 15a, l. 7; *Lieh-kuo chih-chuan*, vol. 1, *chüan* 1, p. 26a, l. 6; *Hai-fu shan-t'ang tz'u-kao*, *chüan* 1, p. 45, l. 4; *Ch'üan-Han chih-chuan*, vol. 2, *chüan* 3, p. 11a, l. 9; *Shuang-lieh chi*, scene 6, p. 16, l. 9; *San-pao t'ai-chien Hsi-yang chi t'ung-su yen-i*, vol. 2, ch. 98, p. 1259, ll. 10–11; *Sui-T'ang liang-ch'ao shih-chuan*, *chüan* 1, ch. 1, p. 5b, l. 7; and an abundance of other occurrences, too numerous to list.

5. This five-character expression occurs in *Liu Sheng mi Lien chi*, *chüan* 3, p. 9b, l. 7.

6. An orthographic variant of this four-character expression occurs in *Yüan-ch'ü hsüan wai-pien*, 2:576, l. 5.

7. This four-character expression, the literal meaning of which is "to escape the womb and change the bones," is a variant of one that has already occurred in the *Chin*

P'ing Mei tz'u-hua, vol. 3, ch. 56, p. 11a, l. 1. See Roy, *The Plum in the Golden Vase*, vol. 3, p. 391, l. 43; and chap. 56, n. 40. It occurs in the same form that it does here in *Yüan-ch'ü hsüan*, 1:313, l. 14; *Yüan-ch'ü hsüan wai-pien*, 3:813, ll. 18–19; *Li Yün-ch'ing te-wu sheng-chen*, scene 3, p. 14a, l. 1; and Chüeh-lien's (16th century) commentary on the *Chin-kang k'o-i, [Hsiao-shih] Chin-kang k'o-i [hui-yao chu-chieh]*, 24:728, lower register, ll. 12–13.

8. Variants of this proverbial couplet occur in *Chang Hsieh chuang-yüan*, scene 45, p. 189, l. 5; and *Sha-kou chi*, scene 14, p. 53, l. 2.

9. This formulaic four-character expression occurs in *Lü-ch'uang hsin-hua*, chüan 1, p. 22, l. 5; a song by Lu Chih (cs 1268), *Ch'üan Yüan san-ch'ü*, 1:127, l. 11; *Chin-ming ch'ih Wu Ch'ing feng Ai-ai*, p. 462, l. 15; and *Hai-ling i-shih*, chüan 2, p. 105, l. 7. It also recurs in the *Chin P'ing Mei tz'u-hua*, vol. 4, ch. 67, p. 22b, l. 9; and ch. 78, p. 9a, l. 8.

10. This four-character expression occurs in *Ko tai hsiao*, scene 1, p. 114, ll. 12–13.

11. This four-character expression recurs in the *Chin P'ing Mei tz'u-hua*, vol. 5, ch. 81, p. 9b, l. 5.

12. This date corresponds to the year 1112 in the Western calendar.

13. See Roy, *The Plum in the Golden Vase*, vol. 1, chap. 18, n. 9.

14. Variants of this proverbial couplet occur in *Shui-hu ch'üan-chuan*, vol. 1, ch. 17, p. 251, l. 14; *Huan-yu chi-wen* (Record of things heard during official travels), by Chang I (16th century), in *Shuo-fu hsü*, 9:732, p. 3a, ll. 2–3; and *K'o-tso chui-yü*, chüan 1, p. 10, l. 7.

15. This four-character expression occurs in an anonymous Sung dynasty lyric, *Ch'üan Sung tz'u*, 5:3742, lower register, l. 8.

16. This song suite is by Liu Shou (b. 1466). For the attribution of authorship, see *Ch'üan Ming san-ch'ü*, 1:843. Versions of it are included in ibid., 1:843–46; as well as *Sheng-shih hsin-sheng*, pp. 345–47; *Tz'u-lin chai-yen*, 2:613–18; and *Yung-hsi yüeh-fu*, ts'e 12, pp. 77a–79b.

17. This proverbial injunction is from *The Book of Rites*. See *Li-chi*, p. 3, ll. 15–16; and Legge, *Li Chi: Book of Rites*, 1:81, ll. 24–26. It occurs exactly as in the novel in *[Chi-p'ing chiao-chu] Hsi-hsiang chi*, play no. 3, scene 4, p. 78, l. 10; and *Huang hsiao-tzu*, chüan 1, scene 9, p. 27b, l. 9. Variants also occur in *Kuan-yüan chi*, scene 18, p. 38, l. 1; and *Shuang-lieh chi*, scene 18, p. 52, l. 6.

18. This four-character expression occurs in *Ching-ch'ai chi*, scene 7, p. 17, l. 10. A homophonic variant also occurs in *Shuang-lieh chi*, scene 4, p. 12, l. 11.

19. This line is misquoted from a poem by Tu Fu (712–70) written in 758, *Ch'üan T'ang shih*, vol. 4, chüan 225, p. 2411, l. 1. The original line reads "jaybird," the name of a tower in the Han dynasty imperial park, rather than "water birds."

20. This four-character expression occurs in *I-chien chih*, vol. 2, chih-i (second supplementary record), chüan 6, p. 841, l. 10; *I-k'u kuei lai tao-jen ch'u-kuai*, p. 188, l. 1; an anonymous song in *Tz'u-lin chai-yen*, 1:51, l. 3; and *Pao-chien chi*, scene 33, p. 61, l. 2.

21. This line occurs verbatim in the late Ming collection of vernacular stories entitled *Ku-chang chüeh-ch'en* (Clapping the hands to shake off the dust of the world), pref. dated 1631, 5 vols., in *Ming-Ch'ing shan-pen hsiao-shuo ts'ung-k'an, ch'u-pien*, vol. 1, ch. 1, p. 9a, l. 2. This leads me to believe that it probably occurs in an earlier poem that has not been identified.

22. These two lines are derived from a famous quatrain by Cheng Ku (cs 887), *Ch'üan T'ang shih*, vol. 10, *chüan* 675, p. 7731, l. 10. They occur together in a lyric by Liu Yung (cs 1034), *Ch'üan Sung tz'u*, 1:42, lower register, ll. 15–16; an anonymous Sung dynasty lyric, ibid. 5:3741, upper register, l. 2; *Yüan-ch'ü hsüan wai-pien*, 1:22, l. 9; *Hsüan-ho i-shih*, p. 37, l. 1; and a song suite by Ch'en So-wen (d. c. 1604), *Ch'üan Ming san-ch'ü*, 2:2559, l. 14. The second line also occurs independently in an anonymous song suite in *Sheng-shih hsin-sheng*, p. 559, l. 1; an anonymous song suite in *Tz'u-lin chai-yen*, 2:869, l. 4; an anonymous song published in 1553, *Ch'üan Ming san-ch'ü*, 4:4572, l. 4; an anonymous song suite in *Yung-hsi yüeh-fu, ts'e* 10, p. 44b, l. 8; and *Ssu-hsi chi*, scene 17, p. 43, l. 7.

23. This four-character expression occurs in *San-pao t'ai-chien Hsi-yang chi t'ung-su yen-i*, vol. 1, ch. 33, p. 426, l. 11.

24. See Roy, *The Plum in the Golden Vase*, vol. 3, chap. 59, n. 2.

25. The source of this song is *Pao-chien chi*, scene 33, p. 61, ll. 8–10.

26. These two lines are from a set of songs by Ching Yüan-ch'i (14th century), *Ch'üan Yüan san-ch'ü*, 2:1150, l. 4. Versions are also included in *Tz'u-lin chai-yen*, 1:142, l. 1; and *Yung-hsi yüeh-fu, ts'e* 15b, p. 17b, l. 3.

27. This is an example of a *hsieh-hou yü* that puns on the word *chü*, meaning "saw," and the word *chü*, meaning "line." I have tried to render this by using the word "piece" in two of its related meanings.

28. This four-character expression occurs in an anonymous song suite in *Yung-hsi yüeh-fu, ts'e* 9, p. 65b, l. 10.

29. The source of this song, with considerable textual variation, is *Pao-chien chi*, scene 33, p. 61, ll. 14–16. This song and the preceding one are sung by the protagonist of the drama, Lin Ch'ung, who has been framed and is serving a sentence as an exiled convict who is exposed to the vicissitudes of the winter weather. His prose soliloquy between the two songs emphasizes the contrast between the enjoyment of the snow by the affluent, who appreciate it in the comfort of their well-heated homes, and the discomfort it imposes on the less privileged who are forced to endure its rigors. The quotations from the drama at this juncture are clearly intended to reflect ironically on Hsi-men Ch'ing's sybaritic lifestyle.

30. This couplet is from a poem by Wen T'ing-yün (c. 812–c. 870), *Ch'üan T'ang shih*, vol. 9, *chüan* 578, p. 6721, l. 8. It is also quoted, with some textual variation, in *Hsi-yu chi*, vol. 1, ch. 23, p. 258, ll. 14–15.

31. A variant version of this proverbial couplet occurs in a speech attributed to the Buddhist monk Shao-wu (12th century), *Wu-teng hui-yüan*, vol. 3, *chüan* 20, p. 1326, l. 9.

32. This four-character expression occurs in *Ju-i chün chuan*, p. 9b, ll. 5–6; and recurs in the *Chin P'ing Mei tz'u-hua*, vol. 4, ch. 73, p. 20b, l. 10.

33. This formulaic four-character expression is ubiquitous in Chinese literature. See, e.g., a poem by Po Chü-i (772–846), *Ch'üan T'ang shih*, vol. 7, *chüan* 437, p. 4850, l. 15; *Yüan-ch'ü hsüan*, 2:702, l. 17; *P'i-p'a chi*, scene 29, p. 164, ll. 7–8: an anonymous song suite in *Yung-hsi yüeh-fu, ts'e* 13, p. 77b, l. 10; a song by Huang O (1498–1569), *Ch'üan Ming san-ch'ü*, 2:1759, l. 6; *Hai-fu shan-t'ang tz'u-kao, chüan* 3, p. 179, l. 10; and a song suite by Shen Ching (1553–1610), *Ch'üan Ming san-ch'ü*, 3:3259, l. 9.

34. This four-character expression recurs in the *Chin P'ing Mei tz'u-hua*, vol. 5, ch. 100, p. 12a, l. 11.

35. See Roy, *The Plum in the Golden Vase*, vol. 3, chap. 59, n. 81.

36. For this allusion, see chap. 65, n. 67.

37. This quatrain is derived, with some textual variation in the first and third lines, from one in *Huai-ch'un ya-chi*, *chüan* 10, p. 37a, ll. 3–4.

38. See Roy, *The Plum in the Golden Vase*, vol. 3, chap. 43, n. 30.

39. This proverbial five-character expression occurs in *Yüan-ch'ü hsüan*, 1:328, l. 20; *Yüan-ch'ü hsüan wai-pien*, 1:2, l. 21; and *Hua Kuan So pien Yün-nan chuan*, p. 4b, l. 15. It also recurs in the *Chin P'ing Mei tz'u-hua*, vol. 4, ch. 79, p. 2b, l. 6.

40. These two lines, with a synonymous variant in the second line, occur together in *Yüan-ch'ü hsüan wai-pien*, 2:498, l. 5.

41. This four-character expression, with a synonymous orthographic variant, recurs in the *Chin P'ing Mei tz'u-hua*, vol. 4, ch. 72, p. 16b, l. 2; and ch. 80, p. 5b, l. 3.

42. This four-character expression occurs ubiquitously in Chinese literature. See, e.g., the biography of the Buddhist monk Tao-hsien (9th century), in *Tsu-t'ang chi*, *chüan* 9, p. 215, l. 6; a poem by Huang T'ing-chien (1045–1105), *Ch'üan Sung shih*, 17:11710, l. 12; *I-chien chih*, vol. 3, *san-chih*, *chi* (third record, section six), *chüan* 7, p. 1352, l. 8; *Ju-ju chü-shih yü-lu*, *chia-chi* (first collection), *chüan* 1, p. 7a, l. 12; *Yüan-ch'ü hsüan*, 1:330, l. 4; the early vernacular story *Hua-teng chiao Lien-nü ch'eng-Fo chi* (The girl Lien-nü attains Buddhahood in her bridal palanquin), in *Ch'ing-p'ing shan-t'ang hua-pen*, p. 203, l. 9; *Ching-ch'ai chi*, scene 48, p. 136, l. 10; *P'o-yao chi*, *chüan* 1, scene 1, p. 1a, l. 5; *Hsiao-p'in chi*, p. 73, l. 11; *Shui-hu ch'üan-chuan*, vol. 1, ch. 19, p. 280, l. 5; *Chung-shan lang*, scene 1, p. 238, ll. 8–9; *Yao-shih pen-yüan kung-te pao-chüan*, 14:221, l. 3; a song by Shen Shih (1488–1565), *Ch'üan Ming san-ch'ü*, 2:1369, l. 11; *Ming-feng chi*, scene 11, p. 48, l. 6; a song suite by Ch'in Shih-yung (late 16th century), *Ch'üan Ming san-ch'ü*, 5:6126, l. 11; *Hsi-yu chi*, vol. 2, ch. 51, p. 594, l. 11; a song by Hsüeh Lun-tao (c. 1531–c. 1600), *Ch'üan Ming san-ch'ü*, 3:2713, l. 1; a set of songs by Hu Wen-huan (fl. 1592–1617), ibid., 3:2920, l. 11; *Ta-T'ang Ch'in-wang tz'u-hua*, vol. 1, *chüan* 2, ch. 9, p. 9b, l. 9; *[Hsin-k'o] Shih-shang hua-yen ch'ü-lo t'an-hsiao chiu-ling*, *chüan* 3, p. 16b, lower register, l. 3; and an abundance of other occurrences, too numerous to list.

43. A variant of this four-character expression occurs in the tsa-chü drama *Hei Hsüan-feng chang-i shu-ts'ai* (The Black Whirlwind is chivalrous and openhanded), by Chu Yu-tun (1379–1439), in *Shui-hu hsi-ch'ü chi*, *ti-i chi*, scene 1, p. 97, l. 7. It occurs in the same form as in the novel in *Shui-hu ch'üan-chuan*, vol. 4, ch. 87, p. 1427, l. 9; and *Hsi-yu chi*, vol. 2, ch. 84, p. 956, l. 8.

44. This four-character expression occurs in the early vernacular story *Chang Ku-lao chung-kua ch'ü Wen-nü* (Chang Ku-lao plants melons and weds Wen-nü), in *Ku-chin hsiao-shuo*, vol. 2, *chüan* 33, p. 499, l. 5; *Chi Ya-fan chin-man ch'an-huo*, p. 283, l. 15; *Cheng Chieh-shih li-kung shen-pi kung*, p. 660, l. 13; *San hsien-shen Pao Lung-t'u tuan-yüan*, p. 176, l. 2; *Shih-wu kuan hsi-yen ch'eng ch'iao-huo*, p. 695, l. 10, and an anonymous Ming dynasty song, *Ch'üan Ming san-ch'ü*, 4:4759, l. 7. A homophonic variant also occurs in *Hsi-yu chi*, vol. 1, ch. 15, p. 168, l. 8.

45. See Roy, *The Plum in the Golden Vase*, vol. 2, chap. 30, n. 37.

46. See ibid., chap. 31, n. 24.

47. This four-character expression occurs in *Hsi-yu chi*, vol. 2, ch. 77, p. 883, l. 2.

48. This formulaic four-character expression occurs ubiquitously in Chinese vernacular literature. See, e.g. *Yüan-ch'ü hsüan*, 2:496, l. 18; *Yüan-ch'ü hsüan wai-pien*,

1:6, l. 2; *Hei Hsüan-feng chang-i shu-ts'ai*, scene 3, p. 109, l. 6; *Chin-t'ung Yü-nü Chiao Hung chi*, p. 80, l. 12; the anonymous Yüan-Ming tsa-chü drama *Shou-t'ing hou nu chan Kuan P'ing* (The Marquis of Shou-t'ing angrily executes Kuan P'ing), in *Ku-pen Yüan Ming tsa-chü*, vol. 3, scene 1, p. 4b, l. 5; *T'ao Yüan-ming tung-li shang-chü*, scene 4, p. 13b, l. 1; *Nü ku-ku shuo-fa sheng-t'ang chi*, scene 2, p. 5b, l. 14; the anonymous Yüan-Ming tsa-chü drama *Liang-shan wu-hu ta chieh-lao* (The five tigers of Liang-shan carry out a great jailbreak), in *Ku-pen Yüan Ming tsa-chü*, vol. 3, scene 5, p. 9a, l. 14; *Ch'ang-an ch'eng ssu-ma t'ou-T'ang, hsieh-tzu* (wedge), p. 3a, l. 6; *Sung ta-chiang Yüeh Fei ching-chung*, scene 1, p. 6a, l. 3; the anonymous Ming tsa-chü drama *Wang Wen-hsiu Wei-t'ang ch'i-yü chi* (The story of Wang Wen-hsiu's remarkable encounter in Wei-t'ang), in *Ku-pen Yüan Ming tsa-chü*, vol. 4, scene 1, p. 1b, l. 5; *Chung-shan lang*, scene 3, p. 248, l. 13; *Shui-hu ch'üan-chuan*, vol. 3, ch. 59, p. 985, l. 4; and an abundance of other occurrences, too numerous to list.

49. This formulaic four-character expression occurs ubiquitously in Chinese vernacular literature. See, e.g., *[Chi-p'ing chiao-chu] Hsi-hsiang chi*, play no. 1, scene 2, p. 18, l. 6; *Yüan-ch'ü hsüan*, 2:449, l. 15; *Yüan-ch'ü hsüan wai-pien*, 3:825, l. 9; *Yüeh Fei p'o-lu tung-ch'uang chi, chüan* 2, scene 32, p. 19b, l. 3; *Wang Wen-hsiu Wei-t'ang ch'i-yü chi*, scene 3, p. 6b, l. 4; and an anonymous Ming song suite in *Yung-hsi yüeh-fu, ts'e* 7, p. 21b, l. 3. It also recurs in the *Chin P'ing Mei tz'u-hua*, vol. 5, ch. 84, p. 6b, l. 2.

50. I have been unable to locate any information on this Taoist deity.

51. On this figure, see Stephen F. Teiser, *The Scripture on the Ten Kings and the Making of Purgatory in Medieval Chinese Buddhism* (Honolulu: University of Hawaii Press, 1994), pp. 175–76.

52. This line occurs verbatim in *Pao-chien chi*, scene 42, p. 76, l. 12; and *Shuang-lieh chi*, scene 39, p. 109, l. 8. Variants also occur in a poem written in prison by Su Shih (1037–1101) in 1079, *Su Shih shih-chi*, vol. 3, chüan 19, p. 999, l. 5; a lyric by Chang Feng-i (1527–1613), in *Ch'üan Ming tz'u pu-pien* (A supplement to Complete tz'u lyrics of the Ming), comp. Chou Ming-ch'u and Yeh Yeh, 2 vols. (Hang-chou: Che-chiang ta-hsüeh ch'u-pan she, 2007), 1:488, lower register, ll. 12–13; and the last line of a long poetic lament by the lonely wife of a traveling merchant in *Kuo-se t'ien-hsiang, chüan* 2, p. 37b, upper register, ll. 10–11.

CHAPTER 68

1. The Ch'ang-lo Palace, or Palace of Lasting Joy, was an enormous palace complex built by Emperor Kao-tsu of the Han dynasty (r. 202–195 B.C.) on the ruins of a Ch'in palace, and completed in 200 B.C. Li Fu-jen, or Lady Li (2nd century B.C.), was a favorite of Emperor Wu of the Han dynasty (r. 141–87 B.C.) but died young, leaving the emperor so disconsolate that he composed a rhapsody about her in which he mentions seeing her in his dreams. See *Han-shu* (History of the Former Han dynasty), comp. Pan Ku (32–92), 8 vols. (Peking: Chung-hua shu-chü, 1962), vol. 8, chüan 97a, pp. 3951–56; and *Courtier and Commoner in Ancient China: Selections from the History of the Former Han by Pan Ku*, trans. Burton Watson (New York: Columbia University Press, 1974), pp. 247–51.

2. This is an allusion to the famous literary tale by T'ao Ch'ien (365–427) entitled "The Peach Blossom Spring," in which a fisherman from Wu-ling stumbles upon a

secluded utopia but is unable to find his way back to it after his departure. See Hightower, *The Poetry of T'ao Ch'ien*, pp. 254–58.

3. This poem is by Hu Su (995–1067), *Ch'üan Sung shih*, 4:2098, ll. 3–4.

4. This four-character expression occurs in *Pai Niang-tzu yung-chen Lei-feng T'a*,
p. 424, l. 11; *Hsiu-ju chi*, scene 23, p. 65, ll. 8–9; *Shui-hu ch'üan-chuan*, vol. 2, ch. 51,
p. 846, l. 1; and recurs in the *Chin P'ing Mei tz'u-hua*, vol. 4, ch. 69, p. 7b, l. 4.

5. This four-character expression occurs in *Ch'üan-Han chih-chuan*, vol. 3, *chüan*
3, p. 35b, l. 7; and *San-pao t'ai-chien Hsi-yang chi t'ung-su yen-i*, vol. 1, ch. 20, p. 261,
l. 3.

6. On this work, see *The Flower Ornament Scripture: A Translation of the Avatamsaka Sutra*, trans. Thomas Cleary (Boston: Shambhala, 1987).

7. This text was translated into Chinese by Amoghavajra (705–74).

8. On this ritual, see Charles Orzech, "Saving the Burning-Mouth Hungry Ghost,"
in Donald S. Lopez, Jr., ed., *Religions of China in Practice* (Princeton: Princeton University Press, 1996), pp. 278–83.

9. This couplet is derived from one in *Pao-chien chi*, scene 51, p. 90, l. 11.

10. This five-character expression is taken verbatim from ibid., ll. 21–22.

11. This five character expression is taken verbatim from ibid., l. 22.

12. This four-character expression is of Buddhist origin and literally means the four
categories of living creatures classified according to their mode of birth, i.e., the womb-
born, the egg-born, the moisture-born, and those produced by metamorphosis. These
four terms are independently explained in *Lu-shan Yüan-kung hua*, p. 182, l. 13; and
occur together as in the novel in ibid., p. 186, l. 7; a lyric by Ch'ang-ch'üan-tzu (13th
century), *Ch'üan Chin Yüan tz'u*, 1:588, lower register, l. 13; a commentary in *Chin-
kang ching chi-chu*, p. 103a, l. 4; and *P'u-ching ju-lai yao-shih pao-chüan*, 5:123, ll. 4–5.

13. This couplet is taken verbatim from *Pao-chien chi*, scene 51, p. 90, l. 22.

14. This line is taken verbatim from ibid., scene 51, p. 90, l. 18.

15. The proximate source of this four-character expression is ibid. It is of Buddhist
origin and occurs ubiquitously in Chinese vernacular literature. See, e.g., a poem by
P'ang Yün (d. 808), *Ch'üan T'ang shih pu-pien*, 2:968, l. 3; *Ju-ju chü-shih yü-lu*, *i-chi*
(second collection), *chüan* 1, p. 1b, l. 8; a poem by Wang Ch'u-i (1142–1217), *Ch'üan
Chin shih*, 2:14, l. 1; *Yüan-ch'ü hsüan*, 3:1247, l. 12; *Nü ku-ku shuo-fa sheng-t'ang chi*,
hsieh-tzu (wedge), p. 8b, l. 8; *Fo-shuo Huang-chi chieh-kuo pao-chüan* (Precious volume expounded by the Buddha on the karmic results of the era of the Imperial Ultimate), originally published in 1430, in *Pao-chüan ch'u-chi*, 10:221, l. 2; *[Hsiao-shih]
Chin-kang k'o-i [hui-yao chu-chieh]*, 24:652, lower register, l. 22; and *Ch'ien-t'ang hu-
yin Chi-tien Ch'an-shih yü-lu*, p. 30a, l. 11. It also recurs in the *Chin P'ing Mei tz'u-
hua*, vol. 4, ch. 74, p. 13a, l. 2.

16. In Buddhist eschatology it was believed that at the end of each epoch or kalpa
Maitreya Buddha would descend to the world and convene a Dragon Flower Assembly
at which the faithful would achieve enlightenment and be saved from the impending
catastrophe. See Alan Sponberg and Helen Hardacre, eds., *Maitreya, the Future Buddha* (Cambridge: Cambridge University Press, 1988), passim.

17. The last three characters of this line are also taken verbatim from *Pao-chien chi*,
scene 51, p. 90, l. 18.

18. The last three characters of this line literally mean "to cut down the falling flowers," but the context indicates that this idiom refers to abortions.

19. During the Ming dynasty mandarin squares with the motif of an egret flying through the clouds were badges of rank worn by civil officials of the sixth rank. For further information, see Roy, *The Plum in the Golden Vase*, vol. 3, chap. 51, n. 35.

20. This formulaic four-character expression occurs ubiquitously in Chinese vernacular literature. See, e.g., *Chung-ch'ing li-chi*, vol. 3, *chüan* 6, p. 22a, ll. 2–3; *Shui-hu ch'üan-chuan*, vol. 2, ch. 54, p. 903, l. 1; *Lieh-kuo chih-chuan*, vol. 3, *chüan* 8, p. 53b, l. 2; an anonymous song suite in *Yung-hsi yüeh-fu*, *ts'e* 11, p. 67a, l. 2; the anonymous sixteenth-century literary tale *Ku-Hang hung-mei chi* (The story of the red plum of old Hang-chou), in *Kuo-se t'ien-hsiang*, vol. 3, *chüan* 8, upper register, p. 9a, l. 15; *Chin-lan ssu-yu chuan*, p. 11a, l. 4; *Ch'üan-Han chih-chuan*, vol. 3, *chüan* 1, p. 7a, l. 14; *Ta-T'ang Ch'in-wang tz'u-hua*, vol. 1, *chüan* 3, ch. 18, p. 19a, l. 6; and *Sui-T'ang liang-ch'ao shih-chuan*, *chüan* 5, ch. 48, p. 46b, l. 5.

21. This formulaic four-character expression occurs ubiquitously in Chinese literature. See, e.g., *Han-shu*, vol. 1, *chüan* 6, p. 212, l. 9; an essay entitled *Han erh-tsu yu-lieh lun* (A discussion of the relative merits of the two Han dynasty founding emperors), by Ts'ao Chih (192–232), in *Ts'ao Chih chi chiao-chu* (Ts'ao Chih's collected works collated and annotated), ed. Chao Yu-wen (Peking: Jen-min wen-hsüeh ch'u-pan she, 1984), *chüan* 1, p. 103, l. 5; an essay entitled *San-kuo lun* (A discussion of the Three Kingdoms), by Wang Po (649–76), in *Ch'üan T'ang wen*, vol. 4, *chüan* 182, p. 21b, l. 1; *Chiu T'ang shu*, vol. 7, *chüan* 53, p. 2210, l. 7; *Yüan-ch'ü hsüan*, 2:664, l. 13; *Yüan-ch'ü hsüan wai-pien*, 3:1020, l. 1; *San-kuo chih t'ung-su yen-i*, vol. 2, *chüan* 17, p. 801, l. 4; *T'ang-shu chih-chuan t'ung-su yen-i*, vol. 1, *chüan* 1, p. 10b, ll. 3–4; *Hung-fu chi*, scene 2, p. 2, l. 2; and *Sui-T'ang liang-ch'ao shih-chuan*, *chüan* 1, ch. 6, p. 34b, ll. 8–9.

22. This four-character expression occurs in *Ch'üan-Han chih-chuan*, vol. 3, *chüan* 6, p. 24b, l. 12.

23. This formulaic four-character expression occurs ubiquitously in Chinese vernacular literature. See, e.g., *Yüan-ch'ü hsüan*, 2:577, l. 19; *Ching-ch'ai chi*, scene 15, p. 44, l. 8; the tsa-chü drama *Cho Wen-chün ssu-pen Hsiang-ju* (Cho Wen-chün elopes with [Ssu-ma] Hsiang-ju), by Chu Ch'üan (1378–1448), in *Ming-jen tsa-chü hsüan*, scene 2, p. 121, l. 2; *Nü ku-ku shuo-fa sheng-t'ang chi*, scene 1, p. 4b, l. 6; *P'o-yao chi*, *chüan* 1, scene 5, p. 14a, l. 10; *Wu Lun-ch'üan Pei*, *chüan* 4, scene 28, p. 28a, ll. 1–2; *Huai-hsiang chi*, scene 21, p. 64, l. 8; *Hsiu-ju chi*, scene 35, p. 98, l. 11; and *Huang-Ming k'ai-yün ying-wu chuan*, *chüan* 2, p. 18a, l. 9.

24. This four-character expression occurs in *Mu-tan t'ing*, scene 42, p. 212, l. 11.

25. This four-character expression occurs in *Ming-chu chi*, scene 9, p. 25, l. 11; *Shui-hu ch'üan-chuan*, vol. 4, ch. 91, p. 1479, ll. 15–16; a letter by Kuei Yu-kuang (1507–71) written in 1554, in *Chen-ch'uan hsien-sheng chi* (Collected works of Kuei Yu-kuang), by Kuei Yu-kuang, 2 vols. (Shanghai: Shang-hai ku-chi ch'u-pan she, 1981), vol. 1, *chüan* 8, p. 177, l. 3; and *San-pao t'ai-chien Hsi-yang chi t'ung-su yen-i*, vol. 1, ch. 32, p. 423, l. 11.

26. This four-character expression occurs in an obituary account of the career of Ssu-ma Kuang (1019–86) by Su Shih (1037–1101), in *Su Shih wen-chi*, vol. 2, *chüan* 16, p. 487, ll. 11–12.

27. This four-character expression occurs in *Huang-ch'ao pien-nien kang-mu pei-yao*, vol. 2, *chüan* 25, p. 14b, l. 6.

28. This four-character expression occurs ubiquitously in Chinese literature. See, e.g., *Li-chi*, ch. 40, p. 127, l. 3; *Yu-ming lu* (Records of the realms of the dead and the

living), comp. Liu I-ch'ing (403–44), ed. and annot. Cheng Wan-ch'ing (Peking: Wen-hua i-shu ch'u-pan she, 1988), *chüan* 1, p. 8, l. 3; the biography of Ho-jo Tun (517–65), in *Chou shu* (History of the Chou dynasty [557–81]), comp. Ling-hu Te-fen (583–666), 3 vols. (Peking: Chung-hua shu-chü, 1971), vol. 2, *chüan* 28, p. 475, l. 14; a passage in the collection of anomaly accounts entitled *Kuang-i chi* (Great book of marvels), comp. Tai Fu (cs 757), as quoted in *T'ai-p'ing kuang-chi*, vol. 7, *chüan* 338, p. 2683, l. 12; a passage in the collection of anomaly accounts entitled *Chi-shen lu* (Record of miracu-lous events), comp. Hsü Hsüan (917–92), as quoted in ibid., vol. 8, *chüan* 367, p. 2916, l. 2; a poem by Hsü Chi (1028–1103), *Ch'üan Sung shih*, 11:7593, l. 7; the prose pref-ace to a poem by Chang Lei (1054–1114), ibid., 20:13032, l. 13; a poem by the Buddhist monk Te-hung (1071–1128), ibid., 23:15321, l. 10; *T'ieh-wei shan ts'ung-t'an* (Collected remarks from the Iron Cordon Mountains), by Ts'ai T'ao (d. after 1147) (Peking: Chung-hua shu-chü, 1997), *chüan* 3, p. 59, l. 5; *I-chien chih*, vol. 2, *chih-chia* (first supplementary record), *chüan* 5, p. 747, l. 1; *Huang-ch'ao pien-nien kang-mu pei-yao*, vol. 2, *chüan* 29, p. 12b, l. 8; *[Hsin-pien] Wu-tai shih p'ing-hua*, p. 83, l. 12; *Chien-teng yü-hua*, *chüan* 3, p. 228, l. 5; *Hua-ying chi*, p. 844, l. 25; the long sixteenth-century literary tale *Hsün-fang ya-chi* (Elegant vignettes of fragrant pursuits), in *Kuo-se t'ien-hsiang*, vol. 2, *chüan* 4, lower register, p. 27b, l. 9; the literary tale *Liao-yang hai-shen chuan* (The sea goddess of Liao-yang), by Ts'ai Yü (d. 1541), in *Ku-tai wen-yen tuan-p'ien hsiao-shuo hsüan-chu, erh-chi* (An annotated selection of classic literary tales, second collection), ed. Ch'eng Po-ch'üan (Shanghai: Shang-hai ku-chi ch'u-pan she, 1984), p. 388, l. 6; *Ta-Sung chung-hsing yen-i*, vol. 1, *chüan* 1, p. 32a, l. 9; *Ch'üan-Han chih-chuan*, vol. 3, *chüan* 6, p. 39a, l. 9; *Huang-Ming k'ai-yün ying-wu chuan*, *chüan* 8, p. 5b, l. 3; *Pai-chia kung-an*, *chüan* 3, ch. 23, p. 7a, l. 7; an essay by Li Chih (1527–1602), in his *Fen-shu* (A book to be burned) (Peking: Chung-hua shu-chü, 1961), *chüan* 5, p. 205, ll. 14–15; *Yang-chia fu shih-tai chung-yung yen-i chih-chuan*, vol. 1, *chüan* 4, p. 4b, ll. 9–10; and a host of other occurrences, too numerous to list.

29. For these two types of hangers-on that frequented the pleasure quarters, see Roy, *The Plum in the Golden Vase*, vol. 1, chap. 15, pp. 311–14.

30. This formulaic four-character expression occurs ubiquitously in Chinese ver-nacular literature. See, e.g., *Yüan-ch'ü hsüan*, 4:1443, l. 20; *Sung Ssu-kung ta-nao Chin-hun Chang*, p. 536, l. 3; the tsa-chü drama *Hsiang-nang yüan* (The tragedy of the scent bag), by Chu Yu-tun (1379–1439), author's pref. dated 1433, in *Sheng-Ming tsa-chü, erh-chi* (Tsa-chü dramas of the glorious Ming dynasty, second collection), comp. Shen T'ai (17th century), fac. repr. of 1641 edition (Peking: Chung-kuo hsi-chü ch'u-pan she, 1958), scene 1, p. 6a, l. 8; a song suite by Yang Shen (1488–1559), *Ch'üan Ming san-ch'ü*, 2:1451, l. 5; *Pao-chien chi*, scene 46, p. 84, l. 8; *Hai-fu shan-t'ang tz'u-kao*, *chüan* 3, p. 164, l. 6; *Hsi-yu chi*, vol. 2, ch. 80, p. 919, l. 17; a song by Wang K'o-tu (c. 1526–c. 1594), *Ch'üan Ming san-ch'ü*, 2:2460, l. 7; and the anonymous late Ming ch'uan-ch'i drama *Chin-ch'üeh chi* (The golden sparrow), *Liu-shih chung ch'ü* ed., scene 5, p. 11, l. 3.

31. According to the recollections of a contemporary of the author of the *Chin P'ing Mei*, when he first became a government student in the 1560s, his fellow students were given to wearing this type of bridge-shaped scholar's cap. See *Yün-chien chü-mu ch'ao* (Jottings on matters eyewitnessed in Yün-chien), by Fan Lien (b. 1540), pref. dated 1593, in *Pi-chi hsiao-shuo ta-kuan*, vol. 6, ts'e 13, *chüan* 2, p. 1a, l. 7.

32. An orthographic variant of this four-character expression occurs in the anonymous thirteenth-century prosimetric narrative *Liu Chih-yüan chu-kung-tiao [chiao-chu]* (Medley in various modes on Liu Chih-yüan [collated and annotated]), ed. Lan Li-ming (Ch'eng-tu: Pa-Shu shu-she, 1989), part 3, p. 103, l. 4. It occurs in the same form as in the novel in a lyric by Yü Chien-fa (14th century), *Ch'üan Chin Yüan tz'u*, 2:1143, upper register, ll. 8–9.

33. This four-character expression occurs in *Pao-chien chi*, scene 3, p. 9, l. 24; and recurs in the *Chin P'ing Mei tz'u-hua*, vol. 4, ch. 77, p. 8a, l. 9.

34. See *[Chi-p'ing chiao-chu] Hsi-hsiang chi*, play no. 1, scene 1, p. 5, l. 16.

35. The locus classicus for this four-character expression is the *Chuang-tzu*. See *Chuang-tzu yin-te*, ch. 1, p. 2, l. 11. It occurs ubiquitously in later Chinese literature. See, e.g., the biography of Ts'ui Hao (d. 450), *Wei-shu*, vol. 3, *chüan* 35, p. 812, l. 8; a memorial to the throne by Ling-hu Ch'u (766–837) submitted in 835, *Chiu T'ang shu*, vol. 6, *chüan* 49, p. 2129, l. 6; an essay by Su Hsün (1009–66), *Ch'üan Sung wen*, vol. 22, *chüan* 926, p. 153, l. 2; a poem by Ch'ao Pu-chih (1053–1110), *Ch'üan Sung shih*, 19:12809, ll. 11–12; a poem by the Buddhist monk Huai-shen (1077–1132), ibid., 24:16161, l. 1; *Yüan-shih shih-fan* (Mr. Yüan's precepts for social life), by Yüan Ts'ai (cs 1163), completed in 1178, ed. and annot. Ho Heng-chen and Yang Liu (Tientsin: T'ien-chin ku-chi ch'u-pan she, 1995), *chüan* 1, p. 55, l. 15; a lyric by Feng Tzu-chen (1257–1314) written in 1302, *Ch'üan Chin Yüan tz'u*, 2:919, upper register, l. 1; *Shuang-chu chi*, scene 6, p. 17, l. 8; *Chung-ch'ing li-chi*, *chüan* 6, p. 9b, l. 7; the middle-period vernacular story *Nü han-lin* (The female academician), in *Tsui yü-ch'ing*, 4:1460, upper register, l. 5; *Hung-fu chi*, scene 17, p. 32, l. 4; *Hsi-yu chi*, vol. 2, ch. 96, p. 1085, l. 3; *Ko tai hsiao*, scene 3, p. 141, l. 9; *San-pao t'ai-chien Hsi-yang chi t'ung-su yen-i*, vol. 2, ch. 87, p. 1123, l. 12; *Shih-hou chi*, scene 15, p. 50, l. 9; and an abundance of other occurrences, too numerous to list.

36. These two lines are from the *I-ching* (Book of changes). See *Chou-i yin-te* (A concordance to the *I-ching*) (Taipei: Chinese Materials and Research Aids Service Center, 1966), p. 2. column 1, ll. 19–20. They occur ubiquitously in later Chinese literature. See, e.g., an essay by Chi K'ang (223–62), in *Chi K'ang chi chiao-chu*) (Chi K'ang's collected works collated and annotated), ed. Tai Ming-yang (Peking: Jen-min wen-hsüeh ch'u-pan she, 1962), *chüan* 9, p. 306, ll. 4–5; *Yüeh-fu ku-t'i yao-chieh* (Explanations of the old titles of Music Bureau ballads), by Wu Ching (670–749), as quoted in *Yüeh-fu shih-chi*, vol. 3, *chüan* 76, p. 1079, l. 3; the preface to a long poetic work by Emperor T'ai-tsung (r. 976–97) of the Sung dynasty, *Ch'üan Sung shih*, 1:311, l. 5; a speech attributed to the Buddhist monk Pao-en (1058–1111), *Wu-teng hui-yüan*, vol. 3, *chüan* 14, p. 886, l. 13; *Yu-kuei chi*, scene 36, p. 104, ll. 8–9; an anonymous song in *Yüeh-fu ch'ün-chu*, *chüan* 1, p. 27, l. 4; *San-kuo chih t'ung-su yen-i*, vol. 2, *chüan* 15, p. 699, l. 18; *Shui-hu ch'üan-chuan*, vol. 4, ch. 85, p. 1401, l. 16; and *Sui-T'ang liang-ch'ao shih-chuan*, *chüan* 2, ch. 20, p. 58a, l. 4. The first line occurs independently in *Chuang-tzu yin-te*, ch. 31, p. 86, l. 12; *San-kuo chih* (History of the Three Kingdoms), comp. Ch'en Shou (233–97), 5 vols. (Peking: Chung-hua shu-chü, 1973), vol. 3, *chüan* 21, p. 629, l. 1; a preface by Yang Chiung (650–c. 694), *Ch'üan T'ang wen*, vol. 4, *chüan* 191, p. 6a, l. 9; a note to one of his own poems by Emperor T'ai-tsung (r. 976–97) of the Sung dynasty, *Ch'üan Sung shih*, 1:317, l. 6; a lyric by T'eng Pin (fl. early 14th century), *Ch'üan Chin Yüan tz'u*, 2:812, lower register, l. 2; a song suite by

Ch'iao Chi (d. 1345), *Ch'üan Yüan san-ch'ü*, 1:637, l. 2; a song suite by Yang T'ing-ho (1459–1529) written in 1513, *Ch'üan Ming san-ch'ü* 1:766, l. 1; *Shui-hu ch'üan-chuan*, vol. 3, ch. 57, p. 964, l. 13; a lyric by Hsia Yen (1483–1548), *Ch'üan Ming tz'u*, 2:716, upper register, l. 14; and *Hai-fu shan-t'ang tz'u-kao*, *chüan* 3, p. 179, l. 2. The second line also occurs independently in a note to one of his own poems by Emperor T'ai-tsung (r. 976–97) of the Sung dynasty, *Ch'üan Sung shih*, 1:341, l. 3; a poem by Wen Yen-po (1006–97), ibid., 6:3548, l. 2; *Ching-ch'ai chi*, scene 5, p. 11, l. 12; a song suite by Ch'en Ho (1516–60), *Ch'üan Ming san-ch'ü*, 2:2162, l. 7; a song suite by Yin Shih-tan (1522–82), ibid., 2:2339, l. 1; and *Hai-fu shan-t'ang tz'u-kao*, *chüan* 1, p. 21, l. 9.

37. These two lines are from the same passage in the *I-ching* as the two lines above. See *Chou-i yin-te*, p. 2, column 1, ll. 21–22.

38. See *[Chi-p'ing chiao-chu] Hsi-hsiang chi*, play no. 3, scene 3, p. 70, l. 10.

39. See Roy, *The Plum in the Golden Vase*, vol. 1, chap. 15, n. 1.

40. See ibid., vol. 2, chap. 22, n. 14.

41. See ibid., chap. 37, n. 29.

42. This four-character expression occurs in a list of fanciful names for tortures in *Pao-chien chi*, scene 14, p. 28, l. 18.

43. This four-character expression occurs in ibid.; and *Hsi-yu chi*, vol. 2, ch. 94, p. 1062, l. 2. It also recurs in the *Chin P'ing Mei tz'u-hua*, vol. 5, ch. 87, p. 9a, l. 2. It is said to be the T'ang dynasty name for a type of torture in *Wan-li yeh-huo pien*, vol. 2, *chüan* 18, p. 477, l. 2.

44. This four-character expression occurs in two anonymous song suites describing feats of horsemanship in *Sheng-shih hsin-sheng*, p. 425, l. 9; and p. 461, l. 3. It also occurs in *Hsi-yu chi*, vol. 2, ch. 72, l. 12, where it is elaborately described as a form of torture.

45. Variants of these last two expressions occur together in *Pao-chien chi*, scene 14, p. 28, ll. 15–16.

46. This formulaic four-character expression occurs ubiquitously in Chinese literature. See, e.g., a speech attributed to the Buddhist monk Cheng-hsien (1084–1159), *Wu-teng hui-yüan*, vol. 3, *chüan* 20, p. 1316, l. 15; an encomium by the Buddhist monk Tsung-kao (1089–1163), in *Ta-hui P'u-chüeh ch'an-shih yü-lu* (The recorded sayings of the Ch'an Master Ta-hui P'u-chüeh), *Taishō shinshū daizōkyō*, vol. 47, no. 1998, *chüan* 12, p. 860, lower register, l. 14; a letter by Chu Hsi (1130–1200), *Hui-an hsien-sheng Chu Wen-kung wen-chi*, *chüan* 60, p. 6b, l. 13; *Yüan-ch'ü hsüan*, 3:1170, ll. 2–3; *Shui-hu ch'üan-chuan*, vol. 2, ch. 43, p. 697, l. 3; *Pao-chien chi*, scene 51, p. 91, l. 4; and *Hsi-yu chi*, vol. 2, ch. 68, p. 782, l. 5.

47. See Roy, *The Plum in the Golden Vase*, vol. 3, chap. 59, n. 39.

48. This four-character expression occurs in a lyric by Chao I-fu (1189–1256), *Ch'üan Sung tz'u*, 4:2675, upper register, l. 12; an anonymous Sung dynasty lyric, ibid., 5:3799, upper register, l. 10; the early vernacular story *Yang Ssu-wen Yen-shan feng ku-jen* (Yang Ssu-wen encounters an old acquaintance in Yen-shan), in *Ku-chin hsiao-shuo*, vol. 2, *chüan* 24, p. 368, l. 8; and a lyric by Ch'ü Yu (1341–1427), *Ch'üan Ming tz'u*, 1:182, upper register, l. 3.

49. This four-character expression occurs in a song suite by Chao Yen-hui (14th century), *Ch'üan Yüan san-ch'ü*, 2:1232, l. 10; and an anonymous song suite in *Sheng-shih hsin-sheng*, p. 493, l. 11.

50. The proximate source of this poem, with some insignificant textual variations, is *Shui-hu ch'üan-chuan*, vol. 3, ch. 81, p. 1335, l. 17–p. 1336, l. 1.

51. This four-character expression recurs in the *Chin P'ing Mei tz'u-hua*, vol. 4, ch. 69, p. 6b, l. 5.

52. The Chinese text here splits the character for "infatuation" into its left and right components, which are then used as a slang term for the same word.

53. See Roy, *The Plum in the Golden Vase*, vol. 2, chap. 32, n. 12.

54. These two four-character expressions occur together in reverse order in *[Chi-p'ing chiao-chu] Hsi-hsiang chi*, play no. 4, scene 1, p. 143, l. 15–p. 144, l. 1. They also occur in reverse order in *[Hsin-k'o] Shih-shang hua-yen ch'ü-lo t'an-hsiao chiu-ling*, *chüan* 1, p. 13b, lower register, ll. 3–4. The second of these expressions, which has already occurred in the *Chin P'ing Mei tz'u-hua*, vol. 3, ch. 52, p. 2b, l. 4, also recurs in ibid., vol. 4, ch. 80, p. 5a, l. 2; and vol. 5, ch. 93, p. 13b, l. 7.

55. This line occurs in a quatrain by Lo Yin (833–909), *Ch'üan T'ang shih*, vol. 10, *chüan* 663, p. 7601, l. 13; and *Su Wu mu-yang chi*, *chüan* 2, scene 24, p. 20a, l. 6.

56. These six lines are derived from a lyric in the long literary tale entitled *Chiao Hung chuan* (The Story of Chiao-niang and Fei-hung), by Sung Yüan (14th century), in *Ku-tai wen-yen tuan-p'ien hsiao-shuo hsüan-chu, erh-chi*, p. 289, ll. 13–14. The first two lines occur there verbatim, and, although there is considerable textual variation in the remaining four lines, the similarities are such as to make the derivation unmistakable. The same lyric also occurs in the dramatic version of the above work *Chin-t'ung Yü-nü Chiao Hung chi*, p. 33, ll. 7–9.

57. These six characters are taken verbatim from *Ju-i chün chuan*, p. 11a, l. 6.

58. This formulaic four-character expression occurs ubiquitously in Chinese vernacular literature. See, e.g., a lyric by Chou Pang-yen (1056–1121), *Ch'üan Sung tz'u*, 2:629, lower register, l. 11; a lyric by Wang Chi-ch'ang (12th century), *Ch'üan Chin Yüan tz'u*, 1:561, lower register, ll. 14–15; *Kuan-shih-yin p'u-sa pen-hsing ching*, p. 52b, l. 3; *Cheng Chieh-shih li-kung shen-pi kung*, p. 667, l. 10; the early vernacular story *Feng-yüeh Jui-hsien T'ing* (The romance in the Jui-hsien Pavilion), in *Ch'ing-p'ing shan-t'ang hua-pen*, p. 42, l. 4; *Wu-chieh Ch'an-shih ssu Hung-lien chi*, p. 141, l. 2; *Hsiao-p'in chi*, p. 76, l. 5; *Chung-ch'ing li-chi*, vol. 3, *chüan* 7, p. 5b, l. 6; a set of songs by T'ang Yin (1470–1524), *Ch'üan Ming san-ch'ü*, 1:1062, l. 1; *Liu Ch'i-ch'ing shih-chiu Wan-chiang lou chi*, p. 3, l. 10; *Tu Li-niang mu-se huan-hun*, p. 535, l. 27; the middle-period vernacular story *Hsin-ch'iao shih Han Wu mai ch'un-ch'ing* (Han Wu-niang sells her charms at New Bridge Market), in *Ku-chin hsiao-shuo*, vol. 1, *chüan* 3, p. 66, l. 5; the middle-period vernacular story *Yüeh-ming Ho-shang tu Liu Ts'ui* (The monk Yüeh-ming converts Liu Ts'ui), in ibid., vol. 2, *chüan* 29, p. 431, l. 8; *Jen hsiao-tzu lieh-hsing wei shen*, p. 573, l. 7; a song suite by Huang O (1498–1569), *Ch'üan Ming san-ch'ü*, 2:1760, l. 8; *Pai-chia kung-an*, *chüan* 10, ch. 94, p. 10b, l. 3; a literary tale in *Yüan-chu chih-yü: hsüeh-ch'uang t'an-i*, *chüan* 2, p. 64, ll. 6–7; and an abundance of other occurrences, too numerous to list. It also recurs in the *Chin P'ing Mei tz'u-hua*, vol. 4, ch. 73, p. 21a, l. 3; and vol. 5, ch. 98, p. 8a, l. 5.

59. This four-character expression occurs in *Ta-T'ang Ch'in-wang tz'u-hua*, vol. 2, *chüan* 8, ch. 62, p. 52a, l. 7.

60. This formulaic four-character expression occurs ubiquitously in Chinese vernacular fiction. See, e.g., the long literary tale *Yu hsien-k'u* (Excursion to the dwelling

of the goddesses), by Chang Cho (cs 675) (Shanghai: Chung-kuo ku-tien wen-hsüeh
ch'u-pan she, 1955), p. 2, l. 11; a lyric by Liu Yung (cs 1034), *Ch'üan Sung tz'u*, 1:13,
lower register, l. 2; a lyric by Yang Wu-chiu (1097–1171), ibid., 2:1199, lower register,
l. 7; *Wu-wang fa Chou p'ing-hua*, p. 84, l. 7; *Yüan-ch'ü hsüan*, 4:1690, l. 4; *Yüan-ch'ü
hsüan wai-pien*, 3:771, l. 1; *Yu-kuei chi*, scene 17, p. 44, ll. 2–3; *Feng-yüeh Nan-lao chi*,
scene 1, p. 3b, l. 9; *Chin-ch'ai chi*, scene 17, p. 35, l. 17; *Wu Lun-ch'üan Pei, chüan* 1,
scene 4, p. 15b, ll. 2–3; the middle-period vernacular story *Ts'ao Po-ming ts'o-k'an tsang
chi* (The story of Ts'ao Po-ming and the mistaken identification of the booty), in *Ch'ing-
p'ing shan-t'ang hua-pen*, p. 207, l. 6; *Huai-hsiang chi*, scene 24, p. 73, l. 10; a lyric by
Yang Shen (1488–1559), *Ch'üan Ming tz'u*, 2:783, upper register, l. 14; a lyric by
Huang O (1498–1569), ibid., 2:864, lower register, l. 14; *Pao-chien chi*, scene 28, p. 51,
l. 7; *Huan-sha chi*, scene 16, p. 51, l. 10; *Hua-shen san-miao chuan*, p. 8b, l. 9; *Hai-fu
shan-t'ang tz'u-kao, chüan* 3, p. 155, l. 13; *Mu-lien chiu-mu ch'üan-shan hsi-wen, chüan*
3, p. 22b, l. 2; the ch'uan-ch'i drama *Fu-jung chi* (The story of the hibiscus painting), by
Chiang Chi (late 16th century), in *Ku-pen hsi-ch'ü ts'ung-k'an, wu-chi*, item 6, *chüan* 1,
scene 13, p. 41a, l. 4; a set of songs by Hsüeh Lun-tao (c. 1531–c. 1600), *Ch'üan Ming
san-ch'ü*, 3:2772, l. 10; and an abundance of other occurrences, too numerous to list.

61. This four-character expression occurs in *Yüan-ch'ü hsüan wai-pien*, 2:412, l. 9;
2:587, l. 3; and *Hai-fu shan-t'ang tz'u-kao, chüan* 3, p. 182, l. 13.

62. This formulaic four-character expression occurs ubiquitously in Chinese literature. See, e.g., a quatrain by Li Po (701–62), *Ch'üan T'ang shih*, vol. 3, *chüan* 164,
p. 1703, l. 10; a poem by Liu Yü-hsi (772–842) written in 824, ibid., vol. 6, *chüan* 363,
p. 4100, l. 13; a lyric by Chang Lun (12th century), *Ch'üan Sung tz'u*, 3:1424, lower
register, ll. 1–2; a lyric by Chang Hung-fan (1238–80), *Ch'üan Chin Yüan tz'u*, 2:731,
lower register, ll. 1–2; a song suite by Chu Yu-tun (1379–1439), *Ch'üan Ming san-
ch'ü*, 1:354, l. 12; *Chien-teng yü-hua, chüan* 5, p. 300, l. 1; a lyric by Ma Hung (15th
century), *Ch'üan Ming tz'u*, 1:250, upper register, l. 7; *Pao-chien chi*, scene 28, p. 52,
l. 21; *Liu sheng mi Lien chi, chüan* 2, p. 16a, l. 13; *San-pao t'ai-chien Hsi-yang chi
t'ung-su yen-i*, vol. 1, ch. 48, p. 624, l. 2; and an abundance of other occurrences, too
numerous to list.

63. This formulaic four-character expression occurs ubiquitously in Chinese vernacular literature. See, e.g., *Yüan-ch'ü hsüan*, 4:1562, l. 10; *Yüan-ch'ü hsüan wai-pien*,
1:72, l. 20; *Chin-t'ung Yü-nü Chiao Hung chi*, p. 24, l. 2; *Ch'ien-chin chi*, scene 22,
p. 72, l. 5; a song suite by Ch'en To (fl. early 16th century), *Ch'üan Ming san-ch'ü*,
1:599, l. 11; *Ch'üan-Han chih-chuan*, vol. 2, *chüan* 2, p. 33b, l. 9; and an abundance
of other occurrences, too numerous to list.

64. This formulaic four-character expression occurs ubiquitously in Chinese vernacular literature. See, e.g., *Hsiao Sun-t'u*, scene 10, p. 297, l. 7; *Chiao Hung chuan*,
p. 289, l. 7; *Cheng Chieh-shih li-kung shen-pi kung*, p. 666, l. 9; a song by Chung Ssu-
ch'eng (c. 1279–c. 1360), *Ch'üan Yüan san-ch'ü*, 2:1358, l. 3; *Chieh-chih-erh chi*,
p. 255, l. 13; *P'ei Hsiu-niang yeh-yu Hsi-hu chi*, p. 348, l. 26; an anonymous song suite
in *Yung-hsi yüeh-fu, ts'e* 8, p. 71a, l. 5; *Hsi-yu chi*, vol. 1, ch. 9, p. 90, l. 5; and *Pai-chia
kung-an, chüan* 10, ch. 93, p. 10a, l. 8.

65. This four-character expression occurs in close conjunction with the preceding
line in *Hsiao Sun-t'u*, scene 10, p. 297, l. 7. It also occurs in an anonymous Yüan dynasty song suite, *Ch'üan Yüan san-ch'ü*, 2:1880, l. 4; and a song suite by Wang Chih-
teng (1535–1612), *Ch'üan Ming san-ch'ü*, 3:2914, ll. 11–12.

66. This four-character expression occurs in a song suite by Chu T'ing-yü (14th century), *Ch'üan Yüan san-ch'ü*, 2:1205, l. 6; and two anonymous song suites in *Yung-hsi yüeh-fu*, ts'e 9, p. 67b, ll. 4–5; and ts'e 13, p. 50b, l. 8.

67. This four-character expression occurs in *Chien-teng hsin-hua*, chüan 2, p. 58, l. 6; and recurs in the *Chin P'ing Mei tz'u-hua*, vol. 5, ch. 97, p. 7b, l. 2.

68. This four-character expression occurs in *Kuan-yüan chi*, scene 21, p. 44, l. 9; and *Ch'un-wu chi*, scene 18, p. 49, l. 10.

69. This four-character expression occurs in an anonymous set of songs published in 1471. See *Ch'üan Ming san-ch'ü*, 4:4515, l. 13.

70. This formulaic four-character expression occurs ubiquitously in Chinese literature. See, e.g., a poem by Po Chü-i (772–846), *Ch'üan T'ang shih pu-pien*, vol. 2, chüan 28, p. 1082, l. 7; a poem by Li She (early 9th century), *Ch'üan T'ang shih*, vol. 7, chüan 477, p. 5424, l. 15; a poem by Lo Yin (833–909), ibid., vol. 10, chüan 665, p. 7610, l. 13; *Yüan-ch'ü hsüan*, 2:782, l. 20; a song suite from the lost tsa-chü drama *Han Ts'ai-yün ssu-chu Fu-jung T'ing* (Han Ts'ai-yün performs music in the Hibiscus Pavilion), by Wang Shih-fu (13th century), in *Yüan-jen tsa-chü kou-ch'en*, p. 26, l. 2; *Chiang Shih yüeh-li chi*, chüan 3, scene 26, p. 9a, ll. 1–2; and two anonymous song suites in *Yung-hsi yüeh-fu*, ts'e 5, p. 17b, ll. 5–6; and ts'e 11, p. 13b, l. 10.

71. On this deity, see Anne S. Goodrich, *Peking Paper Gods: A Look at Home Worship* (Nettetal: Steyler Verlag, 1991), pp. 85–86.

72. Variants of this proverbial expression occur in a speech attributed to the Buddhist monk Shan-hui (805–81), *Tsu-t'ang chi*, chüan 7, p. 154, l. 20; *Yeh-k'o ts'ung-shu* (Collected writings of a rustic sojourner), by Wang Mao (1151–1213) (Peking: Chung-hua shu-chü, 1987), chüan 29, p. 335, l. 7; *Yüan-ch'ü hsüan*, 4:1467, l. 20; Chüeh-lien's (16th century) commentary to the *Chin-kang k'o-i, [Hsiao-shih] Chin-kang k'o-i [hui-yao chu-chieh]*, 24:721, upper register, ll. 21–22; and a set of songs by Chin Luan (1494–1583), *Ch'üan Ming san-ch'ü*, 2:1606, l. 7. It also recurs in the *Chin P'ing Mei tz'u-hua*, vol. 5, ch. 87, p. 8b, l. 7.

73. There is a sixteenth-century figure of this name who was executed for conspiracy and corruption in 1565. See Liu Chung-kuang, "Chin P'ing Mei jen-wu k'ao-lun," pp. 168–71; and *Ming shih*, vol. 26, chüan 307, pp. 7899–7900.

74. This idiomatic four-character expression recurs in the *Chin P'ing Mei tz'u-hua*, vol. 5, ch. 88, p. 10a, l. 2.

75. There is a famous literary tale, which occurs in a number of versions, about a T'ang palace lady who indicates her loneliness by writing a poem on a red leaf and dropping it into a stream that flows through the palace grounds, from which it is rescued by a young scholar who is much taken with the sentiments expressed. He responds by writing a poem of his own upon another leaf and then dropping it upstream so that it will float into the palace grounds. Years later, a contingent of palace ladies is released from service and the scholar becomes married to one of them, who discovers the leaf with her original poem in her husband's possession. It turns out that she also had recovered the poem he wrote in response, so they feel that it is the exchange of red leaves that has brought them together. The best-known version of this tale is entitled *Liu-hung chi* (Red leaves on the water) and is included in *Ch'ing-so kao-i*, chüan 5, pp. 46–49, where it is attributed to Chang Shih (fl. mid-11th century). It has been translated in *The Golden Casket: Chinese Novellas of Two Millennia*, trans. Wolfgang Bauer and Herbert Franke, trans. from the German by Christopher Levenson

(New York: Harcourt Brace and World, 1964), pp. 171–76. The last five characters of this line occur verbatim in *Liu-hung chi*, p. 48, l. 9; and *[Hsin-k'o] Shih-shang hua-yen ch'ü-lo t'an-hsiao chiu-ling*, chüan 1, p. 3a, lower register, l. 10. A synonymous variant of these five characters also occurs in *Yen-chih chi*, chüan 1, scene 16, p. 22a, l. 11; and *Chu-fa chi*, chüan 1, scene 9, p. 18b, l. 2. A variant of the entire couplet occurs in the *Chin P'ing Mei tz'u-hua*, vol. 5, ch. 97, p. 9b, ll. 10–11.

76. This line is very similar to one in a quatrain attributed to Ts'ui Hu (cs 796), *Ch'üan T'ang shih*, vol. 6, chüan 366, p. 4148, l. 9.

CHAPTER 69

1. See Roy, *The Plum in the Golden Vase*, 1:460, n. 32.
2. See chap. 68, n. 75.
3. See Roy, *The Plum in the Golden Vase*, vol. 1, chap. 3, n. 29.
4. See ibid., vol. 2, chap. 23, n. 14.
5. See ibid., vol. 1, chap. 8, n. 35.
6. This poem is from *Huai-ch'un ya-chi*, chüan 9, p. 21b, ll. 3–6. The multiple allusions in this poem to famous tales of romantic love, and even to instances of sexual restraint, are undoubtedly intended to reflect ironically on the sordid affair between Hsi-men Ch'ing and Lady Lin that is consummated in this chapter.
7. Variants of this proverbial couplet occur in *Yüan-ch'ü hsüan*, 2:545, l. 17; and *Ming-feng chi*, scene 11, p. 47, l. 12.
8. This four-character expression occurs in a statement attributed to Tung Chung-shu (c. 179–c. 114 B.C.), in *Han-shu*, vol. 3, chüan 24a, p. 1137, l. 7. It occurs ubiquitously in later Chinese literature. See, e.g., a song suite by Ch'ien Lin (14th century), *Ch'üan Yüan san-ch'ü*, 2:1030, l. 13; *Chien-teng yü-hua*, chüan 3, p. 213, l. 10; *Chung-ch'ing li-chi*, vol. 2, chüan 6, p. 12b, l. 5; *Wu Lun-ch'üan Pei*, chüan 1, scene 6, p. 29a, l. 1; the ch'uan-ch'i drama *Yü-ching t'ai* (The jade mirror stand), by Chu Ting (16th century), *Liu-shih chung ch'ü* ed. (Taipei: K'ai-ming shu-tien, 1970), scene 6, p. 12, l. 12; the collection of literary tales entitled *Mi-teng yin-hua* (Tales told while searching for a lamp), by Shao Ching-chan (16th century), author's pref. dated 1592, in *Chien-teng hsin-hua [wai erh-chung]*, chüan 1, p. 325, l. 11; and *Ta-T'ang Ch'in-wang tz'u-hua*, vol. 1, chüan 3, ch. 22, p. 57a, l. 10. It also recurs in the *Chin P'ing Mei tz'u-hua*, vol. 5, ch. 91, p. 5b, l. 4.
9. This formulaic four-character expression occurs ubiquitously in Chinese literature. See, e.g., a preface to a poetry anthology compiled by Yüan Chieh (719–72), written in 760, in *T'ang-jen hsüan T'ang-shih [shih-chung]* (Anthologies of T'ang poetry selected by T'ang figures [ten examples]) (Peking: Chung-hua shu-chü, 1959), p. 27, ll. 4–5; a poem by Hsüeh Feng (cs 841), *Ch'üan T'ang shih*, vol. 8, chüan 548, p. 6321, l. 1; a speech attributed to Chao K'uang-yin (927–76), the founding emperor of the Sung dynasty (r. 960–76), in 961, in *Hsü Tzu-chih t'ung-chien ch'ang-pien* (Long draft of A continuation of the Comprehensive mirror for aid in government), comp. Li T'ao (1115–84), 34 vols. (Peking: Chung-hua shu-chü, 1979–93), vol. 2, chüan 2, p. 50, l. 3; *Yüan-ch'ü hsüan*, 2:447, l. 12; *Yüan-ch'ü hsüan wai-pien*, 3:1027, l. 6; *Wang Ai-hu ta-nao Tung-p'ing fu*, scene 1, p. 1b, l. 14; a song by Chia Chung-ming (1343–c. 1422), *Ch'üan Ming san-ch'ü*, 1:187, l. 11; *Wu Lun-ch'üan Pei*, chüan 4, scene 28,

p. 27a, l. 7; a song by Ch'ang Lun (1493–1526), *Ch'üan Ming san-ch'ü*, 2:1547, l. 8; *Ju-i chün chuan*, p. 6b, l. 10; *Shui-hu ch'üan-chuan*, vol. 3, ch. 78, p. 1297, l. 3; *Pao-chien chi*, scene 33, p. 61, ll. 11–12; *Lieh-kuo chih-chuan*, vol. 1, *chüan* 3, p. 80a, l. 13; a set of songs by Hsüeh Lun-tao (c. 1531–c. 1600), *Ch'üan Ming san-ch'ü*, 3:2697, l. 12; and an abundance of other occurrences, too numerous to list.

10. Variants of this formulaic couplet occur in *Chao-shih ku-erh chi*, *chüan* 2, scene 35, p. 24b, l. 6; *P'o-yao chi*, *chüan* 1, scene 11, p. 30a, l. 7; *[Hsin-pien] Liu Chih-yüan huan-hsiang Pai-t'u chi*, p. 37, ll. 11–12; *Hsiu-ju chi*, scene 31, p. 87, l. 11; and *Yü-ching t'ai*, scene 32, p. 88, l. 4. It occurs in the same form as in the novel in a song suite by Liu Shih-chung (14th century), *Ch'üan Yüan san-ch'ü*, 1:674, l. 6; *Yüan-ch'ü hsüan*, 1:351, l. 1; *P'i-p'a chi*, scene 3, p. 14, l. 6; *Pai-t'u chi*, scene 24, p. 66, l. 2; *Huan-sha chi*, scene 34, p. 122, l. 5; and *Hai-ling i-shih*, p. 154, l. 4. The first line also occurs independently in a song by Jen Yü (14th century), *Ch'üan Yüan san-ch'ü*, 1:1006, l. 2; and the second line in a song suite by Ch'en To (fl. early 16th century), *Ch'üan Ming san-ch'ü*, 1:649, l. 7.

11. See Roy, *The Plum in the Golden Vase*, vol. 1, chap. 3, n. 7.

12. This formulaic four-character expression occurs ubiquitously in Chinese vernacular literature. See, e.g., a quatrain by Su Sung (1020–1101), *Ch'üan Sung shih*, 10:6416, l. 16; a poem by Chang Po-tuan (11th century), ibid., 10:6468, l. 2; *Yüan-ch'ü hsüan*, 3:971, l. 18; a set of songs by Wang Ai-shan (14th century), *Ch'üan Yüan san-ch'ü*, 2:1190, l. 6; a song suite by T'ang Shih (14th–15th centuries), ibid., 2:1507, l. 1; a song suite by Chu Yu-tun (1379–1439), *Ch'üan Ming san-ch'ü*, 1:369, l. 4; a song suite in the front matter of the 1498 edition of *Hsi-hsiang chi*, p. 1b, l. 1; *[Hsin-tseng] Ch'iu-po i-chuan lun* ([Newly added] Treatise on the single meaningful glance), by Lai-feng Tao-jen, included as part of the front matter in ibid., p. 8b, l. 15; a set of songs by Chang Lien (cs 1544), *Ch'üan Ming san-ch'ü*, 2:1679, l. 4; *Tung-t'ien hsüan-chi*, scene 1, p. 6b, l. 1; *Hai-fu shan-t'ang tz'u-kao*, *chüan* 3, p. 160, l. 2; and an abundance of other occurrences, too numerous to list.

13. This four-character expression occurs in *Sha-kou chi*, scene 2, p. 2, l. 5; *San-kuo chih t'ung-su yen-i*, vol. 1, *chüan* 12, p. 571, l. 5; and recurs in the *Chin P'ing Mei tz'u-hua*, vol. 4, ch. 69, p. 7b, l. 5.

14. Orthographic variants of this four-character expression occur ubiquitously in Chinese vernacular literature. See, e.g., *Tung Chieh-yüan Hsi-hsiang chi*, *chüan* 3, p. 69, l. 14; and *chüan* 7, p. 151, l. 3; *[Chi-p'ing chiao-chu] Hsi-hsiang chi*, play no. 1, scene 4, p. 42, l. 4; a song suite by Ma Chih-yüan (c. 1250–c. 1325), *Ch'üan Yüan san-ch'ü*, 1:265, l. 4; *Yüan-ch'ü hsüan*, 2:642, ll. 8–9; *Yüan-ch'ü hsüan wai-pien*, 1:45, l. 18; *Shui-hu ch'üan-chuan*, vol. 1, ch. 7, p. 114, l. 12; *Nan Hsi-hsiang chi* (Li Jih-hua), scene 10, p. 28, l. 10; verse 82 of a suite of one hundred songs to the tune "Hsiao-t'ao hung" that retells the story of the *Ying-ying chuan* by a Ming dynasty figure named Wang Yen-chen, *Yung-hsi yüeh-fu*, ts'e 19, p. 48a, l. 8; a song suite by Liang Ch'en-yü (1519–91) written in 1561, *Ch'üan Ming san-ch'ü*, 2:2219, l. 3; *Seng-ni kung-fan*, scene 1, p. 335, l. 3; and *Mu-tan t'ing*, scene 28, p. 148, l. 11.

15. This four-character expression recurs in the *Chin P'ing Mei tz'u-hua*, vol. 5, ch. 81, p. 5b, l. 4; and ch. 91, p. 5b, l. 8.

16. Wang Ching-ch'ung (d. 949) is a historical figure, but, far from being an exemplar of integrity and righteousness, he served under three successive regimes during the Five Dynasties period and was disloyal to each of them in turn, finally burning

himself to death when he realized that he faced inevitable defeat. See his biography in *Hsin Wu-tai shih* (New history of the Five Dynasties), comp. Ou-yang Hsiu (1007–72), 3 vols. (Peking: Chung-hua shu-chü, 1974), vol. 2, *chüan* 53, pp. 603–605. The introduction of his name in this episode is thus clearly intended to be ironic.

17. This three-character expression occurs in *[Chi-p'ing chiao-chu] Hsi-hsiang chi*, play no. 5, scene 4, p. 197, l. 11; *Chang Yü-hu su nü-chen kuan chi*, p. 18a, l. 2; and *Chin-t'ung Yü-nü Chiao Hung chi*, p. 32, l. 3.

18. This four-character expression recurs in the *Chin P'ing Mei tz'u-hua*, vol. 4, ch. 78, p. 9a, l. 1.

19. The asterism Hsüan-yüan, which roughly corresponds to the constellation Leo, is traditionally said to represent the empress.

20. This formulaic four-character expression occurs ubiquitously in Chinese vernacular literature. See, e.g., a song suite by Kuan Han-ch'ing (13th century), *Ch'üan Yüan san-ch'ü*, 1:169, l. 2; *T'ien-pao i-shih chu-kung-tiao*, p. 174, l. 4; *Yüan-ch'ü hsüan wai-pien*, 3:983, ll. 11–12; *Chin-yin chi*, *chüan* 4, scene 38, p. 11b, l. 8; *Chien-teng yü-hua*, *chüan* 5, p. 294, l. 2; *Shang Lu san-yüan chi*, *chüan* 1, scene 7, p. 8a, l. 3; an anonymous set of songs in *Yung-hsi yüeh-fu*, *ts'e* 17, p. 57b, l. 5; *Tung-t'ien hsüan-chi*, scene 4, p. 13b, ll. 12–13; *Chin-tiao chi*, *chüan* 4, scene 41, p. 21a, l. 5; *Hsi-yu chi*, vol. 2, ch. 54, p. 626, ll. 10–11; and a song suite by Wang Chih-teng (1535–1612), *Ch'üan Ming san-ch'ü*, 3:2914, l. 3.

21. An orthographic variant of this four-character expression occurs in *Shui-hu ch'üan-chuan*, vol. 1, ch. 7, p. 113, l. 9.

22. Variants of this four-character expression occur in *Chu-tzu yü-lei* (Classified sayings of Master Chu), comp. Li Ching-te (13th century), 8 vols. (Taipei: Cheng-chung shu-chü, 1982), vol. 7, *chüan* 116, p. 10a, l. 4; *Shui-hu ch'üan-chuan*, vol. 4, ch. 104, p. 1597, l. 16; and *Hsi-yu chi*, vol. 1, ch. 44, p. 509, l. 3. It occurs in the same form as in the novel in *Hsi-kua chi*, scene 6, p. 622, l. 1; and the anonymous fifteenth-century ch'uan-ch'i drama *Ts'ai-lou chi* (The gaily colored tower), ed. Huang Shang (Shanghai: Shang-hai ku-tien wen-hsüeh ch'u-pan she, 1956), scene 6, p. 19, ll. 18–19. It also recurs in the *Chin P'ing Mei tz'u-hua*, vol. 5, ch. 86, p. 10b, l. 1.

23. This four-character expression occurs ubiquitously in Chinese literature. See, e.g., *Shih-chi*, vol. 2, *chüan* 10, p. 427, l. 13; *Ta-T'ang hsi-yü chi [chiao-chu]* (Great T'ang record of the western regions [edited and annotated]), by Hsüan-tsang (602–64), ed. and annot. Chi Hsien-lin et al., originally completed in 646 (Peking: Chung-hua shu-chü, 1985), *chüan* 2, p. 243, l. 9; a memorial by Po Chü-i (772–846), *Ch'üan T'ang wen*, vol. 14, *chüan* 671, p. 19a. ll. 8–9; *I-chien chih*, vol. 1, *i-chih* (second record), *chüan* 15, p. 313, l. 12; *Ju-ju chü-shih yü-lu*, chia-chi (first collection), *chüan* 1, p. 6a, l. 3; *Tung Chieh-yüan Hsi-hsiang chi*, *chüan* 1, p. 18, ll. 9–10; *Chung-ch'ing li-chi*, vol. 2, *chüan* 6, p. 13b, l. 5; *San-kuo chih t'ung-su yen-i*, vol. 1, *chüan* 8, p. 375, l. 19; *Ju-i chün chuan*, p. 19b, ll. 5–6; *Shui-hu ch'üan-chuan*, vol. 4, ch. 97, p. 1529, l. 7; *T'ang-shu chih-chuan t'ung-su yen-i*, vol. 1, *chüan* 5, p. 45a, l. 12; *Lieh-kuo chih-chuan*, vol. 1, *chüan* 3, p. 10b, ll. 2–3; *Pai-chia kung-an*, *chüan* 9, ch. 82, p. 15a, l. 9; and *San-pao t'ai-chien Hsi-yang chi t'ung-su yen-i*, vol. 2, ch. 68, p. 876, l. 8. It also recurs in the *Chin P'ing Mei tz'u-hua*, vol. 5, ch. 92, p. 15b, l. 1.

24. This four-character expression occurs ubiquitously in Chinese literature. See, e.g., a memorial to the throne written by Wang Seng-ta (423–58) in 456, in *Sung shu*, vol. 7, *chüan* 75, p. 1957, l. 3; a memorial by Liu Yü-hsi (772–842) written in 800, in

Liu Yü-hsi chi chien-cheng (An annotated edition of Liu Yü-hsi's collected works), annot. Ch'ü T'ui-yüan, 3 vols. (Shanghai: Shang-hai ku-chi ch'u-pan she, 1989), vol. 1, *chüan* 11, p. 295, l. 9; the ch'uan-ch'i drama *Chiao-hsiao chi* (The story of the mermaid silk handkerchief), by Shen Ch'ing (15th century), in *Ku-pen hsi-ch'ü ts'ung-k'an*, *ch'u-chi*, item 91, *chüan* 2, scene 25, p. 25a, l. 8; *Pao-chien chi*, scene 18, p. 36, l. 10; *Hsi-yu chi*, vol. 2, ch. 97, p. 1101, l. 3; *Fu-jung chi*, *chüan* 2, scene 27, p. 37b, l. 8; and *Yang-chia fu shih-tai chung-yung yen-i chih-chuan*, vol. 1, *chüan* 2, p. 29a, l. 8.

25. This four-character expression occurs in the anonymous Yüan-Ming tsa-chü drama *Han Yüan-shuai an-tu Ch'en-ts'ang* (Han Hsin surreptitiously emerges at Ch'en-ts'ang), in *Ku-pen Yüan Ming tsa-chü*, vol. 2, scene 3, p. 16b, l. 6; and the allegorical Taoist drama on internal alchemy entitled *Hsing-t'ien Feng-yüeh t'ung-hsüan chi* (The Master of Breeze and Moonlight utilizes his Heaven-bestowed nature to penetrate the mysteries), by Lan Mao (1403–76), pref. dated 1454, in *Ku-pen hsi-ch'ü ts'ung-k'an*, *wu-chi*, item 1, scene 10, p. 26a, l. 7.

26. This four-character expression occurs in *Chien-teng yü-hua*, *chüan* 5, p. 287, ll. 12–13; *Shuang-chu chi*, scene 38, p. 132, l. 2; and *Huai-ch'un ya-chi*, *chüan* 9, p. 24a, l. 10. It also recurs in the *Chin P'ing Mei tz'u-hua*, vol. 4, ch. 71, p. 9a, l. 8; and vol. 5, ch. 82, p. 2b, l. 3.

27. This four-character expression recurs in the *Chin P'ing Mei tz'u-hua*, vol. 4, ch. 78, p. 29b, l. 2; and vol. 5, ch. 81, p. 4b, l. 6.

28. This formulaic four-character expression occurs in *San-kuo chih p'ing-hua*, p. 1, l. 13; *Ts'ui Tai-chao sheng-ssu yüan-chia*, p. 94, l. 12; the early vernacular story *Wan Hsiu-niang ch'ou-pao shan-t'ing-erh* (Wan Hsiu-niang gets her revenge with a toy pavilion), in *Ching-shih t'ung-yen*, *chüan* 37, p. 560, l. 17; and *Chang Yü-hu su nü-chen kuan chi*, p. 20b, l. 8. It also recurs in the *Chin P'ing Mei tz'u-hua*, vol. 4, ch. 78, p. 24a, ll. 1–2; and vol. 5, ch. 82, p. 3a, l. 7.

29. This four-character expression recurs in the *Chin P'ing Mei tz'u-hua*, vol. 4, ch. 75, p. 30b, l. 8.

30. This four-character expression occurs in *Mencius*. See *Meng-tzu yin-te*, Book 1A, ch. 7, p. 4, l. 1. It also occurs in a poem by the Buddhist monk Te-hung (1071–1128), *Ch'üan Sung shih*, 23:15375, l. 9; *Tu Li-niang mu-se huan-hun*, p. 536, l. 3; and *Sui-T'ang liang-ch'ao shih-chuan*, *chüan* 5, ch. 47, p. 42b, l. 5.

31. This four-character expression occurs in a lyric by Liu Yung (cs 1034), *Ch'üan Sung tz'u*, 1:43, upper register, l. 15, and an anonymous set of songs in *Tz'u-lin i-chih* (A branch from the forest of song), comp. Huang Wen-hua (16th century), originally published in 1573, fac. repr. in *Shan-pen hsi-ch'ü ts'ung-k'an*, vol. 4, *chüan* 1, p. 12a, middle register, ll. 8–9.

32. This four-character expression occurs in *Chang Yü-hu su nü-chen kuan chi*, p. 16b, l. 10; *Hsin-ch'iao shih Han Wu mai ch'un-ch'ing*, p. 74, l. 2; and *Hai-ling i-shih*, p. 70, l. 10. It also recurs in the *Chin P'ing Mei tz'u-hua*, vol. 5, ch. 98, p. 8a, l. 1; and ch. 99, p. 3a, l. 1.

33. This line, with one insignificant variant, is from the final line of a quatrain in *Huai-ch'un ya-chi*, *chüan* 10, p. 35a, l. 15.

34. This four-character expression occurs in *Ta-T'ang Ch'in-wang tz'u-hua*, vol. 1, *chüan* 1, p. 1b, l. 5.

35. See Roy, *The Plum in the Golden Vase*, vol. 1, chap. 13, n. 11.

36. This poem, with some textual variation, is taken from *Huai-ch'un ya-chi, chüan* 10, p. 34b, ll. 12–16.

37. This formulaic four-character expression occurs ubiquitously in Chinese vernacular literature. See, e.g., a speech attributed to the Buddhist monk Hsi-mu (9th century), *Wu-teng hui-yüan,* vol. 1, *chüan* 4, p. 246, l. 3; a poem by the Buddhist monk Tao-ning (1053–1113), *Ch'üan Sung shih,* 19:12900, l. 9; an anonymous Yüan dynasty song, *Ch'üan Yüan san-ch'ü,* 2:1669, l. 12; *Yüan-ch'ü hsüan,* 3:939, l. 3; *Pai-she chi, chüan* 2, scene 18, p. 22a, l. 8; *Chung-ch'ing li-chi, chüan* 6, p. 22a, l. 6; *Ch'ien-chin chi,* scene 5, p. 10, l. 5; *Ch'en Hsün-chien Mei-ling shih-ch'i chi,* p. 125, l. 3; *Jen hsiao-tzu lieh-hsing wei shen,* p. 579, l.13; an anonymous set of songs published in 1553, *Ch'üan Ming san-ch'ü,* 4:4552, l. 6; *Ta-Sung chung-hsing yen-i,* vol. 2, *chüan* 8, p. 23a, ll. 3–4; *Wang Wen-hsiu Wei-t'ang ch'i-yü chi,* scene 3, p. 5b, l. 9; *Hsün-ch'in chi,* scene 32, p. 102, l. 8; and *Sui-T'ang liang-ch'ao shih-chuan, chüan* 6, ch. 55, p. 25b, l. 2.

38. This formulaic four-character expression occurs ubiquitously in Chinese literature. See, e.g., a poem by the Buddhist monk Chiao-jan (8th century) written in 778, *Ch'üan T'ang shih,* vol. 12, *chüan* 821, p. 9260, l. 5; a poem by Huang T'ing-chien (1045–1105), *Ch'üan Sung shih,* 17:11615, l. 7; a quatrain by Mi Fu (1051–1107), ibid., 18:12255, l. 4; a lyric by Huang Shang (1044–1130), *Ch'üan Sung tz'u,* 1:382, lower register, l. 1; a lyric by Yeh Meng-te (1077–1148), ibid., 2:775, lower register, l. 3; a lyric by Wang I-sun (13th century), ibid., 5:3364, lower register, l. 7; a lyric by Ch'iu Yüan (1247–1326), ibid., 5:3404, upper register, l. 2; *[Chi-p'ing chiao-chu] Hsi-hsiang chi,* play no. 1, scene 3, p. 32, l. 14; *Yüan-ch'ü hsüan,* 3:1161, l. 2; *Yüan-ch'ü hsüan wai-pien,* 3:776, l. 19; *Fu Lu Shou san-hsing tu-shih,* p. 585, l. 7; *Chien-teng yü-hua, chüan* 1, p. 148, l. 12; *Ch'ung-mo-tzu tu-pu Ta-lo T'ien,* scene 1, p. 1b, l. 3; *Hsing-t'ien Feng-yüeh t'ung-hsüan chi,* scene 6, p. 15b, l. 8; a lyric by Hsü Tuan-pen (fl. late 15th century), *Ch'üan Ming tz'u,* 2:631, upper register, l. 13; *Chung-ch'ing li-chi, chüan* 6, p. 29b, l. 5; a song suite by Yang T'ing-ho (1459–1529), *Ch'üan Ming san-ch'ü,* 1:767, l. 9; *Tung-t'ien hsüan-chi,* scene 1, p. 4b, l. 4; a lyric by Kung Yung-ch'ing (1500–63), *Ch'üan Ming tz'u pu-pien,* 1:335, lower register, l. 10; *Hsi-yu chi,* vol. 1, ch. 25, p. 284, l. 11; *T'ou-pi chi, chüan* 2, scene 25, p. 13b, l. 8; the ch'uan-ch'i drama *Hu-fu chi* (The story of the tiger tally), by Chang Feng-i (1527–1613), in *Ku-pen hsi-ch'ü ts'ung-k'an, ch'u-chi,* item 63, *chüan* 1, scene 18, p. 26b, l. 6; *Ta-T'ang Ch'in-wang tz'u-hua,* vol. 2, *chüan* 5, ch. 38, p. 58a, l. 10; and an abundance of other occurrences, too numerous to list. It also recurs in the *Chin P'ing Mei tz'u-hua,* vol. 5, ch. 100, p. 11a, l. 6.

39. A variant of this proverbial couplet occurs in the *Chin P'ing Mei tz'u-hua,* vol. 5, ch. 85, p. 5a, ll. 8–9.

40. This formulaic four-character expression occurs ubiquitously in Chinese vernacular literature. See, e.g., *Yüan-ch'ü hsüan,* 1:211, l. 18; *Sha-kou chi,* scene 3, p. 5, l. 9; *Ching-ch'ai chi,* scene 23, p. 71, l. 10; *P'i-p'a chi,* scene 16, p. 97, l. 4; *Wu Lun-ch'üan Pei, chüan* 1, scene 2, p. 5a, l. 1; *Yü-huan chi,* scene 6, p. 13, l. 1; *Ching-chung chi,* scene 5, p. 9, l. 10; *Ch'ien-chin chi,* scene 23, p. 74, l. 11; *Yüeh Fei p'o-lu tung-ch'uang chi, chüan* 1, scene 14, p. 20b, l. 4; *Huai-hsiang chi,* scene 19, p. 54, l. 4; *San-yüan chi,* scene 3, p. 6, l. 5; *Chiang Shih yüeh-li chi, chüan* 1, scene 4, p. 5a, l. 8; *Shui-hu ch'üan-chuan,* vol. 1, ch. 3, p. 47, l. 6; *Yen-chih chi, chüan* 1, scene 3, p. 4a, l. 11; *Hsi-yu chi,* vol. 1, ch. 23, p. 264, l. 16; and an abundance of other occurrences,

too numerous to list. It also recurs in the *Chin P'ing Mei tz'u-hua*, vol. 4, ch. 72, p. 21a, l. 5; and vol. 5, ch. 95, p. 8a, l. 7.

41. See Roy, *The Plum in the Golden Vase*, vol. 1, chap. 12, n. 37.

42. This four-character expression occurs in *Shih-wu kuan hsi-yen ch'eng ch'iao-huo*, p. 698, l. 13.

43. This four-character expression occurs in *Pai-chia kung-an, chüan* 9, ch. 75, p. 7b, l. 11.

44. This formulaic four-character expression occurs ubiquitously in Chinese vernacular literature. See, e.g., *Shih Hung-chao lung-hu chün-ch'en hui*, p. 213, l. 11; *Pai Niang-tzu yung-chen Lei-feng T'a*, p. 426, l. 4; *P'i-p'a chi*, scene 11, p. 73, l. 14; *Pai-she chi, chüan* 1, scene 4, p. 8b, l. 4; *Yüeh Fei p'o-lu tung-ch'uang chi, chüan* 1, scene 12, p. 16a, l. 8; *Shui-hu ch'üan-chuan*, vol. 1, ch. 17, p. 251, l. 1; *Hsiu-ju chi*, scene 11, p. 28, l. 11; *Wang Lan-ch'ing chen-lieh chuan*, scene 2, p. 4b, l. 14; *Nü han-lin*, 4:1487, l. 12; *Pa-i chi*, scene 14, p. 33, l. 3; and an abundance of other occurrences, too numerous to list.

45. This four-character expression occurs in *Yüan-ch'ü hsüan*, 4:1734, l. 12; and *Hsi-yu chi*, vol. 1, ch. 3, p. 32, ll. 11–12. It also recurs in the *Chin P'ing Mei tz'u-hua*, vol. 5, ch. 91, p. 3a, l. 6.

46. Variants of this proverbial couplet occur in *Yüan-ch'ü hsüan*, 2:543, ll. 12–13; and 598, l. 15; *P'o-yao chi, chüan* 1, scene 5, p. 19a, l. 10; and *Shui-hu ch'üan-chuan*, vol. 1, ch. 8, p. 130, l. 14; and ch. 19, p. 275, ll. 13–14.

47. This four-character expression recurs in the *Chin P'ing Mei tz'u-hua*, vol. 5, ch. 87, p. 7a, l. 10.

48. This formulaic epistolary expression occurs ubiquitously in Chinese vernacular literature. See, e.g., *[Hsin-pien] Wu-tai shih p'ing-hua*, p. 214, l. 1; *Yüan-ch'ü hsüan wai-pien*, 3:836, l. 5; *Ching-ch'ai chi*, scene 22, p. 68, ll. 10–11; *Shui-hu ch'üan-chuan*, vol. 4, ch. 89, p. 1458, l. 4; *Nan Sung chih-chuan*, vol. 1, *chüan* 1, p. 12a, l. 6; *Chin-lan ssu-yu chuan*, p. 22b, l. 6; *Ch'üan-Han chih-chuan*, vol. 2, *chüan* 2, p. 27a, l. 11; *Hsi-yu chi*, vol. 1, ch. 29, p. 330, l. 14; and *Ts'an-T'ang Wu-tai shih yen-i chuan*, ch. 24, p. 90, l. 26. It also recurs in the *Chin P'ing Mei tz'u-hua*, vol. 4, ch. 69, p. 19a, l. 3; and ch. 76, p. 21a, l. 10.

49. This four-character expression recurs in the *Chin P'ing Mei tz'u-hua*, vol. 4, ch. 78, p. 9a, l. 1.

50. Mi Fu (1052–1107) is one of the most renowned artists and calligraphers of the Northern Sung dynasty. For a study of his work as a calligrapher, see Lothar Ledderose, *Mi Fu and the Classical Tradition of Chinese Calligraphy* (Princeton: Princeton University Press, 1979).

51. For the expression "carry rings and knot grass," see Roy, *The Plum in the Golden Vase*, vol. 1, chap. 17, n. 42.

52. This formulaic reduplicative expression occurs ubiquitously in Chinese vernacular literature. See, e.g., *Chang Hsieh chuang-yüan*, scene 24, p. 123, l. 14; the early vernacular story *Yang Wen lan-lu hu chuan* (The story of Yang Wen, the road-blocking tiger), in *Ch'ing-p'ing shan-t'ang hua-pen*, p. 177, l. 9; *Wu-wang fa Chou p'ing-hua*, p. 61, l. 11; *Yüan-ch'ü hsüan*, 3:1241, l. 18; *Sha-kou chi*, scene 34, p. 117, l. 9; *Ching-ch'ai chi*, scene 43, p. 125, l. 11; *Yu-kuei chi*, scene 22, p. 63, l. 10; *P'o-yao chi, chüan*, 2, scene 16, p. 2b, l. 10; *Shui-hu ch'üan-chuan*, vol. 4, ch. 104, p. 1597, l. 4; *Lien-huan chi, chüan* 2, scene 20, p. 48, l. 9; *Ch'ien-t'ang hu-yin Chi-tien Ch'an-shih yü-lu*, p. 7b,

l. 7; *Yü-chüeh chi*, scene 16, p. 49, l. 5; *Ming-feng chi*, scene 33, p. 137, ll. 9–10; *Hsi-yu chi*, vol. 1, ch. 15, p. 175, ll. 11–12; *Mu-tan t'ing*, scene 55, p. 274, l. 7; and an abundance of other occurrences, too numerous to list.

53. This four-character expression occurs in *Ta-Sung chung-hsing yen-i*, vol. 1, *chüan* 2, p. 2b, l. 11; *San Sui p'ing-yao chuan*, *chüan* 3, ch. 14, p. 55a, l. 8; *Hsi-yu chi*, vol. 1, ch. 18, p. 207, l. 15; *Pai-chia kung-an*, *chüan* 1, ch. 1, p. 12a, l. 10; and *Ta-T'ang Ch'in-wang tz'u-hua*, vol. 1, *chüan* 3, ch. 22, p. 62a, l. 4.

54. This formulaic four-character expression occurs ubiquitously in Chinese vernacular literature. See, e.g., *Cho Chi Pu chuan-wen* (Story of the apprehension of Chi Pu), in *Tun-huang pien-wen chi*, 1:58, l. 10; an anecdote about Feng Shun-ch'ing (10th century), in the lost work *Wang-shih chien-wen chi* (Record of things seen and heard by Mr. Wang), comp. Wang Jen-yü (880–942), as quoted in *T'ai-p'ing kuang-chi*, vol. 6, *chüan* 257, p. 2004, l. 14; *Kuan-shih-yin p'u-sa pen-hsing ching*, p. 24a, l. 7; *San hsien-shen Pao Lung-t'u tuan-yüan*, p. 180, l. 14; *Yü Chung-chü t'i-shih yü shang-huang*, p. 74, l. 16; *San-kuo chih t'ung-su yen-i*, vol. 1, *chüan* 3, p. 124, l. 21; *Shui-hu ch'üan-chuan*, vol. 1, ch. 15, p. 221, l. 9; *San Sui p'ing-yao chuan*, *chüan* 4, ch. 18, p. 19b, l. 9; *Nan Sung chih-chuan*, vol. 2, *chüan* 9, p. 23b, l. 4; *Pei Sung chih-chuan*, vol. 2, *chüan* 4, p. 24b, l. 1; *Ch'üan-Han chih-chuan*, vol. 2, *chüan* 3, p. 21b, l. 2; *Ts'an-T'ang Wu-tai shih yen-i chuan*, ch. 35, p. 139, l. 21; *Pai-chia kung-an*, *chüan* 2, ch. 11, p. 11a, ll. 1–2; *San-pao t'ai-chien Hsi-yang chi t'ung-su yen-i*, vol. 2, ch. 62, p. 801, l. 11; *Hai-ling i-shih*, p. 117, l. 9; *Yang-chia fu shih-tai chung-yung yen-i chih-chuan*, vol. 1, *chüan* 1, p. 27a, l. 3; *Ta-T'ang Ch'in-wang tz'u-hua*, vol. 1, *chüan* 2, ch. 10, p. 24a, l. 1; and *Sui-T'ang liang-ch'ao shih-chuan*, *chüan* 1, p. 24a, l. 9. It also recurs in the *Chin P'ing Mei tz'u-hua*, vol. 5, ch. 100, p. 14b, l. 2.

55. It should be noted that, unlike American pigs, the typical Chinese pig is black, so this idiomatic expression is equivalent to the pot calling the kettle black.

56. Variants of this proverbial expression occur in *Yüan-ch'ü hsüan*, 3:1249, l. 16; 4:1528, l. 1; and *K'o-tso chui-yü*, *chüan* 1, p. 10, l. 11.

57. According to legend, in 206 B.C., when Liu Pang (256–195 B.C.), the founding emperor of the Han dynasty, was struggling for hegemony with Hsiang Yü (232–202 B.C.), his commander Han Hsin (d. 196 B.C.) won a decisive victory by making a show of repairing the cliffside roadways in a certain mountainous area of what is now Szechwan province, while secretly sending his armies out to make a surprise attack in the area of Ch'en-ts'ang, in what is now Shensi province. This couplet occurs ubiquitously in Chinese vernacular literature. See, e.g., a speech attributed to the Buddhist monk Chih-yü (1185–1269), in *Hsü-t'ang Ho-shang yü-lu*, *chüan* 1, p. 989, upper register, l. 26; *Ch'ien-Han shu p'ing-hua* (The p'ing-hua on the history of the Former Han dynasty), originally published in 1321–23 (Shanghai: Ku-tien wen-hsüeh ch'u-pan she, 1955), p. 12, ll. 12–13; *San-kuo chih p'ing-hua*, p. 4, ll. 2–3; *Yüan-ch'ü hsüan*, 1:81, l. 4; and 3:1280, l. 14; *Han Yüan-shuai an-tu Ch'en-ts'ang*, scene 2, p. 12b, l.13; *Ch'ien-chin chi*, scene 28, p. 96, l. 9; *Ch'üan-Han chih-chuan*, vol. 2, *chüan* 2, p. 2b, l. 1; *Huang-Ming k'ai-yün ying-wu chuan*, *chüan* 8, p. 9a, l. 2; and *San-pao t'ai-chien Hsi-yang chi t'ung-su yen-i*, vol. 2, ch. 92, p. 1184, l. 11. The first line of the couplet occurs independently in *Han Yüan-shuai an-tu Ch'en-ts'ang*, hsieh-tzu (wedge), p. 10b, l. 8; and the second line of the couplet occurs independently in ibid., scene 2, p. 11b, l. 4; and *San-kuo chih t'ung-su yen-i*, vol. 2, *chüan* 20, p. 929, l. 6.

58. Variants of this proverbial couplet occur in *[Hsiao-shih] Chen-k'ung sao-hsin pao-chüan*, 19:92, l. 4–93, l. 1; *Hsi-yu chi*, vol. 2, ch. 99, p. 1122, l. 6; and *San-pao t'ai-chien Hsi-yang chi t'ung-su yen-i*, vol. 1, ch. 13, p. 159, l. 10.

59. Variants of this idiomatic expression, in which the positions of the words "ghosts" and "spirits" are reversed, occur in *Yüan-ch'ü hsüan wai-pien*, 3:1016, l. 1; and *Han Yüan-shuai an-tu Ch'en-ts'ang*, scene 1, p. 5a, ll. 6–7. It occurs in the same form as in the novel in *Ch'ien-Han shu p'ing-hua*, p. 8, l. 5; *Yüan-ch'ü hsüan*, 2:735, l. 19; *San-kuo chih t'ung-su yen-i*, vol. 1, *chüan* 8, p. 383, l. 7; *Shui-hu ch'üan-chuan*, vol. 1, ch. 20, p. 289, l. 6; *Lieh-kuo chih-chuan*, vol. 2, *chüan* 6, p. 12a, l. 10; *Huang-Ming k'ai-yün ying-wu chuan*, *chüan* 6, p. 13b, ll. 6–7; *San-pao t'ai-chien Hsi-yang chi t'ung-su yen-i*, vol. 2, ch. 63, p. 816, l. 12; and the novel *Tung-yu chi: shang-tung pa-hsien chuan* (Journey to the east: the story of the eight immortals of the upper realm), comp. Wu Yüan-t'ai (16th century), appendix dated 1596, fac. repr. of Chien-yang edition published by Yü Hsiang-tou (c. 1550–1637), in *Ku-pen Hsiao-shuo ts'ung-k'an, ti san-shih chiu chi* (Collectanea of rare editions of traditional fiction, thirty-ninth series) (Peking: Chung-hua shu-chü, 1991), vol. 1, *chüan* 1, p. 28a, l. 10.

60. The Flower-washing Stream is the name of a waterway outside the city of Ch'eng-tu, on the banks of which the famous T'ang poet Tu Fu (712–70) made his home while a refugee in Szechwan.

61. This four-character expression occurs in a poem by Ch'ien Wei-yen (962–1034), *Ch'üan Sung shih*, 2:1067, l. 4; a lyric by Yen Shu (991–1055), *Ch'üan Sung tz'u*, 1:108, lower register, l. 17; a poem by Liu Ch'ang (1019–68), *Ch'üan Sung shih*, 9:5871, l. 15; a poem by Tsou Hao (1060–1111), ibid., 21:14034, l. 9; a quatrain by the Buddhist monk Huai-shen (1077–1132), ibid., 24:16130, l. 12; a lyric by Li Shih (b. 1108, cs 1151), *Ch'üan Sung tz'u*, 2:1296, lower register, l. 16; a lyric by Mao Ch'ien (b. c. 1116), ibid., 2:1368, upper register, l. 3; and a lyric by Lu Yu (1125–1210), ibid., 3:1601, lower register, l. 3.

62. This is the final couplet of a quatrain by Chang Shu (cs 891), *Ch'üan T'ang shih*, vol. 10, *chüan* 690, p. 7923, l. 11.

63. On the allusion behind this line, see Roy, *The Plum in the Golden Vase*, vol. 1, chap. 6, n. 28. Lines very similar to this one occur in a poem by Ts'ao T'ang (c. 802–c. 866), *Ch'üan T'ang shih*, vol. 10, *chüan* 640, p. 7338, l. 10; *Yüan-ch'ü hsüan*, 4:1366, l. 2; *Chung-ch'ing li-chi*, *chüan* 6, p. 22b, l. 3; and *Huai-hsiang chi*, scene 16, p. 46, l. 2.

64. This line is taken verbatim from a poem by Liu Yü-hsi (772–842), *Ch'üan T'ang shih*, vol. 6, *chüan* 361, p. 4081, l. 9.

65. This couplet is taken verbatim from a quatrain by Ts'ui Chiao (fl. early 9th century), ibid., vol. 8, *chüan* 505, p. 5744, l. 13. It also occurs in *Lien-huan chi*, scene 25, p. 65, l. 12; and *Hai-ling i-shih*, p. 121, l. 12. The last line occurs independently in *Chin-chien chi*, scene 24, p. 77, l. 12. The proximate source of this entire quatrain, with some textual variation, is probably *Yü-chüeh chi*, scene 16, p. 52, ll. 2–3. It also recurs, with some textual variation in the *Chin P'ing Mei tz'u-hua*, vol. 5, ch. 83, p. 5a, ll. 10–11.

CHAPTER 70

1. The Han dynasty figure Li Kuang (d. 119 B.C.), though a famous general, was once forced by a drunken watchman to stay overnight at the Pa-ling relay station against his will. See Watson, *Records of the Grand Historian of China*, 2:145–46.

2. This four-character expression, the literal meaning of which is "Spring equipped with legs," occurs, with its two components in reverse order, in *K'ai-yüan T'ien-pao*

i-shih (Forgotten events of the K'ai-yüan [713–41] and T'ien-pao [742–56] reign periods), comp. Wang Jen-yü (880–942), in *K'ai-yüan T'ien-pao i-shih shih-chung* (Ten works dealing with forgotten events of the K'ai-yüan and T'ien-pao reign periods), ed. Ting Ju-ming (Shanghai: Shang-hai ku-chi ch'u-pan she), *chüan* 3, p. 102, l. 8. It occurs ubiquitously in the form given in the novel in later Chinese literature. See, e.g., a quatrain by Li P'eng (12th century), *Ch'üan Sung shih*, 24:15957, l. 13; a lyric by Hung K'uo (1117–84), *Ch'üan Sung tz'u*, 2:1369, upper register, l. 16; a lyric by Shen Tuan-chieh (12th century), ibid., 3:1682, lower register, l. 3; a poem by Yang Wan-li (1127–1206), *Ch'üan Sung shih*, 42:26576, l. 1; a lyric by Chang Tzu (1153–1211), *Ch'üan Sung tz'u*, 3:2137, lower register, l. 10; a lyric by Tu Tung (cs 1214), ibid., 4:2695, upper register, l. 7; a lyric by Li Tseng-po (1198–c. 1265), ibid., 4:2824, lower register, l. 1; a lyric by Ch'en Chu (1214–97), ibid., 4:3037, lower register, l. 8; a lyric by Wang Yüeh (1423–98), *Ch'üan Ming tz'u*, 1:310, lower register, l. 6; a lyric by Min Kuei (1430–1511), *Ch'üan Ming tz'u pu-pien*, 1:107, lower register, l. 1; a lyric by Wang Hung-ju (d. 1519), ibid., 1:137, upper register, ll. 9–10; a lyric by Wang Chiu-ssu (1468–1551), *Ch'üan Ming tz'u*, 2:482, lower register, l. 1; a lyric by Ch'en T'ing (cs 1502), ibid., 2:551, lower register, l. 9; a lyric by Hsiang Ch'iao (1493–1552), *Ch'üan Ming tz'u pu-pien*, 1:297, upper register, l. 7; a lyric by Ch'en Fei (cs 1535), *Ch'üan Ming tz'u*, 2:959, upper register, l. 2; a lyric by Hu Kao (cs 1550), *Ch'üan Ming tz'u pu-pien*, 1:451, upper register, l. 2; a lyric by Sung No (1530–85), ibid., 1:494, upper register, l. 6; a lyric by Wang T'ing-no (fl. 1593–1611), *Ch'üan Ming tz'u*, 3:1218, lower register, l. 13; and *Mu-tan t'ing*, scene 8, p. 34, l. 7.

3. This four-character expression occurs in a letter by Lou Yüeh (1137–1213), in *Kung-k'uei chi* (Collected works of Kung-k'uei [Lou Yüeh]), 112 *chüan*, *Ssu-pu ts'ung-k'an* (Collectanea of [facsimile reproductions from] the four treasuries) ed. (Shanghai: Shang-wu yin-shu kuan, 1929), *chüan* 61, p. 9b, l. 3; *Huan-tai chi*, *chüan* 2, scene 32, p. 27b, l. 2; *Chung-ch'ing li-chi*, *chüan* 6, p. 24b, l. 11; *Lieh-kuo chih-chuan*, vol. 3, *chüan* 8, p. 36b, l. 11; and *Sui-T'ang liang-ch'ao shih-chuan*, *chüan* 3, ch. 21, p. 6a, l. 4.

4. This four-character expression occurs in *Hsüeh Jen-kuei cheng-Liao shih-lüeh*, p. 12, l. 6; *Shui-hu ch'üan-chuan*, vol. 3, ch. 82, p. 1357, l. 9; *San-pao t'ai-chien Hsi-yang chi t'ung-su yen-i*, vol. 1, ch. 33, p. 432, l. 9; and *Ch'eng-yün chuan*, *chüan* 2, p. 1a, l. 4. It also recurs in the *Chin P'ing Mei tz'u-hua*, vol. 4, ch. 76, p. 6b, l. 4.

5. This four-character expression occurs in *Hsi-yu chi*, vol. 2, ch. 56, p. 650, l. 15.

6. This four-character expression occurs in ibid., ch. 87, p. 991, l. 15.

7. This four-character expression occurs in *Shuang-chu chi*, scene 28, p. 94, ll. 4–5.

8. Meng Ch'ang-ling (fl. early 12th century) is a historical figure who held the post of commissioner of waterways and undertook numerous construction projects that required great expenditures of money and labor. See Liu Chung-kuang, "Chin P'ing Mei jen-wu k'ao-lun," pp. 130–31.

9. There is a sixteenth-century figure of this name who passed the *chin-shih* examinations in 1521. See *Ming-Ch'ing chin-shih t'i-ming pei-lu so-yin* (Index to Ming-Ch'ing stele lists of *chin-shih* degrees), comp. Chu Pao-chiung and Hsieh P'ei-lin, 3 vols. (Shanghai: Shang-hai ku-chi ch'u-pan she, 1980), 3:2507, l. 5.

10. Cheng Chü-chung (1059–1123) is a historical figure. For his biography, see *Sung shih*, vol. 32, *chüan* 351, pp. 11103–5.

11. Ts'ai Hsing (fl. early 12th century) is a historical figure. For his appointment as director of the Palace Administration, see *Sung shih*, vol. 39, *chüan* 472, p. 13731, l. 15; and *Hsüan-ho i-shih*, p. 32, l. 13.

12. Lin Ling-su (d. c. 1125) is a historical figure who looms large in the history of Sung religion as the founder of the Shen-hsiao, or Divine Empyrean, school of Taoism. For his biography, see *Sung shih*, vol. 39, *chüan* 462, pp. 13528–30; *Lin Ling-su chuan* (The story of Lin Ling-su), by Keng Yen-hsi (fl. early 12th century), in *Pin-t'ui lu* (Records written after my guests have left), by Chao Yü-shih (1175–1231) (Taipei: Kuang-wen shu-chü, 1970), *chüan* 1, pp. 5a–8a; the long hagiography by Chao Ting (1085–1147), in *Li-shih chen-hsien t'i-tao t'ung-chien* (Comprehensive mirror of immortals who embodied the Tao through the ages), comp. Chao Tao-i (fl. 1294–1307), in *Cheng-t'ung Tao-tsang*, *ts'e* 148, *chüan* 53, pp. 1a–16a; and *Hsüan-ho i-shih*, pp. 22–28, and 66–71.

13. See Schuyler Cammann, *China's Dragon Robes* (New York: Ronald Press, 1952), p. 15; and *Chung-kuo i-kuan fu-shih ta tz'u-tien* (Comprehensive dictionary of Chinese costume and its decorative motifs), comp. Chou Hsün and Kao Ch'un-ming (Shanghai: Shang-hai tz'u-shu ch'u-pan she, 1996), p. 592.

14. For the conferral of this title on Lin Ling-su, see *Lin Ling-su chuan*, p. 6a, l. 5; *Li-shih chen-hsien t'i-tao t'ung-chien*, *chüan* 53, p. 6a, l. 4; and *Hsüan-ho i-shih*, p. 25, l. 1.

15. For the conferral of this title on Lin Ling-su, see *Lin Ling-su chuan*, p. 5b, l. 4; *Li-shih chen-hsien t'i-tao t'ung-chien*, *chüan* 53, p. 7a, ll. 8–9; *Hsüan-ho i-shih*, p. 23, l. 10; and *Sung shih*, vol. 39, *chüan* 462, p. 13529, l. 11.

16. This title was conferred on Lin Ling-su in the fifth month of the year 1118. See ibid., vol. 2, *chüan* 21, p. 400, ll. 3–4.

17. Chia Hsiang (fl. early 12th century), Ho Hsin (fl. early 12th century), and Lan Ts'ung-hsi (fl. early 12th century) are all historical figures. See Liu Chung-kuang, "Chin P'ing mei jen-wu k'ao-lun," pp. 133–35.

18. For a detailed description of this palace that was constructed in 1113–14, see *Sung shih*, vol. 7, *chüan* 85, pp. 2100–2101.

19. Chang Pang-ch'ang (1081–1127) is a historical figure. For his biography, see ibid., vol. 39, *chüan* 475, pp. 13789–93.

20. Pai Shih-chung (d. 1127), is a historical figure. For his biography see ibid., vol. 33, *chüan* 371, pp. 11517–18.

21. Lin Shu (d. c. 1126) is a historical figure. For his biography see ibid., vol. 32, *chüan* 351, pp. 11110–12.

22. Chang Ko (1068–1113) is a historical figure. For his biography see ibid., *chüan* 353, pp. 11144–45.

23. A person of this name is mentioned in *Hsüan-ho i-shih*, p. 38, l. 5.

24. Variants of these two lines occur together in *Pai-she chi*, *chüan* 2, scene 21, p. 18b, ll. 9–10; and *Shui-hu ch'üan-chuan*, vol. 3, ch. 88, p. 1443, l. 3. The first line occurs independently in the same form as in the novel in *Yüan-ch'ü hsüan*, 4:1515, l. 9; *Shuang-chu chi*, scene 21, p. 65, ll. 2–3; and *Shui-hu ch'üan-chuan*, vol. 3, ch. 71, p. 1200, l. 6.

25. This four-character expression occurs in a famous quatrain by Liu Yü-hsi (772–842) written in 816. See *Ch'üan T'ang shih*, vol. 6, *chüan* 365, p. 4116, l. 10. It occurs

ubiquitously in later Chinese literature. See, e.g., a poem by Lo Yin (833–909), ibid., vol. 10, *chüan* 658, p. 7559, l. 14; a long poem by Emperor T'ai-tsung of the Sung dynasty (r. 976–97), *Ch'üan Sung shih*, 1:343, l. 3; a poem by Chang Yung (946–1015), ibid., 1:530, l. 14; a poem by Ch'en Yao-sou (961–1017), ibid., 2:984, l. 5; a poem by Chao Pien (1008–84), ibid., 6:4210, l. 2; a poem by Ssu-ma Kuang (1019–86), ibid., 9:6186, l. 5; a lyric by Ch'iu Ch'u-chi (1148–1227), *Ch'üan Chin Yüan tz'u*, 1:455, upper register, l. 7; a lyric by Chang Yeh (13th–14th centuries), ibid., 2:902, lower register, l. 10; a lyric by Sung Chiung (1292–1344), ibid., 2:1052, upper register, l. 11; *Sha-kou chi*, scene 21, p. 77, l. 9; *Liang-shan wu-hu ta chieh-lao*, scene 4, p. 7b, l. 2; and an abundance of other occurrences, too numerous to list.

26. This was a huge temple complex, the most important Buddhist establishment in K'ai-feng. For the details of its history, see the material collected in *Tung-ching meng-hua lu chu* (Commentary on A Dream of past splendors in the Eastern Capital), comp. Teng Chih-ch'eng (Peking: Shang-wu yin-shu kuan, 1959), pp. 91–95.

27. This is a quotation from *Mencius* where it is described as being a proverbial saying of his time. See *Meng-tzu yin-te*, Book 2A, ch. 1, p. 10, l. 9. The same saying, with one insignificant variant is quoted in *Han-shu*, vol. 5, *chüan* 41, p. 2089, l. 5. It occurs in the same form as in the novel in *Ming-hsin pao-chien*, *chüan* 2, p. 6a, l. 8; *Yang-chia fu shih-tai chung-yung yen-i chih-chuan*, vol. 1, *chüan* 4, p. 27a, ll. 4–5; and *Sui-T'ang liang-ch'ao shih-chuan*, *chüan* 2, ch. 20, p. 53b, l. 1.

28. This four-character expression occurs in a document by Liu I-hsin (404–39), in *Sung shu*, vol. 8, *chüan* 95, p. 2333, ll. 2–3; *K'ai-ho chi*, p. 235, l. 1; a memorial by Ch'in Kuan (1049–1100) written in 1080, in *Huai-hai chi chien-chu* (Ch'in Kuan's collected works collated and annotated), ed. Hsü P'ei-chün, 3 vols. (Shanghai: Shang-hai ku-chi ch'u-pan she, 1994), vol. 2, *chüan* 17, p. 648, l. 14; a set of songs by K'ang Hai (1475–1541), *Ch'üan Ming san-ch'ü*, 1:1122, ll. 1–2; *Shui-hu ch'üan-chuan*, vol. 3, ch. 63, p. 1075, l. 9; *Lieh-kuo chih-chuan*, vol. 1, *chüan* 3, p. 35b, ll. 3–4; *Chin-tiao chi*, *chüan* 3, scene 31, p. 21a, l. 8; *Huang-Ming k'ai-yün ying-wu chuan*, *chüan* 1, p. 4a, l. 8; and *San-pao t'ai-chien Hsi-yang chi t'ung-su yen-i*, vol. 1, ch. 4, p. 50, l. 14.

29. See Roy, *The Plum in the Golden Vase*, vol. 2, chap. 35, n. 12.

30. See ibid., chap. 30, n. 16.

31. Consort Liu (1088–1121) is a historical figure. For data about her, and the fact that she lived for a time in the home of Ho Hsin, see *Sung shih*, vol. 25, *chüan* 243, p. 8644, l. 8–p. 8645, l. 4; and Liu Chung-kuang, "*Chin P'ing Mei* jen-wu k'ao-lun," pp. 138–40.

32. This statement is from the *Hsi-tz'u* (Attached commentary) in the *I-ching* (Book of Changes). See *Chou-i yin-te*, p. 42, column 1, ll. 12–13. It also occurs in *Han-shu*, vol. 8, *chüan* 99b, p. 4116, l. 12; *[Hsin-pien] Wu-tai shih p'ing-hua*, p. 30, l. 4; *Tuan-fa chi*, *chüan* 2, scene 36, p. 40b, l. 8; and recurs in the *Chin P'ing Mei tz'u-hua*, vol. 4, ch. 76, p. 25a, l. 4. The first four characters of this seven-character expression also occur independently in *Hou-Han shu*, vol. 4, *chüan* 29, p. 1017, ll. 11–12; *Hsüan-ho i-shih*, p. 39, l. 9; *San-kuo chih t'ung-su yen-i*, vol. 2, *chüan* 15, p. 700, l. 21; *Nan Sung chih-chuan*, vol. 1, *chüan* 8, p. 14a, l. 12; *Mu-lien chiu-mu ch'üan-shan hsi-wen*, *chüan* 1, p. 71, l. 3; *Ch'üan-Han chih-chuan*, vol. 3, *chüan* 4, p. 13b, ll. 8–9; *Pai-chia kung-an*, *chüan* 2, ch. 16, p. 20b, l. 3; and *Yang-chia fu shih-tai chung-yung yen-i chih-chuan*, *chüan* 7, p. 37a, ll. 7–8.

33. This was a type of hat worn by eunuchs in the Ming dynasty that was made of stiff gauze with a raised back in the shape of three mountains. See *Chung-kuo i-kuan fu-shih ta tz'u-tien*, p. 69.

34. Consort Feng (fl. mid 11th century–early 12th century) is a historical figure who was the consort of Emperor Jen-tsung (r. 1022–63) and resided in the palace for five reigns. See *Sung shih*, vol. 25, *chüan* 242, p. 8623, ll. 7–10.

35. The Chinese term *t'ou-nao chiu* that I have translated as "pick-me-up" literally means "drink that goes to the head." During the Ming dynasty this referred to a concoction of diced meat and other ingredients doused with heated wine and was commonly served as a pick-me-up on cold mornings. See *Yung-ch'uang hsiao-p'in* (Minor essays from the portable kiosk), by Chu Kuo-chen (1557–1632), author's postface dated 1622, 2 vols. (Peking: Chung-hua shu-chü, 1959), vol. 2, *chüan* 17, p. 398, l. 13–p. 399, l. 5.

36. This four-character expression occurs in *Hsing-t'ien feng-yüeh t'ung-hsüan chi*, scene 5, p. 14b, l. 6.

37. This four-character expression is an abbreviation of a six-character saying about the importance of environment in *Mencius*. See *Meng-tzu yin-te*, Book 7A, ch. 36, p. 54, l. 2.

38. This four-character expression occurs in a remark attributed to Ou-yang Hsiu (1007–72) in a fragment of the lost work *Mu-fu yen-hsien lu* (Anecdotes recorded during a private secretary's leisure hours), comp. Pi Chung-hsün (11th century), in *Shuo-fu san-chung*, 5:1900, p. 1b, l. 8. It is quoted as proverbial in Hu San-hsing's (1230–1302) commentary to the *Tzu-chih t'ung-chien*, vol. 4, *chüan* 286, p. 9343, l. 10; and occurs in *[Chiao-ting] Yüan-k'an tsa-chü san-shih chung* (A collated edition of Thirty tsa-chü dramas printed during the Yüan dynasty), ed. Cheng Ch'ien (Taipei: Shih-chieh shu-chü, 1962), p. 91, l. 4; *Yüan-ch'ü hsüan*, 2:554, ll. 17–18; *Yüan-ch'ü hsüan wai-pien*, 1:208, l. 4; *Ming-hsin pao-chien*, *chüan* 2, p. 2b, ll. 4–5; *San-pao t'ai-chien Hsi-yang chi t'ung-su yen-i*, vol. 2, ch. 52, p. 674, l. 4; and *Ta-T'ang Ch'in-wang tz'u-hua*, vol. 1, *chüan* 3, ch. 23, p. 70b, l. 1. It also recurs in the *Chin P'ing Mei tz'u-hua*, vol. 5, ch. 81, p. 8b, l. 9; and ch. 90. p. 5a, l. 5.

39. This proverbial saying occurs in *Ming-hsin pao-chien*, *chüan* 1, p. 13b, l. 12; and a set of songs by Chin Luan (1494–1583), *Ch'üan Ming san-ch'ü*, 2:1586, l. 1.

40. Synonymous variants of this four-character expression occur in *Lu-shan Yüan-kung hua*, p. 172, l. 11; and *Yang-chia fu shih-tai chung-yung yen-i chih-chuan*, vol. 2, *chüan* 7, p. 24a, l. 6. In the same form as in the novel, it occurs ubiquitously in Chinese vernacular literature. See, e.g., *Tung Chieh-yüan Hsi-hsiang chi*, *chüan* 2, p. 50, l. 1; *San-kuo chih t'ung-su yen-i*, vol. 1, *chüan* 1, p. 4, l. 4; *Shui-hu ch'üan-chuan*, vol. 3, ch. 61, p. 1027, l. 2; *Lien-huan chi*, *chüan* 2, scene 16, p. 38, l. 11; *Nan Sung chih-chuan*, vol. 1, *chüan* 6, p. 27b, l. 9; *Pei Sung chih-chuan*, vol. 2, *chüan* 5, p. 9a, l. 1; *Lieh-kuo chih-chuan*, vol. 1, *chüan* 2, p. 9b, l. 11; *Hua-shen san-miao chuan*, p. 54a, l. 2; *Hsi-yu chi*, vol. 1, ch. 41, p. 470, l. 10; *Huang-Ming k'ai-yün ying-wu chuan*, *chüan* 1, p. 23b, l. 4; *Ta-T'ang Ch'in-wang tz'u-hua*, vol. 2, *chüan* 5, ch. 36, p. 36b, l. 6; and *Sui-T'ang liang-ch'ao shih-chuan*, *chüan* 9, ch. 82, p. 11b, l. 4.

41. This four-character expression occurs in *San-yüan chi*, scene 32, p. 84, l. 8; and *Huang-Ming k'ai-yün ying-wu chuan*, *chüan* 2, p. 10a, l. 8.

42. See Roy, *The Plum in the Golden Vase*, vol. 1, chap. 7, n. 16.

43. This was the centrally located gate in the south wall of the city of K'ai-feng.

44. These two lines occur in close proximity to each other in *Shui-hu ch'üan-chuan*, vol. 3, ch. 55, p. 918, ll. 12–13.

45. These two lines occur together in *Lieh-kuo chih-chuan*, vol. 3, *chüan* 8, p. 4b, ll. 6–7; *San-pao t'ai-chien Hsi-yang chi t'ung-su yen-i*, vol. 1, ch. 15, p. 196, l. 10; and *Sui-T'ang liang-ch'ao shih-chuan*, *chüan* 2, ch. 12, p. 6b, ll. 3–4. They occur together with a variant in the second line in *San-kuo chih t'ung-su yen-i*, vol. 1, *chüan* 5, p. 247, ll. 11–12; *Ts'an-T'ang Wu-tai shih yen-i chuan*, ch. 60, p. 228, ll. 3–4; and *Ta-T'ang Ch'in-wang tz'u-hua*, vol. 1, *chüan* 1, ch. 3, p. 26b, l. 6. The first line also occurs independently in *Yüan-ch'ü hsüan wai-pien*, 2:509, l. 18; and *Ch'üan-Han chih-chuan*, vol. 2, *chüan* 4, p. 25b, l. 12.

46. See Roy, *The Plum in the Golden Vase*, vol. 2, chap. 32, n. 16.

47. This formulaic four-character expression occurs ubiquitously in Chinese vernacular literature. See, e.g., *Kuan-shih-yin p'u-sa pen-hsing ching*, p. 3b, l. 8; *Meng-liang lu* (Record of the millet dream), comp. Wu Tzu-mu (13th century), pref. dated 1274, in *Tung-ching meng-hua lu [wai ssu-chung]*, *chüan* 2, p. 150, l. 5; *Yüan-ch'ü hsüan wai-pien*, 2:366, l. 4; *Yu-kuei chi*, scene 3, p. 3, l. 6; *Chin-ch'ai chi*, scene 30, p. 55, l. 20; a song suite by Ch'iu Ju-ch'eng (15th century), *Ch'üan Ming san-ch'ü*, 2:2403, l. 4; *San-kuo chih t'ung-su yen-i*, vol. 1, *chüan* 1, p. 5, l. 3; *Shui-hu ch'üan-chuan*, vol. 1, ch. 13, p. 189, ll. 16–17; *Lien-huan chi*, *chüan* 1, scene 12, p. 29, l. 7; *Ta-Sung chung-hsing yen-i*, vol. 2, *chüan* 6, p. 49b, l. 4; *Nan Sung chih-chuan*, vol. 1, *chüan* 5, p. 9a, l. 12; *Pei Sung chih-chuan*, vol. 2, *chüan* 4, p. 2a, l. 10; *Lieh-kuo chih-chuan*, vol. 1, *chüan* 3, p. 77b, l. 8; *Pai-p'ao chi*, *chüan* 1, scene 19, p. 31a, l. 8; *Ching-chung chi*, scene 6, p. 13, l. 4; *Yen-chih chi*, *chüan* 2, scene 27, p. 11b, l. 6; *Ts'an-T'ang Wu-tai shih yen-i chuan*, ch. 26, p. 103, l. 6; *Hsi-yu chi*, vol. 1, ch. 4, p. 45, l. 2; *Pai-chia kung-an*, *chüan* 3, ch. 26, p. 15a, l. 4; *San-pao t'ai-chien Hsi-yang chi t'ung-su yen-i*, vol. 1, ch. 8, p. 102, l. 9; *Ch'eng-yün chuan*, *chüan* 4, p. 5a, l. 3; *Tung-yu chi: shang-tung pa-hsien chuan*, *chüan* 1, p. 25b, l. 9; *Ta-T'ang Ch'in-wang tz'u-hua*, vol. 1, *chüan* 1, ch. 1, p. 9a, l. 2; *Sui-T'ang liang-ch'ao shih-chuan*, *chüan* 1, ch. 6, p. 33a, l. 9; and an abundance of other occurrences, too numerous to list.

48. See Roy, *The Plum in the Golden Vase*, vol. 2, chap. 21, n. 7.

49. During the Sung dynasty this type of headgear was a badge of exalted rank and could only be worn by imperial princes and the three highest officials in the bureaucracy. See *Sung shih*, vol. 11, *chüan* 152, p. 3558, ll. 4–6.

50. Wang Tsu-tao (d. 1108) is a historical figure. For his biography, see ibid., vol. 32, *chüan* 348, pp. 11040–42.

51. There is a sixteenth-century figure of this name who passed the *chin-shih* examinations in 1511. See *Ming-Ch'ing chin-shih t'i-ming pei-lu*, 3:2499, l. 1.

52. A person of this name and with a similar title figures briefly in *Hsüan-ho i-shih*, p. 51, ll. 5 and 10.

53. A person of this name and with a similar title figures briefly in ibid., p. 51, ll. 5 and 10.

54. This formulaic four-character expression occurs together with the following line in *Yüan-ch'ü hsüan*, 3:985, l. 10; *Wu Lun-ch'üan Pei*, *chüan* 1, scene 6, p. 29a, l. 6; and *Chiao-hsiao chi*, *chüan* 1, scene 11, p. 25a, l. 1. It occurs independently in *Yüan-ch'ü hsüan wai-pien*, 3:990, l. 1; the anonymous Ming tsa-chü drama *Wu Ch'i ti Ch'in kua shuai-yin* (Wu Ch'i resists Ch'in and accepts the commander's seal), in *Ku-pen Yüan*

Ming tsa-chü, vol. 2, scene 4, p. 12b, l. 5; *Sung ta-chiang Yüeh Fei ching-chung,* scene 1, p. 4b, ll. 4–5; *Huai-ch'un ya-chi, chüan* 10, p. 20b, l. 2; *Ts'an-T'ang Wu-tai shih yen-i chuan,* ch. 33, p. 132, l. 2; *Mu-lien chiu-mu ch'üan-shan hsi-wen, chüan* 3, p. 79a, l. 6; and a set of songs by Liu Hsiao-tsu (1522–89), *Ch'üan Ming san-ch'ü,* 2:2321, l. 5.

55. In addition to the occurrences in conjunction with the preceding line referred to in the previous note, this formulaic four-character expression occurs independently in *Yüan-ch'ü hsüan,* 2:824, l. 9; a song by Sun Chou-ch'ing (14th century), *Ch'üan Yüan san-ch'ü,* 2:1064, l. 2; *Yü-huan chi,* scene 15, p. 51, l. 9; an anonymous song suite in *Tz'u-lin chai-yen,* 2:1001, l. 9; an anonymous song suite in *Yung-hsi yüeh-fu, ts'e* 9, p. 37a, l. 2; a lyric by Min Kuei (1430–1511), *Ch'üan Ming tz'u pu-pien,* 1:106, upper register, l. 14; a lyric by Liu Chieh (1476–1555), ibid., 1:213, upper register, ll. 8–9; a lyric by Sun Ch'eng-en (1485–1565), *Ch'üan Ming tz'u,* 2:749, upper register, ll. 15–16; *Hai-fu shan-t'ang tz'u-kao, chüan* 1, p. 10, l. 2; and a lyric by Hsia Shu-fang (fl. late 16th century), *Ch'üan Ming tz'u,* 3:1158, upper register, ll. 2–3.

56. This formulaic four-character expression occurs in a poem by Wen Yen-po (1006–97), *Ch'üan Sung shih,* 6:3509, l. 6; a poem by Ssu-ma kuang (1019–86), ibid., 9:6123, l. 10; *Ching-ch'ai chi,* scene 19, p. 60, l. 1; the Yüan-Ming hsi-wen drama *Pai-yüeh t'ing chi* (Moon prayer pavilion), in *Ku-pen hsi-ch'ü ts'ung-k'an, ch'u-chi,* item 9, *chüan* 1, scene 25, p. 42a, l. 3; *Chao-shih ku-erh chi, chüan* 2, scene 41, p. 38a, l. 3; *Chin-ch'ai chi,* scene 18, p. 37, l. 14; *P'o-yao chi, chüan* 1, scene 5, p. 16a, l. 8; *Wu Lun-ch'üan Pei, chüan* 4, scene 27, p. 25a, l. 2; *Huai-hsiang chi,* scene 2, p. 3, l. 3; a song suite by Ch'en To (fl. early 16th century), *Ch'üan Ming san-ch'ü,* 1:570, l. 5; a song suite by Wang Chiu-ssu (1468–1551), ibid., 1:942, l. 9; an anonymous song suite in *Yung-hsi yüeh-fu, ts'e* 8, p. 16b, l. 7; a song suite by Ch'en So-wen (d. c. 1604), *Ch'üan Ming san-ch'ü,* 2:2541, l. 4; and *Ch'un-wu chi,* scene 11, p. 27, l. 3.

57. These two lines, with minor textual variations, occur in reverse order in *Shih-jen yü-hsieh* (Jade splinters from the poets), comp. Wei Ch'ing-chih (13th century), pref. dated 1244, 2 vols. (Shanghai: Ku-tien wen-hsüeh ch'u-pan she, 1958), vol. 1, *chüan* 4, p. 102, l. 9.

58. An identical line, except for the omission of the character for "newly," occurs in a song suite by Chang K'o-chiu (1270–1348), *Ch'üan Yüan san-ch'ü,* 1:995, l. 2.

59. This four-character expression occurs in *Yüan-ch'ü hsüan,* 2:804, l. 7; an anonymous Yüan dynasty song suite, *Ch'üan Yüan san-ch'ü,* 2:1825, l. 3; a lyric written in 1380 by Lin Ta-t'ung (cs 1371), *Ch'üan Ming tz'u pu-pien,* 1:15, upper register, l. 11; the tsa-chü drama *Lü Tung-pin hua-yüeh shen-hsien hui* (Lü Tung-pin arranges a meeting with divine immortals amid flowers and moonlight), by Chu Yu-tun (1379–1439), completed in 1435, in *Ku-pen Yüan Ming tsa-chü,* vol. 2, scene 1, p. 2a, l. 3; a set of anonymous songs published in 1471, *Ch'üan Ming san-ch'ü,* 4:4517, l. 10; an anonymous song in *Tz'u-lin chai-yen,* 1:66, l. 10; a song suite by Ch'en To (fl. early 16th century), *Ch'üan Ming san-ch'ü,* 1:654, l. 5; a song by Shen Shih (1488–1565), ibid., 2:1362, l. 3; a song suite by Chang Lien (cs 1544), ibid., 2:1688, l. 11; the Ming tsa-chü drama *Tu-lo yüan Ssu-ma ju-hsiang* (In Tu-lo Garden Ssu-ma Kuang becomes grand councilor), by Sang Shao-liang (16th century), in *Ku-pen Yüan Ming tsa-chü,* vol. 2, scene 2, p. 4a, l. 14; and two anonymous song suites in *Ch'ün-yin lei-hsüan,* 3:1937, l. 6; and 4:2492, l. 7.

60. The four-character expression for a puppet show occurs in a song by Ch'iao Chi (d. 1345), *Ch'üan Yüan san-ch'ü,* 1:634, l. 7; *Han Hsiang-tzu chiu-tu Wen-kung*

sheng-hsien chi, chüan 1, scene 1, p. 1a, l. 5; *Hai-fu shan-t'ang tz'u-kao, chüan* 1, p. 19, l. 6; and a lyric by Wu Ch'eng-en (c. 1500–82), *Ch'üan Ming tz'u,* 2:989, upper register, l. 12.

61. The term that I have translated as "singing girls" actually reads *Hsüeh-erh,* the name of a favorite concubine of Li Mi (582–618), who was renowned for her ability to set verse to music and then perform it. See *Pei-meng so-yen* (Trivial accounts of northern dreams), comp. Sun Kuang-hsien (d. 968) (Peking: Chung-hua shu-chü, 1960), appendix, *chüan* 2, p. 168, ll. 4–5. Her name later became used as a generic term for singing girls.

62. This four-character expression occurs in a poem by Mei Yao-ch'en (1002–60), *Ch'üan Sung shih,* 5:3086, l. 2; a lyric by Ch'ao Pu-chih (1053–1110), *Ch'üan Sung tz'u,* 1:582, lower register, l. 14; a lyric by Ts'ao Tsu (cs 1121), ibid., 2:805, upper register, l. 14; a lyric by Hung Tzu-k'uei (1176–1236), ibid., 4:2465, upper register, l. 7; a song by Jen Yü (14th century), *Ch'üan Yüan san-ch'ü,* 1:1006, l. 6; a lyric by Chang Yü-niang (14th century), *Ch'üan Chin Yüan tz'u,* 2:873, upper register, l. 14; and a lyric by Li Tung-yang (1447–1516), *Ch'üan Ming tz'u,* 2:377, upper register, l. 3.

63. This four-character expression first appears in a ballad by Emperor Wu of the Liang dynasty (r. 502–49), *Yüeh-fu shih-chi,* vol. 4, *chüan* 86, p. 1204, l. 7, where it refers to twelve gold hairpins on the head of a single woman. Later it came to be used for groups of female entertainers with gold pins in their hair. See, e.g., a poem by Po Chü-i (772–846), *Ch'üan T'ang shih,* vol. 7, *chüan* 457, p. 5184, l. 11; a set of quatrains by Sung Pai (936–1012), *Ch'üan Sung shih,* 1:285, l. 8; a poem by Yü Tzu-chih (11th century), ibid., 11:7375, l. 14; a lyric by Ch'ao Pu-chih (1053–1110), *Ch'üan Sung tz'u,* 1:553, lower register, l. 12; a lyric by Chu Tun-ju (1081–1159), ibid., 2:844, upper register, ll. 1–2; a lyric by Huang Kung-tu (1109–56), ibid., 2:1329, lower register, l. 17; a song by Chang K'o-chiu (1270–1348), *Ch'üan Yüan san-ch'ü,* 1:889, ll. 1–2; a song by Chung Ssu-ch'eng (c. 1279–c. 1360), ibid., 2:1356, l. 2; a set of songs by Wang Yüan-heng (14th century), ibid., 2:1380, l. 10; *Yüan-ch'ü hsüan,* 2:479, l. 11; *Yüan-ch'ü hsüan wai-pien,* 2:407, l. 3; *[Hsin-pien] Wu-tai shih p'ing-hua,* p. 115, l. 14; *P'i-p'a chi,* scene 18, p. 109, l. 7; *Ssu-shih hua-yüeh sai chiao-jung,* scene 2, p. 4a, l. 9; a song by Chu Yu-tun (1379–1439), *Ch'üan Ming san-ch'ü,* 1:318, l. 8; *P'o-yao chi, chüan* 2, scene 29, p. 41b, l. 10; *Chin-ch'ai chi,* scene 32, p. 59, l. 12; *Jen chin shu ku-erh hsün-mu,* scene 3, p. 10a, l. 13; a song by Ch'en To (fl. early 16th century), *Ch'üan Ming san-ch'ü,* 1:518, l. 4; a song by Wang P'an (d. 1530), ibid., 1:1045, l. 1; *Chiang Shih yüeh-li chi, chüan* 4, scene 36, p. 7b, l. 10; *Lien-huan chi, chüan* 1, scene 3, p. 5, l. 8; a set of songs by Yang Shen (1488–1559), *Ch'üan Ming san-ch'ü,* 2:1407, l. 9; *Huan-sha chi,* scene 4, p. 9, ll. 10–11; *Hai-ling i-shih,* p. 96, l. 2; and an abundance of other occurrences, too numerous to list.

64. This four-character expression occurs in a poem by Po Chü-i (772–846), *Ch'üan T'ang shih,* vol. 7, *chüan* 426, p. 4694, l. 13; a poem by Wen T'ing-yün (c. 812–c. 870) written in 846, ibid., vol. 9, *chüan* 576, p. 6704, l. 13; a poem by Wei Chuang (836–910), ibid., vol. 10, *chüan* 695, p. 8001, l. 7; a poem by Huang T'ao (cs 895), ibid., *chüan* 705, p. 8109, l. 9; a quatrain attributed to Lü Tung-pin (9th century), ibid., vol. 12, *chüan* 858, p. 9697, l. 14; a poem by Li Fang (925–96), *Ch'üan Sung shih,* 1:186, l. 6; a poem by Wang Yü-ch'eng (954–1001), ibid., 2:806, l. 5; a poem by Sun Chin (969–1017), ibid., 2:1254, l. 4; a quatrain by Ch'iu Ch'u-chi (1148–1227), *Ch'üan Chin shih,* 2:162, l. 8; *Yüan-ch'ü hsüan,* 3:1056, l. 18; and *Ta-Sung chung-hsing yen-i,* vol. 1, *chüan* 4, p. 51a, l. 2.

65. This four-character expression occurs in a poem by Ssu-ma Kuang (1019–86), *Ch'üan Sung shih*, 9:6030, l. 5; a lyric by Ma Yü (1123–83), *Ch'üan Chin Yüan tz'u*, 1:382, lower register, l. 7; a lyric by Ch'ang-ch'üan-tzu (13th century), ibid., 1:588, upper register, ll. 10–11; a lyric by Liu Min-chung (1243–1318), ibid., 2:761, upper register, l. 8; a lyric by P'eng Ssu (13th century), *Ch'üan Sung tz'u*, 4:2526, lower register, l. 11; a lyric by Chiang Chieh (cs 1274), ibid., 5:3444, lower register, l. 1; a lyric by Sa-tu-la (cs 1327), *Ch'üan Chin Yüan tz'u*, 2:1090, lower register, l. 11; *Yüan-ch'ü hsüan*, 2:778, l. 1; and a song suite by Li Chih-yüan (14th century), *Ch'üan Yüan san-ch'ü*, 2:1258, l. 11.

66. This entire passage of descriptive parallel prose, with some textual variation, is taken from *Pao-chien chi*, scene 3, p. 8, ll. 1–10.

67. These two lines occur together at the beginning of a song suite by Ch'iu Ju-ch'eng (15th century), *Ch'üan Ming san-ch'ü*, 2:2403, l. 11.

68. This four-character expression occurs in a fragment from the lost ch'uan-ch'i drama *Chung-hsiao chi* (A story of loyalty and filiality), by Shih P'an (1531–1623), preserved in *Ch'ün-yin lei-hsüan*, 1:270, l. 9.

69. This four-character expression is from chapter 73 of the *Tao-te ching* (Book of the Way and its power). See *Lao Tzu Tao Te Ching*, trans. D. C. Lau (New York: Penguin Books, 1963), p. 135, l. 15. It is followed by the words, "Though the mesh is not fine, nothing ever slips through." Thus this four-character expression functions like a *hsieh-hou yü* in that it immediately evokes the words that follow in the original context. It occurs ubiquitously in later Chinese literature. See, e.g., the biography of Huang-fu Mi (215–282) in *Chin shu*, vol. 5, *chüan* 51, p. 1411, l. 13; the biography of Yüan Ch'eng (d. 519) in *Wei-shu*, vol. 2, *chüan* 19, p. 477, l. 12; the biography of Chu Tz'u (742–84) in *Hsin T'ang shu* (New history of the T'ang dynasty), comp. Ou-yang Hsiu (1007–72) and Sung Ch'i (998–1061), 20 vols. (Peking: Chung-hua shu-chü, 1975), vol. 20, *chüan* 225, p. 6448, l. 12; the eighth-century prosimetric work *Wu Tzu-hsü pien-wen* (The story of Wu Tzu-hsü), in *Tun-huang pien-wen chi*, 1:4, l. 8; a poem attributed to Lü Tung-pin (9th century), *Ch'üan T'ang shih*, vol. 12, *chüan* 858, p. 9700, l. 1; a poem by T'ien Hsi (940–1004), *Ch'üan Sung shih*, 1:482, l. 13; *Kuan-shih-yin p'u-sa pen-hsing ching*, p. 88a, l. 9; a quatrain by Hou Shan-yüan (12th century), *Ch'üan Chin shih*, 2:332, l. 17; *Yüan-shih shih-fan*, *chüan* 2, p. 88, l. 1; *Liu Chih-yüan chu-kung-tiao [chiao-chu]*, part 2, p. 56, ll. 9–10; *Yüan-ch'ü hsüan*, 1:126, l. 9; *Yüan-ch'ü hsüan wai-pien*, 2:644, l. 3; *Shih-wu kuan hsi-yen ch'eng ch'iao-huo*, p. 700, l. 4; *Ming-hsin pao-chien*, *chüan* 1, p. 2b, l. 3; *Wu Lun-ch'üan Pei*, *chüan* 3, scene 17, p. 12b, l. 6; *T'ao Yüan-ming tung-li shang-chü*, scene 2, p. 6b, l. 10; a song suite by Wang Yang-ming (1472–1529), *Ch'üan Ming san-ch'ü*, 1:1102, l. 4; a set of songs written by Li K'ai-hsien (1502–68) in 1531, *Li K'ai-hsien chi* (The collected works of Li K'ai-hsien), by Li K'ai-hsien (1502–68), ed. Lu Kung, 3 vols. (Peking: Chung-hua shu-chü, 1959), 3:906, l. 11; *Jen chin shu ku-erh hsün-mu*, scene 2, p. 7b, l. 3; *Jen hsiao-tzu lieh-hsing wei shen*, p. 582, l. 5; *Hsün-ch'in chi*, scene 33, p. 112, l. 2; *Pao-chien chi*, scene 34, p. 62, l. 21; *Lieh-kuo chih-chuan*, vol. 2, *chüan* 5, p. 97a, l. 9; *Ts'an-T'ang Wu-tai shih yen-i chuan*, ch. 25, p. 97, l. 27; *Hai-fu shan-t'ang tz'u-kao*, *chüan* 4, p. 190, l. 15; *Chin-tiao chi*, *chüan* 2, scene 10, p. 5b, l. 9; the ch'uan-ch'i drama *Ko-i chi* (The hempen garment), by Ku Ta-tien (1541–96), in *Ku-pen hsi-ch'ü ts'ung-k'an*, *wu-chi*, item 3, *chüan* 2, scene 26, p. 21a, l. 2; and *San-pao t'ai-chien Hsi-yang chi t'ung-su yen-i*, vol. 1, ch. 45, p. 578, l. 14.

70. Variants of this four-character expression occur in a speech by the Buddhist monk Ch'i-wen (10th century), *Wu-teng hui-yüan*, vol. 2, *chüan* 8, p. 476, l. 4; a

speech by the Buddhist monk K'o-ch'in (1063–1135), in *Yüan-wu Fo-kuo ch'an-shih yü-lu* (Recorded sayings of Ch'an Master Yüan-wu Fo-Kuo), pref. dated 1134, in *Taishō shinshū daizōkyō*, vol. 47, no. 1997, *chüan* 7, p. 744, upper register, l. 16; *Chu-tzu yü-lei*, vol. 1, *chüan* 5, p. 2a, l. 13; *Ts'ang-lang shih-hua [chiao-shih]* (Ts'ang-lang's remarks on poetry collated and annotated), by Yen Yü (13th century), ed. and annot. Kuo Shao-yü (Peking: Jen-min wen-hsüeh ch'u-pan she, 1962), p. 111, l. 5; and a fragment from the lost ch'uan-ch'i drama *Chung-hsiao chi*, preserved in *Ch'ün-yin lei-hsüan*, 1:271, l. 4.

71. This four-character expression occurs together with the preceding line in a fragment from the lost ch'uan-ch'i drama *Chung-hsiao chi*, preserved in *Ch'ün-yin lei-hsüan*, 1:271, l. 4.

72. See Roy, *The Plum in the Golden Vase*, vol. 3, chap. 41, n. 24.

73. See ibid., chap. 59, n. 57.

74. Wang Mang (45 B.C.–A.D. 23), who deposed the Han emperor in A.D. 9 and ruled as founder of the Hsin dynasty from then until his death in A.D. 23, is the most notorious usurper in Chinese history.

75. Tung Cho (d. 192) was a ruthless dictator who aspired to usurp the throne but was assassinated before he succeeded. He was grossly obese, and while his corpse was exposed in the marketplace, the guards made a lamp out of his punctured navel, which burned until the dawn of the next day. See his biography in *Hou-Han shu*, vol. 8, *chüan* 72, p. 2332, ll. 2–3.

76. This four-character expression occurs in *Wu Lun-ch'üan Pei*, *chüan* 3, scene 16, p. 4b, l. 3; *Pao-chien chi*, scene 3, p. 9, l. 23; and a fragment of the lost ch'uan-ch'i drama *Chung-hsiao chi*, preserved in *Ch'ün-yin lei-hsüan*, 1:270, l. 4.

77. It is said that Emperor Hsüan-tsung of the T'ang dynasty (r. 712–56) often wrote the names of people he was considering for appointment to the position of grand councilor in his own hand and placed them on his desk. On one occasion, when the crown prince came into his presence, he hid the names under a golden goblet and asked the crown prince if he could guess who they were. When the crown prince guessed correctly, the emperor rewarded him with a goblet of wine. See *Tz'u Liu-shih chiu-wen* (An addendum to Liu Fang's [cs 741] old reminiscences), by Li Te-yü (787–850), in *K'ai-yüan T'ien-pao i-shih shih-chung*, p. 5, ll. 9–11.

78. This four-character expression first occurs in the *Shu-ching* (Book of documents). See *The Shoo King or The Book of Historical Documents*, trans. James Legge (Hong Kong: University of Hong Kong Press, 1960), p. 527. It occurs ubiquitously in later Chinese literature. See, e.g., the lost work *Kuang-i chi* (Great book of marvels), by Tai Fu (cs 757), as quoted in *T'ai-p'ing kuang-chi*, vol. 8, *chüan* 380, p. 3024, l. 3; a poem by Yüan Chen (775–831), *Ch'üan T'ang shih*, vol. 6, *chüan* 419, p. 4613, l. 8; a poem by Fu Pi (1004–83), *Ch'üan Sung shih*, 5:3367, l. 12; a poem by Shao Yung (1011–77) written in 1072, ibid., 7:4696, l. 13; a poem by Lu Yu (1125–1210), ibid., 41:25558, l. 3; *Yüan-ch'ü hsüan*, 1:10, l. 1; *Yüan-ch'ü hsüan wai-pien*, 2:369, l. 16; the prose preface to a song suite by Wang Yüan-ting (14th century), *Ch'üan Yüan san-ch'ü*, 1:690, l. 5; a set of songs by Hsüeh Ang-fu (14th century), ibid., 1:705, l. 13; *Ching-ch'ai chi*, scene 19, p. 58, l. 4; *Wu Lun-ch'üan Pei*, *chüan* 4, scene 27, p. 23a, ll. 5–6; *San-yüan chi*, scene 31, p. 82, l. 3; *Shuang-chu chi*, scene 26, p. 83, l. 11; *Hsiu-ju chi*, scene 4, p. 9, l. 12; *Ming-feng chi*, scene 4, p. 14, l. 10; *Hai-fu shan-t'ang tz'u-kao*, *chüan* 1, p. 34, l. 2; a set of songs by Wu Ch'eng-en (c. 1500–1582), *Ch'üan Ming san-ch'ü*,

2:1798, l. 5; *Mu-lien chiu-mu ch'üan-shan hsi-wen, chüan* 3, p. 79a, l. 1; *Su Ying huang-hou ying-wu chi, chüan* 1, scene 2, p. 1b, l. 1; *Pa-i chi*, scene 6, p. 10, l. 9; *Chin-tiao chi, chüan* 2, scene 17, p. 23b, l. 3; *Huang-Ming k'ai-yün ying-wu chuan, chüan* 1, p. 9b, l. 10; *Shuang-lieh chi*, scene 38, p. 104, l. 5; *Mu-tan t'ing*, scene 53, p. 264, l. 4; and an abundance of other occurrences, too numerous to list.

79. During the T'ang dynasty gold fish-shaped ornaments were worn at the waist as emblems of rank by imperial princes and high officials. This four-character expression is derived from a line in a poem by Han Yü (768–824) that reads, "A gold fish is suspended from the jade girdle." See *Ch'üan T'ang shih*, vol. 5, *chüan* 342, p. 3836, l. 9. It occurs ubiquitously in later Chinese literature. See, e.g., a lyric by Chiang Han (fl. early 12th century), *Ch'üan Sung tz'u*, 2:8915, upper register, l. 4; a lyric by Shih Hao (1106–94), ibid., 2:1251, lower register, l. 10; a lyric by K'ang Yü-chih (12th century), ibid., 2:1304, lower register, l. 12; a lyric by Hsin Ch'i-chi (1140–1207), ibid., 3:1876, upper register, l. 7; a lyric by Chao Shih-hsia (cs 1175) written in 1167, ibid., 3:2088, upper register, l. 8; a lyric by Liu Kuo (1154–1206), ibid., 3:2143, lower register, l. 2; *Huang-ch'ao pien-nien kang-mu pei-yao*, vol. 2, *chüan* 30, p. 13a, l. 7; a lyric by Li Chün-ming (1176–c. 1256), *Ch'üan Chin Yüan tz'u*, 1:65, upper register, l. 12; a lyric by Yüan Hao-wen (1190–1257), ibid., 1:131, upper register, ll. 4–5; a lyric by Liu Min-chung (1243–1318), ibid., 2:751, lower register, l. 14; a song by Chang K'o-chiu (1270–1348), *Ch'üan Yüan san-ch'ü*, 1:772, l. 11; *Yüan-ch'ü hsüan wai-pien*, 2:372, l. 7; the Ming tsa-chü drama *Tu Tzu-mei ku-chiu yu-ch'un* (Tu Fu buys wine for a spring excursion), by Wang Chiu-ssu (1468–1551), in *Sheng-Ming tsa-chü, erh-chi*, scene 2, p. 10b, l. 9; *Ming-chu chi*, scene 29, p. 90, l. 9; a lyric by Hsia Yen (1483–1548), *Ch'üan Ming tz'u*, 2:723, upper register, l. 3; a song suite by Wu T'ing-han (cs 1521), *Ch'üan Ming san-ch'ü*, 2:1792, l. 5; a song suite by Chang Lien (cs 1544), ibid., 2:1704, l. 2; *Pao-chien chi*, scene 11, p. 24, l. 15; *Shuang-lieh chi*, scene 37, p. 101, l. 4; and an abundance of other occurrences, too numerous to list. It also recurs in the *Chin P'ing Mei tz'u-hua*, vol. 4, ch. 71, p. 15b, ll. 5–6.

80. A synonymous variant of this proverbial expression occurs in *Pai-p'ao chi, chüan* 2, scene 42, p. 25b, l. 10. It occurs in the same form as in the novel in *Ku-ch'eng chi, chüan* 2, scene 28, p. 25a, l. 1; and *Pao-chien chi*, scene 38, p. 67, ll. 18–19.

81. These two lines are derived from a proclamation issued in 617 by the rebel Li Mi (582–619) denouncing Yang Kuang (569–618), the last emperor of the Sui dynasty (r. 604–18). See *Chiu T'ang shu*, vol. 7, *chüan* 53, p. 2215, l. 15. Versions very close to that in the novel occur in *Wu Lun-ch'üan Pei, chüan* 3, scene 16, p. 4a, ll. 4–5; *Mu-lien chiu-mu ch'üan-shan hsi-wen, chüan* 2, p. 18a, ll. 4–5; and a fragment of the lost ch'uan-ch'i drama *Chung-hsiao chi*, preserved in *Ch'ün-yin lei-hsüan*, 1:269, ll. 7–8.

82. This formulaic four-character expression occurs ubiquitously in Chinese vernacular literature. See, e.g., *Chao-shih ku-erh chi, chüan* 2, scene 33, p. 21a, ll. 3–4; *Chin-yin chi, chüan* 4, scene 42, p. 25a, l. 4; *Yen-chih chi, chüan* 2, scene 41, p. 36b, l. 3; *Lieh-kuo chih-chuan*, vol. 1, *chüan* 3, p. 29b, l. 8; *Hsi-yu chi*, vol. 2, ch. 77, p. 885, l. 13; *Ts'ao-lu chi, chüan* 3, scene 39, p. 23a, l. 10; *Shih-i chi, chüan* 1, scene 1, p. 1a, l. 6; and *Ta-T'ang Ch'in-wang tz'u-hua*, vol. 2, *chüan* 8, ch. 60, p. 34b, l. 5.

83. This song suite is taken, with minor textual variation, from *Pao-chien chi*, scene 51, p. 89, l. 15–p. 90, l. 6. Although the *Chin P'ing Mei* has often been described as a work of realism, or even of naturalism, this scene is one of the numerous deliberate violations of the illusion of verisimilitude in order to emphasize a political point on the

part of the author, since the presentation of such a scathing attack on the character of the person for whom it is performed would have been inconceivable in real life.

84. This list of names represents a deliberate mixing of the terms of administrative geography of the Sung and Ming dynasties.

85. For a line drawing of what such a building might have looked like, see Liang Ssu-ch'eng, *A Pictorial History of Chinese Architecture*, ed. Wilma Fairbank (Cambridge: MIT Press, 1985), p. 11, fig. 8.

86. This formulaic four-character expression occurs in a poem by Li Ching (916–61), Emperor Yüan-tsung of the Southern T'ang dynasty (r. 943–61), written in 947. See *Ch'üan T'ang shih*, vol. 1, *chüan* 8, p. 71, l. 1. It occurs ubiquitously in later Chinese literature. See, e.g., a poem by Kuo Hsiang-cheng (1035–1113), *Ch'üan Sung shih*, 13:8946, l. 11; a quatrain by the Buddhist monk Tzu-ch'un (d. 1119), ibid., 21:13864, l. 15; a lyric by Wang Chih-tao (1093–1169), *Ch'üan Sung tz'u*, 2:1162, upper register, l. 13; a lyric by Lu Tsu-kao (cs 1199), ibid., 4:2409, lower register, l. 15; a lyric by Hao Ta-t'ung (1140–1212), *Ch'üan Chin Yüan tz'u*, 1:423, upper register, l. 13; a song by Chang K'o-chiu (1270–1348), *Ch'üan Yüan san-ch'ü*, 1:825, l. 8; *Yüan-ch'ü hsüan wai-pien*, 3:780, l. 16; *Chiao-hsiao chi, chüan* 1, scene 3, p. 3b, l. 1; a song suite by Yang Hsün-chi (1458–1546), *Ch'üan Ming san-ch'ü*, 1:741, l. 9; *Liu sheng mi Lien chi, chüan* 2, p. 5a, l. 11; *Pa-i chi*, scene 2, p. 2, l. 3; *Chin-tiao chi, chüan* 1, scene 2, p. 3b, l. 3; *Su Ying huang-hou ying-wu chi, chüan* 1, scene 2, p. 3b, l. 1; *Yü-ching t'ai*, scene 14, p. 36, l. 11; and a host of other occurrences, too numerous to list.

87. This line is probably derived from a virtually identical line occurring in a similar context in *Shui-hu ch'üan-chuan*, vol. 1, ch. 7, p. 119, l. 11.

88. See Roy, *The Plum in the Golden Vase*, vol. 2, chap. 30, n. 30.

89. This four-character expression occurs in the prose preface to a lyric by Liu Chiang-sun (b. 1257), *Ch'üan Sung tz'u*, 5:3529, upper register, l. 10; and *Yüeh Fei p'o-lu tung-ch'uang chi, chüan* 2, scene 27, p. 11b, l. 6.

90. For the "six traitors" see Roy, *The Plum in the Golden Vase*, vol. 1, introduction, n. 53.

91. The proximate source of this quatrain is *Hsüan-ho i-shih*, p. 92, ll. 3–4.

CHAPTER 71

1. Legend has it that, during the Spring and Autumn Period (722–481 B.C.), when Po Ya played the zither his friend Chung Tzu-ch'i was so attuned to his playing that when he thought of Mount T'ai as he played, his friend would exclaim over the lofty mountains, and when he thought of rushing rivers, his friend would exclaim over the flowing waters. Po Ya appreciated this mutual understanding so much that when Chung Tzu-ch'i died, he smashed his zither and never played it again. This story first occurs in *Lü-shih ch'un-ch'iu* (The spring and autumn annals of Mr. Lü), comp. Lü Pu-wei (d. 235 B.C.), in *Chu-tzu chi-ch'eng* (A corpus of the philosophers), 8 vols. (Hong Kong: Chung-hua shu-chü, 1978), vol. 6, *chüan* 14, p. 140, ll. 7–10. The four-character expression "lofty mountains and flowing waters" occurs ubiquitously in later Chinese literature. See, e.g., a poem by Mou Jung (fl. early 9th century), *Ch'üan T'ang shih*, vol. 7, *chüan* 467, p. 5314, l. 12; a quatrain by Wang An-shih (1021–86), *Ch'üan Sung shih*, 10:6739, l. 6; a quatrain by Su Shih (1037–1101), ibid., 14:9633, l. 17; a

lyric by the Buddhist monk Chung-shu (fl. late 11th century), *Ch'üan Sung tz'u pu-chi*, p. 10, lower register, l. 10; a lyric by Wang Chih-tao (1093–1169), *Ch'üan Sung tz'u*, 2:1159, lower register, l. 11; *Tung Chieh-yüan Hsi-hsiang chi*, *chüan* 4, p. 82, l. 9; a lyric by Sung Te-fang (1183–1247), *Ch'üan Chin Yüan tz'u*, 2:1196, upper register, l. 2; a speech attributed to the Buddhist monk Chih-yü (1185–1269), *Hsü-t'ang Ho-shang yü-lu*, *chüan* 1, p. 987, lower register, l. 2; a prose postface by Wen T'ien-hsiang (1236–83), *Wen T'ien-hsiang ch'üan-chi*, *chüan* 10, p. 385, l. 2; *Yüan-ch'ü hsüan*, 2:723, l. 14; *Yüan-ch'ü hsüan wai-pien*, 2:506, ll. 10–11; a set of songs by Hsüeh Ang-fu (14th century), *Ch'üan Yüan san-ch'ü*, 1:706, l. 13; a lyric by Hu Yen (1361–1443), *Ch'üan Ming tz'u*, 1:207, lower register, l. 14; *Chien-teng yü-hua*, *chüan* 2, p. 180, l. 10; *Shen-hsiang ch'üan-pien*, *chüan* 636, p. 53b, l. 4; *Hua-ying chi*, p. 886, l. 23; *Nan Hsi-hsiang chi* (Li Jih-hua), scene 18, p. 50, l. 4; *Nan Hsi-hsiang chi* (Lu Ts'ai), *chüan* 1, scene 18, p. 370, l. 6; a song suite by Chin Luan (1494–1583), *Ch'üan Ming san-ch'ü*, 2:1641, ll. 8–9; *Hai-fu shan-t'ang tz'u-kao*, *chüan* 2b, p. 136, l. 8; *Fu-jung chi*, *chüan* 2, scene 20, p. 16a, ll. 8–9; and a host of other occurrences, too numerous to list.

2. This line occurs verbatim in a poem by Chang Ching-hsiu (cs 1067), *Ch'üan Sung shih*, 14:9742, ll. 1–2. This anonymous poem is the opening verse of *Hsüan-ho i-shih*. See ibid., p. 1, ll. 3–6.

3. This four-character expression recurs in the *Chin P'ing Mei tz'u-hua*, vol. 4, ch. 72, p. 9b, l. 7.

4. The flying fish python robe was the second of three grades of python robes bestowed upon high officials in the sixteenth century. See Cammann, *China's Dragon Robes*, p. 17; and Sophie Volpp, "The Gift of a Python Robe: The Circulation of Objects in *Jin Ping Mei*," *Harvard Journal of Asiatic Studies*, vol. 65, no. 1 (June 2005), p. 147.

5. A variant of this proverbial saying occurs in *Hsi-yu chi*, vol. 1, ch. 32, p. 366, l. 1. The second line occurs independently in *San-kuo chih p'ing-hua*, p. 7, l. 6; *Shui-hu ch'üan-chuan*, vol. 1, ch. 19, p. 273, l. 12; and *Hsi-yu chi*, vol. 1, ch. 4, p. 42, l. 14.

6. This four-character expression occurs in *Sui-T'ang liang-ch'ao shih-chuan*, *chüan* 5, ch. 47, p. 39a, l. 6.

7. The song suite that follows dramatizes a famous incident in which Chao K'uang-yin (927–76), the founding emperor of the Sung dynasty (r. 960–76), while still in the process of consolidating his rule, pays an unexpected visit one snowy winter night to the home of his chief advisor Chao P'u (922–92), to discuss the strategy to be followed in order to subdue his rivals. See his biography in *Sung shih*, vol. 25, *chüan* 256, p. 8932, ll. 9–13; and *Nan Sung chih-chuan*, vol. 2, *chüan* 10, pp. 11a–12a. This passage presents an idealized picture of the relations that ought to obtain between a Confucian sovereign and his trusted ministers.

8. This four-character expression occurs in a poem by P'an Ta-lin (11th century), *Ch'üan Sung shih*, 20:13433, l. 10; a lyric by Chiang K'uei (1155–1221), *Ch'üan Sung tz'u*, 3:2178, lower register, l. 17; a song suite by Wang Po-ch'eng (fl. late 13th century), *Ch'üan Yüan san-ch'ü*, 1:328, l. 13; *Yüan-ch'ü hsüan wai-pien*, 3:719, l. 7; a lyric by Hsiao Hsien (1431–1506), *Ch'üan Ming tz'u pu-pien*, 1:107, lower register, l. 15; and *Han Hsiang-tzu chiu-tu Wen-kung sheng-hsien chi*, *chüan* 1, scene 6, p. 11b, l. 2.

9. Wan-sui shan, or Myriad Years Mount, was the Ming dynasty name for the artificial mountain, now commonly called Coal Hill, just north of the Forbidden City in Peking.

10. See Roy, *The Plum in the Golden Vase*, vol. 1, chap. 15, n. 13.

11. For a description of this palace, construction on which was begun in 199 B.C., see *The Grand Scribe's Records*, vol. 2: *The Basic Annals of Han China*, ed. William H. Nienhauser, Jr. (Bloomington: Indiana University Press, 2002), p. 74, n. 503.

12. It is said that Emperor Kao-tsu (r. 618–26), the founder of the T'ang dynasty, while stationed in T'ai-yüan in 617, was tricked, while drunk, into spending the night in the Chin-yang Palace with two imperial concubines of the last ruler of the Sui dynasty. When he found out that he had unwittingly committed this capital offense, he was motivated to initiate his successful revolt against the ruling dynasty. See *Hsin T'ang shu*, vol. 1, *chüan* 1, p. 2, l. 11–p. 3, l. 3; and Howard J. Wechsler, "The founding of the T'ang dynasty: Kao-tsu (reign 618–26)," in *The Cambridge History of China*, vol. 3: *Sui and T'ang China, 589–906, Part I*, ed. Denis Twitchett (Cambridge: Cambridge University Press, 1979), p. 155. This incident is further elaborated upon in *Sui-T'ang liang-ch'ao shih-chuan, chüan* 1, ch. 9, pp. 52a–57b.

13. This four-character expression occurs in *[Chi-p'ing chiao-chu] Hsi hsiang chi*, play no. 2, scene 1, p. 49, l. 5; an anonymous Yüan dynasty song suite, *Ch'üan Yüan san-ch'ü*, 2:1781, l. 2; *P'u-tung Ts'ui Chang chu-yü shih-chi* (Collection of poetic gems about [the affair of] Ts'ui [Ying-ying] and Chang [Chün-jui] in P'u-tung), included as part of the front matter in the 1498 edition of *Hsi-hsiang chi*, p. 19b, l. 17; a set of songs by Ch'en To (fl. early 16th century), *Ch'üan Ming san-ch'ü*, 1:523, l. 13; an anonymous song suite in *Yung-hsi yüeh-fu*, ts'e 16, p. 18a, l. 4; *Chin-tiao chi, chüan* 4, scene 38, p. 14b, l. 6; a song by Ch'in Shih-yung (16th century), *Ch'üan Ming san-ch'ü*, 2:2130, l. 4; and a song suite by Ch'en So-wen (d. c. 1604), ibid., 2:2486, ll. 2–3.

14. Fu Yüeh (late 12th century B.C.) is the name of a legendary convict laborer who was raised to the status of chief minister by Wu Ting, the seventeenth ruler of the Shang dynasty (r. late 12th century B.C.). See *Shih-chi*, vol. 1, *chüan* 3, p. 102, ll. 12–15; and *The Grand Scribe's Records*, vol. 1: *The Basic Annals of Pre-Han China*, ed. William H. Nienhauser, Jr. (Bloomington: Indiana University Press, 1994), p. 48, ll. 1–13.

15. See Roy, *The Plum in The Golden Vase*, vol. 2, chap. 21, n. 67.

16. The sage rulers Yü, and T'ang, and King Wen and his son King Wu, are the legendary founders of what are traditionally believed to be the three earliest Chinese dynasties, the Hsia, Shang, and Chou.

17. See Roy, *The Plum in the Golden Vase*, vol. 1, preface, n. 22.

18. Fang Hsüan-ling (578–648), Tu Ju-hui (585–630), Hsiao Ho (d. 193 B.C.), and Ts'ao Shen (d. 190 B.C.) were famous officials who helped to found the T'ang and Han dynasties.

19. An anecdote attributing such a remark to Chao P'u (922–92) occurs in *Ho-lin yü-lu* (Jade dew from Ho-lin), by Lo Ta-ching (cs 1226), originally completed in 1252 (Peking: Chung-hua shu-chü, 1983), *i-pien* (second section), *chüan* 1, p. 128, ll. 3–7.

20. The influential, though unconventional, scholar Ma Jung (79–166) is said to have suspended a crimson curtain in his reception hall, in front of which he instructed his pupils, while behind it he kept a band of female musicians for his entertainment. See his biography in *Hou-Han shu*, vol. 7, *chüan* 60a, p. 1972, ll. 8–9.

21. This five-character expression is from a lyric by Su Shih (1037–1101), *Ch'üan Sung tz'u*, 1:278, lower register, l. 6. It occurs ubiquitously in later Chinese literature. See, e.g., *Yüan-ch'ü hsüan*, 2:447, l. 13; *Yüan-ch'ü hsüan wai-pien*, 2:370, l. 4; a song by Ch'en To (fl. early 16th century), *Ch'üan Ming san-ch'ü*, 1:566, l. 4; *Chieh-chih-erh*

chi, p. 245, l. 6; an anonymous set of songs in *Yung-hsi yüeh-fu*, *ts'e* 19, p. 6b, l. 1; *Lien-huan chi*, *chüan* 2, scene 23, p. 59, l. 9; a song suite by K'ang Wu (early 16th century), *Ch'üan Ming san-ch'ü*, 2:1279, l. 11; a song suite by Chin Luan (1494–1583), ibid., 2:1631, l. 5; *San-pao t'ai-chien Hsi-yang chi t'ung-su yen-i*, vol. 2, ch. 81, p. 1040, l. 14; and an abundance of other occurrences, too numerous to list.

22. This four-character expression occurs ubiquitously in Chinese literature. See, e.g., *Hsüan-kuai lu*, *chüan* 1, p. 12, l. 14; *Shen-hsien kan-yü chuan* (Biographies of persons who had contacts and encounters with gods and immortals), comp. Tu Kuang-t'ing (850–933), in *Yün-chi ch'i-ch'ien*, *chüan* 112, p. 695, left column, ll. 21–22; the prose commentary to a long poem by Emperor T'ai-tsung of the Sung dynasty (r. 976–97), *Ch'üan Sung shih*, 1:336, l. 4; a lyric by Wang Che (1112–70), *Ch'üan Chin Yüan tz'u*, 1:184, lower register, l. 14; a poem by Ma Yü (1123–83), *Ch'üan Chin shih*, 1:303, l. 10; a set of quatrains by Ch'iu Ch'u-chi (1148–1227), ibid., 2:165, l. 10; *Chin-ming ch'ih Wu Ch'ing feng Ai-ai*, p. 469, l. 11; *Nan-chi hsing tu-t'o Hai-t'ang hsien*, scene 2, p. 3b, l. 6; *Shen-hsiang ch'üan-pien*, *chüan* 634, p. 16a, l. 9; *San-kuo chih t'ung-su yen-i*, vol. 1, *chüan* 8, p. 360, l. 12; a song suite by Chang Lien (cs 1544), *Ch'üan Ming san-ch'ü*, 2:1692, l. 14; *Mi-teng yin-hua*, p. 350, l. 3; and an abundance of other occurrences, too numerous to list.

23. The proverbial sayings quoted in these two lines first occur in a speech attributed to Sung Hung (1st century A.D.) in reply to Emperor Kuang-wu (r. 25–57), the founder of the Later Han dynasty, when the Emperor tried to persuade him to divorce his wife in order to marry a princess. See his biography in *Hou-Han shu*, vol. 4, *chüan* 26, p. 905, l. 2. They occur together frequently in Chinese vernacular literature, sometimes in reverse order. See, e.g., *Ming-hsin pao-chien*, *chüan* 2, p. 13b, l. 15; *Ching-ch'ai chi*, scene 19, p. 59, l. 10; *P'i-p'a chi*, scene 36, p. 202, l. 6; the anonymous early Ming tsa-chü drama *Lung-men yin-hsiu* (The beauty concealed at Lung-men), in *Ku-pen Yüan Ming tsa-chü*, vol. 3, scene 4, p. 10b, ll. 3–4; the early Ming tsa-chü drama *Yü-ch'iao hsien-hua* (A casual dialogue between a fisherman and a woodcutter), in *Ku-pen yüan Ming tsa-chü*, vol. 4, scene 2, p. 7a, l. 8; *Chin-ch'ai chi*, scene 42, p. 73, l. 1; *Wu Lun-ch'üan Pei*, *chüan* 2, scene 10, p. 9b, l. 3; and *Ch'üan-Han chih-chuan*, vol. 3, *chüan* 3, p. 1a, l. 11. The second saying also occurs independently in *San-pao t'ai-chien Hsi-yang chi t'ung-su yen-i*, vol. 2, ch. 57, p. 735, ll. 12–13.

24. This proverbial saying has already occurred in the *Chin P'ing Mei tz'u-hua*, vol. 1, ch. 2, p. 2b, l. 7. See Roy, *The Plum in the Golden Vase*, vol. 1, chap. 2, p. 45, l. 31.

25. This is probably an expanded version of a proverbial saying that has already occurred in the *Chin P'ing Mei tz'u-hua*, vol. 2, ch. 31, p. 13a, l. 5. See Roy, *The Plum in the Golden Vase*, vol. 2, chap. 31, p. 234, l. 37; and n. 40.

26. T'ai-chia was the third ruler of the Shang dynasty (c. 1570–1045 B.C.) and I Yin was a famous minister who served under the first three rulers of the dynasty. Legend has it that he had sufficient prestige to exile T'ai-chia for his failings as a ruler, and to act as regent for three years, before replacing him on the throne when he repented his errors. See *Shih-chi*, vol. 1, *chüan* 3, pp. 93–99; and Nienhauser, *The Grand Scribe's Records*, vol. 1: *The Basic Annals of Pre-Han China*, pp. 42–46.

27. See above, chap. 64, n. 37.

28. This four-character expression occurs in *Nan Hsi-hsiang chi* (Lu Ts'ai), *chüan* 1, scene 9, p. 349, ll. 7–8.

29. This four-character expression occurs in *Ming-feng chi*, scene 30, p. 124, l. 2.

30. The five-character expressions quoted in these two lines occur together ubiquitously in Chinese vernacular literature. See, e.g., *Chang Hsieh chuang-yüan*, scene 16,
p. 85, l. 13; *Chi Ya-fan chin-man ch'an-huo*, p. 284, l. 8; *Pai Niang-tzu yung-chen Lei-
feng T'a*, p. 430, l. 9; *Chang Yü-hu su nü-chen kuan chi*, p. 20b, ll. 1–2; *K'an p'i-hsüeh
tan-cheng Erh-lang Shen*, p. 247, l. 4; two anonymous Yüan dynasty song suites, *Ch'üan
Yüan san-ch'ü*, 2:1678, l. 1; and 2:1847, l. 12; *Chin-yin chi, chüan* 3, scene 29, p. 26b,
l. 3; *Lien-huan chi, chüan* 2, scene 24, p. 62, l. 11; *Nü han-lin*, 4:1490, l. 1; *Shui-hu
ch'üan-chuan*, vol. 1, ch. 21, p. 313, l. 9; and *Pai-chia kung-an, chüan* 5, ch. 48, p. 17a,
l. 9. They also occur in truncated form in *Hsi-yu chi*, vol. 2, ch. 63, p. 726, l. 12; and
the first expression occurs independently in *Hsiao Sun-t'u*, scene 16, p. 313, l. 3.

31. This five-character expression occurs in *Shen-hsiang ch'üan-pien, chüan* 624,
p. 3a, ll. 7–8.

32. This formulaic four-character expression occurs ubiquitously in Chinese vernacular literature. See, e.g., a song suite by Ching Kan-ch'en (13th century), *Ch'üan
Yüan san-ch'ü*, 1:140, l. 1; a song suite by Liu T'ing-hsin (14th century), ibid., 2:1436,
l. 8; an anonymous Yüan dynasty song suite, ibid., 2:1877, l. 5; *Yüan-ch'ü hsüan*,
3:1163, l. 9; *Yüan-ch'ü hsüan wai-pien*, 1:2, l. 20; a song suite by Chu Yün-ming (1460–
1526), *Ch'üan Ming san-ch'ü*, 1:782, l. 5; a song suite by Ch'ang Lun (1493–1526),
ibid., 2:1553, l. 13; *Shuang-lieh chi*, scene 25, p. 70, l. 12; and an abundance of other
occurrences, too numerous to list.

33. At the time in question, T'ai-yüan, the capital of the short-lived kingdom of
Northern Han (951–79), was ruled by Liu Chün (926–68), who reigned from 954 to
968.

34. Ch'ien Ch'u (929–88) was the last ruler of the kingdom of Wu-yüeh (895–978)
and reigned from 947 to 978, when he surrendered to the Sung.

35. See Roy, *The Plum in the Golden Vase*, vol. 1, preface, n. 28.

36. Liu Ch'ang (943–80) was the last ruler of the kingdom of Southern Han (917–71)
and reigned from 958 to 971, when he surrendered to the Sung.

37. See Roy, *The Plum in the Golden Vase*, vol. 2, chap. 27, n. 43.

38. This four-character expression occurs in a song suite by Liu Shih-chung (14th
century), *Ch'üan Yüan san-ch'ü*, 1:669, l. 9; *Yüan-ch'ü hsüan wai-pien*, 2:406, l. 20; and
San-yüan chi, scene 30, p. 80, l. 6.

39. This formulaic five-character expression occurs in *Yüan-ch'ü hsüan*, 3:969, l. 14;
Yüan-ch'ü hsüan wai-pien, 2:541, l. 7; a song suite by Wang Chiu-ssu (1468–1551),
Ch'üan Ming san-ch'ü, 1:970, l. 4; and an anonymous song suite in *Yung-hsi yüeh-fu*,
ts'e 9, p. 46b, l. 4.

40. This formulaic five-character expression occurs in *Yüan-ch'ü hsüan*, 3:969, l. 14;
Yüan-ch'ü hsüan wai-pien, 2:541, l. 7; *Shui-hu ch'üan-chuan*, vol. 2, ch. 51, p. 837, l. 3;
and an anonymous song suite in *Yung-hsi yüeh-fu, ts'e* 9, p. 46b, l. 4.

41. In the drama from which this song suite is taken, during the interim between the
preceding song and the following one, Chao P'u recommends the names of four generals to the emperor, who has them summoned into his presence. The four lines of the
following song are addressed to these generals, one after the other.

42. This line is addressed to Ts'ao Pin (931–99), a historical figure. For his biography, see *Sung shih*, vol. 26, *chüan* 258, pp. 8977–83; and Herbert Franke, ed., *Sung
Biographies*, 4 vols. (Wiesbaden: Franz Steiner Verlag, 1976), 3:1060–62.

43. This line is addressed to Shih Shou-hsin (928–84), a historical figure. For his biography, see *Sung shih*, vol. 25, *chüan* 250, pp. 8809–11; and Franke, *Sung Biographies*, 2:873–75.

44. This line is addressed to Wang Ch'üan-pin (908–76), a historical figure. For his biography, see *Sung shih*, vol. 25, *chüan* 255, pp. 8919–24; and Franke, *Sung Biographies*, 3:1109–12. For a picture of these cliffside roadways, see Joseph Needham, Wang Ling, and Lu Gwei-djen, *Science and Civilisation in China*, vol. 4, part 3: *Civil Engineering and Nautics* (Cambridge: Cambridge University Press, 1971), fig. 713.

45. This line is addressed to P'an Mei (925–91), a historical figure. For his biography, see *Sung shih*, vol. 26, *chüan* 258, pp. 8990–93; and Franke, *Sung Biographies*, 2:818–21.

46. *Liu-t'ao* (The six tactics) and *San-lüeh* (The three strategies) are the titles of two classic works on military strategy, probably dating from the third century B.C. and the first century B.C.. These two works are translated and discussed in Ralph D. Sawyer, trans., *The Seven Military Classics of Ancient China* (Boulder, Colo.: Westview Press, 1993), pp. 19–105, 277–306. The two titles frequently occur together in later Chinese literature where they are used as a general reference to works on military strategy. See, e.g., a requiem by Huang T'ao (cs 895), *Ch'üan T'ang wen*, vol. 17, *chüan* 826, p. 24b, l. 9; the prose preface to a poem by Emperor T'ai-tsung of the Sung dynasty (r. 976–97), *Ch'üan Sung shih*, 1:310, l. 16; a lyric by Ko Li-fang (cs 1138), *Ch'üan Sung tz'u*, 2:1345, lower register, l. 6; a poem by Yeh-lü Ch'u-ts'ai (1190–1244), *Yüan shih hsüan*, *ch'u-chi*, 1:344, l. 13; *Ch'i-kuo ch'un-ch'iu p'ing-hua*, p. 54, l. 3; *Ch'in ping liu-kuo p'ing-hua* (The p'ing-hua on the annexation of the Six States by Ch'in), originally published in 1321–23 (Shanghai: Ku-tien wen-hsüeh ch'u-pan she, 1955), p. 47, l. 3; *Yüan-ch'ü hsüan*, 2:815, l. 14; *Yüan-ch'ü hsüan wai-pien*, 2:347, l. 5; *Yu-kuei chi*, scene 4, p. 7, l. 1; a song suite attributed to T'ang Shih (14th–15th centuries), *Ch'üan Yüan san-ch'ü*, 2:1490, l. 14; *Sung Kung-ming p'ai chiu-kung pa-kua chen*, scene 1, p. 1a, l. 3; a lyric by Han Yung (1422–78), *Ch'üan Ming tz'u*, 1:303, lower register, l. 15; *Yü-huan chi*, scene 21, p. 79, l. 8; *Shui-hu ch'üan-chuan*, vol. 1, ch. 14, p. 206, l. 2; *Pai-p'ao chi*, *chüan* 1, scene 19, p. 13b, l. 8; *Ch'en Hsün-chien Mei-ling shih-ch'i chi*, p. 122, l. 4; *Lieh-kuo chih-chuan*, vol. 3, *chüan* 8, p. 3a, l. 12; *Hsi-yu chi*, vol. 1, ch. 33, p. 376, l. 8; *San-pao t'ai-chien Hsi-yang chi t'ung-su yen-i*, vol. 1, ch. 48, p. 623, l. 2; *Yang-chia fu shih-tai chung-yung yen-i chih-chuan*, vol. 1, *chüan* 1, p. 21a, l. 7; *Ta-T'ang Ch'in-wang tz'u-hua*, vol. 1, *chüan* 4, ch. 25, p. 9a, l. 2; and a host of other occurrences, too numerous to list.

47. This formulaic four-character expression occurs ubiquitously in Chinese vernacular literature. See, e.g., *[Chiao-ting] Yüan-k'an tsa-chü san-shih chung*, p. 399, l. 13; *Yüan-ch'ü hsüan*, 1:10, l. 1; *Yüan-ch'ü hsüan wai-pien*, 1:45, l. 17; *Ch'i-kuo ch'un-ch'iu p'ing-hua*, p. 7, l. 5; *Ch'in ping liu-kuo p'ing-hua*, p. 31, l. 11; *Hsüeh Jen-kuei cheng-Liao shih-lüeh*, p. 68, l. 9; the tsa-chü drama *Kuan Yün-ch'ang i-yung tz'u-chin* (Kuan Yün-ch'ang righteously and heroically refuses gold), by Chu Yu-tun (1379–1439), originally completed in 1416, in *Ming-jen tsa-chü hsüan*, scene 2, p. 152, l. 4; *Shou-t'ing hou nu chan Kuan P'ing*, scene 1, p. 4a, l. 10; *Ch'ang-an ch'eng ssu-ma t'ou-T'ang, hsieh-tzu* (wedge), p. 4b, l. 3; *Pai-t'u chi*, scene 27, p. 72, l. 7; *Chin-ch'ai chi*, scene 13, p. 27, l. 16; *Yü-huan chi*, scene 23, p. 87, l. 10; *Yüeh Fei p'o-lu tung-ch'uang chi*, *chüan* 1, scene 9, p. 12b, l. 2; *San-kuo chih t'ung-su yen-i*, vol. 2, *chüan* 19, p. 876,

l. 22; *Huai-hsiang chi*, scene 36, p. 121, l. 3; *Nan Hsi-hsiang chi* (Li Jih-hua), scene 15, p. 40, l. 2; *Shui-hu ch'üan-chuan*, vol. 2, ch. 50, p. 830, l. 9; *Pai-p'ao chi*, *chüan* 2, scene 21, p. 2a, l. 10; *T'ang-shu chih-chuan t'ung-su yen-i*, vol. 1, *chüan* 4, p. 29a, l. 8; *Nan Sung chih-chuan*, vol. 2, *chüan* 9, p. 11a, l. 7; *Lieh-kuo chih-chuan*, vol. 3, *chüan* 8, p. 7b, ll. 3–4; *Huan-sha chi*, scene 8, p. 26, l. 5; *Chu-fa chi*, *chüan* 2, scene 20, p. 12a, l. 1; *Shuang-lieh chi*, scene 18, p. 53, l. 1; *Huang-Ming k'ai-yün ying-wu chuan*, *chüan* 2, p. 6b, l. 3; *San-pao t'ai-chien Hsi-yang chi t'ung-su yen-i*, vol. 1, ch. 22, p. 290, l. 14; *I-hsia chi*, scene 13, p. 33, l. 11; *Ta-T'ang Ch'in-wang tz'u-hua*, vol. 1, *chüan* 2, ch. 11, p. 25b, l. 10; *Sui-T'ang liang-ch'ao shih-chuan*, *chüan* 9, p. 59a, l. 5; and an abundance of other occurrences, too numerous to list.

48. On the term paracoda, see Dale R. Johnson, *Yuarn Music Dramas: Studies in Prosody and Structure and a Complete Catalogue of Northern Arias in the Dramatic Style* (Ann Arbor: Center for Chinese Studies, University of Michigan, 1980), p. 28.

49. This four-character expression occurs in *Lu-shan Yüan-kung hua*, p. 188, l. 2; Hsing Ping's (932–1010) commentary on Book 2, paragraph 2, of the *Lun-yü*, in *Shih-san ching chu-shu* (The thirteen classics with their commentaries), comp. Juan Yüan (1764–1849), 2 vols. (Peking: Chung-hua shu-chü, 1982), 2:2461, lower register, column 13; *Yüan-ch'ü hsüan wai-pien*, 2:440, l. 17; *San-kuo chih t'ung-su yen-i*, vol. 1, *chüan* 6, p. 273, l. 3; *Shui-hu ch'üan-chuan*, vol. 2, ch. 42, p. 679, l. 12; *Yü-chüeh chi*, scene 13, p. 40, l. 7; *Ch'üan-Han chih-chuan*, vol. 3, *chüan* 6, p. 7b, l. 12; the anonymous Ming tsa-chü drama *Erh-lang Shen so Ch'i-t'ien Ta-sheng* (Erh-lang Shen confines the Great Sage Equal to Heaven), in *Ming-jen tsa-chü hsüan*, scene 2, p. 716, l. 11; and *Hsi-yu chi*, vol. 1, ch. 19, p. 218, l. 6.

50. This formulaic four-character expression occurs ubiquitously in Chinese vernacular literature. See, e.g., *Yüan-ch'ü hsüan*, 2:608, l. 11; *Yüan-ch'ü hsüan wai-pien*, 2:495, ll. 3–4; *Sung ta-chiang Yüeh Fei ching-chung*, scene 3, p. 10b, l. 14; *Sung Kung-ming p'ai chiu-kung pa-kua chen*, scene 3, p. 9a, l. 10; *Huang-hua Yü tieh-ta Ts'ai Ko-ta*, scene 2, p. 8b, l. 7; *San-kuo chih t'ung-su yen-i*, vol. 1, *chüan* 1, p. 48, l. 3; *Shui-hu ch'üan-chuan*, vol. 3, ch. 83, p. 1376, l. 2; *Tung-t'ien hsüan-chi*, scene 3, p. 11b, l. 12; *T'ang-shu chih-chuan t'ung-su yen-i*, vol. 4, *chüan* 2, p. 23b, l. 2; *Ta-Sung chung-hsing yen-i*, vol. 1, *chüan* 2, p. 35b, l. 9; *Pei Sung chih-chuan*, vol. 3, *chüan* 8, p. 3b, l. 12; *Hung-fu chi*, scene 31, p. 65, l. 5; *Erh-lang Shen so Ch'i-t'ien Ta-sheng*, scene 1, p. 708, l. 1; *Fu-jung chi*, *chüan* 2, scene 21, p. 22a, l. 8; a song suite by Ch'iu Ju-ch'eng (16th century), *Ch'üan Ming san-ch'ü*, 2:2402, l. 12; *Ts'an-T'ang Wu-tai shih yen-i chuan*, ch. 54, p. 209, l. 19; *Chin-tiao chi*, *chüan* 4, scene 37, p. 12a, l. 6; *San-pao t'ai-chien Hsi-yang chi t'ung-su yen-i*, vol. 1, ch. 16, p. 203, l. 11; *Mu-tan t'ing*, scene 45, p. 224, l. 14; *Yang-chia fu shih-tai chung-yung yen-i chih-chuan*, vol. 2, *chüan* 5, p. 10b, l. 7; *Ta-T'ang Ch'in-wang tz'u-hua*, vol. 1, *chüan* 1, ch. 4, p. 42a, l. 6; *Sui-T'ang liang-ch'ao shih-chuan*, *chüan* 1, ch. 4, p. 21b, l. 1; and an abundance of other occurrences, too numerous to list.

51. This four-character expression occurs in the anonymous Yüan-Ming tsa-chü drama *Yün chi-mou Sui Ho p'ien Ying Pu* (Employing a stratagem Sui Ho tricks Ying Pu), in *Ku-pen Yüan Ming tsa-chü*, vol. 2, scene 3, p. 10a, ll. 7–8; *Lü-weng san-hua Han-tan tien*, scene 3, p. 7a, l. 5; and *Yang-chia fu shih-tai chung-yung yen-i chih-chuan*, vol. 1, *chüan* 4, p. 13a, l. 9.

52. This four-character expression occurs in *Yu-kuei chi*, scene 12, p. 36, l. 3.

53. See Roy, *The Plum in the Golden Vase*, vol. 1, chap. 3, n. 11.

54. This four-character expression occurs in *Lieh-kuo chih-chuan*, vol. 3, *chüan* 8, p. 10b, l. 7.

55. The nine terrains are enumerated and discussed in chapter 11 of *Sun-tzu's Art of War*, traditionally attributed to Sun Wu (6th century B.C.). See the translation of this work in Sawyer, *The Seven Military Classics of Ancient China*, pp. 178–82.

56. This line has been inadvertently omitted from the text of the novel. The five types of secret agents are enumerated and discussed in chapter 13 of *Sun-tzu's Art of War*. See ibid., pp. 184–86.

57. These two lines are derived from ibid., chapter 7, p. 170.

58. This four-character expression occurs in *Sun-tzu's Art of War*. See *Shih-i chia chu Sun-tzu (Sun-tzu* with eleven commentaries) (Peking: Chung-hua shu-chü, 1962), chap. 5, p. 69, l. 7; and Sawyer, *The Seven Military Classics of Ancient China*, p. 165, ll. 12–13.

59. This four-character expression occurs in a document by Tu Mu (803–52), *Ch'üan T'ang wen*, vol. 16, *chüan* 748, p. 16a, l. 7; a lyric by Hsin Ch'i-chi (1140–1207), *Ch'üan Sung tz'u*, 3:1937, upper register, l. 11; *Yüan-ch'ü hsüan wai-pien*, 1:183, ll. 4–5; *Yü-ch'iao hsien-hua*, scene 3, p. 9a, l. 9; *Shen-hsiang ch'üan-pien*, *chüan* 637, p. 19a, l. 7; *Chü-ting chi*, *chüan* 1, scene 11, p. 26a, l. 10; *Yü-tsan chi*, scene 15, p. 54, l. 3; *Chin-tiao chi*, *chüan* 3, scene 31, p. 22a, l. 6; and *Yang-chia fu shih-tai chung-yung yen-i chih-chuan*, vol. 1, *chüan* 2, p. 5b, l. 5.

60. This song suite is from scene 3 of the tsa-chü drama entitled *Feng-yün hui* (The meeting of wind and cloud), by Lo Kuan-chung (14th century), see *Yüan-ch'ü hsüan wai-pien*, 2:625–29. Versions of it are also preserved in the anthologies *Sheng-shih hsin-sheng*, pp. 50–54; *Tz'u-lin chai-yen*, 2:814–22; and *Yung-hsi yüeh-fu*, ts'e 2, pp. 3b–6a. It is also quoted in extenso in *Tz'u-nüeh* (Pleasantries on lyrical verse), by Li K'ai-hsien (1502–68), in *Chung-kuo ku-tien hsi-ch'ü lun-chu chi-ch'eng* (A corpus of critical works on classical Chinese drama), comp. Chung-kuo hsi-ch'ü yen-chiu yüan (The Chinese Academy of Dramatic Arts), 10 vols. (Peking: Chung-kuo hsi-chü ch'u-pan she, 1959), 3:316–18. The text as given in the novel is closer to those in the above anthologies than to those in the dramatic version or in *Tz'u-nüeh*. In some cases, where the text in the dramatic version is superior to that in the novel, I have amended the translation accordingly. The introduction at this point in the narrative of such an idealized picture of the relationship between a sage emperor and his loyal officials is clearly intended to reflect ironically on the situation depicted in the novel. For an analysis of this ironic contrast, see Katherine Carlitz, "The Role of Drama in the *Chin P'ing Mei*: The Relationship between Fiction and Drama as a Guide to the Viewpoint of a Sixteenth-Century Chinese Novel," Ph.D. dissertation, University of Chicago, 1978, pp. 321–24.

61. A synonymous variant of this proverbial couplet occurs in *Ming-feng chi*, scene 37, p. 154, l. 7.

62. This four-character expression recurs in the *Chin P'ing Mei tz'u-hua*, vol. 4, ch. 78, p. 7b, ll. 5–6.

63. These two lines are a quotation from the *Lun-yü* (The analects of Confucius), where they occur twice. See *Lun-yü yin-te*, Book 8, p. 15, paragraph 14; and Book 14, p. 29, paragraph 26. They are also quoted in *Ming-hsin pao-chien*, *chüan* 1, p. 9b, l. 15; *Shih-pa kuo Lin-t'ung tou-pao*, scene 3, p. 691, l. 5; and *[Hsin-k'o] Shih-shang hua-yen ch'ü-lo t'an-hsiao chiu-ling*, *chüan* 2, p. 3a, lower register, l. 10. The first line also occurs independently in *Shui-hu ch'üan-chuan*, vol. 1, ch. 19, p. 279, l. 8.

64. Variants of this proverbial saying occur in a speech by the Buddhist monk Ju-min (d. 920), *Wu-teng hui-yüan*, vol. 1, *chüan* 4, p. 239, l. 3; and a lyric by Hsin Ch'i-chi (1140–1207), *Ch'üan Sung tz'u*, 3:1894, lower register, l. 9.

65. This line recurs in the *Chin P'ing Mei tz'u-hua*, vol. 5, ch. 97, p. 11a, ll. 5–6.

66. Variants of this proverbial saying occur in *Mi-teng yin-hua*, *chüan* 1, p. 321, l. 3; and *San-pao t'ai-chien Hsi-yang chi t'ung-su yen-i*, vol. 1, ch. 19, p. 250, l. 5.

67. This four-character expression occurs in *Hsi-hu yu-lan chih-yü* (Supplement to the Guide to the West Lake), comp. T'ien Ju-ch'eng (cs 1526) (Peking: Chung-hua shu-chü, 1958), *chüan* 25, p. 458, l. 5; *Ku-Hang hung-mei chi*, p. 2a, l. 14; *Pai-chia kung-an*, *chüan* 5, ch. 44, p. 4b, ll. 2–3; and *Yang-chia fu shih-tai chung-yung yen-i chih-chuan*, vol. 2, *chüan* 6, p. 24a, l. 5. It also recurs in the *Chin P'ing Mei tz'u-hua*, vol. 4, ch. 78, p. 9b, l. 4; and ch. 79, p. 6a, l. 9.

68. The proximate source of these two lines is *Shui-hu ch'üan-chuan*, vol. 1, ch. 3, p. 48, ll. 5–6.

69. This phrase occurs in *Huai-ch'un ya-chi*, *chüan* 10, p. 26a, ll. 10–11.

70. This four-character expression occurs in *Tung Yung yü-hsien chuan*, p. 241, l. 3; *Pei Sung chih-chuan*, vol. 2, *chüan* 4, p. 18b, l. 9; *Lieh-kuo chih-chuan*, vol. 2, *chüan* 4, p. 15a, ll. 7–8; *Pai-chia kung-an*, *chüan* 5, ch. 48, p. 17b, l. 11; *Yang-chia fu shih-tai chung-yung yen-i chih-chuan*, vol. 1, *chüan* 2, p. 2b, ll. 7–8; and *Sui-T'ang liang-ch'ao shih-chuan*, *chüan* 10, ch. 92, p. 11a, l. 5.

71. This formulaic four-character expression occurs ubiquitously in Chinese vernacular literature. See, e.g., a song by Pai P'u (1226–c. 1306), *Ch'üan Yüan san-ch'ü*, 1:195, l. 13; a song by Ma Chih-yüan (c. 1250–c. 1325), ibid., 1:249, l. 1; a song by Kuan Yüan-shih (1286–1324), ibid., 1:358, l. 6; a song suite by T'ang Shih (14th–15th centuries), ibid., 2:1491, l. 14; a song suite by Ch'en To (fl. early 16th century), *Ch'üan Ming san-ch'ü*, 1:578, l. 9; and an abundance of other occurrences, too numerous to list.

72. This four-character expression occurs in *K'an p'i-hsüeh tan-cheng Erh-lang shen*, p. 248, l. 4.

73. This four-character expression occurs in *P'ei Hsiu-niang yeh-yu Hsi-hu chi*, p. 344, l. 30; and recurs in the *Chin P'ing Mei tz'u-hua*, vol. 5, ch. 93, p. 13b, l. 2.

74. This formulaic four-character expression occurs ubiquitously in Chinese literature. See, e.g., an anecdote from the lost collection of literary tales entitled *Ho-tung chi* (Records from east of the river), comp. Hsüeh Yü-ssu (9th century), as quoted in *T'ai-p'ing kuang-chi*, vol. 6, *chüan* 281, p. 2244, ll. 5–6; the anonymous eleventh-century literary tale entitled *Su Hsiao-ch'ing*, in Hu Shih-ying, *Hua-pen hsiao-shuo kai-lun*, 1:354, ll. 7–8; the title to a set of quatrains by Ch'eng Chü (1078–1144), *Ch'üan Sung shih*, 25:16367, l. 1; the prose preface to a lyric written in 1144 by Hsiang Tzu-yin (1085–1152), *Ch'üan Sung tz'u*, 2:953, upper register, l. 12; *T'ieh-wei shan ts'ung-t'an*, *chüan* 3, p. 58, l. 9; *I-chien chih*, vol. 2, *ting-chih* (fourth record), *chüan* 4, p. 567, l. 10; *Tung Chieh-yüan Hsi-hsiang chi*, *chüan* 1, p. 12, l. 10; the prose preface to a lyric by Wang Yün (1228–1304), *Ch'üan Chin Yüan tz'u*, 2:685, upper register, l. 3; *Hsüan-ho i-shih*, p. 66, l. 1; *Chiao Hung chuan*, p. 283, l. 14; *Chien-teng hsin-hua*, *chüan* 2, p. 46, l. 8; *Chien-teng yü-hua*, *chüan* 1, p. 148, l. 12; *Chieh-chih-erh chi*, p. 246, l. 16; *Pei Sung chih-chuan*, vol. 2, *chüan* 6, p. 5a, l. 6; *Huang-Ming k'ai-yün ying-wu chuan*, *chüan* 2, p. 7a, l. 3; *Pai-chia kung-an*, *chüan* 4, ch. 37, p. 13b, l. 8; and a host of other occurrences, too numerous to list.

75. This formulaic four-character expression occurs ubiquitously in Chinese literature. See, e.g., *Han chi* (Records of the Former Han dynasty), comp. Hsün Yüeh (148–
209), originally completed in 200, in *Liang Han chi* (Two records of the Former and
Later Han dynasties), ed. Chang Lieh, 2 vols. (Peking: Chung-hua shu-chü, 2005),
vol. 1, *chüan* 30, p. 531, l. 4; *Shu-i chi* (Accounts of strange things), comp. Tsu Ch'ung-
chih (429–500), in *Ku hsiao-shuo kou-ch'en* (Rescued fragments of early fiction), comp.
Lu Hsün (Peking: Jen-min wen-hsüeh ch'u-pan she, 1955), p. 162, l. 12; Yü Hsin's
(513–81) preface to his *Ai Chiang-nan fu* (Lament for the South), in *Yü Tzu-shan chi
chu* (Annotated edition of the works of Yü Hsin), annot. Ni Fan (17th century), originally published in 1687, 3 vols. (Peking: Chung-hua shu-chü, 1980), vol. 1, *chüan* 2,
p. 94, l. 12; *Yen-shih chia-hsün [chi-chieh]*, *chüan* 3, ch. 8, p. 178, l. 14; an interlinear
comment on a poem by Yüan Chen (775–831), *Ch'üan T'ang shih*, vol. 6, *chüan* 419,
p. 4620, l. 6; the T'ang dynasty literary tale entitled *Liu I chuan* (The story of Liu I), by
Li Ch'ao-wei (fl. late 8th century), in *T'ang Sung ch'uan-ch'i chi*, p. 51, l. 10; the literary tale entitled *Miao-nü* from the lost work *T'ung-yu chi* (Records of penetrating the
unseen), comp. Ch'en Shao (fl. late 8th century), as quoted in *T'ai-p'ing kuang-chi*,
vol. 2, *chüan* 67, p. 417, l. 1; the prose preface to a poem by Sung Hsiang (996–1066),
Ch'üan Sung shih, 4:2280, l. 10; the literary tale entitled *Wen Wan*, in *Ch'ing-so kao-i*,
chüan 7, p. 154, l. 8; *Su Hsiao-ch'ing*, 1:353, l. 29; *Chien-teng yü-hua*, *chüan* 2, p. 200,
l. 3; *Hsiao-p'in chi*, p. 47, l. 3; *Chung-ch'ing li-chi*, *chüan* 6, p. 38b, l. 1; *Hua-ying chi*,
p. 927, ll. 21–22; *Liao-yang hai-shen chuan*, p. 387, l. 14; *Ta-Sung chung-hsing yen-i*,
vol. 1, *chüan* 1, p. 32b, l. 1; *T'ang-shu chih-chuan t'ung-su yen-i*, vol. 1, *chüan* 5, p. 45a,
l. 9; *Huai-ch'un ya-chi*, *chüan* 10, p. 20a, l. 13; *Pai-chia kung-an*, *chüan* 4, ch. 37,
p. 14b, l. 2; and an abundance of other occurrences, too numerous to list. It also recurs
in the *Chin P'ing Mei tz'u-hua*, vol. 4, ch. 79, p. 20a, l. 3.

76. The proximate source of this quatrain, with some textual variation, is *Huai-ch'un
ya-chi*, *chüan* 10, p. 37b, ll. 11–12.

77. This four-character expression occurs in the literary tale *Huo Hsiao-yü chuan*
(The story of Huo Hsiao-yü), by Chiang Fang (early 9th century), in *T'ang Sung
ch'uan-ch'i chi*, p. 71, l. 1; a lyric by Chu Tun-ju (1081–1159), *Ch'üan Sung tz'u*,
2:847, upper register, l. 10; a lyric by Wang Shen (1155–1227), ibid., 3:2196, lower
register, l. 8; a lyric by Ch'iu Yüan (1247–1326), ibid., 5:3403, lower register, l. 13; a
lyric by Chang Chih-han (fl. late 13th century), *Ch'üan Chin Yüan tz'u*, 2:717, upper
register, l. 18; a lyric by Wang Hsing (1331–95), *Ch'üan Ming tz'u*, 1:150, lower register, l. 15; *P'o-yao chi*, *chüan* 1, scene 11, p. 30b, l. 8; *Hsiao-p'in chi*, p. 23, l. 1; *Chung-
shan lang*, scene 3, p. 253, l. 1; and an anonymous song suite in *Yung-hsi yüeh-fu*, ts'e
10, p. 36b, l. 6. It also recurs in the *Chin P'ing Mei tz'u-hua*, vol. 4, ch. 78, p. 28b. l. 5;
and vol. 5, ch. 81, p. 8b, l. 10.

78. For Hung-niang, see Roy, *The Plum in the Golden Vase*, vol. 1, chap. 8, n. 10.
Versions of this couplet recur in the *Chin P'ing Mei tz'u-hua*, vol. 4, ch. 78, p. 30a, ll.
8–9; and vol. 5, ch. 83, p. 8a, l. 3.

79. The proximate source of this line is *Shui-hu ch'üan-chuan*, vol. 3, ch. 82,
p. 1347, l. 11.

80. This couplet is from a poem by Ts'en Shen (c. 715–c. 770). See Roy, *The Plum
in the Golden Vase*, vol. 3, chap. 60, n. 23.

81. This four-character expression is derived from a line in *Tung-tu fu* (Rhapsody on
the Eastern Capital), by Pan Ku (32–92), in *Wen-hsüan* (Selections of refined literature),

comp. Hsiao T'ung (501–31), 3 vols., fac. repr. (Peking: Chung-hua shu-chü, 1981), vol. 1, *chüan* 1, p. 22b, l. 4. It occurs in the same form as in the novel in an edict issued in 1035 by Emperor Jen-tsung of the Sung dynasty (r. 1022–63), *Hsü Tzu-chih t'ung-chien ch'ang-pien*, vol. 9, *chüan* 116, p. 2730, l. 1; and a preface by Kao Ch'i (1336–74), in *Kao Ch'ing-ch'iu chi* (The collected works of Kao Ch'i), ed. Hsü Ch'eng-yü and Shen Pei-tsung, 2 vols. (Shanghai: Shang-hai ku-chi ch'u-pan she, 1985), 2:902, l. 10.

82. The proximate source of these six lines, with some textual variation, is *Shui-hu ch'üan-chuan*, vol. 3, ch. 82, p. 1358, ll. 16–17.

83. The proximate source of the preceding clause is *Hsüan-ho i-shih*, p. 44, l. 14.

84. The proximate source of these two lines is ibid., p. 44, l. 14–p. 45, l. 1.

85. This formulaic four-character expression occurs ubiquitously in Chinese vernacular literature. See, e.g., a song by Ma Chih-yüan (c. 1250–c. 1325), *Ch'üan Yüan san-ch'ü*, 1:251, l. 14; *Yüan-ch'ü hsüan*, 1:94, l. 13; *Yüan-ch'ü hsüan wai-pien*, 2:350, l. 12; a lyric by Liang Yin (1303–89), *Ch'üan Ming tz'u*, 1:36, lower register, l. 9; *Wu Lun-ch'üan Pei*, *chüan* 2, scene 10, p. 6a, l. 5; *Ch'ien-chin chi*, scene 26, p. 85, l. 9; *Ming-chu chi*, scene 23, p. 66, l. 1; an anonymous song suite in *Sheng-shih hsin-sheng*, p. 423, l. 10; *Shui-hu ch'üan-chuan*, vol. 4, ch. 110, p. 1647, l. 6; *Hsiu-ju chi*, scene 34, p. 98, l. 3; *Chang Tzu-fang mu-tao chi*, p. 108, l. 8; a lyric by Hsia Yen (1483–1548), *Ch'üan Ming tz'u*, 2:707, lower register, l. 3; a lyric by Yang I (1488–1564), ibid., 2:909, lower register, l. 3; *Su Ying huang-hou ying-wu chi*, *chüan* 1, scene 7, p. 14b, l. 2; a set of songs by Hsüeh Lun-tao (c. 1531–c. 1600), *Ch'üan Ming san-ch'ü*, 3:2778, l. 3; *Ta-T'ang Ch'in-wang tz'u-hua*, vol. 1, *chüan* 3, ch. 21, p. 50a, l. 3; and an abundance of other occurrences, too numerous to list.

86. This reduplicative four-character expression occurs in a lyric written in 1358 by Ling Yün-han (14th century), *Ch'üan Chin Yüan tz'u*, 2:1150, lower register, l. 4.

87. This four-character expression occurs in a poem by Chang Shao (10th century), *Ch'üan T'ang shih*, vol. 12, *chüan* 887, p. 10024, l. 10.

88. This reduplicative four-character expression occurs in *Chin-tiao chi*, *chüan* 2, scene 16, p. 21b, l. 3; *San-pao t'ai-chien Hsi-yang chi t'ung-su yen-i*, vol. 2, ch. 70, p. 906, l. 13; and *Chieh-hsia chi*, scene 12, p. 27, l. 8.

89. A synonymous orthographic variant of this reduplicative four-character expression occurs in *Lieh-tzu* (4th century). See *Lieh-tzu chi-shih* (A critical edition of *Lieh-tzu*), ed. Yang Po-chün (Hong Kong: T'ai-p'ing shu-chü, 1965), *chüan* 5, p. 105, l. 10. It occurs in the same form as in the novel in the preface to a poem by the Buddhist monk Te-hung (1071–1128), *Ch'üan Sung shih*, 23:15348, l. 8; *Hsiang-nang chi*, scene 15, p. 41, l. 12; and *Wu Lun-ch'üan Pei*, *chüan* 2, scene 10, p. 6a, l. 4.

90. This formulaic four-character expression occurs ubiquitously in Chinese literature. See, e.g., a lyric by Liu Yung (cs 1034), *Ch'üan Sung tz'u*, 1:25, upper register, ll. 8–9; a lyric by Ch'ao Tuan-li (1046–1113), ibid., 1:421, lower register, ll. 3–4; a lyric by Wang Yüan-liang (13th century), *Ch'üan Sung tz'u pu-chi*, p. 85, upper register, l. 12; a song suite by K'ung Wen-ch'ing (13th century), *Ch'üan Yüan san-ch'ü*, 1:529, l. 10; *T'ien-pao i-shih chu-kung-tiao*, p. 187, l. 6; a lyric by Yü Chi (1272–1348), *Ch'üan Chin Yüan tz'u*, 2:863, lower register, l. 8; a lyric written in 1358 by Ling Yün-han (14th century), ibid., 2:1149, lower register, l. 11; *Yüan-ch'ü hsüan*, 2:623, l. 16; *Yüan-ch'ü hsüan wai-pien*, 2:548, l. 4; a lyric written in 1377 by Liu Ping (14th century), *Ch'üan Ming tz'u*, 1:135, lower register, l. 7; *Ch'ien-chin chi*, scene 22, p. 69, l. 7; an anonymous song suite in *Sheng-shih hsin-sheng*, p. 423, ll. 10–11; a lyric by Hsia Yen

(1483–1548), *Ch'üan Ming tz'u*, 2:703, lower register, ll. 12–13; *K'ung Shu-fang shuang-yü shan-chui chuan*, p. 64, l. 12; an anonymous song suite in *Yung-hsi yüeh-fu*, *ts'e* 11, p. 4a, ll. 6–7; and a song suite by Huang O (1498–1569), *Ch'üan Ming san-ch'ü*, 2:1760, l. 7.

91. This reduplicative four-character expression occurs in an anonymous Yüan dynasty song, *Ch'üan Yüan san-ch'ü*, 2:1669, l. 10; *Hsing-t'ien Feng-yüeh t'ung-hsüan chi*, scene 6, p. 15b, l. 5; *K'u-kung wu-tao chüan*, p. 158, l. 3; an anonymous song suite in *Yung-hsi yüeh-fu*, *ts'e* 3, p. 27b, l. 2; and *Hsi-yu chi*, vol. 1, ch. 1, p. 4, l. 4.

92. An orthographic variant of this reduplicative four-character expression occurs in *Wu Lun-ch'üan Pei*, chüan 2, scene 10, p. 6a, l. 6.

93. This four-character expression occurs ubiquitously in Chinese popular literature. See, e.g., *I-chien chih*, vol. 2, ting-chih (4th record), chüan 10, p. 620, l. 9; *San-kuo chih p'ing-hua*, p. 2, l. 6; *Yüan-ch'ü hsüan*, 4:1465, l. 16; the tsa-chü drama *Ch'ing-ho hsien chi-mu ta-hsien* (In Ch'ing-ho district a stepmother acts very virtuously), by Chu Yu-tun (1379–1439), completed in 1434, in *Ming-jen tsa-chü hsüan*, p. 233, l. 7; *Shui-hu ch'üan-chuan*, vol. 3, ch. 72, p. 1214, l. 16; an anonymous song suite in *Yung-hsi yüeh-fu*, *ts'e* 4, p. 52b, l. 5; *K'uei-kuan Yao Pien tiao Chu-ko*, p. 311, ll. 3–4; and *Ta-T'ang Ch'in-wang tz'u-hua*, vol. 1, chüan 2, ch. 14, p. 51b, l. 8.

94. This formulaic reduplicative four-character expression occurs ubiquitously in Chinese literature. See, e.g., an anonymous ballad from the Chin dynasty (265–420), *Yüeh-fu shih-chi*, vol. 2, chüan 47, p. 684, ll. 2–3; a lyric by P'an Lang (d. 1009), *Ch'üan Sung tz'u*, 1:5, lower register, l. 14; a poem by Chang Yung (946–1015), *Ch'üan Sung shih*, 1:528, l. 11; a lyric by Yen Shu (991–1055), *Ch'üan Sung tz'u*, 1:100, upper register, l. 16; a quatrain by Wang An-shih (1021–86), *Ch'üan Sung shih*, 10:6685, l. 17; a set of quatrains by Liu Yen (1048–1102), ibid., 18:12041, l. 17; a lyric by Hung K'uo (1117–84), *Ch'üan Sung tz'u*, 2:1371, lower register, l. 17; a lyric by Wang Ch'ien-ch'iu (12th century), ibid., 3:1468, lower register, l. 2; a lyric by Hsin Ch'i-chi (1140–1207), ibid., 3:1922, upper register, l. 15; a quatrain by Lu Yu (1125–1210), *Ch'üan Sung shih*, 41:25704, l. 15; *Feng-yüeh Nan-lao chi*, scene 4, p. 8b, l. 8; *Shui-hu ch'üan-chuan*, vol. 4, ch. 104, p. 1592, ll. 10–11; a set of songs by Ch'en To (fl. early 16th century), *Ch'üan Ming san-ch'ü*, 1:469, l. 3; a song suite by K'ang Hai (1475–1541), ibid., 1:1225, l. 7; a lyric by Ch'en T'ing (cs 1502), *Ch'üan Ming tz'u*, 2:554, lower register, l. 5; *Ming-chu chi*, scene 26, p. 81, l. 2; *Tu Tzu-mei ku-chiu yu-ch'un*, scene 3, p. 13b, l. 6; a song suite by Ku Ying-hsiang (1483–1565), *Ch'üan Ming san-ch'ü*, 2:1334, l. 11; *Yü-chüeh chi*, scene 12, p. 36, l. 5; *Ts'an-T'ang Wu-tai shih yen-i chuan*, ch. 37, p. 150, l. 16; a song by Hsüeh Lun-tao (c. 1531–c. 1600), *Ch'üan Ming san-ch'ü*, 3:2805, l. 11; *Yang-chia fu shih-tai chung-yung yen-i chih-chuan*, vol. 1, chüan 2, p. 5a, l. 1; *Ta-T'ang Ch'in-wang tz'u-hua*, vol. 1, chüan 2, ch. 13, p. 46b, ll. 1–2; *Sui-T'ang liang-ch'ao shih-chuan*, chüan 4, ch. 34, p. 19b, l. 2; and an abundance of other occurrences, too numerous to list.

95. This formulaic reduplicative four-character expression occurs ubiquitously in Chinese vernacular literature. See, e.g., a set of quatrains by Li Mi-hsün (1089–1153), *Ch'üan Sung shih*, 30:19330, l. 16; a lyric by Wang Chih (1135–89), *Ch'üan Sung tz'u*, 3:1641, lower register, l. 6; a song by Pang Che (14th century), *Ch'üan Yüan san-ch'ü*, 2:1289, l. 6; *Chiang Shih yüeh-li chi*, chüan 4, scene 38, p. 13a, l. 8; *Tung-t'ien hsüan-chi*, scene 2, p. 8b, ll. 12–13; *T'ou-pi chi*, chüan 1, scene 5, p. 13a, l. 2; *Chieh-hsia chi*, scene 12, p. 28, l. 5; and *Chin-chien chi*, scene 5, p. 10, l. 12.

96. This reduplicative four-character expression occurs in *Wu Lun-ch'üan Pei*, *chüan* 2, scene 10, p. 6b, l. 1.

97. This reduplicative four-character expression occurs in a lyric by Chang Pi (10th century), *Ch'üan T'ang shih*, vol. 12, *chüan* 898, p. 10148, l. 16; a lyric written in 1197 by Chao Shih-hsia (cs 1175), *Ch'üan Sung tz'u*, 3:2091, upper register, l. 3; *Wu Lun-ch'üan Pei*, *chüan* 2, scene 10, p. 6b, l. 1; and *Hsi-yu chi*, vol. 1, ch. 12, p. 132, l. 16.

98. This four-character expression occurs in *Wu Lun-ch'üan Pei*, *chüan* 2, scene 10, p. 6b, l. 1.

99. This reduplicative four-character expression occurs in ibid., l. 2.

100. This four-character expression recurs in the *Chin P'ing Mei tz'u-hua*, vol. 4, ch. 71, p. 14b, l. 11.

101. This reduplicative four-character expression occurs in *Wu Lun-ch'üan Pei*, *chüan* 2, scene 10, p. 6a, l. 8.

102. This reduplicative four-character expression occurs in *Hai-ling i-shih*, p. 60, l. 5.

103. This formulaic four-character expression occurs ubiquitously in Chinese literature. See, e.g., a poem by Ts'en Shen (c. 715–c. 770), *Ch'üan T'ang shih*, vol. 3, *chüan* 199, p. 2058, ll. 3–4; a poem by Ch'eng Lang-chung (fl. early 12th century), *Ch'üan Sung shih*, 31:20084, l. 12; a set of quatrains by Hou Shan-yüan (12th century), *Ch'üan Chin shih*, 2:307, l. 10; a lyric by Lu Ping (fl. early 13th century), *Ch'üan Sung tz'u*, 3:2161, lower register, l. 14; a song suite by Liu T'ing-hsin (14th century), *Ch'üan Yüan san-ch'ü*, 2:1435, l. 12; a song by T'ang Fu (14th century), *Ch'üan Ming san-ch'ü*, 1:218, l. 6; a song suite by Wang T'ien (15th century), ibid., 1:1012, l. 9; a song suite by K'ang Wu (early 16th century), ibid., 2:1279, l. 9; *Shui-hu ch'üan-chuan*, vol. 2, ch. 30, p. 462, l. 12; the middle-period vernacular story *K'uai-tsui Li Ts'ui-lien chi* (The story of the sharp-tongued Li Ts'ui-lien), in *Ch'ing-p'ing shan-t'ang hua-pen*, p. 57, l. 6; *Chin-lan ssu-yu chuan*, p. 15b, l. 3; *Ch'üan-Han chih-chuan*, vol. 2, *chüan* 4, p. 20b, l. 3; *Hsi-yu chi*, vol. 2, ch. 68, p. 780, l. 15; and *Huang-Ming k'ai-yün ying-wu chuan*, *chüan* 1, p. 2b, ll. 9–10.

104. This reduplicative four-character expression is ultimately derived from a passage in Book 8 of the *Lun-yü* (The analects of Confucius), where the two duplicated characters occur in adjacent statements. See *Lun-yü yin-te*, Book 8, p. 15, paragraph 19, l. 1. It occurs in the same form as in the novel in a treatise by Wang Pao (1st century B.C.), *Wen-hsüan*, vol. 3, *chüan* 51, p. 12a, l. 8; a letter by Sun Ch'u (d. 293), ibid., vol. 2, *chüan* 43, p. 10a, l. 4; a rhapsody by Chang Hsieh (fl. late 3rd century), ibid., *chüan* 35, p. 16a, l. 5; a sacrificial text composed in 785 by Lu Chih (754–805), *Ch'üan T'ang wen*, vol. 10, *chüan* 475, p. 29a, l. 3; an anonymous lyric from the Yüan dynasty, *Ch'üan Chin Yüan tz'u*, 2:1270, upper register, ll. 6–7; *Hsiao-p'in chi*, p. 84, l. 10; *Chin-tiao chi*, *chüan* 2, scene 17, p. 22b, l. 9; an anonymous song suite in *Yung-hsi yüeh-fu*, ts'e 6, p. 3a, l. 9; and *Hsi-yu chi*, vol. 1, ch. 30, p. 228, l. 3.

105. The proximate source of the above passage of descriptive parallel prose, with some textual variation, is *Shui-hu ch'üan-chuan*, vol. 3, ch. 82, p. 1357, l. 15–p. 1358, l. 10. In a few cases I have amended the text to accord with that in the above source.

106. This four-character expression occurs ubiquitously in Chinese vernacular literature. See, e.g., *Sha-kou chi*, scene 8, p. 25, l. 12; *Hsiang-nang chi*, scene 10, p. 26, l. 12; *Yüeh Fei p'o-lu tung-ch'uang chi*, *chüan* 2, scene 33, p. 13a, l. 7; *Ching-chung chi*, scene 35, p. 89, l. 12; *Ts'ao-lu chi*, *chüan* 2, scene 23, p. 19a, l. 1; and an abundance of other occurrences, too numerous to list.

107. See Roy, *The Plum in the Golden Vase*, vol. 2, chap. 39, n. 28.

108. On Indigo Field jade, see ibid., chap. 36, n. 22. This line occurs in *K'an p'i-hsüeh tan-cheng Erh-lang Shen*, p. 245, l. 12; and *Shui-hu ch'üan-chuan*, vol. 4, ch. 88, p. 1439, l. 13.

109. The ultimate source of this line, with one textual variant, is a quatrain by Su Shih (1037–1101) composed in 1093. See *Su Shih shih-chi*, vol. 6, *chüan* 36, p. 1955, l. 13. This line is quoted in the same form as in the novel in *Cho Wen-chün ssu-pen Hsiang-ju*, scene 1, p. 115, l. 11; *Wu Lun-ch'üan Pei*, *chüan* 2, scene 10, p. 6b, l. 7; and *Mu-lien chiu-mu ch'üan-shan hsi-wen*, *chüan* 1, p. 18a, l. 4.

110. This four-character expression occurs in a similar line in *Hsi-yu chi*, vol. 1, ch. 39, p. 448, l. 1.

111. This formulaic four-character expression occurs in a quatrain attributed to Lü Tung-pin (9th century), *Ch'üan T'ang shih*, vol. 12, *chüan* 858, p. 9699, l. 4; a lyric by Ch'eng Pi (1164–1242), *Ch'üan Sung tz'u*, 4:2289, lower register, l. 16; *Ming-chu chi*, scene 23, p. 66, l. 2; a song suite by Wu Kuo-pao (cs 1550), *Ch'üan Ming san-ch'ü*, 2:2270, l. 10; and a lyric by Wu Ch'eng-en (c. 1500–82), *Ch'üan Ming tz'u*, 2:978, lower register, l. 11.

112. The proximate source of this quatrain is *Shui-hu ch'üan-chuan*, vol. 3, ch. 82, p. 1358, ll. 10–11. The ultimate source of the last line, like the second line, is a quatrain by Su Shih (1037–1101) composed in 1093. See *Su Shih shih-chi*, vol. 6, *chüan* 36, p. 1955, l. 14. This line is quoted independently in *Yüan-ch'ü hsüan wai-pien*, 2:357, l. 4; an anonymous song suite in *Yung-hsi yüeh-fu*, ts'e 4, p. 54b, ll. 7–8; and *Hu-fu chi*, *chüan* 2, scene 24, p. 6a, ll. 6–7; and quoted as part of the original poem by Su Shih in *Wu Lun-ch'üan Pei*, *chüan* 2, scene 10, p. 6b, l. 7; *San-yüan chi*, scene 23, p. 60, l. 3; *Mu-lien chiu-mu ch'üan-shan hsi-wen*, *chüan* 1, p. 18a, l. 4; and *Ch'üan-Han chih-chuan*, vol. 2, *chüan* 4, p. 20b, l. 5.

113. The first of these two lines occurs independently in a poem by Yen Chen-ch'ing (709–85), *Ch'üan T'ang shih pu-pien*, 2:928, l. 7; a poem by Cheng Hsieh (1022–72), *Ch'üan Sung shih*, 10:6820, l. 3; and *Huang-Ming k'ai-yün ying-wu chuan*, *chüan* 1, p. 16b, l. 14. The second line occurs independently in *San-kuo chih p'ing-hua*, p. 11, l. 14; and *Huang-Ming k'ai-yün ying-wu chuan*, *chüan* 2, p. 15b, l. 12. The two lines occur together in *Shih Hung-chao lung-hu chün-ch'en hui*, p. 221, l. 8; *Yüan-ch'ü hsüan wai-pien*, 2:618, l. 14; and *Ch'üan-Han chih-chuan*, vol. 2, *chüan* 1, p. 2b, l. 12.

114. This four-character expression occurs in *Ch'ao-yeh ch'ien-tsai*, *chüan* 5, p. 110, l. 9; and *Wu-wang fa Chou p'ing-hua*, p. 2, l. 2.

115. Wen T'ung (1018–79) was a famous artist who was called "The Ink Master" for his skill at calligraphy, and particularly for his black-and-white inkwash paintings of bamboo.

116. Hsüeh Chi (649–713) was a high-ranking scholar official who was famous for his calligraphy.

117. On Meng Ch'ang, see Roy, *The Plum in the Golden Vase*, vol. 2, chap. 27, n. 43.

118. Ch'en Shu-pao (553–604) was the last emperor of the Ch'en dynasty (r. 582–89). The proximate source of these twelve lines, with some textual variation, is *Hsüan-ho i-shih*, p. 10, ll. 6–8.

119. The proximate source of this paragraph, with some textual variation, is ibid., ll. 13–14. The names of the last two reign periods have been inadvertently omitted in the

novel, but I have supplied them on the basis of the historical record and the cited passage in *Hsüan-ho i-shih*.

120. This four-character expression occurs in *Shui-hu ch'üan-chuan*, vol. 3, ch. 59, p. 990. l. 16; *Chang Tzu-fang mu-tao chi*, p. 102, l. 5; and an anonymous song suite in *Yung-hsi yüeh-fu*, *ts'e* 4, p. 54a, ll. 9–10.

121. This ceremony is mentioned in *Shui-hu ch'üan-chuan*, vol. 4, ch. 93, p. 1497, l. 12; *Hsi-yu chi*, vol. 1, ch. 39, p. 450, l. 10; *San-pao t'ai-chien Hsi-yang chi t'ung-su yen-i*, vol. 1, ch. 18, p. 236, l. 14; and the treatise on court ceremonial in *Ming shih*, vol. 5, *chüan* 53, p. 1351, l. 6.

122. The proximate source of this passage is *Hsüan-ho i-shih*, p. 45, ll. 1–2.

123. This statement is in error, since, in the time scheme of the novel, this event takes place in celebration of the winter solstice of the year 1117, at which time Emperor Hui-tsung would have been on the throne for only seventeen rather than twenty years.

124. This four-character expression occurs in *Yü-ch'iao hsien-hua*, scene 4, p. 12a, l. 6; and *Pa-i chi*, scene 14, p. 31, l. 12.

125. This four-character expression occurs in *Hsi-yu chi*, vol. 1, ch. 45, p. 519, l. 16; and *Yang-chia fu shih-tai chung-yung yen-i chih-chuan*, vol. 2, *chüan* 7, p. 20b, l. 9.

126. This formulaic Chinese equivalent of "Long Live the King" occurs ubiquitously in Chinese vernacular literature. See, e.g., *Yüan-ch'ü hsüan*, 2:646, l. 9; *Yüan-ch'ü hsüan wai-pien*, 1:141, l. 21; *[Hsin-pien] Wu-tai shih p'ing-hua*, p. 200, l. 10; *Ching-ch'ai chi*, scene 17, p. 54, l. 5; *Pai-yüeh t'ing chi*, *chüan* 2, scene 43, p. 43a, l. 2; *P'i-p'a chi*, scene 15, p. 88, l. 7; *Wu Lun-ch'üan Pei*, *chüan* 3, scene 18, p. 16b, l. 7; *Ch'ien-chin chi*, scene 26, p. 85, l. 6; *San-yüan chi*, scene 36, p. 97, l. 8; *Yü-huan chi*, scene 25, p. 93, l. 5; *Ming-chu chi*, scene 34, p. 109, l. 7; *Hsiu-ju chi*, scene 34, p. 96, l. 7; *Ts'ao-lu chi*, *chüan* 4, scene 54, p. 28a, l. 9; *Chin-tiao chi*, *chüan* 2, scene 17, p. 26a, l. 2; *Pao-chien chi*, scene 50, p. 88, ll. 24–25; *Ming-feng chi*, scene 15, p. 67, l. 2; *Tu-lo yüan Ssu-ma ju-hsiang*, scene 4, p. 9b, l. 11; *Ssu-hsi chi*, scene 29, p. 73, ll. 3–4; *Mu-lien chiu-mu ch'üan-shan hsi-wen*, *chüan* 1, p. 3a, l. 8; *T'ou-pi chi*, *chüan* 2, scene 34, p. 32a, l. 10; *Shuang-lieh chi*, scene 6, p. 18, l. 5; *Fu-jung chi*, *chüan* 2, scene 30, p. 51b, l. 9; *San-pao t'ai-chien Hsi-yang chi t'ung-su yen-i*, vol. 1, ch. 9, p. 108, l. 8; *[Hsin-k'o] Shih-shang hua-yen ch'ü-lo t'an-hsiao chiu-ling*, *chüan* 2, p. 21b, lower register, l. 8; and a host of other occurrences, too numerous to list.

127. The first of these two formulaic four-character expressions occurs as early as the first century A.D. in a memorial by Tu Shih (d. 38), see *Hou-Han shu*, vol. 4, *chüan* 31, p. 1096, l. 9. It occurs ubiquitously in later Chinese literature. See, e.g., a memorial submitted in 121 by Hsü Ch'ung (fl. early 2nd century), *Ch'üan Shang-ku San-tai Ch'in Han San-kuo Liu-ch'ao wen*, vol. 1: *Ch'üan Hou-Han wen* (Complete prose of the Later Han dynasty), *chüan* 49, p. 5b, l. 5; a memorial submitted in 223 by Ts'ao Chih (192–232), *Ts'ao Chih chi chiao-chu*, *chüan* 2, p. 269, l. 8; a memorial submitted in 274 by Ch'en Shou (233–97), *San-kuo chih*, vol. 4, *chüan* 35, p. 931, l. 11; a memorial submitted in 1060 by Wang An-shih (1021–86), *Ch'üan Sung wen*, vol. 32, *chüan* 1381, p. 340, l. 13; *Ch'in p'ing liu-kuo p'ing-hua*, p. 30, l. 9; *Hsüan-ho i-shih*, p. 7, l. 12; *P'i-p'a chi*, scene 15, p. 89, ll. 3–4; *San-kuo chih t'ung-su yen-i*, vol. 2, *chüan* 15, p. 701, l. 10; *Huai-hsiang chi*, scene 3, p. 6, l. 8; *Huan-sha chi*, scene 18, p. 62, l. 11; *Hai-fu shan-t'ang tz'u-kao*, *chüan* 4, p. 186, l. 5; *Hsi-yu chi*, vol. 1, ch. 45, p. 517, l. 11; *San-pao t'ai-chien Hsi-yang chi t'ung-su yen-i*, vol. 2, ch. 61, p. 784, l. 11; *Yang-chia fu shih-tai chung-yung*

yen-i chih-chuan, vol. 1, *chüan* 2, p. 8a, l. 3; and a host of other occurrences, too numerous to list. The two expressions occur together in *Yu-kuei chi*, scene 4, p. 5, l. 12; *Wu Lun-ch'üan Pei*, *chüan* 3, scene 16, p. 3b, l. 6; *Shuang-chu chi*, scene 26, p. 83, l. 2; *Shui-hu ch'üan-chuan*, vol. 4, ch. 89, p. 1458, l. 11; *Hsiu-ju chi*, scene 34, p. 96, l. 7; *Pao-chien chi*, scene 6, p. 16, ll. 5–6; *Nan Sung chih-chuan*, vol. 2, *chüan* 10, p. 22a, l. 11; *Lieh-kuo chih-chuan*, vol. 1, *chüan* 1, p. 11b, l. 4; *Ming-feng chi*, scene 15, p. 65, l. 2; *T'ou-pi chi*, *chüan* 2, scene 23, p. 10a, l. 5; *Pu-fu lao*, scene 5, p. 329, ll. 11–12; *Ch'üan-Han chih-chuan*, vol. 3, *chüan* 4, p. 18a, l. 13; *Huang-Ming k'ai-yün ying-wu chuan*, *chüan* 5, p. 25b, l. 12; *Pa-i chi*, scene 13, p. 29, l. 7; *Shuang-lieh chi*, scene 6, p. 18, l. 6; and a host of other occurrences, too numerous to list. The second expression also occurs independently in *Tung-yu chi: shang-tung pa-hsien chuan*, *chüan* 2, p. 43a, l. 2.

128. This four-character expression occurs in an anonymous set of Sung dynasty lyrics, *Ch'üan Sung tz'u*, 5:3727, lower register, l. 11; an anonymous song suite in *Sheng-shih hsin-sheng*, p. 87, l. 8; *Lieh-kuo chih-chuan*, vol. 1, *chüan* 2, p. 24a, l. 10; and *Ch'üan-Han chih-chuan*, vol. 2, *chüan*, 3, p. 32b, ll. 10–11.

129. This four-character expression occurs in *P'ei Hsing Ch'uan-ch'i*, p. 103, l. 6; and *Sui-T'ang liang-ch'ao shih-chuan*, *chüan* 12, ch. 115, p. 21a, l. 4.

130. This four-character expression occurs ubiquitously in Chinese literature. See, e.g., a poem by Lu Hsiang (8th century), *Ch'üan T'ang shih*, vol. 2, *chüan* 122, p. 1219, ll. 13–14; a poem written in 778 by Chang Chü (8th century), ibid., vol. 5, *chüan* 281, p. 3193, l. 12; a poem by Fan Hsün (8th century), ibid., *chüan* 307, p. 3489, l. 13; a set of quatrains by Ho Ning (898–955), ibid., vol. 11, *chüan* 735, p. 8395, l. 4; a speech by an unidentified monk in 1124 during an exchange with the Buddhist monk K'o-ch'in (1063–1135), *Yüan-wu Fo-kuo ch'an-shih yü-lu*, *chüan* 4, p. 732, lower register, l. 13; *Yüan-ch'ü hsüan*, 4:1456, l. 4; *Yüan-ch'ü hsüan wai-pien*, 1:77, l. 17; *Ch'ien-Han shu p'ing-hua*, p. 71, l. 1; a song suite by T'ang Shih (14th–15th centuries), *Ch'üan Yüan san-ch'ü*, 2:1485, l. 12; *Huang T'ing-tao yeh-tsou Liu-hsing ma*, scene 1, p. 85, l. 4; *Han Yüan-shuai an-tu Ch'en-ts'ang*, scene 3, p. 16b, l. 9: an anonymous set of songs published in 1471, *Ch'üan Ming san-ch'ü*, 4:4499, l. 10; an anonymous song suite in *Sheng-shih hsin-sheng*, p. 87, l. 9; *Ch'ing feng-nien Wu-kuei nao Chung K'uei*, scene 1, p. 2a, l. 4; *Shui-hu ch'üan-chuan*, vol. 3, ch. 82, p. 1360, l. 1; a song suite by Yang Hsün-chi (1458–1546), *Ch'üan Ming san-ch'ü*, 1:741, ll. 5–6; and an abundance of other occurrences, too numerous to list.

131. This four-character expression occurs in *Huang-ch'ao pien-nien kang-mu pei-yao*, vol. 2, *chüan* 28, p. 17b, l. 5; and *Hsüan-ho i-shih*, p. 25, l. 14.

132. The Scarlet Empyrean Tower was the name of a lofty building in the Mount Ken Imperial Park. See Hargett, "Huizong's Magic Marchmount: The Genyue Pleasure Park of Kaifeng," p. 21, ll. 1–21; and a set of one hundred quatrains celebrating the most noteworthy sights in the Mount Ken Imperial Park, jointly composed in 1122 at the behest of Emperor Hui-tsung (r. 1100–1125) by Li Chih (fl. early 12th century) and Ts'ao Tsu (cs 1121), *Ch'üan Sung shih*, 26:17030, ll. 4–5.

133. This is an allusion to a passage in *Chuang-tzu* in which a border guard at Hua wishes Emperor Yao (3rd millennium B.C.) long life, riches, and many sons. See *Chuang-tzu yin-te*, ch. 12, p. 30, ll. 1–3; and Watson, *The Complete Works of Chuang Tzu*, ch. 12, p. 130, ll. 1–11.

134. Variants of all or part of this formula for ending a document submitted to the throne occur ubiquitously in Chinese literature. See, e.g., a memorial submitted with

a poem in 1044 by Sung Ch'i (998–1061), *Ch'üan Sung shih*, 4:2511, l. 8; a memorial submitted in 1085 by Ssu-ma Kuang (1019–86), *Ch'üan Sung wen*, vol. 28, *chüan* 1202, p. 214, l. 1; a memorial submitted with a poem by Tseng Kung (1019–83), *Ch'üan Sung shih*, 8:5567, l. 8; a memorial submitted with a poem by Su Sung (1020–1101), ibid., 10:6311, l. 11; *P'i-p'a chi*, scene 15, p. 90, ll. 3–4; *Wu Lun-ch'üan Pei*, *chüan* 2, scene 10, p. 7b, l. 8; and *chüan* 3, scene 16, p. 5b, l. 3; *Pai-p'ao chi*, *chüan* 1, scene 16, p. 27b, ll. 7–8; *Ta-Sung chung-hsing yen-i*, vol. 1, *chüan* 2, p. 19b, ll. 1–2; *Lieh-kuo chih-chuan*, vol. 1, *chüan* 3, p. 3a, ll. 5–6; and *T'ou-pi chi*, *chüan* 2, scene 23, p. 10a, l. 6.

135. On this seal, see *T'ieh-wei shan ts'ung-t'an*, *chüan* 1, p. 8, ll. 9–12; *Huang-ch'ao pien-nien kang-mu pei-yao*, vol. 2, *chüan* 28, p. 18a, ll. 3–5; and *Hsüan-ho i-shih*, p. 27, l. 8.

136. Variants of this formulaic couplet occur in *Hsüan-ho i-shih*, p. 45, l. 2; *Chü-ting chi*, *chüan* 1, scene 7, p. 14b, l. 10; *Shui-hu ch'üan-chuan*, vol. 2, ch. 54, ll. 8–9; and vol. 3, ch. 78, p. 1294, l. 14; *Hsi-yu chi*, vol. 1, ch. 11, p. 123, l. 14; and vol. 2, ch. 85, ll. 5–6. It occurs in the same form as in the novel in *Shui-hu ch'üan-chuan*, vol. 1, ch. 1, p. 2, l. 3; and vol. 3, ch. 74, p. 1250, l. 4.

137. The proximate source of these three lines is *Hsüan-ho i-shih*, p. 45, ll. 2–3.

138. This four-character expression occurs ubiquitously in Chinese vernacular literature. See, e.g., *Yüan-ch'ü hsüan*, 1:349, l. 5; *Ch'in ping liu-kuo p'ing-hua*, p. 25, l. 14; *[Hsin-pien] Wu-tai shih p'ing-hua*, p. 116, l. 1; *K'an p'i-hsüeh tan-cheng Erh-lang Shen*, p. 255, ll. 11–12; *Shui-hu ch'üan-chuan*, vol. 2, ch. 53, p. 883, l. 5; *Li Yüan Wu-chiang chiu chu-she*, p. 327, ll. 7–8; *Ch'üan-Han chih-chuan*, vol. 2, *chüan* 2, p. 27b, l. 1; *San-pao t'ai-chien Hsi-yang chi t'ung-su yen-i*, vol. 1, ch. 16, p. 200, l. 10; and *Ta-T'ang Ch'in-wang tz'u-hua*, vol. 1, *chüan* 2, ch. 12, p. 35b, l. 7.

139. This four-character expression occurs ubiquitously in Chinese vernacular literature. See, e.g., *K'an p'i-hsüeh tan-cheng Erh-lang Shen*, p. 261, l. 2; *Yü-huan chi*, scene 34, p. 126, l. 8; *Shui-hu ch'üan-chuan*, vol. 4, ch. 110, p. 1647, l. 5; and *Ta-T'ang Ch'in-wang tz'u-hua*, vol. 1, *chüan* 2, ch. 12, p. 35b, l. 7.

140. This four-character expression occurs in *Han-shu*, vol. 1, *chüan* 9, p. 281, ll. 11–12; the early alchemical text *Ts'an-t'ung ch'i* (The kinship of the three), attributed to Wei Po-yang (2nd century), in *Shuo-fu san-chung*, 3:340, ch. 16, p. 9b, l. 9; *T'ang-shu chih-chuan t'ung-su yen-i*, vol. 1, *chüan* 4, p. 9b, l. 4; *Hsi-yu chi*, vol. 1, ch. 12, p. 129, l. 5; *Ch'üan-Han chih-chuan*, vol. 3, *chüan* 2, p. 22a, l. 11; *Ch'eng-yün chuan*, *chüan* 3, p. 11a, l. 5; *Yang-chia fu shih-tai chung-yung yen-i chih-chuan*, vol. 2, *chüan* 7, p. 34b, l. 9; and *Sui-T'ang liang-ch'ao shih-chuan*, *chüan* 3, ch. 29, p. 53a, l. 1.

141. This four-character expression occurs in a lyric by Wen T'ien-hsiang (1236–82), *Ch'üan Sung tz'u*, 5:3306, lower register, l. 5; *Chung-ch'ing li-chi*, vol. 3, *chüan* 7, p. 8b, l. 8; and *Shui-hu ch'üan-chuan*, vol. 3, ch. 65, p. 1107, l. 6.

142. Similar lines with the same meaning occur in a quatrain by Chia Tao (779–843), *Ch'üan T'ang shih pu-pien*, 1:395, l. 4; and *Chin-yin chi*, *chüan* 2, scene 11, p. 1a, l. 5.

143. Variants of lines 1–2 and 5–6 above occur in *I-k'u kuei lai tao-jen ch'u-kuai*, p. 194, l. 5; and a close variant of all six lines occurs in *Ch'ien-t'ang meng*, p. 3b, ll. 3–5.

144. This four-character expression occurs in a set of songs published in 1553, *Ch'üan Ming san-ch'ü*, 4:4606, l. 12; *Han Hsiang-tzu chiu-tu Wen-kung sheng-hsien chi*, *chüan* 2, scene 15, p. 3a, l. 1; and *Hsi-yu chi*, vol. 1, ch. 40, p. 465, l. 5.

145. This four-character expression occurs in *Yüan-ch'ü hsüan wai-pien*, 2:684, l. 19; *Lieh-kuo chih-chuan*, vol. 3, *chüan* 7, p. 44a, l. 6; and *Hsi-yu chi*, vol. 1, ch. 40, p. 464, l. 17. These six lines, with some textual variation, occur together in *Ch'ien-t'ang meng*, p. 3b, ll. 7–9.

146. This four-character expression occurs in *San-kuo chih t'ung-su yen-i*, vol. 1, *chüan* 1, p. 26, l. 10; *Pei Sung chih-chuan*, vol. 2, *chüan* 3, p. 1b, l. 5; *Ch'üan-Han chih-chuan*, vol. 3, *chüan* 1, p. 33a, l. 3, and *Ts'an-T'ang Wu-tai shih yen-i chuan*, ch. 5, p. 13, l. 5.

147. This formulaic four-character expression occurs ubiquitously in Chinese literature. See, e.g., a poem by Shao Yung (1011–77), *Ch'üan Sung shih*, 7:4522, l. 5; a poem by Ko Sheng-chung (1072–1144), ibid., 24:15626, l. 1; a lyric by the wife of Hsü Chün-pao (13th century), *Ch'üan Sung tz'u*, 5:3420, upper register, l. 6; [*Chi-p'ing chiao-chu*] *Hsi-hsiang chi*, play no. 2, hsieh-tzu (wedge), p. 67, l. 8; a lyric by Emperor Jen-tsung of the Ming dynasty (r. 1424–25), *Ch'üan Ming tz'u*, 1:248, upper register, l. 2; *Ch'ing-ho hsien chi-mu ta-hsien*, p. 235, ll. 1–2; *Yüeh Fei p'o-lu tung-ch'uang chi*, *chüan* 1, scene 2, p. 2a, l. 5; *Ch'ien-chin chi*, scene 28, p. 96, l. 12; *Lien-huan chi*, *chüan* 1, scene 10, p. 23, l. 6; *T'ang-shu chih-chuan t'ung-su yen-i*, vol. 1, *chüan* 5, p. 15b, l. 2; *Pai-p'ao chi*, *chüan* 1, scene 20, p. 33a, l. 3; *Lieh-kuo chih-chuan*, vol. 2, *chüan* 4, p. 47b, l. 13; *Huang-Ming k'ai-yün ying-wu chuan*, *chüan* 5, p. 10b, l. 13; *Ts'ao-lu chi*, *chüan* 2, scene 21, p. 13b, l. 2; *I-hsia chi*, scene 6, p. 12, l. 1; *Ta-T'ang Ch'in-wang tz'u-hua*, vol. 1, *chüan* 3, ch. 18, p. 18a, l. 6; *Sui-T'ang liang-ch'ao shih-chuan*, *chüan* 9, ch. 89b, p. 54b, l. 6; and a host of other occurrences, too numerous to list.

148. This four-character expression occurs in *Yüan-ch'ü hsüan*, 4:1366, l. 12.

149. A synonymous variant of this line occurs in *Shui-hu ch'üan-chuan*, vol. 2, ch. 52, p. 866, l. 3.

150. Variants of this couplet occur in *I-k'u kuei lai tao-jen ch'u-kuai*, p. 194, ll. 5–6; *Ch'ien-t'ang meng*, p. 3b, ll. 6–7; and *Ch'en Hsün-chien Mei-ling shih-ch'i chi*, p. 125, l. 14.

151. This four-character expression occurs in *Hsi-yu chi*, vol. 1, ch. 26, p. 299, l. 15.

152. This formulaic four-character expression occurs ubiquitously in Chinese vernacular literature. See, e.g., *Yüan-ch'ü hsüan wai-pien*, 1:209, l. 7; *Hsiang-nang yüan*, scene 2, p. 12b, l. 2; a song suite written in 1531 by Li K'ai-hsien (1502–68), *Ch'üan Ming san-ch'ü*, 2:1848, l. 4; *Yao-shih pen-yüan kung-te pao-chüan*, 14:200, l. 4; *San-yüan chi*, scene 14, p. 40, l. 6; *Chin-tiao chi*, *chüan* 3, scene 20, p. 2a, l. 10; *Hsi-yu chi*, vol. 1, ch. 22, p. 250, l. 5; and *San-pao t'ai-chien Hsi-yang chi t'ung-su yen-i*, vol. 1, ch. 9, p. 115, l. 1.

153. A synonymous variant of this line occurs in *Pai-p'ao chi*, *chüan* 2, scene 28, p. 10a, l. 3.

154. This formulaic four-character expression occurs ubiquitously in Chinese literature. See, e.g., a poem by Li Ying (cs 856), *Ch'üan T'ang shih*, vol. 9, *chüan* 590, p. 6849, l. 2; a lyric by Ch'iu Ch'u-chi (1148–1227), *Ch'üan Chin Yüan tz'u*, 1:462, lower register, l. 15; a lyric by Liu K'o-chuang (1187–1269), *Ch'üan Sung tz'u*, 4:2627, lower register, l. 11; *Yüan-ch'ü hsüan wai-pien*, 3:842, l. 20; a song suite by Ch'ang Lun (1493–1526), *Ch'üan Ming san-ch'ü*, 2:1553, l. 4; a lyric written in 1529 by Yang Shen (1488–1559), *Ch'üan Ming tz'u*, 2:790, lower register, l. 5; an anonymous song suite in *Yung-hsi yüeh-fu*, ts'e 8, p. 71a, l. 2; *Ming-feng chi*, scene 8, p. 30, l. 12; *Mu-lien chiu-mu*

ch'üan-shan hsi-wen, chüan 1, p. 85a, 1. 6; and a literary tale in *Yüan-chu chih-yü: hsüeh-ch'uang t'an-i, chüan* 1, p. 18, 1. 2.

CHAPTER 72

1. This four-character expression is from the third paragraph of the second section of the *Hsi-tz'u* (Attached commentary) in the *I-ching* (Book of changes). See *Chou-i yin-te*, p. 46, column 2, 1. 3. It also occurs in a lyric by Lü Hsi-chou (c. 1501–c. 1554), *Ch'üan Ming tz'u pu-pien*, 1:366, upper register, 1. 5.

2. This four-character expression occurs in a set of songs by Chu Ch'üan (1378–1448), *Ch'üan Ming san-ch'ü*, 1:261, 1. 3.

3. This four-character expression is derived from a passage in the *I-ching* (Book of changes), in which the two constituents occur in reverse order. See *Chou-i yin-te*, p. 24, column 2, 1. 20. It occurs in the same form as in the novel in a poem quoted in *Ju-i chün chuan*, p. 2b, 1. 1; and *Sui-T'ang liang-ch'ao shih-chuan, chüan* 10, ch. 92, p. 8a, 1. 5.

4. This four-character expression occurs in a song suite by Hu Wen-huan (fl. 1592–1617), *Ch'üan Ming san-ch'ü*, 3:2944, 1. 3.

5. This four-character expression occurs in a lyric written in 1253 by Li Mao-ying (1201–57), *Ch'üan Sung tz'u*, 4:2870, upper register, 1. 10; a lyric by Liu Chih-yüan (13th century), *Ch'üan Chin Yüan tz'u*, 1:576, upper register, 1. 13; a song suite by Shen Ho (13th century), *Ch'üan Yüan san-ch'ü*, 1:531, 1. 12; and *Ming-chu chi*, scene 22, p. 65, 1. 7.

6. The proximate source of lines 1–2 and 5–6 of this poem, with minor textual variations, is a lyric in the version of *Huai-ch'un ya-chi* in *Yen-chü pi-chi* (A miscellany for leisured hours), ed. Ho Ta-lun (fl. early 17th century), 2 vols., fac. repr. of Ming ed. in *Ming-Ch'ing shan-pen hsiao-shuo ts'ung-k'an, ti-erh chi*, vol. 2, *chüan* 10, upper register, p. 27b, ll. 13–15. This lyric does not occur in any of the other extant versions of this literary tale, none of which, including this one, is complete.

7. No such incident occurs in the supplied chapter 55, which is not by the original author of the novel, although a similar event in which Ch'en Ching-chi had been caught out in P'an Chin-lien's room, by Hsiao-yü rather than Ju-i, is alluded to there. See Roy, *The Plum in the Golden Vase*, vol. 3, chap. 55, n. 48.

8. See ibid., vol. 1, chap. 18, n. 12.

9. A variant of this line occurs in *Hsi-yu chi*, vol. 2, ch. 61, p. 698, 1. 4.

10. A synonymous variant of this four-character expression occurs in the *Chin P'ing Mei tz'u-hua*, vol. 5, ch. 95, p. 10b, 1. 10.

11. This four-character expression recurs in ibid., vol. 4, ch. 75, p. 16a, 1. 2.

12. An orthographic variant of this four-character expression occurs in ibid., ch. 80, p. 2b, 1. 7.

13. This four-character expression occurs in *Hsiu-ju chi*, scene 18, p. 49, 1. 8; and *Hsi-yu chi*, vol. 1, ch. 18, p. 206, 1. 15. It also recurs in the *Chin P'ing Mei tz'u-hua*, vol. 4, ch. 75, p. 21a, 1. 2; and p. 23a, 1. 5.

14. An orthographic variant of this four-character expression occurs in ibid., ch. 79, p. 13a, 1. 1; and vol. 5, ch. 83, p. 4a, 1. 1.

15. See Roy, *The Plum in the Golden Vase*, vol. 2, chap. 33, n. 13.

16. A variant of this proverbial saying occurs in *Yüan-ch'ü hsüan*, 4:1440, 1. 20; and 4:1470, 1. 4.

17. This reduplicative four-character expression recurs in the *Chin P'ing Mei tz'u-hua*, vol. 5, ch. 93, p. 6a, l. 6.

18. This four-character expression occurs in an anonymous poem from the T'ang dynasty, *Ch'üan T'ang shih*, vol. 11, *chüan* 785, p. 8857, l. 5; and a lyric by Han Pang-ch'i (1479–1556), *Ch'üan Ming tz'u*, 2:622, lower register, l. 8.

19. The proximate source of this poem is *Huai-ch'un ya-chi*, *chüan* 10, p. 11a, ll. 8–9.

20. See Roy, *The Plum in the Golden Vase*, vol. 1, chap. 7, n. 16.

21. This proverbial saying occurs in the anonymous Yüan-Ming tsa-chü drama *Wei Cheng kai-chao* (Wei Cheng alters the rescript), in *Ku-pen Yüan Ming tsa-chü*, vol. 3, scene 1, p. 3a, ll. 9–10.

22. This proverbial saying is quoted approvingly by Confucius in the *Lun-yü* (The analects of Confucius). See *Lun-yü yin-te*, Book 13, p. 25, paragraph 11. It is also quoted in *San-kuo chih t'ung-su yen-i*, vol. 1, *chüan* 9, p. 422, ll. 21–22.

23. The text here actually reads "the twenty-eighth," but I have emended it in order to bring it into conformity with the time scheme of the novel.

24. This four-character expression occurs in a lyric by Liu Chen (cs 1202), *Ch'üan Sung tz'u*, 4:2476, upper register, l. 1; *Yüan-ch'ü hsüan*, 3:1106, l. 6; *Pai-t'u chi*, scene 7, p. 22, l. 11; *Huai-hsiang chi*, scene 7, p. 16, l. 9; a song suite by Wang Chiu-ssu (1468–1551), *Ch'üan Ming san-ch'ü*, 1:950, l. 1; and an anonymous song suite in *Yung-hsi yüeh-fu*, ts'e 6, p. 86a, l. 10.

25. This formulaic four-character expression occurs in *Chang Yü-hu su nü-chen kuan chi*, p. 18a, l. 11; *Hua-teng chiao Lien-nü ch'eng-Fo chi*, p. 194, l. 13; and *Shui-hu ch'üan-chuan*, vol. 2, ch. 50, p. 830, l. 12. It also recurs in the *Chin P'ing Mei tz'u-hua*, vol. 4, ch. 72, p. 11b, l. 7.

26. This four-character expression occurs in *P'ei Hsiu-niang yeh-yu Hsi-hu chi*, p. 348, l. 27; and *Tung-yu chi: shang-tung pa-hsien chuan*, *chüan* 1, p. 58a, l. 4.

27. This four-character expression occurs in *Cheng Chieh-shih li-kung shen-pi kung*, p. 667, l. 6; and *[Hsin-tseng] Ch'iu-po i-chuan lun*, p. 8b, l. 4.

28. This four-character expression occurs in a song suite by Ch'eng K'o-chung (16th century), in *Ch'üan Ming san-ch'ü*, 3:3080, l. 9.

29. This four-character expression occurs in *Ju-i chün chuan*, p. 7b, l. 3.

30. For the fact that Ssu-ma Hsiang-ju (179–117 B.C.) suffered from diabetes, see his biography in Watson, *Records of the Grand Historian of China*, 2:330, l. 2.

31. For the allusion behind this line, see Roy, *The Plum in the Golden Vase*, vol. 2, chap. 39, n. 1. These two lines are derived, with some textual modification, from a quatrain by Li Shang-yin (c. 813–58). See *Ch'üan T'ang shih*, vol. 8, *chüan* 539, p. 6163, l. 12.

32. This four-character expression occurs in a letter written in 1187 by Chu Hsi (1130–1200), *Hui-an hsien-sheng Chu Wen-kung wen-chi*, *chüan* 48, p. 1b, l. 5; *Hsiao-p'in chi*, p. 30, l. 2; and *Hsi-yu chi*, vol. 1, ch. 5, p. 51, l. 9.

33. This figure is probably based on one who appears in *Shui-hu ch'üan-chuan*, vol. 2, ch. 37, p. 589, ll. 15–16, and elsewhere. The historical Ts'ai Ching (1046–1126) did not have a ninth son of this name.

34. This formulaic four-character expression occurs in *Lu-shan Yüan-kung hua*, p. 167, l. 9; *Ta-T'ang San-tsang ch'ü-ching shih-hua* (Prosimetric account of how the monk Tripitaka of the great T'ang [made a pilgrimage] to procure sutras), printed in the 13th century but probably older (Shanghai: Chung-kuo ku-tien wen-hsüeh ch'u-pan

she, 1955), episode 5, p. 10, l. 3; *Yüan-ch'ü hsüan*, 4:1636, l. 18; *Yu-kuei chi*, scene 35, p. 100, l. 9; *Pai-she chi, chüan* 1, scene 5, p. 11a, l. 7; *P'o-yao chi, chüan* 2, scene 17, p. 4a, l. 2; *Yüeh Fei p'o-lu tung-ch'uang chi, chüan* 1, scene 13, p. 18a, l. 10; *Chiang Shih yüeh-li chi, chüan* 4, scene 37, p. 9a, l. 4; *Huan-sha chi*, scene 26, p. 92, l. 5; *Ch'üan-Han chih-chuan*, vol. 3, *chüan* 3, p. 16b, l. 6; and a host of other occurrences, too numerous to list.

35. This four-character expression is derived from a passage in *Shih-chi*, vol. 3, *chüan* 18, p. 877, l. 5. Variants of it occur in a poem by Lo Yin (833–909), *Ch'üan T'ang shih*, vol. 10, *chüan* 662, p. 7587, l. 14; a quatrain by Wang An-shih (1021–86), *Ch'üan Sung shih*, 10:6741, l. 13; a lyric by Wang Yün (1228–1304), *Ch'üan Chin Yüan tz'u*, 2:661, lower register, ll. 5–6; and *Yüan-ch'ü hsüan*, 1:82, ll. 18–19. It occurs in the same form as in the novel in a lyric by Liu Yung (cs 1034), *Ch'üan Sung tz'u*, 1:57, upper register, l. 15; a song suite attributed to a Ming dynasty singing girl surnamed Ts'ao, *Ch'üan Ming san-ch'ü*, 2:2175, l. 8; and *San-pao t'ai-chien Hsi-yang chi t'ung-su yen-i*, vol. 1, ch. 36, p. 461, l. 7.

36. A variant of this formulaic four-character expression occurs in a quatrain attributed to Tu Kuang-t'ing (850–933), *Ch'üan T'ang shih*, vol. 12, *chüan* 854, p. 9666, l. 8. It occurs in the same form as in the novel in an anonymous song included in *Tun-huang ch'ü chiao-lu* (Collated record of songs from Tun-huang), comp. Jen Erh-pei (Shanghai: Shang-hai wen-i lien-ho ch'u-pan she, 1955), p. 12, l. 14; *P'i-p'a chi*, scene 3, p. 16, l. 16; *Ts'ai-lou chi*, scene 6, p. 20, l. 9; *Shui-hu ch'üan-chuan*, vol. 1, ch. 21, p. 306, l. 2; *Hsi-yu chi*, vol. 1, ch. 23, p. 263, l. 17; and *Yü-ching t'ai*, scene 5, p. 11, l. 4. It also recurs in the *Chin P'ing Mei tz'u-hua*, vol. 4, ch. 74, p. 5b, l. 6; vol. 5, ch. 86, p. 4a, l. 2; ch. 91, p. 9a, ll. 5 and 10; and p. 10a, l. 4; and ch. 96, p. 1b, l. 6.

37. This four-character expression occurs in a lyric by Ch'in Kuan (1049–1100), *Ch'üan Sung tz'u*, 1:455, lower register, l. 16; a poem by Hua Chen (b. 1051, cs 1079), *Ch'üan Sung shih*, 18:12314, l. 11; a lyric by Shih Hao (1106–94), *Ch'üan Sung tz'u*, 2:1273, upper register, l. 3; a lyric by Chao Pi-hsiang (1245–94), ibid., 5:3383, upper register, l. 2; a lyric by Ch'iu Yüan (1247–1326), ibid., 5:3397, lower register, ll. 7–8; and a lyric by Chang K'en (14th century), *Ch'üan Ming tz'u*, 1:201, lower register, ll. 1–2.

38. This formulaic four-character expression occurs in *Shui-hu ch'üan-chuan*, vol. 4, ch. 90, p. 1473, l. 2; and *Kuei-chien chiao-ch'ing*, 4:1548, l. 8.

39. This four-character expression occurs in a lyric by Chao Ch'ang-ch'ing (12th century), *Ch'üan Sung tz'u*, 3:1811, lower register, ll. 2–3.

40. This four-character expression occurs in a letter by Lu Chiu-yüan (1139–92), in *Hsiang-shan hsien-sheng ch'üan-chi* (Complete works of Master Hsiang-shan [Lu Chiu-yüan]), 36 *chüan*, Ssu-pu ts'ung-k'an ed., *chüan* 14, p. 4a, l. 6; *Yüan-ch'ü hsüan*, 1:373, l. 10; *Hsüan-ho i-shih*, p. 59, l. 2; and *Hsiao-p'in chi*, p. 94, l. 13.

41. This four-character expression occurs in *Ch'ün-yin lei-hsüan*, 4:2486, l. 5.

42. This four-character expression is derived from a passage in the *Shu-ching* (Book of documents), which Legge translates as: "The hen does not announce the morning. The crowing of a hen in the morning indicates the subversion of the family." See Legge, *The Shoo King or The Book of Historical Documents*, pp. 302–3. It occurs in the same form as in the novel in *Chiu Wu-tai shih* (Old history of the Five Dynasties), comp. Hsüeh Chü-cheng (912–981) et al., 6 vols. (Peking: Chung-hua shu-chü, 1976), vol. 2, *chüan* 34, p. 479, l. 5; *Hsin T'ang shu*, vol. 11, *chüan* 76, p. 3470, ll. 10–11; *Ch'eng-yün chuan, chüan* 2, p. 13a, l. 3; and *Shih-hou chi*, scene 11, p. 36, l. 7.

43. This line is derived from one in a lyric by Su Shih (1037–1101), *Ch'üan Sung tz'u*, 1:284, lower register, l. 12.

44. According to an anecdote in a work attributed to Liu Tsung-yüan (773–819), during the K'ai-huang reign period (581–600) of the Sui dynasty (581–618) a certain Chao Shih-hsiung fell into a drunken stupor beside a tavern in the woods on the slope of Mount Lo-fu and dreamed that he had an assignation with a lovely female companion, but when he awakened at dawn, he found that he had only been sleeping under a plum tree that had shed its white blossoms on him during the night. See *Lung-ch'eng lu* (Records of Lung-ch'eng), attributed to Liu Tsung-yüan (773–819), in *Pai-ch'uan hsüeh-hai, i-chi* (second collection), *chüan* 1, p. 3a, l. 11–p. 3b, l. 7.

45. This four-character expression is derived from a line in the song entitled *Ho-po* (The River Earl), one of the *Chiu-ko* (Nine songs) in the *Ch'u-tz'u* (Songs of Ch'u), comp. Wang I (d. 158). See *Ch'u-tz'u pu-chu [fu so-yin]* (Songs of Ch'u with supplementary annotation [and a concordance]), comp. Hung Hsing-tsu (1090–1155) (Kyoto: Chūbun shuppan-sha, 1972), *chüan* 2, p. 18b, ll. 8–9. It occurs in the same form as in the novel in a poem by Liu Ch'ang (1019–68), *Ch'üan Sung shih*, 9:5860, l. 13; a poem by Huang T'ing-chien (1045–1105), ibid., 17:11555, l. 6; a lyric by Chang Yüan-kan (1091–c. 1162), *Ch'üan Sung tz'u*, 2:1075, upper register, ll. 5–6; a lyric by Ch'iu Yüan (1247–1326), ibid., 5:3403, lower register, l. 13; a lyric by Liu Chiang-sun (b. 1257), ibid., 5:3527, lower register, l. 8; a song by A-lu-wei (14th century), *Ch'üan Yüan san-ch'ü*, 1:684, l. 11; *Yüan-ch'ü hsüan*, 3:1045, l. 4; *Lü Tung-pin hua-yüeh shen-hsien hui*, scene 1, p. 2a, l. 2; an anonymous song suite in *Yung-hsi yüeh-fu, ts'e* 11, p. 4a, l. 7; and a host of other occurrences, too numerous to list.

46. This four-character expression occurs in a song suite by Chu Yu-tun (1379–1439), *Ch'üan Ming san-ch'ü*, 1:369, l. 14.

47. This formulaic four-character expression occurs in a song suite by Wang Chung-yüan (13th century), *Ch'üan Yüan san-ch'ü*, 2:1105, l. 4; a song suite by Li Ai-shan (14th century), ibid., 2:1188, l. 10; a song suite by T'ung-t'ung (14th century), ibid., 2:1261, l. 10; *Yüan-ch'ü hsüan*, 4:1359, l. 4; *Yüan-ch'ü hsüan wai-pien*, 2:384, l. 17; an anonymous song suite in *Yung-hsi yüeh-fu, ts'e* 6, p. 1b, l. 1; and an abundance of other occurrences, too numerous to list.

48. This formulaic four-character expression occurs in a lyric by Yang Wu-chiu (1097–1171), *Ch'üan Sung tz'u*, 2:1202, lower register, l. 8; a lyric by Chang Yen (1248–1322), ibid., 5:3502, upper register, l. 7; a lyric by Yü Chi (1272–1348), *Ch'üan Chin Yüan tz'u*, 2:863, upper register, l. 13; *Yüan-ch'ü hsüan*, 3:1095, l. 11; a set of songs by Chu Yu-tun (1379–1439), *Ch'üan Ming san-ch'ü*, 1:266, l. 7; a lyric by Ku Hsün (1418–1505), *Ch'üan Ming tz'u*, 1:293, upper register, l. 14; a song suite by Hsia Yen (1482–1548), *Ch'üan Ming san-ch'ü*, 2:1303, l. 11; a set of song lyrics by Li K'ai-hsien (1502–68) written in 1531, *Li K'ai-hsien chi*, 3:905, l. 6; *Pao-chien chi*, scene 1, p. 5, ll. 7–8; *Huan-sha chi*, scene 1, p. 1, l. 4; and *Hai-fu shan-t'ang tz'u-kao, chüan* 1, p. 23, l. 11.

49. An orthographic variant of this four-character expression occurs in a lyric by Wei Hsiang (1033–1105), *Ch'üan Sung tz'u*, 1:219, upper register, ll. 4–5; and a song by Ao-tun Chou-ch'ing (13th century), *Ch'üan Yüan san-ch'ü*, 1:152, l. 6.

50. An orthographic variant of this four-character expression occurs in *Yüan-ch'ü hsüan*, 4:1359, l. 4.

51. This four-character expression occurs in *Ming-feng chi*, scene 4, p. 15, l. 9.

52. It was an ancient Chinese belief that if the bodies of young girls were marked with a red paste made from gecko wall lizards that had been fed cinnabar and then pulverized into a mash, it would serve to protect their chastity. See *Po-wu chih* (A treatise on curiosities), comp. Chang Hua (232–300), ed. Fan Ning (Peking: Chung-hua shu-chü, 1980), *chüan* 4, p. 51, ll. 1–2.

53. This four-character expression occurs in *T'ien-pao i-shih chu-kung-tiao*, p. 152, l. 1.

54. This four-character expression occurs in a lyric by Hsin Ch'i-chi (1140–1207), *Ch'üan Sung tz'u*, 3:1880, upper register, l. 5; and a lyric by Ch'eng Kai (12th century), ibid., 3:1992, upper register, l. 11.

55. This four-character expression occurs in a poem by Hsü Yin (cs 894), *Ch'üan T'ang shih*, vol. 11, *chüan* 709, p. 8166, l. 6; a lyric by Niu Ch'iao (cs 878), ibid., vol. 12, *chüan* 892, p. 10080, l. 13; a lyric by Chou Pang-yen (1056–1121), *Ch'üan Sung tz'u*, 2:620, upper register, l. 10; a lyric by Lü Sheng-chi (12th century), ibid., 3:1754, lower register, l. 7; a lyric by Chao Shan-k'uo (12th century), ibid., 3:1986, lower register, l. 16; a quatrain by Wang Che (1112–70), *Ch'üan Chin shih*, 1:184, l. 10; a song by Chang K'o-chiu (1270–1348), *Ch'üan Yüan san-ch'ü*, 1:786, l. 8; *Ch'ung-mo-tzu tu-pu Ta-lo T'ien*, scene 4, p. 13a, l. 12; and an abundance of other occurrences, too numerous to list.

56. This four-character expression is derived from the third line of a quatrain attributed to Liu Yü-hsi (772–842) in an anecdote in *Pen-shih shih* (The original incidents of poems), comp. Meng Ch'i (cs 875), pref. dated 886 (Peking: Chung-hua shu-chü, 1959), *chüan* 1, p. 11, ll. 8–10.

57. A nearly synonymous line, with one textual variant, occurs in *Shuang-chu chi*, scene 5, p. 12, l. 1.

58. This four-character expression occurs in *Yüan-ch'ü hsüan*, 4:1358, l. 14; and *T'ien-pao i-shih chu-kung-tiao*, p. 152, l. 1.

59. The above song suite on the winter season is by Liu Tui (fl. early 15th century), though the version of the text given in the novel is badly garbled, and the last song in the suite has been omitted. Versions of this suite are preserved in *Tz'u-lin chai-yen*, 2:598–603; and *Yung-hsi yüeh-fu*, ts'e 11, pp. 27b–29a; and a reconstructed version can be found in *Yüan-jen tsa-chü kou-ch'en*, pp. 123–27, where the question of its provenance is also discussed. Despite the fact that it is badly garbled, the version in the novel is closer to that in *Tz'u-lin chai-yen* than to that in *Yung-hsi yüeh-fu*, and I have emended the text accordingly.

60. This subject refers to a passage in *Chuang-tzu* in which the Yellow Emperor is said to have inquired about the Way from a herd boy, who replied that it was not much different from herding horses. See *Chuang-tzu yin-te*, ch. 24, p. 65, l. 21–p. 66, l. 8; and Watson, *The Complete Works of Chuang Tzu*, ch. 24, pp. 264–66.

61. This subject refers to the story of Fu Sheng (3rd–2nd century B.C.), a scholar who is said to have hidden a copy of the *Shang-shu* (Book of documents) in the wall of his home at the time that it was proscribed during the burning of the books in the reign of Ch'in Shih Huang-ti (r. 221–210 B.C.), from which an incomplete text was reconstructed during the reign of Emperor Wen of the Han dynasty (r. 180–157 B.C.). See *Shih-chi*, vol. 10, *chüan* 121, pp. 3124–25; and Watson, *Records of the Grand Historian of China*, 2:406–7.

62. This subject is derived from an episode in the biography of Ping Chi (1st century B.C.), a much-admired chancellor who is said to have noticed once that an ox was panting as he passed it in the street and stopped to inquire about it because he felt that the heat that caused the ox to pant was an indication of irregularity in the relations of yin and yang, and that it was the chancellor's responsibility to see that these cosmic forces were properly harmonized. See *Han-shu*, vol. 7, *chüan* 74, pp. 3147–48; and Watson, *Courtier and Commoner in Ancient China: Selections from the History of the Former Han by Pan Ku*, pp. 192–93.

63. Sung Ching is probably an abbreviated reference to Sung Tzu-ching, or Sung Ch'i (998–1061), who was responsible, together with Ou-yang Hsiu (1007–72), for the compilation of the *Hsin T'ang shu* (New history of the T'ang dynasty). According to an anecdote in *Ch'ü-wei chiu-wen* (Old stories heard in Ch'ü-wei), by Chu Pien (d. 1144), in *Pi-chi hsiao-shuo ta-kuan*, vol. 4, *ts'e* 8, *chüan* 6, p. 3b, ll. 2–7, Sung Ch'i, who was something of a bon vivant, was not above surrounding himself with singing girls as he toiled at the compilation of his history late at night.

64. The ultimate source of this four-character expression is a famous quatrain by Su Shih (1037–1101) written in 1073. See *Su Shih shih-chi*, vol. 2, *chüan* 9, p. 430, l. 8. It occurs ubiquitously in later Chinese literature. See, e.g., a lyric by Ch'in Kuan (1049–1100), *Ch'üan Sung tz'u*, 1:483, lower register, l. 6; a lyric by Yang Wu-chiu (1097–1171), ibid., 2:1177, lower register, ll. 10–11; a lyric by Wang Shih-p'eng (1112–71), ibid., 2:1352, lower register, l. 10; a lyric by Yao Shu-yao (cs 1154), ibid., 3:1552, upper register, l. 16; a lyric by Hsin Ch'i-chi (1140–1207), ibid., 3:1951, lower register, l. 12; a song by Yang Kuo (13th century), *Ch'üan Yüan san-ch'ü*, 1:8, ll. 1–2; a song suite by Kuan Yün-shih (1286–1324), ibid., 1:378, l. 11; a lyric by Ku Hsün (1418–1505), *Ch'üan Ming tz'u*, 1:293, upper register, l. 15; a lyric by Wang Chiu-ssu (1468–1551), ibid., 2:488, lower register, l. 9; *Ku-Hang hung-mei chi*, p. 11a, l. 1; a song by Liang Ch'en-yü (1519–91), *Ch'üan Ming san-ch'ü*, 2:2190, l. 4; a song by Ch'en So-wen (d. c. 1604), ibid., 2:2499, l. 1; and an abundance of other occurrences, too numerous to list.

65. This four-character expression occurs in *Shui-hu ch'üan-chuan*, vol. 1, ch. 2, p. 17, ll. 14–15; and *Ta-T'ang Ch'in-wang tz'u-hua*, vol. 1, *chüan* 1, ch. 5, p. 48, l. 6. It also recurs in the *Chin P'ing Mei tz'u-hua*, vol. 4, ch. 78, p. 9a, ll. 8–9.

66. This four-character expression occurs in a song suite from an early version of *Ts'ai-lou chi* that is preserved in *Sheng-shih hsin-sheng*, p. 419, l. 5; an anonymous song suite in *Yung-hsi yüeh-fu*, *ts'e* 1, p. 23a, l. 2; and *Pao-chien chi*, scene 22, p. 42, l. 3.

67. On Liu-an tea, see Roy, *The Plum in the Golden Vase*, vol. 2, chap. 23, n. 3.

68. This four-character expression recurs in the *Chin P'ing Mei tz'u-hua*, vol. 4, ch. 77, p. 11a, l. 8.

69. This four-character expression occurs in *Nan Hsi-hsiang chi* (Li Jih-hua), scene 30, p. 88, l. 1.

70. This four-character expression occurs in a song suite by Shang Tao (cs 1212), *Ch'üan Yüan san-ch'ü*, 1:24, l. 5; *Yüan-ch'ü hsüan wai-pien*, 2:411, l. 12; a song suite by Ch'en To (fl. early 16th century), *Ch'üan Ming san-ch'ü*, 1:588, l. 3; a song by Wang Chiu-ssu (1468–1551), ibid., 1:862, l. 13; a song suite by Chu Ying-ch'en (16th century), ibid., 2:1271, l. 13; a song suite by Wu Kuo-pao (cs 1550), ibid., 2:2279, l. 7; *Liu Sheng mi Lien chi*, *chüan* 2, p. 37b, l. 11; and an abundance of other occurrences, too numerous to list.

71. These two lines occur together in *San-pao t'ai-chien Hsi-yang chi t'ung-su yen-i*, vol. 1, ch. 8, p. 99, l. 3.

72. This poem is derived, with some textual variation, from the first and last couplets of a poem in *Huai-ch'un ya-chi*, *chüan* 10, p. 38a, ll. 10 and 13. The same poem has already appeared in its entirety in the *Chin P'ing Mei tz'u-hua*, vol. 3, ch. 59, p. 8a, ll. 1–4; and is translated in Roy, *The Plum in the Golden Vase*, vol. 3, chap. 59, p. 465, ll. 18–33.

73. On this type of chair, see Roy, *The Plum in the Golden Vase*, vol. 2, chap. 34, n. 4.

74. Variants of this proverbial expression occur in *Huan-tai chi*, *chüan* 2, scene 22, p. 4b, l. 1; and *San-pao t'ai-chien Hsi-yang chi t'ung-su yen-i*, vol. 1, ch. 26, p. 343, ll. 14–15.

75. This four-character expression occurs ubiquitously in Chinese literature. See, e.g., an essay by Ts'ai Yung (132–92) as quoted in his biography in *Hou-Han shu*, vol. 7, *chüan* 60b, p. 1986, l. 5; a memorial by Ch'en Chien (d. 485) as quoted in his biography in *Wei-shu*, vol. 3, *chüan* 34, p. 803, l. 7; a poem by Mei Yao-ch'en (1002–60), *Ch'üan Sung shih*, 5:3064, l. 2; the prose preface to a set of poems by Shih Chieh (1005–45), ibid., 5:3394, l. 13; a poem by Ou-yang Hsiu (1007–72) written in 1046, ibid., 6:3609, l. 7; a lyric by Wang Che (1112–70), *Ch'üan Chin Yüan tz'u*, 1:239, lower register, l. 4; a lyric by Ch'en Te-wu (13th century), *Ch'üan Sung tz'u*, 5:3452, upper register, l. 11; [*Chi-p'ing chiao-chu*] *Hsi-hsiang chi*, play no. 5, scene 2, p. 183, l. 15; *Yüan-ch'ü hsüan*, 2:424, l. 16; *Wei Cheng kai-chao*, scene 4, p. 17a, l. 7; *Chien-teng hsin-hua*, *chüan* 1, p. 12, ll. 1–2; *Chien-teng yü-hua*, *chüan* 5, p. 301, l. 7; *Hsiao-p'in chi*, p. 59. l. 10; *Huang-chi chin-tan chiu-lien cheng-hsin kuei-chen huan-hsiang pao-chüan*, 8:119, ll. 3–4; *Hua-ying chi*, p. 855, l. 10; *Pai-p'ao chi*, *chüan* 2, scene 31, p. 14a, l. 4; *Hung-fu chi*, scene 34, p. 74, l. 9; *Lieh-kuo chih-chuan*, vol. 1, *chüan* 2, p. 51b, l. 4; *Chin-tiao chi*, *chüan* 3, scene 27, p. 16b, ll. 1–2; *Mu-lien chiu-mu ch'üan-shan hsi-wen*, *chüan* 2, p. 48b, l. 2; *San-pao t'ai-chien Hsi-yang chi t'ung-su yen-i*, vol. 1, ch. 9, p. 109, l. 8; *Sui-T'ang liang-ch'ao shih-chuan*, *chüan* 4, ch. 32, p. 10a, l. 6; and an abundance of other occurrences, too numerous to list.

76. This four-character expression is from the *Ch'ien-tzu wen* (Thousand-character text), by Chou Hsing-ssu (d. 521), in *Dai Kan-Wa jiten* (Great Chinese–Japanese dictionary), comp. Morohashi Tetsuji, 13 vols. (Tokyo: Taishōkan shoten, 1960), 2:523, upper register, l. 1. It occurs ubiquitously in later Chinese literature. See, e.g., a speech attributed to the Buddhist monk Wen-sui (834–96), *Wu-teng hui-yüan*, vol. 2, *chüan* 13, p. 814, l. 13; a speech attributed to the Buddhist monk Tao-k'uang (10th century), *Tsu-t'ang chi*, *chüan* 13, p. 289, l. 11; a speech attributed to the Buddhist monk Shan-ning (11th century), *Wu-teng hui-yüan*, vol. 3, *chüan* 16, p. 1060, l. 11; *Yüan-ch'ü hsüan*, 2:467, ll. 15–16; *Yüan-ch'ü hsüan wai-pien*, 1:211, l. 20; *Mu-lien chiu-mu ch'üan-shan hsi-wen*, *chüan* 1, p. 62a, l. 8; *P'u-ching ju-lai yao-shih pao-chüan*, 5:172, l. 4; and *Ta-T'ang Ch'in-wang tz'u-hua*, vol. 1, *chüan* 2, ch. 14, p. 53a, l. 1.

77. This proverbial expression occurs in a speech attributed to the Buddhist monk Wu-yin (884–960), *Tsu-t'ang chi*, *chüan* 12, p. 270, l. 8; and a speech attributed to the Buddhist monk Hsing-yin (11th century), *Wu-teng hui-yüan*, *chüan* 15, p. 998, l. 6. It also recurs in the *Chin P'ing Mei tz'u-hua*, vol. 5, ch. 96, p. 8b, l. 9.

78. This formulaic four-character expression occurs ubiquitously in Chinese literature. See, e.g., a speech attributed to Kuo Hsiao-k'o (7th century), *Chiu T'ang shu*,

vol. 8, *chüan* 83, p. 2773, l. 9; a speech attributed to Chu Hsi (1130–1200), *Chu-tzu yü-lei*, vol. 1, *chüan* 13, p. 13b, l. 2; a lyric by Kung Ta-ming (1168–1238), *Ch'üan Sung tz'u*, 4:2312, lower register, l. 13; *Ho-lin yü-lu, i-pien* (second section), *chüan* 6, p. 220, l. 3; *T'ien-pao i-shih chu-kung-tiao*, p. 237, l. 6; *Yüan-ch'ü hsüan*, 3:1263, ll. 9–10; *Yüan-ch'ü hsüan wai-pien*, 3:1001, l. 21; *Ching-ch'ai chi*, scene 14, p. 41, l. 11; *Pai-yüeh t'ing chi*, *chüan* 2, scene 43, p. 42a, ll. 2–3; *Hsiang-nang yüan*, scene 2, p. 14a, l. 7; *Hsing-t'ien Feng-yüeh t'ung-hsüan chi*, p. 6a, l. 4; *San-kuo chih t'ung-su yen-i*, vol. 1, *chüan* 1, p. 42, l. 4; *Lien-huan chi*, *chüan* 1, scene 12, p. 30, l. 12; *Huai-hsiang chi*, scene 29, p. 94, l. 6; *Ta-Sung chung-hsing yen-i*, vol. 1, *chüan* 1, p. 44b, l. 8; *Nan Sung chih-chuan*, vol. 1, *chuan* 8, p. 16b, l. 8; *Ming-feng chi*, scene 21, p. 88, ll. 8–9; *Ch'üan-Han chih-chuan*, vol. 3, *chüan* 4, p. 22b, l. 13; *Hsi-yu chi*, vol. 1, ch. 15, p. 172, l. 11; *Ko tai hsiao*, scene 3, p. 144, l. 4; *Ts'an-T'ang Wu-tai shih yen-i chuan*, ch. 13, p. 43, l. 16; *Yang-chia fu shih-tai chung-yung yen-i chih-chuan*, vol. 2, *chüan* 5, p. 4a, ll. 5–6; *Ta-T'ang Ch'in-wang tz'u-hua*, vol. 1, *chüan* 2, ch. 9, p. 8b, ll. 5–6; and an abundance of other occurrences, too numerous to list.

79. This four-character expression recurs in the *Chin P'ing Mei tz'u-hua*, vol. 4, ch. 76, p. 4a, l. 10.

CHAPTER 73

1. This poem, with some textual variants, has already occurred in the *Chin P'ing Mei tz'u-hua*, vol. 2, chap. 22, p. 1a, ll. 3–6. See Roy, The Plum in the Golden Vase, vol. 2, chap. 22, n. 5.

2. See ibid., vol. 3, chap. 51, n. 27.

3. This four-character expression occurs in *Fo-yin shih ssu t'iao Ch'in-niang*, p. 238, l. 3; *Chien-teng yü-hua*, *chüan* 5, p. 295, l. 4; and *Mu-tan t'ing*, scene 10, p. 48, l. 9.

4. This four-character expression occurs in *Ch'ien-t'ang hu-yin Chi-tien Ch'an-shih yü-lu*, p. 47b, l. 5; and recurs in the Chin P'ing Mei tz'u-hua, vol. 5, ch. 88, p. 9a, l. 7.

5. This four-character expression, which is of Buddhist origin, refers to the fate of humans whose bad karma condemns them to be reborn as animals. It occurs ubiquitously in Chinese literature. See, e.g., the biography of the Buddhist monk P'u-yüan (748–834), *Tsu-t'ang chi*, chüan 16, p. 353, l. 11; a speech by the Buddhist monk I-hsüan (d. 867), *Ku tsun-su yü-lu*, *chüan* 4, p. 104a, lower register, l. 10; the biography of the Buddhist monk Pen-chi (840–901), *Wu-teng hui-yüan*, vol. 2, *chüan* 13. p. 788, l. 2; a poem by the Buddhist monk Ch'ang-ch'a (d. 961), *Ch'üan T'ang shih pu-pien*, vol. 3, chüan 43, p. 1379, l. 6; a poem by Chiang I-kung (10th century), *Ch'üan T'ang shih*, vol. 12, *chüan* 870, p. 9872, l. 9; a quatrain by Han Wei (1017–98), *Ch'üan Sung shih*, 8:5286, l. 10; *Ju-ju chü-shih yü-lu*, chia-chi (first collection), *chüan* 1, p. 4a, l. 9; [*Hsiao-shih*] *Chin-kang k'o-i* [*hui-yao chu-chieh*], *chüan* 1, p. 658, middle register, l. 5; a lyric by Ch'ang-ch'üan-tzu (13th century), *Ch'üan Chin Yüan tz'u*, 1:592, upper register, l. 2; *Wu Lun-ch'üan Pei*, *chüan* 3, scene 17, p. 10b, l. 6; *Chung-shan lang*, scene 3, p. 253, l. 6; an anonymous song suite in *Yung-hsi yüeh-fu*, ts'e 6, p. 63a, l. 9; *Hsi-yu chi*, vol. 1, ch. 7, p. 71, l. 14; *Fen-shu*, *chüan* 4, p. 166, l. 10; and an abundance of other occurrences, too numerous to list.

6. This four-character expression recurs twice in the *Chin P'ing Mei tz'u-hua*, vol. 4, ch. 78, p. 16b, l. 8; and p. 28b, l. 8.

7. This formulaic four-character expression occurs ubiquitously in Chinese vernacular literature. See, e.g., a lyric written in 1380 by Lin Ta-t'ung (cs 1371), *Ch'üan Ming tz'u pu-pien*, 1:15, upper register, l. 3; *Chin-t'ung Yü-nü Chiao Hung chi*, p. 78, l. 6; an anonymous song suite in *Sheng-shih hsin-sheng*, p. 67, l. 5; a lyric written in 1514 by Ku Lin (1476–1545), *Ch'üan Ming tz'u*, 2:593, upper register, l. 16; a song suite by Ch'en To (fl. early 16th century), *Ch'üan Ming san-ch'ü*, 1:642, ll. 10–11; and *Shih Chen-jen ssu-sheng so pai-yüan*, scene 2, p. 7b, l. 11.

8. Versions of this anonymous song suite are preserved in *Sheng-shih hsin-sheng*, pp. 291–93; *Tz'u-lin chai-yen*, 2:1050–53; *Yung-hsi yüeh-fu*, ts'e 9, pp. 52a–53b; and *Ch'ün-yin lei-hsüan*, 3:1936–39.

9. This four-character expression occurs in *[Chi-p'ing chiao-chu] Hsi-hsiang chi*, play no. 2, scene 1, p. 48, l. 5; *Shih-wu kuan hsi-yen ch'eng ch'iao-huo*, p. 697, l. 14; and *[Hsin-tseng] Ch'iu-po i-chuan lun*, p. 8a, l. 9.

10. Versions of this anonymous song suite are preserved in *Sheng-shih hsin-sheng*, pp. 285–87; *Tz'u-lin chai-yen*, 2:1038–41; *Yung-hsi yüeh-fu*, ts'e 9, pp. 79b-80b; and *Ch'ün-yin lei-hsüan*, 3:1949–51.

11. This four-character expression comes from the last line of a famous quatrain by Tu Mu (803–52), *Ch'üan T'ang shih*, vol. 8, *chüan* 523, p. 5982, l. 8. It alludes to the legend of Nung-yü and Hsiao-shih, for which see Roy, *The Plum in the Golden Vase*, vol. 1, chap. 12, n. 3. It occurs ubiquitously in later Chinese literature. See, e.g., a lyric by Wei Fu-jen (11th century), the wife of Tseng Pu (1036–1107), *Ch'üan Sung tz'u*, 1:268, lower register, l. 3; a lyric by Ho Meng-kuei (b. 1228, cs 1265), ibid., 5:3150, upper register, l. 9; a lyric by Pai P'u (1226–c. 1306), *Ch'üan Chin Yüan tz'u*, 2:638, upper register, l. 7; a lyric by Chang Hung-fan (1238–80), ibid., 2:730, upper register, l. 10; *[Chi-p'ing chiao-chu] Hsi-hsiang chi*, play no. 4, scene 4, p. 168, l. 12; a song by Hsü Tsai-ssu (14th century), *Ch'üan Yüan san-ch'ü*, 2:1059, l. 11; a lyric by Liu Chi (1311–75), *Ch'üan Ming tz'u*, 1:91, lower register, l. 12; a lyric by Chang Yüan (1474–1524), *Ch'üan Ming tz'u pu-pien*, 1:181, upper register, l. 2; a lyric by Wen Cheng-ming (1470–1559), *Ch'üan Ming tz'u*, 2:504, upper register, ll. 6–7; a set of songs by K'ang Hai (1475–1541), Ch'üan Ming san-ch'ü, 1:1168, ll. 2–3; a lyric by Tai Kuan (cs 1508), *Ch'üan Ming tz'u*, 2:663, upper register, l. 11; a lyric by Yang Shen (1488–1559), ibid., 2:787. upper register, ll. 5–6; *Fu-jung chi, chüan* 2, scene 25, p. 32b, l. 9; *Mu-tan t'ing*, scene 35, p. 183, l. 6; and an abundance of other occurrences, too numerous to list.

12. This formulaic four-character expression that refers to the tokens exchanged by separated lovers occurs in a song suite by Tseng Jui (c. 1260–c. 1330), *Ch'üan Yüan san-ch'ü*, 1:511, l. 14; *Yüan-ch'ü hsüan*, 3:1222, l. 1; *Yüan-ch'ü hsüan wai-pien*, 3:787, l. 21; *Chin-ch'ai chi*, scene 44, p. 78, l. 16; and a set of songs by Wang Chiu-ssu (1468–1551), *Ch'üan Ming san-ch'ü*, 1:895, l. 11.

13. This four-character expression occurs in *Hai-fu shan-t'ang tz'u-kao, chüan* 3, p. 160, l. 2.

14. According to Chinese legend, the red spots on the surface of the azalea blossom were bloodstains left by the cuckoo, who called so vociferously that it coughed up drops of blood. This image came to be applied to the blood produced by the rupturing of the hymen upon the defloration of a virgin.

15. Chu Pa-chieh is the name of one of the principal characters in the *Hsi-yu chi*, a pig, proverbial for his ugliness, who symbolizes the human appetites. A variant of this line occurs in the *Chin P'ing Mei tz'u-hua*, vol. 4, ch. 76, p. 21b. l. 11–p. 22a, l. 1.

16. For the story behind this allusion, see Roy, *The Plum in the Golden Vase*, vol. 3, chap. 55, n. 24.

17. Legend has it that Wen Ch'iao (288–329) once presented a jade mirror stand as an engagement present from an intended bridegroom in the course of deceiving his great aunt into letting him marry her daughter. See *Shih-shuo Hsin-yü: A New Account of Tales of the World*, by Liu I-ch'ing, trans. Richard B. Mather (Minneapolis: University of Minnesota Press, 1976), p. 445, item 9.

18. See Roy, *The Plum in the Golden Vase*, vol. 1, chap. 3, n. 29.

19. This four-character expression occurs in *Hsiu-ju chi*, scene 24, p. 67, l. 6; and an anonymous song suite in *Yung-hsi yüeh-fu*, ts'e 14, p. 53a, l. 1.

20. This line occurs in a song by Wang Chiu-ssu (1468–1551), *Ch'üan Ming san-ch'ü*, 1:924, l. 2.

21. This line occurs in [*Chi-p'ing chiao-chu*] *Hsi-hsiang chi*, play no. 4, scene 4, p. 166, l. 11.

22. A synonymous variant of this line occurs in *Yüan-ch'ü hsüan*, 3:984, l. 18; and *Chin-t'ung Yü-nü Chiao Hung chi*, p. 40, l. 14.

23. This song suite is by Ch'en To (fl. early 16th century), see *Ch'üan Ming san-ch'ü*, 1:573–74. Versions of it are also preserved in *Tz'u-lin chai-yen*, 2:859–63: *Yung-hsi yüeh-fu*, ts'e 14, pp. 9a–10a; *Nan-pei kung tz'u-chi*, vol. 4, chüan 6, pp. 702–3; *Ch'ün-yin lei-hsüan*, 3:1954–57; and *Wu-sao ho-pien*, ts'e 4, chüan 4, pp. 95b–97b.

24. A more common variant of this four-character expression that means "showing its fangs and brandishing its claws" occurs in *Yüan-ch'ü hsüan*, 4:1710, l. 5; and *Shui-hu ch'üan-chuan*, vol. 2, ch. 43, p. 699, l. 3. I suspect that the version given in the novel may be a copyist's error for the above variant, which is the more logical of the two.

25. This four-character expression occurs in *Chin-yin chi*, chüan 3, scene 29, p. 28a, l. 2; *Shuang-chu chi*, scene 2, p. 4, l. 7; and with an orthographic variant, in *Shui-hu ch'üan-chuan*, vol. 2, ch. 34, p. 534, l. 2.

26. This short song suite is preserved in *Sheng-shih hsin-sheng*, pp. 522–23; *Tz'u-lin chai-yen*, 1:257–58; *Yung-hsi yüeh-fu*, ts'e 16, pp. 26a–26b; and *Ch'ün-yin lei-hsüan*, 4:2077–78, where it is said to be by Chia Chung-ming (1343–c. 1422).

27. See Roy, *The Plum in the Golden Vase*, vol. 2, chap. 22, n. 14.

28. This song suite is by Ching Kan-ch'en (13th century). See *Ch'üan Yüan san-ch'ü*, 1:139–41. Versions of it are preserved in *Sheng-shih hsin-sheng*, pp. 76–79; *Tz'u-lin chai-yen*, 2:1109–14; *Yung-hsi yüeh-fu*, ts'e 1, pp. 19b–21a; *Nan-pei kung tz'u-chi*, vol. 4, chüan 6, pp. 614–16; and *Ch'ün-yin lei-hsüan*, 3:1980–83.

29. This colloquial expression has already occurred in the *Chin P'ing Mei tz'u-hua*, vol. 1, ch. 12, p. 13b, l. 10; but I translated it differently in that context. See Roy, *The Plum in the Golden Vase*, vol. 1, chap. 12, p. 244, ll. 23–24.

30. Squire Sun Ju-ch'üan and his servant Chu Chi are characters from *Ching-ch'ai chi*. Sun is a loutish, half-witted oaf who has nothing going for him but his inherited wealth, and who depends on his servant Chu Chi for advice in everything he undertakes. See, e.g., *Ching-ch'ai chi*, scene 7.

31. A synonymous variant of this proverbial expression recurs in the *Chin P'ing Mei tz'u-hua*, vol. 3, ch. 76, p. 14b, l. 1.

32. This line occurs in the same form as in the novel in [*Chiao-ting*] *Yüan-k'an tsa-chü san-shih chung*, p. 326, l. 2; and in a variant form in *Yüan-ch'ü hsüan*, 3:1137, ll. 14–15.

33. See Roy, *The Plum in the Golden Vase*, vol. 3, chap. 43, n. 13.

34. These two lines recur in the *Chin P'ing Mei tz'u-hua*, vol. 4, ch. 75, p. 11a, ll. 5–6.

35. A variant of this colloquial expression occurs in *Yüan-ch'ü hsüan*, 1:209, l. 21.

36. See Roy, *The Plum in the Golden Vase*, vol. 2, chap. 32, n. 82.

37. The recitation that follows at this point is a truncated and somewhat garbled version of the early vernacular story *Wu-chieh Ch'an-shih ssu Hung-lien chi*. I have relied upon the text of this story in making certain necessary emendations.

38. This quatrain is derived from the opening poem of the story cited in the preceding note, although the second couplet has been considerably altered.

39. This four-character expression occurs ubiquitously in Chinese Buddhist and vernacular literature. See, e.g., a speech attributed to the Buddhist monk I-hsüan (d. 867), *Wu-teng hui-yüan*, vol. 2, *chüan* 11, p. 649, l. 5; a gatha by the Buddhist monk Hsiao-ts'ung (d. 1030), ibid., vol. 3, *chüan* 15, p. 986, l. 5; a gatha by the Buddhist monk Huai-shen (1077–1132), *Ch'üan Sung shih*, 24:16147, l. 15; *Yüan-ch'ü hsüan*, 1:295, l. 21; *Fo-shuo Huang-chi chieh-kuo pao-chüan*, 10:244, ll. 5–6; *Huang-chi chin-tan chiu-lien cheng-hsin kuei-chen huan-hsiang pao-chüan*, 8:307, ll. 3–4; *Yüeh-ming Ho-shang tu Liu Ts'ui*, p. 435, l. 13; *P'u-ching ju-lai yao-shih pao-chüan*, 5:54, l. 10; and *Hsi-yu chi*, vol. 1, ch. 12, p. 134, l. 11. It also recurs in the *Chin P'ing Mei tz'u-hua*, vol. 4, ch. 75, p. 24b, l. 9.

40. This four-character expression occurs in a lyric by Hou Shan-yüan (12th century), *Ch'üan Chin Yüan tz'u*, 1:515, upper register, l. 14; and *Huan-sha chi*, scene 33, p. 120, l. 8.

41. This four-character expression occurs in *I-chien chih*, vol. 3, *chih-chih*, *ting* (second record, section 4), *chüan* 3, p. 990, l. 9; *Hsing-t'ien Feng-yüeh t'ung-hsüan chi*, scene 6, p. 17a, l. 5; *Hua-ying chi*, p. 876, l. 11; and *Mu-lien chiu-mu ch'üan-shan hsi-wen*, *chüan* 1, p. 48b, l. 4.

42. This four-character expression occurs in *Fo-shuo Wu-liang shou ching* (*Sukhāvatīvyūha*), trans. Sanghavarman in 252, in *Taishō shinshū daizōkyō*, vol. 12, no. 360, *chüan* 2, p. 276, lower register, l. 9; *Ju-ju chü-shih yü-lu, i-chi* (second collection), *chüan* 2, p. 1a, l. 13; and *Chieh-hsia chi*, scene 14, p. 34, l. 1.

43. This four-character expression, which is of Buddhist origin, occurs ubiquitously in Chinese literature. See, e.g., *Ju-ju chü-shih yü-lu, chia-chi* (first collection), *chüan* 2, p. 4a, l. 9; *Kuan-shih-yin p'u-sa pen-hsing ching*, p. 122b, l. 10; *Yüan-ch'ü hsüan*, 3:1241, l. 14; a statement attributed to Emperor Jen-tsung of the Yüan dynasty (r. 1311–20) in *Yüan shih*, vol. 2, *chüan* 26, p. 594, l. 2; a lyric by Wang Wei-i (d. 1326), *Ch'üan Chin Yüan tz'u*, 2:1257, lower register, l. 11; *Hsiao-p'in chi*, p. 37, l. 3; *Fo-shuo Huang-chi chieh-kuo pao-chüan*, 10:269, l. 6; *Huang-chi chin-tan chiu-lien cheng-hsin kuei-chen huan-hsiang pao-chüan*, 8:283, l. 2; *Cheng-hsin ch'u-i wu hsiu cheng tzu-tsai pao-chüan*, 3:92, l. 4; *Yüeh-ming Ho-shang tu Liu Ts'ui*, p. 437, l. 13; *Yao-shih pen-yüan kung-te pao-chüan*, 14:343, l. 1; *Tung-t'ien hsüan-chi*, scene 1, p. 7a, l. 3; *P'u-ming ju-lai wu-wei liao-i pao-chüan*, 4:382, l. 5; *Mu-lien chiu-mu ch'üan-shan hsi-wen*, *chüan* 1, p. 7a, l. 7; *Hsi-yu chi*, vol. 1, ch. 11, p. 121, l. 7; *San-pao t'ai-chien Hsi-yang chi t'ung-su yen-i*, vol. 1, ch. 4, p 49, l. 7; a reference to the teaching of Bodhidharma (fl. 470–528) in *Hsü Fen-shu* (Supplement to A book to be burned), by Li Chih (1527–1602) (Peking: Chung-hua shu-chü, 1961), *chüan* 4, p. 96, l. 4; and an abundance of other occurrences, too numerous to list.

44. This four-character expression occurs in *Shui-hu ch'üan-chuan*, vol. 2, ch. 44, p. 714, l. 5.

45. This four-character expression occurs in *San-kuo chih t'ung-su yen-i*, vol. 1, *chüan* 1, p. 21, l. 15; *Lieh-kuo chih-chuan*, vol. 3, *chüan* 8, p. 1b, ll. 6–7; and *San-pao ta'i-chien Hsi-yang chi t'ung-su yen-i*, vol. 1, ch. 15, p. 195, ll. 2–3.

46. This four-character expression occurs in *Shen-hsiang ch'üan-pien*, *chüan* 641, p. 29b, l. 6; and *Huang-Ming k'ai-yün ying-wu chuan*, *chüan* 6, p. 18b, l. 10.

47. This proverbial expression occurs ubiquitously in Chinese vernacular literature. See, e.g., *Yüan-ch'ü hsüan*, 3:1158, l. 21; *Sha-kou chi*, scene 10, p. 32, l. 4; *[Yüan-pen] Wang chuang-yüan Ching-ch'ai chi* ([Original edition of] Top graduate Wang and the Thorn hairpin), in *Ku-pen hsi-ch'ü ts'ung-k'an*, ch'u-chi, item no, 13, *chüan* 2, scene 28, p. 5a, l. 9; *P'i-p'a chi*, scene 16, p. 102, l. 9; *Ch'ien-chin chi*, scene 21, p. 67, l. 5; *Nan Hsi-hsiang chi* (Li Jih-hua), scene 24, p. 71, l. 7; *Hsiu-ju chi*, scene 26, p. 74, l. 6; *Yüeh-ming Ho-shang tu Liu Ts'ui*, p. 430, l. 12; *Ming-feng chi*, scene 23, p. 98, ll. 11–12; *Mu-lien chiu-mu ch'üan-shan hsi-wen*, *chüan* 2, p. 74a, l. 5; *Hsi-yu chi*, vol. 1, ch. 33, p. 378, ll. 11–12; and *San-pao t'ai-chien Hsi-yang chi t'ung-su yen-i*, vol. 1, ch. 19, p. 252, l. 8.

48. This four-character expression is derived from a passage in *chüan* 2, section 3, of the *Hsi-tz'u* (Attached commentary) in the *I-ching* (Book of changes). See *Chou-i yin-te*, p. 46, column 1, l. 23. It occurs ubiquitously in later Chinese literature. See, e.g., a dirge by P'an Yüeh (247–300), *Wen-hsüan*, vol. 3, *chüan* 57, p. 5a, l. 1; an epitaph by Yang Chiung (650–c. 694), *Ch'üan T'ang wen*, vol. 5, *chüan* 294, p. 19a, l. 9; a poem by Po Chü-i (772–846), *Ch'üan T'ang shih*, vol. 7, *chüan* 462, p. 5252, l. 10; a poem by Hsüeh Feng (cs 841), ibid., vol. 8, *chüan* 548, p. 6321, l. 3; a poem by Fang Kan (c. 809–c. 885), ibid., vol. 10, *chüan* 651, p. 7478, l. 5; *Sou-shen chi* (In search of the supernatural), comp. Kou Tao-hsing (10th century), in *Tun-huang pien-wen chi*, 2:883, l. 7; a poem by Shao Yung (1011–77), *Ch'üan Sung shih*, 7:4532, l. 5; a quatrain by Wang An-shang (11th century), ibid., 13:8713, l. 11; a lyric by Wang Che (1112–70), *Ch'üan Chin Yüan tz'u*, 1:248, upper register, l. 8; the poetical exegesis of the *Diamond Sutra* by the Buddhist monk Tao-ch'uan (fl. 1127–63), *Chin-kang pan-jo-po-lo-mi ching chu* (Commentary on the *Vajracchedikā prajñāpāramitā sutra*), by Tao-ch'uan (fl. 1127–63), pref. dated 1179, in *[Shinzan] Dai Nihon zokuzōkyō*, vol. 24, no. 461, p. 555, middle register, l. 11; *Liu Chih-yüan chu-kung-tiao [chiao-chu]*, part 11, p. 112, l. 3; *Wu-wang fa Chou p'ing-hua*, p. 23, l. 9; *Pai Niang-tzu yung-chen Lei-feng T'a*, p. 430, l. 10; *Chang Yü-hu wu-su nü-chen kuan*, scene 4, p. 624, ll. 4–5; *Chung-ch'ing li-chi*, *chüan* 7, p. 25b, l. 10; *Lieh-kuo chih-chuan*, vol. 3, *chüan* 8, p. 12a, ll. 9–10; *San-pao t'ai-chien Hsi-yang chi t'ung-su yen-i*, vol. 1, ch. 9, p. 115, l. 9; *Sui-T'ang liang-ch'ao shih-chuan*, *chüan* 11, ch. 101, p. 2a, l. 2; and an abundance of other occurrences, too numerous to list.

49. This four-character expression occurs in a lyric by Ko T'an (cs 1154, d. 1182), *Ch'üan Sung tz'u*, 3:1548, upper register, l. 8; *Fo-yin shih ssu t'iao Ch'in-niang*, p. 238, l. 3; *Shui-hu ch'üan-chuan*, vol. 3, ch. 69, p. 1172, l. 12; and *Pai-chia kung-an*, *chüan* 7, ch. 63, p. 23b, l. 11.

50. This four-character expression occurs in the middle-period vernacular story *Hsien-yün An Juan-san ch'ang yüan-chai* (In Idle Cloud Nunnery Juan the Third repays his debt of love), in *Ku-chin hsiao-shuo*, vol. 1, *chüan* 4, p. 91, l. 15; and *Hsi-yu chi*, vol. 1, ch. 27, p. 307, l. 2.

51. This four-character expression occurs ubiquitously in Chinese vernacular literature. See, e.g., *Ch'ing-so kao-i, hou-chi* (second collection), *chüan* 3, p. 116, l. 9; *Ch'i-kuo ch'un-ch'iu p'ing-hua*, p. 6, ll. 1–2; *San-kuo chih p'ing-hua*, p. 126, l. 8; *Feng-yüeh Jui-hsien T'ing*, p. 44, l. 11; *Erh-lang Shen so Ch'i-t'ien Ta-sheng*, scene 1, p. 705, l. 1; *Yün chi-mou Sui Ho p'ien Ying Pu*, scene 2, p. 5a, l. 1; *Ch'ing feng-nien Wu-kuei nao Chung K'uei, hsieh-tzu* (wedge), p. 1a, l. 7; *Yüeh-ming Ho-shang tu Liu Ts'ui*, p. 431, ll. 6–7; *Ming-feng chi*, scene 33, p. 136, l. 11; *Ch'üan-Han chih-chuan*, vol. 2, *chüan* 3, p. 37a, l. 10; *Pai-chia kung-an, chüan* 2, ch. 12, p. 15a, l. 9; *Yang-chia fu shih-tai chung-yung yen-i chih-chuan*, vol. 1, *chüan* 3, p. 18b, ll. 3–4; and *Sui-T'ang liang-ch'ao shih-chuan, chüan* 9, ch. 87, p. 38b, l. 3. It also recurs in the *Chin P'ing Mei tz'u-hua*, vol. 5, ch. 95, p. 5a, l. 6.

52. This four-character expression occurs ubiquitously in Chinese vernacular literature. See, e.g., *Yüan-ch'ü hsüan*, 3:1102, l. 9; *Sha-kou chi*, scene 24, p. 91, l. 2; *Shuang-chu chi*, scene 40, p. 144, l. 10; *Chiao-hsiao chi, chüan* 1, scene 13, p. 28b, l. 4; *Yüeh-ming Ho-shang tu Liu Ts'ui*, p. 433, l. 3; *Ch'ien-t'ang hu-yin Chi-tien Ch'an-shih yü-lu*, p. 11b, l. 10; and *San-pao t'ai-chien Hsi-yang chi t'ung-su yen-i*, vol. 2, ch. 92, p. 1188, l. 10. It also recurs in the *Chin P'ing Mei tz'u-hua*, vol. 4, ch. 73, p. 13a, l. 4; and vol. 5, ch. 86, p. 3b, l. 4.

53. This four-character expression occurs ubiquitously in Chinese vernacular literature. See, e.g., *Yüeh Fei p'o-lu tung-ch'uang chi, chüan* 2, scene 26, p. 9a, l. 1; *Shui-hu ch'üan-chuan*, vol. 1, ch. 16, p. 226, l. 15; *Yüeh-ming Ho-shang tu Liu Ts'ui*, p. 432, l. 3; *Ts'ao-lu chi, chüan* 3, scene 36, p. 19a, l. 9; *Su Ying huang-hou ying-wu chi, chüan* 1, scene 10, p. 20a, l. 9; *Yang-chia fu shih-tai chung-yung yen-i chih-chuan*, vol. 2, *chüan* 6, p. 1a, l. 10; and *Ta-T'ang Ch'in-wang tz'u-hua*, vol. 2, *chüan* 5, ch. 33, p. 9a, l. 10.

54. See Roy, *The Plum in the Golden Vase*, vol. 3, chap. 57, n. 29.

55. A virtually identical line, with one textual variant, occurs in *Chien-teng hsin-hua, chüan* 3, p. 72, l. 15.

56. This four-character expression occurs in the middle-period vernacular story *Lao Feng T'ang chih-chien Han Wen-ti* (The elderly Feng T'ang straightforwardly admonishes Emperor Wen of the Han dynasty), in *Ch'ing-p'ing shan-t'ang hua-pen*, p. 293, l. 15; and *Lieh-kuo chih-chuan*, vol. 2, *chüan* 6, p. 34b, l. 6.

57. This formulaic four-character expression occurs in *Lü Tung-pin hua-yüeh shen-hsien hui*, scene 4, p. 9a, l. 2; *Yüeh-ming Ho-shang tu Liu Ts'ui*, p. 435, l. 13; and *Mu-lien chiu-mu ch'üan-shan hsi-wen, chüan* 2, p. 60a, l. 7.

58. The story that Su Shih (1037–1101) was a reincarnation of the Buddhist monk Wu-chieh was already current during the early twelfth century and may have originated with Su Shih himself. *See Leng-chai yeh-hua* (Evening talk from a cold studio), by Hui-hung (1071–1128), in *Pi-chi hsiao-shuo ta-kuan*, vol. 4, *ts'e* 8, *chüan* 7, p. 2a, l. 11–p. 2b, l. 6; and *Ch'un-chu chi-wen* (Record of hearsay from a spring islet), by Ho Wei (1077–1145) (Peking: Chung-hua shu-chü, 1983), *chüan* 1, p. 5, l. 8–p. 6, l. 2. Both of these authors were personally acquainted with Su Shih.

59. This formulaic four-character expression occurs in *Shuang-chu chi*, scene 44, p. 157, l. 9; *San Sui p'ing-yao chuan, chüan* 3, ch. 12, p. 22b, l. 4; and *Yen-chih chi, chüan* 2, scene 36, p. 24a, l. 8.

60. A very similar line occurs in *Ch'ien-t'ang hu-yin Chi-tien Ch'an-shih yü-lu*, p. 54a, l. 1.

61. See Roy, *The Plum in the Golden Vase*, vol. 3, chap. 55, n. 43.

62. Although the four poems above are all from *Wu-chieh Ch'an-shih ssu Hung-lien chi*, this poem, with some textual variation, is taken from *Yüeh-ming Ho-shang tu Liu Ts'ui*, p. 433, ll. 6–7. The same poem also occurs in *San-pao t'ai-chien Hsi-yang chi t'ung-su yen-i*, vol. 2, ch. 92, p. 1188, ll. 12–15.

63. This formulaic four-character expression occurs ubiquitously in Chinese vernacular literature. See, e.g., a lyric by Yin Chih-p'ing (1169–1251), *Ch'üan Chin Yüan tz'u*, 2:1182, upper register, l. 15; *Chang Hsieh chuang-yüan*, scene 10, p. 56, l. 8; a song suite by Pai P'u (1226–c. 1306), *Ch'üan Yüan san-ch'ü*, 1:207, l. 5; *Yüan-ch'ü hsüan*, 3:1102, l. 1; *Yüan-ch'ü hsüan wai-pien*, 2:417, l. 18; an anonymous song suite in *Sheng-shih hsin-sheng*, p. 124, l. 2; *San Sui p'ing-yao chuan*, chüan 1, ch. 2, p. 14a, l. 7; an anonymous song suite in *Yung-hsi yüeh-fu*, ts'e 19, p. 22a, l. 7; *Yang-chia fu shih-tai chung-yung yen-i chih-chuan*, vol. 1, chüan 3, p. 43b, l. 6; and *Ta-T'ang Ch'in-wang tz'u-hua*, vol. 1, chüan 3, ch. 20, p. 37a, l. 7.

64. This formulaic four-character expression occurs ubiquitously in Chinese vernacular literature. See, e.g., a lyric by Ts'ai Shen (1088–1156), *Ch'üan Sung tz'u*, 2:1011, upper register, l. 16; a lyric by Tseng Ti (1109–80), ibid., 2:1316, lower register, l. 14; a lyric by Fan Ch'eng-ta (1126–93), ibid., 3:1616, lower register, ll. 13–14; a lyric by Hsin Ch'i-chi (1140–1207), ibid., 3:1879, lower register, l. 5; a lyric by Liu Ping-chung (13th century), *Ch'üan Chin Yüan tz'u*, 2:618, lower register, l. 6; [*Chi-p'ing chiao-chu*] *Hsi-hsiang chi*, play no. 1, scene 3, p. 32, l. 15; a lyric by Yü Chi (1272–1348), *Ch'üan Chin Yüan tz'u*, 2:863, lower register, l. 17; a lyric by Chang Yeh (13th–14th centuries), ibid., 2:897, upper register, l. 9; *Yüan-ch'ü hsüan wai-pien*, 2:350, l. 4; a lyric by Ch'ü Yu (1341–1427), *Ch'üan Ming tz'u*, 1:171, upper register, l. 1; *Ch'ien-t'ang meng*, p. 1a, l. 8; *Liang-shan wu-hu ta chieh-lao*, scene 4, p. 7b, l. 14; *Huai-hsiang chi*, scene 26, p. 83, l. 2; a set of songs by Huang O (1498–1569), *Ch'üan Ming san-ch'ü*, 2:1746, l. 9; a lyric by Kao Lien (late 16th century), *Ch'üan Ming tz'u*, 3:1174, lower register, l. 11; *Ta-T'ang Ch'in-wang tz'u-hua*, vol. 1, chüan 3, ch. 19, p. 31b, l. 1; and an abundance of other occurrences, too numerous to list. It also recurs in the *Chin P'ing Mei tz'u-hua*, vol. 5, ch. 89, p. 12b, l. 6.

65. See Roy, *The Plum in the Golden Vase*, vol. 2, appendix, n. 3.

66. This four-character expression occurs in an anonymous set of songs published in 1553, *Ch'üan Ming san-ch'ü*, 5:6154, l. 6.

67. This line occurs in an anonymous set of songs in *Yung-hsi yüeh-fu*, ts'e 15b, p. 26b, l. 9.

68. See Roy, *The Plum in the Golden Vase*, vol. 2, chap. 21, n. 2.

69. This four-character expression occurs in a poem by the Buddhist monk Cheng-chüeh (1091–1157), *Ch'üan Sung shih*, 31:19747, l. 6; and *Ming-feng chi*, scene 35, p. 147, l. 10.

70. This formulaic reduplicative expression occurs ubiquitously in Chinese vernacular literature. See, e.g., *Tung Chieh-yüan Hsi-hsiang chi*, chüan 6, p. 126, l. 4; a set of songs by Liu T'ing-hsin (14th century), *Ch'üan Yüan san-ch'ü*, 2:1430, l. 4; a song suite by Yang No (14th–15th centuries), *Ch'üan Ming san-ch'ü*, 1:204, l. 10; an anonymous song suite in *Sheng-shih hsin-sheng*, p. 530, ll. 11–12; an anonymous set of songs in *Yung-hsi yüeh-fu*, ts'e 15b, p. 26a, l. 6; *Pu-fu lao*, scene 4, p. 321, l. 14; *Hsi-yu chi*, vol. 1, ch. 14, p. 161, l. 10; and an abundance of other occurrences, too numerous to list.

71. See Roy, *The Plum in the Golden Vase*, vol. 1, chap. 8, n. 19.

72. This six-character expression occurs in *[Hsiao-shih] Chen-k'ung sao-hsin pao-chüan*, 19:46, l. 4.

73. This four-character expression occurs in a set of lyrics by Pei Ch'iung (c. 1297–1379), *Ch'üan Ming tz'u*, 1:23, upper register, l. 15.

74. This formulaic four-character expression occurs ubiquitously in Chinese vernacular literature. See, e.g., *Yüan-ch'ü hsüan*, 3:1278, l. 17; *Ching-ch'ai chi*, scene 15, p. 47, l. 7; a song suite by T'ang Fu (14th century), *Ch'üan Ming san-ch'ü*, 1:230, l. 6; *Yü-huan chi*, scene 12, p. 42, l. 6; *Feng-yüeh Nan-lao chi*, hsieh-tzu (wedge), p. 1a, l. 7; and an abundance of other occurrences, too numerous to list.

75. This entire line occurs in an anonymous song suite in *Sheng-shih hsin-sheng*, p. 287, l. 3.

76. This formulaic four-character expression occurs ubiquitously in Chinese vernacular literature. See, e.g., a lyric by Chang Lun (12th century), *Ch'üan Sung tz'u*, 3:1424, upper register, l. 8; a song suite by Liu T'ing-hsin (14th century), *Ch'üan Yüan san-ch'ü*, 2:1446, l. 6; *Yüan-ch'ü hsüan*, 4:1622, l. 6; *Yüan-ch'ü hsüan wai-pien*, 3:802, l. 6; *San-kuo chih t'ung-su yen-i*, vol. 1, chüan 10, p. 473, ll. 1–2; *Shui-hu ch'üan-chuan*, vol. 3, ch. 69, p. 1171, l. 10; *Wang Wen-hsiu Wei-t'ang ch'i-yü chi*, scene 4, p. 9a, l. 1; and *Hsi-yu chi*, vol. 1, ch. 38, p. 438, l. 7.

77. This reduplicative four-character expression occurs in *Nan Hsi-hsiang chi* (Li Jih-hua), scene 19, p. 54, l. 6; *Hsi-yu chi*, vol. 2, ch. 80, p. 917, l. 2; and *Sui-T'ang liang-ch'ao shih-chuan*, chüan 6, ch. 57, p. 40a, l. 7.

78. A synonymous variant of this four-character expression occurs in *Yüan-ch'ü hsüan*, 3:1274, l. 13. It occurs in the same form as in the novel in *Ssu-sheng yüan*, play no. 4, scene 3, p. 75, l. 5.

79. This four-character expression occurs in *Huai-ch'un ya-chi*, chüan 10, p. 34a, ll. 7–8; and *Hsün-fang ya-chi*, p. 8b, l. 4. It also recurs in the *Chin P'ing Mei tz'u-hua*, vol. 4, ch. 75, p. 5a, ll. 9–10.

80. This four-character expression recurs in the *Chin P'ing Mei tz'u-hua*, vol. 4, ch. 79, p. 6b, l. 2.

81. This formulaic four-character expression occurs ubiquitously in Chinese vernacular literature. See, e.g., *Ch'ing-so kao-i*, chüan 4, p. 38, l. 11; a quatrain by Pi Chung-yu (1047–1121), *Ch'üan Sung shih*, 18:11935, l. 4; *Yüan-ch'ü hsüan*, 3:1269, l. 11; *Hsin-ch'iao shih Han Wu mai ch'un-ch'ing*, p. 69, l. 1; *T'ang-shu chih-chuan t'ung-su yen-i*, vol. 1, chüan 1, p. 18a, ll. 5–6; *Ch'üan-Han chih-chuan*, vol. 2, chüan 6, p. 28b, l. 10; and *Sui-T'ang liang-ch'ao shih-chuan*, chüan 2, ch. 12, p. 6b, l. 4.

82. The locus classicus for this four-character expression is a remonstrance addressed to Liu Pi (213–154 B.C.), the Prince of Wu, by Mei Ch'eng (d. 141 B.C.), as quoted in *Han-shu*, vol. 5, chüan 51, p. 2359, l. 11. It occurs ubiquitously in later Chinese literature. See, e.g., *Ta-Tai Li-chi chu-tzu so-yin* (A concordance to the *Book of rites of the elder Tai*) (Taipei: T'ai-wan Shang-wu yin-shu kuan, 1992), chüan 5, section 5, p. 35, ll. 16–17; a speech attributed to Fang Hsüan-ling (578–648) in 626, as quoted in *Tzu-chih t'ung-chien*, vol. 3, chüan 191, p. 6005, l. 10; a passage of literary criticism in *T'ang kuo-shih pu* (Supplement to the History of the T'ang), comp. Li Chao (early 9th century) (Shanghai: Ku-tien wen-hsüeh ch'u-pan she, 1957), chüan 3, p. 55, l. 9; the prose commentary to a long poem by Emperor T'ai-tsung of the Sung dynasty (r. 976–97), *Ch'üan Sung shih*, 1:326, l. 5; a memorial by Ssu-ma Kuang

(1019–86) submitted in 1056, *Ssu-ma Kuang tsou-i* (The memorials of Ssu-ma Kuang), ed. Wang Ken-lin (T'ai-yüan: Shan-hsi Jen-min ch'u-pan she, 1986), *chüan* 1, p. 10, l. 14; a passage of poetic criticism by Yeh Meng-te (1077–1148), in *Sung shih-hua ch'üan-pien* (Complete compendium of Sung dynasty talks on poetry), ed. Wu Wen-chih, 10 vols. (Nanking: Chiang-su ku-chi ch'u-pan she, 1998), 3:2688, l. 2; a poem by the Buddhist monk Cheng-chüeh (1091–1157), *Ch'üan Sung shih*, 31:19888, l. 17; [*Hsin-pien*] *Wu-tai shih p'ing-hua*, p. 83, l. 3; *Shen-hsiang ch'üan-pien*, *chüan* 631, p. 35a, l. 6; *Ju-i chün chuan*, p. 13b, l. 4; and *Huang-Ming k'ai-yün ying-wu chuan*, *chüan* 7, p. 33a, l. 7.

83. This six-character expression recurs in the *Chin P'ing Mei tz'u-hua*, vol. 4, ch. 79. p. 9a, l. 10.

84. Variants of this idiomatic expression occur in *Yüan-ch'ü hsüan*, 1:9, l. 19; 4:1370, l. 16; and 4:1373, l. 14; *Yüan-ch'ü hsüan wai-pien*, 1:29, l. 8; *I-k'u kuei lai tao-jen ch'u-kuai*, p. 192, l. 13; *Yu-kuei chi*, scene 7, p. 15, ll. 7–8; *San-pao t'ai-chien Hsi-yang chi t'ung-su yen-i*, vol. 2, ch. 85, p. 1092, l. 7; and the *Chin P'ing Mei tz'u-hua*, vol. 5, ch. 95, p. 10b, l. 1.

85. This line is derived from the last line of the *Ch'ih-pi fu* (Rhapsody on the Red Cliff), written in 1082 by Su Shih (1037–1101). See *Su Shih wen-chi*, vol. 1, *chüan* 1, p. 6, l. 15. The same line is also quoted without attribution in *Huai-ch'un ya-chi*, *chüan* 10, p. 26a, l. 13.

CHAPTER 74

1. Tun-hsün was the ancient name of a small state in Southeast Asia, the exact location of which has not been determined, but which is thought to have been somewhere near the southern coast of what is now Myanmar, or Burma.

2. This poem is by T'an Yung-chih (10th century). See *Ch'üan T'ang shih*, vol. 11, *chüan* 764, p. 8671, ll. 8–9; and *Ch'üan Sung shih*, 1:42, ll. 10–11. For an illuminating discussion of this poem and its relevance to the contents of chapter 74, see Indira Satyendra, "Toward a Poetics of the Chinese Novel: A Study of the Prefatory Poems in the *Chin P'ing Mei tz'u-hua*," Ph.D. dissertation, University of Chicago, 1989, pp. 99–101.

3. This four-character expression occurs in an anonymous set of songs published in 1553. See, *Ch'üan Ming san-ch'ü*, 4:4607, l. 2.

4. This four-character expression occurs in *Cho Wen-chün ssu-pen Hsiang-ju*, scene 4, p. 134, l. 7.

5. This four-character expression occurs in *Ch'ien-t'ang meng*, p. 3b, l. 15.

6. This four-character expression occurs in a statement attributed to Hui-neng (638–713), the Sixth Patriarch of Ch'an Buddhism, *Tsu-t'ang chi*, *chüan* 2, p. 61, l. 4; a set of quatrains about Hui-neng by Huang Shang (1043–1129), *Ch'üan Sung shih*, 16:11114, l. 8; a poem by Li Chih-i (1047–1117), ibid., 17:11214. l. 13; a speech attributed to the Buddhist monk Hui-hui (1097–1183), *Wu-teng hui-yüan*, vol. 3, *chüan* 14, p. 914, l. 9; a song suite by Chu Yu-tun (1379–1439), *Ch'üan Ming san-ch'ü*, 1:357, l. 5; *K'u-kung wu-tao chüan*, 1:185, l. 1; *Tu-lo yüan Ssu-ma ju-hsiang*, scene 1, p. 3a, l. 12; and an abundance of other occurrences, too numerous to list. It also recurs twice in the *Chin P'ing Mei tz'u-hua*, vol. 5, ch. 89, p. 5a, l. 5; and ch. 91, p. 4a, l. 4.

7. This four-character expression occurs in *Chin-ch'ai chi*, scene 63, p. 108, l. 11; and *K'uai-tsui Li Ts'ui-lien chi*, p. 65, l. 1.

8. This formulaic four-character expression occurs in *Shui-hu ch'üan-chuan*, vol. 3, ch. 67, p. 1136, ll. 5–6; and *Hsi-yu chi*, vol. 1, ch. 15, p. 175, l. 3.

9. The following song suite is selectively quoted from *Nan Hsi-hsiang chi* (Li Jih-hua), scene 17, p. 44, l. 2–p. 45, l. 11, with the prose dialogue omitted, and is ultimately derived from *[Chi-p'ing chiao-chu] Hsi-hsiang chi*, play no. 2, scene 3, p. 71, l. 11– p. 73, l. 12. It portrays a situation in which the heroine Ts'ui Ying-ying's maidservant Hung-niang comes to invite the hero Chang Chün-jui to a party in his honor hosted by Ying-ying's mother as a reward for his part in rescuing them from attacking rebels. Hung-niang erroneously expects the occasion to be a wedding feast, as originally promised by Ying-ying's mother, and so encourages the hero to anticipate the consummation of his desires. Much of the wording is the same in the two versions, but there are also many discrepancies.

10. This formulaic four-character expression occurs in *Yüan-ch'ü hsüan*, 4:1656, l. 12; *[Chi-p'ing chiao-chu] Hsi-hsiang chi*, play no. 1, scene 3, p. 34, l. 9; *Hua-shen san-miao chuan*, p. 24b, l. 9; and recurs in the *Chin P'ing Mei tz'u-hua*, vol. 5, ch. 82, p. 6a, l. 8.

11. This four-character expression occurs in *Yu-kuei chi*, scene 18, p. 46, l. 3; and *Han Hsiang-tzu chiu-tu Wen-kung sheng-hsien chi*, chüan 2, scene 22, p. 12b, l. 10.

12. This formulaic reduplicative expression occurs in an anonymous set of songs on the story of the *Hsi-hsiang chi* published in 1471, *Ch'üan Ming san-ch'ü*, 4:4512, l. 9; a set of song lyrics by Li K'ai-hsien (1502–68) written in 1531, *Li K'ai-hsien chi*, 3:917, l. 12; a song by Huang O (1498–1569), *Ch'üan Ming san-ch'ü*, 2:1752, l. 13; *T'ien-yüan ch'i-yü*, vol. 3, chüan 8, p. 5a, l. 5; and *Seng-ni kung-fan*, scene 3, p. 343. l. 13.

13. This four-character expression occurs in a poem by Wei Hsiang (1033–1105), *Ch'üan Sung shih*, 13:8515, l. 10; a lyric by Chu Tun-ju (1081–1159), *Ch'üan Sung tz'u*, 2:863, lower register, l. 11; a lyric by Lu Tsu-kao (cs 1199), ibid., 4:2409, lower register, l. 16; and a song by T'ang Yin (1470–1524), *Ch'üan Ming san-ch'ü*, 1:1064, l. 10.

14. This four-character expression occurs in a song suite by Wu Hung-tao (14th century), *Ch'üan Yüan san-ch'ü*, 1:736, l. 13.

15. This formulaic four-character expression occurs in *[Chi-p'ing chiao-chu] Hsi-hsiang chi*, play no. 1, scene 1, p. 5, l. 11; a song by Tseng Jui (c. 1260–c. 1330), *Ch'üan Yüan san-ch'ü*, 1:490, l. 10; *P'u-tung Ts'ui Chang chu-yü shih-chi*, p. 15a, l. 15; an anonymous set of songs on the story of the *Hsi-hsiang chi* published in 1553, *Ch'üan Ming san-ch'ü*, 4:4643, l. 14; a song suite by Ch'en Ho (1516–60), ibid., 2:2161, l. 6; *Yü-tsan chi*, scene 17, p. 64, l. 19; *Yen-chih chi*, chüan 2, scene 23, p. 6a, l. 5; *T'ou-pi chi*, chüan 1, scene 7, p. 21a, l. 4; *Pu-fu lao*, scene 1, p. 301, ll. 11–12; a set of songs by Liu Hsiao-tsu (1522–89), *Ch'üan Ming san-ch'ü*, 2:2312, l. 9; a song suite by Ch'en So-wen (d. c. 1604), ibid., 2:2552, l. 11; and an abundance of other occurrences, too numerous to list.

16. This four-character expression is an alternate version of one that occurs three times in song no. 35 in the *Shih-ching* (Book of Songs). See Roy, *The Plum in the Golden Vase*, vol. 1, chap. 8, n. 1. It occurs ubiquitously in later Chinese literature. See, e.g., a song by Kuan Han-ch'ing (13th century), *Ch'üan Yüan san-ch'ü*, 1:160, l. 11; a song suite by K'ang Wen-yüan (14th century), ibid., 2:1120, l. 7; a song by Chia

Ku (14th century), ibid., 2:1332, l. 8; *Yüan-ch'ü hsüan*, 2:539, l. 14; *Yüan-ch'ü hsüan wai-pien*, 2:574, l. 5; a song suite by Chu Yu-tun (1379–1439), *Ch'üan Ming san-ch'ü*, 1:362, l. 4; *P'u-tung Ts'ui Chang chu-yü shih-chi*, p. 19b, l. 12; a song suite by T'ang Yin (1470–1524), *Ch'üan Ming san-ch'ü*, 1:1087, l. 9; *Nan Hsi-hsiang chi* (Li Jih-hua), scene 34, p. 98, l. 12; a song suite by Chin Luan (1494–1583), *Ch'üan Ming san-ch'ü*, 2:1639, l. 14; and an abundance of other occurrences, too numerous to list.

17. "Plucking the cassia" is a conventional idiom for passing the civil service examinations.

18. This four-character expression alludes to the story of Nung-yü and Hsiao-shih. See Roy, *The Plum in the Golden Vase*, vol. 1, chap. 12, n. 3. It occurs in *Yüan-ch'ü hsüan*, 4:1331, l. 4; *Yüan-ch'ü hsüan wai-pien*, 3:896, l. 14; a song suite by Ch'en To (fl. early 16th century), *Ch'üan Ming san-ch'ü*, 1:661, l. 2; an anonymous song suite in *Yung-hsi yüeh-fu*, ts'e 6, p. 49a, l. 3; *Yü-ching t'ai*, scene 4, p. 8, l. 8; and *I-hsia chi*, scene 9, p. 22, l. 1.

19. The ultimate source of this line is a famous quatrain by Tu Mu (803–52). *Ch'üan T'ang shih*, vol. 8, *chüan* 524, p. 6002, l. 11. It is quoted verbatim in a song by Lu Chih (cs 1268), *Ch'üan Yüan san-ch'ü*, 1:112, ll. 7–8; a set of songs by Ch'en To (fl. early 16th century), *Ch'üan Ming san-ch'ü*, 1:524, l. 7; a set of songs by Yang T'ing-ho (1459–1529), ibid., 1:758, ll. 11–12; a lyric by Hsia Yang (16th century), *Ch'üan Ming tz'u*, 2:441, upper register, ll. 11–12; and an anonymous song suite in *Yung-hsi yüeh-fu*, ts'e 9, p. 72a, l. 4.

20. This formulaic four-character expression occurs ubiquitously in Chinese literature. See, e.g., a poem by the Buddhist monk Te-hung (1071–1128), *Ch'üan Sung shih*, 23:15219, l. 15; a poem by Lu Yu (1125–1210), ibid., 39:24450, l. 17; a lyric by Wan-yen Shu (1172–1232), *Ch'üan Chin Yüan tz'u*, 1:45, lower register, l. 8; a lyric by Li Mao-ying (1201–57), *Ch'üan Sung tz'u*, 4:2872, lower register, l. 1; a lyric by Liu Min-chung (1243–1318), *Ch'üan Chin Yüan tz'u*, 2:757, upper register, ll. 5–6; a song by Chang K'o-chiu (1270–1348), *Ch'üan Yüan san-ch'ü*, 1:772, l. 11; *Yüan-ch'ü hsüan*, 1:247, l. 18; *Yüan-ch'ü hsüan wai-pien*, 2:568, l. 7; *Ching-ch'ai chi*, scene 14, p. 43, l. 1; *Chin-t'ung Yü-nü Chiao Hung chi*, p. 53, l. 11; *Huang T'ing-tao yeh-tsou Liu-hsing ma*, scene 1, p. 87, l. 13; *P'i-p'a chi*, scene 2, p. 6, l. 8; *Pai-she chi*, *chüan* 1, scene 3, p. 6a, l. 2; the anonymous Yüan-Ming tsa-chü drama *Meng-mu san-i* (The mother of Mencius moves three times), in *Ku-pen Yüan Ming tsa-chü*, vol. 2, scene 3, p. 10, l. 2; *P'o-yao chi*, *chüan* 2, scene 25, p. 26a, l. 10; *Chung-ch'ing li-chi*, *chüan* 6, p. 36a, l. 12; a song suite by Wang Chiu-ssu (1468–1551), *Ch'üan Ming san-ch'ü*, 1:966, l. 5; a lyric by Chu Yen-t'ai (16th century), *Ch'üan Ming tz'u*, 2:633, upper register, l. 15; a lyric by Meng Ssu (16th century), ibid., 2:972, lower register, l. 10; *Su Ying huang-hou ying-wu chi*, *chüan* 2, scene 24, p. 11a, l. 8; *Fu-jung chi*, *chüan* 2, scene 17, p. 6b, ll. 3–4; and a host of other occurrences, too numerous to list.

21. This expression is quoted as a proverbial saying in *Sun-p'u* (Monograph on bamboo shoots), comp. Tsan-ning (919–1001), in *Shuo-fu san-chung*, 8:4857, *chüan* 2, p. 17a, l. 9. It occurs ubiquitously in later Chinese literature. See, e.g., [Chi-p'ing chiao-chu] *Hsi-hsiang chi*, play no. 2, scene 4, p. 78, l. 12; *Yüan-ch'ü hsüan*, 1:86, l. 2; *Yüan-ch'ü hsüan wai-pien*, 1:230, ll. 8–9; *Huang hsiao-tzu*, *chüan* 2, scene 19, p. 17a, l. 5; *Hsiang-nang chi*, scene 5, p. 15, ll. 2–3; *San-pao t'ai-chien Hsi-yang chi t'ung-su yen-i*, vol. 1, ch. 24, p. 308, l. 8; and an abundance of other occurrences, too numerous to list.

22. For the ultimate source of this song suite see note 9 above. It is also preserved in *Ch'ün-yin lei-hsüan*, 3:1342–44; and, in the same truncated form as in the novel, in *Wu-yü ts'ui-ya* (A florilegium of song lyrics from Wu), comp. Chou Chih-piao (fl. early 17th century), pref. dated 1616, fac. repr. in *Shan-pen hsi-ch'ü ts'ung-k'an*, 13:694–97; and *Nan-yin san-lai* (Three kinds of southern sound), comp. Ling Meng-ch'u (1580–1644), 4 *ts'e*, fac. repr. of late Ming edition (Shanghai: Shang-hai ku-chi shu-tien, 1963), *ts'e* 3, pp. 72b-74a. For an illuminating discussion of the ironic significance of this song suite, and the cluster of other allusions surrounding it at this point in the novel, see Carlitz, "The Role of Drama in the *Chin P'ing Mei*: The Relationship between Fiction and Drama as a Guide to the Viewpoint of a Sixteenth-Century Chinese Novel," pp. 216–34.

23. This ch'uan-ch'i drama by Yao Mao-liang (15th century) tells the story of two historical paragons of loyalty from the T'ang dynasty who sacrifice their lives in defending the city of Sui-yang during the rebellion of An Lu-shan (d. 757).

24. This is the opening line of the song suite from the final scene of *Hsi-hsiang chi*, in which Chang Chün-jui returns in triumph from the capital after passing the examinations. See *[Chi-p'ing chiao-chu] Hsi-hsiang chi*, play no. 5, scene 4, p. 195, l. 8.

25. These two lines are quoted from a poem by Tu Fu (712–70), although the text has been somewhat garbled. See *Ch'üan T'ang shih*, vol. 4, *chüan* 224, p. 2400, l. 8. The first line probably alludes to Huan Tien (d. 201), who became known for riding a piebald horse when he was first appointed as a censor. See his biography in *Hou-Han shu*, vol. 5, *chüan* 37, p. 1258, ll. 6–7. The second line alludes to Ch'ih Ch'ao (336–77) who served as an adjutant to Huan Wen (312–73) and was known for his heavily bewhiskered face. See his biography in *Chin shu*, vol. 6, *chüan* 67, p. 1803, ll. 4–5.

26. This is the last line of a famous poem by Po Chü-i (772–846) written in 815 when he was serving as the marshall of Chiang-chou, another name for Chiu-chiang, of which the guest of honor in the novel, Ts'ai Hsiu, was currently the prefect. See *Ch'üan T'ang shih*, vol. 7, *chüan* 435, p. 4822, l. 8. This line is quoted verbatim in the prelude to an anonymous Sung dynasty lyric, *Ch'üan Sung tz'u*, 5:3649, upper register, l. 11; *Yüan-ch'ü hsüan*, 3:893, l. 10; and *Yüan-ch'ü hsüan wai-pien*, 3:792, l. 6; and is alluded to twice in *[Chi-p'ing chiao-chu] Hsi-hsiang chi*, play no. 2, scene 4, p. 81, l. 13; and play no. 4, scene 3, p. 160, l. 15.

27. The source of this song suite has not been identified, but the same line, with one insignificant textual variant, also occurs in *San-pao t'ai-chien Hsi-yang chi t'ung-su yen-i*, vol. 1, ch. 35, p. 451, l. 15.

28. The first couplet of this poem has already occurred in the novel. See Roy, *The Plum in the Golden Vase*, vol. 3, chap. 48, p. 158, ll. 5–8; and the sources cited in ibid., chap. 48, n. 18. The third line occurs independently in *T'ien-pao i-shih chu-kung-tiao*, p. 151, l. 8; a set of songs by Ch'en Ts'ao-an (1247–c. 1320), *Ch'üan Yüan san-ch'ü*, 1:145, l. 7; a song suite by T'ung-t'ung (14th century), ibid., 2:1261, ll. 11–12; *Yüan-ch'ü hsüan*, 1:798, l. 20; *Yüan-ch'ü hsüan wai-pien*, 2:382, l. 1; a song suite by Ch'ang Lun (1493–1526), *Ch'üan Ming san-ch'ü*, 2:1558, l. 6; and an anonymous song suite in *Yung-hsi yüeh-fu*, *ts'e* 4, p. 44a, ll. 4–5. The poem as a whole, with one variant in the fourth line, occurs in *Wu-wang fa Chou p'ing-hua*, p. 19, ll. 13–14; *Hsüan-ho i-shih*, p. 52, ll. 7–8; and *Shui-hu ch'üan-chuan*, vol. 1, ch. 2, p. 25, ll. 13–14.

29. This four-character expression occurs in *Pai-chia kung-an*, *chüan* 1, p. 6b, l. 7.

30. See Roy, *The Plum in the Golden Vase*, vol. 2, chap. 21, n. 52.

31. The recitation that follows is the earliest extant version of a story that was further elaborated in a variety of literary genres during the later Ming and Ch'ing dynasties. For an important study of the evolution of this tale, see Beata Grant, "The Spiritual Saga of Woman Huang: From Pollution to Purification," in *Ritual Opera, Operatic Ritual: "Mu-lien Rescues His Mother" in Chinese Popular Culture*, ed. David Johnson (Berkeley: Chinese Popular Culture Project, 1989), pp. 224–311.

32. This four-character expression occurs in *[Hsiao-shih] Chin-kang k'o-i [hui-yao chu-chieh]*, *chüan* 1, p. 651, lower register, l. 18.

33. This four-character expression occurs in *Ju-ju chü-shih yü-lu, i-chi* (second collection), *chüan* 1, p. 4a. l. 14; a quatrain by Wang Ch'u-i (1142–1217), *Ch'üan Chin shih*, 2:47, l. 9; a lyric by Li Tao-ch'un (late 13th century), *Ch'üan Chin Yüan tz'u*, 2:1227, lower register, ll. 1–2; *[Hsiao-shih] Chin-kang k'o-i [hui-yao chu-chieh]*, *chüan* 1, p. 651, lower register, l. 18; and *Yao-shih pen-yüan kung-te pao-chüan*, 14:315, l. 3.

34. This four-character expression also occurs in *Cheng-hsin ch'u-i wu hsiu cheng tzu-tsai pao-chüan*, 3:43, l. 3.

35. This four-character expression for perfect enlightenment also occurs in a poem by Wang Ch'u-i (1142–1217), *Ch'üan Chin shih*, 2:13, l. 10.

36. This formulaic four-character expression occurs in a poem by Wang An-shih (1021–86), *Ch'üan Sung shih*, 10:6620, l. 9; a lyric by Chao Ch'ang-ch'ing (12th century), *Ch'üan Sung tz'u*, 3:1806, upper register, l. 11; *Kuan-shih-yin p'u-sa pen-hsing ching*, p. 17a, l. 6; a lyric by Shu Hsün (14th century), *Ch'üan Chin Yüan tz'u*, 2:1089, upper register, l. 5; *Shen-hsiang ch'üan-pien*, *chüan* 631, p. 17a, ll. 5–6; and *Cheng-hsin ch'u-i wu hsiu cheng tzu-tsai pao-chüan*, 3:46, l. 1.

37. This four-character expression also occurs in *K'u-kung wu-tao chüan*, 1:96, l. 3.

38. This four-character expression also occurs in a lyric by Ma Yü (1123–83), *Ch'üan Chin Yüan tz'u*, 1:278, upper register, l. 5; an anonymous lyric from the Chin-Yüan period, ibid., 2:1274, upper register, l. 5; and *Han Hsiang-tzu chiu-tu Wen-kung sheng-hsien chi*, *chüan* 1, scene 11, p. 22a, l. 7.

39. This line also occurs in *Wei-wei pu-tung T'ai-shan shen-ken chieh-kuo pao-chüan*, 3:440, l. 2.

40. This couplet recurs as part of the funeral obsequies for Hsi-men Ch'ing in the *Chin P'ing Mei tz'u-hua*, vol. 4, ch. 80, p. 7a, l. 9. The above five sentences occur, with minor textual variation, in *Ju-ju chü-shih yü-lu, chia-chi* (first collection), *chüan* 1, p. 3b, l. 12–p. 4a, l. 1; and *[Hsiao-shih] Chin-kang k'o-i [hui-yao chu-chieh]*, *chüan* 1, p. 656, upper register, l. 21–lower register, l. 8.

41. These two lines are taken verbatim from a poem by Liu Yü-hsi (772–842), *Ch'üan T'ang shih*, vol. 6, *chüan* 357, p. 4015, l. 3.

42. For the famous parable of the burning house, see *The Lotus Sutra*, trans. Burton Watson (New York: Columbia University Press, 1993), pp. 56–79.

43. This formulaic four-character expression occurs ubiquitously in Chinese literature. See, e.g., a statement attributed to the Buddhist monk Chih-hsien (d. 898), *Tsu-t'ang chi*, *chüan* 19, p. 420, l. 16; *Tun-huang pien-wen chi*, 2:669, l. 9; an anonymous Yüan dynasty song, *Ch'üan Yüan san-ch'ü*, 2:1695, l. 6; a set of songs by T'ang Yin (1470–1524), *Ch'üan Ming san-ch'ü*, 1:1070, l. 10; an anonymous song suite in *Yung-hsi yüeh-fu*, ts'e 7. p. 26a, l. 6; and an abundance of other occurrences, too numerous to list.

44. This quatrain is attributed to Hsü Shou-hsin (1033–1108), *Ch'üan Sung shih*, 12:8381, l. 8. A variant of the last couplet occurs in *Mu-lien chiu-mu ch'üan-shan*

hsi-wen, chüan 1, p. 11a, ll. 2–3. The entire text of the recitation up to this point also occurs, with minor textual variation, in *Pao-chien chi*, scene 41, p. 74, ll. 20–26.

45. This four-character expression occurs in *K'ung-ts'ung-tzu* (The K'ung family masters' anthology), probably comp. Wang Su (195–256), in *Pai-tzu ch'üan-shu* (Complete works of the hundred philosophers), fac. repr., 8 vols. (Hang-chou: Che-chiang jen-min ch'u-pan she, 1984), vol. 1, *chüan* 1, ch. 9, p. 10a, ll. 7–8; a memorial by Han Tzu-hsi (d. 541), in *Wei-shu*, vol. 4, *chüan* 60, p. 1335, l. 15; and a memorial by Chu Hsi (1130–1200) submitted in 1180, in *Hui-an hsien-sheng Chu Wen-kung wen-chi*, *chüan* 11, p. 13b, l. 4.

46. This four-character expression occurs in a poem by Han Wo (844–923), *Ch'üan T'ang shih*, vol. 10, *chüan* 682, p. 7821, l. 8.

47. Close variants of this couplet occur in *Huang T'ing-tao yeh-tsou Liu-hsing ma*, scene 2, p. 96, ll. 6–7; the prosimetric tz'u-hua narrative *Shih Kuan-shou ch'i Liu Tu-sai shang-yüan shih-wu yeh k'an-teng chuan* (Story of how Shih Kuan-shou's wife Liu Tu-sai went to view the lantern festival on the fifteenth day of the new year), in *Ming Ch'eng-hua shuo-ch'ang tz'u-hua ts'ung-k'an*, ts'e 9, p. 8a, ll. 7–8; *Yao-shih pen-yüan kung-te pao-chüan*, 14:210, ll. 1–2; and *San-pao t'ai-chien Hsi-yang chi t'ung-su yen-i*, vol. 1, ch. 47, p. 610, l. 6.

48. This formulaic four-character expression occurs ubiquitously in Chinese vernacular literature. See, e.g., *Yüan-ch'ü hsüan*, 1:369, l. 7; *Yüan-ch'ü hsüan wai-pien*, 1:27, l. 17; *K'an p'i-hsüeh tan-cheng Erh-lang Shen*, p. 249, l. 7; *Hsiang-nang yüan*, scene 4, p. 27a, l. 4; *San-kuo chih t'ung-su yen-i*, vol. 2, *chüan* 19, p. 915, l. 6; *Shui-hu ch'üan-chuan*, vol. 1, ch. 1, p. 7, l. 9; a set of songs by Ch'en To (fl. early 16th century), *Ch'üan Ming san-ch'ü*, 1:510, l. 7; *Ming-chu chi*, scene 5, p. 12, l. 9; *Hung-fu chi*, scene 19, p. 38, l. 12; *Ssu-hsi chi*, scene 31, p. 76, l. 12; *Hai-fu shan-t'ang tz'u-kao, chüan* 4, p. 187, l. 13; *Sui-T'ang liang-ch'ao shih-chuan, chüan* 5, ch. 49, p. 51b, l. 6; and a host of other occurrences, too numerous to list.

49. For the Dragon Flower Assembly, see ch. 68, n. 16 above. Very similar lines occur in a poem by Wang Kang (11th century), *Ch'üan Sung shih*, 7:4908, l. 13; and *Yüan-ch'ü hsüan wai-pien*, 2:691, ll. 10–11. A virtually identical line also recurs in the *Chin P'ing Mei tz'u-hua*, vol. 5, ch. 88, p. 9a, l. 6.

50. A synonymous variant of this four-character expression occurs in *Shen-i fu* (Rhapsody on the divine wonders [of physiognomy]), attributed to Ch'en T'uan (895–989), in *Shen-hsiang ch'üan-pien, chüan* 636, p. 53b, l. 8; and *Yüan-ch'ü hsüan*, 2:623, l. 17. It occurs in the same form as in the novel in *Mu-lien chiu-mu ch'üan-shan hsi-wen, chüan* 1, p. 11b, l. 8.

51. This formulaic four-character expression occurs ubiquitously in Chinese literature. See, e.g., a poem by the Buddhist monk K'uei-chi (d. 682), *Ch'üan T'ang shih pu-pien*, 2:688, l. 9; the prose commentary to a long poem by Emperor T'ai-tsung of the Sung dynasty (r. 976–97), *Ch'üan Sung shih*, 1:326, l. 6; a poem by Shao Yung (1011–77), ibid., 7:4701, l. 5; a lyric by Chang Kang (1083–1166), *Ch'üan Sung tz'u*, 2:923, upper register, l. 7; a lyric by Wang Che (1112–70), *Ch'üan Chin Yüan tz'u*, 1:186, lower register, l. 13; a quatrain by T'an Ch'u-tuan (1123–85), *Ch'üan Chin shih*, 1:340, l. 16; a set of quatrains by Ch'iu Ch'u-chi (1148–1227), ibid., 2:168, l. 6; *Kuan-shih-yin p'u-sa pen-hsing ching*, p. 22a, l. 2; *Yüan-ch'ü hsüan*, 2:792, ll. 14–15; *Chang Ku-lao chung-kua ch'ü Wen-nü*, p. 491, l. 1; a set of songs by Lu Chih (cs 1268), *Ch'üan Yüan san-ch'ü*, 1:114, l. 8; a song suite by Kuan Han-ch'ing (13th century), ibid., 1:178,

l. 1; a lyric by Ku Hsün (1418–1505), *Ch'üan Ming tz'u*, 1:280, lower register, l. 16; *Shuang-chu chi*, scene 24, p. 74, l. 12; a set of songs by Li K'ai-hsien (1502–68), the author's pref. to which is dated 1544, *Li K'ai-hsien chi*, 3:873, l. 6; a song suite by Wang Yin (16th century) written in 1569, *Ch'üan Ming san-ch'ü*, 3:2679, l. 13; *Yü-chüeh chi*, scene 29, p. 89, l. 2; *Hsi-yu chi*, vol. 1, ch. 11, p. 115, l. 3; and a host of other occurrences, too numerous to list. It also recurs in the *Chin P'ing mei tz'u-hua*, vol. 5, ch. 91, p. 1a, l. 4.

52. A version of this quatrain, with minor textual variations, occurs in *[Hsiao-shih] Chin-kang k'o-i [hui-yao chu-chieh]*, *chüan* 3, p. 678, middle register, ll. 19–20. It occurs in the same form as in the novel in *Pao-chien chi*, scene 41, p. 75, ll. 7–8.

53. This four-character expression occurs in *Tun-huang pien-wen chi*, 2:775, l. 9; and a lyric by Ma Yü (1123–83), *Ch'üan Chin Yüan tz'u*, 1:396, lower register, l. 14.

54. This four-character expression occurs in a poem attributed to Lü Tung-pin (9th century), *Ch'üan T'ang shih*, vol. 12, *chüan* 858, p. 9704, l. 13; *Tun-huang pien-wen chi*, 2:775, l. 10; a set of songs in *Tun-huang ch'ü chiao-lu*, p. 150, l. 1; a poem by Wang Che (1112–70), *Ch'üan Chin shih*, 1:194, l. 10; *Tung Chieh-yüan Hsi-hsiang chi*, *chüan* 8, p. 161, l. 6; a lyric by Ma Yü (1123–83), *Ch'üan Chin Yüan tz'u*, 1:395, upper register, l. 14; a lyric by Hou Shan-yüan (12th century), ibid., 1:514, lower register, ll. 14–15; a lyric by Ch'ang-ch'üan-tzu (13th century), ibid., 1:587, lower register, ll. 5–6; and a song suite by Yao Shou-chung (13th century), *Ch'üan Yüan san-ch'ü*, 1:321, l. 4.

55. This line occurs verbatim in *P'o-hsieh hsien-cheng yao-shih chüan*, 2:332, ll. 2–3; *Cheng-hsin ch'u-i wu hsiu cheng tzu-tsai pao-chüan*, 3:14, ll. 3–4; and *Wei-wei pu-tung T'ai-shan shen-ken chieh-kuo pao-chüan*, 3:573, l. 4. The entire quatrain, with an insignificant textual variation in the second line, occurs in *[Hsiao-shih] Chin-kang k'o-i [hui-yao chu-chieh]*, *chüan* 3, p. 685, upper register, ll. 23–24. It occurs in the same form as in the novel in *Pao-chien chi*, scene 41, p. 75, ll. 6–7.

56. This formulaic four-character expression occurs ubiquitously in Chinese literature. See, e.g., *Ch'ien-fu lun* (The comments of a recluse), by Wang Fu (c. 90–165) (Shanghai: Shang-hai ku-chi ch'u-pan she, 1978), *chüan* 1, ch. 4, p. 36, l. 11; a poem by Li Ch'iao (644–713), *Ch'üan T'ang shih*, vol. 2, *chüan* 57, p. 690, l. 7; a poem by Ch'en Tzu-ang (661–702), ibid., vol. 2, *chüan* 83, p. 902, l. 12; a quatrain by Li Ch'ün-yü (c. 813–c. 861), ibid., vol. 9, *chüan* 570, p. 6610, l. 8; the literary tale *Tung-ch'eng lao-fu chuan* (The old man of the eastern wall), by Ch'en Hung-tsu (9th century), in *T'ang Sung ch'uan-ch'i chi*, p. 118, l. 13; a poem by Shao Yung (1011–77), *Ch'üan Sung shih*, 7:4468, l. 7; a poem by Su Shih (1037–1101), *Su Shih shih-chi*, vol. 1, *chüan* 1, p. 26, l. 5; a lyric by Han Shih-chung (1089–1151), *Ch'üan Sung tz'u*, 2:1032, upper register, l. 14; a quatrain by Ma Yü (1123–83), *Ch'üan Chin shih*, 1:251, l. 4; a song by Lu Chih (cs 1268), *Ch'üan Yüan san-ch'ü*, 1:114, l. 13; *Yüan-ch'ü hsüan*, 1:259, l. 8; *Yüan-ch'ü hsüan wai-pien*, 1:328, l. 4; *Shih Hung-chao lung-hu chün-ch'en hui*, p. 234, l. 1; *K'an p'i-hsüeh tan-cheng Erh-lang Shen*, p. 246, l. 15; *Yu-kuei chi*, scene 14, p. 39, l. 4; a song by Chu Yu-tun (1379–1439), *Ch'üan Ming san-ch'ü*, 1:301, l. 6; *Chin-ch'ai chi*, scene 67, p. 121, l. 18; *P'o-yao chi*, *chüan* 1, scene 11, p. 33b, l. 4; *Shen-hsiang ch'üan-pien*, *chüan* 632, p. 28a, l. 4; *K'u-kung wu-tao chüan*, 1:89, l. 3; *Pao-chien chi*, scene 5, p. 13, l. 23; *Mu-lien chiu-mu ch'üan-shan hsi-wen*, *chüan* 1, p. 10b, ll. 6–7; and an abundance of other occurrences, too numerous to list. It also recurs in the *Chin P'ing Mei tz'u-hua*, vol. 5, ch. 91, p. 7a, ll. 8–9.

57. Variants of this four-character expression occur in a famous rhapsody entitled *Ch'i-fa* (Seven stimuli), by Mei Ch'eng (d. 141 B.C.), in *Wen-hsüan*, vol. 2, *chüan* 34, p. 5b, l. 2; the biography of Wang Ying (d. 516), in *Nan shih* (History of the Southern dynasties), comp. Li Yen-shou (7th century), completed in 659, 6 vols. (Peking: Chung-hua shu-chü, 1975), vol. 2, *chüan* 23, p. 621, l. 11; *Wu Tzu-hsü pien-wen*, 1:20, l. 14; and *Yang-chia fu shih-tai chung-yung yen-i chih-chuan*, vol. 1, *chüan* 4, p. 43b, l. 8. It occurs in the same form as in the novel in *Shui-hu ch'üan-chuan*, vol. 3, ch. 58, p. 972, l. 13.

58. This formulaic four-character expression occurs in *Yü Chung-chü t'i-shih yü shang-huang*, p. 67, l. 15; *K'u-kung wu-tao chüan*, 1:90, l. 2; *Shui-hu ch'üan-chuan*, vol. 1, ch. 12, p. 179, l. 4; *Hsi-yu chi*, vol. 1, ch. 16, p. 188, l. 3; *San-pao t'ai-chien Hsi-yang chi t'ung-su yen-i*, vol. 1, ch. 26, p. 343, l. 11; and an abundance of other occurrences, too numerous to list.

59. A variant of this four-character expression occurs in *K'u-kung wu-tao chüan*, 1:90, l. 3. It occurs in the same form as in the novel in *Hsi-yu chi*, vol. 2, ch. 75, p. 864, l. 1.

60. This four-character expression occurs ubiquitously in Chinese literature. See, e.g., *Hsi-i hsien-sheng chuan* (Biography of Master Hsi-i [Ch'en T'uan]), by P'ang Chüeh (11th century), in *Ch'ing-so kao-i, ch'ien-chi, chüan* 8, p. 72, l. 5; *Kuan-shih-yin p'u-sa pen-hsing ching*, p. 40b, l. 6; a lyric by Wang Che (1112–70), *Ch'üan Chin Yüan tz'u*, 1:238, upper register, l. 8; a lyric by Ma Yü (1123–83), ibid., 1:341, upper register, l. 10; a lyric by Wang Tan-kuei (12th century), ibid., 1:490, upper register, l. 12; *Yüan-ch'ü hsüan*, 4:1343, l. 15; *Yüan-ch'ü hsüan wai-pien*, 3:829, l. 1; a set of songs by Chang Ch'üan-i (14th century), *Ch'üan Ming san-ch'ü*, 1:234, ll. 13–14; *Hsiao-p'in chi*, p. 88, l. 5; *Shuang-chu chi*, scene 44, p. 157, l. 10; *Li Yün-ch'ing te-wu sheng-chen*, scene 4, p. 16b, l. 7; *K'u-kung wu-tao chüan*, 1:91, l. 1; a set of songs written by Li K'ai-hsien (1502–68) in 1531, *Li K'ai-hsien chi*, 3:912, l. 10; *Yao-shih pen-yüan kung-te pao-chüan*, 14:361, l. 4; *Ku-Hang hung-mei chi*, p. 5a, l. 6; *Ts'an-T'ang Wu-tai shih yen-i chuan*, ch. 3, p. 6, l. 15; and an abundance of other occurrences, too numerous to list. It also recurs in the *Chin P'ing Mei tz'u-hua*, vol. 4, ch. 75, p. 1b, l. 5.

61. The above two sentences are similar in meaning to, and contain some of the same wording as, a passage in *K'u-kung wu-tao chüan*, 1:90. l. 2–91. l. 2.

62. This four-character expression occurs in a song suite by Chu Ying-ch'en (16th century), *Ch'üan Ming san-ch'ü*, 2:1269, l. 13.

63. This four-character expression occurs in *Ju-ju chü-shih yü-lu, chia-chi* (first collection), *chüan* 1, p. 1a, l. 11; and *[Hsiao-shih] Chen-k'ung pao-chüan*, 19:265, ll. 6–7.

64. This couplet occurs in *[Hsiao-shih] Chin-kang k'o-i [hui-yao chu-chieh]*, *chüan* 8, p. 743, upper register, l. 18.

65. This song occurs in *Pao-chien chi*, scene 41, p. 74, ll. 6–8.

66. Four-character variants of this expression occur in Philip B. Yampolsky's recension of the Tun-huang manuscript of *The Platform Sutra of the Sixth Patriarch* (New York: Columbia University Press, 1967), p. 25, l. 2; *Lu-shan Yüan-kung hua*, p. 183, ll. 13–14; *[Hsiao-shih] Chin-kang k'o-i [hui-yao chu-chieh]*, *chüan* 1, p. 467, upper register, l. 16; and *Kuan-shih-yin p'u-sa pen-hsing ching*, p. 125b, l. 5. It occurs in the same form as in the novel in a set of quatrains by Ko Sheng-chung (1072–1144), *Ch'üan Sung shih*, 24:15696, l. 11; a gatha by the Buddhist monk Huai-shen (1077–1132),

ibid., 24;16117, l. 3; a set of poems by the Sung dynasty poet Chang Yün-hsin, ibid., 72:45438, l. 16; *Yüan-ch'ü hsüan wai-pien*, 3:959, l. 16; and *San-pao t'ai-chien Hsi-yang chi t'ung-su yen-i*, vol. 1, ch. 2, p. 18, l. 14.

67. This expression occurs in an encomium composed in 1118 by the Buddhist monk Te-hung (1071–1128), *Ch'üan Sung shih*, 23:15349, l. 14; and *[Hsiao-shih] Chin-kang k'o-i [hui-yao chu-chieh]*, *chüan* 2, p. 671, upper register, l. 10.

68. These two clauses occur in ibid., *chüan* 1, p. 653, middle register, l. 13.

69. Versions of the formulaic invocation embodied in this sentence occur near the beginning of ibid., *chüan* 1, p. 652, lower register, ll. 7–8, 14, and 21–22; *Fo-shuo Huang-chi chieh-kuo pao-chüan*, 10:224, l. 7–225, l. 3; *Yao-shih pen-yüan kung-te pao-chüan*, 14:197, l. 5–198, l. 4; *P'u-ming ju-lai wu-wei liao-i pao-chüan*, 4:379, l, 6–380, l. 2; and *[Hsiao-shih] Chen-k'ung sao-hsin pao-chüan*, 18:399, ll. 1–4.

70. This quatrain has already appeared in the novel. See Roy, *The Plum in the Golden Vase*, vol. 3, chap. 51, p. 246, ll. 29–36; and n. 51.

71. This four-character expression occurs in *Seng-ni kung-fan*, scene 1, p. 336, l. 6.

72. Versions of this introductory couplet occur in *Fo-shuo Huang-chi chieh-kuo pao-chüan*, 10:228, l. 5; *Yao-shih pen-yüan kung-te pao-chüan*, 14:201, l. 2; and *P'u-ching ju-lai yao-shih pao-chüan*, 5:23, ll. 2–3.

73. This formulaic four-character expression occurs ubiquitously in Chinese literature. See, e.g., a Taoist ritual text by Tu Kuang-t'ing (850–933), *Ch'üan T'ang wen*, vol. 19, *chüan* 927, p. 2b, l. 7; a speech attributed to the Buddhist monk Kuang-yün (10th century), *Tsu-t'ang chi*, *chüan* 13, p. 292, l. 3; a quatrain by Emperor T'ai-tsung of the Sung dynasty (r. 976–97), *Ch'üan Sung shih*, 1:420, l. 13; a poem by Su Shih (1037–1101) written in 1095, *Su Shih shih-chi*, vol. 7, *chüan* 39, p. 2127, l. 6; *Yüan-ch'ü hsüan*, 2:584, l. 16; *Yüan-ch'ü hsüan wai-pien*, 1:58, ll. 19–20; a song by Chia Chung-ming (1343–c. 1422), *Ch'üan Ming san-ch'ü*, 1:182, l. 3; *Chien-teng hsin-hua*, *chüan* 1, p. 12, l. 1; a song by Chu Yu-tun (1379–1439), *Ch'üan Ming san-ch'ü*, 1:288, l. 2; *Su Wu mu-yang chi*, *chüan* 1, scene 10, p. 25a, l. 1; *Ku-ch'eng chi*, *chüan* 1, scene 12, p. 22a, l. 6; *Yü-huan chi*, scene 15, p. 51, l. 10; a lyric by Ch'en Hsün (1385–1462), *Ch'üan Ming tz'u*, 1:246, lower register, l. 14; a lyric by Ku Hsün (1418–1505), ibid., 1:294, lower register, l. 9; a song suite by Ch'en To (fl. early 16th century), *Ch'üan Ming san-ch'ü*, 1:657, l. 7; *Tung-t'ien hsüan-chi*, scene 4, p. 12b, l. 2; *Ssu-hsi chi*, scene 29, p. 72, l. 9; *Hai-fu shan-t'ang tz'u-kao*, *chüan* 2a, p. 99, l. 5; *Mu-lien chiu-mu ch'üan-shan hsi-wen*, *chüan* 3, p. 72a, l. 7; *Ch'üan-Han chih-chuan*, vol. 3, *chüan* 1, p. 3b, l. 10; *Hsi-yu chi*, vol. 1, ch. 37, p. 422, l. 13; and an abundance of other occurrences, too numerous to list.

74. This formulaic four-character expression occurs ubiquitously in Chinese literature. See, e.g., a lyric said to have circulated in 1125 that allegedly foretold the collapse of the Northern Sung dynasty, in *Ch'ing-yeh lu* (Anecdotes recorded on clear nights), comp. Yü Wen-pao (13th century), *Shuo-fu san-chung*, 4:1735, p. 3a, l. 4; the same poem as quoted without attribution in *Hsüan-ho i-shih*, p. 71, l. 11; *Meng-liang lu*, *chüan* 14, p. 247, l. 6; *Yüan-ch'ü hsüan wai-pien*, 2:561, l. 5; *Sha-kou chi*, scene 35, p. 120, l. 4; a song suite by Chu Yu-tun (1379–1439), *Ch'üan-Ming san-ch'ü*, 1:346, l. 7; *Fo-shuo Huang-chi chieh-kuo pao-chüan*, 10:394, l. 6; *Li Yün-ch'ing te-wu sheng-chen*, scene 4, p. 16b, l. 12; *Meng-mu san-i*, scene 1, p. 1a, ll. 10–11; *Chin-tiao chi*, *chüan* 2, scene 17, p. 23b, l. 5; *Mu-lien chiu-mu ch'üan-shan hsi-wen*, *chüan* 1, p. 21b, l. 6; *Ch'eng-yün chuan*, *chüan* 1, p. 1a, l. 8; *Kuan-yüan chi*, scene 30, p. 65, l. 3; *Pa-i*

chi, scene 2, p. 3, l. 3; *Ch'üan-Han chih-chuan*, vol. 3, *chüan* 1, p. 4a, l. 8; *Hsi-yu chi*, vol. 1, ch. 37, p. 431, l. 6; *San-pao t'ai-chien Hsi-yang chi t'ung-su yen-i*, vol. 1, ch. 2, p. 24, l. 14; a set of songs by Hsüeh Lun-tao (c. 1531–c. 1600), *Ch'üan Ming san-ch'ü*, 3:2743, ll. 9–10; *Yang-chia fu shih-tai chung-yung yen-i chih-chuan*, vol. 2, *chüan* 8, p. 1a, l. 5; *Sui-T'ang liang-ch'ao shih-chuan*, *chüan* 12, ch. 119, p. 37a, l. 5; and an abundance of other occurrences, too numerous to list.

75. This formulaic four-character expression occurs ubiquitously in Chinese vernacular literature, with variant orthographies for the first syllable but essentially the same meaning. See, e.g., *Yüan-ch'ü hsüan*, 2:683, l. 9; and 4:1587, l. 3; *Lo-yang san-kuai chi*, p. 66, ll. 8 and 14; *Nü ku-ku shuo-fa sheng-t'ang chi*, scene 3, p. 9b, l. 13; *Shih Chen-jen ssu-sheng so pai-yüan*, scene 3, p. 9b, l. 13; the anonymous Ming tsa-chü drama *Chu sheng-shou wan-kuo lai-ch'ao* (In order to celebrate the emperor's birthday a myriad states come to pay homage), in *Ku-pen Yüan Ming tsa-chü*, vol. 4, scene 1, p. 1a, l. 5; *Hsiu-ju chi*, scene 31, p. 86, l. 6; a song suite by Ch'en To (fl. early 16th century), *Ch'üan Ming san-ch'ü*, 1:627, l. 8; *Liu-ch'ing jih-cha* (Daily jottings worthy of preservation), by T'ien I-heng (1524–c. 1574), pref. dated 1572, fac. repr. of 1609 ed. (Shanghai: Shang-hai ku-chi ch'u-pan she, 1985), *chüan* 27, p. 10a, l. 2; *Mu-lien chiu-mu ch'üan-shan hsi-wen*, *chüan* 1, p. 31b, l. 1; *Hsi-yu chi*, vol. 1, ch. 8, p. 85, l. 16; and *San-pao t'ai-chien Hsi-yang chi t'ung-su yen-i*, vol. 1, ch. 2, p. 25, l. 12. It also recurs, in the alternate orthography, in the *Chin P'ing Mei tz'u-hua*, vol. 4, ch. 74, p. 14a, l. 3.

76. This four-character expression occurs in *Fo-ting-hsin Kuan-shih-yin p'u-sa ta t'o-lo-ni ching* (Kuan-shih-yin Bodhisattva's great Dhāranā sutra of the Buddha's essence), 3 fascicles, in *Tun-huang pao-tsang* (Treasures from Tun-huang), comp. Huang Yung-wu, 140 vols. (Taipei: Hsin-wen-feng ch'u-pan kung-ssu, 1981–86), vol. 132, p. 66, upper register, l. 9; a lyric by Ma Yü (1123–83), *Ch'üan Chin Yüan tz'u*, 1:353, lower register, ll. 4–5; and *Yüan-ch'ü hsüan wai-pien*, 2:420, l. 15.

77. This formulaic four-character expression occurs ubiquitously in Chinese literature. See, e.g., *P'ei Hsing Ch'uan-ch'i*, p. 78, l. 11; *I-chien chih*, vol. 1, *i-chih* (second collection), *chüan* 11, p. 275, ll. 4–5; *Tung Chieh-yüan Hsi-hsiang chi*, *chüan* 8, p. 160, l. 7; *Liu Chih-yüan chu-kung-tiao [chiao-chu]*, part 1, p. 19, l. 1; *San-kuo chih p'ing-hua*, p. 34, l. 4; *Yüan-ch'ü hsüan wai-pien*, 1:134, l. 2; *Shih Hung-chao lung-hu chün-ch'en hui*, p. 220, l. 15; *Chi Ya-fan chin-man ch'an-huo*, p. 276, l. 1; *Hsi-hu san-t'a chi*, p. 28, l. 16; *Pai Niang-tzu yung-chen Lei-feng T'a*, p. 430, l. 6; *K'an p'i-hsüeh tan-cheng Erh-lang Shen*, p. 245, l. 5; *Pai-yüeh t'ing chi*, *chüan* 2, scene 43, p. 41a, l. 1; the middle-period vernacular story *Ho-t'ung wen-tzu chi* (The story of the contract), in *Ch'ing-p'ing shan-t'ang hua-pen*, p. 35, l. 8; *K'uai-tsui Li Ts'ui-lien chi*, p. 53, l. 5; *San-kuo chih t'ung-su yen-i*, vol. 1, *chüan* 4, p. 158, l. 18; *Chiang Shih yüeh-li chi*, *chüan* 4, scene 39, p. 17a, l. 2; *Shui-hu ch'üan-chuan*, vol. 1, ch. 2, p. 26, l. 9; *Lien-huan chi*, *chüan* 2, scene 30, p. 76, l. 3; *Ts'ao-lu chi*, *chüan* 4, scene 47, p. 16a, l. 1; *Hsi-yu chi*, vol. 1, ch. 12, p. 132, l. 5; *San-pao t'ai-chien Hsi-yang chi t'ung-su yen-i*, vol. 1, ch. 16, p. 208, l. 7; *Ta-T'ang Ch'in-wang tz'u-hua*, vol. 2, *chüan* 6, ch. 42, p. 18b, l. 5; and an abundance of other occurrences, too numerous to list. It also recurs three times in the *Chin P'ing Mei tz'u-hua*, vol. 5, ch. 91, p. 8a, l. 6; p. 8b, l. 1; and p. 9b, l. 1.

78. This four-character expression occurs in *T'an-shih wu-wei pao-chüan*, 1:346, l. 4; *P'o-hsieh hsien-cheng yao-shih chüan*, 2:26, l. 1; *Cheng-hsin ch'u-i wu hsiu cheng tzu-tsai pao-chüan*, 3:23, l. 4; *Wei-wei pu-tung T'ai-shan shen-ken chieh-kuo pao-chüan*,

3:396, l. 4; *Yao-shih pen-yüan kung-te pao-chüan*, 14:356, l. 3; and *[Hsiao-shih] Chen-k'ung pao-chüan*, 19:295, l. 2. It also recurs in the *Chin P'ing Mei tz'u-hua*, vol. 4, ch. 74, p. 17a, l. 10.

79. This four-character expression occurs in *Ling-pao wu-liang tu-jen shang-p'in miao-ching*, chüan 1, p. 5a, l. 6; *Sou-shen chi* (Kou Tao-hsing), 2:875, ll. 11–12; a long poem by Emperor T'ai-tsung of the Sung dynasty (r. 976–97), *Ch'üan Sung shih*, 1:386, l. 11; *Wu-wang fa Chou p'ing-hua*, p. 3, l. 7; *Shui-hu ch'üan-chuan*, vol. 2, ch. 33, p. 514, l. 14; *Tu Li-niang mu-se huan-hun*, 2:536, l. 19; and *Ta-T'ang Ch'in-wang tz'u-hua*, vol. 1, chüan 1, ch. 5, p. 57a, l. 7. It also recurs in the *Chin P'ing Mei tz'u-hua*, vol. 4, ch. 74, p. 14b, ll. 7–8.

80. This four-character expression occurs in *Ta-T'ang San-tsang ch'ü-ching shih-hua*, episode 2, p. 2, l. 1; *Sha-kou chi*, scene 10, p. 30, l. 9; *Ming-chu chi*, scene 35, p. 112, l. 10; and *Yü-ching t'ai*, scene 31, p. 85, l. 1.

81. This five-character expression occurs in *Ta Mu-kan-lien ming-chien chiu-mu pien-wen* (Transformation text on Mahāmaudgalyāyana rescuing his mother from the underworld), dated 921, in *Tun-huang pien-wen chi*, 2:721, l. 11.

82. This four-character expression occurs in *Ta-T'ang San-tsang ch'ü-ching shih-hua*, episode 10, p. 23, l. 5; and *San Sui p'ing-yao chuan*, chüan 1, ch. 1, p. 5a, l. 8.

83. On this proverbial couplet, see above, chap. 62, n. 48.

84. This line occurs verbatim in *[Hsiao-shih] Chen-k'ung sao-hsin pao-chüan*, 18:539, l. 2.

85. This five-character expression occurs in *T'ien-pao i-shih chu-kung-tiao*, p. 249, l. 11; and *Hai-fu shan-t'ang tz'u-kao*, chüan 3, p. 151, l. 5.

86. See Roy, *The Plum in the Golden Vase*, vol. 1, chap. 5, n. 24.

87. This four-character expression occurs in *Hua-teng chiao Lien-nü ch'eng-Fo chi*, p. 205, l. 10; *Hsiang-nang chi*, scene 23, p. 65, l. 1; and *Shui-hu ch'üan-chuan*, vol. 3, ch. 84, p. 1392, l. 13.

88. This formulaic four-character expression occurs ubiquitously in Chinese vernacular literature. See, e.g., *Yüan-ch'ü hsüan*, 3:1070, l. 9; *Sha-kou chi*, scene 20, p. 75, l. 1; *Hua-teng chiao Lien-nü ch'eng-Fo chi*, p. 193, l. 13; *Shih-wu kuan hsi-yen ch'eng ch'iao-huo*, p. 706, l. 1; *Pao-tzu Ho-shang tzu huan-su*, p. 119, l. 21; *Nü ku-ku shuo-fa sheng-t'ang chi*, scene 3, p. 9b, l. 13; *Nan Hsi-hsiang chi* (Lu Ts'ai), chüan 1, scene 17, p. 366, l. 1; *Shih Chen-jen ssu-sheng so pai-yüan*, scene 3, p. 9b, l. 13; *Seng-ni kung-fan*, scene 1, p. 333, l. 4; *Hsi-yu chi*, vol. 1, ch. 27, p. 312, l. 1; *Mu-lien chiu-mu ch'üan-shan hsi-wen*, chüan 1, p. 42b, l. 5; *P'u-ching ju-lai yao-shih pao-chüan*, 5:67, l. 5; *Pai-chia kung-an*, chüan 2, ch. 16, p. 21a, l. 4; *San-pao t'ai-chien Hsi-yang chi t'ung-su yen-i*, vol. 1, ch. 14, p. 182, l. 1; and an abundance of other occurrences, too numerous to list. It also recurs in the *Chin P'ing Mei tz'u-hua*, vol. 4, ch. 74, p. 16a, l. 1; and p. 16b, l. 4.

89. See Roy, *The Plum in the Golden Vase*, vol. 1, chap. 5, n. 24.

90. See ibid., vol. 2, chap. 26, n. 14.

91. This four-character expression occurs in *Chü-ting chi*, chüan 1, scene 9, p. 22b, l. 2.

92. This formulaic four-character expression occurs ubiquitously in Chinese vernacular literature. See, e.g., a lyric by Chu Tun-ju (1081–1159), *Ch'üan Sung tz'u*, 2:839, lower register, l. 4; *Chang Hsieh chuang-yüan*, scene 11, p. 62, l. 7; *Yüan-ch'ü hsüan wai-pien*, 2:417, l. 18; *Cheng Chieh-shih li-kung shen-pi kung*, p. 660, l. 8; *Liang-shan wu-hu ta chieh-lao*, scene 2, p. 3b, l. 4; *P'o-yao chi*, chüan 1, scene 12, p. 34b, l. 5;

an anonymous song suite in *Sheng-shih hsin-sheng*, p. 531, l. 9; an anonymous song-suite in *Yung-hsi yüeh-fu*, ts'e 6, p. 13a, ll. 1–2; and *Huang-Ming k'ai-yün ying-wu chuan*, *chüan* 1, p. 15b, l. 5.

93. This four-character expression occurs in *[Hsiao-shih] Chin-kang k'o-i [hui-yao chu-chieh]*, *chüan* 9, p. 753, upper register, l. 12; and p. 755, upper register, l. 8.

94. This sentence occurs in ibid., *chüan* 9, p. 753, middle register, l. 1.

95. This formulaic four-character expression occurs ubiquitously in Chinese vernacular literature. See, e.g., a poem by Ma Yü (1123–83), *Ch'üan Chin shih*, 1:293, l. 12; a poem by Liu Ch'u-hsüan (1147–1203), ibid., 2:121, l. 14; a lyric by Wang Ch'u-i (1142–1217), *Ch'üan Chin Yüan tz'u*, 1:444, lower register, l. 10; *Cheng-hsin ch'u-i wu hsiu cheng tzu-tsai pao-chüan*, 3:19, l. 3; *P'u-ming ju-lai wu-wei liao-i pao-chüan*, 4:487, ll. 2–3; *P'u-ching ju-lai yao-shih pao-chüan*, 5:141, ll. 9–10; and *San-pao t'ai-chien Hsi-yang chi t'ung-su yen-i*, vol. 1, ch. 2, p. 18, l. 7.

96. This four-character expression occurs in *K'u-kung wu-tao chüan*, 1:211, l. 1; *Wei-wei pu-tung T'ai-shan shen-ken chieh-kuo pao-chüan*, 3:444, l. 3; and *Yao-shih pen-yüan kung-te pao-chüan*, 14:210, l. 3.

97. This formulaic four-character expression occurs ubiquitously in Chinese literature. See, e.g., a poem by the Buddhist monk Hsi-ch'ien (700–790), *Ch'üan T'ang shih pu-pien*, 2:925, ll. 11–12; a statement attributed to the Buddhist monk I-hsüan (d. 867), *Ku tsun-su yü-lu*, *chüan* 4, p. 105b, upper register, ll. 8–9; the Buddhist compendium *Tsung-ching lu* (The mirror of the source), comp. Yen-shou (904–75), in *Taishō shinshū daizōkyō*, vol. 48, no. 2016, p. 421, lower register, l. 8; a poem by Huang T'ing-chien (1045–1105), *Ch'üan Sung shih*, 17:11708, l. 8; a speech attributed to the Buddhist monk Tao-k'ai (1043–1118), *Wu-teng hui-yüan*, vol. 3, *chüan* 14, p. 883, l. 7; a lyric by Wang Che (1112–70), *Ch'üan Chin Yüan tz'u*, 1:171, upper register, l. 2; a lyric by Ma Yü (1123–83), ibid., 1:289, upper register, l. 15; a lyric by Hou Shan-yüan (12th century), ibid., 1:506, lower register, l. 4; a lyric by Ch'ang-ch'üan-tzu (13th century), ibid., 1:584, upper register, l. 10; *[Hsiao-shih] Chin-kang k'o-i [hui-yao chu-chieh]*, *chüan* 7, p. 727, lower register, l. 24; *Chang Hsieh chuang-yüan*, scene 12, p. 68, l. 9; a song suite by Tseng Jui (c. 1260–c. 1330), *Ch'üan Yüan san-ch'ü*, 1:517, l. 8; *Yüan-ch'ü hsüan*, 4:1329, l. 9; *Hsing-t'ien Feng-yüeh t'ung-hsüan chi*, p. 5b, ll. 7–8; *Yao-shih pen-yüan kung-te pao-chüan*, 14:307, l. 4; *P'u-ming ju-lai wu-wei liao-i pao-chüan*, 4:477, l. 2; *Mu-lien chiu-mu ch'üan-shan hsi-wen*, *chüan* 2, p. 16b, l. 1; *[Hsiao-shih] Chen-k'ung sao-hsin pao-chüan*, 18:414, l. 4; and an abundance of other occurrences, too numerous to list.

98. This four-character expression occurs in *[Hsiao-shih] Chin-kang k'o-i [hui-yao chu-chieh]*, *chüan* 9, p. 755, upper register, l. 18; *Huang-chi chin-tan chiu-lien cheng-hsin kuei-chen huan-hsiang pao-chüan*, 8:479, l. 2; *P'u-ming ju-lai wu-wei liao-i pao-chüan*, 4:525, l. 6; and *[Hsiao-shih] Chen-k'ung sao-hsin pao-chüan*, 19:255, ll. 3–4.

99. This sentence occurs in *Huang-chi chin-tan chiu-lien cheng-hsin kuei-chen huan-hsiang pao-chüan*, 8:479, l. 2.

100. This four-character expression occurs in ibid., 8:479, l. 3.

101. This four-character expression occurs in *P'u-ming ju-lai wu-wei liao-i pao-chüan*, 4:504, l. 4; *P'u-ching ju-lai yao-shih pao-chüan*, 5:127, l. 8; *[Hsiao-shih] Chen-k'ung sao-hsin pao-chüan*, 19:229, l. 3; and *[Hsiao-shih] Chen-k'ung pao-chüan*, 19:278, l. 7.

102. This entire line occurs verbatim in *Yao-shih pen-yüan kung-te pao-chüan*, 14:216, l. 4.

103. This formulaic four-character expression occurs ubiquitously in Chinese literature. See, e.g., a quatrain by Chang Fang-p'ing (1007–1091), *Ch'üan Sung shih*,
6:3849, l. 7; a poem by Su Che (1039–1112), ibid., 15:10131, l. 15; a poem by Wang
Che (1112–70), *Ch'üan Chin shih*, 1:144, l. 8; a lyric by Ma Yü (1123–83), *Ch'üan
Chin Yüan tz'u*, 1:331, lower register, l. 9; a lyric by T'an Ch'u-tuan (1123–85), ibid.,
1:399, lower register, l. 10; a lyric by Wang Ch'u-i (1142–1217), ibid., 1:435, lower
register, l. 15; *Yüan-ch'ü hsüan*, 3:1073, ll. 13–14; *Yüan-ch'ü hsüan wai-pien*, 2:691,
l. 14; *[Hsiao-shih] Chin-kang k'o-i [hui-yao chu-chieh]*, *chüan* 7, p. 733, lower register,
l. 7; a lyric by Chu Yün-ming (1460–1526), *Ch'üan Ming tz'u*, 2:419, lower register, l.
8; *Yüeh-ming Ho-shang tu Liu Ts'ui*, p. 433, l. 12; *P'u-ming ju-lai wu-wei liao-i pao-
chüan*, 4:573, l. 2; *Ch'ien-t'ang hu-yin Chi-tien Ch'an-shih yü-lu*, p. 7a, l. 9; *Hsi-yu chi*,
vol. 1, ch. 7, p. 70, l. 14; and a host of other occurrences, too numerous to list.

104. Versions of this formulaic invocation, usually involving the numbers 1 through
10, with considerable textual variation, occur in *Huang-chi chin-tan chiu-lien cheng-
hsin kuei-chen huan-hsiang pao-chüan*, 8:480, ll. 1–5; *K'u-kung wu-tao chüan*, 1:204,
l. 4–206, l. 2; *T'an-shih wu-wei pao-chüan*, 1:534, l. 3–535, l. 3; *P'o-hsieh hsien-cheng
yao-shih chüan*, 2:503, l. 4–504, l. 3; *Cheng-hsin ch'u-i wu hsiu cheng tzu-tsai pao-
chüan*, 3:336, ll. 2–4; *Wei-wei pu-tung T'ai-shan shen-ken chieh-kuo pao-chüan*, 3:361,
l. 3–362, l. 1; *Yao-shih pen-yüan kung-te pao-chüan*, 14:383, l. 1–384, l. 2; and *[Hsiao-
shih] Chen-k'ung sao-hsin pao-chüan*, 19:250, l. 4–251, l. 4. The last line also occurs
independently in a gatha by the Buddhist monk K'o-ch'in (1063–1135), *Ch'üan Sung
shih*, 22:14418, l. 2; a gatha by the Buddhist monk Ch'ing-yüan (1067–1120), ibid.,
22:14716, ll. 12–13; *Yüan-wu Fo-kuo ch'an-shih yü-lu*, *chüan* 7, p. 743, lower register,
ll. 26–27; a poem by Wang Che (1112–70), *Ch'üan Chin shih*, 1:232, l. 13; *P'u-ming
ju-lai wu-wei liao-i pao-chüan*, 4:598, l. 7; *[Hsiao-shih] Chen-k'ung pao-chüan*, 19:299,
l. 13; and an abundance of other occurrences, too numerous to list.

105. An orthographic variant of this four-character expression occurs in an admonition made in 1388 by Chu Yüan-chang (1328–98), the founding emperor (r. 1368–98)
of the Ming dynasty, to Liu Ching (1340–1402), the second son of Liu Chi (1311–75).
See *Liu Chi chi* (Liu Chi's collected works), ed. Lin Chia-li (Hang-chou: Che-chiang
ku-chi ch'u-pan she, 1999), p. 668. l. 10.

106. This formulaic four-character expression occurs ubiquitously in Chinese vernacular literature. See, e.g., a lyric by Chou Pang-yen (1056–1121), *Ch'üan Sung tz'u*,
2:610, lower register, l. 3; a lyric by Wang Chih-tao (1093–1169), ibid., 2:1138, upper
register, l. 6; a song by Kuan Yün-shih (1286–1324), *Ch'üan Yüan san-ch'ü*, 1:365, l. 3;
a song by Chang K'o-chiu (1270–1348), ibid., 1:888, l. 4; a song suite by Chi Tzu-an
(14th century), ibid., 2:1458, l. 11; a song suite by T'ang Shih (14th-15th centuries),
ibid., 2:1491, l. 1; *Yüan-ch'ü hsüan*, 1:188, l. 3; a lyric by Ch'ü Yu (1341–1427), *Ch'üan
Ming tz'u pu-pien*, 1:50, upper register, l. 16; *Chien-teng yü-hua*, *chüan* 4, p. 271, l. 14;
Cho Wen-chün ssu-pen Hsiang-ju, scene 2, p. 120, l. 3; a lyric by Hsia Yen (1482–1548),
Ch'üan Ming tz'u, 2:699, upper register, l. 8; *Kuan-yüan chi*, scene 21, p. 43, l. 12; a
song suite by Shen Ching (1553–1610), *Ch'üan Ming san-ch'ü*, 3:3281, l. 8; and an
abundance of other occurrences, too numerous to list.

107. This formulaic four-character expression occurs ubiquitously in Chinese literature. See, e.g., an epitaph by Yang Chiung (650–c. 694), *Ch'üan T'ang wen*, vol. 5,
chüan 196, p. 1b, l. 1; a lyric by Ma Yü (1123–83), *Ch'üan Chin Yüan tz'u*, 1:395,
upper register, l. 13; a lyric by Hsü Yu-jen (1287–1364), ibid, 2:971, lower register, ll.

14–15; a song suite by T'ang Shih (14th–15th centuries), *Ch'üan Yüan san-ch'ü*, 2:1506, l. 12; *Yüan-ch'ü hsüan*, 2:480, l. 16; *T'ao Yüan-ming tung-li shang-chü*, scene 4, p. 14b, l. 5; *Ssu-shih hua-yüeh sai chiao-jung*, scene 1, p. 2b, l. 12; *Yü-huan chi*, scene 11, p. 37, l. 7; a song suite by Ch'en To (fl. early 16th century), *Ch'üan Ming san-ch'ü*, 1:572, l. 2; a lyric by Kuei Hua (1476–1527), *Ch'üan Ming tz'u*, 2:752, upper register, l. 7; a set of songs written in 1507 by K'ang Hai (1475–1541), *Ch'üan Ming san-ch'ü*, 1:1173, l. 13; *Chiang Shih yüeh-li chi*, chüan 4, scene 40, p. 20b, l. 8; *Yen-chih chi*, chüan 1, scene 9, p. 13b, l. 7; *Mu-lien chiu-mu ch'üan-shan hsi-wen*, chüan 3, p. 33b, l. 6; and *Mu-tan t'ing*, scene 53, p. 264, l. 8.

108. This formulaic four-character expression occurs ubiquitously in Chinese vernacular literature. See, e.g., a speech recorded in the biography of the Buddhist monk I-ts'un (822–908), in *Tsu-t'ang chi*, chüan 7, p. 169, l. 4; a speech attributed to the Buddhist monk Hsing-nien (926–93), *Wu-teng hui-yüan*, vol. 2, chüan 11, p. 681, l. 1; a letter by Chu Hsi (1130–1200), in *Hui-an hsien-sheng Chu Wen-kung wen-chi*, chüan 29, p. 15a, l. 4; *[Chi-p'ing chiao-chu] Hsi-hsiang chi*, play no. 4, scene 4, p. 166, ll. 7–8; a set of songs by Liu T'ing-hsin (14th century), *Ch'üan Yüan san-ch'ü*, 2:1431, l. 4; *Yüan-ch'ü hsüan*, 1:343, l. 20; *K'an p'i-hsüeh tan-cheng Erh-lang Shen*, p. 252, l. 14; *Shui-hu ch'üan-chuan*, vol. 2, ch. 29, p. 448, l. 12; a set of songs by Li K'ai-hsien (1502–68) written in 1531, *Li K'ai-hsien chi*, 3:918, l. 10; *Pao-chien chi*, scene 49, p. 88, l. 6; *Yü-chüeh chi*, scene 29, p. 87, l. 12; *Hai-fu shan-t'ang tz'u-kao*, chüan 3, p. 167, l. 8; *Hsi-yu chi*, vol. 2, ch. 67, p. 768, l. 13; a set of songs by Hsüeh Lun-tao (c. 1531–c. 1600), *Ch'üan Ming san-ch'ü*, 3:2819, l. 9; *Shih-hou chi*, scene 10, p. 32, l. 9; *Ta-T'ang Ch'in-wang tz'u-hua*, vol. 1, chüan 2, ch. 11, p. 28b, l. 8; and an abundance of other occurrences, too numerous to list.

109. Versions of the above four songs are preserved in the same order as that in which they occur in the novel in *Tz'u-lin chai-yen*, 1:38–40, where they are attributed to an otherwise unknown author named Chang Shan-fu. They are also preserved, but in a different order, in *Yung-hsi yüeh-fu*, ts'e 15b, pp. 23b–24a. The version in the novel is closest to that in *Yung-hsi yüeh-fu*.

110. This line occurs verbatim in *Yüeh-i t'u Ch'i*, scene 3, p. 10b, l. 5.

111. This four-character expression occurs ubiquitously in Chinese literature. See, e.g., a poem written in 1100 by Su Shih (1037–1101), *Su Shih shih-chi*, vol. 7, chüan 43, p. 2366, l. 11; a lyric by Chang Yüan-kan (1091–c. 1162), *Ch'üan Sung tz'u*, 2:1076, lower register, ll. 7–8; a lyric by Ni Ch'eng (cs 1138), ibid., 2:1332, upper register, l. 7; a lyric by Yüan Ch'ü-hua (cs 1145), ibid., 3:1500, lower register, l. 12; a lyric by Fan Tuan-ch'en (cs 1154), ibid., 3:1561, lower register, l. 4; a lyric by Chang Hsiao-hsiang (1132–69), ibid., 3:1688, upper register, l. 13; a lyric by Wu Ch'ien (1196–1262), ibid., 4:2761, upper register, l. 11; a lyric by Li Tseng-po (1198–c. 1265), ibid., 4:2819, upper register, ll. 5–6; a lyric by P'u Tao-yüan (1260–1336), *Ch'üan Chin Yüan tz'u*, 2:835, lower register, l. 8; a lyric by Ch'en To (fl. early 16th century), *Ch'üan Ming tz'u*, 2:473, upper register, l. 8; a lyric by Ch'en T'ing (cs 1502), ibid., 2:557, upper register, l. 11; a song suite by Ku Ting-ch'en (1473–1540), *Ch'üan Ming san-ch'ü*, 1:1106, l. 2; a song suite by Wu Kuo-pao (cs 1550), ibid., 2:2290, l. 5; and an abundance of other occurrences, too numerous to list.

112. This four-character expression occurs in an anonymous Sung dynasty lyric, *Ch'üan Sung tz'u*, 5:3660, lower register, l. 13.

CHAPTER 75

1. A variant of this four-character expression in which the first two characters are reversed occurs in *Yüan-ch'ü hsüan*, 1:297, l. 3; and 3:1073, l. 9. It occurs in the same form as in the novel in a lyric by Chang Chi-hsien (1092–1126), *Ch'üan Sung tz'u*, 2:756, lower register, l. 8; and a poem by Liu Ch'u-hsüan (1147–1203), *Ch'üan Chin shih*, 2:119, l. 5.

2. This four-character expression occurs in *Kuan-shih-yin p'u-sa pen-hsing ching*, p. 9a, ll. 2–3; and a lyric by Ch'ang-ch'üan-tzu (13th century), *Ch'üan Chin Yüan tz'u*, 1:589, lower register, l. 11.

3. The first and last couplets of this poem occur in the opening quatrain of *Yüeh-ming Ho-shang tu Liu Ts'ui*, p. 428, l. 2.

4. These two four-character lines occur in *P'u-sa ying-lo ching* (Sutra of the bodhisattva's necklace), trans. Chu Fo-nien (4th century), in *Taishō shinshū daizōkyō*, vol. 16, no. 656, *chüan* 8, ch. 24, p. 78, lower register, ll. 6–7. They occur frequently in later Chinese literature. See, e.g., *Yüan-ch'ü hsüan*, 1:299, l. 9; the early vernacular story *Yin-chih chi-shan* (A secret good deed accumulates merit), in *Ch'ing-p'ing shan-t'ang hua-pen*, p. 119, l. 4; *Ming-hsin pao-chien*, *chüan* 1, p. 1a, l. 5; *Chao-shih ku-erh chi*, *chüan* 2, scene 40, p. 34a, l. 6; *Yü-huan chi*, scene 31, p. 111, l. 1; *Jen chin shu ku-erh hsün-mu*, scene 1, p. 3a, l. 12; *Pa-i chi*, scene 39, p. 82, l. 10; *Chiao-hsiao chi*, *chüan* 2, scene 29, p. 37b, l. 1; *San-pao t'ai-chien Hsi-yang chi t'ung-su yen-i*, vol. 2, ch. 87, p. 1124, l. 15; and an abundance of other occurrences, too numerous to list. They occur together in reverse order in *[Hsin-pien] Liu Chih-yüan huan-hsiang Pai-t'u chi*, p. 35a, l. 12; *Shuang-chu chi*, scene 44, p. 160, l. 2; and, with a synonymous variant, in *P'u-ching ju-lai yao-shih pao-chüan*, 5:63, l. 4. The first line occurs independently in *Hua-teng chiao Lien-nü ch'eng-Fo chi*, p. 205, l. 15; and the second line occurs independently in *Mu-lien chiu-mu ch'üan-shan hsi-wen*, *chüan* 2, p. 20b, l. 10.

5. This four-character expression is an abbreviated version of a passage in the *Kuan-tzu*. See *Kuan-tzu chiao-cheng* (The *Kuan-tzu* collated and corrected), ed. and annot. Tai Wang (1837–73), in *Chu-tzu chi-ch'eng*, *chüan* 21, ch. 67, p. 349, l. 16. It occurs often in later Chinese literature. See, e.g., *Ta-pan nieh-p'an ching* (The Mahāparinirvānasūtra), trans. Dharmakṣema (fl. 385–433), in *Taishō shinshū daizōkyō*, vol. 12, no. 374, *chüan* 12, p. 437, middle register, ll. 20–21; a poem by the Buddhist monk I-po (741–821), *Ch'üan T'ang shih pu-pien*, 1:389, l. 4; a speech attributed to Bodhidharma (fl. 470–528), in *Tsu-t'ang chi*, *chüan* 2, p. 45, l. 22; a memorial submitted in 986 by Chao P'u (922–92), as quoted in *Shao-shih wen-chien lu* (Record of things heard and seen by Mr. Shao), by Shao Po-wen (1056–1134), author's preface dated 1132 (Peking: Chung-hua shu-chü, 1983), *chüan* 6, p. 49, l. 1; the prose commentary to a long poem by Emperor T'ai-tsung (r. 976–97) of the Sung dynasty, *Ch'üan Sung shih*, 1:335, l. 13; a speech quoted in *Yün-chi ch'i-ch'ien*, *chüan* 89, p. 545, right-hand column, ll. 2–3; a poem by Huang Lü (cs 1057), *Ch'üan Sung shih*, 11:7483, l. 16; *Yüan-shih shih-fan*, *chüan* 2, p. 92, ll. 8–9; *Yüan-ch'ü hsüan*, 4:1749, l. 21; *Hsiao-p'in chi*, p. 91, l. 13; *Shui-hu ch'üan-chuan*, vol. 2, ch. 45, p. 731, l. 5; *Yao-shih pen-yüan kung-te pao-chüan*, 14:301, l. 5; and the popular Taoist work *Hsüan-t'ien shang-ti ch'ui-chieh wen* (Admonitions of the Supreme Sovereign of the Mysterious Celestial Realm), in *Kuo-se t'ien-hsiang*, vol. 2, *chüan* 4, upper register, p. 53a, l. 2.

6. This formulaic four-character expression occurs ubiquitously in Chinese vernacular literature. See, e.g., *Yüan-ch'ü hsüan wai-pien*, 3:951, l. 20; *Wu-chieh Ch'an-shih ssu Hung-lien chi*, p. 137, l. 14; *Yüeh-ming Ho-shang tu Liu-ts'ui*, p. 428, l. 3; *Nü ku-ku shuo-fa sheng-t'ang chi*, scene 3, p. 9b, l. 13; and *Hsi-yu chi*, vol. 1, ch. 9, p. 93, l. 7. It also recurs in the *Chin P'ing Mei tz'u-hua*, vol. 5, ch. 88, p. 9a, l. 1.

7. These two lines, with one textual variant, occur in *Yüeh-ming Ho-shang tu Liu Ts'ui*, p. 428, l. 3.

8. The locus classicus of this four-character expression is a passage in the *Shu-ching* (Book of documents). See Legge, *The Shoo King or The Book of Historical Documents*, p. 158, line 5 of the Chinese text. It occurs ubiquitously in later Chinese literature. See, e.g., *Mo-tzu yin-te*, ch. 16, p. 26, ll. 2–3; a proclamation issued in 617 by Li Mi (582–619), as quoted in his biography in *Chiu T'ang shu*, vol. 7, *chüan* 53, p. 2215, l. 14; the prose preface to a set of poems by Yü Ch'ung (1033–81), *Ch'üan Sung shih*, 12:8361, l. 17; *Ho-lin yü-lu, ping-pien* (third section), *chüan* 1, p. 239, l. 4; a legal judgment issued by Hu Ying (cs 1232), in *Ming-kung shu-p'an ch'ing-ming chi* (A collection of enlightened judgments by famous gentlemen), pref. dated 1261, 2 vols. (Peking: Chung-hua shu-chü, 1987), vol. 2, *chüan* 14, p. 541, l. 11; a treatise composed in 1375 by Chu Yüan-chang (1328–98), the founding emperor (r. 1368–98) of the Ming dynasty, in *Ming T'ai-tsu chi* (Collected works of Emperor T'ai-tsu of the Ming dynasty), ed. Hu Shih-o (Ho-fei: Huang-shan shu-she, 1991), *chüan* 10, p. 216, l. 4; *Hua-ying chi*, p. 888, l. 20; the author's preface to *Ta-Sung chung-hsing yen-i*, vol. 1, p. 1b, l. 1; the author's preface to *Mu-lien chiu-mu ch'üan-shan hsi-wen*, p. 1b, l. 2; and an abundance of other occurrences, too numerous to list.

9. These ten lines occur in *Ming-hsin pao-chien*, *chüan* 2, p. 3b, ll. 6–8.

10. This formulaic four-character expression occurs ubiquitously in Chinese vernacular literature. See, e.g., *Yüan-ch'ü hsüan*, 2:479, ll. 8–9; *Yüan-ch'ü hsüan wai-pien*, 1:146, l. 10; *Nü ku-ku shuo-fa sheng-t'ang chi*, scene 3, p. 9b, l. 13; *Shih Chen-jen ssu-sheng so pai-yüan*, scene 1, p. 2b, l. 9; *Huang-chi chin-tan chiu-lien cheng-hsin kuei-chen huan-hsiang pao-chüan*, 8:73, l. 1; *San-yüan chi*, scene 33, p. 87, l. 8; *Shui-hu ch'üan-chuan*, vol. 1, ch. 17, p. 249, l. 4; *P'u-ming ju-lai wu-wei liao-i pao-chüan*, 4:402, l. 4; *P'u-ching ju-lai yao-shih pao-chüan*, 5:49, l. 4; *Mu-tan t'ing*, scene 23, p. 117, l. 6; and a host of other occurrences, too numerous to list.

11. The above four lines occur verbatim in *Yüeh-ming Ho-shang tu Liu Ts'ui*, p. 428, l. 3.

12. This four-character expression occurs in *Fo-ting hsin Kuan-shih-yin p'u-sa ta t'o-lo-ni ching*, p. 67, lower register, l. 8; *Chi Ya-fan chin-man ch'an-huo*, p. 275, l. 6; *Cheng Chieh-shih li-kung shen-pi kung*, p. 668, l. 3; *Chang Yü-hu wu-su nü-chen kuan*, scene 3, p. 613, l. 2; *Yüeh-ming Ho-shang tu Liu Ts'ui*, p. 433, l. 16; Chüeh-lien's (16th century) commentary on the *Chin-kang k'o-i, [Hsiao-shih] Chin-kang k'o-i [hui-yao chu-chieh]*, *chüan* 9, p. 754, middle register, l. 16; *San-pao t'ai-chien Hsi-yang chi t'ung-su yen-i*, vol. 1, ch. 11, p. 138, l. 14; and *Shih-hou chi*, scene 25, p. 87, l. 11.

13. These two lines occur in reverse order in *Yin-shan cheng-yao* (Correct essentials of nutrition), by Hu-ssu-hui (fl. early 14th century), completed in 1330 (Peking: Jen-min wei-sheng ch'u-pan she, 1986), *chüan* 1, p. 8, l. 8; and *San-pao t'ai-chien Hsi-yang chi t'ung-su yen-i*, vol. 1, ch. 11, p. 138, l. 2.

14. This paragraph on prenatal education reads like a paraphrase of a well-known passage in *Lieh-nü chuan* (Biographies of exemplary women), comp. Liu Hsiang (79–8 B.C.) (Taipei: Chung-hua shu-chü, 1972), *chüan* 1, p. 4a, l. 13–p. 4b, l. 5; and *The Position of Women in Early China According to the Lieh Nü Chuan*, trans. Albert Richard O'Hara (Taipei: Mei Ya Publications, 1971), p. 23, l. 20–p. 24, l. 9.

15. This formulaic four-character expression occurs in *Yüan-ch'ü hsüan*, 1:251, l. 12; and an anonymous song suite in *Yung-hsi yüeh-fu, ts'e* 9, p. 66a, l. 7.

16. For the phrase "carry rings and knot grass," see Roy, *The Plum in the Golden vase*, vol. 1, chap. 17, n. 42. This four-character expression recurs in the *Chin P'ing Mei tz'u-hua*, vol. 4, ch. 78, p. 1a, l. 9.

17. See Roy, *The Plum in the Golden Vase*, vol. 1, chap. 18, n. 9.

18. This four-character expression occurs in *Chang Hsieh chuang-yüan*, scene 19, p. 99, l. 14; an anonymous song quoted in *Tz'u-nüeh*, 3:281, l. 13; and an anonymous song suite in *Ch'ün-yin lei-hsüan*, 3:1940, l. 7. It also recurs in the *Chin P'ing Mei tz'u-hua*, vol. 4, ch. 77, p. 13b, l. 7; and vol. 5, ch. 91, p. 10b, l. 9.

19. See Roy, *The Plum in the Golden Vase*, vol. 1, chap. 11, nn. 13, 14, and 15.

20. The locus classicus for this couplet is a quatrain attributed to Ch'en Shu-pao (553–604), the last emperor of the Ch'en dynasty (r. 582–89), *Hsien-Ch'in Han Wei Chin Nan-pei ch'ao shih*, 3:2521, l. 11. It has become proverbial, and versions of it occur often in later Chinese literature. See, e.g., *Yüan-ch'ü hsüan wai-pien*, 3:814, l. 11; *San hsien-shen Pao Lung-t'u tuan-yüan*, p. 171, l. 9; *Chin-yin chi, chüan* 3, scene 25, p. 17b, l. 8; *Pai-she chi, chüan* 1, scene 11, p. 23a, l. 8; *P'o-yao chi, chüan* 1, scene 2, p. 5a, l. 3; *Yü-huan chi*, scene 17, p. 67, l. 2; *Hsin-ch'iao shih Han Wu mai ch'un-ch'ing*, p. 70, l. 12; *Pai-p'ao chi, chüan* 1, scene 10, p. 14b, l. 3; *Yü-chüeh chi*, scene 29, p. 88, l. 3; and *Su Ying huang-hou ying-wu chi, chüan* 2, scene 24, p. 12b, ll. 2–3.

21. This topic probably refers to the subject matter of play no. 3, scene 2, of *Hsi-hsiang chi*. See *[Chi-p'ing chiao-chu] Hsi-hsiang chi*, pp. 108–114; and *The Moon and the Zither: The Story of the Western Wing*, by Wang Shifu; trans. Stephen H. West and Wilt L. Idema (Berkeley: University of California Press, 1991), pp. 290–304.

22. This song by Ch'en To (fl. early 16th century) has already appeared in the novel. See Roy, *The Plum in the Golden Vase*, vol. 3, chap. 44, pp. 68, ll. 15–20; and p. 70, ll. 30–41; and the sources cited in n. 10.

23. This four-character expression occurs in a song suite by Chu Ying-ch'en (16th century), *Ch'üan Ming san-ch'ü*, 2:1268, l. 7; and *Mu-lien chiu-mu ch'üan-shan hsi-wen, chüan* 1, p. 56a, l. 2.

24. This line occurs in *Sha-kou chi*, scene 9, p. 27, l. 10.

25. This four-character expression occurs in *Ming-feng chi*, scene 34, p. 144, l. 7.

26. Variants of this line occur in a poem by Liu Pan (1023–89), *Ch'üan Sung shih*, 11:7103, l. 7; and an anonymous lyric from the Sung dynasty, *Ch'üan Sung tz'u*, 5:3836, lower register, l. 6.

27. This four-character expression occurs in *K'an p'i-hsüeh tan-cheng Erh-lang Shen*, p. 247, l. 8.

28. This four-character expression occurs in *Yüan-ch'ü hsüan*, 4:1688, ll. 8–9; *Yüan-ch'ü hsüan wai-pien*, 3:785, l. 19; a song by Sheng Ts'ung-chou (14th century), *Ch'üan Ming san-ch'ü*, 1:249, l. 8; a song suite by Chu Yu-tun (1379–1439), ibid., 1:368, l. 4;

and two anonymous song suites in *Yung-hsi yüeh-fu*, *ts'e* 8, p. 84b, l. 1; and *ts'e* 12, p. 53a, l. 6.

29. These four songs are by Ch'en To (fl. early 16th century), *Ch'üan Ming san-ch'ü*, 1:475–76. They are also preserved in *Nan-pei kung tz'u-chi*, vol. 2, *chüan* 4, pp. 234–35; and *Wu-sao ho-pien*, *ts'e* 4, *chüan* 4, pp. 31a–32a.

30. This four-character expression recurs in the *Chin P'ing Mei tz'u-hua*, vol. 5, ch. 84, p. 5b, l. 1.

31. This was the characteristic facial makeup of the clown in traditional Chinese drama.

32. Variants of this couplet occur in a speech attributed to the Buddhist monk Shun-te (868–937), in *Tsu-t'ang chi*, *chüan* 14, p. 312, l. 8; and *Shui-hu ch'üan-chuan*, vol. 1, ch. 21, p. 306, l. 12.

33. This idiomatic expression recurs in the *Chin P'ing Mei tz'u-hua*, vol. 4, ch. 75, p. 22a, l. 3.

34. This four-character expression recurs in ibid., vol. 4, ch. 75, p. 22a, l. 3; and p. 22b, l. 10.

35. This four-character expression is derived from a line in a famous essay by Han Yü (768–824). See *Han Ch'ang-li wen-chi chiao-chu*, *chüan* 1, p. 15, l. 6. It occurs ubiquitously in later Chinese literature. See, e.g., a lyric by Emperor Hui-tsung of the Sung dynasty (r. 1100–25), *Ch'üan Sung tz'u*, 2:898, upper register, l. 9; *Chu-tzu yü-lei*, vol. 2, *chüan* 20, p. 14a, l. 6; *Yüan-ch'ü hsüan*, 1:102, l. 17; *Hsiao-p'in chi*, p. 16, l. 2; an anonymous song suite in *Sheng-shih hsin-sheng*, p. 456, l. 7; *Ko tai hsiao*, scene 1, p. 119, ll. 9–10; *San-pao t'ai-chien Hsi-yang-chi t'ung-su yen-i*, vol. 2, ch. 77, p. 997, l. 13; and *Mu-tan t'ing*, scene 41, p. 208, ll. 5–6.

36. This four-character expression occurs in *Yüan-ch'ü hsüan*, 4:1692, l. 9; *Yüan-ch'ü hsüan wai-pien*, 1:215, l. 5; *Chin-ming ch'ih Wu Ch'ing feng Ai-ai*, p. 468, l. 16; *Shui-hu ch'üan-chuan*, vol. 3, ch. 65, p. 1106, l. 11; *Ssu-yu Chai ts'ung-shuo* (Collected observations from the Four Friends Studio), by Ho Liang-chün (1506–73) (Peking: Chung-hua shu-chü, 1959), *chüan* 8, p. 66, l. 12; and *Hsi-yu chi*, vol. 2, ch. 68, p.779, l. 12.

37. This formulaic four-character expression occurs ubiquitously in Chinese ver-nacular literature. See, e.g., *Yüan-ch'ü hsüan*, 2:611, l. 8; *Yüan-ch'ü hsüan wai-pien*, 2:635, l. 17; *Shui-hu ch'üan-chuan*, vol. 3, ch. 75, p. 1257, l. 11; *Hsi-yu chi*, vol. 1, ch. 31, p. 358, l. 12; and an abundance of other occurrences, too numerous to list.

38. This four-character expression occurs in *Ju-i chün chuan*, p. 9b, l. 2; and recurs in the *Chin P'ing Mei tz'u-hua*, vol. 4, ch. 79, p. 9a, l. 7.

39. This four-character expression occurs in *Yu-kuei chi*, scene 29, p. 89, l. 9; *Liang-shan wu-hu ta chieh-lao*, scene 4, p. 7a, ll. 12–13; and *Hsi-yu chi*, vol. 1, ch. 23, p. 256, l. 13.

40. Variants of this proverbial expression occur in a set of songs by Ma Chih-yüan (c. 1250–c. 1325), *Ch'üan Yüan san-ch'ü*, 1:254, ll. 2–3; *Ming-hsin Pao-chien*, *chüan* 2, p. 4a, l. 13; *Shui-hu ch'üan-chuan*, vol. 1, ch. 2, p. 29, ll. 7–8; and *Kuan-yüan chi*, scene 8, p. 14, l. 6. It occurs in the same form as in the novel in a speech attributed to the Buddhist monk Chih-yü (1185–1269), in *Hsü-t'ang Ho-shang yü-lu*, *chüan* 1, p. 991, lower register, l. 12. It recurs in the *Chin P'ing Mei tz'u-hua*, vol. 4, ch. 75, p. 24a, l. 2.

41. Variants of this four-character expression occur in *Wu Tzu-hsü pien-wen*, p. 18, l. 12; and *Hsin T'ang shu*, vol. 3, *chüan* 34, p. 882, l. 7. It occurs in the same form as

in the novel in a set of songs by Li K'ai-hsien (1502–68) written in 1531, *Li K'ai-hsien chi*, 3:914, l. 14; an anonymous song suite in *Yung-hsi yüeh-fu*, ts'e 5, p. 22b, ll. 5–6; *Pao-chien chi*, scene 6, p. 17, l. 9; *Hai-fu shan-t'ang tz'u-kao, chüan* 3, p. 147, l. 10; and *Ta-T'ang Ch'in-wang tz'u-hua*, vol. 1, *chüan* 2, ch. 9, p. 3b, l. 8.

42. This formulaic four-character expression occurs ubiquitously in Chinese vernacular literature. See, e.g., *Yüan-ch'ü hsüan*, 1:165, l. 21; a song suite by T'ang Shih (14th-15th centuries), *Ch'üan Ming san-ch'ü*, 1:102, l. 8; a set of songs by Chu Yu-tun (1379–1439), ibid., 1:330, l. 15; *Nü ku-ku shuo-fa sheng-t'ang chi*, scene 2, p. 7b, l. 11; and an abundance of other occurrences, too numerous to list.

43. A variant of this proverbial couplet, in which the two lines occur in reverse order, is recorded in a speech attributed to the Buddhist monk Jen-yung (11th century), *Wu-teng hui-yüan*, vol. 3, *chüan* 19, p. 1237, l. 9.

44. This reduplicative compound occurs ubiquitously in Chinese vernacular literature. See, e.g., a lyric by Chang Hsiao-hsiang (1132–69), *Ch'üan Sung tz'u*, 3:1697, lower register, l. 6; *Kuan-shih-yin p'u-sa pen-hsing ching*, p. 25a, l. 6; a song by Chou Wen-chih (d. 1334), *Ch'üan Yüan san-ch'ü*, 1:552, l. 6; a set of songs by Liu T'ing-hsin (14th century), ibid., 2:1430, l. 13; *Sha-kou chi*, scene 14, p. 48, ll. 1–2; *Chin-ming ch'ih Wu Ch'ing feng Ai-ai*, p. 468, l. 5; *Nü ku-ku shuo-fa sheng-t'ang chi*, scene 3, p. 13a, l. 6; *Chin-t'ung Yü-nü Chiao Hung chi*, p. 39, l. 6; *Fo-shuo Huang-chi chieh-kuo pao-chüan*, 10:267, l. 6; *Wu Lun-ch'üan Pei, chüan* 1, scene 4, p. 15b, l. 7; *Yüeh Fei p'o-lu tung-ch'uang chi, chüan* 1, scene 19, p. 31a, l. 1; *[Hsiao-shih] Chen-k'ung pao-chüan*, 19:285, l. 8; *Ssu-hsi chi*, scene 18, p. 46, ll. 10–11; *Yen-chih chi, chüan* 2, scene 37, p. 27a, l. 1; *Hsi-yu chi*, vol. 1, ch. 4, p. 39, l. 4; *Hai-ling i-shih*, p. 110, l. 8; and an abundance of other occurrences, too numerous to list.

45. A variant of this proverbial saying occurs in a quatrain by the Buddhist monk Chih-yü (1185–1269), *Hsü-t'ang Ho-shang yü-lu, chüan* 5, p. 1022, middle register, l. 6.

46. Variants of this line occur in *Shih Hung-chao lung-hu chün-ch'en hui*, p. 230, l. 1; *Chang Ku-lao chung-kua ch'ü Wen-nü*, p. 496, l. 9; *Ch'en Hsün-chien Mei-ling shih-ch'i chi*, p. 131, l. 13; and *Shui-hu ch'üan-chuan*, vol. 1, ch. 3, p. 51, l. 6.

47. This line has already occurred in the *Chin P'ing Mei tz'u-hua*, vol. 1, ch. 8, p. 11a, ll. 6–7. See Roy, *The Plum in the Golden Vase*, vol. 1, chap. 8, p. 165, ll. 28–29.

48. This line occurs verbatim in an anonymous lyric in *Ch'üan Chin Yüan tz'u*, 2:1297, lower register, l. 9; and *Yüan-ch'ü hsüan*, 3:1043, l. 19; and 3:1101, ll. 11–12.

49. This expression recurs in the *Chin P'ing Mei tz'u-hua*, vol. 5, ch. 92, p. 12a, l. 4.

50. This four-character expression occurs in *Yüan-shih shih-fan, chüan* 2, p. 115, l. 23; a document composed by Chu Hsi (1130–1200), *Hui-an hsien-sheng Chu Wen-kung wen-chi, pieh-chi* (separate collection), *chüan* 9, p. 13a, l. 8; *Yüan-ch'ü hsüan*, 1:342, l. 8; *Jen-tsung jen-mu chuan* (The story of how Emperor Jen-tsung [r. 1022–63] reclaimed his mother), fac. repr. in *Ming Ch'eng-hua shuo-ch'ang tz'u-hua ts'ung-k'an*, ts'e 4, p. 6a, ll. 11–12; *Pai-chia kung-an, chüan* 9, ch. 83, p. 16a, l. 1; and *Hsi-yu chi*, vol. 2, ch. 98, p. 1111, l. 8. It also recurs in the *Chin P'ing Mei tz'u-hua*, vol. 5, ch. 85, p. 9b, ll. 4–5; and ch. 86, p. 1b, l. 3.

51. An orthographic variant of this four-character expression occurs in a song by Kao Ying-ch'i (16th century), *Ch'üan Ming san-ch'ü*, 2:2299, l. 3.

52. This four-character expression occurs ubiquitously in Chinese literature. See, e.g., *Han-shu*, vol. 8, *chüan* 94b, p. 3834, l. 2; a speech attributed to K'ung Yen (d. 370)

in his biography in *Chin shu*, vol. 7, *chüan* 78, p. 2060, l. 7; a memorial by Wang Jung (468–94), *Ch'üan Shang-ku San-tai Ch'in Han San-kuo Liu-ch'ao wen, Ch'üan Ch'i wen* (Complete prose of the Ch'i dynasty), *chüan* 12, p. 5a, l. 5; a memorial by Yüan Fu (d. 540), *Pei shih*, vol. 2, *chüan* 16, p. 611, ll. 13–14; a speech attributed to Wei Cheng (580–643) in *Tzu-chih t'ung-chien*, vol. 3, *chüan* 193, p. 6076, l. 11; *Chin-yin chi, chüan* 2, scene 19, p. 28a, l. 9; *San-yüan chi*, scene 20, p. 54, ll. 8–9; *Shuang-chu chi*, scene 13, p. 37, l. 1; *T'ang-shu chih-chuan t'ung-su yen-i*, vol. 2, *chüan* 6, p. 42b, l. 6; *Lieh-kuo chih-chuan*, vol. 3, *chüan* 7, p. 42a, l. 2; *Mu-lien chiu-mu ch'üan-shan hsi-wen, chüan* 1, p. 46a, l. 10; *P'u-ching ju-lai yao-shih pao-chüan*, 5:107, l. 8; *Huang-Ming k'ai-yün ying-wu chuan, chüan* 2, p. 2b, l. 7; *Hsi-yu chi*, vol. 2, ch. 76, p. 867, l. 11; *Pai-chia kung-an, chüan* 3, ch. 21, p. 3a, ll. 6–7; *San-pao t'ai-chien Hsi-yang chi t'ung-su yen-i*, vol. 1, ch. 25, p. 323, l. 15; *Ta-T'ang Ch'in-wang tz'u-hua*, vol. 2, *chüan* 8, ch. 64, p. 69a, l. 5; *Sui-T'ang liang-ch'ao shih-chuan, chüan* 8, ch. 77, p. 36a, l. 7; and an abundance of other occurrences, too numerous to list.

53. See, Roy, *The Plum in the Golden Vase*, vol. 2, chap. 26, n. 12.

54. This four-character expression occurs in a lyric by Ko Ch'ang-keng (1134–1229), *Ch'üan Sung tz'u*, 4:2569, lower register, l. 2; and an anonymous song suite from the Yüan dynasty, *Ch'üan Yüan san-ch'ü*, 2:1656, l. 1.

55. This four-character expression occurs in *Huang-hua Yü tieh-ta Ts'ai Ko-ta*, scene 1, p. 2a, l. 9.

56. This formulaic four-character expression occurs ubiquitously in Chinese vernacular literature. See, e.g., *Shuang-chu chi*, scene 14, p. 40, ll. 9–10; a song suite by Ch'en To (fl. early 16th century), *Ch'üan Ming san-ch'ü*, 1:609, l. 8; *Ts'an-T'ang Wu-tai shih yen-i-chuan*, ch. 15, p. 51, ll. 6–7; *Mu-tan t'ing*, scene 48, p. 237, l. 8; a set of songs by Hsüeh Lun-tao (c. 1531–c. 1600), *Ch'üan Ming san-ch'ü*, 3:2791, l. 3; and an abundance of other occurrences, too numerous to list. It also recurs in the *Chin P'ing Mei tz'u-hua*, vol. 5, ch. 93, p. 11b, l. 9.

57. This four-character expression for the expendability of a wife or concubine occurs in *Yüan-ch'ü hsüan*, 1:291, ll. 19–20; 2:560, l. 15; and *Yüan-ch'ü hsüan wai-pien*, 3:825, l. 14.

58. This idiomatic expression recurs in the *Chin P'ing Mei tz'u-hua*, vol. 5, ch. 86, p. 6a, l. 5.

59. A variant of this four-character expression occurs in *Pei Sung chih-chuan, chüan* 5, p. 25a, l. 7.

60. For this allusion, see chap. 72, n. 44 above. A virtually identical line recurs in the *Chin P'ing Mei tz'u-hua*, vol. 4, ch. 77, p. 6b, l. 2.

CHAPTER 76

1. This line is from a lyric by Huang T'ing-chien (1045–1105), *Ch'üan Sung tz'u*, 1:395, upper register, l. 9. It occurs frequently in later Chinese literature. See, e.g., a lyric by Liu Ping-chung (13th century), *Ch'üan Chin Yüan tz'u*, 2:615, lower register, ll. 6–7; a lyric by Hsia Yen (1482–1548), *Ch'üan Ming tz'u*, 2:690, lower register, ll. 4–5; a song by Liang Ch'en-yü (1519–91), *Ch'üan Ming san-ch'ü*, 2:2178, l. 5; *Kuan-yüan chi*, scene 11, p. 21, l. 1; and an abundance of other occurrences, too numerous to list.

2. Consort Chen (183–221) was a famous beauty who was taken as consort by Ts'ao P'i (187–226), Emperor Wen of the Wei dynasty (r. 220–26), and posthumously raised to the status of empress. For her biography see *San-kuo chih*, vol. 1, *chüan* 5, pp. 159–63; and *Empresses and Consorts: Selections from Chen Shou's Records of the Three States with Pei Songzhi's Commentary*, trans. Robert Joe Cutter and William Gordon Crowell (Honolulu: University of Hawai'i Press, 1999), pp. 95–106.

3. See Roy, *The Plum in the Golden Vase*, vol. 2, chap. 26, n. 23.

4. This formulaic four-character expression occurs in *Tung Chieh-yüan Hsi-hsiang chi*, *chüan* 5, p. 108, l. 1; *Yang Wen lan-lu hu chuan*, p. 170, l. 9; and *Nan Hsi-hsiang chi* (Li Jih-hua), scene 34, p. 96, l. 11.

5. A variant of this proverbial saying occurs in *Chi-le pien* (Chicken ribs collection), by Chuang Ch'o (c. 1090–c. 1150), pref. dated 1133 (Peking: Chung-hua shu-chü, 1983), *chüan* 1, p. 18, l. 7; and *[Chiao-ting] Yüan-k'an tsa-chü san-shih chung*, p. 399, l. 1. It occurs in the same form as in the novel in the lost collection of anecdotes entitled *T'ung-yu chi* (Accounts of communication with the nether world), comp. Ch'en Shao (8th century), as quoted in *T'ai-p'ing kuang-chi*, vol. 8, *chüan* 363, p. 2886, ll. 2–3; and *Yeh-k'o ts'ung-shu*, *chüan* 29, p. 335, ll. 10–11, where it is suggested that the word *chi* (cock or rooster) may be intended to pun with the word *chi* (imperial favorite or concubine). Such a line does occur in an anonymous song suite in *Yung-hsi yüeh-fu*, ts'e 5, p. 22, l. 3. A variant of this saying also recurs in the *Chin P'ing Mei tz'u-hua*, vol. 5, ch. 86, p. 10b, l. 11.

6. Variants of this proverbial couplet occur ubiquitously in Chinese vernacular literature. See, e.g., *Chang Hsieh chuang-yüan*, scene 9, p. 51, ll. 1–2; *Yüan-ch'ü hsüan wai-pien*, 3:946, ll. 2–3; *Sha-kou chi*, scene 6, p. 20, ll. 9–10; *P'i-p'a chi*, scene 33, p. 185, l. 10; *Hsiang-nang chi*, scene 22, p. 61, l. 9; *Shuang-chu chi*, scene 33, p. 114, l. 7; *Shui-hu ch'üan-chuan*, vol. 2, ch. 28, p. 438, l. 3; *Ming-chu chi*, scene 25, p. 75, l. 5; *Ch'en Hsün-chien Mei-ling shih-ch'i chi*, p. 127, l. 7; *Pai-p'ao chi*, *chüan* 2, scene 29, p. 10b, l. 9; *Ssu-hsi chi*, scene 37, p. 94, ll. 9–10; *Huan-sha chi*, scene 13, p. 42, l. 9; *Kuan-yüan chi*, scene 11, p. 22, l. 11; *T'ou-pi chi*, *chüan* 1, scene 4, p. 12a, l. 4; *Shuang-lieh chi*, scene 8, p. 24, l. 4; *Hsi-yu chi*, vol. 1, ch. 28, p. 322, l. 6; *San-pao t'ai-chien Hsi-yang chi t'ung-su yen-i*, vol. 1, ch. 36, p. 470, l. 1; *Han-tan meng chi*, scene 4, p. 2301, l. 2; *I-hsia chi*, scene 10, p. 23, l. 7; and *Ta-T'ang Ch'in-wang tz'u-hua*, vol. 1, *chüan* 2, ch. 14, p. 52b, l. 1. A variant also recurs in the *Chin P'ing Mei tz'u-hua*, vol. 5, ch. 90, p. 12a, l. 2.

7. See Roy, *The Plum in the Golden Vase*, vol. 1, chap. 12, n. 40.

8. This four-character expression occurs in *Yüan-ch'ü hsüan*, 1:64, l. 18; *Yüan-ch'ü hsüan wai-pien*, 1:324, l. 7; *Hei Hsüan-feng chang-i shu-ts'ai*, scene 1, p. 97, l. 7; *Seng-ni kung-fan*, scene 4, p. 346, l. 8; and *Hsi-yu chi*, vol. 1, ch. 19, p. 215, l. 4.

9. Variants of these two lines occur in a speech attributed to the Buddhist monk Fa-yen (d. 1104) in *Ta-hui P'u-chüeh ch'an-shih tsung-men wu-k'u* (Arsenal of the Ch'an Master Ta-hui P'u-chüeh's sect), comp. Tao-ch'ien (12th century), originally completed in 1140, in *Taishō shinshū daizōkyō*, vol. 47, no. 1998b, p. 952, upper register, ll. 6–8; and a statement attributed to Chang Shang-ying (1043–1121) in *Ming-hsin pao-chien*, *chüan* 2, p. 2b, ll. 11–12.

10. This couplet recurs in the *Chin P'ing Mei tz'u-hua*, vol. 4, ch. 79, p. 12a, l. 6.

11. This formulaic four-character expression occurs ubiquitously in Chinese vernacular literature. See, e.g., a poem by Yang Wan-li (1127–1206), *Ch'üan Sung shih*,

42:26480, l. 7; a lyric by Pai P'u (1226–c. 1306), *Ch'üan Chin Yüan tz'u*, 2:646, lower register, l. 3; a song by Chang K'o-chiu (1270–1348), *Ch'üan Yüan san-ch'ü*, 1:900, l. 10; *Yüan-ch'ü hsüan*, 4:1627, l. 14; *Chin-t'ung Yü-nü Chiao Hung chi*, p. 32, l. 12; *Jen chin shu ku-erh hsün-mu*, scene 3, p. 11a, l. 3; *Shui-hu ch'üan-chuan*, vol. 3, ch. 75, p. 1254, l. 10; an anonymous song suite in *Yung-hsi yüeh-fu*, ts'e 8, p. 78a, l. 9; and *[Hsiao-shih] Chen-k'ung sao-hsin pao-chüan*, 19:224, ll. 2–3.

12. This four-character expression occurs in two sets of songs by Hsüeh Lun-tao (c. 1531–c. 1600), *Ch'üan Ming san-ch'ü*, 3:2802, l. 13; and 3:2834, l. 9.

13. A variant of this proverbial saying is quoted as being current in Nanking in the late sixteenth century in *K'o-tso chui-yü*, *chüan* 1, p. 10, l. 13.

14. This is an example of a *hsieh-hou yü*, in which the second part of a common saying is left out but implied. The second part of this saying, which is clearly implied here, is "but you've done a complete about-face." See Roy, *The Plum in the Golden Vase*, vol. 1, chap. 19, p. 387, ll. 36–37.

15. This four-character expression occurs in *Ta-Sung chung-hsing yen-i*, vol. 1, *chüan* 3, p. 21b, l. 1.

16. This four-character expression occurs in *Hai-ling i-shih*, p. 63, l. 10.

17. This four-character expression occurs in *Chiao Hung chuan*, p. 291, l. 3.

18. For this drama, see above, chap. 65, n. 91.

19. This is the fourth of the four short plays that constituted the lost fifteenth-century ch'uan-ch'i drama *Ssu-chieh chi*, which is not extant in its complete form, although excerpts from it are available in various late Ming anthologies. For an illuminating discussion of the plot of this play and the ironic function performed by its introduction at this point in the narrative, see Carlitz, "The Role of Drama in the *Chin P'ing Mei*," pp. 213–16.

20. This four-character expression occurs in *Shuang-lieh chi*, scene 21, p. 62, l. 3.

21. This four-character expression occurs in a statement by the Buddhist monk Tsung-kao (1089–1163), in *Ta-hui P'u-chüeh ch'an-shih yü-lu tsung-men wu-k'u*, p. 947, upper register, l. 18; a lyric by Shen Ying (cs 1160), *Ch'üan Sung tz'u*, 3:1657 upper register, l. 8; *Yüan-ch'ü hsüan*, 2:455, l. 19; and a song suite by Wang T'ing-hsiang (1474–1544), *Ch'üan Ming san-ch'ü*, 1:1108, l. 8.

22. This proverbial saying occurs in *Yüan-ch'ü hsüan*, 3:1032, l. 8; and 4:1362, ll. 19–20.

23. A variant of this couplet, in which the two lines occur in reverse order, is recorded in *Ku-chin t'an-kai* (A representative selection of anecdotes ancient and modern), comp. Feng Meng-lung (1574–1646), pref. dated 1620 (Fu-chou: Hai-hsia wen-i ch'u-pan she, 1985), *chüan* 29, p. 905, ll. 5–6.

24. This four-character expression occurs in *Hsiu-ju chi*, scene 19, p. 54, l. 1; *Hsi-yu chi*, vol. 1, ch. 30, p. 339, l. 7; and *San-pao t'ai-chien Hsi-yang chi t'ung-su yen-i*, vol. 1, ch. 40, p. 519, l. 5.

25. This four-character expression occurs in *Yüan-ch'ü hsüan*, 2:573, l. 6; 2:637, l. 20; and *Ts'an-T'ang Wu-tai shih yen-i chuan*, ch. 46, p. 183, l. 4.

26. For a description of this condiment, see Hu, *Food Plants of China*, pp. 106–7.

27. A synonymous variant of this four-character expression occurs in a poem by Yüan Chen (775–831), *Ch'üan T'ang shih*, vol. 6, *chüan* 413, p. 4574, l. 1; and *Chieh-an Lao-jen man-pi* (Casual notes by the Old Man of Self-restraint Studio), comp. Li Hsü (1505–93) (Peking: Chung-hua shu-chü, 1982), *chüan* 6, p. 222, l. 5. It occurs in

the same form as in the novel in a speech by the Buddhist monk Cheng-chüeh (1091–1157), as quoted in *Wan-sung Lao-jen p'ing-ch'ang T'ien-t'ung Chüeh ho-shang sung-ku Ts'ung-jung An lu* (A record from the Ts'ung-jung Monastery of the comments by the Old Man of Myriad Pines Studio on the poetic eulogies of the past by the monk Cheng-chüeh of the T'ien-t'ung Monastery), by the Buddhist monk Hsing-hsiu (1166–1246), in *Taishō shinshū daizōkyō*, vol. 48, no. 2004, *chüan* 3, p. 253, upper register, l. 21.

28. This four-character expression occurs in *Liu Chih-yüan chu-kung-tiao [chiao-chu]*, part 12, p. 154, l. 10.

29. See Roy, *The Plum in the Golden Vase*, vol. 1, chap. 9, n. 18.

30. This four-character expression occurs in *Hsi-yu chi*, vol. 1, ch. 39, p. 456, l. 9.

31. This four-character expression occurs in *Wang Wen-hsiu Wei-t'ang ch'i-yü chi*, scene 4, p. 9a, ll. 7–8; and *Han-tan meng chi*, scene 4, p. 2300, ll. 11–12.

32. See Roy, *The Plum in the Golden Vase*, vol. 2, chap. 34, n. 11.

33. A variant of this proverbial expression occurs in *K'uai-tsui Li Ts'ui-lien chi*, p. 63, l. 16.

34. A variant of this couplet occurs in the *Chin P'ing Mei tz'u-hua*, vol. 5, ch. 86, p. 8a, l. 5.

35. This quatrain has already appeared in the novel. See *Chin P'ing Mei tz'u-hua*, vol. 1, ch. 11, p. 11b, ll. 3–4; and Roy, *The Plum in the Golden Vase*, vol. 1, chap. 11, p. 223, ll. 26–33.

36. On this institution, see Charles O. Hucker, *A Dictionary of Official Titles in Imperial China* (Stanford: Stanford University Press, 1985), pp. 383–84, no. 4685.

37. This colloquial expression is the equivalent of "locking the barn door after the horse has fled."

38. See Roy, *The Plum in the Golden Vase*, vol. 3, chap. 52, n. 20.

39. See above, chap. 73, n. 15.

40. See Roy, *The Plum in the Golden Vase*, vol. 3, chap. 42, n. 10.

41. This example of Ying Po-chüeh's familiarity with the argot of the licensed quarters is intentionally opaque, and the commentators are not agreed on its interpretation. My translation is thus merely tentative. For my understanding of the tail end of the remark, see Roy, *The Plum in the Golden Vase*, vol. 2, chap. 32, n. 15.

42. This four-character expression occurs in a speech attributed to the Buddhist monk K'o-wen (1025–1102), *Ku tsun-su yü-lu*, *chüan* 43, p.364b, lower register, l. 4; a gatha by the Buddhist monk K'o-ch'in (1063–1135), *Ch'üan Sung shih*, 22:14420, l. 3; an encomium by the Buddhist monk Cheng-chüeh (1091–1157), ibid., 31:19860, l. 11; and a lyric written in 1246 by Li Tseng-po (1198–c. 1265), *Ch'üan Sung tz'u*, 4:2807, lower register, l. 8.

43. Variants of this proverbial couplet occur in *Pao Lung-t'u tuan pai-hu ching chuan* (The story of how Academician Pao judged the case of the white tiger demon), originally published in the 1470s, fac. repr. in *Ming Ch'eng-hua shuo-ch'ang tz'u-hua ts'ung-k'an*, ts'e 8, p. 5b, l. 12; *Huan-tai chi*, *chüan* 1, scene 14, p. 40b, l. 3; *Shui-hu ch'üan-chuan*, vol. 2, ch. 45, p. 745, l. 6; *Ts'ao Po-ming ts'o-k'an tsang chi*, p. 211, l. 14; and *Ch'un-wu chi*, scene 25, p. 68, l. 3. It occurs in the same form as in the novel in *Yüan-ch'ü hsüan*, 4:1371, l. 16; *Sha-kou chi*, scene 2, p. 4, l. 3; *P'i-p'a chi*, scene 28, p. 161, l. 5; *Ming-hsin pao-chien*, *chüan* 2, p. 2a, ll. 4–5; *Hsiang-nang chi*, scene 33, p. 101, l. 6; *Shang Lu san-yüan chi*, *chüan* 1, scene 12, p. 17a, l. 7; *Jen hsiao-tzu lieh-hsing wei shen*, p. 577, l. 9; *Mu-lien chiu-mu ch'üan-shan hsi-wen*, *chüan* 1, p. 73a, l. 6; *Pai-chia*

kung-an, chüan 7, ch. 59, p. 12a, l. 6; and *Ta-T'ang Ch'in-wang tz'u-hua*, vol. 1, *chüan* 2, ch. 10, p. 14b, ll. 2–3. It also recurs in the *Chin P'ing Mei tz'u-hua*, vol. 4, ch. 80, p. 12a, ll. 3–4.

44. This expression recurs in the *Chin P'ing Mei tz'u-hua*, vol. 5, ch. 100, p. 14a, ll. 5–6.

45. This line is a truncated form of two adjacent lines in the *Shih-ching* (Book of songs). See *Mao-shih yin-te* (Concordance to the Mao version of the *Book of Songs*) (Tokyo: Japan Council for East Asian Studies, 1962), song no. 255, p. 67, l. 5. These two lines are quoted ubiquitously in later Chinese literature. See, e.g., the prose commentary to a long poem by Emperor T'ai-tsung (r. 976–97) of the Sung dynasty, *Ch'üan Sung shih*, 1:322, l. 14; a poem by Hsü Chi (1028–1103), ibid., 11:7641, l. 11; *[Chi-p'ing chiao-chu] Hsi-hsiang chi*, play no. 2, scene 5, p. 91, l. 8; *Ta-Sung chung-hsing yen-i*, vol. 1, *chüan* 2, p. 5b, l. 11; *Sui-T'ang liang-ch'ao shih-chuan*, *chüan* 11, ch. 110, p. 60a, l. 7; and an abundance of other occurrences, too numerous to list.

46. This line is derived from a line in *Chuang-tzu*, which Burton Watson translates: "The friendship of a gentleman, they say, is insipid as water." See *Chuang-tzu yin-te*, ch. 20, p. 53, ll. 5–6; and Watson, *The Complete Works of Chuang Tzu*, ch. 20, p. 215, ll. 19–20.

47. Common variants of this couplet occur in *Yüan-ch'ü hsüan*, 2:454, l. 3; *Yüan-ch'ü hsüan wai-pien*, 2:382, l. 17; *Wei Feng-hsiang ku Yü-huan chi*, *chüan* 1, scene 4, p. 5b, l. 5; *Chiang Shih yüeh-li chi*, *chüan* 1, scene 9, p. 15a, l. 1; and *Yü-chüeh chi*, scene 22, p. 69, l. 12. It occurs in the same form as in the novel in *Shui-hu ch'üan-chuan*, vol. 1, ch. 22, p. 334, l. 14; and the second line occurs independently in *Wei Feng-hsiang ku Yü-huan chi*, *chüan* 1, scene 6, p. 14a, l. 1.

CHAPTER 77

1. This refers to Hsiao Yen (464–549), Emperor Wu (r. 502–49) of the Liang dynasty (502–57).

2. P'an Yü-nu (d. 502) was the favorite consort of Hsiao Pao-chüan (484–502), the feckless teenage ruler (r. 498–502) of the Southern Ch'i dynasty (479–502). She was a famous beauty, and after Hsiao Pao-chüan's assassination, Hsiao Yen, the founding ruler of the Liang dynasty, wanted to take her as a concubine but was dissuaded by one of his officials, and had her put to death.

3. This poem is by Lu Kuei-meng (fl. 865–881) and was written in response to one by his friend P'i Jih-hsiu (c. 834–c. 883). See *Ch'üan T'ang shih*, vol. 9, *chüan* 624, p. 7175, ll. 3–4. For P'i Jih-hsiu's poem, see ibid., *chüan* 613, p. 7070, ll. 4–5. The title of the original poem is "Wild Plum Blossoms Glimpsed during a Journey."

4. This four-character expression occurs in *Yu-kuei chi*, scene 38, p. 109, l. 3.

5. This four-character expression, with the meaning in which it is used in the novel, occurs in an autobiographical statement by Li Ts'ung-k'o (886–936), the last emperor (r. 934–36) of the Later T'ang dynasty (923–36), *Chiu Wu-tai shih*, vol. 2, *chüan* 46, p. 628, l. 8; *San-kuo chih t'ung-su yen-i*, vol. 2, *chüan* 17, p. 802, l. 21; *San-pao t'ai-chien Hsi-yang chi t'ung-su yen-i*, vol. 1, ch. 22, p. 287, l. 10; and *Ta-T'ang Ch'in-wang tz'u-hua*, vol. 1, *chüan* 1, ch. 7, p. 77a, ll. 5–6.

6. This expression recurs in the *Chin P'ing Mei tz'u-hua*, vol. 4, ch. 78, p. 17a, l. 4.

7. This formulaic four-character expression occurs in a lyric by Li Tseng-po (1198–c. 1265) composed in 1257, *Ch'üan Sung tz'u*, 4:2826, lower register, l. 2; *Yüan-ch'ü hsüan*, 1:152, l. 20; *Yüan-ch'ü hsüan wai-pien*, 2:692, l. 11; a lyric by Tung Chi (fl. late 14th century), *Ch'üan Ming tz'u*, 1:137, upper register, l. 12; *Ch'ien-chin chi*, scene 24, p. 77, l. 12; and *Shui-hu ch'üan-chuan*, vol. 3, ch. 71, p. 1205, l. 4. It also recurs in the *Chin P'ing Mei tz'u-hua*, vol. 5, ch. 96, p. 2b, ll. 1–2; and a synonymous variant occurs in ibid., vol. 5, ch. 89, p. 10b, l. 1.

8. This couplet occurs verbatim in *Tung Yung yü-hsien chuan*, p. 236, l. 12.

9. This four-character expression occurs in *Yüan-ch'ü hsüan*, 4:1718, l. 7.

10. This four-character expression occurs in a lyric by Hung K'uo (1117–84), *Ch'üan Sung tz'u*, 2:1389, upper register, l. 4; and *Pai-t'u chi*, scene 2, p. 2, l. 7.

11. This four-character expression occurs in a lyric by Wang Chih-tao (1093–1169), *Ch'üan Sung tz'u*, 2:1162, lower register, l. 10; a lyric by Chou Tuan-ch'en (13th century), ibid., 4:2651, upper register, l. 14; a song suite by Chou Wen-chih (d. 1334), *Ch'üan Yüan san-ch'ü*, 1:561, l. 6; and a lyric by Wu Ching-k'uei (1292–1355), *Ch'üan Chin Yüan tz'u*, 2:1048, lower register, ll. 2–3.

12. This formulaic four-character expression occurs ubiquitously in Chinese vernacular literature. See, e.g., *Yüan-ch'ü hsüan*, 3:861, l. 1; *Yüan-ch'ü hsüan wai-pien*, 1:117, l. 18; *Lü-weng san-hua Han-tan tien*, scene 3, p. 7b, l. 4; a song by Chang Ming-shan (14th century), *Ch'üan Yüan san-ch'ü*, 2:1283, l. 14; *Liang-shan wu-hu ta chieh-lao*, scene 2, p. 3a, l. 4; *Ssu-shih hua-yüeh sai chiao-jung*, scene 4, p. 9a, ll. 4–5; an anonymous song suite in *Sheng-shih hsin-sheng*, p. 418, l. 6; *Pao-chien chi*, scene 33, p. 61, l. 11; *Han Hsiang-tzu chiu-tu Wen-kung sheng-hsien chi*, chüan 2, scene 31, p. 29b, l. 3; and a host of other occurrences, too numerous to list.

13. The proximate source of this passage of descriptive parallel prose, with some textual variation, is *Shui-hu ch'üan-chuan*, vol. 1, ch. 10, p. 154, ll. 5–7.

14. This four-character expression occurs in *Chien-teng yü-hua*, chüan 5, p. 287, l. 12; and recurs in the *Chin P'ing Mei tz'u-hua*, vol. 5, ch. 82, p. 2b, l. 2.

15. For this allusion, see above, chap. 72, n. 44.

16. See Roy, *The Plum in the Golden Vase*, vol. 1, chap. 2, n. 47.

17. See ibid., chap. 8, n. 41.

18. This four-character expression occurs in *Yu-yang tsa-tsu* (Assorted notes from Yu-yang), comp. Tuan Ch'eng-shih (803–63) (Peking: Chung-hua shu-chü, 1981), *ch'ien-chi* (first collection), chüan 19, p. 184, l. 4; *Tu-yang tsa-pien* (Miscellaneous records from Tu-yang), compiled by Su O (9th century), originally completed in 876, in *Pi-chi hsiao-shuo ta-kuan*, vol. 1, ts'e 1, chüan 2, p. 4a, l. 8; *Ch'un-chu chi-wen*, chüan 9, p. 132, l. 5; *I-chien chih*, vol. 4, *pu* (supplement), chüan 12, p. 1663, l. 3; *Tu Li-niang mu-se huan-hun*, p. 535, l. 20; *Hsün-fang ya-chi*, vol. 2, chüan 4, p. 14b, l. 12; and *Ku-hang hung-mei chi*, chüan 8, p. 11b, l. 11. It also recurs in the *Chin P'ing Mei tz'u-hua*, vol. 5, ch. 84. p. 4a, l. 5.

19. The ultimate source of these four lines, with insignificant textual variation, is a quatrain by Lo Yin (833–909), *Ch'üan T'ang shih*, vol. 10, chüan 659, p. 7570, l. 8. It is quoted in the same form as in the novel, but without attribution, in *Hou-ts'un Ch'ien-chia shih chiao-chu* (Liu K'o-chuang's poems by a thousand authors edited and annotated), comp. Liu K'o-chuang (1187–1269), ed. and annot. Hu Wen-nung and Wang

Hao-sou (Kuei-yang: Kuei-chou jen-min ch'u-pan she, 1986), *chüan* 13, p. 376, ll. 4–5; and is also quoted without attribution in the popular primer *Shen-t'ung shih* (Poems by infant prodigies), traditionally attributed to Wang Chu (cs 1100), in *Chung-kuo ku-tai meng-hsüeh shu ta-kuan* (A corpus of traditional Chinese primers), comp. Lu Yang-t'ao (Shanghai: T'ung-chi ta-hsüeh ch'u-pan she, 1995), p. 273, right-hand column, ll. 12–15; which means that it would have been familiar to any literate person in six-teenth-century China. It also occurs in *Pai-t'u chi*, scene 17, p. 52, l. 4; *San-yüan chi*, scene 3, p. 5, ll. 3–4; *Ts'ai-lou chi*, scene 9, p. 25, ll. 20–21; *Shui-hu ch'üan-chuan*, vol. 1, ch. 24, p. 360, l. 8; *Tung Yung yü-hsien chuan*, p. 236, ll. 4–5; and *San Sui p'ing-yao chuan*, *chüan* 1, ch. 2, p. 14b, ll. 3–4. The first line also occurs independently in a song suite by Chu Yün-ming (1460–1526), *Ch'üan Ming san-ch'ü*, 1:780, l. 5; the last two lines occur independently in *Mu-lien chiu-mu ch'üan-shan hsi-wen*, *chüan* 1, p. 86a, l. 7; and the last line occurs independently in a lyric by Ku Hsün (1418–1505), *Ch'üan Ming tz'u*, 1:286, upper register, l. 2.

20. This four-character expression occurs in *Ta-T'ang Ch'in-wang tz'u-hua*, vol. 2, *chüan* 6, ch. 46, p. 49b, l. 5.

21. The locus classicus for this four-character expression is a line in the *Shih-ching* (Book of songs). See *Mao-shih yin-te*, song no, 41, p. 9. It occurs ubiquitously in later Chinese literature. See, e.g., a lyric by Hsiang Tzu-yin (1085–1152), *Ch'üan Sung tz'u*, 2:962, upper register, l. 6; *I-chien chih*, vol. 4, *pu* (supplement), *chüan* 20, p. 1740, l. 1; *P'o-yao chi*, *chüan* 2, scene 26, p. 30a, l. 5; a song suite by Wang Chiu-ssu (1468–1551), *Ch'üan Ming san-ch'ü*, 1:952, l. 8; *Wang Lan-ch'ing chen-lieh chuan*, scene 4, p. 9a, l. 7; and an anonymous song-suite in *Yung-hsi yüeh-fu*, ts'e 11, p. 71b, l. 4.

22. This four-character expression occurs in an epitaph for Li Po (701–62) written by Fan Ch'uan-cheng (cs 794), *Ch'üan T'ang wen*, vol. 13, *chüan* 614, p. 13b, l. 2; *Yü-huan chi*, scene 5, p. 11, l. 8; and *Liu sheng mi Lien chi*, *chüan* 3, p. 16a, l. 5.

23. This four-character expression for the separation of lovers is derived from a line in a famous poem by Po Chü-i (772–846), *Ch'üan T'ang shih*, vol. 7, *chüan* 427, p. 4707, l. 12. It occurs frequently in Chinese vernacular literature. See, e.g., a song suite by Shang Tao (cs 1212), *Ch'üan Yüan san-ch'ü*, 1:27, l. 5; *[Chi-p'ing chiao-chu] Hsi-hsiang chi*, play no. 4, scene 4, p. 167, l. 14; *Yüan-ch'ü hsüan*, 1:343, l. 4; *Yüan-ch'ü hsüan wai-pien*, 3:787, l. 21; *Hsüan-ho i-shih*, p. 55, l. 6; a set of songs by Wang Yüan-heng (14th century), *Ch'üan Yüan san-ch'ü*, 2:1378, l. 11; a set of songs by Liu T'ing-hsin (14th century), ibid., 2:1431, l. 6; an anonymous song suite in *Sheng-shih hsin-sheng*, p. 414, l. 10; a song suite by Ch'en To (fl. early 16th century), *Ch'üan Ming san-ch'ü*, 1:581, l. 9; an anonymous song suite in *Yung-hsi yüeh-fu*, ts'e 7, p. 20a, l. 4; *Hai-fu shan-t'ang tz'u-kao*, *chüan* 2b, p. 136, ll. 9–10; and a host of other occurrences, too numerous to list.

24. This four-character expression refers to the lack of news, since fish and geese are legendary bearers of messages. It occurs ubiquitously in Chinese literature. See, e.g., a poem by Tai Shu-lun (732–89), *Ch'üan T'ang shih*, vol. 5, *chüan* 273, p. 3072, l. 8; a quatrain by Chu Shu-chen (fl. 1078–1138), *Ch'üan Sung shih*, 28:17975, l. 10; a lyric by Hung Hsi-wen (1282–1366), *Ch'üan Chin Yüan tz'u*, 2:944, upper register, l. 15; *Yüan-ch'ü hsüan*, 4:1573, l. 6; *Yüan-ch'ü hsüan wai-pien*, 1:214, l. 6; a song by Chao Hsien-hung (14th century), *Ch'üan Yüan san-ch'ü*, 2:1179, l. 7; *Hsiang-nang yüan*, scene 2, p. 13b, l. 3; *Chien-teng yü-hua*, *chüan* 3, p. 226, l. 13; *Chin-ch'ai chi*, scene 43, p. 75, l. 21; *Ch'ien-chin chi*, scene 45, p. 141, l. 3; *San-yüan chi*, scene 16, p. 44, l. 12;

Shuang-chu chi, scene 41, p. 149, l. 2; a set of songs by Ch'en To (fl. early 16th century), *Ch'üan Ming san-ch'ü*, 1:506, l. 14; a song suite by Wang P'an (d. 1530), ibid., 1:1051, l. 6; a song suite by Liang Ch'en-yü (1519–91), ibid., 2:2205, l. 13; a song suite by Wu Kuo-pao (cs 1550), ibid., 2:2284, ll. 8–9; *Han Hsiang-tzu chiu-tu Wen-kung sheng-hsien chi, chüan* 1, scene 13, p. 33b, l. 8; *Chin-lan ssu-yu chuan*, p. 9a, l. 14; *Ssu-hsi chi*, scene 34, p. 85, l. 11; a set of songs by Hsüeh Lun-tao (c. 1531–c. 1600), *Ch'üan Ming san-ch'ü*, 3:2789, l. 5; and an abundance of other occurrences, too numerous to list.

25. This five-character expression occurs in a song by Kuan Han-ch'ing (13th century), *Ch'üan Yüan san-ch'ü*, 1:159, l. 5; a song by an anonymous Yüan dynasty author, ibid., 2:1732, l. 1; *[Chi-p'ing chiao-chu] Hsi-hsiang chi*, play no. 1, scene 4, p. 41, l. 9; and an anonymous song suite in *Yung-hsi yüeh-fu, ts'e* 9, p. 17b, ll. 6–7.

26. An orthographic variant of this four-character expression occurs in *Tung Chieh-yüan Hsi-hsiang chi, chüan* 1, p. 16, l. 3. It occurs in the same form as in the novel in two anonymous song suites in *Yung-hsi yüeh-fu, ts'e* 4, p. 57b, l. 1; and *ts'e* 14, p. 30a, l. 1.

27. This four-character expression occurs in a lyric by Ch'ao Tuan-li (1046–1113), *Ch'üan Sung tz'u*, 1:440, upper register, l. 2.

28. This formulaic four-character expression occurs, with some orthographic variation, in a song suite by Wang T'ing-hsiu (13th century), *Ch'üan Yüan san-ch'ü*, 1:317, l. 12; a song suite by Chao Ming-tao (14th century), ibid., 1:333, l. 10; *Lü-weng san-hua Han-tan tien*, scene 2, p. 3b, l. 11; a song suite by Ch'en To (fl. early 16th century), *Ch'üan Ming san-ch'ü*, 1:655, ll. 10–11; three anonymous song suites in *Yung-hsi yüeh-fu, ts'e* 1, p. 15a, ll. 1–2; *ts'e* 2, p. 49b, ll. 7–8; and *ts'e* 5, p. 19a, l. 5; *Hsi-yu chi*, vol. 2, ch. 77, p. 889, l. 12; and a song suite by Ku Yang-ch'ien (1537–1604), *Ch'üan Ming san-ch'ü*, 3:3041, l. 10.

29. Tu Fu (712–70), Han Yü (768–824), and Liu Tsung-yüan (773–819) are three of the most famous literary figures of the T'ang dynasty.

30. On these two lines, see Roy, *The Plum in the Golden Vase*, vol. 2, Appendix, n. 3.

31. For this allusion, see ibid., vol. 3, chap. 54, n. 13. This five-character line occurs in a song suite by Chao Ming-tao (14th century), *Ch'üan Yüan san-ch'ü*, 1:334, l. 5; a song suite by Chao Yen-hui (14th century), ibid., 2:1233, l. 10; a song suite by T'ang Shih (14th-15th centuries), ibid., 2:1490, l. 1; an anonymous song suite from the Yüan dynasty, ibid., 2:1855, l. 7; and an anonymous song suite in *Yung-hsi yüeh-fu, ts'e* 3, p. 28a, l. 10.

32. For this allusion, see Roy, *The Plum in the Golden Vase*, vol. 2, chap. 38, n. 34.

33. This five-character expression occurs in *Yüan-ch'ü hsüan wai-pien*, 3:763, l. 1; a set of songs by Yün K'an-tzu (14th century), in *Yüeh-fu ch'ün-chu, chüan* 4, p. 207, l. 11; and a song suite by Hu Wen-huan (fl. 1592–1617), *Ch'üan Ming san-ch'ü*, 3:2937, l. 9.

34. This four-character expression occurs in a set of lyrics attributed to Emperor Yang of the Sui dynasty (r. 604–18) in an apocryphal ninth-century work entitled *Sui Yang-ti hai-shan chi* (Record of the artificial mountains and lakes created by Emperor Yang of the Sui dynasty), included in *Ch'ing-so kao-i, hou-chi* (second collection), *chüan* 5, part 1, p. 138, l. 15; a lyric by Liu Yung (cs 1034), *Ch'üan Sung tz'u*, 1:28, lower register, l. 12; a lyric by Ou-yang Hsiu (1007–72), ibid., 1:138, lower register, l. 4; a lyric by Chu Tun-ju (1081–1159), ibid., 2:849, upper register, l. 7; a set of quatrains

by Emperor Hui-tsung of the Sung dynasty (r. 1100–25), *Ch'üan Sung shih*, 26:17045, l. 13; a quatrain written in 1175 by Chao Shih-hsia (cs 1175), *Ch'üan Sung tz'u*, 3:2076, lower register, l. 12; a lyric by Ch'en Yün-p'ing (13th century), ibid., 5:3126, lower register, l. 11; a lyric by the poetess Chang Hung-ch'iao (14th century), *Ch'üan Ming tz'u*, 1:195. lower register, l. 14; two anonymous song suites in *Sheng-shih hsin-sheng*, p. 547, l. 2; and p. 557, l. 1; and a lyric by the singing girl Hsü Ching-hung (16th century), *Ch'üan Ming tz'u*, 3:1042, lower register, l. 11.

35. This four-character expression occurs in a poem by Ch'iu Ch'u-chi (1148–1227), *Ch'üan Chin shih*, 2:154, l. 9; *Yüan-ch'ü hsüan wai-pien*, 3:857, l. 13; *Pai-t'u chi*, scene 3, p. 5, l. 10; a set of songs published in 1471, *Ch'üan Ming san-ch'ü*, 4:4511, l. 8; and an anonymous set of songs in *Yung-hsi yüeh-fu*, ts'e 20, p. 43b, l. 8.

36. This four-character expression occurs in *Chin-ming ch'ih Wu Ch'ing feng Ai-ai*, p. 464, l. 15; a song suite by T'ang Yin (1470–1524), *Ch'üan Ming san-ch'ü*, 1:1090, l. 8; a set of songs by Wu Kuo-pao (cs 1550), ibid., 2:2262, l. 3; and *Ch'ün-yin lei-hsüan*, 3:1726, l. 8.

37. A synonymous variant of this four-character expression occurs in a song suite by Shang Tao (cs 1212), *Ch'üan Yüan san-ch'ü*, 1:22, l. 7; a song suite by Wang T'ing-hsiu (13th century), ibid., 1:318, l. 2; a song suite by Chao Ming-tao (14th century), ibid., 1:334, l. 3; a set of songs by Chao Hsien-hung (14th century), ibid., 2:1179, l. 8; a song suite by T'ang Shih (14th-15th centuries), ibid., 2:1489, l. 4; *Yüan-ch'ü hsüan*, 2:583, l. 19; *Yüan-ch'ü hsüan wai-pien*, 1:30, l. 3; an anonymous song in *Yüeh-fu ch'ün-chu*, *chüan* 1, p. 33, l. 10; an anonymous song suite published in 1471, *Ch'üan Ming san-ch'ü*, 4:4534, l. 12; and a host of other occurrences, too numerous to list. It occurs in the same form as in the novel in *[Chi-p'ing chiao-chu] Hsi-hsiang chi*, play no. 1, scene 4, p. 42, l. 4; *Yüan-ch'ü hsüan wai-pien*, 1:55, l. 21; the tsa-chü drama *T'ung-lo Yüan Yen Ch'ing po-yü* (In T'ung-lo Tavern Yen Ch'ing gambles for fish), in *Shui-hu hsi-ch'ü chi, ti-i chi*, scene 4, p. 30, l. 5; a song suite by Li Tung-yang (1447–1516), *Ch'üan Ming san-ch'ü*, 1:427, l. 6; a set of songs by Ch'in Shih-yung (16th century), ibid., 5:6110, l. 9; *Hai-fu shan-t'ang tz'u-kao*, *chüan* 3, p. 161, l. 4; *Hsi-yu chi*, vol. 1, ch. 23, p. 260, l. 10; and a host of other occurrences, too numerous to list.

38. This four-character expression occurs in a song suite by T'ang shih (14th-15th centuries), *Ch'üan Yüan san-ch'ü*, 2:1547, l. 8.

39. This formulaic four-character expression occurs ubiquitously in Chinese vernacular literature. See, e.g., a set of quatrains by Chu Shu-chen (fl. 1078–1138), as quoted in *Hsi-hu yu-lan chih-yü*, *chüan* 16, p. 313, l. 14; *Tsui-weng t'an-lu* (The old drunkard's selection of tales), comp. Lo Yeh (13th century) (Taipei: Shih-chieh shu-chü, 1972), *chi-chi* (6th collection), *chüan* 1, p. 55, l. 4; *T'ien-pao i-shih chu-kung-tiao*, p. 159, l. 7; a song suite by T'ang Shih (14th-15th centuries), *Ch'üan Yüan san-ch'ü*, 2:1547, l. 6; an anonymous set of songs in the fourteenth-century anthology of songs entitled *Li-yüan an-shih yüeh-fu hsin-sheng* (Model new song lyrics from the Pear Garden), modern ed. ed. Sui Shu-sen (Peking: Chung-hua shu-chü, 1958), *chüan* 3, p. 105, l. 2; *Yang Wen lan-lu hu chuan*, p. 170, l. 1; *Ch'ien-t'ang meng*, p. 3b, l. 17; *Lien-huan chi*, *chüan* 2, scene 21, p. 55, l. 1; an anonymous song suite in *Sheng-shih hsin-sheng*, p. 96, l. 12–p. 97, l. 1; an anonymous song suite in *Feng-yüeh chin-nang [chien-chiao]*, p. 57, l. 2; an anonymous set of songs in *Yung-hsi yüeh-fu*, ts'e 17, p. 49b, l. 10; *Yen-chih chi*, *chüan* 1, scene 8, p. 12a, l. 3; an anonymous song suite in *Nan-kung tz'u-chi*, vol. 1, *chüan* 3, p. 162, l. 8; a set of songs by Hsüeh Lun-tao (c. 1531–c. 1600),

Ch'üan Ming san-ch'ü, 3:2832, l. 6; *Ta-T'ang Ch'in-wang tz'u-hua*, vol. 2, *chüan* 6, ch. 43, p. 23a, l. 1; and a host of other occurrences, too numerous to list.

40. This formulaic four-character expression occurs ubiquitously in Chinese vernacular literature. See, e.g., a lyric by Ch'en Liang (1143–94), *Ch'üan Sung tz'u*, 3:2105, upper register, l. 15; a lyric by Chang Yen (1248–1322), ibid., 5:3494, lower register, l. 16; *Yüan-ch'ü hsüan*, 4:1443, l. 20; *Yüan-ch'ü hsüan wai-pien*, 2:385, l. 19; an anonymous Yüan dynasty song suite, *Ch'üan Yüan san-ch'ü*, 2:1841, l. 5; *Fo-yin shih ssu t'iao Ch'in-niang*, p. 236, l. 13; a lyric by Ni Ch'ien (cs 1439), *Ch'üan Ming tz'u*, 1:268, lower register, l. 4; *Ming-chu chi*, scene 6, p. 16, l. 6; a song suite by Chu Ying-ch'en (16th century), *Ch'üan Ming san-ch'ü*, 2:1274, l. 11; a song suite by Chou Jui (16th century), ibid., 2:1506, l. 12; the middle-period vernacular story *Feng Po-yü feng-yüeh hsiang-ssu hsiao-shuo* (The story of Feng Po-yü: a tale of romantic longing), in *Hsiung Lung-feng ssu-chung hsiao-shuo*, p. 45, l. 8; *T'ang-shu chih-chuan t'ung-su yen-i*, vol. 1, *chüan* 2, p. 49a, l. 4; *Lieh-kuo chih-chuan*, vol. 3, *chüan* 8, p. 52a, l. 11; *Yü-chüeh chi*, scene 2, p. 3, l. 6; *Hsün-fang ya-chi*, p. 51b, l. 13; *Mu-lien chiu-mu ch'üan-shan hsi-wen*, *chüan* 3, p. 22b, l. 4; *Ch'üan-Han chih-chuan*, vol. 2, *chüan* 1, p. 5b, l. 8; *Shuang-lieh chi*, scene 36, p. 98, l. 11; a set of songs by Hsüeh Lun-tao (c. 1531–c. 1600), *Ch'üan Ming san-ch'ü*, 3:2810, l. 7; and an abundance of other occurrences, too numerous to list.

41. This four-character expression occurs in a song suite by T'ang Shih (14th–15th centuries), *Ch'üan Yüan san-ch'ü*, 2:1548, l. 14.

42. A synonymous variant of this line occurs in a speech by the Buddhist monk Hui-leng (854–932), *Tsu-t'ang chi*, *chüan* 10, p. 238, l. 26. It occurs in the same form as in the novel in a poem by Hsü Chi (1028–1103), *Ch'üan Sung shih*, 11:7711, l. 11; *Yüan-ch'ü hsüan*, 2:437, ll. 1–2; *Yüan-ch'ü hsüan wai-pien*, 1:140, ll. 9–10; *Chao Po-sheng ch'a-ssu yü Jen-tsung*, p. 165, l. 2; *Ching-ch'ai chi*, scene 16, p. 49, l. 6; *Chin-yin chi*, *chüan* 3, scene 20, p. 5a, l. 7; *Ts'ai-lou chi*, scene 12, p. 49, l. 19; an anonymous set of songs in *Yung-hsi yüeh-fu*, ts'e 19, p. 57b, ll. 4–5; *Mu-lien chiu-mu ch'üan-shan hsi-wen*, *chüan* 3, p. 76a, l. 3; and an abundance of other occurrences, too numerous to list.

43. Versions of this song suite are preserved in *Sheng-shih hsin-sheng*, pp. 282–84; *Tz'u-lin chai-yen*, 2:1032–36; *Yung-hsi yüeh-fu*, ts'e 9, pp. 78a–79b; and *Ch'ün-yin lei-hsüan*, 3:1943–46.

44. This four-character expression occurs in a lyric by Liu Kuo (1154–1206), *Ch'üan Sung tz'u*, 3:2143, upper register, l. 6; a lyric by Wei Liao-weng (1178–1237), ibid., 4:2374, upper register, l. 12; a lyric by Chang Chi (13th century), ibid., 4:2553, upper register, l. 2; a lyric by Li Tseng-po (1198–c. 1265), ibid., 4:2813, upper register, l.15; a lyric by Fang Yüeh (1199–1262), ibid., 4:2837, lower register, l. 15; *[Chi-p'ing chiao-chu] Hsi-hsiang chi*, play no. 2, scene 5, p. 92, l. 13; and a song by Chang K'o-chiu (1270–1348), *Ch'üan Yüan san-ch'ü*, 1:774, l. 6.

45. See Roy, *The Plum in the Golden Vase*, vol. 2, chap. 27, n. 17.

46. See ibid., vol. 1, chap. 3, n. 29.

47. The proximate source of this poem, with considerable textual variation, is *Huai-ch'un ya-chi*, *chüan* 9, p. 30b, ll. 8–11.

48. This four-character expression, which is usually used to describe hesitant speech, occurs in *Chin-yin chi*, *chüan* 2, scene 12, p. 5b, l. 11–p. 6a, l. 1; *Mu-lien chiu-mu ch'üan-shan hsi-wen*, *chüan* 3, p. 36b, l. 9; *Tzu-ch'ai chi*, scene 42, p. 158, l. 13; and *Hai-ling i-shih*, p. 114, l. 12.

49. This four-character expression occurs in *Jen hsiao-tzu lieh-hsing wei shen*, p. 574, l. 1.

50. The proximate source of this quatrain, with some textual variation, is the version of *Huai-ch'un ya-chi*, in *Yen-ch'ü pi-chi* (Ho Ta-lun), vol. 2, *chüan* 10, p. 19a, ll. 9–10.

51. For a picture of this kind of headgear, see Huang Lin et al., eds., *Chin P'ing Mei ta tz'u-tien* (Great dictionary of the *Chin P'ing Mei*) (Ch'eng-tu: Pa-Shu shu-she, 1991), p. 937.

52. This four-character expression occurs in *Pao-chien chi*, scene 41, p. 75, l. 16; and *Ts'an-T'ang Wu-tai shih yen-i chuan*, ch. 18, p. 68, l. 3. It also recurs in the *Chin P'ing Mei tz'u-hua*, vol. 4, ch. 78, p. 23b, l. 7; and vol. 5, ch. 82, p. 7b, l. 9.

53. This four-character expression occurs in a set of songs by Tseng Jui (c. 1260–c. 1330), *Ch'üan Yüan san-ch'ü*, 1:478, l. 11; and a song suite by Shen Ching (1553–1610), *Ch'üan Ming san-ch'ü*, 3:3280, l. 7.

54. This four-character expression occurs ubiquitously in Chinese literature. See, e.g., *Chuang-tzu yin-te*, ch. 13, p. 36, l. 12; *Hsün-tzu yin-te*, ch. 26, p. 98, l. 3; a poem by Li Yüan-li (d. 672), *Ch'üan T'ang shih pu-pien*, vol. 2, p. 684, l. 9; the literary tale *Li-wa chuan* (The story of Li Wa), by Po Hsing-chien (776–826), in *T'ang Sung ch'uan-ch'i chi*, p. 104, l. 12; a poem by Yang P'an (cs 1046), *Ch'üan Sung shih*, 8:5039, l. 14; a poem by the Buddhist monk Liao-yüan (1032–98), ibid., 12:8334, l. 3; a poem by Su Shih (1037–1101), *Su Shih shih-chi*, vol. 2, *chüan* 11, p. 530, l. 3; a lyric by Huang T'ing-chien (1045–1105), *Ch'üan Sung tz'u*, 1:406, upper register, l. 3; *Yüan-shih shih-fan*, *chüan* 1, p. 56, ll. 3–4; *I-chien chih*, vol. 1, chia-chih (first record), *chüan* 10, p. 87, l. 6; a lyric by Hsin Ch'i-chi (1140–1207), *Ch'üan Sung tz'u*, 3:1909, upper register, ll. 14–15; a lyric by Liu Kuo (1154–1206), ibid., 3:2145, upper register, l. 13; *Chung-ch'ing li-chi*, *chüan* 6, p. 32b, l. 5; *Hua-shen san-miao chuan*, p. 4a, l. 2; *Ts'an-T'ang Wu-tai shih yen-i chuan*, ch. 55, p. 213, l. 25; *Hsi-yu chi*, vol. 1, ch. 27, p. 312, l. 11; *San-pao t'ai-chien Hsi-yang chi t'ung-su yen-i*, vol. 1, ch. 38, p. 498, l. 1; *Sui-T'ang liang-ch'ao shih-chuan*, *chüan* 12, ch. 113, p. 8b, l. 6; and a host of other occurrences, too numerous to list.

55. This formulaic couplet occurs ubiquitously in Chinese vernacular literature. See, e.g., *Wu-wang fa Chou P'ing-hua*, p. 7, ll. 5–6; *Huan-men tzu-ti ts'o li-shen*, scene 2, p. 221, l. 6; *Yüan-ch'ü hsüan*, 2:534, l. 8; *Ching-ch'ai chi*, scene 7, p. 18, l. 7; *Ch'ien-t'ang meng*, p. 3b, ll. 13–14; *San-kuo chih t'ung-su yen-i*, vol. 1, *chüan* 9, p. 433, ll. 13–14; *Shui-hu ch'üan-chuan*, vol. 2, ch. 32, p. 505, l. 3; *San Sui p'ing-yao chuan*, *chüan* 1, ch. 1, p. 7b, ll. 7–8; *Wang Lan-ch'ing chen-lieh chuan*, scene 3, p. 6a, ll. 11–12; *Nan Sung chih-chuan*, vol. 2, *chüan* 9, p. 11b, ll. 11–12; *Huan-sha chi*, scene 22, p. 76, l. 2; *Chin-lan ssu-yu chuan*, p. 24a, l. 13; *Hsi-yu chi*, vol. 1, ch. 9, p. 91, l. 5; *Hai-ling i-shih*, p. 83, ll. 4–5; *Sui-T'ang liang-ch'ao shih-chuan*, *chüan* 7, ch. 68, p. 41b, ll. 4–5; and an abundance of other occurrences, too numerous to list.

56. This four-character expression occurs in *Hsüan-ho i-shih*, p. 48, l. 2; *Yüan-ch'ü hsüan wai-pien*, 1:131, l. 18; *Sung Ssu-kung ta-nao Chin-hun Chang*, p. 536, l. 1; *Yü Chung-chü t'i-shih yü shang-huang*, p. 68, l. 9; *Yü-huan chi*, scene 6, p. 13, l. 10; a song suite by Chang Lien (cs 1544), *Ch'üan Ming san-ch'ü*, 2:1707, l. 9; *Chu-fa chi*, *chüan* 2, scene 17, p. 2a, l. 8; *Hai-ling i-shih*, p. 62, l. 8; and *[Hsin-k'o] Shih-shang hua-yen ch'ü-lo t'an-hsiao chiu-ling*, *chüan* 1, p. 5a, lower register, l. 9.

57. This line, like the following one, refers to the difficulty of distinguishing between one's memory of events one has experienced in a dreaming or a waking state. It

is based on a story in *Lieh-tzu* in which a minister of the state of Cheng is called upon to decide a case in which two men lay claim to a dead deer, though neither one of them is sure whether their claims are based on memories from a dreaming or a waking state. See *Lieh-tzu chi-shih, chüan* 3, pp. 66–67; and *The Book of Lieh-tzu*, trans. A. C. Graham (London: John Murray, 1960), pp. 69–70. For the allusion in the following line, see Roy, *The Plum in the Golden Vase*, vol. 3, chap. 56, n. 2.

58. These two lines are derived, with some textual variation, from the opening couplet of a quatrain on the subject of dreams by Po Chü-i (772–846). See *Ch'üan T'ang shih*, vol. 7, *chüan* 451, p. 5098, l. 3. Variants of this couplet occur in *Hsüan-ho i-shih*, p. 22, l. 14; *[Hsin-pien] Wu-tai shih p'ing-hua*, p. 163, l. 14; *San hsien-shen Pao Lung-t'u tuan-yüan*, p. 174, l. 2; *K'an p'i-hsüeh tan-cheng Erh-lang Shen*, p. 258, l. 14; *Huang hsiao-tzu, chüan* 2, scene 19, p. 17a, ll. 3–4; *Ch'en Hsün-chien Mei-ling shih-ch'i chi*, p. 124, l. 10; *Chieh-chih-erh chi*, p. 254, l. 1; and the *Chin P'ing Mei tz'u-hua*, vol. 5, ch. 94, p. 6a, ll. 2–3.

59. This quatrain is derived, with some textual variation to fit the context, from one in *Huai-ch'un ya-chi, chüan* 10, p. 13a, ll. 5–6.

60. This four-character expression recurs in the *Chin P'ing Mei tz'u-hua*, vol. 5, ch. 94, p. 2b, l. 6.

61. This four-character expression occurs in *San-kuo chih t'ung-su yen-i*, vol. 1, *chüan* 4, p. 181, l. 17; *Ming-feng chi*, scene 6, p. 23, l. 9; and *Yü-chüeh chi*, scene 21, p. 67, l. 1.

62. The locus classicus for this four-character expression is a passage in the *Tso-chuan* under the year 494 B.C. See *The Ch'un Ts'ew with the Tso Chuen*, trans. James Legge (Hong Kong: Hong Kong University Press, 1960), p. 793, l. 7. It occurs frequently in later Chinese literature. See, e.g., *Meng-tzu yin-te*, Book 4B, ch. 20, p. 31, l. 18; a dirge by P'an Yüeh (247–300), in *Wen-hsüan*, vol. 3, *chüan* 56, p. 27a, l. 4; a memorial by Han Yü (768–824), *Han Ch'ang-li wen-chi chiao-chu, chüan* 8, p. 345, l. 1; *Lieh-kuo chih-chuan*, vol. 1, *chüan* 2, p. 6a, l. 13; and *San-pao t'ai-chien Hsi-yang chi t'ung-su yen-i*, vol. 2, ch. 57, p. 737, l. 2.

63. This four-character expression occurs ubiquitously in Chinese literature. See, e.g., *Chan-kuo ts'e* (Intrigues of the Warring States), comp. Liu Hsiang (79–8 B.C.), 3 vols. (Shanghai: Shang-hai ku-chi ch'u-pan she, 1985), vol. 1, *chüan* 3, p. 75, ll. 8–9; *Han Fei tzu so-yin* (A concordance to *Han Fei tzu*) (Peking: Chung-hua shu-chü, 1982), ch. 31, p. 795, l. 21; *Shih-chi*, vol. 7, *chüan* 68, p. 2231, l. 12; *Han chi, chüan* 30, p. 527, ll. 2–3; the biography of She-ti Shih-wen (6th-7th centuries), *Pei shih*, vol. 6, *chüan* 54, p. 1957, l. 14; an essay by Ch'üan Te-yü (759–818), *Ch'üan T'ang wen*, vol. 10, *chüan* 488, p. 17b, l. 5; an anonymous ninth-century song, *Ch'üan T'ang shih*, vol. 12, *chüan* 874, p. 9898, l. 12; a literary tale included in *Ch'ing-so kao-i, pieh-chi* (supplementary collection), *chüan* 3, p. 200, l. 14; *Ming-kung shu-p'an ch'ing-ming chi*, vol. 2, *chüan* 12, p. 449, l. 13; *Shih-i chi, chüan* 2, scene 24, p. 15a, l. 4; *T'ou-pi chi, chüan* 2, scene 35, p. 34a, l. 5; *Ts'an-T'ang Wu-tai shih yen-i chuan*, ch. 58, p. 221, l. 10; and *San-pao t'ai-chien Hsi-yang chi t'ung-su yen-i*, vol. 1, ch. 50, p. 644, l. 8.

64. This four-character expression occurs in a memorial by Liu Yü-hsi (772–842), *Ch'üan T'ang wen*, vol. 13, *chüan* 602, p. 14b, l. 7; a memorial by Su Shih (1037–1101), *Su Shih wen-chi*, vol. 2, *chüan* 24, p. 704, l. 6; *Shuang-chu chi*, scene 5, p. 12, l. 5; the literary tale entitled *Chung-shan lang chuan* (The tale of the wolf of Chung-shan), by Ma Chung-hsi (1446–1512), in *Ku-tai wen-yen tuan-p'ien hsiao-shuo hsüan-chi*,

erh-chi, p. 369, l. 9; *Huai-hsiang chi*, scene 3, p. 5, l. 10; *Chu-fa chi*, chüan 1, scene 2, p. 2b, l. 6; and a literary tale in *Yüan-chu chih-yü: hsüeh-ch'uang t'an-i*, chüan 1, p. 10, l. 8.

65. This four-character expression occurs under the year 618 in *Tzu-chih t'ung-chien*, vol. 3, chüan 186, p. 5835, ll. 10–11. It also occurs in *Chiu T'ang shu*, vol. 7, chüan 64, p. 2436, l. 13; *T'ieh-wei shan ts'ung-t'an*, chüan 1, p. 3, l. 11; *Yüan-shih shih-fan*, chüan 3, p. 121, ll. 13–14; *Hsiang-nang chi*, scene 11, p. 31, ll. 3–4; *Ch'üan-Han chih-chuan*, vol. 3, chüan 1, p. 21b, l. 4; *Ta-T'ang Ch'in-wang tz'u-hua*, vol. 1, chüan 1, ch. 3, p. 30b, l. 8; and *Sui-T'ang liang-ch'ao shih-chuan*, chüan 1, ch. 9, p. 55b, l. 1.

66. This four-character expression occurs in *Shui-hu ch'üan-chuan*, vol. 4, ch. 103. p. 1586, l. 7; *Ta-Sung chung-hsing yen-i*, vol. 1, chüan 1, p. 10b, l. 10; *T'ang-shu chih-chuan t'ung-su yen-i*, vol. 1, chüan 4, p. 16a, l. 12; *Ts'ao-lu chi*, chüan 2, scene 25, p. 23b, l. 5; *Yü-ching t'ai*, scene 28, p. 74, l. 11; and *Sui-T'ang liang-ch'ao shih-chuan*, chüan 4, ch. 38, p. 48b, l. 9.

67. This four-character expression occurs in *Liu sheng mi Lien chi*, chüan 3, p. 10b, l. 13.

68. This four-character expression occurs in *Ta-Sung chung-hsing yen-i*, vol. 1, chüan 1, p. 39a, l. 2.

69. This four-character expression occurs in *Lieh-kuo chih-chuan*, vol. 2, chüan 6, p. 71a, ll. 1–2.

70. Variants of this couplet occur in a gatha by the Buddhist monk Tao-ning (1053–1113), *Ch'üan Sung shih*, 19:12895, ll. 3–4; *Wu-teng hui-yüan*, vol. 3, chüan 17, p. 1157, l. 2; the thirteenth-century encyclopedia *Shih-lin kuang-chi* (Expansive gleanings from the forest of affairs), fac. repr. of 14th-century ed. (Peking: Chung-hua shu-chü, 1963), ch'ien-chi, chüan 9, p. 9a, l. 14; a comment by Yü Yen (1258–1314), *Sung shih-hua ch'üan-pien*, 10:10417, l. 2; *Ming-hsin pao-chien*, chüan 2, p. 2b, ll. 8–9; and *Hsün-ch'in chi*, scene 33, p. 110, l. 4. Variants of the second line also occur independently in *Yüan-ch'ü hsüan*, 2:749, l. 3; *Yüan-ch'ü hsüan wai-pien*, 2:376, ll. 3–4; *P'i-p'a chi*, scene 38, p. 212, ll. 12–13; a set of songs by Su Tzu-wen (16th century), *Ch'üan Ming san-ch'ü*, 4:4010, l. 8; and the *Chin P'ing Mei tz'u-hua*, vol. 5, ch. 81, p. 3b, l. 9; and ch. 90, p. 10b, ll. 5–6. The second line occurs in the same form as in the novel in *Ming-kung shu-p'an ch'ing-ming chi*, vol.1, chüan 2, p. 61, l. 10; and a set of quatrains by Sung Wu (1260–c. 1336), in *Yüan shih hsüan, ch'u-chi*, 2:1298, l. 4.

CHAPTER 78

1. This poem on the winter solstice employs the language of traditional Chinese correlative thinking, according to which all the phenomena marking the changes of the seasons are interrelated. The best way to understand it is to read the monograph entitled "The Chinese Cosmic Magic Known as Watching for the Ethers," in Derk Bodde, *Essays on Chinese Civilization*, ed. Charles Le Blanc and Dorothy Borei (Princeton: Princeton University Press, 1981), pp. 351–72.

2. The Eight Spirits are variously defined in different sources, and there is no consensus as to their identification.

3. The above poem is by the poetess Chu Shu-chen (fl. 1078–1138), *Ch'üan Sung shih*, 28:17990, ll. 3–4. The significance of its placement at this point in the novel is

discussed in Satyendra, "Toward a Poetics of the Chinese Novel: A Study of the Prefatory Poems in the *Chin P'ing Mei tz'u-hua*," pp. 111–12.

4. This four-character expression occurs in *San-kuo chih t'ung-su yen-i*, vol. 2, *chüan* 14, p. 671, l. 13; *Nü han-lin*, 4:1480, upper register, l. 1; and *Hsi-yu chi*, vol. 2, ch. 64, p. 730, l. 4. It also recurs in the *Chin P'ing Mei tz'u-hua*, vol. 4, ch. 78, p. 21a, l. 3.

5. The proximate source of these two lines is a passage in *Huai-ch'un ya-chi*, *chüan* 10, p, 5a, l. 1.

6. This line is derived from ibid., *chüan* 10, p. 6a, l. 1. Two characters required to preserve the parallelism have been omitted in the novel, but I have resupplied them in my translation.

7. This year corresponds to the year 1118 in the Western calendar.

8. This four-character expression recurs in the *Chin P'ing Mei tz'u-hua*, vol. 4, ch. 78, p. 9a, l. 9.

9. This formulaic four-character expression occurs ubiquitously in Chinese vernacular literature. See, e.g., a song suite by T'ung-t'ung (14th century), *Ch'üan Yüan san-ch'ü*, 2:1261, l. 9; *Shui-hu ch'üan-chuan*, vol. 3, ch. 82, p. 1359, l. 1; an anonymous song suite in *Sheng-shih hsin-sheng*, p. 424, l. 8; a song suite by Ning-chai (16th century), *Ch'üan Ming san-ch'ü*, 2:2430, l. 9; a lyric by Wang T'ing-hsiang (1474–1544), *Ch'üan Ming tz'u*, 2:524, upper register, l. 15; and an anonymous song suite in *Yung-hsi yüeh-fu*, *ts'e* 2, p. 39b, l. 3.

10. This four-character expression occurs in a poem by Ch'iang Chih (1022–76), *Ch'üan Sung shih*, 10:6920, l. 10; and a lyric written in 1358 by Ling Yün-han (14th century), *Ch'üan Ming tz'u*, 1:156, upper register, ll. 13–14. It also recurs in the *Chin P'ing Mei tz'u-hua*, vol. 4, ch. 78, p. 16a, l. 7.

11. This four-character expression occurs in *Fo-shuo Huang-chi chieh-kuo pao-chüan*, 10:350, l. 4; *K'uai-tsui Li Ts'ui-lien chi*, p. 56, l. 16; *Yüeh-ming Ho-shang tu Liu Ts'ui*, p. 440, l. 2; *San-ming t'ung-hui* (Comprehensive compendium on the three fates), comp. Wan Min-ying (cs 1550), in *[Ying-yin Wen-yüan ko] Ssu-k'u ch'üan-shu* ([Facsimile reprint of the Wen-yüan ko Imperial Library copy of the] Complete library of the four treasuries), 1,500 vols. (Taipei: T'ai-wan Shang-wu yin-shu kuan, 1986), vol. 810, *chüan* 1, p. 10, l. 4; *Han Hsiang-tzu chiu-tu Wen-kung sheng-hsien chi*, *chüan* 1, scene 6, p. 10a, l. 9; *Ming-feng chi*, scene 37, p. 154, l. 10; and *Mu-lien chiu-mu ch'üan-shan hsi-wen*, *chüan* 2, p. 9a, l. 1.

12. On this couplet, see Roy, *The Plum in the Golden Vase*, vol. 2, chap. 28, n. 17.

13. According to legend, in ancient times one Shang-ling Mu-tzu, who had been married for five years without offspring, composed a sad lament when his relatives proposed that he abandon his wife and marry another. See *Ku-chin chu*, *chüan* 2, p. 11, ll. 8–10.

14. This quatrain, with some textual variation, is derived from one in *Huai-ch'un ya-chi*, *chüan* 10, p. 37a, ll. 12–13.

15. This idiomatic expression occurs in *[Chi-p'ing chiao-chu] Hsi-hsiang chi*, play no. 4, *hsieh-tzu* (wedge), p. 140, l. 8; *Yüan-ch'ü hsüan*, 3:1165, ll. 1–2; *T'ung-lo yüan Yen Ch'ing po-yü*, scene 2, p. 25, l. 18; *Hai-ling i-shih*, p. 91, l. 12; and an abundance of other occurrences, too numerous to list.

16. This is Chao K'uang-yin (927–76), the founding emperor of the Sung dynasty (r. 960–76).

17. See Roy, *The Plum in the Golden Vase*, vol. 3, chap. 47, n. 4.

18. This four-character expression occurs ubiquitously in Chinese literature. See, e.g., a lyric by Feng Yen-ssu (903–960), *Ch'üan T'ang shih*, vol. 12, *chüan* 898, p. 10159, l. 6; a quatrain by Su Shih (1037–1101), *Su Shih shih-chi*, vol. 4, *chüan* 22, p. 1187, l. 4, and p. 1197, n. 74; a lyric by Li Mi-hsün (1089–1153), *Ch'üan Sung tz'u*, 2:1056, upper register, l. 13; an anonymous quatrain quoted in *I-chien chih*, vol. 3, *san-chih, chi* (third record, section six), *chüan* 7, p. 1353, l. 6; an anonymous twelfth-century quatrain quoted in *Ho-lin yü-lu*, *chüan* 5, p. 79, l. 10; a lyric by Wang Chi (cs 1151), *Ch'üan Chin Yüan tz'u*, 1:34, lower register, ll. 15–16; a lyric by Yüan Hao-wen (1190–1257), ibid., 1:106, upper register, ll. 2–3; a lyric by Liu Ch'en-weng (1232–97), *Ch'üan Sung tz'u*, 4:3217, upper register, l. 3; a lyric by Chao Pi-hsiang (1245–94), ibid., 4:3382, upper register, l. 13; *T'ien-pao i-shih chu-kung-tiao*, p. 151, l. 6; a set of quatrains by Sung Wu (1260–c. 1336), *Yüan shih hsüan, ch'u-chi*, 2:1298, l. 10; *Yüan-ch'ü hsüan*, 1:10, l. 13; *Yüan-ch'ü hsüan wai-pien*, 2:581, l. 14; a set of songs by Chung Ssu-ch'eng (c. 1279–c. 1360), *Ch'üan Yüan san-ch'ü*, 2:1354, l. 10; *Chao-shih ku-erh chi*, *chüan* 1, scene 2, p. 2a, l. 5; *Wu Lun-ch'üan Pei*, *chüan* 2, scene 12, p. 18b, l. 5; an anonymous song suite in *Sheng-shih hsin-sheng*, p. 228, l. 11; a lyric by Wang Hung-ju (cs 1487, d. 1519), *Ch'üan Ming tz'u pu-pien*, 1:139, lower register, l. 9; a song suite by Ch'en To (fl. early 16th century), *Ch'üan Ming san-ch'ü*, 1:653, l. 6; *Hsiu-ju chi*, scene 4, p. 11, l. 10; a set of songs by K'ang Hai (1475–1541), *Ch'üan Ming san-ch'ü*, 1:1165, l. 2; verse 54 of a suite of one hundred songs to the tune "Hsiao-t'ao hung" that retells the story of the *Ying-ying chuan* by a Ming dynasty figure named Wang Yen-chen, *Yung-hsi yüeh-fu*, ts'e 19, p. 43b, l. 6; a lyric by Ch'en Ju-lun (cs 1532), *Ch'üan Ming tz'u*, 2:923, upper register, l. 3; *Chin-lan ssu-yu chuan*, p. 9b, l. 15; *Tzu-ch'ai chi*, scene 16, p. 65, l. 4; *Pa-i chi*, scene 2, p. 1, l. 11; a song suite by Shen Ching (1553–1610), *Ch'üan Ming san-ch'ü*, 3:3294, l. 2; and an abundance of other occurrences, too numerous to list.

19. This four-character expression occurs in *Shui-hu ch'üan-chuan*, vol. 2, ch. 45, p. 737, l. 7.

20. This line is derived from *Ju-i chün chuan*, p. 13b, l. 9.

21. This magical form of military formation is described in very similar terms in *Ch'i-kuo ch'un-ch'iu p'ing-hua*, p. 59, ll. 2–5; *Pei Sung chih-chuan*, vol. 3, *chüan* 7, p. 13b, ll. 7–9; *Tung-yu chi: shang-tung pa-hsien chuan*, *chüan* 2, p. 12a, ll. 1–4; and *Yang-chia fu shih-tai chung-yung yen-i chih-chuan*, vol. 1, *chüan* 4, p. 32b, ll. 7–10.

22. This four-character expression occurs in a poem by Chao Ting-ch'en (cs 1091), *Ch'üan Sung shih*, 22:14882, l. 7; a poem by Fan Ch'eng-ta (1126–93), ibid., 41:25988, l. 9; and a lyric by Wu Wen-ying (13th century), *Ch'üan Sung tz'u*, 4:2902, upper register, l. 10.

23. This idiomatic expression for a dangerously seductive woman occurs ubiquitously in Chinese vernacular literature. See, e.g., an anonymous Yüan dynasty song, *Ch'üan Yüan san-ch'ü*, 2:1690, l. 9; *Yüan-ch'ü hsüan*, 1:264, l. 11; *Hsiu-ju chi*, scene 20, p. 57, l. 3; *Yüeh-ming Ho-shang tu Liu Ts'ui*, p. 438, l. 11; *Hsi-yu chi*, vol. 2, ch. 54, p. 630, l. 9; *Ssu-sheng yüan*, p. 24, l. 5; *Shuang-lieh chi*, scene 3, p. 8, l. 4; *Chü-ting chi*, *chüan* 2, scene 16, p. 36b, l. 1; *Han Hsiang-tzu chiu-tu Wen-kung sheng-hsien chi*, *chüan* 1, scene 11, p. 22a, l. 9; and *Mu-tan t'ing*, scene 20, p. 99, l. 13.

24. This formulaic four-character expression occurs ubiquitously in Chinese vernacular literature. See, e.g., a poem by Yüan Hao-wen (1190–1257), *Yüan I-shan shih-*

chi chien-chu (Yüan Hao-wen's poetry collection annotated), annot. Shih Kuo-ch'i (Peking: Jen-min wen-hsüeh ch'u-pan she, 1958), *chüan* 4, p. 204, l. 7; a lyric by Wei Ch'u (1231–92), *Ch'üan Chin Yüan tz'u*, 2:701, upper register, ll. 11–12; *[Chi-p'ing chiao-chu] Hsi-hsiang chi*, play no. 4, scene 2, p. 149, l. 9; *Yüan-ch'ü hsüan*, 1:343, ll. 19–20; *T'ien-pao i-shih chu-kung-tiao*, p. 174, l. 3; a song by Hsü Yen (d. 1301), *Ch'üan Yüan san-ch'ü*, 1:82, l. 10; a song suite by Tseng Jui (c. 1260–c. 1330), ibid., 1:508, l. 13; a song suite by Chao Hsien-hung (14th century), ibid., 2:1183, l. 10; a set of songs by Wang Ai-shan (14th century), ibid., 2:1192, l. 3; *Feng-yüeh Jui-hsien T'ing*, p. 42, l. 4; *P'u-tung Ts'ui Chang chu-yü shih-chi*, p. 18a, l. 4; *P'u-tung Ts'ui Chang Hai-weng shih-chi*, p. 23b, l. 13; a set of songs by Chu Yün-ming (1460–1526), *Ch'üan Ming san-ch'ü*, 1:774, l. 7; *Lien-huan chi, chüan* 2, scene 23, p. 60, l. 6; *Chieh-chih-erh chi*, p. 256, l. 5; *Huan-sha chi*, scene 28, p. 102, l. 2; *Yen-chih chi, chüan* 1, scene 16, p. 22a, l. 7; and a host of other occurrences, too numerous to list.

25. See Roy, *The Plum in the Golden Vase*, vol. 1, chap. 13, n. 23.

26. This four-character expression occurs in *Shui-hu ch'üan-chuan*, vol. 3, ch. 55, p. 921, l. 3; *Ts'an-T'ang Wu-tai shih yen-i chuan*, ch. 40, p. 162, l. 13; *Yang-chia fu shih-tai chung-yung yen-i chih-chuan*, vol. 1, *chüan* 2, p. 27b, l. 2; and *Ta-T'ang Ch'in-wang tz'u-hua*, vol. 2, *chüan* 6, ch. 43, p. 25a, ll. 3–4.

27. This four-character expression occurs in a lyric by Wang Shen (1155–1227), *Ch'üan Sung tz'u*, 3:2198, upper register, l. 4; *Shui-hu ch'üan-chuan*, vol. 2, ch. 42, p. 677, l. 3; a song by Liu Liang-ch'en (1482–1551), *Ch'üan Ming san-ch'ü*, 2:1314, l. 14; and two songs by Hsüeh Lun-tao (c. 1531–c. 1600), ibid., 3:2701, ll. 12–13; and 3:2772, l. 11. It also recurs in the *Chin P'ing Mei tz'u-hua*, vol. 5, ch. 98, p. 9a, l. 5.

28. This four-character expression occurs ubiquitously in Chinese literature. See, e.g., a lyric by Po Chü-i (772–846), *Ch'üan T'ang shih*, vol. 12, *chüan* 890, p. 10057, l. 3; a lyric by Su Shih (1037–1101), *Ch'üan Sung tz'u*, 1:297, lower register, l. 7; a lyric by Mao Ch'ien (12th century), ibid., 2:1367, upper register, l. 15; a lyric by Chang Hsiao-hsiang (1132–69), ibid., 3:1697, lower register, l. 1; a lyric by Chang Yü-niang (14th century), *Ch'üan Chin Yüan tz'u*, 2:870, lower register, l. 11; a lyric by Ch'ü Yu (1341–1427), *Ch'üan Ming tz'u*, 1:166, lower register, l. 3; *Hsiang-nang chi*, scene 13, p. 36, l. 2; *Hsin-ch'iao shih Han wu mai ch'un-ch'ing*, p. 63, l. 3; *Pai-p'ao chi, chüan* 1, scene 18, p. 29b, l. 7; a lyric by Yang Shen (1488–1559), *Ch'üan Ming tz'u*, 2:808, lower register, l. 6; and *Huai-ch'un ya-chi, chüan* 10, p. 38a, l. 7.

29. This four-character expression occurs in *Yüan-ch'ü hsüan*, 3:1210, l. 6; *Hei Hsüan-feng chang-i shu-ts'ai*, scene 3, p. 107, l. 20; and *Hsi-yu chi*, vol. 1, ch. 19, p. 213, ll. 4–5.

30. A variant of this couplet has already occurred in the *Chin P'ing Mei tz'u-hua*, vol. 2, ch. 37, p. 10b, ll. 4–5. See Roy, *The Plum in the Golden Vase*, vol. 2, chap. 37, p. 377, ll. 21–24.

31. A variant of this couplet recurs in the *Chin P'ing Mei tz'u-hua*, vol. 5, ch. 93, p. 13b, ll. 9–10.

32. This formulaic four-character expression occurs in *San-kuo chih t'ung-su yen-i*, vol. 1, *chüan* 12, p. 538, l. 5; *Yen-chih chi, chüan* 2, scene 23, p. 5a, l. 11; *Chü-ting chi, chüan* 1, scene 6, p. 11b, l. 10; *Hsi-yu chi*, vol. 2, ch. 74, p. 849, l. 8; *San-pao t'ai-chien Hsi-yang chi t'ung-su yen-i*, vol. 1, ch. 46, p. 595, l. 11; and *Ta-T'ang Ch'in-wang tz'u-hua*, vol. 1, *chüan* 2, ch. 9, p. 12a, l. 2.

33. See Roy, *The Plum in the Golden Vase*, vol. 1, chap. 6, n. 28.

34. This quatrain is derived, with considerable textual variation, from one in *Huai-ch'un ya-chi*, vol. 10, p. 19b, ll. 8–9.

35. This formulaic four-character expression occurs in a song suite by Chao Yen-hui (14th century), *Ch'üan Yüan san-ch'ü*, 2:1232, l. 14; *Han Yüan-shuai an-tu Ch'en-ts'ang*, scene 1, p. 4a, ll. 6–7; *Yü-huan chi*, scene 22, p. 84, l. 9; *San-kuo chih t'ung-su yen-i*, vol. 1, *chüan* 1, p. 41, l. 18; and a set of songs by Ch'en To (fl. early 16th century), *Ch'üan Ming san-ch'ü*, 1:545, ll. 3–4.

36. This formulaic four-character expression occurs in *Cho Chi Pu chuan-wen*, 1:61, l. 2; a poem by Ma Yü (1123–83), *Ch'üan Chin shih*, 1:324, l. 11; a quatrain by the Buddhist monk Chih-yü (1185–1269), *Ch'üan Sung shih*, 57:35920, l. 12; and *San Sui p'ing-yao chuan*, *chüan* 1, ch. 5, p. 53b, l. 9.

37. The proximate source of this quatrain is *Huai-ch'un ya-chi*, *chüan* 10, p. 9b, ll. 7–8.

38. This four-character expression occurs in *Ju-i chün chuan*, p. 9b, l. 1.

39. A virtually synonymous version of this line, with one textual variant, occurs in a quatrain in *Chung-ch'ing li-chi*, *chüan* 6, p. 32b, l. 7.

40. This line is probably derived from a similar one in a quatrain in *Huai-ch'un ya-chi*, *chüan* 10, p. 36a, l. 6.

41. The proximate source of the last three lines of this quatrain is one in ibid., *chüan* 10, p. 35a, ll. 14–15.

42. Variants of this *hsieh-hou yü* occur in *Shih-yü sheng-sou: Chung-yüan shih-yü* (Market argot and slang: The market argot of the Central Plain), published in the Lung-ch'ing reign period (1567–72), in *Han-shang huan wen-ts'un* (Literary remains of the Han-shang Studio), by Ch'ien Nan-yang (Shanghai: Shang-hai wen-i ch'u-pan she, 1980), p. 167, lower register, l. 6; the late Ming compilation *Hsin-ch'i teng-mi: Chiang-hu ch'iao-yü* (Novel and unusual lantern riddles: Witticisms current in the demimonde), in ibid., p. 170, upper register, l. 1; and *[Hsin-k'o] Shih-shang hua-yen ch'ü-lo t'an-hsiao chiu-ling*, *chüan* 2, p. 16a, upper register, ll. 1–2. The second line also occurs independently in a set of songs by Liu Hsiao-tsu (1522–89), *Ch'üan Ming san-ch'ü*, 2:2314, l. 14.

43. Variants of this line occur in *[Chiao-ting] Yüan-k'an tsa-chü san-shih chung*, p. 94, l. 5; *Shih-yü sheng-sou: Chung-yüan shih-yü*, p. 165, lower register, l. 9; and a song suite by Su Tzu-wen (16th century), *Ch'ün-yin lei-hsüan*, 4:2038, l. 4.

44. On this song suite, see Roy, *The Plum in the Golden Vase*, vol. 1, chap. 15, n. 20; and appendix 2, pp. 437–41.

45. A variant of this idiomatic expression occurs in the *Chin P'ing Mei tz'u-hua*, vol. 5, ch. 86, p. 9b, l. 3.

46. Variants of this idiomatic expression occur in *[Chi-p'ing chiao-chu] Hsi-hsiang chi*, play no. 3, scene 3, p. 123, l. 10; *Yüan-ch'ü hsüan*, 3:990, ll. 1–2; *Sha-kou chi*, scene 12, p. 43, ll. 4–5; *Chin-t'ung Yü-nü Chiao Hung chi*, p. 33, l. 4; *Hsiu-ju chi*, scene 21, p. 62, l. 2; and *K'ung Shu-fang shuang-yü shan-chui chuan*, p. 66, ll. 3–4.

47. See Roy, *The Plum in the Golden Vase*, vol. 2, chap. 29, n. 106.

48. This formulaic four-character expression occurs ubiquitously in Chinese vernacular literature. See, e.g., a poem by Meng Chiao (751–814), *Ch'üan T'ang shih*, vol. 6., *chüan* 379, p. 4254, l. 11; *Yüan-ch'ü hsüan*, 1:222, l. 11; *Yu-kuei chi*, scene 7, p. 15, ll. 2–3; *Shih-wu kuan hsi-yen ch'eng ch'iao-huo*, p. 694, l. 15; *Fo-shuo Huang-chi*

chieh-kuo pao-chüan, 10:330, l. 1; and *Yang-chia fu shih-tai chung-yung yen-i chih-chuan*, vol. 2, *chüan* 7, p. 13b, l. 2.

49. Variants of this idiomatic expression occur ubiquitously in Chinese literature. See, e.g., *Chuang-tzu yin-te*, ch. 12, p. 31, ll. 18–19; *Shih-chi*, vol. 2, *chüan* 8, p. 381, l. 3; *Shuo-yüan chu-tzu so-yin*, ch. 2, p. 13, l. 3; a letter by Su Shih (1037–1101), *Su Shih wen-chi*, vol. 4, *chüan* 48, p. 1398, ll. 14–15; *Tung Chieh-yüan Hsi-hsiang chi*, *chüan* 2, p. 51, l. 12; *Yüan-ch'ü hsüan*, 3:1178, l. 15; *P'i-p'a chi*, scene 30, p. 173, l. 9; *Hsiao-p'in chi*, p. 86, ll. 12–13; *Chin-ch'ai chi*, scene 45, p. 80, ll. 11–12; *Wu Lun-ch'üan Pei*, *chüan* 1, scene 6, p. 31a, l. 3; *Ch'ien-chin chi*, scene 2, p. 3, l. 3; *Shuang-chu chi*, scene 9, p. 25, l. 1; *Huai-hsiang chi*, scene 12, p. 32, l. 4; and *Lieh-kuo chih-chuan*, vol. 3, *chüan* 8, p. 13b, l. 6. It occurs in the same form as in the novel in the prose commentary to a quatrain by the Buddhist monk I-ch'ing (1032–83), *Ch'üan Sung shih*, 12:8208, ll. 13–14; *Sha-kou chi*, scene 19, p. 72, l. 5; *San-yüan chi*, scene 5, p. 12, ll. 4–5; *San-kuo chih t'ung-su yen-i*, vol. 1, *chüan* 5, p. 217, l. 9; *Ch'ien-t'ang hu-yin Chi-tien Ch'an-shih yü-lu*, p. 6b, ll. 3–4; *San Sui p'ing-yao chuan*, *chüan* 1, ch. 1, p. 5b, l. 6; *Hsi-yu chi*, vol. 1, ch. 47, p. 541, l. 9; and *Ch'un-wu chi*, scene 23, p. 65, ll. 1–2.

50. This idiomatic expression recurs in the *Chin P'ing Mei tz'u-hua*, vol. 5, ch. 96, p. 4b, l. 8.

51. This four-character expression recurs in ibid., ch. 92, p. 11b, ll. 7–8.

52. A synonymous variant of this idiomatic expression occurs in *Pai-she chi*, *chüan* 2, scene 17, p. 10a, l. 9.

53. These two lines occur in *Chang Yü-hu su nü-chen kuan chi*, p. 20b, l. 8. They also recur in the *Chin P'ing Mei tz'u-hua*, vol. 5, ch. 82, p. 3a, l. 7.

54. This couplet is from a poem by Chu Shu-chen (fl. 1078–1138), *Ch'üan Sung shih*, 28:17954, l. 15.

55. These two lines are derived from a passage in the *Lun-yü* (The analects of Confucius). See *Lun-yü yin-te*, Book 20, paragraph 2, l. 5.

56. See Roy, *The Plum in the Golden Vase*, vol. 2, chap. 30, n. 16.

57. These two structures are mentioned together in *Hsüan-ho i-shih*, p. 26, l. 9.

58. See ibid., p. 30, l. 13.

59. The locus classicus for this four-character expression is the *Shu-ching*. See Legge, *The Shoo King or The Book of Historical Documents*, p. 349, l. 6 of the Chinese text. It also occurs in *Tung-ching meng-hua lu*, *chüan* 3, p. 19, l. 7; and *Huai-ch'un ya-chi*, *chüan* 9, p. 23a, ll. 7–8.

60. This four-character expression occurs in a song on the subject of antiques by Ch'en To (fl. early 16th century), *Ch'üan Ming san-ch'ü*, 1:545, l. 3.

61. This four-character expression occurs in *Hsüan-ho i-shih*, p. 30, ll. 6–7. It refers to the stone drums traditionally dated to the reign of King Hsüan of the Chou dynasty (r. 827–782 B.C.).

62. These two lines refer to the brazen colossi in the shape of immortals holding out their hands to catch the dew that were erected by Emperor Wu of the Han dynasty (r. 141–87 B.C.). See Roy, *The Plum in the Golden Vase*, vol. 2, chap. 30, n. 1.

63. For a definitive study of Emperor Hui-tsung's passion for collecting antique artifacts of all kinds, see Patricia Buckley Ebrey, *Accumulating Culture: The Collections of Emperor Huizong* (Seattle: University of Washington Press, 2008).

64. This four-character expression occurs ubiquitously in Chinese literature. See, e.g., *San-kuo chih*, vol. 2, *chüan*, 14, p. 434, l. 15; *Chiu T'ang shu*, vol. 8, *chüan* 67,

p. 2476, l. 12; *Tzu-chih t'ung-chien*, vol. 3, *chüan* 184, p. 5754, l. 6; *Mo-chi* (Records of silence), comp. Wang Chih (d. c. 1154) (Peking: Chung-hua shu-chü, 1981), *chüan* 1, p. 2, l. 2; *[Hsin-pien] Wu-tai shih p'ing-hua*, p. 84, l. 13; *Hsing-t'ien Feng-yüeh t'ung-hsüan chi*, scene 14, p. 34b, l. 2; *San-kuo chih t'ung-su yen-i*, vol. 1, *chüan* 6, p. 250, l. 15; *Hung-fu chi*, scene 27, p. 58, l. 1; *Ta-Sung chung-hsing yen-i*, vol. 1, *chüan* 2, p. 43b, ll. 7–8; *T'ang-shu chih-chuan t'ung-su yen-i*, vol. 1, *chüan* 1, p. 26b, l. 6; *Nan Sung chih-chuan*, vol. 1, *chüan*, 4, p. 22a, l. 9; *Pei Sung chih-chuan*, vol. 3, *chüan* 10, p. 11a, l. 4; *Lieh-kuo chih-chuan*, vol. 1, *chüan* 3, p. 5a, ll. 6–7; *Ch'üan-Han chih-chuan*, vol. 2, *chüan* 5, p. 14a, l. 1; *Huang-Ming k'ai-yün ying-wu chuan*, *chüan* 2, p. 5a, l. 12; *Ch'eng-yün chuan*, *chüan* 2, p. 18b, l. 4; *Ts'an-T'ang Wu-tai shih yen-i chuan*, ch. 55, p. 212, l. 5; *Yang-chia fu shih-tai chung-yung yen-i chih-chuan*, vol. 1, *chüan* 1, p. 27a, l. 2; *Ta-T'ang Ch'in-wang tz'u-hua*, vol. 1, *chüan* 3, ch. 18, p. 15a, ll. 6–7; *Sui-T'ang liang-ch'ao shih-chuan*, *chüan* 2, ch. 13, p. 12a, l. 4; and a host of other occurrences, too numerous to list.

65. This statement is derived from a famous line in the biography of Han Hsin (d. 196 B.C.) in *Shih-chi*, vol. 8, *chüan* 92, p. 2629, ll. 9–10, where it refers to the conquest of the empire.

66. This four-character expression occurs in *Yu-kuei chi*, scene 8, p. 23, ll. 3–4; *P'i-p'a chi*, scene 3, p. 14, l. 7; *Lieh-kuo chih-chuan*, vol. 1, *chüan* 2, p. 31b, l. 2; *Yen-chih chi*, *chüan* 1, scene 9, p. 12b, l. 3; and *Hsi-yu chi*, vol. 1, ch. 30, p. 342, l. 3.

67. These two lines occur together in *Ch'ien-t'ang meng*, p. 3b, ll. 16–17.

68. This four-character expression occurs in *Yüan-ch'ü hsüan wai-pien*, 2:386, l. 17; and *Hai-fu shan-t'ang tz'u-kao*, *chüan* 3, p. 156, l. 2.

69. These twelve lines are very close to formulaic passages of descriptive parallel prose in *P'i-p'a chi*, scene 3, p. 14, ll. 7–10; and *Ch'ien-t'ang meng*, p. 3b, l. 17–p. 4a, l. 5.

70. These four lines, with slight textual variation, occur in *Ch'ien-t'ang meng*, p. 4a, ll. 6–7.

71. These two lines occur in ibid., p. 4a, l. 5; *Wu Lun-ch'üan Pei*, *chüan* 2, scene 10, p. 9b l. 5; and *Ch'en Hsün-chien Mei-ling shih-ch'i chi*, p. 122, l. 5.

72. See Roy, *The Plum in the Golden Vase*, vol. 1, chap. 15, n. 14.

73. This four-character expression occurs in *Chin-t'ung Yü-nü Chiao Hung chi*, p. 32, l. 7.

74. This formulaic four-character expression occurs ubiquitously in Chinese vernacular literature. See, e.g., a lyric by Li Ch'u-ch'üan (1134–89), *Ch'üan Sung tz'u*, 3:1735, lower register, l. 13; a lyric written in 1230 by Liu Chen (cs 1202), ibid., 4:2473, upper register, l. 13; a lyric by Yüan Hao-wen (1190–1257), *Ch'üan Chin Yüan tz'u*, 1:114, upper register, l. 6; a lyric by Wei Ch'u (1231–92), ibid., 2:704, upper register, l. 7; a lyric by Yü Chi (1272–1348), ibid., 2:868, upper register, l. 2; a set of songs by Wang Yüan-heng (14th century), *Ch'üan Yüan san-ch'ü*, 2:1384, ll. 13–14; *Chiao Hung chuan*, p. 298, ll. 3–4; *Yu-kuei chi*, scene 28, p. 88, l. 11; a lyric by Chu Yu-tun (1379–1439), *Ch'üan Ming tz'u*, 1:238, lower register, l. 9; *Wu Lun-ch'üan Pei*, *chüan* 4, scene 29, p. 36a, ll. 4–5; *Ming-chu chi*, scene 1, p. 1, l. 6; a song suite by Chang Lien (cs 1544), *Ch'üan Ming san-ch'ü*, 2:1695, l. 7; *Yen-chih chi*, *chüan* 1, scene 2, p. 4a, l. 1; *Hai-fu shan-t'ang tz'u-kao*, *chüan* 4, p. 193, l. 14; the author's preface to *Mu-lien chiu-mu ch'üan-shan hsi-wen*, dated 1582, p. 2a, l. 1; *Ch'üan-Han chih-chuan*, vol. 2, *chüan* 1, p. 6a, l. 7; and an abundance of other occurrences, too numerous to list.

75. See Roy, *The Plum in the Golden Vase*, vol. 3, chap. 43, n. 63.

76. On this couplet, see ibid., chap. 43, n. 64.

77. This tsa-chü drama is by Chu Yu-tun (1379–1439). See *Ch'üan Ming tsa-chü* (Complete tsa-chü plays of the Ming dynasty), 12 vols. (Taipei: Ting-wen shu-chü, 1979), 4:1745–68. For good discussions of the ironic significance of the introduction of this play at this point in the narrative, see Carlitz, *The Rhetoric of Chin p'ing mei*, pp. 119–21; and W. L. Idema, *The Dramatic Oeuvre of Chu Yu-tun (1379–1439)* (Leiden: E. J. Brill, 1985), pp. 174–75.

78. This song suite by Ts'ao Meng-hsiu (15th century) consists entirely of a paean of praise for the reigning Ming emperor. See *Ch'üan Ming san-ch'ü*, 2:2417–18. It may also be found in *Sheng-shih hsin-sheng*, pp. 75–76; *Tz'u-lin chai-yen*, 2:1106–09; and *Yung-hsi yüeh-fu, ts'e* 1, pp. 3b–4b.

79. This formulaic four-character expression occurs ubiquitously in Chinese vernacular literature. See, e.g., a quatrain in *[Hsiao-shih] Chin-kang k'o-i [hui-yao chu-chieh]*, *chüan* 8, p. 738, upper register, l. 18; *Kuan-shih-yin p'u-sa pen-hsing ching*, p. 19a, l. 4; *Hsiao Sun-t'u*, scene 9, p. 285, l. 3; *Yüan-ch'ü hsüan*, 1:75, l. 6; *Ch'in ping liu-kuo p'ing-hua*, p. 54, l. 7; a song suite by Chou Wen-chih (d. 1334), *Ch'üan Yüan san-ch'ü*, 1:563, l. 12; *Cheng Chieh-shih li-kung shen-pi kung*, p. 657, l. 6; *Ching-ch'ai chi*, scene 14, p. 43, l. 4; a song suite by Wang Yüeh (1423–98), *Ch'üan Ming san-ch'ü*, 1:404, l. 3; *Fo-shuo Huang-chi chieh-kuo pao-chüan*, 10:357, l. 1; *Huang-chi chin-tan chiu-lien cheng-hsin kuei-chen huan-hsiang pao-chüan*, 8:147, ll. 1–2; *Yüeh Fei p'o-lu tung-ch'uang chi*, *chüan* 2, scene 29, p. 13a, l. 8; *T'an-shih wu-wei pao-chüan*, 1:547, l. 4; *Chiang Shih yüeh-li chi*, *chüan* 1, scene 2, p. 2b, l. 6; *Chang Tzu-fang mu-tao chi*, p. 106, l. 5; *Yao-shih pen-yüan kung-te pao-chüan*, 14:265, l. 1; *Pao-chien chi*, scene 4, p. 12, ll. 7–8; *Hai-fu shan-t'ang tz'u-kao*, *chüan* 1, p. 13, l. 2; *Hsi-yu chi*, vol. 1, ch. 1, p. 7, l. 13; a song suite by Yin Shih-tan (1522–82), *Ch'üan Ming san-ch'ü*, 2:2344, l. 3; a set of songs by Hsüeh Lun-tao (c. 1531–c. 1600), ibid., 3:2765, l. 11; *Ta-T'ang Ch'in-wang tz'u-hua*, vol. 1, *chüan* 4, ch. 30, p. 50b, l. 4; and an abundance of other occurrences, too numerous to list.

80. This four-character expression occurs in an admonition by Chang Hua (232–300), *Wen-hsüan*, vol. 3, *chüan* 56, p. 3a, l. 7; a couplet by Li P'ing (10th century), *Ch'üan T'ang shih*, vol. 11, *chüan* 795, p. 8950, l. 8; a poem written in 1096 by Ho Chu (1052–1125), *Ch'üan Sung shih*, 19:12508, l. 7; and *San-ming t'ung-hui*, *chüan* 2, p. 109b, l. 3.

81. This four-character expression occurs in *Ch'üan-Han chih-chuan*, vol. 3, *chüan* 2, p. 11a, ll. 4–5; and *Ts'an-T'ang Wu-tai shih yen-i chuan*, ch. 47, p. 191, l. 26.

82. This four-character expression occurs independently in *Huai-hsiang chi*, scene 25, p. 78, l. 1.

83. This couplet is derived from one in *[Chi-p'ing chiao-chu] Hsi-hsiang chi*, play no. 1, scene 1, p. 9, l. 1.

84. This four-character expression occurs in a lyric by Yang Wu-chiu (1097–1171), *Ch'üan Sung tz'u*, 2:1198, lower register, l. 10; and a lyric by Chang K'o-chiu (1270–1348), *Ch'üan Yüan san-ch'ü*, 1:763, ll. 4–5.

85. Lü-chu (d. 300) was the favorite concubine of Shih Ch'ung (249–300). She committed suicide by jumping from a tower after his death.

86. Lo-fu is the heroine of an anonymous Music Bureau ballad, possibly dating from the Later Han dynasty, in which she resolutely refuses the advances of an official who

has been attracted to her while she is picking mulberries, on the grounds that both of them are already married. The last five characters of the preceding line are a verbatim quote from this ballad. See *Yüeh-fu shih-chi*, vol. 2, *chüan* 28, p. 411, l. 5. This quatrain is derived, with some textual variation, from one in the version of *Huai-ch'un ya-chi* included in *Yen-chü pi-chi* (Ho Ta-lun), vol. 2, *chüan* 9, p. 15a ll. 14–15. It is not found in the other extant versions of this tale.

CHAPTER 79

1. This poem is by Shao Yung (1011–77). See *Ch'üan Sung shih*, 7:4505, ll. 6–7. A slightly different version of it has already occurred in the novel as the opening verse of chapter 26. See Roy, *The Plum in the Golden Vase*, vol. 2, ch. 26, p. 100, ll. 6–21; and n. 1.

2. The locus classicus for this four-character expression is the *Shu-ching* (Book of Documents). See Legge, *The Shoo King or the Book of Historical Documents*, p. 186, l. 9 of the Chinese text. It also occurs in the commentary to a long poem by Emperor T'ai-tsung of the Sung dynasty (r. 976–97), *Ch'üan Sung shih*, 1:321, l. 14.

3. The locus classicus for these two lines is the *Shu-ching* (Book of Documents). See Legge, *The Shoo King or the Book of Historical Documents*, p. 198, ll. 4–6 of the Chinese text. They are quoted verbatim in the commentary to a long poem by Emperor T'ai-tsung of the Sung dynasty (r. 976–97), *Ch'üan Sung shih*, 1:321, l. 6; *Chang Hsieh chuang-yüan*, scene 16, p. 83, l. 4; and *Ming-hsin pao-chien*, *chüan* 1, p. 1a, ll. 3–4.

4. This four-character expression occurs in the preface to the *Chin P'ing Mei tz'u-hua*, p. 5a, ll. 5–6. See Roy, *The Plum in the Golden Vase*, vol. 1, preface, p. 4, l. 43–p. 5, l. 1.

5. This four-character expression occurs in a song suite by Kuan Yün-shih (1286–1324), *Ch'üan Yüan san-ch'ü*, 1:384, l. 5; *Yüan-ch'ü hsüan*, 3:998, l. 7; an anonymous song in *T'ai-ho cheng-yin p'u* (Formulary for the correct sounds of great harmony), comp. Chu Ch'üan (1378–1448), in *Chung-kuo ku-tien hsi-ch'ü lun-chu chi-ch'eng*, 3:97, l. 2; a lyric by Ku Hsün (1418–1505), *Ch'üan Ming tz'u*, 1:294, lower register, l. 9; a song suite by Ch'en To (fl. early 16th century), *Ch'üan Ming san-ch'ü*, 1:647, l. 9; and an anonymous song suite in *Yung-hsi yüeh-fu*, *ts'e* 1, p. 32a, l. 1.

6. This four-character expression occurs in a lyric by Yüan T'ao (12th century), *Ch'üan Sung tz'u*, 2:986, upper register, l. 15; *Shui-hu ch'üan-chuan*, vol. 2, ch. 33, p. 516, l. 10; a song suite by Ch'en To (fl. early 16th century), *Ch'üan Ming san-ch'ü*, 1:672, l. 2; an anonymous song suite in *Sheng-shih hsin-sheng*, p. 73, l. 12; and an anonymous song suite in *Yung-hsi yüeh-fu*, *ts'e* 9, p. 5b, l. 6.

7. A variant of this couplet has already occurred in the novel. See Roy, *The Plum in the Golden Vase*, vol. 3, chap. 42, p. 23, ll. 28–31; and n. 6.

8. Variants of this idiomatic saying occur in *[Hsin-pien] Liu Chih-yüan huan-hsiang Pai-t'u chi*, p. 25b, l. 13; *Yü-huan chi*, scene 17, p. 63, l. 10; and *I-hsia chi*, scene 27, p. 72, l. 10.

9. This four-character expression occurs ubiquitously in Chinese vernacular literature. See, e.g., *Hsiao-p'in chi*, p. 57, l. 8; *Ta-Sung chung-hsing yen-i*, vol. 1, *chüan* 2, p. 21b, l. 6; *T'ang-shu chih-chuan t'ung-su yen-i*, vol. 1, *chüan* 5, p. 38a, l. 7; *Nan Sung*

chih-chuan, vol. 1, *chüan* 4, p. 14b, l. 11; *Pei Sung chih-chuan,* vol. 2, *chüan* 1, p. 15a, l. 2; *Lieh-kuo chih-chuan,* vol. 3, *chüan* 7, p. 28b, l. 3; *Tung-yu chi: shang-tung pa-hsien chuan, chüan* 2, p. 30a, l. 9; *Hua-shen san-miao chuan,* p. 33a, l. 9; *Ch'üan-Han chih-chuan,* vol. 3, *chüan* 3, p. 33b, l. 10; *Huang-Ming k'ai-yün ying-wu chuan, chüan* 1, p. 20a, l. 5; *Pai-chia kung-an, chüan* 5, ch. 49, p. 25b, l. 8; and *San-pao t'ai-chien Hsi-yang chi t'ung-su yen-i,* vol. 2, ch. 61, p. 791, l. 10.

10. See Roy, *The Plum in the Golden Vase,* vol. 1, chap. 19, n. 17.

11. This four-character expression occurs in *Chang Hsieh chuang-yüan,* scene 39, p. 170, l. 10; an anonymous Yüan dynasty song suite, *Ch'üan Yüan san-ch'ü,* 2:1877, l. 14; *Shui-hu ch'üan-chuan,* vol. 1, ch. 2, p. 17, l. 8; *Shen Hsiao-kuan i-niao hai ch'i-ming,* p. 396, l. 14; *Huan-sha chi,* scene 9, p. 26, l. 11; and a set of songs by Wu Kuo-pao (cs 1550), *Ch'üan Ming san-ch'ü,* 2:2264, l. 14.

12. This formulaic four-character expression occurs ubiquitously in Chinese vernacular literature. See, e.g., a poem written in 1087 by Su Shih (1037–1101), *Su Shih shih-chi,* vol. 5, *chüan* 28, p. 1476, l. 10; a lyric by Chi I (1193–1269), *Ch'üan Chin Yüan tz'u,* 2:1220, upper register, ll. 5–6; a song attributed to Yao Sui (1238–1313), *Ch'üan Yüan san-ch'ü,* 1:212, l. 9; a song suite by T'ung-t'ung (14th century), ibid., 2:1262, l. 4; *Yüan-ch'ü hsüan,* 2:800, l. 5; a set of songs by Ch'en To (fl. early 16th century), *Ch'üan Ming san-ch'ü,* 1:502, l. 5; a song suite by Ch'ang Lun (1493–1526), ibid., 2:1529, l. 3; *Hsin-ch'iao shih Han Wu mai ch'un-ch'ing,* p. 74, l. 3; *Hai-fu shan-t'ang tz'u-kao, chüan* 2b, p. 128, ll. 7–8; *Hai-ling i-shih,* p. 162, l. 11; *Sui-T'ang liang-ch'ao shih-chuan, chüan* 1, ch. 9, p. 56b, l. 8; and an abundance of other occurrences, too numerous to list. It also recurs in the *Chin P'ing Mei tz'u-hua,* vol. 5, ch. 99, p. 3a, l. 2.

13. This reduplicative four-character expression occurs in an anonymous song from the Yüan dynasty, *Ch'üan Yüan san-ch'ü,* 2:1669, l. 11; an anonymous song suite from the Yüan dynasty, ibid., 2:1804, l. 9; *Yüan-ch'ü hsüan,* 4:1652, l. 12; an anonymous song suite in *Yung-hsi yüeh-fu, ts'e* 3, p. 27b, l. 4; and an anonymous song in ibid., *ts'e* 19, p. 59a, l. 2.

14. The site of this apparition is the place where Wu Sung had inadvertently killed Li Wai-ch'uan in chapter 9, a death for which Hsi-men Ch'ing, Wu Sung's intended victim, was indirectly responsible. See Roy, *The Plum in the Golden Vase,* vol. 1, chap. 9, pp. 184–85.

15. On this couplet, see ibid., vol. 2, chap. 27, n. 4.

16. The depleted supply of the aphrodisiac remaining in the cylindrical pillbox (an obvious phallic symbol) is emblematic of Hsi-men Ch'ing's depleted virility.

17. This four-character expression occurs in *Ju-i chün chuan,* p. 15a, l. 6.

18. This detail, along with many others, the most significant of which is the administration of medicine (aphrodisiac/poison) to an incapacitated victim, recalls the scene in chapter 5 in which P'an Chin-lien murders her first husband, Wu Chih. There are a number of verbal correspondences. See the *Chin P'ing Mei tz'u-hua,* vol. 1, chap. 5, pp. 6a–8a; and Roy, *The Plum in the Golden Vase,* vol. 1, chap. 5, pp. 104–7.

19. This four-character expression occurs in *Pei Sung chih-chuan,* vol. 2, *chüan* 6, p. 11b, l. 6.

20. This four-character expression occurs in *Hsi-yu chi,* vol. 2, ch. 81, p. 928, l. 17.

21. This four-character expression occurs in *Ju-i chün chuan,* p. 13b, l. 1.

22. This clause occurs verbatim in ibid., p. 18a, l. 5.

23. Much of the language in these two paragraphs echoes that used by the author in the famous description of the scene in the grape arbor in chapter 27, except that, significantly, the roles of P'an Chin-lien and Hsi-men Ch'ing have been reversed.

24. At this point in the narrative the attentive reader will be reminded of Hsi-men Ch'ing's appearance on his way home from the assignation with Wang Liu-erh at the beginning of this episode. Swaying drunkenly on his runaway horse, dressed in purple, with a scarf wrapped around his neck, he has become the personification of a bloated penis with a constricting satin band tied around its root. In the course of ingesting the Indian monk's medicine, he has gradually come to replicate the appearance of that emblematic figure from whom he acquired the aphrodisiac in chapter 49, whose complexion is there described in identical words as being "the color of purple liver." See the *Chin P'ing Mei tz'u-hua*, vol. 3, chap. 49, p. 13a, l. 2; and Roy, *The Plum in the Golden Vase*, vol. 3, chap. 49, p. 193, l. 35.

25. The act of putting a restorative red date into the mouth of the fainting Hsi-men Ch'ing is obviously intended to parallel the act of putting a glob of aphrodisiac ointment into the mouth of his urethra a little while before.

26. This four-character expression occurs in *Han Fei tzu so-yin*, ch. 13, p. 750, l. 4; a letter by Li Po (701–62), *Ch'üan T'ang wen*, vol. 8, *chüan* 348, p. 13b, l. 9; and *San-pao t'ai-chien Hsi-yang chi t'ung-su yen-i*, vol. 1, ch. 9, p. 110, l. 15.

27. These are the very words uttered by P'an Chin-lien at the climax of the episode in the grape arbor in chapter 27. See the *Chin P'ing Mei tz'u-hua*, vol. 2, chap. 27, p. 12b, ll. 10–11; and Roy, *The Plum in the Golden Vase*, vol. 2, chap. 27, p. 149, ll. 12–13.

28. This is a quotation from *Chuang-tzu*. See *Chuang-tzu yin-te*, ch. 6, p. 15, l. 7.

29. This formulaic saying echoes and fulfills its earlier use as a predictive device in chapter 6 of the novel. See Roy, *The Plum in the Golden Vase*, vol. 1, chap. 6, p. 117, ll. 3–6. Its proximate source is *Shui-hu ch'üan-chuan*, vol. 1, ch. 26, p. 407, l. 5.

30. These two four-character expressions occur in an anonymous song suite in *Yung-hsi yüeh-fu*, ts'e 4, p. 34b, l. 9.

31. This four-character expression occurs in *Yüan-ch'ü hsüan*, 4:1465, ll. 7–8; and *Mu-lien chiu-mu ch'üan-shan hsi-wen*, *chüan* 1, p. 70a, l. 1.

32. The proximate source of this descriptive passage of rhyming prose, with minor textual variants, is *Chang Yü-hu su nü-chen kuan chi*, p. 19a, l. 9–p. 19b, l. 2. The last two lines may ultimately be derived from the final couplet of a quatrain that is variously attributed to the late-ninth-century figures Tu Kuang-t'ing and Cheng Ao. See *Ch'üan T'ang shih*, vol. 12, *chüan* 854, p. 9666, l. 14; and *chüan* 855, p. 9672, l. 3.

33. This four-character expression occurs ubiquitously in Chinese vernacular literature. See, e.g., a poem written in 1073 by Su Shih (1037–1101), *Su Shih shih-chi*, vol. 2, *chüan* 9, p. 447, l. 1; a lyric by Teng Su (1091–1133), *Ch'üan Sung tz'u*, 2:1107, upper register, l. 4; a poem by Wang Che (1112–70), *Ch'üan Chin shih*, 1:192, l. 11; a quatrain by the Buddhist monk Chung-jen (d. 1203), *Wu-teng hui-yüan*, vol. 3, *chüan* 19, p. 1291, l. 7; a set of poems by Hao Ta-t'ung (1140–1212), *Ch'üan Chin shih*, 2:4, l. 10; *Ching-ch'ai chi*, scene 7, p. 16, l. 4; *Ts'ao Po-ming ts'o-k'an tsang chi*, p. 206, l. 15; *San-pao t'ai-chien Hsi-yang chi t'ung-su yen-i*, vol. 2, ch. 95, p. 1222, l. 8; *Ta-T'ang Ch'in-wang tz'u-hua*, vol. 1, *chüan* 7, ch. 54, p. 44a, l. 4; and *[Hsin-k'o] Shih-shang hua-yen ch'ü-lo t'an-hsiao chiu-ling*, *chüan* 4, p. 2a, upper register, l. 10.

34. This four-character expression occurs in a literary tale in *Yüan-chu chih-yü: hsüeh-ch'uang t'an-i*, *chüan* 1, p. 40, l. 11.

35. This quatrain is attributed to Lü Tung-pin (9th century). See *Ch'üan T'ang shih*, vol. 12, *chüan* 858, p. 9702, l. 12. It is quoted without attribution in *Shui-hu ch'üan-chuan*, vol. 2, ch. 44, p. 723, l. 7; and *Hsin-ch'iao shih Han Wu mai ch'un-ch'ing*, p. 73, l. 6. Both of these works are known to have been drawn upon by the author of the *Chin P'ing Mei tz'u-hua*.

36. On this couplet see Roy, *The Plum in the Golden Vase*, vol. 3, chap. 54, n. 42.

37. This four-character expression occurs in the title of a poem by Mei Yao-ch'en (1002–60), *Ch'üan Sung shih*, 5:2800, l. 11; a passage of poetic criticism by Chou Tzu-chih (1083–1155), *Sung shih-hua ch'üan-pien*, 3:2833, l. 3; *I-chien chih*, vol. 1, *ping-chih* (third record), *chüan* 1, p. 364, l. 10; *Hsüan-ho i-shih*, p. 111, l. 1; and the middle-period vernacular story *Cheng Yüan-ho*, in *Tsui yü-ch'ing*, 4:1441, upper register, l. 3.

38. See Roy, *The Plum in the Golden Vase*, vol. 2, chap. 29, p. 175, ll. 4–5.

39. This four-character expression occurs in *Shang Lu san-yüan chi*, *chüan* 1, scene 12, p. 17a, l. 10; *Pai-p'ao chi*, *chüan* 1, scene 14, p. 20a, l. 3; *Su Ying huang-hou ying-wu chi*, *chüan* 2, scene 25, p. 13b, ll. 2–3; an anonymous song suite in *Yung-hsi yüeh-fu*, *ts'e* 8, p. 78b, l. 3; and a set of songs by Hsüeh Kang (c. 1535–95), *Ch'üan Ming san-ch'ü*, 3:2970, l. 2.

40. This four-character expression occurs in *Shen-hsiang ch'üan-pien*, *chüan* 642, p. 24a, ll. 8–9.

41. This four-character expression occurs ubiquitously in Chinese literature. See, e.g., a speech attributed to the Buddhist monk Fa-ch'ang (1005–81), *Wu-teng hui-yüan*, vol. 3, *chüan* 16, p. 1024, l. 15; a letter by Chu Hsi (1130–1200), *Hui-an hsien-sheng Chu Wen-kung wen-chi*, *chüan* 26, p. 5a, l. 6; a song by Wang Ho-ch'ing (13th century), *Ch'üan Yüan san-ch'ü*, 1:43, l. 7; a song suite by Ching Kan-ch'en (13th century), ibid., 1:139, l. 12; *[Chiao-ting] Yüan-k'an tsa-chü san-shih chung*, p. 93, l. 5; *Yüan-ch'ü hsüan*, 3:963, l. 19; *Yüan-ch'ü hsüan wai-pien*, 3:716, l. 18; a song suite by T'ang Fu (14th century), *Ch'üan Ming san-ch'ü*, 1:229, l. 1; *Hsiang-nang chi*, scene 23, p. 63, l. 8; *San-kuo chih t'ung-su yen-i*, *chüan* 8, p. 390, l. 15; *Wang Lan-ch'ing chen-lieh chuan*, scene 3, p. 5a, l. 10; *Chiang Shih yüeh-li chi*, *chüan* 1, scene 14, p. 24b, l. 7; *Yü-huan chi*, scene 22, p. 83, l. 5; and *Mu-lien chiu-mu ch'üan-shan hsi-wen*, *chüan* 2, p. 28a, l. 9.

42. These four characters occur in a poem attributed to Sun Ssu-miao (581–682), *Ch'üan T'ang shih pu-pien*, 2:686, ll. 13–14.

43. This four-character expression occurs in a poem by Li Po (701–62), *Ch'üan T'ang shih*, vol. 3, *chüan* 166, p. 1715, l. 9; a poem by Huang T'ing-chien (1045–1105), *Ch'üan Sung shih*, 17:11513, l. 5; a lyric by Liu Kuo (1154–1206), *Ch'üan Sung tz'u*, 3:2144, upper register, ll. 7–8; a lyric by Ch'ü Yu (1341–1427), *Ch'üan Ming tz'u*, 1:167, lower register, l. 6; a lyric by Chang Ch'e (15th century), ibid., 1:224, upper register, l. 1; *Lien-huan chi*, *chüan* 1, scene 13, p. 33, l. 4; a song suite by Chu Ying-ch'en (16th century), *Ch'üan Ming san-ch'ü*, 2:1273, l. 12; *Yü-huan chi*, scene 10, p. 31, l. 11; and a lyric by Wang Ts'ai (1508–84), *Ch'üan Ming tz'u pu-pien*, 1:404, upper register, ll. 1–2.

44. See Roy, *The Plum in the Golden Vase*, vol. 1, chap. 17, n. 14.

45. This quatrain is derived, with one insignificant textual variant, from one in *Pao-chien chi*, scene 10, p. 22, ll. 4–5.

46. This four-character expression occurs in a quatrain by Chou Mo (10th century), *Ch'üan Sung shih*, 1:251, l. 12; *Chien-teng yü-hua*, *chüan* 4, p. 255, l. 10; and *San-pao t'ai-chien Hsi-yang chi t'ung-su yen-i*, vol. 1, ch. 20, p. 259, l. 4.

47. Kuei-ku tzu (the Master of the Demon Gorge) is a legendary Taoist sage, said to have lived in the fourth century B.C. Sources differ as to his real name, but it is said in some of them to have been Wang Ch'an, the name that is given in the novel. See, e.g., *Ch'i-kuo ch'un-ch'iu p'ing-hua*, p. 74, l. 7; and *Yüan-ch'ü hsüan*, 2:733, l. 4.

48. Death Knell and Condoler are baleful stars. See above, chap. 61, n. 64.

49. The proximate source of these six lines is *Pao-chien chi*, scene 10, p. 22, ll. 9–10.

50. The proximate source of this quatrain is ibid., ll. 23–24.

51. There is a temple to this goddess on the peak of Mount T'ai that even today remains an important pilgrimage site. See the map in Naquin and Yü, eds., *Pilgrims and Sacred Sites in China*, p. 40. For a succinct study of her cult, see ibid., pp. 334–38.

52. This idiomatic expression occurs in *Hsi-yu chi*, vol. 2, ch. 70, p. 804, l. 9.

53. This four-character expression occurs ubiquitously in Chinese literature. See, e.g., *I-chien chih*, vol. 2, *chih-chih, chia* (second record, section 1), *chüan* 3, p. 733, l. 7; *Yüan-ch'ü hsüan*, 3:1149, l. 2; *Hsiao-p'in chi*, p. 1, l. 13; *Chung-ch'ing li-chi, chüan* 6, p. 29a, l. 9; *Yüeh Fei p'o-lu tung-ch'uang chi, chüan* 2, scene 38, p. 29a, l. 4; *Hsiang-nang chi*, scene 4, p. 11, l. 10; *Hua-ying chi*, p. 864, l. 9; *Shui-hu ch'üan-chuan*, vol. 2, ch. 52, p. 859, l. 8; *Hua-shen san-miao chuan*, p. 53a, ll. 1–2; *T'ien-yüan ch'i-yü, chüan* 8, p. 14a, l. 1; *Hsi-yu chi*, vol. 1, ch. 38, p. 434, l. 4; *Pai-chia kung-an, chüan* 1, ch. 2, p. 14b, l. 7; *San-pao t'ai-chien Hsi-yang chi t'ung-su yen-i*, vol. 1, ch. 46, p. 595, l. 3; *Mu-tan t'ing*, scene 32, p. 173, l. 10; and an abundance of other occurrences, too numerous to list.

54. See Roy, *The Plum in the Golden Vase*, vol. 1, chap. 20, n. 35.

55. This line occurs in *[Hsin-k'o] Shih-shang hua-yen ch'ü-lo t'an-hsiao chiu-ling, chüan* 4, p. 10b, upper register, l. 10.

56. This four-character expression occurs in *Chung-ch'ing li-chi, chüan* 7, p. 27a, l. 10.

57. This four-character expression for marital fidelity occurs in *Ching-ch'ai chi*, scene 32, p. 100, l. 9; *P'i-p'a chi*, scene 22, p. 133, l. 11; *Huang hsiao-tzu, chüan* 1, scene 6, p. 10b, l. 9; *Nan Hsi-hsiang chi* (Lu Ts'ai), scene 35, p. 409, l. 10; and *I-hsia chi*, scene 9, p. 22, l. 4.

58. This four-character expression occurs in *Ching-ch'ai chi*, scene 21, p. 65, l. 9.

59. This four-character expression occurs in *Yüan-ch'ü hsüan*, 2:642, l. 5; *Yüan-ch'ü hsüan wai-pien*, 1:9, l. 8; *Yün chi-mou Sui Ho p'ien Ying Pu*, scene 3, p. 8b, l. 9; an anonymous song suite in *Yung-hsi yüeh-fu, ts'e* 6, p. 19b, l. 1; and an abundance of other occurrences, too numerous to list.

60. For an explanation of the term *hsiang-huo* (ministerial fire), see Nigel Wiseman and Feng Ye, *A Practical Dictionary of Chinese Medicine* (Brookline, Mass.: Paradigm Publications, 2002), p. 396.

61. This proverbial couplet occurs ubiquitously in Chinese vernacular literature. See, e.g., *Kuan-shih-yin p'u-sa pen-hsing ching*, p. 18b, l. 9; *[Chiao-ting] Yüan-k'an tsa-chü san-shih chung*, p. 22, l. 1; *[Chi-p'ing chiao-chu] Hsi-hsiang chi*, play no. 5, scene 4, p. 200, ll. 1–2; *Yüan-ch'ü hsüan*, 4:1651, l. 17; *Hsüan-ho i-shih*, p. 54, l. 6; *Ming-hsin pao-chien, chüan* 2, p. 4a, l. 4; *Ching-ch'ai chi*, scene 34, p. 105, l. 7; *Liang-shan wu-hu ta chieh-lao*, scene 4, p. 7b, l. 13; *Shang Lu san-yüan chi, chüan* 1, scene 14, p. 20b, l. 9; and *Shui-hu ch'üan-chuan*, vol. 1, ch. 21, p. 317, l. 17. It also recurs in the *Chin P'ing Mei tz'u-hua*, vol. 5, ch. 87, p. 10a, l. 3; and ch. 99, p. 8b, ll. 4–5. The first line

occurs independently in *Yüan-ch'ü hsüan wai-pien*, 2:382, l. 2; and the second line occurs independently in *Yüan-ch'ü hsüan*, 1:396, l. 13; *Yüan-ch'ü hsüan wai-pien*, 2:4, l. 2; *Chin-yin chi, chüan* 2, scene 16, p. 19b, l. 5; *Ch'ien-chin chi*, scene 41, p. 134, l. 2; *Chang Tzu-fang mu-tao chi*, p. 109, l. 10; *Pai-p'ao chi, chüan* 1, scene 14, p. 20a, l. 10; and *San-pao t'ai-chien Hsi-yang chi t'ung-su yen-i*, vol. 1, ch. 17, p. 221, l. 5.

62. On Teng T'ung (2nd century B.C.) and the Copper Mountains see Roy, *The Plum in the Golden Vase*, vol. 3, chap. 56, n. 4.

63. This formulaic four-character expression occurs ubiquitously in Chinese vernacular literature. See, e.g., *Yüan-ch'ü hsüan*, 2:801, l. 8; an anonymous Yüan dynasty song, *Ch'üan Yüan san-ch'ü*, 2:1886, l. 8; *Chin-t'ung Yü-nü Chiao Hung chi*, p. 7, l. 1; *Shih-pa kuo Lin-t'ung tou-pao*, scene 2, p. 685, l. 8; *Wu Lun-ch'üan Pei, chüan* 1, scene 6, p. 30b, l. 4; *T'an-shih wu-wei pao-chüan*, 1:517, l. 1; *Tung Yung yü-hsien chuan*, p. 238, l. 15; and *Ch'üan-Han chih-chuan*, vol. 2, chüan 5, p. 27a, l. 8.

64. This four-character expression occurs in *Shih-pa kuo Lin-t'ung tou-pao*, scene 4, p. 701, l. 12.

65. This formulaic four-character expression occurs ubiquitously in Chinese vernacular literature. See, e.g., *Ju-ju chü-shih yü-lu, chia-chi* (first collection), *chüan* 1, p. 5b, ll. 9–10; *Yüan-ch'ü hsüan*, 2:462, l.8; *Yüan-ch'ü hsüan wai-pien*, 3:753, ll. 13–14; *San-kuo chih t'ung-su yen-i*, vol. 2, *chüan* 18, p. 838, ll. 5–6; *Shui-hu ch'üan-chuan*, vol. 1, ch. 11, p. 169, l. 11; *Huang T'ing-tao yeh-tsou Liu-hsing ma*, scene 3, p. 106, l. 3; the tsa-chü drama *Chung-shan lang yüan-pen* (Yüan-pen on the wolf of Chung-shan), by Wang Chiu-ssu (1468–1551), in *Ming-jen tsa-chü hsüan*, p. 264, l. 6; *Lieh-kuo chih-chuan*, vol. 2, *chüan* 4, p. 48a, l. 6; *Pai-chia kung-an, chüan* 3, ch. 27, p. 17a, l. 7; *Yang-chia fu shih-tai chung-yung yen-i chih-chuan*, vol. 2, *chüan* 8, p. 22a, l. 1; *Ta-T'ang Ch'in-wang tz'u-hua*, vol. 2, *chüan* 6, ch. 45, p. 41a, l. 7; and a host of other occurrences, too numerous to list. It also recurs in the *Chin P'ing Mei tz'u-hua*, vol. 5, ch. 95, p. 5b, l. 6.

66. This four-character expression occurs in *Wang K'uei*, 4:1511, upper register, l. 7; *K'an p'i-hsüeh tan-cheng Erh-lang Shen*, p. 258, l. 1; and *Chiao-hsiao chi, chüan* 1, scene 10, p. 22b, l. 4.

67. A variant of this proverbial couplet occurs in *Hsün-ch'in chi*, scene 17, p. 58, ll. 6–7. The second line occurs independently in *Ming-hsin pao-chien, chüan* 2, p. 14a, l. 4.

68. The last line of this verse is from a quatrain by Fan Chung-yen (989–1052), *Ch'üan Sung shih*, 3:1918, l. 3.

CHAPTER 80

1. On this four-character expression, see Roy, *The Plum in the Golden Vase*, vol. 1, chap. 13, n. 16.

2. This proverbial couplet occurs frequently in Chinese vernacular literature. See, e.g., the author's commentary to a quatrain by the Buddhist monk I-ch'ing (1032–1083), *Ch'üan Sung shih*, 12:8217, l. 12; *Chang Hsieh chuang-yüan*, scene 34, p. 159, l. 7; *Yüan-ch'ü hsüan wai-pien*, 1:24, l. 8; a song suite by Sun Shu-shun (14th century), *Ch'üan Yüan san-ch'ü*, 2:1137, l. 5; *Sha-kou chi*, scene 16, p. 57, l. 8; *Ming-hsin pao-chien, chüan* 2, p. 3a, l. 13; *Pai-t'u chi*, scene 10, p. 33, l. 6; *P'i-p'a chi*, scene 40, p. 220,

ll. 1–2; *Chin-yin chi, chüan* 1, scene 10, p. 23a, l. 8; *Huan-tai chi, chüan* 2, scene 33, p. 31b, l. 3; *P'o-yao chi, chüan* 2, scene 28, p. 41a, l. 3; *Chiang Shih yüeh-li chi, chüan* 1, scene 9, p. 14b, l. 8; *Hsün-ch'in chi*, scene 25, p. 84, ll. 2–3; *Shui-hu ch'üan-chuan*, vol. 2, ch. 37, p. 590, l. 16; *Chin-tiao chi, chüan* 3, scene 32, p. 28a, l. 7; and *San-pao t'ai-chien Hsi-yang chi t'ung-su yen-i*, vol. 2, ch. 85, p. 1093, l. 2. The first line also occurs independently in an anonymous song suite in *Yung-hsi yüeh-fu*, ts'e 4, p. 42b, l. 9; and the second line in *Yüan-ch'ü hsüan*, 4:1362, l. 2; *Yüan-ch'ü hsüan wai-pien*, 1:45, l. 14; *Ch'ung-mo-tzu tu-pu Ta-lo T'ien*, scene 2, p. 4b, l. 14; *P'o-yao chi, chüan* 2, scene 28, p. 39a, l. 4; *Yü-huan chi*, scene 31, p. 113, l. 10; and *Hai-fu shan-t'ang tz'u-kao, chüan* 2a, p. 70, l. 8.

3. This formulaic four-character expression occurs ubiquitously in Chinese literature. See, e.g., a quatrain by Chao Ch'ung-sen (12th century), *Ch'üan Sung shih*, 38:23717, l. 11; a poem by Wen T'ien-hsiang (1236–83), ibid., 68:42993, l. 17; a song by Kuan Yün-shih (1286–1324), *Ch'üan Yüan san-ch'ü*, 1:368, l. 2; a set of songs by Wang Yüan-heng (14th century), ibid., 2:1387, l. 5; *Yüan-ch'ü hsüan*, 2:453, l. 15; *Yüan-ch'ü hsüan wai-pien*, 2:670, l. 19; *Yü-ch'iao hsien-hua*, scene 1, p. 1a, l. 10; *Chin-yin chi, chüan* 1, scene 2, p. 2b, l. 8; a set of songs by Wang Chiu-ssu (1468–1551), *Ch'üan Ming san-ch'ü*, 1:903, l. 7; a parallel prose couplet by Li K'ai-hsien (1502–68) published in 1552, *Li K'ai-hsien ch'üan-chi* (The complete works of Li K'ai-hsien), ed. and annot. Pu Chien, 3 vols. (Peking: Wen-hua i-shu ch'u-pan she, 2004), 3:1440, l. 6; *Han Hsiang-tzu chiu-tu Wen-kung sheng-hsien chi, chüan* 1, scene 6, p. 10a, l. 8; a lyric written in 1573 by Feng Wei-min (1511–80), *Hai-fu shan-t'ang tz'u-kao, chüan* 2a, p. 73, ll. 2–3; a song suite by Yin Shih-tan (1522–82), *Ch'üan Ming san-ch'ü*, 2:2340, l. 15; a song suite written in 1594 by Wang K'o-tu (c. 1526–c. 1594), ibid., 2:2471, l. 13; a lyric by Ch'en Shih-yüan (1516–96), *Ch'üan Ming tz'u*, 3:1027, lower register, l. 16; and a song suite by Ch'en So-wen (d. c. 1604), *Ch'üan Ming san-ch'ü*, 2:2548, l. 9.

4. This four-character expression occurs in a famous document entitled *P'eng-tang lun* (On factions) composed by Ou-yang Hsiu (1007–72) in 1044. See *Ou-yang Yung-shu chi*, vol. 1, *chüan* 17, p. 22, l. 9.

5. See Roy, *The Plum in the Golden Vase*, vol. 2, chap. 21, n. 2.

6. This four-character expression occurs in *Lieh-kuo chih-chuan*, vol. 3, *chüan* 8, p. 68b, l. 4.

7. This four-character expression occurs in *Hsi-yu chi*, vol. 2, ch. 93, p. 1051, l. 7.

8. This four-character expression occurs in *Yüeh Fei p'o-lu tung-ch'uang chi, chüan* 2, scene 40, p. 33b, l. 10.

9. As pointed out on pages xxxvii–xxxviii of my introduction, this parodic eulogy is a piece of sustained double entendre, intended to suggest none too subtly that Hsi-men Ch'ing is nothing but a prick, and that his sycophantic friends are like his testicles.

10. This proverbial saying recurs in the *Chin P'ing Mei tz'u-hua*, vol. 5, ch. 86, p. 11a, l. 11. The second line recurs independently in ibid., p. 10b, l. 8. Variants of the second line also occur in *Ching-ch'u T'ang tsa-chih* (Miscellaneous records from the Ching-ch'u Hall), by Ni Ssu (1174–1220), in *Shuo-fu san-chung*, 6:3482, p. 7a, l. 9; and *Hai-fu shan-t'ang tz'u-kao, chüan* 3, p. 178, l. 4.

11. Variants of this proverbial saying occur in *Chang Hsieh chuang-yüan*, scene 33, p. 157, l. 5; *Yüan-ch'ü hsüan*, 2:651, l. 8; *Sung Ssu-kung ta-nao Chin-hun Chang*,

p. 530, ll. 15–16; *Shih-wu kuan hsi-yen ch'eng ch'iao-huo*, p. 704, l. 6; *Shui-hu ch'üan-chuan*, vol. 1, ch. 6, p. 100, l. 17; *Tung-t'ien hsüan-chi*, scene 1, p. 5b, l. 8; and *Hsi-yu chi*, vol. 2, ch. 96, p. 1088, l. 9.

12. This four-character expression occurs in *Feng-yüeh Nan-lao chi*, scene 4, p. 9a, l. 3; the anonymous Ming ch'uan-ch'i drama *Wang Chao-chün ch'u-sai ho-jung chi* (Wang Chao-chün is sent abroad to make a marriage alliance with the Huns), in *Ku-pen hsi-ch'ü ts'ung-k'an, erh-chi* (Collectanea of rare editions of traditional drama, second series) (Shanghai: Shang-wu yin-shu kuan, 1955), item 7, *chüan* 2, scene 30, p. 28b, ll. 5–6; a fragment of the lost ch'uan-ch'i drama *Hsi-kua chi* (The watermelon story), in *Feng-yüeh chin-nang [chien-chiao]*, p. 624, l. 5; and *Shih-i chi, chüan* 1, scene 9, p. 16b, l. 1.

13. This four-character expression occurs in *Wu Tzu-hsü pien-wen*, p. 8, l. 2; *T'ien-pao i-shih chu-kung-tiao*, p. 220, l. 8; *Ming-chu chi*, scene 17, p. 46, l. 6; *Wang Chao-chün ch'u-sai ho-jung chi, chüan* 1, scene 6, p. 14b, l. 5; and *Han Hsiang-tzu chiu-tu Wen-kung sheng-hsien chi, chüan* 2, scene 21, p. 11b, l. 1.

14. This four-character expression recurs in the *Chin P'ing Mei tz'u-hua*, vol. 5, ch. 100, p.7a, l. 8.

15. This four-character expression occurs in *Hsi-yu chi*, vol. 1, ch. 44, p. 515, l. 10.

16. See Roy, *The Plum in the Golden Vase*, vol. 2, chap. 38, n. 19.

17. This proverbial saying occurs in *Yüan-ch'ü hsüan*, 2:812, l. 10.

18. For a succinct discussion of the ironic significance of the introduction of this play at this point in the novel, see Carlitz, *The Rhetoric of Chin p'ing mei*, p. 99.

19. A synonymous variant of this four-character expression occurs in *Shui-hu ch'üan-chuan*, vol. 2, ch. 35, p. 548, l. 5; *Ta-Sung chung-hsing yen-i*, vol. 1, *chüan* 1, p. 19b, ll. 10–11; *T'ang-shu chih-chuan t'ung-su yen-i*, vol. 1, *chüan* 1, p. 20b, l. 2; *Pei Sung chih-chuan*, vol. 2, *chüan* 4, p. 4a, l. 10; *Lieh-kuo chih-chuan*, vol. 1, *chüan* 1, p. 29b, ll. 6–7; *Hsi-yu chi*, vol. 1, ch. 21, p. 243, l. 12; *Tung-yu chi: shang-tung pa-hsien chuan, chüan* 2, p. 36b, ll. 4–5; *San-pao t'ai-chien Hsi-yang chi t'ung-su yen-i*, vol. 1, ch. 3, p. 37, l. 14; *Yang-chia fu shih-tai chung-yung yen-i chih-chuan*, vol. 2, *chüan* 7, p. 26a, l. 6; and *Sui-T'ang liang-ch'ao shih-chuan, chüan* 3, ch. 29, p. 52a, l. 6. It occurs in the same form as in the novel in *[Hsin-pien] Wu-tai shih p'ing-hua*, p. 48, l. 3; *San-kuo chih t'ung-su yen-i*, vol. 1, *chüan* 3, p. 104, l. 23; *Nan Sung chih-chuan*, vol. 1, *chüan* 7, p. 10a, l. 8; *Pei Sung chih-chuan*, vol. 3, *chüan* 7, p. 26a, l. 2; *Ts'an-T'ang Wu-tai shih yen-i chuan*, ch. 11, p. 38, l. 25; and *Ch'üan-Han chih-chuan*, vol. 3, *chüan* 4, p. 40a, l. 2.

20. This couplet, with one textual variant, is from a poem by Chu Shu-chen (fl. 1078–1138), *Ch'üan Sung shih*, 28:17950, l. 11.

21. A version of this anonymous song, with some textual variation, is preserved in *Yung-hsi yüeh-fu, ts'e* 17, pp. 44b–45a.

22. This four-character expression occurs in a work of Taoist exegesis entitled *Tao-te chen-ching chih-kuei* (A reconsideration of the meaning of the *Tao-te ching*), attributed to Yen Chün-p'ing (1st century B.C.), in *Cheng-t'ung Tao-tsang, ts'e* 376, *chüan* 8, p. 11a, l. 9; and a fragment of the lost ch'uan-ch'i drama *Hui-wen chi* (The story of the palindrome), in *Feng-yüeh chin-nang [chien-chiao]*, p. 687, l. 9.

23. This quatrain, with insignificant textual variation, has already appeared in the novel as the closing poem of chap. 65.

24. The above twenty-two lines, with minor textual variation, have already occurred in the novel. See the *Chin P'ing Mei tz'u-hua*, vol. 3, ch. 51, p. 17b, ll. 2–7; and Roy, *The Plum in the Golden Vase*, vol. 3, chap. 51, pp. 245–46.

25. These two lines have already occurred in the *Chin P'ing Mei tz'u-hua*, vol. 4, ch. 74, p. 11b, ll. 8–9.

26. This four-character expression occurs in *Chin-yin chi*, *chüan* 2, scene 13, p. 8a, l. 3; and *[Hsiao-shih] Chen-k'ung pao-chüan*, 18:538, l. 4.

27. These are the four elements of which all things are made according to Buddhist doctrine. See above, chap. 65, n. 21.

28. This four-character expression occurs ubiquitously in Chinese vernacular literature. See, e.g., *Tung Chieh-yüan Hsi-hsiang chi*, *chüan* 5, p. 103, l. 9; *[Hsin-pien] Wu-tai shih p'ing-hua*, p. 163, l. 5; a lyric by Li Tao-ch'un (fl. late 13th century), *Ch'üan Chin Yüan tz'u*, 2:1232, lower register, l. 12; *Nao Fan-lou to-ch'ing Chou Sheng-hsien*, p. 272, l. 2; *Shui-hu ch'üan-chuan*, vol. 1, ch. 5, p. 84, l. 2; *Jen hsiao-tzu lieh-hsing wei shen*, p. 582, l. 10; and *San Sui p'ing-yao chuan*, *chüan* 4, ch. 20, p. 42a, l. 5.

29. This four-character expression occurs in a letter by Hsiao Chu (1013–73), *Ch'üan Sung wen*, vol. 24, *chüan* 1029, p. 377, l. 6; a lyric by Hsieh Chin (1369–1415), *Ch'üan Ming tz'u*, 1:212, lower register, l. 5; *Huan-tai chi*, *chüan* 2, scene 22, p. 5b, l. 5; *Chin-tiao chi*, *chüan* 4, scene 42, p. 26b, l. 6; *San-pao t'ai-chien Hsi-yang chi t'ung-su yen-i*, vol. 2, ch. 74, p. 950, l. 6; and a set of songs by Hsüeh Lun-tao (c. 1531–c. 1600), *Ch'üan Ming san-ch'ü*, 3:2857, l. 5.

30. A virtually synonymous variant of these two lines occurs in *T'ai-kung chia-chiao* (Family teachings of T'ai-kung), in Chou Feng-wu, *Tun-huang hsieh-pen T'ai-kung chia-chiao yen-chiu* (A study of the Tun-huang manuscripts of the *T'ai-kung chia-chiao*) (Taipei: Ming-wen shu-chü, 1986), p. 58, l. 16. They occur together in the same form as in the novel in a speech attributed to the Buddhist monk Yen-chao (896–973), *Wu-teng hui-yüan*, vol. 2, *chüan* 11, p. 677, ll. 4–5; *Ju-ju chü-shih yü-lu*, *chia-chi* (first collection), *chüan* 1, p. 9b, l. 7; *Kuan-shih-yin p'u-sa pen-hsing ching*, p. 37a, l. 6; *Pai Niang-tzu yung-chen Lei-feng T'a*, p. 422, l. 8; *Sha-kou chi*, scene 25, p. 97, ll. 9–10; and *San-pao t'ai-chien Hsi-yang chi t'ung-su yen-i*, vol. 2, ch. 84, p. 1082, l. 15. The first line also occurs independently in a gatha by the Buddhist monk Tao-ning (1053–1113), *Ch'üan Sung shih*, 19:12904, l. 7; a gatha by the Buddhist monk Ying-tuan (1069–1129), ibid., 22:14953, l. 7; *Ming-feng chi*, scene 7, p. 28, l. 7; and a set of songs by Hsüeh Lun-tao (c. 1531–c. 1600), *Ch'üan Ming san-ch'ü*, 3:2802, l. 12.

31. An orthographic variant of this four-character expression occurs in *Yu-kuei chi*, scene 34, p. 99, l. 6; and a song suite by Ch'en To (fl. early 16th century), *Ch'üan Ming san-ch'ü*, 1:621, l. 6. It occurs in the same form as in the novel in *[Chiao-ting] Yüan-k'an tsa-chü san-shih chung*, p. 398, l. 8; *Yüan-ch'ü hsüan*, 1:347, ll. 5–6; *Yüan-ch'ü hsüan wai-pien*, 3:845, l. 17; *Chin-t'ung Yü-nü Chiao Hung chi*, p. 58, l. 1; *Yü-huan chi*, scene 16, p. 58, l. 10; *Wang Ai-hu ta-nao Tung-p'ing fu*, scene 2, p. 3b, l. 2; *Ch'ang-an ch'eng ssu-ma t'ou-T'ang*, scene 2, p. 7b, l. 5; *Hai-fu shan-t'ang tz'u-kao*, *chüan* 2a, p. 81, l. 13; *Hsi-yu chi*, vol. 2, ch. 80, p. 912, l. 10; a set of songs by Liu Hsiao-tsu (1522–89), *Ch'üan Ming san-ch'ü*, 2:2321, l. 12; *Mu-tan t'ing*, scene 32, p. 170, l. 10; *Shih-hou chi*, scene 10, p. 30, l. 8; and an abundance of other occurrences, too numerous to list. It also recurs in the *Chin P'ing Mei tz'u-hua*, vol. 5, ch. 83, p. 1b, l. 7.

32. This four-character expression occurs in *San-pao t'ai-chien Hsi-yang chi t'ung-su yen-i*, vol. 2, ch. 83, p. 1068, l. 14; and recurs in the *Chin P'ing Mei tz'u-hua*, vol. 5, ch. 86, p. 1b, l. 7.

33. This idiomatic expression recurs in ibid., ch. 87, p. 7b, l. 8.

34. Variants of this proverbial expression occur in *Ming-kung shu-p'an ch'ing-ming chi*, vol. 2, *chüan* 12, p. 461, l. 8; *San-pao t'ai-chien Hsi-yang chi t'ung-su yen-i*, vol. 2, ch. 89, p. 1152, ll. 5–6; and *Liu-yüan hui-hsüan chiang-hu fang-yü* (Slang expressions current in the demimonde selected from the six licensed brothels [of Chin-ling]), in *Han-shang huan wen-ts'un*, p. 160, lower register, l. 13.

35. Versions of this poem, with considerable textual variation, and completely different first, seventh, and eighth lines, occur in *Ts'ao Po-ming ts'o-k'an tsang chi*, p. 206, l. 15–p. 207, l. 3; and *[Hsin-k'o] Shih-shang hua-yen ch'ü-lo t'an-hsiao chiu-ling*, *chüan* 4, p. 2a, upper register, l. 10–p. 2b, l. 4.

36. This four-character expression occurs in a song suite by Ch'en So-wen (d. c. 1604), *Ch'üan Ming san-ch'ü*, 2:2575, l. 14.

37. This couplet is taken verbatim from the last two lines of a quatrain by Huang T'ing-chien (1045–1105), *Ch'üan Sung shih*, 17:11708, l. 6.

38. This quatrain is taken, with insignificant textual variation, from one in *Huai-ch'un ya-chi*, *chüan* 10, p. 13b, ll. 1–2.

39. This four-character expression is from the famous rhapsody by Su Shih (1037–1101) entitled *Ch'ih-pi fu*, p. 6, l. 13. It also occurs in a lyric by Ts'ao Kuan (cs 1154), *Ch'üan Sung tz'u*, 3:1540, lower register, l. 15; *Liu-ch'ing jih-cha*, vol. 2, *chüan* 22, p. 5b, l. 7; *Hsi-yu chi*, vol. 1, ch. 3, p. 30, l. 11; and *Mu-lien chiu-mu ch'üan-shan hsi-wen*, *chüan* 3, p. 82a, l. 10.

40. This formulaic four-character expression occurs ubiquitously in Chinese vernacular literature. See, e.g. *Yüan-ch'ü hsüan*, 3:1215, ll. 15–16; *Shih-wu kuan hsi-yen ch'eng ch'iao-huo*, p. 692, l. 1; *Sha-kou chi*, scene 19, p. 73, l. 5; *Ching-ch'ai chi*, scene 39, p. 116, l. 5; *Pai-t'u chi*, scene 31, p. 81, l. 8; *P'o-yao chi*, *chüan* 2, scene 25, p. 26a, l. 7; *Huan-tai chi*, *chüan* 1, scene 20, p. 54a, l. 8; *Tung Yung yü-hsien chuan*, p. 241, l. 5; *Yao-shih pen-yüan kung-te pao-chüan*, 14:300, l. 5; *Hu-fu chi*, *chüan* 1, scene 16, p. 24a, l. 6; *Hsi-yu chi*, vol. 1, ch. 35, p. 401, l. 16; *Chin-tiao chi*, *chüan* 3, scene 31, p. 21b, l. 1; *Ta-T'ang Ch'in-wang tz'u-hua*, vol. 1, *chüan* 2, ch. 12, p. 37b, l. 7; and an abundance of other occurrences, too numerous to list.

41. This four-character expression occurs in *Chieh-hsia chi*, scene 17, p. 42, ll. 8–9.

42. This four-character expression occurs ubiquitously in Chinese vernacular literature. See, e.g., *Yüan-ch'ü hsüan*, 1:299, l. 3; *Yüan-ch'ü hsüan wai-pien*, 3:808, l. 9; *Chin-yin chi*, *chüan* 2, scene 18, p. 26a, l. 1; *San-kuo chih t'ung-su yen-i*, *chüan* 1, p. 40, l. 7; *Shui-hu ch'üan-chuan*, vol. 1, ch. 16, p. 225, l. 9; *Shang Lu san-yüan chi*, *chüan* 1, scene 13, p. 18b, ll. 7–8; and an abundance of other occurrences, too numerous to list.

43. This four-character expression occurs in a set of poems by Shao Yung (1011–77), *Ch'üan Sung shih*, 7:4678, l. 10; and *San-pao t'ai-chien Hsi-yang chi t'ung-su yen-i*, vol. 2, ch. 59, p. 755, l. 5.

44. The locus classicus for this four-character expression is a passage in *Mencius*. See *Meng-tzu yin-te*, Book 3B, ch. 7, p. 24, l. 13. It also occurs in the biography of Shih K'uang-han (902–41), in *Chiu Wu-tai shih*, vol. 4, *chüan* 88, p. 1151, l. 14; and *Yüan-ch'ü hsüan wai-pien*, 2:635, l. 2.

45. This four-character expression occurs in *Chin-chien chi*, scene 30, p. 93, l. 7.

46. This four-character expression occurs in a speech attributed to the Buddhist monk Chih-yü (1185–1269), *Hsü-t'ang Ho-shang yü-lu*, *chüan* 1, p. 991, upper register, l. 17; and *Cheng Yüan-ho*, 4:1441, ll. 10–11.

47. This four-character expression occurs ubiquitously in Chinese vernacular literature. See, e.g., a speech attributed to the Sung dynasty Buddhist monk Wei-su, *Wu-teng
hui-yüan*, vol. 2, *chüan* 10, p. 638, l. 7; *Meng-liang lu*, *chüan* 18, p. 294, l. 4; *Yü-ch'iao
hsien-hua*, scene 3, p. 8a, l. 6; *Pai-she chi*, *chüan* 1, scene 10, p. 19a, l. 9; *Shen-hsiang
ch'üan-pien*, *chüan* 632, p. 11a, l. 5; and *San-pao t'ai-chien Hsi-yang chi t'ung-su yen-i*,
vol. 2, ch. 53, p. 680, l. 2.

BIBLIOGRAPHY

PRIMARY SOURCES

The Book of Lieh-tzu. Translated by A. C. Graham. London: John Murray, 1960.

Cha-ch'uan Hsiao Ch'en pien Pa-wang 霅川蕭琛貶霸王 (In Cha-ch'uan Hsiao Ch'en rebukes the Hegemon-King). In *Ch'ing-p'ing shan-t'ang hua-pen*, pp. 313–22.

Chan-kuo ts'e 戰國策 (Intrigues of the Warring States). Compiled by Liu Hsiang 劉向 (79–8 B.C.). 3 vols. Shanghai: Shang-hai ku-chi ch'u-pan she, 1985.

Chang Hsieh chuang-yüan 張協狀元 (Top graduate Chang Hsieh). In *Yung-lo ta-tien hsi-wen san-chung chiao-chu*, pp. 1–217.

Chang Ku-lao chung-kua ch'ü Wen-nü 張古老種瓜娶文女 (Chang Ku-lao plants melons and weds Wen-nü). In *Ku-chin hsiao-shuo*, vol. 2, *chüan* 33, pp. 487–502.

Chang Sheng ts'ai-luan teng chuan 張生彩鸞燈傳 (The story of Chang Sheng and the painted phoenix lanterns). In *Hsiung Lung-feng ssu-chung hsiao-shuo*, pp. 1–13.

Chang Tzu-fang mu-tao chi 長子房慕道記 (The story of Chang Liang's pursuit of the Way). In *Ch'ing-p'ing shan-t'ang hua-pen*, pp. 102–13.

Chang Yü-hu su nü-chen kuan chi 張于湖宿女貞觀記 (Chang Yü-hu spends the night in a Taoist nunnery). In *Yen-chü pi-chi* (Lin Chin-yang), vol. 2, *chüan* 6, pp. 6b–24b, lower register.

Ch'ang-an ch'eng ssu-ma t'ou-T'ang 長安城四馬投唐 (In Ch'ang-an city four horsemen surrender to the T'ang). In *Ku-pen Yüan Ming tsa-chü*, vol. 3.

Chao Po-sheng ch'a-ssu yü Jen-tsung 趙伯昇茶肆遇仁宗 (Chao Po-sheng encounters Emperor Jen-tsung in a tea shop), in *Ku-chin hsiao-shuo*, vol. 1, *chüan* 11, pp. 165–74.

Chao-shih ku-erh 趙氏孤兒 (The orphan of Chao). By Chi Chün-hsiang 紀君祥 (13th century). In *Yüan-ch'ü hsüan*, 4:1476–98.

Chao-shih ku-erh chi 趙氏孤兒記 (The story of the orphan of Chao). In *Ku-pen hsi-ch'ü ts'ung-k'an, ch'u-chi*, item 16.

Chao T'ai-tsu ch'ien-li sung Ching-niang 趙太祖千里送京娘 (Chao T'ai-tsu escorts Ching-niang on a thousand-li journey). In *Ching-shih t'ung-yen*, *chüan* 21, pp. 289–306.

Ch'ao-yeh ch'ien-tsai 朝野僉載 (Comprehensive record of affairs within and without the court). Compiled by Chang Cho 張鷟 (cs 675). Peking: Chung-hua shu-chü, 1979.

Chen-ch'uan hsien-sheng chi 震川先生集 (Collected works of Kuei Yu-kuang). By Kuei Yu-kuang 歸有光 (1507–71). 2 vols. Shanghai: Shang-hai ku-chi ch'u-pan she, 1981.

Chen-chung chi 枕中記 (The world inside a pillow). By Shen Chi-chi 沈既濟 (d. c. 786). In *Traditional Chinese Stories: Themes and Variations*, pp. 435–38.

Ch'en Hsün-chien Mei-ling shih-ch'i chi 陳巡檢梅嶺失妻記 (Police chief Ch'en loses his wife in crossing the Mei-ling Range). In *Ch'ing-p'ing shan-t'ang hua-pen*, pp. 121–36.

Ch'en Liang chi [tseng-ting pen] 陳亮集[增訂本] (Collected works of Ch'en Liang [augmented and revised edition]). Edited by Teng Kuang-ming 鄧廣銘. 2 vols. Peking: Chung-hua shu-chü, 1987.

Cheng Chieh-shih li-kung shen-pi kung 鄭節使立功神臂弓 (Commissioner Cheng wins merit with his magic bow). In *Hsing-shih heng-yen*, vol. 2, *chüan* 31, pp. 656–73.

Cheng-hsin ch'u-i wu hsiu cheng tzu-tsai pao-chüan 正信除疑無修證自在寶卷 (Precious volume of self-determination needing neither cultivation nor verification which rectifies belief and dispels doubt). By Lo Ch'ing 羅清 (1442–1527). Originally published in 1509. In *Pao-chüan ch'u-chi*, 3:1–339.

Cheng-t'ung Tao-tsang 正通道藏 (The Cheng-t'ung [1436–49] Taoist canon). Shanghai: Shang-wu yin-shu kuan, 1926.

Cheng Yüan-ho 鄭元和. In *Tsui yü-ch'ing*, pp. 1411–50, upper register.

Ch'eng-yün chuan 承運傳 (The story of the assumption of the mandate [by the Yung-lo emperor]). In *Ku-pen hsiao-shuo ts'ung-k'an, ti-pa chi*, vol. 3.

Chi K'ang chi chiao-chu 嵇康集校注 (Chi K'ang's collected works collated and annotated). Edited by Tai Ming-yang 戴明揚. Peking: Jen-min wen-hsüeh ch'u-pan she, 1962.

Chi-le pien 雞肋編 (Chicken ribs collection). By Chuang Ch'o 莊綽 (c. 1090–c. 1150). Preface dated 1133. Peking: Chung-hua shu chü, 1983.

[Chi-p'ing chiao-chu] Hsi-hsiang chi [集評校注]西廂記 (The romance of the western chamber [with collected commentary and critical annotation]). Edited and annotated by Wang Chi-ssu 王季思. Shanghai: Shang-hai ku-chi ch'u-pan she, 1987.

Chi Ya-fan chin-man ch'an-huo 計押番金鰻產禍 (Duty Group Leader Chi's golden eel engenders catastrophe). In *Ching-shih t'ung-yen*, *chüan* 20, pp. 274–88.

Ch'i-fa 七發 (Seven stimuli). By Mei Ch'eng 枚乘 (d. 141 B.C.). In *Wen-hsüan*, vol. 2, *chüan* 34, pp. 1a–13b.

Ch'i-kuo ch'un-ch'iu p'ing-hua 七國春秋平話 (The p'ing-hua on the events of the seven states). Originally published in 1321–23. Shanghai: Ku-tien wen-hsüeh ch'u-pan she, 1955.

Ch'i-tung yeh-yü 齊東野語 (Rustic words of a man from eastern Ch'i). By Chou Mi 周密 (1232–98). Preface dated 1291. Peking: Chung-hua shu-chü, 1983.

Chia-hsüan tz'u pien-nien chien-chu 稼軒詞編年箋注 (The lyrics of Hsin Ch'i-chi [1140–1207] arranged chronologically and annotated). Edited by Teng Kuang-ming 鄧廣銘. Shanghai: Shang-hai ku-chi ch'u-pan she, 1978.

Chiang Shih yüeh-li chi 姜詩躍鯉記 (The story of Chiang Shih and the leaping carp). By Ch'en P'i-chai 陳羆齋 (fl. early 16th century). In *Ku-pen hsi-ch'ü ts'ung-k'an, ch'u-chi*, item 36.

Chiao-hsiao chi 鮫綃記 (The Story of the mermaid silk handkerchief). By Shen Ch'ing 沈鯖 (15th century). In *Ku-pen hsi-ch'ü ts'ung-k'an, ch'u-chi*, item 91.

Chiao Hung chuan 嬌紅傳 (The Story of Chiao-niang and Fei-hung). By Sung Yüan 宋遠 (14th century). In *Ku-tai wen-yen tuan-p'ien hsiao-shuo hsüan-chu, erh-chi*, pp. 280–323.

[Chiao-ting] Yüan-k'an tsa-chü san-shih chung [校訂]元刊雜劇三十種 (A collated edition of Thirty tsa-chü dramas printed during the Yüan dynasty). Edited by Cheng Ch'ien 鄭騫. Taipei: Shih-chieh shu-chü, 1962.

Ch'iao Chi chi 喬吉集 (The collected works of Ch'iao Chi [d. 1345]). Edited and annotated by Li Hsiu-sheng 李修生 et al. T'ai-yüan: Shan-hsi jen-min ch'u-pan she, 1988.

Chieh-an Lao-jen man-pi 戒庵老人漫筆 (Casual notes by the Old Man of Self-Restraint Studio). Compiled by Li Hsü 李詡 (1505–93). Peking: Chung-hua shu-chü, 1982.

Chieh-chih-erh chi 戒指兒記 (The story of the ring). In *Ch'ing-p'ing shan-t'ang hua-pen*, pp. 241–71.

Chieh-hsia chi 節俠記 (The steadfast knight errant). By Hsü San-chieh 許三階 (fl. late 16th century). *Liu-shih chung ch'ü* edition. Taipei: K'ai-ming shu-tien, 1970.

Chien-chieh lu 鑒誡錄 (A register of object lessons). Compiled by Ho Kuang-yüan 何光遠 (10th century). In *Shuo-k'u*, 1:279–302.

Chien-teng hsin-hua 剪燈新話 (New wick-trimming tales). By Ch'ü Yu 瞿佑 (1341–1427). In *Chien-teng hsin-hua [wai erh-chung]*, pp. 1–119.

Chien-teng hsin-hua [wai erh-chung] 剪燈新話[外二種] (New wick-trimming tales [plus two other works]). Edited and annotated by Chou I 周夷. Shanghai: Ku-tien wen-hsüeh ch'u-pan she, 1957.

Chien-teng yü-hua 剪燈餘話 (More wick-trimming tales). By Li Ch'ang-ch'i 李昌祺 (1376–1452). Author's preface dated 1420. In *Chien-teng hsin-hua [wai erh-chung]*, pp. 121–312.

Ch'ien-chin chi 千金記 (The thousand pieces of gold). By Shen Ts'ai 沈采 (15th century). *Liu-shih chung ch'ü* edition. Taipei: K'ai-ming shu-tien, 1970.

Ch'ien-fu lun 潛夫論 (The comments of a recluse). By Wang Fu 王符 (c. 90–165). Shanghai: Shang-hai ku-chi ch'u-pan she, 1978.

Ch'ien-Han shu p'ing-hua 前漢書平話 (The p'ing-hua on the history of the Former Han dynasty). Originally published in 1321–23. Shanghai: Ku-tien wen-hsüeh ch'u-pan she, 1955.

Ch'ien-t'ang hu-yin Chi-tien Ch'an-shih yü-lu 錢塘湖隱濟顛禪師語錄 (The recorded sayings of the lakeside recluse of Ch'ien-t'ang, the Ch'an master Crazy Chi [Tao-chi (1148–1209)]). Fac. repr. of 1569 edition. In *Ku-pen hsiao-shuo ts'ung-k'an, ti-pa chi*, vol. 1.

Ch'ien-t'ang meng 錢塘夢 (The dream in Ch'ien-t'ang). Included as part of the front matter in the 1498 edition of the *Hsi-hsiang chi*, pp. 1a–4b.

Ch'ien-tzu wen 千字文 (Thousand-character text). By Chou Hsing-ssu 周興嗣 (d. 521). In *Dai Kan-Wa jiten*, 2:522–23.

Ch'ih-pi fu 赤壁賦 (Rhapsody on the Red Cliff). By Su Shih 蘇軾 (1037–1101). In *Su Shih wen-chi*, vol. 1, *chüan* 1, pp. 5–6.

Chin-ch'ai chi 金釵記 (The gold hairpin). Manuscript dated 1431. Modern edition edited by Liu Nien-tzu 劉念茲. Canton: Kuang-tung jen-min ch'u-pan she, 1985.

Chin-chien chi 金箋記 (The brocade note). By Chou Lü-ching 周履靖 (1549–1640). *Liu-shih chung ch'ü* edition. Taipei: K'ai-ming shu-tien, 1970.

Chin-ch'üeh chi 金雀記 (The golden sparrow). *Liu-shih chung ch'ü* edition. Taipei: K'ai-ming shu-tien, 1970.

Chin-kang ching chi-chu 金剛經集注 (The *Vajracchedikā prajñāpāramitā* sutra with collected commentaries). Compiled by the Yung-lo 永樂 emperor of the Ming dynasty (r. 1402–24). Preface dated 1424. Fac. repr. of original edition. Shanghai: Shang-hai ku-chi ch'u-pan she, 1984.

Chin-kang pan-jo-po-lo-mi ching chu 金剛般若波羅密經注 (Commentary on the *Vajracchedikā prajñāpāramitā* sutra). By Tao-ch'uan 道川 (fl. 1127–63). Preface dated 1179. In *[Shinzan] Dai Nihon zokuzōkyō*, vol. 24, no. 461, pp. 535–65.

Chin-lan ssu-yu chuan 金蘭四友傳 (The story of the four ardent friends). In *Kuo-se t'ien-hsiang*, vol. 3, *chüan* 9, upper register, pp. 1a–26b.

Chin-ming ch'ih Wu Ch'ing feng Ai-ai 金明池吳清逢愛愛 (Wu Ch'ing meets Ai-ai at Chin-ming Pond). In *Ching-shih t'ung-yen*, *chüan* 30, pp. 459–71.

Chin P'ing Mei tz'u–hua 金瓶每詞話 (Story of the plum in the golden vase). Preface dated 1618. 5 vols. Fac. repr. Tokyo: Daian, 1963.

Chin shu 晉書 (History of the Chin dynasty [265–420]). Compiled by Fang Hsüan-ling 房玄齡(578–648) et al. 10 vols. Peking: Chung-hua shu-chü, 1974.

Chin-tiao chi 金貂記 (The golden sable). In *Ku-pen hsi-ch'ü ts'ung-k'an, ch'u-chi*, item 41.

Chin-t'ung Yü-nü Chiao Hung chi 金童玉女嬌紅記 (The Golden Lad and the Jade Maiden: The story of Chiao-niang and Fei-hung). Attributed to Liu Tui 劉兌 (fl. early 15th century). In *Ming-jen tsa-chü hsüan*, pp. 1–83.

Chin-yin chi 金印記 (The golden seal). By Su Fu-chih 蘇復之 (14th century). In *Ku-pen hsi-ch'ü ts'ung-k'an, ch'u-chi*, item 27.

Ch'in ping liu-kuo p'ing-hua 秦併六國平話 (The p'ing-hua on the annexation of the Six States by Ch'in). Originally published 1321–23. Shanghai: Ku-tien wen-hsüeh ch'u-pan she, 1955.

Chinese Poems. Translated by Arthur Waley. London: Allen and Unwin, 1956.

Ching-ch'ai chi 荊釵記 (The thorn hairpin). *Liu-shih chung ch'ü* edition. Taipei: K'ai-ming shu-tien, 1970.

Ching-ch'u T'ang tsa-chih 經鉏堂雜誌 (Miscellaneous records from the Ching-ch'u Hall). By Ni Ssu 倪思 (1174–1220). In *Shuo-fu san-chung*, 6:3479–84.

Ching-chung chi 精忠記 (A tale of perfect loyalty). *Liu-shih chung ch'ü* edition. Taipei: K'ai-ming shu-tien, 1970.

Ching-shih t'ung-yen 警世通言 (Common words to warn the world). Edited by Feng Meng-lung 馮夢龍 (1574–1646). First published 1624. Peking: Tso-chia ch'u-pan she, 1957.

Ch'ing feng-nien Wu-kuei nao Chung K'uei 慶豐年五鬼鬧鍾馗 (Celebrating a prosperous year, the Five Devils plague Chung K'uei). In *Ku-pen Yüan Ming tsa-chü*, vol. 4.

Ch'ing-ho hsien chi-mu ta-hsien 清河縣繼母大賢 (In Ch'ing-ho district a stepmother acts very virtuously). By Chu Yu-tun 朱有燉 (1379–1439). Completed in 1434. In *Ming-jen tsa-chü hsüan*, pp. 217–36.

Ch'ing-i lu 清異錄 (Records of the unusual). Attributed to T'ao Ku 陶穀 (903–70). In *Shuo-fu*, vol. 2, *chüan* 61, pp. 1a–71b.

Ch'ing-p'ing shan-t'ang hua-pen 清平山堂話本 (Stories printed by the Ch'ing-p'ing Shan-t'ang). Edited by T'an Cheng-pi 譚正璧. Shanghai: Ku-tien wen-hsüeh ch'u-pan she, 1957.

Ch'ing-shih 情史 (Histories of love). Compiled by Feng Meng-lung 馮夢龍 (1574–1646). Originally published between 1628 and 1632. 2 vols. Shen-yang: Ch'un-feng wen-i ch'u-pan she, 1986.

Ch'ing-so kao-i 青瑣高議 (Lofty sentiments from the green latticed windows). Compiled by Liu Fu 劉斧 (fl. 1040–1113). Shanghai: Ku-tien wen-hsüeh ch'u-pan she, 1958.

Ch'ing-yeh lu 清夜錄 (Anecdotes recorded on clear nights). Compiled by Yü Wen-pao 俞文豹 (13th century). In *Shuo-fu san-chung*, 4:1734–39.

Chiu-pien nan chiu-kung p'u 舊編南九宮譜 (Formulary for the old repertory of the nine southern musical modes). Compiled by Chiang Hsiao 蔣孝(16th century). Preface dated 1549. Fac. repr. in *Shan-pen hsi-ch'ü ts'ung-k'an*, vol. 26.

Chiu T'ang shu 舊唐書 (Old history of the T'ang dynasty). Compiled by Liu Hsü 劉昫 (887–946) et al. 16 vols. Peking: Chung-hua shu-chü, 1975.

Chiu-t'ien sheng-shen chang ching 九天生神章經 (Scripture of the stanzas of the vitalizing spirits of the Nine Heavens). In *Cheng-t'ung Tao-tsang, ts'e* 165.

Chiu Wu-tai shih 舊五代史 (Old history of the Five Dynasties). Compiled by Hsüeh Chü-cheng 薛居正 (912–981) et al. 6 vols. Peking: Chung-hua shu-chü, 1976.

Cho Chi Pu chuan-wen 捉季布傳文 (Story of the apprehension of Chi Pu). In *Tun-huang pien-wen chi*, 1:51–84.

Cho Wen-chün ssu-pen Hsiang-ju 卓文君私奔相如 (Cho Wen-chün elopes with [Ssuma] Hsiang-ju). By Chu Ch'üan 朱權 (1378–1448). In *Ming-jen tsa-chü hsüan*, pp. 113–39.

Ch'o-keng lu 輟耕錄 (Notes recorded during respites from the plough). By T'ao Tsung-i 陶宗儀 (c. 1316–c. 1403). Preface dated 1366. Peking: Chung-hua shu-chü, 1980.

Chou-i yin-te 周易引得 (A concordance to the *I-ching*). Taipei: Chinese Materials and Research Aids Service Center, 1966.

Chou shu 周書 (History of the Chou dynasty [557–81]). Compiled by Ling-hu Te-fen 令狐德棻(583–666). 3 vols. Peking: Chung-hua shu-chü, 1971.

Chu-fa chi 祝髮記 (Taking the tonsure). By Chang Feng-i 張鳳翼 (1527–1613). Completed in 1586. In *Ku-pen hsi-ch'ü ts'ung-k'an, ch'u-chi*, item 61.

Chu Hsi's Family Rituals: A Twelfth-Century Chinese Manual for the Performance of Cappings, Weddings, Funerals, and Ancestral Rites. Translated and annotated by Patricia Buckley Ebrey. Princeton: Princeton University Press, 1991.

Chu-kung-tiao liang-chung 諸宮調兩種 (Two exemplars of the medley in various modes). Edited and annotated by Ling Ching-yen 凌景埏 and Hsieh Po-yang 謝伯陽. N.p.: Ch'i-Lu shu-she, 1988.

Chu sheng-shou wan-kuo lai-ch'ao 祝聖壽萬國來朝 (In order to celebrate the emperor's birthday a myriad states come to pay homage). In *Ku-pen Yüan Ming tsa-chü*, vol. 4.

Chu-tzu chi-ch'eng 諸子集成 (A corpus of the philosophers). 8 vols. Hong Kong: Chung-hua shu-chü, 1978.

Chu-tzu yü-lei 朱子語類 (Classified sayings of Master Chu). Compiled by Li Ching-te 李靖德 (13th century). 8 vols. Taipei: Cheng-chung shu-chü, 1982.

Ch'u-tz'u pu-chu [fu so-yin] 楚辭補注[附索引] (Songs of Ch'u with supplementary annotation [and a concordance]). Compiled by Hung Hsing-tsu 洪興祖 (1090–1155). Kyoto: Chūbun shuppan-sha, 1972.

Chuang-tzu yin-te 莊子引得 (A concordance to *Chuang-tzu*). Cambridge: Harvard University Press, 1956.

Ch'un-chu chi-wen 春渚紀聞 (Record of hearsay from a spring islet). By Ho Wei 何薳 (1077–1145). Peking: Chung-hua shu-chü, 1983.

The Ch'un Ts'ew with the Tso Chuen. Translated by James Legge. Hong Kong: Hong Kong University Press, 1960.

Ch'un-wu chi 春蕪記 (The story of the scented handkerchief). By Wang Ling 汪錂 (fl. early 17th century). *Liu-shih chung ch'ü* edition. Taipei: K'ai-ming shu-tien, 1970.

Chung-ch'ing li-chi 鍾情麗集 (A pleasing tale of passion). In *Yen-chü pi-chi* (Lin Chin-yang), vol. 2, *chüan* 6, pp. 1a–40b, and vol. 3, *chüan* 7, pp. 1a–30a, upper register.

Chung-hua tao-chiao ta tz'u-tien 中華道教大辭典 (Encyclopedia of the Chinese Taoist religion). Compiled by Hu Fu-ch'en 胡孚琛 et al. Peking: Chung-kuo she-hui k'o-hsüeh ch'u-pan she, 1995.

Chung-kuo i-kuan fu-shih ta tz'u-tien 中國衣冠服飾大辭典 (Comprehensive dictionary of Chinese costume and its decorative motifs). Compiled by Chou Hsün 周汛 and Kao Ch'un-ming 高春明. Shanghai: Shang-hai tz'u-shu ch'u-pan she, 1996.

Chung-kuo ku-tai meng-hsüeh shu ta-kuan 中國古代蒙學書大觀 (A corpus of traditional Chinese primers). Compiled by Lu Yang-t'ao 陸養濤. Shanghai: T'ung-chi ta-hsüeh ch'u-pan she, 1995.

Chung-kuo ku-tien hsi-ch'ü lun-chu chi-ch'eng 中國古典戲曲論著集成 (A corpus of critical works on classical Chinese drama). Compiled by Chung-kuo hsi-ch'ü yen-chiu yüan 中國戲曲研究院 (The Chinese Academy of Dramatic Arts). 10 vols. Peking: Chung-kuo hsi-chü ch'u-pan she, 1959.

Chung-kuo mei-shu chia jen-ming tz'u-tien 中國美術家人名辭典 (Biographical dictionary of Chinese artists). Compiled by Yü Chien-hua 俞劍華. Shanghai: Jen-min mei-shu ch'u-pan she, 1981.

Chung-shan lang 中山狼 (The wolf of Chung-shan). By K'ang Hai 康海 (1475–1541). In *Ming-jen tsa-chü hsüan*, pp. 237–59.

Chung-shan lang chuan 中山狼傳 (The tale of the wolf of Chung-shan). By Ma Chung-hsi 馬中錫 (1446–1512). In *Ku-tai wen-yen tuan-p'ien hsiao-shuo hsüan-chi, erh-chi*, pp. 367–71.

Chung-shan lang yüan-pen 中山狼院本 (Yüan-pen on the wolf of Chung-shan). By Wang Chiu-ssu 王九思 (1468–1551). In *Ming-jen tsa-chü hsüan*, pp. 261–68.

Ch'ung-mo-tzu tu-pu Ta-lo T'ien 沖漠子獨步大羅天 (Ch'ung-mo tzu ascends to the Grand Veil Heaven). By Chu Ch'üan 朱權 (1378–1448). In *Ku-pen Yüan Ming tsa-chü*, vol. 2.

Chü-ting chi 舉鼎記 (Lifting the tripod). In *Ku-pen hsi-ch'ü ts'ung-k'an, ch'u-chi*, item 39.

Ch'ü-wei chiu-wen 曲洧舊聞 (Old stories heard in Ch'ü-wei). By Chu Pien 朱弁 (d. 1144). In *Pi-chi hsiao-shuo ta-kuan*, vol. 4, ts'e 8.

Ch'üan Chin shih 全金詩 (Complete poetry of the Chin dynasty [1115–1234]). Compiled by Hsüeh Jui-chao 薛瑞兆 and Kuo Ming-chih 郭明志. 4 vols. Tientsin: Nan-k'ai ta-hsüeh ch'u-pan she, 1995.

Ch'üan Chin Yüan tz'u 全金元詞 (Complete lyrics of the Chin and Yüan dynasties). Compiled by T'ang Kuei-chang 唐圭璋. 2 vols. Peking: Chung-hua shu-chü, 1979.

Ch'üan-Han chih-chuan 全漢志傳 (Chronicle of the entire Han dynasty). 12 *chüan*. Chien-yang: K'o-ch'in chai, 1588. Fac. repr. in *Ku-pen hsiao-shuo ts'ung-k'an, ti-wu chi*, vols. 2–3.

Ch'üan Ming san-ch'ü 全明散曲 (Complete nondramatic song lyrics of the Ming). Compiled by Hsieh Po-yang 謝伯陽. 5 vols. Chi-nan: Ch'i-Lu shu-she, 1994.

Ch'üan Ming tsa-chü 全明雜劇 (Complete tsa-chü plays of the Ming dynasty). 12 vols. Taipei: Ting-wen shu-chü, 1979.

Ch'üan Ming tz'u 全明詞 (Complete tz'u lyrics of the Ming). Compiled by Jao Tsung-i 饒宗頤 and Chang Chang 張璋. 6 vols. Peking: Chung-hua shu-chü, 2004.

Ch'üan Ming tz'u pu-pien 全明詞補編 (A supplement to Complete *tz'u* lyrics of the Ming). Compiled by Chou Ming-ch'u 周明初 and Yeh Yeh 葉曄. 2 vols. Hang-chou: Che-chiang ta-hsüeh ch'u-pan she, 2007.

Ch'üan Shang-ku San-tai Ch'in Han San-kuo Liu-ch'ao wen 全上古三代秦漢三國六朝文 (Complete Prose from High Antiquity, the Three Dynasties, Ch'in, Han, the Three Kingdoms, and the Six Dynasties). Compiled by Yen K'o-chün 嚴可均 (1762–1843). 5 vols. Peking: Chung-hua shu-chü, 1965.

Ch'üan Sung shih 全宋詩 (Complete poetry of the Sung). Compiled by Fu Hsüan-ts'ung 傅璇琮 et al. 72 vols. Peking: Pei-ching ta-hsüeh ch'u-pan she, 1991–98.

Ch'üan Sung tz'u 全宋詞 (Complete *tz'u* lyrics of the Sung). Compiled by T'ang Kuei-chang 唐圭璋. 5 vols. Hong Kong: Chung-hua shu-chü, 1977.

Ch'üan Sung tz'u pu-chi 全宋詞補輯 (Supplement to Complete *tz'u* lyrics of the Sung). Compiled by K'ung Fan-li 孔凡禮. Peking: Chung-hua shu-chü, 1981.

Ch'üan Sung wen 全宋文 (Complete prose of the Sung). Compiled by Tseng Tsao-chuang 曾棗莊, Liu Lin 劉琳 et al. 50 vols. Ch'eng-tu: Pa-Shu shu-she, 1988–94.

Ch'üan T'ang shih 全唐詩 (Complete poetry of the T'ang). 12 vols. Peking: Chung-hua shu-chü, 1960.

Ch'üan T'ang shih pu-pien 全唐詩補編 (A supplement to the Complete poetry of the T'ang). Compiled by Ch'en Shang-chün 陳尚君. 3 vols. Peking: Chung-hua shu-chü, 1992.

Ch'üan T'ang wen 全唐文 (Complete prose of the T'ang). 20 vols. Kyoto: Chūbun shuppan-sha, 1976.

Ch'üan Yüan san-ch'ü 全元散曲 (Complete nondramatic song lyrics of the Yüan). Compiled by Sui Shu-sen 隋樹森. 2 vols. Peking: Chung-hua shu-chü, 1964.

Ch'ün-yin lei-hsüan 群音類選 (An anthology of songs categorized by musical type). Compiled by Hu Wen-huan 胡文煥 (fl. 1592–1617). 4 vols. Fac. repr. Peking: Chung-hua shu-chü, 1980.

The Complete Works of Chuang Tzu. Translated by Burton Watson. New York: Columbia University Press, 1968.

Courtier and Commoner in Ancient China: Selections from the History of the Former Han by Pan Ku. Translated by Burton Watson. New York: Columbia University Press, 1974.

Dai Kan-Wa jiten 大漢和辭典 (Great Chinese-Japanese dictionary). Compiled by Morohashi Tetsuji 諸橋轍次. 13 vols. Tokyo: Taishūkan shoten, 1960

Empresses and Consorts: Selections from Chen Shou's Records of the Three States with Pei Songzhi's Commentary. Translated by Robert Joe Cutter and William Gordon Crowell. Honolulu: University of Hawai'i Press, 1999.

Erh-lang Shen so Ch'i-t'ien Ta-sheng 二郎神鎖齊天大聖 (Erh-lang Shen confines the Great Sage Equal to Heaven). In *Ming-jen tsa-chü hsüan*, pp. 703–30.

Family Instructions for the Yen Clan. By Yen Chih-t'ui (531–91). Translated by Teng Ssu-yü. Leiden: E. J. Brill, 1968.

Fen-shu 焚書 (A book to be burned). By Li Chih 李贄 (1527–1602). Peking: Chung-hua shu-chü, 1961.

Feng Po-yü feng-yüeh hsiang-ssu hsiao-shuo 馮伯玉風月相思小説 (The story of Feng Po-yü: a tale of romantic longing). In *Hsiung Lung-feng ssu-chung hsiao-shuo*, pp. 31–49.

Feng-yüeh chin-nang [chien-chiao] 風月錦囊箋校 (Brocade pouch of romantic verse [annotated and collated]). Annotated and collated by Sun Ch'ung-t'ao 孫崇濤 and Huang Shih-chung 黃仕忠. Originally published in 1553. Peking: Chung-hua shu-chü, 2000.

Feng-yüeh hsiang-ssu 風月相思 (A tale of romantic longing). In *Ch'ing-p'ing shan-t'ang hua-pen*, pp. 79–94.

Feng-yüeh Jui-hsien T'ing 風月瑞仙亭 (The romance in the Jui-hsien Pavilion). In *Ch'ing-p'ing shan-t'ang hua-pen*, pp. 38–45.

Feng-yüeh Nan-lao chi 風月南牢記 (Romance in the South Prison). In *Ku-pen Yüan Ming tsa-chü*, vol. 4.

Feng-yün hui 風雲會 (The meeting of wind and cloud). By Lo Kuan-chung 羅貫中 (14th century). In *Yüan-ch'ü hsüan wai-pien*, 2:617–32.

The Flower Ornament Scripture: A Translation of the Avatamsaka Sutra. Translated by Thomas Cleary. Boston: Shambala, 1987.

Fo-mu ta k'ung-ch'üeh ming-wang ching 佛母大孔雀明王經 (Sutra of the Peacock King). Translated into Chinese by Amoghavajra (705–74). In *Taishō shinshū daizōkyō*, vol. 19, no. 982, pp. 415–39.

Fo-shuo Huang-chi chieh-kuo pao-chüan 佛說皇極結果寶卷 (Precious volume expounded by the Buddha on the karmic results of the era of the Imperial Ultimate). Originally published in 1430. In *Pao-chüan ch'u-chi*, 10:219–406.

Fo-shuo Wu-liang shou ching 佛說無量壽經 (*Sukhāvatīvyūha*). Translated by Sangha-varman in the year 252. In *Taishō shinshū daizōkyō*, vol. 12, no. 360, pp. 265–79.

Fo-ting-hsin Kuan-shih-yin p'u-sa ta t'o-lo-ni ching 佛頂心觀世音菩薩大陀羅尼經 (Kuan-shih-yin Bodhisattva's great Dhāranī sutra of the Buddha's essence). 3 fascicles. In *Tun-huang pao-tsang*,132: 65–71.

Fo-yin shih ssu t'iao Ch'in-niang 佛印師四調琴娘 (The priest Fo-yin teases Ch'in-niang four times). In *Hsing-shih heng-yen*, vol. 1, *chüan*, 12, pp. 232–40.

Fu-jung chi 芙蓉記 (The story of the hibiscus painting). By Chiang Chi 江楫 (late 16th century). In *Ku-pen hsi-ch'ü ts'ung-k'an, wu-chi*, item 6.

Fu Lu Shou san-hsing tu-shih 福祿壽三星度世 (The three stellar deities of Fortune, Emolument, and Longevity visit the mundane world). In *Ching-shih t'ung-yen*, *chüan* 39, pp. 583–91.

Fu-mu en chung ching chiang-ching wen 父母恩重經講經文 (Sutra lecture on the Sutra on the importance of parental kindness). Dated 927. In *Tun-huang pien-wen chi*, 2:672–94.

Fu-mu en chung ching chiang-ching wen 父母恩重經講經文 (Sutra lecture on the Sutra on the importance of parental kindness). In *Tun-huang pien-wen chi*, 2:695–700.

A Gallery of Chinese Immortals. Translated by Lionel Giles. London: John Murray, 1948.

The Golden Casket: Chinese Novellas of Two Millennia. Translated by Wolfgang Bauer and Herbert Franke; translated from the German by Christopher Levenson. New York: Harcourt Brace and World, 1964.

The Grand Scribe's Records. Volume 1: *The Basic Annals of Pre-Han China.* Edited by William H. Nienhauser, Jr. Bloomington: Indiana University Press, 1994.

The Grand Scribe's Records. Volume 2: *The Basic Annals of Han China.* Edited by William H. Nienhauser, Jr. Bloomington: Indiana University Press, 2002.

Hai-fu shan-t'ang tz'u-kao 海浮山堂詞稿 (Draft lyrics from Hai-fu shan-t'ang). By Feng Wei-min 馮惟敏 (1511–80). Preface dated 1566. Shanghai: Shang-hai ku-chi ch'u-pan she, 1981.

Hai-ling i-shih 海陵佚史 (The debauches of Emperor Hai-ling of the Chin dynasty [r. 1149–61]). In *Ssu wu-hsieh hui-pao*, vol. 1.

Han Ch'ang-li wen-chi chiao-chu 韓昌黎文集校注 (The prose works of Han Yü 韓愈 [768–824] with critical annotation). Edited by Ma T'ung-po 馬通伯. Shanghai: Ku-tien wen-hsüeh ch'u-pan she, 1957.

Han chi 漢紀 (Records of the Former Han dynasty). Compiled by Hsün Yüeh 荀悅 (148–209). Originally completed in the year 200. In *Liang Han chi*, vol. 1.

Han erh-tsu yu-lieh lun 漢二祖優劣論 (A discussion of the relative merits of the two Han dynasty founding emperors). By Ts'ao Chih 曹植 (192–232). In *Ts'ao Chih chi chiao-chu, chüan* 1, pp. 102–5.

Han Fei tzu so-yin 韓非子索引 (A concordance to *Han Fei tzu*). Peking: Chung-hua shu-chü, 1982.

Han Hsiang-tzu chiu-tu Wen-kung sheng-hsien chi 韓湘子九度文公昇仙記 (Han Hsiang-tzu nine times endeavors to induce Han Yü to ascend to the realm of the immortals). In *Ku-pen hsi-ch'ü ts'ung-k'an, ch'u-chi*, item 47.

Han-shang huan wen-ts'un 漢上宦文存 (Literary remains of the Han-shang Studio). By Ch'ien Nan-yang 錢南揚. Shanghai: Shang-hai wen-i ch'u-pan she, 1980.

Han-shu 漢書 (History of the Former Han dynasty). Compiled by Pan Ku 班固 (32–92). 8 vols. Peking: Chung-hua shu-chü, 1962.

Han-tan meng chi 邯鄲夢記 (The dream at Han-tan). By T'ang Hsien-tsu 湯顯祖 (1550–1616). Author's preface dated 1601. In *T'ang Hsien-tsu chi*, 4:2277–2432.

Han Wu-ti nei-chuan 漢武帝內傳 (Esoteric traditions regarding Emperor Wu of the Han dynasty). Traditionally attributed to Pan Ku 班固 (32–92) but more probably dating from the fifth or sixth century. In *Ts'ung-shu chi-ch'eng*, 1st series, vol. 3436.

Han Yüan-shuai an-tu Ch'en-ts'ang 韓元帥暗度陳倉 (Han Hsin surreptitiously emerges at Ch'en-ts'ang). In *Ku-pen Yüan Ming tsa-chü*, vol. 2.

Hei Hsüan-feng chang-i shu-ts'ai 黑旋風仗義疏財 (The Black Whirlwind is chivalrous and openhanded). By Chu Yu-tun 朱有燉 (1379–1439). In *Shui-hu hsi-ch'ü chi, ti-i chi*, pp. 95–112.

Ho-lin yü-lu 鶴林玉露 (Jade dew from Ho-lin). By Lo Ta-ching 羅大經 (cs 1226). Originally completed in 1252. Peking: Chung-hua shu-chü, 1983.

Ho-t'ung wen-tzu chi 合同文字記 (The story of the contract). In *Ch'ing-p'ing shan-t'ang hua-pen*, pp. 33–38.

Hou-cheng lu 侯鯖錄 (A patrician potpourri). By Chao Ling-chih 趙令畤 (1051–1134). In *Pi-chi hsiao-shuo ta-kuan*, vol. 4, ts'e 8.

Hou-Han shu 後漢書 (History of the Later Han dynasty). Compiled by Fan Yeh 范曄 (398–445). 12 vols. Peking: Chung-hua shu-chü, 1965.

Hou-ts'un Ch'ien-chia shih chiao-chu 後村千家詩校注 (Liu K'o-chuang's Poems by a thousand authors edited and annotated). Compiled by Liu K'o-chuang 劉克莊 (1187–1269). Edited and annotated by Hu Wen-nung 胡問儂 and Wang Hao-sou 王皓叟. Kuei-yang: Kuei-chou jen-min ch'u-pan she, 1986.

Hsi-hsiang chi 西廂記 (The romance of the western chamber). Fac. repr. of 1498 edition. Taipei: Shih-chieh shu-chü, 1963.

Hsi-hsiang hui-pien 西廂匯編 (Collected versions of the *Romance of the western chamber*). Compiled by Huo Sung-lin 霍松林. Chi-nan: Shan-tung wen-i ch'u-pan she, 1987.

Hsi-hu Lao-jen Fan-sheng lu 西湖老人繁勝錄 (The Old Man of West Lake's Record of luxuriant splendor). In *Tung-ching meng-hua lu [wai ssu-chung]*, pp. 111–28.

Hsi-hu san-t'a chi 西湖三塔記 (The three pagodas at West Lake). In *Ch'ing-p'ing shan-t'ang hua-pen*, pp. 22–32.

Hsi-hu yu-lan chih-yü 西湖遊覽志餘 (Supplement to the Guide to the West Lake). Compiled by T'ien Ju-ch'eng 田汝成 (cs 1526). Peking: Chung-hua shu-chü, 1958.

Hsi-i hsien-sheng chuan 希夷先生傳 (Biography of Master Hsi-i [Ch'en T'uan]). By P'ang Chüeh 龐覺 (11th century). In *Ch'ing-so kao-i, ch'ien-chi* (first collection), *chüan* 8, pp. 72–74.

Hsi-kua chi 西瓜記 (The watermelon story). In *Feng-yüeh chin-nang [chien-chiao]*, pp. 616–32.

Hsi-yu chi 西遊記 (The journey to the west). 2 vols. Peking: Tso-chia ch'u-pan she, 1954.

Hsiang-nang chi 香囊記 (The scent bag). By Shao Ts'an 邵璨 (15th century). *Liu-shih chung ch'ü* edition. Taipei: K'ai-ming shu-tien, 1970.

Hsiang-nang yüan 香囊怨 (The tragedy of the scent bag). By Chu Yu-tun 朱有燉 (1379–1439). Author's preface dated 1433. In *Sheng-Ming tsa-chü, erh-chi*.

Hsiang-shan hsien-sheng ch'üan-chi 象山先生全集 (Complete works of Master Hsiang-shan [Lu Chiu-yüan]). By Lu Chiu-yüan (1139–92). 36 *chüan. Ssu-pu ts'ung-k'an* edition. Shanghai: Shang-wu yin-shu kuan, 1929.

Hsiao-ching 孝經 (The classic of filial piety). In *Shih-san ching ching-wen*.

The Hsiao Ching. Translated by Mary Lelia Makra. New York: St. John's University Press, 1971.

Hsiao fu-jen chin-ch'ien tseng nien-shao 小夫人金錢贈年少 (The merchant's wife offers money to a young clerk). In *Ching-shih t'ung-yen, chüan* 16, pp. 222–33.

Hsiao-p'in chi 效顰集 (Emulative frowns collection). By Chao Pi 趙弼 (fl. early 15th century). Author's postface dated 1428. Shanghai: Ku-tien wen-hsüeh ch'u-pan she, 1957.

[Hsiao-shih] Chen-k'ung pao-chüan [銷釋]真空寶卷 ([Clearly presented] Precious volume on [the teaching of the Patriarch] Chen-k'ung). In *Pao-chüan ch'u-chi*, 19:261–300.

[Hsiao-shih] Chen-k'ung sao-hsin pao-chüan [銷釋]真空掃心寶卷 ([Clearly presented] Precious volume on [the Patriarch] Chen-k'ung's [instructions for] sweeping clear the mind). Published in 1584. In *Pao-chüan ch'u-chi*, 18:385–19:259.

[Hsiao-shih] Chin-kang k'o-i [hui-yao chu-chieh] [銷釋]金剛科儀[會要註解] ([Clearly presented] liturgical exposition of the Diamond sutra [with critical commentary]). Edited and annotated by Chüeh-lien 覺連. Preface dated 1551. In *[Shinzan] Dai Nihon zoku zōkyō*, 24:650–756.

Hsiao Sun-t'u 小孫屠 (Little Butcher Sun). In *Yung-lo ta-tien hsi-wen san-chung chiao-chu*, pp. 257–324.

Hsiao T'ien-hsiang pan-yeh ch'ao-yüan 小天香半夜朝元 (Little Heavenly Fragrance ascends to paradise at midnight). By Chu Yu-tun 朱有燉 (1379–1439). In *Ch'üan Ming tsa-chü*, vol. 4:1745–68.

Hsien-Ch'in Han Wei Chin Nan-pei ch'ao shih 先秦漢魏晉南北朝詩 (Complete poetry of the Pre-Ch'in, Han, Wei, Chin, and Northern and Southern dynasties). Compiled by Lu Ch'in-li 逯欽立. 3 vols. Peking: Chung-hua shu-chü, 1983.

Hsien-yün An Juan-san ch'ang yüan-chai 閑雲菴阮三償冤債 (In Idle Cloud Nunnery Juan the Third repays his debt of love). In *Ku-chin hsiao-shuo*, vol. 1, *chüan* 4, pp. 80–94.

Hsin-ch'i teng-mi: Chiang-hu ch'iao-yü 新奇燈謎:江湖俏語 (Novel and unusual lantern riddles: Witticisms current in the demimonde). In *Han-shang huan wen-ts'un*, pp. 168–74.

Hsin-ch'iao shih Han Wu mai ch'un-ch'ing 新橋市韓五賣春情 (Han Wu-niang sells her charms at New Bridge Market). In *Ku-chin hsiao-shuo*, vol. 1, *chüan* 3, pp. 62–79.

[*Hsin-k'an ch'üan-hsiang*] *Ying-ko hsiao-i chuan* [新刊全相]鶯哥孝義傳 ([Newly printed fully illustrated] Story of the filial and righteous parrot). In *Ming Ch'eng-hua shuo-ch'ang tz'u-hua ts'ung-k'an*, ts'e 10.

[*Hsin-k'o hsiu-hsiang p'i-p'ing*] *Chin P'ing Mei* [新刻繡像批評]金瓶梅 ([Newly cut illustrated commentarial edition] of the *Chin P'ing Mei*). 2 vols. Chi-nan: Ch'i-Lu shu-she, 1989.

[*Hsin-k'o*] *Shih-shang hua-yen ch'ü-lo t'an-hsiao chiu-ling* [新刻]時尚華筵趣樂談笑酒令 ([Newly printed] Currently fashionable jokes and drinking games to be enjoyed at formal banquets). 4 *chüan*. Ming edition published by the Wen-te T'ang.

[*Hsin-pien*] *Liu Chih-yüan huan-hsiang Pai-t'u chi* [新編]劉知遠還鄉白兔記 ([Newly compiled] Liu Chih-yüan's return home: The white rabbit). In *Ming Ch'eng-hua shuo-ch'ang tz'u-hua ts'ung-k'an*, ts'e 12.

[*Hsin-pien shuo-ch'ang ch'üan-hsiang*] *Shih-lang fu-ma chuan* [新編 説唱全相]石郎駙馬傳 ([Newly compiled prosimetric fully illustrated] Story of the imperial son-in-law Shih Ching-t'ang [892–942]). Originally published in 1471. In *Ming Ch'eng-hua shuo-ch'ang tz'u-hua ts'ung-k'an*, ts'e 2.

[*Hsin-pien*] *Wu-tai shih p'ing-hua* [新編]五代史平話 ([Newly compiled] p'ing-hua on the history of the Five Dynasties). Originally published in the 14th century. Shanghai: Chung-kuo ku-tien wen-hsüeh ch'u-pan she, 1954.

Hsin T'ang shu 新唐書 (New history of the T'ang dynasty). Compiled by Ou-yang Hsiu 歐陽修(1007–72) and Sung Ch'i 宋祁(998–1061). 20 vols. Peking: Chung-hua shu-chü, 1975.

[*Hsin-tseng*] *Ch'iu-po i-chuan lun* [新增]秋波一轉論 ([Newly added] Treatise on the single meaningful glance). By Lai-feng Tao-jen 來鳳道人. Included as part of the front matter in the 1498 edition of the *Hsi-hsiang chi*, pp. 8a–8b.

Hsin Wu-tai shih 新五代史 (New history of the Five Dynasties). Compiled by Ou-yang Hsiu 歐陽修 (1007–72). 3 vols. Peking: Chung-hua shu-chü, 1974.

Hsing-shih heng-yen 醒世恆言 (Constant words to awaken the world). Edited by Feng Meng-lung 馮夢龍 (1574–1646). First published in 1627. 2 vols. Hong Kong: Chung-hua shu-chü, 1958.

Hsing-t'ien Feng-yüeh t'ung-hsüan chi 性天風月通玄記 (The Master of Breeze and Moonlight utilizes his Heaven-bestowed nature to penetrate the mysteries). By Lan Mao 蘭茂(1403–76). Preface dated 1454. In *Ku-pen hsi-ch'ü ts'ung-k'an, wu-chi*, item 1.

Hsiu-ju chi 繡襦記 (The embroidered jacket). By Hsü Lin 徐霖 (1462–1538). *Liu-shih chung ch'ü* edition. Taipei: K'ai-ming shu-tien, 1970.

Hsiung Lung-feng ssu-chung hsiao-shuo 熊龍峯四種小説 (Four vernacular stories published by Hsiung Lung-feng 熊龍峯 [fl. c. 1590]). Edited by Wang Ku-lu 王古魯. Shanghai: Ku-tien wen-hsüeh ch'u-pan she, 1958.

Hsü Fen-shu 續焚書 (Supplement to A book to be burned). By Li Chih 李贄 (1527–1602). Peking: Chung-hua shu-chü, 1961.

Hsü-t'ang Ho-shang yü-lu 虛堂和尚語錄 (Recorded sayings of the Monk Hsü-t'ang). In *Taishō shinshū daizōkyō*, vol. 47, no. 2000, pp. 984–1064.

Hsü Tsang-ching 續藏經 (Continuation of the Buddhist canon). 150 vols. Fac. repr. Hong Kong: Hsiang-kang ying-yin *Hsü Tsang-ching* wei-yüan hui, 1967.

Hsü Tzu-chih t'ung-chien ch'ang-pien 續資治通鑑長編 (Long draft of A continuation of the Comprehensive mirror for aid in government). Compiled by Li T'ao 李燾 (1115–84). 34 vols. Peking: Chung-hua shu-chü, 1979–93.

Hsüan-ho i-shih 宣和遺事 (Forgotten events of the Hsüan-ho reign period [1119–25]). Shanghai: Shang-hai ku-tien wen-hsüeh ch'u-pan she, 1955.

Hsüan-kuai lu 玄怪錄 (Accounts of mysteries and anomalies). By Niu Seng-ju 牛僧孺 (779–847). In *Hsüan-kuai lu; Hsü Hsüan-kuai lu*, pp. 1–133.

Hsüan-kuai lu; Hsü Hsüan-kuai lu 玄怪錄;續玄怪錄 (Accounts of mysteries and anomalies; Continuation of Accounts of mysteries and anomalies). By 牛僧孺 (779–847) and Li Fu-yen 李復言 (9th century). Peking: Chung-hua shu-chü, 1982.

Hsüan-t'ien shang-ti ch'ui-chieh wen 玄天上帝垂誡文 (Admonitions of the Supreme Sovereign of the Mysterious Celestial Realm). In *Kuo-se t'ien-hsiang*, vol. 2, *chüan* 4, upper register, pp. 51b–53b.

Hsüeh Jen-kuei cheng-Liao shih-lüeh 薛仁貴征遼事略 (A brief account of Hsüeh Jen-kuei's campaign in Liao-tung). Shanghai: Ku-tien wen-hsüeh ch'u-pan she, 1957.

Hsün-ch'in chi 尋親記 (The quest for the father). *Liu-shih chung ch'ü* edition. Taipei: K'ai-ming shu-tien, 1970.

Hsün-fang ya-chi 尋芳雅集 (Elegant vignettes of fragrant pursuits). In *Kuo-se t'ien-hsiang*, vol. 2, *chüan* 4, pp. 1a–57a, lower register.

Hsün-tzu yin-te 荀子引得 (A concordance to *Hsün-tzu*). Taipei: Chinese Materials and Research Aids Service Center, 1966.

Hu-fu chi 虎符記 (The story of the tiger tally). In *Ku-pen hsi-ch'ü ts'ung-k'an, ch'u-chi*, item 63.

Hua Kuan So pien Yün-nan chuan 花關索貶雲南傳 (The story of how Hua Kuan So was exiled to Yün-nan). Originally published in 1478. Fac. repr. in *Ming Ch'eng-hua shuo-ch'ang tz'u-hua ts'ung-k'an*, ts'e 1.

Hua-shen san-miao chuan 花神三妙傳 (The flower god and the three beauties). In *Kuo-se t'ien-hsiang*, vol. 2., *chüan* 6, lower register, pp. 1a–61a.

Hua-teng chiao Lien-nü ch'eng-Fo chi 花燈轎蓮女成佛記 (The girl Lien-nü attains Buddhahood in her bridal palanquin). In *Ch'ing-p'ing shan-t'ang hua-pen*, pp. 193–205.

Hua-ying chi 花影集 (Flower shadows collection). By T'ao Fu 陶輔 (1441–c. 1523). Author's preface dated 1523. In *Ming-Ch'ing hsi-chien hsiao-shuo ts'ung-k'an*, pp. 831–940.

Huai-ch'un ya-chi 懷春雅集 (Elegant vignettes of spring yearning). In *Yen-chü pi-chi* (Ho Ta-lun), vol. 2, *chüan* 9, pp. 1a–37a, and *chüan* 10, pp. 1a–27b, upper register.

Huai-ch'un ya-chi 懷春雅集 (Elegant vignettes of spring yearning). In *Yen-chü pi-chi* (Lin Chin-yang), vol. 3, *chüan* 9, pp. 16b–32a, and *chüan* 10, pp. 1a–39b, upper register.

Huai-hai chi chien-chu 淮海集箋注 (Ch'in Kuan's collected works collated and annotated). Edited by Hsü P'ei-chün 徐培均. 3 vols. Shanghai: Shang-hai ku-chi ch'u-pan she, 1994.

Huai-hsiang chi 懷香記 (The stolen perfume). By Lu Ts'ai 陸采 (1497–1537). *Liu-shih chung ch'ü* edition. Taipei: K'ai-ming shu-tien, 1970.

Huan-men tzu-ti ts'o li-shen 宦門子弟錯立身 (The scion of an official's family opts for the wrong career). In *Yung-lo ta-tien hsi-wen san-chung chiao-chu*, pp. 219–55.

Huan-sha chi 浣紗記 (The girl washing silk). By Liang Ch'en-yü 梁辰魚 (1519–1591). *Liu-shih chung ch'ü* edition. Taipei: K'ai-ming shu-tien, 1970.

Huan-tai chi 還帶記 (The return of the belts). By Shen Ts'ai 沈采 (15th century). In *Ku-pen hsi-ch'ü ts'ung-k'an, ch'u-chi*, item 32.

Huan-yu chi-wen 宦遊紀聞 (Record of things heard during official travels). By Chang I 張誼 (16th century). In *Shuo-fu hsü*, 9:731–34.

Huang-ch'ao pien-nien kang-mu pei-yao 皇朝編年綱目備要 (Chronological outline of the significant events of the imperial [Sung] dynasty). Compiled by Ch'en Chün 陳均 (c. 1165–c. 1236). Preface dated 1229. 2 vols. Fac. repr. Taipei: Ch'eng-wen ch'u-pan she, 1966.

Huang-chi chin-tan chiu-lien cheng-hsin kuei-chen huan-hsiang pao-chüan 皇極金丹九蓮正信皈真還鄉寶卷 (Precious volume of the golden elixir and nine-petaled lotus of the Imperial Ultimate period that leads to rectifying belief, reverting to the real, and returning to our true home). Originally published in 1498. In *Pao-chüan ch'u-chi*, 8:1–482.

Huang hsiao-tzu 黃孝子 (The filial son Huang [Chüeh-ching]黃覺經). In *Ku-pen hsi-ch'ü ts'ung-k'an, ch'u-chi*, item 23.

Huang-hua Yü tieh-ta Ts'ai Ko-ta 黃花峪跌打蔡紇縫 (Ts'ai the Blister gets his come-uppance in Chrysanthemum Valley). In *Ch'ün-yin lei-hsüan*, 3:1835–67.

Huang-Ming k'ai-yün ying-wu chuan 皇明開運英武傳 (Chronicle of the heroic military exploits that initiated the reign of the imperial Ming dynasty). Nanking: Yang Ming-feng, 1591. Fac. repr. in *Ku-pen hsiao-shuo ts'ung-k'an, ti san-shih liu chi*, vol. 1.

Huang T'ing-tao yeh-tsou Liu-hsing ma 黃廷道夜走流星馬 (Huang T'ing-tao steals the horse Shooting Star by night). By Huang Yüan-chi 黃元吉 (14th century). In *Ming-jen tsa-chü hsüan*, pp. 85–111.

Hui-an hsien-sheng Chu Wen-kung wen-chi 晦庵先生朱文公集 (The collected literary works of Chu Hsi 朱熹 [1130–1200]). *Ssu-pu pei-yao* edition. Shanghai: Chung-hua shu-chü, 1936.

Hung-fu chi 紅拂記 (The story of Red Duster). By Chang Feng-i 張鳳翼 (1527–1613). *Liu-shih chung ch'ü* edition. Taipei: K'ai-ming shu-tien, 1970.

Huo Hsiao-yü chuan 霍小玉傳 (The story of Huo Hsiao-yü). By Chiang Fang 蔣防 (early 9th century). In *T'ang Sung ch'uan-ch'i chi*, pp. 68–78.

I-chien chih 夷堅志 (Records of I-chien). Compiled by Hung Mai 洪邁 (1123–1202). 4 vols. Peking: Chung-hua shu-chü, 1981.

I-hsia chi 義俠記 (The righteous knight-errant). By Shen Ching 沈璟 (1553–1610). *Liu-shih chung ch'ü* edition. Taipei: K'ai-ming shu-tien, 1970.

I-k'u kuei lai tao-jen ch'u-kuai 一窟鬼癩道人除怪 (A mangy Taoist exorcises a lair of demons). In *Ching-shih t'ung-yen*, *chüan* 14, pp. 185–98.

Jen chin shu ku-erh hsün-mu 認金梳孤兒尋母 (Identifying the gold [hairpins] and the [jade] comb an orphan seeks his mother). In *Ku-pen Yüan-Ming tsa-chü*, vol. 3.

Jen hsiao-tzu lieh-hsing wei shen 任孝子烈性爲神 (The apotheosis of Jen the filial son). In *Ku-chin hsiao-shuo*, vol. 2, *chüan* 38, pp. 571–86.

Jen-tsung jen-mu chuan 仁宗認母傳 (The story of how Emperor Jen-tsung [r. 1022–63] reclaimed his mother). Fac. repr. in *Ming Ch'eng-hua shuo-ch'ang tz'u-hua ts'ung-k'an*, ts'e 4.

Ju-i chün chuan 如意君傳 (The tale of Lord As You Like It). Japanese movable type edition, colophon dated 1880.

Ju-ju chü-shih yü-lu 如如居士語錄 (The recorded sayings of layman Ju-ju). By Yen Ping 顏丙 (d. 1212). Preface dated 1194. Photocopy of manuscript in the Kyoto University Library.

Jung-chai sui-pi 容齋隨筆 (Miscellaneous notes from the Tolerant Study). By Hung Mai 洪邁(1123–1202). 2 vols. Shanghai: Shang-hai ku-chi ch'u-pan she, 1978.

Jung-yü T'ang pen Shui-hu chuan 容與堂本水滸傳 (The Jung-yü T'ang edition of the *Shui-hu chuan*). Originally published in 1610. 2 vols. Shanghai: Shang-hai ku-chi ch'u-pan she, 1988.

K'ai-ho chi 開河記 (The opening of the canal). In *T'ang Sung ch'uan-ch'i chi*, pp. 232–45.

K'ai-yüan T'ien-pao i-shih 開元天寶遺事 (Forgotten events of the K'ai-yüan [713–41] and T'ien-pao [742–56] reign periods). Compiled by Wang Jen-yü 王仁裕 (880–942). In *K'ai-yüan T'ien-pao i-shih shih-chung*, pp. 65–109.

K'ai-yüan T'ien-pao i-shih shih-chung 開元天寶遺事十種 (Ten works dealing with forgotten events of the K'ai-yüan [713–21] and T'ien-pao [742–56] reign periods). Edited by Ting Ju-ming 丁如明. Shanghai: Shang-hai ku-chi ch'u-pan she, 1985.

K'an p'i-hsüeh tan-cheng Erh-lang Shen 勘皮靴單證二郎神 (Investigation of a leather boot convicts Erh-lang Shen). In *Hsing-shih heng-yen*, vol. 1, *chüan* 13, pp. 241–63.

Kao Ch'ing-ch'iu chi 高青丘集 (The collected works of Kao Ch'i [1336–74]). Edited by Hsü Ch'eng-yü 徐澄宇 and Shen Pei-tsung 沈北宗. 2 vols. Shanghai: Shang-hai ku-chi ch'u-pan she, 1985.

Ko-i chi 葛衣記 (The hempen garment). By Ku Ta-tien 顧大典 (1541–96). In *Ku-pen hsi-ch'ü ts'ung-k'an, wu-chi*, item 3.

Ko tai hsiao 歌代嘯 (A song in place of a shriek). Attributed to Hsü Wei 徐渭 (1521–93). In *Ssu-sheng yüan*, pp. 107–68.

K'o-tso chui-yü 客座贅語 (Superfluous words of a sojourner). By Ku Ch'i-yüan 顧起元 (1565–1628). Author's colophon dated 1618. Peking: Chung-hua shu-chü, 1987.

Ku-chang chüeh-ch'en 鼓掌絕塵 (Clapping the hands to shake off the dust of the world). Preface dated 1631. 5 vols. In *Ming-Ch'ing shan-pen hsiao-shuo ts'ung-k'an, ch'u-pien*.

Ku-ch'eng chi 古城記 (The reunion at Ku-ch'eng). In *Ku-pen hsi-ch'ü ts'ung-k'an, ch'u-chi*, item 25.

Ku-chin chu 古今註 (Notes on things ancient and modern). By Ts'ui Pao 崔豹 (fl. late 3rd century). Shanghai: Shang-wu yin-shu kuan, 1956.

Ku-chin hsiao-shuo 古今小説 (Stories old and new). Edited by Feng Meng-lung 馮夢龍(1574–1646). 2 vols. Peking: Jen-min wen-hsüeh ch'u-pan she, 1958.

Ku-chin t'an-kai 古今譚概 (A representative selection of anecdotes ancient and modern). Compiled by Feng Meng-lung 馮夢龍 (1574–1646). Preface dated 1620. Fuchou: Hai-hsia wen-i ch'u-pan she, 1985.

Ku-chin t'u-shu chi-ch'eng 古今圖書集成 (A comprehensive corpus of books and illustrations ancient and modern), presented to the emperor in 1725. Fac. repr. Taipei: Wen-hsing shu-tien, 1964.

Ku-Hang hung-mei chi 古杭紅梅記 (The story of the red plum of old Hang-chou). In *Kuo-se t'ien-hsiang*, vol. 3, *chüan* 8, upper register, pp. 1a–18b.

Ku hsiao-shuo kou-ch'en 古小説鉤沉 (Rescued fragments of early fiction). Compiled by Lu Hsün 魯迅. Peking: Jen-min wen-hsüeh ch'u-pan she, 1955.

Ku-pen hsi-ch'ü ts'ung-k'an, ch'u-chi 古本戲曲叢刊, 初集 (Collectanea of rare editions of traditional drama, first series). Shanghai: Shang-wu yin-shu kuan, 1954.

Ku-pen hsi-ch'ü ts'ung-k'an, erh-chi 古本戲曲叢刊, 二集 (Collectanea of rare editions of traditional drama, second series). Shanghai: Shang-wu yin-shu kuan, 1955.

Ku-pen hsi-ch'ü ts'ung-k'an, wu-chi 古本戲曲叢刊, 五集 (Collectanea of rare editions of traditional drama, fifth series). Shanghai: Shang-hai ku-chi ch'u-pan she, 1986.

Ku-pen hsiao-shuo ts'ung-k'an, ti-erh chi 古本小説叢刊, 第二集 (Collectanea of rare editions of traditional fiction, second series). Peking: Chung-hua shu-chü, 1990.

Ku-pen hsiao-shuo ts'ung-k'an, ti erh-shih liu chi 古本小説叢刊, 第二十六集 (Collectanea of rare editions of traditional fiction, twenty-sixth series). Peking: Chung-hua shu-chü, 1991.

Ku-pen hsiao-shuo ts'ung-k'an, ti-liu chi 古本小説叢刊, 第六集 (Collectanea of rare editions of traditional fiction, sixth series). Peking: Chung-hua shu-chü, 1990.

Ku-pen hsiao-shuo ts'ung-k'an, ti-pa chi 古本小説叢刊, 第八集 (Collectanea of rare editions of traditional fiction, eighth series). Peking: Chung-hua shu-chü, 1990.

Ku-pen hsiao-shuo ts'ung-k'an, ti san-shih ch'i chi 古本小説叢刊, 第三十七集 (Collectanea of rare editions of traditional fiction, thirty-seventh series). Peking: Chung-hua shu-chü, 1991.

Ku-pen hsiao-shuo ts'ung-k'an, ti san-shih chiu chi 古本小説叢刊, 第三十九集 (Collectanea of rare editions of traditional fiction, thirty-ninth series). Peking: Chung-hua shu-chü, 1991.

Ku-pen hsiao-shuo ts'ung-k'an, ti san-shih liu chi 古本小説叢刊, 第三十六集 (Collectanea of rare editions of traditional fiction, thirty-sixth series). Peking: Chung-hua shu-chü, 1991.

Ku-pen hsiao-shuo ts'ung-k'an, ti san-shih ssu chi 古本小説叢刊, 第三十四集 (Collectanea of rare editions of traditional fiction, thirty-fourth series). Peking: Chung-hua shu-chü, 1991.

Ku-pen hsiao-shuo ts'ung-k'an, ti shih-erh chi 古本小説叢刊, 第十二集 (Collectanea of rare editions of traditional fiction, twelfth series). Peking: Chung-hua shu-chü, 1991.

Ku-pen hsiao-shuo ts'ung-k'an, ti-ssu chi 古本小説叢刊, 第四集 (Collectanea of rare editions of traditional fiction, fourth series). Peking: Chung-hua shu-chü, 1990.

Ku-pen hsiao-shuo ts'ung-k'an, ti-wu chi 古本小説叢刊, 第五集 (Collectanea of rare editions of traditional fiction, fifth series). Peking: Chung-hua shu-chü, 1990.

Ku-pen Yüan Ming tsa-chü 孤本元明雜劇 (Unique editions of Yüan and Ming tsa-chü drama). Edited by Wang Chi-lieh 王季烈. 4 vols. Peking: Chung-kuo hsi-chü ch'u-pan she, 1958.

Ku-tai wen-yen tuan-p'ien hsiao-shuo hsüan-chu, erh-chi 古代文言短篇小説選注, 二 集 (An annotated selection of classic literary tales, second collection). Edited by Ch'eng Po-ch'üan 成伯泉. Shanghai: Shang-hai ku-chi ch'u-pan she, 1984.

Ku tsun-su yü-lu 古尊宿語錄 (The recorded sayings of eminent monks of old). Compiled by Tse Tsang-chu 賾藏主 (13th century). In *Hsü Tsang-ching*, 118:79a–418a.

K'u-kung wu-tao chüan 苦功悟道卷 (Precious volume on awakening to the Way through bitter toil). By Lo Ch'ing 羅清 (1442–1527). Originally published in 1509. In *Pao-chüan ch'u-chi*, 1:1–293.

K'uai-tsui Li Ts'ui-lien chi 快嘴李翠蓮集 (The story of the sharp-tongued Li Ts'ui-lien). In *Ch'ing-p'ing shan-t'ang hua-pen*, pp. 52–67.

Kuan-shih-yin p'u-sa pen-hsing ching 觀世音菩薩本行經 (Sutra on the deeds of the bodhisattva Avalokiteśvara). Also known as *Hsiang-shan pao-chüan* 香山寶卷 (Precious scroll on Hsiang-shan). Attributed to P'u-ming 普明 (fl. early 12th century). N.p., n.d. (probably 19th century).

Kuan-tzu chiao-cheng 管子校正 (The *Kuan-tzu* collated and corrected). Edited and annotated by Tai Wang 戴望 (1837–73). In *Chu-tzu chi-ch'eng*, 5:1–427.

Kuan-yüan chi 灌園記 (The story of the gardener). By Chang Feng-i 張鳳翼 (1527–1613). *Liu-shih chung ch'ü* edition. Taipei: K'ai-ming shu-tien, 1970.

Kuan Yün-ch'ang i-yung tz'u-chin 關雲長義勇辭金 (Kuan Yün-ch'ang righteously and heroically refuses gold). By Chu Yu-tun 朱有燉 (1379–1439). Originally completed in 1416. In *Ming-jen tsa-chü hsüan*, pp. 141–68.

Kuang Ch'ün-fang p'u 廣羣芳譜 (An enlarged version of the Monograph on fragrant plants). Compiled by Wang Hao 汪灝 (cs 1703) et al. Presented to the throne in 1708. 4 vols. Shanghai: Shang-hai shu-tien, 1985.

Kuei-chien chiao-ch'ing 貴賤交情 (An intimate bond between the exalted and the humble). In *Tsui-yü ch'ing*, 4:1524–64, upper register.

K'uei-kuan Yao Pien tiao Chu-ko 夔關姚卞弔諸葛 (At K'uei-kuan Yao Pien commemorates Chu-ko Liang). In *Ch'ing-p'ing shan-t'ang hua-pen*, pp. 304–12.

Kung-k'uei chi 攻媿集 (Collected works of Kung-k'uei [Lou Yüeh]). By Lou Yüeh 樓鑰 (1137–1213). 112 *chüan*. *Ssu-pu ts'ung-k'an* edition. Shanghai: Shang-wu yin-shu kuan, 1929.

K'ung Shu-fang shuang-yü shan-chui chuan 孔淑芳雙魚扇墜傳 (The story of K'ung Shu-fang and the pair of fish-shaped fan pendants), in *Hsiung Lung-feng ssu-chung hsiao-shuo*, pp. 63–70.

K'ung-ts'ung-tzu 孔叢子 (The K'ung family masters' anthology). Probably compiled by Wang Su 王肅 (195–256). In *Pai-tzu ch'üan-shu*, vol. 1.

Kuo-ch'ao hsien-cheng lu 國朝獻徵錄 (A corpus of primary biographical sources for the Ming dynasty). Compiled by Chiao Hung 焦竑 (1541–1620). Originally published in 1616. 8 vols. Fac. repr. Taipei: Hsüeh-sheng shu-chü, 1965.

Kuo-se t'ien-hsiang 國色天香 (Celestial fragrance of national beauties). Compiled by Wu Ching-so 吳敬所 (fl. late 16th century). Preface dated 1587. 3 vols. Fac. repr. in *Ming-Ch'ing shan-pen hsiao-shuo ts'ung-k'an, ti-erh chi*.

Lao Feng T'ang chih-chien Han Wen-ti 老馮唐直諫漢文帝 (The elderly Feng T'ang straightforwardly admonishes Emperor Wen of the Han dynasty). In *Ch'ing-p'ing shan-t'ang hua-pen*, pp. 289–96.

Lao Tzu Tao Te Ching. Translated by D. C. Lau. New York: Penguin Books, 1963.

Leng-chai yeh-hua 冷齋夜話 (Evening talk from a cold studio). By Hui-hung 惠洪 (1071–1128). In *Pi-chi hsiao-shuo ta-kuan*, vol. 4, *ts'e* 8.

Li-chi 禮記 (The book of rites). In *Shih-san ching ching-wen*.

Li Chi: Book of Rites. Translated by James Legge. 2 vols. New Hyde Park, N.Y.: University Books, 1967.

Li K'ai-hsien chi 李開先集 (The collected works of Li K'ai-hsien). By Li K'ai-hsien (1502–68). Edited by Lu Kung 路工. 3 vols. Peking: Chung-hua shu-chü, 1959.

Li K'ai-hsien ch'üan-chi 李開先全集 (The complete works of Li K'ai-hsien). Edited and annotated by Pu Chien 卜鍵. 3 vols. Peking: Wen-hua i-shu ch'u-pan she, 2004.

Li-shih chen-hsien t'i-tao t'ung-chien 歷世真仙體道通鑑 (Comprehensive mirror of immortals who embodied the Tao through the ages). Compiled by Chao Tao-i 趙道一 (fl. 1294–1307). In *Cheng-t'ung Tao-tsang, ts'e* 139–48.

Li-wa chuan 李娃傳 (The story of Li Wa). By Po Hsing-chien 白行簡 (776–826). In *T'ang Sung ch'uan-ch'i chi*, pp. 97–108.

Li-yüan an-shih yüeh-fu hsin-sheng 梨園按試樂府新聲 (Model new songs from the Pear Garden). Modern edition edited by Sui Shu-sen 隋樹森. Peking: Chung-hua shu-chü, 1958.

Li Yüan Wu-chiang chiu chu-she 李元吳江救朱蛇 (Li Yüan saves a red snake on the Wu River). In *Ch'ing-p'ing shan-t'ang hua-pen*, pp. 324–34.

Li Yün-ch'ing te-wu sheng-chen 李雲卿得悟昇真 (Li Yün-ch'ing attains enlightenment and achieves transcendence). In *Ku-pen Yüan Ming tsa-chü*, vol. 4.

Liang Han chi 兩漢紀 (Two records of the Former and Later Han dynasties). Edited by Chang Lieh 張烈. 2 vols. Peking: Chung-hua shu-chü, 2005.

Liang-shan wu-hu ta chieh-lao 梁山五虎大劫牢 (The five tigers of Liang-shan carry out a great jailbreak). In *Ku-pen Yüan Ming tsa-chü*, vol. 3.

Liao-yang hai-shen chuan 遼陽海神傳 (The sea goddess of Liao-yang). By Ts'ai Yü 蔡羽 (d. 1541). In *Ku-tai wen-yen tuan-p'ien hsiao-shuo hsüan-chu, erh-chi*, pp. 381–89.

Lieh-kuo chih-chuan 列國志傳 (Chronicle of the feudal states). By Yü Shao-yü 余邵魚 (fl. mid 16th century). 8 *chüan*. Chien-yang: San-t'ai kuan, 1606. Fac. repr. in *Ku-pen hsiao-shuo ts'ung-k'an, ti-liu chi*, vols. 1–3.

Lieh-nü chuan 列女傳 (Biographies of exemplary women). Compiled by Liu Hsiang 劉向 (79–8 B.C.) Taipei: Chung-hua shu-chü, 1972.

Lieh-tzu chi-shih 列子集釋 (A critical edition of *Lieh-tzu*). Edited by Yang Po-chün 楊伯峻. Hong Kong: T'ai-p'ing shu-chü, 1965.

Lien-huan chi 連環記 (A stratagem of interlocking rings). By Wang Chi 王濟 (1474–1540). Peking: Chung-hua shu-chü, 1988.

Lin Ling-su chuan 林靈素傳 (The story of Lin Ling-su). By Keng Yen-hsi 耿延禧 (fl. early 12th century). In *Pin-t'ui lu*, *chüan* 1, pp. 5a–8a.

Ling-pao ling-chiao chi-tu chin-shu 靈寶領教濟度金書 (The golden book of salvation according to the Ling-pao tradition). Compiled by Lin Ling-chen 林靈真 (1239–1302). In *Cheng-t'ung Tao-tsang, ts'e* 208–63.

Ling-pao wu-liang tu-jen shang-ching ta-fa 靈寶無量度人上經大法 (Great rites of the preeminent scripture of the Numinous Treasure that saves innumerable human beings). Compiled ca. 1200. In *Cheng-t'ung Tao-tsang, ts'e* 85–99.

Ling-pao wu-liang tu-jen shang-p'in miao-ching 靈寶無量度人上品妙經 (Most excellent and mysterious scripture of the Numinous Treasure that saves innumerable human beings). In *Cheng-t'ung Tao-tsang, ts'e* 1–13.

Ling-pao yü-chien 靈寶玉鑑 (Jade mirror of the Numinous Treasure). Probably compiled in the twelfth century. In *Cheng-t'ung Tao-tsang, ts'e* 302–311.

Liu Chi chi 劉基集 (Liu Chi's collected works). Edited by Lin Chia-li 林家驪. Hang-chou: Che-chiang ku-chi ch'u-pan she, 1999.

Liu Ch'i-ch'ing shih-chiu Wan-chiang Lou chi 柳耆卿詩酒翫江樓記 (Liu Ch'i-ch'ing indulges in poetry and wine in the Riverside Pavilion). In *Ch'ing-p'ing shan-t'ang hua-pen*, pp. 1–5.

Liu Chih-yüan chu-kung-tiao [chiao-chu] 劉知遠諸公調[校注] (Medley in various modes on Liu Chih-yüan [collated and annotated]). Edited by Lan Li-ming 藍立蓂. Ch'eng-tu: Pa-Shu shu-she, 1989.

Liu-ch'ing jih-cha 留青日札 (Daily jottings worthy of preservation). By T'ien I-heng 田藝蘅(1524–c. 1574). Preface dated 1572. Fac. repr. of 1609 edition. Shanghai: Shang-hai ku-chi ch'u-pan she, 1985.

Liu Ho-tung chi 柳河東集 (The collected works of Liu Tsung-yüan [773–819]). 2 vols. Peking: Chung-hua shu-chü, 1961.

Liu-hung chi 流紅記 (Red leaves on the water). By Chang Shih 張實 (fl. mid-11th century). In *Ch'ing-so kao-i, chüan* 5, pp. 46–49.

Liu I chuan 柳毅傳 (The story of Liu I). By Li Ch'ao-wei 李朝威 (fl. late 8th century). In *T'ang Sung ch'uan-ch'i chi*, pp. 51–63.

Liu sheng mi Lien chi 劉生覓蓮記 (The story of Liu I-ch'un's 劉一春 quest of Sun Pi-lien 孫碧蓮). In *Kuo-se t'ien-hsiang*, vol. 1, *chüan* 2, pp. 1a–40b, and *chüan* 3, pp. 1a–41b, lower register.

Liu-shih chung ch'ü 六十種曲 (Sixty ch'uan-ch'i dramas). Compiled by Mao Chin 毛晉(1599–1659). 60 vols. Taipei: K'ai-ming shu-tien, 1970.

Liu Wen-lung ling-hua ching 劉文龍菱花鏡 (Liu Wen-lung's caltrop-patterned mirror). In *Sung-Yüan hsi-wen chi-i*, pp. 214–18.

Liu Yü-hsi chi chien-cheng 劉禹錫集箋證 (An annotated edition of Liu Yü-hsi's collected works). Annotated by Ch'ü T'ui-yüan 瞿蛻園. 3 vols. Shanghai: Shang-hai ku-chi ch'u-pan she, 1989.

Liu-yüan hui-hsüan chiang-hu fang-yü 六院彙選江湖方語 (Slang expressions current in the demimonde selected from the six licensed brothels [of Chin-ling]). In *Han-shang huan wen-ts'un*, pp. 158–65.

The Lotus Sutra. Translated by Burton Watson. New York: Columbia University Press, 1993.

Lo-yang san-kuai chi 洛陽三怪記 (The three monsters of Lo-yang). In *Ch'ing-p'ing shan-t'ang hua-pen*, pp. 67–78.

Lu-shan Yüan-kung hua 廬山遠公話 (Story of Hui-yüan 慧遠 [334–416] of Mount Lu). In *Tun-huang pien-wen chi*, 1:167–93.

Lun-yü yin-te 論語引得 (A concordance to the *Analects*). Taipei: Chinese Materials and Research Aids Service Center, 1966.

Lung-ch'eng lu 龍城錄 (Records of Lung-ch'eng). Attributed to Liu Tsung-yüan 柳宗元 (773–819). In *Pai-ch'uan hsüeh-hai, i-chi* (second collection), pp. 1a–6b.

Lung-men yin-hsiu 龍門隱秀 (The beauty concealed at Lung-men). In *Ku-pen Yüan Ming tsa-chü*, vol. 3.

Lü-ch'uang hsin-hua 綠窗新話 (New tales of the green gauze windows). Compiled by Huang-tu Feng-yüeh Chu-jen 皇都風月主人 (13th century). Edited by Chou I 周夷. Shanghai: Ku-tien wen-hsüeh ch'u-pan she, 1957.

Lü-shih ch'un-ch'iu 呂氏春秋 (The spring and autumn annals of Mr. Lü). Compiled by Lü Pu-wei 呂不韋 (d. 235 B.C.). In *Chu-tzu chi-ch'eng*, 6:1–346.

Lü Tung-pin fei-chien chan Huang-lung 呂洞賓飛劍斬黃龍 (Lü Tung-pin beheads Huang-lung with his flying sword). In *Hsing-shih heng-yen*, vol. 2, *chüan* 21, pp. 453–66.

Lü Tung-pin hua-yüeh shen-hsien hui 呂洞賓花月神仙會 (Lü Tung-pin arranges a meeting with divine immortals amid flowers and moonlight). By Chu Yu-tun 朱有燉 (1379–1439). In *Ku-pen Yüan Ming tsa-chü*, vol. 2.

Lü-weng san-hua Han-tan tien 呂翁三化邯鄲店 (Lü Tung-pin's three efforts to convert [student Lu] at the Han-tan inn). In *Ku-pen Yüan Ming tsa-chü*, vol. 4.

Mao-shih yin-te 毛詩引得 (Concordance to the Mao version of the *Book of Songs*). Tokyo: Japan Council for East Asian Studies, 1962.

Mencius. Translated by D. C. Lau. Baltimore: Penguin Books, 1970.

Meng Chiang nü pien-wen 孟姜女變文 (The story of Meng Chiang). In *Tun-huang pien-wen chi*, 1:32–34.

Meng-liang lu 夢粱錄 (Record of the millet dream). Compiled by Wu Tzu-mu 吳自牧 (13th century). Preface dated 1274. In *Tung-ching meng-hua lu [wai ssu-chung]*, pp. 129–328.

Meng-mu san-i 孟母三移 (The mother of Mencius moves three times). In *Ku-pen Yüan Ming tsa-chü*, vol. 2.

Meng-tzu yin-te 孟子引得 (A Concordance to *Meng-tzu*). Taipei: Chinese Materials and Research Aids Service Center, 1966.

Mi-teng yin-hua 覓燈因話 (Tales told while searching for a lamp). By Shao Ching-chan 邵景詹(16th century). Author's preface dated 1592. In *Chien-teng hsin-hua [wai erh-chung]*, pp. 313–51.

Ming Ch'eng-hua shuo-ch'ang tz'u-hua ts'ung-k'an 明成化說唱詞話叢刊 (Corpus of prosimetric tz'u-hua narratives published in the Ch'eng-hua reign period [1465–87] of the Ming dynasty). 12 *ts'e*. Shanghai: Shanghai Museum, 1973.

Ming-Ch'ing chin-shih t'i-ming pei-lu so-yin 明清進士題名碑錄索引 (Index to Ming Ch'ing stele lists of *chin-shih* degrees). Compiled by Chu Pao-chiung 朱保炯 and Hsieh P'ei-lin 謝沛霖. 3 vols. Shanghai: Shang-hai ku-chi ch'u-pan she, 1980.

Ming-Ch'ing hsi-chien hsiao-shuo ts'ung-k'an 明清稀見小説叢刊 (Collectanea of rare works of fiction from the Ming-Ch'ing period). Chi-nan: Ch'i-Lu shu-she, 1996.

Ming-Ch'ing shan-pen hsiao-shuo ts'ung-k'an, ch'u-pien 明清善本小説叢刊, 初編 (Collectanea of rare editions of Ming-Ch'ing fiction, first series). Taipei: T'ien-i ch'u-pan she, 1985.

Ming-Ch'ing shan-pen hsiao-shuo ts'ung-k'an, ti-erh chi 明清善本小説叢刊, 第二輯 (Collectanea of rare editions of Ming-Ch'ing fiction, second series). Taipei: T'ien-i ch'u-pan she, 1985.

Ming-Ch'ing su-yü tz'u-shu chi-ch'eng 明清俗語辭書集成 (A corpus of Ming and Ch'ing glossaries to common expressions). Compiled by Nagasawa Kikuya 長澤規矩也. 3 vols. Shanghai: Shang-hai ku-chi ch'u pan she, 1989.

Ming-chu chi 明珠記 (The luminous pearl). By Lu Ts'ai 陸采 (1497–1537). *Liu-shih chung ch'ü* edition. Taipei: K'ai-ming shu-tien, 1970.

Ming-feng chi 鳴鳳記 (The singing phoenix). *Liu-shih chung ch'ü* edition. Taipei: K'ai-ming shu-tien, 1970.

Ming-hsin pao-chien 明心寶鑑 (A precious mirror to illuminate the mind). Microfilm copy of a Ming edition in the East Asian Library, University of Chicago.

Ming-jen chuan-chi tzu-liao so-yin 明人傳記資料索引 (Index to biographical materials on Ming figures). Taipei: Kuo-li chung-yang t'u-shu kuan, 1978.

Ming-jen tsa-chü hsüan 明人雜劇選 (An anthology of Ming tsa-chü drama). Compiled by Chou I-pai 周貽白. Peking: Jen-min wen-hsüeh ch'u-pan she, 1958.

Ming-kung shu-p'an ch'ing-ming chi 名公書判清明集 (A collection of enlightened judgments by famous gentlemen). Preface dated 1261. 2 vols. Peking: Chung-hua shu-chü, 1987.

Ming pao-ying lun 明報應論 (A treatise on karmic retribution). By Hui-yüan 慧遠 (334–416). Written in the year 402. In *Ch'üan Shang-ku San-tai Ch'in Han San-kuo Liu-ch'ao wen*, vol. 3, *Ch'üan Chin wen* (Complete prose of the Chin dynasty), *chüan* 162, pp. 3a–5a.

Ming shih 明史(History of the Ming dynasty). Compiled by Chang T'ing-yü 張廷玉 (1672–1755) et al. 28 vols. Peking: Chung-hua shu-chü, 1974.

Ming T'ai-tsu chi 明太祖集 (Collected works of Emperor T'ai-tsu of the Ming dynasty). Edited by Hu Shih-o 胡士尊. Ho-fei: Huang-shan shu-she, 1991.

Ming t'ung-chien 明通鑑 (Comprehensive mirror of government under the Ming dynasty). Compiled by Hsia Hsieh 夏燮 (1799–1875). 4 vols. Peking: Chung-hua shu-chü, 1959.

Mo-chi 默記 (Records of silence). Compiled by Wang Chih 王銍 (d. c. 1154). Peking: Chung-hua shu-chü, 1981.

Mo-tzu yin-te 墨子引得 (A concordance to *Mo-tzu*). Peking: Yenching University Press, 1948.

The Moon and the Zither: The Story of the Western Wing. By Wang Shifu; translated by Stephen H. West and Wilt L. Idema. Berkeley: University of California Press, 1991.

Mu-fu yen-hsien lu 幙府燕閑錄 (Anecdotes recorded during a private secretary's leisure hours). Compiled by Pi Chung-hsün 畢仲詢 (11th century). In *Shuo-fu san-chung*, 5:1900–02.

Mu-lien chiu-mu ch'üan-shan hsi-wen 目連救母勸善戲文 (An exhortatory drama on how Maudgalyāyana rescued his mother from the underworld). By Cheng Chih-chen 鄭之珍(1518–95). Author's preface dated 1582. In *Ku-pen hsi-ch'ü ts'ung-k'an*, *ch'u-chi*, item 67.

Mu-tan t'ing 牡丹亭 (The peony pavilion). By T'ang Hsien-tsu 湯顯祖 (1550–1616). Edited and annotated by Hsü Shuo-fang 徐朔方 and Yang Hsiao-mei 楊笑梅. Peking: Chung-hua shu-chü, 1959.

Nan-chi hsing tu-t'o Hai-t'ang hsien 南極星度脫海棠仙 (The Southern Pole Star delivers the Flowering Crab Apple Immortal). By Chu Yu-tun 朱有燉 (1379–1439). Originally completed in 1439. In *Ku-pen Yüan Ming tsa-chü*, vol. 2.

Nan-ching: The Classic of Difficult Issues. Translated by Paul U. Unschuld. Berkeley: University of California Press, 1986.

Nan Hsi-hsiang chi 南西廂記 (A southern version of the *Romance of the western chamber*). Usually attributed to Li Jih-hua 李日華 (fl. early 16th century). *Liu-shih chung ch'ü* edition. Taipei: K'ai-ming shu-tien, 1970).

Nan Hsi-hsiang chi 南西廂記 (A southern version of the *Romance of the western chamber*). By Lu Ts'ai 陸采 (1497–1537). In *Hsi-hsiang hui-pien*, pp. 323–416.

Nan-k'o meng chi 南柯夢記 (The dream of the southern branch). By T'ang Hsien-tsu 湯顯祖 (1550–1616). Completed in 1600. Edited and annotated by Ch'ien Nan-yang 錢南揚. Peking: Jen-min wen-hsüeh ch'u-pan she, 1981.

Nan-kung tz'u-chi 南宮詞紀 (Anthology of southern-style lyrics). Compiled by Ch'en So-wen 陳所聞 (d. c. 1604). In *Nan-pei kung tz'u-chi*, vols. 1–2.

Nan-pei kung tz'u-chi 南北宮詞紀 (Anthology of southern- and northern-style song lyrics). Compiled by Ch'en So-wen 陳所聞 (d. c. 1604); edited by Chao Ching-shen 趙景深. 4 vols. Peking: Chung-hua shu-chü, 1959.

Nan shih 南史 (History of the Southern dynasties). Compiled by Li Yen-shou 李延壽 (7th century). Completed in 659. 6 vols. Peking: Chung-hua shu-chü, 1975.

Nan Sung chih-chuan 南宋志傳 (Chronicle of the Sung conquest of the south). Attributed to Hsiung Ta-mu 熊大木 (mid-16th century). 10 *chüan*. Nanking: Shih-te t'ang, 1593. Fac. repr. in *Ku-pen hsiao-shuo ts'ung-k'an, ti san-shih ssu chi*, vols. 1–2.

Nan-yin san-lai 南音三籟 (Three kinds of southern sound). Compiled by Ling Meng-ch'u 凌濛初(1580–1644). 4 *ts'e*. Fac. repr. of late Ming edition. Shanghai: Shang-hai ku-chi shu-tien, 1963.

Nao Fan-lou to-ch'ing Chou Sheng-hsien 鬧樊樓多情周勝仙 (The disturbance in the Fan Tavern and the passionate Chou Sheng-hsien). In *Hsing-shih heng-yen*, vol. 1, *chüan* 14, pp. 264–76.

Nü han-lin 女翰林 (The female academician). In *Tsui yü-ch'ing*, 4:1450–1503, upper register.

Nü ku-ku shuo-fa sheng-t'ang chi 女姑姑說法陞堂記 (The nun who took the pulpit to expound the dharma). In *Ku-pen Yüan Ming tsa-chü*, vol. 3.

Ou-yang Yung-shu chi 歐陽永叔集 (The collected works of Ou-yang Hsiu 歐陽修 [1007–72]). 3 vols. Shanghai: Shang-wu yin-shu kuan, 1958.

Pa-hsiang pien 八相變 (Pien-wen on the eight aspects [of Śākyamuni Buddha's life]. In *Tun-huang pien-wen chi*, 1:329–42.

Pa-i chi 八義記 (The story of the eight righteous heroes). *Liu-shih chung ch'ü* edition. Taipei: K'ai-ming shu-tien, 1970.

Pai-chia kung-an 百家公案 (A hundred court cases). 1594 edition. Fac. repr. in *Ku-pen hsiao-shuo ts'ung-k'an, ti-erh chi*, vol. 4.

Pai-ch'uan hsüeh-hai 百川學海 (A sea of knowledge fed by a hundred streams). Compiled by Tso Kuei 左圭 (13th century). Preface dated 1273. Fac. repr. of original edition. Peking: Chung-kuo shu-tien, 1990.

Pai Niang-tzu yung-chen Lei-feng T'a 白娘子永鎮雷峰塔 (The White Maiden is eternally imprisoned under Thunder Peak Pagoda). In *Ching-shih t'ung-yen*, *chüan* 28, pp. 420–48.

Pai-p'ao chi 白袍記 (Story of the white robe). In *Ku-pen hsi-ch'ü ts'ung-k'an, ch'u-chi*, item 46.

Pai-she chi 白蛇記 (The story of the white snake). By Cheng Kuo-hsüan 鄭國軒 (14th century). In *Ku-pen hsi-ch'ü ts'ung-k'an, ch'u-chi*, item 43.

Pai-t'u chi 白兔記 (The white rabbit). *Liu-shih chung ch'ü* edition. Taipei: K'ai-ming shu-tien, 1970.

Pai-tzu ch'üan-shu 百子全書 (Complete works of the hundred philosophers). Fac. repr. 8 vols. Hang-chou: Che-chiang jen-min ch'u-pan she, 1984.

Pai-yüeh t'ing chi 拜月亭記 (Moon prayer pavilion). In *Ku-pen hsi-ch'ü ts'ung-k'an*, *ch'u-chi*, item 9.

Pao-chien chi 寶劍記 (The story of the precious sword). By Li K'ai-hsien 李開先 (1502–68). In *Shui-hu hsi-ch'ü chi, ti-erh chi*, pp. 1–98.

Pao-chüan ch'u-chi 寶卷初集 (Precious volumes, first collection). Compiled by Chang Hsi-shun 張希舜 et al. 40 vols. T'ai-yüan: Shan-hsi jen-min ch'u-pan she, 1994.

Pao Lung-t'u tuan pai-hu ching chuan 包龍圖斷白虎精傳 (The story of how Academician Pao judged the case of the white tiger demon). Originally published in the 1470s. Fac. repr. in *Ming Ch'eng-hua shuo-ch'ang tz'u-hua ts'ung-k'an*, ts'e 8.

Pao-tzu Ho-shang tzu huan-su 豹子和尚自還俗 (The Leopard Monk returns to lay life). By Chu Yu-tun 朱有燉 (1379–1439). Preface dated 1433. In *Shui-hu hsi-ch'ü chi, ti-i chi*, pp. 115–26.

Pei-meng so-yen 北夢瑣言 (Trivial accounts of northern dreams). Compiled by Sun Kuang-hsien 孫光憲 (d. 968). Peking: Chung-hua shu-chü, 1960.

Pei shih 北史 (History of the Northern dynasties [386–618]). Compiled by Li Yen-shou 李延壽 (7th century). 10 vols. Peking: Chung-hua shu-chü, 1974.

Pei Sung chih-chuan 北宋志傳 (Chronicle of the Sung conquest of the north). Attributed to Hsiung Ta-mu 熊大木 (mid-16th century). 10 chüan. Nanking: Shih-te t'ang, 1593. Fac. repr. in *Ku-pen hsiao-shuo ts'ung-k'an, ti san-shih ssu chi*, vols. 2–3.

P'ei Hsing Ch'uan-ch'i 裴鉶傳奇 (P'ei Hsing's [825–80] Tales of the marvelous). Edited and annotated by Chou Leng-ch'ieh 周楞伽. Shanghai: Shang-hai ku-chi ch'u-pan she, 1980).

P'ei Hsiu-niang yeh-yu Hsi-hu chi 裴秀娘夜游西湖記 (P'ei Hsiu-niang's night outing on the West Lake). In Hu Shih-ying, *Hua-pen hsiao-shuo kai-lun*, 1:343–49.

Pen-shih shih 本事詩 (The original incidents of poems). Compiled by Meng Ch'i 孟棨 (cs 875). Preface dated 886. Peking: Chung-hua shu-chü, 1959.

P'eng-lai hsien-sheng chuan 蓬萊先生傳 (The story of Mr. P'eng-lai). In *Hsiao-p'in chi*, pp. 69–76.

Pi-chi hsiao-shuo ta-kuan 筆記小說大觀 (Great collectanea of note-form literature). 17 vols. Yang-chou: Chiang-su Kuang-ling ku-chi k'o-yin she, 1984.

P'i-p'a chi 琵琶記 (The lute). By Kao Ming 高明 (d. 1359). Edited by Ch'ien Nan-yang 錢南揚. Peking: Chung-hua shu-chü, 1961.

Pin-t'ui lu 賓退錄 (Records written after my guests have left). By Chao Yü-shih 趙與時 (1175–1231). Taipei: Kuang-wen shu-chü, 1970.

The Plum in the Golden Vase or, Chin P'ing Mei. Volume 1: *The Gathering*. Translated by David Tod Roy. Princeton: Princeton University Press, 1993.

The Plum in the Golden Vase or, Chin P'ing Mei. Volume 2: *The Rivals*. Translated by David Tod Roy. Princeton: Princeton University Press, 2001.

The Plum in the Golden Vase or, Chin P'ing Mei. Volume 3: *The Aphrodisiac*. Translated by David Tod Roy. Princeton: Princeton University Press, 2006.

The Poetry of Li Shang-yin. Translated by James J. Y. Liu. Chicago: University of Chicago Press, 1969.

The Poetry of T'ao Ch'ien. Translated by James Robert Hightower. London: Oxford University Press, 1970.

The Position of Women in Early China According to the Lieh Nü Chuan. Translated by Albert Richard O'Hara. Taipei: Mei Ya Publications, 1971.

Po-wu chih 博物志 (A treatise on curiosities). Compiled by Chang Hua 張華 (232–300). Edited by Fan Ning 范寧. Peking: Chung-hua shu-chü, 1980.

P'o-hsieh hsien-cheng yao-shih chüan 破邪顯正鑰匙卷 (Precious volume on the key to refuting heresy and presenting evidence [for correct doctrine]). By Lo Ch'ing 羅清 (1442–1527). Originally published in 1509. In *Pao-chüan ch'u-chi*, 2:1–508.

P'o-yao chi 破窯記 (The dilapidated kiln). In *Ku-pen hsi-ch'ü ts'ung-k'an, ch'u-chi*, item 19.

Pu-fu lao 不伏老 (Refusal to submit to old age). By Feng Wei-min 馮惟敏 (1511–80). In *Ming-jen tsa-chü hsüan*, pp. 297–332.

P'u-ching ju-lai yao-shih pao-chüan 普靜如來鑰匙寶卷 (Precious volume of the Tathāgatha P'u-ching: the Buddha of the Key [to salvation]). By P'u-ching 普靜 (d. 1586). In *Pao-chüan ch'u-chi*, 5:21–186.

P'u-ming ju-lai wu-wei liao-i pao-chüan 普明如來無為了義寶卷 (Precious volume of the Tathāgatha P'u-ming who thoroughly comprehends the meaning of Nonactivism). By P'u-ming 普明 (d. 1562). Completed in 1558. In *Pao-chüan ch'u-chi*, 4:373–605.

P'u-sa ying-lo ching 菩薩瓔珞經 (Sutra of the bodhisattva's necklace). Translated by Chu Fo-nien 竺佛念 (4th century). In *Taishō shinshū daizōkyō*, vol. 16, no. 656, pp. 1–126.

P'u-tung Ts'ui Chang chu-yü shih-chi 浦東崔張珠玉詩集 (Collection of poetic gems about [the affair of] Ts'ui [Ying-ying] and Chang [Chün-jui] in P'u-tung). Included as part of the front matter in the 1498 edition of *Hsi-hsiang chi*, pp. 13a–21a.

P'u-tung Ts'ui Chang Hai-weng shih-chi 浦東崔張海翁詩集 (Hai-weng's set of poems about [the affair] of Ts'ui [Ying-ying] and Chang [Chün-jui] in P'u-tung). Included as part of the front matter in the 1498 edition of *Hsi-hsiang chi*, pp. 21b–25a.

Records of the Grand Historian of China. Translated by Burton Watson. 2 vols. New York: Columbia University Press, 1961.

San-chiao yüan-liu sou-shen ta-ch'üan 三教源流搜神大全 (Complete compendium on the pantheons of the three religions). Preface dated 1593. Fac. repr. Taipei: Lien-ching ch'u-pan shih-yeh kung-ssu, 1980.

San hsien-shen Pao Lung-t'u tuan-yüan 三現身包龍圖斷冤 (After three ghostly manifestations Academician Pao rights an injustice). In *Ching-shih t'ung-yen, chüan* 13, pp. 169–84.

San-kuo chih 三國志 (History of the Three Kingdoms). Compiled by Ch'en Shou 陳壽 (233–97). 5 vols. Peking: Chung-hua shu-chü, 1973.

San-kuo chih p'ing-hua 三國志平話 (The p'ing-hua on the history of the Three Kingdoms). Originally published in 1321–23. Shanghai: Ku-tien wen-hsüeh ch'u-pan she, 1955.

San-kuo chih t'ung-su yen-i 三國志通俗演義 (The romance of the Three Kingdoms). Attributed to Lo Kuan-chung 羅貫中 (14th century). Preface dated 1522. 2 vols. Shanghai: Shang-hai ku-chi ch'u-pan she, 1980.

San-kuo lun 三國論 (A discussion of the Three Kingdoms), By Wang Po 王勃 (649–76). In *Ch'üan T'ang wen*, vol. 4, *chüan* 182, pp. 18b–21b.

San-ming t'ung-hui 三命通會 (Comprehensive compendium on the three fates). Compiled by Wan Min-ying 萬民英 (cs 1550). In *[Ying-yin Wen-yüan ko] Ssu-k'u ch'üan-shu*, 810:1–691.

San-pao t'ai-chien Hsi-yang chi t'ung-su yen-i 三寶太監西洋記通俗演義 (The romance of Eunuch Cheng Ho's expedition to the Western Ocean). By Lo Mao-teng 羅懋登. Author's preface dated 1597. 2 vols. Shanghai: Shang-hai ku-chi ch'u-pan she, 1985.

San Sui p'ing-yao chuan 三遂平妖傳 (The three Sui quash the demons' revolt). Fac. repr. Tokyo: Tenri daigaku shuppan-bu, 1981.

San-ts'ai t'u-hui 三才圖會 (Assembled illustrations from the three realms). Compiled by Wang Ch'i 王圻 (c. 1535–c. 1614). Preface dated 1609. 6 vols. Fac. repr. Taipei: Ch'eng-wen ch'u-pan she, 1970.

San-tung ch'ün-hsien lu 三洞群仙錄 (Records of the immortals of the three caverns). Compiled by Ch'en Pao-kuang 陳葆光 (12th century). Preface dated 1154. In *Cheng-t'ung Tao-tsang, ts'e* 992–95.

San-yüan chi 三元記 (Feng Ching 馮京 [1021–94] wins first place in three examinations). By Shen Shou-hsien 沈受先 (15th century). *Liu-shih chung ch'ü* edition. Taipei: K'ai-ming shu-tien, 1970.

Seng-ni kung-fan 僧尼共犯 (A monk and a nun violate their vows). By Feng Wei-min 馮惟敏(1511–80). In *Ming-jen tsa-chü hsüan*, pp. 333–50.

The Seven Military Classics of Ancient China. Translated by Ralph D. Sawyer. Boulder, Colo.: Westview Press, 1993.

Sha-kou chi 殺狗記 (The stratagem of killing a dog). *Liu-shih chung ch'ü* edition. Taipei: K'ai-ming shu-tien, 1970.

Shan-pen hsi-ch'ü ts'ung-k'an 善本戲曲叢刊 (Collectanea of rare editions of works on dramatic prosody). Taipei: Hsüeh-sheng shu-chü, 1984–87.

Shang-ch'ing ling-pao ta-fa 上清靈寶大法 (Great rites of the Upper Clarity Numinous Treasure). Compiled by Chin Yün-chung 金允中 (13th century). In *Cheng-t'ung Tao-tsang, ts'e* 963–72.

Shang Lu san-yüan chi 商輅三元記 (Shang Lu [1414–86] wins first place in three examinations). In *Ku-pen hsi-ch'ü ts'ung-k'an, ch'u-chi*, item 28.

Shao-shih wen-chien lu 邵氏聞見錄 (Record of things heard and seen by Mr. Shao). By Shao Po-wen 邵伯溫 (1056–1134). Author's preface dated 1132. Peking: Chung-hua shu-chü, 1983.

Shen-hsiang ch'üan-pien 神相全編 (Complete compendium on effective physiognomy). Compiled by Yüan Chung-ch'e 袁忠徹 (1376–1458). In *Ku-chin t'u-shu chi-ch'eng*, section 17, *i-shu tien, chüan* 631–44.

Shen Hsiao-kuan i-niao hai ch'i-ming 沈小官一鳥害七命 (Master Shen's bird destroys seven lives). In *Ku-chin hsiao-shuo*, vol. 2, *chüan* 26, pp. 391–403.

Shen-hsien kan-yü chuan 神仙感遇傳 (Biographies of persons who had contacts and encounters with gods and immortals). Compiled by Tu Kuang-t'ing 杜光庭 (850–933). In *Yün-chi ch'i-ch'ien* 雲笈七籤, *chüan* 112.

Shen-i fu 神異賦 (Rhapsody on the divine wonders [of physiognamy]). Attributed to Ch'en T'uan 陳摶 (895–989). In *Shen-hsiang ch'üan-pien, chüan* 636, pp. 1a–54a.

Shen-t'ung shih 神童詩 (Poems by infant prodigies). Traditionally attributed to Wang Chu 汪洙 (cs 1100). In *Chung-kuo ku-tai meng-hsüeh shu ta-kuan*, pp. 263–80.

Sheng-Ming tsa-chü, erh-chi 盛明雜劇, 二集 (Tsa-chü dramas of the glorious Ming dynasty, second collection). Compiled by Shen T'ai 沈泰 (17th century). Fac. repr. of 1641 edition. Peking: Chung-kuo hsi-chü ch'u-pan she, 1958.

Sheng-shih hsin-sheng 盛世新聲 (New songs of a surpassing age). Preface dated 1517. Fac. repr. Peking: Wen-hsüeh ku-chi k'an-hsing she, 1955.

Shih Chen-jen ssu-sheng so pai-yüan 時真人四聖鎖白猿 (Perfected Man Shih and the four generals subdue the white gibbon). In *Ku-pen Yüan Ming tsa-chü*, vol. 4.

Shih-chi 史記 (Records of the historian). By Ssu-ma Ch'ien 司馬遷 (145–c. 90 B.C.). 10 vols. Peking: Chung-hua shu-chü, 1972.

Shih-hou chi 獅吼記 (The lion's roar). By Wang T'ing-no 汪廷訥 (fl. 1593–1611). *Liu-shih chung ch'ü* edition. Taipei: K'ai-ming shu-tien, 1970.

Shih Hung-chao lung-hu chün-ch'en hui 史弘肇龍虎君臣會 (Shih Hung-chao: The meeting of dragon and tiger, ruler and minister). In *Ku-chin hsiao-shuo*, vol. 1, *chüan* 15, pp. 212–38.

Shih-i chi 十義記 (The story of ten righteous persons). In *Ku-pen hsi-ch'ü ts'ung-k'an*, *ch'u-chi*, item 42.

Shih-i chi 拾遺記 (Salvaged records of the marvelous). Compiled by Wang Chia 王嘉 (4th century). Edited and annotated by Ch'i Chih-p'ing 齊治平. Peking: Chung-hua shu-chü, 1981.

Shih-i chia chu Sun-tzu 十一家注孫子 (*Sun-tzu* with eleven commentaries). Peking: Chung-hua shu-chü, 1962.

Shih-jen yü-hsieh 詩人玉屑 (Jade splinters from the poets). Compiled by Wei Ch'ing-chih 魏慶之 (13th century). Preface dated 1244. 2 vols. Shanghai: Ku-tien wen-hsüeh ch'u-pan she, 1958.

Shih Kuan-shou ch'i Liu Tu-sai shang-yüan shih-wu yeh k'an-teng chuan 師官受妻劉都賽上元十五夜看燈傳 (Story of how Shih Kuan-shou's wife Liu Tu-sai went to view the lantern festival on the fifteenth day of the new year). Fac. repr. in *Ming Ch'eng-hua shuo-ch'ang tz'u-hua ts'ung-k'an*, ts'e 9.

Shih-lin kuang-chi 事林廣記 (Expansive gleanings from the forest of affairs). Fac. repr. of 14th-century edition. Peking: Chung-hua shu-chü, 1963.

Shih-pa kuo Lin-t'ung tou-pao 十八國臨潼鬥寶 (Eighteen states compete to present the most outstanding treasure). In *Ming-jen tsa-chü hsüan*, pp. 663–702.

Shih-san ching ching-wen 十三經經文 (The texts of the thirteen classics). Taipei: K'ai-ming shu-tien, 1955.

Shih-san ching chu-shu 十三經注疏 (The thirteen classics with their commentaries). Compiled by Juan Yüan 阮元 (1764–1849). 2 vols. Peking: Chung-hua shu-chü, 1982.

Shih-shuo Hsin-yü: A New Account of Tales of the World. By Liu I-ch'ing; translated by Richard B. Mather. Minneapolis: University of Minnesota Press, 1976.

Shih-wu kuan hsi-yen ch'eng ch'iao-huo 十五貫戲言成巧禍 (Fifteen strings of cash: a casual jest leads to uncanny disaster). In *Hsing-shih heng-yen*, vol. 2, *chüan* 33, pp. 691–706.

Shih-yü sheng-sou: Chung-yüan shih-yü 市語聲嗽:中原市語 (Market argot and slang: The market argot of the Central Plain). Published in the Lung-ch'ing reign period (1567–72). In *Han-shang huan wen-ts'un*, pp. 165–68.

[Shinzan] Dai Nihon zokuzōkyō [新纂]大日本續藏經 ([Newly compiled] great Japanese continuation of the Buddhist canon). 100 vols. Tokyo: Kokusho kankōkai, 1977.

The Shoo King or The Book of Historical Documents. Translated by James Legge. Hong Kong: University of Hong Kong Press, 1960.

Shou-t'ing hou nu chan Kuan P'ing 壽亭侯怒斬關平 (The Marquis of Shou-t'ing angrily executes Kuan P'ing). In *Ku-pen Yüan Ming tsa-chü*, vol. 3.

Shu-i chi 述異記 (Accounts of strange things). Compiled by Tsu Ch'ung-chih 祖沖之 (429–500). In *Ku hsiao-shuo kou-ch'en*, pp. 137–65.

Shuang-chu chi 雙珠記 (The pair of pearls). By Shen Ch'ing 沈鯖 (15th century). *Liu-shih chung ch'ü* edition. Taipei: K'ai-ming shu-tien, 1970.

Shuang-chung chi 雙忠記 (The loyal pair). By Yao Mao-liang 姚茂良 (15th century). In *Ku-pen hsi-ch'ü ts'ung-k'an, ch'u-chi*, item 33.

Shuang-lieh chi 雙烈記 (The heroic couple). By Chang Ssu-wei 張四維 (late 16th century). *Liu-shih chung ch'ü* edition. Taipei: K'ai-ming shu-tien, 1970.

Shui-hu chih-chuan p'ing-lin 水湖志傳評林 (The chronicle of the *Outlaws of the Marsh* with a forest of commentary). Edited by Yü Hsiang-tou 余象斗 (c. 1550–1637). 25 *chüan*. Chien-yang: Shuang-feng t'ang, 1594. Fac. repr. in *Ku-pen hsiao-shuo ts'ung-k'an, ti shih-erh chi*, vols. 1–3.

Shui-hu ch'üan-chuan 水滸全傳 (Variorum edition of the *Outlaws of the Marsh*). Edited by Cheng Chen-to 鄭振鐸 et al. 4 vols. Hong Kong: Chung-hua shu-chü, 1958.

Shui-hu hsi-ch'ü chi, ti-erh chi 水滸戲曲集, 第二集 (Corpus of drama dealing with the *Shui-hu* cycle, second series). Edited by Fu Hsi-hua 傅惜華. Shanghai: Ku-tien wen-hsüeh ch'u-pan she, 1958.

Shui-hu hsi-ch'ü chi, ti-i chi 水滸戲曲集, 第一集 (Corpus of drama dealing with the *Shui-hu* cycle, first series). Edited by Fu Hsi-hua 傅惜華 and Tu Ying-t'ao 杜穎陶. Shanghai: Ku-tien wen-hsüeh ch'u-pan she, 1957.

Shuo-fu 說郛 (The frontiers of apocrypha). Compiled by T'ao Tsung-i 陶宗儀 (c. 1360–c. 1403). 2 vols. Taipei: Hsin-hsing shu-chü, 1963.

Shuo-fu hsü 說郛續 (The frontiers of apocrypha continued). Compiled by T'ao T'ing 陶珽 (cs 1610). Fac. repr. of Ming ed. In *Shuo-fu san-chung*, vols. 9–10.

Shuo-fu san-chung 說郛三種 (The frontiers of apocrypha: Three recensions). 10 vols. Shanghai: Shang-hai ku-chi ch'u-pan she, 1988.

Shuo-k'u 說庫 (A treasury of literary tales). Compiled by Wang Wen-ju 王文濡 (fl. early 20th century). Originally published in 1915. Fac. repr. 2 vols. Taipei: Hsin-hsing shu-chü, 1963.

Shuo-yüan chu-tzu so-yin 說苑逐字索引 (A concordance to the *Shuo-yüan*). Taipei: T'ai-wan Shang-wu yin-shu kuan, 1992.

The Songs of the South. Translated by David Hawkes. New York: Penguin Books, 1985.

Sou-shen chi 搜神記 (In search of the supernatural). Compiled by Kou Tao-hsing 句道興 (10th century). In *Tun-huang pien-wen chi*, 2:865–89.

Ssu-ch'ao wen-chien lu 四朝聞見錄 (A record of things heard and seen during four reigns). By Yeh Shao-weng 葉紹翁 (c. 1175–c. 1230). Peking: Chung-hua shu-chü, 1997.

Ssu-hsi chi 四喜記(The four occasions for delight). By Hsieh Tang 謝讜 (1512–69). *Liu-shih chung ch'ü* edition. Taipei: K'ai-ming shu-tien, 1970.

Ssu-ma Kuang tsou-i 司馬光奏議 (The memorials of Ssu-ma Kuang). Edited by Wang Ken-lin 王根林. T'ai-yüan: Shan-hsi Jen-min ch'u-pan she, 1986.

Ssu-pu pei-yao 四部備要 (Collectanea of works from the four treasuries). Shanghai: Chung-hua shu-chü, 1936.

Ssu-pu ts'ung-k'an 四部叢刊 (Collectanea of [facsimile reproductions from] the four treasuries). Shanghai: Shang-wu yin-shu kuan, 1929.

Ssu-sheng yüan 四聲猿 (Four cries of a gibbon). By Hsü Wei 徐渭 (1521–93). Originally published in 1588. Edited and annotated by Chou Chung-ming 周中明. Shanghai: Shang-hai ku-chi ch'u-pan she, 1984.

Ssu-shih hua-yüeh sai chiao-jung 四時花月賽嬌容 (The flowers and moonlight of the four seasons compete in loveliness). By Chu Yu-tun 朱有燉 (1379–1439). In *Ku-pen Yüan Ming tsa-chü*, vol. 2.

Ssu wu-hsieh hui-pao 思無邪匯寶(No depraved thoughts collectanea). Compiled by Ch'en Ch'ing-hao 陳慶浩 and Wang Ch'iu-kuei 王秋桂. 45 vols. Taipei: Encyclopedia Britannica, 1995–97.

Ssu-yu Chai ts'ung-shuo 四友齋叢說 (Collected observations from the Four Friends Studio). By Ho Liang-chün 何良俊 (1506–73). Peking: Chung-hua shu-chü, 1959.

Su Ch'ang-kung Chang-t'ai Liu chuan 蘇長公章臺柳傳 (The story of Su Shih [1037–1101] and the courtesan Chang-t'ai Liu). In *Hsiung Lung-feng ssu-chung hsiao-shuo*, pp. 23–28.

Su Hsiao-ch'ing 蘇小卿. In Hu Shih-ying, *Hua-pen Hsiao-shuo kai-lun*, 1:352–55.

Su Shih shih-chi 蘇軾詩集 (Collected poetry of Su Shih). By Su Shih 蘇軾 (1037–1101). 8 vols. Peking: Chung-hua shu-chü, 1982.

Su Shih wen-chi 蘇軾文集 (Collected prose of Su Shih). By Su Shih 蘇軾 (1037–1101). 6 vols. Peking: Chung-hua shu-chü, 1986.

Su-shui chi-wen 涑水記聞 (Things heard by a man from Su-shui). Compiled by Ssu-ma Kuang 司馬光 (1019–86). Peking: Chung-hua shu-chü, 1989.

Su Wu mu-yang chi 蘇武牧羊記 (Su Wu herds sheep). In *Ku-pen hsi-ch'ü ts'ung-k'an, ch'u-chi*, item 20.

Su Ying huang-hou ying-wu chi 蘇英皇后鸚鵡記 (The story of Empress Su Ying's parrot). In *Ku-pen hsi-ch'ü ts'ung-k'an, ch'u-chi*, item 45.

Sui shu 隋書 (History of the Sui dynasty [581–618]). Compiled by Wei Cheng 魏徵 (580–643) et al. 6 vols. Peking: Chung-hua shu-chü, 1973.

Sui-T'ang liang-ch'ao shih-chuan 隋唐兩朝史傳 (Historical chronicle of the Sui and T'ang dynasties). 12 *chüan*. Su-chou: Kung Shao-shan, 1619. Microfilm of unique copy in Sonkeikaku Bunko, Tokyo.

Sui Yang-ti hai-shan chi 隋煬帝海山記 (Record of the artificial mountains and lakes created by Emperor Yang of the Sui dynasty). In *Ch'ing-so kao-i, hou-chi* (second collection), *chüan* 5, pp. 133–44.

Sun-p'u 筍譜 (Monograph on bamboo shoots). Compiled by Tsan-ning 贊寧 (919–1001). In *Shuo-fu san-chung*, 8:4838–57.

Sun-tzu's Art of War. Traditionally attributed to Sun Wu 孫武 (6th century B.C.). Translated in Sawyer, *The Seven Military Classics of Ancient China*, pp. 145–86.

Sung-ch'ao yen-i i-mou lu 宋朝燕翼詒謀錄 (Secret writings on the politics of Sung monarchs). Compiled by Wang Yung 王栐 (fl. early 13th century). Originally published in 1227. In *Pai-ch'uan hsüeh-hai, ting-chi* (fourth collection), pp. 302–31.

Sung Kung-ming p'ai chiu-kung pa-kua chen 宋公明排九宮八卦陣 (Sung Chiang deploys the nine-palace eight-trigram battle formation). In *Ku-pen Yüan Ming tsa-chü*, vol. 3.

Sung shih 宋史 (History of the Sung dynasty). Compiled by T'o-t'o 脫脫 (1313–55) et al. 40 vols. Peking: Chung-hua shu-chü, 1977.

Sung-shih chi-shih pen-mo 宋史紀事本末 (Sung historical materials topically arranged). Compiled by Ch'en Pang-chan 陳邦瞻 (cs 1598, d. 1623). Originally published in 1605. 4 vols. Peking: Chung-hua shu-chü, 1955.

Sung shih-hua ch'üan-pien 宋詩話全編 (Complete compendium of Sung dynasty talks on poetry). Edited by Wu Wen-chih 吳文治. 10 vols. Nanking: Chiang-su ku-chi ch'u-pan she, 1998.

Sung shu 宋書 (History of the Liu-Sung dynasty [420–79]). Compiled by Shen Yüeh 沈約 (441–513). 8 vols. Peking: Chung-hua shu-chü, 1074.

Sung Ssu-kung ta-nao Chin-hun Chang 宋四公大鬧禁魂張 (Sung the Fourth raises hell with Tightwad Chang). In *Ku-chin hsiao-shuo*, vol. 2, *chüan* 36, pp. 525–50.

Sung ta-chiang Yüeh Fei ching-chung 宋大將岳飛精忠 (The perfect loyalty of the Sung general-in-chief Yüeh Fei). In *Ku-pen Yüan Ming tsa-chü*, vol. 3.

Sung-Yüan hsi-wen chi-i 宋元戲文輯佚 (Collected fragments of Sung and Yüan hsi-wen drama). Compiled by Ch'ien Nan-yang 錢南揚. Shanghai: Shang-hai ku-tien wen-hsüeh ch'u-pan she, 1956.

Ta-hui P'u-chüeh ch'an-shih tsung-men wu-k'u 大慧普覺禪師宗門武庫 (Arsenal of the Ch'an Master Ta-hui P'u-chüeh's sect). Compiled by Tao-ch'ien 道謙 (12th century). Originally completed in 1140. In *Taishō shinshū daizōkyō*, vol. 47, no. 1998b, pp. 943–57.

Ta-hui P'u-chüeh ch'an-shih yü-lu 大慧普覺禪師語錄 (The recorded sayings of the Ch'an Master Ta-hui P'u-chüeh). By Tsung-kao 宗杲 (1089–1163). In *Taishō shinshū daizōkyō*, vol. 47, no. 1998, pp. 811–957.

Ta-pan nieh-p'an ching 大般涅槃經 (The Mahāparinirvāṇasūtra). Translated by Dharmakṣema (fl. 385–433). In *Taishō shinshū daizōkyō*, vol. 12, no. 374, pp. 365–603.

Ta-Sung chung-hsing yen-i 大宋中興演義 (The romance of the restoration of the great Sung dynasty). By Hsiung Ta-mu 熊大木 (mid-16th century). 8 *chüan*. Chien-yang: Ch'ing-pai t'ang, 1552. Fac. repr. in *Ku-pen hsiao-shuo ts'ung-k'an, ti san-shih ch'i chi*, vols. 1–3.

Ta-Tai Li-chi chu-tzu so-yin 大戴禮記逐字索引 (A concordance to the *Book of rites of the elder Tai*). Taipei: T'ai-wan Shang-wu yin-shu kuan, 1992.

Ta-T'ang Ch'in-wang tz'u-hua 大唐秦王詞話 (Prosimetric story of the Prince of Ch'in of the Great T'ang). 2 vols. Fac. repr. of early 17th-century edition. Peking: Wen-hsüeh ku-chi k'an-hsing she, 1956.

Ta-T'ang hsi-yü chi [chiao-chu] 大唐西域記[校註] (Great T'ang record of the western regions [edited and annotated]). By Hsüan-tsang 玄奘 (602–64). Edited and annotated by Chi Hsien-lin 季羨林 et al. Originally completed in 646. Peking: Chung-hua shu-chü, 1985.

Ta-T'ang San-tsang ch'ü-ching shih-hua 大唐三藏取經詩話 (Prosimetric account of how the monk Tripitaka of the great T'ang [made a pilgrimage] to procure sutras). Printed in the 13th century but probably older. Shanghai: Chung-kuo ku-tien wen-hsüeh ch'u-pan she, 1955.

Taishō shinshū daizōkyō 大正新修大藏經 (The newly edited great Buddhist canon compiled in the Taishō reign period [1912–26]). 85 vols. Tokyo: Taishō issaikyō kankōkai, 1922–32.

T'ai-ho cheng-yin p'u 太和正音譜 (Formulary for the correct sounds of great harmony). Compiled by Chu Ch'üan 朱權 (1378–1448). In *Chung-kuo ku-tien hsi-ch'ü lun-chu chi-ch'eng*, 3:1–231.

T'ai-hsia hsin-tsou 太霞新奏 (New songs from the empyreal clouds). Compiled by Feng Meng-lung 馮夢龍 (1574–1646). Originally published in 1627. Fac. repr. Fu-chou: Hai-hsia wen-i ch'u-pan she, 1986.

T'ai-kung chia-chiao 太公家教 (Family teachings of T'ai-kung). In Chou Feng-wu. *Tun-huang hsieh-pen T'ai-kung chia-chiao yen-chiu*, pp. 9–28.

T'ai-p'ing kuang-chi 太平廣記 (Extensive gleanings from the reign of Great Tranquility). Compiled by Li Fang 李昉 (925–96) et al. First printed in 981. 10 vols. Peking: Chung-hua shu-chü, 1961.

T'ai-shang chiu-chen miao-chieh chin-lu tu-ming pa-tsui miao-ching 太上九真妙戒金錄度命拔罪妙經 (Scripture of the golden register for the redemption of sins and for salvation [including] the marvelous precepts of the nine perfected). In *Cheng-t'ung Tao-tsang, ts'e* 77.

T'ai-shang Tao-chün shuo chieh-yüan pa-tu miao-ching 太上道君說解冤拔度妙經 (Marvelous scripture for delivery from enmity and salvation enunciated by the Most High Lord of the Tao). In *Cheng-t'ung Tao-tsang, ts'e* 181.

T'ai-tzu ch'eng-tao ching 太子成道經 (Sutra on how the crown prince [Śākyamuni] attained the Way). In *Tun-huang pien-wen chi*, 1:285–300.

T'an-shih wu-wei pao-chüan 嘆世無爲寶卷 (Precious volume on Nonactivism in lamentation for the world). By Lo Ch'ing 羅清 (1442–1527). Originally published in 1509. In *Pao-chüan ch'u-chi*, 1:295–572.

T'ang Hsien-tsu chi 湯顯祖集 (Collected works of T'ang Hsien-tsu [1550–1616]). Edited by Hsü Shuo-fang 徐朔方 and Ch'ien Nan-yang 錢南揚. 4 vols. Peking: Chung-hua shu-chü, 1962.

T'ang-jen hsüan T'ang-shih [shih-chung] 唐人選唐詩[十種] (Anthologies of T'ang poetry selected by T'ang figures [ten examples]). Peking: Chung-hua shu-chü, 1959.

T'ang kuo-shih pu 唐國史補 (Supplement to the History of the T'ang). Compiled by Li Chao 李肇 (early 9th century). Shanghai: Ku-tien wen-hsüeh ch'u-pan she, 1957.

T'ang-shu chih-chuan t'ung-su yen-i 唐書志傳通俗演義 (The romance of the chronicles of the T'ang dynasty). By Hsiung Ta-mu 熊大木 (mid-16th century). 8 *chüan*. Chien-yang: Ch'ing-chiang t'ang, 1553. Fac. repr. in *Ku-pen hsiao-shuo ts'ung-k'an, ti-ssu chi*, vols. 1–2.

T'ang Sung ch'uan-ch'i chi 唐宋傳奇集 (An anthology of literary tales from the T'ang and Sung dynasties). Edited by Lu Hsün 魯迅. Peking: Wen-hsüeh ku-chi k'an-hsing she, 1958.

Tao-te chen-ching chih-kuei 道德真經指歸 (A reconsideration of the meaning of the Tao-te ching). Attributed to Yen Chün-p'ing 嚴君平 (1st century B.C.). In *Cheng-t'ung Tao-tsang, ts'e* 375–77.

T'ao Yüan-ming tung-li shang-chü 陶淵明東籬賞菊 (T'ao Yüan-ming enjoys the chrysanthemums by the eastern hedge). In *Ku-pen Yüan Ming tsa-chü*, vol. 3.

Ti-ching ching-wu lüeh 帝京景物略 (A brief account of the sights of the imperial capital). Compiled by Liu T'ung 劉侗 (cs 1634) and Yü I-cheng 于奕正 (d. c. 1635). Preface dated 1635. Peking: Ku-chi ch'u-pan she, 1980.

T'ieh-wei shan ts'ung-t'an 鐵圍山叢談 (Collected remarks from the Iron Cordon Mountains). By Ts'ai T'ao 蔡絛 (d. after 1147). Peking: Chung-hua shu-chü, 1997.

T'ien-kung k'ai-wu 天工開物 (The exploitation of the works of nature). By Sung Ying-hsing 宋應星 (1587–c. 1666). Hong Kong: Chung-hua shu-chü, 1978.

T'ien-kung k'ai-wu: Chinese Technology in the Seventeenth Century. Translated by E-tu Zen Sun and Shiou-chuan Sun. University Park: Pennsylvania State University Press, 1966.

T'ien-pao i-shih chu-kung-tiao 天寶遺事諸宮調 (Medley in various modes on the forgotten events of the T'ien-pao [742–56] reign period). By Wang Po-ch'eng 王伯成 (fl. late 13th century). In *Chu-kung-tiao liang-chung*, pp. 88–256.

T'ien-yüan ch'i-yü 天緣奇遇 (Celestial destinies remarkably fulfilled). In *Kuo-se t'ien-hsiang*, vol. 3, *chüan* 7, pp. 1a–29b; and *chüan* 8, pp. 1a–30b, lower register.

T'ou-pi chi 投筆記 (Throwing down the brush). In *Ku-pen hsi-ch'ü ts'ung-k'an, ch'u-chi*, item 38.

Traditional Chinese Stories: Themes and Variations. Edited by Y. W. Ma and Joseph S. M. Lau. New York; Columbia University Press, 1978.

Ts'ai-lou chi 彩樓記 (The gaily colored tower). Edited by Huang Shang 黃裳. Shanghai: Shang-hai ku-tien wen-hsüeh ch'u-pan she, 1956.

Ts'an-T'ang Wu-tai shih yen-i chuan 殘唐五代史演義傳 (Romance of the late T'ang and Five Dynasties). Peking: Pao-wen t'ang shu-tien, 1983.

Ts'an-t'ung ch'i 參同契 (The kinship of the three). Attributed to Wei Po-yang 魏伯陽 (2nd century). In *Shuo-fu san-chung*, 3:336–46.

Tsang-tu 葬度 (Funeral considerations). By Wang Wen-lu 王文祿 (b. 1503). In *Shuo-fu hsü*, 10:1435–38.

Ts'ang-lang shih-hua [chiao-shih] 滄浪詩話[校釋] (Ts'ang-lang's remarks on poetry collated and annotated). By Yen Yü 嚴羽 (13th century). Edited and annotated by Kuo Shao-yü 郭紹虞. Peking: Jen-min wen-hsüeh ch'u-pan she, 1962.

Tsao-chiao Lin Ta-wang chia-hsing 皂角林大王假形 (A feat of impersonation by the King of Tsao-chiao Wood), in *Ching-shih t'ung-yen*, *chüan* 36, pp. 546–55.

Ts'ao Chih chi chiao-chu 曹植集校注 (Ts'ao Chih's collected works collated and annotated). Edited by Chao Yu-wen 趙幼文. Peking: Jen-min wen-hsüeh ch'u-pan she, 1984.

Ts'ao-lu chi 草廬記 (The story of the thatched hut). In *Ku-pen hsi-ch'ü ts'ung-k'an, ch'u-chi*, item 26.

Ts'ao Po-ming ts'o-k'an tsang chi 曹伯明錯勘贓記 (The story of Ts'ao Po-ming and the mistaken identification of the booty). In *Ch'ing-p'ing shan-t'ang hua-pen*, pp. 206–11.

Tseng Chi-heng 曾季衡. By P'ei Hsing 裴鉶 (825–80). In *P'ei Hsing Ch'uan-ch'i*, pp. 78–79.

Tseng-ting nan chiu-kung ch'ü-p'u 增定南九宮曲譜 (An augmented and corrected edition of the formulary for songs composed in the nine southern musical modes). Compiled by Shen Ching 沈璟 (1553–1610). Originally published in 1606. Fac. repr. of late Ming edition. In *Shan-pen hsi-ch'ü ts'ung-k'an*, vols. 27–28.

Ts'o-jen shih 錯認屍 (The wrongly identified corpse). In *Ch'ing-p'ing shan-t'ang hua-pen*, pp. 212–35.

Tsu-t'ang chi 祖堂集 (Patriarchal hall collection). Edited by Wu Fu-hsiang 吳福祥 and Ku Chih-ch'uan 顧之川. Originally published in 952. Ch'ang-sha: Yüeh-lu shu-she, 1996.

Tsui-weng t'an-lu 醉翁談錄 (The old drunkard's selection of tales). Compiled by Lo Yeh 羅燁 (13th century). Taipei: Shih-chieh shu-chü, 1972.

Tsui yü-ch'ing 最娛情 (Superlative delights). Preface dated 1647. Fac. repr. In *Ku-pen hsiao-shuo ts'ung-k'an, ti erh-shih liu chi*, 4:1411–1566.

Ts'ui Tai-chao sheng-ssu yüan-chia 崔待詔生死冤家 (Artisan Ts'ui and his ghost wife). In *Ching-shih t'ung-yen*, *chüan* 8, pp. 90–104.

Ts'ui Ya-nei pai-yao chao-yao 崔衙內白鷂招妖 (The white falcon of Minister Ts'ui's son embroils him with demons). In *Ching-shih t'ung-yen*, *chüan* 19, pp. 261–73.

Tsung-ching lu 宗鏡錄 (The mirror of the source). Compiled by Yen-shou 延壽 (904–75). In *Taishō shinshū daizōkyō*, vol. 48, no. 2016, pp. 415–957.

Ts'ung-shu chi-ch'eng 叢書集成 (A corpus of works from collectanea). 1st series. Shanghai: Shang-wu yin-shu kuan, 1935–37.

Tu-ch'eng chi-sheng 都城紀勝 (A record of the splendors of the capital city). By Kuan-yüan Nai-te Weng 灌園耐得翁 (13th century). Author's preface dated 1235. In *Tung-ching meng-hua lu [wai ssu-chung]*, pp. 89–110.

Tu Li-niang mu-se huan-hun 杜麗娘慕色還魂 (Tu Li-niang yearns for love and returns to life). In Hu Shih-ying, *Hua-pen hsiao-shuo kai-lun*, 2:533–37.

Tu-lo yüan Ssu-ma ju-hsiang 獨樂園司馬入相 (In Tu-lo Garden Ssu-ma Kuang becomes grand councilor). By Sang Shao-liang 桑紹良 (16th century). In *Ku-pen Yüan Ming tsa-chü*, vol. 2.

Tu Tzu-mei ku-chiu yu-ch'un 杜子美沽酒遊春 (Tu Fu buys wine for a spring excursion). By Wang Chiu-ssu 王九思 (1468–1551). In *Sheng-Ming tsa-chü, erh-chi*.

Tu-yang tsa-pien 杜陽雜編 (Miscellaneous records from Tu-yang). Compiled by Su O 蘇鶚 (9th century). Originally completed in 876. In *Pi-chi hsiao-shuo ta-kuan*, vol. 1, *ts'e* 1, pp. 141–52.

Tuan-fa chi 斷髮記 (The severed tresses). By Li K'ai-hsien 李開先 (1502–68). In *Ku-pen hsi-ch'ü ts'ung-k'an, wu-chi*, item 2.

Tun-huang ch'ü chiao-lu 敦煌曲校錄 (Collated record of songs from Tun-huang). Compiled by Jen Erh-pei 任二北. Shanghai: Shang-hai wen-i lien-ho ch'u-pan she, 1955.

Tun-huang pao-tsang 敦煌寶藏 (Treasures from Tun-huang). Compiled by Huang Yung-wu 黃永武. 140 vols. Taipei: Hsin-wen-feng ch'u-pan kung-ssu, 1981–86.

Tun-huang pien-wen chi 敦煌變文集 (Collection of pien-wen from Tun-huang). Edited by Wang Chung-min 王重民 et al. 2 vols. Peking: Jen-min wen-hsüeh ch'u-pan she, 1984.

Tung-ch'eng lao-fu chuan 東城老父傳 (The old man of the eastern wall). By Ch'en Hung-tsu 陳鴻祖 (9th century). In *T'ang Sung ch'uan-ch'i chi*, pp. 117–22.

Tung Chieh-yüan Hsi-hsiang chi 董解元西廂記 (Master Tung's Western chamber romance). Edited and annotated by Ling Ching-yen 凌景埏. Peking: Jen-min wen-hsüeh ch'u-pan she, 1962.

Tung-ching meng-hua lu 東京夢華錄 (A dream of past splendors in the Eastern Capital). Compiled by Meng Yüan-lao 孟元老 (12th century). Preface dated 1147. In *Tung-ching meng-hua lu [wai ssu-chung]*, pp. 1–87.

Tung-ching meng-hua lu chu 東京夢華錄注 (Commentary on A dream of past splendors in the Eastern Capital). Compiled by Teng Chih-ch'eng 鄧之誠. Peking: Shang-wu yin-shu kuan, 1959.

Tung-ching meng-hua lu [wai ssu-chung] 東京夢話錄[外四種] (A dream of past splendors in the Eastern Capital [plus four other works]). Compiled by Meng Yüan-lao 孟元老 (12th century) et al. Shanghai: Shang-hai ku-chi wen-hsüeh ch'u-pan she, 1956.

Tung-ku so chien 東谷所見 (Observations of Tung-ku). By Li Chih-yen 李之彥 (13th century). Author's preface dated 1268. In *Shuo-fu san-chung*, 6:3419–29.

Tung-t'ien hsüan-chi 洞天玄記 (Mysterious record of the grotto heaven). Attributed to Yang Shen 楊慎 (1488–1559). In *Ku-pen Yüan Ming tsa-chü*, vol. 2.

Tung-tu fu 東都賦 (Rhapsody on the Eastern Capital). By Pan Ku 班固 (32–92). In *Wen-hsüan*, vol. 1, *chüan* 1, pp. 19a-29b.

Tung-yu chi: shang-tung pa-hsien chuan 東遊記:上洞八仙傳 (Journey to the east: the story of the eight immortals of the upper realm). Compiled by Wu Yüan-t'ai 吳元泰 (16th century). Appendix dated 1596. Fac. repr. of Chien-yang edition published by Yü Hsiang-tou 余象斗(c. 1550–1637). In *Ku-pen Hsiao-shuo ts'ung-k'an, ti san-shih chiu chi*, 1:1–260.

Tung Yung yü-hsien chuan 董永遇仙傳 (The story of Tung Yung's encounter with an immortal). In *Ch'ing-p'ing shan-t'ang hua-pen*, pp. 235–44.

T'ung-lo Yüan Yen Ch'ing po-yü 同樂院燕青博魚 (In T'ung-lo Tavern Yen Ch'ing gambles for fish). In *Shui-hu hsi-ch'ü chi, ti-i chi*, pp. 16–30.

Tzu-ch'ai chi 紫釵記 (The story of the purple hairpin). By T'ang Hsien-tsu 湯顯祖 (1550–1616); edited and annotated by Hu Shih-ying 胡士瑩. Peking: Jen-min wen-hsüeh ch'u-pan she, 1982.

Tzu-chih t'ung-chien 資治通鑑 (Comprehensive mirror for aid in government). Compiled by Ssu-ma Kuang 司馬光 (1019–86). 4 vols. Peking: Ku-chi ch'u-pan she, 1957.

Tz'u-lin chai-yen 詞林摘艷 (Select flowers from the forest of song). Compiled by Chang Lu 張祿. Preface dated 1525. 2 vols. Fac. repr. Peking: Wen-hsüeh ku-chi k'an-hsing she, 1955.

Tz'u-lin i-chih 詞林一枝 (A branch from the forest of song). Compiled by Huang Wen-hua 黃文華 (16th century). Originally published in 1573. Fac. repr. in *Shan-pen hsi-ch'ü ts'ung-k'an*, vol. 4.

Tz'u Liu-shih chiu-wen 次柳氏舊聞 (An addendum to Liu Fang's [cs 741] old reminiscences). By Li Te-yü 李德裕 (787–850). In *K'ai-yüan T'ien-pao i-shih shih-chung*, pp. 1–13.

Tz'u-nüeh 詞謔 (Pleasantries on lyrical verse). By Li K'ai-hsien 李開先 (1502–68). In *Chung-kuo ku-tien hsi-ch'ü lun-chu chi-ch'eng*, 3:257–418.

Tz'u-pei shui-ch'an fa 慈悲水懺法 (Litany of the compassionate water of samādhi). In *Taishō shinshū daizōkyō*, vol. 45, no. 1910, pp. 967–78.

Wan Hsiu-niang ch'ou-pao shan-t'ing-erh 萬秀娘仇報山亭兒 (Wan Hsiu-niang gets her revenge with a toy pavilion). In *Ching-shih t'ung-yen*, *chüan* 37, pp. 556–71.

Wan-li yeh-huo pien 萬曆野獲編 (Private gleanings of the Wan-li reign period [1573–1620]). By Shen Te-fu 沈德符 (1578–1642). Author's preface dated 1619. 3 vols. Peking: Chung-hua shu-chü, 1980.

Wan-shu tsa-chi 宛署雜記 (Miscellaneous records concerning the magistracy of Wan-p'ing). By Shen Pang 沈榜. Preface dated 1592. Peking: Pei-ching ku-chi ch'u-pan-she, 1980.

Wan-sung Lao-jen p'ing-ch'ang T'ien-t'ung Chüeh ho-shang sung-ku Ts'ung-jung An lu 萬松老人評唱天童覺和尚頌古從容庵錄 (A record from the Ts'ung-jung Monastery of the comments by the Old Man of Myriad Pines Studio on the poetic eulogies of the past by the monk Cheng-chüeh of the T'ien-t'ung Monastery). By the Buddhist monk Hsing-hsiu 行秀 (1166–1246). In *Taishō shinshū daizōkyō*, vol. 48, no. 2004, pp. 226–92.

Wang Ai-hu ta-nao Tung-p'ing fu 王矮虎大鬧東平府 (Short-legged Tiger Wang creates a ruckus in Tung-p'ing prefecture). In *Ku-pen Yüan Ming tsa-chü*, vol. 3.

Wang Chao-chün ch'u-sai ho-jung chi 王昭君出塞和戎記 (Wang Chao-chün is sent abroad to make a marriage alliance with the Huns). In *Ku-pen hsi-ch'ü ts'ung-k'an, erh-chi,* item 7.

Wang K'uei 王魁 (The story of Wang K'uei). In *Tsui yü-ch'ing,* pp.1503–21, upper register.

Wang Lan-ch'ing chen-lieh chuan 王蘭卿貞烈傳 (The story of Wang Lan-ch'ing's heroic refusal to remarry). By K'ang Hai 康海 (1475–1541). In *Ku-pen Yüan Ming tsa-chü,* vol. 2.

Wang Wen-hsiu Wei-t'ang ch'i-yü chi 王文秀渭塘奇遇記 (The story of Wang Wen-hsiu's remarkable encounter in Wei-t'ang). In *Ku-pen Yüan Ming tsa-chü,* vol. 4.

Wei Cheng kai-chao 魏徵改詔 (Wei Cheng alters the rescript). In *Ku-pen Yüan Ming tsa-chü,* vol. 3.

Wei Feng-hsiang ku Yü-huan chi 韋鳳翔古玉環記 (The old version of Wei Kao 韋皋 [746–806] and the story of the jade ring). In *Ku-pen hsi-ch'ü ts'ung-k'an, ch'u-chi,* item 22.

Wei-shu 魏書 (History of the Northern Wei dynasty [338–534]). Compiled by Wei Shou 魏收 (506–72). 8 vols. Peking: Chung-hua shu-chü, 1974.

Wei-wei pu-tung T'ai-shan shen-ken chieh-kuo pao-chüan 巍巍不動太山深根結果寶卷 (Precious volume of deeply rooted karmic fruits, majestic and unmoved like Mount T'ai). By Lo Ch'ing 羅清 (1442–1527). Originally published in 1509. In *Pao-chüan ch'u-chi,* 3:341–647.

Wen-hsüan 文選 (Selections of refined literature). Compiled by Hsiao T'ung 蕭統 (501–31). 3 vols. Fac. repr. Peking: Chung-hua shu-chü, 1981.

Wen T'ien-hsiang ch'üan-chi 文天祥全集 (The complete works of Wen Tian-hsiang [1236–83]). Edited and annotated by Hsiung Fei 熊飛, Ch'i Shen-ch'i 漆身起, and Huang Shun-ch'iang 黃順強. Nan-ch'ang: Chiang-hsi jen-min ch'u-pan she, 1987.

Wu Ch'i ti Ch'in kua shuai-yin 吳起敵秦掛帥印 (Wu Ch'i resists Ch'in and accepts the commander's seal). In *Ku-pen Yüan Ming tsa-chü,* vol. 2.

Wu-chieh Ch'an-shih ssu Hung-lien chi 五戒禪師私紅蓮記 (The Ch'an Master Wu-chieh defiles Hung-lien). In *Ch'ing-p'ing shan-t'ang hua-pen,* pp. 136–54.

Wu Lun-ch'üan Pei 伍倫全備 (Wu Lun-ch'üan 伍倫全 and Wu Lun-pei 伍倫備, or the five cardinal human relationships completely exemplified). By Ch'iu Chün 邱濬 (1421–95). In *Ku-pen hsi-ch'ü ts'ung-k'an, ch'u-chi,* item 37.

Wu-sao ho-pien 吳騷合編 (Combined anthology of the songs of Wu). Compiled by Chang Ch'i 張琦 (fl. early 17th century) and Chang Hsü-ch'u 張旭初 (fl. early 17th century). Preface dated 1637. 4 *ts'e.* Fac. repr. Shanghai: Shang-wu yin-shu kuan, 1934.

Wu-teng hui-yüan 五燈會元 (The essentials of the five lamps). Compiled by P'u-chi 普濟(1179–1253). 3 vols. Peking: Chung-hua shu-chü, 1984.

Wu Tzu-hsü pien-wen 伍子胥變文 (The story of Wu Tzu-hsü). In *Tun-huang pien-wen chi,* 1:1–31.

Wu-wang fa Chou p'ing-hua 武王伐紂平話 (The p'ing-hua on King Wu's conquest of King Chou). Originally published in 1321–23. Shanghai: Chung-kuo ku-tien wen-hsüeh ch'u-pan she, 1955.

Wu-yü ts'ui-ya 吳歈萃雅 (A florilegium of song lyrics from Wu). Compiled by Chou Chih-piao 周之標 (fl. early 17th cent.). Preface dated 1616. Fac. repr. in *Shan-pen hsi-ch'ü ts'ung-k'an,* vols. 12–13.

Wu Yüeh ch'un-ch'iu chu-tzu so-yin 吳越春秋逐字索引 (A concordance to the *Wu Yüeh ch'un-ch'iu*). Hong Kong: Shang-wu yin-shu kuan, 1993.

Xunzi: A Translation and Study of the Complete Works. Translated by John Knoblock. 3 vols. Stanford: Stanford University Press, 1988–94.

Ya-su chi-yen 雅俗稽言 (A study of expressions both cultivated and vulgar). Compiled by Chang Ts'un-shen 張存紳 (17th century). Preface dated 1623. In *Ming-Ch'ing su-yü tz'u-shu chi-ch'eng,* 2:1695–2106.

Yang-chia fu shih-tai chung-yung yen-i chih-chuan 楊家府世代忠勇演義志傳 (Popular chronicle of the generations of loyal and brave exploits of the Yang household). Preface dated 1606. 2 vols. Fac. repr. Taipei: Kuo-li chung-yang t'u-shu kuan, 1971.

Yang Ssu-wen Yen-shan feng ku-jen 楊思溫燕山逢故人 (Yang Ssu-wen encounters an old acquaintance in Yen-shan). In *Ku-chin hsiao-shuo,* vol. 2, *chüan* 24, pp. 366–81.

Yang Wen lan-lu hu chuan 楊溫攔路虎傳 (The story of Yang Wen, the road-blocking tiger). In *Ch'ing-p'ing shan-t'ang hua-pen,* pp. 169–86.

Yao-shih pen-yüan kung-te pao-chüan 藥師本願功德寶卷 (Precious volume on the original vows and merit of the Healing Buddha). Published in 1544. In *Pao-chüan ch'u-chi,* 14:189–385.

Yeh-k'o ts'ung-shu 野客叢書 (Collected writings of a rustic sojourner). By Wang Mao 王楙(1151–1213). Peking: Chung-hua shu-chü, 1987.

Yen-chih chi 胭脂記 (The story of the rouge). By T'ung Yang-chung 童養中 (16th century). In *Ku-pen hsi-ch'ü ts'ung-k'an, ch'u-chi,* item 49.

Yen-chü pi-chi 燕居筆記 (A miscellany for leisured hours). Edited by Ho Ta-lun 何大掄 (fl. early 17th century). 2 vols. Fac. repr. of Ming edition. In *Ming-Ch'ing shan-pen hsiao-shuo ts'ung-k'an, ti-erh chi.*

Yen-chü pi-chi 燕居筆記 (A miscellany for leisured hours). Edited by Lin Chin-yang 林近陽 (fl. early 17th century). 3 vols. Fac. repr. of Ming edition. In *Ming-Ch'ing shan-pen hsiao-shuo ts'ung-k'an, ch'u-pien.*

Yen P'ing-chung erh-t'ao sha san-shih 晏平仲二桃殺三士 (Yen P'ing-chung kills three stalwarts with two peaches). In *Ku-chin hsiao-shuo,* vol. 2, *chüan* 25, pp. 384–90.

Yen-shih chia-hsün [chi-chieh] 顏氏家訓[集解] (Family Instructions for the Yen clan [with collected commentaries]). By Yen Chih-t'ui 顏之推 (531–91). Edited by Wang Li-ch'i 王利器. Shanghai: Shang-hai ku-chi ch'u-pan she, 1980.

Yen-tzu fu 鷰子賦 (Rhapsody on the swallow). In *Tun-huang pien-wen chi,* 1:249–54.

Yin-chih chi-shan 陰隲積善 (A secret good deed accumulates merit). In *Ch'ing-p'ing shan-t'ang hua-pen,* pp. 115–19.

Yin-shan cheng-yao 飲膳正要 (Correct essentials of nutrition). By Hu-ssu-hui 忽思慧 (fl. early 14th century). Completed in 1330. Peking: Jen-min wei-sheng ch'u-pan she, 1986.

Ying-hsüeh ts'ung-shuo 螢雪叢說 (Collected observations compiled by the light shed by fireflies and reflected from the snow). By Yü Ch'eng 俞成 (12th century). Author's preface dated 1200. In *Pai-ch'uan hsüeh-hai, ting-chi* (fourth collection), pp. 332–42.

[Ying-yin Wen-yüan ko] Ssu-k'u ch'üan-shu [景印文淵閣]四庫全書 ([Facsimile reprint of the Wen-yüan ko Imperial Library copy of the] Complete library of the four treasuries). 1,500 vols. Taipei: T'ai-wan Shang-wu yin-shu kuan, 1986.

Yu hsien-k'u 游仙窟 (Excursion to the dwelling of the goddesses). By Chang Cho 張鷟 (cs 675). Shanghai: Chung-kuo ku-tien wen-hsüeh ch'u-pan she, 1955.

Yu-kuei chi 幽閨記 (Tale of the secluded chambers). *Liu-shih chung ch'ü* edition. Taipei: K'ai-ming shu-tien, 1970.

Yu-ming lu 幽明錄 (Records of the realms of the dead and the living). Compiled by Liu I-ch'ing 劉義慶 (403–44). Edited and annotated by Cheng Wan-ch'ing 鄭晚晴. Peking: Wen-hua i-shu ch'u-pan she, 1988.

Yu-yang tsa-tsu 酉陽雜俎 (Assorted notes from Yu-yang). Compiled by Tuan Ch'eng-shih 段成式 (803–63). Peking: Chung-hua shu-chü, 1981.

Yung-ch'uang hsiao-p'in 湧幢小品 (Minor essays from the portable kiosk). By Chu Kuo-chen 朱國禎 (1557–1632). Author's postface dated 1622. 2 vols. Peking: Chung-hua shu-chü, 1959.

Yung-hsi yüeh-fu 雍熙樂府 (Songs of a harmonious era). Preface dated 1566. 20 *ts'e*. Fac. repr. Shanghai: Shang-wu yin-shu kuan, 1934.

Yung-lo ta-tien hsi-wen san-chung chiao-chu 永樂大典戲文三種校注 (An annotated recension of the three hsi-wen preserved in the *Yung-lo ta-tien*). Edited and annotated by Ch'ien Nan-yang 錢南揚. Peking: Chung-hua shu-chü, 1979.

Yü-ch'iao hsien-hua 漁樵閑話 (A casual dialogue between a fisherman and a woodcutter). In *Ku-pen yüan Ming tsa-chü*, vol. 4.

Yü-ching t'ai 玉鏡臺 (The jade mirror stand). By Chu Ting 朱鼎 (16th century). *Liu-shih chung ch'ü* edition. Taipei: K'ai-ming shu-tien, 1970.

Yü Chung-chü t'i-shih yü shang-huang 俞仲舉題詩遇上皇 (Yü Chung-chü composes a poem and meets the retired emperor, Sung Kao-tsung [r. 1127–62]). In *Ching-shih t'ung-yen*, chüan 6, pp. 63–76.

Yü-chüeh chi 玉玦記 (The jade thumb-ring). By Cheng Jo-yung 鄭若庸 (16th century). *Liu-shih chung ch'ü* edition. Taipei: K'ai-ming shu-tien, 1970.

Yü-huan chi 玉環記 (The story of the jade ring). *Liu-shih chung ch'ü* edition. Taipei: K'ai-ming shu-tien, 1970.

Yü-tsan chi 玉簪記 (The story of the jade hairpin). By Kao Lien 高濂 (1527–c. 1603). Probably written in 1570. Edited and annotated by Huang Shang 黃裳. Shanghai: Shang-hai ku-tien wen-hsüeh ch'u-pan she, 1956.

Yü Tzu-shan chi chu 庾子山集注 (Annotated edition of the works of Yü Hsin). Annotated by Ni Fan 倪璠 (17th century). Originally published in 1687. 3 vols. Peking: Chung-hua shu-chü, 1980.

Yüan-chu chih-yü: hsüeh-ch'uang t'an-i 鴛渚誌餘:雪窗談異 (Supplementary guide to Mandarin Duck Island: tales of the unusual from the snowy window). Peking: Chung-hua shu-chü, 1997.

Yüan-ch'ü hsüan 元曲選 (An anthology of Yüan tsa-chü drama). Compiled by Tsang Mao-hsün 臧懋循 (1550–1620). 4 vols. Peking: Chung-hua shu-chü, 1979.

Yüan-ch'ü hsüan wai-pien 元曲選外編 (A supplementary anthology of Yüan tsa-chü drama). Compiled by Sui Shu-sen 隋樹森. 3 vols. Peking: Chung-hua shu-chü, 1961.

Yüan I-shan shih-chi chien-chu 元遺山詩集箋注 (Yüan Hao-wen's poetry collection annotated). Annotated by Shih Kuo-ch'i 施國祁. Peking: Jen-min wen-hsüeh ch'u-pan she, 1958.

Yüan-jen tsa-chü kou-ch'en 元人雜劇鈎沉 (Rescued fragments from tsa-chü drama by Yüan authors). Compiled by Chao Ching-shen 趙景深. Shanghai: Shang-hai ku-tien wen-hsüeh ch'u-pan she, 1956.

[Yüan-pen] Wang chuang-yüan Ching-ch'ai chi [原本]王狀元荊釵記 ([Original edition of] Top graduate Wang and the Thorn hairpin). In *Ku-pen hsi-ch'ü ts'ung-k'an, ch'u-chi,* item 13.

Yüan shih 元史 (History of the Yüan dynasty). Compiled by Sung Lien 宋濂 (1310–81) et al. 15 vols. Peking: Chung-hua shu-chü, 1976.

Yüan shih hsüan, ch'u-chi 元詩選, 初集 (An anthology of Yüan poetry, first collection). Compiled by Ku Ssu-li 顧嗣立 (1665–1722). 3 vols. Peking: Chung-hua shu-chü, 1987.

Yüan-shih shih-fan 袁氏世范 (Mr. Yüan's precepts for social life). By Yüan Ts'ai 袁采 (cs 1163). Completed in 1178. Edited and annotated by Ho Heng-chen 賀恒禎 and Yang Liu 楊柳. Tientsin: T'ien-chin ku-chi ch'u-pan she, 1995.

Yüan-wu Fo-kuo ch'an-shih yü-lu 圓悟佛果禪師語錄 (Recorded sayings of Ch'an Master Yüan-wu Fo-Kuo). Preface dated 1134. In *Taishō shinshū daizōkyō,* vol. 47, no. 1997, pp. 713–810.

Yüeh Fei p'o-lu tung-ch'uang chi 岳飛破虜東窗記 (Yüeh Fei defeats the barbarians: the plot at the eastern window). By Chou Li 周禮 (15th century). In *Ku-pen hsi-ch'ü ts'ung-k'an, ch'u-chi,* item 21.

Yüeh-fu ch'ün-chu 樂府群珠 (A string of lyric pearls). Modern edition edited by Lu Ch'ien 盧前. Shanghai: Shang-wu yin-shu kuan, 1957.

Yüeh-fu shih-chi 樂府詩集 (Collection of Music Bureau ballads). Compiled by Kuo Mao-ch'ien 郭茂倩 (12th century). 4 vols. Peking: Chung-hua shu-chü, 1979.

Yüeh I t'u Ch'i 樂毅圖齊 (Yüeh I attacks Ch'i). In *Ku-pen Yüan Ming tsa-chü,* vol. 2.

Yüeh-ming Ho-shang tu Liu Ts'ui 月明和尚度柳翠 (The monk Yüeh-ming converts Liu Ts'ui). In *Ku-chin hsiao-shuo,* vol. 2, *chüan* 29, pp. 428–41.

Yün-chi ch'i ch'ien 雲笈七簽 (Seven lots from the bookbag of the clouds). Compiled by Chang Chün-fang 張君房 (c. 965–c. 1045). Edited and annotated by Chiang Li-sheng 蔣力生 et al. Peking: Hua-hsia ch'u-pan she, 1996.

Yün chi-mou Sui Ho p'ien Ying Pu 運機謀隨何騙英布 (Employing a stratagem Sui Ho tricks Ying Pu). In *Ku-pen Yüan Ming tsa-chü,* vol. 2.

Yün-chien chü-mu ch'ao 雲間據目抄 (Jottings on matters eyewitnessed in Yün-chien). By Fan Lien 范濂 (b. 1540). Preface dated 1593. In *Pi-chi hsiao-shuo ta-kuan,* vol. 6, *ts'e* 13.

SECONDARY SOURCES

Birnbaum, Raoul. *The Healing Buddha.* Boston: Shambhala, 1989.

Bodde, Derk. "The Chinese Cosmic Magic Known as Watching for the Ethers." In Bodde, *Essays on Chinese Civilization,* pp. 351–72.

———. *Essays on Chinese Civilization.* Edited by Charles Le Blanc and Dorothy Borei. Princeton: Princeton University Press, 1981.

Bokenkamp, Stephen R. *Early Daoist Scriptures.* Berkeley: University of California Press. 1997.

Cammann, Schuyler. *China's Dragon Robes.* New York: Ronald Press, 1952.

Campany, Robert Ford. *To Live as Long as Heaven and Earth: A Translation and Study of Ge Hong's Traditions of Divine Transcendents.* Berkeley: University of California Press, 2002.

Carlitz, Katherine. *The Rhetoric of Chin p'ing mei*. Bloomington: Indiana University Press, 1986.

——. "The Role of Drama in the *Chin P'ing Mei*: The Relationship between Fiction and Drama as a Guide to the Viewpoint of a Sixteenth-Century Chinese Novel." Ph.D. dissertation, University of Chicago, 1978.

Chao Wei-pang. "The Chinese Science of Fate Calculation." *Folklore Studies* 5 (1946): 279–315.

Chou Feng-wu 周鳳五. *Tun-huang hsieh-pen T'ai-kung chia-chiao yen-chiu* 敦煌寫本太公家教研究 (A study of the Tun-huang manuscripts of the *T'ai-kung chia-chiao*). Taipei: Ming-wen shu-chü, 1986.

Chou Hsi-pao 周錫保. *Chung-kuo ku-tai fu-shih shih* 中國古代服飾史 (History of traditional Chinese costume). Peking: Chung-kuo hsi-chü ch'u-pan she, 1984.

Chou Pao-chu 周寶珠. *Sung-tai Tung-ching yen-chiu* 宋代東京研究 (A study of the Eastern Capital during the Sung dynasty). K'ai-feng: Ho-nan ta-hsüeh ch'u-pan she, 1992.

Cole, Alan. *Mothers and Sons in Chinese Buddhism*. Stanford: Stanford University Press, 1998.

Davis, Edward L. *Society and the Supernatural in Song China*. Honolulu: University of Hawai'i Press, 2001.

Dean, Kenneth. *Taoist Ritual and the Popular Cults of Southeast China*. Princeton: Princeton University Press, 1993.

de Bruyn, Pierre-Henry. "Wudang Shan: The Origins of a Major Center of Modern Taoism." In Lagerwey, ed. *Religion and Chinese Society*, 2:553–90.

De Groot, J. J. M. *The Religious System of China*. 6 vols. Taipei: Ch'eng Wen Publishing company, 1972.

Ebrey, Patricia Buckley. *Accumulating Culture: The Collections of Emperor Huizong*. Seattle: University of Washington Press, 2008.

Franke, Herbert, ed. *Sung Biographies*. 4 vols. Wiesbaden: Franz Steiner Verlag, 1976.

Frankel, Hans H. "T'ang Literati: A Composite Biography." In Arthur F. Wright and Denis Twitchett, eds. *Confucian Personalities*, pp. 65–83.

Goodrich, Anne S. *Peking Paper Gods: A Look at Home Worship*. Nettetal: Steyler Verlag, 1991.

Goodrich, L. Carrington, and Chaoying Fang, eds. *Dictionary of Ming Biography*. 2 vols. New York: Columbia University Press, 1976.

Grant, Beata. "The Spiritual Saga of Woman Huang: from Pollution to Purification." In David Johnson, ed. *Ritual Opera, Operatic Ritual: "Mu-lien Rescues His Mother" in Chinese Popular Culture*, pp. 224–311.

Hargett, James M. "Huizong's Magic Marchmount: The Genyue Pleasure Park of Kaifeng." *Monumenta Serica* 38 (1988–89): 1–48.

Hou, Ching-lang. *Monnaies d'offrande et la notion de tresorerie dans la religion chinoise*. Paris: College de France, Institut des Hautes Etudes Chinoises, 1975.

Hu Shih-ying 胡士瑩. *Hua-pen hsiao-shuo kai-lun* 話本小説概論 (A comprehensive study of promptbook fiction). 2 vols. Peking: Chung-hua shu-chü, 1980.

Hu, Shiu-ying. *Food Plants of China*. Hong Kong: The Chinese University Press, 2005.

Huang Lin 黃霖 et al. eds. *Chin P'ing Mei ta tz'u-tien* 金瓶梅大辭典 (Great dictionary of the *Chin P'ing Mei*). Ch'eng-tu: Pa-Shu shu-she, 1991.

Hucker, Charles O. A *Dictionary of Official Titles in Imperial China*. Stanford: Stanford University Press, 1985.

Hymes, Robert. *Way and Byway: Taoism, Local Religion, and Models of Divinity in Sung and Modern China*. Berkeley: University of California Press, 2002.

Idema, W. L. *The Dramatic Oeuvre of Chu Yu-tun (1379–1439)*. Leiden: E. J. Brill, 1985.

Johnson, Dale R. *Yuarn Music Dramas: Studies in Prosody and Structure and a Complete Catalogue of Northern Arias in the Dramatic Style*. Ann Arbor: Center for Chinese Studies, University of Michigan, 1980.

Johnson, David. ed. *Ritual Opera, Operatic Ritual: "Mu-lien Rescues His Mother" in Chinese Popular Culture*. Berkeley: Chinese Popular Culture Project, 1989.

Kohn, Livia. *God of the Dao: Lord Lao in History and Myth*. Ann Arbor: Center for Chinese Studies, University of Michigan, 1998.

Lagerwey, John. "The Pilgrimage to Wu-tang Shan." In Susan Naquin and Chün-fang Yü, eds. *Pilgrims and Sacred Sites in China*, pp. 293–332.

———. *Taoist Ritual in Chinese Society and History*. New York: Macmillan, 1987.

———, ed. *Religion and Chinese Society*. 2 vols. Hong Kong: The Chinese University Press and École francaise d'Extrême-Orient, 2004.

Ledderose, Lothar. *Mi Fu and the Classical Tradition of Chinese Calligraphy*. Princeton: Princetoan University Press, 1979

Liang Ssu-ch'eng. *A Pictorial History of Chinese Architecture*. Edited by Wilma Fairbank. Cambridge: MIT Press, 1985.

Linrothe, Rob, and Jeff Watt. *Demonic Divine: Himalayan Art and Beyond*. Chicago: Serindia Publications, 2004.

Liu Chung-kuang 劉中光. "*Chin P'ing Mei* jen-wu k'ao-lun" 金瓶梅人物考論 (A study of the historical figures in the *Chin P'ing Mei*). In Yeh Kuei-t'ung et al., *Chin P'ing Mei tso-che chih mi*, pp. 105–224.

Lopez, Donald S., Jr. *Elaborations on Emptiness: Uses of the Heart Sutra*. Princeton: Princeton University Press, 1996.

———, ed. *Religions of China in Practice*. Princeton: Princeton University Press, 1996.

Lu Ko 魯歌 and Ma Cheng 馬征. *Chin P'ing Mei* jen-wu ta-ch'üan 金瓶梅人物大全 (Great compendium of the characters in the *Chin P'ing Mei*). Ch'ang-ch'un: Chi-lin wen-shih ch'u-pan she, 1991.

Mei Chieh 梅節. *Chin P'ing Mei* tz'u-hua chiao-tu chi 金瓶梅詞話校讀記 (Collation notes on the text of the *Chin P'ing Mei tz'u-hua*). Peking: Pei-ching t'u-shu kuan ch'u-pan she, 2004.

Naquin, Susan, and Chün-fang Yü, eds. *Pilgrims and Sacred Sites in China*. Berkeley: University of California Press, 1992.

Needham, Joseph, Wang Ling, and Lu Gwei-djen. *Science and Civilisation in China*, vol. 4, part 3, *Civil Engineering and Nautics*. Cambridge: Cambridge University Press, 1971.

Orzech, Charles. "Saving the Burning-Mouth Hungry Ghost." In Donald S. Lopez Jr., ed. *Religions of China in Practice*, pp. 278–83.

Owen, Stephen. *The Poetry of Meng Chiao and Han Yü*. New Haven: Yale University Press, 1975.

Robinet, Isabelle. *Taoist Meditation: The Mao-shan Tradition of Great Purity*. Translated by Julian F. Pas and Norman J. Girardot. Albany: State University of New York Press, 1993.

Roy, David T. "The Case for T'ang Hsien-tsu's Authorship of the *Jin Ping Mei*. *Chinese Literature: Essays, Articles, Reviews*. 8, 1 & 2 (July 1986): 31–62.

Saso, Michael. *The Teachings of Taoist Master Chuang*. New Haven: Yale University Press, 1978.

Satyendra, Indira. "Toward a Poetics of the Chinese Novel: A Study of the Prefatory Poems in the *Chin P'ing Mei tz'u-hua*." Ph.D. dissertation, University of Chicago, 1989.

Schafer, Edward H. *The Golden Peaches of Samarkand: A Study of T'ang Exotics*. Berkeley: University of California Press, 1963.

Schipper, Kristofer, and Franciscus Verellen, eds. *The Taoist Canon: A Historical Companion to the Daozang*. 3 vols. Chicago: University of Chicago Press, 2004.

Sponberg, Alan, and Helen Hardacre, eds. *Maitreya, the Future Buddha*. Cambridge: Cambridge University Press, 1988.

Stone, Charles R. *The Fountainhead of Chinese Erotica: The Lord of Perfect Satisfaction (Ruyijun zhuan)*. Honolulu: University of Hawai'i Press, 2003.

Strickmann, Michel. "Saintly Fools and Chinese Masters (Holy Fools)." *Asia Major*, Third Series, 7, 1 (1994): 35–57.

Teiser, Stephen F. *The Scripture on the Ten Kings and the Making of Purgatory in Medieval Chinese Buddhism*. Honolulu: University of Hawaii Press, 1994.

Ting Lang 丁朗. *Chin P'ing Mei yü Pei-ching* 金瓶梅與北京 (*Chin P'ing Mei* and Peking). Peking: Chung-kuo she-hui ch'u-pan she, 1996.

Ts'ai Tun-yung 蔡敦勇. *Chin P'ing Mei chü-ch'ü p'in-t'an* 金瓶梅劇曲品探 (A critical evaluation of the drama and song quoted in the *Chin P'ing Mei*). Nanking: Chiang-su wen-i ch'u-pan she, 1989.

Twitchett, Denis, ed. *The Cambridge History of China*. Volume 3: *Sui and T'ang China, 589–906, Part I*. Cambridge: Cambridge University Press, 1979.

Unschuld, Paul U. *Huang Di nei jing su wen: Nature, Knowledge, Imagery in an Ancient Chinese Medical Text*. Berkeley: University of California Press, 2003.

Volpp, Sophie. "The Gift of a Python Robe: The Circulation of Objects in *Jin Ping Mei*." *Harvard Journal of Asiatic Studies* 65, 1 (June 2005): 133–58.

Wang Kang 王崗. *Lang-man ch'ing-kan yü tsung-chiao ching-shen: wan Ming wen-hsüeh yü wen-hua ssu-ch'ao* 浪漫情感與宗教精神:晚明文學與文化思潮 (Romantic feeling and religious consciousness: trends in late Ming literature and culture). Hong Kong: T'ien-ti t'u-shu yu-hsien kung-ssu, 1999.

Wechsler, Howard J. "The Founding of the T'ang Dynasty: Kao-tsu (reign 618–26)." In Denis Twitchett, ed. *The Cambridge History of China*. Volume 3: *Sui and T'ang China, 589–906, Part I*, pp. 150–88.

Wiseman, Nigel, and Feng Ye. *A Practical Dictionary of Chinese Medicine*. Brookline, Mass.: Paradigm Publications, 2002.

Wright, Arthur F., and Denis Twitchett, eds. *Confucian Personalities*. Stanford: Stanford University Press, 1962.

Yampolsky, Philip B. *The Platform Sutra of the Sixth Patriarch*. New York: Columbia University Press, 1967.

Yeh Kuei-t'ung 葉桂桐 et al., eds. *Chin P'ing Mei tso-che chih mi* 金瓶梅作者之謎 (The riddle of the authorship of the *Chin P'ing Mei*). N.p.: Ning-hsia jen-min ch'u-pan she, 1988.

Yifa. *The Origins of Buddhist Monastic Codes in China.* Honolulu: University of Hawai'i Press, 2002.

Yü, Chün-fang. *Kuan-yin: The Chinese Transformation of Avalokiteśvara.* New York: Columbia University Press, 2001.

INDEX

Ch'en Cheng-hui 陳正彙 (early 12th cent.),
146, 149, 575, 732n.84

Ch'en Chien 陳建 (d. 485), 796n.75

Ch'en Ching-chi 陳經濟, 41–42, 55–56, 79,
84–86, 89, 92, 95, 98, 104, 107, 117–18,
122–23, 129, 133, 136–37, 143, 148, 158,
179–80, 183–84, 188, 192–93, 208–10, 239,
342–43, 354, 378, 387, 464, 475–76, 479,
514–15, 519–20, 528, 546, 567, 569, 578,
581–83, 599, 616, 619, 628, 641, 648,
657–58, 662–63, 665, 668–70, 673–79, 684,
790n.7

Ch'en Ch'ing-hao 陳慶浩, 698n.42

Ch'en Chu 陳著 (1214–97), 738n.38, 762n.2

Ch'en Chün 陳均 (c. 1165–c. 1236), 690n.9

Ch'en Fei 陳棐 (cs 1535), 762n.2

Ch'en Ho 陳鶴 (1516–60), 750n.36, 806n.15

Ch'en Hsiang 陳襄 (1017–80), 713n.1

Ch'en Hsün 陳循 (1385–1462), 813n.73

Ch'en Hsün-chien Mei-ling shih-ch'i chi 陳巡
檢梅嶺失妻記, 717n.37, 720n.16, 758n.37,
777n.46, 789n.150, 823n.46, 825n.6,
835n.58, 842n.71

Ch'en Hung-tsu 陳鴻祖 (9th cent.), 811n.56

Ch'en Ju-lun 陳如綸 (cs 1532), 838n.18

Ch'en Kuan 陳瓘 (1057–1122), 149, 732n.84,
734n.98

Ch'en Liang 陳亮 (1143–94), 709n.33,
731n.73, 737n.25, 833n.40

Ch'en Liang chi [tseng-ting pen] 陳亮集[增訂
本], 709n.33, 731n.73

Ch'en Pang-chan 陳邦瞻 (cs 1598, d. 1623),
723n.5

Ch'en Pao-kuang 陳葆光 (12th cent.),
735n.9

Ch'en P'i-chai 陳羆齋 (early 16th cent.),
697n.40

Ch'en Shang-chün 陳尚君, 699n.56

Ch'en Shao 陳劭 (late 8th cent.), 781n.75,
825n.5

Ch'en Shih-yüan 陳士元 (1516–96), 850n.3

Ch'en Shou 陳壽 (233–97), 749n.36,
786n.127

Ch'en Shu-pao 陳叔寶 (553–604), 333,
785n.118, 821n.20

Ch'en So-wen 陳所聞 (d. c. 1604), 699n.57,
743n.22, 767n.56, 774n.13, 795n.64,
806n.15, 850n.3, 853n.36

Ch'en Ssu-chen 陳四箴, 145, 575, 732n.81

Ch'en Te-wu 陳德武 (13th cent.), 713n.1,
796n.75

Ch'en T'ing 陳霆 (cs 1502), 762n.2, 783n.94,
818n.111

Ch'en To 陳鐸 (early 16th cent.), 701n.88,
711n.45, 740nn.61, 62, 741n.4, 752n.63,
755n.10, 767nn.56, 59, 768n.63, 774nn.13,
21, 780n.71, 783n.94, 795n.70, 798n.7,
799n.23, 807nn.18, 19, 810n.48, 813n.73,
814n.75, 818nn.107, 111, 821n.22,
822n.29, 824n.56, 830n.23, 831nn.24, 28,
838n.18, 840n.35, 841n.60, 844nn.5, 6,
845n.12, 852n.31

Ch'en-ts'ang 陳倉, 274, 757n.25, 760n.57

Ch'en Ts'ao-an 陳草庵 (1247–c. 1320),
808n.28

Ch'en Tsung-shan 陳宗善, 297, 302

Ch'en T'uan 陳摶 (895–989), 810n.50,
812n.60

Ch'en Tzu-ang 陳子昂 (661–702), 811n.56

Ch'en Yao-sou 陳堯叟 (961–1017), 764n.25

Ch'en Yü 陳餘 (d. 204 B.C.), 724n.7

Ch'en Yün-p'ing 陳允平 (13th cent.), 832n.34

Cheng Ai-hsiang 鄭愛香, 219–28 233–36,
238, 553–54, 556–61

Cheng Ai-yüeh 鄭愛月, 8, 24, 97–99, 108,
117, 141, 164, 180, 182–83, 192, 194, 211,
213, 219–39, 426, 429, 530–31, 533–36,
544, 551–63, 567, 581, 616, 623–24,
628–29, 650–51, 676

Cheng Ao 鄭遨 (late 9th cent.), 846n.32

Cheng, Auntie 鄭媽, 219–20, 222–23,
226–28, 232–33, 237, 552, 563, 650

Cheng Chen-to 鄭振鐸 (1898–1958), 689n.4

Cheng Chi 鄭紀, 100

Cheng Chieh-shih li-kung shen-pi kung 鄭節
使立功神臂弓, 709n.30, 711n.47, 727n.40,
744n.44, 751n.58, 752n.64, 791n.27,
815n.92, 820n.12, 843n.79

Cheng Ch'ien 鄭騫 (b. 1906), 765n.38

Cheng Chih-chen 鄭之珍 (1518–95), 693n.19

Cheng-chou 鄭州, 425

Cheng Ch'un 鄭春, 97–98, 103, 141, 180,
182, 188–89, 192, 194, 219–22, 224, 228,
235–36, 238–39, 354, 356–57, 376, 379,
426, 435–36, 609–10

Cheng Chü-chung 鄭居中, 280, 285, 297,
686, 762n.10

Cheng-chüeh 正覺 (1091–1157), 707n.21,
803n.69, 805n.82, 827nn.27, 42

Cheng Feng 鄭奉, 97–98, 103, 141, 164, 171,
173, 189, 221, 236, 354, 356–57, 376, 379,
426, 534, 616, 624, 628